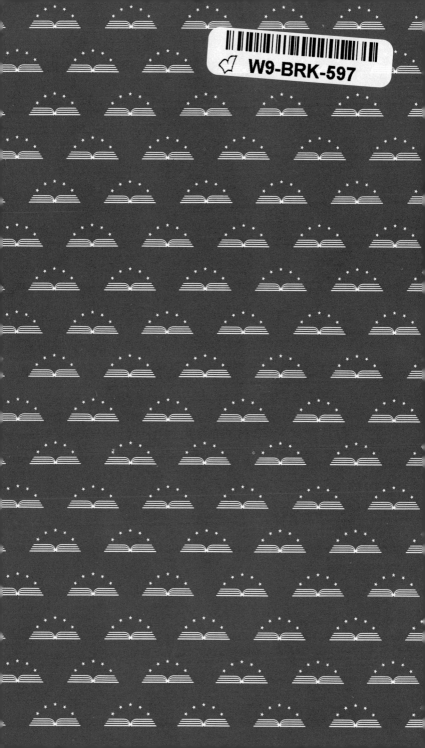

EDITH WHARTON

EDITH WHARTON

NOVELS

The House of Mirth

The Reef

The Custom of the Country

The Age of Innocence

THE LIBRARY OF AMERICA

Library of Congress Catalog Card Number: 85–19816
For cataloging information, see end of *Notes* section.
ISBN 0–940450–31–3

Third Printing
The Library of America—30

R. W. B. LEWIS

WROTE THE NOTES AND SELECTED

THE TEXTS FOR THIS VOLUME

Grateful acknowledgement is made to the National Endowment for the Humanities and the Ford Foundation for their generous financial support of this series.

Contents

THE HOUSE OF MIRTH

I

Selden paused in surprise. In the afternoon rush of the Grand Central Station his eyes had been refreshed by the sight of Miss Lily Bart.

It was a Monday in early September, and he was returning to his work from a hurried dip into the country; but what was Miss Bart doing in town at that season? If she had appeared to be catching a train, he might have inferred that he had come on her in the act of transition between one and another of the country-houses which disputed her presence after the close of the Newport season; but her desultory air perplexed him. She stood apart from the crowd, letting it drift by her to the platform or the street, and wearing an air of irresolution which might, as he surmised, be the mask of a very definite purpose. It struck him at once that she was waiting for some one, but he hardly knew why the idea arrested him. There was nothing new about Lily Bart, yet he could never see her without a faint movement of interest: it was characteristic of her that she always roused speculation, that her simplest acts seemed the result of far-reaching intentions.

An impulse of curiosity made him turn out of his direct line to the door, and stroll past her. He knew that if she did not wish to be seen she would contrive to elude him; and it amused him to think of putting her skill to the test.

"Mr. Selden—what good luck!"

She came forward smiling, eager almost, in her resolve to intercept him. One or two persons, in brushing past them, lingered to look; for Miss Bart was a figure to arrest even the suburban traveller rushing to his last train.

Selden had never seen her more radiant. Her vivid head, relieved against the dull tints of the crowd, made her more conspicuous than in a ball-room, and under her dark hat and veil she regained the girlish smoothness, the purity of tint, that she was beginning to lose after eleven years of late hours and indefatigable dancing. Was it really eleven years, Selden found himself wondering, and had she indeed reached the

3

nine-and-twentieth birthday with which her rivals credited her?

"What luck!" she repeated. "How nice of you to come to my rescue!"

He responded joyfully that to do so was his mission in life, and asked what form the rescue was to take.

"Oh, almost any—even to sitting on a bench and talking to me. One sits out a cotillion—why not sit out a train? It is n't a bit hotter here than in Mrs. Van Osburgh's conservatory—and some of the women are not a bit uglier."

She broke off, laughing, to explain that she had come up to town from Tuxedo, on her way to the Gus Trenors' at Bellomont, and had missed the three-fifteen train to Rhinebeck.

"And there is n't another till half-past five." She consulted the little jewelled watch among her laces. "Just two hours to wait. And I don't know what to do with myself. My maid came up this morning to do some shopping for me, and was to go on to Bellomont at one o'clock, and my aunt's house is closed, and I don't know a soul in town." She glanced plaintively about the station. "It *is* hotter than Mrs. Van Osburgh's, after all. If you can spare the time, do take me somewhere for a breath of air."

He declared himself entirely at her disposal: the adventure struck him as diverting. As a spectator, he had always enjoyed Lily Bart; and his course lay so far out of her orbit that it amused him to be drawn for a moment into the sudden intimacy which her proposal implied.

"Shall we go over to Sherry's for a cup of tea?"

She smiled assentingly, and then made a slight grimace.

"So many people come up to town on a Monday—one is sure to meet a lot of bores. I 'm as old as the hills, of course, and it ought not to make any difference; but if *I 'm* old enough, you 're not," she objected gaily. "I 'm dying for tea—but is n't there a quieter place?"

He answered her smile, which rested on him vividly. Her discretions interested him almost as much as her imprudences: he was so sure that both were part of the same carefully-elaborated plan. In judging Miss Bart, he had always made use of the "argument from design."

"The resources of New York are rather meagre," he said; "but I 'll find a hansom first, and then we 'll invent something."

He led her through the throng of returning holiday-makers, past sallow-faced girls in preposterous hats, and flat-chested women struggling with paper bundles and palm-leaf fans. Was it possible that she belonged to the same race? The dinginess, the crudity of this average section of womanhood made him feel how highly specialized she was.

A rapid shower had cooled the air, and clouds still hung refreshingly over the moist street.

"How delicious! Let us walk a little," she said as they emerged from the station.

They turned into Madison Avenue and began to stroll northward. As she moved beside him, with her long light step, Selden was conscious of taking a luxurious pleasure in her nearness: in the modelling of her little ear, the crisp upward wave of her hair—was it ever so slightly brightened by art?—and the thick planting of her straight black lashes. Everything about her was at once vigorous and exquisite, at once strong and fine. He had a confused sense that she must have cost a great deal to make, that a great many dull and ugly people must, in some mysterious way, have been sacrificed to produce her. He was aware that the qualities distinguishing her from the herd of her sex were chiefly external: as though a fine glaze of beauty and fastidiousness had been applied to vulgar clay. Yet the analogy left him unsatisfied, for a coarse texture will not take a high finish; and was it not possible that the material was fine, but that circumstance had fashioned it into a futile shape?

As he reached this point in his speculations the sun came out, and her lifted parasol cut off his enjoyment. A moment or two later she paused with a sigh.

"Oh, dear, I 'm so hot and thirsty—and what a hideous place New York is!" She looked despairingly up and down the dreary thoroughfare. "Other cities put on their best clothes in summer, but New York seems to sit in its shirt-sleeves." Her eyes wandered down one of the side-streets. "Some one has had the humanity to plant a few trees over there. Let us go into the shade."

"I am glad my street meets with your approval," said Selden as they turned the corner.

"Your street? Do you live here?"

She glanced with interest along the new brick and limestone house-fronts, fantastically varied in obedience to the American craving for novelty, but fresh and inviting with their awnings and flower-boxes.

"Ah, yes—to be sure: *The Benedick*. What a nice-looking building! I don't think I 've ever seen it before." She looked across at the flat-house with its marble porch and pseudo-Georgian façade. "Which are your windows? Those with the awnings down?"

"On the top floor—yes."

"And that nice little balcony is yours? How cool it looks up there!"

He paused a moment. "Come up and see," he suggested. "I can give you a cup of tea in no time—and you won't meet any bores."

Her colour deepened—she still had the art of blushing at the right time—but she took the suggestion as lightly as it was made.

"Why not? It 's too tempting—I 'll take the risk," she declared.

"Oh, I 'm not dangerous," he said in the same key. In truth, he had never liked her as well as at that moment. He knew she had accepted without afterthought: he could never be a factor in her calculations, and there was a surprise, a refreshment almost, in the spontaneity of her consent.

On the threshold he paused a moment, feeling for his latch-key.

"There 's no one here; but I have a servant who is supposed to come in the mornings, and it 's just possible he may have put out the tea-things and provided some cake."

He ushered her into a slip of a hall hung with old prints. She noticed the letters and notes heaped on the table among his gloves and sticks; then she found herself in a small library, dark but cheerful, with its walls of books, a pleasantly faded Turkey rug, a littered desk, and, as he had foretold, a tea-tray on a low table near the window. A breeze had sprung up, swaying inward the muslin curtains, and bringing a fresh scent of mignonette and petunias from the flower-box on the balcony.

Lily sank with a sigh into one of the shabby leather chairs.

"How delicious to have a place like this all to one's self! What a miserable thing it is to be a woman." She leaned back in a luxury of discontent.

Selden was rummaging in a cupboard for the cake.

"Even women," he said, "have been known to enjoy the privileges of a flat."

"Oh, governesses—or widows. But not girls—not poor, miserable, marriageable girls!"

"I even know a girl who lives in a flat."

She sat up in surprise. "You do?"

"I do," he assured her, emerging from the cupboard with the sought-for cake.

"Oh, I know—you mean Gerty Farish." She smiled a little unkindly. "But I said *marriageable*—and besides, she has a horrid little place, and no maid, and such queer things to eat. Her cook does the washing and the food tastes of soap. I should hate that, you know."

"You should n't dine with her on wash-days," said Selden, cutting the cake.

They both laughed, and he knelt by the table to light the lamp under the kettle, while she measured out the tea into a little tea-pot of green glaze. As he watched her hand, polished as a bit of old ivory, with its slender pink nails, and the sapphire bracelet slipping over her wrist, he was struck with the irony of suggesting to her such a life as his cousin Gertrude Farish had chosen. She was so evidently the victim of the civilization which had produced her, that the links of her bracelet seemed like manacles chaining her to her fate.

She seemed to read his thought. "It was horrid of me to say that of Gerty," she said with charming compunction. "I forgot she was your cousin. But we 're so different, you know: she likes being good, and I like being happy. And besides, she is free and I am not. If I were, I daresay I could manage to be happy even in her flat. It must be pure bliss to arrange the furniture just as one likes, and give all the horrors to the ash-man. If I could only do over my aunt's drawing-room I know I should be a better woman."

"Is it so very bad?" he asked sympathetically.

She smiled at him across the tea-pot which she was holding up to be filled.

"That shows how seldom you come there. Why don't you come oftener?"

"When I do come, it's not to look at Mrs. Peniston's furniture."

"Nonsense," she said. "You don't come at all—and yet we get on so well when we meet."

"Perhaps that's the reason," he answered promptly. "I'm afraid I haven't any cream, you know—shall you mind a slice of lemon instead?"

"I shall like it better." She waited while he cut the lemon and dropped a thin disk into her cup. "But that is not the reason," she insisted.

"The reason for what?"

"For your never coming." She leaned forward with a shade of perplexity in her charming eyes. "I wish I knew—I wish I could make you out. Of course I know there are men who don't like me—one can tell that at a glance. And there are others who are afraid of me: they think I want to marry them." She smiled up at him frankly. "But I don't think you dislike me—and you can't possibly think I want to marry you."

"No—I absolve you of that," he agreed.

"Well, then——?"

He had carried his cup to the fireplace, and stood leaning against the chimney-piece and looking down on her with an air of indolent amusement. The provocation in her eyes increased his amusement—he had not supposed she would waste her powder on such small game; but perhaps she was only keeping her hand in; or perhaps a girl of her type had no conversation but of the personal kind. At any rate, she was amazingly pretty, and he had asked her to tea and must live up to his obligations.

"Well, then," he said with a plunge, "perhaps *that's* the reason."

"What?"

"The fact that you don't want to marry me. Perhaps I don't regard it as such a strong inducement to go and see you." He felt a slight shiver down his spine as he ventured this, but her laugh reassured him.

"Dear Mr. Selden, that was n't worthy of you. It 's stupid of you to make love to me, and it is n't like you to be stupid." She leaned back, sipping her tea with an air so enchantingly judicial that, if they had been in her aunt's drawing-room, he might almost have tried to disprove her deduction.

"Don't you see," she continued, "that there are men enough to say pleasant things to me, and that what I want is a friend who won't be afraid to say disagreeable ones when I need them? Sometimes I have fancied you might be that friend—I don't know why, except that you are neither a prig nor a bounder, and that I should n't have to pretend with you or be on my guard against you." Her voice had dropped to a note of seriousness, and she sat gazing up at him with the troubled gravity of a child.

"You don't know how much I need such a friend," she said. "My aunt is full of copy-book axioms, but they were all meant to apply to conduct in the early fifties. I always feel that to live up to them would include wearing book-muslin with gigot sleeves. And the other women—my best friends—well, they use me or abuse me; but they don't care a straw what happens to me. I 've been about too long—people are getting tired of me; they are beginning to say I ought to marry."

There was a moment's pause, during which Selden meditated one or two replies calculated to add a momentary zest to the situation; but he rejected them in favour of the simple question: "Well, why don't you?"

She coloured and laughed. "Ah, I see you *are* a friend after all, and that is one of the disagreeable things I was asking for."

"It was n't meant to be disagreeable," he returned amicably. "Is n't marriage your vocation? Is n't it what you 're all brought up for?"

She sighed. "I suppose so. What else is there?"

"Exactly. And so why not take the plunge and have it over?"

She shrugged her shoulders. "You speak as if I ought to marry the first man who came along."

"I did n't mean to imply that you are as hard put to it as

that. But there must be some one with the requisite qualifi-
cations."

She shook her head wearily. "I threw away one or two
good chances when I first came out—I suppose every girl
does; and you know I am horribly poor—and very expensive.
I must have a great deal of money."

Selden had turned to reach for a cigarette-box on the
mantelpiece.

"What 's become of Dillworth?" he asked.

"Oh, his mother was frightened—she was afraid I should
have all the family jewels reset. And she wanted me to promise that I would n't do over the drawing-room."

"The very thing you are marrying for!"

"Exactly. So she packed him off to India."

"Hard luck—but you can do better than Dillworth."

He offered the box, and she took out three or four cigarettes, putting one between her lips and slipping the others
into a little gold case attached to her long pearl chain.

"Have I time? Just a whiff, then." She leaned forward,
holding the tip of her cigarette to his. As she did so, he
noted, with a purely impersonal enjoyment, how evenly the
black lashes were set in her smooth white lids, and how the
purplish shade beneath them melted into the pure pallour of
the cheek.

She began to saunter about the room, examining the book-
shelves between the puffs of her cigarette-smoke. Some of the
volumes had the ripe tints of good tooling and old morocco,
and her eyes lingered on them caressingly, not with the appreciation of the expert, but with the pleasure in agreeable tones
and textures that was one of her inmost susceptibilities. Suddenly her expression changed from desultory enjoyment to
active conjecture, and she turned to Selden with a question.

"You collect, don't you—you know about first editions and
things?"

"As much as a man may who has no money to spend. Now
and then I pick up something in the rubbish heap; and I go
and look on at the big sales."

She had again addressed herself to the shelves, but her eyes
now swept them inattentively, and he saw that she was preoccupied with a new idea.

"And Americana—do you collect Americana?"

Selden stared and laughed.

"No, that 's rather out of my line. I 'm not really a collector, you see; I simply like to have good editions of the books I am fond of."

She made a slight grimace. "And Americana are horribly dull, I suppose?"

"I should fancy so—except to the historian. But your real collector values a thing for its rarity. I don't suppose the buyers of Americana sit up reading them all night—old Jefferson Gryce certainly did n't."

She was listening with keen attention. "And yet they fetch fabulous prices, don't they? It seems so odd to want to pay a lot for an ugly badly-printed book that one is never going to read! And I suppose most of the owners of Americana are not historians either?"

"No; very few of the historians can afford to buy them. They have to use those in the public libraries or in private collections. It seems to be the mere rarity that attracts the average collector."

He had seated himself on an arm of the chair near which she was standing, and she continued to question him, asking which were the rarest volumes, whether the Jefferson Gryce collection was really considered the finest in the world, and what was the largest price ever fetched by a single volume.

It was so pleasant to sit there looking up at her, as she lifted now one book and then another from the shelves, fluttering the pages between her fingers, while her drooping profile was outlined against the warm background of old bindings, that he talked on without pausing to wonder at her sudden interest in so unsuggestive a subject. But he could never be long with her without trying to find a reason for what she was doing, and as she replaced his first edition of La Bruyère and turned away from the bookcases, he began to ask himself what she had been driving at. Her next question was not of a nature to enlighten him. She paused before him with a smile which seemed at once designed to admit him to her familiarity, and to remind him of the restrictions it imposed.

"Don't you ever mind," she asked suddenly, "not being rich enough to buy all the books you want?"

He followed her glance about the room, with its worn furniture and shabby walls.

"Don't I just? Do you take me for a saint on a pillar?"

"And having to work—do you mind that?"

"Oh, the work itself is not so bad—I 'm rather fond of the law."

"No; but the being tied down: the routine—don't you ever want to get away, to see new places and people?"

"Horribly—especially when I see all my friends rushing to the steamer."

She drew a sympathetic breath. "But do you mind enough—to marry to get out of it?"

Selden broke into a laugh. "God forbid!" he declared.

She rose with a sigh, tossing her cigarette into the grate.

"Ah, there 's the difference—a girl must, a man may if he chooses." She surveyed him critically. "Your coat 's a little shabby—but who cares? It does n't keep people from asking you to dine. If I were shabby no one would have me: a woman is asked out as much for her clothes as for herself. The clothes are the background, the frame, if you like: they don't make success, but they are a part of it. Who wants a dingy woman? We are expected to be pretty and well-dressed till we drop—and if we can't keep it up alone, we have to go into partnership."

Selden glanced at her with amusement: it was impossible, even with her lovely eyes imploring him, to take a sentimental view of her case.

"Ah, well, there must be plenty of capital on the look-out for such an investment. Perhaps you 'll meet your fate to-night at the Trenors'."

She returned his look interrogatively.

"I thought you might be going there—oh, not in that capacity! But there are to be a lot of your set—Gwen Van Osburgh, the Wetheralls, Lady Cressida Raith—and the George Dorsets."

She paused a moment before the last name, and shot a query through her lashes; but he remained imperturbable.

"Mrs. Trenor asked me; but I can't get away till the end of the week; and those big parties bore me."

"Ah, so they do me," she exclaimed.

"Then why go?"

"It's part of the business—you forget! And besides, if I did n't, I should be playing bézique with my aunt at Richfield Springs."

"That's almost as bad as marrying Dillworth," he agreed, and they both laughed for pure pleasure in their sudden intimacy.

She glanced at the clock.

"Dear me! I must be off. It's after five."

She paused before the mantelpiece, studying herself in the mirror while she adjusted her veil. The attitude revealed the long slope of her slender sides, which gave a kind of wild-wood grace to her outline—as though she were a captured dryad subdued to the conventions of the drawing-room; and Selden reflected that it was the same streak of sylvan freedom in her nature that lent such savour to her artificiality.

He followed her across the room to the entrance-hall; but on the threshold she held out her hand with a gesture of leave-taking.

"It's been delightful; and now you will have to return my visit."

"But don't you want me to see you to the station?"

"No; good bye here, please."

She let her hand lie in his a moment, smiling up at him adorably.

"Good bye, then—and good luck at Bellomont!" he said, opening the door for her.

On the landing she paused to look about her. There were a thousand chances to one against her meeting anybody, but one could never tell, and she always paid for her rare indiscretions by a violent reaction of prudence. There was no one in sight, however, but a char-woman who was scrubbing the stairs. Her own stout person and its surrounding implements took up so much room that Lily, to pass her, had to gather up her skirts and brush against the wall. As she did so, the woman paused in her work and looked up curiously, resting her clenched red fists on the wet cloth she had just drawn from her pail. She had a broad sallow face, slightly pitted with small-pox, and thin straw-coloured hair through which her scalp shone unpleasantly.

"I beg your pardon," said Lily, intending by her politeness to convey a criticism of the other's manner.

The woman, without answering, pushed her pail aside, and continued to stare as Miss Bart swept by with a murmur of silken linings. Lily felt herself flushing under the look. What did the creature suppose? Could one never do the simplest, the most harmless thing, without subjecting one's self to some odious conjecture? Half way down the next flight, she smiled to think that a char-woman's stare should so perturb her. The poor thing was probably dazzled by such an unwonted apparition. But *were* such apparitions unwonted on Selden's stairs? Miss Bart was not familiar with the moral code of bachelors' flat-houses, and her colour rose again as it occurred to her that the woman's persistent gaze implied a groping among past associations. But she put aside the thought with a smile at her own fears, and hastened downward, wondering if she should find a cab short of Fifth Avenue.

Under the Georgian porch she paused again, scanning the street for a hansom. None was in sight, but as she reached the sidewalk she ran against a small glossy-looking man with a gardenia in his coat, who raised his hat with a surprised exclamation.

"Miss Bart? Well—of all people! This *is* luck," he declared; and she caught a twinkle of amused curiosity between his screwed-up lids.

"Oh, Mr. Rosedale—how are you?" she said, perceiving that the irrepressible annoyance on her face was reflected in the sudden intimacy of his smile.

Mr. Rosedale stood scanning her with interest and approval. He was a plump rosy man of the blond Jewish type, with smart London clothes fitting him like upholstery, and small sidelong eyes which gave him the air of appraising people as if they were bric-a-brac. He glanced up interrogatively at the porch of the Benedick.

"Been up to town for a little shopping, I suppose?" he said, in a tone which had the familiarity of a touch.

Miss Bart shrank from it slightly, and then flung herself into precipitate explanations.

"Yes—I came up to see my dress-maker. I am just on my way to catch the train to the Trenors'."

"Ah—your dress-maker; just so," he said blandly. "I did n't know there were any dress-makers in the Benedick."

"The Benedick?" She looked gently puzzled. "Is that the name of this building?"

"Yes, that 's the name: I believe it 's an old word for bachelor, is n't it? I happen to own the building—that 's the way I know." His smile deepened as he added with increasing assurance: "But you must let me take you to the station. The Trenors are at Bellomont, of course? You 've barely time to catch the five-forty. The dress-maker kept you waiting, I suppose."

Lily stiffened under the pleasantry.

"Oh, thanks," she stammered; and at that moment her eye caught a hansom drifting down Madison Avenue, and she hailed it with a desperate gesture.

"You 're very kind; but I could n't think of troubling you," she said, extending her hand to Mr. Rosedale; and heedless of his protestations, she sprang into the rescuing vehicle, and called out a breathless order to the driver.

II

IN THE HANSOM she leaned back with a sigh.

Why must a girl pay so dearly for her least escape from routine? Why could one never do a natural thing without having to screen it behind a structure of artifice? She had yielded to a passing impulse in going to Lawrence Selden's rooms, and it was so seldom that she could allow herself the luxury of an impulse! This one, at any rate, was going to cost her rather more than she could afford. She was vexed to see that, in spite of so many years of vigilance, she had blundered twice within five minutes. That stupid story about her dress-maker was bad enough—it would have been so simple to tell Rosedale that she had been taking tea with Selden! The mere statement of the fact would have rendered it innocuous. But, after having let herself be surprised in a falsehood, it was doubly stupid to snub the witness of her discomfiture. If she had had the presence of mind to let Rosedale drive her to the station, the concession might have purchased his silence. He had his race's accuracy in the appraisal of values, and to be seen walking down the platform at the crowded afternoon hour in the company of Miss Lily Bart would have been money in his pocket, as he might himself have phrased it. He knew, of course, that there would be a large house-party at Bellomont, and the possibility of being taken for one of Mrs. Trenor's guests was doubtless included in his calculations. Mr. Rosedale was still at a stage in his social ascent when it was of importance to produce such impressions.

The provoking part was that Lily knew all this—knew how easy it would have been to silence him on the spot, and how difficult it might be to do so afterward. Mr. Simon Rosedale was a man who made it his business to know everything about every one, whose idea of showing himself to be at home in society was to display an inconvenient familiarity with the habits of those with whom he wished to be thought intimate. Lily was sure that within twenty-four hours the story of her visiting her dress-maker at the Benedick would be in active circulation among Mr. Rosedale's acquaintances. The worst of it was that she had always snubbed and ignored him. On his first appearance—when her improvident cousin, Jack Stepney, had obtained for him (in return for favours too easily guessed) a card to one of the vast impersonal Van Osburgh "crushes"—Rosedale, with that mixture of artistic sensibility and business astuteness which characterizes his race, had instantly gravitated toward Miss Bart. She understood his motives, for her own course was guided by as nice calculations. Training and experience had taught her to be hospitable to newcomers, since the most unpromising might be useful later on, and there were plenty of available *oubliettes* to swallow them if they were not. But some intuitive repugnance, getting the better of years of social discipline, had made her push Mr. Rosedale into his *oubliette* without a trial. He had left behind only the ripple of amusement which his speedy despatch had caused among her friends; and though later (to shift the metaphor) he reappeared lower down the stream, it was only in fleeting glimpses, with long submergences between.

Hitherto Lily had been undisturbed by scruples. In her little set Mr. Rosedale had been pronounced "impossible," and Jack Stepney roundly snubbed for his attempt to pay his debts in dinner invitations. Even Mrs. Trenor, whose taste for variety had led her into some hazardous experiments, resisted Jack's attempts to disguise Mr. Rosedale as a novelty, and declared that he was the same little Jew who had been served up and rejected at the social board a dozen times within her memory; and while Judy Trenor was obdurate there was small chance of Mr. Rosedale's penetrating beyond the outer limbo of the Van Osburgh crushes. Jack gave up the contest with a laughing "You 'll see," and, sticking manfully to his guns, showed himself with Rosedale at the fashionable restaurants, in company with the personally vivid if socially obscure ladies who are available for such purposes. But the attempt had hitherto been vain, and as Rosedale undoubtedly paid for the dinners, the laugh remained with his debtor.

Mr. Rosedale, it will be seen, was thus far not a factor to be feared—unless one put one's self in his power. And this was precisely what Miss Bart had done. Her clumsy fib had let him see that she had something to conceal; and she was sure he had a score to settle with her. Something in his smile

told her he had not forgotten. She turned from the thought
with a little shiver, but it hung on her all the way to the
station, and dogged her down the platform with the persistency of Mr. Rosedale himself.

She had just time to take her seat before the train started;
but having arranged herself in her corner with the instinctive
feeling for effect which never forsook her, she glanced about
in the hope of seeing some other member of the Trenors'
party. She wanted to get away from herself, and conversation
was the only means of escape that she knew.

Her search was rewarded by the discovery of a very blond
young man with a soft reddish beard, who, at the other end
of the carriage, appeared to be dissembling himself behind an
unfolded newspaper. Lily's eye brightened, and a faint smile
relaxed the drawn lines of her mouth. She had known that
Mr. Percy Gryce was to be at Bellomont, but she had not
counted on the luck of having him to herself in the train; and
the fact banished all perturbing thoughts of Mr. Rosedale.
Perhaps, after all, the day was to end more favourably than it
had begun.

She began to cut the pages of a novel, tranquilly studying
her prey through downcast lashes while she organized a
method of attack. Something in his attitude of conscious absorption told her that he was aware of her presence: no one
had ever been quite so engrossed in an evening paper! She
guessed that he was too shy to come up to her, and that she
would have to devise some means of approach which should
not appear to be an advance on her part. It amused her to
think that any one as rich as Mr. Percy Gryce should be shy;
but she was gifted with treasures of indulgence for such idiosyncrasies, and besides, his timidity might serve her purpose
better than too much assurance. She had the art of giving self-
confidence to the embarrassed, but she was not equally sure
of being able to embarrass the self-confident.

She waited till the train had emerged from the tunnel and
was racing between the ragged edges of the northern suburbs.
Then, as it lowered its speed near Yonkers, she rose from her
seat and drifted slowly down the carriage. As she passed Mr.
Gryce, the train gave a lurch, and he was aware of a slender
hand gripping the back of his chair. He rose with a start, his

ingenuous face looking as though it had been dipped in crimson: even the reddish tint in his beard seemed to deepen.

The train swayed again, almost flinging Miss Bart into his arms. She steadied herself with a laugh and drew back; but he was enveloped in the scent of her dress, and his shoulder had felt her fugitive touch.

"Oh, Mr. Gryce, is it you? I'm so sorry—I was trying to find the porter and get some tea."

She held out her hand as the train resumed its level rush, and they stood exchanging a few words in the aisle. Yes—he was going to Bellomont. He had heard she was to be of the party—he blushed again as he admitted it. And was he to be there for a whole week? How delightful!

But at this point one or two belated passengers from the last station forced their way into the carriage, and Lily had to retreat to her seat.

"The chair next to mine is empty—do take it," she said over her shoulder; and Mr. Gryce, with considerable embarrassment, succeeded in effecting an exchange which enabled him to transport himself and his bags to her side.

"Ah—and here is the porter, and perhaps we can have some tea."

She signalled to that official, and in a moment, with the ease that seemed to attend the fulfilment of all her wishes, a little table had been set up between the seats, and she had helped Mr. Gryce to bestow his encumbering properties beneath it.

When the tea came he watched her in silent fascination while her hands flitted above the tray, looking miraculously fine and slender in contrast to the coarse china and lumpy bread. It seemed wonderful to him that any one should perform with such careless ease the difficult task of making tea in public in a lurching train. He would never have dared to order it for himself, lest he should attract the notice of his fellow-passengers; but, secure in the shelter of her conspicuousness, he sipped the inky draught with a delicious sense of exhilaration.

Lily, with the flavour of Selden's caravan tea on her lips, had no great fancy to drown it in the railway brew which seemed such nectar to her companion; but, rightly judging that one of the charms of tea is the fact of drinking it together, she proceeded to give the last touch to Mr. Gryce's enjoyment by smiling at him across her lifted cup.

"Is it quite right—I have n't made it too strong?" she asked solicitously; and he replied with conviction that he had never tasted better tea.

"I daresay it is true," she reflected; and her imagination was fired by the thought that Mr. Gryce, who might have sounded the depths of the most complex self-indulgence, was perhaps actually taking his first journey alone with a pretty woman.

It struck her as providential that she should be the instrument of his initiation. Some girls would not have known how to manage him. They would have over-emphasized the novelty of the adventure, trying to make him feel in it the zest of an escapade. But Lily's methods were more delicate. She remembered that her cousin Jack Stepney had once defined Mr. Gryce as the young man who had promised his mother never to go out in the rain without his overshoes; and acting on this hint, she resolved to impart a gently domestic air to the scene, in the hope that her companion, instead of feeling that he was doing something reckless or unusual, would merely be led to dwell on the advantage of always having a companion to make one's tea in the train.

But in spite of her efforts, conversation flagged after the tray had been removed, and she was driven to take a fresh measurement of Mr. Gryce's limitations. It was not, after all, opportunity but imagination that he lacked: he had a mental palate which would never learn to distinguish between railway tea and nectar. There was, however, one topic she could rely on: one spring that she had only to touch to set his simple machinery in motion. She had refrained from touching it because it was a last resource, and she had relied on other arts to stimulate other sensations; but as a settled look of dulness began to creep over his candid features, she saw that extreme measures were necessary.

"And how," she said, leaning forward, "are you getting on with your Americana?"

His eye became a degree less opaque: it was as though an incipient film had been removed from it, and she felt the pride of a skilful operator.

"I 've got a few new things," he said, suffused with plea-sure, but lowering his voice as though he feared his fellow-passengers might be in league to despoil him.

She returned a sympathetic enquiry, and gradually he was drawn on to talk of his latest purchases. It was the one subject which enabled him to forget himself, or allowed him, rather, to remember himself without constraint, because he was at home in it, and could assert a superiority that there were few to dispute. Hardly any of his acquaintances cared for Ameri-cana, or knew anything about them; and the consciousness of this ignorance threw Mr. Gryce's knowledge into agreeable relief. The only difficulty was to introduce the topic and to keep it to the front; most people showed no desire to have their ignorance dispelled, and Mr. Gryce was like a merchant whose warehouses are crammed with an unmarketable com-modity.

But Miss Bart, it appeared, really did want to know about Americana; and moreover, she was already sufficiently in-formed to make the task of farther instruction as easy as it was agreeable. She questioned him intelligently, she heard him submissively; and, prepared for the look of lassitude which usually crept over his listeners' faces, he grew eloquent under her receptive gaze. The "points" she had had the pres-ence of mind to glean from Selden, in anticipation of this very contingency, were serving her to such good purpose that she began to think her visit to him had been the luckiest incident of the day. She had once more shown her talent for profiting by the unexpected, and dangerous theories as to the advis-ability of yielding to impulse were germinating under the sur-face of smiling attention which she continued to present to her companion.

Mr. Gryce's sensations, if less definite, were equally agree-able. He felt the confused titillation with which the lower organisms welcome the gratification of their needs, and all his senses floundered in a vague well-being, through which Miss Bart's personality was dimly but pleasantly perceptible.

Mr. Gryce's interest in Americana had not originated with himself: it was impossible to think of him as evolving any taste of his own. An uncle had left him a collection already noted among bibliophiles; the existence of the collection was the only fact that had ever shed glory on the name of Gryce, and the nephew took as much pride in his inheritance as though it had been his own work. Indeed, he gradually came to regard it as such, and to feel a sense of personal complacency when he chanced on any reference to the Gryce Americana. Anxious as he was to avoid personal notice, he took, in the printed mention of his name, a pleasure so exquisite and excessive that it seemed a compensation for his shrinking from publicity.

To enjoy the sensation as often as possible, he subscribed to all the reviews dealing with book-collecting in general, and American history in particular, and as allusions to his library abounded in the pages of these journals, which formed his only reading, he came to regard himself as figuring prominently in the public eye, and to enjoy the thought of the interest which would be excited if the persons he met in the street, or sat among in travelling, were suddenly to be told that he was the possessor of the Gryce Americana.

Most timidities have such secret compensations, and Miss Bart was discerning enough to know that the inner vanity is generally in proportion to the outer self-depreciation. With a more confident person she would not have dared to dwell so long on one topic, or to show such exaggerated interest in it; but she had rightly guessed that Mr. Gryce's egoism was a thirsty soil, requiring constant nurture from without. Miss Bart had the gift of following an undercurrent of thought while she appeared to be sailing on the surface of conversation; and in this case her mental excursion took the form of a rapid survey of Mr. Percy Gryce's future as combined with her own. The Gryces were from Albany, and but lately introduced to the metropolis, where the mother and son had come, after old Jefferson Gryce's death, to take possession of his house in Madison Avenue—an appalling house, all brown stone without and black walnut within, with the Gryce library in a fire-proof annex that looked like a mausoleum. Lily, however, knew all about them: young Mr. Gryce's arrival had fluttered the maternal breasts of New York, and when a girl has no mother to palpitate for her she must needs be on the alert for herself. Lily, therefore, had not only contrived to put herself in the young man's way, but had made the acquaintance

of Mrs. Gryce, a monumental woman with the voice of a pulpit orator and a mind preoccupied with the iniquities of her
servants, who came sometimes to sit with Mrs. Peniston and
learn from that lady how she managed to prevent the kitchen-
maid's smuggling groceries out of the house. Mrs. Gryce had
a kind of impersonal benevolence: cases of individual need
she regarded with suspicion, but she subscribed to Institutions when their annual reports showed an impressive surplus. Her domestic duties were manifold, for they extended
from furtive inspections of the servants' bedrooms to unannounced descents to the cellar; but she had never allowed herself many pleasures. Once, however, she had had a special
edition of the Sarum Rule printed in rubric and presented to
every clergyman in the diocese; and the gilt album in which
their letters of thanks were pasted formed the chief ornament
of her drawing-room table.

Percy had been brought up in the principles which so excellent a woman was sure to inculcate. Every form of prudence and suspicion had been grafted on a nature originally
reluctant and cautious, with the result that it would have
seemed hardly needful for Mrs. Gryce to extract his promise
about the overshoes, so little likely was he to hazard himself
abroad in the rain. After attaining his majority, and coming
into the fortune which the late Mr. Gryce had made out of a
patent device for excluding fresh air from hotels, the young
man continued to live with his mother in Albany; but on
Jefferson Gryce's death, when another large property passed
into her son's hands, Mrs. Gryce thought that what she called
his "interests" demanded his presence in New York. She accordingly installed herself in the Madison Avenue house, and
Percy, whose sense of duty was not inferior to his mother's,
spent all his week days in the handsome Broad Street office
where a batch of pale men on small salaries had grown grey
in the management of the Gryce estate, and where he was
initiated with becoming reverence into every detail of the art
of accumulation.

As far as Lily could learn, this had hitherto been Mr.
Gryce's only occupation, and she might have been pardoned
for thinking it not too hard a task to interest a young man
who had been kept on such low diet. At any rate, she felt

herself so completely in command of the situation that she
yielded to a sense of security in which all fear of Mr. Rosedale, and of the difficulties on which that fear was contingent,
vanished beyond the edge of thought.

The stopping of the train at Garrisons would not have distracted her from these thoughts, had she not caught a sudden
look of distress in her companion's eye. His seat faced toward
the door, and she guessed that he had been perturbed by the
approach of an acquaintance; a fact confirmed by the turning
of heads and general sense of commotion which her own entrance into a railway-carriage was apt to produce.

She knew the symptoms at once, and was not surprised to
be hailed by the high notes of a pretty woman, who entered
the train accompanied by a maid, a bull-terrier, and a footman
staggering under a load of bags and dressing-cases.

"Oh, Lily—are you going to Bellomont? Then you can't
let me have your seat, I suppose? But I *must* have a seat in
this carriage—porter, you must find me a place at once. Can't
some one be put somewhere else? I want to be with my
friends. Oh, how do you do, Mr. Gryce? Do please make him
understand that I must have a seat next to you and Lily."

Mrs. George Dorset, regardless of the mild efforts of a traveller with a carpet-bag, who was doing his best to make room
for her by getting out of the train, stood in the middle of the
aisle, diffusing about her that general sense of exasperation
which a pretty woman on her travels not infrequently creates.

She was smaller and thinner than Lily Bart, with a restless
pliability of pose, as if she could have been crumpled up and
run through a ring, like the sinuous draperies she affected.
Her small pale face seemed the mere setting of a pair of dark
exaggerated eyes, of which the visionary gaze contrasted curiously with her self-assertive tone and gestures; so that, as one
of her friends observed, she was like a disembodied spirit who
took up a great deal of room.

Having finally discovered that the seat adjoining Miss
Bart's was at her disposal, she possessed herself of it with a
farther displacement of her surroundings, explaining meanwhile that she had come across from Mount Kisco in her
motor-car that morning, and had been kicking her heels for an
hour at Garrisons, without even the alleviation of a cigarette,

her brute of a husband having neglected to replenish her case before they parted that morning.

"And at this hour of the day I don't suppose you 've a single one left, have you, Lily?" she plaintively concluded.

Miss Bart caught the startled glance of Mr. Percy Gryce, whose own lips were never defiled by tobacco.

"What an absurd question, Bertha!" she exclaimed, blushing at the thought of the store she had laid in at Lawrence Selden's.

"Why, don't you smoke? Since when have you given it up? What—you never—— And you don't either, Mr. Gryce? Ah, of course—how stupid of me—I understand."

And Mrs. Dorset leaned back against her travelling cushions with a smile which made Lily wish there had been no vacant seat beside her own.

III

BRIDGE AT Bellomont usually lasted till the small hours; and when Lily went to bed that night she had played too long for her own good.

Feeling no desire for the self-communion which awaited her in her room, she lingered on the broad stairway, looking down into the hall below, where the last card-players were grouped about the tray of tall glasses and silver-collared decanters which the butler had just placed on a low table near the fire.

The hall was arcaded, with a gallery supported on columns of pale yellow marble. Tall clumps of flowering plants were grouped against a background of dark foliage in the angles of the walls. On the crimson carpet a deer-hound and two or three spaniels dozed luxuriously before the fire, and the light from the great central lantern overhead shed a brightness on the women's hair and struck sparks from their jewels as they moved.

There were moments when such scenes delighted Lily, when they gratified her sense of beauty and her craving for the external finish of life; there were others when they gave a sharper edge to the meagreness of her own opportunities. This was one of the moments when the sense of contrast was uppermost, and she turned away impatiently as Mrs. George Dorset, glittering in serpentine spangles, drew Percy Gryce in her wake to a confidential nook beneath the gallery.

It was not that Miss Bart was afraid of losing her newly-acquired hold over Mr. Gryce. Mrs. Dorset might startle or dazzle him, but she had neither the skill nor the patience to effect his capture. She was too self-engrossed to penetrate the recesses of his shyness, and besides, why should she care to give herself the trouble? At most it might amuse her to make sport of his simplicity for an evening—after that he would be merely a burden to her, and knowing this, she was far too experienced to encourage him. But the mere thought of that other woman, who could take a man up and toss him aside as she willed, without having to regard him as a possible factor in her plans, filled Lily Bart with envy. She had been

26

bored all the afternoon by Percy Gryce—the mere thought seemed to waken an echo of his droning voice—but she could not ignore him on the morrow, she must follow up her success, must submit to more boredom, must be ready with fresh compliances and adaptabilities, and all on the bare chance that he might ultimately decide to do her the honour of boring her for life.

It was a hateful fate—but how escape from it? What choice had she? To be herself, or a Gerty Farish. As she entered her bedroom, with its softly-shaded lights, her lace dressing-gown lying across the silken bedspread, her little embroidered slippers before the fire, a vase of carnations filling the air with perfume, and the last novels and magazines lying uncut on a table beside the reading-lamp, she had a vision of Miss Farish's cramped flat, with its cheap conveniences and hideous wall-papers. No; she was not made for mean and shabby surroundings, for the squalid compromises of poverty. Her whole being dilated in an atmosphere of luxury; it was the background she required, the only climate she could breathe in. But the luxury of others was not what she wanted. A few years ago it had sufficed her: she had taken her daily meed of pleasure without caring who provided it. Now she was beginning to chafe at the obligations it imposed, to feel herself a mere pensioner on the splendour which had once seemed to belong to her. There were even moments when she was conscious of having to pay her way.

For a long time she had refused to play bridge. She knew she could not afford it, and she was afraid of acquiring so expensive a taste. She had seen the danger exemplified in more than one of her associates—in young Ned Silverton, for instance, the charming fair boy now seated in abject rapture at the elbow of Mrs. Fisher, a striking divorcée with eyes and gowns as emphatic as the head-lines of her "case." Lily could remember when young Silverton had stumbled into their circle, with the air of a strayed Arcadian who has published charming sonnets in his college journal. Since then he had developed a taste for Mrs. Fisher and bridge, and the latter at least had involved him in expenses from which he had been more than once rescued by harassed maiden sisters, who treasured the sonnets, and went without sugar in their tea to keep their darling afloat. Ned's case was familiar to Lily: she had seen his charming eyes—which had a good deal more poetry in them than the sonnets—change from surprise to amusement, and from amusement to anxiety, as he passed under the spell of the terrible god of chance; and she was afraid of discovering the same symptoms in her own case.

For in the last year she had found that her hostesses expected her to take a place at the card-table. It was one of the taxes she had to pay for their prolonged hospitality, and for the dresses and trinkets which occasionally replenished her insufficient wardrobe. And since she had played regularly the passion had grown on her. Once or twice of late she had won a large sum, and instead of keeping it against future losses, had spent it in dress or jewelry; and the desire to atone for this imprudence, combined with the increasing exhilaration of the game, drove her to risk higher stakes at each fresh venture. She tried to excuse herself on the plea that, in the Trenor set, if one played at all one must either play high or be set down as priggish or stingy; but she knew that the gambling passion was upon her, and that in her present surroundings there was small hope of resisting it.

Tonight the luck had been persistently bad, and the little gold purse which hung among her trinkets was almost empty when she returned to her room. She unlocked the wardrobe, and taking out her jewel-case, looked under the tray for the roll of bills from which she had replenished the purse before going down to dinner. Only twenty dollars were left: the discovery was so startling that for a moment she fancied she must have been robbed. Then she took paper and pencil, and seating herself at the writing-table, tried to reckon up what she had spent during the day. Her head was throbbing with fatigue, and she had to go over the figures again and again; but at last it became clear to her that she had lost three hundred dollars at cards. She took out her cheque-book to see if her balance was larger than she remembered, but found she had erred in the other direction. Then she returned to her calculations; but figure as she would, she could not conjure back the vanished three hundred dollars. It was the sum she had set aside to pacify her dress-maker—unless she should decide to use it as a sop to the jeweller. At any rate, she had so many uses for it that its very insufficiency had caused her to play high in the hope of doubling it. But of course she had lost—she who needed every penny, while Bertha Dorset, whose husband showered money on her, must have pocketed at least five hundred, and Judy Trenor, who could have afforded to lose a thousand a night, had left the table clutching such a heap of bills that she had been unable to shake hands with her guests when they bade her good night.

A world in which such things could be seemed a miserable place to Lily Bart; but then she had never been able to understand the laws of a universe which was so ready to leave her out of its calculations.

She began to undress without ringing for her maid, whom she had sent to bed. She had been long enough in bondage to other people's pleasure to be considerate of those who depended on hers, and in her bitter moods it sometimes struck her that she and her maid were in the same position, except that the latter received her wages more regularly.

As she sat before the mirror brushing her hair, her face looked hollow and pale, and she was frightened by two little lines near her mouth, faint flaws in the smooth curve of the cheek.

"Oh, I must stop worrying!" she exclaimed. "Unless it's the electric light——" she reflected, springing up from her seat and lighting the candles on the dressing-table.

She turned out the wall-lights, and peered at herself between the candle-flames. The white oval of her face swam out waveringly from a background of shadows, the uncertain light blurring it like a haze; but the two lines about the mouth remained.

Lily rose and undressed in haste.

"It is only because I am tired and have such odious things to think about," she kept repeating; and it seemed an added injustice that petty cares should leave a trace on the beauty which was her only defence against them.

But the odious things were there, and remained with her. She returned wearily to the thought of Percy Gryce, as a wayfarer picks up a heavy load and toils on after a brief rest. She was almost sure she had "landed" him: a few days' work and she would win her reward. But the reward itself seemed unpalatable just then: she could get no zest from the thought of victory. It would be a rest from worry, no more—and how little that would have seemed to her a few years earlier! Her ambitions had shrunk gradually in the desiccating air of failure. But why had she failed? Was it her own fault or that of destiny?

She remembered how her mother, after they had lost their money, used to say to her with a kind of fierce vindictiveness: "But you 'll get it all back—you 'll get it all back, with your face." . . . The remembrance roused a whole train of association, and she lay in the darkness reconstructing the past out of which her present had grown.

A house in which no one ever dined at home unless there was "company"; a door-bell perpetually ringing; a hall-table showered with square envelopes which were opened in haste, and oblong envelopes which were allowed to gather dust in the depths of a bronze jar; a series of French and English maids giving warning amid a chaos of hurriedly-ransacked wardrobes and dress-closets; an equally changing dynasty of nurses and footmen; quarrels in the pantry, the kitchen and the drawing-room; precipitate trips to Europe, and returns with gorged trunks and days of interminable unpacking; semi-annual discussions as to where the summer should be spent, grey interludes of economy and brilliant reactions of expense—such was the setting of Lily Bart's first memories.

Ruling the turbulent element called home was the vigorous and determined figure of a mother still young enough to dance her ball-dresses to rags, while the hazy outline of a neutral-tinted father filled an intermediate space between the butler and the man who came to wind the clocks. Even to the eyes of infancy, Mrs. Hudson Bart had appeared young; but Lily could not recall the time when her father had not been bald and slightly stooping, with streaks of grey in his hair, and a tired walk. It was a shock to her to learn afterward that he was but two years older than her mother.

Lily seldom saw her father by daylight. All day he was "down town"; and in winter it was long after nightfall when she heard his fagged step on the stairs and his hand on the school-room door. He would kiss her in silence, and ask one or two questions of the nurse or the governess; then Mrs.

Bart's maid would come to remind him that he was dining out, and he would hurry away with a nod to Lily. In summer, when he joined them for a Sunday at Newport or Southampton, he was even more effaced and silent than in winter. It seemed to tire him to rest, and he would sit for hours staring at the sea-line from a quiet corner of the verandah, while the clatter of his wife's existence went on unheeded a few feet off. Generally, however, Mrs. Bart and Lily went to Europe for the summer, and before the steamer was half way over Mr. Bart had dipped below the horizon. Sometimes his daughter heard him denounced for having neglected to forward Mrs. Bart's remittances; but for the most part he was never mentioned or thought of till his patient stooping figure presented itself on the New York dock as a buffer between the magnitude of his wife's luggage and the restrictions of the American custom-house.

(In this desultory yet agitated fashion life went on through Lily's teens: a zig-zag broken course down which the family craft glided on a rapid current of amusement, tugged at by the underflow of a perpetual need—the need of more money. Lily could not recall the time when there had been money enough, and in some vague way her father seemed always to blame for the deficiency. It could certainly not be the fault of Mrs. Bart, who was spoken of by her friends as a " wonderful manager." Mrs. Bart was famous for the unlimited effect she produced on limited means; and to the lady and her acquaintances there was something heroic in living as though one were much richer than one's bank-book denoted.) .

Lily was naturally proud of her mother's aptitude in this line: she had been brought up in the faith that, whatever it cost, one must have a good cook, and be what Mrs. Bart called "decently dressed." Mrs. Bart's worst reproach to her husband was to ask him if he expected her to "live like a pig"; and his replying in the negative was always regarded as a justification for cabling to Paris for an extra dress or two, and telephoning to the jeweller that he might, after all, send home the turquoise bracelet which Mrs. Bart had looked at that morning.

Lily knew people who "lived like pigs," and their appearance and surroundings justified her mother's repugnance to that form of existence. They were mostly cousins, who inhabited dingy houses with engravings from Cole's Voyage of Life on the drawing-room walls, and slatternly parlour-maids who said "I 'll go and see" to visitors calling at an hour when all right-minded persons are conventionally if not actually out. The disgusting part of it was that many of these cousins were rich, so that Lily imbibed the idea that if people lived like pigs it was from choice, and through the lack of any proper standard of conduct. This gave her a sense of reflected superiority, and she did not need Mrs. Bart's comments on the family frumps and misers to foster her naturally lively taste for splendour.

Lily was nineteen when circumstances caused her to revise her view of the universe.

The previous year she had made a dazzling début fringed by a heavy thunder-cloud of bills. The light of the début still lingered on the horizon, but the cloud had thickened; and suddenly it broke. The suddenness added to the horror; and there were still times when Lily relived with painful vividness every detail of the day on which the blow fell. She and her mother had been seated at the luncheon-table, over the *chaufroix* and cold salmon of the previous night's dinner: it was one of Mrs. Bart's few economies to consume in private the expensive remnants of her hospitality. Lily was feeling the pleasant languor which is youth's penalty for dancing till dawn; but her mother, in spite of a few lines about the mouth, and under the yellow waves on her temples, was as alert, determined and high in colour as if she had risen from an untroubled sleep.

In the centre of the table, between the melting *marrons glacés* and candied cherries, a pyramid of American Beauties lifted their vigorous stems; they held their heads as high as Mrs. Bart, but their rose-colour had turned to a dissipated purple, and Lily's sense of fitness was disturbed by their reappearance on the luncheon-table.

"I really think, mother," she said reproachfully, " we might afford a few fresh flowers for luncheon. Just some jonquils or lilies-of-the-valley——"

Mrs. Bart stared. Her own fastidiousness had its eye fixed on the world, and she did not care how the luncheon-table looked when there was no one present at it but the family. But she smiled at her daughter's innocence.

"Lilies-of-the-valley," she said calmly, "cost two dollars a dozen at this season."

Lily was not impressed. She knew very little of the value of money.

"It would not take more than six dozen to fill that bowl," she argued.

"Six dozen what?" asked her father's voice in the doorway.

The two women looked up in surprise; though it was a Saturday, the sight of Mr. Bart at luncheon was an unwonted one. But neither his wife nor his daughter was sufficiently interested to ask an explanation.

Mr. Bart dropped into a chair, and sat gazing absently at the fragment of jellied salmon which the butler had placed before him.

"I was only saying," Lily began, "that I hate to see faded flowers at luncheon; and mother says a bunch of lilies-of-the-valley would not cost more than twelve dollars. May n't I tell the florist to send a few every day?"

She leaned confidently toward her father: he seldom refused her anything, and Mrs. Bart had taught her to plead with him when her own entreaties failed.

Mr. Bart sat motionless, his gaze still fixed on the salmon, and his lower jaw dropped; he looked even paler than usual, and his thin hair lay in untidy streaks on his forehead. Suddenly he looked at his daughter and laughed. The laugh was so strange that Lily coloured under it: she disliked being ridiculed, and her father seemed to see something ridiculous in the request. Perhaps he thought it foolish that she should trouble him about such a trifle.

"Twelve dollars—twelve dollars a day for flowers? Oh, certainly, my dear—give him an order for twelve hundred." He continued to laugh.

Mrs. Bart gave him a quick glance.

"You need n't wait, Poleworth—I will ring for you," she said to the butler.

The butler withdrew with an air of silent disapproval, leaving the remains of the *chaufroix* on the sideboard.

"What is the matter, Hudson? Are you ill?" said Mrs. Bart severely.

She had no tolerance for scenes which were not of her own making, and it was odious to her that her husband should make a show of himself before the servants.

"Are you ill?" she repeated.

"Ill?——No, I'm ruined," he said.

Lily made a frightened sound, and Mrs. Bart rose to her feet.

"Ruined——?" she cried; but controlling herself instantly, she turned a calm face to Lily.

"Shut the pantry door," she said.

Lily obeyed, and when she turned back into the room her father was sitting with both elbows on the table, the plate of salmon between them, and his head bowed on his hands.

Mrs. Bart stood over him with a white face which made her hair unnaturally yellow. She looked at Lily as the latter approached: her look was terrible, but her voice was modulated to a ghastly cheerfulness.

"Your father is not well—he does n't know what he is saying. It is nothing—but you had better go upstairs; and don't talk to the servants," she added.

Lily obeyed; she always obeyed when her mother spoke in that voice. She had not been deceived by Mrs. Bart's words: she knew at once that they were ruined. In the dark hours which followed, that awful fact overshadowed even her father's slow and difficult dying. To his wife he no longer counted: he had become extinct when he ceased to fulfil his purpose, and she sat at his side with the provisional air of a traveller who waits for a belated train to start. Lily's feelings were softer: she pitied him in a frightened ineffectual way. But the fact that he was for the most part unconscious, and that his attention, when she stole into the room, drifted away from her after a moment, made him even more of a stranger than in the nursery days when he had never come home till after dark. She seemed always to have seen him through a blur—first of sleepiness, then of distance and indifference—and now the fog had thickened till he was almost indistinguishable. If she could have performed any little services for him, or have exchanged with him a few of those affecting

words which an extensive perusal of fiction had led her to
connect with such occasions, the filial instinct might have
stirred in her; but her pity, finding no active expression, remained in a state of spectatorship, overshadowed by her
mother's grim unflagging resentment. Every look and act of
Mrs. Bart's seemed to say: "You are sorry for him now—but
you will feel differently when you see what he has done
to us."

It was a relief to Lily when her father died.

Then a long winter set in. There was a little money left, but
to Mrs. Bart it seemed worse than nothing—the mere mockery of what she was entitled to. What was the use of living if
one had to live like a pig? She sank into a kind of furious
apathy, a state of inert anger against fate. Her faculty for
"managing" deserted her, or she no longer took sufficient
pride in it to exert it. It was well enough to "manage" when
by so doing one could keep one's own carriage; but when
one's best contrivance did not conceal the fact that one had
to go on foot, the effort was no longer worth making.

Lily and her mother wandered from place to place, now
paying long visits to relations whose house-keeping Mrs. Bart
criticized, and who deplored the fact that she let Lily breakfast in bed when the girl had no prospects before her, and
now vegetating in cheap continental refuges, where Mrs. Bart
held herself fiercely aloof from the frugal tea-tables of her
companions in misfortune. She was especially careful to avoid
her old friends and the scenes of her former successes. To be
poor seemed to her such a confession of failure that it
amounted to disgrace; and she detected a note of condescension in the friendliest advances.

Only one thought consoled her, and that was the contemplation of Lily's beauty. She studied it with a kind of passion,
as though it were some weapon she had slowly fashioned for
her vengeance. It was the last asset in their fortunes, the nucleus around which their life was to be rebuilt. She watched
it jealously, as though it were her own property and Lily its
mere custodian; and she tried to instil into the latter a sense
of the responsibility that such a charge involved. She followed
in imagination the career of other beauties, pointing out to
her daughter what might be achieved through such a gift, and

dwelling on the awful warning of those who, in spite of it, had failed to get what they wanted: to Mrs. Bart, only stupidity could explain the lamentable dénouement of some of her examples. She was not above the inconsistency of charging fate, rather than herself, with her own misfortunes; but she inveighed so acrimoniously against love-matches that Lily would have fancied her own marriage had been of that nature, had not Mrs. Bart frequently assured her that she had been "talked into it"—by whom, she never made clear.

Lily was duly impressed by the magnitude of her opportunities. The dinginess of her present life threw into enchanting relief the existence to which she felt herself entitled. To a less illuminated intelligence Mrs. Bart's counsels might have been dangerous; but Lily understood that beauty is only the raw material of conquest, and that to convert it into success other arts are required. She knew that to betray any sense of superiority was a subtler form of the stupidity her mother denounced, and it did not take her long to learn that a beauty needs more tact than the possessor of an average set of features.

Her ambitions were not as crude as Mrs. Bart's. It had been among that lady's grievances that her husband—in the early days, before he was too tired—had wasted his evenings in what she vaguely described as "reading poetry"; and among the effects packed off to auction after his death were a score or two of dingy volumes which had struggled for existence among the boots and medicine bottles of his dressing-room shelves. There was in Lily a vein of sentiment, perhaps transmitted from this source, which gave an idealizing touch to her most prosaic purposes. She liked to think of her beauty as a power for good, as giving her the opportunity to attain a position where she should make her influence felt in the vague diffusion of refinement and good taste. She was fond of pictures and flowers, and of sentimental fiction, and she could not help thinking that the possession of such tastes ennobled her desire for worldly advantages. She would not indeed have cared to marry a man who was merely rich: she was secretly ashamed of her mother's crude passion for money. Lily's preference would have been for an English nobleman with political ambitions and vast estates; or, for second choice, an Italian prince with a castle in the Apennines and an hereditary office in the Vatican. Lost causes had a romantic charm for her, and she liked to picture herself as standing aloof from the vulgar press of the Quirinal, and sacrificing her pleasure to the claims of an immemorial tradition. . . .

How long ago and how far off it all seemed! Those ambitions were hardly more futile and childish than the earlier ones which had centred about the possession of a French jointed doll with real hair. Was it only ten years since she had wavered in imagination between the English earl and the Italian prince? Relentlessly her mind travelled on over the dreary interval. . . .

After two years of hungry roaming Mrs. Bart had died—died of a deep disgust. She had hated dinginess, and it was her fate to be dingy. Her visions of a brilliant marriage for Lily had faded after the first year.

"People can't marry you if they don't see you—and how can they see you in these holes where we're stuck?" That was the burden of her lament; and her last adjuration to her daughter was to escape from dinginess if she could.

"Don't let it creep up on you and drag you down. Fight your way out of it somehow—you're young and can do it," she insisted.

She had died during one of their brief visits to New York, and there Lily at once became the centre of a family council composed of the wealthy relatives whom she had been taught to despise for living like pigs. It may be that they had an inkling of the sentiments in which she had been brought up, for none of them manifested a very lively desire for her company; indeed, the question threatened to remain unsolved till Mrs. Peniston with a sigh announced: "I'll try her for a year."

Every one was surprised, but one and all concealed their surprise, lest Mrs. Peniston should be alarmed by it into reconsidering her decision.

Mrs. Peniston was Mr. Bart's widowed sister, and if she was by no means the richest of the family group, its other members nevertheless abounded in reasons why she was clearly destined by Providence to assume the charge of Lily. In the first place she was alone, and it would be charming for her to have a young companion. Then she sometimes travelled, and Lily's familiarity with foreign customs—deplored as a misfortune by her more conservative relatives—would at least enable her to act as a kind of courier. But as a matter of fact Mrs. Peniston had not been affected by these considerations. She had taken the girl simply because no one else would have her, and because she had the kind of moral *mauvaise honte* which makes the public display of selfishness difficult, though it does not interfere with its private indulgence. It would have been impossible for Mrs. Peniston to be heroic on a desert island, but with the eyes of her little world upon her she took a certain pleasure in her act.

She reaped the reward to which disinterestedness is entitled, and found an agreeable companion in her niece. She had expected to find Lily headstrong, critical and "foreign"—for even Mrs. Peniston, though she occasionally went abroad, had the family dread of foreignness—but the girl showed a pliancy, which, to a more penetrating mind than her aunt's, might have been less reassuring than the open selfishness of youth. Misfortune had made Lily supple instead of hardening her, and a pliable substance is less easy to break than a stiff one.

Mrs. Peniston, however, did not suffer from her niece's adaptability. Lily had no intention of taking advantage of her aunt's good nature. She was in truth grateful for the refuge offered her: Mrs. Peniston's opulent interior was at least not externally dingy. But dinginess is a quality which assumes all manner of disguises; and Lily soon found that it was as latent in the expensive routine of her aunt's life as in the makeshift existence of a continental pension.

Mrs. Peniston was one of the episodical persons who form the padding of life. It was impossible to believe that she had herself ever been a focus of activities. The most vivid thing about her was the fact that her grandmother had been a Van Alstyne. This connection with the well-fed and industrious stock of early New York revealed itself in the glacial neatness of Mrs. Peniston's drawing-room and in the excellence of her cuisine. She belonged to the class of old New Yorkers who have always lived well, dressed expensively, and done little else; and to these inherited obligations Mrs. Peniston faithfully conformed. She had always been a looker-on at life, and her mind resembled one of those little mirrors which her Dutch ancestors were accustomed to affix to their upper windows, so that from the depths of an impenetrable domesticity they might see what was happening in the street.

Mrs. Peniston was the owner of a country-place in New Jersey, but she had never lived there since her husband's death—a remote event, which appeared to dwell in her memory chiefly as a dividing point in the personal reminiscences that formed the staple of her conversation. She was a woman who remembered dates with intensity, and could tell at a moment's notice whether the drawing-room curtains had been renewed before or after Mr. Peniston's last illness.

Mrs. Peniston thought the country lonely and trees damp, and cherished a vague fear of meeting a bull. To guard against such contingencies she frequented the more populous watering-places, where she installed herself impersonally in a hired house and looked on at life through the matting screen of her verandah. In the care of such a guardian, it soon became clear to Lily that she was to enjoy only the material advantages of good food and expensive clothing; and, though far from underrating these, she would gladly have exchanged them for what Mrs. Bart had taught her to regard as opportunities. She sighed to think what her mother's fierce energies would have accomplished, had they been coupled with Mrs. Peniston's resources. Lily had abundant energy of her own, but it was restricted by the necessity of adapting herself to her aunt's habits. She saw that at all costs she must keep Mrs. Peniston's favour till, as Mrs. Bart would have phrased it, she could stand on her own legs. Lily had no mind for the vagabond life of the poor relation, and to adapt herself to Mrs. Peniston she had, to some degree, to assume that lady's passive attitude. She had fancied at first that it would be easy to draw her aunt into the whirl of her own activities, but there was a static force in Mrs. Peniston against which her niece's efforts spent themselves in vain. To attempt to bring her into active relation with life was like tugging at a piece of furniture which has been screwed to the floor. She did not, indeed, expect Lily to remain equally immovable: she had all the American guardian's indulgence for the volatility of youth.

She had indulgence also for certain other habits of her niece's. It seemed to her natural that Lily should spend all her money on dress, and she supplemented the girl's scanty income by occasional "handsome presents" meant to be applied to the same purpose. Lily, who was intensely practical, would have preferred a fixed allowance; but Mrs. Peniston liked the periodical recurrence of gratitude evoked by unexpected cheques, and was perhaps shrewd enough to perceive that such a method of giving kept alive in her niece a salutary sense of dependence.

Beyond this, Mrs. Peniston had not felt called upon to do anything for her charge: she had simply stood aside and let her take the field. Lily had taken it, at first with the confidence of assured possessorship, then with gradually narrowing demands, till now she found herself actually struggling for a foothold on the broad space which had once seemed her own for the asking. How it happened she did not yet know. Sometimes she thought it was because Mrs. Peniston had been too passive, and again she feared it was because she herself had not been passive enough. Had she shown an undue eagerness for victory? Had she lacked patience, pliancy and dissimulation? Whether she charged herself with these faults or absolved herself from them, made no difference in the sum-total of her failure. Younger and plainer girls had been married off by dozens, and she was nine-and-twenty, and still Miss Bart.

She was beginning to have fits of angry rebellion against fate, when she longed to drop out of the race and make an independent life for herself. But what manner of life would it be? She had barely enough money to pay her dress-makers' bills and her gambling debts; and none of the desultory interests which she dignified with the name of tastes was pronounced enough to enable her to live contentedly in obscurity. Ah, no—she was too intelligent not to be honest with herself. She knew that she hated dinginess as much as her mother had hated it, and to her last breath she meant to fight against it, dragging herself up again and again above its flood till she gained the bright pinnacles of success which presented such a slippery surface to her clutch.

IV

THE NEXT MORNING, on her breakfast tray, Miss Bart found a note from her hostess.

"Dearest Lily," it ran, "if it is not too much of a bore to be down by ten, will you come to my sitting-room to help me with some tiresome things?"

Lily tossed aside the note and subsided on her pillows with a sigh. It *was* a bore to be down by ten—an hour regarded at Bellomont as vaguely synchronous with sunrise—and she knew too well the nature of the tiresome things in question. Miss Pragg, the secretary, had been called away, and there would be notes and dinner-cards to write, lost addresses to hunt up, and other social drudgery to perform. It was understood that Miss Bart should fill the gap in such emergencies, and she usually recognized the obligation without a murmur.

Today, however, it renewed the sense of servitude which the previous night's review of her cheque-book had produced. Everything in her surroundings ministered to feelings of ease and amenity. The windows stood open to the sparkling freshness of the September morning, and between the yellow boughs she caught a perspective of hedges and parterres leading by degrees of lessening formality to the free undulations of the park. Her maid had kindled a little fire on the hearth, and it contended cheerfully with the sunlight which slanted across the moss-green carpet and caressed the curved sides of an old marquetry desk. Near the bed stood a table holding her breakfast tray, with its harmonious porcelain and silver, a handful of violets in a slender glass, and the morning paper folded beneath her letters. There was nothing new to Lily in these tokens of a studied luxury; but, though they formed a part of her atmosphere, she never lost her sensitiveness to their charm. Mere display left her with a sense of superior distinction; but she felt an affinity to all the subtler manifestations of wealth.

Mrs. Trenor's summons, however, suddenly recalled her state of dependence, and she rose and dressed in a mood of irritability that she was usually too prudent to indulge. She knew that such emotions leave lines on the face as well as in the character, and she had meant to take warning by the little creases which her midnight survey had revealed.

The matter-of-course tone of Mrs. Trenor's greeting deepened her irritation. If one did drag one's self out of bed at such an hour, and come down fresh and radiant to the monotony of note-writing, some special recognition of the sacrifice seemed fitting. But Mrs. Trenor's tone showed no consciousness of the fact.

"Oh, Lily, that 's nice of you," she merely sighed across the chaos of letters, bills and other domestic documents which gave an incongruously commercial touch to the slender elegance of her writing-table.

"There are such lots of horrors this morning," she added, clearing a space in the centre of the confusion and rising to yield her seat to Miss Bart.

Mrs. Trenor was a tall fair woman, whose height just saved her from redundancy. Her rosy blondness had survived some forty years of futile activity without showing much trace of ill-usage except in a diminished play of feature. It was difficult to define her beyond saying that she seemed to exist only as a hostess, not so much from any exaggerated instinct of hospitality as because she could not sustain life except in a crowd. The collective nature of her interests exempted her from the ordinary rivalries of her sex, and she knew no more personal emotion than that of hatred for the woman who presumed to give bigger dinners or have more amusing house-parties than herself. As her social talents, backed by Mr. Trenor's bank-account, almost always assured her ultimate triumph in such competitions, success had developed in her an unscrupulous good nature toward the rest of her sex, and in Miss Bart's utilitarian classification of her friends, Mrs. Trenor ranked as the woman who was least likely to "go back" on her.

"It was simply inhuman of Pragg to go off now," Mrs. Trenor declared, as her friend seated herself at the desk. "She says her sister is going to have a baby—as if that were anything to having a house-party! I 'm sure I shall get most horribly mixed up and there will be some awful rows. When I was down at Tuxedo I asked a lot of people for next week, and I 've mislaid the list and can't remember who is coming. And this week is going to be a horrid failure too—and Gwen

Van Osburgh will go back and tell her mother how bored people were. I did n't mean to ask the Wetheralls—that was a blunder of Gus's. They disapprove of Carry Fisher, you know. As if one could help having Carry Fisher! It *was* foolish of her to get that second divorce—Carry always overdoes things—but she said the only way to get a penny out of Fisher was to divorce him and make him pay alimony. And poor Carry has to consider every dollar. It 's really absurd of Alice Wetherall to make such a fuss about meeting her, when one thinks of what society is coming to. Some one said the other day that there was a divorce and a case of appendicitis in every family one knows. Besides, Carry is the only person who can keep Gus in a good humour when we have bores in the house. Have you noticed that *all* the husbands like her? All, I mean, except her own. It 's rather clever of her to have made a specialty of devoting herself to dull people—the field is such a large one, and she has it practically to herself. She finds compensations, no doubt—I know she borrows money of Gus—but then I 'd *pay* her to keep him in a good humour, so I can't complain, after all."

Mrs. Trenor paused to enjoy the spectacle of Miss Bart's efforts to unravel her tangled correspondence.

"But it is n't only the Wetheralls and Carry," she resumed, with a fresh note of lament. "The truth is, I 'm awfully disappointed in Lady Cressida Raith."

"Disappointed? Had n't you known her before?"

"Mercy, no—never saw her till yesterday. Lady Skiddaw sent her over with letters to the Van Osburghs, and I heard that Maria Van Osburgh was asking a big party to meet her this week, so I thought it would be fun to get her away, and Jack Stepney, who knew her in India, managed it for me. Maria was furious, and actually had the impudence to make Gwen invite herself here, so that they should n't be *quite* out of it—if I 'd known what Lady Cressida was like, they could have had her and welcome! But I thought any friend of the Skiddaws' was sure to be amusing. You remember what fun Lady Skiddaw was? There were times when I simply had to send the girls out of the room. Besides, Lady Cressida is the Duchess of Beltshire's sister, and I naturally supposed she was the same sort; but you never can tell in those English families.

They are so big that there 's room for all kinds, and it turns out that Lady Cressida is the moral one—married a clergyman and does missionary work in the East End. Think of my taking such a lot of trouble about a clergyman's wife, who wears Indian jewelry and botanizes! She made Gus take her all through the glass-houses yesterday, and bothered him to death by asking him the names of the plants. Fancy treating Gus as if he were the gardener!"

Mrs. Trenor brought this out in a *crescendo* of indignation.

"Oh, well, perhaps Lady Cressida will reconcile the Wetheralls to meeting Carry Fisher," said Miss Bart pacifically.

"I 'm sure I hope so! But she is boring all the men horribly, and if she takes to distributing tracts, as I hear she does, it will be too depressing. The worst of it is that she would have been so useful at the right time. You know we have to have the Bishop once a year, and she would have given just the right tone to things. I always have horrid luck about the Bishop's visits," added Mrs. Trenor, whose present misery was being fed by a rapidly rising tide of reminiscence; "last year, when he came, Gus forgot all about his being here, and brought home the Ned Wintons and the Farleys—five divorces and six sets of children between them!"

"When is Lady Cressida going?" Lily enquired.

Mrs. Trenor cast up her eyes in despair. "My dear, if one only knew! I was in such a hurry to get her away from Maria that I actually forgot to name a date, and Gus says she told some one she meant to stop here all winter."

"To stop here? In this house?"

"Don't be silly—in America. But if no one else asks her— you know they *never* go to hotels."

"Perhaps Gus only said it to frighten you."

"No—I heard her tell Bertha Dorset that she had six months to put in while her husband was taking the cure in the Engadine. You should have seen Bertha look vacant! But it 's no joke, you know—if she stays here all the autumn she 'll spoil everything, and Maria Van Osburgh will simply exult."

At this affecting vision Mrs. Trenor's voice trembled with self-pity.

"Oh, Judy—as if any one were ever bored at Bellomont!"

Miss Bart tactfully protested. "You know perfectly well that, if Mrs. Van Osburgh were to get all the right people and leave you with all the wrong ones, you 'd manage to make things go off, and she would n't."

Such an assurance would usually have restored Mrs. Trenor's complacency; but on this occasion it did not chase the cloud from her brow.

"It is n't only Lady Cressida," she lamented. "Everything has gone wrong this week. I can see that Bertha Dorset is furious with me."

"Furious with you? Why?"

"Because I told her that Lawrence Selden was coming; but he would n't, after all, and she 's quite unreasonable enough to think it 's my fault."

Miss Bart put down her pen and sat absently gazing at the note she had begun.

"I thought that was all over," she said.

"So it is, on his side. And of course Bertha has n't been idle since. But I fancy she 's out of a job just at present—and some one gave me a hint that I had better ask Lawrence. Well, I *did* ask him—but I could n't make him come; and now I suppose she 'll take it out of me by being perfectly nasty to every one else."

"Oh, she may take it out of *him* by being perfectly charming—to some one else."

Mrs. Trenor shook her head dolefully. "She knows he would n't mind. And who else is there? Alice Wetherall won't let Lucius out of her sight. Ned Silverton can't take his eyes off Carry Fisher—poor boy! Gus is bored by Bertha, Jack Stepney knows her too well—and—well, to be sure, there 's Percy Gryce!"

She sat up smiling at the thought.

Miss Bart's countenance did not reflect the smile.

"Oh, she and Mr. Gryce would not be likely to hit it off."

"You mean that she 'd shock him and he 'd bore her? Well, that 's not such a bad beginning, you know. But I hope she won't take it into her head to be nice to him, for I asked him here on purpose for you."

Lily laughed. "*Merci du compliment!* I should certainly have no show against Bertha."

"Do you think I am uncomplimentary? I 'm not really, you know. Every one knows you 're a thousand times handsomer and cleverer than Bertha; but then you 're not nasty. And for always getting what she wants in the long run, commend me to a nasty woman."

Miss Bart stared in affected reproval. "I thought you were so fond of Bertha."

"Oh, I am—it 's much safer to be fond of dangerous people. But she *is* dangerous—and if I ever saw her up to mischief it 's now. I can tell by poor George's manner. That man is a perfect barometer—he always knows when Bertha is going to——"

"To fall?" Miss Bart suggested.

"Don't be shocking! You know he believes in her still. And of course I don't say there 's any real harm in Bertha. Only she delights in making people miserable, and especially poor George."

"Well, he seems cut out for the part—I don't wonder she likes more cheerful companionship."

"Oh, George is not as dismal as you think. If Bertha did n't worry him he would be quite different. Or if she 'd leave him alone, and let him arrange his life as he pleases. But she does n't dare lose her hold of him on account of the money, and so when *he* is n't jealous she pretends to be."

Miss Bart went on writing in silence, and her hostess sat following her train of thought with frowning intensity.

"Do you know," she exclaimed after a long pause, "I believe I 'll call up Lawrence on the telephone and tell him he simply *must* come?"

"Oh, don't," said Lily, with a quick suffusion of colour. The blush surprised her almost as much as it did her hostess, who, though not commonly observant of facial changes, sat staring at her with puzzled eyes.

"Good gracious, Lily, how handsome you are!——Why? Do you dislike him so much?"

"Not at all; I like him. But if you are actuated by the benevolent intention of protecting me from Bertha—I don't think I need your protection."

Mrs. Trenor sat up with an exclamation. "Lily!——*Percy?* Do you mean to say you 've actually done it?"

Miss Bart smiled. "I only mean to say that Mr. Gryce and I are getting to be very good friends."

"H'm — I see." Mrs. Trenor fixed a rapt eye upon her. "You know they say he has eight hundred thousand a year — and spends nothing, except on some rubbishy old books. And his mother has heart-disease and will leave him a lot more. *Oh, Lily, do go slowly*," her friend adjured her.

Miss Bart continued to smile without annoyance. "I should n't, for instance," she remarked, "be in any haste to tell him that he had a lot of rubbishy old books."

"No, of course not; I know you 're wonderful about getting up people's subjects. But he 's horribly shy, and easily shocked, and — and —— "

"Why don't you say it, Judy? I have the reputation of being on the hunt for a rich husband?"

"Oh, I don't mean that; he would n't believe it of you — at first," said Mrs. Trenor, with candid shrewdness. "But you know things are rather lively here at times — I must give Jack and Gus a hint — and if he thought you were what his mother would call fast — oh, well, you know what I mean. Don't wear your scarlet *crêpe-de-chine* for dinner, and don't smoke if you can help it, Lily dear!"

Lily pushed aside her finished work with a dry smile. "You 're very kind, Judy: I 'll lock up my cigarettes and wear that last year's dress you sent me this morning. And if you are really interested in my career, perhaps you 'll be kind enough not to ask me to play bridge again this evening."

"Bridge? Does he mind bridge, too? Oh, Lily, what an awful life you 'll lead! But of course I won't — why did n't you give me a hint last night? There 's nothing I would n't do, you poor duck, to see you happy!"

And Mrs. Trenor, glowing with her sex's eagerness to smooth the course of true love, enveloped Lily in a long embrace.

"You 're quite sure," she added solicitously, as the latter extricated herself, "that you would n't like me to telephone for Lawrence Selden?"

"Quite sure," said Lily.

The next three days demonstrated to her own complete satisfaction Miss Bart's ability to manage her affairs without extraneous aid.

As she sat, on the Saturday afternoon, on the terrace at Bellomont, she smiled at Mrs. Trenor's fear that she might go too fast. If such a warning had ever been needful, the years had taught her a salutary lesson, and she flattered herself that she now knew how to adapt her pace to the object of pursuit. In the case of Mr. Gryce she had found it well to flutter ahead, losing herself elusively and luring him on from depth to depth of unconscious intimacy. The surrounding atmosphere was propitious to this scheme of courtship. Mrs. Trenor, true to her word, had shown no signs of expecting Lily at the bridge-table, and had even hinted to the other card-players that they were to betray no surprise at her unwonted defection. In consequence of this hint, Lily found herself the centre of that feminine solicitude which envelops a young woman in the mating season. A solitude was tacitly created for her in the crowded existence of Bellomont, and her friends could not have shown a greater readiness for self-effacement had her wooing been adorned with all the attributes of romance. In Lily's set this conduct implied a sympathetic comprehension of her motives, and Mr. Gryce rose in her esteem as she saw the consideration he inspired.

The terrace at Bellomont on a September afternoon was a spot propitious to sentimental musings, and as Miss Bart stood leaning against the balustrade above the sunken garden, at a little distance from the animated group about the tea-table, she might have been lost in the mazes of an inarticulate happiness. In reality, her thoughts were finding definite utterance in the tranquil recapitulation of the blessings in store for her. From where she stood she could see them embodied in the form of Mr. Gryce, who, in a light overcoat and muffler, sat somewhat nervously on the edge of his chair, while Carry Fisher, with all the energy of eye and gesture with which nature and art had combined to endow her, pressed on him the duty of taking part in the task of municipal reform.

Mrs. Fisher's latest hobby was municipal reform. It had been preceded by an equal zeal for socialism, which had in turn replaced an energetic advocacy of Christian Science. Mrs. Fisher was small, fiery and dramatic; and her hands and eyes were admirable instruments in the service of whatever cause she happened to espouse. She had, however, the fault common to enthusiasts of ignoring any slackness of response on the part of her hearers, and Lily was amused by her unconsciousness of the resistance displayed in every angle of Mr. Gryce's attitude. Lily herself knew that his mind was divided between the dread of catching cold if he remained out of doors too long at that hour, and the fear that, if he retreated to the house, Mrs. Fisher might follow him up with a paper to be signed. Mr. Gryce had a constitutional dislike to what he called "committing himself," and tenderly as he cherished his health, he evidently concluded that it was safer to stay out of reach of pen and ink till chance released him from Mrs. Fisher's toils. Meanwhile he cast agonized glances in the direction of Miss Bart, whose only response was to sink into an attitude of more graceful abstraction. She had learned the value of contrast in throwing her charms into relief, and was fully aware of the extent to which Mrs. Fisher's volubility was enhancing her own repose.

She was roused from her musings by the approach of her cousin Jack Stepney who, at Gwen Van Osburgh's side, was returning across the garden from the tennis court.

The couple in question were engaged in the same kind of romance in which Lily figured, and the latter felt a certain annoyance in contemplating what seemed to her a caricature of her own situation. Miss Van Osburgh was a large girl with flat surfaces and no high lights: Jack Stepney had once said of her that she was as reliable as roast mutton. His own taste was in the line of less solid and more highly-seasoned diet; but hunger makes any fare palatable, and there had been times when Mr. Stepney had been reduced to a crust.

Lily considered with interest the expression of their faces: the girl's turned toward her companion's like an empty plate held up to be filled, while the man lounging at her side already betrayed the encroaching boredom which would presently crack the thin veneer of his smile.

"How impatient men are!" Lily reflected. "All Jack has to do to get everything he wants is to keep quiet and let that girl marry him; whereas I have to calculate and contrive, and retreat and advance, as if I were going through an intricate dance, where one misstep would throw me hopelessly out of time."

As they drew nearer she was whimsically struck by a kind of family likeness between Miss Van Osburgh and Percy Gryce. There was no resemblance of feature. Gryce was handsome in a didactic way—he looked like a clever pupil's drawing from a plaster-cast—while Gwen's countenance had no more modelling than a face painted on a toy balloon. But the deeper affinity was unmistakable: the two had the same prejudices and ideals, and the same quality of making other standards non-existent by ignoring them. This attribute was common to most of Lily's set: they had a force of negation which eliminated everything beyond their own range of perception. Gryce and Miss Van Osburgh were, in short, made for each other by every law of moral and physical correspondence——"Yet they would n't look at each other," Lily mused, "they never do. Each of them wants a creature of a different race, of Jack's race and mine, with all sorts of intuitions, sensations and perceptions that they don't even guess the existence of. And they always get what they want."

She stood talking with her cousin and Miss Van Osburgh, till a slight cloud on the latter's brow advised her that even cousinly amenities were subject to suspicion, and Miss Bart, mindful of the necessity of not exciting enmities at this crucial point of her career, dropped aside while the happy couple proceeded toward the tea-table.

Seating herself on the upper step of the terrace, Lily leaned her head against the honeysuckles wreathing the balustrade. The fragrance of the late blossoms seemed an emanation of the tranquil scene, a landscape tutored to the last degree of rural elegance. In the foreground glowed the warm tints of the gardens. Beyond the lawn, with its pyramidal pale-gold maples and velvety firs, sloped pastures dotted with cattle; and through a long glade the river widened like a lake under the silver light of September. Lily did not want to join the circle about the tea-table. They represented the future she had chosen, and she was content with it, but in no haste to anticipate its joys. The certainty that she could marry Percy Gryce when she pleased had lifted a heavy load from her mind, and her money troubles were too recent for their removal not to leave a sense of relief which a less discerning intelligence might have taken for happiness. Her vulgar cares were at an end. She would be able to arrange her life as she pleased, to soar into that empyrean of security where creditors cannot penetrate. She would have smarter gowns than Judy Trenor, and far, far more jewels than Bertha Dorset. She would be free forever from the shifts, the expedients, the humiliations of the relatively poor. Instead of having to flatter, she would be flattered; instead of being grateful, she would receive thanks. There were old scores she could pay off as well as old benefits she could return. And she had no doubts as to the extent of her power. She knew that Mr. Gryce was of the small chary type most inaccessible to impulses and emotions. He had the kind of character in which prudence is a vice, and good advice the most dangerous nourishment. But Lily had known the species before: she was aware that such a guarded nature must find one huge outlet of egoism, and she determined to be to him what his Americana had hitherto been: the one possession in which he took sufficient pride to spend money on it. She knew that this generosity to self is one of the forms of meanness, and she resolved so to identify herself with her husband's vanity that to gratify her wishes would be to him the most exquisite form of self-indulgence. The system might at first necessitate a resort to some of the very shifts and expedients from which she intended it should free her; but she felt sure that in a short time she would be able to play the game in her own way. How should she have distrusted her powers? Her beauty itself was not the mere ephemeral possession it might have been in the hands of inexperience: her skill in enhancing it, the care she took of it, the use she made of it, seemed to give it a kind of permanence. She felt she could trust it to carry her through to the end.

And the end, on the whole, was worth while. Life was not the mockery she had thought it three days ago. There was room for her, after all, in this crowded selfish world of pleasure whence, so short a time since, her poverty had seemed to exclude her. These people whom she had ridiculed and yet envied were glad to make a place for her in the charmed circle about which all her desires revolved. They were not as brutal and self-engrossed as she had fancied—or rather, since it would no longer be necessary to flatter and humour them, that side of their nature became less conspicuous. Society is a revolving body which is apt to be judged according to its place in each man's heaven; and at present it was turning its illuminated face to Lily.

In the rosy glow it diffused her companions seemed full of amiable qualities. She liked their elegance, their lightness, their lack of emphasis: even the self-assurance which at times was so like obtuseness now seemed the natural sign of social ascendency. They were lords of the only world she cared for, and they were ready to admit her to their ranks and let her lord it with them. Already she felt within her a stealing allegiance to their standards, an acceptance of their limitations, a disbelief in the things they did not believe in, a contemptuous pity for the people who were not able to live as they lived.

The early sunset was slanting across the park. Through the boughs of the long avenue beyond the gardens she caught the flash of wheels, and divined that more visitors were approaching. There was a movement behind her, a scattering of steps and voices: it was evident that the party about the tea-table was breaking up. Presently she heard a tread behind her on the terrace. She supposed that Mr. Gryce had at last found means to escape from his predicament, and she smiled at the significance of his coming to join her instead of beating an instant retreat to the fire-side.

She turned to give him the welcome which such gallantry deserved; but her greeting wavered into a blush of wonder, for the man who had approached her was Lawrence Selden.

"You see I came after all," he said; but before she had time to answer, Mrs. Dorset, breaking away from a lifeless colloquy with her host, had stepped between them with a little gesture of appropriation.

V

THE OBSERVANCE of Sunday at Bellomont was chiefly marked by the punctual appearance of the smart omnibus destined to convey the household to the little church at the gates. Whether any one got into the omnibus or not was a matter of secondary importance, since by standing there it not only bore witness to the orthodox intentions of the family, but made Mrs. Trenor feel, when she finally heard it drive away, that she had somehow vicariously made use of it.

It was Mrs. Trenor's theory that her daughters actually did go to church every Sunday; but their French governess's convictions calling her to the rival fane, and the fatigues of the week keeping their mother in her room till luncheon, there was seldom any one present to verify the fact. Now and then, in a spasmodic burst of virtue—when the house had been too uproarious over night—Gus Trenor forced his genial bulk into a tight frock-coat and routed his daughters from their slumbers; but habitually, as Lily explained to Mr. Gryce, this parental duty was forgotten till the church bells were ringing across the park, and the omnibus had driven away empty.

Lily had hinted to Mr. Gryce that this neglect of religious observances was repugnant to her early traditions, and that during her visits to Bellomont she regularly accompanied Muriel and Hilda to church. This tallied with the assurance, also confidentially imparted, that, never having played bridge before, she had been "dragged into it" on the night of her arrival, and had lost an appalling amount of money in consequence of her ignorance of the game and of the rules of betting. Mr. Gryce was undoubtedly enjoying Bellomont. He liked the ease and glitter of the life, and the lustre conferred on him by being a member of this group of rich and conspicuous people. But he thought it a very materialistic society; there were times when he was frightened by the talk of the men and the looks of the ladies, and he was glad to find that Miss Bart, for all her ease and self-possession, was not at home in so ambiguous an atmosphere. For this reason he had been especially pleased to learn that she would, as usual, attend the young Trenors to church on Sunday morning; and as he paced the gravel sweep before the door, his light over-coat on his arm and his prayer-book in one carefully-gloved hand, he reflected agreeably on the strength of character which kept her true to her early training in surroundings so subversive to religious principles.

For a long time Mr. Gryce and the omnibus had the gravel sweep to themselves; but, far from regretting this deplorable indifference on the part of the other guests, he found himself nourishing the hope that Miss Bart might be unaccompanied. The precious minutes were flying, however; the big chestnuts pawed the ground and flecked their impatient sides with foam; the coachman seemed to be slowly petrifying on the box, and the groom on the doorstep; and still the lady did not come. Suddenly, however, there was a sound of voices and a rustle of skirts in the doorway, and Mr. Gryce, restoring his watch to his pocket, turned with a nervous start; but it was only to find himself handing Mrs. Wetherall into the carriage.

The Wetheralls always went to church. They belonged to the vast group of human automata who go through life without neglecting to perform a single one of the gestures executed by the surrounding puppets. It is true that the Bellomont puppets did not go to church; but others equally important did—and Mr. and Mrs. Wetherall's circle was so large that God was included in their visiting-list. They ap-peared, therefore, punctual and resigned, with the air of people bound for a dull "At Home," and after them Hilda and Muriel straggled, yawning and pinning each other's veils and ribbons as they came. They had promised Lily to go to church with her, they declared, and Lily was such a dear old duck that they did n't mind doing it to please her, though they could n't fancy what had put the idea in her head, and though for their own part they would much rather have played lawn tennis with Jack and Gwen, if she had n't told them she was coming. The Misses Trenor were followed by Lady Cressida Raith, a weather-beaten person in Liberty silk and ethnological trinkets, who, on seeing the omnibus, ex-pressed her surprise that they were not to walk across the park; but at Mrs. Wetherall's horrified protest that the church was a mile away, her ladyship, after a glance at the height of the other's heels, acquiesced in the necessity of driving, and poor Mr. Gryce found himself rolling off between four ladies for whose spiritual welfare he felt not the least concern.

It might have afforded him some consolation could he have known that Miss Bart had really meant to go to church. She had even risen earlier than usual in the execution of her purpose. She had an idea that the sight of her in a grey gown of devotional cut, with her famous lashes drooped above a prayer-book, would put the finishing touch to Mr. Gryce's subjugation, and render inevitable a certain incident which she had resolved should form a part of the walk they were to take together after luncheon. Her intentions in short had never been more definite; but poor Lily, for all the hard glaze of her exterior, was inwardly as malleable as wax. Her faculty for adapting herself, for entering into other people's feelings, if it served her now and then in small contingencies, hampered her in the decisive moments of life. She was like a water-plant in the flux of the tides, and today the whole current of her mood was carrying her toward Lawrence Selden. Why had he come? Was it to see herself or Bertha Dorset? It was the last question which, at that moment, should have engaged her. She might better have contented herself with thinking that he had simply responded to the despairing summons of his hostess, anxious to interpose him between herself and the ill-humour of Mrs. Dorset. But Lily had not rested till she learned from Mrs. Trenor that Selden had come of his own accord.

"He did n't even wire me—he just happened to find the trap at the station. Perhaps it 's not over with Bertha after all," Mrs. Trenor musingly concluded; and went away to arrange her dinner-cards accordingly.

Perhaps it was not, Lily reflected; but it should be soon, unless she had lost her cunning. If Selden had come at Mrs. Dorset's call, it was at her own that he would stay. So much the previous evening had told her. Mrs. Trenor, true to her simple principle of making her married friends happy, had placed Selden and Mrs. Dorset next to each other at dinner; but, in obedience to the time-honoured traditions of the match-maker, she had separated Lily and Mr. Gryce, sending

in the former with George Dorset, while Mr. Gryce was coupled with Gwen Van Osburgh.

George Dorset's talk did not interfere with the range of his
neighbour's thoughts. He was a mournful dyspeptic, intent
on finding out the deleterious ingredients of every dish and
diverted from this care only by the sound of his wife's voice.
On this occasion, however, Mrs. Dorset took no part in the
general conversation. She sat talking in low murmurs with
Selden, and turning a contemptuous and denuded shoulder
toward her host, who, far from resenting his exclusion,
plunged into the excesses of the *menu* with the joyous irresponsibility of a free man. To Mr. Dorset, however, his
wife's attitude was a subject of such evident concern that,
when he was not scraping the sauce from his fish, or scooping
the moist bread-crumbs from the interior of his roll, he sat
straining his thin neck for a glimpse of her between the
lights.

Mrs. Trenor, as it chanced, had placed the husband and
wife on opposite sides of the table, and Lily was therefore
able to observe Mrs. Dorset also, and by carrying her glance
a few feet farther, to set up a rapid comparison between Lawrence Selden and Mr. Gryce. It was that comparison which
was her undoing. Why else had she suddenly grown interested in Selden? She had known him for eight years or more:
ever since her return to America he had formed a part of her
background. She had always been glad to sit next to him at
dinner, had found him more agreeable than most men, and
had vaguely wished that he possessed the other qualities needful to fix her attention; but till now she had been too busy
with her own affairs to regard him as more than one of the
pleasant accessories of life. Miss Bart was a keen reader of her
own heart, and she saw that her sudden preoccupation with
Selden was due to the fact that his presence shed a new light
on her surroundings. Not that he was notably brilliant or exceptional; in his own profession he was surpassed by more
than one man who had bored Lily through many a weary
dinner. It was rather that he had preserved a certain social
detachment, a happy air of viewing the show objectively, of
having points of contact outside the great gilt cage in which
they were all huddled for the mob to gape at. How alluring

the world outside the cage appeared to Lily, as she heard its door clang on her! In reality, as she knew, the door never clanged: it stood always open; but most of the captives were like flies in a bottle, and having once flown in, could never regain their freedom. It was Selden's distinction that he had never forgotten the way out.

That was the secret of his way of readjusting her vision. Lily, turning her eyes from him, found herself scanning her little world through his retina: it was as though the pink lamps had been shut off and the dusty daylight let in. She looked down the long table, studying its occupants one by one, from Gus Trenor, with his heavy carnivorous head sunk between his shoulders, as he preyed on a jellied plover, to his wife, at the opposite end of the long bank of orchids, suggestive, with her glaring good-looks, of a jeweller's window lit by electricity. And between the two, what a long stretch of vacuity! How dreary and trivial these people were! Lily reviewed them with a scornful impatience: Carry Fisher, with her shoulders, her eyes, her divorces, her general air of embodying a "spicy paragraph"; young Silverton, who had meant to live on proof-reading and write an epic, and who now lived on his friends and had become critical of truffles; Alice Wetherall, an animated visiting-list, whose most fervid convictions turned on the wording of invitations and the engraving of dinner-cards; Wetherall, with his perpetual nervous nod of acquiescence, his air of agreeing with people before he knew what they were saying; Jack Stepney, with his confident smile and anxious eyes, half way between the sheriff and an heiress; Gwen Van Osburgh, with all the guileless confidence of a young girl who has always been told that there is no one richer than her father.

Lily smiled at her classification of her friends. How different they had seemed to her a few hours ago! Then they had symbolized what she was gaining, now they stood for what she was giving up. That very afternoon they had seemed full of brilliant qualities; now she saw that they were merely dull in a loud way. Under the glitter of their opportunities she saw the poverty of their achievement. It was not that she wanted them to be more disinterested; but she would have liked them to be more picturesque. And she had a shamed recollection

of the way in which, a few hours since, she had felt the cen-
tripetal force of their standards. She closed her eyes an instant, and the vacuous routine of the life she had chosen
stretched before her like a long white road without dip or
turning: it was true she was to roll over it in a carriage instead
of trudging it on foot, but sometimes the pedestrian enjoys
the diversion of a short cut which is denied to those on
wheels.

She was roused by a chuckle which Mr. Dorset seemed to
eject from the depths of his lean throat.

"I say, do look at her," he exclaimed, turning to Miss Bart
with lugubrious merriment—"I beg your pardon, but do just
look at my wife making a fool of that poor devil over there!
One would really suppose she was gone on him—and it 's all
the other way round, I assure you."

Thus adjured, Lily turned her eyes on the spectacle which
was affording Mr. Dorset such legitimate mirth. It certainly
appeared, as he said, that Mrs. Dorset was the more active
participant in the scene: her neighbour seemed to receive her
advances with a temperate zest which did not distract him
from his dinner. The sight restored Lily's good humour, and
knowing the peculiar disguise which Mr. Dorset's marital
fears assumed, she asked gaily: "Are n't you horribly jealous
of her?"

Dorset greeted the sally with delight. "Oh, abominably—
you 've just hit it—keeps me awake at night. The doctors tell
me that 's what has knocked my digestion out—being so in-
fernally jealous of her.—I can't eat a mouthful of this stuff,
you know," he added suddenly, pushing back his plate with a
clouded countenance; and Lily, unfailingly adaptable, accorded her radiant attention to his prolonged denunciation of
other people's cooks, with a supplementary tirade on the toxic
qualities of melted butter.

It was not often that he found so ready an ear; and, being
a man as well as a dyspeptic, it may be that as he poured his
grievances into it he was not insensible to its rosy symmetry.
At any rate he engaged Lily so long that the sweets were
being handed when she caught a phrase on her other side,
where Miss Corby, the comic woman of the company, was
bantering Jack Stepney on his approaching engagement. Miss

Corby's rôle was jocularity: she always entered the conversation with a handspring.

"And of course you 'll have Sim Rosedale as best man!" Lily heard her fling out as the climax of her prognostications; and Stepney responded, as if struck: "Jove, that 's an idea. What a thumping present I 'd get out of him!"

Sim Rosedale! The name, made more odious by its diminutive, obtruded itself on Lily's thoughts like a leer. It stood for one of the many hated possibilities hovering on the edge of life. If she did not marry Percy Gryce, the day might come when she would have to be civil to such men as Rosedale. *If she did not marry him?* But she meant to marry him—she was sure of him and sure of herself. She drew back with a shiver from the pleasant paths in which her thoughts had been straying, and set her feet once more in the middle of the long white road. . . . When she went upstairs that night she found that the late post had brought her a fresh batch of bills. Mrs. Peniston, who was a conscientious woman, had forwarded them all to Bellomont.

Miss Bart, accordingly, rose the next morning with the most earnest conviction that it was her duty to go to church. She tore herself betimes from the lingering enjoyment of her breakfast-tray, rang to have her grey gown laid out, and despatched her maid to borrow a prayer-book from Mrs. Trenor.

But her course was too purely reasonable not to contain the germs of rebellion. No sooner were her preparations made than they roused a smothered sense of resistance. A small spark was enough to kindle Lily's imagination, and the sight of the grey dress and the borrowed prayer-book flashed a long light down the years. She would have to go to church with Percy Gryce every Sunday. They would have a front pew in the most expensive church in New York, and his name would figure handsomely in the list of parish charities. In a few years, when he grew stouter, he would be made a warden. Once in the winter the rector would come to dine, and her husband would beg her to go over the list and see that no *divorcées* were included, except those who had showed signs of penitence by being re-married to the very wealthy. There was nothing especially arduous in this round of reli-

gious obligations; but it stood for a fraction of that great bulk
of boredom which loomed across her path. And who could
consent to be bored on such a morning? Lily had slept well,
and her bath had filled her with a pleasant glow, which was
becomingly reflected in the clear curve of her cheek. No lines
were visible this morning, or else the glass was at a happier
angle.

And the day was the accomplice of her mood: it was a day
for impulse and truancy. The light air seemed full of powdered gold; below the dewy bloom of the lawns the wood-
lands blushed and smouldered, and the hills across the river
swam in molten blue. Every drop of blood in Lily's veins
invited her to happiness.

The sound of wheels roused her from these musings, and
leaning behind her shutters she saw the omnibus take up its
freight. She was too late, then—but the fact did not alarm
her. A glimpse of Mr. Gryce's crestfallen face even suggested
that she had done wisely in absenting herself, since the disappointment he so candidly betrayed would surely whet his
appetite for the afternoon walk. That walk she did not mean
to miss; one glance at the bills on her writing-table was
enough to recall its necessity. But meanwhile she had the
morning to herself, and could muse pleasantly on the disposal
of its hours. She was familiar enough with the habits of Bellomont to know that she was likely to have a free field till
luncheon. She had seen the Wetheralls, the Trenor girls and
Lady Cressida packed safely into the omnibus; Judy Trenor
was sure to be having her hair shampooed; Carry Fisher had
doubtless carried off her host for a drive; Ned Silverton was
probably smoking the cigarette of young despair in his bedroom; and Kate Corby was certain to be playing tennis with
Jack Stepney and Miss Van Osburgh. Of the ladies, this left
only Mrs. Dorset unaccounted for, and Mrs. Dorset never
came down till luncheon: her doctors, she averred, had forbidden her to expose herself to the crude air of the morning.

To the remaining members of the party Lily gave no special
thought; wherever they were, they were not likely to interfere
with her plans. These, for the moment, took the shape of
assuming a dress somewhat more rustic and summerlike in
style than the garment she had first selected, and rustling

downstairs, sunshade in hand, with the disengaged air of a lady in quest of exercise. The great hall was empty but for the knot of dogs by the fire, who, taking in at a glance the outdoor aspect of Miss Bart, were upon her at once with lavish offers of companionship. She put aside the ramping paws which conveyed these offers, and assuring the joyous volunteers that she might presently have a use for their company, sauntered on through the empty drawing-room to the library at the end of the house. The library was almost the only surviving portion of the old manor-house of Bellomont: a long spacious room, revealing the traditions of the mother-country in its classically-cased doors, the Dutch tiles of the chimney, and the elaborate hob-grate with its shining brass urns. A few family portraits of lantern-jawed gentlemen in tie-wigs, and ladies with large head-dresses and small bodies, hung between the shelves lined with pleasantly-shabby books: books mostly contemporaneous with the ancestors in question, and to which the subsequent Trenors had made no perceptible additions. The library at Bellomont was in fact never used for reading, though it had a certain popularity as a smoking-room or a quiet retreat for flirtation. It had occurred to Lily, however, that it might on this occasion have been resorted to by the only member of the party in the least likely to put it to its original use. She advanced noiselessly over the dense old rug scattered with easy-chairs, and before she reached the middle of the room she saw that she had not been mistaken. Lawrence Selden was in fact seated at its farther end; but though a book lay on his knee, his attention was not engaged with it, but directed to a lady whose lace-clad figure, as she leaned back in an adjoining chair, detached itself with exaggerated slimness against the dusky leather of the upholstery.

Lily paused as she caught sight of the group; for a moment she seemed about to withdraw, but thinking better of this, she announced her approach by a slight shake of her skirts which made the couple raise their heads, Mrs. Dorset with a look of frank displeasure, and Selden with his usual quiet smile. The sight of his composure had a disturbing effect on Lily; but to be disturbed was in her case to make a more brilliant effort at self-possession.

"Dear me, am I late?" she asked, putting a hand in his as he advanced to greet her.

"Late for what?" enquired Mrs. Dorset tartly. "Not for luncheon, certainly—but perhaps you had an earlier engagement?"

"Yes, I had," said Lily confidingly.

"Really? Perhaps I am in the way, then? But Mr. Selden is entirely at your disposal." Mrs. Dorset was pale with temper, and her antagonist felt a certain pleasure in prolonging her distress.

"Oh, dear, no—do stay," she said good-humouredly. "I don't in the least want to drive you away."

"You're awfully good, dear, but I never interfere with Mr. Selden's engagements."

The remark was uttered with a little air of proprietorship not lost on its object, who concealed a faint blush of annoyance by stooping to pick up the book he had dropped at Lily's approach. The latter's eyes widened charmingly and she broke into a light laugh.

"But I have no engagement with Mr. Selden! My engagement was to go to church; and I'm afraid the omnibus has started without me. *Has* it started, do you know?"

She turned to Selden, who replied that he had heard it drive away some time since.

"Ah, then I shall have to walk; I promised Hilda and Muriel to go to church with them. It's too late to walk there, you say? Well, I shall have the credit of trying, at any rate—and the advantage of escaping part of the service. I'm not so sorry for myself, after all!"

And with a bright nod to the couple on whom she had intruded, Miss Bart strolled through the glass doors and carried her rustling grace down the long perspective of the garden walk.

She was taking her way churchward, but at no very quick pace; a fact not lost on one of her observers, who stood in the doorway looking after her with an air of puzzled amusement. The truth is that she was conscious of a somewhat keen shock of disappointment. All her plans for the day had been built on the assumption that it was to see her that Selden had come to Bellomont. She had expected, when she came downstairs, to find him on the watch for her; and she had found him, instead, in a situation which might well denote that he had been on the watch for another lady. Was it possible, after all, that he had come for Bertha Dorset? The latter had acted on the assumption to the extent of appearing at an hour when she never showed herself to ordinary mortals, and Lily, for the moment, saw no way of putting her in the wrong. It did not occur to her that Selden might have been actuated merely by the desire to spend a Sunday out of town: women never learn to dispense with the sentimental motive in their judgments of men. But Lily was not easily disconcerted; competition put her on her mettle, and she reflected that Selden's coming, if it did not declare him to be still in Mrs. Dorset's toils, showed him to be so completely free from them that he was not afraid of her proximity.

These thoughts so engaged her that she fell into a gait hardly likely to carry her to church before the sermon, and at length, having passed from the gardens to the wood-path beyond, so far forgot her intention as to sink into a rustic seat at a bend of the walk. The spot was charming, and Lily was not insensible to the charm, or to the fact that her presence enhanced it; but she was not accustomed to taste the joys of solitude except in company, and the combination of a handsome girl and a romantic scene struck her as too good to be wasted. No one, however, appeared to profit by the opportunity; and after a half hour of fruitless waiting she rose and wandered on. She felt a stealing sense of fatigue as she walked; the sparkle had died out of her, and the taste of life was stale on her lips. She hardly knew what she had been seeking, or why the failure to find it had so blotted the light from her sky: she was only aware of a vague sense of failure, of an inner isolation deeper than the loneliness about her.

Her footsteps flagged, and she stood gazing listlessly ahead, digging the ferny edge of the path with the tip of her sunshade. As she did so a step sounded behind her, and she saw Selden at her side.

"How fast you walk!" he remarked. "I thought I should never catch up with you."

She answered gaily: "You must be quite breathless! I've been sitting under that tree for an hour."

"Waiting for me, I hope?" he rejoined; and she said with a vague laugh:

"Well—waiting to see if you would come."

"I seize the distinction, but I don't mind it, since doing the one involved doing the other. But were n't you sure that I should come?"

"If I waited long enough—but you see I had only a limited time to give to the experiment."

"Why limited? Limited by luncheon?"

"No; by my other engagement."

"Your engagement to go to church with Muriel and Hilda?"

"No; but to come home from church with another person."

"Ah, I see; I might have known you were fully provided with alternatives. And is the other person coming home this way?"

Lily laughed again. "That 's just what I don't know; and to find out, it is my business to get to church before the service is over."

"Exactly; and it is my business to prevent your doing so; in which case the other person, piqued by your absence, will form the desperate resolve of driving back in the omnibus."

Lily received this with fresh appreciation; his nonsense was like the bubbling of her inner mood. "Is that what you would do in such an emergency?" she enquired.

Selden looked at her with solemnity. "I am here to prove to you," he cried, " what I am capable of doing in an emergency!"

"Walking a mile in an hour—you must own that the omnibus would be quicker!"

"Ah—but will he find you in the end? That 's the only test of success."

They looked at each other with the same luxury of enjoyment that they had felt in exchanging absurdities over his tea-table; but suddenly Lily's face changed, and she said: "Well, if it is, he has succeeded."

Selden, following her glance, perceived a party of people advancing toward them from the farther bend of the path. Lady Cressida had evidently insisted on walking home, and the rest of the church-goers had thought it their duty to accompany her. Lily's companion looked rapidly from one to the other of the two men of the party; Wetherall walking respectfully at Lady Cressida's side with his little sidelong look of nervous attention, and Percy Gryce bringing up the rear with Mrs. Wetherall and the Trenors.

"Ah—now I see why you were getting up your Americana!" Selden exclaimed with a note of the freest admiration; but the blush with which the sally was received checked whatever amplifications he had meant to give it.

That Lily Bart should object to being bantered about her suitors, or even about her means of attracting them, was so new to Selden that he had a momentary flash of surprise, which lit up a number of possibilities; but she rose gallantly to the defence of her confusion, by saying, as its object approached: "That was why I was waiting for you—to thank you for having given me so many points!"

"Ah, you can hardly do justice to the subject in such a short time," said Selden, as the Trenor girls caught sight of Miss Bart; and while she signalled a response to their boisterous greeting, he added quickly: "Won't you devote your afternoon to it? You know I must be off tomorrow morning. We 'll take a walk, and you can thank me at your leisure."

VI

THE AFTERNOON was perfect. A deeper stillness possessed the air, and the glitter of the American autumn was tempered by a haze which diffused the brightness without dulling it.

In the woody hollows of the park there was already a faint chill; but as the ground rose the air grew lighter, and ascending the long slopes beyond the high-road, Lily and her companion reached a zone of lingering summer. The path wound across a meadow with scattered trees; then it dipped into a lane plumed with asters and purpling sprays of bramble, whence, through the light quiver of ash-leaves, the country unrolled itself in pastoral distances.

Higher up, the lane showed thickening tufts of fern and of the creeping glossy verdure of shaded slopes; trees began to overhang it, and the shade deepened to the checkered dusk of a beech-grove. The boles of the trees stood well apart, with only a light feathering of undergrowth; the path wound along the edge of the wood, now and then looking out on a sunlit pasture or on an orchard spangled with fruit.

Lily had no real intimacy with nature, but she had a passion for the appropriate and could be keenly sensitive to a scene which was the fitting background of her own sensations. The landscape outspread below her seemed an enlargement of her present mood, and she found something of herself in its calmness, its breadth, its long free reaches. On the nearer slopes the sugar-maples wavered like pyres of light; lower down was a massing of grey orchards, and here and there the lingering green of an oak-grove. Two or three red farm-houses dozed under the apple-trees, and the white wooden spire of a village church showed beyond the shoulder of the hill; while far below, in a haze of dust, the high-road ran between the fields.

"Let us sit here," Selden suggested, as they reached an open ledge of rock above which the beeches rose steeply between mossy boulders.

Lily dropped down on the rock, glowing with her long climb. She sat quiet, her lips parted by the stress of the ascent, her eyes wandering peacefully over the broken ranges of the landscape. Selden stretched himself on the grass at her feet, tilting his hat against the level sun-rays, and clasping his hands behind his head, which rested against the side of the rock. He had no wish to make her talk; her quick-breathing silence seemed a part of the general hush and harmony of things. In his own mind there was only a lazy sense of pleasure, veiling the sharp edges of sensation as the September haze veiled the scene at their feet. But Lily, though her attitude was as calm as his, was throbbing inwardly with a rush of thoughts. There were in her at the moment two beings, one drawing deep breaths of freedom and exhilaration, the other gasping for air in a little black prison-house of fears. But gradually the captive's gasps grew fainter, or the other paid less heed to them: the horizon expanded, the air grew stronger, and the free spirit quivered for flight.

She could not herself have explained the sense of buoyancy which seemed to lift and swing her above the sun-suffused world at her feet. Was it love, she wondered, or a mere fortuitous combination of happy thoughts and sensations? How much of it was owing to the spell of the perfect afternoon, the scent of the fading woods, the thought of the dulness she had fled from? Lily had no definite experience by which to test the quality of her feelings. She had several times been in love with fortunes or careers, but only once with a man. That was years ago, when she first came out, and had been smitten with a romantic passion for a young gentleman named Herbert Melson, who had blue eyes and a little wave in his hair. Mr. Melson, who was possessed of no other negotiable securities, had hastened to employ these in capturing the eldest Miss Van Osburgh: since then he had grown stout and wheezy, and was given to telling anecdotes about his children. If Lily recalled this early emotion it was not to compare it with that which now possessed her; the only point of comparison was the sense of lightness, of emancipation, which she remembered feeling, in the whirl of a waltz or the seclusion of a conservatory, during the brief course of her youthful romance. She had not known again till today that lightness, that glow of freedom; but now it was something more than a blind groping of the blood. The peculiar charm of her feeling for Selden was that she understood it; she could put her finger on every link of the chain that was drawing them together. Though his popularity was of the quiet kind, felt rather than actively expressed among his friends, she had never mistaken his inconspicuousness for obscurity. His reputed cultivation was generally regarded as a slight obstacle to easy intercourse, but Lily, who prided herself on her broad-minded recognition of literature, and always carried an Omar Khayam in her travelling-bag, was attracted by this attribute, which she felt would have had its distinction in an older society. It was, moreover, one of his gifts to look his part; to have a height which lifted his head above the crowd, and the keenly-modelled dark features which, in a land of amorphous types, gave him the air of belonging to a more specialized race, of carrying the impress of a concentrated past. Expansive persons found him a little dry, and very young girls thought him sarcastic; but this air of friendly aloofness, as far removed as possible from any assertion of personal advantage, was the quality which piqued Lily's interest. Everything about him accorded with the fastidious element in her taste, even to the light irony with which he surveyed what seemed to her most sacred. She admired him most of all, perhaps, for being able to convey as distinct a sense of superiority as the richest man she had ever met.

It was the unconscious prolongation of this thought which led her to say presently, with a laugh: "I have broken two engagements for you today. How many have you broken for me?"

"None," said Selden calmly. "My only engagement at Bellomont was with you."

She glanced down at him, faintly smiling.

"Did you really come to Bellomont to see me?"

"Of course I did."

Her look deepened meditatively. "Why?" she murmured, with an accent which took all tinge of coquetry from the question.

"Because you 're such a wonderful spectacle: I always like to see what you are doing."

"How do you know what I should be doing if you were not here?"

Selden smiled. "I don't flatter myself that my coming has deflected your course of action by a hair's breadth."

"That 's absurd—since, if you were not here, I could obviously not be taking a walk with you."

"No; but your taking a walk with me is only another way of making use of your material. You are an artist and I happen to be the bit of colour you are using today. It 's a part of your cleverness to be able to produce premeditated effects extemporaneously."

Lily smiled also: his words were too acute not to strike her sense of humour. It was true that she meant to use the accident of his presence as part of a very definite effect; or that, at least, was the secret pretext she had found for breaking her promise to walk with Mr. Gryce. She had sometimes been accused of being too eager—even Judy Trenor had warned her to go slowly. Well, she would not be too eager in this case; she would give her suitor a longer taste of suspense. Where duty and inclination jumped together, it was not in Lily's nature to hold them asunder. She had excused herself from the walk on the plea of a headache: the horrid headache which, in the morning, had prevented her venturing to church. Her appearance at luncheon justified the excuse. She looked languid, full of a suffering sweetness; she carried a scent-bottle in her hand. Mr. Gryce was new to such manifestations; he wondered rather nervously if she were delicate, having far-reaching fears about the future of his progeny. But sympathy won the day, and he besought her not to expose herself: he always connected the outer air with ideas of exposure.

Lily had received his sympathy with languid gratitude, urging him, since she should be such poor company, to join the rest of the party who, after luncheon, were starting in automobiles on a visit to the Van Osburghs at Peekskill. Mr. Gryce was touched by her disinterestedness, and, to escape from the threatened vacuity of the afternoon, had taken her advice and departed mournfully, in a dust-hood and goggles: as the motor-car plunged down the avenue she smiled at his resemblance to a baffled beetle.

Selden had watched her manœuvres with lazy amusement. She had made no reply to his suggestion that they should spend the afternoon together, but as her plan unfolded itself he felt fairly confident of being included in it. The house was empty when at length he heard her step on the stair and strolled out of the billiard-room to join her. She had on a hat and walking-dress, and the dogs were bounding at her feet.

"I thought, after all, the air might do me good," she explained; and he agreed that so simple a remedy was worth trying.

The excursionists would be gone at least four hours; Lily and Selden had the whole afternoon before them, and the sense of leisure and safety gave the last touch of lightness to her spirit. With so much time to talk, and no definite object to be led up to, she could taste the rare joys of mental vagrancy.

She felt so free from ulterior motives that she took up his charge with a touch of resentment.

"I don't know," she said, " why you are always accusing me of premeditation."

"I thought you confessed to it: you told me the other day that you had to follow a certain line—and if one does a thing at all it is a merit to do it thoroughly."

"If you mean that a girl who has no one to think for her is obliged to think for herself, I am quite willing to accept the imputation. But you must find me a dismal kind of person if you suppose that I never yield to an impulse."

"Ah, but I don't suppose that: have n't I told you that your genius lies in converting impulses into intentions?"

"My genius?" she echoed with a sudden note of weariness. "Is there any final test of genius but success? And I certainly have n't succeeded."

Selden pushed his hat back and took a side-glance at her. "Success—what is success? I shall be interested to have your definition."

"Success?" She hesitated. "Why, to get as much as one can out of life, I suppose. It 's a relative quality, after all. Is n't that your idea of it?"

"My idea of it? God forbid!" He sat up with sudden energy, resting his elbows on his knees and staring out upon the mellow fields. "My idea of success," he said, "is personal freedom."

"Freedom? Freedom from worries?"

"From everything—from money, from poverty, from ease and anxiety, from all the material accidents. To keep a kind of republic of the spirit—that's what I call success."

She leaned forward with a responsive flash. "I know—I know—it's strange; but that's just what I've been feeling today."

He met her eyes with the latent sweetness of his. "Is the feeling so rare with you?" he said.

She blushed a little under his gaze. "You think me horribly sordid, don't you? But perhaps it's rather that I never had any choice. There was no one, I mean, to tell me about the republic of the spirit."

"There never is—it's a country one has to find the way to one's self."

"But I should never have found my way there if you had n't told me."

"Ah, there are sign-posts—but one has to know how to read them."

"Well, I have known, I have known!" she cried with a glow of eagerness. "Whenever I see you, I find myself spelling out a letter of the sign—and yesterday—last evening at dinner—I suddenly saw a little way into your republic."

Selden was still looking at her, but with a changed eye. Hitherto he had found, in her presence and her talk, the æsthetic amusement which a reflective man is apt to seek in desultory intercourse with pretty women. His attitude had been one of admiring spectatorship, and he would have been almost sorry to detect in her any emotional weakness which should interfere with the fulfilment of her aims. But now the hint of this weakness had become the most interesting thing about her. He had come on her that morning in a moment of disarray; her face had been pale and altered, and the diminution of her beauty had lent her a poignant charm. *That is how she looks when she is alone!* had been his first thought; and the second was to note in her the change which his coming produced. It was the danger-point of their intercourse that he could not doubt the spontaneity of her liking. From whatever angle he viewed their dawning intimacy, he could not see it as part of her scheme of life; and to be the unforeseen element in a career so accurately planned was stimulating even to a man who had renounced sentimental experiments.

"Well," he said, "did it make you want to see more? Are you going to become one of us?"

He had drawn out his cigarettes as he spoke, and she reached her hand toward the case.

"Oh, do give me one—I have n't smoked for days!"

"Why such unnatural abstinence? Everybody smokes at Bellomont."

"Yes—but it is not considered becoming in a *jeune fille à marier*; and at the present moment I am a *jeune fille à marier*."

"Ah, then I 'm afraid we can't let you into the republic."

"Why not? Is it a celibate order?"

"Not in the least, though I 'm bound to say there are not many married people in it. But you will marry some one very rich, and it 's as hard for rich people to get into as the kingdom of heaven."

"That 's unjust, I think, because, as I understand it, one of the conditions of citizenship is not to think too much about money, and the only way not to think about money is to have a great deal of it."

"You might as well say that the only way not to think about air is to have enough to breathe. That is true enough in a sense; but your lungs are thinking about the air, if you are not. And so it is with your rich people—they may not be thinking of money, but they 're breathing it all the while; take them into another element and see how they squirm and gasp!"

Lily sat gazing absently through the blue rings of her cigarette-smoke.

"It seems to me," she said at length, "that you spend a good deal of your time in the element you disapprove of."

Selden received this thrust without discomposure. "Yes; but I have tried to remain amphibious: it 's all right as long as one's lungs can work in another air. The real alchemy consists in being able to turn gold back again into something else; and that 's the secret that most of your friends have lost."

Lily mused. "Don't you think," she rejoined after a moment, "that the people who find fault with society are too apt to regard it as an end and not a means, just as the people who despise money speak as if its only use were to be kept in bags and gloated over? Is n't it fairer to look at them both as opportunities, which may be used either stupidly or intelligently, according to the capacity of the user?"

"That is certainly the sane view; but the queer thing about society is that the people who regard it as an end are those who are in it, and not the critics on the fence. It 's just the other way with most shows—the audience may be under the illusion, but the actors know that real life is on the other side of the footlights. The people who take society as an escape from work are putting it to its proper use; but when it becomes the thing worked for it distorts all the relations of life." Selden raised himself on his elbow. "Good heavens!" he went on, "I don't underrate the decorative side of life. It seems to me the sense of splendour has justified itself by what it has produced. The worst of it is that so much human nature is used up in the process. If we 're all the raw stuff of the cosmic effects, one would rather be the fire that tempers a sword than the fish that dyes a purple cloak. And a society like ours wastes such good material in producing its little patch of purple! Look at a boy like Ned Silverton—he 's really too good to be used to refurbish anybody's social shabbiness. There 's a lad just setting out to discover the universe: is n't it a pity he should end by finding it in Mrs. Fisher's drawing-room?"

"Ned is a dear boy, and I hope he will keep his illusions long enough to write some nice poetry about them; but do you think it is only in society that he is likely to lose them?"

Selden answered her with a shrug. "Why do we call all our generous ideas illusions, and the mean ones truths? Is n't it a sufficient condemnation of society to find one's self accepting such phraseology? I very nearly acquired the jargon at Silverton's age, and I know how names can alter the colour of beliefs."

She had never heard him speak with such energy of affirmation. His habitual touch was that of the eclectic, who lightly turns over and compares; and she was moved by this sudden glimpse into the laboratory where his faiths were formed.

"Ah, you are as bad as the other sectarians," she exclaimed;

" why do you call your republic a republic? It is a close corporation, and you create arbitrary objections in order to keep people out."

"It is not *my* republic; if it were, I should have a *coup d'état* and seat you on the throne."

"Whereas, in reality, you think I can never even get my foot across the threshold? Oh, I understand what you mean. You despise my ambitions—you think them unworthy of me!"

Selden smiled, but not ironically. "Well, is n't that a tribute? I think them quite worthy of most of the people who live by them."

She had turned to gaze on him gravely. "But is n't it possible that, if I had the opportunities of these people, I might make a better use of them? Money stands for all kinds of things—its purchasing quality is n't limited to diamonds and motor-cars."

"Not in the least: you might expiate your enjoyment of them by founding a hospital."

"But if you think they are what I should really enjoy, you must think my ambitions are good enough for me."

Selden met this appeal with a laugh. "Ah, my dear Miss Bart, I am not divine Providence, to guarantee your enjoying the things you are trying to get!"

"Then the best you can say for me is, that after struggling to get them I probably shan't like them?" She drew a deep breath. "What a miserable future you foresee for me!"

"Well—have you never foreseen it for yourself?"

The slow colour rose to her cheek, not a blush of excitement but drawn from the deep wells of feeling; it was as if the effort of her spirit had produced it.

"Often and often," she said. "But it looks so much darker when you show it to me!"

He made no answer to this exclamation, and for a while they sat silent, while something throbbed between them in the wide quiet of the air. But suddenly she turned on him with a kind of vehemence.

"Why do you do this to me?" she cried. "Why do you make the things I have chosen seem hateful to me, if you have nothing to give me instead?"

The words roused Selden from the musing fit into which he had fallen. He himself did not know why he had led their talk along such lines; it was the last use he would have imagined himself making of an afternoon's solitude with Miss Bart. But it was one of those moments when neither seemed to speak deliberately, when an indwelling voice in each called to the other across unsounded depths of feeling.

"No, I have nothing to give you instead," he said, sitting up and turning so that he faced her. "If I had, it should be yours, you know."

She received this abrupt declaration in a way even stranger than the manner of its making: she dropped her face on her hands and he saw that for a moment she wept.

It was for a moment only, however; for when he leaned nearer and drew down her hands with a gesture less passionate than grave, she turned on him a face softened but not disfigured by emotion, and he said to himself, somewhat cruelly, that even her weeping was an art.

The reflection steadied his voice as he asked, between pity and irony: "Is n't it natural that I should try to belittle all the things I can't offer you?"

Her face brightened at this, but she drew her hand away, not with a gesture of coquetry, but as though renouncing something to which she had no claim.

"But you belittle *me*, don't you," she returned gently, "in being so sure they are the only things I care for?"

Selden felt an inner start; but it was only the last quiver of his egoism. Almost at once he answered quite simply: "But you do care for them, don't you? And no wishing of mine can alter that."

He had so completely ceased to consider how far this might carry him, that he had a distinct sense of disappointment when she turned on him a face sparkling with derision.

"Ah," she cried, "for all your fine phrases you 're really as great a coward as I am, for you would n't have made one of them if you had n't been so sure of my answer."

The shock of this retort had the effect of crystallizing Selden's wavering intentions.

"I am not so sure of your answer," he said quietly. "And I do you the justice to believe that you are not either."

It was her turn to look at him with surprise; and after a moment—"Do you want to marry me?" she asked.

He broke into a laugh. "No, I don't want to—but perhaps I should if you did!"

"That 's what I told you—you 're so sure of me that you can amuse yourself with experiments." She drew back the hand he had regained, and sat looking down on him sadly.

"I am not making experiments," he returned. "Or if I am, it is not on you but on myself. I don't know what effect they are going to have on me—but if marrying you is one of them, I will take the risk."

She smiled faintly. "It would be a great risk, certainly—I have never concealed from you how great."

"Ah, it 's you who are the coward!" he exclaimed.

She had risen, and he stood facing her with his eyes on hers. The soft isolation of the falling day enveloped them: they seemed lifted into a finer air. All the exquisite influences of the hour trembled in their veins, and drew them to each other as the loosened leaves were drawn to the earth.

"It 's you who are the coward," he repeated, catching her hands in his.

She leaned on him for a moment, as if with a drop of tired wings: he felt as though her heart were beating rather with the stress of a long flight than the thrill of new distances. Then, drawing back with a little smile of warning—"I shall look hideous in dowdy clothes; but I can trim my own hats," she declared.

They stood silent for a while after this, smiling at each other like adventurous children who have climbed to a forbidden height from which they discover a new world. The actual world at their feet was veiling itself in dimness, and across the valley a clear moon rose in the denser blue.

Suddenly they heard a remote sound, like the hum of a giant insect, and following the high-road, which wound whiter through the surrounding twilight, a black object rushed across their vision.

Lily started from her attitude of absorption; her smile faded and she began to move toward the lane.

"I had no idea it was so late! We shall not be back till after dark," she said, almost impatiently.

Selden was looking at her with surprise: it took him a moment to regain his usual view of her; then he said, with an uncontrollable note of dryness: "That was not one of our party; the motor was going the other way."

"I know—I know——" She paused, and he saw her redden through the twilight. "But I told them I was not well—that I should not go out. Let us go down!" she murmured.

Selden continued to look at her; then he drew his cigarette-case from his pocket and slowly lit a cigarette. It seemed to him necessary, at that moment, to proclaim, by some habitual gesture of this sort, his recovered hold on the actual: he had an almost puerile wish to let his companion see that, their flight over, he had landed on his feet.

She waited while the spark flickered under his curved palm; then he held out the cigarettes to her.

She took one with an unsteady hand, and putting it to her lips, leaned forward to draw her light from his. In the indistinctness the little red gleam lit up the lower part of her face, and he saw her mouth tremble into a smile.

"Were you serious?" she asked, with an odd thrill of gaiety which she might have caught up, in haste, from a heap of stock inflections, without having time to select the just note.

Selden's voice was under better control. "Why not?" he returned. "You see I took no risks in being so." And as she continued to stand before him, a little pale under the retort, he added quickly: "Let us go down."

VII

IT SPOKE MUCH for the depth of Mrs. Trenor's friendship
that her voice, in admonishing Miss Bart, took the same
note of personal despair as if she had been lamenting the collapse of a house-party.

"All I can say is, Lily, that I can't make you out!" She
leaned back, sighing, in the morning abandon of lace and
muslin, turning an indifferent shoulder to the heaped-up importunities of her desk, while she considered, with the eye of
a physician who has given up the case, the erect exterior of
the patient confronting her.

"If you had n't told me you were going in for him seriously—but I 'm sure you made that plain enough from the
beginning! Why else did you ask me to let you off bridge,
and to keep away Carry and Kate Corby? I don't suppose you
did it because he amused you; we could none of us imagine
your putting up with him for a moment unless you meant to
marry him. And I 'm sure everybody played fair! They all
wanted to help it along. Even Bertha kept her hands off—I
will say that—till Lawrence came down and you dragged him
away from her. After that she had a right to retaliate—why
on earth did you interfere with her? You 've known Lawrence
Selden for years—why did you behave as if you had just discovered him? If you had a grudge against Bertha it was a
stupid time to show it—you could have paid her back just as
well after you were married! I told you Bertha was dangerous.
She was in an odious mood when she came here, but Lawrence's turning up put her in a good humour, and if you 'd
only let her think he came for *her* it would have never occurred to her to play you this trick. Oh, Lily, you 'll never do
anything if you 're not serious!"

Miss Bart accepted this exhortation in a spirit of the purest
impartiality. Why should she have been angry? It was the
voice of her own conscience which spoke to her through Mrs.
Trenor's reproachful accents. But even to her own conscience
she must trump up a semblance of defence.

"I only took a day off—I thought he meant to stay on all
this week, and I knew Mr. Selden was leaving this morning."

Mrs. Trenor brushed aside the plea with a gesture which laid bare its weakness.

"He did mean to stay—that 's the worst of it. It shows that he 's run away from you; that Bertha 's done her work and poisoned him thoroughly."

Lily gave a slight laugh. "Oh, if he 's running I 'll overtake him!"

Her friend threw out an arresting hand. "Whatever you do, Lily, do nothing!"

Miss Bart received the warning with a smile. "I don't mean, literally, to take the next train. There are ways——" But she did not go on to specify them.

Mrs. Trenor sharply corrected the tense. "There *were* ways—plenty of them! I did n't suppose you needed to have them pointed out. But don't deceive yourself—he 's thoroughly frightened. He has run straight home to his mother, and she 'll protect him!"

"Oh, to the death," Lily agreed, dimpling at the vision.

"How you can *laugh*——" her friend rebuked her; and she dropped back to a soberer perception of things with the question: "What was it Bertha really told him?"

"Don't ask me—horrors! She seemed to have raked up everything. Oh, you know what I mean—of course there is n't anything, *really*; but I suppose she brought in Prince Varigliano—and Lord Hubert—and there was some story of your having borrowed money of old Ned Van Alstyne: did you ever?"

"He is my father's cousin," Miss Bart interposed.

"Well, of course she left *that* out. It seems Ned told Carry Fisher; and she told Bertha, naturally. They 're all alike, you know: they hold their tongues for years, and you think you 're safe, but when their opportunity comes they remember everything."

Lily had grown pale: her voice had a harsh note in it. "It was some money I lost at bridge at the Van Osburghs'. I repaid it, of course."

"Ah, well, they would n't remember that; besides, it was the idea of the gambling debt that frightened Percy. Oh, Bertha knew her man—she knew just what to tell him!"

In this strain Mrs. Trenor continued for nearly an hour to

admonish her friend. Miss Bart listened with admirable equanimity. Her naturally good temper had been disciplined by years of enforced compliance, since she had almost always had to attain her ends by the circuitous path of other people's; and, being naturally inclined to face unpleasant facts as soon as they presented themselves, she was not sorry to hear an impartial statement of what her folly was likely to cost, the more so as her own thoughts were still insisting on the other side of the case. Presented in the light of Mrs. Trenor's vigorous comments, the reckoning was certainly a formidable one, and Lily, as she listened, found herself gradually reverting to her friend's view of the situation. Mrs. Trenor's words were moreover emphasized for her hearer by anxieties which she herself could scarcely guess. Affluence, unless stimulated by a keen imagination, forms but the vaguest notion of the practical strain of poverty. Judy knew it must be "horrid" for poor Lily to have to stop to consider whether she could afford real lace on her petticoats, and not to have a motor-car and a steam-yacht at her orders; but the daily friction of unpaid bills, the daily nibble of small temptations to expenditure, were trials as far out of her experience as the domestic problems of the char-woman. Mrs. Trenor's unconsciousness of the real stress of the situation had the effect of making it more galling to Lily. While her friend reproached her for missing the opportunity to eclipse her rivals, she was once more battling in imagination with the mounting tide of indebtedness from which she had so nearly escaped. What wind of folly had driven her out again on those dark seas?

If anything was needed to put the last touch to her self-abasement it was the sense of the way her old life was opening its ruts again to receive her. Yesterday her fancy had fluttered free pinions above a choice of occupations; now she had to drop to the level of the familiar routine, in which moments of seeming brilliancy and freedom alternated with long hours of subjection.

She laid a deprecating hand on her friend's. "Dear Judy! I'm sorry to have been such a bore, and you are very good to me. But you must have some letters for me to answer—let me at least be useful."

She settled herself at the desk, and Mrs. Trenor accepted her resumption of the morning's task with a sigh which implied that, after all, she had proved herself unfit for higher uses.

The luncheon table showed a depleted circle. All the men but Jack Stepney and Dorset had returned to town (it seemed to Lily a last touch of irony that Selden and Percy Gryce should have gone in the same train), and Lady Cressida and the attendant Wetheralls had been despatched by motor to lunch at a distant country-house. At such moments of diminished interest it was usual for Mrs. Dorset to keep her room till the afternoon; but on this occasion she drifted in when luncheon was half over, hollowed-eyed and drooping, but with an edge of malice under her indifference.

She raised her eyebrows as she looked about the table. "How few of us are left! I do so enjoy the quiet—don't you, Lily? I wish the men would always stop away—it 's really much nicer without them. Oh, you don't count, George: one does n't have to talk to one's husband. But I thought Mr. Gryce was to stay for the rest of the week?" she added enquiringly. "Did n't he intend to, Judy? He 's such a nice boy—I wonder what drove him away? He is rather shy, and I 'm afraid we may have shocked him: he has been brought up in such an old-fashioned way. Do you know, Lily, he told me he had never seen a girl play cards for money till he saw you doing it the other night? And he lives on the interest of his income, and always has a lot left over to invest!"

Mrs. Fisher leaned forward eagerly. "I do believe it is some one's duty to educate that young man. It is shocking that he has never been made to realize his duties as a citizen. Every wealthy man should be compelled to study the laws of his country."

Mrs. Dorset glanced at her quietly. "I think he *has* studied the divorce laws. He told me he had promised the Bishop to sign some kind of a petition against divorce."

Mrs. Fisher reddened under her powder, and Stepney said with a laughing glance at Miss Bart: "I suppose he is thinking of marriage, and wants to tinker up the old ship before he goes aboard."

His betrothed looked shocked at the metaphor, and George Dorset exclaimed with a sardonic growl: "Poor devil! It is n't the ship that will do for him, it 's the crew."

"Or the stowaways," said Miss Corby brightly. "If I contemplated a voyage with him I should try to start with a
friend in the hold."

Miss Van Osburgh's vague feeling of pique was struggling
for appropriate expression. "I 'm sure I don't see why you
laugh at him; I think he 's very nice," she exclaimed; "and, at
any rate, a girl who married him would always have enough
to be comfortable."

She looked puzzled at the redoubled laughter which hailed
her words, but it might have consoled her to know how
deeply they had sunk into the breast of one of her hearers.

Comfortable! At that moment the word was more eloquent
to Lily Bart than any other in the language. She could not
even pause to smile over the heiress's view of a colossal fortune as a mere shelter against want: her mind was filled with
the vision of what that shelter might have been to her. Mrs.
Dorset's pin-pricks did not smart, for her own irony cut
deeper: no one could hurt her as much as she was hurting
herself, for no one else—not even Judy Trenor—knew the
full magnitude of her folly.

She was roused from these unprofitable considerations by a
whispered request from her hostess, who drew her apart as
they left the luncheon-table.

"Lily, dear, if you 've nothing special to do, may I tell
Carry Fisher that you intend to drive to the station and fetch
Gus? He will be back at four, and I know she has it in her
mind to meet him. Of course I 'm very glad to have him
amused, but I happen to know that she has bled him rather
severely since she 's been here, and she is so keen about going
to fetch him that I fancy she must have got a lot more bills
this morning. It seems to me," Mrs. Trenor feelingly concluded, "that most of her alimony is paid by other women's
husbands!"

Miss Bart, on her way to the station, had leisure to muse
over her friend's words, and their peculiar application to herself. Why should she have to suffer for having once, for a few
hours, borrowed money of an elderly cousin, when a woman
like Carry Fisher could make a living unrebuked from the
good-nature of her men friends and the tolerance of their
wives? It all turned on the tiresome distinction between what

a married woman might, and a girl might not, do. Of course it was shocking for a married woman to borrow money—and Lily was expertly aware of the implication involved—but still, it was the mere *malum prohibitum* which the world decries but condones, and which, though it may be punished by private vengeance, does not provoke the collective disapprobation of society. To Miss Bart, in short, no such opportunities were possible. She could of course borrow from her women friends—a hundred here or there, at the utmost—but they were more ready to give a gown or a trinket, and looked a little askance when she hinted her preference for a cheque. Women are not generous lenders, and those among whom her lot was cast were either in the same case as herself, or else too far removed from it to understand its necessities. The result of her meditations was the decision to join her aunt at Richfield. She could not remain at Bellomont without playing bridge, and being involved in other expenses; and to continue her usual series of autumn visits would merely prolong the same difficulties. She had reached a point where abrupt retrenchment was necessary, and the only cheap life was a dull life. She would start the next morning for Richfield.

At the station she thought Gus Trenor seemed surprised, and not wholly unrelieved, to see her. She yielded up the reins of the light runabout in which she had driven over, and as he climbed heavily to her side, crushing her into a scant third of the seat, he said: "Halloo! It is n't often you honour me. You must have been uncommonly hard up for something to do."

The afternoon was warm, and propinquity made her more than usually conscious that he was red and massive, and that beads of moisture had caused the dust of the train to adhere unpleasantly to the broad expanse of cheek and neck which he turned to her; but she was aware also, from the look in his small dull eyes, that the contact with her freshness and slenderness was as agreeable to him as the sight of a cooling beverage.

The perception of this fact helped her to answer gaily: "It 's not often I have the chance. There are too many ladies to dispute the privilege with me."

"The privilege of driving me home? Well, I 'm glad you

won the race, anyhow. But I know what really happened—
my wife sent you. Now did n't she?"

He had the dull man's unexpected flashes of astuteness, and
Lily could not help joining in the laugh with which he had
pounced on the truth.

"You see, Judy thinks I 'm the safest person for you to be
with; and she 's quite right," she rejoined.

"Oh, is she, though? If she is, it 's because you would n't
waste your time on an old hulk like me. We married men have
to put up with what we can get: all the prizes are for the
clever chaps who 've kept a free foot. Let me light a cigar,
will you? I 've had a beastly day of it."

He drew up in the shade of the village street, and passed
the reins to her while he held a match to his cigar. The little
flame under his hand cast a deeper crimson on his puffing
face, and Lily averted her eyes with a momentary feeling of
repugnance. And yet some women thought him handsome!

As she handed back the reins, she said sympathetically:
"Did you have such a lot of tiresome things to do?"

"I should say so—rather!" Trenor, who was seldom listened to, either by his wife or her friends, settled down into
the rare enjoyment of a confidential talk. "You don't know
how a fellow has to hustle to keep this kind of thing going."
He waved his whip in the direction of the Bellomont acres,
which lay outspread before them in opulent undulations.
"Judy has no idea of what she spends—not that there is n't
plenty to keep the thing going," he interrupted himself, "but
a man has got to keep his eyes open and pick up all the tips
he can. My father and mother used to live like fighting-cocks
on their income, and put by a good bit of it too—luckily for
me—but at the pace we go now, I don't know where I
should be if it were n't for taking a flyer now and then. The
women all think—I mean Judy thinks—I 've nothing to do
but to go down town once a month and cut off coupons, but
the truth is it takes a devilish lot of hard work to keep the
machinery running. Not that I ought to complain to-day,
though," he went on after a moment, "for I did a very neat
stroke of business, thanks to Stepney's friend Rosedale: by
the way, Miss Lily, I wish you 'd try to persuade Judy to be
decently civil to that chap. He 's going to be rich enough to

buy us all out one of these days, and if she 'd only ask him to dine now and then I could get almost anything out of him. The man is mad to know the people who don't want to know him, and when a fellow 's in that state there is nothing he won't do for the first woman who takes him up."

Lily hesitated a moment. The first part of her companion's discourse had started an interesting train of thought, which was rudely interrupted by the mention of Mr. Rosedale's name. She uttered a faint protest.

"But you know Jack did try to take him about, and he was impossible."

"Oh, hang it—because he 's fat and shiny, and has a shoppy manner! Well, all I can say is that the people who are clever enough to be civil to him now will make a mighty good thing of it. A few years from now he 'll be in it whether we want him or not, and then he won't be giving away a half-a-million tip for a dinner."

Lily's mind had reverted from the intrusive personality of Mr. Rosedale to the train of thought set in motion by Trenor's first words. This vast mysterious Wall Street world of "tips" and "deals"—might she not find in it the means of escape from her dreary predicament? She had often heard of women making money in this way through their friends: she had no more notion than most of her sex of the exact nature of the transaction, and its vagueness seemed to diminish its indelicacy. She could not, indeed, imagine herself, in any extremity, stooping to extract a "tip" from Mr. Rosedale; but at her side was a man in possession of that precious commodity, and who, as the husband of her dearest friend, stood to her in a relation of almost fraternal intimacy.

In her inmost heart Lily knew it was not by appealing to the fraternal instinct that she was likely to move Gus Trenor; but this way of explaining the situation helped to drape its crudity, and she was always scrupulous about keeping up appearances to herself. Her personal fastidiousness had a moral equivalent, and when she made a tour of inspection in her own mind there were certain closed doors she did not open.

As they reached the gates of Bellomont she turned to Trenor with a smile.

"The afternoon is so perfect—don't you want to drive me

a little farther? I 've been rather out of spirits all day, and it 's so restful to be away from people, with some one who won't mind if I 'm a little dull."

She looked so plaintively lovely as she proffered the request, so trustfully sure of his sympathy and understanding, that Trenor felt himself wishing that his wife could see how other women treated him—not battered wire-pullers like Mrs. Fisher, but a girl that most men would have given their boots to get such a look from.

"Out of spirits? Why on earth should you ever be out of spirits? Is your last box of Doucet dresses a failure, or did Judy rook you out of everything at bridge last night?"

Lily shook her head with a sigh. "I have had to give up Doucet; and bridge too—I can't afford it. In fact I can't afford any of the things my friends do, and I am afraid Judy often thinks me a bore because I don't play cards any longer, and because I am not as smartly dressed as the other women. But you will think me a bore too if I talk to you about my worries, and I only mention them because I want you to do me a favour—the very greatest of favours."

Her eyes sought his once more, and she smiled inwardly at the tinge of apprehension that she read in them.

"Why, of course—if it 's anything I can manage——" He broke off, and she guessed that his enjoyment was disturbed by the remembrance of Mrs. Fisher's methods.

"The greatest of favours," she rejoined gently. "The fact is, Judy is angry with me, and I want you to make my peace."

"Angry with you? Oh, come, nonsense——" his relief broke through in a laugh. "Why, you know she 's devoted to you."

"She is the best friend I have, and that is why I mind having to vex her. But I daresay you know what she has wanted me to do. She has set her heart—poor dear—on my marrying—marrying a great deal of money."

She paused with a slight falter of embarrassment, and Trenor, turning abruptly, fixed on her a look of growing intelligence.

"A great deal of money? Oh, by Jove—you don't mean Gryce? What—you do? Oh, no, of course I won't mention it—you can trust me to keep my mouth shut—but Gryce—

good Lord, *Gryce!* Did Judy really think you could bring yourself to marry that portentous little ass? But you could n't, eh? And so you gave him the sack, and that 's the reason why he lit out by the first train this morning?" He leaned back, spreading himself farther across the seat, as if dilated by the joyful sense of his own discernment. "How on earth could Judy think you would do such a thing? *I* could have told her you 'd never put up with such a little milksop!"

Lily sighed more deeply. "I sometimes think," she murmured, "that men understand a woman's motives better than other women do."

"Some men—I 'm certain of it! I could have *told* Judy," he repeated, exulting in the implied superiority over his wife.

"I thought you would understand; that 's why I wanted to speak to you," Miss Bart rejoined. "I *can't* make that kind of marriage; it 's impossible. But neither can I go on living as all the women in my set do. I am almost entirely dependent on my aunt, and though she is very kind to me she makes me no regular allowance, and lately I 've lost money at cards, and I don't dare tell her about it. I have paid my card debts, of course, but there is hardly anything left for my other expenses, and if I go on with my present life I shall be in horrible difficulties. I have a tiny income of my own, but I 'm afraid it 's badly invested, for it seems to bring in less every year, and I am so ignorant of money matters that I don't know if my aunt's agent, who looks after it, is a good adviser." She paused a moment, and added in a lighter tone: "I did n't mean to bore you with all this, but I want your help in making Judy understand that I can't, at present, go on living as one must live among you all. I am going away tomorrow to join my aunt at Richfield, and I shall stay there for the rest of the autumn, and dismiss my maid and learn how to mend my own clothes."

At this picture of loveliness in distress, the pathos of which was heightened by the light touch with which it was drawn, a murmur of indignant sympathy broke from Trenor. Twenty-four hours earlier, if his wife had consulted him on the subject of Miss Bart's future, he would have said that a girl with extravagant tastes and no money had better marry the first rich man she could get; but with the subject of discussion at his side, turning to him for sympathy, making him feel that he understood her better than her dearest friends, and confirming the assurance by the appeal of her exquisite nearness, he was ready to swear that such a marriage was a desecration, and that, as a man of honour, he was bound to do all he could to protect her from the results of her disinterestedness. This impulse was reinforced by the reflection that if she had married Gryce she would have been surrounded by flattery and approval, whereas, having refused to sacrifice herself to expediency, she was left to bear the whole cost of her resistance. Hang it, if he could find a way out of such difficulties for a professional sponge like Carry Fisher, who was simply a mental habit corresponding to the physical titillations of the cigarette or the cock-tail, he could surely do as much for a girl who appealed to his highest sympathies, and who brought her troubles to him with the trustfulness of a child.

Trenor and Miss Bart prolonged their drive till long after sunset; and before it was over he had tried, with some show of success, to prove to her that, if she would only trust him, he could make a handsome sum of money for her without endangering the small amount she possessed. She was too genuinely ignorant of the manipulations of the stock-market to understand his technical explanations, or even perhaps to perceive that certain points in them were slurred; the haziness enveloping the transaction served as a veil for her embarrassment, and through the general blur her hopes dilated like lamps in a fog. She understood only that her modest investments were to be mysteriously multiplied without risk to herself; and the assurance that this miracle would take place within a short time, that there would be no tedious interval for suspense and reaction, relieved her of her lingering scruples.

Again she felt the lightening of her load, and with it the release of repressed activities. Her immediate worries conjured, it was easy to resolve that she would never again find herself in such straits, and as the need of economy and self-denial receded from her foreground she felt herself ready to meet any other demand which life might make. Even the immediate one of letting Trenor, as they drove homeward, lean a little nearer and rest his hand reassuringly on hers, cost her only a momentary shiver of reluctance. It was part of the game to make him feel that her appeal had been an uncalculated impulse, provoked by the liking he inspired; and the renewed sense of power in handling men, while it consoled her wounded vanity, helped also to obscure the thought of the claim at which his manner hinted. He was a coarse dull man who, under all his show of authority, was a mere supernumerary in the costly show for which his money paid: surely, to a clever girl, it would be easy to hold him by his vanity, and so keep the obligation on his side.

VIII

THE FIRST thousand dollar cheque which Lily received with a blotted scrawl from Gus Trenor strengthened her self-confidence in the exact degree to which it effaced her debts.

The transaction had justified itself by its results: she saw now how absurd it would have been to let any primitive scruple deprive her of this easy means of appeasing her creditors. Lily felt really virtuous as she dispensed the sum in sops to her tradesmen, and the fact that a fresh order accompanied each payment did not lessen her sense of disinterestedness. How many women, in her place, would have given the orders without making the payment!

She had found it reassuringly easy to keep Trenor in a good humour. To listen to his stories, to receive his confidences and laugh at his jokes, seemed for the moment all that was required of her, and the complacency with which her hostess regarded these attentions freed them of the least hint of ambiguity. Mrs. Trenor evidently assumed that Lily's growing intimacy with her husband was simply an indirect way of returning her own kindness.

"I'm so glad you and Gus have become such good friends," she said approvingly. "It's too delightful of you to be so nice to him, and put up with all his tiresome stories. I know what they are, because I had to listen to them when we were engaged—I'm sure he is telling the same ones still. And now I shan't always have to be asking Carry Fisher here to keep him in a good-humour. She's a perfect vulture, you know; and she has n't the least moral sense. She is always getting Gus to speculate for her, and I'm sure she never pays when she loses."

Miss Bart could shudder at this state of things without the embarrassment of a personal application. Her own position was surely quite different. There could be no question of her not paying when she lost, since Trenor had assured her that she was certain not to lose. In sending her the cheque he had explained that he had made five thousand for her out of Rosedale's "tip," and had put four thousand back in the same venture, as there was the promise of another "big rise"; she understood therefore that he was now speculating with her own money, and that she consequently owed him no more than the gratitude which such a trifling service demanded. She vaguely supposed that, to raise the first sum, he had borrowed on her securities; but this was a point over which her curiosity did not linger. It was concentrated, for the moment, on the probable date of the next "big rise."

The news of this event was received by her some weeks later, on the occasion of Jack Stepney's marriage to Miss Van Osburgh. As a cousin of the bridegroom, Miss Bart had been asked to act as bridesmaid; but she had declined on the plea that, since she was much taller than the other attendant virgins, her presence might mar the symmetry of the group. The truth was, she had attended too many brides to the altar: when next seen there she meant to be the chief figure in the ceremony. She knew the pleasantries made at the expense of young girls who have been too long before the public, and she was resolved to avoid such assumptions of youthfulness as might lead people to think her older than she really was.

The Van Osburgh marriage was celebrated in the village church near the paternal estate on the Hudson. It was the "simple country wedding" to which guests are convoyed in special trains, and from which the hordes of the uninvited have to be fended off by the intervention of the police. While these sylvan rites were taking place, in a church packed with fashion and festooned with orchids, the representatives of the press were threading their way, note-book in hand, through the labyrinth of wedding presents, and the agent of a cinematograph syndicate was setting up his apparatus at the church door. It was the kind of scene in which Lily had often pictured herself as taking the principal part, and on this occasion the fact that she was once more merely a casual spectator, instead of the mystically veiled figure occupying the centre of attention, strengthened her resolve to assume the latter part before the year was over. The fact that her immediate anxieties were relieved did not blind her to a possibility of their recurrence; it merely gave her enough buoyancy to rise once more above her doubts and feel a renewed faith in her beauty, her power, and her general fitness to attract a brilliant destiny. It could not be that one conscious of such aptitudes for mastery and enjoyment was doomed to a perpetuity of failure; and her mistakes looked easily reparable in the light of her restored self-confidence.

A special appositeness was given to these reflections by the discovery, in a neighbouring pew, of the serious profile and neatly-trimmed beard of Mr. Percy Gryce. There was something almost bridal in his own aspect: his large white gardenia had a symbolic air that struck Lily as a good omen. After all, seen in an assemblage of his kind he was not ridiculous-looking: a friendly critic might have called his heaviness weighty, and he was at his best in the attitude of vacant passivity which brings out the oddities of the restless. She fancied he was the kind of man whose sentimental associations would be stirred by the conventional imagery of a wedding, and she pictured herself, in the seclusion of the Van Osburgh conservatories, playing skilfully upon sensibilities thus prepared for her touch. In fact, when she looked at the other women about her, and recalled the image she had brought away from her own glass, it did not seem as though any special skill would be needed to repair her blunder and bring him once more to her feet.

The sight of Selden's dark head, in a pew almost facing her, disturbed for a moment the balance of her complacency. The rise of her blood as their eyes met was succeeded by a contrary motion, a wave of resistance and withdrawal. She did not wish to see him again, not because she feared his influence, but because his presence always had the effect of cheapening her aspirations, of throwing her whole world out of focus. Besides, he was a living reminder of the worst mistake in her career, and the fact that he had been its cause did not soften her feelings toward him. She could still imagine an ideal state of existence in which, all else being superadded, intercourse with Selden might be the last touch of luxury; but in the world as it was, such a privilege was likely to cost more than it was worth.

"Lily, dear, I never saw you look so lovely! You look as if something delightful had just happened to you!"

The young lady who thus formulated her admiration of her brilliant friend did not, in her own person, suggest such happy possibilities. Miss Gertrude Farish, in fact, typified the mediocre and the ineffectual. If there were compensating qualities in her wide frank glance and the freshness of her smile, these were qualities which only the sympathetic observer would perceive before noticing that her eyes were of a workaday grey and her lips without haunting curves. Lily's own view of her wavered between pity for her limitations and impatience at her cheerful acceptance of them. To Miss Bart, as to her mother, acquiescence in dinginess was evidence of stupidity; and there were moments when, in the consciousness of her own power to look and to be so exactly what the occasion required, she almost felt that other girls were plain and inferior from choice. Certainly no one need have confessed such acquiescence in her lot as was revealed in the "useful" colour of Gerty Farish's gown and the subdued lines of her hat: it is almost as stupid to let your clothes betray that you know you are ugly as to have them proclaim that you think you are beautiful.

Of course, being fatally poor and dingy, it was wise of Gerty to have taken up philanthropy and symphony concerts; but there was something irritating in her assumption that existence yielded no higher pleasures, and that one might get as much interest and excitement out of life in a cramped flat as in the splendours of the Van Osburgh establishment. Today, however, her chirping enthusiasms did not irritate Lily. They seemed only to throw her own exceptionalness into becoming relief, and give a soaring vastness to her scheme of life.

"Do let us go and take a peep at the presents before every one else leaves the dining-room!" suggested Miss Farish, linking her arm in her friend's. It was characteristic of her to take a sentimental and unenvious interest in all the details of a wedding: she was the kind of person who always kept her handkerchief out during the service, and departed clutching a box of wedding-cake.

"Is n't everything beautifully done?" she pursued, as they entered the distant drawing-room assigned to the display of Miss Van Osburgh's bridal spoils. "I always say no one does things better than cousin Grace! Did you ever taste anything more delicious than that *mousse* of lobster with champagne sauce? I made up my mind weeks ago that I would n't miss this wedding, and just fancy how delightfully it all came about. When Lawrence Selden heard I was coming, he insisted on fetching me himself and driving me to the station, and when we go back this evening I am to dine with him at Sherry's. I really feel as excited as if I were getting married myself!"

Lily smiled: she knew that Selden had always been kind to his dull cousin, and she had sometimes wondered why he wasted so much time in such an unremunerative manner; but now the thought gave her a vague pleasure.

"Do you see him often?" she asked.

"Yes; he is very good about dropping in on Sundays. And now and then we do a play together; but lately I have n't seen much of him. He does n't look well, and he seems nervous and unsettled. The dear fellow! I do wish he would marry some nice girl. I told him so today, but he said he did n't care for the really nice ones, and the other kind did n't care for him—but that was just his joke, of course. He could never marry a girl who *was n't* nice. Oh, my dear, did you ever see such pearls?"

They had paused before the table on which the bride's jewels were displayed, and Lily's heart gave an envious throb as she caught the refraction of light from their surfaces—the milky gleam of perfectly matched pearls, the flash of rubies relieved against contrasting velvet, the intense blue rays of sapphires kindled into light by surrounding diamonds: all these precious tints enhanced and deepened by the varied art of their setting. The glow of the stones warmed Lily's veins like wine. More completely than any other expression of wealth they symbolized the life she longed to lead, the life of fastidious aloofness and refinement in which every detail should have the finish of a jewel, and the whole form a harmonious setting to her own jewel-like rareness.

"Oh, Lily, do look at this diamond pendant—it 's as big as a dinner-plate! Who can have given it?" Miss Farish bent short-sightedly over the accompanying card. "*Mr. Simon Rosedale.* What, that horrid man? Oh, yes—I remember he 's a friend of Jack's, and I suppose cousin Grace had to ask him here today; but she must rather hate having to let Gwen accept such a present from him."

Lily smiled. She doubted Mrs. Van Osburgh's reluctance, but was aware of Miss Farish's habit of ascribing her own delicacies of feeling to the persons least likely to be encumbered by them.

"Well, if Gwen does n't care to be seen wearing it she can always exchange it for something else," she remarked.

"Ah, here is something so much prettier," Miss Farish continued. "Do look at this exquisite white sapphire. I 'm sure the person who chose it must have taken particular pains. What is the name? Percy Gryce? Ah, then I 'm not surprised!" She smiled significantly as she replaced the card. "Of course you 've heard that he 's perfectly devoted to Evie Van Osburgh? Cousin Grace is so pleased about it—it 's quite a romance! He met her first at the George Dorsets', only about six weeks ago, and it 's just the nicest possible marriage for dear Evie. Oh, I don't mean the money—of course she has plenty of her own—but she 's such a quiet stay-at-home kind of girl, and it seems he has just the same tastes; so they are exactly suited to each other."

Lily stood staring vacantly at the white sapphire on its velvet bed. Evie Van Osburgh and Percy Gryce? The names rang derisively through her brain. *Evie Van Osburgh?* The youngest, dumpiest, dullest of the four dull and dumpy daughters whom Mrs. Van Osburgh, with unsurpassed astuteness, had "placed" one by one in enviable niches of existence! Ah, lucky girls who grow up in the shelter of a mother's love—a mother who knows how to contrive opportunities without conceding favours, how to take advantage of propinquity without allowing appetite to be dulled by habit! The cleverest girl may miscalculate where her own interests are concerned, may yield too much at one moment and withdraw too far at the next: it takes a mother's unerring vigilance and foresight to land her daughters safely in the arms of wealth and suitability.

Lily's passing light-heartedness sank beneath a renewed sense of failure. Life was too stupid, too blundering! Why should Percy Gryce's millions be joined to another great fortune, why should this clumsy girl be put in possession of powers she would never know how to use?

She was roused from these speculations by a familiar touch

on her arm, and turning saw Gus Trenor beside her. She felt a thrill of vexation: what right had he to touch her? Luckily Gerty Farish had wandered off to the next table, and they were alone.

Trenor, looking stouter than ever in his tight frock-coat, and unbecomingly flushed by the bridal libations, gazed at her with undisguised approval.

"By Jove, Lily, you do look a stunner!" He had slipped insensibly into the use of her Christian name, and she had never found the right moment to correct him. Besides, in her set all the men and women called each other by their Christian names; it was only on Trenor's lips that the familiar address had an unpleasant significance.

"Well," he continued, still jovially impervious to her annoyance, "have you made up your mind which of these little trinkets you mean to duplicate at Tiffany's tomorrow? I 've got a cheque for you in my pocket that will go a long way in that line!"

Lily gave him a startled look: his voice was louder than usual, and the room was beginning to fill with people. But as her glance assured her that they were still beyond ear-shot a sense of pleasure replaced her apprehension.

"Another dividend?" she asked, smiling and drawing near him in the desire not to be overheard.

"Well, not exactly: I sold out on the rise and I 've pulled off four thou' for you. Not so bad for a beginner, eh? I suppose you 'll begin to think you 're a pretty knowing speculator. And perhaps you won't think poor old Gus such an awful ass as some people do."

"I think you the kindest of friends; but I can't thank you properly now."

She let her eyes shine into his with a look that made up for the hand-clasp he would have claimed if they had been alone—and how glad she was that they were not! The news filled her with the glow produced by a sudden cessation of physical pain. The world was not so stupid and blundering after all: now and then a stroke of luck came to the unluckiest. At the thought her spirits began to rise: it was characteristic of her that one trifling piece of good fortune should give wings to all her hopes. Instantly came the reflection that Percy

Gryce was not irretrievably lost; and she smiled to think of the excitement of recapturing him from Evie Van Osburgh. What chance could such a simpleton have against her if she chose to exert herself? She glanced about, hoping to catch a glimpse of Gryce; but her eyes lit instead on the glossy countenance of Mr. Rosedale, who was slipping through the crowd with an air half obsequious, half obtrusive, as though, the moment his presence was recognized, it would swell to the dimensions of the room.

Not wishing to be the means of effecting this enlargement, Lily quickly transferred her glance to Trenor, to whom the expression of her gratitude seemed not to have brought the complete gratification she had meant it to give.

"Hang thanking me—I don't want to be thanked, but I *should* like the chance to say two words to you now and then," he grumbled. "I thought you were going to spend the whole autumn with us, and I 've hardly laid eyes on you for the last month. Why can't you come back to Bellomont this evening? We 're all alone, and Judy is as cross as two sticks. Do come and cheer a fellow up. If you say yes I 'll run you over in the motor, and you can telephone your maid to bring your traps from town by the next train."

Lily shook her head with a charming semblance of regret. "I wish I could—but it 's quite impossible. My aunt has come back to town, and I must be with her for the next few days."

"Well, I 've seen a good deal less of you since we 've got to be such pals than I used to when you were Judy's friend," he continued with unconscious penetration.

"When I was Judy's friend? Am I not her friend still? Really, you say the most absurd things! If I were always at Bellomont you would tire of me much sooner than Judy— but come and see me at my aunt's the next afternoon you are in town; then we can have a nice quiet talk, and you can tell me how I had better invest my fortune."

It was true that, during the last three or four weeks, she had absented herself from Bellomont on the pretext of having other visits to pay; but she now began to feel that the reckoning she had thus contrived to evade had rolled up interest in the interval.

The prospect of the nice quiet talk did not appear as all-sufficing to Trenor as she had hoped, and his brows continued to lower as he said: "Oh, I don't know that I can promise you a fresh tip every day. But there's one thing you might do for me; and that is, just to be a little civil to Rosedale. Judy has promised to ask him to dine when we get to town, but I can't induce her to have him at Bellomont, and if you would let me bring him up now it would make a lot of difference. I don't believe two women have spoken to him this afternoon, and I can tell you he's a chap it pays to be decent to."

Miss Bart made an impatient movement, but suppressed the words which seemed about to accompany it. After all, this was an unexpectedly easy way of acquitting her debt; and had she not reasons of her own for wishing to be civil to Mr. Rosedale?

"Oh, bring him by all means," she said smiling; "perhaps I can get a tip out of him on my own account."

Trenor paused abruptly, and his eyes fixed themselves on hers with a look which made her change colour.

"I say, you know—you'll please remember he's a blooming bounder," he said; and with a slight laugh she turned toward the open window near which they had been standing.

The throng in the room had increased, and she felt a desire for space and fresh air. Both of these she found on the terrace, where only a few men were lingering over cigarettes and liqueur, while scattered couples strolled across the lawn to the autumn-tinted borders of the flower-garden.

As she emerged, a man moved toward her from the knot of smokers, and she found herself face to face with Selden. The stir of the pulses which his nearness always caused was increased by a slight sense of constraint. They had not met since their Sunday afternoon walk at Bellomont, and that episode was still so vivid to her that she could hardly believe him to be less conscious of it. But his greeting expressed no more than the satisfaction which every pretty woman expects to see reflected in masculine eyes; and the discovery, if distasteful to her vanity, was reassuring to her nerves. Between the relief of her escape from Trenor, and the vague apprehension of her meeting with Rosedale, it was pleasant to rest a moment on the sense of complete understanding which Lawrence Selden's manner always conveyed.

"This is luck," he said smiling. "I was wondering if I should be able to have a word with you before the special snatches us away. I came with Gerty Farish, and promised not to let her miss the train, but I am sure she is still extracting sentimental solace from the wedding presents. She appears to regard their number and value as evidence of the disinterested affection of the contracting parties."

There was not the least trace of embarrassment in his voice, and as he spoke, leaning slightly against the jamb of the window, and letting his eyes rest on her in the frank enjoyment of her grace, she felt with a faint chill of regret that he had gone back without an effort to the footing on which they had stood before their last talk together. Her vanity was stung by the sight of his unscathed smile. She longed to be to him something more than a piece of sentient prettiness, a passing diversion to his eye and brain; and the longing betrayed itself in her reply.

"Ah," she said, "I envy Gerty that power she has of dressing up with romance all our ugly and prosaic arrangements! I have never recovered my self-respect since you showed me how poor and unimportant my ambitions were."

The words were hardly spoken when she realized their infelicity. It seemed to be her fate to appear at her worst to Selden.

"I thought, on the contrary," he returned lightly, "that I had been the means of proving they were more important to you than anything else."

It was as if the eager current of her being had been checked by a sudden obstacle which drove it back upon itself. She looked at him helplessly, like a hurt or frightened child: this real self of hers, which he had the faculty of drawing out of the depths, was so little accustomed to go alone!

The appeal of her helplessness touched in him, as it always did, a latent chord of inclination. It would have meant nothing to him to discover that his nearness made her more brilliant, but this glimpse of a twilight mood to which he alone had the clue seemed once more to set him in a world apart with her.

"At least you can't think worse things of me than you say!" she exclaimed with a trembling laugh; but before he could answer, the flow of comprehension between them was abruptly stayed by the reappearance of Gus Trenor, who advanced with Mr. Rosedale in his wake.

"Hang it, Lily, I thought you 'd given me the slip: Rosedale and I have been hunting all over for you!"

His voice had a note of conjugal familiarity: Miss Bart fancied she detected in Rosedale's eye a twinkling perception of the fact, and the idea turned her dislike of him to repugnance.

She returned his profound bow with a slight nod, made more disdainful by the sense of Selden's surprise that she should number Rosedale among her acquaintances. Trenor had turned away, and his companion continued to stand before Miss Bart, alert and expectant, his lips parted in a smile at whatever she might be about to say, and his very back conscious of the privilege of being seen with her.

It was the moment for tact; for the quick bridging over of gaps; but Selden still leaned against the window, a detached observer of the scene, and under the spell of his observation Lily felt herself powerless to exert her usual arts. The dread of Selden's suspecting that there was any need for her to propitiate such a man as Rosedale checked the trivial phrases of politeness. Rosedale still stood before her in an expectant attitude, and she continued to face him in silence, her glance just level with his polished baldness. The look put the finishing touch to what her silence implied.

He reddened slowly, shifting from one foot to the other, fingered the plump black pearl in his tie, and gave a nervous twist to his moustache; then, running his eye over her, he drew back, and said, with a side-glance at Selden: "Upon my soul, I never saw a more ripping get-up. Is that the last creation of the dress-maker you go to see at the Benedick? If so, I wonder all the other women don't go to her too!"

The words were projected sharply against Lily's silence, and she saw in a flash that her own act had given them their emphasis. In ordinary talk they might have passed unheeded; but following on her prolonged pause they acquired a special meaning. She felt, without looking, that Selden had immediately seized it, and would inevitably connect the allusion with her visit to himself. The consciousness increased her irritation against Rosedale, but also her feeling that now, if ever, was the moment to propitiate him, hateful as it was to do so in Selden's presence.

"How do you know the other women don't go to my dress-maker?" she returned. "You see I'm not afraid to give her address to my friends!"

Her glance and accent so plainly included Rosedale in this privileged circle that his small eyes puckered with gratification, and a knowing smile drew up his moustache.

"By Jove, you need n't be!" he declared. "You could give 'em the whole outfit and win at a canter!"

"Ah, that's nice of you; and it would be nicer still if you would carry me off to a quiet corner, and get me a glass of lemonade or some innocent drink before we all have to rush for the train."

She turned away as she spoke, letting him strut at her side through the gathering groups on the terrace, while every nerve in her throbbed with the consciousness of what Selden must have thought of the scene.

But under her angry sense of the perverseness of things, and the light surface of her talk with Rosedale, a third idea persisted: she did not mean to leave without an attempt to discover the truth about Percy Gryce. Chance, or perhaps his own resolve, had kept them apart since his hasty withdrawal from Bellomont; but Miss Bart was an expert in making the most of the unexpected, and the distasteful incidents of the last few minutes—the revelation to Selden of precisely that part of her life which she most wished him to ignore—increased her longing for shelter, for escape from such humiliating contingencies. Any definite situation would be more tolerable than this buffeting of chances, which kept her in an attitude of uneasy alertness toward every possibility of life.

Indoors there was a general sense of dispersal in the air, as of an audience gathering itself up for departure after the principal actors had left the stage; but among the remaining groups, Lily could discover neither Gryce nor the youngest Miss Van Osburgh. That both should be missing struck her with foreboding; and she charmed Mr. Rosedale by proposing that they should make their way to the conservatories at the farther end of the house. There were just enough people left in the long suite of rooms to make their progress conspicuous, and Lily was aware of being followed by looks of amusement and interrogation, which glanced off as harmlessly from her indifference as from her companion's self-satisfaction. She cared very little at that moment about being seen with Rosedale: all her thoughts were centred on the object of her search. The latter, however, was not discoverable in the conservatories, and Lily, oppressed by a sudden conviction of failure, was casting about for a way to rid herself of her now superfluous companion, when they came upon Mrs. Van Osburgh, flushed and exhausted, but beaming with the consciousness of duty performed.

She glanced at them a moment with the benign but vacant eye of the tired hostess, to whom her guests have become mere whirling spots in a kaleidoscope of fatigue; then her attention became suddenly fixed, and she seized on Miss Bart with a confidential gesture.

"My dear Lily, I have n't had time for a word with you, and now I suppose you are just off. Have you seen Evie? She 's been looking everywhere for you: she wanted to tell you her little secret; but I daresay you have guessed it already. The engagement is not to be announced till next week—but you are such a friend of Mr. Gryce's that they both wished you to be the first to know of their happiness."

IX

IN MRS. PENISTON'S youth, fashion had returned to town in October; therefore on the tenth day of the month the blinds of her Fifth Avenue residence were drawn up, and the eyes of the Dying Gladiator in bronze who occupied the drawing-room window resumed their survey of that deserted thoroughfare.

The first two weeks after her return represented to Mrs. Peniston the domestic equivalent of a religious retreat. She "went through" the linen and blankets in the precise spirit of the penitent exploring the inner folds of conscience; she sought for moths as the stricken soul seeks for lurking infirmities. The topmost shelf of every closet was made to yield up its secret, cellar and coal-bin were probed to their darkest depths and, as a final stage in the lustral rites, the entire house was swathed in penitential white and deluged with expiatory soapsuds.

It was on this phase of the proceedings that Miss Bart entered on the afternoon of her return from the Van Osburgh wedding. The journey back to town had not been calculated to soothe her nerves. Though Evie Van Osburgh's engagement was still officially a secret, it was one of which the innumerable intimate friends of the family were already possessed; and the trainful of returning guests buzzed with allusions and anticipations. Lily was acutely aware of her own part in this drama of innuendo: she knew the exact quality of the amusement the situation evoked. The crude forms in which her friends took their pleasure included a loud enjoyment of such complications: the zest of surprising destiny in the act of playing a practical joke. Lily knew well enough how to bear herself in difficult situations. She had, to a shade, the exact manner between victory and defeat: every insinuation was shed without an effort by the bright indifference of her manner. But she was beginning to feel the strain of the attitude; the reaction was more rapid, and she lapsed to a deeper self-disgust.

As was always the case with her, this moral repulsion found a physical outlet in a quickened distaste for her surroundings.

She revolted from the complacent ugliness of Mrs. Peniston's black walnut, from the slippery gloss of the vestibule tiles, and the mingled odour of sapolio and furniture-polish that met her at the door.

The stairs were still carpetless, and on the way up to her room she was arrested on the landing by an encroaching tide of soapsuds. Gathering up her skirts, she drew aside with an impatient gesture; and as she did so she had the odd sensation of having already found herself in the same situation but in different surroundings. It seemed to her that she was again descending the staircase from Selden's rooms; and looking down to remonstrate with the dispenser of the soapy flood, she found herself met by a lifted stare which had once before confronted her under similar circumstances. It was the char-woman of the Benedick who, resting on crimson elbows, examined her with the same unflinching curiosity, the same apparent reluctance to let her pass. On this occasion, how-ever, Miss Bart was on her own ground.

"Don't you see that I wish to go by? Please move your pail," she said sharply.

The woman at first seemed not to hear; then, without a word of excuse, she pushed back her pail and dragged a wet floor-cloth across the landing, keeping her eyes fixed on Lily while the latter swept by. It was insufferable that Mrs. Penis-ton should have such creatures about the house; and Lily en-tered her room resolved that the woman should be dismissed that evening.

Mrs. Peniston, however, was at the moment inaccessible to remonstrance: since early morning she had been shut up with her maid, going over her furs, a process which formed the culminating episode in the drama of household renovation. In the evening also Lily found herself alone, for her aunt, who rarely dined out, had responded to the summons of a Van Alstyne cousin who was passing through town. The house, in its state of unnatural immaculateness and order, was as dreary as a tomb, and as Lily, turning from her brief repast between shrouded sideboards, wandered into the newly-uncovered glare of the drawing-room she felt as though she were buried alive in the stifling limits of Mrs. Peniston's existence.

She usually contrived to avoid being at home during the season of domestic renewal. On the present occasion, however, a variety of reasons had combined to bring her to town; and foremost among them was the fact that she had fewer invitations than usual for the autumn. She had so long been accustomed to pass from one country-house to another, till the close of the holidays brought her friends to town, that the unfilled gaps of time confronting her produced a sharp sense of waning popularity. It was as she had said to Selden—people were tired of her. They would welcome her in a new character, but as Miss Bart they knew her by heart. She knew herself by heart too, and was sick of the old story. There were moments when she longed blindly for anything different, anything strange, remote and untried; but the utmost reach of her imagination did not go beyond picturing her usual life in a new setting. She could not figure herself as anywhere but in a drawing-room, diffusing elegance as a flower sheds perfume.

Meanwhile, as October advanced she had to face the alternative of returning to the Trenors or joining her aunt in town. Even the desolating dulness of New York in October, and the soapy discomforts of Mrs. Peniston's interior, seemed preferable to what might await her at Bellomont; and with an air of heroic devotion she announced her intention of remaining with her aunt till the holidays.

Sacrifices of this nature are sometimes received with feelings as mixed as those which actuate them; and Mrs. Peniston remarked to her confidential maid that, if any of the family were to be with her at such a crisis (though for forty years she had been thought competent to see to the hanging of her own curtains), she would certainly have preferred Miss Grace to Miss Lily. Grace Stepney was an obscure cousin, of adaptable manners and vicarious interests, who "ran in" to sit with Mrs. Peniston when Lily dined out too continuously; who played bézique, picked up dropped stitches, read out the deaths from the Times, and sincerely admired the purple satin drawing-room curtains, the Dying Gladiator in the window, and the seven-by-five painting of Niagara which represented the one artistic excess of Mr. Peniston's temperate career.

Mrs. Peniston, under ordinary circumstances, was as much

bored by her excellent cousin as the recipient of such services usually is by the person who performs them. She greatly preferred the brilliant and unreliable Lily, who did not know one end of a crochet-needle from the other, and had frequently wounded her susceptibilities by suggesting that the drawing-room should be "done over." But when it came to hunting for missing napkins, or helping to decide whether the back-stairs needed re-carpeting, Grace's judgment was certainly sounder than Lily's: not to mention the fact that the latter resented the smell of beeswax and brown soap, and behaved as though she thought a house ought to keep clean of itself, without extraneous assistance.

Seated under the cheerless blaze of the drawing-room chandelier—Mrs. Peniston never lit the lamps unless there was "company"—Lily seemed to watch her own figure retreating down vistas of neutral-tinted dulness to a middle age like Grace Stepney's. When she ceased to amuse Judy Trenor and her friends she would have to fall back on amusing Mrs. Peniston; whichever way she looked she saw only a future of servitude to the whims of others, never the possibility of asserting her own eager individuality.

A ring at the door-bell, sounding emphatically through the empty house, roused her suddenly to the extent of her boredom. It was as though all the weariness of the past months had culminated in the vacuity of that interminable evening. If only the ring meant a summons from the outer world—a token that she was still remembered and wanted!

After some delay a parlour-maid presented herself with the announcement that there was a person outside who was asking to see Miss Bart; and on Lily's pressing for a more specific description, she added:

"It 's Mrs. Haffen, Miss; she won't say what she wants."

Lily, to whom the name conveyed nothing, opened the door upon a woman in a battered bonnet, who stood firmly planted under the hall-light. The glare of the unshaded gas shone familiarly on her pock-marked face and the reddish baldness visible through thin strands of straw-coloured hair. Lily looked at the char-woman in surprise.

"Do you wish to see me?" she asked.

"I should like to say a word to you, Miss." The tone was

neither aggressive nor conciliatory: it revealed nothing of the speaker's errand. Nevertheless, some precautionary instinct warned Lily to withdraw beyond ear-shot of the hovering parlour-maid.

She signed to Mrs. Haffen to follow her into the drawing-room, and closed the door when they had entered.

"What is it that you wish?" she enquired.

The char-woman, after the manner of her kind, stood with her arms folded in her shawl. Unwinding the latter, she produced a small parcel wrapped in dirty newspaper.

"I have something here that you might like to see, Miss Bart." She spoke the name with an unpleasant emphasis, as though her knowing it made a part of her reason for being there. To Lily the intonation sounded like a threat.

"You have found something belonging to me?" she asked, extending her hand.

Mrs. Haffen drew back. "Well, if it comes to that, I guess it 's mine as much as anybody's," she returned.

Lily looked at her perplexedly. She was sure, now, that her visitor's manner conveyed a threat; but, expert as she was in certain directions, there was nothing in her experience to prepare her for the exact significance of the present scene. She felt, however, that it must be ended as promptly as possible.

"I don't understand; if this parcel is not mine, why have you asked for me?"

The woman was unabashed by the question. She was evidently prepared to answer it, but like all her class she had to go a long way back to make a beginning, and it was only after a pause that she replied: "My husband was janitor to the Benedick till the first of the month; since then he can't get nothing to do."

Lily remained silent and she continued: "It was n't no fault of our own, neither: the agent had another man he wanted the place for, and we was put out, bag and baggage, just to suit his fancy. I had a long sickness last winter, and an operation that ate up all we 'd put by; and it 's hard for me and the children, Haffen being so long out of a job."

After all, then, she had come only to ask Miss Bart to find a place for her husband; or, more probably, to seek the young lady's intervention with Mrs. Peniston. Lily had such an air of always getting what she wanted that she was used to being appealed to as an intermediary, and, relieved of her vague apprehension, she took refuge in the conventional formula.

"I am sorry you have been in trouble," she said.

"Oh, that we have, Miss, and it 's on'y just beginning. If on'y we 'd 'a got another situation—but the agent, he 's dead against us. It ain't no fault of ours, neither, but——"

At this point Lily's impatience overcame her. "If you have anything to say to me——" she interposed.

The woman's resentment of the rebuff seemed to spur her lagging ideas.

"Yes, Miss; I 'm coming to that," she said. She paused again, with her eyes on Lily, and then continued, in a tone of diffuse narrative: "When we was at the Benedick I had charge of some of the gentlemen's rooms; leastways, I swep' 'em out on Saturdays. Some of the gentlemen got the greatest sight of letters: I never saw the like of it. Their waste-paper baskets 'd be fairly brimming, and papers falling over on the floor. Maybe havin' so many is how they get so careless. Some of 'em is worse than others. Mr. Selden, Mr. Lawrence Selden, he was always one of the carefullest: burnt his letters in winter, and tore 'em in little bits in summer. But sometimes he 'd have so many he 'd just bunch 'em together, the way the others did, and tear the lot through once—like this."

While she spoke she had loosened the string from the parcel in her hand, and now she drew forth a letter which she laid on the table between Miss Bart and herself. As she had said, the letter was torn in two; but with a rapid gesture she laid the torn edges together and smoothed out the page.

A wave of indignation swept over Lily. She felt herself in the presence of something vile, as yet but dimly conjectured—the kind of vileness of which people whispered, but which she had never thought of as touching her own life. She drew back with a motion of disgust, but her withdrawal was checked by a sudden discovery: under the glare of Mrs. Peniston's chandelier she had recognized the hand-writing of the letter. It was a large disjointed hand, with a flourish of masculinity which but slightly disguised its rambling weakness, and the words, scrawled in heavy ink on pale-tinted note-paper, smote on Lily's ear as though she had heard them spoken.

At first she did not grasp the full import of the situation. She understood only that before her lay a letter written by Bertha Dorset, and addressed, presumably, to Lawrence Selden. There was no date, but the blackness of the ink proved the writing to be comparatively recent. The packet in Mrs. Haffen's hand doubtless contained more letters of the same kind—a dozen, Lily conjectured from its thickness. The letter before her was short, but its few words, which had leapt into her brain before she was conscious of reading them, told a long history—a history over which, for the last four years, the friends of the writer had smiled and shrugged, viewing it merely as one among the countless "good situations" of the mundane comedy. Now the other side presented itself to Lily, the volcanic nether side of the surface over which conjecture and innuendo glide so lightly till the first fissure turns their whisper to a shriek. Lily knew that there is nothing society resents so much as having given its protection to those who have not known how to profit by it: it is for having betrayed its connivance that the body social punishes the offender who is found out. And in this case there was no doubt of the issue. The code of Lily's world decreed that a woman's husband should be the only judge of her conduct: she was technically above suspicion while she had the shelter of his approval, or even of his indifference. But with a man of George Dorset's temper there could be no thought of condonation—the possessor of his wife's letters could overthrow with a touch the whole structure of her existence. And into what hands Bertha Dorset's secret had been delivered! For a moment the irony of the coincidence tinged Lily's disgust with a confused sense of triumph. But the disgust prevailed—all her instinctive resistances, of taste, of training, of blind inherited scruples, rose against the other feeling. Her strongest sense was one of personal contamination.

She moved away, as though to put as much distance as possible between herself and her visitor. "I know nothing of these letters," she said; "I have no idea why you have brought them here."

Mrs. Haffen faced her steadily. "I 'll tell you why, Miss. I brought 'em to you to sell, because I ain't got no other way of raising money, and if we don't pay our rent by tomorrow night we 'll be put out. I never done anythin' of the kind before, and if you 'd speak to Mr. Selden or to Mr. Rosedale about getting Haffen taken on again at the Benedick—I seen you talking to Mr. Rosedale on the steps that day you come out of Mr. Selden's rooms——"

The blood rushed to Lily's forehead. She understood now—Mrs. Haffen supposed her to be the writer of the letters. In the first leap of her anger she was about to ring and order the woman out; but an obscure impulse restrained her. The mention of Selden's name had started a new train of thought. Bertha Dorset's letters were nothing to her—they might go where the current of chance carried them! But Selden was inextricably involved in their fate. Men do not, at worst, suffer much from such exposure; and in this instance the flash of divination which had carried the meaning of the letters to Lily's brain had revealed also that they were appeals—repeated and therefore probably unanswered—for the renewal of a tie which time had evidently relaxed. Nevertheless, the fact that the correspondence had been allowed to fall into strange hands would convict Selden of negligence in a matter where the world holds it least pardonable; and there were graver risks to consider where a man of Dorset's ticklish balance was concerned.

If she weighed all these things it was unconsciously: she was aware only of feeling that Selden would wish the letters rescued, and that therefore she must obtain possession of them. Beyond that her mind did not travel. She had, indeed, a quick vision of returning the packet to Bertha Dorset, and of the opportunities the restitution offered; but this thought lit up abysses from which she shrank back ashamed.

Meanwhile Mrs. Haffen, prompt to perceive her hesitation, had already opened the packet and ranged its contents on the table. All the letters had been pieced together with strips of thin paper. Some were in small fragments, the others merely torn in half. Though there were not many, thus spread out they nearly covered the table. Lily's glance fell on a word here and there—then she said in a low voice: "What do you wish me to pay you?"

Mrs. Haffen's face reddened with satisfaction. It was clear that the young lady was badly frightened, and Mrs. Haffen was the woman to make the most of such fears. Anticipating an easier victory than she had foreseen, she named an exorbitant sum.

But Miss Bart showed herself a less ready prey than might have been expected from her imprudent opening. She refused to pay the price named, and after a moment's hesitation, met it by a counter-offer of half the amount.

Mrs. Haffen immediately stiffened. Her hand travelled toward the outspread letters, and folding them slowly, she made as though to restore them to their wrapping.

"I guess they 're worth more to you than to me, Miss, but the poor has got to live as well as the rich," she observed sententiously.

Lily was throbbing with fear, but the insinuation fortified her resistance.

"You are mistaken," she said indifferently. "I have offered all I am willing to give for the letters; but there may be other ways of getting them."

Mrs. Haffen raised a suspicious glance: she was too experienced not to know that the traffic she was engaged in had perils as great as its rewards, and she had a vision of the elaborate machinery of revenge which a word of this commanding young lady's might set in motion.

She applied the corner of her shawl to her eyes, and murmured through it that no good came of bearing too hard on the poor, but that for her part she had never been mixed up in such a business before, and that on her honour as a Christian all she and Haffen had thought of was that the letters must n't go any farther.

Lily stood motionless, keeping between herself and the char-woman the greatest distance compatible with the need of speaking in low tones. The idea of bargaining for the letters was intolerable to her, but she knew that, if she appeared to weaken, Mrs. Haffen would at once increase her original demand.

She could never afterward recall how long the duel lasted, or what was the decisive stroke which finally, after a lapse of time recorded in minutes by the clock, in hours by the precipitate beat of her pulses, put her in possession of the letters; she knew only that the door had finally closed, and that she stood alone with the packet in her hand.

She had no idea of reading the letters; even to unfold Mrs. Haffen's dirty newspaper would have seemed degrading. But what did she intend to do with its contents? The recipient of the letters had meant to destroy them, and it was her duty to carry out his intention. She had no right to keep them—to do so was to lessen whatever merit lay in having secured their possession. But how destroy them so effectually that there should be no second risk of their falling in such hands? Mrs. Peniston's icy drawing-room grate shone with a forbidding lustre: the fire, like the lamps, was never lit except when there was company.

Miss Bart was turning to carry the letters upstairs when she heard the opening of the outer door, and her aunt entered the drawing-room. Mrs. Peniston was a small plump woman, with a colourless skin lined with trivial wrinkles. Her grey hair was arranged with precision, and her clothes looked excessively new and yet slightly old-fashioned. They were always black and tightly fitting, with an expensive glitter: she was the kind of woman who wore jet at breakfast. Lily had never seen her when she was not cuirassed in shining black, with small tight boots, and an air of being packed and ready to start; yet she never started.

She looked about the drawing-room with an expression of minute scrutiny. "I saw a streak of light under one of the blinds as I drove up: it's extraordinary that I can never teach that woman to draw them down evenly."

Having corrected the irregularity, she seated herself on one of the glossy purple arm-chairs; Mrs. Peniston always sat on a chair, never in it. Then she turned her glance to Miss Bart.

"My dear, you look tired; I suppose it's the excitement of the wedding. Cornelia Van Alstyne was full of it: Molly was there, and Gerty Farish ran in for a minute to tell us about it. I think it was odd, their serving melons before the *consommé*: a wedding breakfast should always begin with *consommé*. Molly didn't care for the bridesmaids' dresses. She had it straight from Julia Melson that they cost three hundred dollars apiece at Céleste's, but she says they didn't look it. I'm glad you decided not to be a bridesmaid; that shade of salmon-pink would n't have suited you."

Mrs. Peniston delighted in discussing the minutest details of festivities in which she had not taken part. Nothing would have induced her to undergo the exertion and fatigue of attending the Van Osburgh wedding, but so great was her interest in the event that, having heard two versions of it, she now prepared to extract a third from her niece. Lily, however, had been deplorably careless in noting the particulars of the entertainment. She had failed to observe the colour of Mrs. Van Osburgh's gown, and could not even say whether the old Van Osburgh Sèvres had been used at the bride's table: Mrs. Peniston, in short, found that she was of more service as a listener than as a narrator.

"Really, Lily, I don't see why you took the trouble to go to the wedding, if you don't remember what happened or whom you saw there. When I was a girl I used to keep the *menu* of every dinner I went to, and write the names of the people on the back; and I never threw away my cotillion favours till after your uncle's death, when it seemed unsuitable to have so many coloured things about the house. I had a whole closet-full, I remember; and I can tell to this day what balls I got them at. Molly Van Alstyne reminds me of what I was at that age; it 's wonderful how she notices. She was able to tell her mother exactly how the wedding-dress was cut, and we knew at once, from the fold in the back, that it must have come from Paquin."

Mrs. Peniston rose abruptly, and, advancing to the ormolu clock surmounted by a helmeted Minerva, which throned on the chimney-piece between two malachite vases, passed her lace handkerchief between the helmet and its visor.

"I knew it—the parlour-maid never dusts there!" she exclaimed, triumphantly displaying a minute spot on the handkerchief; then, reseating herself, she went on: "Molly thought Mrs. Dorset the best-dressed woman at the wedding. I 've no doubt her dress *did* cost more than any one else's, but I can't quite like the idea—a combination of sable and *point de Milan*. It seems she goes to a new man in Paris, who won't take an order till his client has spent a day with him at his villa at Neuilly. He says he must study his subject's home life—a most peculiar arrangement, I should say! But Mrs. Dorset told Molly about it herself: she said the villa was full of the most exquisite things and she was really sorry to leave. Molly said she never saw her looking better; she was in tremendous spirits, and said she had made a match between Evie Van Osburgh and Percy Gryce. She really seems to have a very good influence on young men. I hear she is interesting herself now in that silly Silverton boy, who has had his head turned by Carry Fisher, and has been gambling so dreadfully. Well, as I was saying, Evie is really engaged: Mrs. Dorset had her to stay with Percy Gryce, and managed it all, and Grace Van Osburgh is in the seventh heaven—she had almost despaired of marrying Evie."

Mrs. Peniston again paused, but this time her scrutiny addressed itself, not to the furniture, but to her niece.

"Cornelia Van Alstyne was so surprised: she had heard that you were to marry young Gryce. She saw the Wetheralls just after they had stopped with you at Bellomont, and Alice Wetherall was quite sure there was an engagement. She said that when Mr. Gryce left unexpectedly one morning, they all thought he had rushed to town for the ring."

Lily rose and moved toward the door.

"I believe I *am* tired: I think I will go to bed," she said; and Mrs. Peniston, suddenly distracted by the discovery that the easel sustaining the late Mr. Peniston's crayon-portrait was not exactly in line with the sofa in front of it, presented an absent-minded brow to her kiss.

In her own room Lily turned up the gas-jet and glanced toward the grate. It was as brilliantly polished as the one below, but here at least she could burn a few papers with less risk of incurring her aunt's disapproval. She made no immediate motion to do so, however, but dropping into a chair looked wearily about her. Her room was large and comfortably-furnished—it was the envy and admiration of poor Grace Stepney, who boarded; but, contrasted with the light tints and luxurious appointments of the guest-rooms where so many weeks of Lily's existence were spent, it seemed as dreary as a prison. The monumental wardrobe and bedstead of black walnut had migrated from Mr. Peniston's bedroom, and the magenta "flock" wall-paper, of a pattern dear to the early 'sixties, was hung with large steel engravings of an anecdotic character. Lily had tried to mitigate this charmless background by a few frivolous touches, in the shape of a lace-decked toilet table and a little painted desk surmounted by photographs; but the futility of the attempt struck her as she looked about the room. What a contrast to the subtle elegance of the setting she had pictured for herself—an apartment which should surpass the complicated luxury of her friends' surroundings by the whole extent of that artistic sensibility which made her feel herself their superior; in which every tint and line should combine to enhance her beauty and give distinction to her leisure! Once more the haunting sense of physical ugliness was intensified by her mental depression, so that each piece of the offending furniture seemed to thrust forth its most aggressive angle.

Her aunt's words had told her nothing new; but they had revived the vision of Bertha Dorset, smiling, flattered, victorious, holding her up to ridicule by insinuations intelligible to every member of their little group. The thought of the ridicule struck deeper than any other sensation: Lily knew every turn of the allusive jargon which could flay its victims without the shedding of blood. Her cheek burned at the recollection, and she rose and caught up the letters. She no longer meant to destroy them: that intention had been effaced by the quick corrosion of Mrs. Peniston's words.

Instead, she approached her desk, and lighting a taper, tied and sealed the packet; then she opened the wardrobe, drew out a despatch-box, and deposited the letters within it. As she did so, it struck her with a flash of irony that she was indebted to Gus Trenor for the means of buying them.

X

T HE AUTUMN dragged on monotonously. Miss Bart had received one or two notes from Judy Trenor, reproaching her for not returning to Bellomont; but she replied evasively, alleging the obligation to remain with her aunt. In truth, however, she was fast wearying of her solitary existence with Mrs. Peniston, and only the excitement of spending her newly-acquired money lightened the dulness of the days.

All her life Lily had seen money go out as quickly as it came in, and whatever theories she cultivated as to the prudence of setting aside a part of her gains, she had unhappily no saving vision of the risks of the opposite course. It was a keen satisfaction to feel that, for a few months at least, she would be independent of her friends' bounty, that she could show herself abroad without wondering whether some penetrating eye would detect in her dress the traces of Judy Trenor's refurbished splendour. The fact that the money freed her temporarily from all minor obligations obscured her sense of the greater one it represented, and having never before known what it was to command so large a sum, she lingered delectably over the amusement of spending it.

It was on one of these occasions that, leaving a shop where she had spent an hour of deliberation over a dressing-case of the most complicated elegance, she ran across Miss Farish, who had entered the same establishment with the modest object of having her watch repaired. Lily was feeling unusually virtuous. She had decided to defer the purchase of the dressing-case till she should receive the bill for her new opera-cloak, and the resolve made her feel much richer than when she had entered the shop. In this mood of self-approval she had a sympathetic eye for others, and she was struck by her friend's air of dejection.

Miss Farish, it appeared, had just left the committee-meeting of a struggling charity in which she was interested. The object of the association was to provide comfortable lodgings, with a reading-room and other modest distractions, where young women of the class employed in down town offices might find a home when out of work, or in need of rest, and the first year's financial report showed so deplorably small a balance that Miss Farish, who was convinced of the urgency of the work, felt proportionately discouraged by the small amount of interest it aroused. The other-regarding sentiments had not been cultivated in Lily, and she was often bored by the relation of her friend's philanthropic efforts, but today her quick dramatizing fancy seized on the contrast between her own situation and that represented by some of Gerty's "cases." These were young girls, like herself; some perhaps pretty, some not without a trace of her finer sensibilities. She pictured herself leading such a life as theirs—a life in which achievement seemed as squalid as failure—and the vision made her shudder sympathetically. The price of the dressing-case was still in her pocket; and drawing out her little gold purse she slipped a liberal fraction of the amount into Miss Farish's hand.

The satisfaction derived from this act was all that the most ardent moralist could have desired. Lily felt a new interest in herself as a person of charitable instincts: she had never before thought of doing good with the wealth she had so often dreamed of possessing, but now her horizon was enlarged by the vision of a prodigal philanthropy. Moreover, by some obscure process of logic, she felt that her momentary burst of generosity had justified all previous extravagances, and excused any in which she might subsequently indulge. Miss Farish's surprise and gratitude confirmed this feeling, and Lily parted from her with a sense of self-esteem which she naturally mistook for the fruits of altruism.

About this time she was farther cheered by an invitation to spend the Thanksgiving week at a camp in the Adirondacks. The invitation was one which, a year earlier, would have provoked a less ready response, for the party, though organized by Mrs. Fisher, was ostensibly given by a lady of obscure origin and indomitable social ambitions, whose acquaintance Lily had hitherto avoided. Now, however, she was disposed to coincide with Mrs. Fisher's view, that it did n't matter who gave the party, as long as things were well done; and doing things well (under competent direction) was Mrs. Wellington Bry's strong point. The lady (whose consort was known as "Welly" Bry on the Stock Exchange and in sporting circles)

had already sacrificed one husband, and sundry minor considerations, to her determination to get on; and, having obtained a hold on Carry Fisher, she was astute enough to
perceive the wisdom of committing herself entirely to that
lady's guidance. Everything, accordingly, was well done, for
there was no limit to Mrs. Fisher's prodigality when she was
not spending her own money, and as she remarked to her
pupil, a good cook was the best introduction to society. If the
company was not as select as the *cuisine*, the Welly Brys at
least had the satisfaction of figuring for the first time in the
society columns in company with one or two noticeable
names; and foremost among these was of course Miss Bart's.
The young lady was treated by her hosts with corresponding
deference; and she was in the mood when such attentions are
acceptable, whatever their source. Mrs. Bry's admiration was
a mirror in which Lily's self-complacency recovered its lost
outline. No insect hangs its nest on threads as frail as those
which will sustain the weight of human vanity; and the sense
of being of importance among the insignificant was enough
to restore to Miss Bart the gratifying consciousness of power.
If these people paid court to her it proved that she was
still conspicuous in the world to which they aspired; and
she was not above a certain enjoyment in dazzling them by
her fineness, in developing their puzzled perception of her
superiorities.

Perhaps, however, her enjoyment proceeded more than she
was aware from the physical stimulus of the excursion, the
challenge of crisp cold and hard exercise, the responsive thrill
of her body to the influences of the winter woods. She returned to town in a glow of rejuvenation, conscious of a
clearer colour in her cheeks, a fresh elasticity in her muscles.
The future seemed full of a vague promise, and all her apprehensions were swept out of sight on the buoyant current of
her mood.

A few days after her return to town she had the unpleasant
surprise of a visit from Mr. Rosedale. He came late, at the
confidential hour when the tea-table still lingers by the fire in
friendly expectancy; and his manner showed a readiness to
adapt itself to the intimacy of the occasion.

Lily, who had a vague sense of his being somehow connected with her lucky speculations, tried to give him the welcome he expected; but there was something in the quality of his geniality which chilled her own, and she was conscious of marking each step in their acquaintance by a fresh blunder.

Mr. Rosedale—making himself promptly at home in an adjoining easy-chair, and sipping his tea critically, with the comment: "You ought to go to my man for something really good"—appeared totally unconscious of the repugnance which kept her in frozen erectness behind the urn. It was perhaps her very manner of holding herself aloof that appealed to his collector's passion for the rare and unattainable. He gave, at any rate, no sign of resenting it and seemed prepared to supply in his own manner all the ease that was lacking in hers.

His object in calling was to ask her to go to the opera in his box on the opening night, and seeing her hesitate he said persuasively: "Mrs. Fisher is coming, and I've secured a tremendous admirer of yours, who'll never forgive me if you don't accept."

As Lily's silence left him with this allusion on his hands, he added with a confidential smile: "Gus Trenor has promised to come to town on purpose. I fancy he'd go a good deal farther for the pleasure of seeing you."

Miss Bart felt an inward motion of annoyance: it was distasteful enough to hear her name coupled with Trenor's, and on Rosedale's lips the allusion was peculiarly unpleasant.

"The Trenors are my best friends—I think we should all go a long way to see each other," she said, absorbing herself in the preparation of fresh tea.

Her visitor's smile grew increasingly intimate. "Well, I wasn't thinking of Mrs. Trenor at the moment—they say Gus doesn't always, you know." Then, dimly conscious that he had not struck the right note, he added, with a well-meant effort at diversion: "How's your luck been going in Wall Street, by the way? I hear Gus pulled off a nice little pile for you last month."

Lily put down the tea-caddy with an abrupt gesture. She felt that her hands were trembling, and clasped them on her knee to steady them; but her lip trembled too, and for a moment she was afraid the tremor might communicate itself to her voice. When she spoke, however, it was in a tone of perfect lightness.

"Ah, yes—I had a little bit of money to invest, and Mr. Trenor, who helps me about such matters, advised my putting it in stocks instead of a mortgage, as my aunt's agent wanted me to do; and as it happened, I made a lucky 'turn'—is that what you call it? For you make a great many yourself, I believe."

She was smiling back at him now, relaxing the tension of her attitude, and admitting him, by imperceptible gradations of glance and manner, a step farther toward intimacy. The protective instinct always nerved her to successful dissimulation, and it was not the first time she had used her beauty to divert attention from an inconvenient topic.

When Mr. Rosedale took leave, he carried with him, not only her acceptance of his invitation, but a general sense of having comported himself in a way calculated to advance his cause. He had always believed he had a light touch and a knowing way with women, and the prompt manner in which Miss Bart (as he would have phrased it) had "come into line," confirmed his confidence in his powers of handling the skittish sex. Her way of glossing over the transaction with Trenor he regarded at once as a tribute to his own acuteness, and a confirmation of his suspicions. The girl was evidently nervous, and Mr. Rosedale, if he saw no other means of advancing his acquaintance with her, was not above taking advantage of her nervousness.

He left Lily to a passion of disgust and fear. It seemed incredible that Gus Trenor should have spoken of her to Rosedale. With all his faults, Trenor had the safeguard of his traditions, and was the less likely to overstep them because they were so purely instinctive. But Lily recalled with a pang that there were convivial moments when, as Judy had confided to her, Gus "talked foolishly": in one of these, no doubt, the fatal word had slipped from him. As for Rosedale, she did not, after the first shock, greatly care what conclusions he had drawn. Though usually adroit enough where her own interests were concerned, she made the mistake, not uncommon to persons in whom the social habits are instinctive, of supposing that the inability to acquire them quickly implies a general dulness. Because a blue-bottle bangs irrationally against a window-pane, the drawing-room naturalist may forget that under less artificial conditions it is capable of measuring distances and drawing conclusions with all the accuracy needful to its welfare; and the fact that Mr. Rosedale's drawing-room manner lacked perspective made Lily class him with Trenor and the other dull men she knew, and assume that a little flattery, and the occasional acceptance of his hospitality, would suffice to render him innocuous. However, there could be no doubt of the expediency of showing herself in his box on the opening night of the opera; and after all, since Judy Trenor had promised to take him up that winter, it was as well to reap the advantage of being first in the field.

For a day or two after Rosedale's visit, Lily's thoughts were dogged by the consciousness of Trenor's shadowy claim, and she wished she had a clearer notion of the exact nature of the transaction which seemed to have put her in his power; but her mind shrank from any unusual application, and she was always helplessly puzzled by figures. Moreover she had not seen Trenor since the day of the Van Osburgh wedding, and in his continued absence the trace of Rosedale's words was soon effaced by other impressions.

When the opening night of the opera came, her apprehensions had so completely vanished that the sight of Trenor's ruddy countenance in the back of Mr. Rosedale's box filled her with a sense of pleasant reassurance. Lily had not quite reconciled herself to the necessity of appearing as Rosedale's guest on so conspicuous an occasion, and it was a relief to find herself supported by any one of her own set—for Mrs. Fisher's social habits were too promiscuous for her presence to justify Miss Bart's.

To Lily, always inspirited by the prospect of showing her beauty in public, and conscious tonight of all the added enhancements of dress, the insistency of Trenor's gaze merged itself in the general stream of admiring looks of which she felt herself the centre. Ah, it was good to be young, to be radiant, to glow with the sense of slenderness, strength and elasticity, of well-poised lines and happy tints, to feel one's self lifted to a height apart by that incommunicable grace which is the bodily counterpart of genius!

All means seemed justifiable to attain such an end, or rather, by a happy shifting of lights with which practice had familiarized Miss Bart, the cause shrank to a pin-point in the general brightness of the effect. But brilliant young ladies, a little blinded by their own effulgence, are apt to forget that the modest satellite drowned in their light is still performing its own revolutions and generating heat at its own rate. If Lily's poetic enjoyment of the moment was undisturbed by the base thought that her gown and opera cloak had been indirectly paid for by Gus Trenor, the latter had not sufficient poetry in his composition to lose sight of these prosaic facts. He knew only that he had never seen Lily look smarter in her life, that there was n't a woman in the house who showed off good clothes as she did, and that hitherto he, to whom she owed the opportunity of making this display, had reaped no return beyond that of gazing at her in company with several hundred other pairs of eyes.

It came to Lily therefore as a disagreeable surprise when, in the back of the box, where they found themselves alone between two acts, Trenor said, without preamble, and in a tone of sulky authority: "Look here, Lily, how is a fellow ever to see anything of you? I 'm in town three or four days in the week, and you know a line to the club will always find me, but you don't seem to remember my existence nowadays unless you want to get a tip out of me."

The fact that the remark was in distinctly bad taste did not make it any easier to answer, for Lily was vividly aware that it was not the moment for that drawing up of her slim figure and surprised lifting of the brows by which she usually quelled incipient signs of familiarity.

"I 'm very much flattered by your wanting to see me," she returned, essaying lightness instead, "but, unless you have mislaid my address, it would have been easy to find me any afternoon at my aunt's—in fact, I rather expected you to look me up there."

If she hoped to mollify him by this last concession the attempt was a failure, for he only replied, with the familiar lowering of the brows that made him look his dullest when he was angry: "Hang going to your aunt's, and wasting the afternoon listening to a lot of other chaps talking to you! You know I'm not the kind to sit in a crowd and jaw—I'd always rather clear out when that sort of circus is going on. But why can't we go off somewhere on a little lark together—a nice quiet little expedition like that drive at Bellomont, the day you met me at the station?"

He leaned unpleasantly close in order to convey this suggestion, and she fancied she caught a significant aroma which explained the dark flush on his face and the glistening dampness of his forehead.

The idea that any rash answer might provoke an unpleasant outburst tempered her disgust with caution, and she answered with a laugh: "I don't see how one can very well take country drives in town, but I am not always surrounded by an admiring throng, and if you will let me know what afternoon you are coming I will arrange things so that we can have a nice quiet talk."

"Hang talking! That's what you always say," returned Trenor, whose expletives lacked variety. "You put me off with that at the Van Osburgh wedding—but the plain English of it is that, now you've got what you wanted out of me, you'd rather have any other fellow about."

His voice had risen sharply with the last words, and Lily flushed with annoyance, but she kept command of the situation and laid a persuasive hand on his arm.

"Don't be foolish, Gus; I can't let you talk to me in that ridiculous way. If you really want to see me, why should n't we take a walk in the Park some afternoon? I agree with you that it's amusing to be rustic in town, and if you like I'll meet you there, and we'll go and feed the squirrels, and you shall take me out on the lake in the steam-gondola."

She smiled as she spoke, letting her eyes rest on his in a way that took the edge from her banter and made him suddenly malleable to her will.

"All right, then: that's a go. Will you come tomorrow? Tomorrow at three o'clock, at the end of the Mall? I'll be there sharp, remember; you won't go back on me, Lily?"

But to Miss Bart's relief the repetition of her promise was cut short by the opening of the box door to admit George Dorset.

Trenor sulkily yielded his place, and Lily turned a brilliant smile on the newcomer. She had not talked with Dorset since their visit at Bellomont, but something in his look and manner told her that he recalled the friendly footing on which they had last met. He was not a man to whom the expression of admiration came easily: his long sallow face and distrustful eyes seemed always barricaded against the expansive emotions. But, where her own influence was concerned, Lily's intuitions sent out thread-like feelers, and as she made room for him on the narrow sofa she was sure he found a dumb pleasure in being near her. Few women took the trouble to make themselves agreeable to Dorset, and Lily had been kind to him at Bellomont, and was now smiling on him with a divine renewal of kindness.

"Well, here we are, in for another six months of caterwauling," he began complainingly. "Not a shade of difference between this year and last, except that the women have got new clothes and the singers have n't got new voices. My wife 's musical, you know—puts me through a course of this every winter. It is n't so bad on Italian nights—then she comes late, and there 's time to digest. But when they give Wagner we have to rush dinner, and I pay up for it. And the draughts are damnable—asphyxia in front and pleurisy in the back. There 's Trenor leaving the box without drawing the curtain! With a hide like that draughts don't make any difference. Did you ever watch Trenor eat? If you did, you 'd wonder why he 's alive; I suppose he 's leather inside too.—But I came to say that my wife wants you to come down to our place next Sunday. Do for heaven's sake say yes. She 's got a lot of bores coming—intellectual ones, I mean; that 's her new line, you know, and I 'm not sure it ain't worse than the music. Some of 'em have long hair, and they start an argument with the soup, and don't notice when things are handed to them. The consequence is the dinner gets cold, and I have dyspepsia. That silly ass Silverton brings them to the house—he writes poetry, you know, and Bertha and he are getting tremendously thick. She could write better than any of 'em if she chose, and I don't blame her for wanting clever fellows about; all I say is: 'Don't let me see 'em eat!' "

The gist of this strange communication gave Lily a distinct thrill of pleasure. Under ordinary circumstances, there would have been nothing surprising in an invitation from Bertha Dorset; but since the Bellomont episode an unavowed hostility had kept the two women apart. Now, with a start of inner wonder, Lily felt that her thirst for retaliation had died out. *If you would forgive your enemy*, says the Malay proverb, *first inflict a hurt on him*; and Lily was experiencing the truth of the apothegm. If she had destroyed Mrs. Dorset's letters, she might have continued to hate her; but the fact that they remained in her possession had fed her resentment to satiety.

She uttered a smiling acceptance, hailing in the renewal of the tie an escape from Trenor's importunities.

XI

MEANWHILE the holidays had gone by and the season was beginning. Fifth Avenue had become a nightly torrent of carriages surging upward to the fashionable quarters about the Park, where illuminated windows and outspread awnings betokened the usual routine of hospitality. Other tributary currents crossed the main stream, bearing their freight to the theatres, restaurants or opera; and Mrs. Peniston, from the secluded watch-tower of her upper window, could tell to a nicety just when the chronic volume of sound was increased by the sudden influx setting toward a Van Osburgh ball, or when the multiplication of wheels meant merely that the opera was over, or that there was a big supper at Sherry's.

Mrs. Peniston followed the rise and culmination of the season as keenly as the most active sharer in its gaieties; and, as a looker-on, she enjoyed opportunities of comparison and generalization such as those who take part must proverbially forego. No one could have kept a more accurate record of social fluctuations, or have put a more unerring finger on the distinguishing features of each season: its dulness, its extravagance, its lack of balls or excess of divorces. She had a special memory for the vicissitudes of the "new people" who rose to the surface with each recurring tide, and were either submerged beneath its rush or landed triumphantly beyond the reach of envious breakers; and she was apt to display a remarkable retrospective insight into their ultimate fate, so that, when they had fulfilled their destiny, she was almost always able to say to Grace Stepney—the recipient of her prophecies—that she had known exactly what would happen.

This particular season Mrs. Peniston would have characterized as that in which everybody "felt poor" except the Welly Brys and Mr. Simon Rosedale. It had been a bad autumn in Wall Street, where prices fell in accordance with that peculiar law which proves railway stocks and bales of cotton to be more sensitive to the allotment of executive power than many estimable citizens trained to all the advantages of self-government. Even fortunes supposed to be independent of the market either betrayed a secret dependence on it, or suffered from a sympathetic affection: fashion sulked in its country-houses, or came to town incognito, general entertainments were discountenanced, and informality and short dinners became the fashion.

But society, amused for a while at playing Cinderella, soon wearied of the hearthside rôle, and welcomed the Fairy God-mother in the shape of any magician powerful enough to turn the shrunken pumpkin back again into the golden coach. The mere fact of growing richer at a time when most people's investments are shrinking, is calculated to attract envious attention; and according to Wall Street rumours, Welly Bry and Rosedale had found the secret of performing this miracle.

Rosedale, in particular, was said to have doubled his fortune, and there was talk of his buying the newly-finished house of one of the victims of the crash, who, in the space of twelve short months, had made the same number of millions, built a house in Fifth Avenue, filled a picture-gallery with old masters, entertained all New York in it, and been smuggled out of the country between a trained nurse and a doctor, while his creditors mounted guard over the old masters, and his guests explained to each other that they had dined with him only because they wanted to see the pictures. Mr. Rosedale meant to have a less meteoric career. He knew he should have to go slowly, and the instincts of his race fitted him to suffer rebuffs and put up with delays. But he was prompt to perceive that the general dulness of the season afforded him an unusual opportunity to shine, and he set about with patient industry to form a background for his growing glory. Mrs. Fisher was of immense service to him at this period. She had set off so many newcomers on the social stage that she was like one of those pieces of stock scenery which tell the experienced spectator exactly what is going to take place. But Mr. Rosedale wanted, in the long run, a more individual environment. He was sensitive to shades of difference which Miss Bart would never have credited him with perceiving, because he had no corresponding variations of manner; and it was becoming more and more clear to him that Miss Bart herself possessed precisely the complementary qualities needed to round off his social personality.

Such details did not fall within the range of Mrs. Peniston's vision. Like many minds of panoramic sweep, hers was apt to overlook the *minutiæ* of the foreground, and she was much more likely to know where Carry Fisher had found the Welly Brys' *chef* for them, than what was happening to her own niece. She was not, however, without purveyors of information ready to supplement her deficiencies. Grace Stepney's mind was like a kind of moral fly-paper, to which the buzzing items of gossip were drawn by a fatal attraction, and where they hung fast in the toils of an inexorable memory. Lily would have been surprised to know how many trivial facts concerning herself were lodged in Miss Stepney's head. She was quite aware that she was of interest to dingy people, but she assumed that there is only one form of dinginess, and that admiration for brilliancy is the natural expression of its inferior state. She knew that Gerty Farish admired her blindly, and therefore supposed that she inspired the same sentiments in Grace Stepney, whom she classified as a Gerty Farish without the saving traits of youth and enthusiasm.

In reality, the two differed from each other as much as they differed from the object of their mutual contemplation. Miss Farish's heart was a fountain of tender illusions, Miss Stepney's a precise register of facts as manifested in their relation to herself. She had sensibilities which, to Lily, would have seemed comic in a person with a freckled nose and red eye-lids, who lived in a boarding-house and admired Mrs. Peniston's drawing-room; but poor Grace's limitations gave them a more concentrated inner life, as poor soil starves certain plants into intenser efflorescence. She had in truth no abstract propensity to malice: she did not dislike Lily because the latter was brilliant and predominant, but because she thought that Lily disliked her. It is less mortifying to believe one's self unpopular than insignificant, and vanity prefers to assume that indifference is a latent form of unfriendliness. Even such scant civilities as Lily accorded to Mr. Rosedale would have made Miss Stepney her friend for life; but how could she foresee that such a friend was worth cultivating? How, moreover, can a young woman who has never been ignored measure the pang which this injury inflicts? And, lastly, how could Lily, accustomed to choose between a

pressure of engagements, guess that she had mortally offended Miss Stepney by causing her to be excluded from one
of Mrs. Peniston's infrequent dinner-parties?

Mrs. Peniston disliked giving dinners, but she had a high
sense of family obligation, and on the Jack Stepneys' return
from their honeymoon she felt it incumbent upon her to light
the drawing-room lamps and extract her best silver from the
Safe Deposit vaults. Mrs. Peniston's rare entertainments were
preceded by days of heart-rending vacillation as to every detail
of the feast, from the seating of the guests to the pattern of
the table-cloth, and in the course of one of these preliminary
discussions she had imprudently suggested to her cousin
Grace that, as the dinner was a family affair, she might be
included in it. For a week the prospect had lighted up Miss
Stepney's colourless existence; then she had been given to
understand that it would be more convenient to have her
another day. Miss Stepney knew exactly what had happened.
Lily, to whom family reunions were occasions of unalloyed
dulness, had persuaded her aunt that a dinner of "smart" people would be much more to the taste of the young couple,
and Mrs. Peniston, who leaned helplessly on her niece in social matters, had been prevailed upon to pronounce Grace's
exile. After all, Grace could come any other day; why should
she mind being put off?

It was precisely because Miss Stepney could come any other
day—and because she knew her relations were in the secret
of her unoccupied evenings—that this incident loomed
gigantically on her horizon. She was aware that she had Lily
to thank for it; and dull resentment was turned to active
animosity.

Mrs. Peniston, on whom she had looked in a day or two
after the dinner, laid down her crochet-work and turned
abruptly from her oblique survey of Fifth Avenue.

"Gus Trenor?—Lily and Gus Trenor?" she said, growing
so suddenly pale that her visitor was almost alarmed.

"Oh, cousin Julia . . . of course I don't mean . . ."

"I don't know what you *do* mean," said Mrs. Peniston, with
a frightened quiver in her small fretful voice. "Such things
were never heard of in my day. And my own niece! I 'm not
sure I understand you. Do people say he 's in love with her?"

Mrs. Peniston's horror was genuine. Though she boasted an unequalled familiarity with the secret chronicles of society, she had the innocence of the school-girl who regards wickedness as a part of "history," and to whom it never occurs that the scandals she reads of in lesson-hours may be repeating themselves in the next street. Mrs. Peniston had kept her imagination shrouded, like the drawing-room furniture. She knew, of course, that society was "very much changed," and that many women her mother would have thought "peculiar" were now in a position to be critical about their visiting-lists; she had discussed the perils of divorce with her rector, and had felt thankful at times that Lily was still unmarried; but the idea that any scandal could attach to a young girl's name, above all that it could be lightly coupled with that of a married man, was so new to her that she was as much aghast as if she had been accused of leaving her carpets down all summer, or of violating any of the other cardinal laws of housekeeping.

Miss Stepney, when her first fright had subsided, began to feel the superiority that greater breadth of mind confers. It was really pitiable to be as ignorant of the world as Mrs. Peniston!

She smiled at the latter's question. "People always say unpleasant things—and certainly they're a great deal together. A friend of mine met them the other afternoon in the Park—quite late, after the lamps were lit. It's a pity Lily makes herself so conspicuous."

"*Conspicuous!*" gasped Mrs. Peniston. She bent forward, lowering her voice to mitigate the horror. "What sort of things do they say? That he means to get a divorce and marry her?"

Grace Stepney laughed outright. "Dear me, no! He would hardly do that. It—it's a flirtation—nothing more."

"A flirtation? Between my niece and a married man? Do you mean to tell me that, with Lily's looks and advantages, she could find no better use for her time than to waste it on a fat stupid man almost old enough to be her father?" This argument had such a convincing ring that it gave Mrs. Peniston sufficient reassurance to pick up her work, while she waited for Grace Stepney to rally her scattered forces.

But Miss Stepney was on the spot in an instant. "That's the worst of it—people say she is n't wasting her time! Every one knows, as you say, that Lily is too handsome and—and charming—to devote herself to a man like Gus Trenor unless——"

"Unless?" echoed Mrs. Peniston.

Her visitor drew breath nervously. It was agreeable to shock Mrs. Peniston, but not to shock her to the verge of anger. Miss Stepney was not sufficiently familiar with the classic drama to have recalled in advance how bearers of bad tidings are proverbially received, but she now had a rapid vision of forfeited dinners and a reduced wardrobe as the possible consequence of her disinterestedness. To the honour of her sex, however, hatred of Lily prevailed over more personal considerations. Mrs. Peniston had chosen the wrong moment to boast of her niece's charms.

"Unless," said Grace, leaning forward to speak with low-toned emphasis, "unless there are material advantages to be gained by making herself agreeable to him."

She felt that the moment was tremendous, and remembered suddenly that Mrs. Peniston's black brocade, with the cut jet fringe, would have been hers at the end of the season.

Mrs. Peniston put down her work again. Another aspect of the same idea had presented itself to her, and she felt that it was beneath her dignity to have her nerves racked by a dependent relative who wore her old clothes.

"If you take pleasure in annoying me by mysterious insinuations," she said coldly, "you might at least have chosen a more suitable time than just as I am recovering from the strain of giving a large dinner."

The mention of the dinner dispelled Miss Stepney's last scruples. "I don't know why I should be accused of taking pleasure in telling you about Lily. I was sure I should n't get any thanks for it," she returned with a flare of temper. "But I have some family feeling left, and as you are the only person who has any authority over Lily, I thought you ought to know what is being said of her."

"Well," said Mrs. Peniston, " what I complain of is that you have n't told me yet what *is* being said."

"I did n't suppose I should have to put it so plainly. People say that Gus Trenor pays her bills."

"Pays her bills—her bills?" Mrs. Peniston broke into a laugh. "I can't imagine where you can have picked up such rubbish. Lily has her own income—and I provide for her very handsomely——"

"Oh, we all know that," interposed Miss Stepney drily. "But Lily wears a great many smart gowns——"

"I like her to be well-dressed—it 's only suitable!"

"Certainly; but then there are her gambling debts besides."

Miss Stepney, in the beginning, had not meant to bring up this point; but Mrs. Peniston had only her own incredulity to blame. She was like the stiff-necked unbelievers of Scripture, who must be annihilated to be convinced.

"Gambling debts? Lily?" Mrs. Peniston's voice shook with anger and bewilderment. She wondered whether Grace Stepney had gone out of her mind. "What do you mean by her gambling debts?"

"Simply that if one plays bridge for money in Lily's set one is liable to lose a great deal—and I don't suppose Lily always wins."

"Who told you that my niece played cards for money?"

"Mercy, cousin Julia, don't look at me as if I were trying to turn you against Lily! Everybody knows she is crazy about bridge. Mrs. Gryce told me herself that it was her gambling that frightened Percy Gryce—it seems he was really taken with her at first. But, of course, among Lily's friends it 's quite the custom for girls to play for money. In fact, people are inclined to excuse her on that account——"

"To excuse her for what?"

"For being hard up—and accepting attentions from men like Gus Trenor—and George Dorset——"

Mrs. Peniston gave another cry. "George Dorset? Is there any one else? I should like to know the worst, if you please."

"Don't put it in that way, cousin Julia. Lately Lily has been a good deal with the Dorsets, and he seems to admire her—but of course that 's only natural. And I 'm sure there is no truth in the horrid things people say; but she *has* been spending a great deal of money this winter. Evie Van

Osburgh was at Céleste's ordering her trousseau the other day—yes, the marriage takes place next month—and she told me that Céleste showed her the most exquisite things she was just sending home to Lily. And people say that Judy Trenor has quarrelled with her on account of Gus; but I'm sure I'm sorry I spoke, though I only meant it as a kindness."

Mrs. Peniston's genuine incredulity enabled her to dismiss Miss Stepney with a disdain which boded ill for that lady's prospect of succeeding to the black brocade; but minds impenetrable to reason have generally some crack through which suspicion filters, and her visitor's insinuations did not glide off as easily as she had expected. Mrs. Peniston disliked scenes, and her determination to avoid them had always led her to hold herself aloof from the details of Lily's life. In her youth, girls had not been supposed to require close supervision. They were generally assumed to be taken up with the legitimate business of courtship and marriage, and interference in such affairs on the part of their natural guardians was considered as unwarrantable as a spectator's suddenly joining in a game. There had of course been "fast" girls even in Mrs. Peniston's early experience; but their fastness, at worst, was understood to be a mere excess of animal spirits, against which there could be no graver charge than that of being "unladylike." The modern fastness appeared synonymous with immorality, and the mere idea of immorality was as offensive to Mrs. Peniston as a smell of cooking in the drawing-room: it was one of the conceptions her mind refused to admit.

She had no immediate intention of repeating to Lily what she had heard, or even of trying to ascertain its truth by means of discreet interrogation. To do so might be to provoke a scene; and a scene, in the shaken state of Mrs. Peniston's nerves, with the effects of her dinner not worn off, and her mind still tremulous with new impressions, was a risk she deemed it her duty to avoid. But there remained in her thoughts a settled deposit of resentment against her niece, all the denser because it was not to be cleared by explanation or discussion. It was horrible of a young girl to let herself be talked about; however unfounded the charges against her, she must be to blame for their having been made. Mrs. Peniston felt as if there had been a contagious illness in the house, and she was doomed to sit shivering among her contaminated furniture.

XII

M ISS BART had in fact been treading a devious way, and none of her critics could have been more alive to the fact than herself; but she had a fatalistic sense of being drawn from one wrong turning to another, without ever perceiving the right road till it was too late to take it.

Lily, who considered herself above narrow prejudices, had not imagined that the fact of letting Gus Trenor make a little money for her would ever disturb her self-complacency. And the fact in itself still seemed harmless enough; only it was a fertile source of harmful complications. As she exhausted the amusement of spending the money these complications became more pressing, and Lily, whose mind could be severely logical in tracing the causes of her ill-luck to others, justified herself by the thought that she owed all her troubles to the enmity of Bertha Dorset. This enmity, however, had apparently expired in a renewal of friendliness between the two women. Lily's visit to the Dorsets had resulted, for both, in the discovery that they could be of use to each other; and the civilized instinct finds a subtler pleasure in making use of its antagonist than in confounding him. Mrs. Dorset was, in fact, engaged in a new sentimental experiment, of which Mrs. Fisher's late property, Ned Silverton, was the rosy victim; and at such moments, as Judy Trenor had once remarked, she felt a peculiar need of distracting her husband's attention. Dorset was as difficult to amuse as a savage; but even his self-engrossment was not proof against Lily's arts, or rather these were especially adapted to soothe an uneasy egoism. Her experience with Percy Gryce stood her in good stead in ministering to Dorset's humours, and if the incentive to please was less urgent, the difficulties of her situation were teaching her to make much of minor opportunities.

Intimacy with the Dorsets was not likely to lessen such difficulties on the material side. Mrs. Dorset had none of Judy Trenor's lavish impulses, and Dorset's admiration was not likely to express itself in financial "tips," even had Lily cared to renew her experiences in that line. What she required, for the moment, of the Dorsets' friendship, was simply its social sanction. She knew that people were beginning to talk of her; but this fact did not alarm her as it had alarmed Mrs. Peniston. In her set such gossip was not unusual, and a handsome girl who flirted with a married man was merely assumed to be pressing to the limit of her opportunities. It was Trenor himself who frightened her. Their walk in the Park had not been a success. Trenor had married young, and since his marriage his intercourse with women had not taken the form of the sentimental small-talk which doubles upon itself like the paths in a maze. He was first puzzled and then irritated to find himself always led back to the same starting-point, and Lily felt that she was gradually losing control of the situation. Trenor was in truth in an unmanageable mood. In spite of his understanding with Rosedale he had been somewhat heavily "touched" by the fall in stocks; his household expenses weighed on him, and he seemed to be meeting, on all sides, a sullen opposition to his wishes, instead of the easy good luck he had hitherto encountered.

Mrs. Trenor was still at Bellomont, keeping the town-house open, and descending on it now and then for a taste of the world, but preferring the recurrent excitement of week-end parties to the restrictions of a dull season. Since the holidays she had not urged Lily to return to Bellomont, and the first time they met in town Lily fancied there was a shade of coldness in her manner. Was it merely the expression of her displeasure at Miss Bart's neglect, or had disquieting rumours reached her? The latter contingency seemed improbable, yet Lily was not without a sense of uneasiness. If her roaming sympathies had struck root anywhere, it was in her friendship with Judy Trenor. She believed in the sincerity of her friend's affection, though it sometimes showed itself in self-interested ways, and she shrank with peculiar reluctance from any risk of estranging it. But, aside from this, she was keenly conscious of the way in which such an estrangement would react on herself. The fact that Gus Trenor was Judy's husband was at times Lily's strongest reason for disliking him, and for resenting the obligation under which he had placed her.

To set her doubts at rest, Miss Bart, soon after the New Year, "proposed" herself for a week-end at Bellomont. She had learned in advance that the presence of a large party would protect her from too great assiduity on Trenor's part, and his wife's telegraphic "come by all means" seemed to assure her of her usual welcome.

Judy received her amicably. The cares of a large party always prevailed over personal feelings, and Lily saw no change in her hostess's manner. Nevertheless, she was soon aware that the experiment of coming to Bellomont was destined not to be successful. The party was made up of what Mrs. Trenor called "poky people"—her generic name for persons who did not play bridge—and, it being her habit to group all such obstructionists in one class, she usually invited them together, regardless of their other characteristics. The result was apt to be an irreducible combination of persons having no other quality in common than their abstinence from bridge, and the antagonisms developed in a group lacking the one taste which might have amalgamated them, were in this case aggravated by bad weather, and by the ill-concealed boredom of their host and hostess. In such emergencies, Judy would usually have turned to Lily to fuse the discordant elements; and Miss Bart, assuming that such a service was expected of her, threw herself into it with her accustomed zeal. But at the outset she perceived a subtle resistance to her efforts. If Mrs. Trenor's manner toward her was unchanged, there was certainly a faint coldness in that of the other ladies. An occasional caustic allusion to "your friends the Wellington Brys," or to "the little Jew who has bought the Greiner house—some one told us you knew him, Miss Bart,"—showed Lily that she was in disfavour with that portion of society which, while contributing least to its amusement, has assumed the right to decide what forms that amusement shall take. The indication was a slight one, and a year ago Lily would have smiled at it, trusting to the charm of her personality to dispel any prejudice against her. But now she had grown more sensitive to criticism and less confident in her power of disarming it. She knew, moreover, that if the ladies at Bellomont permitted themselves to criticize her friends openly, it was a proof that they were not afraid of subjecting her to the same treatment behind her back. The nervous dread lest anything in Trenor's manner should seem to justify their disapproval made her seek every pretext for avoiding him, and she left Bellomont conscious of having failed in every purpose which had taken her there.

In town she returned to preoccupations which, for the moment, had the happy effect of banishing troublesome thoughts. The Welly Brys, after much debate, and anxious counsel with their newly acquired friends, had decided on the bold move of giving a general entertainment. To attack society collectively, when one's means of approach are limited to a few acquaintances, is like advancing into a strange country with an insufficient number of scouts; but such rash tactics have sometimes led to brilliant victories, and the Brys had determined to put their fate to the touch. Mrs. Fisher, to whom they had entrusted the conduct of the affair, had decided that *tableaux vivants* and expensive music were the two baits most likely to attract the desired prey, and after prolonged negotiations, and the kind of wire-pulling in which she was known to excel, she had induced a dozen fashionable women to exhibit themselves in a series of pictures which, by a farther miracle of persuasion, the distinguished portrait painter, Paul Morpeth, had been prevailed upon to organize.

Lily was in her element on such occasions. Under Morpeth's guidance her vivid plastic sense, hitherto nurtured on no higher food than dress-making and upholstery, found eager expression in the disposal of draperies, the study of attitudes, the shifting of lights and shadows. Her dramatic instinct was roused by the choice of subjects, and the gorgeous reproductions of historic dress stirred an imagination which only visual impressions could reach. But keenest of all was the exhilaration of displaying her own beauty under a new aspect: of showing that her loveliness was no mere fixed quality, but an element shaping all emotions to fresh forms of grace.

Mrs. Fisher's measures had been well-taken, and society, surprised in a dull moment, succumbed to the temptation of Mrs. Bry's hospitality. The protesting minority were forgotten in the throng which abjured and came; and the audience was almost as brilliant as the show.

Lawrence Selden was among those who had yielded to the proffered inducements. If he did not often act on the accepted social axiom that a man may go where he pleases, it was because he had long since learned that his pleasures were mainly to be found in a small group of the like-minded. But he enjoyed spectacular effects, and was not insensible to the part money plays in their production: all he asked was that the very rich should live up to their calling as stage-managers, and not spend their money in a dull way. This the Brys could certainly not be charged with doing. Their recently built house, whatever it might lack as a frame for domesticity, was almost as well-designed for the display of a festal assemblage as one of those airy pleasure-halls which the Italian architects improvised to set off the hospitality of princes. The air of improvisation was in fact strikingly present: so recent, so rapidly-evoked was the whole *mise-en-scène* that one had to touch the marble columns to learn they were not of cardboard, to seat one's self in one of the damask-and-gold arm-chairs to be sure it was not painted against the wall.

Selden, who had put one of these seats to the test, found himself, from an angle of the ball-room, surveying the scene with frank enjoyment. The company, in obedience to the decorative instinct which calls for fine clothes in fine surroundings, had dressed rather with an eye to Mrs. Bry's background than to herself. The seated throng, filling the immense room without undue crowding, presented a surface of rich tissues and jewelled shoulders in harmony with the festooned and gilded walls, and the flushed splendours of the Venetian ceiling. At the farther end of the room a stage had been constructed behind a proscenium arch curtained with folds of old damask; but in the pause before the parting of the folds there was little thought of what they might reveal, for every woman who had accepted Mrs. Bry's invitation was engaged in trying to find out how many of her friends had done the same.

Gerty Farish, seated next to Selden, was lost in that indiscriminate and uncritical enjoyment so irritating to Miss Bart's finer perceptions. It may be that Selden's nearness had something to do with the quality of his cousin's pleasure; but Miss Farish was so little accustomed to refer her enjoyment of such scenes to her own share in them, that she was merely conscious of a deeper sense of contentment.

"Was n't it dear of Lily to get me an invitation? Of course

it would never have occurred to Carry Fisher to put me on the list, and I should have been so sorry to miss seeing it all—and especially Lily herself. Some one told me the ceiling was by Veronese—you would know, of course, Lawrence. I suppose it 's very beautiful, but his women are so dreadfully fat. Goddesses? Well, I can only say that if they 'd been mortals and had to wear corsets, it would have been better for them. I think our women are much handsomer. And this room is wonderfully becoming—every one looks so well! Did you ever see such jewels? Do look at Mrs. George Dorset's pearls—I suppose the smallest of them would pay the rent of our Girls' Club for a year. Not that I ought to complain about the club; every one has been so wonderfully kind. Did I tell you that Lily had given us three hundred dollars? Was n't it splendid of her? And then she collected a lot of money from her friends—Mrs. Bry gave us five hundred, and Mr. Rosedale a thousand. I wish Lily were not so nice to Mr. Rosedale, but she says it 's no use being rude to him, because he does n't see the difference. She really can't bear to hurt people's feelings—it makes me so angry when I hear her called cold and conceited! The girls at the club don't call her that. Do you know she has been there with me twice?—yes, Lily! And you should have seen their eyes! One of them said it was as good as a day in the country just to look at her. And she sat there, and laughed and talked with them—not a bit as if she were being *charitable*, you know, but as if she liked it as much as they did. They 've been asking ever since when she 's coming back; and she 's promised me——oh!"

Miss Farish's confidences were cut short by the parting of the curtain on the first *tableau*—a group of nymphs dancing across flower-strewn sward in the rhythmic postures of Botticelli's Spring. *Tableaux vivants* depend for their effect not only on the happy disposal of lights and the delusive interposition of layers of gauze, but on a corresponding adjustment of the mental vision. To unfurnished minds they remain, in spite of every enhancement of art, only a superior kind of wax-works; but to the responsive fancy they may give magic glimpses of the boundary world between fact and imagination. Selden's mind was of this order: he could yield to vision-making influences as completely as a child to the spell of a fairy-tale. Mrs. Bry's *tableaux* wanted none of the qualities which go to the producing of such illusions, and under Morpeth's organizing hand the pictures succeeded each other with the rhythmic march of some splendid frieze, in which the fugitive curves of living flesh and the wandering light of young eyes have been subdued to plastic harmony without losing the charm of life.

The scenes were taken from old pictures, and the participators had been cleverly fitted with characters suited to their types. No one, for instance, could have made a more typical Goya than Carry Fisher, with her short dark-skinned face, the exaggerated glow of her eyes, the provocation of her frankly-painted smile. A brilliant Miss Smedden from Brooklyn showed to perfection the sumptuous curves of Titian's Daughter, lifting her gold salver laden with grapes above the harmonizing gold of rippled hair and rich brocade, and a young Mrs. Van Alstyne, who showed the frailer Dutch type, with high blue-veined forehead and pale eyes and lashes, made a characteristic Vandyck, in black satin, against a curtained archway. Then there were Kauffmann nymphs garlanding the altar of Love; a Veronese supper, all sheeny textures, pearl-woven heads and marble architecture; and a Watteau group of lute-playing comedians, lounging by a fountain in a sunlit glade.

Each evanescent picture touched the vision-building faculty in Selden, leading him so far down the vistas of fancy that even Gerty Farish's running commentary—"Oh, how lovely Lulu Melson looks!" or: "That must be Kate Corby, to the right there, in purple"—did not break the spell of the illusion. Indeed, so skilfully had the personality of the actors been subdued to the scenes they figured in that even the least imaginative of the audience must have felt a thrill of contrast when the curtain suddenly parted on a picture which was simply and undisguisedly the portrait of Miss Bart.

Here there could be no mistaking the predominance of personality—the unanimous "Oh!" of the spectators was a tribute, not to the brush-work of Reynolds's "Mrs. Lloyd" but to the flesh and blood loveliness of Lily Bart. She had shown her artistic intelligence in selecting a type so like her own that she could embody the person represented without ceasing to be herself. It was as though she had stepped, not out of, but into, Reynolds's canvas, banishing the phantom of his dead beauty by the beams of her living grace. The impulse to show herself in a splendid setting—she had thought for a moment of representing Tiepolo's Cleopatra—had yielded to the truer instinct of trusting to her unassisted beauty, and she had purposely chosen a picture without distracting accessories of dress or surroundings. Her pale draperies, and the background of foliage against which she stood, served only to relieve the long dryad-like curves that swept upward from her poised foot to her lifted arm. The noble buoyancy of her attitude, its suggestion of soaring grace, revealed the touch of poetry in her beauty that Selden always felt in her presence, yet lost the sense of when he was not with her. Its expression was now so vivid that for the first time he seemed to see before him the real Lily Bart, divested of the trivialities of her little world, and catching for a moment a note of that eternal harmony of which her beauty was a part.

"Deuced bold thing to show herself in that get-up; but, gad, there is n't a break in the lines anywhere, and I suppose she wanted us to know it!"

These words, uttered by that experienced connoisseur, Mr. Ned Van Alstyne, whose scented white moustache had brushed Selden's shoulder whenever the parting of the curtains presented any exceptional opportunity for the study of the female outline, affected their hearer in an unexpected way. It was not the first time that Selden had heard Lily's beauty lightly remarked on, and hitherto the tone of the comments had imperceptibly coloured his view of her. But now it woke only a motion of indignant contempt. This was the world she lived in, these were the standards by which she was fated to be measured! Does one go to Caliban for a judgment on Miranda?

In the long moment before the curtain fell, he had time to feel the whole tragedy of her life. It was as though her beauty, thus detached from all that cheapened and vulgarized it, had held out suppliant hands to him from the world in which he and she had once met for a moment, and where he felt an overmastering longing to be with her again.

He was roused by the pressure of ecstatic fingers. "Was n't

she too beautiful, Lawrence? Don't you like her best in that
simple dress? It makes her look like the real Lily—the Lily I
know."

He met Gerty Farish's brimming gaze. "The Lily *we*
know," he corrected; and his cousin, beaming at the implied
understanding, exclaimed joyfully: "I 'll tell her that! She always says you dislike her."

The performance over, Selden's first impulse was to seek
Miss Bart. During the interlude of music which succeeded the
tableaux, the actors had seated themselves here and there in
the audience, diversifying its conventional appearance by the
varied picturesqueness of their dress. Lily, however, was not
among them, and her absence served to protract the effect she
had produced on Selden: it would have broken the spell to
see her too soon in the surroundings from which accident had
so happily detached her. They had not met since the day of
the Van Osburgh wedding, and on his side the avoidance had
been intentional. Tonight, however, he knew that, sooner or
later, he should find himself at her side; and though he let the
dispersing crowd drift him whither it would, without making
an immediate effort to reach her, his procrastination was not
due to any lingering resistance, but to the desire to luxuriate
a moment in the sense of complete surrender.

Lily had not an instant's doubt as to the meaning of the
murmur greeting her appearance. No other *tableau* had been
received with that precise note of approval: it had obviously
been called forth by herself, and not by the picture she im-
personated. She had feared at the last moment that she was
risking too much in dispensing with the advantages of a more
sumptuous setting, and the completeness of her triumph gave
her an intoxicating sense of recovered power. Not caring to
diminish the impression she had produced, she held herself
aloof from the audience till the movement of dispersal before
supper, and thus had a second opportunity of showing herself
to advantage, as the throng poured slowly into the empty
drawing-room where she was standing.

She was soon the centre of a group which increased and
renewed itself as the circulation became general, and the individual comments on her success were a delightful prolon-

gation of the collective applause. At such moments she lost something of her natural fastidiousness, and cared less for the quality of the admiration received than for its quantity. Differences of personality were merged in a warm atmosphere of praise, in which her beauty expanded like a flower in sunlight; and if Selden had approached a moment or two sooner he would have seen her turning on Ned Van Alstyne and George Dorset the look he had dreamed of capturing for himself.

Fortune willed, however, that the hurried approach of Mrs. Fisher, as whose aide-de-camp Van Alstyne was acting, should break up the group before Selden reached the threshold of the room. One or two of the men wandered off in search of their partners for supper, and the others, noticing Selden's approach, gave way to him in accordance with the tacit free-masonry of the ball-room. Lily was therefore standing alone when he reached her; and finding the expected look in her eye, he had the satisfaction of supposing he had kindled it. The look did indeed deepen as it rested on him, for even in that moment of self-intoxication Lily felt the quicker beat of life that his nearness always produced. She read, too, in his answering gaze the delicious confirmation of her triumph, and for the moment it seemed to her that it was for him only she cared to be beautiful.

Selden had given her his arm without speaking. She took it in silence, and they moved away, not toward the supper-room, but against the tide which was setting thither. The faces about her flowed by like the streaming images of sleep: she hardly noticed where Selden was leading her, till they passed through a glass doorway at the end of the long suite of rooms and stood suddenly in the fragrant hush of a garden. Gravel grated beneath their feet, and about them was the transparent dimness of a midsummer night. Hanging lights made emerald caverns in the depths of foliage, and whitened the spray of a fountain falling among lilies. The magic place was deserted: there was no sound but the plash of the water on the lily-pads, and a distant drift of music that might have been blown across a sleeping lake.

Selden and Lily stood still, accepting the unreality of the scene as a part of their own dream-like sensations. It would not have surprised them to feel a summer breeze on their faces, or to see the lights among the boughs reduplicated in the arch of a starry sky. The strange solitude about them was no stranger than the sweetness of being alone in it together.

At length Lily withdrew her hand, and moved away a step, so that her white-robed slimness was outlined against the dusk of the branches. Selden followed her, and still without speaking they seated themselves on a bench beside the fountain.

Suddenly she raised her eyes with the beseeching earnestness of a child. "You never speak to me—you think hard things of me," she murmured.

"I think of you at any rate, God knows!" he said.

"Then why do we never see each other? Why can't we be friends? You promised once to help me," she continued in the same tone, as though the words were drawn from her unwillingly.

"The only way I can help you is by loving you," Selden said in a low voice.

She made no reply, but her face turned to him with the soft motion of a flower. His own met it slowly, and their lips touched.

She drew back and rose from her seat. Selden rose too, and they stood facing each other. Suddenly she caught his hand and pressed it a moment against her cheek.

"Ah, love me, love me—but don't tell me so!" she sighed with her eyes in his; and before he could speak she had turned and slipped through the arch of boughs, disappearing in the brightness of the room beyond.

Selden stood where she had left him. He knew too well the transiency of exquisite moments to attempt to follow her; but presently he reëntered the house and made his way through the deserted rooms to the door. A few sumptuously-cloaked ladies were already gathered in the marble vestibule, and in the coat-room he found Van Alstyne and Gus Trenor.

The former, at Selden's approach, paused in the careful selection of a cigar from one of the silver boxes invitingly set out near the door.

"Hallo, Selden, going too? You 're an Epicurean like myself, I see: you don't want to see all those goddesses gobbling terrapin. Gad, what a show of good-looking women; but not one of 'em could touch that little cousin of mine. Talk of jewels—what 's a woman want with jewels when she 's got herself to show? The trouble is that all these fal-bals they wear cover up their figures when they 've got 'em. I never knew till tonight what an outline Lily has."

"It 's not her fault if everybody don't know it now," growled Trenor, flushed with the struggle of getting into his fur-lined coat. "Damned bad taste, I call it—no, no cigar for me. You can't tell what you 're smoking in one of these new houses—likely as not the *chef* buys the cigars. Stay for supper? Not if I know it! When people crowd their rooms so that you can't get near any one you want to speak to, I 'd as soon sup in the elevated at the rush hour. My wife was dead right to stay away: she says life 's too short to spend it in breaking in new people."

XIII

LILY WOKE from happy dreams to find two notes at her bed-side.

One was from Mrs. Trenor, who announced that she was coming to town that afternoon for a flying visit, and hoped Miss Bart would be able to dine with her. The other was from Selden. He wrote briefly that an important case called him to Albany, whence he would be unable to return till the evening, and asked Lily to let him know at what hour on the following day she would see him.

Lily, leaning back among her pillows, gazed musingly at his letter. The scene in the Brys' conservatory had been like a part of her dreams; she had not expected to wake to such evidence of its reality. Her first movement was one of annoyance: this unforeseen act of Selden's added another complication to life. It was so unlike him to yield to such an irrational impulse! Did he really mean to ask her to marry him? She had once shown him the impossibility of such a hope, and his subsequent behaviour seemed to prove that he had accepted the situation with a reasonableness somewhat mortifying to her vanity. It was all the more agreeable to find that this reasonableness was maintained only at the cost of not seeing her; but, though nothing in life was as sweet as the sense of her power over him, she saw the danger of allowing the episode of the previous night to have a sequel. Since she could not marry him, it would be kinder to him, as well as easier for herself, to write a line amicably evading his request to see her: he was not the man to mistake such a hint, and when next they met it would be on their usual friendly footing.

Lily sprang out of bed, and went straight to her desk. She wanted to write at once, while she could trust to the strength of her resolve. She was still languid from her brief sleep and the exhilaration of the evening, and the sight of Selden's writing brought back the culminating moment of her triumph: the moment when she had read in his eyes that no philosophy was proof against her power. It would be pleasant to have that sensation again . . . no one else could give it to her in its fulness; and she could not bear to mar her mood of luxurious retrospection by an act of definite refusal. She took up her pen and wrote hastily: *"Tomorrow at four;"* murmuring to herself, as she slipped the sheet into its envelope: "I can easily put him off when tomorrow comes."

Judy Trenor's summons was very welcome to Lily. It was the first time she had received a direct communication from Bellomont since the close of her last visit there, and she was still visited by the dread of having incurred Judy's displeasure. But this characteristic command seemed to reëstablish their former relations; and Lily smiled at the thought that her friend had probably summoned her in order to hear about the Brys' entertainment. Mrs. Trenor had absented herself from the feast, perhaps for the reason so frankly enunciated by her husband, perhaps because, as Mrs. Fisher somewhat differently put it, she "could n't bear new people when she had n't discovered them herself." At any rate, though she remained haughtily at Bellomont, Lily suspected in her a devouring eagerness to hear of what she had missed, and to learn exactly in what measure Mrs. Wellington Bry had surpassed all previous competitors for social recognition. Lily was quite ready to gratify this curiosity, but it happened that she was dining out. She determined, however, to see Mrs. Trenor for a few moments, and ringing for her maid she despatched a telegram to say that she would be with her friend that evening at ten.

She was dining with Mrs. Fisher, who had gathered at an informal feast a few of the performers of the previous evening. There was to be plantation music in the studio after dinner—for Mrs. Fisher, despairing of the republic, had taken up modelling, and annexed to her small crowded house a spacious apartment, which, whatever its uses in her hours of plastic inspiration, served at other times for the exercise of an indefatigable hospitality. Lily was reluctant to leave, for the dinner was amusing, and she would have liked to lounge over a cigarette and hear a few songs; but she could not break her engagement with Judy, and shortly after ten she asked her hostess to ring for a hansom, and drove up Fifth Avenue to the Trenors'.

She waited long enough on the doorstep to wonder that

Judy's presence in town was not signalized by a greater promptness in admitting her; and her surprise was increased when, instead of the expected footman, pushing his shoulders into a tardy coat, a shabby care-taking person in calico let her into the shrouded hall. Trenor, however, appeared at once on the threshold of the drawing-room, welcoming her with unusual volubility while he relieved her of her cloak and drew her into the room.

"Come along to the den; it 's the only comfortable place in the house. Does n't this room look as if it was waiting for the body to be brought down? Can't see why Judy keeps the house wrapped up in this awful slippery white stuff—it 's enough to give a fellow pneumonia to walk through these rooms on a cold day. You look a little pinched yourself, by the way: it 's rather a sharp night out. I noticed it walking up from the club. Come along, and I 'll give you a nip of brandy, and you can toast yourself over the fire and try some of my new Egyptians—that little Turkish chap at the Embassy put me on to a brand that I want you to try, and if you like 'em I 'll get out a lot for you: they don't have 'em here yet, but I 'll cable."

He led her through the house to the large room at the back, where Mrs. Trenor usually sat, and where, even in her absence, there was an air of occupancy. Here, as usual, were flowers, newspapers, a littered writing-table, and a general aspect of lamp-lit familiarity, so that it was a surprise not to see Judy's energetic figure start up from the arm-chair near the fire.

It was apparently Trenor himself who had been occupying the seat in question, for it was overhung by a cloud of cigar smoke, and near it stood one of those intricate folding tables which British ingenuity has devised to facilitate the circulation of tobacco and spirits. The sight of such appliances in a drawing-room was not unusual in Lily's set, where smoking and drinking were unrestricted by considerations of time and place, and her first movement was to help herself to one of the cigarettes recommended by Trenor, while she checked his loquacity by asking, with a surprised glance: "Where 's Judy?"

Trenor, a little heated by his unusual flow of words, and

perhaps by prolonged propinquity with the decanters, was bending over the latter to decipher their silver labels.

"Here, now, Lily, just a drop of cognac in a little fizzy water—you do look pinched, you know: I swear the end of your nose is red. I'll take another glass to keep you company—Judy?—Why, you see, Judy's got a devil of a headache—quite knocked out with it, poor thing—she asked me to explain—make it all right, you know—Do come up to the fire, though; you look dead-beat, really. Now do let me make you comfortable, there's a good girl."

He had taken her hand, half-banteringly, and was drawing her toward a low seat by the hearth; but she stopped and freed herself quietly.

"Do you mean to say that Judy's not well enough to see me? Does n't she want me to go upstairs?"

Trenor drained the glass he had filled for himself, and paused to set it down before he answered.

"Why, no—the fact is, she's not up to seeing anybody. It came on suddenly, you know, and she asked me to tell you how awfully sorry she was—if she'd known where you were dining she'd have sent you word."

"She did know where I was dining; I mentioned it in my telegram. But it does n't matter, of course. I suppose if she's so poorly she won't go back to Bellomont in the morning, and I can come and see her then."

"Yes: exactly—that's capital. I'll tell her you'll pop in to-morrow morning. And now do sit down a minute, there's a dear, and let's have a nice quiet jaw together. You won't take a drop, just for sociability? Tell me what you think of that cigarette. Why, don't you like it? What are you chucking it away for?"

"I am chucking it away because I must go, if you'll have the goodness to call a cab for me," Lily returned with a smile.

She did not like Trenor's unusual excitability, with its too evident explanation, and the thought of being alone with him, with her friend out of reach upstairs, at the other end of the great empty house, did not conduce to a desire to prolong their *tête-à-tête*.

But Trenor, with a promptness which did not escape her, had moved between herself and the door.

"Why must you go, I should like to know? If Judy 'd been here you 'd have sat gossiping till all hours—and you can't even give me five minutes! It 's always the same story. Last night I could n't get near you—I went to that damned vulgar party just to see you, and there was everybody talking about you, and asking me if I 'd ever seen anything so stunning, and when I tried to come up and say a word, you never took any notice, but just went on laughing and joking with a lot of asses who only wanted to be able to swagger about afterward, and look knowing when you were mentioned."

He paused, flushed by his diatribe, and fixing on her a look in which resentment was the ingredient she least disliked. But she had regained her presence of mind, and stood composedly in the middle of the room, while her slight smile seemed to put an ever increasing distance between herself and Trenor.

Across it she said: "Don't be absurd, Gus. It 's past eleven, and I must really ask you to ring for a cab."

He remained immovable, with the lowering forehead she had grown to detest.

"And supposing I won't ring for one—what 'll you do then?"

"I shall go upstairs to Judy if you force me to disturb her."

Trenor drew a step nearer and laid his hand on her arm. "Look here, Lily: won't you give me five minutes of your own accord?"

"Not tonight, Gus: you——"

"Very good, then: I 'll take 'em. And as many more as I want." He had squared himself on the threshold, his hands thrust deep in his pockets. He nodded toward the chair on the hearth.

"Go and sit down there, please: I 've got a word to say to you."

Lily's quick temper was getting the better of her fears. She drew herself up and moved toward the door.

"If you have anything to say to me, you must say it another time. I shall go up to Judy unless you call a cab for me at once."

He burst into a laugh. "Go upstairs and welcome, my dear; but you won't find Judy. She ain't there."

Lily cast a startled look upon him. "Do you mean that Judy is not in the house—not in town?" she exclaimed.

"That 's just what I do mean," returned Trenor, his bluster sinking to sullenness under her look.

"Nonsense—I don't believe you. I am going upstairs," she said impatiently.

He drew unexpectedly aside, letting her reach the threshold unimpeded.

"Go up and welcome; but my wife is at Bellomont."

But Lily had a flash of reassurance. "If she had n't come she would have sent me word——"

"She did; she telephoned me this afternoon to let you know."

"I received no message."

"I did n't send any."

The two measured each other for a moment, but Lily still saw her opponent through a blur of scorn that made all other considerations indistinct.

"I can't imagine your object in playing such a stupid trick on me; but if you have fully gratified your peculiar sense of humour I must again ask you to send for a cab."

It was the wrong note, and she knew it as she spoke. To be stung by irony it is not necessary to understand it, and the angry streaks on Trenor's face might have been raised by an actual lash.

"Look here, Lily, don't take that high and mighty tone with me." He had again moved toward the door, and in her instinctive shrinking from him she let him regain command of the threshold. "I *did* play a trick on you; I own up to it; but if you think I 'm ashamed you 're mistaken. Lord knows I 've been patient enough—I 've hung round and looked like an ass. And all the while you were letting a lot of other fellows make up to you . . . letting 'em make fun of me, I daresay . . . I 'm not sharp, and can't dress my friends up to look funny, as you do . . . but I can tell when it 's being done to me . . . I can tell fast enough when I 'm made a fool of . . ."

"Ah, I should n't have thought that!" flashed from Lily; but her laugh dropped to silence under his look.

"No; you would n't have thought it; but you 'll know

better now. That 's what you 're here for tonight. I 've been waiting for a quiet time to talk things over, and now I 've got it I mean to make you hear me out."

His first rush of inarticulate resentment had been followed by a steadiness and concentration of tone more disconcerting to Lily than the excitement preceding it. For a moment her presence of mind forsook her. She had more than once been in situations where a quick sword-play of wit had been needful to cover her retreat; but her frightened heart-throbs told her that here such skill would not avail.

To gain time she repeated: "I don't understand what you want."

Trenor had pushed a chair between herself and the door. He threw himself in it, and leaned back, looking up at her.

"I 'll tell you what I want: I want to know just where you and I stand. Hang it, the man who pays for the dinner is generally allowed to have a seat at table."

She flamed with anger and abasement, and the sickening need of having to conciliate where she longed to humble.

"I don't know what you mean—but you must see, Gus, that I can't stay here talking to you at this hour——"

"Gad, you go to men's houses fast enough in broad daylight—strikes me you 're not always so deuced careful of appearances."

The brutality of the thrust gave her the sense of dizziness that follows on a physical blow. Rosedale had spoken then—this was the way men talked of her— She felt suddenly weak and defenceless: there was a throb of self-pity in her throat. But all the while another self was sharpening her to vigilance, whispering the terrified warning that every word and gesture must be measured.

"If you have brought me here to say insulting things——" she began.

Trenor laughed. "Don't talk stage-rot. I don't want to insult you. But a man 's got his feelings—and you 've played with mine too long. I did n't begin this business—kept out of the way, and left the track clear for the other chaps, till you rummaged me out and set to work to make an ass of me—and an easy job you had of it, too. That 's the trouble—it was too easy for you—you got reckless—thought you could turn me inside out, and chuck me in the gutter like an empty purse. But, by gad, that ain't playing fair: that's dodging the rules of the game. Of course I know now what you wanted— it was n't my beautiful eyes you were after—but I tell you what, Miss Lily, you 've got to pay up for making me think so——"

He rose, squaring his shoulders aggressively, and stepped toward her with a reddening brow; but she held her footing, though every nerve tore at her to retreat as he advanced.

"Pay up?" she faltered. "Do you mean that I owe you money?"

He laughed again. "Oh, I 'm not asking for payment in kind. But there 's such a thing as fair play—and interest on one's money—and hang me if I 've had as much as a look from you——"

"Your money? What have I to do with your money? You advised me how to invest mine . . . you must have seen I knew nothing of business . . . you told me it was all right——"

"It *was* all right—it is, Lily: you 're welcome to all of it, and ten times more. I 'm only asking for a word of thanks from you." He was closer still, with a hand that grew formidable; and the frightened self in her was dragging the other down.

"I *have* thanked you; I 've shown I was grateful. What more have you done than any friend might do, or any one accept from a friend?"

Trenor caught her up with a sneer. "I don't doubt you 've accepted as much before—and chucked the other chaps as you 'd like to chuck me. I don't care how you settled your score with them—if you fooled 'em I 'm that much to the good. Don't stare at me like that—I know I 'm not talking the way a man is supposed to talk to a girl—but, hang it, if you don't like it you can stop me quick enough—you know I 'm mad about you—damn the money, there 's plenty more of it—if *that* bothers you . . . I was a brute, Lily—Lily!— just look at me——"

Over and over her the sea of humiliation broke—wave crashing on wave so close that the moral shame was one with the physical dread. It seemed to her that self-esteem would

have made her invulnerable—that it was her own dishonour
which put a fearful solitude about her.

His touch was a shock to her drowning consciousness. She
drew back from him with a desperate assumption of scorn.

"I 've told you I don't understand—but if I owe you
money you shall be paid——"

Trenor's face darkened to rage: her recoil of abhorrence
had called out the primitive man.

"Ah—you 'll borrow from Selden or Rosedale—and take
your chances of fooling them as you 've fooled me! Unless—
unless you 've settled your other scores already—and I 'm the
only one left out in the cold!"

She stood silent, frozen to her place. The words—the
words were worse than the touch! Her heart was beating all
over her body—in her throat, her limbs, her helpless useless
hands. Her eyes travelled despairingly about the room—they
lit on the bell, and she remembered that help was in call. Yes,
but scandal with it—a hideous mustering of tongues. No, she
must fight her way out alone. It was enough that the servants
knew her to be in the house with Trenor—there must be
nothing to excite conjecture in her way of leaving it.

She raised her head, and achieved a last clear look at him.

"I am here alone with you," she said. "What more have you
to say?"

To her surprise, Trenor answered the look with a speechless
stare. With his last gust of words the flame had died out,
leaving him chill and humbled. It was as though a cold air
had dispersed the fumes of his libations, and the situation
loomed before him black and naked as the ruins of a fire. Old
habits, old restraints, the hand of inherited order, plucked
back the bewildered mind which passion had jolted from its
ruts. Trenor's eye had the haggard look of the sleep-walker
waked on a deathly ledge.

"Go home! Go away from here"——he stammered, and
turning his back on her walked toward the hearth.

The sharp release from her fears restored Lily to immediate
lucidity. The collapse of Trenor's will left her in control, and
she heard herself, in a voice that was her own yet outside
herself, bidding him ring for the servant, bidding him give
the order for a hansom, directing him to put her in it when

it came. Whence the strength came to her she knew not; but
an insistent voice warned her that she must leave the house
openly, and nerved her, in the hall before the hovering care-
taker, to exchange light words with Trenor, and charge him
with the usual messages for Judy, while all the while she
shook with inward loathing. On the doorstep, with the street
before her, she felt a mad throb of liberation, intoxicating as
the prisoner's first draught of free air; but the clearness of
brain continued, and she noted the mute aspect of Fifth
Avenue, guessed at the lateness of the hour, and even observed a man's figure—was there something half-familiar in
its outline?—which, as she entered the hansom, turned from
the opposite corner and vanished in the obscurity of the side
street.

But with the turn of the wheels reaction came, and shuddering darkness closed on her. "I can't think—I can't think,"
she moaned, and leaned her head against the rattling side of
the cab. She seemed a stranger to herself, or rather there were
two selves in her, the one she had always known, and a new
abhorrent being to which it found itself chained. She had
once picked up, in a house where she was staying, a translation of the *Eumenides*, and her imagination had been seized
by the high terror of the scene where Orestes, in the cave of
the oracle, finds his implacable huntresses asleep, and snatches
an hour's repose. Yes, the Furies might sometimes sleep, but
they were there, always there in the dark corners, and now
they were awake and the iron clang of their wings was in her
brain . . . She opened her eyes and saw the streets passing—
the familiar alien streets. All she looked on was the same and
yet changed. There was a great gulf fixed between today and
yesterday. Everything in the past seemed simple, natural, full
of daylight—and she was alone in a place of darkness and
pollution.—Alone! It was the loneliness that frightened her.
Her eyes fell on an illuminated clock at a street corner, and
she saw that the hands marked the half hour after eleven.
Only half-past eleven—there were hours and hours left of the
night! And she must spend them alone, shuddering sleepless
on her bed. Her soft nature recoiled from this ordeal, which
had none of the stimulus of conflict to goad her through it.
Oh, the slow cold drip of the minutes on her head! She had

a vision of herself lying on the black walnut bed—and the darkness would frighten her, and if she left the light burning the dreary details of the room would brand themselves forever on her brain. She had always hated her room at Mrs. Peniston's—its ugliness, its impersonality, the fact that nothing in it was really hers. To a torn heart uncomforted by human nearness a room may open almost human arms, and the being to whom no four walls mean more than any others, is, at such hours, expatriate everywhere.

Lily had no heart to lean on. Her relation with her aunt was as superficial as that of chance lodgers who pass on the stairs. But even had the two been in closer contact, it was impossible to think of Mrs. Peniston's mind as offering shelter or comprehension to such misery as Lily's. As the pain that can be told is but half a pain, so the pity that questions has little healing in its touch. What Lily craved was the darkness made by enfolding arms, the silence which is not solitude, but compassion holding its breath.

She started up and looked forth on the passing streets. Gerty!—they were nearing Gerty's corner. If only she could reach there before this labouring anguish burst from her breast to her lips—if only she could feel the hold of Gerty's arms while she shook in the ague-fit of fear that was coming upon her! She pushed up the door in the roof and called the address to the driver. It was not so late—Gerty might still be waking. And even if she were not, the sound of the bell would penetrate every recess of her tiny apartment, and rouse her to answer her friend's call.

XIV

GERTY FARISH, the morning after the Wellington Brys' entertainment, woke from dreams as happy as Lily's. If they were less vivid in hue, more subdued to the half-tints of her personality and her experience, they were for that very reason better suited to her mental vision. Such flashes of joy as Lily moved in would have blinded Miss Farish, who was accustomed, in the way of happiness, to such scant light as shone through the cracks of other people's lives.

Now she was the centre of a little illumination of her own: a mild but unmistakable beam, compounded of Lawrence Selden's growing kindness to herself and the discovery that he extended his liking to Lily Bart. If these two factors seem incompatible to the student of feminine psychology, it must be remembered that Gerty had always been a parasite in the moral order, living on the crumbs of other tables, and content to look through the window at the banquet spread for her friends. Now that she was enjoying a little private feast of her own, it would have seemed incredibly selfish not to lay a plate for a friend; and there was no one with whom she would rather have shared her enjoyment than Miss Bart.

As to the nature of Selden's growing kindness, Gerty would no more have dared to define it than she would have tried to learn a butterfly's colours by knocking the dust from its wings. To seize on the wonder would be to brush off its bloom, and perhaps see it fade and stiffen in her hand: better the sense of beauty palpitating out of reach, while she held her breath and watched where it would alight. Yet Selden's manner at the Brys' had brought the flutter of wings so close that they seemed to be beating in her own heart. She had never seen him so alert, so responsive, so attentive to what she had to say. His habitual manner had an absent-minded kindliness which she accepted, and was grateful for, as the liveliest sentiment her presence was likely to inspire; but she was quick to feel in him a change implying that for once she could give pleasure as well as receive it.

And it was so delightful that this higher degree of sympathy should be reached through their interest in Lily Bart!

Gerty's affection for her friend—a sentiment that had learned
to keep itself alive on the scantiest diet—had grown to active
adoration since Lily's restless curiosity had drawn her into the
circle of Miss Farish's work. Lily's taste of beneficence had
wakened in her a momentary appetite for well-doing. Her
visit to the Girls' Club had first brought her in contact with
the dramatic contrasts of life. She had always accepted with
philosophic calm the fact that such existences as hers were
pedestalled on foundations of obscure humanity. The dreary
limbo of dinginess lay all around and beneath that little illuminated circle in which life reached its finest efflorescence, as
the mud and sleet of a winter night enclose a hot-house filled
with tropical flowers. All this was in the natural order of
things, and the orchid basking in its artificially created atmosphere could round the delicate curves of its petals undisturbed by the ice on the panes.

But it is one thing to live comfortably with the abstract
conception of poverty, another to be brought in contact with
its human embodiments. Lily had never conceived of these
victims of fate otherwise than in the mass. That the mass was
composed of individual lives, innumerable separate centres of
sensation, with her own eager reachings for pleasure, her own
fierce revulsions from pain—that some of these bundles of
feeling were clothed in shapes not so unlike her own, with
eyes meant to look on gladness, and young lips shaped for
love—this discovery gave Lily one of those sudden shocks of
pity that sometimes decentralize a life. Lily's nature was incapable of such renewal: she could feel other demands only
through her own, and no pain was long vivid which did not
press on an answering nerve. But for the moment she was
drawn out of herself by the interest of her direct relation with
a world so unlike her own. She had supplemented her first
gift by personal assistance to one or two of Miss Farish's most
appealing subjects, and the admiration and interest her presence excited among the tired workers at the club ministered
in a new form to her insatiable desire to please.

Gerty Farish was not a close enough reader of character to
disentangle the mixed threads of which Lily's philanthropy
was woven. She supposed her beautiful friend to be actuated
by the same motive as herself—that sharpening of the moral

vision which makes all human suffering so near and insistent that the other aspects of life fade into remoteness. Gerty lived by such simple formulas that she did not hesitate to class her friend's state with the emotional "change of heart" to which her dealings with the poor had accustomed her; and she rejoiced in the thought that she had been the humble instrument of this renewal. Now she had an answer to all criticisms of Lily's conduct: as she had said, she knew "the real Lily," and the discovery that Selden shared her knowledge raised her placid acceptance of life to a dazzled sense of its possibilities—a sense farther enlarged, in the course of the afternoon, by the receipt of a telegram from Selden asking if he might dine with her that evening.

While Gerty was lost in the happy bustle which this announcement produced in her small household, Selden was at one with her in thinking with intensity of Lily Bart. The case which had called him to Albany was not complicated enough to absorb all his attention, and he had the professional faculty of keeping a part of his mind free when its services were not needed. This part—which at the moment seemed dangerously like the whole—was filled to the brim with the sensations of the previous evening. Selden understood the symptoms: he recognized the fact that he was paying up, as there had always been a chance of his having to pay up, for the voluntary exclusions of his past. He had meant to keep free from permanent ties, not from any poverty of feeling, but because, in a different way, he was, as much as Lily, the victim of his environment. There had been a germ of truth in his declaration to Gerty Farish that he had never wanted to marry a "nice" girl: the adjective connoting, in his cousin's vocabulary, certain utilitarian qualities which are apt to preclude the luxury of charm. Now it had been Selden's fate to have a charming mother: her graceful portrait, all smiles and Cashmere, still emitted a faded scent of the undefinable quality. His father was the kind of man who delights in a charming woman: who quotes her, stimulates her, and keeps her perennially charming. Neither one of the couple cared for money, but their disdain of it took the form of always spending a little more than was prudent. If their house was shabby, it was exquisitely kept; if there were good books on the

shelves there were also good dishes on the table. Selden senior had an eye for a picture, his wife an understanding of
old lace; and both were so conscious of restraint and discrimination in buying that they never quite knew how it was that
the bills mounted up.) .

Though many of Selden's friends would have called his parents poor, he had grown up in an atmosphere where restricted means were felt only as a check on aimless profusion:
where the few possessions were so good that their rarity gave
them a merited relief, and abstinence was combined with elegance in a way exemplified by Mrs. Selden's knack of wearing her old velvet as if it were new. A man has the advantage
of being delivered early from the home point of view, and
before Selden left college he had learned that there are as
many different ways of going without money as of spending
it. Unfortunately, he found no way as agreeable as that practised at home; and his views of womankind in especial were
tinged by the remembrance of the one woman who had given
him his sense of "values." It was from her that he inherited
his detachment from the sumptuary side of life: the stoic's
carelessness of material things, combined with the Epicurean's
pleasure in them. Life shorn of either feeling appeared to him
a diminished thing; and nowhere was the blending of the two
ingredients so essential as in the character of a pretty woman.

It had always seemed to Selden that experience offered a
great deal besides the sentimental adventure, yet he could vividly conceive of a love which should broaden and deepen till
it became the central fact of life. What he could not accept,
in his own case, was the makeshift alternative of a relation
that should be less than this: that should leave some portions
of his nature unsatisfied, while it put an undue strain on others. He would not, in other words, yield to the growth of an
affection which might appeal to pity yet leave the understanding untouched: sympathy should no more delude him than a
trick of the eyes, the grace of helplessness than a curve of the
cheek.

But now—that little *but* passed like a sponge over all his
vows. His reasoned-out resistances seemed for the moment so
much less important than the question as to when Lily would
receive his note! He yielded himself to the charm of trivial

preoccupations, wondering at what hour her reply would be sent, with what words it would begin. As to its import he had no doubt—he was as sure of her surrender as of his own. And so he had leisure to muse on all its exquisite details, as a hard worker, on a holiday morning, might lie still and watch the beam of light travel gradually across his room. But if the new light dazzled, it did not blind him. He could still discern the outline of facts, though his own relation to them had changed. He was no less conscious than before of what was said of Lily Bart, but he could separate the woman he knew from the vulgar estimate of her. His mind turned to Gerty Farish's words, and the wisdom of the world seemed a groping thing beside the insight of innocence. *Blessed are the pure in heart, for they shall see God*—even the hidden god in their neighbour's breast! Selden was in the state of impassioned self-absorption that the first surrender to love produces. His craving was for the companionship of one whose point of view should justify his own, who should confirm, by deliberate observation, the truth to which his intuitions had leaped. He could not wait for the midday recess, but seized a moment's leisure in court to scribble his telegram to Gerty Farish.

Reaching town, he was driven direct to his club, where he hoped a note from Miss Bart might await him. But his box contained only a line of rapturous assent from Gerty, and he was turning away disappointed when he was hailed by a voice from the smoking room.

"Hallo, Lawrence! Dining here? Take a bite with me— I 've ordered a canvas-back."

He discovered Trenor, in his day clothes, sitting, with a tall glass at his elbow, behind the folds of a sporting journal.

Selden thanked him, but pleaded an engagement.

"Hang it, I believe every man in town has an engagement tonight. I shall have the club to myself. You know how I 'm living this winter, rattling round in that empty house. My wife meant to come to town today, but she 's put it off again, and how is a fellow to dine alone in a room with the looking-glasses covered, and nothing but a bottle of Harvey sauce on the side-board? I say, Lawrence, chuck your engagement and take pity on me—it gives me the blue devils to dine alone, and there's nobody but that canting ass Wetherall in the club."

"Sorry, Gus—I can't do it."

As Selden turned away, he noticed the dark flush on Trenor's face, the unpleasant moisture of his intensely white forehead, the way his jewelled rings were wedged in the creases of his fat red fingers. Certainly the beast was predominating—the beast at the bottom of the glass. And he had heard this man's name coupled with Lily's! Bah—the thought sickened him; all the way back to his rooms he was haunted by the sight of Trenor's fat creased hands——

On his table lay the note: Lily had sent it to his rooms. He knew what was in it before he broke the seal—a grey seal with *Beyond!* beneath a flying ship. Ah, he would take her beyond—beyond the ugliness, the pettiness, the attrition and corrosion of the soul——

Gerty's little sitting-room sparkled with welcome when Selden entered it. Its modest "effects," compact of enamel paint and ingenuity, spoke to him in the language just then sweetest to his ear. It is surprising how little narrow walls and a low ceiling matter, when the roof of the soul has suddenly been raised. Gerty sparkled too; or at least shone with a tempered radiance. He had never before noticed that she had "points"—really, some good fellow might do worse . . . Over the little dinner (and here, again, the effects were wonderful) he told her she ought to marry—he was in a mood to pair off the whole world. She had made the caramel custard with her own hands? It was sinful to keep such gifts to herself. He reflected with a throb of pride that Lily could trim her own hats—she had told him so the day of their walk at Bellomont.

He did not speak of Lily till after dinner. During the little repast he kept the talk on his hostess, who, fluttered at being the centre of observation, shone as rosy as the candle-shades she had manufactured for the occasion. Selden evinced an extraordinary interest in her household arrangements: complimented her on the ingenuity with which she had utilized every inch of her small quarters, asked how her servant managed about afternoons out, learned that one may improvise delicious dinners in a chafing-dish, and uttered thoughtful generalizations on the burden of a large establishment.

When they were in the sitting-room again, where they fitted as snugly as bits in a puzzle, and she had brewed the coffee, and poured it into her grandmother's egg-shell cups, his eye, as he leaned back, basking in the warm fragrance, lighted on a recent photograph of Miss Bart, and the desired transition was effected without an effort. The photograph was well enough—but to catch her as she had looked last night! Gerty agreed with him—never had she been so radiant. But could photography capture that light? There had been a new look in her face—something different; yes, Selden agreed there had been something different. The coffee was so exquisite that he asked for a second cup: such a contrast to the watery stuff at the club! Ah, your poor bachelor with his impersonal club fare, alternating with the equally impersonal *cuisine* of the dinner-party! A man who lived in lodgings missed the best part of life—he pictured the flavourless solitude of Trenor's repast, and felt a moment's compassion for the man . . . But to return to Lily—and again and again he returned, questioning, conjecturing, leading Gerty on, draining her inmost thoughts of their stored tenderness for her friend.

At first she poured herself out unstintingly, happy in this perfect communion of their sympathies. His understanding of Lily helped to confirm her own belief in her friend. They dwelt together on the fact that Lily had had no chance. Gerty instanced her generous impulses—her restlessness and discontent. The fact that her life had never satisfied her proved that she was made for better things. She might have married more than once—the conventional rich marriage which she had been taught to consider the sole end of existence—but when the opportunity came she had always shrunk from it. Percy Gryce, for instance, had been in love with her—every one at Bellomont had supposed them to be engaged, and her dismissal of him was thought inexplicable. This view of the Gryce incident chimed too well with Selden's mood not to be instantly adopted by him, with a flash of retrospective contempt for what had once seemed the obvious solution. If rejection there had been—and he wondered now that he had ever doubted it!—then he held the key to the secret, and the hillsides of Bellomont were lit up, not with sunset, but with dawn. It was he who had wavered and disowned the face of opportunity—and the joy now warming his breast might have been a familiar inmate if he had captured it in its first flight.

It was at this point, perhaps, that a joy just trying its wings in Gerty's heart dropped to earth and lay still. She sat facing Selden, repeating mechanically: "No, she has never been understood——" and all the while she herself seemed to be sitting in the centre of a great glare of comprehension. The little confidential room, where a moment ago their thoughts had touched elbows like their chairs, grew to unfriendly vastness, separating her from Selden by all the length of her new vision of the future—and that future stretched out interminably, with her lonely figure toiling down it, a mere speck on the solitude.

"She is herself with a few people only; and you are one of them," she heard Selden saying. And again: "Be good to her, Gerty, won't you?" and: "She has it in her to become whatever she is believed to be—you 'll help her by believing the best of her?"

The words beat on Gerty's brain like the sound of a language which has seemed familiar at a distance, but on approaching is found to be unintelligible. He had come to talk to her of Lily—that was all! There had been a third at the feast she had spread for him, and that third had taken her own place. She tried to follow what he was saying, to cling to her own part in the talk—but it was all as meaningless as the boom of waves in a drowning head, and she felt, as the drowning may feel, that to sink would be nothing beside the pain of struggling to keep up.

Selden rose, and she drew a deep breath, feeling that soon she could yield to the blessed waves.

"Mrs. Fisher's? You say she was dining there? There 's music afterward; I believe I had a card from her." He glanced at the foolish pink-faced clock that was drumming out this hideous hour. "A quarter past ten? I might look in there now; the Fisher evenings are amusing. I have n't kept you up too late, Gerty? You look tired—I 've rambled on and bored you." And in the unwonted overflow of his feelings, he left a cousinly kiss upon her cheek.

At Mrs. Fisher's, through the cigar-smoke of the studio, a dozen voices greeted Selden. A song was pending as he entered, and he dropped into a seat near his hostess, his eyes roaming in search of Miss Bart. But she was not there, and the discovery gave him a pang out of all proportion to its seriousness; since the note in his breast-pocket assured him that at four the next day they would meet. To his impatience it seemed immeasurably long to wait, and half-ashamed of the impulse, he leaned to Mrs. Fisher to ask, as the music ceased, if Miss Bart had not dined with her.

"Lily? She 's just gone. She had to run off, I forget where. Was n't she wonderful last night?"

"Who 's that? Lily?" asked Jack Stepney, from the depths of a neighbouring arm-chair. "Really, you know, I 'm no prude, but when it comes to a girl standing there as if she was up at auction—I thought seriously of speaking to cousin Julia."

"You did n't know Jack had become our social censor?" Mrs. Fisher said to Selden with a laugh; and Stepney spluttered, amid the general derision: "But she 's a cousin, hang it, and when a man 's married— *Town Talk* was full of her this morning."

"Yes: lively reading that was," said Mr. Ned Van Alstyne, stroking his moustache to hide the smile behind it. "Buy the dirty sheet? No, of course not; some fellow showed it to me—but I 'd heard the stories before. When a girl 's as good-looking as that she 'd better marry; then no questions are asked. In our imperfectly organized society there is no provision as yet for the young woman who claims the privileges of marriage without assuming its obligations."

"Well, I understand Lily is about to assume them in the shape of Mr. Rosedale," Mrs. Fisher said with a laugh.

"Rosedale—good heavens!" exclaimed Van Alstyne, dropping his eye-glass. "Stepney, that 's your fault for foisting the brute on us."

"Oh, confound it, you know, we don't *marry* Rosedale in our family," Stepney languidly protested; but his wife, who sat in oppressive bridal finery at the other side of the room, quelled him with the judicial reflection: "In Lily's circumstances it's a mistake to have too high a standard."

"I hear even Rosedale has been scared by the talk lately," Mrs. Fisher rejoined; "but the sight of her last night sent him off his head. What do you think he said to me after her *tableau*? 'My God, Mrs. Fisher, if I could get Paul Morpeth to paint her like that, the picture'd appreciate a hundred per cent in ten years.'"

"By Jove, — but isn't she about somewhere?" exclaimed Van Alstyne, restoring his glass with an uneasy glance.

"No; she ran off while you were all mixing the punch down stairs. Where was she going, by the way? What's on tonight? I hadn't heard of anything."

"Oh, not a party, I think," said an inexperienced young Farish who had arrived late. "I put her in her cab as I was coming in, and she gave the driver the Trenors' address."

"The Trenors'?" exclaimed Mrs. Jack Stepney. "Why, the house is closed — Judy telephoned me from Bellomont this evening."

"Did she? That's queer. I'm sure I'm not mistaken. Well, come now, Trenor's there, anyhow — I — oh, well — the fact is, I've no head for numbers," he broke off, admonished by the nudge of an adjoining foot, and the smile that circled the room.

In its unpleasant light Selden had risen and was shaking hands with his hostess. The air of the place stifled him, and he wondered why he had stayed in it so long.

On the doorstep he stood still, remembering a phrase of Lily's: "It seems to me you spend a good deal of time in the element you disapprove of."

Well — what had brought him there but the quest of her? It was her element, not his. But he would lift her out of it, take her beyond! That *Beyond!* on her letter was like a cry for rescue. He knew that Perseus's task is not done when he has loosed Andromeda's chains, for her limbs are numb with bondage, and she cannot rise and walk, but clings to him with dragging arms as he beats back to land with his burden. Well, he had strength for both — it was her weakness which had put the strength in him. It was not, alas, a clean rush of waves they had to win through, but a clogging morass of old associations and habits, and for the moment its vapours were in his throat. But he would see clearer, breathe freer in her presence: she was at once the dead weight at his breast and the spar which should float them to safety. He smiled at the whirl of metaphor with which he was trying to build up a defence against the influences of the last hour. It was pitiable that he, who knew the mixed motives on which social judgments depend, should still feel himself so swayed by them. How could he lift Lily to a freer vision of life, if his own view of her was to be coloured by any mind in which he saw her reflected?

The moral oppression had produced a physical craving for air, and he strode on, opening his lungs to the reverberating coldness of the night. At the corner of Fifth Avenue Van Alstyne hailed him with an offer of company.

"Walking? A good thing to blow the smoke out of one's head. Now that women have taken to tobacco we live in a bath of nicotine. It would be a curious thing to study the effect of cigarettes on the relation of the sexes. Smoke is almost as great a solvent as divorce: both tend to obscure the moral issue."

Nothing could have been less consonant with Selden's mood than Van Alstyne's after-dinner aphorisms, but as long as the latter confined himself to generalities his listener's nerves were in control. Happily Van Alstyne prided himself on his summing up of social aspects, and with Selden for audience was eager to show the sureness of his touch. Mrs. Fisher lived in an East side street near the Park, and as the two men walked down Fifth Avenue the new architectural developments of that versatile thoroughfare invited Van Alstyne's comment.

"That Greiner house, now—a typical rung in the social ladder! The man who built it came from a *milieu* where all the dishes are put on the table at once. His façade is a complete architectural meal; if he had omitted a style his friends might have thought the money had given out. Not a bad purchase for Rosedale, though: attracts attention, and awes the Western sight-seer. By and bye he'll get out of that phase, and want something that the crowd will pass and the few pause before. Especially if he marries my clever cousin——"

Selden dashed in with the query: "And the Wellington Brys'? Rather clever of its kind, don't you think?"

They were just beneath the wide white façade, with its rich restraint of line, which suggested the clever corseting of a redundant figure.

"That's the next stage: the desire to imply that one has been to Europe, and has a standard. I'm sure Mrs. Bry thinks her house a copy of the *Trianon*; in America every marble house with gilt furniture is thought to be a copy of the *Trianon*. What a clever chap that architect is, though—how he takes his client's measure! He has put the whole of Mrs. Bry in his use of the composite order. Now for the Trenors, you remember, he chose the Corinthian: exuberant, but based on the best precedent. The Trenor house is one of his best things—does n't look like a banqueting-hall turned inside out. I hear Mrs. Trenor wants to build out a new ball-room, and that divergence from Gus on that point keeps her at Bellomont. The dimensions of the Brys' ball-room must rankle: you may be sure she knows 'em as well as if she'd been there last night with a yard-measure. Who said she was in town, by the way? That Farish boy? She is n't, I know; Mrs. Stepney was right; the house is dark, you see: I suppose Gus lives in the back."

He had halted opposite the Trenors' corner, and Selden perforce stayed his steps also. The house loomed obscure and uninhabited; only an oblong gleam above the door spoke of provisional occupancy.

"They've bought the house at the back: it gives them a hundred and fifty feet in the side street. There's where the ball-room's to be, with a gallery connecting it: billiard-room and so on above. I suggested changing the entrance, and carrying the drawing-room across the whole Fifth Avenue front; you see the front door corresponds with the windows——"

The walking-stick which Van Alstyne swung in demonstration dropped to a startled "Hallo!" as the door opened and two figures were seen silhouetted against the hall-light. At the same moment a hansom halted at the curb-stone, and one of the figures floated down to it in a haze of evening draperies; while the other, black and bulky, remained persistently projected against the light.

For an immeasurable second the two spectators of the incident were silent; then the house-door closed, the hansom
rolled off, and the whole scene slipped by as if with the turn
of a stereopticon.

Van Alstyne dropped his eye-glass with a low whistle.

"A—hem—nothing of this, eh, Selden? As one of the family, I know I may count on you—appearances are deceptive—and Fifth Avenue is so imperfectly lighted——"

"Goodnight," said Selden, turning sharply down the side
street without seeing the other's extended hand.

Alone with her cousin's kiss, Gerty stared upon her
thoughts. He had kissed her before—but not with another
woman on his lips. If he had spared her that she could have
drowned quietly, welcoming the dark flood as it submerged
her. But now the flood was shot through with glory, and it
was harder to drown at sunrise than in darkness. Gerty hid
her face from the light, but it pierced to the crannies of her
soul. She had been so contented, life had seemed so simple
and sufficient—why had he come to trouble her with new
hopes? And Lily—Lily, her best friend! Woman-like, she accused the woman. Perhaps, had it not been for Lily, her fond
imagining might have become truth. Selden had always liked
her—had understood and sympathized with the modest independence of her life. He, who had the reputation of weighing all things in the nice balance of fastidious perceptions, had
been uncritical and simple in his view of her: his cleverness
had never overawed her because she had felt at home in his
heart. And now she was thrust out, and the door barred
against her by Lily's hand! Lily, for whose admission there
she herself had pleaded! The situation was lighted up by a
dreary flash of irony. She knew Selden—she saw how the
force of her faith in Lily must have helped to dispel his hesitations. She remembered, too, how Lily had talked of him—
she saw herself bringing the two together, making them
known to each other. On Selden's part, no doubt, the wound
inflicted was inconscient; he had never guessed her foolish
secret; but Lily—Lily must have known! When, in such matters, are a woman's perceptions at fault? And if she knew,
then she had deliberately despoiled her friend, and in mere

wantonness of power, since, even to Gerty's suddenly flaming jealousy, it seemed incredible that Lily should wish to be Selden's wife. Lily might be incapable of marrying for money, but she was equally incapable of living without it, and Selden's eager investigations into the small economies of house-keeping made him appear to Gerty as tragically duped as herself.

She remained long in her sitting-room, where the embers were crumbling to cold grey, and the lamp paled under its gay shade. Just beneath it stood the photograph of Lily Bart, looking out imperially on the cheap gim-cracks, the cramped furniture of the little room. Could Selden picture her in such an interior? Gerty felt the poverty, the insignificance of her surroundings: she beheld her life as it must appear to Lily. And the cruelty of Lily's judgments smote upon her memory. She saw that she had dressed her idol with attributes of her own making. When had Lily ever really felt, or pitied, or understood? All she wanted was the taste of new experiences: she seemed like some cruel creature experimenting in a laboratory.

The pink-faced clock drummed out another hour, and Gerty rose with a start. She had an appointment early the next morning with a district visitor on the East side. She put out her lamp, covered the fire, and went into her bedroom to undress. In the little glass above her dressing-table she saw her face reflected against the shadows of the room, and tears blotted the reflection. What right had she to dream the dreams of loveliness? A dull face invited a dull fate. She cried quietly as she undressed, laying aside her clothes with her habitual precision, setting everything in order for the next day, when the old life must be taken up as though there had been no break in its routine. Her servant did not come till eight o'clock, and she prepared her own tea-tray and placed it beside the bed. Then she locked the door of the flat, extinguished her light and lay down. But on her bed sleep would not come, and she lay face to face with the fact that she hated Lily Bart. It closed with her in the darkness like some formless evil to be blindly grappled with. Reason, judgment, renunciation, all the sane daylight forces, were beaten back in the sharp struggle for self-preservation. She wanted happiness—

wanted it as fiercely and unscrupulously as Lily did, but without Lily's power of obtaining it. And in her conscious impotence she lay shivering, and hated her friend——

A ring at the door-bell caught her to her feet. She struck a light and stood startled, listening. For a moment her heart beat incoherently, then she felt the sobering touch of fact, and remembered that such calls were not unknown in her charitable work. She flung on her dressing-gown to answer the summons, and unlocking her door, confronted the shining vision of Lily Bart.

Gerty's first movement was one of revulsion. She shrank back as though Lily's presence flashed too sudden a light upon her misery. Then she heard her name in a cry, had a glimpse of her friend's face, and felt herself caught and clung to.

"Lily—what is it?" she exclaimed.

Miss Bart released her, and stood breathing brokenly, like one who has gained shelter after a long flight.

"I was so cold—I could n't go home. Have you a fire?"

Gerty's compassionate instincts, responding to the swift call of habit, swept aside all her reluctances. Lily was simply some one who needed help—for what reason, there was no time to pause and conjecture: disciplined sympathy checked the wonder on Gerty's lips, and made her draw her friend silently into the sitting-room and seat her by the darkened hearth.

"There is kindling wood here: the fire will burn in a minute."

She knelt down, and the flame leapt under her rapid hands. It flashed strangely through the tears which still blurred her eyes, and smote on the white ruin of Lily's face. The girls looked at each other in silence; then Lily repeated: "I could n't go home."

"No—no—you came here, dear! You 're cold and tired— sit quiet, and I 'll make you some tea."

Gerty had unconsciously adopted the soothing note of her trade: all personal feeling was merged in the sense of ministry, and experience had taught her that the bleeding must be stayed before the wound is probed.

Lily sat quiet, leaning to the fire: the clatter of cups behind her soothed her as familiar noises hush a child whom silence has kept wakeful. But when Gerty stood at her side with the tea she pushed it away, and turned an estranged eye on the familiar room.

"I came here because I could n't bear to be alone," she said.

Gerty set down the cup and knelt beside her.

"Lily! Something has happened—can't you tell me?"

"I could n't bear to lie awake in my room till morning. I hate my room at Aunt Julia's—so I came here——"

She stirred suddenly, broke from her apathy, and clung to Gerty in a fresh burst of fear.

"Oh, Gerty, the furies . . . you know the noise of their wings—alone, at night, in the dark? But you don't know—there is nothing to make the dark dreadful to you——"

The words, flashing back on Gerty's last hours, struck from her a faint derisive murmur; but Lily, in the blaze of her own misery, was blinded to everything outside it.

"You 'll let me stay? I shan't mind when daylight comes—Is it late? Is the night nearly over? It must be awful to be sleepless—everything stands by the bed and stares——"

Miss Farish caught her straying hands. "Lily, look at me! Something has happened—an accident? You have been frightened—what has frightened you? Tell me if you can—a word or two—so that I can help you."

Lily shook her head.

"I am not frightened: that 's not the word. Can you imagine looking into your glass some morning and seeing a disfigurement—some hideous change that has come to you while you slept? Well, I seem to myself like that—I can't bear to see myself in my own thoughts—I hate ugliness, you know—I 've always turned from it—but I can't explain to you—you would n't understand."

She lifted her head and her eyes fell on the clock.

"How long the night is! And I know I shan't sleep tomorrow. Some one told me my father used to lie sleepless and think of horrors. And he was not wicked, only unfortunate—and I see now how he must have suffered, lying alone with his thoughts! But I am bad—a bad girl—all my thoughts are bad—I have always had bad people about me. Is that any excuse? I thought I could manage my own life—I was proud—proud! but now I 'm on their level——"

Sobs shook her, and she bowed to them like a tree in a dry storm.

Gerty knelt beside her, waiting, with the patience born of experience, till this gust of misery should loosen fresh speech. She had first imagined some physical shock, some peril of the crowded streets, since Lily was presumably on her way home from Carry Fisher's; but she now saw that other nerve-centres were smitten, and her mind trembled back from conjecture.

Lily's sobs ceased, and she lifted her head.

"There are bad girls in your slums. Tell me—do they ever pick themselves up? Ever forget, and feel as they did before?"

"Lily! you must n't speak so—you 're dreaming."

"Don't they always go from bad to worse? There 's no turning back—your old self rejects you, and shuts you out."

She rose, stretching her arms as if in utter physical weariness. "Go to bed, dear! You work hard and get up early. I 'll watch here by the fire, and you 'll leave the light, and your door open. All I want is to feel that you are near me." She laid both hands on Gerty's shoulders, with a smile that was like sunrise on a sea strewn with wreckage.

"I can't leave you, Lily. Come and lie on my bed. Your hands are frozen—you must undress and be made warm." Gerty paused with sudden compunction. "But Mrs. Peniston—it 's past midnight! What will she think?"

"She goes to bed. I have a latch-key. It does n't matter—I can't go back there."

"There 's no need to: you shall stay here. But you must tell me where you have been. Listen, Lily—it will help you to speak!" She regained Miss Bart's hands, and pressed them against her. "Try to tell me—it will clear your poor head. Listen—you were dining at Carry Fisher's." Gerty paused and added with a flash of heroism: "Lawrence Selden went from here to find you."

At the word, Lily's face melted from locked anguish to the open misery of a child. Her lips trembled and her gaze widened with tears.

"He went to find me? And I missed him! Oh, Gerty, he

tried to help me. He told me—he warned me long ago—he foresaw that I should grow hateful to myself!"

The name, as Gerty saw with a clutch at the heart, had loosened the springs of self-pity in her friend's dry breast, and tear by tear Lily poured out the measure of her anguish. She had dropped sideways in Gerty's big arm-chair, her head buried where lately Selden's had leaned, in a beauty of abandonment that drove home to Gerty's aching senses the inevitableness of her own defeat. Ah, it needed no deliberate purpose on Lily's part to rob her of her dream! To look on that prone loveliness was to see in it a natural force, to recognize that love and power belong to such as Lily, as renunciation and service are the lot of those they despoil. But if Selden's infatuation seemed a fatal necessity, the effect that his name produced shook Gerty's steadfastness with a last pang. Men pass through such superhuman loves and outlive them: they are the probation subduing the heart to human joys. How gladly Gerty would have welcomed the ministry of healing: how willingly have soothed the sufferer back to tolerance of life! But Lily's self-betrayal took this last hope from her. The mortal maid on the shore is helpless against the siren who loves her prey: such victims are floated back dead from their adventure.

Lily sprang up and caught her with strong hands. "Gerty, you know him—you understand him—tell me; if I went to him, if I told him everything—if I said: 'I am bad through and through—I want admiration, I want excitement, I want money—' yes, *money!* That's my shame, Gerty—and it's known, it's said of me—it's what men think of me— If I said it all to him—told him the whole story—said plainly: 'I've sunk lower than the lowest, for I've taken what they take, and not paid as they pay'—oh, Gerty, you know him, you can speak for him: if I told him everything would he loathe me? Or would he pity me, and understand me, and save me from loathing myself?"

Gerty stood cold and passive. She knew the hour of her probation had come, and her poor heart beat wildly against its destiny. As a dark river sweeps by under a lightning flash, she saw her chance of happiness surge past under a flash of temptation. What prevented her from saying: "He is like other men"? She was not so sure of him, after all! But to do so would have been like blaspheming her love. She could not put him before herself in any light but the noblest: she must trust him to the height of her own passion.

"Yes: I know him; he will help you," she said; and in a moment Lily's passion was weeping itself out against her breast.

There was but one bed in the little flat, and the two girls lay down on it side by side when Gerty had unlaced Lily's dress and persuaded her to put her lips to the warm tea. The light extinguished, they lay still in the darkness, Gerty shrinking to the outer edge of the narrow couch to avoid contact with her bed-fellow. Knowing that Lily disliked to be caressed, she had long ago learned to check her demonstrative impulses toward her friend. But tonight every fibre in her body shrank from Lily's nearness: it was torture to listen to her breathing, and feel the sheet stir with it. As Lily turned, and settled to completer rest, a strand of her hair swept Gerty's cheek with its fragrance. Everything about her was warm and soft and scented: even the stains of her grief became her as rain-drops do the beaten rose. But as Gerty lay with arms drawn down her side, in the motionless narrowness of an effigy, she felt a stir of sobs from the breathing warmth beside her, and Lily flung out her hand, groped for her friend's, and held it fast.

"Hold me, Gerty, hold me, or I shall think of things," she moaned; and Gerty silently slipped an arm under her, pillowing her head in its hollow as a mother makes a nest for a tossing child. In the warm hollow Lily lay still and her breathing grew low and regular. Her hand still clung to Gerty's as if to ward off evil dreams, but the hold of her fingers relaxed, her head sank deeper into its shelter, and Gerty felt that she slept.

XV

WHEN LILY WOKE she had the bed to herself, and the winter light was in the room.

She sat up, bewildered by the strangeness of her surroundings; then memory returned, and she looked about her with a shiver. In the cold slant of light reflected from the back wall of a neighbouring building, she saw her evening dress and opera cloak lying in a tawdry heap on a chair. Finery laid off is as unappetizing as the remains of a feast, and it occurred to Lily that, at home, her maid's vigilance had always spared her the sight of such incongruities. Her body ached with fatigue, and with the constriction of her attitude in Gerty's bed. All through her troubled sleep she had been conscious of having no space to toss in, and the long effort to remain motionless made her feel as if she had spent her night in a train.

This sense of physical discomfort was the first to assert itself; then she perceived, beneath it, a corresponding mental prostration, a languor of horror more insufferable than the first rush of her disgust. The thought of having to wake every morning with this weight on her breast roused her tired mind to fresh effort. She must find some way out of the slough into which she had stumbled: it was not so much compunction as the dread of her morning thoughts that pressed on her the need of action. But she was unutterably tired; it was weariness to think connectedly. She lay back, looking about the poor slit of a room with a renewal of physical distaste. The outer air, penned between high buildings, brought no freshness through the window; steam-heat was beginning to sing in a coil of dingy pipes, and a smell of cooking penetrated the crack of the door.

The door opened, and Gerty, dressed and hatted, entered with a cup of tea. Her face looked sallow and swollen in the dreary light, and her dull hair shaded imperceptibly into the tones of her skin.

She glanced shyly at Lily, asking in an embarrassed tone how she felt; Lily answered with the same constraint, and raised herself up to drink the tea.

"I must have been over-tired last night; I think I had a

nervous attack in the carriage," she said, as the drink brought clearness to her sluggish thoughts.

"You were not well; I am so glad you came here," Gerty returned.

"But how am I to get home? And Aunt Julia——?"

"She knows; I telephoned early, and your maid has brought your things. But won't you eat something? I scrambled the eggs myself."

Lily could not eat; but the tea strengthened her to rise and dress under her maid's searching gaze. It was a relief to her that Gerty was obliged to hasten away: the two kissed silently, but without a trace of the previous night's emotion.

Lily found Mrs. Peniston in a state of agitation. She had sent for Grace Stepney and was taking digitalis. Lily breasted the storm of enquiries as best she could, explaining that she had had an attack of faintness on her way back from Carry Fisher's; that, fearing she would not have strength to reach home, she had gone to Miss Farish's instead; but that a quiet night had restored her, and that she had no need of a doctor.

This was a relief to Mrs. Peniston, who could give herself up to her own symptoms, and Lily was advised to go and lie down, her aunt's panacea for all physical and moral disorders. In the solitude of her own room she was brought back to a sharp contemplation of facts. Her daylight view of them necessarily differed from the cloudy vision of the night. The winged furies were now prowling gossips who dropped in on each other for tea. But her fears seemed the uglier, thus shorn of their vagueness; and besides, she had to act, not rave. For the first time she forced herself to reckon up the exact amount of her debt to Trenor; and the result of this hateful computation was the discovery that she had, in all, received nine thousand dollars from him. The flimsy pretext on which it had been given and received shrivelled up in the blaze of her shame: she knew that not a penny of it was her own, and that to restore her self-respect she must at once repay the whole amount. The inability thus to solace her outraged feelings gave her a paralyzing sense of insignificance. She was realizing for the first time that a woman's dignity may cost more to keep up than her carriage; and that the maintenance of a moral attribute should be dependent on dollars and cents, made the world appear a more sordid place than she had conceived it.

After luncheon, when Grace Stepney's prying eyes had been removed, Lily asked for a word with her aunt. The two ladies went upstairs to the sitting-room, where Mrs. Peniston seated herself in her black satin arm-chair tufted with yellow buttons, beside a bead-work table bearing a bronze box with a miniature of Beatrice Cenci in the lid. Lily felt for these objects the same distaste which the prisoner may entertain for the fittings of the court-room. It was here that her aunt received her rare confidences, and the pink-eyed smirk of the turbaned Beatrice was associated in her mind with the gradual fading of the smile from Mrs. Peniston's lips. That lady's dread of a scene gave her an inexorableness which the greatest strength of character could not have produced, since it was independent of all considerations of right or wrong; and knowing this, Lily seldom ventured to assail it. She had never felt less like making the attempt than on the present occasion; but she had sought in vain for any other means of escape from an intolerable situation.

Mrs. Peniston examined her critically. "You 're a bad colour, Lily: this incessant rushing about is beginning to tell on you," she said.

Miss Bart saw an opening. "I don't think it 's that, Aunt Julia; I 've had worries," she replied.

"Ah," said Mrs. Peniston, shutting her lips with the snap of a purse closing against a beggar.

"I 'm sorry to bother you with them," Lily continued, "but I really believe my faintness last night was brought on partly by anxious thoughts——"

"I should have said Carry Fisher's cook was enough to account for it. She has a woman who was with Maria Melson in 1891—the spring of the year we went to Aix—and I remember dining there two days before we sailed, and feeling *sure* the coppers had n't been scoured."

"I don't think I ate much; I can't eat or sleep." Lily paused, and then said abruptly: "The fact is, Aunt Julia, I owe some money."

Mrs. Peniston's face clouded perceptibly, but did not

express the astonishment her niece had expected. She was silent, and Lily was forced to continue: "I have been foolish——"

"No doubt you have: extremely foolish," Mrs. Peniston interposed. "I fail to see how any one with your income, and no expenses—not to mention the handsome presents I've always given you——"

"Oh, you've been most generous, Aunt Julia; I shall never forget your kindness. But perhaps you don't quite realize the expense a girl is put to nowadays——"

"I don't realize that *you* are put to any expense except for your clothes and your railway fares. I expect you to be handsomely dressed; but I paid Céleste's bill for you last October."

Lily hesitated: her aunt's implacable memory had never been more inconvenient. "You were as kind as possible; but I have had to get a few things since——"

"What kind of things? Clothes? How much have you spent? Let me see the bill—I daresay the woman is swindling you."

"Oh, no, I think not: clothes have grown so frightfully expensive; and one needs so many different kinds, with country visits, and golf and skating, and Aiken and Tuxedo——"

"Let me see the bill," Mrs. Peniston repeated.

Lily hesitated again. In the first place, Mme. Céleste had not yet sent in her account, and secondly, the amount it represented was only a fraction of the sum that Lily needed.

"She hasn't sent in the bill for my winter things, but I *know* it's large; and there are one or two other things; I've been careless and imprudent—I'm frightened to think of what I owe——"

She raised the troubled loveliness of her face to Mrs. Peniston, vainly hoping that a sight so moving to the other sex might not be without effect upon her own. But the effect produced was that of making Mrs. Peniston shrink back apprehensively.

"Really, Lily, you are old enough to manage your own affairs, and after frightening me to death by your performance of last night you might at least choose a better time to worry me with such matters." Mrs. Peniston glanced at the clock, and swallowed a tablet of digitalis. "If you owe Céleste another thousand, she may send me her account," she added, as though to end the discussion at any cost.

"I am very sorry, Aunt Julia; I hate to trouble you at such a time; but I have really no choice—I ought to have spoken sooner—I owe a great deal more than a thousand dollars."

"A great deal more? Do you owe two? She must have robbed you!"

"I told you it was not only Céleste. I—there are other bills—more pressing—that must be settled."

"What on earth have you been buying? Jewelry? You must have gone off your head," said Mrs. Peniston with asperity. "But if you have run into debt, you must suffer the consequences, and put aside your monthly income till your bills are paid. If you stay quietly here until next spring, instead of racing about all over the country, you will have no expenses at all, and surely in four or five months you can settle the rest of your bills if I pay the dress-maker now."

Lily was again silent. She knew she could not hope to extract even a thousand dollars from Mrs. Peniston on the mere plea of paying Céleste's bill: Mrs. Peniston would expect to go over the dress-maker's account, and would make out the cheque to her and not to Lily. And yet the money must be obtained before the day was over!

"The debts I speak of are—different—not like tradesmen's bills," she began confusedly; but Mrs. Peniston's look made her almost afraid to continue. Could it be that her aunt suspected anything? The idea precipitated Lily's avowal.

"The fact is, I 've played cards a good deal—bridge; the women all do it; girls too—it 's expected. Sometimes I 've won—won a good deal—but lately I 've been unlucky—and of course such debts can't be paid off gradually——"

She paused: Mrs. Peniston's face seemed to be petrifying as she listened.

"Cards—you 've played cards for money? It 's true, then: when I was told so I would n't believe it. I won't ask if the other horrors I was told were true too; I 've heard enough for the state of my nerves. When I think of the example you 've had in this house! But I suppose it 's your foreign bringing-up—no one knew where your mother picked up her friends. And her Sundays were a scandal—that I know."

Mrs. Peniston wheeled round suddenly. "You play cards on Sunday?"

Lily flushed with the recollection of certain rainy Sundays at Bellomont and with the Dorsets.

"You 're hard on me, Aunt Julia: I have never really cared for cards, but a girl hates to be thought priggish and superior, and one drifts into doing what the others do. I 've had a dreadful lesson, and if you 'll help me out this time I promise you——"

Mrs. Peniston raised her hand warningly. "You need n't make any promises: it 's unnecessary. When I offered you a home I did n't undertake to pay your gambling debts."

"Aunt Julia! You don't mean that you won't help me?"

"I shall certainly not do anything to give the impression that I countenance your behaviour. If you really owe your dress-maker, I will settle with her—beyond that I recognize no obligation to assume your debts."

Lily had risen, and stood pale and quivering before her aunt. Pride stormed in her, but humiliation forced the cry from her lips: "Aunt Julia, I shall be disgraced—I——" But she could go no farther. If her aunt turned such a stony ear to the fiction of the gambling debts, in what spirit would she receive the terrible avowal of the truth?

"I consider that you *are* disgraced, Lily: disgraced by your conduct far more than by its results. You say your friends have persuaded you to play cards with them; well, they may as well learn a lesson too. They can probably afford to lose a little money—and at any rate, I am not going to waste any of mine in paying them. And now I must ask you to leave me—this scene has been extremely painful, and I have my own health to consider. Draw down the blinds, please; and tell Jennings I will see no one this afternoon but Grace Stepney."

Lily went up to her own room and bolted the door. She was trembling with fear and anger—the rush of the furies' wings was in her ears. She walked up and down the room with blind irregular steps. The last door of escape was closed—she felt herself shut in with her dishonour——

Suddenly her wild pacing brought her before the clock on the chimney-piece. Its hands stood at half-past three, and she remembered that Selden was to come to her at four. She had meant to put him off with a word—but now her heart leaped at the thought of seeing him. Was there not a promise of rescue in his love? As she had lain at Gerty's side the night before, she had thought of his coming, and of the sweetness of weeping out her pain upon his breast. Of course she had meant to clear herself of its consequences before she met him—she had never really doubted that Mrs. Peniston would come to her aid. And she had felt, even in the full storm of her misery, that Selden's love could not be her ultimate refuge; only it would be so sweet to take a moment's shelter there, while she gathered fresh strength to go on.

But now his love was her only hope, and as she sat alone with her wretchedness the thought of confiding in him became as seductive as the river's flow to the suicide. The first plunge would be terrible—but afterward, what blessedness might come! She remembered Gerty's words: "I know him—he will help you"; and her mind clung to them as a sick person might cling to a healing relic. Oh, if he really understood—if he would help her to gather up her broken life, and put it together in some new semblance in which no trace of the past should remain! He had always made her feel that she was worthy of better things, and she had never been in greater need of such solace. Once and again she shrank at the thought of imperilling his love by her confession: for love was what she needed—it would take the glow of passion to weld together the shattered fragments of her self-esteem. But she recurred to Gerty's words and held fast to them. She was sure that Gerty knew Selden's feeling for her, and it had never dawned upon her blindness that Gerty's own judgment of him was coloured by emotions far more ardent than her own.

Four o'clock found her in the drawing-room: she was sure that Selden would be punctual. But the hour came and passed—it moved on feverishly, measured by her impatient heart-beats. She had time to take a fresh survey of her wretchedness, and to fluctuate anew between the impulse to confide in Selden and the dread of destroying his illusions. But as the minutes passed the need of throwing herself on his comprehension became more urgent: she could not bear the weight of her misery alone. There would be a perilous moment, perhaps: but could she not trust to her beauty to bridge it over, to land her safe in the shelter of his devotion?

But the hour sped on and Selden did not come. Doubtless he had been detained, or had misread her hurriedly scrawled note, taking the four for a five. The ringing of the door-bell a few minutes after five confirmed this supposition, and made Lily hastily resolve to write more legibly in future. The sound of steps in the hall, and of the butler's voice preceding them, poured fresh energy into her veins. She felt herself once more the alert and competent moulder of emergencies, and the remembrance of her power over Selden flushed her with sudden confidence. But when the drawing-room door opened it was Rosedale who came in.

The reaction caused her a sharp pang, but after a passing movement of irritation at the clumsiness of fate, and at her own carelessness in not denying the door to all but Selden, she controlled herself and greeted Rosedale amicably. It was annoying that Selden, when he came, should find that particular visitor in possession, but Lily was mistress of the art of ridding herself of superfluous company, and to her present mood Rosedale seemed distinctly negligible.

His own view of the situation forced itself upon her after a few moments' conversation. She had caught at the Brys' entertainment as an easy impersonal subject, likely to tide them over the interval till Selden appeared, but Mr. Rosedale, tenaciously planted beside the tea-table, his hands in his pockets, his legs a little too freely extended, at once gave the topic a personal turn.

"Pretty well done—well, yes, I suppose it was: Welly Bry's got his back up and don't mean to let go till he's got the hang of the thing. Of course, there were things here and there—things Mrs. Fisher could n't be expected to see to—the champagne was n't cold, and the coats got mixed in the coat-room. I would have spent more money on the music. But that 's my character: if I want a thing I 'm willing to pay: I don't go up to the counter, and then wonder if the article 's worth the price. I would n't be satisfied to entertain like the Welly Brys; I 'd want something that would look more easy and natural, more as if I took it in my stride. And it takes just two things to do that, Miss Bart: money, and the right woman to spend it."

He paused, and examined her attentively while she affected to rearrange the tea-cups.

"I 've got the money," he continued, clearing his throat, "and what I want is the woman—and I mean to have her too."

He leaned forward a little, resting his hands on the head of his walking-stick. He had seen men of Ned Van Alstyne's type bring their hats and sticks into a drawing-room, and he thought it added a touch of elegant familiarity to their appearance.

Lily was silent, smiling faintly, with her eyes absently resting on his face. She was in reality reflecting that a declaration would take some time to make, and that Selden must surely appear before the moment of refusal had been reached. Her brooding look, as of a mind withdrawn yet not averted, seemed to Mr. Rosedale full of a subtle encouragement. He would not have liked any evidence of eagerness.

"I mean to have her too," he repeated, with a laugh intended to strengthen his self-assurance. "I generally *have* got what I wanted in life, Miss Bart. I wanted money, and I 've got more than I know how to invest; and now the money does n't seem to be of any account unless I can spend it on the right woman. That 's what I want to do with it: I want my wife to make all the other women feel small. I 'd never grudge a dollar that was spent on that. But it is n't every woman can do it, no matter how much you spend on her. There was a girl in some history book who wanted gold shields, or something, and the fellows threw 'em at her, and she was crushed under 'em: they killed her. Well, that 's true enough: some women looked buried under their jewelry. What I want is a woman who 'll hold her head higher the more diamonds I put on it. And when I looked at you the other night at the Brys', in that plain white dress, looking as if you had a crown on, I said to myself: 'By gad, if she had one she 'd wear it as if it grew on her.' "

Still Lily did not speak, and he continued, warming with his theme: "Tell you what it is, though, that kind of woman costs more than all the rest of 'em put together. If a woman 's going to ignore her pearls, they want to be better than any-body else's—and so it is with everything else. You know what I mean—you know it 's only the showy things that are cheap. Well, I should want my wife to be able to take the earth for granted if she wanted to. I know there 's one thing vulgar about money, and that 's the thinking about it; and my wife would never have to demean herself in that way." He paused, and then added, with an unfortunate lapse to an earlier man-ner: "I guess you know the lady I 've got in view, Miss Bart."

Lily raised her head, brightening a little under the chal-lenge. Even through the dark tumult of her thoughts, the clink of Mr. Rosedale's millions had a faintly seductive note. Oh, for enough of them to cancel her one miserable debt! But the man behind them grew increasingly repugnant in the light of Selden's expected coming. The contrast was too gro-tesque: she could scarcely suppress the smile it provoked. She decided that directness would be best.

"If you mean me, Mr. Rosedale, I am very grateful—very much flattered; but I don't know what I have ever done to make you think——"

"Oh, if you mean you 're not dead in love with me, I 've got sense enough left to see that. And I ain't talking to you as if you were—I presume I know the kind of talk that 's expected under those circumstances. I 'm confoundedly gone on you—that 's about the size of it—and I 'm just giving you a plain business statement of the consequences. You 're not very fond of me—*yet*—but you 're fond of luxury, and style, and amusement, and of not having to worry about cash. You like to have a good time, and not to have to settle for it; and what I propose to do is to provide for the good time and do the settling."

He paused, and she returned with a chilling smile: "You are mistaken in one point, Mr. Rosedale: whatever I enjoy I am prepared to settle for."

She spoke with the intention of making him see that, if his words implied a tentative allusion to her private affairs, she was prepared to meet and repudiate it. But if he recognized her meaning it failed to abash him, and he went on in the same tone: "I did n't mean to give offence; excuse me if I 've spoken too plainly. But why ain't you straight with me—why do you put up that kind of bluff? You know there 've been times when you were bothered—damned bothered—and as a girl gets older, and things keep moving along, why, before she knows it, the things she wants are liable to move past her and not come back. I don't say it 's anywhere near that with you yet; but you 've had a taste of bothers that a girl like yourself ought never to have known about, and what I 'm offering you is the chance to turn your back on them once for all."

The colour burned in Lily's face as he ended; there was no mistaking the point he meant to make, and to permit it to pass unheeded was a fatal confession of weakness, while to resent it too openly was to risk offending him at a peril-ous moment. Indignation quivered on her lip; but it was quelled by the secret voice which warned her that she must not quarrel with him. He knew too much about her, and even at the moment when it was essential that he should show himself at his best, he did not scruple to let her see how much he knew. How then would he use his power when her expression of contempt had dispelled his one mo-tive for restraint? (Her whole future might hinge on her way of answering him: she had to stop and consider that, in the stress of her other anxieties, as a breathless fugitive may have to pause at the cross-roads and try to decide coolly which turn to take.)

"You are quite right, Mr. Rosedale. I *have* had bothers; and I am grateful to you for wanting to relieve me of them. It is not always easy to be quite independent and self-respecting when one is poor and lives among rich people; I have been careless about money, and have worried about my bills. But I should be selfish and ungrateful if I made that a reason for accepting all you offer, with no better return to make than the desire to be free from my anxieties. You must give me time—time to think of your kindness—and of what I could give you in return for it——"

She held out her hand with a charming gesture in which dismissal was shorn of its rigour. Its hint of future leniency made Rosedale rise in obedience to it, a little flushed with his unhoped-for success, and disciplined by the tradition of his blood to accept what was conceded, without undue haste to press for more. Something in his prompt acquiescence frightened her; she felt behind it the stored force of a patience that might subdue the strongest will. But at least they had parted amicably, and he was out of the house without meeting Selden—Selden, whose continued absence now smote her with a new alarm. Rosedale had remained over an hour, and she understood that it was now too late to hope for Selden. He would write explaining his absence, of course; there would be a note from him by the late post. But her confession would have to be postponed; and the chill of the delay settled heavily on her fagged spirit.

It lay heavier when the postman's last ring brought no note for her, and she had to go upstairs to a lonely night—a night as grim and sleepless as her tortured fancy had pictured it to Gerty. She had never learned to live with her own thoughts, and to be confronted with them through such hours of lucid misery made the confused wretchedness of her previous vigil seem easily bearable.

Daylight disbanded the phantom crew, and made it clear to her that she would hear from Selden before noon; but the day passed without his writing or coming. Lily remained at home, lunching and dining alone with her aunt, who complained of flutterings of the heart, and talked icily on general topics. Mrs. Peniston went to bed early, and when she had gone Lily sat down and wrote a note to Selden. She was about to ring for a messenger to despatch it when her eye fell on a paragraph in the evening paper which lay at her elbow: "Mr. Lawrence Selden was among the passengers sailing this afternoon for Havana and the West Indies on the Windward Liner Antilles."

She laid down the paper and sat motionless, staring at her note. She understood now that he was never coming—that he had gone away because he was afraid that he might come. She rose, and walking across the floor stood gazing at herself for a long time in the brightly-lit mirror above the mantelpiece. The lines in her face came out terribly—she looked old; and when a girl looks old to herself, how does she look to other people? She moved away, and began to wander aimlessly about the room, fitting her steps with mechanical precision between the monstrous roses of Mrs. Peniston's

Axminster. Suddenly she noticed that the pen with which she had written to Selden still rested against the uncovered inkstand. She seated herself again, and taking out an envelope, addressed it rapidly to Rosedale. Then she laid out a sheet of paper, and sat over it with suspended pen. It had been easy enough to write the date, and "Dear Mr. Rosedale"—but after that her inspiration flagged. She meant to tell him to come to her, but the words refused to shape themselves. At length she began: "I have been thinking——" then she laid the pen down, and sat with her elbows on the table and her face hidden in her hands.

Suddenly she started up at the sound of the door-bell. It was not late—barely ten o'clock—and there might still be a note from Selden, or a message—or he might be there himself, on the other side of the door! The announcement of his sailing might have been a mistake—it might be another Lawrence Selden who had gone to Havana—all these possibilities had time to flash through her mind, and build up the conviction that she was after all to see or hear from him, before the drawing-room door opened to admit a servant carrying a telegram.

Lily tore it open with shaking hands, and read Bertha Dorset's name below the message: "Sailing unexpectedly tomorrow. Will you join us on a cruise in Mediterranean?"

BOOK II

I

IT CAME VIVIDLY to Selden on the Casino steps that Monte Carlo had, more than any other place he knew, the gift of accommodating itself to each man's humour.

His own, at the moment, lent it a festive readiness of welcome that might well, in a disenchanted eye, have turned to paint and facility. So frank an appeal for participation—so outspoken a recognition of the holiday vein in human nature—struck refreshingly on a mind jaded by prolonged hard work in surroundings made for the discipline of the senses. As he surveyed the white square set in an exotic coquetry of architecture, the studied tropicality of the gardens, the groups loitering in the foreground against mauve mountains which suggested a sublime stage-setting forgotten in a hurried shifting of scenes—as he took in the whole outspread effect of light and leisure, he felt a movement of revulsion from the last few months of his life.

The New York winter had presented an interminable perspective of snow-burdened days, reaching toward a spring of raw sunshine and furious air, when the ugliness of things rasped the eye as the gritty wind ground into the skin. Selden, immersed in his work, had told himself that external conditions did not matter to a man in his state, and that cold and ugliness were a good tonic for relaxed sensibilities. When an urgent case summoned him abroad to confer with a client in Paris, he broke reluctantly with the routine of the office; and it was only now that, having despatched his business, and slipped away for a week in the south, he began to feel the renewed zest of spectatorship that is the solace of those who take an objective interest in life.

The multiplicity of its appeals—the perpetual surprise of its contrasts and resemblances! All these tricks and turns of the show were upon him with a spring as he descended the Casino steps and paused on the pavement at its doors. He had not been abroad for seven years—and what changes the renewed contact produced! If the central depths were untouched, hardly a pin-point of surface remained the same.

And this was the very place to bring out the completeness of the renewal. The sublimities, the perpetuities, might have left him as he was: but this tent pitched for a day's revelry spread a roof of oblivion between himself and his fixed sky.

It was mid-April, and one felt that the revelry had reached its climax and that the desultory groups in the square and gardens would soon dissolve and re-form in other scenes. Meanwhile the last moments of the performance seemed to gain an added brightness from the hovering threat of the curtain. The quality of the air, the exuberance of the flowers, the blue intensity of sea and sky, produced the effect of a closing *tableau*, when all the lights are turned on at once. This impression was presently heightened by the way in which a consciously conspicuous group of people advanced to the middle front, and stood before Selden with the air of the chief performers gathered together by the exigencies of the final effect. Their appearance confirmed the impression that the show had been staged regardless of expense, and emphasized its resemblance to one of those "costume-plays" in which the protagonists walk through the passions without displacing a drapery. The ladies stood in unrelated attitudes calculated to isolate their effects, and the men hung about them as irrelevantly as stage heroes whose tailors are named in the programme. It was Selden himself who unwittingly fused the group by arresting the attention of one of its members.

"Why, Mr. Selden!" Mrs. Fisher exclaimed in surprise; and with a gesture toward Mrs. Jack Stepney and Mrs. Wellington Bry, she added plaintively: "We 're starving to death because we can't decide where to lunch."

Welcomed into their group, and made the confidant of their difficulty, Selden learned with amusement that there were several places where one might miss something by not lunching, or forfeit something by lunching; so that eating actually became a minor consideration on the very spot consecrated to its rites.

"Of course one gets the best things at the *Terrasse*—but that looks as if one had n't any other reason for being there: the Americans who don't know any one always rush for the best food. And the Duchess of Beltshire has taken up Bécassin's lately," Mrs. Bry earnestly summed up.

Mrs. Bry, to Mrs. Fisher's despair, had not progressed beyond the point of weighing her social alternatives in public. She could not acquire the air of doing things because she wanted to, and making her choice the final seal of their fitness.

Mr. Bry, a short pale man, with a business face and leisure clothes, met the dilemma hilariously.

"I guess the Duchess goes where it's cheapest, unless she can get her meal paid for. If you offered to blow her off at the *Terrasse* she'd turn up fast enough."

But Mrs. Jack Stepney interposed. "The Grand Dukes go to that little place at the Condamine. Lord Hubert says it's the only restaurant in Europe where they can cook peas."

Lord Hubert Dacey, a slender shabby-looking man, with a charming worn smile, and the air of having spent his best years in piloting the wealthy to the right restaurant, assented with gentle emphasis: "It's quite that."

"Peas?" said Mr. Bry contemptuously. "Can they cook terrapin? It just shows," he continued, "what these European markets are, when a fellow can make a reputation cooking peas!"

Jack Stepney intervened with authority. "I don't know that I quite agree with Dacey: there's a little hole in Paris, off the Quai Voltaire—but in any case, I can't advise the Condamine *gargote*; at least not with ladies."

Stepney, since his marriage, had thickened and grown prudish, as the Van Osburgh husbands were apt to do; but his wife, to his surprise and discomfiture, had developed an earth-shaking fastness of gait which left him trailing breathlessly in her wake.

"That's where we'll go then!" she declared, with a heavy toss of her plumage. "I'm so tired of the *Terrasse*: it's as dull as one of mother's dinners. And Lord Hubert has promised to tell us who all the awful people are at the other place— has n't he, Carry? Now, Jack, don't look so solemn!"

"Well," said Mrs. Bry, "all I want to know is who their dress-makers are."

"No doubt Dacey can tell you that too," remarked Stepney, with an ironic intention which the other received with the light murmur, "I can at least *find out*, my dear fellow"; and

Mrs. Bry having declared that she could n't walk another step, the party hailed two or three of the light phaetons which hover attentively on the confines of the gardens, and rattled off in procession toward the Condamine.

Their destination was one of the little restaurants overhanging the boulevard which dips steeply down from Monte Carlo to the low intermediate quarter along the quay. From the window in which they presently found themselves installed, they overlooked the intense blue curve of the harbour, set between the verdure of twin promontories: to the right, the cliff of Monaco, topped by the mediæval silhouette of its church and castle, to the left the terraces and pinnacles of the gambling-house. Between the two, the waters of the bay were furrowed by a light coming and going of pleasure-craft, through which, just at the culminating moment of luncheon, the majestic advance of a great steam-yacht drew the company's attention from the peas.

"By Jove, I believe that 's the Dorsets back!" Stepney exclaimed; and Lord Hubert, dropping his single eye-glass, corroborated: "It 's the Sabrina—yes."

"So soon? They were to spend a month in Sicily," Mrs. Fisher observed.

"I guess they feel as if they had: there 's only one up-to-date hotel in the whole place," said Mr. Bry disparagingly.

"It was Ned Silverton's idea—but poor Dorset and Lily Bart must have been horribly bored." Mrs. Fisher added in an undertone to Selden: "I do hope there has n't been a row."

"It 's most awfully jolly having Miss Bart back," said Lord Hubert, in his mild deliberate voice; and Mrs. Bry added ingenuously: "I daresay the Duchess will dine with us, now that Lily 's here."

"The Duchess admires her immensely: I 'm sure she 'd be charmed to have it arranged," Lord Hubert agreed, with the professional promptness of the man accustomed to draw his profit from facilitating social contacts: Selden was struck by the businesslike change in his manner.

"Lily has been a tremendous success here," Mrs. Fisher continued, still addressing herself confidentially to Selden. "She looks ten years younger—I never saw her so handsome. Lady Skiddaw took her everywhere in Cannes, and the

Crown Princess of Macedonia had her to stop for a week at Cimiez. People say that was one reason why Bertha whisked the yacht off to Sicily: the Crown Princess did n't take much notice of her, and she could n't bear to look on at Lily's triumph."

Selden made no reply. He was vaguely aware that Miss Bart was cruising in the Mediterranean with the Dorsets, but it had not occurred to him that there was any chance of running across her on the Riviera, where the season was virtually at an end. As he leaned back, silently contemplating his filigree cup of Turkish coffee, he was trying to put some order in his thoughts, to tell himself how the news of her nearness was really affecting him. He had a personal detachment enabling him, even in moments of emotional high-pressure, to get a fairly clear view of his feelings, and he was sincerely surprised by the disturbance which the sight of the Sabrina had produced in him. He had reason to think that his three months of engrossing professional work, following on the sharp shock of his disillusionment, had cleared his mind of its sentimental vapours. The feeling he had nourished and given prominence to was one of thankfulness for his escape: he was like a traveller so grateful for rescue from a dangerous accident that at first he is hardly conscious of his bruises. Now he suddenly felt the latent ache, and realized that after all he had not come off unhurt.

An hour later, at Mrs. Fisher's side in the Casino gardens, he was trying to find fresh reasons for forgetting the injury received in the contemplation of the peril avoided. The party had dispersed with the loitering indecision characteristic of social movements at Monte Carlo, where the whole place, and the long gilded hours of the day, seem to offer an infinity of ways of being idle. Lord Hubert Dacey had finally gone off in quest of the Duchess of Beltshire, charged by Mrs. Bry with the delicate negotiation of securing that lady's presence at dinner, the Stepneys had left for Nice in their motor-car, and Mr. Bry had departed to take his place in the pigeon-shooting match which was at the moment engaging his highest faculties.

Mrs. Bry, who had a tendency to grow red and stertorous after luncheon, had been judiciously prevailed upon by Carry

Fisher to withdraw to her hotel for an hour's repose; and
Selden and his companion were thus left to a stroll propitious
to confidences. The stroll soon resolved itself into a tranquil
session on a bench overhung with laurel and Banksian roses,
from which they caught a dazzle of blue sea between marble
balusters, and the fiery shafts of cactus-blossoms shooting me-
teor-like from the rock. The soft shade of their niche, and the
adjacent glitter of the air, were conducive to an easy lounging
mood, and to the smoking of many cigarettes; and Selden,
yielding to these influences, suffered Mrs. Fisher to unfold to
him the history of her recent experiences. She had come
abroad with the Welly Brys at the moment when fashion flees
the inclemency of the New York spring. The Brys, intoxicated
by their first success, already thirsted for new kingdoms, and
Mrs. Fisher, viewing the Riviera as an easy introduction to
London society, had guided their course thither. She had affiliations of her own in every capital, and a facility for picking
them up again after long absences; and the carefully dissemi-
nated rumour of the Brys' wealth had at once gathered about
them a group of cosmopolitan pleasure-seekers.

"But things are not going as well as I expected," Mrs.
Fisher frankly admitted. "It's all very well to say that everybody with money can get into society; but it would be truer
to say that *nearly* everybody can. And the London market is
so glutted with new Americans that, to succeed there now,
they must be either very clever or awfully queer. The Brys are
neither. *He* would get on well enough if she'd let him alone;
they like his slang and his brag and his blunders. But Louisa
spoils it all by trying to repress him and put herself forward.
If she'd be natural herself—fat and vulgar and bouncing—it
would be all right; but as soon as she meets anybody smart
she tries to be slender and queenly. She tried it with the
Duchess of Beltshire and Lady Skiddaw, and they fled. I've
done my best to make her see her mistake—I've said to her
again and again: 'Just let yourself go, Louisa'; but she keeps
up the humbug even with me—I believe she keeps on being
queenly in her own room, with the door shut.

"The worst of it is," Mrs. Fisher went on, "that she thinks
it's all *my* fault. When the Dorsets turned up here six weeks
ago, and everybody began to make a fuss about Lily Bart, I

could see Louisa thought that if she 'd had Lily in tow instead
of me she would have been hob-nobbing with all the royalties
by this time. She does n't realize that it 's Lily's beauty that
does it: Lord Hubert tells me Lily is thought even handsomer
than when he knew her at Aix ten years ago. It seems she was
tremendously admired there. An Italian Prince, rich and the
real thing, wanted to marry her; but just at the critical moment a good-looking step-son turned up, and Lily was silly
enough to flirt with him while her marriage-settlements with
the step-father were being drawn up. Some people said the
young man did it on purpose. You can fancy the scandal:
there was an awful row between the men, and people began
to look at Lily so queerly that Mrs. Peniston had to pack up
and finish her cure elsewhere. Not that *she* ever understood:
to this day she thinks that Aix did n't suit her, and mentions
her having been sent there as proof of the incompetence of
French doctors. That 's Lily all over, you know: she works
like a slave preparing the ground and sowing her seed; but
the day she ought to be reaping the harvest she over-sleeps
herself or goes off on a picnic."

Mrs. Fisher paused and looked reflectively at the deep
shimmer of sea between the cactus-flowers. "Sometimes," she
added, "I think it 's just flightiness—and sometimes I think
it 's because, at heart, she despises the things she 's trying for.
And it 's the difficulty of deciding that makes her such an
interesting study." She glanced tentatively at Selden's motionless profile, and resumed with a slight sigh: "Well, all I can
say is, I wish she 'd give *me* some of her discarded opportunities. I wish we could change places now, for instance. She
could make a very good thing out of the Brys if she managed
them properly, and I should know just how to look after
George Dorset while Bertha is reading Verlaine with Neddy
Silverton."

She met Selden's sound of protest with a sharp derisive
glance. "Well, what 's the use of mincing matters? We all
know that 's what Bertha brought her abroad for. When Bertha wants to have a good time she has to provide occupation
for George. At first I thought Lily was going to play her cards
well *this* time, but there are rumours that Bertha is jealous of
her success here and at Cannes, and I should n't be surprised

if there were a break any day. Lily's only safeguard is that
Bertha needs her badly—oh, very badly. The Silverton affair
is in the acute stage: it's necessary that George's attention
should be pretty continuously distracted. And I'm bound to
say Lily *does* distract it: I believe he'd marry her tomorrow if
he found out there was anything wrong with Bertha. But you
know him—he's as blind as he's jealous; and of course
Lily's present business is to keep him blind. A clever woman
might know just the right moment to tear off the bandage:
but Lily is n't clever in that way, and when George does open
his eyes she'll probably contrive not to be in his line of
vision."

Selden tossed away his cigarette. "By Jove—it's time for
my train," he exclaimed, with a glance at his watch; adding,
in reply to Mrs. Fisher's surprised comment—"Why, I
thought of course you were at Monte!"—a murmured word
to the effect that he was making Nice his head-quarters.

"The worst of it is, she snubs the Brys now," he heard
irrelevantly flung after him.

Ten minutes later, in the high-perched bedroom of an hotel
overlooking the Casino, he was tossing his effects into a couple of gaping portmanteaux, while the porter waited outside
to transport them to the cab at the door. It took but a brief
plunge down the steep white road to the station to land him
safely in the afternoon express for Nice; and not till he was
installed in the corner of an empty carriage, did he exclaim to
himself, with a reaction of self-contempt: "What the deuce
am I running away from?"

The pertinence of the question checked Selden's fugitive
impulse before the train had started. It was ridiculous to be
flying like an emotional coward from an infatuation his reason had conquered. He had instructed his bankers to forward
some important business letters to Nice, and at Nice he
would quietly await them. He was already annoyed with himself for having left Monte Carlo, where he had intended to
pass the week which remained to him before sailing; but it
would now be difficult to return on his steps without an appearance of inconsistency from which his pride recoiled. In
his inmost heart he was not sorry to put himself beyond the
probability of meeting Miss Bart. Completely as he had

detached himself from her, he could not yet regard her merely as a social instance; and viewed in a more personal way she was not likely to be a reassuring object of study. Chance encounters, or even the repeated mention of her name, would send his thoughts back into grooves from which he had resolutely detached them; whereas, if she could be entirely excluded from his life, the pressure of new and varied impressions, with which no thought of her was connected, would soon complete the work of separation. Mrs. Fisher's conversation had, indeed, operated to that end; but the treatment was too painful to be voluntarily chosen while milder remedies were untried; and Selden thought he could trust himself to return gradually to a reasonable view of Miss Bart, if only he did not see her.

Having reached the station early, he had arrived at this point in his reflections before the increasing throng on the platform warned him that he could not hope to preserve his privacy; the next moment there was a hand on the door, and he turned to confront the very face he was fleeing.

Miss Bart, glowing with the haste of a precipitate descent upon the train, headed a group composed of the Dorsets, young Silverton and Lord Hubert Dacey, who had barely time to spring into the carriage, and envelop Selden in ejaculations of surprise and welcome, before the whistle of departure sounded. The party, it appeared, were hastening to Nice in response to a sudden summons to dine with the Duchess of Beltshire and to see the water-fête in the bay; a plan evidently improvised—in spite of Lord Hubert's protesting "Oh, I say, you know,"—for the express purpose of defeating Mrs. Bry's endeavour to capture the Duchess.

During the laughing relation of this manœuvre, Selden had time for a rapid impression of Miss Bart, who had seated herself opposite to him in the golden afternoon light. Scarcely three months had elapsed since he had parted from her on the threshold of the Brys' conservatory; but a subtle change had passed over the quality of her beauty. Then it had had a transparency through which the fluctuations of the spirit were sometimes tragically visible; now its impenetrable surface suggested a process of crystallization which had fused her whole being into one hard brilliant substance. The change had

struck Mrs. Fisher as a rejuvenation: to Selden it seemed like
that moment of pause and arrest when the warm fluidity of
youth is chilled into its final shape.

He felt it in the way she smiled on him, and in the readiness and competence with which, flung unexpectedly into
his presence, she took up the thread of their intercourse as
though that thread had not been snapped with a violence
from which he still reeled. Such facility sickened him—but
he told himself that it was with the pang which precedes recovery. Now he would really get well—would eject the last
drop of poison from his blood. Already he felt himself
calmer in her presence than he had learned to be in the
thought of her. Her assumptions and elisions, her short-cuts
and long *détours*, the skill with which she contrived to meet
him at a point from which no inconvenient glimpses of the
past were visible, suggested what opportunities she had had
for practising such arts since their last meeting. He felt that
she had at last arrived at an understanding with herself: had
made a pact with her rebellious impulses, and achieved a
uniform system of self-government, under which all vagrant
tendencies were either held captive or forced into the service
of the state.

And he saw other things too in her manner: saw how it
had adjusted itself to the hidden intricacies of a situation in
which, even after Mrs. Fisher's elucidating flashes, he still felt
himself agrope. Surely Mrs. Fisher could no longer charge
Miss Bart with neglecting her opportunities! To Selden's exasperated observation she was only too completely alive to
them. She was "perfect" to every one: subservient to Bertha's
anxious predominance, good-naturedly watchful of Dorset's
moods, brightly companionable to Silverton and Dacey, the
latter of whom met her on an evident footing of old admiration, while young Silverton, portentously self-absorbed,
seemed conscious of her only as of something vaguely obstructive. And suddenly, as Selden noted the fine shades of
manner by which she harmonized herself with her surroundings, it flashed on him that, to need such adroit handling, the
situation must indeed be desperate. She was on the edge of
something—that was the impression left with him. He
seemed to see her poised on the brink of a chasm, with one

graceful foot advanced to assert her unconsciousness that the
ground was failing her.

On the Promenade des Anglais, where Ned Silverton hung
on him for the half hour before dinner, he received a deeper
impression of the general insecurity. Silverton was in a mood
of Titanic pessimism. How any one could come to such a
damned hole as the Riviera—any one with a grain of imagination—with the whole Mediterranean to choose from: but
then, if one's estimate of a place depended on the way they
broiled a spring chicken! Gad! what a study might be made
of the tyranny of the stomach—the way a sluggish liver or
insufficient gastric juices might affect the whole course of the
universe, overshadow everything in reach—chronic dyspepsia
ought to be among the "statutory causes"; a woman's life
might be ruined by a man's inability to digest fresh bread.
Grotesque? Yes—and tragic—like most absurdities. There's
nothing grimmer than the tragedy that wears a comic
mask. . . . Where was he? Oh—the reason they chucked
Sicily and rushed back? Well—partly, no doubt, Miss Bart's
desire to get back to bridge and smartness. Dead as a stone
to art and poetry—the light never *was* on sea or land for her!
And of course she persuaded Dorset that the Italian food was
bad for him. Oh, she could make him believe anything— *anything!* Mrs. Dorset was aware of it—oh, perfectly: nothing
she did n't see! But she could hold her tongue—she 'd had
to, often enough. Miss Bart was an intimate friend—she
would n't hear a word against her. Only it hurts a woman's
pride—there are some things one does n't get used to . . .
All this in confidence, of course? Ah—and there were the
ladies signalling from the balcony of the hotel. . . . He
plunged across the Promenade, leaving Selden to a meditative
cigar.

The conclusions it led him to were fortified, later in the
evening, by some of those faint corroborative hints that gen-
erate a light of their own in the dusk of a doubting mind.
Selden, stumbling on a chance acquaintance, had dined with
him, and adjourned, still in his company, to the brightly lit
Promenade, where a line of crowded stands commanded the
glittering darkness of the waters. The night was soft and persuasive. Overhead hung a summer sky furrowed with the rush

of rockets; and from the east a late moon, pushing up beyond the lofty bend of the coast, sent across the bay a shaft of brightness which paled to ashes in the red glitter of the illuminated boats. Down the lantern-hung Promenade, snatches of band-music floated above the hum of the crowd and the soft tossing of boughs in dusky gardens; and between these gardens and the backs of the stands there flowed a stream of people in whom the vociferous carnival mood seemed tempered by the growing languor of the season.

Selden and his companion, unable to get seats on one of the stands facing the bay, had wandered for a while with the throng, and then found a point of vantage on a high garden-parapet above the Promenade. Thence they caught but a triangular glimpse of the water, and of the flashing play of boats across its surface; but the crowd in the street was under their immediate view, and seemed to Selden, on the whole, of more interest than the show itself. After a while, however, he wearied of his perch and, dropping alone to the pavement, pushed his way to the first corner and turned into the moonlit silence of a side street. Long garden-walls overhung by trees made a dark boundary to the pavement; an empty cab trailed along the deserted thoroughfare, and presently Selden saw two persons emerge from the opposite shadows, signal to the cab, and drive off in it toward the centre of the town. The moonlight touched them as they paused to enter the carriage, and he recognized Mrs. Dorset and young Silverton.

Beneath the nearest lamp-post he glanced at his watch and saw that the time was close on eleven. He took another cross street, and without breasting the throng on the Promenade, made his way to the fashionable club which overlooks that thoroughfare. Here, amid the blaze of crowded baccarat tables, he caught sight of Lord Hubert Dacey, seated with his habitual worn smile behind a rapidly dwindling heap of gold. The heap being in due course wiped out, Lord Hubert rose with a shrug, and joining Selden, adjourned with him to the deserted terrace of the club. It was now past midnight, and the throng on the stands was dispersing, while the long trails of red-lit boats scattered and faded beneath a sky repossessed by the tranquil splendour of the moon.

Lord Hubert looked at his watch. "By Jove, I promised to

join the Duchess for supper at the *London House*; but it 's past twelve, and I suppose they 've all scattered. The fact is, I lost them in the crowd soon after dinner, and took refuge here, for my sins. They had seats on one of the stands, but of course they could n't stop quiet: the Duchess never can. She and Miss Bart went off in quest of what they call adventures—gad, it ain't their fault if they don't have some queer ones!" He added tentatively, after pausing to grope for a cigarette: "Miss Bart 's an old friend of yours, I believe? So she told me.—Ah, thanks—I don't seem to have one left." He lit Selden's proffered cigarette, and continued, in his high-pitched drawling tone: "None of my business, of course, but I did n't introduce her to the Duchess. Charming woman, the Duchess, you understand; and a very good friend of mine; but *rather* a liberal education."

Selden received this in silence, and after a few puffs Lord Hubert broke out again: "Sort of thing one can't communicate to the young lady—though young ladies nowadays are so competent to judge for themselves; but in this case—I 'm an old friend too, you know . . . and there seemed no one else to speak to. The whole situation 's a little mixed, as I see it—but there used to be an aunt somewhere, a diffuse and innocent person, who was great at bridging over chasms she did n't see . . . Ah, in New York, is she? Pity New York 's such a long way off!"

II

M ISS BART, emerging late the next morning from her cabin, found herself alone on the deck of the Sabrina. The cushioned chairs, disposed expectantly under the wide awning, showed no signs of recent occupancy, and she presently learned from a steward that Mrs. Dorset had not yet appeared, and that the gentlemen—separately—had gone ashore as soon as they had breakfasted. Supplied with these facts, Lily leaned awhile over the side, giving herself up to a leisurely enjoyment of the spectacle before her. Unclouded sunlight enveloped sea and shore in a bath of purest radiancy. The purpling waters drew a sharp white line of foam at the base of the shore; against its irregular eminences, hotels and villas flashed from the greyish verdure of olive and eucalyptus; and the background of bare and finely-pencilled mountains quivered in a pale intensity of light.

How beautiful it was—and how she loved beauty! She had always felt that her sensibility in this direction made up for certain obtusenesses of feeling of which she was less proud; and during the last three months she had indulged it passionately. The Dorsets' invitation to go abroad with them had come as an almost miraculous release from crushing difficulties; and her faculty for renewing herself in new scenes, and casting off problems of conduct as easily as the surroundings in which they had arisen, made the mere change from one place to another seem, not merely a postponement, but a solution of her troubles. Moral complications existed for her only in the environment that had produced them; she did not mean to slight or ignore them, but they lost their reality when they changed their background. She could not have remained in New York without repaying the money she owed to Trenor; to acquit herself of that odious debt she might even have faced a marriage with Rosedale; but the accident of placing the Atlantic between herself and her obligations made them dwindle out of sight as if they had been milestones and she had travelled past them.

Her two months on the Sabrina had been especially calculated to aid this illusion of distance. She had been plunged into new scenes, and had found in them a renewal of old hopes and ambitions. The cruise itself charmed her as a romantic adventure. She was vaguely touched by the names and scenes amid which she moved, and had listened to Ned Silverton reading Theocritus by moonlight, as the yacht rounded the Sicilian promontories, with a thrill of the nerves that confirmed her belief in her intellectual superiority. But the weeks at Cannes and Nice had really given her more pleasure. The gratification of being welcomed in high company, and of making her own ascendency felt there, so that she found herself figuring once more as the "beautiful Miss Bart" in the interesting journal devoted to recording the least movements of her cosmopolitan companions—all these experiences tended to throw into the extreme background of memory the prosaic and sordid difficulties from which she had escaped.

If she was faintly aware of fresh difficulties ahead, she was sure of her ability to meet them: it was characteristic of her to feel that the only problems she could not solve were those with which she was familiar. Meanwhile she could honestly be proud of the skill with which she had adapted herself to somewhat delicate conditions. She had reason to think that she had made herself equally necessary to her host and hostess; and if only she had seen any perfectly irreproachable means of drawing a financial profit from the situation, there would have been no cloud on her horizon. The truth was that her funds, as usual, were inconveniently low; and to neither Dorset nor his wife could this vulgar embarrassment be safely hinted. Still, the need was not a pressing one; she could worry along, as she had so often done before, with the hope of some happy change of fortune to sustain her; and meanwhile life was gay and beautiful and easy, and she was conscious of figuring not unworthily in such a setting.

She was engaged to breakfast that morning with the Duchess of Beltshire, and at twelve o'clock she asked to be set ashore in the gig. Before this she had sent her maid to enquire if she might see Mrs. Dorset; but the reply came back that the latter was tired, and trying to sleep. Lily thought she understood the reason of the rebuff. Her hostess had not been included in the Duchess's invitation, though she herself had made the most loyal efforts in that direction. But her grace was impervious to hints, and invited or omitted as she chose. It was not Lily's fault if Mrs. Dorset's complicated attitudes did not fall in with the Duchess's easy gait. The Duchess, who seldom explained herself, had not formulated her objection beyond saying: "She 's rather a bore, you know. The only one of your friends I like is that little Mr. Bry— *he 's* funny—" but Lily knew enough not to press the point, and was not altogether sorry to be thus distinguished at her friend's expense. Bertha certainly *had* grown tiresome since she had taken to poetry and Ned Silverton.

On the whole, it was a relief to break away now and then from the Sabrina; and the Duchess's little breakfast, organized by Lord Hubert with all his usual virtuosity, was the pleasanter to Lily for not including her travelling-companions. Dorset, of late, had grown more than usually morose and incalculable, and Ned Silverton went about with an air that seemed to challenge the universe. The freedom and lightness of the ducal intercourse made an agreeable change from these complications, and Lily was tempted, after luncheon, to adjourn in the wake of her companions to the hectic atmosphere of the Casino. She did not mean to play; her diminished pocket-money offered small scope for the adventure; but it amused her to sit on a divan, under the doubtful protection of the Duchess's back, while the latter hung above her stakes at a neighbouring table.

The rooms were packed with the gazing throng which, in the afternoon hours, trickles heavily between the tables, like the Sunday crowd in a lion-house. In the stagnant flow of the mass, identities were hardly distinguishable; but Lily presently saw Mrs. Bry cleaving her determined way through the doors, and, in the broad wake she left, the light figure of Mrs. Fisher bobbing after her like a row-boat at the stern of a tug. Mrs. Bry pressed on, evidently animated by the resolve to reach a certain point in the rooms; but Mrs. Fisher, as she passed Lily, broke from her towing-line, and let herself float to the girl's side.

"Lose her?" she echoed the latter's query, with an indifferent glance at Mrs. Bry's retreating back. "I daresay—it does n't matter: I *have* lost her already." And, as Lily exclaimed, she added: "We had an awful row this morning. You know, of course, that the Duchess chucked her at dinner last night, and she thinks it was my fault—my want of management. The worst of it is, the message—just a mere word by telephone—came so late that the dinner had to be paid for; and Bécassin *had* run it up—it had been so drummed into him that the Duchess was coming!" Mrs. Fisher indulged in a faint laugh at the remembrance. "Paying for what she does n't get rankles so dreadfully with Louisa: I can't make her see that it 's one of the preliminary steps to getting what you have n't paid for—and as I was the nearest thing to smash, she smashed me to atoms, poor dear!"

Lily murmured her commiseration. Impulses of sympathy came naturally to her, and it was instinctive to proffer her help to Mrs. Fisher.

"If there 's anything I can do—if it 's only a question of meeting the Duchess! I heard her say she thought Mr. Bry amusing——"

But Mrs. Fisher interposed with a decisive gesture. "My dear, I have my pride: the pride of my trade. *I* could n't manage the Duchess, and I can't palm off your arts on Louisa Bry as mine. I 've taken the final step: I go to Paris tonight with the Sam Gormers. *They 're* still in the elementary stage; an Italian Prince is a great deal more than a Prince to them, and they 're always on the brink of taking a courier for one. To save them from that is my present mission." She laughed again at the picture. "But before I go I want to make my last will and testament—I want to leave you the Brys."

"Me?" Miss Bart joined in her amusement. "It 's charming of you to remember me, dear; but really——"

"You 're already so well provided for?" Mrs. Fisher flashed a sharp glance at her. "*Are* you, though, Lily—to the point of rejecting my offer?"

Miss Bart coloured slowly. "What I really meant was, that the Brys would n't in the least care to be so disposed of."

Mrs. Fisher continued to probe her embarrassment with an unflinching eye. "What you really meant was that you 've snubbed the Brys horribly; and you know that they know it——"

"Carry!"

"Oh, on certain sides Louisa bristles with perceptions. If you'd even managed to have them asked once on the Sabrina—especially when royalties were coming! But it's not too late," she ended earnestly, "it's not too late for either of you."

Lily smiled. "Stay over, and I'll get the Duchess to dine with them."

"I shan't stay over—the Gormers have paid for my *salon-lit*," said Mrs. Fisher with simplicity. "But get the Duchess to dine with them all the same."

Lily's smile again flowed into a slight laugh: her friend's importunity was beginning to strike her as irrelevant. "I'm sorry I have been negligent about the Brys——" she began.

"Oh, as to the Brys—it's you I'm thinking of," said Mrs. Fisher abruptly. She paused, and then, bending forward, with a lowered voice: "You know we all went on to Nice last night when the Duchess chucked us. It was Louisa's idea—I told her what I thought of it."

Miss Bart assented. "Yes—I caught sight of you on the way back, at the station."

"Well, the man who was in the carriage with you and George Dorset—that horrid little Dabham who does 'Society Notes from the Riviera'—had been dining with us at Nice. And he's telling everybody that you and Dorset came back alone after midnight."

"Alone—? When he was with us?" Lily laughed, but her laugh faded into gravity under the prolonged implication of Mrs. Fisher's look. "We *did* come back alone—if that's so very dreadful! But whose fault was it? The Duchess was spending the night at Cimiez with the Crown Princess; Bertha got bored with the show, and went off early, promising to meet us at the station. We turned up on time, but she did n't—she did n't turn up at all!"

Miss Bart made this announcement in the tone of one who presents, with careless assurance, a complete vindication; but Mrs. Fisher received it in a manner almost inconsequent. She seemed to have lost sight of her friend's part in the incident: her inward vision had taken another slant.

"Bertha never turned up at all? Then how on earth did she get back?"

"Oh, by the next train, I suppose; there were two extra ones for the *fête*. At any rate, I know she 's safe on the yacht, though I have n't yet seen her; but you see it was not my fault," Lily summed up.

"Not your fault that Bertha did n't turn up? My poor child, if only you don't have to pay for it!" Mrs. Fisher rose—she had seen Mrs. Bry surging back in her direction. "There 's Louisa, and I must be off—oh, we 're on the best of terms externally; we 're lunching together; but at heart it 's *me* she 's lunching on," she explained; and with a last hand-clasp and a last look, she added: "Remember, I leave her to you; she 's hovering now, ready to take you in."

Lily carried the impression of Mrs. Fisher's leave-taking away with her from the Casino doors. She had accomplished, before leaving, the first step toward her reinstatement in Mrs. Bry's good graces. An affable advance—a vague murmur that they must see more of each other—an allusive glance to a near future that was felt to include the Duchess as well as the Sabrina—how easily it was all done, if one possessed the knack of doing it! She wondered at herself, as she had so often wondered, that, possessing the knack, she did not more consistently exercise it. But sometimes she was forgetful— and sometimes, could it be that she was proud? Today, at any rate, she had been vaguely conscious of a reason for sinking her pride, had in fact even sunk it to the point of suggesting to Lord Hubert Dacey, whom she ran across on the Casino steps, that he might really get the Duchess to dine with the Brys, if *she* undertook to have them asked on the Sabrina. Lord Hubert had promised his help, with the readiness on which she could always count: it was his only way of ever reminding her that he had once been ready to do so much more for her. Her path, in short, seemed to smooth itself before her as she advanced; yet the faint stir of uneasiness persisted. Had it been produced, she wondered, by her chance meeting with Selden? She thought not—time and change seemed so completely to have relegated him to his proper distance. The sudden and exquisite reaction from her anxieties had had the effect of throwing the recent past so far back that even Selden, as part of it, retained a certain air of unreality. And he had made it so clear that they were not to meet again; that he had merely dropped down to Nice for a day or two, and had almost his foot on the next steamer. No—that part of the past had merely surged up for a moment on the fleeing surface of events; and now that it was submerged again, the uncertainty, the apprehension persisted.

They grew to sudden acuteness as she caught sight of George Dorset descending the steps of the Hôtel de Paris and making for her across the square. She had meant to drive down to the quay and regain the yacht; but she now had the immediate impression that something more was to happen first.

"Which way are you going? Shall we walk a bit?" he began, putting the second question before the first was answered, and not waiting for a reply to either before he directed her silently toward the comparative seclusion of the lower gardens.

She detected in him at once all the signs of extreme nervous tension. The skin was puffed out under his sunken eyes, and its sallowness had paled to a leaden white against which his irregular eyebrows and long reddish moustache were relieved with a saturnine effect. His appearance, in short, presented an odd mixture of the bedraggled and the ferocious.

He walked beside her in silence, with quick precipitate steps, till they reached the embowered slopes to the east of the Casino; then, pulling up abruptly, he said: "Have you seen Bertha?"

"No—when I left the yacht she was not yet up."

He received this with a laugh like the whirring sound in a disabled clock. "Not yet up? Had she gone to bed? Do you know at what time she came on board? This morning at seven!" he exclaimed.

"At seven?" Lily started. "What happened—an accident to the train?"

He laughed again. "They missed the train—all the trains—they had to drive back."

"Well——?" She hesitated, feeling at once how little even this necessity accounted for the fatal lapse of hours.

"Well, they could n't get a carriage at once—at that time of night, you know—" the explanatory note made it almost seem as though he were putting the case for his wife—"and when they finally did, it was only a one-horse cab, and the horse was lame!"

"How tiresome! I see," she affirmed, with the more earnestness because she was so nervously conscious that she did not; and after a pause she added: "I 'm so sorry—but ought we to have waited?"

"Waited for the one-horse cab? It would scarcely have carried the four of us, do you think?"

She took this in what seemed the only possible way, with a laugh intended to sink the question itself in his humorous treatment of it. "Well, it would have been difficult; we should have had to walk by turns. But it would have been jolly to see the sunrise."

"Yes: the sunrise *was* jolly," he agreed.

"Was it? You saw it, then?"

"I saw it, yes; from the deck. I waited up for them."

"Naturally—I suppose you were worried. Why did n't you call on me to share your vigil?"

He stood still, dragging at his moustache with a lean weak hand. "I don't think you would have cared for its *dénouement*," he said with sudden grimness.

Again she was disconcerted by the abrupt change in his tone, and as in one flash she saw the peril of the moment, and the need of keeping her sense of it out of her eyes.

"*Dénouement*—is n't that too big a word for such a small incident? The worst of it, after all, is the fatigue which Bertha has probably slept off by this time."

She clung to the note bravely, though its futility was now plain to her in the glare of his miserable eyes.

"Don't—don't——!" he broke out, with the hurt cry of a child; and while she tried to merge her sympathy, and her resolve to ignore any cause for it, in one ambiguous murmur of deprecation, he dropped down on the bench near which they had paused, and poured out the wretchedness of his soul.

It was a dreadful hour—an hour from which she emerged shrinking and seared, as though her lids had been scorched by its actual glare. It was not that she had never had premonitory glimpses of such an outbreak; but rather because, here and there throughout the three months, the surface of life had shown such ominous cracks and vapours that her fears had always been on the alert for an upheaval. There had been moments when the situation had presented itself under a homelier yet more vivid image—that of a shaky vehicle, dashed by unbroken steeds over a bumping road, while she cowered within, aware that the harness wanted mending, and wondering what would give way first. Well—everything had given way now; and the wonder was that the crazy outfit had held together so long. Her sense of being involved in the crash, instead of merely witnessing it from the road, was intensified by the way in which Dorset, through his furies of denunciation and wild reactions of self-contempt, made her feel the need he had of her, the place she had taken in his life. But for her, what ear would have been open to his cries? And what hand but hers could drag him up again to a footing of sanity and self-respect? All through the stress of the struggle with him, she had been conscious of something faintly maternal in her efforts to guide and uplift him. But for the present, if he clung to her, it was not in order to be dragged up, but to feel some one floundering in the depths with him: he wanted her to suffer with him, not to help him to suffer less.

Happily for both, there was little physical strength to sustain his frenzy. It left him, collapsed and breathing heavily, to an apathy so deep and prolonged that Lily almost feared the passers-by would think it the result of a seizure, and stop to offer their aid. But Monte Carlo is, of all places, the one where the human bond is least close, and odd sights are the least arresting. If a glance or two lingered on the couple, no intrusive sympathy disturbed them; and it was Lily herself who broke the silence by rising from her seat. With the clearing of her vision the sweep of peril had extended, and she saw that the post of danger was no longer at Dorset's side.

"If you won't go back, I must—don't make me leave you!" she urged.

But he remained mutely resistant, and she added: "What are you going to do? You really can't sit here all night."

"I can go to an hotel. I can telegraph my lawyers." He sat up, roused by a new thought. "By Jove, Selden's at Nice—I'll send for Selden!"

Lily, at this, reseated herself with a cry of alarm. "No, no, *no!*" she protested.

He swung round on her distrustfully. "Why not Selden? He's a lawyer, is n't he? One will do as well as another in a case like this."

"As badly as another, you mean. I thought you relied on *me* to help you."

"You do—by being so sweet and patient with me. If it had n't been for you I'd have ended the thing long ago. But now it's got to end." He rose suddenly, straightening himself with an effort. "You can't want to see me ridiculous."

She looked at him kindly. "That's just it." Then, after a moment's pondering, almost to her own surprise she broke out with a flash of inspiration: "Well, go over and see Mr. Selden. You'll have time to do it before dinner."

"Oh, *dinner*——" he mocked her; but she left him with the smiling rejoinder: "Dinner on board, remember; we'll put it off till nine if you like."

It was past four already; and when a cab had dropped her at the quay, and she stood waiting for the gig to put off for her, she began to wonder what had been happening on the yacht. Of Silverton's whereabouts there had been no mention. Had he returned to the Sabrina? Or could Bertha—the dread alternative sprang on her suddenly—could Bertha, left to herself, have gone ashore to rejoin him? Lily's heart stood still at the thought. All her concern had hitherto been for young Silverton, not only because, in such affairs, the woman's instinct is to side with the man, but because his case made a peculiar appeal to her sympathies. He was so desperately in earnest, poor youth, and his earnestness was of so different a quality from Bertha's, though hers too was desperate enough. The difference was that Bertha was in earnest only about herself, while he was in earnest about her. But now, at the actual crisis, this difference seemed to throw the weight of destitution on Bertha's side, since at least he had her to suffer for, and she had only herself. At any rate, viewed less ideally, all the disadvantages of such a situation were for the woman; and it was to Bertha that Lily's sympathies now went out. She was not fond of Bertha Dorset, but neither was she without a sense of obligation, the heavier for having so little per-

sonal liking to sustain it. Bertha had been kind to her, they
had lived together, during the last months, on terms of easy
friendship, and the sense of friction of which Lily had recently
become aware seemed to make it the more urgent that she
should work undividedly in her friend's interest.

It was in Bertha's interest, certainly, that she had despatched Dorset to consult with Lawrence Selden. Once the
grotesqueness of the situation accepted, she had seen at a
glance that it was the safest in which Dorset could find himself. Who but Selden could thus miraculously combine the
skill to save Bertha with the obligation of doing so? The consciousness that much skill would be required made Lily rest
thankfully in the greatness of the obligation. Since he would
have to pull Bertha through she could trust him to find a way;
and she put the fulness of her trust in the telegram she managed to send him on her way to the quay.

Thus far, then, Lily felt that she had done well; and the
conviction strengthened her for the task that remained. She
and Bertha had never been on confidential terms, but at such
a crisis the barriers of reserve must surely fall: Dorset's wild
allusions to the scene of the morning made Lily feel that
they were down already, and that any attempt to rebuild
them would be beyond Bertha's strength. She pictured the
poor creature shivering behind her fallen defences and awaiting with suspense the moment when she could take refuge
in the first shelter that offered. If only that shelter had not
already offered itself elsewhere! As the gig traversed the
short distance between the quay and the yacht, Lily grew
more than ever alarmed at the possible consequences of her
long absence. What if the wretched Bertha, finding in all the
long hours no soul to turn to—but by this time Lily's eager
foot was on the side-ladder, and her first step on the Sabrina
showed the worst of her apprehensions to be unfounded; for
there, in the luxurious shade of the after-deck, the wretched
Bertha, in full command of her usual attenuated elegance,
sat dispensing tea to the Duchess of Beltshire and Lord
Hubert.

The sight filled Lily with such surprise that she felt that
Bertha, at least, must read its meaning in her look, and she
was proportionately disconcerted by the blankness of the look

returned. But in an instant she saw that Mrs. Dorset had, of necessity, to look blank before the others, and that, to mitigate the effect of her own surprise, she must at once produce some simple reason for it. The long habit of rapid transitions made it easy for her to exclaim to the Duchess: "Why, I thought you 'd gone back to the Princess!" and this sufficed for the lady she addressed, if it was hardly enough for Lord Hubert.

At least it opened the way to a lively explanation of how the Duchess was, in fact, going back the next moment, but had first rushed out to the yacht for a word with Mrs. Dorset on the subject of tomorrow's dinner—the dinner with the Brys, to which Lord Hubert had finally insisted on dragging them.

"To save my neck, you know!" he explained, with a glance that appealed to Lily for some recognition of his promptness; and the Duchess added, with her noble candour: "Mr. Bry has promised him a tip, and he says if we go he 'll pass it on to us."

This led to some final pleasantries, in which, as it seemed to Lily, Mrs. Dorset bore her part with astounding bravery, and at the close of which Lord Hubert, from half way down the side-ladder, called back, with an air of numbering heads: "And of course we may count on Dorset too?"

"Oh, count on him," his wife assented gaily. She was keeping up well to the last—but as she turned back from waving her adieux over the side, Lily said to herself that the mask must drop and the soul of fear look out.

Mrs. Dorset turned back slowly; perhaps she wanted time to steady her muscles; at any rate, they were still under perfect control when, dropping once more into her seat behind the tea-table, she remarked to Miss Bart with a faint touch of irony: "I suppose I ought to say good morning."

If it was a cue, Lily was ready to take it, though with only the vaguest sense of what was expected of her in return. There was something unnerving in the contemplation of Mrs. Dorset's composure, and she had to force the light tone in which she answered: "I tried to see you this morning, but you were not yet up."

"No—I got to bed late. After we missed you at the station

I thought we ought to wait for you till the last train." She spoke very gently, but with just the least tinge of reproach.

"You missed us? You waited for us at the station?" Now indeed Lily was too far adrift in bewilderment to measure the other's words or keep watch on her own. "But I thought you did n't get to the station till after the last train had left!"

Mrs. Dorset, examining her between lowered lids, met this with the immediate query: "Who told you that?"

"George—I saw him just now in the gardens."

"Ah, is that George's version? Poor George—he was in no state to remember what I told him. He had one of his worst attacks this morning, and I packed him off to see the doctor. Do you know if he found him?"

Lily, still lost in conjecture, made no reply, and Mrs. Dorset settled herself indolently in her seat. "He 'll wait to see him; he was horribly frightened about himself. It 's very bad for him to be worried, and whenever anything upsetting happens, it always brings on an attack."

This time Lily felt sure that a cue was being pressed on her; but it was put forth with such startling suddenness, and with so incredible an air of ignoring what it led up to, that she could only falter out doubtfully: "Anything upsetting?"

"Yes—such as having you so conspicuously on his hands in the small hours. You know, my dear, you 're rather a big responsibility in such a scandalous place after midnight."

At that—at the complete unexpectedness and the inconceivable audacity of it—Lily could not restrain the tribute of an astonished laugh.

"Well, really—considering it was you who burdened him with the responsibility!"

Mrs. Dorset took this with an exquisite mildness. "By not having the superhuman cleverness to discover you in that frightful rush for the train? Or the imagination to believe that you 'd take it without us—you and he all alone—instead of waiting quietly in the station till we *did* manage to meet you?"

Lily's colour rose: it was growing clear to her that Bertha was pursuing an object, following a line she had marked out for herself. Only, with such a doom impending, why waste time in these childish efforts to avert it? The puerility of the attempt disarmed Lily's indignation: did it not prove how horribly the poor creature was frightened?

"No; by our simply all keeping together at Nice," she returned.

"Keeping together? When it was you who seized the first opportunity to rush off with the Duchess and her friends? My dear Lily, you are not a child to be led by the hand!"

"No—nor to be lectured, Bertha, really; if that 's what you are doing to me now."

Mrs. Dorset smiled on her reproachfully. "Lecture you—I? Heaven forbid! I was merely trying to give you a friendly hint. But it 's usually the other way round, is n't it? I 'm expected to take hints, not to give them: I 've positively lived on them all these last months."

"Hints—from me to you?" Lily repeated.

"Oh, negative ones merely—what not to be and to do and to see. And I think I 've taken them to admiration. Only, my dear, if you 'll let me say so, I did n't understand that one of my negative duties was *not* to warn you when you carried your imprudence too far."

A chill of fear passed over Miss Bart: a sense of remembered treachery that was like the gleam of a knife in the dusk. But compassion, in a moment, got the better of her instinctive recoil. What was this outpouring of senseless bitterness but the tracked creature's attempt to cloud the medium through which it was fleeing? It was on Lily's lips to exclaim: "You poor soul, don't double and turn—come straight back to me, and we 'll find a way out!" But the words died under the impenetrable insolence of Bertha's smile. Lily sat silent, taking the brunt of it quietly, letting it spend itself on her to the last drop of its accumulated falseness; then, without a word, she rose and went down to her cabin.

III

Miss Bart's telegram caught Lawrence Selden at the door of his hotel; and having read it, he turned back to wait for Dorset. The message necessarily left large gaps for conjecture; but all that he had recently heard and seen made these but too easy to fill in. On the whole he was surprised; for though he had perceived that the situation contained all the elements of an explosion, he had often enough, in the range of his personal experience, seen just such combinations subside into harmlessness. Still, Dorset's spasmodic temper, and his wife's reckless disregard of appearances, gave the situation a peculiar insecurity; and it was less from the sense of any special relation to the case than from a purely professional zeal, that Selden resolved to guide the pair to safety. Whether, in the present instance, safety for either lay in repairing so damaged a tie, it was no business of his to consider: he had only, on general principles, to think of averting a scandal, and his desire to avert it was increased by his fear of its involving Miss Bart. There was nothing specific in this apprehension; he merely wished to spare her the embarrassment of being ever so remotely connected with the public washing of the Dorset linen.

How exhaustive and unpleasant such a process would be, he saw even more vividly after his two hours' talk with poor Dorset. If anything came out at all, it would be such a vast unpacking of accumulated moral rags as left him, after his visitor had gone, with the feeling that he must fling open the windows and have his room swept out. But nothing should come out; and happily for his side of the case, the dirty rags, however pieced together, could not, without considerable difficulty, be turned into a homogeneous grievance. The torn edges did not always fit—there were missing bits, there were disparities of size and colour, all of which it was naturally Selden's business to make the most of in putting them under his client's eye. But to a man in Dorset's mood the completest demonstration could not carry conviction, and Selden saw that for the moment all he could do was to soothe and temporize, to offer sympathy and to counsel prudence. He let

Dorset depart charged to the brim with the sense that, till their next meeting, he must maintain a strictly noncommittal attitude; that, in short, his share in the game consisted for the present in looking on. Selden knew, however, that he could not long keep such violences in equilibrium; and he promised to meet Dorset, the next morning, at an hotel in Monte Carlo. Meanwhile he counted not a little on the reaction of weakness and self-distrust that, in such natures, follows on every unwonted expenditure of moral force; and his telegraphic reply to Miss Bart consisted simply in the injunction: "Assume that everything is as usual."

On this assumption, in fact, the early part of the following day was lived through. Dorset, as if in obedience to Lily's imperative bidding, had actually returned in time for a late dinner on the yacht. The repast had been the most difficult moment of the day. Dorset was sunk in one of the abysmal silences which so commonly followed on what his wife called his "attacks" that it was easy, before the servants, to refer it to this cause; but Bertha herself seemed, perversely enough, little disposed to make use of this obvious means of protection. She simply left the brunt of the situation on her husband's hands, as if too absorbed in a grievance of her own to suspect that she might be the object of one herself. To Lily this attitude was the most ominous, because the most perplexing, element in the situation. As she tried to fan the weak flicker of talk, to build up, again and again, the crumbling structure of "appearances," her own attention was perpetually distracted by the question: "What on earth can she be driving at?" There was something positively exasperating in Bertha's attitude of isolated defiance. If only she would have given her friend a hint they might still have worked together successfully; but how could Lily be of use, while she was thus obstinately shut out from participation? To be of use was what she honestly wanted; and not for her own sake but for the Dorsets'. She had not thought of her own situation at all: she was simply engrossed in trying to put a little order in theirs. But the close of the short dreary evening left her with a sense of effort hopelessly wasted. She had not tried to see Dorset alone: she had positively shrunk from a renewal of his confidences. It was Bertha whose confidence she sought, and who should as eagerly have invited her own; and Bertha, as if in the infatuation of self-destruction, was actually pushing away her rescuing hand.

Lily, going to bed early, had left the couple to themselves; and it seemed part of the general mystery in which she moved that more than an hour should elapse before she heard Bertha walk down the silent passage and regain her room. The morrow, rising on an apparent continuance of the same conditions, revealed nothing of what had occurred between the confronted pair. One fact alone outwardly proclaimed the change they were all conspiring to ignore; and that was the non-appearance of Ned Silverton. No one referred to it, and this tacit avoidance of the subject kept it in the immediate foreground of consciousness. But there was another change, perceptible only to Lily; and that was that Dorset now avoided her almost as pointedly as his wife. Perhaps he was repenting his rash outpourings of the previous day; perhaps only trying, in his clumsy way, to conform to Selden's counsel to behave "as usual." Such instructions no more make for easiness of attitude than the photographer's behest to "look natural"; and in a creature as unconscious as poor Dorset of the appearance he habitually presented, the struggle to maintain a pose was sure to result in queer contortions.

It resulted, at any rate, in throwing Lily strangely on her own resources. She had learned, on leaving her room, that Mrs. Dorset was still invisible, and that Dorset had left the yacht early; and feeling too restless to remain alone, she too had herself ferried ashore. Straying toward the Casino, she attached herself to a group of acquaintances from Nice, with whom she lunched, and in whose company she was returning to the rooms when she encountered Selden crossing the square. She could not, at the moment, separate herself definitely from her party, who had hospitably assumed that she would remain with them till they took their departure; but she found time for a momentary pause of enquiry, to which he promptly returned: "I 've seen him again—he 's just left me."

She waited before him anxiously. "Well? what has happened? What *will* happen?"

"Nothing as yet—and nothing in the future, I think."

"It 's over, then? It 's settled? You 're sure?"

He smiled. "Give me time. I 'm not sure—but I 'm a good deal surer." And with that she had to content herself, and hasten on to the expectant group on the steps.

Selden had in fact given her the utmost measure of his sureness, had even stretched it a shade to meet the anxiety in her eyes. And now, as he turned away, strolling down the hill toward the station, that anxiety remained with him as the visible justification of his own. It was not, indeed, anything specific that he feared: there had been a literal truth in his declaration that he did not think anything would happen. What troubled him was that, though Dorset's attitude had perceptibly changed, the change was not clearly to be accounted for. It had certainly not been produced by Selden's arguments, or by the action of his own soberer reason. Five minutes' talk sufficed to show that some alien influence had been at work, and that it had not so much subdued his resentment as weakened his will, so that he moved under it in a state of apathy, like a dangerous lunatic who has been drugged. Temporarily, no doubt, however exerted, it worked for the general safety: the question was how long it would last, and by what kind of reaction it was likely to be followed. On these points Selden could gain no light; for he saw that one effect of the transformation had been to shut him off from free communion with Dorset. The latter, indeed, was still moved by the irresistible desire to discuss his wrong; but, though he revolved about it with the same forlorn tenacity, Selden was aware that something always restrained him from full expression. His state was one to produce first weariness and then impatience in his hearer; and when their talk was over, Selden began to feel that he had done his utmost, and might justifiably wash his hands of the sequel.

It was in this mind that he had been making his way back to the station when Miss Bart crossed his path; but though, after his brief word with her, he kept mechanically on his course, he was conscious of a gradual change in his purpose. The change had been produced by the look in her eyes; and in his eagerness to define the nature of that look, he dropped into a seat in the gardens, and sat brooding upon the question. It was natural enough, in all conscience, that she should

appear anxious: a young woman placed, in the close intimacy
of a yachting-cruise, between a couple on the verge of disaster, could hardly, aside from her concern for her friends, be
insensible to the awkwardness of her own position. The worst
of it was that, in interpreting Miss Bart's state of mind, so
many alternative readings were possible; and one of these, in
Selden's troubled mind, took the ugly form suggested by Mrs.
Fisher. If the girl was afraid, was she afraid for herself or for
her friends? And to what degree was her dread of a catastrophe intensified by the sense of being fatally involved in it?
The burden of offence lying manifestly with Mrs. Dorset, this
conjecture seemed on the face of it gratuitously unkind; but
Selden knew that in the most one-sided matrimonial quarrel
there are generally counter-charges to be brought, and that
they are brought with the greater audacity where the original
grievance is so emphatic. Mrs. Fisher had not hesitated to
suggest the likelihood of Dorset's marrying Miss Bart if "anything happened"; and though Mrs. Fisher's conclusions were
notoriously rash, she was shrewd enough in reading the signs
from which they were drawn. Dorset had apparently shown
marked interest in the girl, and this interest might be used to
cruel advantage in his wife's struggle for rehabilitation. Selden
knew that Bertha would fight to the last round of powder:
the rashness of her conduct was illogically combined with a
cold determination to escape its consequences. She could be
as unscrupulous in fighting for herself as she was reckless in
courting danger, and whatever came to her hand at such moments was likely to be used as a defensive missile. He did not,
as yet, see clearly just what course she was likely to take, but
his perplexity increased his apprehension, and with it the
sense that, before leaving, he must speak again with Miss
Bart. Whatever her share in the situation—and he had always
honestly tried to resist judging her by her surroundings—
however free she might be from any personal connection with
it, she would be better out of the way of a possible crash; and
since she had appealed to him for help, it was clearly his business to tell her so.

This decision at last brought him to his feet, and carried
him back to the gambling rooms, within whose doors he had
seen her disappearing; but a prolonged exploration of the

crowd failed to put him on her traces. He saw instead, to his surprise, Ned Silverton loitering somewhat ostentatiously about the tables; and the discovery that this actor in the drama was not only hovering in the wings, but actually inviting the exposure of the footlights, though it might have seemed to imply that all peril was over, served rather to deepen Selden's sense of foreboding. Charged with this impression he returned to the square, hoping to see Miss Bart move across it, as every one in Monte Carlo seemed inevitably to do at least a dozen times a day; but here again he waited vainly for a glimpse of her, and the conclusion was slowly forced on him that she had gone back to the Sabrina. It would be difficult to follow her there, and still more difficult, should he do so, to contrive the opportunity for a private word; and he had almost decided on the unsatisfactory alternative of writing, when the ceaseless diorama of the square suddenly unrolled before him the figures of Lord Hubert and Mrs. Bry.

Hailing them at once with his question, he learned from Lord Hubert that Miss Bart had just returned to the Sabrina in Dorset's company; an announcement so evidently disconcerting to him that Mrs. Bry, after a glance from her companion, which seemed to act like the pressure on a spring, brought forth the prompt proposal that he should come and meet his friends at dinner that evening—"At Bécassin's—a little dinner to the Duchess," she flashed out before Lord Hubert had time to remove the pressure.

Selden's sense of the privilege of being included in such company brought him early in the evening to the door of the restaurant, where he paused to scan the ranks of diners approaching down the brightly lit terrace. There, while the Brys hovered within over the last agitating alternatives of the *menu*, he kept watch for the guests from the Sabrina, who at length rose on the horizon in company with the Duchess, Lord and Lady Skiddaw and the Stepneys. From this group it was easy for him to detach Miss Bart on the pretext of a moment's glance into one of the brilliant shops along the terrace, and to say to her, while they lingered together in the white dazzle of a jeweller's window: "I stopped over to see you—to beg of you to leave the yacht."

The eyes she turned on him showed a quick gleam of her former fear. "To leave—? What do you mean? What has happened?"

"Nothing. But if anything should, why be in the way of it?"

The glare from the jeweller's window, deepening the pallour of her face, gave to its delicate lines the sharpness of a tragic mask. "Nothing will, I am sure; but while there's even a doubt left, how can you think I would leave Bertha?"

The words rang out on a note of contempt—was it possibly of contempt for himself? Well, he was willing to risk its renewal to the extent of insisting, with an undeniable throb of added interest: "You have yourself to think of, you know—" to which, with a strange fall of sadness in her voice, she answered, meeting his eyes: "If you knew how little difference that makes!"

"Oh, well, nothing *will* happen," he said, more for his own reassurance than for hers; and "Nothing, nothing, of course!" she valiantly assented, as they turned to overtake their companions.

In the thronged restaurant, taking their places about Mrs. Bry's illuminated board, their confidence seemed to gain support from the familiarity of their surroundings. Here were Dorset and his wife once more presenting their customary faces to the world, she engrossed in establishing her relation with an intensely new gown, he shrinking with dyspeptic dread from the multiplied solicitations of the *menu*. The mere fact that they thus showed themselves together, with the utmost openness the place afforded, seemed to declare beyond a doubt that their differences were composed. How this end had been attained was still matter for wonder, but it was clear that for the moment Miss Bart rested confidently in the result; and Selden tried to achieve the same view by telling himself that her opportunities for observation had been ampler than his own.

Meanwhile, as the dinner advanced through a labyrinth of courses, in which it became clear that Mrs. Bry had occasionally broken away from Lord Hubert's restraining hand, Selden's general watchfulness began to lose itself in a particular study of Miss Bart. It was one of the days when she was so handsome that to be handsome was enough, and all the rest—her grace, her quickness, her social felicities—seemed the overflow of a bounteous nature. But what especially struck him was the way in which she detached herself, by a hundred undefinable shades, from the persons who most abounded in her own style. It was in just such company, the fine flower and complete expression of the state she aspired to, that the differences came out with special poignancy, her grace cheapening the other women's smartness as her finely-discriminated silences made their chatter dull. The strain of the last hours had restored to her face the deeper eloquence which Selden had lately missed in it, and the bravery of her words to him still fluttered in her voice and eyes. Yes, she was matchless—it was the one word for her; and he could give his admiration the freer play because so little personal feeling remained in it. His real detachment from her had taken place, not at the lurid moment of disenchantment, but now, in the sober after-light of discrimination, where he saw her definitely divided from him by the crudeness of a choice which seemed to deny the very differences he felt in her. It was before him again in its completeness—the choice in which she was content to rest: in the stupid costliness of the food and the showy dulness of the talk, in the freedom of speech which never arrived at wit and the freedom of act which never made for romance. The strident setting of the restaurant, in which their table seemed set apart in a special glare of publicity, and the presence at it of little Dabham of the "Riviera Notes," emphasized the ideals of a world where conspicuousness passed for distinction, and the society column had become the roll of fame.

It was as the immortalizer of such occasions that little Dabham, wedged in modest watchfulness between two brilliant neighbours, suddenly became the centre of Selden's scrutiny. How much did he know of what was going on, and how much, for his purpose, was still worth finding out? His little eyes were like tentacles thrown out to catch the floating intimations with which, to Selden, the air at moments seemed thick; then again it cleared to its normal emptiness, and he could see nothing in it for the journalist but leisure to note the elegance of the ladies' gowns. Mrs. Dorset's, in particular, challenged all the wealth of Mr. Dabham's vocabulary: it had surprises and subtleties worthy of what he would have called "the literary style." At first, as Selden had noticed, it had been almost too preoccupying to its wearer; but now she was in full command of it, and was even producing her effects with unwonted freedom. Was she not, indeed, too free, too fluent, for perfect naturalness? And was not Dorset, to whom his glance had passed by a natural transition, too jerkily wavering between the same extremes? Dorset indeed was always jerky; but it seemed to Selden that tonight each vibration swung him farther from his centre.

The dinner, meanwhile, was moving to its triumphant close, to the evident satisfaction of Mrs. Bry, who, throned in apoplectic majesty between Lord Skiddaw and Lord Hubert, seemed in spirit to be calling on Mrs. Fisher to witness her achievement. Short of Mrs. Fisher her audience might have been called complete; for the restaurant was crowded with persons mainly gathered there for the purpose of spectator-ship, and accurately posted as to the names and faces of the celebrities they had come to see. Mrs. Bry, conscious that all her feminine guests came under that heading, and that each one looked her part to admiration, shone on Lily with all the pent-up gratitude that Mrs. Fisher had failed to deserve. Sel-den, catching the glance, wondered what part Miss Bart had played in organizing the entertainment. She did, at least, a great deal to adorn it; and as he watched the bright security with which she bore herself, he smiled to think that he should have fancied her in need of help. Never had she appeared more serenely mistress of the situation than when, at the mo-ment of dispersal, detaching herself a little from the group about the table, she turned with a smile and a graceful slant of the shoulders to receive her cloak from Dorset.

The dinner had been protracted over Mr. Bry's exceptional cigars and a bewildering array of liqueurs, and many of the other tables were empty; but a sufficient number of diners still lingered to give relief to the leave-taking of Mrs. Bry's distinguished guests. This ceremony was drawn out and com-plicated by the fact that it involved, on the part of the Duch-ess and Lady Skiddaw, definite farewells, and pledges of speedy reunion in Paris, where they were to pause and replenish their wardrobes on the way to England. The quality of Mrs. Bry's hospitality, and of the tips her husband had presumably imparted, lent to the manner of the English ladies a general effusiveness which shed the rosiest light over their hostess's future. In its glow Mrs. Dorset and the Stepneys were also visibly included, and the whole scene had touches of intimacy worth their weight in gold to the watchful pen of Mr. Dabham.

A glance at her watch caused the Duchess to exclaim to her sister that they had just time to dash for their train, and the flurry of this departure over, the Stepneys, who had their motor at the door, offered to convey the Dorsets and Miss Bart to the quay. The offer was accepted, and Mrs. Dorset moved away with her husband in attendance. Miss Bart had lingered for a last word with Lord Hubert, and Stepney, on whom Mr. Bry was pressing a final, and still more expensive, cigar, called out: "Come on, Lily, if you 're going back to the yacht."

Lily turned to obey; but as she did so, Mrs. Dorset, who had paused on her way out, moved a few steps back toward the table.

"Miss Bart is not going back to the yacht," she said in a voice of singular distinctness.

A startled look ran from eye to eye; Mrs. Bry crimsoned to the verge of congestion, Mrs. Stepney slipped nervously behind her husband, and Selden, in the general turmoil of his sensations, was mainly conscious of a longing to grip Dabham by the collar and fling him out into the street.

Dorset, meanwhile, had stepped back to his wife's side. His face was white, and he looked about him with cowed angry eyes. "Bertha!—Miss Bart . . . this is some misunderstanding . . . some mistake . . ."

"Miss Bart remains here," his wife rejoined incisively. "And, I think, George, we had better not detain Mrs. Stepney any longer."

Miss Bart, during this brief exchange of words, remained in admirable erectness, slightly isolated from the embarrassed group about her. She had paled a little under the shock of the insult, but the discomposure of the surrounding faces was not reflected in her own. The faint disdain of her smile seemed to lift her high above her antagonist's reach, and it was not till she had given Mrs. Dorset the full measure of the distance between them that she turned and extended her hand to her hostess.

"I am joining the Duchess tomorrow," she explained, "and it seemed easier for me to remain on shore for the night."

She held firmly to Mrs. Bry's wavering eye while she gave this explanation, but when it was over Selden saw her send a tentative glance from one to another of the women's faces. She read their incredulity in their averted looks, and in the mute wretchedness of the men behind them, and for a miserable half-second he thought she quivered on the brink of failure. Then, turning to him with an easy gesture, and the pale bravery of her recovered smile—"Dear Mr. Selden," she said, "you promised to see me to my cab."

Outside, the sky was gusty and overcast, and as Lily and Selden moved toward the deserted gardens below the restaurant, spurts of warm rain blew fitfully against their faces. The fiction of the cab had been tacitly abandoned; they walked on in silence, her hand on his arm, till the deeper shade of the gardens received them, and pausing beside a bench, he said: "Sit down a moment."

She dropped to the seat without answering, but the electric lamp at the bend of the path shed a gleam on the struggling misery of her face. Selden sat down beside her, waiting for her to speak, fearful lest any word he chose should touch too roughly on her wound, and kept also from free utterance by the wretched doubt which had slowly renewed itself within him. What had brought her to this pass? What weakness had placed her so abominably at her enemy's mercy? And why should Bertha Dorset have turned into an enemy at the very moment when she so obviously needed the support of her sex? Even while his nerves raged at the subjection of husbands to their wives, and at the cruelty of women to their kind, reason obstinately harped on the proverbial relation between smoke and fire. The memory of Mrs. Fisher's hints, and the corroboration of his own impressions, while they deepened his pity also increased his constraint, since, whichever way he sought a free outlet for sympathy, it was blocked by the fear of committing a blunder.

Suddenly it struck him that his silence must seem almost as accusatory as that of the men he had despised for turning from her; but before he could find the fitting word she had cut him short with a question.

"Do you know of a quiet hotel? I can send for my maid in the morning."

"An hotel—*here*—that you can go to alone? It's not possible."

She met this with a pale gleam of her old playfulness. "What *is*, then? It's too wet to sleep in the gardens."

"But there must be some one——"

"Some one to whom I can go? Of course—any number—but at *this* hour? You see my change of plan was rather sudden——"

"Good God—if you'd listened to me!" he cried, venting his helplessness in a burst of anger.

She still held him off with the gentle mockery of her smile. "But haven't I?" she rejoined. "You advised me to leave the yacht, and I'm leaving it."

He saw then, with a pang of self-reproach, that she meant neither to explain nor to defend herself; that by his miserable silence he had forfeited all chance of helping her, and that the decisive hour was past.

She had risen, and stood before him in a kind of clouded majesty, like some deposed princess moving tranquilly to exile.

"Lily!" he exclaimed, with a note of despairing appeal; but—"Oh, not now," she gently admonished him; and then, in all the sweetness of her recovered composure: "Since I must find shelter somewhere, and since you're so kindly here to help me——"

He gathered himself up at the challenge. "You will do as I tell you? There's but one thing, then; you must go straight to your cousins, the Stepneys."

"Oh—" broke from her with a movement of instinctive resistance; but he insisted: "Come—it's late, and you must appear to have gone there directly."

He had drawn her hand into his arm, but she held him back with a last gesture of protest. "I can't—I can't—not that—you don't know Gwen: you must n't ask me!"

"I *must* ask you—you must obey me," he persisted, though infected at heart by her own fear.

Her voice sank to a whisper: "And if she refuses?"—but, "Oh, trust me—trust me!" he could only insist in return; and yielding to his touch, she let him lead her back in silence to the edge of the square.

In the cab they continued to remain silent through the brief drive which carried them to the illuminated portals of the Stepneys' hotel. Here he left her outside, in the darkness of the raised hood, while his name was sent up to Stepney, and he paced the showy hall, awaiting the latter's descent. Ten minutes later the two men passed out together between the gold-laced custodians of the threshold; but in the vestibule Stepney drew up with a last flare of reluctance.

"It 's understood, then?" he stipulated nervously, with his hand on Selden's arm. "She leaves tomorrow by the early train—and my wife 's asleep, and can't be disturbed."

IV

THE BLINDS of Mrs. Peniston's drawing-room were drawn down against the oppressive June sun, and in the sultry twilight the faces of her assembled relatives took on a fitting shadow of bereavement.

They were all there: Van Alstynes, Stepneys and Melsons—even a stray Peniston or two, indicating, by a greater latitude in dress and manner, the fact of remoter relationship and more settled hopes. The Peniston side was, in fact, secure in the knowledge that the bulk of Mr. Peniston's property "went back"; while the direct connection hung suspended on the disposal of his widow's private fortune and on the uncertainty of its extent. Jack Stepney, in his new character as the richest nephew, tacitly took the lead, emphasizing his importance by the deeper gloss of his mourning and the subdued authority of his manner; while his wife's bored attitude and frivolous gown proclaimed the heiress's disregard of the insignificant interests at stake. Old Ned Van Alstyne, seated next to her in a coat that made affliction dapper, twirled his white moustache to conceal the eager twitch of his lips; and Grace Stepney, red-nosed and smelling of crape, whispered emotionally to Mrs. Herbert Melson: "I could n't *bear* to see the Niagara anywhere else!"

A rustle of weeds and quick turning of heads hailed the opening of the door, and Lily Bart appeared, tall and noble in her black dress, with Gerty Farish at her side. The women's faces, as she paused interrogatively on the threshold, were a study in hesitation. One or two made faint motions of recognition, which might have been subdued either by the solemnity of the scene, or by the doubt as to how far the others meant to go; Mrs. Jack Stepney gave a careless nod, and Grace Stepney, with a sepulchral gesture, indicated a seat at her side. But Lily, ignoring the invitation, as well as Jack Stepney's official attempt to direct her, moved across the room with her smooth free gait, and seated herself in a chair which seemed to have been purposely placed apart from the others.

It was the first time that she had faced her family since her return from Europe, two weeks earlier; but if she perceived any uncertainty in their welcome, it served only to add a tinge of irony to the usual composure of her bearing. The shock of dismay with which, on the dock, she had heard from Gerty Farish of Mrs. Peniston's sudden death, had been mitigated, almost at once, by the irrepressible thought that now, at last, she would be able to pay her debts. She had looked forward with considerable uneasiness to her first encounter with her aunt. Mrs. Peniston had vehemently opposed her niece's departure with the Dorsets, and had marked her continued disapproval by not writing during Lily's absence. The certainty that she had heard of the rupture with the Dorsets made the prospect of the meeting more formidable; and how should Lily have repressed a quick sense of relief at the thought that, instead of undergoing the anticipated ordeal, she had only to enter gracefully on a long-assured inheritance? It had been, in the consecrated phrase, "always understood" that Mrs. Peniston was to provide handsomely for her niece; and in the latter's mind the understanding had long since crystallized into fact.

"She gets everything, of course—I don't see what we're here for," Mrs. Jack Stepney remarked with careless loudness to Ned Van Alstyne; and the latter's deprecating murmur—"Julia was always a just woman"—might have been interpreted as signifying either acquiescence or doubt.

"Well, it's only about four hundred thousand," Mrs. Stepney rejoined with a yawn; and Grace Stepney, in the silence produced by the lawyer's preliminary cough, was heard to sob out: "They won't find a towel missing—I went over them with her the very day——"

Lily, oppressed by the close atmosphere, and the stifling odour of fresh mourning, felt her attention straying as Mrs. Peniston's lawyer, solemnly erect behind the Buhl table at the end of the room, began to rattle through the preamble of the will.

"It's like being in church," she reflected, wondering vaguely where Gwen Stepney had got such an awful hat. Then she noticed how stout Jack had grown—he would soon be almost as plethoric as Herbert Melson, who sat a few feet off, breathing puffily as he leaned his black-gloved hands on his stick.

"I wonder why rich people always grow fat—I suppose it's because there's nothing to worry them. If I inherit, I shall have to be careful of my figure," she mused, while the lawyer droned on through a labyrinth of legacies. The servants came first, then a few charitable institutions, then several remoter Melsons and Stepneys, who stirred consciously as their names rang out, and then subsided into a state of impassiveness befitting the solemnity of the occasion. Ned Van Alstyne, Jack Stepney, and a cousin or two followed, each coupled with the mention of a few thousands: Lily wondered that Grace Stepney was not among them. Then she heard her own name— "to my niece Lily Bart ten thousand dollars—" and after that the lawyer again lost himself in a coil of unintelligible periods, from which the concluding phrase flashed out with startling distinctness: "and the residue of my estate to my dear cousin and name-sake, Grace Julia Stepney."

There was a subdued gasp of surprise, a rapid turning of heads, and a surging of sable figures toward the corner in which Miss Stepney wailed out her sense of unworthiness through the crumpled ball of a black-edged handkerchief.

Lily stood apart from the general movement, feeling herself for the first time utterly alone. No one looked at her, no one seemed aware of her presence; she was probing the very depths of insignificance. And under her sense of the collective indifference came the acuter pang of hopes deceived. Disinherited—she had been disinherited—and for Grace Stepney! She met Gerty's lamentable eyes, fixed on her in a despairing effort at consolation, and the look brought her to herself. There was something to be done before she left the house: to be done with all the nobility she knew how to put into such gestures. She advanced to the group about Miss Stepney, and holding out her hand said simply: "Dear Grace, I am so glad."

The other ladies had fallen back at her approach, and a space created itself about her. It widened as she turned to go, and no one advanced to fill it up. She paused a moment, glancing about her, calmly taking the measure of her situation. She heard some one ask a question about the date of the will; she caught a fragment of the lawyer's answer— something about a sudden summons, and an "earlier instrument." Then the tide of dispersal began to drift past her; Mrs. Jack Stepney and Mrs. Herbert Melson stood on the doorstep awaiting their motor; a sympathizing group escorted Grace Stepney to the cab it was felt to be fitting she should take, though she lived but a street or two away; and Miss Bart and Gerty found themselves almost alone in the purple drawing-room, which more than ever, in its stuffy dimness, resembled a well-kept family vault, in which the last corpse had just been decently deposited.

In Gerty Farish's sitting-room, whither a hansom had carried the two friends, Lily dropped into a chair with a faint sound of laughter: it struck her as a humorous coincidence that her aunt's legacy should so nearly represent the amount of her debt to Trenor. The need of discharging that debt had reasserted itself with increased urgency since her return to America, and she spoke her first thought in saying to the anxiously hovering Gerty: "I wonder when the legacies will be paid."

But Miss Farish could not pause over the legacies; she broke into a larger indignation. "Oh, Lily, it's unjust; it's cruel—Grace Stepney must *feel* she has no right to all that money!"

"Any one who knew how to please Aunt Julia has a right to her money," Miss Bart rejoined philosophically.

"But she was devoted to you—she led every one to think——" Gerty checked herself in evident embarrassment, and Miss Bart turned to her with a direct look. "Gerty, be honest: this will was made only six weeks ago. She had heard of my break with the Dorsets?"

"Every one heard, of course, that there had been some disagreement—some misunderstanding——"

"Did she hear that Bertha turned me off the yacht?"

"Lily!"

"That was what happened, you know. She said I was trying to marry George Dorset. She did it to make him think she was jealous. Isn't that what she told Gwen Stepney?"

"I don't know—I don't listen to such horrors."

"I *must* listen to them—I must know where I stand." She paused, and again sounded a faint note of derision. "Did you notice the women? They were afraid to snub me while they thought I was going to get the money—afterward they scuttled off as if I had the plague." Gerty remained silent, and she continued: "I stayed on to see what would happen. They took their cue from Gwen Stepney and Lulu Melson—I saw them watching to see what Gwen would do.—Gerty, I must know just what is being said of me."

"I tell you I don't listen——"

"One hears such things without listening." She rose and laid her resolute hands on Miss Farish's shoulders. "Gerty, are people going to cut me?"

"Your *friends*, Lily—how can you think it?"

"Who are one's friends at such a time? Who, but you, you poor trustful darling? And heaven knows what *you* suspect me of!" She kissed Gerty with a whimsical murmur. "You 'd never let it make any difference—but then you 're fond of criminals, Gerty! How about the irreclaimable ones, though? For I 'm absolutely impenitent, you know."

She drew herself up to the full height of her slender majesty, towering like some dark angel of defiance above the troubled Gerty, who could only falter out: "Lily, Lily—how can you laugh about such things?"

"So as not to weep, perhaps. But no—I 'm not of the tearful order. I discovered early that crying makes my nose red, and the knowledge has helped me through several painful episodes." She took a restless turn about the room, and then, reseating herself, lifted the bright mockery of her eyes to Gerty's anxious countenance.

"I should n't have minded, you know, if I 'd got the money—" and at Miss Farish's protesting "Oh!" she repeated calmly: "Not a straw, my dear; for, in the first place, they would n't have quite dared to ignore me; and if they had, it would n't have mattered, because I should have been independent of them. But now—!" The irony faded from her eyes, and she bent a clouded face upon her friend.

"How can you talk so, Lily? Of course the money ought to have been yours, but after all that makes no difference. The important thing——" Gerty paused, and then continued firmly: "The important thing is that you should clear yourself—should tell your friends the whole truth."

"The whole truth?" Miss Bart laughed. "What is truth? Where a woman is concerned, it 's the story that 's easiest to believe. In this case it 's a great deal easier to believe Bertha Dorset's story than mine, because she has a big house and an opera box, and it 's convenient to be on good terms with her."

Miss Farish still fixed her with an anxious gaze. "But what *is* your story, Lily? I don't believe any one knows it yet."

"My story?—I don't believe I know it myself. You see I never thought of preparing a version in advance as Bertha did—and if I had, I don't think I should take the trouble to use it now."

But Gerty continued with her quiet reasonableness: "I don't want a version prepared in advance—but I want you to tell me exactly what happened from the beginning."

"From the beginning?" Miss Bart gently mimicked her. "Dear Gerty, how little imagination you good people have! Why, the beginning was in my cradle, I suppose—in the way I was brought up, and the things I was taught to care for. Or no—I won't blame anybody for my faults: I 'll say it was in my blood, that I got it from some wicked pleasure-loving ancestress, who reacted against the homely virtues of New Amsterdam, and wanted to be back at the court of the Charleses!" And as Miss Farish continued to press her with troubled eyes, she went on impatiently: "You asked me just now for the truth—well, the truth about any girl is that once she 's talked about she 's done for; and the more she explains her case the worse it looks.—My good Gerty, you don't happen to have a cigarette about you?"

In her stuffy room at the hotel to which she had gone on landing, Lily Bart that evening reviewed her situation. It was the last week in June, and none of her friends were in town. The few relatives who had stayed on, or returned, for the reading of Mrs. Peniston's will, had taken flight again that afternoon to Newport or Long Island; and not one of them had made any proffer of hospitality to Lily. For the first time in her life she found herself utterly alone except for Gerty Farish. Even at the actual moment of her break with the Dorsets she had not had so keen a sense of its consequences, for the Duchess of Beltshire, hearing of the catastrophe from Lord Hubert, had instantly offered her protection, and under her sheltering wing Lily had made an almost triumphant progress to London. There she had been sorely tempted to linger on in a society which asked of her only to amuse and charm it, without enquiring too curiously how she had acquired her gift for doing so; but Selden, before they parted, had pressed on her the urgent need of returning at once to her aunt, and Lord Hubert, when he presently reappeared in London, abounded in the same counsel. Lily did not need to be told that the Duchess's championship was not the best road to social rehabilitation, and as she was besides aware that her noble defender might at any moment drop her in favour of a new *protégée*, she reluctantly decided to return to America. But she had not been ten minutes on her native shore before she realized that she had delayed too long to regain it. The Dorsets, the Stepneys, the Brys—all the actors and witnesses in the miserable drama—had preceded her with their version of the case; and, even had she seen the least chance of gaining a hearing for her own, some obscure disdain and reluctance would have restrained her. She knew it was not by explanations and counter-charges that she could ever hope to recover her lost standing; but even had she felt the least trust in their efficacy, she would still have been held back by the feeling which had kept her from defending herself to Gerty Farish—a feeling that was half pride and half humiliation. For though she knew she had been ruthlessly sacrificed to Bertha Dorset's determination to win back her husband, and though her own relation to Dorset had been that of the merest good-fellowship, yet she had been perfectly aware from the outset that her part in the affair was, as Carry Fisher brutally put it, to distract Dorset's attention from his wife. That was what she was "there for": it was the price she had chosen to pay for three months of luxury and freedom from care. Her habit of resolutely facing the facts, in her rare moments of introspection, did not now allow her to put any false gloss on the situation. She had suffered for the very faithfulness with which she had carried out her part of the tacit compact, but the part was not a handsome one at best, and she saw it now in all the ugliness of failure.

She saw, too, in the same uncompromising light, the train of consequences resulting from that failure; and these became clearer to her with every day of her weary lingering in town. She stayed on partly for the comfort of Gerty Farish's nearness, and partly for lack of knowing where to go. She understood well enough the nature of the task before her. She must set out to regain, little by little, the position she had lost; and the first step in the tedious task was to find out, as soon as possible, on how many of her friends she could count. Her hopes were mainly centred on Mrs. Trenor, who had treasures of easy-going tolerance for those who were amusing or useful to her, and in the noisy rush of whose existence the still small voice of detraction was slow to make itself heard. But Judy, though she must have been apprised of Miss Bart's return, had not even recognized it by the formal note of condolence which her friend's bereavement demanded. Any advance on Lily's side might have been perilous: there was nothing to do but to trust to the happy chance of an accidental meeting, and Lily knew that, even so late in the season, there was always a hope of running across her friends in their frequent passages through town.

To this end she assiduously showed herself at the restaurants they frequented, where, attended by the troubled Gerty, she lunched luxuriously, as she said, on her expectations.

"My dear Gerty, you would n't have me let the head-waiter see that I 've nothing to live on but Aunt Julia's legacy? Think of Grace Stepney's satisfaction if she came in and found us lunching on cold mutton and tea! What sweet shall we have today, dear— *Coupe Jacques* or *Pêches à la Melba*?"

She dropped the *menu* abruptly, with a quick heightening of colour, and Gerty, following her glance, was aware of the advance, from an inner room, of a party headed by Mrs. Trenor and Carry Fisher. It was impossible for these ladies and their companions—among whom Lily had at once distinguished both Trenor and Rosedale—not to pass, in going out, the table at which the two girls were seated; and Gerty's sense of the fact betrayed itself in the helpless trepidation of her manner. Miss Bart, on the contrary, borne forward on the wave of her buoyant grace, and neither shrinking from her friends nor appearing to lie in wait for them, gave to the encounter the touch of naturalness which she could impart to the most strained situations. Such embarrassment as was shown was on Mrs. Trenor's side, and manifested itself in the mingling of exaggerated warmth with imperceptible reservations. Her loudly affirmed pleasure at seeing Miss Bart took the form of a nebulous generalization, which included neither enquiries as to her future nor the expression of a definite wish to see her again. Lily, well-versed in the language of these omissions, knew that they were equally intelligible to the other members of the party: even Rosedale, flushed as he was with the importance of keeping such company, at once took the temperature of Mrs. Trenor's cordiality, and reflected it in his off-hand greeting of Miss Bart. Trenor, red and uncomfortable, had cut short his salutations on the pretext of a word to say to the head-waiter; and the rest of the group soon melted away in Mrs. Trenor's wake.

It was over in a moment—the waiter, *menu* in hand, still hung on the result of the choice between *Coupe Jacques* and *Pêches à la Melba*—but Miss Bart, in the interval, had taken the measure of her fate. Where Judy Trenor led, all the world would follow; and Lily had the doomed sense of the castaway who has signalled in vain to fleeing sails.

In a flash she remembered Mrs. Trenor's complaints of Carry Fisher's rapacity, and saw that they denoted an unexpected acquaintance with her husband's private affairs. In the large tumultuous disorder of the life at Bellomont, where no one seemed to have time to observe any one else, and private aims and personal interests were swept along unheeded in the rush of collective activities, Lily had fancied herself sheltered from inconvenient scrutiny; but if Judy knew when Mrs. Fisher borrowed money of her husband, was she likely to ignore the same transaction on Lily's part? If she was careless of his affections she was plainly jealous of his pocket; and in that fact Lily read the explanation of her rebuff. The immediate result of these conclusions was the passionate resolve to pay back her debt to Trenor. That obligation discharged, she would have but a thousand dollars of Mrs. Peniston's legacy left, and nothing to live on but her own small income, which was considerably less than Gerty Farish's wretched pittance; but this consideration gave way to the imperative claim of her wounded pride. She must be quits with the Trenors first; after that she would take thought for the future.

In her ignorance of legal procrastinations she had supposed that her legacy would be paid over within a few days of the reading of her aunt's will; and after an interval of anxious suspense, she wrote to enquire the cause of the delay. There was another interval before Mrs. Peniston's lawyer, who was also one of the executors, replied to the effect that, some questions having arisen relative to the interpretation of the will, he and his associates might not be in a position to pay the legacies till the close of the twelvemonth legally allotted for their settlement. Bewildered and indignant, Lily resolved to try the effect of a personal appeal; but she returned from her expedition with a sense of the powerlessness of beauty and charm against the unfeeling processes of the law. It seemed intolerable to live on for another year under the weight of her debt; and in her extremity she decided to turn to Miss Stepney, who still lingered in town, immersed in the delectable duty of "going over" her benefactress's effects. It was bitter enough for Lily to ask a favour of Grace Stepney, but the alternative was bitterer still; and one morning she presented herself at Mrs. Peniston's, where Grace, for the facilitation of her pious task, had taken up a provisional abode.

The strangeness of entering as a suppliant the house where she had so long commanded, increased Lily's desire to shorten the ordeal; and when Miss Stepney entered the darkened drawing-room, rustling with the best quality of crape, her visitor went straight to the point: would she be willing to advance the amount of the expected legacy?

Grace, in reply, wept and wondered at the request, bemoaned the inexorableness of the law, and was astonished that Lily had not realized the exact similarity of their positions. Did she think that only the payment of the legacies had been delayed? Why, Miss Stepney herself had not received a penny of her inheritance, and was paying rent—yes, actually!—for the privilege of living in a house that belonged to her. She was sure it was not what poor dear cousin Julia would have wished—she had told the executors so to their faces; but they were inaccessible to reason, and there was nothing to do but to wait. Let Lily take example by her, and be patient—let them both remember how beautifully patient cousin Julia had always been.

Lily made a movement which showed her imperfect assimilation of this example. "But you will have everything, Grace—it would be easy for you to borrow ten times the amount I am asking for."

"Borrow—easy for me to borrow?" Grace Stepney rose up before her in sable wrath. "Do you imagine for a moment that I would raise money on my expectations from cousin Julia, when I know so well her unspeakable horror of every transaction of the sort? Why, Lily, if you must know the truth, it was the idea of your being in debt that brought on her illness—you remember she had a slight attack before you sailed. Oh, I don't know the particulars, of course—I don't *want* to know them—but there were rumours about your affairs that made her most unhappy—no one could be with her without seeing that. I can't help it if you are offended by my telling you this now—if I can do anything to make you realize the folly of your course, and how deeply *she* disapproved of it, I shall feel it is the truest way of making up to you for her loss."

V

IT SEEMED to Lily, as Mrs. Peniston's door closed on her, that she was taking a final leave of her old life. The future stretched before her dull and bare as the deserted length of Fifth Avenue, and opportunities showed as meagrely as the few cabs trailing in quest of fares that did not come. The completeness of the analogy was, however, disturbed as she reached the sidewalk by the rapid approach of a hansom which pulled up at sight of her.

From beneath its luggage-laden top, she caught the wave of a signalling hand; and the next moment Mrs. Fisher, springing to the street, had folded her in a demonstrative embrace.

"My dear, you don't mean to say you're still in town? When I saw you the other day at Sherry's I did n't have time to ask——" She broke off, and added with a burst of frankness: "The truth is I was *horrid*, Lily, and I 've wanted to tell you so ever since."

"Oh——" Miss Bart protested, drawing back from her penitent clasp; but Mrs. Fisher went on with her usual directness: "Look here, Lily, don't let 's beat about the bush: half the trouble in life is caused by pretending there is n't any. That 's not my way, and I can only say I 'm thoroughly ashamed of myself for following the other women's lead. But we 'll talk of that by and bye—tell me now where you 're staying and what your plans are. I don't suppose you 're keeping house in there with Grace Stepney, eh?—and it struck me you might be rather at loose ends."

In Lily's present mood there was no resisting the honest friendliness of this appeal, and she said with a smile: "I *am* at loose ends for the moment, but Gerty Farish is still in town, and she 's good enough to let me be with her whenever she can spare the time."

Mrs. Fisher made a slight grimace. "H'm—that 's a temperate joy. Oh, I know—Gerty 's a trump, and worth all the rest of us put together; but *à la longue* you 're used to a little higher seasoning, are n't you, dear? And besides, I suppose she 'll be off herself before long—the first of August, you say?

Well, look here, you can't spend your summer in town; we 'll talk of that later too. But meanwhile, what do you say to putting a few things in a trunk and coming down with me to the Sam Gormers' tonight?"

And as Lily stared at the breathless suddenness of the suggestion, she continued with her easy laugh: "You don't know them and they don't know you; but that don't make a rap of difference. They 've taken the Van Alstyne place at Roslyn, and I 've got *carte blanche* to bring my friends down there— the more the merrier. They do things awfully well, and there 's to be rather a jolly party there this week——" she broke off, checked by an undefinable change in Miss Bart's expression. "Oh, I don't mean *your* particular set, you know: rather a different crowd, but very good fun. The fact is, the Gormers have struck out on a line of their own: what they want is to have a good time, and to have it in their own way. They gave the other thing a few months' trial, under my distinguished auspices, and they were really doing extremely well—getting on a good deal faster than the Brys, just because they did n't care as much—but suddenly they decided that the whole business bored them, and that what they wanted was a crowd they could really feel at home with. Rather original of them, don't you think so? Mattie Gormer *has* got aspirations still; women always have; but she 's awfully easy-going, and Sam won't be bothered, and they both like to be the most important people in sight, so they 've started a sort of continuous performance of their own, a kind of social Coney Island, where everybody is welcome who can make noise enough and does n't put on airs. *I* think it 's awfully good fun myself—some of the artistic set, you know, any pretty actress that 's going, and so on. This week, for instance, they have Audrey Anstell, who made such a hit last spring in 'The Winning of Winny'; and Paul Morpeth—he 's painting Mattie Gormer—and the Dick Bellingers, and Kate Corby—well, every one you can think of who 's jolly and makes a row. Now don't stand there with your nose in the air, my dear—it will be a good deal better than a broiling Sunday in town, and you 'll find clever people as well as noisy ones—Morpeth, who admires Mattie enormously, always brings one or two of his set."

Mrs. Fisher drew Lily toward the hansom with friendly authority. "Jump in now, there 's a dear, and we 'll drive round to your hotel and have your things packed, and then we 'll have tea, and the two maids can meet us at the train."

It was a good deal better than a broiling Sunday in town—of that no doubt remained to Lily as, reclining in the shade of a leafy verandah, she looked seaward across a stretch of greensward picturesquely dotted with groups of ladies in lace raiment and men in tennis flannels. The huge Van Alstyne house and its rambling dependencies were packed to their fullest capacity with the Gormers' week-end guests, who now, in the radiance of the Sunday forenoon, were dispersing themselves over the grounds in quest of the various distractions the place afforded: distractions ranging from tennis-courts to shooting-galleries, from bridge and whiskey within doors to motors and steam-launches without. Lily had the odd sense of having been caught up into the crowd as carelessly as a passenger is gathered in by an express train. The blonde and genial Mrs. Gormer might, indeed, have figured the conductor, calmly assigning seats to the rush of travellers, while Carry Fisher represented the porter pushing their bags into place, giving them their numbers for the dining-car, and warning them when their station was at hand. The train, meanwhile, had scarcely slackened speed—life whizzed on with a deafening rattle and roar, in which one traveller at least found a welcome refuge from the sound of her own thoughts.

The Gormer *milieu* represented a social out-skirt which Lily had always fastidiously avoided; but it struck her, now that she was in it, as only a flamboyant copy of her own world, a caricature approximating the real thing as the "society play" approaches the manners of the drawing-room. The people about her were doing the same things as the Trenors, the Van Osburghs and the Dorsets: the difference lay in a hundred shades of aspect and manner, from the pattern of the men's waistcoats to the inflexion of the women's voices. Everything was pitched in a higher key, and there was more of each thing: more noise, more colour, more champagne, more familiarity—but also greater good-nature, less rivalry, and a fresher capacity for enjoyment.

Miss Bart's arrival had been welcomed with an uncritical friendliness that first irritated her pride and then brought her to a sharp sense of her own situation—of the place in life which, for the moment, she must accept and make the best of. These people knew her story—of that her first long talk with Carry Fisher had left no doubt: she was publicly branded as the heroine of a "queer" episode—but instead of shrinking from her as her own friends had done, they received her without question into the easy promiscuity of their lives. They swallowed her past as easily as they did Miss Anstell's, and with no apparent sense of any difference in the size of the mouthful: all they asked was that she should—in her own way, for they recognized a diversity of gifts—contribute as much to the general amusement as that graceful actress, whose talents, when off the stage, were of the most varied order. Lily felt at once that any tendency to be "stuck-up," to mark a sense of differences and distinctions, would be fatal to her continuance in the Gormer set. To be taken in on such terms—and into such a world!—was hard enough to the lingering pride in her; but she realized, with a pang of self-contempt, that to be excluded from it would, after all, be harder still. For, almost at once, she had felt the insidious charm of slipping back into a life where every material difficulty was smoothed away. The sudden escape from a stifling hotel in a dusty deserted city to the space and luxury of a great country-house fanned by sea breezes, had produced a state of moral lassitude agreeable enough after the nervous tension and physical discomfort of the past weeks. For the moment she must yield to the refreshment her senses craved—after that she would reconsider her situation, and take counsel with her dignity. Her enjoyment of her surroundings was, indeed, tinged by the unpleasant consideration that she was accepting the hospitality and courting the approval of people she had disdained under other conditions. But she was growing less sensitive on such points: a hard glaze of indifference was fast forming over her delicacies and susceptibilities, and each concession to expediency hardened the surface a little more.

On the Monday, when the party disbanded with uproarious adieux, the return to town threw into stronger relief the charms of the life she was leaving. The other guests were dispersing to take up the same existence in a different setting: some at Newport, some at Bar Harbour, some in the elaborate rusticity of an Adirondack camp. Even Gerty Farish, who welcomed Lily's return with tender solicitude, would soon be preparing to join the aunt with whom she spent her summers on Lake George: only Lily herself remained without plan or purpose, stranded in a backwater of the great current of pleasure. But Carry Fisher, who had insisted on transporting her to her own house, where she herself was to perch for a day or two on the way to the Brys' camp, came to the rescue with a new suggestion.

"Look here, Lily—I'll tell you what it is: I want you to take my place with Mattie Gormer this summer. They're taking a party out to Alaska next month in their private car, and Mattie, who is the laziest woman alive, wants me to go with them, and relieve her of the bother of arranging things; but the Brys want me too—oh, yes, we've made it up: did n't I tell you?—and, to put it frankly, though I like the Gormers best, there's more profit for me in the Brys. The fact is, they want to try Newport this summer, and if I can make it a success for them they—well, they'll make it a success for *me*." Mrs. Fisher clasped her hands enthusiastically. "Do you know, Lily, the more I think of my idea the better I like it— quite as much for you as for myself. The Gormers have both taken a tremendous fancy to you, and the trip to Alaska is— well—the very thing I should want for you just at present."

Miss Bart lifted her eyes with a keen glance. "To take me out of my friends' way, you mean?" she said quietly; and Mrs. Fisher responded with a deprecating kiss: "To keep you out of their sight till they realize how much they miss you."

Miss Bart went with the Gormers to Alaska; and the expedition, if it did not produce the effect anticipated by her friend, had at least the negative advantage of removing her from the fiery centre of criticism and discussion. Gerty Farish had opposed the plan with all the energy of her somewhat inarticulate nature. She had even offered to give up her visit to Lake George, and remain in town with Miss Bart, if the latter would renounce her journey; but Lily could disguise her real distaste for this plan under a sufficiently valid reason.

"You dear innocent, don't you see," she protested, "that Carry is quite right, and that I must take up my usual life, and go about among people as much as possible? If my old friends choose to believe lies about me I shall have to make new ones, that's all; and you know beggars must n't be choosers. Not that I don't like Mattie Gormer—I *do* like her: she's kind and honest and unaffected; and don't you suppose I feel grateful to her for making me welcome at a time when, as you 've yourself seen, my own family have unanimously washed their hands of me?"

Gerty shook her head, mutely unconvinced. She felt not only that Lily was cheapening herself by making use of an intimacy she would never have cultivated from choice, but that, in drifting back now to her former manner of life, she was forfeiting her last chance of ever escaping from it. Gerty had but an obscure conception of what Lily's actual experience had been: but its consequences had established a lasting hold on her pity since the memorable night when she had offered up her own secret hope to her friend's extremity. To characters like Gerty's such a sacrifice constitutes a moral claim on the part of the person in whose behalf it has been made. Having once helped Lily, she must continue to help her; and helping her, must believe in her, because faith is the main-spring of such natures. But even if Miss Bart, after her renewed taste of the amenities of life, could have returned to the barrenness of a New York August, mitigated only by poor Gerty's presence, her worldly wisdom would have counselled her against such an act of abnegation. She knew that Carry Fisher was right: that an opportune absence might be the first step toward rehabilitation, and that, at any rate, to linger on in town out of season was a fatal admission of defeat.

From the Gormers' tumultuous progress across their native continent, she returned with an altered view of her situation. The renewed habit of luxury—the daily waking to an assured absence of care and presence of material ease—gradually blunted her appreciation of these values, and left her more conscious of the void they could not fill. Mattie Gormer's undiscriminating good-nature, and the slap-dash sociability of her friends, who treated Lily precisely as they treated each other—all these characteristic notes of difference began to wear upon her endurance; and the more she saw to criticize in her companions, the less justification she found for making use of them. The longing to get back to her former surroundings hardened to a fixed idea; but with the strengthening of her purpose came the inevitable perception that, to attain it, she must exact fresh concessions from her pride. These, for the moment, took the unpleasant form of continuing to cling to her hosts after their return from Alaska. Little as she was in the key of their *milieu*, her immense social facility, her long habit of adapting herself to others without suffering her own outline to be blurred, the skilled manipulation of all the polished implements of her craft, had won for her an important place in the Gormer group. If their resonant hilarity could never be hers, she contributed a note of easy elegance more valuable to Mattie Gormer than the louder passages of the band. Sam Gormer and his special cronies stood indeed a little in awe of her; but Mattie's following, headed by Paul Morpeth, made her feel that they prized her for the very qualities they most conspicuously lacked. If Morpeth, whose social indolence was as great as his artistic activity, had abandoned himself to the easy current of the Gormer existence, where the minor exactions of politeness were unknown or ignored, and a man could either break his engagements, or keep them in a painting-jacket and slippers, he still preserved his sense of differences, and his appreciation of graces he had no time to cultivate. During the preparations for the Brys' *tableaux* he had been immensely struck by Lily's plastic possibilities—"not the face: too self-controlled for expression; but the rest of her—gad, what a model she'd make!"—and though his abhorrence of the world in which he had seen her was too great for him to think of seeking her there, he was fully alive to the privilege of having her to look at and listen to while he lounged in Mattie Gormer's dishevelled drawing-room.

Lily had thus formed, in the tumult of her surroundings, a little nucleus of friendly relations which mitigated the crudeness of her course in lingering with the Gormers after their return. Nor was she without pale glimpses of her own world, especially since the breaking-up of the Newport season had set the social current once more toward Long Island. Kate

Corby, whose tastes made her as promiscuous as Carry Fisher was rendered by her necessities, occasionally descended on the Gormers, where, after a first stare of surprise, she took Lily's presence almost too much as a matter of course. Mrs. Fisher, too, appearing frequently in the neighbourhood, drove over to impart her experiences and give Lily what she called the latest report from the weather-bureau; and the latter, who had never directly invited her confidence, could yet talk with her more freely than with Gerty Farish, in whose presence it was impossible even to admit the existence of much that Mrs. Fisher conveniently took for granted.

Mrs. Fisher, moreover, had no embarrassing curiosity. She did not wish to probe the inwardness of Lily's situation, but simply to view it from the outside, and draw her conclusions accordingly; and these conclusions, at the end of a confidential talk, she summed up to her friend in the succinct remark: "You must marry as soon as you can."

Lily uttered a faint laugh—for once Mrs. Fisher lacked originality. "Do you mean, like Gerty Farish, to recommend the unfailing panacea of 'a good man's love'?"

"No—I don't think either of my candidates would answer to that description," said Mrs. Fisher after a pause of reflection.

"Either? Are there actually two?"

"Well, perhaps I ought to say one and a half—for the moment."

Miss Bart received this with increasing amusement. "Other things being equal, I think I should prefer a half-husband: who is he?"

"Don't fly out at me till you hear my reasons—George Dorset."

"Oh——" Lily murmured reproachfully; but Mrs. Fisher pressed on unrebuffed. "Well, why not? They had a few weeks' honeymoon when they first got back from Europe, but now things are going badly with them again. Bertha has been behaving more than ever like a madwoman, and George's powers of credulity are very nearly exhausted. They're at their place here, you know, and I spent last Sunday with them. It was a ghastly party—no one else but poor Neddy Silverton, who looks like a galley-slave (they used to talk of my making that poor boy unhappy!)—and after luncheon George carried me off on a long walk, and told me the end would have to come soon."

Miss Bart made an incredulous gesture. "As far as that goes, the end will never come—Bertha will always know how to get him back when she wants him."

Mrs. Fisher continued to observe her tentatively. "Not if he has any one else to turn to! Yes—that's just what it comes to: the poor creature can't stand alone. And I remember him such a good fellow, full of life and enthusiasm." She paused, and went on, dropping her glance from Lily's: "He would n't stay with her ten minutes if he *knew*——"

"Knew——?" Miss Bart repeated.

"What *you* must, for instance—with the opportunities you 've had! If he had positive proof, I mean——"

Lily interrupted her with a deep blush of displeasure. "Please let us drop the subject, Carry: it 's too odious to me." And to divert her companion's attention she added, with an attempt at lightness: "And your second candidate? We must not forget him."

Mrs. Fisher echoed her laugh. "I wonder if you 'll cry out just as loud if I say—Sim Rosedale?"

Miss Bart did not cry out: she sat silent, gazing thoughtfully at her friend. The suggestion, in truth, gave expression to a possibility which, in the last weeks, had more than once recurred to her; but after a moment she said carelessly: "Mr. Rosedale wants a wife who can establish him in the bosom of the Van Osburghs and Trenors."

Mrs. Fisher caught her up eagerly. "And so *you* could—with his money! Don't you see how beautifully it would work out for you both?"

"I don't see any way of making him see it," Lily returned, with a laugh intended to dismiss the subject.

But in reality it lingered with her long after Mrs. Fisher had taken leave. She had seen very little of Rosedale since her annexation by the Gormers, for he was still steadily bent on penetrating to the inner Paradise from which she was now excluded; but once or twice, when nothing better offered, he had turned up for a Sunday, and on these occasions he had left her in no doubt as to his view of her situation. That he still admired her was, more than ever, offensively evident; for in the Gormer circle, where he expanded as in his native element, there were no puzzling conventions to check the full expression of his approval. But it was in the quality of his admiration that she read his shrewd estimate of her case. He enjoyed letting the Gormers see that he had known "Miss Lily"—she was "Miss Lily" to him now—before they had had the faintest social existence: enjoyed more especially impressing Paul Morpeth with the distance to which their intimacy dated back. But he let it be felt that that intimacy was a mere ripple on the surface of a rushing social current, the kind of relaxation which a man of large interests and manifold preoccupations permits himself in his hours of ease.

The necessity of accepting this view of their past relation, and of meeting it in the key of pleasantry prevalent among her new friends, was deeply humiliating to Lily. But she dared less than ever to quarrel with Rosedale. She suspected that her rejection rankled among the most unforgettable of his rebuffs, and the fact that he knew something of her wretched transaction with Trenor, and was sure to put the basest construction on it, seemed to place her hopelessly in his power. Yet at Carry Fisher's suggestion a new hope had stirred in her. Much as she disliked Rosedale, she no longer absolutely despised him. For he was gradually attaining his object in life, and that, to Lily, was always less despicable than to miss it. With the slow unalterable persistency which she had always felt in him, he was making his way through the dense mass of social antagonisms. Already his wealth, and the masterly use he had made of it, were giving him an enviable prominence in the world of affairs, and placing Wall Street under obligations which only Fifth Avenue could repay. In response to these claims, his name began to figure on municipal committees and charitable boards; he appeared at banquets to distinguished strangers, and his candidacy at one of the fashionable clubs was discussed with diminishing opposition. He had figured once or twice at the Trenor dinners, and had learned to speak with just the right note of disdain of the big Van Osburgh crushes; and all he now needed was a wife whose affiliations would shorten the last tedious steps of his ascent. It was with that object that, a year earlier, he had fixed his affections on Miss Bart; but in the interval he had mounted nearer to the goal, while she had lost the power to abbreviate the remaining steps of the way. All this she saw with the clearness of vision that came to her in moments of despondency. It was success that dazzled her—she could distinguish facts plainly enough in the twilight of failure. And the twilight, as she now sought to pierce it, was gradually lighted by a faint spark of reassurance. Under the utilitarian motive of Rosedale's wooing she had felt, clearly enough, the heat of personal inclination. She would not have detested him so heartily had she not known that he dared to admire her. What, then, if the passion persisted, though the other motive had ceased to sustain it? She had never even tried to please him—he had been drawn to her in spite of her manifest disdain. What if she now chose to exert the power which, even in its passive state, he had felt so strongly? What if she made him marry her for love, now that he had no other reason for marrying her?

VI

As became persons of their rising consequence, the Gormers were engaged in building a country-house on Long Island; and it was a part of Miss Bart's duty to attend her hostess on frequent visits of inspection to the new estate. There, while Mrs. Gormer plunged into problems of lighting and sanitation, Lily had leisure to wander, in the bright autumn air, along the tree-fringed bay to which the land declined. Little as she was addicted to solitude, there had come to be moments when it seemed a welcome escape from the empty noises of her life. She was weary of being swept passively along a current of pleasure and business in which she had no share; weary of seeing other people pursue amusement and squander money, while she felt herself of no more account among them than an expensive toy in the hands of a spoiled child.

It was in this frame of mind that, striking back from the shore one morning into the windings of an unfamiliar lane, she came suddenly upon the figure of George Dorset. The Dorset place was in the immediate neighbourhood of the Gormers' newly-acquired estate, and in her motor-flights thither with Mrs. Gormer, Lily had caught one or two passing glimpses of the couple; but they moved in so different an orbit that she had not considered the possibility of a direct encounter.

Dorset, swinging along with bent head, in moody abstraction, did not see Miss Bart till he was close upon her; but the sight, instead of bringing him to a halt, as she had half-expected, sent him toward her with an eagerness which found expression in his opening words.

"Miss Bart!—You'll shake hands, won't you? I've been hoping to meet you—I should have written to you if I'd dared." His face, with its tossed red hair and straggling moustache, had a driven uneasy look, as though life had become an unceasing race between himself and the thoughts at his heels.

The look drew a word of compassionate greeting from Lily, and he pressed on, as if encouraged by her tone: "I wanted to apologize—to ask you to forgive me for the miserable part I played——"

She checked him with a quick gesture. "Don't let us speak of it: I was very sorry for you," she said, with a tinge of disdain which, as she instantly perceived, was not lost on him.

He flushed to his haggard eyes, flushed so cruelly that she repented the thrust. "You might well be; you don't know—you must let me explain. I was deceived: abominably deceived——"

"I am still more sorry for you, then," she interposed, without irony; "but you must see that I am not exactly the person with whom the subject can be discussed."

He met this with a look of genuine wonder. "Why not? Is n't it to you, of all people, that I owe an explanation——"

"No explanation is necessary: the situation was perfectly clear to me."

"Ah——" he murmured, his head drooping again, and his irresolute hand switching at the underbrush along the lane. But as Lily made a movement to pass on, he broke out with fresh vehemence: "Miss Bart, for God's sake don't turn from me! We used to be good friends—you were always kind to me—and you don't know how I need a friend now."

The lamentable weakness of the words roused a motion of pity in Lily's breast. She too needed friends—she had tasted the pang of loneliness; and her resentment of Bertha Dorset's cruelty softened her heart to the poor wretch who was after all the chief of Bertha's victims.

"I still wish to be kind; I feel no ill-will toward you," she said. "But you must understand that after what has happened we can't be friends again—we can't see each other."

"Ah, you *are* kind—you 're merciful—you always were!" He fixed his miserable gaze on her. "But why can't we be friends—why not, when I 've repented in dust and ashes? Is n't it hard that you should condemn me to suffer for the falseness, the treachery of others? I was punished enough at the time—is there to be no respite for me?"

"I should have thought you had found complete respite in the reconciliation which was effected at my expense," Lily began, with renewed impatience; but he broke in imploringly: "Don't put it in that way—when that 's been the worst of my punishment. My God! what could I do—was n't I powerless? You were singled out as a sacrifice: any word I might have said would have been turned against you——"

"I have told you I don't blame you; all I ask you to understand is that, after the use Bertha chose to make of me—after all that her behaviour has since implied—it 's impossible that you and I should meet."

He continued to stand before her, in his dogged weakness. "Is it—need it be? Might n't there be circumstances——?" he checked himself, slashing at the wayside weeds in a wider radius. Then he began again: "Miss Bart, listen—give me a minute. If we 're not to meet again, at least let me have a hearing now. You say we can't be friends after—after what has happened. But can't I at least appeal to your pity? Can't I move you if I ask you to think of me as a prisoner—a prisoner you alone can set free?"

Lily's inward start betrayed itself in a quick blush: was it possible that this was really the sense of Carry Fisher's adumbrations?

"I can't see how I can possibly be of any help to you," she murmured, drawing back a little from the mounting excitement of his look.

Her tone seemed to sober him, as it had so often done in his stormiest moments. The stubborn lines of his face relaxed, and he said, with an abrupt drop to docility: "You *would* see, if you 'd be as merciful as you used to be: and heaven knows I 've never needed it more!"

She paused a moment, moved in spite of herself by this reminder of her influence over him. Her fibres had been softened by suffering, and the sudden glimpse into his mocked and broken life disarmed her contempt for his weakness.

"I am very sorry for you—I would help you willingly; but you must have other friends, other advisers."

"I never had a friend like you," he answered simply. "And besides—can't you see?—you 're the only person"—his voice dropped to a whisper—"the only person who knows."

Again she felt her colour change; again her heart rose in precipitate throbs to meet what she felt was coming.

He lifted his eyes to her entreatingly. "You do see, don't you? You understand? I 'm desperate—I 'm at the end of my tether. I want to be free, and you can free me. I know you can. You don't want to keep me bound fast in hell, do you? You can't want to take such a vengeance as that. You were always kind—your eyes are kind now. You say you 're sorry for me. Well, it rests with you to show it; and heaven knows there 's nothing to keep you back. You understand, of course—there would n't be a hint of publicity—not a sound or a syllable to connect you with the thing. It would never come to that, you know: all I need is to be able to say definitely: 'I know this—and this—and this'—and the fight would drop, and the way be cleared, and the whole abominable business swept out of sight in a second."

He spoke pantingly, like a tired runner, with breaks of exhaustion between his words; and through the breaks she caught, as through the shifting rents of a fog, great golden vistas of peace and safety. For there was no mistaking the definite intention behind his vague appeal; she could have filled up the blanks without the help of Mrs. Fisher's insinuations. Here was a man who turned to her in the extremity of his loneliness and his humiliation: if she came to him at such a moment he would be hers with all the force of his deluded faith. And the power to make him so lay in her hand—lay there in a completeness he could not even remotely conjecture. Revenge and rehabilitation might be hers at a stroke—there was something dazzling in the completeness of the opportunity.

She stood silent, gazing away from him down the autumnal stretch of the deserted lane. And suddenly fear possessed her—fear of herself, and of the terrible force of the temptation. All her past weaknesses were like so many eager accomplices drawing her toward the path their feet had already smoothed. She turned quickly, and held out her hand to Dorset.

"Goodbye—I 'm sorry; there 's nothing in the world that I can do."

"Nothing? Ah, don't say that," he cried; "say what 's true: that you abandon me like the others. You, the only creature who could have saved me!"

"Goodbye—goodby ," she repeated hurriedly; and as she

moved away she heard him cry out on a last note of entreaty:
"At least you 'll let me see you once more?"

Lily, on regaining the Gormer grounds, struck rapidly
across the lawn toward the unfinished house, where she fancied that her hostess might be speculating, not too resignedly,
on the cause of her delay; for, like many unpunctual persons,
Mrs. Gormer disliked to be kept waiting.

As Miss Bart reached the avenue, however, she saw a smart
phaeton with a high-stepping pair disappear behind the
shrubbery in the direction of the gate; and on the doorstep
stood Mrs. Gormer, with a glow of retrospective pleasure on
her open countenance. At sight of Lily the glow deepened to
an embarrassed red, and she said with a slight laugh: "Did
you see my visitor? Oh, I thought you came back by the avenue. It was Mrs. George Dorset—she said she 'd dropped in
to make a neighbourly call."

Lily met the announcement with her usual composure,
though her experience of Bertha's idiosyncrasies would not
have led her to include the neighbourly instinct among them;
and Mrs. Gormer, relieved to see that she gave no sign of
surprise, went on with a deprecating laugh: "Of course what
really brought her was curiosity—she made me take her all
over the house. But no one could have been nicer—no airs,
you know, and so good-natured: I can quite see why people
think her so fascinating."

This surprising event, coinciding too completely with her
meeting with Dorset to be regarded as contingent upon it,
had yet immediately struck Lily with a vague sense of foreboding. It was not in Bertha's habits to be neighbourly, much
less to make advances to any one outside the immediate circle
of her affinities. She had always consistently ignored the
world of outer aspirants, or had recognized its individual
members only when prompted by motives of self-interest; and
the very capriciousness of her condescensions had, as Lily was
aware, given them special value in the eyes of the persons she
distinguished. Lily saw this now in Mrs. Gormer's uncon-
cealable complacency, and in the happy irrelevance with
which, for the next day or two, she quoted Bertha's opinions

and speculated on the origin of her gown. All the secret ambitions which Mrs. Gormer's native indolence, and the attitude of her companions, kept in habitual abeyance, were now germinating afresh in the glow of Bertha's advances; and whatever the cause of the latter, Lily saw that, if they were followed up, they were likely to have a disturbing effect upon her own future.

She had arranged to break the length of her stay with her new friends by one or two visits to other acquaintances as recent; and on her return from this somewhat depressing excursion she was immediately conscious that Mrs. Dorset's influence was still in the air. There had been another exchange of visits, a tea at a country-club, an encounter at a hunt ball; there was even a rumour of an approaching dinner, which Mattie Gormer, with an unnatural effort at discretion, tried to smuggle out of the conversation whenever Miss Bart took part in it.

The latter had already planned to return to town after a farewell Sunday with her friends; and, with Gerty Farish's aid, had discovered a small private hotel where she might establish herself for the winter. The hotel being on the edge of a fashionable neighbourhood, the price of the few square feet she was to occupy was considerably in excess of her means; but she found a justification for her dislike of poorer quarters in the argument that, at this particular juncture, it was of the utmost importance to keep up a show of prosperity. In reality, it was impossible for her, while she had the means to pay her way for a week ahead, to lapse into a form of existence like Gerty Farish's. She had never been so near the brink of insolvency; but she could at least manage to meet her weekly hotel bill, and having settled the heaviest of her previous debts out of the money she had received from Trenor, she had a still fair margin of credit to go upon. The situation, however, was not agreeable enough to lull her to complete unconsciousness of its insecurity. Her rooms, with their cramped outlook down a sallow vista of brick walls and fire-escapes, her lonely meals in the dark restaurant with its surcharged ceiling and haunting smell of coffee—all these material discomforts, which were yet to be accounted as so many privileges soon to be withdrawn, kept constantly before her the disadvantages of her state; and her mind reverted the more insistently to Mrs. Fisher's counsels. Beat about the question as she would, she knew the outcome of it was that she must try to marry Rosedale; and in this conviction she was fortified by an unexpected visit from George Dorset.

She found him, on the first Sunday after her return to town, pacing her narrow sitting-room to the imminent peril of the few knick-knacks with which she had tried to disguise its plush exuberances; but the sight of her seemed to quiet him, and he said meekly that he had n't come to bother her— that he asked only to be allowed to sit for half an hour and talk of anything she liked. In reality, as she knew, he had but one subject: himself and his wretchedness; and it was the need of her sympathy that had drawn him back. But he began with a pretence of questioning her about herself, and as she replied, she saw that, for the first time, a faint realization of her plight penetrated the dense surface of his self-absorption. Was it possible that her old beast of an aunt had actually cut her off? That she was living alone like this because there was no one else for her to go to, and that she really had n't more than enough to keep alive on till the wretched little legacy was paid? The fibres of sympathy were nearly atrophied in him, but he was suffering so intensely that he had a faint glimpse of what other sufferings might mean—and, as she perceived, an almost simultaneous perception of the way in which her particular misfortunes might serve him.

When at length she dismissed him, on the pretext that she must dress for dinner, he lingered entreatingly on the threshold to blurt out: "It 's been such a comfort—do say you 'll let me see you again—" But to this direct appeal it was impossible to give an assent; and she said with friendly decisiveness: "I 'm sorry—but you know why I can't."

He coloured to the eyes, pushed the door shut, and stood before her embarrassed but insistent. "I know how you might, if you would—if things were different—and it lies with you to make them so. It 's just a word to say, and you put me out of my misery!"

Their eyes met, and for a second she trembled again with the nearness of the temptation. "You 're mistaken; I know nothing; I saw nothing," she exclaimed, striving, by sheer force of reiteration, to build a barrier between herself and her peril; and as he turned away, groaning out "You sacrifice us both," she continued to repeat, as if it were a charm: "I know nothing—absolutely nothing."

Lily had seen little of Rosedale since her illuminating talk with Mrs. Fisher, but on the two or three occasions when they had met she was conscious of having distinctly advanced in his favour. There could be no doubt that he admired her as much as ever, and she believed it rested with herself to raise his admiration to the point where it should bear down the lingering counsels of expediency. The task was not an easy one; but neither was it easy, in her long sleepless nights, to face the thought of what George Dorset was so clearly ready to offer. Baseness for baseness, she hated the other least: there were even moments when a marriage with Rosedale seemed the only honourable solution of her difficulties. She did not indeed let her imagination range beyond the day of plighting: after that everything faded into a haze of material well-being, in which the personality of her benefactor remained mercifully vague. She had learned, in her long vigils, that there were certain things not good to think of, certain midnight images that must at any cost be exorcised—and one of these was the image of herself as Rosedale's wife.

Carry Fisher, on the strength, as she frankly owned, of the Brys' Newport success, had taken for the autumn months a small house at Tuxedo; and thither Lily was bound on the Sunday after Dorset's visit. Though it was nearly dinner-time when she arrived, her hostess was still out, and the firelit quiet of the small silent house descended on her spirit with a sense of peace and familiarity. It may be doubted if such an emotion had ever before been evoked by Carry Fisher's surroundings; but, contrasted to the world in which Lily had lately lived, there was an air of repose and stability in the very placing of the furniture, and in the quiet competence of the parlour-maid who led her up to her room. Mrs. Fisher's unconventionality was, after all, a merely superficial divergence from an inherited social creed, while the manners of the Gormer circle represented their first attempt to formulate such a creed for themselves.

It was the first time since her return from Europe that Lily had found herself in a congenial atmosphere, and the stirring of familiar associations had almost prepared her, as she descended the stairs before dinner, to enter upon a group of her old acquaintances. But this expectation was instantly checked by the reflection that the friends who remained loyal were precisely those who would be least willing to expose her to such encounters; and it was hardly with surprise that she found, instead, Mr. Rosedale kneeling domestically on the drawing-room hearth before his hostess's little girl.

Rosedale in the paternal rôle was hardly a figure to soften Lily; yet she could not but notice a quality of homely goodness in his advances to the child. They were not, at any rate, the premeditated and perfunctory endearments of the guest under his hostess's eye, for he and the little girl had the room to themselves; and something in his attitude made him seem a simple and kindly being compared to the small critical creature who endured his homage. Yes, he would be kind—Lily, from the threshold, had time to feel—kind in his gross, unscrupulous, rapacious way, the way of the predatory creature with his mate. She had but a moment in which to consider whether this glimpse of the fireside man mitigated her repugnance, or gave it, rather, a more concrete and intimate form; for at sight of her he was immediately on his feet again, the florid and dominant Rosedale of Mattie Gormer's drawing-room.

It was no surprise to Lily to find that he had been selected as her only fellow-guest. Though she and her hostess had not met since the latter's tentative discussion of her future, Lily knew that the acuteness which enabled Mrs. Fisher to lay a safe and pleasant course through a world of antagonistic forces was not infrequently exercised for the benefit of her friends. It was, in fact, characteristic of Carry that, while she actively gleaned her own stores from the fields of affluence, her real sympathies were on the other side—with the unlucky, the unpopular, the unsuccessful, with all her hungry fellow-toilers in the shorn stubble of success.

Mrs. Fisher's experience guarded her against the mistake of exposing Lily, for the first evening, to the unmitigated impression of Rosedale's personality. Kate Corby and two or three men dropped in to dinner, and Lily, alive to every detail of her friend's method, saw that such opportunities as had been contrived for her were to be deferred till she had, as it were, gained courage to make effectual use of them. She had a sense of acquiescing in this plan with the passiveness of a sufferer resigned to the surgeon's touch; and this feeling of almost lethargic helplessness continued when, after the departure of the guests, Mrs. Fisher followed her upstairs.

"May I come in and smoke a cigarette over your fire? If we talk in my room we shall disturb the child." Mrs. Fisher looked about her with the eye of the solicitous hostess. "I hope you 've managed to make yourself comfortable, dear? Is n't it a jolly little house? It 's such a blessing to have a few quiet weeks with the baby."

Carry, in her rare moments of prosperity, became so expansively maternal that Miss Bart sometimes wondered whether, if she could ever get time and money enough, she would not end by devoting them both to her daughter.

"It 's a well-earned rest: I 'll say that for myself," she continued, sinking down with a sigh of content on the pillowed lounge near the fire. "Louisa Bry is a stern task-master: I often used to wish myself back with the Gormers. Talk of love making people jealous and suspicious—it 's nothing to social ambition! Louisa used to lie awake at night wondering whether the women who called on us called on *me* because I was with her, or on *her* because she was with me; and she was always laying traps to find out what I thought. Of course I had to disown my oldest friends, rather than let her suspect she owed me the chance of making a single acquaintance— when, all the while, that was what she had me there for, and what she wrote me a handsome cheque for when the season was over!"

Mrs. Fisher was not a woman who talked of herself without cause, and the practice of direct speech, far from precluding in her an occasional resort to circuitous methods, served rather, at crucial moments, the purpose of the juggler's chatter while he shifts the contents of his sleeves. Through the haze of her cigarette smoke she continued to gaze meditatively at Miss Bart, who, having dismissed her maid, sat before the toilet-table shaking out over her shoulders the loosened undulations of her hair.

"Your hair 's wonderful, Lily. Thinner—? What does that matter, when it 's so light and alive? So many women's worries seem to go straight to their hair—but yours looks as if there had never been an anxious thought under it. I never saw you look better than you did this evening. Mattie Gormer told me that Morpeth wanted to paint you—why don't you let him?"

Miss Bart's immediate answer was to address a critical glance to the reflection of the countenance under discussion. Then she said, with a slight touch of irritation: "I don't care to accept a portrait from Paul Morpeth."

Mrs. Fisher mused. "N—no. And just now, especially—well, he can do you after you 're married." She waited a moment, and then went on: "By the way, I had a visit from Mattie the other day. She turned up here last Sunday—and with Bertha Dorset, of all people in the world!"

She paused again to measure the effect of this announcement on her hearer, but the brush in Miss Bart's lifted hand maintained its unwavering stroke from brow to nape.

"I never was more astonished," Mrs. Fisher pursued. "I don't know two women less predestined to intimacy—from Bertha's standpoint, that is; for of course poor Mattie thinks it natural enough that she should be singled out—I 've no doubt the rabbit always thinks it is fascinating the anaconda. Well, you know I 've always told you that Mattie secretly longed to bore herself with the really fashionable; and now that the chance has come, I see that she 's capable of sacrificing all her old friends to it."

Lily laid aside her brush and turned a penetrating glance upon her friend. "Including *me*?" she suggested.

"Ah, my dear," murmured Mrs. Fisher, rising to push back a log from the hearth.

"That 's what Bertha means, is n't it?" Miss Bart went on steadily. "For of course she always means something; and before I left Long Island I saw that she was beginning to lay her toils for Mattie."

Mrs. Fisher sighed evasively. "She has her fast now, at any rate. To think of that loud independence of Mattie's being only a subtler form of snobbishness! Bertha can already make her believe anything she pleases—and I 'm afraid she 's begun, my poor child, by insinuating horrors about you."

Lily flushed under the shadow of her drooping hair. "The world is too vile," she murmured, averting herself from Mrs. Fisher's anxious scrutiny.

"It 's not a pretty place; and the only way to keep a footing in it is to fight it on its own terms—and above all, my dear, not alone!" Mrs. Fisher gathered up her floating implications in a resolute grasp. "You 've told me so little that I can only guess what has been happening; but in the rush we all live in there 's no time to keep on hating any one without a cause, and if Bertha is still nasty enough to want to injure you with other people it must be because she 's still afraid of you. From her standpoint there 's only one reason for being afraid of you; and my own idea is that, if you want to punish her, you hold the means in your hand. I believe you can marry George Dorset tomorrow; but if you don't care for that particular form of retaliation, the only thing to save you from Bertha is to marry somebody else."

VII

THE LIGHT projected on the situation by Mrs. Fisher had the cheerless distinctness of a winter dawn. It outlined the facts with a cold precision unmodified by shade or colour, and refracted, as it were, from the blank walls of the surrounding limitations: she had opened windows from which no sky was ever visible. But the idealist subdued to vulgar necessities must employ vulgar minds to draw the inferences to which he cannot stoop; and it was easier for Lily to let Mrs. Fisher formulate her case than to put it plainly to herself. Once confronted with it, however, she went the full length of its consequences; and these had never been more clearly present to her than when, the next afternoon, she set out for a walk with Rosedale.

It was one of those still November days when the air is haunted with the light of summer, and something in the lines of the landscape, and in the golden haze which bathed them, recalled to Miss Bart the September afternoon when she had climbed the slopes of Bellomont with Selden. The importunate memory was kept before her by its ironic contrast to her present situation, since her walk with Selden had represented an irresistible flight from just such a climax as the present excursion was designed to bring about. But other memories importuned her also; the recollection of similar situations, as skilfully led up to, but through some malice of fortune, or her own unsteadiness of purpose, always failing of the intended result. Well, her purpose was steady enough now. She saw that the whole weary work of rehabilitation must begin again, and against far greater odds, if Bertha Dorset should succeed in breaking up her friendship with the Gormers; and her longing for shelter and security was intensified by the passionate desire to triumph over Bertha, as only wealth and predominance could triumph over her. As the wife of Rosedale—the Rosedale she felt it in her power to create—she would at least present an invulnerable front to her enemy.

She had to draw upon this thought, as upon some fiery stimulant, to keep up her part in the scene toward which

Rosedale was too frankly tending. As she walked beside him, shrinking in every nerve from the way in which his look and tone made free of her, yet telling herself that this momentary endurance of his mood was the price she must pay for her ultimate power over him, she tried to calculate the exact point at which concession must turn to resistance, and the price *he* would have to pay be made equally clear to him. But his dapper self-confidence seemed impenetrable to such hints, and she had a sense of something hard and self-contained behind the superficial warmth of his manner.

They had been seated for some time in the seclusion of a rocky glen above the lake, when she suddenly cut short the culmination of an impassioned period by turning upon him the grave loveliness of her gaze.

"I *do* believe what you say, Mr. Rosedale," she said quietly; "and I am ready to marry you whenever you wish."

Rosedale, reddening to the roots of his glossy hair, received this announcement with a recoil which carried him to his feet, where he halted before her in an attitude of almost comic discomfiture.

"For I suppose that is what you do wish," she continued, in the same quiet tone. "And, though I was unable to consent when you spoke to me in this way before, I am ready, now that I know you so much better, to trust my happiness to your hands."

She spoke with the noble directness which she could command on such occasions, and which was like a large steady light thrown across the tortuous darkness of the situation. In its inconvenient brightness Rosedale seemed to waver a moment, as though conscious that every avenue of escape was unpleasantly illuminated.

Then he gave a short laugh, and drew out a gold cigarette-case, in which, with plump jewelled fingers, he groped for a gold-tipped cigarette. Selecting one, he paused to contemplate it a moment before saying: "My dear Miss Lily, I 'm sorry if there 's been any little misapprehension between us— but you made me feel my suit was so hopeless that I had really no intention of renewing it."

Lily's blood tingled with the grossness of the rebuff; but she checked the first leap of her anger, and said in a tone of gentle dignity: "I have no one but myself to blame if I gave you the impression that my decision was final."

Her word-play was always too quick for him, and this reply held him in puzzled silence while she extended her hand and added, with the faintest inflection of sadness in her voice: "Before we bid each other goodbye, I want at least to thank you for having once thought of me as you did."

The touch of her hand, the moving softness of her look, thrilled a vulnerable fibre in Rosedale. It was her exquisite inaccessibleness, the sense of distance she could convey without a hint of disdain, that made it most difficult for him to give her up.

"Why do you talk of saying goodbye? Ain't we going to be good friends all the same?" he urged, without releasing her hand.

She drew it away quietly. "What is your idea of being good friends?" she returned with a slight smile. "Making love to me without asking me to marry you?"

Rosedale laughed with a recovered sense of ease. "Well, that 's about the size of it, I suppose. I can't help making love to you—I don't see how any man could; but I don't mean to ask you to marry me as long as I can keep out of it."

She continued to smile. "I like your frankness; but I am afraid our friendship can hardly continue on those terms."

She turned away, as though to mark that its final term had in fact been reached, and he followed her for a few steps with a baffled sense of her having after all kept the game in her own hands.

"Miss Lily——" he began impulsively; but she walked on without seeming to hear him.

He overtook her in a few quick strides, and laid an entreating hand on her arm. "Miss Lily—don't hurry away like that. You 're beastly hard on a fellow; but if you don't mind speaking the truth I don't see why you should n't allow me to do the same."

She had paused a moment with raised brows, drawing away instinctively from his touch, though she made no effort to evade his words.

"I was under the impression," she rejoined, "that you had done so without waiting for my permission."

"Well—why should n't you hear my reasons for doing it, then? We 're neither of us such new hands that a little plain speaking is going to hurt us. I 'm all broken up on you: there 's nothing new in that. I 'm more in love with you than I was this time last year; but I 've got to face the fact that the situation is changed."

She continued to confront him with the same air of ironic composure. "You mean to say that I 'm not as desirable a match as you thought me?"

"Yes; that 's what I do mean," he answered resolutely. "I won't go into what 's happened. I don't believe the stories about you—I don't *want* to believe them. But they 're there, and my not believing them ain't going to alter the situation."

She flushed to her temples, but the extremity of her need checked the retort on her lip and she continued to face him composedly. "If they are not true," she said, "does n't *that* alter the situation?"

He met this with a steady gaze of his small stock-taking eyes, which made her feel herself no more than some superfine human merchandise. "I believe it does in novels; but I 'm certain it don't in real life. You know that as well as I do: if we 're speaking the truth, let 's speak the whole truth. Last year I was wild to marry you, and you would n't look at me: this year—well, you appear to be willing. Now, what has changed in the interval? Your situation, that 's all. Then you thought you could do better; now——"

"You think you can?" broke from her ironically.

"Why, yes, I do: in one way, that is." He stood before her, his hands in his pockets, his chest sturdily expanded under its vivid waistcoat. "It 's this way, you see: I 've had a pretty steady grind of it these last years, working up my social position. Think it 's funny I should say that? Why should I mind saying I want to get into society? A man ain't ashamed to say he wants to own a racing stable or a picture gallery. Well, a taste for society 's just another kind of hobby. Perhaps I want to get even with some of the people who cold-shouldered me last year—put it that way if it sounds better. Anyhow, I want to have the run of the best houses; and I 'm getting it too, little by little. But I know the quickest way to queer yourself with the right people is to be seen with the wrong ones; and that's the reason I want to avoid mistakes."

Miss Bart continued to stand before him in a silence that might have expressed either mockery or a half-reluctant respect for his candour, and after a moment's pause he went on: "There it is, you see. I'm more in love with you than ever, but if I married you now I'd queer myself for good and all, and everything I've worked for all these years would be wasted."

She received this with a look from which all tinge of resentment had faded. After the tissue of social falsehoods in which she had so long moved it was refreshing to step into the open daylight of an avowed expediency.

"I understand you," she said. "A year ago I should have been of use to you, and now I should be an encumbrance; and I like you for telling me so quite honestly." She extended her hand with a smile.

Again the gesture had a disturbing effect upon Mr. Rosedale's self-command. "By George, you're a dead game sport, you are!" he exclaimed; and as she began once more to move away, he broke out suddenly—"Miss Lily—stop. You know I don't believe those stories—I believe they were all got up by a woman who did n't hesitate to sacrifice you to her own convenience——"

Lily drew away with a movement of quick disdain: it was easier to endure his insolence than his commiseration.

"You are very kind; but I don't think we need discuss the matter farther."

But Rosedale's natural imperviousness to hints made it easy for him to brush such resistance aside. "I don't want to discuss anything; I just want to put a plain case before you," he persisted.

She paused in spite of herself, held by the note of a new purpose in his look and tone; and he went on, keeping his eyes firmly upon her: "The wonder to me is that you've waited so long to get square with that woman, when you've had the power in your hands." She continued silent under the rush of astonishment that his words produced, and he moved a step closer to ask with low-toned directness: "Why don't you use those letters of hers you bought last year?"

Lily stood speechless under the shock of the interrogation. In the words preceding it she had conjectured, at most, an allusion to her supposed influence over George Dorset; nor did the astonishing indelicacy of the reference diminish the likelihood of Rosedale's resorting to it. But now she saw how far short of the mark she had fallen; and the surprise of learning that he had discovered the secret of the letters left her, for the moment, unconscious of the special use to which he was in the act of putting his knowledge.

Her temporary loss of self-possession gave him time to press his point; and he went on quickly, as though to secure completer control of the situation: "You see I know where you stand—I know how completely she's in your power. That sounds like stage-talk, don't it?—but there's a lot of truth in some of those old gags; and I don't suppose you bought those letters simply because you're collecting autographs."

She continued to look at him with a deepening bewilderment: her only clear impression resolved itself into a scared sense of his power.

"You're wondering how I found out about 'em?" he went on, answering her look with a note of conscious pride. "Perhaps you've forgotten that I'm the owner of the Benedick— but never mind about that now. Getting on to things is a mighty useful accomplishment in business, and I've simply extended it to my private affairs. For this *is* partly my affair, you see—at least, it depends on you to make it so. Let's look the situation straight in the eye. Mrs. Dorset, for reasons we need n't go into, did you a beastly bad turn last spring. Everybody knows what Mrs. Dorset is, and her best friends would n't believe her on oath where their own interests were concerned; but as long as they're out of the row it's much easier to follow her lead than to set themselves against it, and you've simply been sacrificed to their laziness and selfishness. Is n't that a pretty fair statement of the case?—Well, some people say you've got the neatest kind of an answer in your hands: that George Dorset would marry you tomorrow, if you'd tell him all you know, and give him the chance to show the lady the door. I daresay he would; but you don't seem to care for that particular form of getting even, and, taking a purely business view of the question, I think you 're right. In a deal like that, nobody comes out with perfectly clean hands, and the only way for you to start fresh is to get Bertha Dorset to back you up, instead of trying to fight her."

He paused long enough to draw breath, but not to give her time for the expression of her gathering resistance; and as he pressed on, expounding and elucidating his idea with the directness of the man who has no doubts of his cause, she found the indignation gradually freezing on her lip, found herself held fast in the grasp of his argument by the mere cold strength of its presentation. There was no time now to wonder how he had heard of her obtaining the letters: all her world was dark outside the monstrous glare of his scheme for using them. And it was not, after the first moment, the horror of the idea that held her spell-bound, subdued to his will; it was rather its subtle affinity to her own inmost cravings. He would marry her tomorrow if she could regain Bertha Dorset's friendship; and to induce the open resumption of that friendship, and the tacit retractation of all that had caused its withdrawal, she had only to put to the lady the latent menace contained in the packet so miraculously delivered into her hands. Lily saw in a flash the advantage of this course over that which poor Dorset had pressed upon her. The other plan depended for its success on the infliction of an open injury, while this reduced the transaction to a private understanding, of which no third person need have the remotest hint. Put by Rosedale in terms of business-like give-and-take, this understanding took on the harmless air of a mutual accommodation, like a transfer of property or a revision of boundary lines. It certainly simplified life to view it as a perpetual adjustment, a play of party politics, in which every concession had its recognized equivalent: Lily's tired mind was fascinated by this escape from fluctuating ethical estimates into a region of concrete weights and measures.

Rosedale, as she listened, seemed to read in her silence not only a gradual acquiescence in his plan, but a dangerously far-reaching perception of the chances it offered; for as she continued to stand before him without speaking, he broke out, with a quick return upon himself: "You see how simple it is, don't you? Well, don't be carried away by the idea that it 's *too* simple. It is n't exactly as if you 'd started in with a clean bill of health. Now we 're talking let 's call things by their right names, and clear the whole business up. You know well enough that Bertha Dorset could n't have touched you if there had n't been—well—questions asked before—little points of interrogation, eh? Bound to happen to a good-looking girl with stingy relatives, I suppose; anyhow, they *did* happen, and she found the ground prepared for her. Do you see where I 'm coming out? You don't want these little questions cropping up again. It 's one thing to get Bertha Dorset into line—but what you want is to keep her there. You can frighten her fast enough—but how are you going to keep her frightened? By showing her that you 're as powerful as she is. All the letters in the world won't do that for you as you are now; but with a big backing behind you, you 'll keep her just where you want her to be. That 's *my* share in the business— that 's what I 'm offering you. You can't put the thing through without me—don't run away with any idea that you can. In six months you 'd be back again among your old worries, or worse ones; and here I am, ready to lift you out of 'em tomorrow if you say so. *Do* you say so, Miss Lily?" he added, moving suddenly nearer.

The words, and the movement which accompanied them, combined to startle Lily out of the state of tranced subservience into which she had insensibly slipped. Light comes in devious ways to the groping consciousness, and it came to her now through the disgusted perception that her would-be accomplice assumed, as a matter of course, the likelihood of her distrusting him and perhaps trying to cheat him of his share of the spoils. This glimpse of his inner mind seemed to present the whole transaction in a new aspect, and she saw that the essential baseness of the act lay in its freedom from risk.

She drew back with a quick gesture of rejection, saying, in a voice that was a surprise to her own ears: "You are mistaken—quite mistaken—both in the facts and in what you infer from them."

Rosedale stared a moment, puzzled by her sudden dash in a direction so different from that toward which she had appeared to be letting him guide her.

"Now what on earth does that mean? I thought we understood each other!" he exclaimed; and to her murmur of "Ah, we do *now*," he retorted with a sudden burst of violence: "I suppose it 's because the letters are to *him*, then? Well, I 'll be damned if I see what thanks you 've got from him!"

VIII

T HE AUTUMN DAYS declined to winter. Once more the leisure world was in transition between country and town, and Fifth Avenue, still deserted at the week-end, showed from Monday to Friday a broadening stream of carriages between house-fronts gradually restored to consciousness.

The Horse Show, some two weeks earlier, had produced a passing semblance of reanimation, filling the theatres and restaurants with a human display of the same costly and high-stepping kind as circled daily about its ring. In Miss Bart's world the Horse Show, and the public it attracted, had ostensibly come to be classed among the spectacles disdained of the elect; but, as the feudal lord might sally forth to join in the dance on his village green, so society, unofficially and incidentally, still condescended to look in upon the scene. Mrs. Gormer, among the rest, was not above seizing such an occasion for the display of herself and her horses; and Lily was given one or two opportunities of appearing at her friend's side in the most conspicuous box the house afforded. But this lingering semblance of intimacy made her only the more conscious of a change in the relation between Mattie and herself, of a dawning discrimination, a gradually formed social standard, emerging from Mrs. Gormer's chaotic view of life. It was inevitable that Lily herself should constitute the first sacrifice to this new ideal, and she knew that, once the Gormers were established in town, the whole drift of fashionable life would facilitate Mattie's detachment from her. She had, in short, failed to make herself indispensable; or rather, her attempt to do so had been thwarted by an influence stronger than any she could exert. That influence, in its last analysis, was simply the power of money: Bertha Dorset's social credit was based on an impregnable bank-account.

Lily knew that Rosedale had overstated neither the difficulty of her own position nor the completeness of the vindication he offered: once Bertha's match in material resources, her superior gifts would make it easy for her to dominate her adversary. An understanding of what such domination would mean, and of the disadvantages accruing from her rejection of it, was brought home to Lily with increasing clearness during the early weeks of the winter. Hitherto, she had kept up a semblance of movement outside the main flow of the social current; but with the return to town, and the concentrating of scattered activities, the mere fact of not slipping back naturally into her old habits of life marked her as being unmistakably excluded from them. If one were not a part of the season's fixed routine, one swung unsphered in a void of social non-existence. Lily, for all her dissatisfied dreaming, had never really conceived the possibility of revolving about a different centre: it was easy enough to despise the world, but decidedly difficult to find any other habitable region. Her sense of irony never quite deserted her, and she could still note, with self-directed derision, the abnormal value suddenly acquired by the most tiresome and insignificant details of her former life. Its very drudgeries had a charm now that she was involuntarily released from them: card-leaving, note-writing, enforced civilities to the dull and elderly, and the smiling endurance of tedious dinners—how pleasantly such obligations would have filled the emptiness of her days! She did indeed leave cards in plenty; she kept herself, with a smiling and valiant persistence, well in the eye of her world; nor did she suffer any of those gross rebuffs which sometimes produce a wholesome reaction of contempt in their victim. Society did not turn away from her, it simply drifted by, preoccupied and inattentive, letting her feel, to the full measure of her humbled pride, how completely she had been the creature of its favour.

She had rejected Rosedale's suggestion with a promptness of scorn almost surprising to herself: she had not lost her capacity for high flashes of indignation. But she could not breathe long on the heights; there had been nothing in her training to develop any continuity of moral strength: what she craved, and really felt herself entitled to, was a situation in which the noblest attitude should also be the easiest. Hitherto her intermittent impulses of resistance had sufficed to maintain her self-respect. If she slipped she recovered her footing, and it was only afterward that she was aware of having recovered it each time on a slightly lower level. She had rejected Rosedale's offer without conscious effort; her whole being had risen against it; and she did not yet perceive that, by the mere act of listening to him, she had learned to live with ideas which would once have been intolerable to her.

To Gerty Farish, keeping watch over her with a tenderer if less discerning eye than Mrs. Fisher's, the results of the struggle were already distinctly visible. She did not, indeed, know what hostages Lily had already given to expediency; but she saw her passionately and irretrievably pledged to the ruinous policy of "keeping up." Gerty could smile now at her own early dream of her friend's renovation through adversity: she understood clearly enough that Lily was not of those to whom privation teaches the unimportance of what they have lost. But this very fact, to Gerty, made her friend the more piteously in want of aid, the more exposed to the claims of a tenderness she was so little conscious of needing.

Lily, since her return to town, had not often climbed Miss Farish's stairs. There was something irritating to her in the mute interrogation of Gerty's sympathy: she felt the real difficulties of her situation to be incommunicable to any one whose theory of values was so different from her own, and the restrictions of Gerty's life, which had once had the charm of contrast, now reminded her too painfully of the limits to which her own existence was shrinking. When at length, one afternoon, she put into execution the belated resolve to visit her friend, this sense of shrunken opportunities possessed her with unusual intensity. The walk up Fifth Avenue, unfolding before her, in the brilliance of the hard winter sunlight, an interminable procession of fastidiously-equipped carriages— giving her, through the little squares of brougham-windows, peeps of familiar profiles bent above visiting-lists, of hurried hands dispensing notes and cards to attendant footmen—this glimpse of the ever-revolving wheels of the great social machine made Lily more than ever conscious of the steepness and narrowness of Gerty's stairs, and of the cramped blind-alley of life to which they led. Dull stairs destined to be mounted by dull people: how many thousands of insignificant figures were going up and down such stairs all over the world at that very moment—figures as shabby and uninteresting as that of the middle-aged lady in limp black who descended Gerty's flight as Lily climbed to it!

"That was poor Miss Jane Silverton—she came to talk things over with me: she and her sister want to do something to support themselves," Gerty explained, as Lily followed her into the sitting-room.

"To support themselves? Are they so hard up?" Miss Bart asked with a touch of irritation: she had not come to listen to the woes of other people.

"I 'm afraid they have nothing left: Ned's debts have swallowed up everything. They had such hopes, you know, when he broke away from Carry Fisher; they thought Bertha Dorset would be such a good influence, because she does n't care for cards, and—well, she talked quite beautifully to poor Miss Jane about feeling as if Ned were her younger brother, and wanting to carry him off on the yacht, so that he might have a chance to drop cards and racing, and take up his literary work again."

Miss Farish paused with a sigh which reflected the perplexity of her departing visitor. "But that is n't all; it is n't even the worst. It seems that Ned has quarrelled with the Dorsets; or at least Bertha won't allow him to see her, and he is so unhappy about it that he has taken to gambling again, and going about with all sorts of queer people. And cousin Grace Van Osburgh accuses him of having had a very bad influence on Freddy, who left Harvard last spring, and has been a great deal with Ned ever since. She sent for Miss Jane, and made a dreadful scene; and Jack Stepney and Herbert Melson, who were there too, told Miss Jane that Freddy was threatening to marry some dreadful woman to whom Ned had introduced him, and that they could do nothing with him because now he 's of age he has his own money. You can fancy how poor Miss Jane felt—she came to me at once, and seemed to think that if I could get her something to do she could earn enough to pay Ned's debts and send him away—I 'm afraid she has no idea how long it would take her to pay for one of his evenings at bridge. And he was horribly in debt when he came back from the cruise—I can't see why he should have spent so much more money under Bertha's influence than Carry's: can you?"

Lily met this query with an impatient gesture. "My dear Gerty, I always understand how people can spend much more money—never how they can spend any less!"

She loosened her furs and settled herself in Gerty's easy-chair, while her friend busied herself with the tea-cups.

"But what can they do—the Miss Silvertons? How do they mean to support themselves?" she asked, conscious that the note of irritation still persisted in her voice. It was the very last topic she had meant to discuss—it really did not interest her in the least—but she was seized by a sudden perverse curiosity to know how the two colourless shrinking victims of young Silverton's sentimental experiments meant to cope with the grim necessity which lurked so close to her own threshold.

"I don't know—I am trying to find something for them. Miss Jane reads aloud very nicely—but it's so hard to find any one who is willing to be read to. And Miss Annie paints a little——"

"Oh, I know—apple-blossoms on blotting-paper; just the kind of thing I shall be doing myself before long!" exclaimed Lily, starting up with a vehemence of movement that threatened destruction to Miss Farish's fragile tea-table.

Lily bent over to steady the cups; then she sank back into her seat. "I'd forgotten there was no room to dash about in—how beautifully one does have to behave in a small flat! Oh, Gerty, I wasn't meant to be good," she sighed out incoherently.

Gerty lifted an apprehensive look to her pale face, in which the eyes shone with a peculiar sleepless lustre.

"You look horribly tired, Lily; take your tea, and let me give you this cushion to lean against."

Miss Bart accepted the cup of tea, but put back the cushion with an impatient hand.

"Don't give me that! I don't want to lean back—I shall go to sleep if I do."

"Well, why not, dear? I'll be as quiet as a mouse," Gerty urged affectionately.

"No—no; don't be quiet; talk to me—keep me awake! I don't sleep at night, and in the afternoon a dreadful drowsiness creeps over me."

"You don't sleep at night? Since when?"

"I don't know—I can't remember." She rose and put the empty cup on the tea-tray. "Another, and stronger, please; if I don't keep awake now I shall see horrors tonight—perfect horrors!"

"But they 'll be worse if you drink too much tea."

"No, no—give it to me; and don't preach, please," Lily returned imperiously. Her voice had a dangerous edge, and Gertie noticed that her hand shook as she held it out to receive the second cup.

"But you look so tired: I 'm sure you must be ill——"

Miss Bart set down her cup with a start. "Do I look ill? Does my face show it?" She rose and walked quickly toward the little mirror above the writing-table. "What a horrid looking-glass—it 's all blotched and discoloured. Any one would look ghastly in it!" She turned back, fixing her plaintive eyes on Gerty. "You stupid dear, why do you say such odious things to me? It 's enough to make one ill to be told one looks so! And looking ill means looking ugly." She caught Gerty's wrists, and drew her close to the window. "After all, I 'd rather know the truth. Look me straight in the face, Gerty, and tell me: am I perfectly frightful?"

"You 're perfectly beautiful now, Lily: your eyes are shining, and your cheeks have grown so pink all of a sudden——"

"Ah, they *were* pale, then—ghastly pale, when I came in? Why don't you tell me frankly that I 'm a wreck? My eyes are bright now because I 'm so nervous—but in the mornings they look like lead. And I can see the lines coming in my face—the lines of worry and disappointment and failure! Every sleepless night leaves a new one—and how can I sleep, when I have such dreadful things to think about?"

"Dreadful things—what things?" asked Gerty, gently detaching her wrists from her friend's feverish fingers.

"What things? Well, poverty, for one—and I don't know any that 's more dreadful." Lily turned away and sank with sudden weariness into the easy-chair near the tea-table. "You asked me just now if I could understand why Ned Silverton spent so much money. Of course I understand—he spends it on living with the rich. You think we live *on* the rich, rather than with them: and so we do, in a sense—but it 's a privilege we have to pay for! We eat their dinners, and drink their wine, and smoke their cigarettes, and use their carriages and their opera-boxes and their private cars—yes, but there 's a tax to pay on every one of those luxuries. The man pays it by big tips to the servants, by playing cards beyond his means, by flowers and presents—and—and—lots of other things that cost; the girl pays it by tips and cards too—oh, yes, I 've had to take up bridge again—and by going to the best dress-makers, and having just the right dress for every occasion, and always keeping herself fresh and exquisite and amusing!"

She leaned back for a moment, closing her eyes, and as she sat there, her pale lips slightly parted, and the lids dropped above her fagged brilliant gaze, Gerty had a startled perception of the change in her face—of the way in which an ashen daylight seemed suddenly to extinguish its artificial brightness. She looked up, and the vision vanished.

"It does n't sound very amusing, does it? And it is n't— I 'm sick to death of it! And yet the thought of giving it all up nearly kills me—it 's what keeps me awake at night, and makes me so crazy for your strong tea. For I can't go on in this way much longer, you know—I 'm nearly at the end of my tether. And then what can I do—how on earth am I to keep myself alive? I see myself reduced to the fate of that poor Silverton woman—slinking about to employment agencies, and trying to sell painted blotting-pads to Women's Exchanges! And there are thousands and thousands of women trying to do the same thing already, and not one of the number who has less idea how to earn a dollar than I have!"

She rose again with a hurried glance at the clock. "It 's late, and I must be off—I have an appointment with Carry Fisher. Don't look so worried, you dear thing—don't think too much about the nonsense I 've been talking." She was before the mirror again, adjusting her hair with a light hand, draw-ing down her veil, and giving a dexterous touch to her furs. "Of course, you know, it has n't come to the employment agencies and the painted blotting-pads yet; but I 'm rather hard-up just for the moment, and if I could find something to do—notes to write and visiting-lists to make up, or that kind of thing—it would tide me over till the legacy is paid.

And Carry has promised to find somebody who wants a kind of social secretary—you know she makes a specialty of the helpless rich."

Miss Bart had not revealed to Gerty the full extent of her anxiety. She was in fact in urgent and immediate need of money: money to meet the vulgar weekly claims which could neither be deferred nor evaded. To give up her apartment, and shrink to the obscurity of a boarding-house, or the provisional hospitality of a bed in Gerty Farish's sitting-room, was an expedient which could only postpone the problem confronting her; and it seemed wiser as well as more agreeable to remain where she was and find some means of earning her living. The possibility of having to do this was one which she had never before seriously considered, and the discovery that, as a bread-winner, she was likely to prove as helpless and ineffectual as poor Miss Silverton, was a severe shock to her self-confidence.

Having been accustomed to take herself at the popular valuation, as a person of energy and resource, naturally fitted to dominate any situation in which she found herself, she vaguely imagined that such gifts would be of value to seekers after social guidance; but there was unfortunately no specific head under which the art of saying and doing the right thing could be offered in the market, and even Mrs. Fisher's resourcefulness failed before the difficulty of discovering a workable vein in the vague wealth of Lily's graces. Mrs. Fisher was full of indirect expedients for enabling her friends to earn a living, and could conscientiously assert that she had put several opportunities of this kind before Lily; but more legitimate methods of bread-winning were as much out of her line as they were beyond the capacity of the sufferers she was generally called upon to assist. Lily's failure to profit by the chances already afforded her might, moreover, have justified the abandonment of farther effort on her behalf; but Mrs. Fisher's inexhaustible good-nature made her an adept at creating artificial demands in response to an actual supply. In the pursuance of this end she at once started on a voyage of discovery in Miss Bart's behalf; and as the result of her explora-

tions she now summoned the latter with the announcement
that she had "found something."

Left to herself, Gerty mused distressfully upon her friend's
plight, and her own inability to relieve it. It was clear to her
that Lily, for the present, had no wish for the kind of help
she could give. Miss Farish could see no hope for her friend
but in a life completely reorganized and detached from its old
associations; whereas all Lily's energies were centred in the
determined effort to hold fast to those associations, to keep
herself visibly identified with them, as long as the illusion
could be maintained. Pitiable as such an attitude seemed to
Gerty, she could not judge it as harshly as Selden, for instance, might have done. She had not forgotten the night of
emotion when she and Lily had lain in each other's arms, and
she had seemed to feel her very heart's blood passing into her
friend. The sacrifice she had made had seemed unavailing
enough; no trace remained in Lily of the subduing influences
of that hour; but Gerty's tenderness, disciplined by long years
of contact with obscure and inarticulate suffering, could wait
on its object with a silent forbearance which took no account
of time. She could not, however, deny herself the solace of
taking anxious counsel with Lawrence Selden, with whom,
since his return from Europe, she had renewed her old relation of cousinly confidence.

Selden himself had never been aware of any change in their
relation. He found Gerty as he had left her, simple, unde-
manding and devoted, but with a quickened intelligence of
the heart which he recognized without seeking to explain it.
To Gerty herself it would once have seemed impossible that
she should ever again talk freely with him of Lily Bart; but
what had passed in the secrecy of her own breast seemed to
resolve itself, when the mist of the struggle cleared, into a
breaking down of the bounds of self, a deflecting of the
wasted personal emotion into the general current of human
understanding.

It was not till some two weeks after her visit from Lily that
Gerty had the opportunity of communicating her fears to Selden. The latter, having presented himself on a Sunday afternoon, had lingered on through the dowdy animation of his

cousin's tea-hour, conscious of something in her voice and eye which solicited a word apart; and as soon as the last visitor was gone Gerty opened her case by asking how lately he had seen Miss Bart.

Selden's perceptible pause gave her time for a slight stir of surprise.

"I have n't seen her at all—I 've perpetually missed seeing her since she came back."

This unexpected admission made Gerty pause too; and she was still hesitating on the brink of her subject when he relieved her by adding: "I 've wanted to see her—but she seems to have been absorbed by the Gormer set since her return from Europe."

"That 's all the more reason: she 's been very unhappy."

"Unhappy at being with the Gormers?"

"Oh, I don't defend her intimacy with the Gormers; but that too is at an end now, I think. You know people have been very unkind since Bertha Dorset quarrelled with her."

"Ah——" Selden exclaimed, rising abruptly to walk to the window, where he remained with his eyes on the darkening street while his cousin continued to explain: "Judy Trenor and her own family have deserted her too—and all because Bertha Dorset has said such horrible things. And she is very poor—you know Mrs. Peniston cut her off with a small legacy, after giving her to understand that she was to have everything."

"Yes—I know," Selden assented curtly, turning back into the room, but only to stir about with restless steps in the circumscribed space between door and window. "Yes—she 's been abominably treated; but it 's unfortunately the precise thing that a man who wants to show his sympathy can't say to her."

His words caused Gerty a slight chill of disappointment. "There would be other ways of showing your sympathy," she suggested.

Selden, with a slight laugh, sat down beside her on the little sofa which projected from the hearth. "What are you thinking of, you incorrigible missionary?" he asked.

Gerty's colour rose, and her blush was for a moment her only answer. Then she made it more explicit by saying: "I am thinking of the fact that you and she used to be great friends—that she used to care immensely for what you thought of her—and that, if she takes your staying away as a sign of what you think now, I can imagine its adding a great deal to her unhappiness."

"My dear child, don't add to it still more—at least to your conception of it—by attributing to her all sorts of susceptibilities of your own." Selden, for his life, could not keep a note of dryness out of his voice; but he met Gerty's look of perplexity by saying more mildly: "But, though you immensely exaggerate the importance of anything I could do for Miss Bart, you can't exaggerate my readiness to do it—if you ask me to." He laid his hand for a moment on hers, and there passed between them, on the current of the rare contact, one of those exchanges of meaning which fill the hidden reservoirs of affection. Gerty had the feeling that he measured the cost of her request as plainly as she read the significance of his reply; and the sense of all that was suddenly clear between them made her next words easier to find.

"I do ask you, then; I ask you because she once told me that you had been a help to her, and because she needs help now as she has never needed it before. You know how dependent she has always been on ease and luxury—how she has hated what was shabby and ugly and uncomfortable. She can't help it—she was brought up with those ideas, and has never been able to find her way out of them. But now all the things she cared for have been taken from her, and the people who taught her to care for them have abandoned her too; and it seems to me that if some one could reach out a hand and show her the other side—show her how much is left in life and in herself——" Gerty broke off, abashed at the sound of her own eloquence, and impeded by the difficulty of giving precise expression to her vague yearning for her friend's retrieval. "I can't help her myself: she 's passed out of my reach," she continued. "I think she 's afraid of being a burden to me. When she was last here, two weeks ago, she seemed dreadfully worried about her future: she said Carry Fisher was trying to find something for her to do. A few days later she wrote me that she had taken a position as private secretary, and that I was not to be anxious, for everything was all right, and she would come in and tell me about it when she had time; but she has never come, and I don't like to go to her, because I am afraid of forcing myself on her when I 'm not wanted. Once, when we were children, and I had rushed up after a long separation, and thrown my arms about her, she said: 'Please don't kiss me unless I ask you to, Gerty'— and she *did* ask me, a minute later; but since then I 've always waited to be asked."

Selden had listened in silence, with the concentrated look which his thin dark face could assume when he wished to guard it against any involuntary change of expression. When his cousin ended, he said with a slight smile: "Since you 've learned the wisdom of waiting, I don't see why you urge me to rush in——" but the troubled appeal of her eyes made him add, as he rose to take leave: "Still, I 'll do what you wish, and not hold you responsible for my failure."

Selden's avoidance of Miss Bart had not been as unintentional as he had allowed his cousin to think. At first, indeed, while the memory of their last hour at Monte Carlo still held the full heat of his indignation, he had anxiously watched for her return; but she had disappointed him by lingering in England, and when she finally reappeared it happened that business had called him to the West, whence he came back only to learn that she was starting for Alaska with the Gormers. The revelation of this suddenly-established intimacy effectually chilled his desire to see her. If, at a moment when her whole life seemed to be breaking up, she could cheerfully commit its reconstruction to the Gormers, there was no reason why such accidents should ever strike her as irreparable. Every step she took seemed in fact to carry her farther from the region where, once or twice, he and she had met for an illumined moment; and the recognition of this fact, when its first pang had been surmounted, produced in him a sense of negative relief. It was much simpler for him to judge Miss Bart by her habitual conduct than by the rare deviations from it which had thrown her so disturbingly in his way; and every act of hers which made the recurrence of such deviations more unlikely, confirmed the sense of relief with which he returned to the conventional view of her.

But Gerty Farish's words had sufficed to make him see how

little this view was really his, and how impossible it was for him to live quietly with the thought of Lily Bart. To hear that she was in need of help—even such vague help as he could offer—was to be at once repossessed by that thought; and by the time he reached the street he had sufficiently convinced himself of the urgency of his cousin's appeal to turn his steps directly toward Lily's hotel.

There his zeal met a check in the unforeseen news that Miss Bart had moved away; but, on his pressing his enquiries, the clerk remembered that she had left an address, for which he presently began to search through his books.

It was certainly strange that she should have taken this step without letting Gerty Farish know of her decision; and Selden waited with a vague sense of uneasiness while the address was sought for. The process lasted long enough for uneasiness to turn to apprehension; but when at length a slip of paper was handed him, and he read on it: "Care of Mrs. Norma Hatch, Emporium Hotel," his apprehension passed into an incredulous stare, and this into the gesture of disgust with which he tore the paper in two, and turned to walk quickly homeward.

IX

W HEN LILY WOKE on the morning after her translation
to the Emporium Hotel, her first feeling was one of
purely physical satisfaction. The force of contrast gave an
added keenness to the luxury of lying once more in a soft-
pillowed bed, and looking across a spacious sunlit room at a
breakfast-table set invitingly near the fire. Analysis and introspection might come later; but for the moment she was not
even troubled by the excesses of the upholstery or the restless
convolutions of the furniture. The sense of being once more
lapped and folded in ease, as in some dense mild medium
impenetrable to discomfort, effectually stilled the faintest note
of criticism.

When, the afternoon before, she had presented herself to
the lady to whom Carry Fisher had directed her, she had been
conscious of entering a new world. Carry's vague present-
ment of Mrs. Norma Hatch (whose reversion to her Christian
name was explained as the result of her latest divorce), left
her under the implication of coming "from the West," with
the not unusual extenuation of having brought a great deal of
money with her. She was, in short, rich, helpless, unplaced:
the very subject for Lily's hand. Mrs. Fisher had not specified
the line her friend was to take; she owned herself unacquainted with Mrs. Hatch, whom she "knew about" through
Melville Stancy, a lawyer in his leisure moments, and the Fal-
staff of a certain section of festive club life. Socially, Mr.
Stancy might have been said to form a connecting link between the Gormer world and the more dimly-lit region on
which Miss Bart now found herself entering. It was, however,
only figuratively that the illumination of Mrs. Hatch's world
could be described as dim: in actual fact, Lily found her
seated in a blaze of electric light, impartially projected from
various ornamental excrescences on a vast concavity of pink
damask and gilding, from which she rose like Venus from her
shell. The analogy was justified by the appearance of the lady,
whose large-eyed prettiness had the fixity of something im-
paled and shown under glass. This did not preclude the immediate discovery that she was some years younger than her

visitor, and that under her showiness, her ease, the aggression
of her dress and voice, there persisted that ineradicable innocence which, in ladies of her nationality, so curiously coexists
with startling extremes of experience.

The environment in which Lily found herself was as
strange to her as its inhabitants. She was unacquainted with
the world of the fashionable New York hotel—a world over-
heated, over-upholstered, and over-fitted with mechanical appliances for the gratification of fantastic requirements, while
the comforts of a civilized life were as unattainable as in a
desert. Through this atmosphere of torrid splendour moved
wan beings as richly upholstered as the furniture, beings without definite pursuits or permanent relations, who drifted on a
languid tide of curiosity from restaurant to concert-hall, from
palm-garden to music-room, from "art exhibit" to dress-
maker's opening. High-stepping horses or elaborately equipped
motors waited to carry these ladies into vague metropolitan
distances, whence they returned, still more wan from the
weight of their sables, to be sucked back into the stifling inertia of the hotel routine. Somewhere behind them, in the
background of their lives, there was doubtless a real past, peopled by real human activities: they themselves were probably
the product of strong ambitions, persistent energies, diversi-
fied contacts with the wholesome roughness of life; yet they
had no more real existence than the poet's shades in limbo.

Lily had not been long in this pallid world without discovering that Mrs. Hatch was its most substantial figure. That
lady, though still floating in the void, showed faint symptoms
of developing an outline; and in this endeavour she was actively seconded by Mr. Melville Stancy. It was Mr. Stancy, a
man of large resounding presence, suggestive of convivial occasions and of a chivalry finding expression in "first-night"
boxes and thousand dollar bonbonnières, who had trans-
planted Mrs. Hatch from the scene of her first development
to the higher stage of hotel life in the metropolis. It was he
who had selected the horses with which she had taken the
blue ribbon at the Show, had introduced her to the photographer whose portraits of her formed the recurring ornament
of "Sunday Supplements," and had got together the group
which constituted her social world. It was a small group still,

with heterogeneous figures suspended in large unpeopled spaces; but Lily did not take long to learn that its regulation was no longer in Mr. Stancy's hands. As often happens, the pupil had outstripped the teacher, and Mrs. Hatch was already aware of heights of elegance as well as depths of luxury beyond the world of the Emporium. This discovery at once produced in her a craving for higher guidance, for the adroit feminine hand which should give the right turn to her correspondence, the right "look" to her hats, the right succession to the items of her *menus*. It was, in short, as the regulator of a germinating social life that Miss Bart's guidance was required; her ostensible duties as secretary being restricted by the fact that Mrs. Hatch, as yet, knew hardly any one to write to.

The daily details of Mrs. Hatch's existence were as strange to Lily as its general tenor. The lady's habits were marked by an Oriental indolence and disorder peculiarly trying to her companion. Mrs. Hatch and her friends seemed to float together outside the bounds of time and space. No definite hours were kept; no fixed obligations existed: night and day flowed into one another in a blur of confused and retarded engagements, so that one had the impression of lunching at the tea-hour, while dinner was often merged in the noisy after-theatre supper which prolonged Mrs. Hatch's vigil till day-light.

Through this jumble of futile activities came and went a strange throng of hangers-on—manicures, beauty-doctors, hair-dressers, teachers of bridge, of French, of "physical development": figures sometimes indistinguishable, by their appearance, or by Mrs. Hatch's relation to them, from the visitors constituting her recognized society. But strangest of all to Lily was the encounter, in this latter group, of several of her acquaintances. She had supposed, and not without relief, that she was passing, for the moment, completely out of her own circle; but she found that Mr. Stancy, one side of whose sprawling existence overlapped the edge of Mrs. Fisher's world, had drawn several of its brightest ornaments into the circle of the Emporium. To find Ned Silverton among the habitual frequenters of Mrs. Hatch's drawing-room was one of Lily's first astonishments; but she soon discovered that he was not Mr. Stancy's most important recruit. It was on little Freddy Van Osburgh, the small slim heir of the Van Osburgh millions, that the attention of Mrs. Hatch's group was centred. Freddy, barely out of college, had risen above the horizon since Lily's eclipse, and she now saw with surprise what an effulgence he shed on the outer twilight of Mrs. Hatch's existence. This, then, was one of the things that young men " went in" for when released from the official social routine; this was the kind of "previous engagement" that so frequently caused them to disappoint the hopes of anxious hostesses. Lily had an odd sense of being behind the social tapestry, on the side where the threads were knotted and the loose ends hung. For a moment she found a certain amusement in the show, and in her own share of it: the situation had an ease and unconventionality distinctly refreshing after her experience of the irony of conventions. But these flashes of amusement were but brief reactions from the long disgust of her days. Compared with the vast gilded void of Mrs. Hatch's existence, the life of Lily's former friends seemed packed with ordered activities. Even the most irresponsible pretty woman of her acquaintance had her inherited obligations, her conventional benevolences, her share in the working of the great civic machine; and all hung together in the solidarity of these traditional functions. The performance of specific duties would have simplified Miss Bart's position; but the vague attendance on Mrs. Hatch was not without its perplexities.

It was not her employer who created these perplexities. Mrs. Hatch showed from the first an almost touching desire for Lily's approval. Far from asserting the superiority of wealth, her beautiful eyes seemed to urge the plea of inexperience: she wanted to do what was "nice," to be taught how to be "lovely." The difficulty was to find any point of contact between her ideals and Lily's.

Mrs. Hatch swam in a haze of indeterminate enthusiasms, of aspirations culled from the stage, the newspapers, the fashion-journals, and a gaudy world of sport still more completely beyond her companion's ken. To separate from these confused conceptions those most likely to advance the lady on her way, was Lily's obvious duty; but its performance was hampered by rapidly-growing doubts. Lily was in fact becoming more and more aware of a certain ambiguity in her situation. It was not that she had, in the conventional sense, any doubt of Mrs. Hatch's irreproachableness. The lady's offences were always against taste rather than conduct; her divorce record seemed due to geographical rather than ethical conditions; and her worst laxities were likely to proceed from a wandering and extravagant good-nature. But if Lily did not mind her detaining her manicure for luncheon, or offering the "Beauty-Doctor" a seat in Freddy Van Osburgh's box at the play, she was not equally at ease in regard to some less apparent lapses from convention. Ned Silverton's relation to Stancy seemed, for instance, closer and less clear than any natural affinities would warrant; and both appeared united in the effort to cultivate Freddy Van Osburgh's growing taste for Mrs. Hatch. There was as yet nothing definable in the situation, which might well resolve itself into a huge joke on the part of the other two; but Lily had a vague sense that the subject of their experiment was too young, too rich and too credulous. Her embarrassment was increased by the fact that Freddy seemed to regard her as coöperating with himself in the social development of Mrs. Hatch: a view that suggested, on his part, a permanent interest in the lady's future. There were moments when Lily found an ironic amusement in this aspect of the case. The thought of launching such a missile as Mrs. Hatch at the perfidious bosom of society was not without its charm: Miss Bart had even beguiled her leisure with visions of the fair Norma introduced for the first time to a family banquet at the Van Osburghs'. But the thought of being personally connected with the transaction was less agreeable; and her momentary flashes of amusement were followed by increasing periods of doubt.

The sense of these doubts was uppermost when, late one afternoon, she was surprised by a visit from Lawrence Selden. He found her alone in the wilderness of pink damask, for in Mrs. Hatch's world the tea-hour was not dedicated to social rites, and the lady was in the hands of her masseuse.

Selden's entrance had caused Lily an inward start of embarrassment; but his air of constraint had the effect of restoring her self-possession, and she took at once the tone of surprise and pleasure, wondering frankly that he should have traced her to so unlikely a place, and asking what had inspired him to make the search.

Selden met this with an unusual seriousness: she had never seen him so little master of the situation, so plainly at the mercy of any obstructions she might put in his way. "I wanted to see you," he said; and she could not resist observing in reply that he had kept his wishes under remarkable control. She had in truth felt his long absence as one of the chief bitternesses of the last months: his desertion had wounded sensibilities far below the surface of her pride.

Selden met the challenge with directness. "Why should I have come, unless I thought I could be of use to you? It is my only excuse for imagining you could want me."

This struck her as a clumsy evasion, and the thought gave a flash of keenness to her answer. "Then you have come now because you think you can be of use to me?"

He hesitated again. "Yes: in the modest capacity of a person to talk things over with."

For a clever man it was certainly a stupid beginning; and the idea that his awkwardness was due to the fear of her attaching a personal significance to his visit, chilled her pleasure in seeing him. Even under the most adverse conditions, that pleasure always made itself felt: she might hate him, but she had never been able to wish him out of the room. She was very near hating him now; yet the sound of his voice, the way the light fell on his thin dark hair, the way he sat and moved and wore his clothes—she was conscious that even these trivial things were inwoven with her deepest life. In his presence a sudden stillness came upon her, and the turmoil of her spirit ceased; but an impulse of resistance to this stealing influence now prompted her to say: "It 's very good of you to present yourself in that capacity; but what makes you think I have anything particular to talk about?"

Though she kept the even tone of light intercourse, the question was framed in a way to remind him that his good offices were unsought; and for a moment Selden was checked by it. The situation between them was one which could have been cleared up only by a sudden explosion of feeling; and their whole training and habit of mind were against the chances of such an explosion. Selden's calmness seemed rather to harden into resistance, and Miss Bart's into a surface of glittering irony, as they faced each other from the opposite corners of one of Mrs. Hatch's elephantine sofas. The sofa in question, and the apartment peopled by its monstrous mates, served at length to suggest the turn of Selden's reply.

"Gerty told me that you were acting as Mrs. Hatch's secretary; and I knew she was anxious to hear how you were getting on."

Miss Bart received this explanation without perceptible softening. "Why did n't she look me up herself, then?" she asked.

"Because, as you did n't send her your address, she was afraid of being importunate." Selden continued with a smile: "You see no such scruples restrained me; but then I have n't as much to risk if I incur your displeasure."

Lily answered his smile. "You have n't incurred it as yet; but I have an idea that you are going to."

"That rests with you, does n't it? You see my initiative does n't go beyond putting myself at your disposal."

"But in what capacity? What am I to do with you?" she asked in the same light tone.

Selden again glanced about Mrs. Hatch's drawing-room; then he said, with a decision which he seemed to have gathered from this final inspection: "You are to let me take you away from here."

Lily flushed at the suddenness of the attack; then she stiffened under it and said coldly: "And may I ask where you mean me to go?"

"Back to Gerty in the first place, if you will; the essential thing is that it should be away from here."

The unusual harshness of his tone might have shown her how much the words cost him; but she was in no state to measure his feelings while her own were in a flame of revolt. To neglect her, perhaps even to avoid her, at a time when she had most need of her friends, and then suddenly and unwarrantably to break into her life with this strange assumption of authority, was to rouse in her every instinct of pride and self-defence.

"I am very much obliged to you," she said, "for taking such

an interest in my plans; but I am quite contented where I am, and have no intention of leaving."

Selden had risen, and was standing before her in an attitude of uncontrollable expectancy.

"That simply means that you don't know where you are!" he exclaimed.

Lily rose also, with a quick flash of anger. "If you have come here to say disagreeable things about Mrs. Hatch——"

"It is only with your relation to Mrs. Hatch that I am concerned."

"My relation to Mrs. Hatch is one I have no reason to be ashamed of. She has helped me to earn a living when my old friends were quite resigned to seeing me starve."

"Nonsense! Starvation is not the only alternative. You know you can always find a home with Gerty till you are independent again."

"You show such an intimate acquaintance with my affairs that I suppose you mean—till my aunt's legacy is paid?"

"I do mean that; Gerty told me of it," Selden acknowledged without embarrassment. He was too much in earnest now to feel any false constraint in speaking his mind.

"But Gerty does not happen to know," Miss Bart rejoined, "that I owe every penny of that legacy."

"Good God!" Selden exclaimed, startled out of his composure by the abruptness of the statement.

"Every penny of it, and more too," Lily repeated; "and you now perhaps see why I prefer to remain with Mrs. Hatch rather than take advantage of Gerty's kindness. I have no money left, except my small income, and I must earn something more to keep myself alive."

Selden hesitated a moment; then he rejoined in a quieter tone: "But with your income and Gerty's—since you allow me to go so far into the details of the situation—you and she could surely contrive a life together which would put you beyond the need of having to support yourself. Gerty, I know, is eager to make such an arrangement, and would be quite happy in it——"

"But I should not," Miss Bart interposed. "There are many reasons why it would be neither kind to Gerty nor wise for myself." She paused a moment, and as he seemed to await a farther explanation, added with a quick lift of her head: "You will perhaps excuse me from giving you these reasons."

"I have no claim to know them," Selden answered, ignoring her tone; "no claim to offer any comment or suggestion beyond the one I have already made. And my right to make that is simply the universal right of a man to enlighten a woman when he sees her unconsciously placed in a false position."

Lily smiled. "I suppose," she rejoined, "that by a false position you mean one outside of what we call society; but you must remember that I had been excluded from those sacred precincts long before I met Mrs. Hatch. As far as I can see, there is very little real difference in being inside or out, and I remember your once telling me that it was only those inside who took the difference seriously."

She had not been without intention in making this allusion to their memorable talk at Bellomont, and she waited with an odd tremor of the nerves to see what response it would bring; but the result of the experiment was disappointing. Selden did not allow the allusion to deflect him from his point; he merely said with completer fulness of emphasis: "The question of being inside or out is, as you say, a small one, and it happens to have nothing to do with the case, except in so far as Mrs. Hatch's desire to be inside may put you in the position I call false."

In spite of the moderation of his tone, each word he spoke had the effect of confirming Lily's resistance. The very apprehensions he aroused hardened her against him: she had been on the alert for the note of personal sympathy, for any sign of recovered power over him; and his attitude of sober impartiality, the absence of all response to her appeal, turned her hurt pride to blind resentment of his interference. The conviction that he had been sent by Gerty, and that, whatever straits he conceived her to be in, he would never voluntarily have come to her aid, strengthened her resolve not to admit him a hair's breadth farther into her confidence. However doubtful she might feel her situation to be, she would rather persist in darkness than owe her enlightenment to Selden.

"I don't know," she said, when he had ceased to speak, " why you imagine me to be situated as you describe; but as you have always told me that the sole object of a bringing-up like mine was to teach a girl to get what she wants, why not assume that that is precisely what I am doing?"

The smile with which she summed-up her case was like a clear barrier raised against farther confidences: its brightness held him at such a distance that he had a sense of being almost out of hearing as he rejoined: "I am not sure that I have ever called you a successful example of that kind of bringing-up."

Her colour rose a little at the implication, but she steeled herself with a light laugh.

"Ah, wait a little longer—give me a little more time before you decide!" And as he wavered before her, still watching for a break in the impenetrable front she presented: "Don't give me up; I may still do credit to my training!" she affirmed.

X

"LOOK AT those spangles, Miss Bart—every one of 'em sewed on crooked."

The tall forewoman, a pinched perpendicular figure, dropped the condemned structure of wire and net on the table at Lily's side, and passed on to the next figure in the line.

There were twenty of them in the work-room, their fagged profiles, under exaggerated hair, bowed in the harsh north light above the utensils of their art; for it was something more than an industry, surely, this creation of ever-varied settings for the face of fortunate womanhood. Their own faces were sallow with the unwholesomeness of hot air and sedentary toil, rather than with any actual signs of want: they were employed in a fashionable millinery establishment, and were fairly well clothed and well paid; but the youngest among them was as dull and colourless as the middle-aged. In the whole work-room there was only one skin beneath which the blood still visibly played; and that now burned with vexation as Miss Bart, under the lash of the forewoman's comment, began to strip the hat-frame of its over-lapping spangles.

To Gerty Farish's hopeful spirit a solution appeared to have been reached when she remembered how beautifully Lily could trim hats. Instances of young lady-milliners establishing themselves under fashionable patronage, and imparting to their "creations" that indefinable touch which the professional hand can never give, had flattered Gerty's visions of the future, and convinced even Lily that her separation from Mrs. Norma Hatch need not reduce her to dependence on her friends.

The parting had occurred a few weeks after Selden's visit, and would have taken place sooner had it not been for the resistance set up in Lily by his ill-starred offer of advice. The sense of being involved in a transaction she would not have cared to examine too closely had soon afterward defined itself in the light of a hint from Mr. Stancy that, if she "saw them through," she would have no reason to be sorry. The implication that such loyalty would meet with a direct reward had hastened her flight, and flung her back, ashamed and penitent, on the broad bosom of Gerty's sympathy. She did not, however, propose to lie there prone, and Gerty's inspiration about the hats at once revived her hopes of profitable activity. Here was, after all, something that her charming listless hands could really do; she had no doubt of their capacity for knotting a ribbon or placing a flower to advantage. And of course only these finishing touches would be expected of her: subordinate fingers, blunt, grey, needle-pricked fingers, would prepare the shapes and stitch the linings, while she presided over the charming little front shop—a shop all white panels, mirrors, and moss-green hangings—where her finished creations, hats, wreaths, aigrettes and the rest, perched on their stands like birds just poising for flight.

But at the very outset of Gerty's campaign this vision of the green-and-white shop had been dispelled. Other young ladies of fashion had been thus "set-up," selling their hats by the mere attraction of a name and the reputed knack of tying a bow; but these privileged beings could command a faith in their powers materially expressed by the readiness to pay their shop-rent and advance a handsome sum for current expenses. Where was Lily to find such support? And even could it have been found, how were the ladies on whose approval she depended to be induced to give her their patronage? Gerty learned that whatever sympathy her friend's case might have excited a few months since had been imperilled, if not lost, by her association with Mrs. Hatch. Once again, Lily had withdrawn from an ambiguous situation in time to save her self-respect, but too late for public vindication. Freddy Van Osburgh was not to marry Mrs. Hatch; he had been rescued at the eleventh hour—some said by the efforts of Gus Trenor and Rosedale—and despatched to Europe with old Ned Van Alstyne; but the risk he had run would always be ascribed to Miss Bart's connivance, and would somehow serve as a summing-up and corroboration of the vague general distrust of her. It was a relief to those who had hung back from her to find themselves thus justified, and they were inclined to insist a little on her connection with the Hatch case in order to show that they had been right.

Gerty's quest, at any rate, brought up against a solid wall of resistance; and even when Carry Fisher, momentarily penitent for her share in the Hatch affair, joined her efforts to Miss Farish's, they met with no better success. Gerty had tried to veil her failure in tender ambiguities; but Carry, always the soul of candour, put the case squarely to her friend.

"I went straight to Judy Trenor; she has fewer prejudices than the others, and besides she 's always hated Bertha Dorset. But what *have* you done to her, Lily? At the very first word about giving you a start she flamed out about some money you 'd got from Gus; I never knew her so hot before. You know she 'll let him do anything but spend money on his friends: the only reason she 's decent to me now is that she knows I 'm not hard up.— He speculated for you, you say? Well, what 's the harm? He had no business to lose. He *did n't* lose? Then what on earth—but I never *could* understand you, Lily!"

The end of it was that, after anxious enquiry and much deliberation, Mrs. Fisher and Gerty, for once oddly united in their effort to help their friend, decided on placing her in the work-room of Mme. Regina's renowned millinery establishment. Even this arrangement was not effected without considerable negotiation, for Mme. Regina had a strong prejudice against untrained assistance, and was induced to yield only by the fact that she owed the patronage of Mrs. Bry and Mrs. Gormer to Carry Fisher's influence. She had been willing from the first to employ Lily in the show-room: as a displayer of hats, a fashionable beauty might be a valuable asset. But to this suggestion Miss Bart opposed a negative which Gerty emphatically supported, while Mrs. Fisher, inwardly unconvinced, but resigned to this latest proof of Lily's unreason, agreed that perhaps in the end it would be more useful that she should learn the trade. To Regina's work-room Lily was therefore committed by her friends, and there Mrs. Fisher left her with a sigh of relief, while Gerty's watchfulness continued to hover over her at a distance.

Lily had taken up her work early in January: it was now two months later, and she was still being rebuked for her inability to sew spangles on a hat-frame. As she returned to her work she heard a titter pass down the tables. She knew she was an object of criticism and amusement to the other workwomen. They were, of course, aware of her history—the exact situation of every girl in the room was known and freely discussed by all the others—but the knowledge did not produce in them any awkward sense of class distinction: it merely explained why her untutored fingers were still blundering over the rudiments of the trade. Lily had no desire that they should recognize any social difference in her; but she had hoped to be received as their equal, and perhaps before long to show herself their superior by a special deftness of touch, and it was humiliating to find that, after two months of drudgery, she still betrayed her lack of early training. Remote was the day when she might aspire to exercise the talents she felt confident of possessing; only experienced workers were entrusted with the delicate art of shaping and trimming the hat, and the forewoman still held her inexorably to the routine of preparatory work.

She began to rip the spangles from the frame, listening absently to the buzz of talk which rose and fell with the coming and going of Miss Haines's active figure. The air was closer than usual, because Miss Haines, who had a cold, had not allowed a window to be opened even during the noon recess; and Lily's head was so heavy with the weight of a sleepless night that the chatter of her companions had the incoherence of a dream.

"I *told* her he'd never look at her again; and he didn't. I wouldn't have, either—I think she acted real mean to him. He took her to the Arion Ball, and had a hack for her both ways. . . . She's taken ten bottles, and her headaches don't seem no better—but she's written a testimonial to say the first bottle cured her, and she got five dollars and her picture in the paper. . . . Mrs. Trenor's hat? The one with the green Paradise? Here, Miss Haines—it'll be ready right off. . . . That was one of the Trenor girls here yesterday with Mrs. George Dorset. How'd I know? Why, Madam sent for me to alter the flower in that Virot hat—the blue tulle: she's tall and slight, with her hair fuzzed out—a good deal like Mamie Leach, on'y thinner. . . ."

On and on it flowed, a current of meaningless sound, on which, startlingly enough, a familiar name now and then floated to the surface. It was the strangest part of Lily's strange experience, the hearing of these names, the seeing the

fragmentary and distorted image of the world she had lived
in reflected in the mirror of the working-girls' minds. She had
never before suspected the mixture of insatiable curiosity and
contemptuous freedom with which she and her kind were discussed in this underworld of toilers who lived on their vanity
and self-indulgence. Every girl in Mme. Regina's work-room
knew to whom the headgear in her hands was destined, and
had her opinion of its future wearer, and a definite knowledge
of the latter's place in the social system. That Lily was a star
fallen from that sky did not, after the first stir of curiosity had
subsided, materially add to their interest in her. She had
fallen, she had "gone under," and true to the ideal of their
race, they were awed only by success—by the gross tangible
image of material achievement. The consciousness of her different point of view merely kept them at a little distance from
her, as though she were a foreigner with whom it was an
effort to talk.

"Miss Bart, if you can't sew those spangles on more regular
I guess you 'd better give the hat to Miss Kilroy."

Lily looked down ruefully at her handiwork. The forewoman was right: the sewing on of the spangles was inexcus-
ably bad. What made her so much more clumsy than usual?
Was it a growing distaste for her task, or actual physical dis-
ability? She felt tired and confused: it was an effort to put her
thoughts together. She rose and handed the hat to Miss
Kilroy, who took it with a suppressed smile.

"I 'm sorry; I 'm afraid I am not well," she said to the
forewoman.

Miss Haines offered no comment. From the first she had
augured ill of Mme. Regina's consenting to include a fashionable apprentice among her workers. In that temple of art no
raw beginners were wanted, and Miss Haines would have
been more than human had she not taken a certain pleasure
in seeing her forebodings confirmed.

"You 'd better go back to binding edges," she said drily.

Lily slipped out last among the band of liberated work-
women. She did not care to be mingled in their noisy dispersal: once in the street, she always felt an irresistible return
to her old standpoint, an instinctive shrinking from all that
was unpolished and promiscuous. In the days—how distant

they now seemed!—when she had visited the Girls' Club with Gerty Farish, she had felt an enlightened interest in the working-classes; but that was because she looked down on them from above, from the happy altitude of her grace and her beneficence. Now that she was on a level with them, the point of view was less interesting.

She felt a touch on her arm, and met the penitent eye of Miss Kilroy.

"Miss Bart, I guess you can sew those spangles on as well as I can when you 're feeling right. Miss Haines did n't act fair to you."

Lily's colour rose at the unexpected advance: it was a long time since real kindness had looked at her from any eyes but Gerty's.

"Oh, thank you: I 'm not particularly well, but Miss Haines was right. I *am* clumsy."

"Well, it 's mean work for anybody with a headache." Miss Kilroy paused irresolutely. "You ought to go right home and lay down. Ever try orangeine?"

"Thank you." Lily held out her hand. "It 's very kind of you—I mean to go home."

She looked gratefully at Miss Kilroy, but neither knew what more to say. Lily was aware that the other was on the point of offering to go home with her, but she wanted to be alone and silent—even kindness, the sort of kindness that Miss Kilroy could give, would have jarred on her just then.

"Thank you," she repeated as she turned away.

She struck westward through the dreary March twilight, toward the street where her boarding-house stood. She had resolutely refused Gerty's offer of hospitality. Something of her mother's fierce shrinking from observation and sympathy was beginning to develop in her, and the promiscuity of small quarters and close intimacy seemed, on the whole, less endurable than the solitude of a hall bedroom in a house where she could come and go unremarked among other workers. For a while she had been sustained by this desire for privacy and independence; but now, perhaps from increasing physical weariness, the lassitude brought about by hours of unwonted confinement, she was beginning to feel acutely the ugliness and discomfort of her surroundings. The day's task done, she dreaded to return to her narrow room, with its blotched wall-paper and shabby paint; and she hated every step of the walk thither, through the degradation of a New York street in the last stages of decline from fashion to commerce.

But what she dreaded most of all was having to pass the chemist's at the corner of Sixth Avenue. She had meant to take another street: she had usually done so of late. But today her steps were irresistibly drawn toward the flaring plate-glass corner; she tried to take the lower crossing, but a laden dray crowded her back, and she struck across the street obliquely, reaching the sidewalk just opposite the chemist's door.

Over the counter she caught the eye of the clerk who had waited on her before, and slipped the prescription into his hand. There could be no question about the prescription: it was a copy of one of Mrs. Hatch's, obligingly furnished by that lady's chemist. Lily was confident that the clerk would fill it without hesitation; yet the nervous dread of a refusal, or even of an expression of doubt, communicated itself to her restless hands as she affected to examine the bottles of per-fume stacked on the glass case before her.

The clerk had read the prescription without comment; but in the act of handing out the bottle he paused.

"You don't want to increase the dose, you know," he re-marked.

Lily's heart contracted. What did he mean by looking at her in that way?

"Of course not," she murmured, holding out her hand.

"That's all right: it's a queer-acting drug. A drop or two more, and off you go—the doctors don't know why."

The dread lest he should question her, or keep the bottle back, choked the murmur of acquiescence in her throat; and when at length she emerged safely from the shop she was almost dizzy with the intensity of her relief. The mere touch of the packet thrilled her tired nerves with the delicious prom-ise of a night of sleep, and in the reaction from her momen-tary fear she felt as if the first fumes of drowsiness were already stealing over her.

In her confusion she stumbled against a man who was hur-rying down the last steps of the elevated station. He drew back, and she heard her name uttered with surprise. It was

Rosedale, fur-coated, glossy and prosperous—but why did she seem to see him so far off, and as if through a mist of splintered crystals? Before she could account for the phenomenon she found herself shaking hands with him. They had parted with scorn on her side and anger upon his; but all trace of these emotions seemed to vanish as their hands met, and she was only aware of a confused wish that she might continue to hold fast to him.

"Why, what 's the matter, Miss Lily? You 're not well!" he exclaimed; and she forced her lips into a pallid smile of reassurance.

"I 'm a little tired—it 's nothing. Stay with me a moment, please," she faltered. That she should be asking this service of Rosedale!

He glanced at the dirty and unpropitious corner on which they stood, with the shriek of the "elevated" and the tumult of trams and waggons contending hideously in their ears.

"We can't stay here; but let me take you somewhere for a cup of tea. The *Longworth* is only a few yards off, and there 'll be no one there at this hour."

A cup of tea in quiet, somewhere out of the noise and ugliness, seemed for the moment the one solace she could bear. A few steps brought them to the ladies' door of the hotel he had named, and a moment later he was seated opposite to her, and the waiter had placed the tea-tray between them.

"Not a drop of brandy or whiskey first? You look regularly done up, Miss Lily. Well, take your tea strong, then; and, waiter, get a cushion for the lady's back."

Lily smiled faintly at the injunction to take her tea strong. It was the temptation she was always struggling to resist. Her craving for the keen stimulant was forever conflicting with that other craving for sleep—the midnight craving which only the little phial in her hand could still. But today, at any rate, the tea could hardly be too strong: she counted on it to pour warmth and resolution into her empty veins.

As she leaned back before him, her lids drooping in utter lassitude, though the first warm draught already tinged her face with returning life, Rosedale was seized afresh by the poignant surprise of her beauty. The dark pencilling of fatigue under her eyes, the morbid blue-veined pallour of the temples, brought out the brightness of her hair and lips, as though all her ebbing vitality were centred there. Against the dull chocolate-coloured background of the restaurant, the purity of her head stood out as it had never done in the most brightly-lit ball-room. He looked at her with a startled uncomfortable feeling, as though her beauty were a forgotten enemy that had lain in ambush and now sprang out on him unawares.

To clear the air he tried to take an easy tone with her. "Why, Miss Lily, I have n't seen you for an age. I did n't know what had become of you."

As he spoke, he was checked by an embarrassing sense of the complications to which this might lead. Though he had not seen her he had heard of her; he knew of her connection with Mrs. Hatch, and of the talk resulting from it. Mrs. Hatch's *milieu* was one which he had once assiduously frequented, and now as devoutly shunned.

Lily, to whom the tea had restored her usual clearness of mind, saw what was in his thoughts and said with a slight smile: "You would not be likely to know about me. I have joined the working classes."

He stared in genuine wonder. "You don't mean——? Why, what on earth are you doing?"

"Learning to be a milliner—at least *trying* to learn," she hastily qualified the statement.

Rosedale suppressed a low whistle of surprise. "Come off—you ain't serious, are you?"

"Perfectly serious. I 'm obliged to work for my living."

"But I understood—I thought you were with Norma Hatch."

"You heard I had gone to her as her secretary?"

"Something of the kind, I believe." He leaned forward to refill her cup.

Lily guessed the possibilities of embarrassment which the topic held for him, and raising her eyes to his, she said suddenly: "I left her two months ago."

Rosedale continued to fumble awkwardly with the tea-pot, and she felt sure that he had heard what had been said of her. But what was there that Rosedale did not hear?

"Was n't it a soft berth?" he enquired, with an attempt at lightness.

"Too soft—one might have sunk in too deep." Lily rested one arm on the edge of the table, and sat looking at him more intently than she had ever looked before. An uncontrollable impulse was urging her to put her case to this man, from whose curiosity she had always so fiercely defended herself.

"You know Mrs. Hatch, I think? Well, perhaps you can understand that she might make things too easy for one."

Rosedale looked faintly puzzled, and she remembered that allusiveness was lost on him.

"It was no place for you, anyhow," he agreed, so suffused and immersed in the light of her full gaze that he found himself being drawn into strange depths of intimacy. He who had had to subsist on mere fugitive glances, looks winged in flight and swiftly lost under covert, now found her eyes settling on him with a brooding intensity that fairly dazzled him.

"I left," Lily continued, "lest people should say I was helping Mrs. Hatch to marry Freddy Van Osburgh—who is not in the least too good for her—and as they still continue to say it, I see that I might as well have stayed where I was."

"Oh, Freddy——" Rosedale brushed aside the topic with an air of its unimportance which gave a sense of the immense perspective he had acquired. "Freddy don't count—but I knew *you* were n't mixed up in that. It ain't your style."

Lily coloured slightly: she could not conceal from herself that the words gave her pleasure. She would have liked to sit there, drinking more tea, and continuing to talk of herself to Rosedale. But the old habit of observing the conventions reminded her that it was time to bring their colloquy to an end, and she made a faint motion to push back her chair.

Rosedale stopped her with a protesting gesture. "Wait a minute—don't go yet; sit quiet and rest a little longer. You look thoroughly played out. And you have n't told me——" He broke off, conscious of going farther than he had meant. She saw the struggle and understood it; understood also the nature of the spell to which he yielded as, with his eyes on her face, he began again abruptly: "What on earth did you mean by saying just now that you were learning to be a milliner?"

"Just what I said. I am an apprentice at Regina's."

"Good Lord—*you*? But what for? I knew your aunt had

turned you down: Mrs. Fisher told me about it. But I understood you got a legacy from her——"

"I got ten thousand dollars; but the legacy is not to be paid
till next summer."

"Well, but—look here: you could *borrow* on it any time
you wanted."

She shook her head gravely. "No; for I owe it already."

"Owe it? The whole ten thousand?"

"Every penny." She paused, and then continued abruptly,
with her eyes on his face: "I think Gus Trenor spoke to you
once about having made some money for me in stocks."

She waited, and Rosedale, congested with embarrassment,
muttered that he remembered something of the kind.

"He made about nine thousand dollars," Lily pursued, in
the same tone of eager communicativeness. "At the time, I
understood that he was speculating with my own money: it
was incredibly stupid of me, but I knew nothing of business.
Afterward I found out that he had *not* used my money—that
what he said he had made for me he had really given me. It
was meant in kindness, of course; but it was not the sort of
obligation one could remain under. Unfortunately I had spent
the money before I discovered my mistake; and so my legacy
will have to go to pay it back. That is the reason why I am
trying to learn a trade."

She made the statement clearly, deliberately, with pauses
between the sentences, so that each should have time to sink
deeply into her hearer's mind. She had a passionate desire
that some one should know the truth about this transaction,
and also that the rumour of her intention to repay the money
should reach Judy Trenor's ears. And it had suddenly occurred to her that Rosedale, who had surprised Trenor's confidence, was the fitting person to receive and transmit her version of the facts. She had even felt a momentary exhilaration
at the thought of thus relieving herself of her detested secret;
but the sensation gradually faded in the telling, and as she
ended her pallour was suffused with a deep blush of misery.

Rosedale continued to stare at her in wonder; but the wonder took the turn she had least expected.

"But see here—if that's the case, it cleans you out altogether?"

He put it to her as if she had not grasped the consequences of her act; as if her incorrigible ignorance of business were about to precipitate her into a fresh act of folly.

"Altogether—yes," she calmly agreed.

He sat silent, his thick hands clasped on the table, his little puzzled eyes exploring the recesses of the deserted restaurant.

"See here—that's fine," he exclaimed abruptly.

Lily rose from her seat with a deprecating laugh. "Oh, no—it's merely a bore," she asserted, gathering together the ends of her feather scarf.

Rosedale remained seated, too intent on his thoughts to notice her movement. "Miss Lily, if you want any backing— I like pluck——" broke from him disconnectedly.

"Thank you." She held out her hand. "Your tea has given me a tremendous backing. I feel equal to anything now."

Her gesture seemed to show a definite intention of dismissal, but her companion had tossed a bill to the waiter, and was slipping his short arms into his expensive overcoat.

"Wait a minute—you've got to let me walk home with you," he said.

Lily uttered no protest, and when he had paused to make sure of his change they emerged from the hotel and crossed Sixth Avenue again. As she led the way westward past a long line of areas which, through the distortion of their paintless rails, revealed with increasing candour the *disjecta membra* of bygone dinners, Lily felt that Rosedale was taking contemptuous note of the neighbourhood; and before the doorstep at which she finally paused he looked up with an air of incredulous disgust.

"This isn't the place? Some one told me you were living with Miss Farish."

"No: I am boarding here. I have lived too long on my friends."

He continued to scan the blistered brown stone front, the windows draped with discoloured lace, and the Pompeian decoration of the muddy vestibule; then he looked back at her face and said with a visible effort: "You'll let me come and see you some day?"

She smiled, recognizing the heroism of the offer to the point of being frankly touched by it. "Thank you—I shall be very glad," she made answer, in the first sincere words she had ever spoken to him.

That evening in her own room Miss Bart—who had fled early from the heavy fumes of the basement dinner-table—sat musing upon the impulse which had led her to unbosom herself to Rosedale. Beneath it she discovered an increasing sense of loneliness—a dread of returning to the solitude of her room, while she could be anywhere else, or in any company but her own. Circumstances, of late, had combined to cut her off more and more from her few remaining friends. On Carry Fisher's part the withdrawal was perhaps not quite involuntary. Having made her final effort on Lily's behalf, and landed her safely in Mme. Regina's work-room, Mrs. Fisher seemed disposed to rest from her labours; and Lily, understanding the reason, could not condemn her. Carry had in fact come dangerously near to being involved in the episode of Mrs. Norma Hatch, and it had taken some verbal ingenuity to extricate herself. She frankly owned to having brought Lily and Mrs. Hatch together, but then she did not know Mrs. Hatch—she had expressly warned Lily that she did not know Mrs. Hatch—and besides, she was not Lily's keeper, and really the girl was old enough to take care of herself. Carry did not put her own case so brutally, but she allowed it to be thus put for her by her latest bosom friend, Mrs. Jack Stepney: Mrs. Stepney, trembling over the narrowness of her only brother's escape, but eager to vindicate Mrs. Fisher, at whose house she could count on the "jolly parties" which had become a necessity to her since marriage had emancipated her from the Van Osburgh point of view.

Lily understood the situation and could make allowances for it. Carry had been a good friend to her in difficult days, and perhaps only a friendship like Gerty's could be proof against such an increasing strain. Gerty's friendship did indeed hold fast; yet Lily was beginning to avoid her also. For she could not go to Gerty's without risk of meeting Selden; and to meet him now would be pure pain. It was pain enough even to think of him, whether she considered him in the distinctness of her waking thoughts, or felt the obsession of his presence through the blur of her tormented nights.

That was one of the reasons why she had turned again to
Mrs. Hatch's prescription. In the uneasy snatches of her natural dreams he came to her sometimes in the old guise of
fellowship and tenderness; and she would rise from the sweet
delusion mocked and emptied of her courage. But in the sleep
which the phial procured she sank far below such half-waking
visitations, sank into depths of dreamless annihilation from
which she woke each morning with an obliterated past.

Gradually, to be sure, the stress of the old thoughts would
return; but at least they did not importune her waking hour.
The drug gave her a momentary illusion of complete renewal,
from which she drew strength to take up her daily work. The
strength was more and more needed as the perplexities of her
future increased. She knew that to Gerty and Mrs. Fisher she
was only passing through a temporary period of probation,
since they believed that the apprenticeship she was serving at
Mme. Regina's would enable her, when Mrs. Peniston's legacy was paid, to realize the vision of the green-and-white
shop with the fuller competence acquired by her preliminary
training. But to Lily herself, aware that the legacy could not
be put to such a use, the preliminary training seemed a wasted
effort. She understood clearly enough that, even if she could
ever learn to compete with hands formed from childhood for
their special work, the small pay she received would not be a
sufficient addition to her income to compensate her for such
drudgery. And the realization of this fact brought her recur-
ringly face to face with the temptation to use the legacy in
establishing her business. Once installed, and in command of
her own work-women, she believed she had sufficient tact and
ability to attract a fashionable *clientèle*; and if the business
succeeded she could gradually lay aside money enough to discharge her debt to Trenor. But the task might take years to
accomplish, even if she continued to stint herself to the utmost; and meanwhile her pride would be crushed under the
weight of an intolerable obligation.

These were her superficial considerations; but under them
lurked the secret dread that the obligation might not always
remain intolerable. She knew she could not count on her continuity of purpose, and what really frightened her was the
thought that she might gradually accommodate herself to

remaining indefinitely in Trenor's debt, as she had accommodated herself to the part allotted her on the Sabrina, and as she had so nearly drifted into acquiescing with Stancy's scheme for the advancement of Mrs. Hatch. Her danger lay, as she knew, in her old incurable dread of discomfort and poverty; in the fear of that mounting tide of dinginess against which her mother had so passionately warned her. And now a new vista of peril opened before her. She understood that Rosedale was ready to lend her money; and the longing to take advantage of his offer began to haunt her insidiously. It was of course impossible to accept a loan from Rosedale; but proximate possibilities hovered temptingly before her. She was quite sure that he would come and see her again, and almost sure that, if he did, she could bring him to the point of offering to marry her on the terms she had previously rejected. Would she still reject them if they were offered? More and more, with every fresh mischance befalling her, did the pursuing furies seem to take the shape of Bertha Dorset; and close at hand, safely locked among her papers, lay the means of ending their pursuit. The temptation, which her scorn of Rosedale had once enabled her to reject, now insistently returned upon her; and how much strength was left her to oppose it?

What little there was must at any rate be husbanded to the utmost; she could not trust herself again to the perils of a sleepless night. Through the long hours of silence the dark spirit of fatigue and loneliness crouched upon her breast, leaving her so drained of bodily strength that her morning thoughts swam in a haze of weakness. The only hope of renewal lay in the little bottle at her bed-side; and how much longer that hope would last she dared not conjecture.

XI

L ILY, lingering for a moment on the corner, looked out on
the afternoon spectacle of Fifth Avenue.

It was a day in late April, and the sweetness of spring was
in the air. It mitigated the ugliness of the long crowded thoroughfare, blurred the gaunt roof-lines, threw a mauve veil
over the discouraging perspective of the side streets, and gave
a touch of poetry to the delicate haze of green that marked
the entrance to the Park.

As Lily stood there, she recognized several familiar faces in
the passing carriages. The season was over, and its ruling
forces had disbanded; but a few still lingered, delaying their
departure for Europe, or passing through town on their return from the South. Among them was Mrs. Van Osburgh,
swaying majestically in her C-spring barouche, with Mrs.
Percy Gryce at her side, and the new heir to the Gryce millions enthroned before them on his nurse's knees. They were
succeeded by Mrs. Hatch's electric victoria, in which that lady
reclined in the lonely splendour of a spring toilet obviously
designed for company; and a moment or two later came
Judy Trenor, accompanied by Lady Skiddaw, who had come
over for her annual tarpon fishing and a dip into "the
street."

This fleeting glimpse of her past served to emphasize the
sense of aimlessness with which Lily at length turned toward
home. She had nothing to do for the rest of the day, nor for
the days to come; for the season was over in millinery as well
as in society, and a week earlier Mme. Regina had notified
her that her services were no longer required. Mme. Regina
always reduced her staff on the first of May, and Miss Bart's
attendance had of late been so irregular—she had so often
been unwell, and had done so little work when she came—
that it was only as a favour that her dismissal had hitherto
been deferred.

Lily did not question the justice of the decision. She was
conscious of having been forgetful, awkward and slow to
learn. It was bitter to acknowledge her inferiority even to herself, but the fact had been brought home to her that as a

bread-winner she could never compete with professional ability. Since she had been brought up to be ornamental, she
could hardly blame herself for failing to serve any practical
purpose; but the discovery put an end to her consoling sense
of universal efficiency.

As she turned homeward her thoughts shrank in anticipation from the fact that there would be nothing to get up for
the next morning. The luxury of lying late in bed was a pleasure belonging to the life of ease; it had no part in the utilitarian existence of the boarding-house. She liked to leave her
room early, and to return to it as late as possible; and she was
walking slowly now in order to postpone the detested approach to her doorstep.

But the doorstep, as she drew near it, acquired a sudden
interest from the fact that it was occupied—and indeed
filled—by the conspicuous figure of Mr. Rosedale, whose
presence seemed to take on an added amplitude from the
meanness of his surroundings.

The sight stirred Lily with an irresistible sense of triumph.
Rosedale, a day or two after their chance meeting, had called
to enquire if she had recovered from her indisposition; but
since then she had not seen or heard from him, and his absence seemed to betoken a struggle to keep away, to let her
pass once more out of his life. If this were the case, his return
showed that the struggle had been unsuccessful, for Lily knew
he was not the man to waste his time in an ineffectual sentimental dalliance. He was too busy, too practical, and above
all too much preoccupied with his own advancement, to indulge in such unprofitable asides.

In the peacock-blue parlour, with its bunches of dried pampas grass, and discoloured steel engravings of sentimental episodes, he looked about him with unconcealed disgust, laying
his hat distrustfully on the dusty console adorned with a
Rogers statuette.

Lily sat down on one of the plush and rosewood sofas, and
he deposited himself in a rocking-chair draped with a starched
antimacassar which scraped unpleasantly against the pink fold
of skin above his collar.

"My goodness—you can't go on living here!" he exclaimed.

Lily smiled at his tone. "I am not sure that I can; but I have gone over my expenses very carefully, and I rather think I shall be able to manage it."

"Be able to manage it? That 's not what I mean—it 's no place for you!"

"It 's what *I* mean; for I have been out of work for the last week."

"Out of work—out of work! What a way for you to talk! The idea of your having to work—it 's preposterous." He brought out his sentences in short violent jerks, as though they were forced up from a deep inner crater of indignation. "It 's a farce—a crazy farce," he repeated, his eyes fixed on the long vista of the room reflected in the blotched glass between the windows.

Lily continued to meet his expostulations with a smile. "I don't know why I should regard myself as an exception——" she began.

"Because you *are*; that 's why; and your being in a place like this is a damnable outrage. I can't talk of it calmly."

She had in truth never seen him so shaken out of his usual glibness; and there was something almost moving to her in his inarticulate struggle with his emotions.

He rose with a start which left the rocking-chair quivering on its beam ends, and placed himself squarely before her.

"Look here, Miss Lily, I 'm going to Europe next week: going over to Paris and London for a couple of months—and I can't leave you like this. I can't do it. I know it 's none of my business—you 've let me understand that often enough; but things are worse with you now than they have been before, and you must see that you 've got to accept help from somebody. You spoke to me the other day about some debt to Trenor. I know what you mean—and I respect you for feeling as you do about it."

A blush of surprise rose to Lily's pale face, but before she could interrupt him he had continued eagerly: "Well, I 'll lend you the money to pay Trenor; and I won't—I—see here, don't take me up till I 've finished. What I mean is, it 'll be a plain business arrangement, such as one man would make with another. Now, what have you got to say against that?"

Lily's blush deepened to a glow in which humiliation and gratitude were mingled; and both sentiments revealed themselves in the unexpected gentleness of her reply.

"Only this: that it is exactly what Gus Trenor proposed; and that I can never again be sure of understanding the plainest business arrangement." Then, realizing that this answer contained a germ of injustice, she added, even more kindly: "Not that I don't appreciate your kindness—that I'm not grateful for it. But a business arrangement between us would in any case be impossible, because I shall have no security to give when my debt to Gus Trenor has been paid."

Rosedale received this statement in silence: he seemed to feel the note of finality in her voice, yet to be unable to accept it as closing the question between them.

In the silence Lily had a clear perception of what was passing through his mind. Whatever perplexity he felt as to the inexorableness of her course—however little he penetrated its motive—she saw that it unmistakably tended to strengthen her hold over him. It was as though the sense in her of unexplained scruples and resistances had the same attraction as the delicacy of feature, the fastidiousness of manner, which gave her an external rarity, an air of being impossible to match. As he advanced in social experience this uniqueness had acquired a greater value for him, as though he were a collector who had learned to distinguish minor differences of design and quality in some long-coveted object.

Lily, perceiving all this, understood that he would marry her at once, on the sole condition of a reconciliation with Mrs. Dorset; and the temptation was the less easy to put aside because, little by little, circumstances were breaking down her dislike for Rosedale. The dislike, indeed, still subsisted; but it was penetrated here and there by the perception of mitigating qualities in him: of a certain gross kindliness, a rather helpless fidelity of sentiment, which seemed to be struggling through the hard surface of his material ambitions.

Reading his dismissal in her eyes, he held out his hand with a gesture which conveyed something of this inarticulate conflict.

"If you'd only let me, I'd set you up over them all—I'd put you where you could wipe your feet on 'em!" he declared;

and it touched her oddly to see that his new passion had not altered his old standard of values.

Lily took no sleeping-drops that night. She lay awake viewing her situation in the crude light which Rosedale's visit had shed on it. In fending off the offer he was so plainly ready to renew, had she not sacrificed to one of those abstract notions of honour that might be called the conventionalities of the moral life? What debt did she owe to a social order which had condemned and banished her without trial? She had never been heard in her own defence; she was innocent of the charge on which she had been found guilty; and the irregularity of her conviction might seem to justify the use of methods as irregular in recovering her lost rights. Bertha Dorset, to save herself, had not scrupled to ruin her by an open falsehood; why should she hesitate to make private use of the facts that chance had put in her way? After all, half the opprobrium of such an act lies in the name attached to it. Call it blackmail and it becomes unthinkable; but explain that it injures no one, and that the rights regained by it were unjustly forfeited, and he must be a formalist indeed who can find no plea in its defence.

The arguments pleading for it with Lily were the old unanswerable ones of the personal situation: the sense of injury, the sense of failure, the passionate craving for a fair chance against the selfish despotism of society. She had learned by experience that she had neither the aptitude nor the moral constancy to remake her life on new lines; to become a worker among workers, and let the world of luxury and pleasure sweep by her unregarded. She could not hold herself much to blame for this ineffectiveness, and she was perhaps less to blame than she believed. Inherited tendencies had combined with early training to make her the highly specialized product she was: an organism as helpless out of its narrow range as the sea-anemone torn from the rock. She had been fashioned to adorn and delight; to what other end does nature round the rose-leaf and paint the humming-bird's breast? And was it her fault that the purely decorative mission is less easily and harmoniously fulfilled among social beings than in the world of nature? That it is apt to be hampered by material necessities or complicated by moral scruples?

These last were the two antagonistic forces which fought out their battle in her breast during the long watches of the night; and when she rose the next morning she hardly knew where the victory lay. She was exhausted by the reaction of a night without sleep, coming after many nights of rest artificially obtained; and in the distorting light of fatigue the future stretched out before her grey, interminable and desolate.

She lay late in bed, refusing the coffee and fried eggs which the friendly Irish servant thrust through her door, and hating the intimate domestic noises of the house and the cries and rumblings of the street. Her week of idleness had brought home to her with exaggerated force these small aggravations of the boarding-house world, and she yearned for that other luxurious world, whose machinery is so carefully concealed that one scene flows into another without perceptible agency.

At length she rose and dressed. Since she had left Mme. Regina's she had spent her days in the streets, partly to escape from the uncongenial promiscuities of the boarding-house, and partly in the hope that physical fatigue would help her to sleep. But once out of the house, she could not decide where to go; for she had avoided Gerty since her dismissal from the milliner's, and she was not sure of a welcome anywhere else.

The morning was in harsh contrast to the previous day. A cold grey sky threatened rain, and a high wind drove the dust in wild spirals up and down the streets. Lily walked up Fifth Avenue toward the Park, hoping to find a sheltered nook where she might sit; but the wind chilled her, and after an hour's wandering under the tossing boughs she yielded to her increasing weariness, and took refuge in a little restaurant in Fifty-ninth Street. She was not hungry, and had meant to go without luncheon; but she was too tired to return home, and the long perspective of white tables showed alluringly through the windows.

The room was full of women and girls, all too much engaged in the rapid absorption of tea and pie to remark her entrance. A hum of shrill voices reverberated against the low ceiling, leaving Lily shut out in a little circle of silence. She felt a sudden pang of profound loneliness. She had lost the sense of time, and it seemed to her as though she had not spoken to any one for days. Her eyes sought the faces about her, craving a responsive glance, some sign of an intuition of her trouble. But the sallow preoccupied women, with their bags and note-books and rolls of music, were all engrossed in their own affairs, and even those who sat by themselves were busy running over proof-sheets or devouring magazines between their hurried gulps of tea. Lily alone was stranded in a great waste of disoccupation.

She drank several cups of the tea which was served with her portion of stewed oysters, and her brain felt clearer and livelier when she emerged once more into the street. She realized now that, as she sat in the restaurant, she had unconsciously arrived at a final decision. The discovery gave her an immediate illusion of activity: it was exhilarating to think that she had actually a reason for hurrying home. To prolong her enjoyment of the sensation she decided to walk; but the distance was so great that she found herself glancing nervously at the clocks on the way. One of the surprises of her unoccupied state was the discovery that time, when it is left to itself and no definite demands are made on it, cannot be trusted to move at any recognized pace. Usually it loiters; but just when one has come to count upon its slowness, it may suddenly break into a wild irrational gallop.

She found, however, on reaching home, that the hour was still early enough for her to sit down and rest a few minutes before putting her plan into execution. The delay did not perceptibly weaken her resolve. She was frightened and yet stimulated by the reserved force of resolution which she felt within herself: she saw it was going to be easier, a great deal easier, than she had imagined.

At five o'clock she rose, unlocked her trunk, and took out a sealed packet which she slipped into the bosom of her dress. Even the contact with the packet did not shake her nerves as she had half-expected it would. She seemed encased in a strong armour of indifference, as though the vigorous exertion of her will had finally benumbed her finer sensibilities.

She dressed herself once more for the street, locked her door and went out. When she emerged on the pavement, the day was still high, but a threat of rain darkened the sky and cold gusts shook the signs projecting from the basement shops along the street. She reached Fifth Avenue and began to walk slowly northward. She was sufficiently familiar with Mrs. Dorset's habits to know that she could always be found at home after five. She might not, indeed, be accessible to visitors, especially to a visitor so unwelcome, and against whom it was quite possible that she had guarded herself by special orders; but Lily had written a note which she meant to send up with her name, and which she thought would secure her admission.

She had allowed herself time to walk to Mrs. Dorset's, thinking that the quick movement through the cold evening air would help to steady her nerves; but she really felt no need of being tranquillized. Her survey of the situation remained calm and unwavering.

As she reached Fiftieth Street the clouds broke abruptly, and a rush of cold rain slanted into her face. She had no umbrella and the moisture quickly penetrated her thin spring dress. She was still half a mile from her destination, and she decided to walk across to Madison Avenue and take the electric car. As she turned into the side street, a vague memory stirred in her. The row of budding trees, the new brick and limestone house-fronts, the Georgian flat-house with flower-boxes on its balconies, were merged together into the setting of a familiar scene. It was down this street that she had walked with Selden, that September day two years ago; a few yards ahead was the doorway they had entered together. The recollection loosened a throng of benumbed sensations— longings, regrets, imaginings, the throbbing brood of the only spring her heart had ever known. It was strange to find herself passing his house on such an errand. She seemed suddenly to see her action as he would see it—and the fact of his own connection with it, the fact that, to attain her end, she must trade on his name, and profit by a secret of his past, chilled her blood with shame. What a long way she had travelled since the day of their first talk together! Even then her feet had been set in the path she was now following—even then she had resisted the hand he had held out.

All her resentment of his fancied coldness was swept away in this overwhelming rush of recollection. Twice he had been ready to help her—to help her by loving her, as he had said—and if, the third time, he had seemed to fail her, whom but herself could she accuse? . . . Well, that part of her life was over; she did not know why her thoughts still clung to it. But the sudden longing to see him remained; it grew to hunger as she paused on the pavement opposite his door. The street was dark and empty, swept by the rain. She had a vision of his quiet room, of the bookshelves, and the fire on the hearth. She looked up and saw a light in his window; then she crossed the street and entered the house.

XII

The library looked as she had pictured it. The green-shaded lamps made tranquil circles of light in the gathering dusk, a little fire flickered on the hearth, and Selden's easy-chair, which stood near it, had been pushed aside when he rose to admit her.

He had checked his first movement of surprise, and stood silent, waiting for her to speak, while she paused a moment on the threshold, assailed by a rush of memories.

The scene was unchanged. She recognized the row of shelves from which he had taken down his La Bruyère, and the worn arm of the chair he had leaned against while she examined the precious volume. But then the wide September light had filled the room, making it seem a part of the outer world: now the shaded lamps and the warm hearth, detaching it from the gathering darkness of the street, gave it a sweeter touch of intimacy.

Becoming gradually aware of the surprise under Selden's silence, Lily turned to him and said simply: "I came to tell you that I was sorry for the way we parted—for what I said to you that day at Mrs. Hatch's."

The words rose to her lips spontaneously. Even on her way up the stairs, she had not thought of preparing a pretext for her visit, but she now felt an intense longing to dispel the cloud of misunderstanding that hung between them.

Selden returned her look with a smile. "I was sorry too that we should have parted in that way; but I am not sure I did n't bring it on myself. Luckily I had foreseen the risk I was taking——"

"So that you really did n't care——?" broke from her with a flash of her old irony.

"So that I was prepared for the consequences," he corrected good-humouredly. "But we 'll talk of all this later. Do come and sit by the fire. I can recommend that arm-chair, if you 'll let me put a cushion behind you."

While he spoke she had moved slowly to the middle of the room, and paused near his writing-table, where the lamp, striking upward, cast exaggerated shadows on the pallour of her delicately-hollowed face.

"You look tired—do sit down," he repeated gently.

She did not seem to hear the request. "I wanted you to know that I left Mrs. Hatch immediately after I saw you," she said, as though continuing her confession.

"Yes—yes; I know," he assented, with a rising tinge of embarrassment.

"And that I did so because you told me to. Before you came I had already begun to see that it would be impossible to remain with her—for the reasons you gave me; but I would n't admit it—I would n't let you see that I understood what you meant."

"Ah, I might have trusted you to find your own way out—don't overwhelm me with the sense of my officiousness!"

His light tone, in which, had her nerves been steadier, she would have recognized the mere effort to bridge over an awkward moment, jarred on her passionate desire to be understood. In her strange state of extra-lucidity, which gave her the sense of being already at the heart of the situation, it seemed incredible that any one should think it necessary to linger in the conventional outskirts of word-play and evasion.

"It was not that—I was not ungrateful," she insisted. But the power of expression failed her suddenly; she felt a tremor in her throat, and two tears gathered and fell slowly from her eyes.

Selden moved forward and took her hand. "You are very tired. Why won't you sit down and let me make you comfortable?"

He drew her to the arm-chair near the fire, and placed a cushion behind her shoulders.

"And now you must let me make you some tea: you know I always have that amount of hospitality at my command."

She shook her head, and two more tears ran over. But she did not weep easily, and the long habit of self-control reasserted itself, though she was still too tremulous to speak.

"You know I can coax the water to boil in five minutes," Selden continued, speaking as though she were a troubled child.

His words recalled the vision of that other afternoon when

they had sat together over his tea-table and talked jestingly of
her future. There were moments when that day seemed more
remote than any other event in her life; and yet she could
always relive it in its minutest detail.

She made a gesture of refusal. "No: I drink too much tea.
I would rather sit quiet—I must go in a moment," she added
confusedly.

Selden continued to stand near her, leaning against the
mantelpiece. The tinge of constraint was beginning to be
more distinctly perceptible under the friendly ease of his manner. Her self-absorption had not allowed her to perceive it at
first; but now that her consciousness was once more putting
forth its eager feelers, she saw that her presence was becoming an embarrassment to him. Such a situation can be saved
only by an immediate outrush of feeling; and on Selden's side
the determining impulse was still lacking.

The discovery did not disturb Lily as it might once have
done. She had passed beyond the phase of well-bred reciproc-
ity, in which every demonstration must be scrupulously proportioned to the emotion it elicits, and generosity of feeling
is the only ostentation condemned. But the sense of loneliness
returned with redoubled force as she saw herself forever shut
out from Selden's inmost self. She had come to him with no
definite purpose; the mere longing to see him had directed
her; but the secret hope she had carried with her suddenly
revealed itself in its death-pang.

"I must go," she repeated, making a motion to rise from
her chair. "But I may not see you again for a long time, and
I wanted to tell you that I have never forgotten the things
you said to me at Bellomont, and that sometimes—sometimes when I seemed farthest from remembering them—they
have helped me, and kept me from mistakes; kept me from
really becoming what many people have thought me."

Strive as she would to put some order in her thoughts, the
words would not come more clearly; yet she felt that she could
not leave him without trying to make him understand that
she had saved herself whole from the seeming ruin of her life.

A change had come over Selden's face as she spoke. Its
guarded look had yielded to an expression still untinged by
personal emotion, but full of a gentle understanding.

"I am glad to have you tell me that; but nothing I have said has really made the difference. The difference is in yourself—it will always be there. And since it *is* there, it can't really matter to you what people think: you are so sure that your friends will always understand you."

"Ah, don't say that—don't say that what you have told me has made no difference. It seems to shut me out—to leave me all alone with the other people." She had risen and stood before him, once more completely mastered by the inner urgency of the moment. The consciousness of his half-divined reluctance had vanished. Whether he wished it or not, he must see her wholly for once before they parted.

Her voice had gathered strength, and she looked him gravely in the eyes as she continued. "Once—twice—you gave me the chance to escape from my life, and I refused it: refused it because I was a coward. Afterward I saw my mistake—I saw I could never be happy with what had contented me before. But it was too late: you had judged me—I understood. It was too late for happiness—but not too late to be helped by the thought of what I had missed. That is all I have lived on—don't take it from me now! Even in my worst moments it has been like a little light in the darkness. Some women are strong enough to be good by themselves, but I needed the help of your belief in me. Perhaps I might have resisted a great temptation, but the little ones would have pulled me down. And then I remembered—I remembered your saying that such a life could never satisfy me; and I was ashamed to admit to myself that it could. That is what you did for me—that is what I wanted to thank you for. I wanted to tell you that I have always remembered; and that I have tried—tried hard . . ."

She broke off suddenly. Her tears had risen again, and in drawing out her handkerchief her fingers touched the packet in the folds of her dress. A wave of colour suffused her, and the words died on her lips. Then she lifted her eyes to his and went on in an altered voice.

"I have tried hard—but life is difficult, and I am a very useless person. I can hardly be said to have an independent existence. I was just a screw or a cog in the great machine I called life, and when I dropped out of it I found I was of no use anywhere else. What can one do when one finds that one only fits into one hole? One must get back to it or be thrown out into the rubbish heap—and you don't know what it's like in the rubbish heap!"

Her lips wavered into a smile—she had been distracted by the whimsical remembrance of the confidences she had made to him, two years earlier, in that very room. Then she had been planning to marry Percy Gryce—what was it she was planning now?

The blood had risen strongly under Selden's dark skin, but his emotion showed itself only in an added seriousness of manner.

"You have something to tell me—do you mean to marry?" he said abruptly.

Lily's eyes did not falter, but a look of wonder, of puzzled self-interrogation, formed itself slowly in their depths. In the light of his question, she had paused to ask herself if her decision had really been taken when she entered the room.

"You always told me I should have to come to it sooner or later!" she said with a faint smile.

"And you have come to it now?"

"I shall have to come to it—presently. But there is something else I must come to first." She paused again, trying to transmit to her voice the steadiness of her recovered smile. "There is some one I must say goodbye to. Oh, not *you*— we are sure to see each other again—but the Lily Bart you knew. I have kept her with me all this time, but now we are going to part, and I have brought her back to you—I am going to leave her here. When I go out presently she will not go with me. I shall like to think that she has stayed with you—and she'll be no trouble, she'll take up no room."

She went toward him, and put out her hand, still smiling. "Will you let her stay with you?" she asked.

He caught her hand, and she felt in his the vibration of feeling that had not yet risen to his lips. "Lily—can't I help you?" he exclaimed.

She looked at him gently. "Do you remember what you said to me once? That you could help me only by loving me? Well—you did love me for a moment; and it helped me. It has always helped me. But the moment is gone—it was I who let it go. And one must go on living. Goodbye."

She laid her other hand on his, and they looked at each other with a kind of solemnity, as though they stood in the presence of death. Something in truth lay dead between them—the love she had killed in him and could no longer call to life. But something lived between them also, and leaped up in her like an imperishable flame: it was the love his love had kindled, the passion of her soul for his.

In its light everything else dwindled and fell away from her. She understood now that she could not go forth and leave her old self with him: that self must indeed live on in his presence, but it must still continue to be hers.

Selden had retained her hand, and continued to scrutinize her with a strange sense of foreboding. The external aspect of the situation had vanished for him as completely as for her: he felt it only as one of those rare moments which lift the veil from their faces as they pass.

"Lily," he said in a low voice, "you must n't speak in this way. I can't let you go without knowing what you mean to do. Things may change—but they don't pass. You can never go out of my life."

She met his eyes with an illumined look. "No," she said. "I see that now. Let us always be friends. Then I shall feel safe, whatever happens."

"Whatever happens? What do you mean? What is going to happen?"

She turned away quietly and walked toward the hearth.

"Nothing at present—except that I am very cold, and that before I go you must make up the fire for me."

She knelt on the hearthrug, stretching her hands to the embers. Puzzled by the sudden change in her tone, he mechanically gathered a handful of wood from the basket and tossed it on the fire. As he did so, he noticed how thin her hands looked against the rising light of the flames. He saw too, under the loose lines of her dress, how the curves of her figure had shrunk to angularity; he remembered long afterward how the red play of the flame sharpened the depression of her nostrils, and intensified the blackness of the shadows which struck up from her cheekbones to her eyes. She knelt there for a few moments in silence; a silence which he dared not break. When she rose he fancied that he saw her draw something from her dress and drop it into the fire; but he hardly noticed the gesture at the time. His faculties seemed tranced, and he was still groping for the word to break the spell.

She went up to him and laid her hands on his shoulders. "Goodbye," she said, and as he bent over her she touched his forehead with her lips.

XIII

THE STREET-LAMPS were lit, but the rain had ceased, and there was a momentary revival of light in the upper sky.

Lily walked on unconscious of her surroundings. She was still treading the buoyant ether which emanates from the high moments of life. But gradually it shrank away from her and she felt the dull pavement beneath her feet. The sense of weariness returned with accumulated force, and for a moment she felt that she could walk no farther. She had reached the corner of Forty-first Street and Fifth Avenue, and she remembered that in Bryant Park there were seats where she might rest.

That melancholy pleasure-ground was almost deserted when she entered it, and she sank down on an empty bench in the glare of an electric street-lamp. The warmth of the fire had passed out of her veins, and she told herself that she must not sit long in the penetrating dampness which struck up from the wet asphalt. But her will-power seemed to have spent itself in a last great effort, and she was lost in the blank reaction which follows on an unwonted expenditure of energy. And besides, what was there to go home to? Nothing but the silence of her cheerless room—that silence of the night which may be more racking to tired nerves than the most discordant noises: that, and the bottle of chloral by her bed. The thought of the chloral was the only spot of light in the dark prospect: she could feel its lulling influence stealing over her already. But she was troubled by the thought that it was losing its power—she dared not go back to it too soon. Of late the sleep it had brought her had been more broken and less profound; there had been nights when she was perpetually floating up through it to consciousness. What if the effect of the drug should gradually fail, as all narcotics were said to fail? She remembered the chemist's warning against increasing the dose; and she had heard before of the capricious and incalculable action of the drug. Her dread of returning to a sleepless night was so great that she lingered on, hoping that excessive weariness would reinforce the waning power of the chloral.

Night had now closed in, and the roar of traffic in Forty-second Street was dying out. As complete darkness fell on the square the lingering occupants of the benches rose and dispersed; but now and then a stray figure, hurrying homeward, struck across the path where Lily sat, looming black for a moment in the white circle of electric light. One or two of these passers-by slackened their pace to glance curiously at her lonely figure; but she was hardly conscious of their scrutiny.

Suddenly, however, she became aware that one of the passing shadows remained stationary between her line of vision and the gleaming asphalt; and raising her eyes she saw a young woman bending over her.

"Excuse me—are you sick?—Why, it 's Miss Bart!" a half-familiar voice exclaimed.

Lily looked up. The speaker was a poorly-dressed young woman with a bundle under her arm. Her face had the air of unwholesome refinement which ill-health and over-work may produce, but its common prettiness was redeemed by the strong and generous curve of the lips.

"You don't remember me," she continued, brightening with the pleasure of recognition, "but I 'd know you anywhere, I 've thought of you such a lot. I guess my folks all know your name by heart. I was one of the girls at Miss Farish's club—you helped me to go to the country that time I had lung-trouble. My name 's Nettie Struther. It was Nettie Crane then—but I daresay you don't remember that either."

Yes: Lily was beginning to remember. The episode of Nettie Crane's timely rescue from disease had been one of the most satisfying incidents of her connection with Gerty's charitable work. She had furnished the girl with the means to go to a sanatorium in the mountains: it struck her now with a peculiar irony that the money she had used had been Gus Trenor's.

She tried to reply, to assure the speaker that she had not forgotten; but her voice failed in the effort, and she felt herself sinking under a great wave of physical weakness. Nettie Struther, with a startled exclamation, sat down and slipped a shabbily-clad arm behind her back.

"Why, Miss Bart, you *are* sick. Just lean on me a little till you feel better."

A faint glow of returning strength seemed to pass into Lily from the pressure of the supporting arm.

"I'm only tired—it is nothing," she found voice to say in a moment; and then, as she met the timid appeal of her companion's eyes, she added involuntarily: "I have been unhappy—in great trouble."

"*You* in trouble? I've always thought of you as being so high up, where everything was just grand. Sometimes, when I felt real mean, and got to wondering why things were so queerly fixed in the world, I used to remember that *you* were having a lovely time, anyhow, and that seemed to show there was a kind of justice somewhere. But you mustn't sit here too long—it's fearfully damp. Don't you feel strong enough to walk on a little ways now?" she broke off.

"Yes—yes; I must go home," Lily murmured, rising.

Her eyes rested wonderingly on the thin shabby figure at her side. She had known Nettie Crane as one of the discouraged victims of over-work and anæmic parentage: one of the superfluous fragments of life destined to be swept prematurely into that social refuse-heap of which Lily had so lately expressed her dread. But Nettie Struther's frail envelope was now alive with hope and energy: whatever fate the future reserved for her, she would not be cast into the refuse-heap without a struggle.

"I am very glad to have seen you," Lily continued, summoning a smile to her unsteady lips. "It will be my turn to think of you as happy—and the world will seem a less unjust place to me too."

"Oh, but I can't leave you like this—you're not fit to go home alone. And I can't go with you either!" Nettie Struther wailed with a start of recollection. "You see, it's my husband's night-shift—he's a motor-man—and the friend I leave the baby with has to step upstairs to get *her* husband's supper at seven. I didn't tell you I had a baby, did I? She'll be four months old day after tomorrow, and to look at her you wouldn't think I'd ever had a sick day. I'd give anything to show you the baby, Miss Bart, and we live right down the street here—it's only three blocks off." She lifted her eyes tentatively to Lily's face, and then added with a burst of courage: "Why won't you get right into the cars and come home with me while I get baby's supper? It's real warm in our kitchen, and you can rest there, and I'll take *you* home as soon as ever she drops off to sleep."

It *was* warm in the kitchen, which, when Nettie Struther's match had made a flame leap from the gas-jet above the table, revealed itself to Lily as extraordinarily small and almost miraculously clean. A fire shone through the polished flanks of the iron stove, and near it stood a crib in which a baby was sitting upright, with incipient anxiety struggling for expression on a countenance still placid with sleep.

Having passionately celebrated her reunion with her offspring, and excused herself in cryptic language for the lateness of her return, Nettie restored the baby to the crib and shyly invited Miss Bart to the rocking-chair near the stove.

"We've got a parlour too," she explained with pardonable pride; "but I guess it's warmer in here, and I don't want to leave you alone while I'm getting baby's supper."

On receiving Lily's assurance that she much preferred the friendly proximity of the kitchen fire, Mrs. Struther proceeded to prepare a bottle of infantile food, which she tenderly applied to the baby's impatient lips; and while the ensuing degustation went on, she seated herself with a beaming countenance beside her visitor.

"You're sure you won't let me warm up a drop of coffee for you, Miss Bart? There's some of baby's fresh milk left over—well, maybe you'd rather just sit quiet and rest a little while. It's too lovely having you here. I've thought of it so often that I can't believe it's really come true. I've said to George again and again: 'I just wish Miss Bart could see me *now*—' and I used to watch for your name in the papers, and we'd talk over what you were doing, and read the descriptions of the dresses you wore. I haven't seen your name for a long time, though, and I began to be afraid you were sick, and it worried me so that George said I'd get sick myself, fretting about it." Her lips broke into a reminiscent smile. "Well, I can't afford to be sick again, that's a fact: the last spell nearly finished me. When you sent me off that time I never thought I'd come back alive, and I didn't much care if I did. You see I didn't know about George and the baby then."

She paused to readjust the bottle to the child's bubbling mouth.

"You precious—don't you be in too much of a hurry! Was it mad with mommer for getting its supper so late? Marry Anto'nette—that 's what we call her: after the French queen in that play at the Garden—I told George the actress reminded me of you, and that made me fancy the name . . . I never thought I 'd get married, you know, and I 'd never have had the heart to go on working just for myself."

She broke off again, and meeting the encouragement in Lily's eyes, went on, with a flush rising under her anæmic skin: "You see I was n't only just *sick* that time you sent me off— I was dreadfully unhappy too. I 'd known a gentleman where I was employed—I don't know as you remember I did typewriting in a big importing firm—and—well—I thought we were to be married: he 'd gone steady with me six months and given me his mother 's wedding ring. But I presume he was too stylish for me—he travelled for the firm, and had seen a great deal of society. Work girls are n't looked after the way you are, and they don't always know how to look after themselves. I did n't . . . and it pretty near killed me when he went away and left off writing . . . It was then I came down sick—I thought it was the end of everything. I guess it would have been if you had n't sent me off. But when I found I was getting well I began to take heart in spite of myself. And then, when I got back home, George came round and asked me to marry him. At first I thought I could n't, because we 'd been brought up together, and I knew he knew about me. But after a while I began to see that that made it easier. I never could have told another man, and I 'd never have married without telling; but if George cared for me enough to have me as I was, I did n't see why I should n't begin over again—and I did."

The strength of the victory shone forth from her as she lifted her irradiated face from the child on her knees.

"But, mercy, I did n't mean to go on like this about myself, with you sitting there looking so fagged out. Only it 's so lovely having you here, and letting you see just how you 've helped me." The baby had sunk back blissfully replete, and

Mrs. Struther softly rose to lay the bottle aside. Then she paused before Miss Bart.

"I only wish I could help *you*—but I suppose there 's nothing on earth I could do," she murmured wistfully.

Lily, instead of answering, rose with a smile and held out her arms; and the mother, understanding the gesture, laid her child in them.

The baby, feeling herself detached from her habitual anchorage, made an instinctive motion of resistance; but the soothing influences of digestion prevailed, and Lily felt the soft weight sink trustfully against her breast. The child's confidence in its safety thrilled her with a sense of warmth and returning life, and she bent over, wondering at the rosy blur of the little face, the empty clearness of the eyes, the vague tendrilly motions of the folding and unfolding fingers. At first the burden in her arms seemed as light as a pink cloud or a heap of down, but as she continued to hold it the weight increased, sinking deeper, and penetrating her with a strange sense of weakness, as though the child entered into her and became a part of herself.

She looked up, and saw Nettie's eyes resting on her with tenderness and exultation.

"Would n't it be too lovely for anything if she could grow up to be just like you? Of course I know she never *could*— but mothers are always dreaming the craziest things for their children."

Lily clasped the child close for a moment and laid her back in her mother's arms.

"Oh, she must not do that—I should be afraid to come and see her too often!" she said with a smile; and then, resisting Mrs. Struther's anxious offer of companionship, and reiterating the promise that of course she would come back soon, and make George's acquaintance, and see the baby in her bath, she passed out of the kitchen and went alone down the tenement stairs.

As she reached the street she realized that she felt stronger and happier: the little episode had done her good. It was the first time she had ever come across the results of her spas-

modic benevolence, and the surprised sense of human fellowship took the mortal chill from her heart.

It was not till she entered her own door that she felt the
reaction of a deeper loneliness. It was long after seven o'clock,
and the light and odours proceeding from the basement made
it manifest that the boarding-house dinner had begun. She
hastened up to her room, lit the gas, and began to dress. She
did not mean to pamper herself any longer, to go without
food because her surroundings made it unpalatable. Since it
was her fate to live in a boarding-house, she must learn to fall
in with the conditions of the life. Nevertheless she was glad
that, when she descended to the heat and glare of the dining-
room, the repast was nearly over.

In her own room again, she was seized with a sudden fever
of activity. For weeks past she had been too listless and indifferent to set her possessions in order, but now she began to
examine systematically the contents of her drawers and cupboard. She had a few handsome dresses left—survivals of her
last phase of splendour, on the Sabrina and in London—but
when she had been obliged to part with her maid she had
given the woman a generous share of her cast-off apparel. The
remaining dresses, though they had lost their freshness, still
kept the long unerring lines, the sweep and amplitude of the
great artist's stroke, and as she spread them out on the bed
the scenes in which they had been worn rose vividly before
her. An association lurked in every fold: each fall of lace and
gleam of embroidery was like a letter in the record of her
past. She was startled to find how the atmosphere of her old
life enveloped her. But, after all, it was the life she had been
made for: every dawning tendency in her had been carefully
directed toward it, all her interests and activities had been
taught to centre around it. She was like some rare flower
grown for exhibition, a flower from which every bud had
been nipped except the crowning blossom of her beauty.

Last of all, she drew forth from the bottom of her trunk a
heap of white drapery which fell shapelessly across her arm.
It was the Reynolds dress she had worn in the Bry *tableaux*.
It had been impossible for her to give it away, but she had
never seen it since that night, and the long flexible folds, as

she shook them out, gave forth an odour of violets which came to her like a breath from the flower-edged fountain where she had stood with Lawrence Selden and disowned her fate. She put back the dresses one by one, laying away with each some gleam of light, some note of laughter, some stray waft from the rosy shores of pleasure. She was still in a state of highly-wrought impressionability, and every hint of the past sent a lingering tremor along her nerves.

She had just closed her trunk on the white folds of the Reynolds dress when she heard a tap at her door, and the red fist of the Irish maid-servant thrust in a belated letter. Carrying it to the light, Lily read with surprise the address stamped on the upper corner of the envelope. It was a business communication from the office of her aunt's executors, and she wondered what unexpected development had caused them to break silence before the appointed time.

She opened the envelope and a cheque fluttered to the floor. As she stooped to pick it up the blood rushed to her face. The cheque represented the full amount of Mrs. Peniston's legacy, and the letter accompanying it explained that the executors, having adjusted the business of the estate with less delay than they had expected, had decided to anticipate the date fixed for the payment of the bequests.

Lily sat down beside the desk at the foot of her bed, and spreading out the cheque, read over and over the *ten thousand dollars* written across it in a steely business hand. Ten months earlier the amount it stood for had represented the depths of penury; but her standard of values had changed in the interval, and now visions of wealth lurked in every flourish of the pen. As she continued to gaze at it, she felt the glitter of the visions mounting to her brain, and after a while she lifted the lid of the desk and slipped the magic formula out of sight. It was easier to think without those five figures dancing before her eyes; and she had a great deal of thinking to do before she slept.

She opened her cheque-book, and plunged into such anxious calculations as had prolonged her vigil at Bellomont on the night when she had decided to marry Percy Gryce. Poverty simplifies book-keeping, and her financial situation was easier to ascertain than it had been then; but she had not yet

learned the control of money, and during her transient phase
of luxury at the Emporium she had slipped back into habits
of extravagance which still impaired her slender balance. A
careful examination of her cheque-book, and of the unpaid
bills in her desk, showed that, when the latter had been settled, she would have barely enough to live on for the next
three or four months; and even after that, if she were to continue her present way of living, without earning any additional money, all incidental expenses must be reduced to the
vanishing point. She hid her eyes with a shudder, beholding
herself at the entrance of that ever-narrowing perspective
down which she had seen Miss Silverton's dowdy figure take
its despondent way.

It was no longer, however, from the vision of material poverty that she turned with the greatest shrinking. She had a
sense of deeper empoverishment—of an inner destitution
compared to which outward conditions dwindled into insignificance. It was indeed miserable to be poor—to look forward to a shabby, anxious middle-age, leading by dreary
degrees of economy and self-denial to gradual absorption in
the dingy communal existence of the boarding-house. But
there was something more miserable still—it was the clutch
of solitude at her heart, the sense of being swept like a stray
uprooted growth down the heedless current of the years. That
was the feeling which possessed her now—the feeling of
being something rootless and ephemeral, mere spin-drift of
the whirling surface of existence, without anything to which
the poor little tentacles of self could cling before the awful
flood submerged them. And as she looked back she saw that
there had never been a time when she had had any real relation to life. Her parents too had been rootless, blown hither
and thither on every wind of fashion, without any personal
existence to shelter them from its shifting gusts. She herself
had grown up without any one spot of earth being dearer to
her than another: there was no centre of early pieties, of grave
endearing traditions, to which her heart could revert and
from which it could draw strength for itself and tenderness
for others. In whatever form a slowly-accumulated past lives
in the blood—whether in the concrete image of the old
house stored with visual memories, or in the conception of

the house not built with hands, but made up of inherited passions and loyalties—it has the same power of broadening and deepening the individual existence, of attaching it by mysterious links of kinship to all the mighty sum of human striving.

Such a vision of the solidarity of life had never before come to Lily. She had had a premonition of it in the blind motions of her mating-instinct; but they had been checked by the disintegrating influences of the life about her. All the men and women she knew were like atoms whirling away from each other in some wild centrifugal dance: her first glimpse of the continuity of life had come to her that evening in Nettie Struther's kitchen.

The poor little working-girl who had found strength to gather up the fragments of her life, and build herself a shelter with them, seemed to Lily to have reached the central truth of existence. It was a meagre enough life, on the grim edge of poverty, with scant margin for possibilities of sickness or mischance, but it had the frail audacious permanence of a bird's nest built on the edge of a cliff—a mere wisp of leaves and straw, yet so put together that the lives entrusted to it may hang safely over the abyss.

Yes—but it had taken two to build the nest; the man's faith as well as the woman's courage. Lily remembered Nettie's words: *I knew he knew about me*. Her husband's faith in her had made her renewal possible—it is so easy for a woman to become what the man she loves believes her to be! Well— Selden had twice been ready to stake his faith on Lily Bart; but the third trial had been too severe for his endurance. The very quality of his love had made it the more impossible to recall to life. If it had been a simple instinct of the blood, the power of her beauty might have revived it. But the fact that it struck deeper, that it was inextricably wound up with inherited habits of thought and feeling, made it as impossible to restore to growth as a deep-rooted plant torn from its bed. Selden had given her of his best; but he was as incapable as herself of an uncritical return to former states of feeling.

There remained to her, as she had told him, the uplifting memory of his faith in her; but she had not reached the age when a woman can live on her memories. As she held Nettie

Struther's child in her arms the frozen currents of youth had loosed themselves and run warm in her veins: the old life-hunger possessed her, and all her being clamoured for its share of personal happiness. Yes—it was happiness she still wanted, and the glimpse she had caught of it made everything else of no account. One by one she had detached herself from the baser possibilities, and she saw that nothing now remained to her but the emptiness of renunciation.

It was growing late, and an immense weariness once more possessed her. It was not the stealing sense of sleep, but a vivid wakeful fatigue, a wan lucidity of mind against which all the possibilities of the future were shadowed forth gigantically. She was appalled by the intense clearness of the vision; she seemed to have broken through the merciful veil which intervenes between intention and action, and to see exactly what she would do in all the long days to come. There was the cheque in her desk, for instance—she meant to use it in paying her debt to Trenor; but she foresaw that when the morning came she would put off doing so, would slip into gradual tolerance of the debt. The thought terrified her—she dreaded to fall from the height of her last moment with Lawrence Selden. But how could she trust herself to keep her footing? She knew the strength of the opposing impulses—she could feel the countless hands of habit dragging her back into some fresh compromise with fate. She felt an intense longing to prolong, to perpetuate, the momentary exaltation of her spirit. If only life could end now—end on this tragic yet sweet vision of lost possibilities, which gave her a sense of kinship with all the loving and foregoing in the world!

She reached out suddenly and, drawing the cheque from her writing-desk, enclosed it in an envelope which she addressed to her bank. She then wrote out a cheque for Trenor, and placing it, without an accompanying word, in an envelope inscribed with his name, laid the two letters side by side on her desk. After that she continued to sit at the table, sorting her papers and writing, till the intense silence of the house reminded her of the lateness of the hour. In the street the noise of wheels had ceased, and the rumble of the "elevated" came only at long intervals through the deep unnatural hush. In the mysterious nocturnal separation from all outward signs of life, she felt herself more strangely confronted with her fate. The sensation made her brain reel, and she tried to shut out consciousness by pressing her hands against her eyes. But the terrible silence and emptiness seemed to symbolize her future—she felt as though the house, the street, the world were all empty, and she alone left sentient in a lifeless universe.

But this was the verge of delirium . . . she had never hung so near the dizzy brink of the unreal. Sleep was what she wanted—she remembered that she had not closed her eyes for two nights. The little bottle was at her bed-side, waiting to lay its spell upon her. She rose and undressed hastily, hungering now for the touch of her pillow. She felt so profoundly tired that she thought she must fall asleep at once; but as soon as she had lain down every nerve started once more into separate wakefulness. It was as though a great blaze of electric light had been turned on in her head, and her poor little anguished self shrank and cowered in it, without knowing where to take refuge.

She had not imagined that such a multiplication of wakefulness was possible: her whole past was reënacting itself at a hundred different points of consciousness. Where was the drug that could still this legion of insurgent nerves? The sense of exhaustion would have been sweet compared to this shrill beat of activities; but weariness had dropped from her as though some cruel stimulant had been forced into her veins.

She could bear it—yes, she could bear it; but what strength would be left her the next day? Perspective had disappeared—the next day pressed close upon her, and on its heels came the days that were to follow—they swarmed about her like a shrieking mob. She must shut them out for a few hours; she must take a brief bath of oblivion. She put out her hand, and measured the soothing drops into a glass; but as she did so, she knew they would be powerless against the supernatural lucidity of her brain. She had long since raised the dose to its highest limit, but tonight she felt she must increase it. She knew she took a slight risk in doing so—she remembered the chemist's warning. If sleep came at all, it might be a sleep without waking. But after all that was but

one chance in a hundred: the action of the drug was incalculable, and the addition of a few drops to the regular dose
would probably do no more than procure for her the rest she
so desperately needed. . . .

She did not, in truth, consider the question very closely—
the physical craving for sleep was her only sustained sensation. Her mind shrank from the glare of thought as instinctively as eyes contract in a blaze of light—darkness, darkness
was what she must have at any cost. She raised herself in bed
and swallowed the contents of the glass; then she blew out
her candle and lay down.

She lay very still, waiting with a sensuous pleasure for the
first effects of the soporific. She knew in advance what form
they would take—the gradual cessation of the inner throb,
the soft approach of passiveness, as though an invisible hand
made magic passes over her in the darkness. The very slowness and hesitancy of the effect increased its fascination: it was
delicious to lean over and look down into the dim abysses of
unconsciousness. Tonight the drug seemed to work more
slowly than usual: each passionate pulse had to be stilled in
turn, and it was long before she felt them dropping into abeyance, like sentinels falling asleep at their posts. But gradually
the sense of complete subjugation came over her, and she
wondered languidly what had made her feel so uneasy and
excited. She saw now that there was nothing to be excited
about—she had returned to her normal view of life. Tomorrow would not be so difficult after all: she felt sure that she
would have the strength to meet it. She did not quite remember what it was that she had been afraid to meet, but the
uncertainty no longer troubled her. She had been unhappy,
and now she was happy—she had felt herself alone, and now
the sense of loneliness had vanished.

She stirred once, and turned on her side, and as she did so,
she suddenly understood why she did not feel herself alone.
It was odd—but Nettie Struther's child was lying on her
arm: she felt the pressure of its little head against her shoulder. She did not know how it had come there, but she felt no
great surprise at the fact, only a gentle penetrating thrill of
warmth and pleasure. She settled herself into an easier position, hollowing her arm to pillow the round downy head, and

holding her breath lest a sound should disturb the sleeping child.

As she lay there she said to herself that there was something she must tell Selden, some word she had found that should make life clear between them. She tried to repeat the word, which lingered vague and luminous on the far edge of thought—she was afraid of not remembering it when she woke; and if she could only remember it and say it to him, she felt that everything would be well.

Slowly the thought of the word faded, and sleep began to enfold her. She struggled faintly against it, feeling that she ought to keep awake on account of the baby; but even this feeling was gradually lost in an indistinct sense of drowsy peace, through which, of a sudden, a dark flash of loneliness and terror tore its way.

She started up again, cold and trembling with the shock: for a moment she seemed to have lost her hold of the child. But no—she was mistaken—the tender pressure of its body was still close to hers: the recovered warmth flowed through her once more, she yielded to it, sank into it, and slept.

XIV

The next morning rose mild and bright, with a promise of summer in the air. The sunlight slanted joyously down Lily's street, mellowed the blistered house-front, gilded the paintless railings of the door-step, and struck prismatic glories from the panes of her darkened window.

When such a day coincides with the inner mood there is intoxication in its breath; and Selden, hastening along the street through the squalor of its morning confidences, felt himself thrilling with a youthful sense of adventure. He had cut loose from the familiar shores of habit, and launched himself on uncharted seas of emotion; all the old tests and measures were left behind, and his course was to be shaped by new stars.

That course, for the moment, led merely to Miss Bart's boarding-house; but its shabby door-step had suddenly become the threshold of the untried. As he approached he looked up at the triple row of windows, wondering boyishly which one of them was hers. It was nine o'clock, and the house, being tenanted by workers, already showed an awakened front to the street. He remembered afterward having noticed that only one blind was down. He noticed too that there was a pot of pansies on one of the window sills, and at once concluded that the window must be hers: it was inevitable that he should connect her with the one touch of beauty in the dingy scene.

Nine o'clock was an early hour for a visit, but Selden had passed beyond all such conventional observances. He only knew that he must see Lily Bart at once—he had found the word he meant to say to her, and it could not wait another moment to be said. It was strange that it had not come to his lips sooner—that he had let her pass from him the evening before without being able to speak it. But what did that matter, now that a new day had come? It was not a word for twilight, but for the morning.

Selden ran eagerly up the steps and pulled the bell; and even in his state of self-absorption it came as a sharp surprise to him that the door should open so promptly. It was still more of a surprise to see, as he entered, that it had been opened by Gerty Farish—and that behind her, in an agitated blur, several other figures ominously loomed.

"Lawrence!" Gerty cried in a strange voice, "how could you get here so quickly?"—and the trembling hand she laid on him seemed instantly to close about his heart.

He noticed the other faces, vague with fear and conjecture—he saw the landlady's imposing bulk sway professionally toward him; but he shrank back, putting up his hand, while his eyes mechanically mounted the steep black walnut stairs, up which he was immediately aware that his cousin was about to lead him.

A voice in the background said that the doctor might be back at any minute—and that nothing, upstairs, was to be disturbed. Some one else exclaimed: "It was the greatest mercy—" then Selden felt that Gerty had taken him gently by the hand, and that they were to be suffered to go up alone.

In silence they mounted the three flights, and walked along the passage to a closed door. Gerty opened the door, and Selden went in after her. Though the blind was down, the irresistible sunlight poured a tempered golden flood into the room, and in its light Selden saw a narrow bed along the wall, and on the bed, with motionless hands and calm unrecognizing face, the semblance of Lily Bart.

That it was her real self, every pulse in him ardently denied. Her real self had lain warm on his heart but a few hours earlier—what had he to do with this estranged and tranquil face which, for the first time, neither paled nor brightened at his coming?

Gerty, strangely tranquil too, with the conscious self-control of one who has ministered to much pain, stood by the bed, speaking gently, as if transmitting a final message.

"The doctor found a bottle of chloral—she had been sleeping badly for a long time, and she must have taken an overdose by mistake. . . . There is no doubt of that—no doubt—there will be no question—he has been very kind. I told him that you and I would like to be left alone with her— to go over her things before any one else comes. I know it is what she would have wished."

Selden was hardly conscious of what she said. He stood

looking down on the sleeping face which seemed to lie like a delicate impalpable mask over the living lineaments he had known. He felt that the real Lily was still there, close to him, yet invisible and inaccessible; and the tenuity of the barrier between them mocked him with a sense of helplessness. There had never been more than a little impalpable barrier between them—and yet he had suffered it to keep them apart! And now, though it seemed slighter and frailer than ever, it had suddenly hardened to adamant, and he might beat his life out against it in vain.

He had dropped on his knees beside the bed, but a touch from Gerty aroused him. He stood up, and as their eyes met he was struck by the extraordinary light in his cousin's face.

"You understand what the doctor has gone for? He has promised that there shall be no trouble—but of course the formalities must be gone through. And I asked him to give us time to look through her things first——"

He nodded, and she glanced about the small bare room. "It won't take long," she concluded.

"No—it won't take long," he agreed.

She held his hand in hers a moment longer, and then, with a last look at the bed, moved silently toward the door. On the threshold she paused to add: "You will find me downstairs if you want me."

Selden roused himself to detain her. "But why are you going? She would have wished——"

Gerty shook her head with a smile. "No: this is what she would have wished——" and as she spoke a light broke through Selden's stony misery, and he saw deep into the hidden things of love.

The door closed on Gerty, and he stood alone with the motionless sleeper on the bed. His impulse was to return to her side, to fall on his knees, and rest his throbbing head against the peaceful cheek on the pillow. They had never been at peace together, they two; and now he felt himself drawn downward into the strange mysterious depths of her tranquillity.

But he remembered Gerty's warning words—he knew that, though time had ceased in this room, its feet were hastening relentlessly toward the door. Gerty had given him this supreme half-hour, and he must use it as she willed.

He turned and looked about him, sternly compelling himself to regain his consciousness of outward things. There was very little furniture in the room. The shabby chest of drawers was spread with a lace cover, and set out with a few gold-topped boxes and bottles, a rose-coloured pin-cushion, a glass tray strewn with tortoise-shell hair-pins—he shrank from the poignant intimacy of these trifles, and from the blank surface of the toilet-mirror above them.

These were the only traces of luxury, of that clinging to the minute observance of personal seemliness, which showed what her other renunciations must have cost. There was no other token of her personality about the room, unless it showed itself in the scrupulous neatness of the scant articles of furniture: a washing-stand, two chairs, a small writing-desk, and the little table near the bed. On this table stood the empty bottle and glass, and from these also he averted his eyes.

The desk was closed, but on its slanting lid lay two letters which he took up. One bore the address of a bank, and as it was stamped and sealed, Selden, after a moment's hesitation, laid it aside. On the other letter he read Gus Trenor's name; and the flap of the envelope was still ungummed.

Temptation leapt on him like the stab of a knife. He staggered under it, steadying himself against the desk. Why had she been writing to Trenor—writing, presumably, just after their parting of the previous evening? The thought unhallowed the memory of that last hour, made a mock of the word he had come to speak, and defiled even the reconciling silence upon which it fell. He felt himself flung back on all the ugly uncertainties from which he thought he had cast loose forever. After all, what did he know of her life? Only as much as she had chosen to show him, and measured by the world's estimate, how little that was! By what right—the letter in his hand seemed to ask—by what right was it he who now passed into her confidence through the gate which death had left unbarred? His heart cried out that it was by right of their last hour together, the hour when she herself had placed the key in his hand. Yes—but what if the letter to Trenor had been written afterward?

He put it from him with sudden loathing, and setting his lips, addressed himself resolutely to what remained of his task. After all, that task would be easier to perform, now that his personal stake in it was annulled.

He raised the lid of the desk, and saw within it a cheque-book and a few packets of bills and letters, arranged with the orderly precision which characterized all her personal habits. He looked through the letters first, because it was the most difficult part of the work. They proved to be few and unimportant, but among them he found, with a strange commotion of the heart, the note he had written her the day after the Brys' entertainment.

"When may I come to you?"—his words overwhelmed him with a realization of the cowardice which had driven him from her at the very moment of attainment. Yes—he had always feared his fate, and he was too honest to disown his cowardice now; for had not all his old doubts started to life again at the mere sight of Trenor's name?

He laid the note in his card-case, folding it away carefully, as something made precious by the fact that she had held it so; then, growing once more aware of the lapse of time, he continued his examination of the papers.

To his surprise, he found that all the bills were receipted; there was not an unpaid account among them. He opened the cheque-book, and saw that, the very night before, a cheque of ten thousand dollars from Mrs. Peniston's executors had been entered in it. The legacy, then, had been paid sooner than Gerty had led him to expect. But, turning another page or two, he discovered with astonishment that, in spite of this recent accession of funds, the balance had already declined to a few dollars. A rapid glance at the stubs of the last cheques, all of which bore the date of the previous day, showed that between four or five hundred dollars of the legacy had been spent in the settlement of bills, while the remaining thousands were comprehended in one cheque, made out, at the same time, to Charles Augustus Trenor.

Selden laid the book aside, and sank into the chair beside the desk. He leaned his elbows on it, and hid his face in his hands. The bitter waters of life surged high about him, their sterile taste was on his lips. Did the cheque to Trenor explain the mystery or deepen it? At first his mind refused to act— he felt only the taint of such a transaction between a man like Trenor and a girl like Lily Bart. Then, gradually, his troubled vision cleared, old hints and rumours came back to him, and out of the very insinuations he had feared to probe, he constructed an explanation of the mystery. It was true, then, that she had taken money from Trenor; but true also, as the contents of the little desk declared, that the obligation had been intolerable to her, and that at the first opportunity she had freed herself from it, though the act left her face to face with bare unmitigated poverty.

That was all he knew—all he could hope to unravel of the story. The mute lips on the pillow refused him more than this—unless indeed they had told him the rest in the kiss they had left upon his forehead. Yes, he could now read into that farewell all that his heart craved to find there; he could even draw from it courage not to accuse himself for having failed to reach the height of his opportunity.

He saw that all the conditions of life had conspired to keep them apart; since his very detachment from the external influences which swayed her had increased his spiritual fastidiousness, and made it more difficult for him to live and love uncritically. But at least he *had* loved her—had been willing to stake his future on his faith in her—and if the moment had been fated to pass from them before they could seize it, he saw now that, for both, it had been saved whole out of the ruin of their lives.

It was this moment of love, this fleeting victory over themselves, which had kept them from atrophy and extinction; which, in her, had reached out to him in every struggle against the influence of her surroundings, and in him, had kept alive the faith that now drew him penitent and reconciled to her side.

He knelt by the bed and bent over her, draining their last moment to its lees; and in the silence there passed between them the word which made all clear.

THE END

THE REEF

I

"UNEXPECTED obstacle. Please don't come till thirtieth. Anna."

All the way from Charing Cross to Dover the train had hammered the words of the telegram into George Darrow's ears, ringing every change of irony on its commonplace syllables: rattling them out like a discharge of musketry, letting them, one by one, drip slowly and coldly into his brain, or shaking, tossing, transposing them like the dice in some game of the gods of malice; and now, as he emerged from his compartment at the pier, and stood facing the wind-swept platform and the angry sea beyond, they leapt out at him as if from the crest of the waves, stung and blinded him with a fresh fury of derision.

"Unexpected obstacle. Please don't come till thirtieth. Anna."

She had put him off at the very last moment, and for the second time: put him off with all her sweet reasonableness, and for one of her usual "good" reasons—he was certain that this reason, like the other, (the visit of her husband's uncle's widow) would be "good"! But it was that very certainty which chilled him. The fact of her dealing so reasonably with their case shed an ironic light on the idea that there had been any exceptional warmth in the greeting she had given him after their twelve years apart.

They had found each other again, in London, some three months previously, at a dinner at the American Embassy, and when she had caught sight of him her smile had been like a red rose pinned on her widow's mourning. He still felt the throb of surprise with which, among the stereotyped faces of the season's diners, he had come upon her unexpected face, with the dark hair banded above grave eyes; eyes in which he had recognized every little curve and shadow as he would have recognized, after half a life-time, the details of a room he had played in as a child. And as, in the plumed starred crowd, she had stood out for him, slender, secluded and different, so he had felt, the instant their glances met, that he as

sharply detached himself for her. All that and more her smile
had said; had said not merely "I remember," but "I remember
just what you remember"; almost, indeed, as though her
memory had aided his, her glance flung back on their recap-
tured moment its morning brightness. Certainly, when their
distracted Ambassadress—with the cry: "Oh, you know Mrs.
Leath? That's perfect, for General Farnham has failed me"—
had waved them together for the march to the dining-room,
Darrow had felt a slight pressure of the arm on his, a pressure
faintly but unmistakably emphasizing the exclamation: "Isn't
it wonderful?—In London—in the season—in a mob?"

Little enough, on the part of most women; but it was a
sign of Mrs. Leath's quality that every movement, every syllable, told with her. Even in the old days, as an intent grave-
eyed girl, she had seldom misplaced her light strokes; and
Darrow, on meeting her again, had immediately felt how
much finer and surer an instrument of expression she had
become.

Their evening together had been a long confirmation of
this feeling. She had talked to him, shyly yet frankly, of what
had happened to her during the years when they had so
strangely failed to meet. She had told him of her marriage to
Fraser Leath, and of her subsequent life in France, where her
husband's mother, left a widow in his youth, had been re-
married to the Marquis de Chantelle, and where, partly in
consequence of this second union, the son had permanently
settled himself. She had spoken also, with an intense eagerness of affection, of her little girl Effie, who was now nine
years old, and, in a strain hardly less tender, of Owen Leath,
the charming clever young step-son whom her husband's
death had left to her care . . .

A porter, stumbling against Darrow's bags, roused him to
the fact that he still obstructed the platform, inert and encumbering as his luggage.

"Crossing, sir?"

Was he crossing? He really didn't know; but for lack of any
more compelling impulse he followed the porter to the luggage van, singled out his property, and turned to march behind it down the gang-way. As the fierce wind shouldered

him, building up a crystal wall against his efforts, he felt anew the derision of his case.

"Nasty weather to cross, sir," the porter threw back at him as they beat their way down the narrow walk to the pier. Nasty weather, indeed; but luckily, as it had turned out, there was no earthly reason why Darrow should cross.

While he pushed on in the wake of his luggage his thoughts slipped back into the old groove. He had once or twice run across the man whom Anna Summers had preferred to him, and since he had met her again he had been exercising his imagination on the picture of what her married life must have been. Her husband had struck him as a characteristic specimen of the kind of American as to whom one is not quite clear whether he lives in Europe in order to cultivate an art, or cultivates an art as a pretext for living in Europe. Mr. Leath's art was water-colour painting, but he practised it furtively, almost clandestinely, with the disdain of a man of the world for anything bordering on the professional, while he devoted himself more openly, and with religious seriousness, to the collection of enamelled snuff-boxes. He was blond and well-dressed, with the physical distinction that comes from having a straight figure, a thin nose, and the habit of looking slightly disgusted—as who should not, in a world where authentic snuff-boxes were growing daily harder to find, and the market was flooded with flagrant forgeries?

Darrow had often wondered what possibilities of communion there could have been between Mr. Leath and his wife. Now he concluded that there had probably been none. Mrs. Leath's words gave no hint of her husband's having failed to justify her choice; but her very reticence betrayed her. She spoke of him with a kind of impersonal seriousness, as if he had been a character in a novel or a figure in history; and what she said sounded as though it had been learned by heart and slightly dulled by repetition. This fact immensely increased Darrow's impression that his meeting with her had annihilated the intervening years. She, who was always so elusive and inaccessible, had grown suddenly communicative and kind: had opened the doors of her past, and tacitly left him to draw his own conclusions. As a result, he had taken leave of her with the sense that he was a being singled out and privileged, to whom she had entrusted something precious to keep. It was her happiness in their meeting that she had given him, had frankly left him to do with as he willed; and the frankness of the gesture doubled the beauty of the gift.

Their next meeting had prolonged and deepened the impression. They had found each other again, a few days later, in an old country house full of books and pictures, in the soft landscape of southern England. The presence of a large party, with all its aimless and agitated displacements, had served only to isolate the pair and give them (at least to the young man's fancy) a deeper feeling of communion, and their days there had been like some musical prelude, where the instruments, breathing low, seem to hold back the waves of sound that press against them.

Mrs. Leath, on this occasion, was no less kind than before; but she contrived to make him understand that what was so inevitably coming was not to come too soon. It was not that she showed any hesitation as to the issue, but rather that she seemed to wish not to miss any stage in the gradual reflowering of their intimacy.

Darrow, for his part, was content to wait if she wished it. He remembered that once, in America, when she was a girl, and he had gone to stay with her family in the country, she had been out when he arrived, and her mother had told him to look for her in the garden. She was not in the garden, but beyond it he had seen her approaching down a long shady path. Without hastening her step she had smiled and signed to him to wait; and charmed by the lights and shadows that played upon her as she moved, and by the pleasure of watching her slow advance toward him, he had obeyed her and stood still. And so she seemed now to be walking to him down the years, the light and shade of old memories and new hopes playing variously on her, and each step giving him the vision of a different grace. She did not waver or turn aside; he knew she would come straight to where he stood; but something in her eyes said "Wait", and again he obeyed and waited.

On the fourth day an unexpected event threw out his calculations. Summoned to town by the arrival in England of her husband's mother, she left without giving Darrow the chance he had counted on, and he cursed himself for a dilatory blunderer. Still, his disappointment was tempered by the certainty of being with her again before she left for France; and they did in fact see each other in London. There, however, the atmosphere had changed with the conditions. He could not say that she avoided him, or even that she was a shade less glad to see him; but she was beset by family duties and, as he thought, a little too readily resigned to them.

The Marquise de Chantelle, as Darrow soon perceived, had the same mild formidableness as the late Mr. Leath: a sort of insistent self-effacement before which every one about her gave way. It was perhaps the shadow of this lady's presence—pervasive even during her actual brief eclipses—that subdued and silenced Mrs. Leath. The latter was, moreover, preoccupied about her step-son, who, soon after receiving his degree at Harvard, had been rescued from a stormy love-affair, and finally, after some months of troubled drifting, had yielded to his step-mother's counsel and gone up to Oxford for a year of supplementary study. Thither Mrs. Leath went once or twice to visit him, and her remaining days were packed with family obligations: getting, as she phrased it, "frocks and governesses" for her little girl, who had been left in France, and having to devote the remaining hours to long shopping expeditions with her mother-in-law. Nevertheless, during her brief escapes from duty, Darrow had had time to feel her safe in the custody of his devotion, set apart for some inevitable hour; and the last evening, at the theatre, between the overshadowing Marquise and the unsuspicious Owen, they had had an almost decisive exchange of words.

Now, in the rattle of the wind about his ears, Darrow continued to hear the mocking echo of her message: "Unexpected obstacle." In such an existence as Mrs. Leath's, at once so ordered and so exposed, he knew how small a complication might assume the magnitude of an "obstacle;" yet, even allowing as impartially as his state of mind permitted for the fact that, with her mother-in-law always, and her stepson intermittently, under her roof, her lot involved a hundred small accommodations generally foreign to the freedom of widowhood—even so, he could not but think that the very ingenuity bred of such conditions might have helped her to find a way out of them. No, her "reason", whatever it was, could, in this case, be nothing but a pretext; unless he leaned to the less flattering alternative that any reason seemed good enough for postponing him! Certainly, if her welcome had meant what he imagined, she could not, for the second time within a few weeks, have submitted so tamely to the disarrangement of their plans; a disarrangement which—his official duties considered—might, for all she knew, result in his not being able to go to her for months.

"Please don't come till thirtieth." The thirtieth—and it was now the fifteenth! She flung back the fortnight on his hands as if he had been an idler indifferent to dates, instead of an active young diplomatist who, to respond to her call, had had to hew his way through a very jungle of engagements! "Please don't come till thirtieth." That was all. Not the shadow of an excuse or a regret; not even the perfunctory "have written" with which it is usual to soften such blows. She didn't want him, and had taken the shortest way to tell him so. Even in his first moment of exasperation it struck him as characteristic that she should not have padded her postponement with a fib. Certainly her moral angles were not draped!

"If I asked her to marry me, she'd have refused in the same language. But thank heaven I haven't!" he reflected.

These considerations, which had been with him every yard of the way from London, reached a climax of irony as he was drawn into the crowd on the pier. It did not soften his feelings to remember that, but for her lack of forethought, he might, at this harsh end of the stormy May day, have been sitting before his club fire in London instead of shivering in the damp human herd on the pier. Admitting the sex's traditional right to change, she might at least have advised him of hers by telegraphing directly to his rooms. But in spite of their exchange of letters she had apparently failed to note his address, and a breathless emissary had rushed from the Embassy to pitch her telegram into his compartment as the train was moving from the station.

Yes, he had given her chance enough to learn where he lived; and this minor proof of her indifference became, as he jammed his way through the crowd, the main point of his grievance against her and of his derision of himself. Half way down the pier the prod of an umbrella increased his exasperation by rousing him to the fact that it was raining. Instantly the narrow ledge became a battle-ground of thrusting, slanting, parrying domes. The wind rose with the rain, and the harried wretches exposed to this double assault wreaked on their neighbours the vengeance they could not take on the elements.

Darrow, whose healthy enjoyment of life made him in general a good traveller, tolerant of agglutinated humanity, felt himself obscurely outraged by these promiscuous contacts. It was as though all the people about him had taken his measure and known his plight; as though they were contemptuously bumping and shoving him like the inconsiderable thing he had become. "She doesn't want you, doesn't want you, doesn't want you," their umbrellas and their elbows seemed to say.

He had rashly vowed, when the telegram was flung into his window: "At any rate I won't turn back"—as though it might cause the sender a malicious joy to have him retrace his steps rather than keep on to Paris! Now he perceived the absurdity of the vow, and thanked his stars that he need not plunge, to no purpose, into the fury of waves outside the harbour.

With this thought in his mind he turned back to look for his porter; but the contiguity of dripping umbrellas made signalling impossible and, perceiving that he had lost sight of the man, he scrambled up again to the platform. As he reached it, a descending umbrella caught him in the collarbone; and the next moment, bent sideways by the wind, it turned inside out and soared up, kite-wise, at the end of a helpless female arm.

Darrow caught the umbrella, lowered its inverted ribs, and looked up at the face it exposed to him.

"Wait a minute," he said; "you can't stay here."

As he spoke, a surge of the crowd drove the owner of the umbrella abruptly down on him. Darrow steadied her with extended arms, and regaining her footing she cried out: "Oh, dear, oh, dear! It's in ribbons!"

Her lifted face, fresh and flushed in the driving rain, woke in him a memory of having seen it at a distant time and in a vaguely unsympathetic setting; but it was no moment to follow up such clues, and the face was obviously one to make its way on its own merits.

Its possessor had dropped her bag and bundles to clutch at the tattered umbrella. "I bought it only yesterday at the Stores; and—yes—it's utterly done for!" she lamented.

Darrow smiled at the intensity of her distress. It was food for the moralist that, side by side with such catastrophes as his, human nature was still agitating itself over its microscopic woes!

"Here's mine if you want it!" he shouted back at her through the shouting of the gale.

The offer caused the young lady to look at him more intently. "Why, it's Mr. Darrow!" she exclaimed; and then, all radiant recognition: "Oh, thank you! We'll share it, if you will."

She knew him, then; and he knew her; but how and where had they met? He put aside the problem for subsequent solution, and drawing her into a more sheltered corner, bade her wait till he could find his porter.

When, a few minutes later, he came back with his recovered property, and the news that the boat would not leave till the tide had turned, she showed no concern.

"Not for two hours? How lucky—then I can find my trunk!"

Ordinarily Darrow would have felt little disposed to involve himself in the adventure of a young female who had lost her trunk; but at the moment he was glad of any pretext for activity. Even should he decide to take the next up train from Dover he still had a yawning hour to fill; and the obvious remedy was to devote it to the loveliness in distress under his umbrella.

"You've lost a trunk? Let me see if I can find it."

It pleased him that she did not return the conventional "Oh, *would* you?" Instead, she corrected him with a laugh— "Not *a* trunk, but *my* trunk; I've no other—" and then added briskly: "You'd better first see to getting your own things on the boat."

This made him answer, as if to give substance to his plans by discussing them: "I don't actually know that I'm going over."

"Not going over?"

"Well . . . perhaps not by this boat." Again he felt a stealing indecision. "I may probably have to go back to London. I'm—I'm waiting . . . expecting a letter . . . (She'll think me a defaulter," he reflected.) "But meanwhile there's plenty of time to find your trunk."

He picked up his companion's bundles, and offered her an arm which enabled her to press her slight person more closely under his umbrella; and as, thus linked, they beat their way back to the platform, pulled together and apart like marionettes on the wires of the wind, he continued to wonder where he could have seen her. He had immediately classed her as a compatriot; her small nose, her clear tints, a kind of sketchy delicacy in her face, as though she had been brightly but lightly washed in with water-colour, all confirmed the evidence of her high sweet voice and of her quick incessant gestures. She was clearly an American, but with the loose native quality strained through a closer woof of manners: the composite product of an enquiring and adaptable race. All this, however, did not help him to fit a name to her, for just such instances were perpetually pouring through the London Embassy, and the etched and angular American was becoming rarer than the fluid type.

More puzzling than the fact of his being unable to identify her was the persistent sense connecting her with something uncomfortable and distasteful. So pleasant a vision as that gleaming up at him between wet brown hair and wet brown boa should have evoked only associations as pleasing; but each effort to fit her image into his past resulted in the same memories of boredom and a vague discomfort . . .

"D ON'T YOU remember me now—at Mrs. Murrett's?"

She threw the question at Darrow across a table of the quiet coffee-room to which, after a vainly prolonged quest for her trunk, he had suggested taking her for a cup of tea.

In this musty retreat she had removed her dripping hat, hung it on the fender to dry, and stretched herself on tiptoe in front of the round eagle-crowned mirror, above the mantel vases of dyed immortelles, while she ran her fingers comb-wise through her hair. The gesture had acted on Darrow's numb feelings as the glow of the fire acted on his circulation; and when he had asked: "Aren't your feet wet, too?" and, after frank inspection of a stout-shod sole, she had answered cheerfully: "No—luckily I had on my new boots," he began to feel that human intercourse would still be tolerable if it were always as free from formality.

The removal of his companion's hat, besides provoking this reflection, gave him his first full sight of her face; and this was so favourable that the name she now pronounced fell on him with a quite disproportionate shock of dismay.

"Oh, Mrs. Murrett's—was it *there*?"

He remembered her now, of course: remembered her as one of the shadowy sidling presences in the background of that awful house in Chelsea, one of the dumb appendages of the shrieking unescapable Mrs. Murrett, into whose talons he had fallen in the course of his headlong pursuit of Lady Ulrica Crispin. Oh, the taste of stale follies! How insipid it was, yet how it clung!

"I used to pass you on the stairs," she reminded him.

Yes: he had seen her slip by—he recalled it now—as he dashed up to the drawing-room in quest of Lady Ulrica. The thought made him steal a longer look. How could such a face have been merged in the Murrett mob? Its fugitive slanting lines, that lent themselves to all manner of tender tilts and foreshortenings, had the freakish grace of some young head of the Italian comedy. The hair stood up from her forehead in a boyish elf-lock, and its colour matched her auburn eyes flecked with black, and the little brown spot on her cheek, between the ear that was meant to have a rose behind it and the chin that should have rested on a ruff. When she smiled, the left corner of her mouth went up a little higher than the right; and her smile began in her eyes and ran down to her lips in two lines of light. He had dashed past that to reach Lady Ulrica Crispin!

"But of course you wouldn't remember me," she was saying. "My name is Viner—Sophy Viner."

Not remember her? But of course he *did*! He was genuinely sure of it now. "You're Mrs. Murrett's niece," he declared.

She shook her head. "No; not even that. Only her reader."

"Her reader? Do you mean to say she ever reads?"

Miss Viner enjoyed his wonder. "Dear, no! But I wrote notes, and made up the visiting-book, and walked the dogs, and saw bores for her."

Darrow groaned. "That must have been rather bad!"

"Yes; but nothing like as bad as being her niece."

"That I can well believe. I'm glad to hear," he added, "that you put it all in the past tense."

She seemed to droop a little at the allusion; then she lifted her chin with a jerk of defiance. "Yes. All is at an end between us. We've just parted in tears—but not in silence!"

"Just parted? Do you mean to say you've been there all this time?"

"Ever since you used to come there to see Lady Ulrica? Does it seem to you so awfully long ago?"

The unexpectedness of the thrust—as well as its doubtful taste—chilled his growing enjoyment of her chatter. He had really been getting to like her—had recovered, under the candid approval of her eye, his usual sense of being a personable young man, with all the privileges pertaining to the state, instead of the anonymous rag of humanity he had felt himself in the crowd on the pier. It annoyed him, at that particular moment, to be reminded that naturalness is not always consonant with taste.

She seemed to guess his thought. "You don't like my saying that you came for Lady Ulrica?" she asked, leaning over the table to pour herself a second cup of tea.

He liked her quickness, at any rate. "It's better," he laughed, "than your thinking I came for Mrs. Murrett!"

"Oh, we never thought anybody came for Mrs. Murrett! It was always for something else: the music, or the cook—when there was a good one—or the other people; generally *one* of the other people."

"I see."

She was amusing, and that, in his present mood, was more to his purpose than the exact shade of her taste. It was odd, too, to discover suddenly that the blurred tapestry of Mrs. Murrett's background had all the while been alive and full of eyes. Now, with a pair of them looking into his, he was conscious of a queer reversal of perspective.

"Who were the ' we'? Were you a cloud of witnesses?"

"There were a good many of us." She smiled. "Let me see—who was there in your time? Mrs. Bolt—and Mademoiselle—and Professor Didymus and the Polish Countess. Don't you remember the Polish Countess? She crystal-gazed, and played accompaniments, and Mrs. Murrett chucked her because Mrs. Didymus accused her of hypnotizing the Professor. But of course you don't remember. We were all invisible to you; but we could see. And we all used to wonder about you——"

Again Darrow felt a redness in the temples. "What about me?"

"Well—whether it was *you* or she who . . ."

He winced, but hid his disapproval. It made the time pass to listen to her.

"And what, if one may ask, was your conclusion?"

"Well, Mrs. Bolt and Mademoiselle and the Countess naturally thought it was *she*; but Professor Didymus and Jimmy Brance—especially Jimmy——"

"Just a moment: who on earth is Jimmy Brance?"

She exclaimed in wonder: "You *were* absorbed—not to remember Jimmy Brance! He must have been right about you, after all." She let her amused scrutiny dwell on him. "But how *could* you? She was false from head to foot!"

"False——?" In spite of time and satiety, the male instinct of ownership rose up and repudiated the charge.

Miss Viner caught his look and laughed. "Oh, I only meant externally! You see, she often used to come to my room after tennis, or to touch up in the evenings, when they were going on; and I assure you she took apart like a puzzle. In fact I used to say to Jimmy—just to make him wild—: 'I'll bet you anything you like there's nothing wrong, because I know she'd never dare un—'" She broke the word in two, and her quick blush made her face like a shallow-petalled rose shading to the deeper pink of the centre.

The situation was saved, for Darrow, by an abrupt rush of memories, and he gave way to a mirth which she as frankly echoed. "Of course," she gasped through her laughter, "I only said it to tease Jimmy——"

Her amusement obscurely annoyed him. "Oh, you're all alike!" he exclaimed, moved by an unaccountable sense of disappointment.

She caught him up in a flash—she didn't miss things! "You say that because you think I'm spiteful and envious? Yes—I *was* envious of Lady Ulrica . . . Oh, not on account of you or Jimmy Brance! Simply because she had almost all the things I've always wanted: clothes and fun and motors, and admiration and yachting and Paris—why, Paris alone would be enough!— And how do you suppose a girl can see that sort of thing about her day after day, and never wonder why some women, who don't seem to have any more right to it, have it all tumbled into their laps, while others are writing dinner invitations, and straightening out accounts, and copying visiting lists, and finishing golf-stockings, and matching ribbons, and seeing that the dogs get their sulphur? One looks in one's glass, after all!"

She launched the closing words at him on a cry that lifted them above the petulance of vanity; but his sense of her words was lost in the surprise of her face. Under the flying clouds of her excitement it was no longer a shallow flower-cup but a darkening gleaming mirror that might give back strange depths of feeling. The girl had stuff in her—he saw it; and she seemed to catch the perception in his eyes.

"That's the kind of education I got at Mrs. Murrett's—and I never had any other," she said with a shrug.

"Good Lord—were you there so long?"

"Five years. I stuck it out longer than any of the others." She spoke as though it were something to be proud of.

"Well, thank God you're out of it now!"

Again a just perceptible shadow crossed her face. "Yes—I'm out of it now fast enough."

"And what—if I may ask—are you doing next?"

She brooded a moment behind drooped lids; then, with a touch of hauteur: "I'm going to Paris: to study for the stage."

"The stage?" Darrow stared at her, dismayed. All his confused contradictory impressions assumed a new aspect at this announcement; and to hide his surprise he added lightly: "Ah—then you *will* have Paris, after all!"

"Hardly Lady Ulrica's Paris. It's not likely to be roses, roses all the way."

"It's not, indeed." Real compassion prompted him to continue: "Have you any—any influence you can count on?"

She gave a somewhat flippant little laugh. "None but my own. I've never had any other to count on."

He passed over the obvious reply. "But have you any idea how the profession is over-crowded? I know I'm trite——"

"I've a very clear idea. But I couldn't go on as I was."

"Of course not. But since, as you say, you'd stuck it out longer than any of the others, couldn't you at least have held on till you were sure of some kind of an opening?"

She made no reply for a moment; then she turned a listless glance to the rain-beaten window. "Oughtn't we be starting?" she asked, with a lofty assumption of indifference that might have been Lady Ulrica's.

Darrow, surprised by the change, but accepting her rebuff as a phase of what he guessed to be a confused and tormented mood, rose from his seat and lifted her jacket from the chairback on which she had hung it to dry. As he held it toward her she looked up at him quickly.

"The truth is, we quarrelled," she broke out, "and I left last night without my dinner—and without my salary."

"Ah—" he groaned, with a sharp perception of all the sordid dangers that might attend such a break with Mrs. Murrett.

"And without a character!" she added, as she slipped her arms into the jacket. "And without a trunk, as it appears—but didn't you say that, before going, there'd be time for another look at the station?"

There was time for another look at the station; but the look again resulted in disappointment, since her trunk was nowhere to be found in the huge heap disgorged by the newly-arrived London express. The fact caused Miss Viner a moment's perturbation; but she promptly adjusted herself to the necessity of proceeding on her journey, and her decision confirmed Darrow's vague resolve to go to Paris instead of retracing his way to London.

Miss Viner seemed cheered at the prospect of his company, and sustained by his offer to telegraph to Charing Cross for the missing trunk; and he left her to wait in the fly while he hastened back to the telegraph office. The enquiry despatched, he was turning away from the desk when another thought struck him and he went back and indited a message to his servant in London: "If any letters with French postmark received since departure forward immediately to Terminus Hotel Gare du Nord Paris."

Then he rejoined Miss Viner, and they drove off through the rain to the pier.

III

ALMOST AS soon as the train left Calais her head had dropped back into the corner, and she had fallen asleep.

Sitting opposite, in the compartment from which he had contrived to have other travellers excluded, Darrow looked at her curiously. He had never seen a face that changed so quickly. A moment since it had danced like a field of daisies in a summer breeze; now, under the pallid oscillating light of the lamp overhead, it wore the hard stamp of experience, as of a soft thing chilled into shape before its curves had rounded: and it moved him to see that care already stole upon her when she slept.

The story she had imparted to him in the wheezing shaking cabin, and at the Calais buffet—where he had insisted on offering her the dinner she had missed at Mrs. Murrett's—had given a distincter outline to her figure. From the moment of entering the New York boarding-school to which a preoccupied guardian had hastily consigned her after the death of her parents, she had found herself alone in a busy and indifferent world. Her youthful history might, in fact, have been summed up in the statement that everybody had been too busy to look after her. Her guardian, a drudge in a big banking house, was absorbed by "the office"; the guardian's wife, by her health and her religion; and an elder sister, Laura, married, unmarried, remarried, and pursuing, through all these alternating phases, some vaguely "artistic" ideal on which the guardian and his wife looked askance, had (as Darrow conjectured) taken their disapproval as a pretext for not troubling herself about poor Sophy, to whom—perhaps for this reason—she had remained the incarnation of remote romantic possibilities.

In the course of time a sudden "stroke" of the guardian's had thrown his personal affairs into a state of confusion from which—after his widely lamented death—it became evident that it would not be possible to extricate his ward's inheritance. No one deplored this more sincerely than his widow, who saw in it one more proof of her husband's life having been sacrificed to the innumerable duties imposed on him,

and who could hardly—but for the counsels of religion—
have brought herself to pardon the young girl for her indirect
share in hastening his end. Sophy did not resent this point of
view. She was really much sorrier for her guardian's death
than for the loss of her insignificant fortune. The latter had
represented only the means of holding her in bondage, and
its disappearance was the occasion of her immediate plunge
into the wide bright sea of life surrounding the island of her
captivity. She had first landed—thanks to the intervention of
the ladies who had directed her education—in a Fifth Avenue
school-room where, for a few months, she acted as a buffer
between three autocratic infants and their bodyguard of
nurses and teachers. The too-pressing attentions of their father's valet had caused her to fly this sheltered spot, against
the express advice of her educational superiors, who implied
that, in their own case, refinement and self-respect had always
sufficed to keep the most ungovernable passions at bay. The
experience of the guardian's widow having been precisely similar, and the deplorable precedent of Laura's career being
present to all their minds, none of these ladies felt any obligation to intervene farther in Sophy's affairs; and she was
accordingly left to her own resources.

A schoolmate from the Rocky Mountains, who was taking
her father and mother to Europe, had suggested Sophy's accompanying them, and "going round" with her while her
progenitors, in the care of the courier, nursed their ailments
at a fashionable bath. Darrow gathered that the "going
round" with Mamie Hoke was a varied and diverting process;
but this relatively brilliant phase of Sophy's career was cut
short by the elopement of the inconsiderate Mamie with a
"matinée idol" who had followed her from New York, and by
the precipitate return of her parents to negotiate for the re-
purchase of their child.

It was then—after an interval of repose with compassionate but impecunious American friends in Paris—that Miss
Viner had been drawn into the turbid current of Mrs. Murrett's career. The impecunious compatriots had found Mrs.
Murrett for her, and it was partly on their account (because
they were such dears, and so unconscious, poor confiding
things, of what they were letting her in for) that Sophy had

stuck it out so long in the dreadful house in Chelsea. The Farlows, she explained to Darrow, were the best friends she had ever had (and the only ones who had ever "been decent" about Laura, whom they had seen once, and intensely admired); but even after twenty years of Paris they were the most incorrigibly inexperienced angels, and quite persuaded that Mrs. Murrett was a woman of great intellectual eminence, and the house at Chelsea "the last of the *salons*"— Darrow knew what she meant? And she hadn't liked to undeceive them, knowing that to do so would be virtually to throw herself back on their hands, and feeling, moreover, after her previous experiences, the urgent need of gaining, at any cost, a name for stability; besides which—she threw it off with a slight laugh—no other chance, in all these years, had happened to come to her.

She had brushed in this outline of her career with light rapid strokes, and in a tone of fatalism oddly untinged by bitterness. Darrow perceived that she classified people according to their greater or less "luck" in life, but she appeared to harbour no resentment against the undefined power which dispensed the gift in such unequal measure. Things came one's way or they didn't; and meanwhile one could only look on, and make the most of small compensations, such as watching "the show" at Mrs. Murrett's, and talking over the Lady Ulricas and other footlight figures. And at any moment, of course, a turn of the kaleidoscope might suddenly toss a bright spangle into the grey pattern of one's days.

This light-hearted philosophy was not without charm to a young man accustomed to more traditional views. George Darrow had had a fairly varied experience of feminine types, but the women he had frequented had either been pronouncedly "ladies" or they had not. Grateful to both for ministering to the more complex masculine nature, and disposed to assume that they had been evolved, if not designed, to that end, he had instinctively kept the two groups apart in his mind, avoiding that intermediate society which attempts to conciliate both theories of life. "Bohemianism" seemed to him a cheaper convention than the other two, and he liked, above all, people who went as far as they could in their own line—liked his "ladies" and their rivals to be equally un-

ashamed of showing for exactly what they were. He had not
indeed—the fact of Lady Ulrica was there to remind him—
been without his experience of a third type; but that experience had left him with a contemptuous distaste for the
woman who uses the privileges of one class to shelter the
customs of another.

As to young girls, he had never thought much about them
since his early love for the girl who had become Mrs. Leath.
That episode seemed, as he looked back on it, to bear no
more relation to reality than a pale decorative design to the
confused richness of a summer landscape. He no longer understood the violent impulses and dreamy pauses of his own
young heart, or the inscrutable abandonments and reluctances
of hers. He had known a moment of anguish at losing her—
the mad plunge of youthful instincts against the barrier of
fate; but the first wave of stronger sensation had swept away
all but the outline of their story, and the memory of Anna
Summers had made the image of the young girl sacred, but
the class uninteresting.

Such generalisations belonged, however, to an earlier stage
of his experience. The more he saw of life the more incalculable he found it; and he had learned to yield to his impressions without feeling the youthful need of relating them to
others. It was the girl in the opposite seat who had roused in
him the dormant habit of comparison. She was distinguished
from the daughters of wealth by her avowed acquaintance
with the real business of living, a familiarity as different as
possible from their theoretical proficiency; yet it seemed to
Darrow that her experience had made her free without hardness and self-assured without assertiveness.

The rush into Amiens, and the flash of the station lights
into their compartment, broke Miss Viner's sleep, and without changing her position she lifted her lids and looked at
Darrow. There was neither surprise nor bewilderment in the
look. She seemed instantly conscious, not so much of where
she was, as of the fact that she was with him; and that fact
seemed enough to reassure her. She did not even turn her
head to look out; her eyes continued to rest on him with a

vague smile which appeared to light her face from within, while her lips kept their sleepy droop.

Shouts and the hurried tread of travellers came to them through the confusing cross-lights of the platform. A head appeared at the window, and Darrow threw himself forward to defend their solitude; but the intruder was only a train hand going his round of inspection. He passed on, and the lights and cries of the station dropped away, merged in a wider haze and a hollower resonance, as the train gathered itself up with a long shake and rolled out again into the darkness.

Miss Viner's head sank back against the cushion, pushing out a dusky wave of hair above her forehead. The swaying of the train loosened a lock over her ear, and she shook it back with a movement like a boy's, while her gaze still rested on her companion.

"You're not too tired?"

She shook her head with a smile.

"We shall be in before midnight. We're very nearly on time." He verified the statement by holding up his watch to the lamp.

She nodded dreamily. "It's all right. I telegraphed Mrs. Farlow that they mustn't think of coming to the station; but they'll have told the *concierge* to look out for me."

"You'll let me drive you there?"

She nodded again, and her eyes closed. It was very pleasant to Darrow that she made no effort to talk or to dissemble her sleepiness. He sat watching her till the upper lashes met and mingled with the lower, and their blent shadow lay on her cheek; then he stood up and drew the curtain over the lamp, drowning the compartment in a bluish twilight.

As he sank back into his seat he thought how differently Anna Summers—or even Anna Leath—would have behaved. She would not have talked too much; she would not have been either restless or embarrassed; but her adaptability, her appropriateness, would not have been nature but "tact." The oddness of the situation would have made sleep impossible, or, if weariness had overcome her for a moment, she would have waked with a start, wondering where she was, and how she had come there, and if her hair were tidy; and nothing short of hairpins and a glass would have restored her self-possession . . .

The reflection set him wondering whether the "sheltered" girl's bringing-up might not unfit her for all subsequent contact with life. How much nearer to it had Mrs. Leath been brought by marriage and motherhood, and the passage of fourteen years? What were all her reticences and evasions but the result of the deadening process of forming a "lady"? The freshness he had marvelled at was like the unnatural whiteness of flowers forced in the dark.

As he looked back at their few days together he saw that their intercourse had been marked, on her part, by the same hesitations and reserves which had chilled their earlier intimacy. Once more they had had their hour together and she had wasted it. As in her girlhood, her eyes had made promises which her lips were afraid to keep. She was still afraid of life, of its ruthlessness, its danger and mystery. She was still the petted little girl who cannot be left alone in the dark . . . His memory flew back to their youthful story, and long-forgotten details took shape before him. How frail and faint the picture was! They seemed, he and she, like the ghostly lovers of the Grecian Urn, forever pursuing without ever clasping each other. To this day he did not quite know what had parted them: the break had been as fortuitous as the fluttering apart of two seed-vessels on a wave of summer air . . .

The very slightness, vagueness, of the memory gave it an added poignancy. He felt the mystic pang of the parent for a child which has just breathed and died. Why had it happened thus, when the least shifting of influences might have made it all so different? If she had been given to him then he would have put warmth in her veins and light in her eyes: would have made her a woman through and through. Musing thus, he had the sense of waste that is the bitterest harvest of experience. A love like his might have given her the divine gift of self-renewal; and now he saw her fated to wane into old age repeating the same gestures, echoing the words she had always heard, and perhaps never guessing that, just outside her glazed and curtained consciousness, life rolled away, a vast blackness starred with lights, like the night landscape beyond the windows of the train.

The engine lowered its speed for the passage through a sleeping station. In the light of the platform lamp Darrow looked across at his companion. Her head had dropped toward one shoulder, and her lips were just far enough apart for the reflection of the upper one to deepen the colour of the other. The jolting of the train had again shaken loose the lock above her ear. It danced on her cheek like the flit of a brown wing over flowers, and Darrow felt an intense desire to lean forward and put it back behind her ear.

IV

As their motor-cab, on the way from the Gare du Nord, turned into the central glitter of the Boulevard, Darrow had bent over to point out an incandescent threshold.

"There!"

Above the doorway, an arch of flame flashed out the name of a great actress, whose closing performances in a play of unusual originality had been the theme of long articles in the Paris papers which Darrow had tossed into their compartment at Calais.

"That's what you must see before you're twenty-four hours older!"

The girl followed his gesture eagerly. She was all awake and alive now, as if the heady rumours of the streets, with their long effervescences of light, had passed into her veins like wine.

"Cerdine? Is that where she acts?" She put her head out of the window, straining back for a glimpse of the sacred threshold. As they flew past it she sank into her seat with a satisfied sigh.

"It's delicious enough just to *know* she's there! I've never seen her, you know. When I was here with Mamie Hoke we never went anywhere but to the music halls, because she couldn't understand any French; and when I came back afterward to the Farlows' I was dead broke, and couldn't afford the play, and neither could they; so the only chance we had was when friends of theirs invited us—and once it was to see a tragedy by a Roumanian lady, and the other time it was for 'L'Ami Fritz' at the Français."

Darrow laughed. "You must do better than that now. 'Le Vertige' is a fine thing, and Cerdine gets some wonderful effects out of it. You must come with me tomorrow evening to see it—with your friends, of course.—That is," he added, "if there's any sort of chance of getting seats."

The flash of a street lamp lit up her radiant face. "Oh, will you really take us? What fun to think that it's tomorrow already!"

It was wonderfully pleasant to be able to give such pleasure. Darrow was not rich, but it was almost impossible for him to picture the state of persons with tastes and perceptions like his own, to whom an evening at the theatre was an unattainable indulgence. There floated through his mind an answer of Mrs. Leath's to his enquiry whether she had seen the play in question. "No. I meant to, of course, but one is so overwhelmed with things in Paris. And then I'm rather sick of Cerdine—one is always being dragged to see her."

That, among the people he frequented, was the usual attitude toward such opportunities. There were too many, they were a nuisance, one had to defend one's self! He even remembered wondering, at the moment, whether to a really fine taste the exceptional thing could ever become indifferent through habit; whether the appetite for beauty was so soon dulled that it could be kept alive only by privation. Here, at any rate, was a fine chance to experiment with such a hunger: he almost wished he might stay on in Paris long enough to take the measure of Miss Viner's receptivity.

She was still dwelling on his promise. "It's too beautiful of you! Oh, don't you *think* you'll be able to get seats?" And then, after a pause of brimming appreciation: "I wonder if you'll think me horrid?—but it may be my only chance; and if you can't get places for us all, wouldn't you perhaps just take *me*? After all, the Farlows may have seen it!"

He had not, of course, thought her horrid, but only the more engaging, for being so natural, and so unashamed of showing the frank greed of her famished youth. "Oh, *you* shall go somehow!" he had gaily promised her; and she had dropped back with a sigh of pleasure as their cab passed into the dimly-lit streets of the Farlows' quarter beyond the Seine . . .

This little passage came back to him the next morning, as he opened his hotel window on the early roar of the Northern Terminus.

The girl was there, in the room next to him. That had been the first point in his waking consciousness. The second was a sense of relief at the obligation imposed on him by this unexpected turn of events. To wake to the necessity of action, to postpone perforce the fruitless contemplation of his private grievance, was cause enough for gratitude, even if the small adventure in which he found himself involved had not, on its own merits, roused an instinctive curiosity to see it through.

When he and his companion, the night before, had reached the Farlows' door in the rue de la Chaise, it was only to find, after repeated assaults on its panels, that the Farlows were no longer there. They had moved away the week before, not only from their apartment but from Paris; and Miss Viner's breach with Mrs. Murrett had been too sudden to permit her letter and telegram to overtake them. Both communications, no doubt, still reposed in a pigeon-hole of the *loge*; but its custodian, when drawn from his lair, sulkily declined to let Miss Viner verify the fact, and only flung out, in return for Darrow's bribe, the statement that the Americans had gone to Joigny.

To pursue them there at that hour was manifestly impossible, and Miss Viner, disturbed but not disconcerted by this new obstacle, had quite simply acceded to Darrow's suggestion that she should return for what remained of the night to the hotel where he had sent his luggage.

The drive back through the dark hush before dawn, with the nocturnal blaze of the Boulevard fading around them like the false lights of a magician's palace, had so played on her impressionability that she seemed to give no farther thought to her own predicament. Darrow noticed that she did not feel the beauty and mystery of the spectacle as much as its pressure of human significance, all its hidden implications of emotion and adventure. As they passed the shadowy colonnade of the Français, remote and temple-like in the paling lights, he felt a clutch on his arm, and heard the cry: "There are things *there* that I want so desperately to see!" and all the way back to the hotel she continued to question him, with shrewd precision and an artless thirst for detail, about the theatrical life of Paris. He was struck afresh, as he listened, by the way in which her naturalness eased the situation of constraint, leaving to it only a pleasant savour of good fellowship. It was the kind of episode that one might, in advance, have characterized as "awkward", yet that was proving, in the event, as much outside such definitions as a sunrise stroll with a dryad in a dew-drenched forest; and Darrow reflected that mankind

would never have needed to invent tact if it had not first invented social complications.

It had been understood, with his good-night to Miss
Viner, that the next morning he was to look up the Joigny
trains, and see her safely to the station; but, while he breakfasted and waited for a time-table, he recalled again her cry of
joy at the prospect of seeing Cerdine. It was certainly a pity,
since that most elusive and incalculable of artists was leaving
the next week for South America, to miss what might be a
last sight of her in her greatest part; and Darrow, having
dressed and made the requisite excerpts from the time-table,
decided to carry the result of his deliberations to his neighbour's door.

It instantly opened at his knock, and she came forth looking as if she had been plunged into some sparkling element
which had curled up all her drooping tendrils and wrapped
her in a shimmer of fresh leaves.

"Well, what do you think of me?" she cried; and with a
hand at her waist she spun about as if to show off some miracle of Parisian dress-making.

"I think the missing trunk has come—and that it was
worth waiting for!"

"You *do* like my dress?"

"I adore it! I always adore new dresses—why, you don't
mean to say it's *not* a new one?"

She laughed out her triumph.

"No, no, no! My trunk hasn't come, and this is only my
old rag of yesterday—but I never knew the trick to fail!"
And, as he stared: "You see," she joyously explained, "I've
always had to dress in all kinds of dreary left-overs, and sometimes, when everybody else was smart and new, it used to
make me awfully miserable. So one day, when Mrs. Murrett
dragged me down unexpectedly to fill a place at dinner, I suddenly thought I'd try spinning around like that, and say to
every one: *'Well, what do you think of me?'* And, do you know,
they were all taken in, including Mrs. Murrett, who didn't
recognize my old turned and dyed rags, and told me afterward it was awfully bad form to dress as if I were somebody
that people would expect to know! And ever since, whenever
I've particularly wanted to look nice, I've just asked people

what they thought of my new frock; and they're always, always taken in!"

She dramatized her explanation so vividly that Darrow felt as if his point were gained.

"Ah, but this confirms your vocation—of course," he cried, "you must see Cerdine!" and, seeing her face fall at this reminder of the change in her prospects, he hastened to set forth his plan. As he did so, he saw how easy it was to explain things to her. She would either accept his suggestion, or she would not: but at least she would waste no time in protestations and objections, or any vain sacrifice to the idols of conformity. The conviction that one could, on any given point, almost predicate this of her, gave him the sense of having advanced far enough in her intimacy to urge his arguments against a hasty pursuit of her friends.

Yes, it would certainly be foolish—she at once agreed—in the case of such dear indefinite angels as the Farlows, to dash off after them without more positive proof that they were established at Joigny, and so established that they could take her in. She owned it was but too probable that they had gone there to "cut down", and might be doing so in quarters too contracted to receive her; and it would be unfair, on that chance, to impose herself on them unannounced. The simplest way of getting farther light on the question would be to go back to the rue de la Chaise, where, at that more conversable hour, the *concierge* might be less chary of detail; and she could decide on her next step in the light of such facts as he imparted.

Point by point, she fell in with the suggestion, recognizing, in the light of their unexplained flight, that the Farlows might indeed be in a situation on which one could not too rashly intrude. Her concern for her friends seemed to have effaced all thought of herself, and this little indication of character gave Darrow a quite disproportionate pleasure. She agreed that it would be well to go at once to the rue de la Chaise, but met his proposal that they should drive by the declaration that it was a " waste" not to walk in Paris; so they set off on foot through the cheerful tumult of the streets.

The walk was long enough for him to learn many things about her. The storm of the previous night had cleared the air, and Paris shone in morning beauty under a sky that was all broad wet washes of white and blue; but Darrow again noticed that her visual sensitiveness was less keen than her feeling for what he was sure the good Farlows—whom he already seemed to know—would have called "the human interest." She seemed hardly conscious of sensations of form and colour, or of any imaginative suggestion, and the spectacle before them—always, in its scenic splendour, so moving to her companion—broke up, under her scrutiny, into a thousand minor points: the things in the shops, the types of character and manner of occupation shown in the passing faces, the street signs, the names of the hotels they passed, the motley brightness of the flower-carts, the identity of the churches and public buildings that caught her eye. But what she liked best, he divined, was the mere fact of being free to walk abroad in the bright air, her tongue rattling on as it pleased, while her feet kept time to the mighty orchestration of the city's sounds. Her delight in the fresh air, in the freedom, light and sparkle of the morning, gave him a sudden insight into her stifled past; nor was it indifferent to him to perceive how much his presence evidently added to her enjoyment. If only as a sympathetic ear, he guessed what he must be worth to her. The girl had been dying for some one to talk to, some one before whom she could unfold and shake out to the light her poor little shut-away emotions. Years of repression were revealed in her sudden burst of confidence; and the pity she inspired made Darrow long to fill her few free hours to the brim.

She had the gift of rapid definition, and his questions as to the life she had led with the Farlows, during the interregnum between the Hoke and Murrett eras, called up before him a queer little corner of Parisian existence. The Farlows themselves—he a painter, she a "magazine writer"—rose before him in all their incorruptible simplicity: an elderly New England couple, with vague yearnings for enfranchisement, who lived in Paris as if it were a Massachusetts suburb, and dwelt hopefully on the "higher side" of the Gallic nature. With equal vividness she set before him the component figures of the circle from which Mrs. Farlow drew the "Inner Glimpses of French Life" appearing over her name in a leading New

England journal: the Roumanian lady who had sent them tickets for her tragedy, an elderly French gentleman who, on the strength of a week's stay at Folkestone, translated English fiction for the provincial press, a lady from Wichita, Kansas, who advocated free love and the abolition of the corset, a clergyman's widow from Torquay who had written an "English Ladies' Guide to Foreign Galleries" and a Russian sculptor who lived on nuts and was "almost certainly" an anarchist. It was this nucleus, and its outer ring of musical, architectural and other American students, which posed successively to Mrs. Farlow's versatile fancy as a centre of "University Life", a "Salon of the Faubourg St. Germain", a group of Parisian "Intellectuals" or a "Cross-section of Montmartre"; but even her faculty for extracting from it the most varied literary effects had not sufficed to create a permanent demand for the "Inner Glimpses", and there were days when—Mr. Farlow's landscapes being equally unmarketable—a temporary withdrawal to the country (subsequently utilized as "Peeps into Château Life") became necessary to the courageous couple.

Five years of Mrs. Murrett's world, while increasing Sophy's tenderness for the Farlows, had left her with few illusions as to their power of advancing her fortunes; and she did not conceal from Darrow that her theatrical projects were of the vaguest. They hung mainly on the problematical goodwill of an ancient comédienne, with whom Mrs. Farlow had a slight acquaintance (extensively utilized in "Stars of the French Footlights" and "Behind the Scenes at the Français"), and who had once, with signs of approval, heard Miss Viner recite the Nuit de Mai.

"But of course I know how much that's worth," the girl broke off, with one of her flashes of shrewdness. "And besides, it isn't likely that a poor old fossil like Mme. Dolle could get anybody to listen to her now, even if she really thought I had talent. But she might introduce me to people; or at least give me a few tips. If I could manage to earn enough to pay for lessons I'd go straight to some of the big people and work with them. I'm rather hoping the Farlows may find me a chance of that kind—an engagement with some American family in Paris who would want to be 'gone

round' with like the Hokes, and who'd leave me time enough
to study."

In the rue de la Chaise they learned little except the exact
address of the Farlows, and the fact that they had sub-let their
flat before leaving. This information obtained, Darrow proposed to Miss Viner that they should stroll along the quays
to a little restaurant looking out on the Seine, and there, over
the *plat du jour*, consider the next step to be taken. The long
walk had given her cheeks a glow indicative of wholesome
hunger, and she made no difficulty about satisfying it in Darrow's company. Regaining the river they walked on in the
direction of Notre Dame, delayed now and again by the
young man's irresistible tendency to linger over the book-
stalls, and by his ever-fresh response to the shifting beauties
of the scene. For two years his eyes had been subdued to the
atmospheric effects of London, to the mysterious fusion of
darkly-piled city and low-lying bituminous sky; and the transparency of the French air, which left the green gardens and
silvery stones so classically clear yet so softly harmonized,
struck him as having a kind of conscious intelligence. Every
line of the architecture, every arch of the bridges, the very
sweep of the strong bright river between them, while contributing to this effect, sent forth each a separate appeal to some
sensitive memory; so that, for Darrow, a walk through the
Paris streets was always like the unrolling of a vast tapestry
from which countless stored fragrances were shaken out.

It was a proof of the richness and multiplicity of the spectacle that it served, without incongruity, for so different a
purpose as the background of Miss Viner's enjoyment. As a
mere drop-scene for her personal adventure it was just as
much in its place as in the evocation of great perspectives of
feeling. For her, as he again perceived when they were seated
at their table in a low window above the Seine, Paris was
"Paris" by virtue of all its entertaining details, its endless ingenuities of pleasantness. Where else, for instance, could one
find the dear little dishes of *hors d'oeuvre*, the symmetrically-
laid anchovies and radishes, the thin golden shells of butter,
or the wood strawberries and brown jars of cream that gave
to their repast the last refinement of rusticity? Hadn't he noticed, she asked, that cooking always expressed the national

character, and that French food was clever and amusing just because the people were? And in private houses, everywhere, how the dishes always resembled the talk—how the very same platitudes seemed to go into people's mouths and come out of them? Couldn't he see just what kind of menu it would make, if a fairy waved a wand and suddenly turned the conversation at a London dinner into joints and puddings? She always thought it a good sign when people liked Irish stew; it meant that they enjoyed changes and surprises, and taking life as it came; and such a beautiful Parisian version of the dish as the *navarin* that was just being set before them was like the very best kind of talk—the kind when one could never tell before-hand just what was going to be said!

Darrow, as he watched her enjoyment of their innocent feast, wondered if her vividness and vivacity were signs of her calling. She was the kind of girl in whom certain people would instantly have recognized the histrionic gift. But experience had led him to think that, except at the creative moment, the divine flame burns low in its possessors. The one or two really intelligent actresses he had known had struck him, in conversation, as either bovine or primitively "jolly". He had a notion that, save in the mind of genius, the creative process absorbs too much of the whole stuff of being to leave much surplus for personal expression; and the girl before him, with her changing face and flexible fancies, seemed destined to work in life itself rather than in any of its counterfeits.

The coffee and liqueurs were already on the table when her mind suddenly sprang back to the Farlows. She jumped up with one of her subversive movements and declared that she must telegraph at once. Darrow called for writing materials, and room was made at her elbow for the parched ink-bottle and saturated blotter of the Parisian restaurant; but the mere sight of these jaded implements seemed to paralyze Miss Viner's faculties. She hung over the telegraph-form with anxiously-drawn brow, the tip of the pen-handle pressed against her lip; and at length she raised her troubled eyes to Darrow's.

"I simply can't think how to say it."

"What—that you're staying over to see Cerdine?"

"But *am* I—am I, really?" The joy of it flamed over her face.

Darrow looked at his watch. "You could hardly get an answer to your telegram in time to take a train to Joigny this afternoon, even if you found your friends could have you."

She mused for a moment, tapping her lip with the pen. "But I must let them know I'm here. I must find out as soon as possible if they *can* have me." She laid the pen down despairingly. "I never *could* write a telegram!" she sighed.

"Try a letter, then, and tell them you'll arrive tomorrow."

This suggestion produced immediate relief, and she gave an energetic dab at the ink-bottle; but after another interval of uncertain scratching she paused again.

"Oh, it's fearful! I don't know what on earth to say. I wouldn't for the world have them know how beastly Mrs. Murrett's been."

Darrow did not think it necessary to answer. It was no business of his, after all. He lit a cigar and leaned back in his seat, letting his eyes take their fill of indolent pleasure. In the throes of invention she had pushed back her hat, loosening the stray lock which had invited his touch the night before. After looking at it for a while he stood up and wandered to the window.

Behind him he heard her pen scrape on.

"I don't want to worry them—I'm so certain they've got bothers of their own." The faltering scratches ceased again. "I wish I weren't such an idiot about writing: all the words get frightened and scurry away when I try to catch them."

He glanced back at her with a smile as she bent above her task like a school-girl struggling with a "composition." Her flushed cheek and frowning brow showed that her difficulty was genuine and not an artless device to draw him to her side. She was really powerless to put her thoughts in writing, and the inability seemed characteristic of her quick impressionable mind, and of the incessant come-and-go of her sensations. He thought of Anna Leath's letters, or rather of the few he had received, years ago, from the girl who had been Anna Summers. He saw the slender firm strokes of the pen, recalled the clear structure of the phrases, and, by an abrupt association of ideas, remembered that, at that very hour, just such a document might be awaiting him at the hotel.

What if it were there, indeed, and had brought him a complete explanation of her telegram? The revulsion of feeling produced by this thought made him look at the girl with sudden impatience. She struck him as positively stupid, and he wondered how he could have wasted half his day with her, when all the while Mrs. Leath's letter might be lying on his table. At that moment, if he could have chosen, he would have left his companion on the spot; but he had her on his hands, and must accept the consequences.

Some odd intuition seemed to make her conscious of his change of mood, for she sprang from her seat, crumpling the letter in her hand.

"I'm too stupid; but I won't keep you any longer. I'll go back to the hotel and write there."

Her colour deepened, and for the first time, as their eyes met, he noticed a faint embarrassment in hers. Could it be that his nearness was, after all, the cause of her confusion? The thought turned his vague impatience with her into a definite resentment toward himself. There was really no excuse for his having blundered into such an adventure. Why had he not shipped the girl off to Joigny by the evening train, instead of urging her to delay, and using Cerdine as a pretext? Paris was full of people he knew, and his annoyance was increased by the thought that some friend of Mrs. Leath's might see him at the play, and report his presence there with a suspiciously good-looking companion. The idea was distinctly disagreeable: he did not want the woman he adored to think he could forget her for a moment. And by this time he had fully persuaded himself that a letter from her was awaiting him, and had even gone so far as to imagine that its contents might annul the writer's telegraphed injunction, and call him to her side at once . . .

V

A T THE PORTER's desk a brief *"Pas de lettres"* fell destructively on the fabric of these hopes.

Mrs. Leath had not written—she had not taken the trouble to explain her telegram. Darrow turned away with a sharp pang of humiliation. Her frugal silence mocked his prodigality of hopes and fears. He had put his question to the porter once before, on returning to the hotel after luncheon; and now, coming back again in the late afternoon, he was met by the same denial. The second post was in, and had brought him nothing.

A glance at his watch showed that he had barely time to dress before taking Miss Viner out to dine; but as he turned to the lift a new thought struck him, and hurrying back into the hall he dashed off another telegram to his servant: "Have you forwarded any letter with French postmark today? Telegraph answer Terminus."

Some kind of reply would be certain to reach him on his return from the theatre, and he would then know definitely whether Mrs. Leath meant to write or not. He hastened up to his room and dressed with a lighter heart.

Miss Viner's vagrant trunk had finally found its way to its owner; and, clad in such modest splendour as it furnished, she shone at Darrow across their restaurant table. In the reaction of his wounded vanity he found her prettier and more interesting than before. Her dress, sloping away from the throat, showed the graceful set of her head on its slender neck, and the wide brim of her hat arched above her hair like a dusky halo. Pleasure danced in her eyes and on her lips, and as she shone on him between the candle-shades Darrow felt that he should not be at all sorry to be seen with her in public. He even sent a careless glance about him in the vague hope that it might fall on an acquaintance.

At the theatre her vivacity sank into a breathless hush, and she sat intent in her corner of their *baignoire*, with the gaze of a neophyte about to be initiated into the sacred mysteries. Darrow placed himself behind her, that he might catch her profile between himself and the stage. He was touched by the youthful seriousness of her expression. In spite of the experiences she must have had, and of the twenty-four years to which she owned, she struck him as intrinsically young; and he wondered how so evanescent a quality could have been preserved in the desiccating Murrett air. As the play progressed he noticed that her immobility was traversed by swift flashes of perception. She was not missing anything, and her intensity of attention when Cerdine was on the stage drew an anxious line between her brows.

After the first act she remained for a few minutes rapt and motionless; then she turned to her companion with a quick patter of questions. He gathered from them that she had been less interested in following the general drift of the play than in observing the details of its interpretation. Every gesture and inflection of the great actress's had been marked and analyzed; and Darrow felt a secret gratification in being appealed to as an authority on the histrionic art. His interest in it had hitherto been merely that of the cultivated young man curious of all forms of artistic expression; but in reply to her questions he found things to say about it which evidently struck his listener as impressive and original, and with which he himself was not, on the whole, dissatisfied. Miss Viner was much more concerned to hear his views than to express her own, and the deference with which she received his comments called from him more ideas about the theatre than he had ever supposed himself to possess.

With the second act she began to give more attention to the development of the play, though her interest was excited rather by what she called "the story" than by the conflict of character producing it. Oddly combined with her sharp apprehension of things theatrical, her knowledge of technical "dodges" and green-room precedents, her glibness about "lines" and "curtains", was the primitive simplicity of her attitude toward the tale itself, as toward something that was "really happening" and at which one assisted as at a street-accident or a quarrel overheard in the next room. She wanted to know if Darrow thought the lovers "really would" be involved in the catastrophe that threatened them, and when he reminded her that his predictions were disqualified by his having already seen the play, she exclaimed: "Oh, then, please don't tell me what's going to happen!" and the next moment was questioning him about Cerdine's theatrical situation and her private history. On the latter point some of her enquiries were of a kind that it is not in the habit of young girls to make, or even to know how to make; but her apparent unconsciousness of the fact seemed rather to reflect on her past associates than on herself.

When the second act was over, Darrow suggested their taking a turn in the *foyer*; and seated on one of its cramped red velvet sofas they watched the crowd surge up and down in a glare of lights and gilding. Then, as she complained of the heat, he led her through the press to the congested *café* at the foot of the stairs, where orangeades were thrust at them between the shoulders of packed *consommateurs*, and Darrow, lighting a cigarette while she sucked her straw, knew the primitive complacency of the man at whose companion other men stare.

On a corner of their table lay a smeared copy of a theatrical journal. It caught Sophy's eye and after poring over the page she looked up with an excited exclamation.

"They're giving *Oedipe* tomorrow afternoon at the Français! I suppose you've seen it heaps and heaps of times?"

He smiled back at her. "You must see it too. We'll go tomorrow."

She sighed at his suggestion, but without discarding it. "How can I? The last train for Joigny leaves at four."

"But you don't know yet that your friends will want you."

"I shall know tomorrow early. I asked Mrs. Farlow to telegraph as soon as she got my letter."

A twinge of compunction shot through Darrow. Her words recalled to him that on their return to the hotel after luncheon she had given him her letter to post, and that he had never thought of it again. No doubt it was still in the pocket of the coat he had taken off when he dressed for dinner. In his perturbation he pushed back his chair, and the movement made her look up at him.

"What's the matter?"

"Nothing. Only—you know I don't fancy that letter can have caught this afternoon's post."

"Not caught it? Why not?"

"Why, I'm afraid it will have been too late." He bent his head to light another cigarette.

She struck her hands together with a gesture which, to his amusement, he noticed she had caught from Cerdine.

"Oh, dear, I hadn't thought of that! But surely it will reach them in the morning?"

"Some time in the morning, I suppose. You know the French provincial post is never in a hurry. I don't believe your letter would have been delivered this evening in any case." As this idea occurred to him he felt himself almost absolved.

"Perhaps, then, I ought to have telegraphed?"

"I'll telegraph for you in the morning if you say so."

The bell announcing the close of the entr'-acte shrilled through the *café*, and she sprang to her feet.

"Oh, come, come! We mustn't miss it!"

Instantly forgetful of the Farlows, she slipped her arm through his and turned to push her way back to the theatre.

As soon as the curtain went up she as promptly forgot her companion. Watching her from the corner to which he had returned, Darrow saw that great waves of sensation were beating deliciously against her brain. It was as though every starved sensibility were throwing out feelers to the mounting tide; as though everything she was seeing, hearing, imagining, rushed in to fill the void of all she had always been denied.

Darrow, as he observed her, again felt a detached enjoyment in her pleasure. She was an extraordinary conductor of sensation: she seemed to transmit it physically, in emanations that set the blood dancing in his veins. He had not often had the opportunity of studying the effects of a perfectly fresh impression on so responsive a temperament, and he felt a fleeting desire to make its chords vibrate for his own amusement.

At the end of the next act she discovered with dismay that in their transit to the *café* she had lost the beautiful pictured programme he had bought for her. She wanted to go back and hunt for it, but Darrow assured her that he would have no trouble in getting her another. When he went out in quest of it she followed him protestingly to the door of the box, and he saw that she was distressed at the thought of his

having to spend an additional franc for her. This frugality
smote Darrow by its contrast to her natural bright profusion;
and again he felt the desire to right so clumsy an injustice.

When he returned to the box she was still standing in the
doorway, and he noticed that his were not the only eyes attracted to her. Then another impression sharply diverted his
attention. Above the fagged faces of the Parisian crowd he
had caught the fresh fair countenance of Owen Leath signalling a joyful recognition.

The young man, slim and eager, had detached himself from
two companions of his own type, and was seeking to push
through the press to his step-mother's friend. The encounter,
to Darrow, could hardly have been more inopportune; it
woke in him a confusion of feelings of which only the uppermost was allayed by seeing Sophy Viner, as if instinctively
warned, melt back into the shadow of their box.

A minute later Owen Leath was at his side. "I was sure it
was you! Such luck to run across you! Won't you come off
with us to supper after it's over? Montmartre, or wherever
else you please. Those two chaps over there are friends of
mine, at the Beaux Arts; both of them rather good fellows—
and we'd be so glad——"

For half a second Darrow read in his hospitable eye the
termination "if you'd bring the lady too"; then it deflected
into: "We'd all be so glad if you'd come."

Darrow, excusing himself with thanks, lingered on for a
few minutes' chat, in which every word, and every tone of his
companion's voice, was like a sharp light flashed into aching
eyes. He was glad when the bell called the audience to their
seats, and young Leath left him with the friendly question:
"We'll see you at Givré later on?"

When he rejoined Miss Viner, Darrow's first care was to
find out, by a rapid inspection of the house, whether Owen
Leath's seat had given him a view of their box. But the young
man was not visible from it, and Darrow concluded that he
had been recognized in the corridor and not at his companion's side. He scarcely knew why it seemed to him so important that this point should be settled; certainly his sense of
reassurance was less due to regard for Miss Viner than to the
persistent vision of grave offended eyes . . .

During the drive back to the hotel this vision was persistently kept before him by the thought that the evening post might have brought a letter from Mrs. Leath. Even if no letter had yet come, his servant might have telegraphed to say that one was on its way; and at the thought his interest in the girl at his side again cooled to the fraternal, the almost fatherly. She was no more to him, after all, than an appealing young creature to whom it was mildly agreeable to have offered an evening's diversion; and when, as they rolled into the illuminated court of the hotel, she turned with a quick movement which brought her happy face close to his, he leaned away, affecting to be absorbed in opening the door of the cab.

At the desk the night porter, after a vain search through the pigeon-holes, was disposed to think that a letter or telegram had in fact been sent up for the gentleman; and Darrow, at the announcement, could hardly wait to ascend to his room. Upstairs, he and his companion had the long dimly-lit corridor to themselves, and Sophy paused on her threshold, gathering up in one hand the pale folds of her cloak, while she held the other out to Darrow.

"If the telegram comes early I shall be off by the first train; so I suppose this is good-bye," she said, her eyes dimmed by a little shadow of regret.

Darrow, with a renewed start of contrition, perceived that he had again forgotten her letter; and as their hands met he vowed to himself that the moment she had left him he would dash down stairs to post it.

"Oh, I'll see you in the morning, of course!"

A tremor of pleasure crossed her face as he stood before her, smiling a little uncertainly.

"At any rate," she said, "I want to thank you now for my good day."

He felt in her hand the same tremor he had seen in her face. "But it's *you*, on the contrary—" he began, lifting the hand to his lips.

As he dropped it, and their eyes met, something passed through hers that was like a light carried rapidly behind a curtained window.

"Good night; you must be awfully tired," he said with a

friendly abruptness, turning away without even waiting to see
her pass into her room. He unlocked his door, and stumbling
over the threshold groped in the darkness for the electric button. The light showed him a telegram on the table, and he
forgot everything else as he caught it up.

"No letter from France," the message read.

It fell from Darrow's hand to the floor, and he dropped
into a chair by the table and sat gazing at the dingy drab and
olive pattern of the carpet. She had not written, then; she had
not written, and it was manifest now that she did not mean
to write. If she had had any intention of explaining her telegram she would certainly, within twenty-four hours, have followed it up by a letter. But she evidently did not intend to
explain it, and her silence could mean only that she had no
explanation to give, or else that she was too indifferent to be
aware that one was needed.

Darrow, face to face with these alternatives, felt a recru-
descence of boyish misery. It was no longer his hurt vanity
that cried out. He told himself that he could have borne an
equal amount of pain, if only it had left Mrs. Leath's image
untouched; but he could not bear to think of her as trivial or
insincere. The thought was so intolerable that he felt a blind
desire to punish some one else for the pain it caused him.

As he sat moodily staring at the carpet its silly intricacies
melted into a blur from which the eyes of Mrs. Leath again
looked out at him. He saw the fine sweep of her brows, and
the deep look beneath them as she had turned from him on
their last evening in London. "This will be good-bye, then,"
she had said; and it occurred to him that her parting phrase
had been the same as Sophy Viner's.

At the thought he jumped to his feet and took down from
its hook the coat in which he had left Miss Viner's letter. The
clock marked the third quarter after midnight, and he knew
it would make no difference if he went down to the post-box
now or early the next morning; but he wanted to clear his
conscience, and having found the letter he went to the door.

A sound in the next room made him pause. He had become
conscious again that, a few feet off, on the other side of a
thin partition, a small keen flame of life was quivering and
agitating the air. Sophy's face came back to him insistently. It

was as vivid now as Mrs. Leath's had been a moment earlier. He recalled with a faint smile of retrospective pleasure the girl's enjoyment of her evening, and the innumerable fine feelers of sensation she had thrown out to its impressions.

It gave him a curiously close sense of her presence to think that at that moment she was living over her enjoyment as intensely as he was living over his unhappiness. His own case was irremediable, but it was easy enough to give her a few more hours of pleasure. And did she not perhaps secretly expect it of him? After all, if she had been very anxious to join her friends she would have telegraphed them on reaching Paris, instead of writing. He wondered now that he had not been struck at the moment by so artless a device to gain more time. The fact of her having practised it did not make him think less well of her; it merely strengthened the impulse to use his opportunity. She was starving, poor child, for a little amusement, a little personal life—why not give her the chance of another day in Paris? If he did so, should he not be merely falling in with her own hopes?

At the thought his sympathy for her revived. She became of absorbing interest to him as an escape from himself and an object about which his thwarted activities could cluster. He felt less drearily alone because of her being there, on the other side of the door, and in his gratitude to her for giving him this relief he began, with indolent amusement, to plan new ways of detaining her. He dropped back into his chair, lit a cigar, and smiled a little at the image of her smiling face. He tried to imagine what incident of the day she was likely to be recalling at that particular moment, and what part he probably played in it. That it was not a small part he was certain, and the knowledge was undeniably pleasant.

Now and then a sound from her room brought before him more vividly the reality of the situation and the strangeness of the vast swarming solitude in which he and she were momentarily isolated, amid long lines of rooms each holding its separate secret. The nearness of all these other mysteries enclosing theirs gave Darrow a more intimate sense of the girl's presence, and through the fumes of his cigar his imagination continued to follow her to and fro, traced the curve of her slim young arms as she raised them to undo her hair, pictured the sliding down of her dress to the waist and then to the knees, and the whiteness of her feet as she slipped across the floor to bed . . .

He stood up and shook himself with a yawn, throwing away the end of his cigar. His glance, in following it, lit on the telegram which had dropped to the floor. The sounds in the next room had ceased, and once more he felt alone and unhappy.

Opening the window, he folded his arms on the sill and looked out on the vast light-spangled mass of the city, and then up at the dark sky, in which the morning planet stood.

VI

AT THE Théâtre Français, the next afternoon, Darrow yawned and fidgeted in his seat.

The day was warm, the theatre crowded and airless, and the performance, it seemed to him, intolerably bad. He stole a glance at his companion, wondering if she shared his feelings. Her rapt profile betrayed no unrest, but politeness might have caused her to feign an interest that she did not feel. He leaned back impatiently, stifling another yawn, and trying to fix his attention on the stage. Great things were going forward there, and he was not insensible to the stern beauties of the ancient drama. But the interpretation of the play seemed to him as airless and lifeless as the atmosphere of the theatre. The players were the same whom he had often applauded in those very parts, and perhaps that fact added to the impression of staleness and conventionality produced by their performance. Surely it was time to infuse new blood into the veins of the moribund art. He had the impression that the ghosts of actors were giving a spectral performance on the shores of Styx.

Certainly it was not the most profitable way for a young man with a pretty companion to pass the golden hours of a spring afternoon. The freshness of the face at his side, reflecting the freshness of the season, suggested dapplings of sunlight through new leaves, the sound of a brook in the grass, the ripple of tree-shadows over breezy meadows . . .

When at length the fateful march of the cothurns was stayed by the single pause in the play, and Darrow had led Miss Viner out on the balcony overhanging the square before the theatre, he turned to see if she shared his feelings. But the rapturous look she gave him checked the depreciation on his lips.

"Oh, why did you bring me out here? One ought to creep away and sit in the dark till it begins again!"

"Is *that* the way they made you feel?"

"Didn't they *you*? . . . As if the gods were there all the while, just behind them, pulling the strings?" Her hands were pressed against the railing, her face shining and darkening under the wing-beats of successive impressions.

Darrow smiled in enjoyment of her pleasure. After all, he *had* felt all that, long ago; perhaps it was his own fault, rather than that of the actors, that the poetry of the play seemed to have evaporated . . . But no, he had been right in judging the performance to be dull and stale: it was simply his companion's inexperience, her lack of occasions to compare and estimate, that made her think it brilliant.

"I was afraid you were bored and wanted to come away."

"*Bored?*" She made a little aggrieved grimace. "You mean you thought me too ignorant and stupid to appreciate it?"

"No; not that." The hand nearest him still lay on the railing of the balcony, and he covered it for a moment with his. As he did so he saw the colour rise and tremble in her cheek.

"Tell me just what you think," he said, bending his head a little, and only half-aware of his words.

She did not turn her face to his, but began to talk rapidly, trying to convey something of what she felt. But she was evidently unused to analyzing her aesthetic emotions, and the tumultuous rush of the drama seemed to have left her in a state of panting wonder, as though it had been a storm or some other natural cataclysm. She had no literary or historic associations to which to attach her impressions: her education had evidently not comprised a course in Greek literature. But she felt what would probably have been unperceived by many a young lady who had taken a first in classics: the ineluctable fatality of the tale, the dread sway in it of the same mysterious "luck" which pulled the threads of her own small destiny. It was not literature to her, it was fact: as actual, as near by, as what was happening to her at the moment and what the next hour held in store. Seen in this light, the play regained for Darrow its supreme and poignant reality. He pierced to the heart of its significance through all the artificial accretions with which his theories of art and the conventions of the stage had clothed it, and saw it as he had never seen it: as life.

After this there could be no question of flight, and he took her back to the theatre, content to receive his own sensations through the medium of hers. But with the continuation of

the play, and the oppression of the heavy air, his attention
again began to wander, straying back over the incidents of
the morning.

He had been with Sophy Viner all day, and he was surprised to find how quickly the time had gone. She had hardly
attempted, as the hours passed, to conceal her satisfaction on
finding that no telegram came from the Farlows. "They'll
have written," she had simply said; and her mind had at once
flown on to the golden prospect of an afternoon at the theatre. The intervening hours had been disposed of in a stroll
through the lively streets, and a repast, luxuriously lingered
over, under the chestnut-boughs of a restaurant in the
Champs Elysées. Everything entertained and interested her,
and Darrow remarked, with an amused detachment, that she
was not insensible to the impression her charms produced.
Yet there was no hard edge of vanity in her sense of her prettiness: she seemed simply to be aware of it as a note in the
general harmony, and to enjoy sounding the note as a singer
enjoys singing.

After luncheon, as they sat over their coffee, she had again
asked an immense number of questions and delivered herself
of a remarkable variety of opinions. Her questions testified to
a wholesome and comprehensive human curiosity, and her
comments showed, like her face and her whole attitude, an
odd mingling of precocious wisdom and disarming ignorance. When she talked to him about "life"—the word was
often on her lips—she seemed to him like a child playing
with a tiger's cub; and he said to himself that some day the
child would grow up—and so would the tiger. Meanwhile,
such expertness qualified by such candour made it impossible
to guess the extent of her personal experience, or to estimate
its effect on her character. She might be any one of a dozen
definable types, or she might—more disconcertingly to her
companion and more perilously to herself—be a shifting and
uncrystallized mixture of them all.

Her talk, as usual, had promptly reverted to the stage. She
was eager to learn about every form of dramatic expression
which the metropolis of things theatrical had to offer, and her
curiosity ranged from the official temples of the art to its less
hallowed haunts. Her searching enquiries about a play whose

production, on one of the latter scenes, had provoked a considerable amount of scandal, led Darrow to throw out laughingly: "To see *that* you'll have to wait till you're married!" and his answer had sent her off at a tangent.

"Oh, I never mean to marry," she had rejoined in a tone of youthful finality.

"I seem to have heard that before!"

"Yes; from girls who've only got to choose!" Her eyes had grown suddenly almost old. "I'd like you to see the only men who've ever wanted to marry me! One was the doctor on the steamer, when I came abroad with the Hokes: he'd been cashiered from the navy for drunkenness. The other was a deaf widower with three grown-up daughters, who kept a clock-shop in Bayswater!—Besides," she rambled on, "I'm not so sure that I believe in marriage. You see I'm all for self-development and the chance to live one's life. I'm awfully modern, you know."

It was just when she proclaimed herself most awfully modern that she struck him as most helplessly backward; yet the moment after, without any bravado, or apparent desire to assume an attitude, she would propound some social axiom which could have been gathered only in the bitter soil of experience.

All these things came back to him as he sat beside her in the theatre and watched her ingenuous absorption. It was on "the story" that her mind was fixed, and in life also, he suspected, it would always be "the story", rather than its remoter imaginative issues, that would hold her. He did not believe there were ever any echoes in her soul . . .

There was no question, however, that what she felt was felt with intensity: to the actual, the immediate, she spread vibrating strings. When the play was over, and they came out once more into the sunlight, Darrow looked down at her with a smile.

"Well?" he asked.

She made no answer. Her dark gaze seemed to rest on him without seeing him. Her cheeks and lips were pale, and the loose hair under her hat-brim clung to her forehead in damp rings. She looked like a young priestess still dazed by the fumes of the cavern.

"You poor child—it's been almost too much for you!"

She shook her head with a vague smile.

"Come," he went on, putting his hand on her arm, "let's jump into a taxi and get some air and sunshine. Look, there are hours of daylight left; and see what a night it's going to be!"

He pointed over their heads, to where a white moon hung in the misty blue above the roofs of the rue de Rivoli.

She made no answer, and he signed to a motor-cab, calling out to the driver: "To the Bois!"

As the carriage turned toward the Tuileries she roused herself. "I must go first to the hotel. There may be a message— at any rate I must decide on something."

Darrow saw that the reality of the situation had suddenly forced itself upon her. "I *must* decide on something," she repeated.

He would have liked to postpone the return, to persuade her to drive directly to the Bois for dinner. It would have been easy enough to remind her that she could not start for Joigny that evening, and that therefore it was of no moment whether she received the Farlows' answer then or a few hours later; but for some reason he hesitated to use this argument, which had come so naturally to him the day before. After all, he knew she would find nothing at the hotel—so what did it matter if they went there?

The porter, interrogated, was not sure. He himself had received nothing for the lady, but in his absence his subordinate might have sent a letter upstairs.

Darrow and Sophy mounted together in the lift, and the young man, while she went into her room, unlocked his own door and glanced at the empty table. For him at least no message had come; and on her threshold, a moment later, she met him with the expected: "No—there's nothing!"

He feigned an unregretful surprise. "So much the better! And now, shall we drive out somewhere? Or would you rather take a boat to Bellevue? Have you ever dined there, on the terrace, by moonlight? It's not at all bad. And there's no earthly use in sitting here waiting."

She stood before him in perplexity.

"But when I wrote yesterday I asked them to telegraph. I

suppose they're horribly hard up, the poor dears, and they thought a letter would do as well as a telegram." The colour had risen to her face. "That's why *I* wrote instead of telegraphing; I haven't a penny to spare myself!"

Nothing she could have said could have filled her listener with a deeper contrition. He felt the red in his own face as he recalled the motive with which he had credited her in his midnight musings. But that motive, after all, had simply been trumped up to justify his own disloyalty: he had never really believed in it. The reflection deepened his confusion, and he would have liked to take her hand in his and confess the injustice he had done her.

She may have interpreted his change of colour as an involuntary protest at being initiated into such shabby details, for she went on with a laugh: "I suppose you can hardly understand what it means to have to stop and think whether one can afford a telegram? But I've always had to consider such things. And I mustn't stay here any longer now—I must try to get a night train for Joigny. Even if the Farlows can't take me in, I can go to the hotel: it will cost less than staying here." She paused again and then exclaimed: "I ought to have thought of that sooner; I ought to have telegraphed yesterday! But I was sure I should hear from them today; and I wanted—oh, I *did* so awfully want to stay!" She threw a troubled look at Darrow. "Do you happen to remember," she asked, " what time it was when you posted my letter?"

VII

DARROW WAS still standing on her threshold. As she put the question he entered the room and closed the door behind him.

His heart was beating a little faster than usual and he had no clear idea of what he was about to do or say, beyond the definite conviction that, whatever passing impulse of expiation moved him, he would not be fool enough to tell her that he had not sent her letter. He knew that most wrongdoing works, on the whole, less mischief than its useless confession; and this was clearly a case where a passing folly might be turned, by avowal, into a serious offense.

"I'm so sorry—so sorry; but you must let me help you . . . You will let me help you?" he said.

He took her hands and pressed them together between his, counting on a friendly touch to help out the insufficiency of words. He felt her yield slightly to his clasp, and hurried on without giving her time to answer.

"Isn't it a pity to spoil our good time together by regretting anything you might have done to prevent our having it?"

She drew back, freeing her hands. Her face, losing its look of appealing confidence, was suddenly sharpened by distrust.

"You didn't forget to post my letter?"

Darrow stood before her, constrained and ashamed, and ever more keenly aware that the betrayal of his distress must be a greater offense than its concealment.

"What an insinuation!" he cried, throwing out his hands with a laugh.

Her face instantly melted to laughter. "Well, then—I *won't* be sorry; I won't regret anything except that our good time is over!"

The words were so unexpected that they routed all his resolves. If she had gone on doubting him he could probably have gone on deceiving her; but her unhesitating acceptance of his word made him hate the part he was playing. At the same moment a doubt shot up its serpent head in his own bosom. Was it not he rather than she who was childishly trustful? Was she not almost too ready to take his word, and dismiss once for all the tiresome question of the letter? Considering what her experiences must have been, such trustfulness seemed open to suspicion. But the moment his eyes fell on her he was ashamed of the thought, and knew it for what it really was: another pretext to lessen his own delinquency.

"Why should our good time be over?" he asked. "Why shouldn't it last a little longer?"

She looked up, her lips parted in surprise; but before she could speak he went on: "I want you to stay with me—I want you, just for a few days, to have all the things you've never had. It's not always May and Paris—why not make the most of them now? You know me—we're not strangers—why shouldn't you treat me like a friend?"

While he spoke she had drawn away a little, but her hand still lay in his. She was pale, and her eyes were fixed on him in a gaze in which there was neither distrust or resentment, but only an ingenuous wonder. He was extraordinarily touched by her expression.

"Oh, do! You must. Listen: to prove that I'm sincere I'll tell you . . . I'll tell you I didn't post your letter . . . I didn't post it because I wanted so much to give you a few good hours . . . and because I couldn't bear to have you go."

He had the feeling that the words were being uttered in spite of him by some malicious witness of the scene, and yet that he was not sorry to have them spoken.

The girl had listened to him in silence. She remained motionless for a moment after he had ceased to speak; then she snatched away her hand.

"You didn't post my letter? You kept it back on purpose? And you tell me so *now*, to prove to me that I'd better put myself under your protection?" She burst into a laugh that had in it all the piercing echoes of her Murrett past, and her face, at the same moment, underwent the same change, shrinking into a small malevolent white mask in which the eyes burned black. "Thank you—thank you most awfully for telling me! And for all your other kind intentions! The plan's delightful—really quite delightful, and I'm extremely flattered and obliged."

She dropped into a seat beside her dressing-table, resting

her chin on her lifted hands, and laughing out at him under the elf-lock which had shaken itself down over her eyes.

Her outburst did not offend the young man; its immediate effect was that of allaying his agitation. The theatrical touch in her manner made his offense seem more venial than he had thought it a moment before.

He drew up a chair and sat down beside her. "After all," he said, in a tone of good-humoured protest, "I needn't have told you I'd kept back your letter; and my telling you seems rather strong proof that I hadn't any very nefarious designs on you."

She met this with a shrug, but he did not give her time to answer. "My designs," he continued with a smile, " were not nefarious. I saw you'd been through a bad time with Mrs. Murrett, and that there didn't seem to be much fun ahead for you; and I didn't see—and I don't yet see—the harm of trying to give you a few hours of amusement between a depressing past and a not particularly cheerful future." He paused again, and then went on, in the same tone of friendly reasonableness: "The mistake I made was not to tell you this at once—not to ask you straight out to give me a day or two, and let me try to make you forget all the things that are troubling you. I was a fool not to see that if I'd put it to you in that way you'd have accepted or refused, as you chose; but that at least you wouldn't have mistaken my intentions.—Intentions!" He stood up, walked the length of the room, and turned back to where she still sat motionless, her elbows propped on the dressing-table, her chin on her hands. "What rubbish we talk about intentions! The truth is I hadn't any: I just liked being with you. Perhaps you don't know how extraordinarily one can like being with you . . . I was depressed and adrift myself; and you made me forget my bothers; and when I found you were going—and going back to dreariness, as I was—I didn't see why we shouldn't have a few hours together first; so I left your letter in my pocket."

He saw her face melt as she listened, and suddenly she unclasped her hands and leaned to him.

"But are *you* unhappy too? Oh, I never understood—I never dreamed it! I thought you'd always had everything in the world you wanted!"

Darrow broke into a laugh at this ingenuous picture of his state. He was ashamed of trying to better his case by an appeal to her pity, and annoyed with himself for alluding to a subject he would rather have kept out of his thoughts. But her look of sympathy had disarmed him; his heart was bitter and distracted; she was near him, her eyes were shining with compassion—he bent over her and kissed her hand.

"Forgive me—do forgive me," he said.

She stood up with a smiling head-shake. "Oh, it's not so often that people try to give me any pleasure—much less two whole days of it! I sha'n't forget how kind you've been. I shall have plenty of time to remember. But this *is* good-bye, you know. I must telegraph at once to say I'm coming."

"To say you're coming? Then I'm not forgiven?"

"Oh, you're forgiven—if that's any comfort."

"It's not, the very least, if your way of proving it is to go away!"

She hung her head in meditation. "But I can't stay.—How *can* I stay?" she broke out, as if arguing with some unseen monitor.

"Why can't you? No one knows you're here . . . No one need ever know."

She looked up, and their eyes exchanged meanings for a rapid minute. Her gaze was as clear as a boy's. "Oh, it's not *that*," she exclaimed, almost impatiently; "it's not people I'm afraid of! They've never put themselves out for me—why on earth should I care about them?"

He liked her directness as he had never liked it before. "Well, then, what is it? Not *me*, I hope?"

"No, not you: I like you. It's the money! With me that's always the root of the matter. I could never yet afford a treat in my life!"

"Is *that* all?" He laughed, relieved by her naturalness. "Look here; since we're talking as man to man—can't you trust me about that too?"

"Trust you? How do you mean? You'd better not trust *me*!" she laughed back sharply. "I might never be able to pay up!"

His gesture brushed aside the allusion. "Money may be the root of the matter; it can't be the whole of it, between friends. Don't you think one friend may accept a small service from another without looking too far ahead or weighing too many chances? The question turns entirely on what you think of me. If you like me well enough to be willing to take a few days' holiday with me, just for the pleasure of the thing, and the pleasure you'll be giving me, let's shake hands on it. If you don't like me well enough we'll shake hands too; only I shall be sorry," he ended.

"Oh, but I shall be sorry too!" Her face, as she lifted it to his, looked so small and young that Darrow felt a fugitive twinge of compunction, instantly effaced by the excitement of pursuit.

"Well, then?" He stood looking down on her, his eyes persuading her. He was now intensely aware that his nearness was having an effect which made it less and less necessary for him to choose his words, and he went on, more mindful of the inflections of his voice than of what he was actually saying: "Why on earth should we say good-bye if we're both sorry to? Won't you tell me your reason? It's not a bit like you to let anything stand in the way of your saying just what you feel. You mustn't mind offending me, you know!"

She hung before him like a leaf on the meeting of cross-currents, that the next ripple may sweep forward or whirl back. Then she flung up her head with the odd boyish movement habitual to her in moments of excitement. "What I feel? Do you want to know what I feel? That you're giving me the only chance I've ever had!"

She turned about on her heel and, dropping into the nearest chair, sank forward, her face hidden against the dressing-table.

Under the folds of her thin summer dress the modelling of her back and of her lifted arms, and the slight hollow between her shoulder-blades, recalled the faint curves of a terra-cotta statuette, some young image of grace hardly more than sketched in the clay. Darrow, as he stood looking at her, reflected that her character, for all its seeming firmness, its flashing edges of "opinion", was probably no less immature. He had not expected her to yield so suddenly to his suggestion, or to confess her yielding in that way. At first he was slightly disconcerted; then he saw how her attitude simplified his own. Her behaviour had all the indecision and awkwardness of inexperience. It showed that she was a child after all; and all he could do—all he had ever meant to do—was to give her a child's holiday to look back to.

For a moment he fancied she was crying; but the next she was on her feet and had swept round on him a face she must have turned away only to hide the first rush of her pleasure.

For a while they shone on each other without speaking; then she sprang to him and held out both hands.

"Is it true? Is it really true? Is it really going to happen to *me*?"

He felt like answering: "You're the very creature to whom it was bound to happen"; but the words had a double sense that made him wince, and instead he caught her proffered hands and stood looking at her across the length of her arms, without attempting to bend them or to draw her closer. He wanted her to know how her words had moved him; but his thoughts were blurred by the rush of the same emotion that possessed her, and his own words came with an effort.

He ended by giving her back a laugh as frank as her own, and declaring, as he dropped her hands: "All that and more too—you'll see!"

VIII

ALL DAY, since the late reluctant dawn, the rain had come down in torrents. It streamed against Darrow's high-perched windows, reduced their vast prospect of roofs and chimneys to a black oily huddle, and filled the room with the drab twilight of an underground aquarium.

The streams descended with the regularity of a third day's rain, when trimming and shuffling are over, and the weather has settled down to do its worst. There were no variations of rhythm, no lyrical ups and downs: the grey lines streaking the panes were as dense and uniform as a page of unparagraphed narrative.

George Darrow had drawn his armchair to the fire. The time-table he had been studying lay on the floor, and he sat staring with dull acquiescence into the boundless blur of rain, which affected him like a vast projection of his own state of mind. Then his eyes travelled slowly about the room.

It was exactly ten days since his hurried unpacking had strewn it with the contents of his portmanteaux. His brushes and razors were spread out on the blotched marble of the chest of drawers. A stack of newspapers had accumulated on the centre table under the "electrolier", and half a dozen paper novels lay on the mantel-piece among cigar-cases and toilet bottles; but these traces of his passage had made no mark on the featureless dulness of the room, its look of being the makeshift setting of innumerable transient collocations. There was something sardonic, almost sinister, in its appearance of having deliberately "made up" for its anonymous part, all in noncommittal drabs and browns, with a carpet and paper that nobody would remember, and chairs and tables as impersonal as railway porters.

Darrow picked up the time-table and tossed it on to the table. Then he rose to his feet, lit a cigar and went to the window. Through the rain he could just discover the face of a clock in a tall building beyond the railway roofs. He pulled out his watch, compared the two time-pieces, and started the hands of his with such a rush that they flew past the hour and he had to make them repeat the circuit more deliberately. He felt a quite disproportionate irritation at the trifling blunder. When he had corrected it he went back to his chair and threw himself down, leaning back his head against his hands. Presently his cigar went out, and he got up, hunted for the matches, lit it again and returned to his seat.

The room was getting on his nerves. During the first few days, while the skies were clear, he had not noticed it, or had felt for it only the contemptuous indifference of the traveller toward a provisional shelter. But now that he was leaving it, was looking at it for the last time, it seemed to have taken complete possession of his mind, to be soaking itself into him like an ugly indelible blot. Every detail pressed itself on his notice with the familiarity of an accidental confidant: whichever way he turned, he felt the nudge of a transient intimacy . . .

The one fixed point in his immediate future was that his leave was over and that he must be back at his post in London the next morning. Within twenty-four hours he would again be in a daylight world of recognized activities, himself a busy, responsible, relatively necessary factor in the big whirring social and official machine. That fixed obligation was the fact he could think of with the least discomfort, yet for some unaccountable reason it was the one on which he found it most difficult to fix his thoughts. Whenever he did so, the room jerked him back into the circle of its insistent associations. It was extraordinary with what a microscopic minuteness of loathing he hated it all: the grimy carpet and wallpaper, the black marble mantel-piece, the clock with a gilt allegory under a dusty bell, the high-bolstered brown-counterpaned bed, the framed card of printed rules under the electric light switch, and the door of communication with the next room. He hated the door most of all . . .

At the outset, he had felt no special sense of responsibility. He was satisfied that he had struck the right note, and convinced of his power of sustaining it. The whole incident had somehow seemed, in spite of its vulgar setting and its inevitable prosaic propinquities, to be enacting itself in some unmapped region outside the pale of the usual. It was not like anything that had ever happened to him before, or in which he had ever pictured himself as likely to be involved; but that, at first, had seemed no argument against his fitness to deal with it.

Perhaps but for the three days' rain he might have got away without a doubt as to his adequacy. The rain had made all the difference. It had thrown the whole picture out of perspective, blotted out the mystery of the remoter planes and the enchantment of the middle distance, and thrust into prominence every commonplace fact of the foreground. It was the kind of situation that was not helped by being thought over; and by the perversity of circumstance he had been forced into the unwilling contemplation of its every aspect . . .

His cigar had gone out again, and he threw it into the fire and vaguely meditated getting up to find another. But the mere act of leaving his chair seemed to call for a greater exertion of the will than he was capable of, and he leaned his head back with closed eyes and listened to the drumming of the rain.

A different noise aroused him. It was the opening and closing of the door leading from the corridor into the adjoining room. He sat motionless, without opening his eyes; but now another sight forced itself under his lowered lids. It was the precise photographic picture of that other room. Everything in it rose before him and pressed itself upon his vision with the same acuity of distinctness as the objects surrounding him. A step sounded on the floor, and he knew which way the step was directed, what pieces of furniture it had to skirt, where it would probably pause, and what was likely to arrest it. He heard another sound, and recognized it as that of a wet umbrella placed in the black marble jamb of the chimney-piece, against the hearth. He caught the creak of a hinge, and instantly differentiated it as that of the wardrobe against the opposite wall. Then he heard the mouse-like squeal of a reluctant drawer, and knew it was the upper one in the chest of drawers beside the bed: the clatter which followed was caused by the mahogany toilet-glass jumping on its loosened pivots . . .

The step crossed the floor again. It was strange how much better he knew it than the person to whom it belonged! Now it was drawing near the door of communication between the two rooms. He opened his eyes and looked. The step had ceased and for a moment there was silence. Then he heard a low knock. He made no response, and after an interval he saw that the door-handle was being tentatively turned. He closed his eyes once more . . .

The door opened, and the step was in the room, coming cautiously toward him. He kept his eyes shut, relaxing his body to feign sleep. There was another pause, then a wavering soft advance, the rustle of a dress behind his chair, the warmth of two hands pressed for a moment on his lids. The palms of the hands had the lingering scent of some stuff that he had bought on the Boulevard . . . He looked up and saw a letter falling over his shoulder to his knee . . .

"Did I disturb you? I'm so sorry! They gave me this just now when I came in."

The letter, before he could catch it, had slipped between his knees to the floor. It lay there, address upward, at his feet, and while he sat staring down at the strong slender characters on the blue-gray envelope an arm reached out from behind to pick it up.

"Oh, don't— *don't!*" broke from him, and he bent over and caught the arm. The face above it was close to his.

"Don't what?"

——"take the trouble," he stammered.

He dropped the arm and stooped down. His grasp closed over the letter, he fingered its thickness and weight and calculated the number of sheets it must contain.

Suddenly he felt the pressure of the hand on his shoulder, and became aware that the face was still leaning over him, and that in a moment he would have to look up and kiss it . . .

He bent forward first and threw the unopened letter into the middle of the fire.

BOOK II

IX

THE LIGHT of the October afternoon lay on an old high-roofed house which enclosed in its long expanse of brick and yellowish stone the breadth of a grassy court filled with the shadow and sound of limes.

From the escutcheoned piers at the entrance of the court a level drive, also shaded by limes, extended to a white-barred gate beyond which an equally level avenue of grass, cut through a wood, dwindled to a blue-green blur against a sky banked with still white slopes of cloud.

In the court, half-way between house and drive, a lady stood. She held a parasol above her head, and looked now at the house-front, with its double flight of steps meeting before a glazed door under sculptured trophies, now down the drive toward the grassy cutting through the wood. Her air was less of expectancy than of contemplation: she seemed not so much to be watching for any one, or listening for an approaching sound, as letting the whole aspect of the place sink into her while she held herself open to its influence. Yet it was no less apparent that the scene was not new to her. There was no eagerness of investigation in her survey: she seemed rather to be looking about her with eyes to which, for some intimate inward reason, details long since familiar had suddenly acquired an unwonted freshness.

This was in fact the exact sensation of which Mrs. Leath was conscious as she came forth from the house and descended into the sunlit court. She had come to meet her step-son, who was likely to be returning at that hour from an afternoon's shooting in one of the more distant plantations, and she carried in her hand the letter which had sent her in search of him; but with her first step out of the house all thought of him had been effaced by another series of impressions.

The scene about her was known to satiety. She had seen Givré at all seasons of the year, and for the greater part of every year, since the far-off day of her marriage; the day when, ostensibly driving through its gates at her husband's side, she had actually been carried there on a cloud of iris-winged visions.

The possibilities which the place had then represented were still vividly present to her. The mere phrase "a French château" had called up to her youthful fancy a throng of romantic associations, poetic, pictorial and emotional; and the serene face of the old house seated in its park among the poplar-bordered meadows of middle France, had seemed, on her first sight of it, to hold out to her a fate as noble and dignified as its own mien.

Though she could still call up that phase of feeling it had long since passed, and the house had for a time become to her the very symbol of narrowness and monotony. Then, with the passing of years, it had gradually acquired a less inimical character, had become, not again a castle of dreams, evoker of fair images and romantic legend, but the shell of a life slowly adjusted to its dwelling: the place one came back to, the place where one had one's duties, one's habits and one's books, the place one would naturally live in till one died: a dull house, an inconvenient house, of which one knew all the defects, the shabbinesses, the discomforts, but to which one was so used that one could hardly, after so long a time, think one's self away from it without suffering a certain loss of identity.

Now, as it lay before her in the autumn mildness, its mistress was surprised at her own insensibility. She had been trying to see the house through the eyes of an old friend who, the next morning, would be driving up to it for the first time; and in so doing she seemed to be opening her own eyes upon it after a long interval of blindness.

The court was very still, yet full of a latent life: the wheeling and rustling of pigeons about the rectangular yews and across the sunny gravel; the sweep of rooks above the lustrous greyish-purple slates of the roof, and the stir of the tree-tops as they met the breeze which every day, at that hour, came punctually up from the river.

Just such a latent animation glowed in Anna Leath. In every nerve and vein she was conscious of that equipoise of bliss which the fearful human heart scarce dares acknowledge. She was not used to strong or full emotions; but she had always known that she should not be afraid of them. She was not afraid now; but she felt a deep inward stillness.

The immediate effect of the feeling had been to send her forth in quest of her step-son. She wanted to stroll back with him and have a quiet talk before they re-entered the house. It was always easy to talk to him, and at this moment he was the one person to whom she could have spoken without fear of disturbing her inner stillness. She was glad, for all sorts of reasons, that Madame de Chantelle and Effie were still at Ouchy with the governess, and that she and Owen had the house to themselves. And she was glad that even he was not yet in sight. She wanted to be alone a little longer; not to think, but to let the long slow waves of joy break over her one by one.

She walked out of the court and sat down on one of the benches that bordered the drive. From her seat she had a diagonal view of the long house-front and of the domed chapel terminating one of the wings. Beyond a gate in the court-yard wall the flower-garden drew its dark-green squares and raised its statues against the yellowing background of the park. In the borders only a few late pinks and crimsons smouldered, but a peacock strutting in the sun seemed to have gathered into his outspread fan all the summer glories of the place.

In Mrs. Leath's hand was the letter which had opened her eyes to these things, and a smile rose to her lips at the mere feeling of the paper between her fingers. The thrill it sent through her gave a keener edge to every sense. She felt, saw, breathed the shining world as though a thin impenetrable veil had suddenly been removed from it.

Just such a veil, she now perceived, had always hung between herself and life. It had been like the stage gauze which gives an illusive air of reality to the painted scene behind it, yet proves it, after all, to be no more than a painted scene.

She had been hardly aware, in her girlhood, of differing from others in this respect. In the well-regulated well-fed Summers world the unusual was regarded as either immoral or ill-bred, and people with emotions were not visited. Sometimes, with a sense of groping in a topsy-turvy universe, Anna had wondered why everybody about her seemed to ignore all the passions and sensations which formed the stuff of great poetry and memorable action. In a community composed entirely of people like her parents and her parents' friends she did not see how the magnificent things one read about could ever have happened. She was sure that if anything of the kind had occurred in her immediate circle her mother would have consulted the family clergyman, and her father perhaps even have rung up the police; and her sense of humour compelled her to own that, in the given conditions, these precautions might not have been unjustified.

Little by little the conditions conquered her, and she learned to regard the substance of life as a mere canvas for the embroideries of poet and painter, and its little swept and fenced and tended surface as its actual substance. It was in the visioned region of action and emotion that her fullest hours were spent; but it hardly occurred to her that they might be translated into experience, or connected with anything likely to happen to a young lady living in West Fifty-fifth Street.

She perceived, indeed, that other girls, leading outwardly the same life as herself, and seemingly unaware of her world of hidden beauty, were yet possessed of some vital secret which escaped her. There seemed to be a kind of freemasonry between them; they were wider awake than she, more alert, and surer of their wants if not of their opinions. She supposed they were "cleverer", and accepted her inferiority good-humouredly, half aware, within herself, of a reserve of unused power which the others gave no sign of possessing.

This partly consoled her for missing so much of what made their "good time"; but the resulting sense of exclusion, of being somehow laughingly but firmly debarred from a share of their privileges, threw her back on herself and deepened the reserve which made envious mothers cite her as a model of ladylike repression.

Love, she told herself, would one day release her from this spell of unreality. She was persuaded that the sublime passion was the key to the enigma; but it was difficult to relate her conception of love to the forms it wore in her experience. Two or three of the girls she had envied for their superior acquaintance with the arts of life had contracted, in the course of time, what were variously described as "romantic" or "foolish" marriages; one even made a runaway match, and languished for a while under a cloud of social reprobation. Here, then, was passion in action, romance converted to reality; yet the heroines of these exploits returned from them untransfigured, and their husbands were as dull as ever when one had to sit next to them at dinner.

Her own case, of course, would be different. Some day she would find the magic bridge between West Fifty-fifth Street and life; once or twice she had even fancied that the clue was in her hand. The first time was when she had met young Darrow. She recalled even now the stir of the encounter. But his passion swept over her like a wind that shakes the roof of the forest without reaching its still glades or rippling its hidden pools. He was extraordinarily intelligent and agreeable, and her heart beat faster when he was with her. He had a tall fair easy presence and a mind in which the lights of irony played pleasantly through the shades of feeling. She liked to hear his voice almost as much as to listen to what he was saying, and to listen to what he was saying almost as much as to feel that he was looking at her; but he wanted to kiss her, and she wanted to talk to him about books and pictures, and have him insinuate the eternal theme of their love into every subject they discussed.

Whenever they were apart a reaction set in. She wondered how she could have been so cold, called herself a prude and an idiot, questioned if any man could really care for her, and got up in the dead of night to try new ways of doing her hair. But as soon as he reappeared her head straightened itself on her slim neck and she sped her little shafts of irony, or flew her little kites of erudition, while hot and cold waves swept over her, and the things she really wanted to say choked in her throat and burned the palms of her hands.

Often she told herself that any silly girl who had waltzed through a season would know better than she how to attract a man and hold him; but when she said "a man" she did not really mean George Darrow.

Then one day, at a dinner, she saw him sitting next to one of the silly girls in question: the heroine of the elopement which had shaken West Fifty-fifth Street to its base. The young lady had come back from her adventure no less silly than when she went; and across the table the partner of her flight, a fat young man with eye-glasses, sat stolidly eating terrapin and talking about polo and investments.

The young woman was undoubtedly as silly as ever; yet after watching her for a few minutes Miss Summers perceived that she had somehow grown luminous, perilous, obscurely menacing to nice girls and the young men they intended eventually to accept. Suddenly, at the sight, a rage of possessorship awoke in her. She must save Darrow, assert her right to him at any price. Pride and reticence went down in a hurricane of jealousy. She heard him laugh, and there was something new in his laugh . . . She watched him talking, talking . . . He sat slightly sideways, a faint smile beneath his lids, lowering his voice as he lowered it when he talked to her. She caught the same inflections, but his eyes were different. It would have offended her once if he had looked at her like that. Now her one thought was that none but she had a right to be so looked at. And that girl of all others! What illusions could he have about a girl who, hardly a year ago, had made a fool of herself over the fat young man stolidly eating terrapin across the table? If that was where romance and passion ended, it was better to take to district visiting or algebra!

All night she lay awake and wondered: "What was she saying to him? How shall I learn to say such things?" and she decided that her heart would tell her—that the next time they were alone together the irresistible word would spring to her lips. He came the next day, and they were alone, and all she found was: "I didn't know that you and Kitty Mayne were such friends."

He answered with indifference that he didn't know it either, and in the reaction of relief she declared: "She's certainly ever so much prettier than she was . . ."

"She's rather good fun," he admitted, as though he had not noticed her other advantages; and suddenly Anna saw in his eyes the look she had seen there the previous evening.

She felt as if he were leagues and leagues away from her. All her hopes dissolved, and she was conscious of sitting rigidly, with high head and straight lips, while the irresistible word fled with a last wing-beat into the golden mist of her illusions . . .

*   *   *

She was still quivering with the pain and bewilderment of this adventure when Fraser Leath appeared. She met him first in Italy, where she was travelling with her parents; and the following winter he came to New York. In Italy he had seemed interesting: in New York he became remarkable. He seldom spoke of his life in Europe, and let drop but the most incidental allusions to the friends, the tastes, the pursuits which filled his cosmopolitan days; but in the atmosphere of West Fifty-fifth Street he seemed the embodiment of a storied past. He presented Miss Summers with a prettily-bound anthology of the old French poets and, when she showed a discriminating pleasure in the gift, observed with his grave smile: "I didn't suppose I should find any one here who would feel about these things as I do." On another occasion he asked her acceptance of a half-effaced eighteenth century pastel which he had surprisingly picked up in a New York auction-room. "I know no one but you who would really appreciate it," he explained.

He permitted himself no other comments, but these conveyed with sufficient directness that he thought her worthy of a different setting. That she should be so regarded by a man living in an atmosphere of art and beauty, and esteeming them the vital elements of life, made her feel for the first time that she was understood. Here was some one whose scale of values was the same as hers, and who thought her opinion worth hearing on the very matters which they both considered of supreme importance. The discovery restored her self-confidence, and she revealed herself to Mr. Leath as she had never known how to reveal herself to Darrow.

As the courtship progressed, and they grew more confidential, her suitor surprised and delighted her by little explosions of revolutionary sentiment. He said: "Shall you mind, I wonder, if I tell you that you live in a dreadfully conventional atmosphere?" and, seeing that she manifestly did not mind: "Of course I shall say things now and then that will horrify your dear delightful parents—I shall shock them awfully, I warn you."

In confirmation of this warning he permitted himself an occasional playful fling at the regular church-going of Mr. and Mrs. Summers, at the innocuous character of the litera-

ture in their library, and at their guileless appreciations in art.
He even ventured to banter Mrs. Summers on her refusal to
receive the irrepressible Kitty Mayne, who, after a rapid passage with George Darrow, was now involved in another and
more flagrant adventure.

"In Europe, you know, the husband is regarded as the only
judge in such matters. As long as he accepts the situation—"
Mr. Leath explained to Anna, who took his view the more
emphatically in order to convince herself that, personally, she
had none but the most tolerant sentiments toward the lady.

The subversiveness of Mr. Leath's opinions was enhanced
by the distinction of his appearance and the reserve of his
manners. He was like the anarchist with a gardenia in his buttonhole who figures in the higher melodrama. Every word,
every allusion, every note of his agreeably-modulated voice,
gave Anna a glimpse of a society at once freer and finer,
which observed the traditional forms but had discarded the
underlying prejudices; whereas the world she knew had discarded many of the forms and kept almost all the prejudices.

In such an atmosphere as his an eager young woman, curious as to all the manifestations of life, yet instinctively desiring that they should come to her in terms of beauty and fine
feeling, must surely find the largest scope for self-expression.
Study, travel, the contact of the world, the comradeship of a
polished and enlightened mind, would combine to enrich her
days and form her character; and it was only in the rare moments when Mr. Leath's symmetrical blond mask bent over
hers, and his kiss dropped on her like a cold smooth pebble,
that she questioned the completeness of the joys he offered.

There had been a time when the walls on which her gaze
now rested had shed a glare of irony on these early dreams.
In the first years of her marriage the sober symmetry of Givré
had suggested only her husband's neatly-balanced mind. It
was a mind, she soon learned, contentedly absorbed in for-
mulating the conventions of the unconventional. West Fifty-
fifth Street was no more conscientiously concerned than Givré
with the momentous question of "what people did"; it was
only the type of deed investigated that was different. Mr.
Leath collected his social instances with the same seriousness
and patience as his snuff-boxes. He exacted a rigid conformity

to his rules of non-conformity and his scepticism had the absolute accent of a dogma. He even cherished certain exceptions to his rules as the book-collector prizes a "defective" first edition. The Protestant church-going of Anna's parents had provoked his gentle sarcasm; but he prided himself on his mother's devoutness, because Madame de Chantelle, in embracing her second husband's creed, had become part of a society which still observes the outward rites of piety.

Anna, in fact, had discovered in her amiable and elegant mother-in-law an unexpected embodiment of the West Fifty-fifth Street ideal. Mrs. Summers and Madame de Chantelle, however strongly they would have disagreed as to the authorized source of Christian dogma, would have found themselves completely in accord on all the momentous minutiæ of drawing-room conduct; yet Mr. Leath treated his mother's foibles with a respect which Anna's experience of him forbade her to attribute wholly to filial affection.

In the early days, when she was still questioning the Sphinx instead of trying to find an answer to it, she ventured to tax her husband with his inconsistency.

"You say your mother won't like it if I call on that amusing little woman who came here the other day, and was let in by mistake; but Madame de Chantelle tells me she lives with her husband, and when mother refused to visit Kitty Mayne you said——"

Mr. Leath's smile arrested her. "My dear child, I don't pretend to apply the principles of logic to my poor mother's prejudices."

"But if you admit that they *are* prejudices——?"

"There are prejudices and prejudices. My mother, of course, got hers from Monsieur de Chantelle, and they seem to me as much in their place in this house as the pot-pourri in your hawthorn jar. They preserve a social tradition of which I should be sorry to lose the least perfume. Of course I don't expect you, just at first, to feel the difference, to see the *nuance*. In the case of little Madame de Vireville, for instance: you point out that she's still under her husband's roof. Very true; and if she were merely a Paris acquaintance—especially if you had met her, as one still might, in the *right kind* of house in Paris—I should be the last to object to your visiting her. But in the country it's different. Even the best provincial society is what you would call narrow: I don't deny it; and if some of our friends met Madame de Vireville at Givré—well, it would produce a bad impression. You're inclined to ridicule such considerations, but gradually you'll come to see their importance; and meanwhile, do trust me when I ask you to be guided by my mother. It is always well for a stranger in an old society to err a little on the side of what you call its prejudices but I should rather describe as its traditions."

After that she no longer tried to laugh or argue her husband out of his convictions. They *were* convictions, and therefore unassailable. Nor was any insincerity implied in the fact that they sometimes seemed to coincide with hers. There were occasions when he really did look at things as she did; but for reasons so different as to make the distance between them all the greater. Life, to Mr. Leath, was like a walk through a carefully classified museum, where, in moments of doubt, one had only to look at the number and refer to one's catalogue; to his wife it was like groping about in a huge dark lumber-room where the exploring ray of curiosity lit up now some shape of breathing beauty and now a mummy's grin.

In the first bewilderment of her new state these discoveries had had the effect of dropping another layer of gauze between herself and reality. She seemed farther than ever removed from the strong joys and pangs for which she felt herself made. She did not adopt her husband's views, but insensibly she began to live his life. She tried to throw a compensating ardour into the secret excursions of her spirit, and thus the old vicious distinction between romance and reality was re-established for her, and she resigned herself again to the belief that "real life" was neither real nor alive.

The birth of her little girl swept away this delusion. At last she felt herself in contact with the actual business of living: but even this impression was not enduring. Everything but the irreducible crude fact of child-bearing assumed, in the Leath household, the same ghostly tinge of unreality. Her husband, at the time, was all that his own ideal of a husband required. He was attentive, and even suitably moved; but as he sat by her bedside, and thoughtfully proffered to her the list of people who had "called to enquire", she looked first at him, and then at the child between them, and wondered at the blundering alchemy of Nature . . .

With the exception of the little girl herself, everything connected with that time had grown curiously remote and unimportant. The days that had moved so slowly as they passed seemed now to have plunged down headlong steeps of time; and as she sat in the autumn sun, with Darrow's letter in her hand, the history of Anna Leath appeared to its heroine like some grey shadowy tale that she might have read in an old book, one night as she was falling asleep . . .

X

Two brown blurs emerging from the farther end of the wood-vista gradually defined themselves as her step-son and an attendant game-keeper. They grew slowly upon the bluish background, with occasional delays and re-effacements, and she sat still, waiting till they should reach the gate at the end of the drive, where the keeper would turn off to his cottage and Owen continue on to the house.

She watched his approach with a smile. From the first days of her marriage she had been drawn to the boy, but it was not until after Effie's birth that she had really begun to know him. The eager observation of her own child had shown her how much she had still to learn about the slight fair boy whom the holidays periodically restored to Givré. Owen, even then, both physically and morally, furnished her with the oddest of commentaries on his father's mien and mind. He would never, the family sighingly recognized, be nearly as handsome as Mr. Leath; but his rather charmingly unbalanced face, with its brooding forehead and petulant boyish smile, suggested to Anna what his father's countenance might have been could one have pictured its neat features disordered by a rattling breeze. She even pushed the analogy farther, and descried in her step-son's mind a quaintly-twisted reflection of her husband's. With his bursts of door-slamming activity, his fits of bookish indolence, his crude revolutionary dogmatizing and his flashes of precocious irony, the boy was not unlike a boisterous embodiment of his father's theories. It was as though Fraser Leath's ideas, accustomed to hang like marionettes on their pegs, should suddenly come down and walk. There were moments, indeed, when Owen's humours must have suggested to his progenitor the gambols of an infant Frankenstein; but to Anna they were the voice of her secret rebellions, and her tenderness to her step-son was partly based on her severity toward herself. As he had the courage she had lacked, so she meant him to have the chances she had missed; and every effort she made for him helped to keep her own hopes alive.

Her interest in Owen led her to think more often of his

mother, and sometimes she would slip away and stand alone before her predecessor's portrait. Since her arrival at Givré the picture—a "full-length" by a once fashionable artist—had undergone the successive displacements of an exiled consort removed farther and farther from the throne; and Anna could not help noting that these stages coincided with the gradual decline of the artist's fame. She had a fancy that if his credit had been in the ascendant the first Mrs. Leath might have continued to throne over the drawing-room mantel-piece, even to the exclusion of her successor's effigy. Instead of this, her peregrinations had finally landed her in the shrouded solitude of the billiard-room, an apartment which no one ever entered, but where it was understood that "the light was better," or might have been if the shutters had not been always closed.

Here the poor lady, elegantly dressed, and seated in the middle of a large lonely canvas, in the blank contemplation of a gilt console, had always seemed to Anna to be waiting for visitors who never came.

"Of course they never came, you poor thing! I wonder how long it took you to find out that they never would?" Anna had more than once apostrophized her, with a derision addressed rather to herself than to the dead; but it was only after Effie's birth that it occurred to her to study more closely the face in the picture, and speculate on the kind of visitors that Owen's mother might have hoped for.

"She certainly doesn't look as if they would have been the same kind as mine: but there's no telling, from a portrait that was so obviously done 'to please the family', and that leaves Owen so unaccounted for. Well, they never came, the visitors; they never came; and she died of it. She died of it long before they buried her: I'm certain of that. Those are stone-dead eyes in the picture . . . The loneliness must have been awful, if even Owen couldn't keep her from dying of it. And to feel it so she must have *had* feelings—real live ones, the kind that twitch and tug. And all she had to look at all her life was a gilt console—yes, that's it, a gilt console screwed to the wall! That's exactly and absolutely what he is!"

She did not mean, if she could help it, that either Effie or Owen should know that loneliness, or let her know it again.

They were three, now, to keep each other warm, and she embraced both children in the same passion of motherhood, as though one were not enough to shield her from her predecessor's fate.

Sometimes she fancied that Owen Leath's response was warmer than that of her own child. But then Effie was still hardly more than a baby, and Owen, from the first, had been almost "old enough to understand": certainly *did* understand now, in a tacit way that yet perpetually spoke to her. This sense of his understanding was the deepest element in their feeling for each other. There were so many things between them that were never spoken of, or even indirectly alluded to, yet that, even in their occasional discussions and differences, formed the unadduced arguments making for final agreement . . .

Musing on this, she continued to watch his approach; and her heart began to beat a little faster at the thought of what she had to say to him. But when he reached the gate she saw him pause, and after a moment he turned aside as if to gain a cross-road through the park.

She started up and waved her sunshade, but he did not see her. No doubt he meant to go back with the game-keeper, perhaps to the kennels, to see a retriever who had hurt his leg. Suddenly she was seized by the whim to overtake him. She threw down the parasol, thrust her letter into her bodice, and catching up her skirts began to run.

She was slight and light, with a natural ease and quickness of gait, but she could not recall having run a yard since she had romped with Owen in his school-days; nor did she know what impulse moved her now. She only knew that run she must, that no other motion, short of flight, would have been buoyant enough for her humour. She seemed to be keeping pace with some inward rhythm, seeking to give bodily expression to the lyric rush of her thoughts. The earth always felt elastic under her, and she had a conscious joy in treading it; but never had it been as soft and springy as today. It seemed actually to rise and meet her as she went, so that she had the feeling, which sometimes came to her in dreams, of skimming miraculously over short bright waves. The air, too, seemed to break in waves against her, sweeping by on its current all the slanted lights and moist sharp perfumes of the failing day. She panted to herself: "This is nonsense!" her blood hummed back: "But it's glorious!" and she sped on till she saw that Owen had caught sight of her and was striding back in her direction. Then she stopped and waited, flushed and laughing, her hands clasped against the letter in her breast.

"No, I'm not mad," she called out; "but there's something in the air today—don't you feel it?—And I wanted to have a little talk with you," she added as he came up to her, smiling at him and linking her arm in his.

He smiled back, but above the smile she saw the shade of anxiety which, for the last two months, had kept its fixed line between his handsome eyes.

"Owen, don't look like that! I don't want you to!" she said imperiously.

He laughed. "You said that exactly like Effie. What do you want me to do? To race with you as I do Effie? But I shouldn't have a show!" he protested, still with the little frown between his eyes.

"Where are you going?" she asked.

"To the kennels. But there's not the least need. The vet has seen Garry and he's all right. If there's anything you wanted to tell me——"

"Did I say there was? I just came out to meet you—I wanted to know if you'd had good sport."

The shadow dropped on him again. "None at all. The fact is I didn't try. Jean and I have just been knocking about in the woods. I wasn't in a sanguinary mood."

They walked on with the same light gait, so nearly of a height that keeping step came as naturally to them as breathing. Anna stole another look at the young face on a level with her own.

"You *did* say there was something you wanted to tell me," her step-son began after a pause.

"Well, there is." She slackened her pace involuntarily, and they came to a pause and stood facing each other under the limes.

"Is Darrow coming?" he asked.

She seldom blushed, but at the question a sudden heat suffused her. She held her head high.

"Yes: he's coming. I've just heard. He arrives tomorrow. But that's not——" She saw her blunder and tried to rectify it. "Or rather, yes, in a way it *is* my reason for wanting to speak to you——"

"Because he's coming?"

"Because he's not yet here."

"It's about him, then?"

He looked at her kindly, half-humourously, an almost fraternal wisdom in his smile.

"About——? No, no: I meant that I wanted to speak today because it's our last day alone together."

"Oh, I see." He had slipped his hands into the pockets of his tweed shooting jacket and lounged along at her side, his eyes bent on the moist ruts of the drive, as though the matter had lost all interest for him.

"Owen——"

He stopped again and faced her. "Look here, my dear, it's no sort of use."

"What's no use?"

"Anything on earth you can any of you say."

She challenged him: "Am *I* one of 'any of you'?"

He did not yield. "Well, then—anything on earth that even *you* can say."

"You don't in the least know what I can say—or what I mean to."

"Don't I, generally?"

She gave him this point, but only to make another. "Yes; but this is particularly. I want to say . . . Owen, you've been admirable all through."

He broke into a laugh in which the odd elder-brotherly note was once more perceptible.

"Admirable," she emphasized. "And so has *she*."

"Oh, and so have you to *her*!" His voice broke down to boyishness. "I've never lost sight of that for a minute. It's been altogether easier for her, though," he threw off presently.

"On the whole, I suppose it has. Well——" she summed up with a laugh, "aren't you all the better pleased to be told you've behaved as well as she?"

"Oh, you know, I've not done it for *you*," he tossed back

at her, without the least note of hostility in the affected lightness of his tone.

"Haven't you, though, perhaps—the least bit? Because, after all, you knew I understood?"

"You've been awfully kind about pretending to."

She laughed. "You don't believe me? You must remember I had your grandmother to consider."

"Yes: and my father—and Effie, I suppose—and the outraged shades of Givré!" He paused, as if to lay more stress on the boyish sneer: "Do you likewise include the late Monsieur de Chantelle?"

His step-mother did not appear to resent the thrust. She went on, in the same tone of affectionate persuasion: "Yes: I must have seemed to you too subject to Givré. Perhaps I have been. But you know that was not my real object in asking you to wait, to say nothing to your grandmother before her return."

He considered. "Your real object, of course, was to gain time."

"Yes—but for whom? Why not for *you*?"

"For me?" He flushed up quickly. "You don't mean——?"

She laid her hand on his arm and looked gravely into his handsome eyes.

"I mean that when your grandmother gets back from Ouchy I shall speak to her——"

"You'll speak to her . . . ?"

"Yes; if only you'll promise to give me time——"

"Time for her to send for Adelaide Painter?"

"Oh, she'll undoubtedly send for Adelaide Painter!"

The allusion touched a spring of mirth in both their minds, and they exchanged a laughing look.

"Only you must promise not to rush things. You must give me time to prepare Adelaide too," Mrs. Leath went on.

"Prepare her too?" He drew away for a better look at her. "Prepare her for what?"

"Why, to prepare your grandmother! For your marriage. Yes, that's what I mean. I'm going to see you through, you know——"

His feint of indifference broke down and he caught her hand. "Oh, you dear divine thing! I didn't dream——"

"I know you didn't." She dropped her gaze and began to walk on slowly. "I can't say you've convinced me of the wisdom of the step. Only I seem to see that other things matter more—and that not missing things matters most. Perhaps I've changed—or *your* not changing has convinced me. I'm certain now that you won't budge. And that was really all I ever cared about."

"Oh, as to not budging—I told you so months ago: you might have been sure of that! And how can you be any surer today than yesterday?"

"I don't know. I suppose one learns something every day——"

"Not at Givré!" he laughed, and shot a half-ironic look at her. "But you haven't really *been* at Givré lately—not for months! Don't you suppose I've noticed that, my dear?"

She echoed his laugh to merge it in an undenying sigh. "Poor Givré . . ."

"Poor empty Givré! With so many rooms full and yet not a soul in it—except of course my grandmother, who *is* its soul!"

They had reached the gateway of the court and stood looking with a common accord at the long soft-hued façade on which the autumn light was dying. "It looks so made to be happy in——" she murmured.

"Yes—today, today!" He pressed her arm a little. "Oh, you darling—to have given it that look for me!" He paused, and then went on in a lower voice: "Don't you feel we owe it to the poor old place to do what we can to give it that look? You, too, I mean? Come, let's make it grin from wing to wing! I've such a mad desire to say outrageous things to it— haven't you? After all, in old times there must have been living people here!"

Loosening her arm from his she continued to gaze up at the house-front, which seemed, in the plaintive decline of light, to send her back the mute appeal of something doomed.

"It *is* beautiful," she said.

"A beautiful memory! Quite perfect to take out and turn over when I'm grinding at the law in New York, and you're——" He broke off and looked at her with a questioning smile. "Come! Tell me. You and I don't have to say things to talk to each other. When you turn suddenly absent-minded and mysterious I always feel like saying: 'Come back. All is discovered'."

She returned his smile. "You know as much as I know. I promise you that."

He wavered, as if for the first time uncertain how far he might go. "I don't know Darrow as much as you know him," he presently risked.

She frowned a little. "You said just now we didn't need to say things——"

"Was *I* speaking? I thought it was your eyes——" He caught her by both elbows and spun her halfway round, so that the late sun shed a betraying gleam on her face. "They're such awfully conversational eyes! Don't you suppose they told me long ago why it's just today you've made up your mind that people have got to live their own lives—even at Givré?"

XI

"THIS IS the south terrace," Anna said. "Should you like to walk down to the river?"

She seemed to listen to herself speaking from a far-off airy height, and yet to be wholly gathered into the circle of consciousness which drew its glowing ring about herself and Darrow. To the aerial listener her words sounded flat and colourless, but to the self within the ring each one beat with a separate heart.

It was the day after Darrow's arrival, and he had come down early, drawn by the sweetness of the light on the lawns and gardens below his window. Anna had heard the echo of his step on the stairs, his pause in the stone-flagged hall, his voice as he asked a servant where to find her. She was at the end of the house, in the brown-panelled sitting-room which she frequented at that season because it caught the sunlight first and kept it longest. She stood near the window, in the pale band of brightness, arranging some salmon-pink geraniums in a shallow porcelain bowl. Every sensation of touch and sight was thrice-alive in her. The grey-green fur of the geranium leaves caressed her fingers and the sunlight wavering across the irregular surface of the old parquet floor made it seem as bright and shifting as the brown bed of a stream.

Darrow stood framed in the door-way of the farthest drawing-room, a light-grey figure against the black and white flagging of the hall; then he began to move toward her down the empty pale-panelled vista, crossing one after another the long reflections which a projecting cabinet or screen cast here and there upon the shining floors.

As he drew nearer, his figure was suddenly displaced by that of her husband, whom, from the same point, she had so often seen advancing down the same perspective. Straight, spare, erect, looking to right and left with quick precise turns of the head, and stopping now and then to straighten a chair or alter the position of a vase, Fraser Leath used to march toward her through the double file of furniture like a general reviewing a regiment drawn up for his inspection. At a certain point, midway across the second room, he always stopped before the mantel-piece of pinkish-yellow marble and looked at himself in the tall garlanded glass that surmounted it. She could not remember that he had ever found anything to straighten or alter in his own studied attire, but she had never known him to omit the inspection when he passed that particular mirror.

When it was over he continued more briskly on his way, and the resulting expression of satisfaction was still on his face when he entered the oak sitting-room to greet his wife . . .

The spectral projection of this little daily scene hung but for a moment before Anna, but in that moment she had time to fling a wondering glance across the distance between her past and present. Then the footsteps of the present came close, and she had to drop the geraniums to give her hand to Darrow . . .

"Yes, let us walk down to the river."

They had neither of them, as yet, found much to say to each other. Darrow had arrived late on the previous afternoon, and during the evening they had had between them Owen Leath and their own thoughts. Now they were alone for the first time and the fact was enough in itself. Yet Anna was intensely aware that as soon as they began to talk more intimately they would feel that they knew each other less well.

They passed out onto the terrace and down the steps to the gravel walk below. The delicate frosting of dew gave the grass a bluish shimmer, and the sunlight, sliding in emerald streaks along the tree-boles, gathered itself into great luminous blurs at the end of the wood-walks, and hung above the fields a watery glory like the ring about an autumn moon.

"It's good to be here," Darrow said.

They took a turn to the left and stopped for a moment to look back at the long pink house-front, plainer, friendlier, less adorned than on the side toward the court. So prolonged yet delicate had been the friction of time upon its bricks that certain expanses had the bloom and texture of old red velvet, and the patches of gold lichen spreading over them looked like the last traces of a dim embroidery. The dome of the chapel, with its gilded cross, rose above one wing, and the other ended in a conical pigeon-house, above which the birds

were flying, lustrous and slatey, their breasts merged in the
blue of the roof when they dropped down on it.

"And this is where you've been all these years."

They turned away and began to walk down a long tunnel
of yellowing trees. Benches with mossy feet stood against the
mossy edges of the path, and at its farther end it widened into
a circle about a basin rimmed with stone, in which the
opaque water strewn with leaves looked like a slab of gold-
flecked agate. The path, growing narrower, wound on circu-
itously through the woods, between slender serried trunks
twined with ivy. Patches of blue appeared above them
through the dwindling leaves, and presently the trees drew
back and showed the open fields along the river.

They walked on across the fields to the tow-path. In a curve
of the wall some steps led up to a crumbling pavilion with
openings choked with ivy. Anna and Darrow seated themselves on the bench projecting from the inner wall of the pavilion and looked across the river at the slopes divided into
blocks of green and fawn-colour, and at the chalk-tinted village lifting its squat church-tower and grey roofs against the
precisely drawn lines of the landscape. Anna sat silent, so intensely aware of Darrow's nearness that there was no surprise
in the touch he laid on her hand. They looked at each other,
and he smiled and said: "There are to be no more obstacles
now."

"Obstacles?" The word startled her. "What obstacles?"

"Don't you remember the wording of the telegram that
turned me back last May? 'Unforeseen obstacle': that was it.
What *was* the earth-shaking problem, by the way? Finding a
governess for Effie, wasn't it?"

"But I gave you my reason: the reason why it *was* an obstacle. I wrote you fully about it."

"Yes, I know you did." He lifted her hand and kissed it.
"How far off it all seems, and how little it all matters today!"

She looked at him quickly. "Do you feel that? I suppose
I'm different. I want to draw all those wasted months into
today—to make them a part of it."

"But they *are*, to me. You reach back and take everything—
back to the first days of all."

She frowned a little, as if struggling with an inarticulate

perplexity. "It's curious how, in those first days, too, some-thing that I didn't understand came between us."

"Oh, in those days we neither of us understood, did we? It's part of what's called the bliss of being young."

"Yes, I thought that, too: thought it, I mean, in looking back. But it couldn't, even then, have been as true of you as of me; and now——"

"Now," he said, "the only thing that matters is that we're sitting here together."

He dismissed the rest with a lightness that might have seemed conclusive evidence of her power over him. But she took no pride in such triumphs. It seemed to her that she wanted his allegiance and his adoration not so much for her-self as for their mutual love, and that in treating lightly any past phase of their relation he took something from its pres-ent beauty. The colour rose to her face.

"Between you and me everything matters."

"Of course!" She felt the unperceiving sweetness of his smile. "That's why," he went on, " 'everything,' for me, is here and now: on this bench, between you and me."

She caught at the phrase. "That's what I meant: it's here and now; we can't get away from it."

"Get away from it? Do you want to? *Again?*"

Her heart was beating unsteadily. Something in her, fitfully and with reluctance, struggled to free itself, but the warmth of his nearness penetrated every sense as the sunlight steeped the landscape. Then, suddenly, she felt that she wanted no less than the whole of her happiness.

" 'Again'? But wasn't it *you*, the last time——?"

She paused, the tremor in her of Psyche holding up the lamp. But in the interrogative light of her pause her compan-ion's features underwent no change.

"The last time? Last spring? But it was you who—for the best of reasons, as you've told me—turned me back from your very door last spring!"

She saw that he was good-humouredly ready to "thresh out," for her sentimental satisfaction, a question which, for his own, Time had so conclusively dealt with; and the sense of his readiness reassured her.

"I wrote as soon as I could," she rejoined. "I explained the delay and asked you to come. And you never even answered my letter."

"It was impossible to come then. I had to go back to my post."

"And impossible to write and tell me so?"

"Your letter was a long time coming. I had waited a week—ten days. I had some excuse for thinking, when it came, that you were in no great hurry for an answer."

"You thought that—really—after reading it?"

"I thought it."

Her heart leaped up to her throat. "Then why are you here today?"

He turned on her with a quick look of wonder. "God knows—if you can ask me that!"

"You see I was right to say I didn't understand."

He stood up abruptly and stood facing her, blocking the view over the river and the checkered slopes. "Perhaps I might say so too."

"No, no: we must neither of us have any reason for saying it again." She looked at him gravely. "Surely you and I needn't arrange the lights before we show ourselves to each other. I want you to see me just as I am, with all my irrational doubts and scruples; the old ones and the new ones too."

He came back to his seat beside her. "Never mind the old ones. They were justified—I'm willing to admit it. With the governess having suddenly to be packed off, and Effie on your hands, and your mother-in-law ill, I see the impossibility of your letting me come. I even see that, at the moment, it was difficult to write and explain. But what does all that matter now? The new scruples are the ones I want to tackle."

Again her heart trembled. She felt her happiness so near, so sure, that to strain it closer might be like a child's crushing a pet bird in its caress. But her very security urged her on. For so long her doubts had been knife-edged: now they had turned into bright harmless toys that she could toss and catch without peril!

"You didn't come, and you didn't answer my letter; and after waiting four months I wrote another."

"And I answered that one; and I'm here."

"Yes." She held his eyes. "But in my last letter I repeated exactly what I'd said in the first—the one I wrote you last June. I told you then that I was ready to give you the answer to what you'd asked me in London; and in telling you that, I told you what the answer was."

"My dearest! My dearest!" Darrow murmured.

"You ignored that letter. All summer you made no sign. And all I ask now is that you should frankly tell me why."

"I can only repeat what I've just said. I was hurt and unhappy and I doubted you. I suppose if I'd cared less I should have been more confident. I cared so much that I couldn't risk another failure. For you'd made me feel that I'd miserably failed. So I shut my eyes and set my teeth and turned my back. There's the whole pusillanimous truth of it!"

"Oh, if it's the *whole* truth——!" She let him clasp her. "There's my torment, you see. I thought that was what your silence meant till I made you break it. Now I want to be sure that I was right."

"What can I tell you to make you sure?"

"You can let me tell *you* everything first." She drew away, but without taking her hands from him. "Owen saw you in Paris," she began.

She looked at him and he faced her steadily. The light was full on his pleasantly-browned face, his grey eyes, his frank white forehead. She noticed for the first time a seal-ring in a setting of twisted silver on the hand he had kept on hers.

"In Paris? Oh, yes . . . So he did."

"He came back and told me. I think you talked to him a moment in a theatre. I asked if you'd spoken of my having put you off—or if you'd sent me any message. He didn't remember that you had."

"In a crush—in a Paris *foyer*? My dear!"

"It was absurd of me! But Owen and I have always been on odd kind of brother-and-sister terms. I think he guessed about us when he saw you with me in London. So he teased me a little and tried to make me curious about you; and when he saw he'd succeeded he told me he hadn't had time to say much to you because you were in such a hurry to get back to the lady you were with."

He still held her hands, but she felt no tremor in his, and

the blood did not stir in his brown cheek. He seemed to be honestly turning over his memories.

"Yes: and what else did he tell you?"

"Oh, not much, except that she was awfully pretty. When I asked him to describe her he said you had her tucked away in a *baignoire* and he hadn't actually seen her; but he saw the tail of her cloak, and somehow knew from that that she was pretty. One *does*, you know . . . I think he said the cloak was pink."

Darrow broke into a laugh. "Of course it was—they always are! So that was at the bottom of your doubts?"

"Not at first. I only laughed. But afterward, when I wrote you and you didn't answer—— Oh, you *do* see?" she appealed to him.

He was looking at her gently. "Yes: I see."

"It's not as if this were a light thing between us. I want you to know me as I am. If I thought that at that moment . . . when you were on your way here, almost——"

He dropped her hand and stood up. "Yes, yes—I understand."

"But do you?" Her look followed him. "I'm not a goose of a girl. I know . . . of course I *know* . . . but there are things a woman feels . . . when what she knows doesn't make any difference. It's not that I want you to explain—I mean about that particular evening. It's only that I want you to have the whole of my feeling. I didn't know what it was till I saw you again. I never dreamed I should say such things to you!"

"I never dreamed I should be here to hear you say them!" He turned back and lifting a floating end of her scarf put his lips to it. "But now that you have, *I* know—*I* know," he smiled down at her.

"You know——?"

"That this is no light thing between us. Now you may ask me anything you please! That was all I wanted to ask *you*."

For a long moment they looked at each other without speaking. She saw the dancing spirit in his eyes turn grave and darken to a passionate sternness. He stooped and kissed her, and she sat as if folded in wings.

XII

IT WAS in the natural order of things that, on the way back to the house, their talk should have turned to the future.

Anna was not eager to define it. She had an extraordinary sensitiveness to the impalpable elements of happiness, and as she walked at Darrow's side her imagination flew back and forth, spinning luminous webs of feeling between herself and the scene about her. Every heightening of emotion produced for her a new effusion of beauty in visible things, and with it the sense that such moments should be lingered over and absorbed like some unrenewable miracle. She understood Darrow's impatience to see their plans take shape. She knew it must be so, she would not have had it otherwise; but to reach a point where she could fix her mind on his appeal for dates and decisions was like trying to break her way through the silver tangle of an April wood.

Darrow wished to use his diplomatic opportunities as a means of studying certain economic and social problems with which he presently hoped to deal in print; and with this in view he had asked for, and obtained, a South American appointment. Anna was ready to follow where he led, and not reluctant to put new sights as well as new thoughts between herself and her past. She had, in a direct way, only Effie and Effie's education to consider; and there seemed, after due reflection, no reason why the most anxious regard for these should not be conciliated with the demands of Darrow's career. Effie, it was evident, could be left to Madame de Chantelle's care till the couple should have organized their life; and she might even, as long as her future step-father's work retained him in distant posts, continue to divide her year between Givré and the antipodes.

As for Owen, who had reached his legal majority two years before, and was soon to attain the age fixed for the taking over of his paternal inheritance, the arrival of this date would reduce his step-mother's responsibility to a friendly concern for his welfare. This made for the prompt realization of Darrow's wishes, and there seemed no reason why the marriage should not take place within the six weeks that remained of his leave.

They passed out of the wood-walk into the open brightness of the garden. The noon sunlight sheeted with gold the bronze flanks of the polygonal yews. Chrysanthemums, russet, saffron and orange, glowed like the efflorescence of an enchanted forest; belts of red begonia purpling to wine-colour ran like smouldering flame among the borders; and above this outspread tapestry the house extended its harmonious length, the soberness of its lines softened to grace in the luminous misty air.

Darrow stood still, and Anna felt that his glance was travelling from her to the scene about them and then back to her face.

"You're sure you're prepared to give up Givré? You look so made for each other!"

"Oh, Givré——" She broke off suddenly, feeling as if her too careless tone had delivered all her past into his hands; and with one of her instinctive movements of recoil she added: "When Owen marries I shall have to give it up."

"When Owen marries? That's looking some distance ahead! I want to be told that meanwhile you'll have no regrets."

She hesitated. Why did he press her to uncover to him her poor starved past? A vague feeling of loyalty, a desire to spare what could no longer harm her, made her answer evasively: "There will probably be no 'meanwhile.' Owen may marry before long."

She had not meant to touch on the subject, for her stepson had sworn her to provisional secrecy; but since the shortness of Darrow's leave necessitated a prompt adjustment of their own plans, it was, after all, inevitable that she should give him at least a hint of Owen's.

"Owen marry? Why, he always seems like a faun in flannels! I hope he's found a dryad. There might easily be one left in these blue-and-gold woods."

"I can't tell you yet where he found his dryad, but she *is* one, I believe: at any rate she'll become the Givré woods better than I do. Only there may be difficulties——"

"Well! At that age they're not always to be wished away."

She hesitated. "Owen, at any rate, has made up his mind to overcome them; and I've promised to see him through."

She went on, after a moment's consideration, to explain that her step-son's choice was, for various reasons, not likely to commend itself to his grandmother. "She must be prepared for it, and I've promised to do the preparing. You know I always *have* seen him through things, and he rather counts on me now."

She fancied that Darrow's exclamation had in it a faint note of annoyance, and wondered if he again suspected her of seeking a pretext for postponement.

"But once Owen's future is settled, you won't, surely, for the sake of what you call seeing him through, ask that I should go away again without you?" He drew her closer as they walked. "Owen will understand, if you don't. Since he's in the same case himself I'll throw myself on his mercy. He'll see that I have the first claim on you; he won't even want you not to see it."

"Owen sees everything: I'm not afraid of that. But his future isn't settled. He's very young to marry—too young, his grandmother is sure to think—and the marriage he wants to make is not likely to convince her to the contrary."

"You don't mean that it's like his first choice?"

"Oh, no! But it's not what Madame de Chantelle would call a good match; it's not even what I call a wise one."

"Yet you're backing him up?"

"Yet I'm backing him up." She paused. "I wonder if you'll understand? What I've most wanted for him, and shall want for Effie, is that they shall always feel free to make their own mistakes, and never, if possible, be persuaded to make other people's. Even if Owen's marriage is a mistake, and has to be paid for, I believe he'll learn and grow in the paying. Of course I can't make Madame de Chantelle see this; but I can remind her that, with his character—his big rushes of impulse, his odd intervals of ebb and apathy—she may drive him into some worse blunder if she thwarts him now."

"And you mean to break the news to her as soon as she comes back from Ouchy?"

"As soon as I see my way to it. She knows the girl and likes her: that's our hope. And yet it may, in the end, prove our danger, make it harder for us all, when she learns the truth, than if Owen had chosen a stranger. I can't tell you more till I've told her: I've promised Owen not to tell any one. All I ask you is to give me time, to give me a few days at any rate. She's been wonderfully 'nice,' as she would call it, about you, and about the fact of my having soon to leave Givré; but that, again, may make it harder for Owen. At any rate, you can see, can't you, how it makes me want to stand by him? You see, I couldn't bear it if the least fraction of my happiness seemed to be stolen from his—as if it were a little scrap of happiness that had to be pieced out with other people's!" She clasped her hands on Darrow's arm. "I want our life to be like a house with all the windows lit: I'd like to string lanterns from the roof and chimneys!"

She ended with an inward tremor. All through her exposition and her appeal she had told herself that the moment could hardly have been less well chosen. In Darrow's place she would have felt, as he doubtless did, that her carefully developed argument was only the disguise of an habitual indecision. It was the hour of all others when she would have liked to affirm herself by brushing aside every obstacle to his wishes; yet it was only by opposing them that she could show the strength of character she wanted him to feel in her.

But as she talked she began to see that Darrow's face gave back no reflection of her words, that he continued to wear the abstracted look of a man who is not listening to what is said to him. It caused her a slight pang to discover that his thoughts could wander at such a moment; then, with a flush of joy she perceived the reason.

In some undefinable way she had become aware, without turning her head, that he was steeped in the sense of her nearness, absorbed in contemplating the details of her face and dress; and the discovery made the words throng to her lips. She felt herself speak with ease, authority, conviction. She said to herself: "He doesn't care what I say—it's enough that I say it—even if it's stupid he'll like me better for it . . ." She knew that every inflexion of her voice, every gesture, every characteristic of her person—its very defects, the fact that her forehead was too high, that her eyes were not large enough, that her hands, though slender, were not small, and that the fingers did not taper—she knew that these deficiencies were so many channels through which her influence streamed to him; that she pleased him in spite of them, perhaps because of them; that he wanted her as she was, and not as she would have liked to be; and for the first time she felt in her veins the security and lightness of happy love.

They reached the court and walked under the limes toward the house. The hall door stood wide, and through the windows opening on the terrace the sun slanted across the black and white floor, the faded tapestry chairs, and Darrow's travelling coat and cap, which lay among the cloaks and rugs piled on a bench against the wall.

The sight of these garments, lying among her own wraps, gave her a sense of homely intimacy. It was as if her happiness came down from the skies and took on the plain dress of daily things. At last she seemed to hold it in her hand.

As they entered the hall her eye lit on an unstamped note conspicuously placed on the table.

"From Owen! He must have rushed off somewhere in the motor."

She felt a secret stir of pleasure at the immediate inference that she and Darrow would probably lunch alone. Then she opened the note and stared at it in wonder.

"Dear," Owen wrote, "after what you said yesterday I can't wait another hour, and I'm off to Francheuil, to catch the Dijon express and travel back with them. Don't be frightened; I won't speak unless it's safe to. Trust me for that—but I had to go."

She looked up slowly.

"He's gone to Dijon to meet his grandmother. Oh, I hope I haven't made a mistake!"

"You? Why, what have you to do with his going to Dijon?"

She hesitated. "The day before yesterday I told him, for the first time, that I meant to see him through, no matter what happened. And I'm afraid he's lost his head, and will be imprudent and spoil things. You see, I hadn't meant to say a word to him till I'd had time to prepare Madame de Chantelle."

She felt that Darrow was looking at her and reading her thoughts, and the colour flew to her face. "Yes: it was when

I heard you were coming that I told him. I wanted him to feel as I felt . . . it seemed too unkind to make him wait!"

Her hand was in his, and his arm rested for a moment on her shoulder.

"It *would* have been too unkind to make him wait."

They moved side by side toward the stairs. Through the haze of bliss enveloping her, Owen's affairs seemed curiously unimportant and remote. Nothing really mattered but this torrent of light in her veins. She put her foot on the lowest step, saying: "It's nearly luncheon time—I must take off my hat . . ." and as she started up the stairs Darrow stood below in the hall and watched her. But the distance between them did not make him seem less near: it was as if his thoughts moved with her and touched her like endearing hands.

In her bedroom she shut the door and stood still, looking about her in a fit of dreamy wonder. Her feelings were unlike any she had ever known: richer, deeper, more complete. For the first time everything in her, from head to foot, seemed to be feeding the same full current of sensation.

She took off her hat and went to the dressing-table to smooth her hair. The pressure of the hat had flattened the dark strands on her forehead; her face was paler than usual, with shadows about the eyes. She felt a pang of regret for the wasted years. "If I look like this today," she said to herself, " what will he think of me when I'm ill or worried?" She began to run her fingers through her hair, rejoicing in its thickness; then she desisted and sat still, resting her chin on her hands.

"I want him to see me as I am," she thought.

Deeper than the deepest fibre of her vanity was the triumphant sense that *as she was*, with her flattened hair, her tired pallor, her thin sleeves a little tumbled by the weight of her jacket, he would like her even better, feel her nearer, dearer, more desirable, than in all the splendours she might put on for him. In the light of this discovery she studied her face with a new intentness, seeing its defects as she had never seen them, yet seeing them through a kind of radiance, as though love were a luminous medium into which she had been bodily plunged.

She was glad now that she had confessed her doubts and

her jealousy. She divined that a man in love may be flattered by such involuntary betrayals, that there are moments when respect for his liberty appeals to him less than the inability to respect it: moments so propitious that a woman's very mistakes and indiscretions may help to establish her dominion. The sense of power she had been aware of in talking to Darrow came back with ten-fold force. She felt like testing him by the most fantastic exactions, and at the same moment she longed to humble herself before him, to make herself the shadow and echo of his mood. She wanted to linger with him in a world of fancy and yet to walk at his side in the world of fact. She wanted him to feel her power and yet to love her for her ignorance and humility. She felt like a slave, and a goddess, and a girl in her teens . . .

XIII

Darrow, late that evening, threw himself into an arm-chair before his fire and mused.

The room was propitious to meditation. The red-veiled lamp, the corners of shadow, the splashes of firelight on the curves of old full-bodied wardrobes and cabinets, gave it an air of intimacy increased by its faded hangings, its slightly frayed and threadbare rugs. Everything in it was harmoniously shabby, with a subtle sought-for shabbiness in which Darrow fancied he discerned the touch of Fraser Leath. But Fraser Leath had grown so unimportant a factor in the scheme of things that these marks of his presence caused the young man no emotion beyond that of a faint retrospective amusement.

The afternoon and evening had been perfect.

After a moment of concern over her step-son's departure, Anna had surrendered herself to her happiness with an impetuosity that Darrow had never suspected in her. Early in the afternoon they had gone out in the motor, traversing miles of sober-tinted landscape in which, here and there, a scarlet vineyard flamed, clattering through the streets of stony villages, coming out on low slopes above the river, or winding through the pale gold of narrow wood-roads with the blue of clear-cut hills at their end. Over everything lay a faint sunshine that seemed dissolved in the still air, and the smell of wet roots and decaying leaves was merged in the pungent scent of burning underbrush. Once, at the turn of a wall, they stopped the motor before a ruined gateway and, stumbling along a road full of ruts, stood before a little old deserted house, fantastically carved and chimneyed, which lay in a moat under the shade of ancient trees. They paced the paths between the trees, found a mouldy Temple of Love on an islet among reeds and plantains, and, sitting on a bench in the stable-yard, watched the pigeons circling against the sunset over their cot of patterned brick. Then the motor flew on into the dusk . . .

When they came in they sat beside the fire in the oak drawing-room, and Darrow noticed how delicately her head stood

out against the sombre panelling, and mused on the enjoyment there would always be in the mere fact of watching her
hands as they moved about among the tea-things . . .

They dined late, and facing her across the table, with its
low lights and flowers, he felt an extraordinary pleasure in
seeing her again in evening dress, and in letting his eyes dwell
on the proud shy set of her head, the way her dark hair
clasped it, and the girlish thinness of her neck above the slight
swell of the breast. His imagination was struck by the quality
of reticence in her beauty. She suggested a fine portrait kept
down to a few tones, or a Greek vase on which the play of
light is the only pattern.

After dinner they went out on the terrace for a look at the
moon-misted park. Through the crepuscular whiteness the
trees hung in blotted masses. Below the terrace, the garden
drew its dark diagrams between statues that stood like muffled conspirators on the edge of the shadow. Farther off, the
meadows unrolled a silver-shot tissue to the mantling of mist
above the river; and the autumn stars trembled overhead like
their own reflections seen in dim water.

He lit his cigar, and they walked slowly up and down the
flags in the languid air, till he put an arm about her, saying:
"You mustn't stay till you're chilled"; then they went back
into the room and drew up their chairs to the fire.

It seemed only a moment later that she said: "It must be
after eleven," and stood up and looked down on him, smiling
faintly. He sat still, absorbing the look, and thinking:
"There'll be evenings and evenings"—till she came nearer,
bent over him, and with a hand on his shoulder said: "Good
night."

He got to his feet and put his arms about her.

"Good night," he answered, and held her fast; and they
gave each other a long kiss of promise and communion.

The memory of it glowed in him still as he sat over his
crumbling fire; but beneath his physical exultation he felt a
certain gravity of mood. His happiness was in some sort the
rallying-point of many scattered purposes. He summed it up
vaguely by saying to himself that to be loved by a woman like
that made "all the difference" . . . He was a little tired of
experimenting on life; he wanted to "take a line", to follow

things up, to centralize and concentrate, and produce results. Two or three more years of diplomacy—with her beside him!—and then their real life would begin: study, travel and book-making for him, and for her—well, the joy, at any rate, of getting out of an atmosphere of bric-à-brac and card-leaving into the open air of competing activities.

The desire for change had for some time been latent in him, and his meeting with Mrs. Leath the previous spring had given it a definite direction. With such a comrade to focus and stimulate his energies he felt modestly but agreeably sure of "doing something". And under this assurance was the lurking sense that he was somehow worthy of his opportunity. His life, on the whole, had been a creditable affair. Out of modest chances and middling talents he had built himself a fairly marked personality, known some exceptional people, done a number of interesting and a few rather difficult things, and found himself, at thirty-seven, possessed of an intellectual ambition sufficient to occupy the passage to a robust and energetic old age. As for the private and personal side of his life, it had come up to the current standards, and if it had dropped, now and then, below a more ideal measure, even these declines had been brief, parenthetic, incidental. In the recognized essentials he had always remained strictly within the limit of his scruples.

From this reassuring survey of his case he came back to the contemplation of its crowning felicity. His mind turned again to his first meeting with Anna Summers and took up one by one the threads of their faintly sketched romance. He dwelt with pardonable pride on the fact that fate had so early marked him for the high privilege of possessing her: it seemed to mean that they had really, in the truest sense of the ill-used phrase, been made for each other.

Deeper still than all these satisfactions was the mere elemental sense of well-being in her presence. That, after all, was what proved her to be the woman for him: the pleasure he took in the set of her head, the way her hair grew on her forehead and at the nape, her steady gaze when he spoke, the grave freedom of her gait and gestures. He recalled every detail of her face, the fine veinings of the temples, the bluish-brown shadows in her upper lids, and the way the reflections of two stars seemed to form and break up in her eyes when he held her close to him . . .

If he had had any doubt as to the nature of her feeling for him those dissolving stars would have allayed it. She was reserved, she was shy even, was what the shallow and effusive would call "cold". She was like a picture so hung that it can be seen only at a certain angle: an angle known to no one but its possessor. The thought flattered his sense of possessorship . . . He felt that the smile on his lips would have been fatuous had it had a witness. He was thinking of her look when she had questioned him about his meeting with Owen at the theatre: less of her words than of her look, and of the effort the question cost her: the reddening of her cheek, the deepening of the strained line between her brows, the way her eyes sought shelter and then turned and drew on him. Pride and passion were in the conflict—magnificent qualities in a wife! The sight almost made up for his momentary embarrassment at the rousing of a memory which had no place in his present picture of himself. Yes! It was worth a good deal to watch that fight between her instinct and her intelligence, and know one's self the object of the struggle . . .

Mingled with these sensations were considerations of another order. He reflected with satisfaction that she was the kind of woman with whom one would like to be seen in public. It would be distinctly agreeable to follow her into drawing-rooms, to walk after her down the aisle of a theatre, to get in and out of trains with her, to say "my wife" of her to all sorts of people. He draped these details in the handsome phrase "She's a woman to be proud of", and felt that this fact somehow justified and ennobled his instinctive boyish satisfaction in loving her.

He stood up, rambled across the room and leaned out for a while into the starry night. Then he dropped again into his armchair with a sigh of deep content.

"Oh, hang it," he suddenly exclaimed, "it's the best thing that's ever happened to me, anyhow!"

The next day was even better. He felt, and knew she felt, that they had reached a clearer understanding of each other. It was as if, after a swim through bright opposing waves, with

a dazzle of sun in their eyes, they had gained an inlet in the
shades of a cliff, where they could float on the still surface
and gaze far down into the depths.

Now and then, as they walked and talked, he felt a thrill of
youthful wonder at the coincidence of their views and their
experiences, at the way their minds leapt to the same point in
the same instant.

"The old delusion, I suppose," he smiled to himself. "Will
Nature never tire of the trick?"

But he knew it was more than that. There were moments
in their talk when he felt, distinctly and unmistakably, the
solid ground of friendship underneath the whirling dance of
his sensations. "How I should like her if I didn't love her!"
he summed it up, wondering at the miracle of such a union.

In the course of the morning a telegram had come from
Owen Leath, announcing that he, his grandmother and Effie
would arrive from Dijon that afternoon at four. The station
of the main line was eight or ten miles from Givré, and Anna,
soon after three, left in the motor to meet the travellers.

When she had gone Darrow started for a walk, planning to
get back late, in order that the reunited family might have the
end of the afternoon to themselves. He roamed the country-
side till long after dark, and the stable-clock of Givré was
striking seven as he walked up the avenue to the court.

In the hall, coming down the stairs, he encountered Anna.
Her face was serene, and his first glance showed him that
Owen had kept his word and that none of her forebodings
had been fulfilled.

She had just come down from the school-room, where
Effie and the governess were having supper; the little girl, she
told him, looked immensely better for her Swiss holiday, but
was dropping with sleep after the journey, and too tired to
make her habitual appearance in the drawing-room before
being put to bed. Madame de Chantelle was resting, but
would be down for dinner; and as for Owen, Anna supposed
he was off somewhere in the park—he had a passion for
prowling about the park at nightfall . . .

Darrow followed her into the brown room, where the tea-
table had been left for him. He declined her offer of tea, but
she lingered a moment to tell him that Owen had in fact kept

his word, and that Madame de Chantelle had come back in the best of humours, and unsuspicious of the blow about to fall.

"She has enjoyed her month at Ouchy, and it has given her a lot to talk about—her symptoms, and the rival doctors, and the people at the hotel. It seems she met your Ambassadress there, and Lady Wantley, and some other London friends of yours, and she's heard what she calls 'delightful things' about you: she told me to tell you so. She attaches great importance to the fact that your grandmother was an Everard of Albany. She's prepared to open her arms to you. I don't know whether it won't make it harder for poor Owen . . . the contrast, I mean . . . There are no Ambassadresses or Everards to vouch for *his* choice! But you'll help me, won't you? You'll help me to help him? To-morrow I'll tell you the rest. Now I must rush up and tuck in Effie . . ."

"Oh, you'll see, we'll pull it off for him!" he assured her; "together, we can't fail to pull it off."

He stood and watched her with a smile as she fled down the half-lit vista to the hall.

XIV

I F DARROW, on entering the drawing-room before dinner, examined its new occupant with unusual interest, it was more on Owen Leath's account than his own.

Anna's hints had roused his interest in the lad's love affair, and he wondered what manner of girl the heroine of the coming conflict might be. He had guessed that Owen's rebellion symbolized for his step-mother her own long struggle against the Leath conventions, and he understood that if Anna so passionately abetted him it was partly because, as she owned, she wanted his liberation to coincide with hers.

The lady who was to represent, in the impending struggle, the forces of order and tradition was seated by the fire when Darrow entered. Among the flowers and old furniture of the large pale-panelled room, Madame de Chantelle had the inanimate elegance of a figure introduced into a "still-life" to give the scale. And this, Darrow reflected, was exactly what she doubtless regarded as her chief obligation: he was sure she thought a great deal of "measure", and approved of most things only up to a certain point.

She was a woman of sixty, with a figure at once young and old-fashioned. Her fair faded tints, her quaint corseting, the *passementerie* on her tight-waisted dress, the velvet band on her tapering arm, made her resemble a "carte de visite" photograph of the middle sixties. One saw her, younger but no less invincibly lady-like, leaning on a chair with a fringed back, a curl in her neck, a locket on her tuckered bosom, toward the end of an embossed morocco album beginning with The Beauties of the Second Empire.

She received her daughter-in-law's suitor with an affability which implied her knowledge and approval of his suit. Darrow had already guessed her to be a person who would instinctively oppose any suggested changes, and then, after one had exhausted one's main arguments, unexpectedly yield to some small incidental reason, and adhere doggedly to her new position. She boasted of her old-fashioned prejudices, talked a good deal of being a grandmother, and made a show of reaching up to tap Owen's shoulder, though his height was little more than hers.

She was full of a small pale prattle about the people she had seen at Ouchy, as to whom she had the minute statistical information of a gazetteer, without any apparent sense of personal differences. She said to Darrow: "They tell me things are very much changed in America . . . Of course in my youth there *was* a Society" . . . She had no desire to return there: she was sure the standards must be so different. "There are charming people everywhere . . . and one must always look on the best side . . . but when one has lived among Traditions it's difficult to adapt one's self to the new ideas . . . These dreadful views of marriage . . . it's so hard to explain them to my French relations . . . I'm thankful to say I don't pretend to understand them myself! But *you're* an Everard— I told Anna last spring in London that one sees that instantly" . . .

She wandered off to the cooking and the service of the hotel at Ouchy. She attached great importance to gastronomic details and to the manners of hotel servants. There, too, there was a falling off, she said. "I don't know, of course; but people say it's owing to the Americans. Certainly my waiter had a way of slapping down the dishes . . . they tell me that many of them are Anarchists . . . belong to Unions, you know." She appealed to Darrow's reported knowledge of economic conditions to confirm this ominous rumour.

After dinner Owen Leath wandered into the next room, where the piano stood, and began to play among the shadows. His step-mother presently joined him, and Darrow sat alone with Madame de Chantelle.

She took up the thread of her mild chat and carried it on at the same pace as her knitting. Her conversation resembled the large loose-stranded web between her fingers: now and then she dropped a stitch, and went on regardless of the gap in the pattern.

Darrow listened with a lazy sense of well-being. In the mental lull of the after-dinner hour, with harmonious memories murmuring through his mind, and the soft tints and shadowy spaces of the fine old room charming his eyes to indolence, Madame de Chantelle's discourse seemed not out of place. He could understand that, in the long run, the atmosphere of Givré might be suffocating; but in his present mood its very limitations had a grace.

Presently he found the chance to say a word in his own behalf; and thereupon measured the advantage, never before particularly apparent to him, of being related to the Everards of Albany. Madame de Chantelle's conception of her native country—to which she had not returned since her twentieth year—reminded him of an ancient geographer's map of the Hyperborean regions. It was all a foggy blank, from which only one or two fixed outlines emerged; and one of these belonged to the Everards of Albany.

The fact that they offered such firm footing—formed, so to speak, a friendly territory on which the opposing powers could meet and treat—helped him through the task of explaining and justifying himself as the successor of Fraser Leath. Madame de Chantelle could not resist such incontestable claims. She seemed to feel her son's hovering and discriminating presence, and she gave Darrow the sense that he was being tested and approved as a last addition to the Leath Collection.

She also made him aware of the immense advantage he possessed in belonging to the diplomatic profession. She spoke of this humdrum calling as a Career, and gave Darrow to understand that she supposed him to have been seducing Duchesses when he was not negotiating Treaties. He heard again quaint phrases which romantic old ladies had used in his youth: "Brilliant diplomatic society . . . social advantages . . . the *entrée* everywhere . . . nothing else *forms* a young man in the same way . . ." and she sighingly added that she could have wished her grandson had chosen the same path to glory.

Darrow prudently suppressed his own view of the profession, as well as the fact that he had adopted it provisionally, and for reasons less social than sociological; and the talk presently passed on to the subject of his future plans.

Here again, Madame de Chantelle's awe of the Career made her admit the necessity of Anna's consenting to an early marriage. The fact that Darrow was "ordered" to South America seemed to put him in the romantic light of a young soldier charged to lead a forlorn hope: she sighed and said: "At such moments a wife's duty is at her husband's side."

The problem of Effie's future might have disturbed her, she added; but since Anna, for a time, consented to leave the little girl with her, that problem was at any rate deferred. She spoke plaintively of the responsibility of looking after her granddaughter, but Darrow divined that she enjoyed the flavour of the word more than she felt the weight of the fact.

"Effie's a perfect child. She's more like my son, perhaps, than dear Owen. She'll never intentionally give me the least trouble. But of course the responsibility will be great . . . I'm not sure I should dare to undertake it if it were not for her having such a treasure of a governess. Has Anna told you about our little governess? After all the worry we had last year, with one impossible creature after another, it seems providential, just now, to have found her. At first we were afraid she was too young; but now we've the greatest confidence in her. So clever and amusing—and *such* a lady! I don't say her education's all it might be . . . no drawing or singing . . . but one can't have everything; and she speaks Italian . . ."

Madame de Chantelle's fond insistence on the likeness between Effie Leath and her father, if not particularly gratifying to Darrow, had at least increased his desire to see the little girl. It gave him an odd feeling of discomfort to think that she should have any of the characteristics of the late Fraser Leath: he had, somehow, fantastically pictured her as the mystical offspring of the early tenderness between himself and Anna Summers.

His encounter with Effie took place the next morning, on the lawn below the terrace, where he found her, in the early sunshine, knocking about golf balls with her brother. Almost at once, and with infinite relief, he saw that the resemblance of which Madame de Chantelle boasted was mainly external. Even that discovery was slightly distasteful, though Darrow was forced to own that Fraser Leath's straight-featured fairness had lent itself to the production of a peculiarly finished image of childish purity. But it was evident that other elements had also gone to the making of Effie, and that another spirit sat in her eyes. Her serious handshake, her "pretty" greeting, were worthy of the Leath tradition, and he guessed her to be more malleable than Owen, more subject to the influences of Givré; but the shout with which she returned to her romp had in it the note of her mother's emancipation.

He had begged a holiday for her, and when Mrs. Leath appeared he and she and the little girl went off for a ramble. Anna wished her daughter to have time to make friends with Darrow before learning in what relation he was to stand to her; and the three roamed the woods and fields till the distant chime of the stable-clock made them turn back for luncheon.

Effie, who was attended by a shaggy terrier, had picked up two or three subordinate dogs at the stable; and as she trotted on ahead with her yapping escort, Anna hung back to throw a look at Darrow.

"Yes," he answered it, "she's exquisite . . . Oh, I see what I'm asking of you! But she'll be quite happy here, won't she? And you must remember it won't be for long . . ."

Anna sighed her acquiescence. "Oh, she'll be happy here. It's her nature to be happy. She'll apply herself to it, conscientiously, as she does to her lessons, and to what she calls 'being good' . . . In a way, you see, that's just what worries me. Her idea of 'being good' is to please the person she's with—she puts her whole dear little mind on it! And so, if ever she's with the wrong person——"

"But surely there's no danger of that just now? Madame de Chantelle tells me that you've at last put your hand on a perfect governess——"

Anna, without answering, glanced away from him toward her daughter.

"It's lucky, at any rate," Darrow continued, "that Madame de Chantelle thinks her so."

"Oh, I think very highly of her too."

"Highly enough to feel quite satisfied to leave her with Effie?"

"Yes. She's just the person for Effie. Only, of course, one never knows . . . She's young, and she might take it into her head to leave us . . ." After a pause she added: "I'm naturally anxious to know what you think of her."

When they entered the house the hands of the hall clock stood within a few minutes of the luncheon hour. Anna led

Effie off to have her hair smoothed and Darrow wandered into the oak sitting-room, which he found untenanted. The sun lay pleasantly on its brown walls, on the scattered books and the flowers in old porcelain vases. In his eyes lingered the vision of the dark-haired mother mounting the stairs with her little fair daughter. The contrast between them seemed a last touch of grace in the complex harmony of things. He stood in the window, looking out at the park, and brooding inwardly upon his happiness . . .

He was roused by Effie's voice and the scamper of her feet down the long floors behind him.

"Here he is! Here he is!" she cried, flying over the threshold.

He turned and stooped to her with a smile, and as she caught his hand he perceived that she was trying to draw him toward some one who had paused behind her in the doorway, and whom he supposed to be her mother.

"*Here* he is!" Effie repeated, with her sweet impatience.

The figure in the doorway came forward and Darrow, looking up, found himself face to face with Sophy Viner. They stood still, a yard or two apart, and looked at each other without speaking.

As they paused there, a shadow fell across one of the terrace windows, and Owen Leath stepped whistling into the room. In his rough shooting clothes, with the glow of exercise under his fair skin, he looked extraordinarily light-hearted and happy. Darrow, with a quick side-glance, noticed this, and perceived also that the glow on the youth's cheek had deepened suddenly to red. He too stopped short, and the three stood there motionless for a barely perceptible beat of time. During its lapse, Darrow's eyes had turned back from Owen's face to that of the girl between them. He had the sense that, whatever was done, it was he who must do it, and that it must be done immediately. He went forward and held out his hand.

"How do you do, Miss Viner?"

She answered: "How do you do?" in a voice that sounded clear and natural; and the next moment he again became aware of steps behind him, and knew that Mrs. Leath was in the room.

To his strained senses there seemed to be another just measurable pause before Anna said, looking gaily about the little group: "Has Owen introduced you? This is Effie's friend, Miss Viner."

Effie, still hanging on her governess's arm, pressed herself closer with a little gesture of appropriation; and Miss Viner laid her hand on her pupil's hair.

Darrow felt that Anna's eyes had turned to him.

"I think Miss Viner and I have met already—several years ago in London."

"I remember," said Sophy Viner, in the same clear voice.

"How charming! Then we're all friends. But luncheon must be ready," said Mrs. Leath.

She turned back to the door, and the little procession moved down the two long drawing-rooms, with Effie waltzing on ahead.

XV

MADAME DE CHANTELLE and Anna had planned, for the afternoon, a visit to a remotely situated acquaintance whom the introduction of the motor had transformed into a neighbour. Effie was to pay for her morning's holiday by an hour or two in the school-room, and Owen suggested that he and Darrow should betake themselves to a distant covert in the desultory quest for pheasants.

Darrow was not an ardent sportsman, but any pretext for physical activity would have been acceptable at the moment; and he was glad both to get away from the house and not to be left to himself.

When he came downstairs the motor was at the door, and Anna stood before the hall mirror, swathing her hat in veils. She turned at the sound of his step and smiled at him for a long full moment.

"I'd no idea you knew Miss Viner," she said, as he helped her into her long coat.

"It came back to me, luckily, that I'd seen her two or three times in London, several years ago. She was secretary, or something of the sort, in the background of a house where I used to dine."

He loathed the slighting indifference of the phrase, but he had uttered it deliberately, had been secretly practising it all through the interminable hour at the luncheon-table. Now that it was spoken, he shivered at its note of condescension. In such cases one was almost sure to overdo . . . But Anna seemed to notice nothing unusual.

"Was she really? You must tell me all about it—tell me exactly how she struck you. I'm so glad it turns out that you know her."

" 'Know' is rather exaggerated: we used to pass each other on the stairs."

Madame de Chantelle and Owen appeared together as he spoke, and Anna, gathering up her wraps, said: "You'll tell me about that, then. Try and remember everything you can."

As he tramped through the woods at his young host's side, Darrow felt the partial relief from thought produced by exercise and the obligation to talk. Little as he cared for shooting, he had the habit of concentration which makes it natural for a man to throw himself wholly into whatever business he has in hand, and there were moments of the afternoon when a sudden whirr in the undergrowth, a vivider gleam against the hazy browns and greys of the woods, was enough to fill the foreground of his attention. But all the while, behind these voluntarily emphasized sensations, his secret consciousness continued to revolve on a loud wheel of thought. For a time it seemed to be sweeping him through deep gulfs of darkness. His sensations were too swift and swarming to be disentangled. He had an almost physical sense of struggling for air, of battling helplessly with material obstructions, as though the russet covert through which he trudged were the heart of a maleficent jungle . . .

Snatches of his companion's talk drifted to him intermittently through the confusion of his thoughts. He caught eager self-revealing phrases, and understood that Owen was saying things about himself, perhaps hinting indirectly at the hopes for which Darrow had been prepared by Anna's confidences. He had already become aware that the lad liked him, and had meant to take the first opportunity of showing that he reciprocated the feeling. But the effort of fixing his attention on Owen's words was so great that it left no power for more than the briefest and most inexpressive replies.

Young Leath, it appeared, felt that he had reached a turning-point in his career, a height from which he could impartially survey his past progress and projected endeavour. At one time he had had musical and literary yearnings, visions of desultory artistic indulgence; but these had of late been superseded by the resolute determination to plunge into practical life.

"I don't want, you see," Darrow heard him explaining, "to drift into what my grandmother, poor dear, is trying to make of me: an adjunct of Givré. I don't want—hang it all!—to slip into collecting sensations as my father collected snuffboxes. I want Effie to have Givré—it's my grandmother's, you know, to do as she likes with; and I've understood lately that if it belonged to me it would gradually gobble me up. I want to get out of it, into a life that's big and ugly and struggling. If I can extract beauty out of *that*, so much the better: that'll prove my vocation. But I want to *make* beauty, not be drowned in the ready-made, like a bee in a pot of honey."

Darrow knew that he was being appealed to for corroboration of these views and for encouragement in the course to which they pointed. To his own ears his answers sounded now curt, now irrelevant: at one moment he seemed chillingly indifferent, at another he heard himself launching out on a flood of hazy discursiveness. He dared not look at Owen, for fear of detecting the lad's surprise at these senseless transitions. And through the confusion of his inward struggles and outward loquacity he heard the ceaseless trip-hammer beat of the question: "What in God's name shall I do?" . . .

To get back to the house before Anna's return seemed his most pressing necessity. He did not clearly know why: he simply felt that he ought to be there. At one moment it occurred to him that Miss Viner might want to speak to him alone—and again, in the same flash, that it would probably be the last thing she would want . . . At any rate, he felt he ought to try to speak to *her*; or at least be prepared to do so, if the chance should occur . . .

Finally, toward four, he told his companion that he had some letters on his mind and must get back to the house and despatch them before the ladies returned. He left Owen with the beater and walked on to the edge of the covert. At the park gates he struck obliquely through the trees, following a grass avenue at the end of which he had caught a glimpse of the roof of the chapel. A grey haze had blotted out the sun and the still air clung about him tepidly. At length the house-front raised before him its expanse of damp-silvered brick, and he was struck afresh by the high decorum of its calm lines and soberly massed surfaces. It made him feel, in the turbid coil of his fears and passions, like a muddy tramp forcing his way into some pure sequestered shrine . . .

By and bye, he knew, he should have to think the complex horror out, slowly, systematically, bit by bit; but for the moment it was whirling him about so fast that he could just clutch at its sharp spikes and be tossed off again. Only one definite immediate fact stuck in his quivering grasp. He must give the girl every chance—must hold himself passive till she had taken them . . .

In the court Effie ran up to him with her leaping terrier.

"I was coming out to meet you—you and Owen. Miss Viner was coming, too, and then she couldn't because she's got such a headache. I'm afraid I gave it to her because I did my division so disgracefully. It's too bad, isn't it? But won't you walk back with me? Nurse won't mind the least bit; she'd so much rather go in to tea."

Darrow excused himself laughingly, on the plea that he had letters to write, which was much worse than having a head-ache, and not infrequently resulted in one.

"Oh, then you can go and write them in Owen's study. That's where gentlemen always write their letters."

She flew on with her dog and Darrow pursued his way to the house. Effie's suggestion struck him as useful. He had pic-tured himself as vaguely drifting about the drawing-rooms, and had perceived the difficulty of Miss Viner's having to seek him there; but the study, a small room on the right of the hall, was in easy sight from the staircase, and so situated that there would be nothing marked in his being found there in talk with her.

He went in, leaving the door open, and sat down at the writing-table. The room was a friendly heterogeneous place, the one repository, in the well-ordered and amply-servanted house, of all its unclassified odds and ends: Effie's croquet-box and fishing rods, Owen's guns and golf-sticks and rac-quets, his step-mother's flower-baskets and gardening imple-ments, even Madame de Chantelle's embroidery frame, and the back numbers of the Catholic Weekly. The early twilight had begun to fall, and presently a slanting ray across the desk showed Darrow that a servant was coming across the hall with a lamp. He pulled out a sheet of note-paper and began to write at random, while the man, entering, put the lamp at his elbow and vaguely "straightened" the heap of newspapers tossed on the divan. Then his steps died away and Darrow sat leaning his head on his locked hands.

Presently another step sounded on the stairs, wavered a moment and then moved past the threshold of the study. Darrow got up and walked into the hall, which was still un-

lighted. In the dimness he saw Sophy Viner standing by the
hall door in her hat and jacket. She stopped at sight of him,
her hand on the door-bolt, and they stood for a second without speaking.

"Have you seen Effie?" she suddenly asked. "She went out
to meet you."

"She *did* meet me, just now, in the court. She's gone on to
join her brother."

Darrow spoke as naturally as he could, but his voice
sounded to his own ears like an amateur actor's in a "light"
part.

Miss Viner, without answering, drew back the bolt. He
watched her in silence as the door swung open; then he said:
"She has her nurse with her. She won't be long."

She stood irresolute, and he added: "I was writing in
there—won't you come and have a little talk? Every one's
out."

The last words struck him as not well-chosen, but there was
no time to choose. She paused a second longer and then
crossed the threshold of the study. At luncheon she had sat
with her back to the window, and beyond noting that she
had grown a little thinner, and had less colour and vivacity,
he had seen no change in her; but now, as the lamplight fell
on her face, its whiteness startled him.

"Poor thing . . . poor thing . . . what in heaven's name
can she suppose?" he wondered.

"Do sit down—I want to talk to you," he said and pushed
a chair toward her.

She did not seem to see it, or, if she did, she deliberately
chose another seat. He came back to his own chair and leaned
his elbows on the blotter. She faced him from the farther side
of the table.

"You promised to let me hear from you now and then," he
began awkwardly, and with a sharp sense of his awkwardness.

A faint smile made her face more tragic. "Did I? There
was nothing to tell. I've had no history—like the happy
countries . . ."

He waited a moment before asking: "You *are* happy here?"

"I *was*," she said with a faint emphasis.

"Why do you say 'was'? You're surely not thinking of

going? There can't be kinder people anywhere." Darrow hardly knew what he was saying; but her answer came to him with deadly definiteness.

"I suppose it depends on you whether I go or stay."

"On me?" He stared at her across Owen's scattered papers. "Good God! What can you think of me, to say that?"

The mockery of the question flashed back at him from her wretched face. She stood up, wandered away, and leaned an instant in the darkening window-frame. From there she turned to fling back at him: "Don't imagine I'm the least bit sorry for anything!"

He steadied his elbows on the table and hid his face in his hands. It was harder, oh, damnably harder, than he had expected! Arguments, expedients, palliations, evasions, all seemed to be slipping away from him: he was left face to face with the mere graceless fact of his inferiority. He lifted his head to ask at random: "You've been here, then, ever since——?"

"Since June; yes. It turned out that the Farlows were hunting for me—all the while—for *this*."

She stood facing him, her back to the window, evidently impatient to be gone, yet with something still to say, or that she expected to hear him say. The sense of her expectancy benumbed him. What in heaven's name could he say to her that was not an offense or a mockery?

"Your idea of the theatre—you gave that up at once, then?"

"Oh, the theatre!" She gave a little laugh. "I couldn't wait for the theatre. I had to take the first thing that offered; I took this."

He pushed on haltingly: "I'm glad—extremely glad— you're happy here . . . I'd counted on your letting me know if there was anything I could do . . . The theatre, now—if you still regret it—if you're not contented here . . . I know people in that line in London—I'm certain I can manage it for you when I get back——"

She moved up to the table and leaned over it to ask, in a voice that was hardly above a whisper: "Then you *do* want me to leave? Is that it?"

He dropped his arms with a groan. "Good heavens! How

can you think such things? At the time, you know, I begged you to let me do what I could, but you wouldn't hear of it . . . and ever since I've been wanting to be of use—to do something, anything, to help you . . ."

She heard him through, motionless, without a quiver of the clasped hands she rested on the edge of the table.

"If you want to help me, then—you can help me to stay here," she brought out with low-toned intensity.

Through the stillness of the pause which followed, the bray of a motor-horn sounded far down the drive. Instantly she turned, with a last white look at him, and fled from the room and up the stairs. He stood motionless, benumbed by the shock of her last words. She was *afraid*, then—afraid of him—sick with fear of him! The discovery beat him down to a lower depth . . .

The motor-horn sounded again, close at hand, and he turned and went up to his room. His letter-writing was a sufficient pretext for not immediately joining the party about the tea-table, and he wanted to be alone and try to put a little order into his tumultuous thinking.

Upstairs, the room held out the intimate welcome of its lamp and fire. Everything in it exhaled the same sense of peace and stability which, two evenings before, had lulled him to complacent meditation. His armchair again invited him from the hearth, but he was too agitated to sit still, and with sunk head and hands clasped behind his back he began to wander up and down the room.

His five minutes with Sophy Viner had flashed strange lights into the shadowy corners of his consciousness. The girl's absolute candour, her hard ardent honesty, was for the moment the vividest point in his thoughts. He wondered anew, as he had wondered before, at the way in which the harsh discipline of life had stripped her of false sentiment without laying the least touch on her pride. When they had parted, five months before, she had quietly but decidedly rejected all his offers of help, even to the suggestion of his trying to further her theatrical aims: she had made it clear that she wished their brief alliance to leave no trace on their lives save that of its own smiling memory. But now that they were unexpectedly confronted in a situation which seemed, to her terrified fancy, to put her at his mercy, her first impulse was to defend her right to the place she had won, and to learn as quickly as possible if he meant to dispute it. While he had pictured her as shrinking away from him in a tremor of self-effacement she had watched his movements, made sure of her opportunity, and come straight down to "have it out" with him. He was so struck by the frankness and energy of the proceeding that for a moment he lost sight of the view of his own character implied in it.

"Poor thing . . . poor thing!" he could only go on saying; and with the repetition of the words the picture of himself as she must see him pitiably took shape again.

He understood then, for the first time, how vague, in comparison with hers, had been his own vision of the part he had played in the brief episode of their relation. The incident had left in him a sense of exasperation and self-contempt, but that, as he now perceived, was chiefly, if not altogether, as it bore on his preconceived ideal of his attitude toward another woman. He had fallen below his own standard of sentimental loyalty, and if he thought of Sophy Viner it was mainly as the chance instrument of his lapse. These considerations were not agreeable to his pride, but they were forced on him by the example of her valiant common-sense. If he had cut a sorry figure in the business, he owed it to her not to close his eyes to the fact any longer . . .

But when he opened them, what did he see? The situation, detestable at best, would yet have been relatively simple if protecting Sophy Viner had been the only duty involved in it. The fact that that duty was paramount did not do away with the contingent obligations. It was Darrow's instinct, in difficult moments, to go straight to the bottom of the difficulty; but he had never before had to take so dark a dive as this, and for the minute he shivered on the brink . . . Well, his first duty, at any rate, was to the girl: he must let her see that he meant to fulfill it to the last jot, and then try to find out how to square the fulfillment with the other problems already in his path . . .

XVI

IN THE OAK ROOM he found Mrs. Leath, her mother-in-law and Effie. The group, as he came toward it down the long drawing-rooms, composed itself prettily about the tea-table. The lamps and the fire crossed their gleams on silver and porcelain, on the bright haze of Effie's hair and on the whiteness of Anna's forehead, as she leaned back in her chair behind the tea-urn.

She did not move at Darrow's approach, but lifted to him a deep gaze of peace and confidence. The look seemed to throw about him the spell of a divine security: he felt the joy of a convalescent suddenly waking to find the sunlight on his face.

Madame de Chantelle, across her knitting, discoursed of their afternoon's excursion, with occasional pauses induced by the hypnotic effect of the fresh air; and Effie, kneeling on the hearth, softly but insistently sought to implant in her terrier's mind some notion of the relation between a vertical attitude and sugar.

Darrow took a chair behind the little girl, so that he might look across at her mother. It was almost a necessity for him, at the moment, to let his eyes rest on Anna's face, and to meet, now and then, the proud shyness of her gaze.

Madame de Chantelle presently enquired what had become of Owen, and a moment later the window behind her opened, and her grandson, gun in hand, came in from the terrace. As he stood there in the lamp-light, with dead leaves and bits of bramble clinging to his mud-spattered clothes, the scent of the night about him and its chill on his pale bright face, he really had the look of a young faun strayed in from the forest.

Effie abandoned the terrier to fly to him. "Oh, Owen, where in the world have you been? I walked miles and miles with Nurse and couldn't find you, and we met Jean and he said he didn't know where you'd gone."

"Nobody knows where I go, or what I see when I get there—that's the beauty of it!" he laughed back at her. "But if you're good," he added, "I'll tell you about it one of these days."

"Oh, now, Owen, now! I don't really believe I'll ever be much better than I am now."

"Let Owen have his tea first," her mother suggested; but the young man, declining the offer, propped his gun against the wall, and, lighting a cigarette, began to pace up and down the room in a way that reminded Darrow of his own caged wanderings. Effie pursued him with her blandishments, and for a while he poured out to her a low-voiced stream of nonsense; then he sat down beside his step-mother and leaned over to help himself to tea.

"Where's Miss Viner?" he asked, as Effie climbed up on him. "Why isn't she here to chain up this ungovernable infant?"

"Poor Miss Viner has a headache. Effie says she went to her room as soon as lessons were over, and sent word that she wouldn't be down for tea."

"Ah," said Owen, abruptly setting down his cup. He stood up, lit another cigarette, and wandered away to the piano in the room beyond.

From the twilight where he sat a lonely music, borne on fantastic chords, floated to the group about the tea-table. Under its influence Madame de Chantelle's meditative pauses increased in length and frequency, and Effie stretched herself on the hearth, her drowsy head against the dog. Presently her nurse appeared, and Anna rose at the same time. "Stop a minute in my sitting-room on your way up," she paused to say to Darrow as she went.

A few hours earlier, her request would have brought him instantly to his feet. She had given him, on the day of his arrival, an inviting glimpse of the spacious book-lined room above stairs in which she had gathered together all the tokens of her personal tastes: the retreat in which, as one might fancy, Anna Leath had hidden the restless ghost of Anna Summers; and the thought of a talk with her there had been in his mind ever since. But now he sat motionless, as if spellbound by the play of Madame de Chantelle's needles and the pulsations of Owen's fitful music.

"She will want to ask me about the girl," he repeated to himself, with a fresh sense of the insidious taint that embittered all his thoughts; the hand of the slender-columned clock on the mantel-piece had spanned a half-hour before shame at his own indecision finally drew him to his feet.

From her writing-table, where she sat over a pile of letters, Anna lifted her happy smile. The impulse to press his lips to it made him come close and draw her upward. She threw her head back, as if surprised at the abruptness of the gesture; then her face leaned to his with the slow droop of a flower. He felt again the sweep of the secret tides, and all his fears went down in them.

She sat down in the sofa-corner by the fire and he drew an armchair close to her. His gaze roamed peacefully about the quiet room.

"It's just like you—it *is* you," he said, as his eyes came back to her.

"It's a good place to be alone in—I don't think I've ever before cared to talk with any one here."

"Let's be quiet, then: it's the best way of talking."

"Yes; but we must save it up till later. There are things I want to say to you now."

He leaned back in his chair. "Say them, then, and I'll listen."

"Oh, no. I want you to tell me about Miss Viner."

"About Miss Viner?" He summoned up a look of faint interrogation.

He thought she seemed surprised at his surprise. "It's important, naturally," she explained, "that I should find out all I can about her before I leave."

"Important on Effie's account?"

"On Effie's account—of course."

"Of course . . . But you've every reason to be satisfied, haven't you?"

"Every apparent reason. We all like her. Effie's very fond of her, and she seems to have a delightful influence on the child. But we know so little, after all—about her antecedents, I mean, and her past history. That's why I want you to try and recall everything you heard about her when you used to see her in London."

"Oh, on that score I'm afraid I sha'n't be of much use. As

I told you, she was a mere shadow in the background of the house I saw her in—and that was four or five years ago . . ."

"When she was with a Mrs. Murrett?"

"Yes; an appalling woman who runs a roaring dinner-factory that used now and then to catch me in its wheels. I escaped from them long ago; but in my time there used to be half a dozen fagged 'hands' to tend the machine, and Miss Viner was one of them. I'm glad she's out of it, poor girl!"

"Then you never really saw anything of her there?"

"I never had the chance. Mrs. Murrett discouraged any competition on the part of her subordinates."

"Especially such pretty ones, I suppose?" Darrow made no comment, and she continued: "And Mrs. Murrett's own opinion—if she'd offered you one—probably wouldn't have been of much value?"

"Only in so far as her disapproval would, on general principles, have been a good mark for Miss Viner. But surely," he went on after a pause, "you could have found out about her from the people through whom you first heard of her?"

Anna smiled. "Oh, we heard of her through Adelaide Painter—;" and in reply to his glance of interrogation she explained that the lady in question was a spinster of South Braintree, Massachusetts, who, having come to Paris some thirty years earlier, to nurse a brother through an illness, had ever since protestingly and provisionally camped there in a state of contemptuous protestation oddly manifested by her never taking the slip-covers off her drawing-room chairs. Her long residence on Gallic soil had not mitigated her hostility toward the creed and customs of the race, but though she always referred to the Catholic Church as the Scarlet Woman and took the darkest views of French private life, Madame de Chantelle placed great reliance on her judgment and experience, and in every domestic crisis the irreducible Adelaide was immediately summoned to Givré.

"It's all the odder because my mother-in-law, since her second marriage, has lived so much in the country that she's practically lost sight of all her other American friends. Besides which, you can see how completely she has identified herself with Monsieur de Chantelle's nationality and adopted French habits and prejudices. Yet when anything goes wrong she always sends for Adelaide Painter, who's more American than the Stars and Stripes, and might have left South Braintree yesterday, if she hadn't, rather, brought it over with her in her trunk."

Darrow laughed. "Well, then, if South Braintree vouches for Miss Viner——"

"Oh, but only indirectly. When we had that odious adventure with Mademoiselle Grumeau, who'd been so highly recommended by Monsieur de Chantelle's aunt, the Chanoinesse, Adelaide was of course sent for, and she said at once: 'I'm not the least bit surprised. I've always told you that what you wanted for Effie was a sweet American girl, and not one of these nasty foreigners.' Unluckily she couldn't, at the moment, put her hand on a sweet American; but she presently heard of Miss Viner through the Farlows, an excellent couple who live in the Quartier Latin and write about French life for the American papers. I was only too thankful to find anyone who was vouched for by decent people; and so far I've had no cause to regret my choice. But I know, after all, very little about Miss Viner; and there are all kinds of reasons why I want, as soon as possible, to find out more—to find out all I can."

"Since you've got to leave Effie I understand your feeling in that way. But is there, in such a case, any recommendation worth half as much as your own direct experience?"

"No; and it's been so favourable that I was ready to accept it as conclusive. Only, naturally, when I found you'd known her in London I was in hopes you'd give me some more specific reasons for liking her as much as I do."

"I'm afraid I can give you nothing more specific than my general vague impression that she seems very plucky and extremely nice."

"You don't, at any rate, know anything specific to the contrary?"

"To the contrary? How should I? I'm not conscious of ever having heard any one say two words about her. I only infer that she must have pluck and character to have stuck it out so long at Mrs. Murrett's."

"Yes, poor thing! She has pluck, certainly; and pride, too; which must have made it all the harder." Anna rose to her feet. "You don't know how glad I am that your impression's on the whole so good. I particularly wanted you to like her."

He drew her to him with a smile. "On that condition I'm prepared to love even Adelaide Painter."

"I almost hope you won't have the chance to—poor Adelaide! Her appearance here always coincides with a catastrophe."

"Oh, then I must manage to meet her elsewhere." He held Anna closer, saying to himself, as he smoothed back the hair from her forehead: "What does anything matter but just *this*?—Must I go now?" he added aloud.

She answered absently: "It must be time to dress"; then she drew back a little and laid her hands on his shoulders. "My love—oh, my dear love!" she said.

It came to him that they were the first words of endearment he had heard her speak, and their rareness gave them a magic quality of reassurance, as though no danger could strike through such a shield.

A knock on the door made them draw apart. Anna lifted her hand to her hair and Darrow stooped to examine a photograph of Effie on the writing-table.

"Come in!" Anna said.

The door opened and Sophy Viner entered. Seeing Darrow, she drew back.

"Do come in, Miss Viner," Anna repeated, looking at her kindly.

The girl, a quick red in her cheeks, still hesitated on the threshold.

"I'm so sorry; but Effie has mislaid her Latin grammar, and I thought she might have left it here. I need it to prepare for tomorrow's lesson."

"Is this it?" Darrow asked, picking up a book from the table.

"Oh, thank you!"

He held it out to her and she took it and moved to the door.

"Wait a minute, please, Miss Viner," Anna said; and as the girl turned back, she went on with her quiet smile: "Effie told us you'd gone to your room with a headache. You mustn't sit up over tomorrow's lessons if you don't feel well."

Sophy's blush deepened. "But you see I have to. Latin's one of my weak points, and there's generally only one page of this book between me and Effie." She threw the words off with a half-ironic smile. "Do excuse my disturbing you," she added.

"You didn't disturb me," Anna answered. Darrow perceived that she was looking intently at the girl, as though struck by something tense and tremulous in her face, her voice, her whole mien and attitude. "You *do* look tired. You'd much better go straight to bed. Effie won't be sorry to skip her Latin."

"Thank you—but I'm really all right," murmured Sophy Viner. Her glance, making a swift circuit of the room, dwelt for an appreciable instant on the intimate propinquity of arm-chair and sofa-corner; then she turned back to the door.

BOOK III

XVII

A T DINNER that evening Madame de Chantelle's slender
monologue was thrown out over gulfs of silence. Owen
was still in the same state of moody abstraction as when Darrow had left him at the piano; and even Anna's face, to her
friend's vigilant eye, revealed not, perhaps, a personal preoccupation, but a vague sense of impending disturbance.

She smiled, she bore a part in the talk, her eyes dwelt on
Darrow's with their usual deep reliance; but beneath the surface of her serenity his tense perceptions detected a hidden
stir.

He was sufficiently self-possessed to tell himself that it was
doubtless due to causes with which he was not directly concerned. He knew the question of Owen's marriage was soon
to be raised, and the abrupt alteration in the young man's
mood made it seem probable that he was himself the centre
of the atmospheric disturbance. For a moment it occurred to
Darrow that Anna might have employed her afternoon in
preparing Madame de Chantelle for her grandson's impending announcement; but a glance at the elder lady's unclouded
brow showed that he must seek elsewhere the clue to Owen's
taciturnity and his step-mother's concern. Possibly Anna had
found reason to change her own attitude in the matter, and
had made the change known to Owen. But this, again, was
negatived by the fact that, during the afternoon's shooting,
young Leath had been in a mood of almost extravagant ex-
pansiveness, and that, from the moment of his late return to
the house till just before dinner, there had been, to Darrow's
certain knowledge, no possibility of a private talk between
himself and his step-mother.

This obscured, if it narrowed, the field of conjecture; and
Darrow's gropings threw him back on the conclusion that he
was probably reading too much significance into the moods
of a lad he hardly knew, and who had been described to him
as subject to sudden changes of humour. As to Anna's fancied
perturbation, it might simply be due to the fact that she had
decided to plead Owen's cause the next day, and had perhaps

already had a glimpse of the difficulties awaiting her. But Darrow knew that he was too deep in his own perplexities to judge the mental state of those about him. It might be, after all, that the variations he felt in the currents of communication were caused by his own inward tremor.

Such, at any rate, was the conclusion he had reached when, shortly after the two ladies left the drawing-room, he bade Owen good-night and went up to his room. Ever since the rapid self-colloquy which had followed on his first sight of Sophy Viner, he had known there were other questions to be faced behind the one immediately confronting him. On the score of that one, at least, his mind, if not easy, was relieved. He had done what was possible to reassure the girl, and she had apparently recognized the sincerity of his intention. He had patched up as decent a conclusion as he could to an incident that should obviously have had no sequel; but he had known all along that with the securing of Miss Viner's peace of mind only a part of his obligation was discharged, and that with that part his remaining duty was in conflict. It had been his first business to convince the girl that their secret was safe with him; but it was far from easy to square this with the equally urgent obligation of safe-guarding Anna's responsibility toward her child. Darrow was not much afraid of accidental disclosures. Both he and Sophy Viner had too much at stake not to be on their guard. The fear that beset him was of another kind, and had a profounder source. He wanted to do all he could for the girl, but the fact of having had to urge Anna to confide Effie to her was peculiarly repugnant to him. His own ideas about Sophy Viner were too mixed and indeterminate for him not to feel the risk of such an experiment; yet he found himself in the intolerable position of appearing to press it on the woman he desired above all others to protect . . .

Till late in the night his thoughts revolved in a turmoil of indecision. His pride was humbled by the discrepancy between what Sophy Viner had been to him and what he had thought of her. This discrepancy, which at the time had seemed to simplify the incident, now turned out to be its most galling complication. The bare truth, indeed, was that he had hardly thought of her at all, either at the time or since, and that he was ashamed to base his judgment of her on his meagre memory of their adventure.

The essential cheapness of the whole affair—as far as his share in it was concerned—came home to him with humiliating distinctness. He would have liked to be able to feel that, at the time at least, he had staked something more on it, and had somehow, in the sequel, had a more palpable loss to show. But the plain fact was that he hadn't spent a penny on it; which was no doubt the reason of the prodigious score it had since been rolling up. At any rate, beat about the case as he would, it was clear that he owed it to Anna—and incidentally to his own peace of mind—to find some way of securing Sophy Viner's future without leaving her installed at Givré when he and his wife should depart for their new post.

The night brought no aid to the solving of this problem; but it gave him, at any rate, the clear conviction that no time was to be lost. His first step must be to obtain from Miss Viner the chance of another and calmer talk; and he resolved to seek it at the earliest hour.

He had gathered that Effie's lessons were preceded by an early scamper in the park, and conjecturing that her governess might be with her he betook himself the next morning to the terrace, whence he wandered on to the gardens and the walks beyond.

The atmosphere was still and pale. The muffled sunlight gleamed like gold tissue through grey gauze, and the beech alleys tapered away to a blue haze blent of sky and forest. It was one of those elusive days when the familiar forms of things seem about to dissolve in a prismatic shimmer.

The stillness was presently broken by joyful barks, and Darrow, tracking the sound, overtook Effie flying down one of the long alleys at the head of her pack. Beyond her he saw Miss Viner seated near the stone-rimmed basin beside which he and Anna had paused on their first walk to the river.

The girl, coming forward at his approach, returned his greeting almost gaily. His first glance showed him that she had regained her composure, and the change in her appearance gave him the measure of her fears. For the first time he saw in her again the sidelong grace that had charmed his eyes in Paris; but he saw it now as in a painted picture.

"Shall we sit down a minute?" he asked, as Effie trotted off.

The girl looked away from him. "I'm afraid there's not much time; we must be back at lessons at half-past nine."

"But it's barely ten minutes past. Let's at least walk a little way toward the river."

She glanced down the long walk ahead of them and then back in the direction of the house. "If you like," she said in a low voice, with one of her quick fluctuations of colour; but instead of taking the way he proposed she turned toward a narrow path which branched off obliquely through the trees.

Darrow was struck, and vaguely troubled, by the change in her look and tone. There was in them an undefinable appeal, whether for help or forbearance he could not tell. Then it occurred to him that there might have been something misleading in his so pointedly seeking her, and he felt a momentary constraint. To ease it he made an abrupt dash at the truth.

"I came out to look for you because our talk of yesterday was so unsatisfactory. I want to hear more about you—about your plans and prospects. I've been wondering ever since why you've so completely given up the theatre."

Her face instantly sharpened to distrust. "I had to live," she said in an off-hand tone.

"I understand perfectly that you should like it here—for a time." His glance strayed down the gold-roofed windings ahead of them. "It's delightful: you couldn't be better placed. Only I wonder a little at your having so completely given up any idea of a different future."

She waited for a moment before answering: "I suppose I'm less restless than I used to be."

"It's certainly natural that you should be less restless here than at Mrs. Murrett's; yet somehow I don't seem to see you permanently given up to forming the young."

"What—exactly—*do* you seem to see me permanently given up to? You know you warned me rather emphatically against the theatre." She threw off the statement without impatience, as though they were discussing together the fate of a third person in whom both were benevolently interested.

Darrow considered his reply. "If I did, it was because you so emphatically refused to let me help you to a start."

She stopped short and faced him. "And you think I may let you now?"

Darrow felt the blood in his cheek. He could not understand her attitude—if indeed she had consciously taken one, and her changes of tone did not merely reflect the involuntary alternations of her mood. It humbled him to perceive once more how little he had to guide him in his judgment of her. He said to himself: "If I'd ever cared a straw for her I should know how to avoid hurting her now"—and his insensibility struck him as no better than a vulgar obtuseness. But he had a fixed purpose ahead and could only push on to it.

"I hope, at any rate, you'll listen to my reasons. There's been time, on both sides, to think them over since——" He caught himself back and hung helpless on the "since": whatever words he chose, he seemed to stumble among reminders of their past.

She walked on beside him, her eyes on the ground. "Then I'm to understand—definitely—that you *do* renew your offer?" she asked.

"With all my heart! If you'll only let me——"

She raised a hand, as though to check him. "It's extremely friendly of you—I *do* believe you mean it as a friend—but I don't quite understand why, finding me, as you say, so well placed here, you should show more anxiety about my future than at a time when I was actually, and rather desperately, adrift."

"Oh, no, not more!"

"If you show any at all, it must, at any rate, be for different reasons.—In fact, it can only be," she went on, with one of her disconcerting flashes of astuteness, "for one of two reasons; either because you feel you ought to help me, or because, for some reason, you think you owe it to Mrs. Leath to let her know what you know of me."

Darrow stood still in the path. Behind him he heard Effie's call, and at the child's voice he saw Sophy turn her head with the alertness of one who is obscurely on the watch. The look was so fugitive that he could not have said wherein it differed from her normal professional air of having her pupil on her mind.

Effie sprang past them, and Darrow took up the girl's challenge.

"What you suggest about Mrs. Leath is hardly worth answering. As to my reasons for wanting to help you, a good deal depends on the words one uses to define rather indefinite things. It's true enough that I want to help you; but the wish isn't due to . . . to any past kindness on your part, but simply to my own interest in you. Why not put it that our friendship gives me the right to intervene for what I believe to be your benefit?"

She took a few hesitating steps and then paused again. Darrow noticed that she had grown pale and that there were rings of shade about her eyes.

"You've known Mrs. Leath a long time?" she asked him suddenly.

He paused with a sense of approaching peril. "A long time—yes."

"She told me you were friends—great friends."

"Yes," he admitted, " we're great friends."

"Then you might naturally feel yourself justified in telling her that you don't think I'm the right person for Effie." He uttered a sound of protest, but she disregarded it. "I don't say you'd *like* to do it. You wouldn't: you'd hate it. And the natural alternative would be to try to persuade me that I'd be better off somewhere else than here. But supposing that failed, and you saw I was determined to stay? *Then* you might think it your duty to tell Mrs. Leath."

She laid the case before him with a cold lucidity. "I should, in your place, I believe," she ended with a little laugh.

"I shouldn't feel justified in telling her, behind your back, if I thought you unsuited for the place; but I should certainly feel justified," he rejoined after a pause, "in telling *you* if I thought the place unsuited to you."

"And that's what you're trying to tell me now?"

"Yes; but not for the reasons you imagine."

"What, then, are your reasons, if you please?"

"I've already implied them in advising you not to give up all idea of the theatre. You're too various, too gifted, too personal, to tie yourself down, at your age, to the dismal drudgery of teaching."

"And is *that* what you've told Mrs. Leath?"

She rushed the question out at him as if she expected to trip him up over it. He was moved by the simplicity of the stratagem.

"I've told her exactly nothing," he replied.

"And what—exactly—do you mean by 'nothing'? You and she were talking about me when I came into her sitting-room yesterday."

Darrow felt his blood rise at the thrust.

"I've told her, simply, that I'd seen you once or twice at Mrs. Murrett's."

"And not that you've ever seen me since?"

"And not that I've ever seen you since . . ."

"And she believes you—she completely believes you?"

He uttered a protesting exclamation, and his flush reflected itself in the girl's cheek.

"Oh, I beg your pardon! I didn't mean to ask you that." She halted, and again cast a rapid glance behind and ahead of her. Then she held out her hand. "Well, then, thank you—and let me relieve your fears. I sha'n't be Effie's governess much longer."

At the announcement, Darrow tried to merge his look of relief into the expression of friendly interest with which he grasped her hand. "You really do agree with me, then? And you'll give me a chance to talk things over with you?"

She shook her head with a faint smile. "I'm not thinking of the stage. I've had another offer: that's all."

The relief was hardly less great. After all, his personal responsibility ceased with her departure from Givré.

"You'll tell me about that, then—won't you?"

Her smile flickered up. "Oh, you'll hear about it soon . . . I must catch Effie now and drag her back to the blackboard."

She walked on for a few yards, and then paused again and confronted him. "I've been odious to you—and not quite honest," she broke out suddenly.

"Not quite honest?" he repeated, caught in a fresh wave of wonder.

"I mean, in seeming not to trust you. It's come over

me again as we talked that, at heart, I've always *known* I
could . . ."

Her colour rose in a bright wave, and her eyes clung to his
for a swift instant of reminder and appeal. For the same space
of time the past surged up in him confusedly; then a veil
dropped between them.

"Here's Effie now!" she exclaimed.

He turned and saw the little girl trotting back to them, her
hand in Owen Leath's.

Even through the stir of his subsiding excitement Darrow
was at once aware of the change effected by the young man's
approach. For a moment Sophy Viner's cheeks burned redder; then they faded to the paleness of white petals. She lost,
however, nothing of the bright bravery which it was her way
to turn on the unexpected. Perhaps no one less familiar with
her face than Darrow would have discerned the tension of the
smile she transferred from himself to Owen Leath, or have
remarked that her eyes had hardened from misty grey to a
shining darkness. But her observer was less struck by this than
by the corresponding change in Owen Leath. The latter,
when he came in sight, had been laughing and talking uncon-
cernedly with Effie; but as his eye fell on Miss Viner his
expression altered as suddenly as hers.

The change, for Darrow, was less definable; but, perhaps
for that reason, it struck him as more sharply significant.
Only—just what did it signify? Owen, like Sophy Viner, had
the kind of face which seems less the stage on which emotions
move than the very stuff they work in. In moments of excitement his odd irregular features seemed to grow fluid, to un-
make and remake themselves like the shadows of clouds on a
stream. Darrow, through the rapid flight of the shadows,
could not seize on any specific indication of feeling: he merely
perceived that the young man was unaccountably surprised at
finding him with Miss Viner, and that the extent of his surprise might cover all manner of implications.

Darrow's first idea was that Owen, if he suspected that the
conversation was not the result of an accidental encounter,
might wonder at his step-mother's suitor being engaged, at
such an hour, in private talk with her little girl's governess.
The thought was so disturbing that, as the three turned back

to the house, he was on the point of saying to Owen: "I came out to look for your mother." But, in the contingency he feared, even so simple a phrase might seem like an awkward attempt at explanation; and he walked on in silence at Miss Viner's side. Presently he was struck by the fact that Owen Leath and the girl were silent also; and this gave a new turn to his thoughts. Silence may be as variously shaded as speech; and that which enfolded Darrow and his two companions seemed to his watchful perceptions to be quivering with cross-threads of communication. At first he was aware only of those that centred in his own troubled consciousness; then it occurred to him that an equal activity of intercourse was going on outside of it. Something was in fact passing mutely and rapidly between young Leath and Sophy Viner; but what it was, and whither it tended, Darrow, when they reached the house, was but just beginning to divine . . .

XVIII

Anna Leath, from the terrace, watched the return of the little group.

She looked down on them, as they advanced across the garden, from the serene height of her unassailable happiness. There they were, coming toward her in the mild morning light, her child, her step-son, her promised husband: the three beings who filled her life. She smiled a little at the happy picture they presented, Effie's gambols encircling it in a moving frame within which the two men came slowly forward in the silence of friendly understanding. It seemed part of the deep intimacy of the scene that they should not be talking to each other, and it did not till afterward strike her as odd that neither of them apparently felt it necessary to address a word to Sophy Viner.

Anna herself, at the moment, was floating in the mid-current of felicity, on a tide so bright and buoyant that she seemed to be one with its warm waves. The first rush of bliss had stunned and dazzled her; but now that, each morning, she woke to the calm certainty of its recurrence, she was growing used to the sense of security it gave.

"I feel as if I could trust my happiness to carry me; as if it had grown out of me like wings." So she phrased it to Darrow, as, later in the morning, they paced the garden-paths together. His answering look gave her the same assurance of safety. The evening before he had seemed preoccupied, and the shadow of his mood had faintly encroached on the great golden orb of their blessedness; but now it was uneclipsed again, and hung above them high and bright as the sun at noon.

Upstairs in her sitting-room, that afternoon, she was thinking of these things. The morning mists had turned to rain, compelling the postponement of an excursion in which the whole party were to have joined. Effie, with her governess, had been despatched in the motor to do some shopping at Francheuil; and Anna had promised Darrow to join him, later in the afternoon, for a quick walk in the rain.

He had gone to his room after luncheon to get some belated letters off his conscience; and when he had left her she had continued to sit in the same place, her hands crossed on her knees, her head slightly bent, in an attitude of brooding retrospection. As she looked back at her past life, it seemed to her to have consisted of one ceaseless effort to pack into each hour enough to fill out its slack folds; but now each moment was like a miser's bag stretched to bursting with pure gold.

She was roused by the sound of Owen's step in the gallery outside her room. It paused at her door and in answer to his knock she called out "Come in!"

As the door closed behind him she was struck by his look of pale excitement, and an impulse of compunction made her say: "You've come to ask me why I haven't spoken to your grandmother!"

He sent about him a glance vaguely reminding her of the strange look with which Sophy Viner had swept the room the night before; then his brilliant eyes came back to her.

"I've spoken to her myself," he said.

Anna started up, incredulous.

"You've spoken to her? When?"

"Just now. I left her to come here."

Anna's first feeling was one of annoyance. There was really something comically incongruous in this boyish surrender to impulse on the part of a young man so eager to assume the responsibilities of life. She looked at him with a faintly veiled amusement.

"You asked me to help you and I promised you I would. It was hardly worth while to work out such an elaborate plan of action if you intended to take the matter out of my hands without telling me."

"Oh, don't take that tone with me!" he broke out, almost angrily.

"That tone? What tone?" She stared at his quivering face. "I might," she pursued, still half-laughing, "more properly make that request of *you*!"

Owen reddened and his vehemence suddenly subsided.

"I meant that I *had* to speak—that's all. You don't give me a chance to explain . . ."

She looked at him gently, wondering a little at her own impatience.

"Owen! Don't I always want to give you every chance? It's because I *do* that I wanted to talk to your grandmother first—that I was waiting and watching for the right moment . . ."

"The right moment? So was I. That's why I've spoken." His voice rose again and took the sharp edge it had in moments of high pressure.

His step-mother turned away and seated herself in her sofa-corner. "Oh, my dear, it's not a privilege to quarrel over! You've taken a load off my shoulders. Sit down and tell me all about it."

He stood before her, irresolute. "I can't sit down," he said.

"Walk about, then. Only tell me: I'm impatient."

His immediate response was to throw himself into the arm-chair at her side, where he lounged for a moment without speaking, his legs stretched out, his arms locked behind his thrown-back head. Anna, her eyes on his face, waited quietly for him to speak.

"Well—of course it was just what one expected."

"She takes it so badly, you mean?"

"All the heavy batteries were brought up: my father, Givré, Monsieur de Chantelle, the throne and the altar. Even my poor mother was dragged out of oblivion and armed with imaginary protests."

Anna sighed out her sympathy. "Well—you were prepared for all that?"

"I thought I was, till I began to hear her say it. Then it sounded so incredibly silly that I told her so."

"Oh, Owen—Owen!"

"Yes: I know. I was a fool; but I couldn't help it."

"And you've mortally offended her, I suppose? That's exactly what I wanted to prevent." She laid a hand on his shoulder. "You tiresome boy, not to wait and let me speak for you!"

He moved slightly away, so that her hand slipped from its place. "You don't understand," he said, frowning.

"I don't see how I can, till you explain. If you thought the time had come to tell your grandmother, why not have asked me to do it? I had my reasons for waiting; but if you'd told me to speak I should have done so, naturally."

He evaded her appeal by a sudden turn. "What *were* your reasons for waiting?"

Anna did not immediately answer. Her step-son's eyes were on her face, and under his gaze she felt a faint disquietude.

"I was feeling my way . . . I wanted to be absolutely sure . . ."

"Absolutely sure of what?"

She delayed again for a just perceptible instant. "Why, simply of *our* side of the case."

"But you told me you were, the other day, when we talked it over before they came back from Ouchy."

"Oh, my dear—if you think that, in such a complicated matter, every day, every hour, doesn't more or less modify one's surest sureness!"

"That's just what I'm driving at. I want to know what has modified yours."

She made a slight gesture of impatience. "What does it matter, now the thing's done? I don't know that I could give any clear reason . . ."

He got to his feet and stood looking down on her with a tormented brow. "But it's absolutely necessary that you should."

At his tone her impatience flared up. "It's not necessary that I should give you any explanation whatever, since you've taken the matter out of my hands. All I can say is that I was trying to help you: that no other thought ever entered my mind." She paused a moment and then added: "If you doubted it, you were right to do what you've done."

"Oh, I never doubted *you*!" he retorted, with a fugitive stress on the pronoun. His face had cleared to its old look of trust. "Don't be offended if I've seemed to," he went on. "I can't quite explain myself, either . . . it's all a kind of tangle, isn't it? That's why I thought I'd better speak at once; or rather why I didn't think at all, but just suddenly blurted the thing out——"

Anna gave him back his look of conciliation. "Well, the how and why don't much matter now. The point is how to deal with your grandmother. You've not told me what she means to do."

"Oh, she means to send for Adelaide Painter."

The name drew a faint note of mirth from him and relaxed both their faces to a smile.

"Perhaps," Anna added, "it's really the best thing for us all."

Owen shrugged his shoulders. "It's too preposterous and humiliating. Dragging that woman into our secrets——!"

"This could hardly be a secret much longer."

He had moved to the hearth, where he stood pushing about the small ornaments on the mantel-shelf; but at her answer he turned back to her.

"You haven't, of course, spoken of it to any one?"

"No; but I intend to now."

She paused for his reply, and as it did not come she continued: "If Adelaide Painter's to be told there's no possible reason why I shouldn't tell Mr. Darrow."

Owen abruptly set down the little statuette between his fingers. "None whatever: I want every one to know."

She smiled a little at his over-emphasis, and was about to meet it with a word of banter when he continued, facing her: "You haven't, as yet, said a word to him?"

"I've told him nothing, except what the discussion of our own plans—his and mine—obliged me to: that you were thinking of marrying, and that I wasn't willing to leave France till I'd done what I could to see you through."

At her first words the colour had rushed to his forehead; but as she continued she saw his face compose itself and his blood subside.

"You're a brick, my dear!" he exclaimed.

"You had my word, you know."

"Yes; yes—I know." His face had clouded again. "And that's all—positively all—you've ever said to him?"

"Positively all. But why do you ask?"

He had a moment's embarrassed hesitation. "It was understood, wasn't it, that my grandmother was to be the first to know?"

"Well—and so she has been, hasn't she, since you've told her?"

He turned back to his restless shifting of the knick-knacks.

"And you're sure that nothing you've said to Darrow could possibly have given him a hint——?"

"Nothing I've said to him—certainly."

He swung about on her. "Why do you put it in that way?"

"In what way?"

"Why—as if you thought some one else might have spoken . . ."

"Some one else? Who else?" She rose to her feet. "What on earth, my dear boy, can you be driving at?"

"I'm trying to find out whether you think he knows anything definite."

"Why should I think so? Do *you*?"

"I don't know. I want to find out."

She laughed at his obstinate insistence. "To test my veracity, I suppose?" At the sound of a step in the gallery she added: "Here he is—you can ask him yourself."

She met Darrow's knock with an invitation to enter, and he came into the room and paused between herself and Owen. She was struck, as he stood there, by the contrast between his happy careless good-looks and her step-son's frowning agitation.

Darrow met her eyes with a smile. "Am I too soon? Or is our walk given up?"

"No; I was just going to get ready." She continued to linger between the two, looking slowly from one to the other. "But there's something we want to tell you first: Owen is engaged to Miss Viner."

The sense of an indefinable interrogation in Owen's mind made her, as she spoke, fix her eyes steadily on Darrow.

He had paused just opposite the window, so that, even in the rainy afternoon light, his face was clearly open to her scrutiny. For a second, immense surprise was alone visible on it: so visible that she half turned to her step-son, with a faint smile for his refuted suspicions. Why, she wondered, should Owen have thought that Darrow had already guessed his secret, and what, after all, could be so disturbing to him in this not improbable contingency? At any rate, his doubt must have been dispelled: there was nothing feigned about Darrow's astonishment. When her eyes turned back to him he was already crossing to Owen with outstretched hand, and she had, through an unaccountable faint flutter of misgiving, a mere confused sense of their exchanging the customary phrases. Her next perception was of Owen's tranquillized look, and of his smiling return of Darrow's congratulatory grasp. She had the eerie feeling of having been overswept by a shadow which there had been no cloud to cast . . .

A moment later Owen had left the room and she and Darrow were alone. He had turned away to the window and stood staring out into the down-pour.

"You're surprised at Owen's news?" she asked.

"Yes: I am surprised," he answered.

"You hadn't thought of its being Miss Viner?"

"Why should I have thought of Miss Viner?"

"You see now why I wanted so much to find out what you knew about her." He made no comment, and she pursued: "Now that you *do* know it's she, if there's anything——"

He moved back into the room and went up to her. His face was serious, with a slight shade of annoyance. "What on earth should there be? As I told you, I've never in my life heard any one say two words about Miss Viner."

Anna made no answer and they continued to face each other without moving. For the moment she had ceased to think about Sophy Viner and Owen: the only thought in her mind was that Darrow was alone with her, close to her, and that, for the first time, their hands and lips had not met.

He glanced back doubtfully at the window. "It's pouring. Perhaps you'd rather not go out?"

She hesitated, as if waiting for him to urge her. "I suppose I'd better not. I ought to go at once to my mother-in-law— Owen's just been telling her," she said.

"Ah." Darrow hazarded a smile. "That accounts for my having, on my way up, heard some one telephoning for Miss Painter!"

At the allusion they laughed together, vaguely, and Anna moved toward the door. He held it open for her and followed her out.

XIX

H E LEFT HER at the door of Madame de Chantelle's sitting-room, and plunged out alone into the rain.

The wind flung about the stripped tree-tops of the avenue and dashed the stinging streams into his face. He walked to the gate and then turned into the high-road and strode along in the open, buffeted by slanting gusts. The evenly ridged fields were a blurred waste of mud, and the russet coverts which he and Owen had shot through the day before shivered desolately against a driving sky.

Darrow walked on and on, indifferent to the direction he was taking. His thoughts were tossing like the tree-tops. Anna's announcement had not come to him as a complete surprise: that morning, as he strolled back to the house with Owen Leath and Miss Viner, he had had a momentary intuition of the truth. But it had been no more than an intuition, the merest faint cloud-puff of surmise; and now it was an attested fact, darkening over the whole sky.

In respect of his own attitude, he saw at once that the discovery made no appreciable change. If he had been bound to silence before, he was no less bound to it now; the only difference lay in the fact that what he had just learned had rendered his bondage more intolerable. Hitherto he had felt for Sophy Viner's defenseless state a sympathy profoundly tinged with compunction. But now he was half-conscious of an obscure indignation against her. Superior as he had fancied himself to ready-made judgments, he was aware of cherishing the common doubt as to the disinterestedness of the woman who tries to rise above her past. No wonder she had been sick with fear on meeting him! It was in his power to do her more harm than he had dreamed . . .

Assuredly he did not want to harm her; but he did desperately want to prevent her marrying Owen Leath. He tried to get away from the feeling, to isolate and exteriorize it sufficiently to see what motives it was made of; but it remained a mere blind motion of his blood, the instinctive recoil from the thing that no amount of arguing can make "straight." His tramp, prolonged as it was, carried him no nearer to enlight-

enment; and after trudging through two or three sallow mud-
stained villages he turned about and wearily made his way
back to Givré. As he walked up the black avenue, making for
the lights that twinkled through its pitching branches, he had
a sudden realisation of his utter helplessness. He might think
and combine as he would; but there was nothing, absolutely
nothing, that he could do . . .

He dropped his wet coat in the vestibule and began to
mount the stairs to his room. But on the landing he was overtaken by a sober-faced maid who, in tones discreetly lowered,
begged him to be so kind as to step, for a moment, into the
Marquise's sitting-room. Somewhat disconcerted by the summons, he followed its bearer to the door at which, a couple
of hours earlier, he had taken leave of Mrs. Leath. It opened
to admit him to a large lamp-lit room which he immediately
perceived to be empty; and the fact gave him time to note,
even through his disturbance of mind, the interesting degree
to which Madame de Chantelle's apartment "dated" and completed her. Its looped and corded curtains, its purple satin
upholstery, the Sèvres jardinières, the rose-wood fire-screen,
the little velvet tables edged with lace and crowded with silver
knick-knacks and simpering miniatures, reconstituted an almost perfect setting for the blonde beauty of the 'sixties. Darrow wondered that Fraser Leath's filial respect should have
prevailed over his æsthetic scruples to the extent of permitting
such an anachronism among the eighteenth century graces of
Givré; but a moment's reflection made it clear that, to its late
owner, the attitude would have seemed exactly in the traditions of the place.

Madame de Chantelle's emergence from an inner room
snatched Darrow from these irrelevant musings. She was already beaded and bugled for the evening, and, save for a
slight pinkness of the eye-lids, her elaborate appearance revealed no mark of agitation; but Darrow noticed that, in recognition of the solemnity of the occasion, she pinched a lace
handkerchief between her thumb and forefinger.

She plunged at once into the centre of the difficulty, appealing to him, in the name of all the Everards, to descend
there with her to the rescue of her darling. She wasn't, she
was sure, addressing herself in vain to one whose person,

whose "tone," whose traditions so brilliantly declared his indebtedness to the principles she besought him to defend. Her own reception of Darrow, the confidence she had at once accorded him, must have shown him that she had instinctively felt their unanimity of sentiment on these fundamental questions. She had in fact recognized in him the one person whom, without pain to her maternal piety, she could welcome as her son's successor; and it was almost as to Owen's father that she now appealed to Darrow to aid in rescuing the wretched boy.

"Don't think, please, that I'm casting the least reflection on Anna, or showing any want of sympathy for her, when I say that I consider her partly responsible for what's happened. Anna is 'modern'—I believe that's what it's called when you read unsettling books and admire hideous pictures. Indeed," Madame de Chantelle continued, leaning confidentially forward, "I myself have always more or less lived in that atmosphere: my son, you know, was very revolutionary. Only he didn't, of course, apply his ideas: they were purely intellectual. That's what dear Anna has always failed to understand. And I'm afraid she's created the same kind of confusion in Owen's mind—led him to mix up things you read about with things you do . . . You know, of course, that she sides with him in this wretched business?"

Developing at length upon this theme, she finally narrowed down to the point of Darrow's intervention. "My grandson, Mr. Darrow, calls me illogical and uncharitable because my feelings toward Miss Viner have changed since I've heard this news. Well! You've known her, it appears, for some years: Anna tells me you used to see her when she was a companion, or secretary or something, to a dreadfully vulgar Mrs. Murrett. And I ask you as a friend, I ask you as one of *us*, to tell me if you think a girl who has had to knock about the world in that kind of position, and at the orders of all kinds of people, is fitted to be Owen's wife . . . I'm not implying anything against her! I *liked* the girl, Mr. Darrow . . . But what's that got to do with it? I don't want her to marry my grandson. If I'd been looking for a wife for Owen, I shouldn't have applied to the Farlows to find me one. That's what Anna won't understand; and what you must help me to make her see."

Darrow, to this appeal, could oppose only the repeated assurance of his inability to interfere. He tried to make Madame
de Chantelle see that the very position he hoped to take in
the household made his intervention the more hazardous. He
brought up the usual arguments, and sounded the expected
note of sympathy; but Madame de Chantelle's alarm had dispelled her habitual imprecision, and, though she had not
many reasons to advance, her argument clung to its point like
a frightened sharp-clawed animal.

"Well, then," she summed up, in response to his repeated
assertions that he saw no way of helping her, "you can, at
least, even if you won't say a word to the others, tell me
frankly and fairly—and quite between ourselves—your personal opinion of Miss Viner, since you've known her so much
longer than we have."

He protested that, if he had known her longer, he had
known her much less well, and that he had already, on this
point, convinced Anna of his inability to pronounce an
opinion.

Madame de Chantelle drew a deep sigh of intelligence.
"Your opinion of Mrs. Murrett is enough! I don't suppose
you pretend to conceal *that*? And heaven knows what other
unspeakable people she's been mixed up with. The only
friends she can produce are called *Hoke* . . . Don't try to
reason with me, Mr. Darrow. There are feelings that go
deeper than facts . . . And I *know* she thought of studying
for the stage . . ." Madame de Chantelle raised the corner of
her lace handkerchief to her eyes. "I'm old-fashioned—like
my furniture," she murmured. "And I thought I could count
on you, Mr. Darrow . . ."

When Darrow, that night, regained his room, he reflected
with a flash of irony that each time he entered it he brought
a fresh troop of perplexities to trouble its serene seclusion.
Since the day after his arrival, only forty-eight hours before,
when he had set his window open to the night, and his hopes
had seemed as many as its stars, each evening had brought its
new problem and its renewed distress. But nothing, as yet,
had approached the blank misery of mind with which he now
set himself to face the fresh questions confronting him.

Sophy Viner had not shown herself at dinner, so that he had had no glimpse of her in her new character, and no means of divining the real nature of the tie between herself and Owen Leath. One thing, however, was clear: whatever her real feelings were, and however much or little she had at stake, if she had made up her mind to marry Owen she had more than enough skill and tenacity to defeat any arts that poor Madame de Chantelle could oppose to her.

Darrow himself was in fact the only person who might possibly turn her from her purpose: Madame de Chantelle, at haphazard, had hit on the surest means of saving Owen—if to prevent his marriage were to save him! Darrow, on this point, did not pretend to any fixed opinion; one feeling alone was clear and insistent in him: he did not mean, if he could help it, to let the marriage take place.

How he was to prevent it he did not know: to his tormented imagination every issue seemed closed. For a fantastic instant he was moved to follow Madame de Chantelle's suggestion and urge Anna to withdraw her approval. If his reticence, his efforts to avoid the subject, had not escaped her, she had doubtless set them down to the fact of his knowing more, and thinking less, of Sophy Viner than he had been willing to admit; and he might take advantage of this to turn her mind gradually from the project. Yet how do so without betraying his insincerity? If he had had nothing to hide he could easily have said: "It's one thing to know nothing against the girl, it's another to pretend that I think her a good match for Owen." But could he say even so much without betraying more? It was not Anna's questions, or his answers to them, that he feared, but what might cry aloud in the intervals between them. He understood now that ever since Sophy Viner's arrival at Givré he had felt in Anna the lurking sense of something unexpressed, and perhaps inexpressible, between the girl and himself . . . When at last he fell asleep he had fatalistically committed his next step to the chances of the morrow.

The first that offered itself was an encounter with Mrs. Leath as he descended the stairs the next morning. She had come down already hatted and shod for a dash to the park lodge, where one of the gatekeeper's children had had an accident. In her compact dark dress she looked more than usually straight and slim, and her face wore the pale glow it took on at any call on her energy: a kind of warrior brightness that made her small head, with its strong chin and closebound hair, like that of an amazon in a frieze.

It was their first moment alone since she had left him, the afternoon before, at her mother-in-law's door; and after a few words about the injured child their talk inevitably reverted to Owen.

Anna spoke with a smile of her "scene" with Madame de Chantelle, who belonged, poor dear, to a generation when "scenes" (in the ladylike and lachrymal sense of the term) were the tribute which sensibility was expected to pay to the unusual. Their conversation had been, in every detail, so exactly what Anna had foreseen that it had clearly not made much impression on her; but she was eager to know the result of Darrow's encounter with her mother-in-law.

"She told me she'd sent for you: she always 'sends for' people in emergencies. That again, I suppose, is *de l'époque.* And failing Adelaide Painter, who can't get here till this afternoon, there was no one but poor you to turn to."

She put it all lightly, with a lightness that seemed to his tight-strung nerves slightly, undefinably over-done. But he was so aware of his own tension that he wondered, the next moment, whether anything would ever again seem to him quite usual and insignificant and in the common order of things.

As they hastened on through the drizzle in which the storm of the night was weeping itself out, Anna drew close under his umbrella, and at the pressure of her arm against his he recalled his walk up the Dover pier with Sophy Viner. The memory gave him a startled vision of the inevitable occasions of contact, confidence, familiarity, which his future relationship to the girl would entail, and the countless chances of betrayal that every one of them involved.

"Do tell me just what you said," he heard Anna pleading; and with sudden resolution he affirmed: "I quite understand your mother-in-law's feeling as she does."

The words, when uttered, seemed a good deal less significant than they had sounded to his inner ear; and Anna replied without surprise: "Of course. It's inevitable that she should. But we shall bring her round in time." Under the dripping dome she raised her face to his. "Don't you remember what you said the day before yesterday? 'Together we can't fail to pull it off for him!' I've told Owen that, so you're pledged and there's no going back."

The day before yesterday! Was it possible that, no longer ago, life had seemed a sufficiently simple business for a sane man to hazard such assurances?

"Anna," he questioned her abruptly, "why are you so anxious for this marriage?"

She stopped short to face him. "Why? But surely I've explained to you—or rather I've hardly had to, you seemed so in sympathy with my reasons!"

"I didn't know, then, who it was that Owen wanted to marry."

The words were out with a spring and he felt a clearer air in his brain. But her logic hemmed him in.

"You knew yesterday; and you assured me then that you hadn't a word to say——"

"Against Miss Viner?" The name, once uttered, sounded on and on in his ears. "Of course not. But that doesn't necessarily imply that I think her a good match for Owen."

Anna made no immediate answer. When she spoke it was to question: "Why don't you think her a good match for Owen?"

"Well—Madame de Chantelle's reasons seem to me not quite as negligible as you think."

"You mean the fact that she's been Mrs. Murrett's secretary, and that the people who employed her before were called Hoke? For, as far as Owen and I can make out, these are the gravest charges against her."

"Still, one can understand that the match is not what Madame de Chantelle had dreamed of."

"Oh, perfectly—if that's all you mean."

The lodge was in sight, and she hastened her step. He strode on beside her in silence, but at the gate she checked him with the question: "Is it really all you mean?"

"Of course," he heard himself declare.

"Oh, then I think I shall convince you—even if I can't, like

Madame de Chantelle, summon all the Everards to my aid!"
She lifted to him the look of happy laughter that sometimes
brushed her with a gleam of spring.

Darrow watched her hasten along the path between the
dripping chrysanthemums and enter the lodge. After she had
gone in he paced up and down outside in the drizzle, waiting
to learn if she had any message to send back to the house;
and after the lapse of a few minutes she came out again.

The child, she said, was badly, though not dangerously,
hurt, and the village doctor, who was already on hand, had
asked that the surgeon, already summoned from Francheuil,
should be told to bring with him certain needful appliances.
Owen had started by motor to fetch the surgeon, but there
was still time to communicate with the latter by telephone.
The doctor furthermore begged for an immediate provision
of such bandages and disinfectants as Givré itself could furnish, and Anna bade Darrow address himself to Miss Viner,
who would know where to find the necessary things, and
would direct one of the servants to bicycle with them to the
lodge.

Darrow, as he hurried off on this errand, had at once perceived the opportunity it offered of a word with Sophy Viner.
What that word was to be he did not know; but now, if ever,
was the moment to make it urgent and conclusive. It was
unlikely that he would again have such a chance of unobserved talk with her.

He had supposed he should find her with her pupil in the
school-room; but he learned from a servant that Effie had
gone to Francheuil with her step-brother, and that Miss
Viner was still in her room. Darrow sent her word that he
was the bearer of a message from the lodge, and a moment
later he heard her coming down the stairs.

XX

For a second, as she approached him, the quick tremor of her glance showed her all intent on the same thought as himself. He transmitted his instructions with mechanical precision, and she answered in the same tone, repeating his words with the intensity of attention of a child not quite sure of understanding. Then she disappeared up the stairs.

Darrow lingered on in the hall, not knowing if she meant to return, yet inwardly sure she would. At length he saw her coming down in her hat and jacket. The rain still streaked the window panes, and, in order to say something, he said: "You're not going to the lodge yourself?"

"I've sent one of the men ahead with the things; but I thought Mrs. Leath might need me."

"She didn't ask for you," he returned, wondering how he could detain her; but she answered decidedly: "I'd better go."

He held open the door, picked up his umbrella and followed her out. As they went down the steps she glanced back at him. "You've forgotten your mackintosh."

"I sha'n't need it."

She had no umbrella, and he opened his and held it out to her. She rejected it with a murmur of thanks and walked on through the thin drizzle, and he kept the umbrella over his own head, without offering to shelter her.

Rapidly and in silence they crossed the court and began to walk down the avenue. They had traversed a third of its length before Darrow said abruptly: "Wouldn't it have been fairer, when we talked together yesterday, to tell me what I've just heard from Mrs. Leath?"

"Fairer——?" She stopped short with a startled look.

"If I'd known that your future was already settled I should have spared you my gratuitous suggestions."

She walked on, more slowly, for a yard or two. "I couldn't speak yesterday. I meant to have told you today."

"Oh, I'm not reproaching you for your lack of confidence. Only, if you *had* told me, I should have been more sure of your really meaning what you said to me yesterday."

She did not ask him to what he referred, and he saw that

her parting words to him lived as vividly in her memory as in his.

"Is it so important that you should be sure?" she finally questioned.

"Not to you, naturally," he returned with involuntary asperity. It was incredible, yet it was a fact, that for the moment his immediate purpose in seeking to speak to her was lost under a rush of resentment at counting for so little in her fate. Of what stuff, then, was his feeling for her made? A few hours earlier she had touched his thoughts as little as his senses; but now he felt old sleeping instincts stir in him . . .

A rush of rain dashed against his face, and, catching Sophy's hat, strained it back from her loosened hair. She put her hands to her head with a familiar gesture . . . He came closer and held his umbrella over her . . .

At the lodge he waited while she went in. The rain continued to stream down on him and he shivered in the dampness and stamped his feet on the flags. It seemed to him that a long time elapsed before the door opened and she reappeared. He glanced into the house for a glimpse of Anna, but obtained none; yet the mere sense of her nearness had completely altered his mood.

The child, Sophy told him, was doing well; but Mrs. Leath had decided to wait till the surgeon came. Darrow, as they turned away, looked through the gates, and saw the doctor's old-fashioned carriage by the road-side.

"Let me tell the doctor's boy to drive you back," he suggested; but Sophy answered: "No; I'll walk," and he moved on toward the house at her side. She expressed no surprise at his not remaining at the lodge, and again they walked on in silence through the rain. She had accepted the shelter of his umbrella, but she kept herself at such a carefully measured distance that even the slight swaying movements produced by their quick pace did not once bring her arm in touch with his; and, noticing this, he perceived that every drop of her blood must be alive to his nearness.

"What I meant just now," he began, " was that you ought to have been sure of my good wishes."

She seemed to weigh the words. "Sure enough for what?"

"To trust me a little farther than you did."

"I've told you that yesterday I wasn't free to speak."

"Well, since you are now, may I say a word to you?"

She paused perceptibly, and when she spoke it was in so low a tone that he had to bend his head to catch her answer. "I can't think what you can have to say."

"It's not easy to say here, at any rate. And indoors I sha'n't know where to say it." He glanced about him in the rain. "Let's walk over to the spring-house for a minute."

To the right of the drive, under a clump of trees, a little stucco pavilion crowned by a balustrade rose on arches of mouldering brick over a flight of steps that led down to a spring. Other steps curved up to a door above. Darrow mounted these, and opening the door entered a small circular room hung with loosened strips of painted paper whereon spectrally faded Mandarins executed elongated gestures. Some black and gold chairs with straw seats and an unsteady table of cracked lacquer stood on the floor of red-glazed tile.

Sophy had followed him without comment. He closed the door after her, and she stood motionless, as though waiting for him to speak.

"Now we can talk quietly," he said, looking at her with a smile into which he tried to put an intention of the frankest friendliness.

She merely repeated: "I can't think what you can have to say."

Her voice had lost the note of half-wistful confidence on which their talk of the previous day had closed, and she looked at him with a kind of pale hostility. Her tone made it evident that his task would be difficult, but it did not shake his resolve to go on. He sat down, and mechanically she followed his example. The table was between them and she rested her arms on its cracked edge and her chin on her interlocked hands. He looked at her and she gave him back his look.

"Have you nothing to say to *me*?" he asked at length.

A faint smile lifted, in the remembered way, the left corner of her narrowed lips.

"About my marriage?"

"About your marriage."

She continued to consider him between half-drawn lids. "What can I say that Mrs. Leath has not already told you?"

"Mrs. Leath has told me nothing whatever but the fact—
and her pleasure in it."

"Well; aren't those the two essential points?"

"The essential points to *you*? I should have thought——"

"Oh, to *you*, I meant," she put in keenly.

He flushed at the retort, but steadied himself and rejoined:
"The essential point to me is, of course, that you should be
doing what's really best for you."

She sat silent, with lowered lashes. At length she stretched
out her arm and took up from the table a little threadbare
Chinese hand-screen. She turned its ebony stem once or twice
between her fingers, and as she did so Darrow was whimsically struck by the way in which their evanescent slight
romance was symbolized by the fading lines on the frail
silk.

"Do you think my engagement to Mr. Leath not really best
for me?" she asked at length.

Darrow, before answering, waited long enough to get his
words into the tersest shape—not without a sense, as he did
so, of his likeness to the surgeon deliberately poising his lan-
cet for a clean incision. "I'm not sure," he replied, "of its
being the best thing for either of you."

She took the stroke steadily, but a faint red swept her face
like the reflection of a blush. She continued to keep her lowered eyes on the screen.

"From whose point of view do you speak?"

"Naturally, that of the persons most concerned."

"From Owen's, then, of course? You don't think me a good
match for him?"

"From yours, first of all. I don't think him a good match
for you."

He brought the answer out abruptly, his eyes on her face.
It had grown extremely pale, but as the meaning of his words
shaped itself in her mind he saw a curious inner light dawn
through her set look. She lifted her lids just far enough for a
veiled glance at him, and a smile slipped through them to her
trembling lips. For a moment the change merely bewildered
him; then it pulled him up with a sharp jerk of apprehension.

"I don't think him a good match for you," he stammered,
groping for the lost thread of his words.

She threw a vague look about the chilly rain-dimmed room. "And you've brought me here to tell me why?"

The question roused him to the sense that their minutes were numbered, and that if he did not immediately get to his point there might be no other chance of making it.

"My chief reason is that I believe he's too young and inexperienced to give you the kind of support you need."

At his words her face changed again, freezing to a tragic coldness. She stared straight ahead of her, perceptibly struggling with the tremor of her muscles; and when she had controlled it she flung out a pale-lipped pleasantry. "But you see I've always had to support myself!"

"He's a boy," Darrow pushed on, "a charming, wonderful boy; but with no more notion than a boy how to deal with the inevitable daily problems . . . the trivial stupid unimportant things that life is chiefly made up of."

"I'll deal with them for him," she rejoined.

"They'll be more than ordinarily difficult."

She shot a challenging glance at him. "You must have some special reason for saying so."

"Only my clear perception of the facts."

"What facts do you mean?"

Darrow hesitated. "You must know better than I," he returned at length, "that the way won't be made easy to you."

"Mrs. Leath, at any rate, has made it so."

"Madame de Chantelle will not."

"How do *you* know that?" she flung back.

He paused again, not sure how far it was prudent to reveal himself in the confidence of the household. Then, to avoid involving Anna, he answered: "Madame de Chantelle sent for me yesterday."

"Sent for you—to talk to you about me?" The colour rose to her forehead and her eyes burned black under lowered brows. "By what right, I should like to know? What have you to do with me, or with anything in the world that concerns me?"

Darrow instantly perceived what dread suspicion again possessed her, and the sense that it was not wholly unjustified caused him a passing pang of shame. But it did not turn him from his purpose.

"I'm an old friend of Mrs. Leath's. It's not unnatural that Madame de Chantelle should talk to me."

She dropped the screen on the table and stood up, turning on him the same small mask of wrath and scorn which had glared at him, in Paris, when he had confessed to his suppression of her letter. She walked away a step or two and then came back.

"May I ask what Madame de Chantelle said to you?"

"She made it clear that she should not encourage the marriage."

"And what was her object in making that clear to *you*?"

Darrow hesitated. "I suppose she thought——"

"That she could persuade you to turn Mrs. Leath against me?"

He was silent, and she pressed him: "Was that it?"

"That was it."

"But if you don't—if you keep your promise——"

"My promise?"

"To say nothing . . . nothing whatever . . ." Her strained look threw a haggard light along the pause.

As she spoke, the whole odiousness of the scene rushed over him. "Of course I shall say nothing . . . you know that . . ." He leaned to her and laid his hand on hers. "You know I wouldn't for the world . . ."

She drew back and hid her face with a sob. Then she sank again into her seat, stretched her arms across the table and laid her face upon them. He sat still, overwhelmed with compunction. After a long interval, in which he had painfully measured the seconds by her hard-drawn breathing, she looked up at him with a face washed clear of bitterness.

"Don't suppose I don't know what you must have thought of me!"

The cry struck him down to a lower depth of self-abasement. "My poor child," he felt like answering, "the shame of it is that I've never thought of you at all!" But he could only uselessly repeat: "I'll do anything I can to help you."

She sat silent, drumming the table with her hand. He saw that her doubt of him was allayed, and the perception made him more ashamed, as if her trust had first revealed to him how near he had come to not deserving it. Suddenly she began to speak.

"You think, then, I've no right to marry him?"

"No right? God forbid! I only meant——"

"That you'd rather I didn't marry any friend of yours." She brought it out deliberately, not as a question, but as a mere dispassionate statement of fact.

Darrow in turn stood up and wandered away helplessly to the window. He stood staring out through its small discoloured panes at the dim brown distances; then he moved back to the table.

"I'll tell you exactly what I meant. You'll be wretched if you marry a man you're not in love with."

He knew the risk of misapprehension that he ran, but he estimated his chances of success as precisely in proportion to his peril. If certain signs meant what he thought they did, he might yet—at what cost he would not stop to think—make his past pay for his future.

The girl, at his words, had lifted her head with a movement of surprise. Her eyes slowly reached his face and rested there in a gaze of deep interrogation. He held the look for a moment; then his own eyes dropped and he waited.

At length she began to speak. "You're mistaken—you're quite mistaken."

He waited a moment longer. "Mistaken——?"

"In thinking what you think. I'm as happy as if I deserved it!" she suddenly proclaimed with a laugh.

She stood up and moved toward the door. "*Now* are you satisfied?" she asked, turning her vividest face to him from the threshold.

XXI

DOWN THE AVENUE there came to them, with the opening of the door, the voice of Owen's motor. It was the signal which had interrupted their first talk, and again, instinctively, they drew apart at the sound. Without a word Darrow turned back into the room, while Sophy Viner went down the steps and walked back alone toward the court.

At luncheon the presence of the surgeon, and the non-appearance of Madame de Chantelle—who had excused herself on the plea of a headache—combined to shift the conversational centre of gravity; and Darrow, under shelter of the necessarily impersonal talk, had time to adjust his disguise and to perceive that the others were engaged in the same re-arrangement. It was the first time that he had seen young Leath and Sophy Viner together since he had learned of their engagement; but neither revealed more emotion than befitted the occasion. It was evident that Owen was deeply under the girl's charm, and that at the least sign from her his bliss would have broken bounds; but her reticence was justified by the tacitly recognized fact of Madame de Chantelle's disapproval. This also visibly weighed on Anna's mind, making her manner to Sophy, if no less kind, yet a trifle more constrained than if the moment of final understanding had been reached. So Darrow interpreted the tension perceptible under the fluent exchange of commonplaces in which he was diligently sharing. But he was more and more aware of his inability to test the moral atmosphere about him: he was like a man in fever testing another's temperature by the touch.

After luncheon Anna, who was to motor the surgeon home, suggested to Darrow that he should accompany them. Effie was also of the party; and Darrow inferred that Anna wished to give her step-son a chance to be alone with his betrothed. On the way back, after the surgeon had been left at his door, the little girl sat between her mother and Darrow, and her presence kept their talk from taking a personal turn. Darrow knew that Mrs. Leath had not yet told Effie of the relation in which he was to stand to her. The premature divulging of Owen's plans had thrown their own into the background, and by common consent they continued, in the little girl's presence, on terms of an informal friendliness.

The sky had cleared after luncheon, and to prolong their excursion they returned by way of the ivy-mantled ruin which was to have been the scene of the projected picnic. This circuit brought them back to the park gates not long before sunset, and as Anna wished to stop at the lodge for news of the injured child Darrow left her there with Effie and walked on alone to the house. He had the impression that she was slightly surprised at his not waiting for her; but his inner restlessness vented itself in an intense desire for bodily movement. He would have liked to walk himself into a state of torpor; to tramp on for hours through the moist winds and the healing darkness and come back staggering with fatigue and sleep. But he had no pretext for such a flight, and he feared that, at such a moment, his prolonged absence might seem singular to Anna.

As he approached the house, the thought of her nearness produced a swift reaction of mood. It was as if an intenser vision of her had scattered his perplexities like morning mists. At this moment, wherever she was, he knew he was safely shut away in her thoughts, and the knowledge made every other fact dwindle away to a shadow. He and she loved each other, and their love arched over them open and ample as the day: in all its sunlit spaces there was no cranny for a fear to lurk. In a few minutes he would be in her presence and would read his reassurance in her eyes. And presently, before dinner, she would contrive that they should have an hour by themselves in her sitting-room, and he would sit by the hearth and watch her quiet movements, and the way the bluish lustre on her hair purpled a little as she bent above the fire.

A carriage drove out of the court as he entered it, and in the hall his vision was dispelled by the exceedingly substantial presence of a lady in a waterproof and a tweed hat, who stood firmly planted in the centre of a pile of luggage, as to which she was giving involved but lucid directions to the footman who had just admitted her. She went on with these directions regardless of Darrow's entrance, merely fixing her small pale eyes on him while she proceeded, in a deep contralto voice, and a fluent French pronounced with the purest Boston

accent, to specify the destination of her bags; and this enabled
Darrow to give her back a gaze protracted enough to take in
all the details of her plain thick-set person, from the square
sallow face beneath bands of grey hair to the blunt boot-toes
protruding under her wide walking skirt.

She submitted to this scrutiny with no more evidence of
surprise than a monument examined by a tourist; but when
the fate of her luggage had been settled she turned suddenly
to Darrow and, dropping her eyes from his face to his feet,
asked in trenchant accents: "What sort of boots have you got
on?"

Before he could summon his wits to the consideration of
this question she continued in a tone of suppressed indignation: "Until Americans get used to the fact that France is under water for half the year they're perpetually risking their
lives by not being properly protected. I suppose you've been
tramping through all this nasty clammy mud as if you'd been
taking a stroll on Boston Common."

Darrow, with a laugh, affirmed his previous experience of
French dampness, and the degree to which he was on his
guard against it; but the lady, with a contemptuous snort,
rejoined: "You young men are all alike——"; to which she
appended, after another hard look at him: "I suppose you're
George Darrow? I used to know one of your mother's cousins, who married a Tunstall of Mount Vernon Street. My
name is Adelaide Painter. Have you been in Boston lately?
No? I'm sorry for that. I hear there have been several new
houses built at the lower end of Commonwealth Avenue and
I hoped you could tell me about them. I haven't been there
for thirty years myself."

Miss Painter's arrival at Givré produced the same effect as
the wind's hauling around to the north after days of languid
weather. When Darrow joined the group about the tea-table
she had already given a tingle to the air. Madame de Chantelle still remained invisible above stairs; but Darrow had the
impression that even through her drawn curtains and bolted
doors a stimulating whiff must have entered.

Anna was in her usual seat behind the tea-tray, and Sophy
Viner presently led in her pupil. Owen was also there, seated,
as usual, a little apart from the others, and following Miss

Painter's massive movements and equally substantial utterances with a smile of secret intelligence which gave Darrow the idea of his having been in clandestine parley with the enemy. Darrow further took note that the girl and her suitor perceptibly avoided each other; but this might be a natural result of the tension Miss Painter had been summoned to relieve.

Sophy Viner would evidently permit no recognition of the situation save that which it lay with Madame de Chantelle to accord; but meanwhile Miss Painter had proclaimed her tacit sense of it by summoning the girl to a seat at her side.

Darrow, as he continued to observe the new-comer, who was perched on her arm-chair like a granite image on the edge of a cliff, was aware that, in a more detached frame of mind, he would have found an extreme interest in studying and classifying Miss Painter. It was not that she said anything remarkable, or betrayed any of those unspoken perceptions which give significance to the most commonplace utterances. She talked of the lateness of her train, of an impending crisis in international politics, of the difficulty of buying English tea in Paris and of the enormities of which French servants were capable; and her views on these subjects were enunciated with a uniformity of emphasis implying complete unconsciousness of any difference in their interest and importance. She always applied to the French race the distant epithet of "those people", but she betrayed an intimate acquaintance with many of its members, and an encyclopaedic knowledge of the domestic habits, financial difficulties and private complications of various persons of social importance. Yet, as she evidently felt no incongruity in her attitude, so she revealed no desire to parade her familiarity with the fashionable, or indeed any sense of it as a fact to be paraded. It was evident that the titled ladies whom she spoke of as Mimi or Simone or Odette were as much "those people" to her as the *bonne* who tampered with her tea and steamed the stamps off her letters (" when, by a miracle, I don't put them in the box myself.") Her whole attitude was of a vast grim tolerance of things-as-they-came, as though she had been some wonderful automatic machine which recorded facts but had not yet been perfected to the point of sorting or labelling them.

All this, as Darrow was aware, still fell short of accounting for the influence she obviously exerted on the persons in contact with her. It brought a slight relief to his state of tension to go on wondering, while he watched and listened, just where the mystery lurked. Perhaps, after all, it was in the fact of her blank insensibility, an insensibility so devoid of egotism that it had no hardness and no grimaces, but rather the freshness of a simpler mental state. After living, as he had, as they all had, for the last few days, in an atmosphere perpetually tremulous with echoes and implications, it was restful and fortifying merely to walk into the big blank area of Miss Painter's mind, so vacuous for all its accumulated items, so echoless for all its vacuity.

His hope of a word with Anna before dinner was dispelled by her rising to take Miss Painter up to Madame de Chantelle; and he wandered away to his own room, leaving Owen and Miss Viner engaged in working out a picture-puzzle for Effie.

Madame de Chantelle—possibly as the result of her friend's ministrations—was able to appear at the dinner-table, rather pale and pink-nosed, and casting tenderly reproachful glances at her grandson, who faced them with impervious serenity; and the situation was relieved by the fact that Miss Viner, as usual, had remained in the school-room with her pupil.

Darrow conjectured that the real clash of arms would not take place till the morrow; and wishing to leave the field open to the contestants he set out early on a solitary walk. It was nearly luncheon-time when he returned from it and came upon Anna just emerging from the house. She had on her hat and jacket and was apparently coming forth to seek him, for she said at once: "Madame de Chantelle wants you to go up to her."

"To go up to her? Now?"

"That's the message she sent. She appears to rely on you to do something." She added with a smile: "Whatever it is, let's have it over!"

Darrow, through his rising sense of apprehension, wondered why, instead of merely going for a walk, he had not jumped into the first train and got out of the way till Owen's affairs were finally settled.

"But what in the name of goodness can I do?" he protested, following Anna back into the hall.

"I don't know. But Owen seems so to rely on you, too——"

"Owen! Is *he* to be there?"

"No. But you know I told him he could count on you."

"But I've said to your mother-in-law all I could."

"Well, then you can only repeat it."

This did not seem to Darrow to simplify his case as much as she appeared to think; and once more he had a movement of recoil. "There's no possible reason for my being mixed up in this affair!"

Anna gave him a reproachful glance. "Not the fact that *I* am?" she reminded him; but even this only stiffened his resistance.

"Why should you be, either—to this extent?"

The question made her pause. She glanced about the hall, as if to be sure they had it to themselves; and then, in a lowered voice: "I don't know," she suddenly confessed; "but, somehow, if *they're* not happy I feel as if we shouldn't be."

"Oh, well——" Darrow acquiesced, in the tone of the man who perforce yields to so lovely an unreasonableness. Escape was, after all, impossible, and he could only resign himself to being led to Madame de Chantelle's door.

Within, among the bric-a-brac and furbelows, he found Miss Painter seated in a redundant purple armchair with the incongruous air of a horseman bestriding a heavy mount. Madame de Chantelle sat opposite, still a little wan and disordered under her elaborate hair, and clasping the handkerchief whose visibility symbolized her distress. On the young man's entrance she sighed out a plaintive welcome, to which she immediately appended: "Mr. Darrow, I can't help feeling that at heart you're with me!"

The directness of the challenge made it easier for Darrow to protest, and he reiterated his inability to give an opinion on either side.

"But Anna declares you have—on hers!"

He could not restrain a smile at this faint flaw in an impartiality so scrupulous. Every evidence of feminine inconsequence in Anna seemed to attest her deeper subjection to the most inconsequent of passions. He had certainly promised her his help—but before he knew what he was promising.

He met Madame de Chantelle's appeal by replying: "If there were anything I could possibly say I should want it to be in Miss Viner's favour."

"You'd want it to be—yes! But could you make it so?"

"As far as facts go, I don't see how I can make it either for or against her. I've already said that I know nothing of her except that she's charming."

"As if that weren't enough—weren't all there *ought* to be!" Miss Painter put in impatiently. She seemed to address herself to Darrow, though her small eyes were fixed on her friend.

"Madame de Chantelle seems to imagine," she pursued, "that a young American girl ought to have a *dossier*—a police-record, or whatever you call it: what those awful women in the streets have here. In our country it's enough to know that a young girl's pure and lovely: people don't immediately ask her to show her bank-account and her visiting-list."

Madame de Chantelle looked plaintively at her sturdy monitress. "You don't expect me not to ask if she's got a family?"

"No; nor to think the worse of her if she hasn't. The fact that she's an orphan ought, with your ideas, to be a merit. You won't have to invite her father and mother to Givré!"

"Adelaide—Adelaide!" the mistress of Givré lamented.

"Lucretia Mary," the other returned—and Darrow spared an instant's amusement to the quaint incongruity of the name—"you know you sent for Mr. Darrow to refute me; and how can he, till he knows what I think?"

"You think it's perfectly simple to let Owen marry a girl we know nothing about?"

"No; but I don't think it's perfectly simple to prevent him."

The shrewdness of the answer increased Darrow's interest in Miss Painter. She had not hitherto struck him as being a person of much penetration, but he now felt sure that her gimlet gaze might bore to the heart of any practical problem.

Madame de Chantelle sighed out her recognition of the difficulty.

"I haven't a word to say against Miss Viner; but she's knocked about so, as it's called, that she must have been mixed up with some rather dreadful people. If only Owen could be made to see that—if one could get at a few facts, I mean. She says, for instance, that she has a sister; but it seems she doesn't even know her address!"

"If she does, she may not want to give it to you. I daresay the sister's one of the dreadful people. I've no doubt that with a little time you could rake up dozens of them: have her 'traced', as they call it in detective stories. I don't think you'd frighten Owen, but you might: it's natural enough he should have been corrupted by those foreign ideas. You might even manage to part him from the girl; but you couldn't keep him from being in love with her. I saw that when I looked them over last evening. I said to myself: 'It's a real old-fashioned American case, as sweet and sound as home-made bread.' Well, if you take his loaf away from him, what are you going to feed him with instead? Which of your nasty Paris poisons do you think he'll turn to? Supposing you succeed in keeping him out of a really bad mess—and, knowing the young man as I do, I rather think that, at this crisis, the only way to do it would be to marry him slap off to somebody else—well, then, who, may I ask, would you pick out? One of your sweet French *ingénues*, I suppose? With as much mind as a minnow and as much snap as a soft-boiled egg. You might hustle him into that kind of marriage; I daresay you could—but if I know Owen, the natural thing would happen before the first baby was weaned."

"I don't know why you insinuate such odious things against Owen!"

"Do you think it would be odious of him to return to his real love when he'd been forcibly parted from her? At any rate, it's what your French friends do, every one of them! Only they don't generally have the grace to go back to an old love; and I believe, upon my word, Owen would!"

Madame de Chantelle looked at her with a mixture of awe and exultation. "Of course you realize, Adelaide, that in suggesting this you're insinuating the most shocking things against Miss Viner?"

"When I say that if you part two young things who are dying to be happy in the lawful way it's ten to one they'll come together in an unlawful one? I'm insinuating shocking things against *you*, Lucretia Mary, in suggesting for a moment that you'll care to assume such a responsibility before your Maker. And you wouldn't, if you talked things straight out with him, instead of merely sending him messages through a miserable sinner like yourself!"

Darrow expected this assault on her adopted creed to provoke in Madame de Chantelle an explosion of pious indignation; but to his surprise she merely murmured: "I don't know what Mr. Darrow'll think of you!"

"Mr. Darrow probably knows his Bible as well as I do," Miss Painter calmly rejoined; adding a moment later, without the least perceptible change of voice or expression: "I suppose you've heard that Gisèle de Folembray's husband accuses her of being mixed up with the Duc d'Arcachon in that business of trying to sell a lot of imitation pearls to Mrs. Homer Pond, the Chicago woman the Duke's engaged to? It seems the jeweller says Gisèle brought Mrs. Pond there, and got twenty-five per cent—which of course she passed on to d'Arcachon. The poor old Duchess is in a fearful state—so afraid her son'll lose Mrs. Pond! When I think that Gisèle is old Bradford Wagstaff's grand-daughter, I'm thankful he's safe in Mount Auburn!"

XXII

IT WAS NOT until late that afternoon that Darrow could claim his postponed hour with Anna. When at last he found her alone in her sitting-room it was with a sense of liberation so great that he sought no logical justification of it. He simply felt that all their destinies were in Miss Painter's grasp, and that, resistance being useless, he could only enjoy the sweets of surrender.

Anna herself seemed as happy, and for more explicable reasons. She had assisted, after luncheon, at another debate between Madame de Chantelle and her confidant, and had surmised, when she withdrew from it, that victory was permanently perched on Miss Painter's banners.

"I don't know how she does it, unless it's by the dead weight of her convictions. She detests the French so that she'd back up Owen even if she knew nothing—or knew too much—of Miss Viner. She somehow regards the match as a protest against the corruption of European morals. I told Owen that was his great chance, and he's made the most of it."

"What a tactician you are! You make me feel that I hardly know the rudiments of diplomacy," Darrow smiled at her, abandoning himself to a perilous sense of well-being.

She gave him back his smile. "I'm afraid I think nothing short of my own happiness is worth wasting any diplomacy on!"

"That's why I mean to resign from the service of my country," he rejoined with a laugh of deep content.

The feeling that both resistance and apprehension were vain was working like wine in his veins. He had done what he could to deflect the course of events: now he could only stand aside and take his chance of safety. Underneath this fatalistic feeling was the deep sense of relief that he had, after all, said and done nothing that could in the least degree affect the welfare of Sophy Viner. That fact took a millstone off his neck.

Meanwhile he gave himself up once more to the joy of Anna's presence. They had not been alone together for two long days, and he had the lover's sense that he had forgotten, or at least underestimated, the strength of the spell she cast. Once more her eyes and her smile seemed to bound his world. He felt that their light would always move with him as the sunset moves before a ship at sea.

The next day his sense of security was increased by a decisive incident. It became known to the expectant household that Madame de Chantelle had yielded to the tremendous impact of Miss Painter's determination and that Sophy Viner had been "sent for" to the purple satin sitting-room.

At luncheon, Owen's radiant countenance proclaimed the happy sequel, and Darrow, when the party had moved back to the oak-room for coffee, deemed it discreet to wander out alone to the terrace with his cigar. The conclusion of Owen's romance brought his own plans once more to the front. Anna had promised that she would consider dates and settle details as soon as Madame de Chantelle and her grandson had been reconciled, and Darrow was eager to go into the question at once, since it was necessary that the preparations for his marriage should go forward as rapidly as possible. Anna, he knew, would not seek any farther pretext for delay; and he strolled up and down contentedly in the sunshine, certain that she would come out and reassure him as soon as the reunited family had claimed its due share of her attention.

But when she finally joined him her first word was for the younger lovers.

"I want to thank you for what you've done for Owen," she began, with her happiest smile.

"Who—I?" he laughed. "Are you confusing me with Miss Painter?"

"Perhaps I ought to say for *me*," she corrected herself. "You've been even more of a help to us than Adelaide."

"My dear child! What on earth have I done?"

"You've managed to hide from Madame de Chantelle that you don't really like poor Sophy."

Darrow felt the pallour in his cheek. "Not like her? What put such an idea into your head?"

"Oh, it's more than an idea—it's a feeling. But what difference does it make, after all? You saw her in such a different setting that it's natural you should be a little doubtful. But when you know her better I'm sure you'll feel about her as I do."

"It's going to be hard for me not to feel about everything as you do."

"Well, then—please begin with my daughter-in-law!"

He gave her back in the same tone of banter: "Agreed: if you'll agree to feel as I do about the pressing necessity of our getting married."

"I want to talk to you about that too. You don't know what a weight is off my mind! With Sophy here for good, I shall feel so differently about leaving Effie. I've seen much more accomplished governesses—to my cost!—but I've never seen a young thing more gay and kind and human. You must have noticed, though you've seen them so little together, how Effie expands when she's with her. And that, you know, is what I want. Madame de Chantelle will provide the necessary restraint." She clasped her hands on his arm. "Yes, I'm ready to go with you now. But first of all—this very moment!—you must come with me to Effie. She knows, of course, nothing of what's been happening; and I want her to be told first about *you*."

Effie, sought throughout the house, was presently traced to the school-room, and thither Darrow mounted with Anna. He had never seen her so alight with happiness, and he had caught her buoyancy of mood. He kept repeating to himself: "It's over—it's over," as if some monstrous midnight hallucination had been routed by the return of day.

As they approached the school-room door the terrier's barks came to them through laughing remonstrances.

"She's giving him his dinner," Anna whispered, her hand in Darrow's.

"Don't forget the gold-fish!" they heard another voice call out.

Darrow halted on the threshold. "Oh—not now!"

"Not now?"

"I mean—she'd rather have you tell her first. I'll wait for you both downstairs."

He was aware that she glanced at him intently. "As you please. I'll bring her down at once."

She opened the door, and as she went in he heard her say: "No, Sophy, don't go! I want you both."

The rest of Darrow's day was a succession of empty and agitating scenes. On his way down to Givré, before he had seen Effie Leath, he had pictured somewhat sentimentally the joy of the moment when he should take her in his arms and receive her first filial kiss. Everything in him that egotistically craved for rest, stability, a comfortably organized middle-age, all the home-building instincts of the man who has sufficiently wooed and wandered, combined to throw a charm about the figure of the child who might—who should—have been his. Effie came to him trailing the cloud of glory of his first romance, giving him back the magic hour he had missed and mourned. And how different the realization of his dream had been! The child's radiant welcome, her unquestioning acceptance of this new figure in the family group, had been all that he had hoped and fancied. If Mother was so awfully happy about it, and Owen and Granny, too, how nice and cosy and comfortable it was going to be for all of them, her beaming look seemed to say; and then, suddenly, the small pink fingers he had been kissing were laid on the one flaw in the circle, on the one point which must be settled before Effie could, with complete unqualified assurance, admit the newcomer to full equality with the other gods of her Olympus.

"And is Sophy awfully happy about it too?" she had asked, loosening her hold on Darrow's neck to tilt back her head and include her mother in her questioning look.

"Why, dearest, didn't you see she was?" Anna had exclaimed, leaning to the group with radiant eyes.

"I think I should like to ask her," the child rejoined, after a minute's shy consideration; and as Darrow set her down her mother laughed: "Do, darling, do! Run off at once, and tell her we expect her to be awfully happy too."

The scene had been succeeded by others less poignant but almost as trying. Darrow cursed his luck in having, at such a moment, to run the gauntlet of a houseful of interested observers. The state of being "engaged", in itself an absurd enough predicament, even to a man only intermittently exposed, became intolerable under the continuous scrutiny of a small circle quivering with participation. Darrow was further-more aware that, though the case of the other couple ought to have made his own less conspicuous, it was rather they who found a refuge in the shadow of his prominence. Ma-dame de Chantelle, though she had consented to Owen's engagement and formally welcomed his betrothed, was nev-ertheless not sorry to show, by her reception of Darrow, of what finely-shaded degrees of cordiality she was capable. Miss Painter, having won the day for Owen, was also free to turn her attention to the newer candidate for her sympathy; and Darrow and Anna found themselves immersed in a warm bath of sentimental curiosity.

It was a relief to Darrow that he was under a positive ob-ligation to end his visit within the next forty-eight hours. When he left London, his Ambassador had accorded him a ten days' leave. His fate being definitely settled and openly published he had no reason for asking to have the time pro-longed, and when it was over he was to return to his post till the time fixed for taking up his new duties. Anna and he had therefore decided to be married, in Paris, a day or two before the departure of the steamer which was to take them to South America; and Anna, shortly after his return to England, was to go up to Paris and begin her own preparations.

In honour of the double betrothal Effie and Miss Viner were to appear that evening at dinner; and Darrow, on leav-ing his room, met the little girl springing down the stairs, her white ruffles and coral-coloured bows making her look like a daisy with her yellow hair for its centre. Sophy Viner was behind her pupil, and as she came into the light Darrow no-ticed a change in her appearance and wondered vaguely why she looked suddenly younger, more vivid, more like the little luminous ghost of his Paris memories. Then it occurred to him that it was the first time she had appeared at dinner since his arrival at Givré, and the first time, consequently, that he had seen her in evening dress. She was still at the age when the least adornment embellishes; and no doubt the mere un-covering of her young throat and neck had given her back her former brightness. But a second glance showed a more precise reason for his impression. Vaguely though he retained such details, he felt sure she was wearing the dress he had seen her in every evening in Paris. It was a simple enough dress, black, and transparent on the arms and shoulders, and he would probably not have recognized it if she had not called his attention to it in Paris by confessing that she hadn't any other. "The same dress? That proves that she's forgotten!" was his first half-ironic thought; but the next moment, with a pang of compunction, he said to himself that she had probably put it on for the same reason as before: simply because she hadn't any other.

He looked at her in silence, and for an instant, above Effie's bobbing head, she gave him back his look in a full bright gaze.

"Oh, there's Owen!" Effie cried, and whirled away down the gallery to the door from which her step-brother was emerging. As Owen bent to catch her, Sophy Viner turned abruptly back to Darrow.

"You, too?" she said with a quick laugh. "I didn't know——" And as Owen came up to them she added, in a tone that might have been meant to reach his ear: "I wish you all the luck that we can spare!"

About the dinner-table, which Effie, with Miss Viner's aid, had lavishly garlanded, the little party had an air of somewhat self-conscious festivity. In spite of flowers, champagne and a unanimous attempt at ease, there were frequent lapses in the talk, and moments of nervous groping for new subjects. Miss Painter alone seemed not only unaffected by the general perturbation but as tightly sealed up in her unconsciousness of it as a diver in his bell. To Darrow's strained attention even Owen's gusts of gaiety seemed to betray an inward sense of insecurity. After dinner, however, at the piano, he broke into a mood of extravagant hilarity and flooded the room with the splash and ripple of his music.

Darrow, sunk in a sofa corner in the lee of Miss Painter's granite bulk, smoked and listened in silence, his eyes moving from one figure to another. Madame de Chantelle, in her armchair near the fire, clasped her little granddaughter to her with the gesture of a drawing-room Niobe, and Anna, seated near them, had fallen into one of the attitudes of vivid calm which seemed to Darrow to express her inmost quality. Sophy Viner, after moving uncertainly about the room, had placed herself beyond Mrs. Leath, in a chair near the piano, where she sat with head thrown back and eyes attached to the musician, in the same rapt fixity of attention with which she had followed the players at the Français. The accident of her having fallen into the same attitude, and of her wearing the same dress, gave Darrow, as he watched her, a strange sense of double consciousness. To escape from it, his glance turned back to Anna; but from the point at which he was placed his eyes could not take in the one face without the other, and that renewed the disturbing duality of the impression. Suddenly Owen broke off with a crash of chords and jumped to his feet.

"What's the use of this, with such a moon to say it for us?"

Behind the uncurtained window a low golden orb hung like a ripe fruit against the glass.

"Yes—let's go out and listen," Anna answered. Owen threw open the window, and with his gesture a fold of the heavy star-sprinkled sky seemed to droop into the room like a drawn-in curtain. The air that entered with it had a frosty edge, and Anna bade Effie run to the hall for wraps.

Darrow said: "You must have one too," and started toward the door; but Sophy, following her pupil, cried back: "We'll bring things for everybody."

Owen had followed her, and in a moment the three reappeared, and the party went out on the terrace. The deep blue purity of the night was unveiled by mist, and the moonlight rimmed the edges of the trees with a silver blur and blanched to unnatural whiteness the statues against their walls of shade.

Darrow and Anna, with Effie between them, strolled to the farther corner of the terrace. Below them, between the fringes of the park, the lawn sloped dimly to the fields above the river. For a few minutes they stood silently side by side, touched to peace beneath the trembling beauty of the sky. When they turned back, Darrow saw that Owen and Sophy Viner, who had gone down the steps to the garden, were also walking in the direction of the house. As they advanced, Sophy paused in a patch of moonlight, between the sharp shadows of the yews, and Darrow noticed that she had thrown over her shoulders a long cloak of some light colour, which suddenly evoked her image as she had entered the restaurant at his side on the night of their first dinner in Paris. A moment later they were all together again on the terrace, and when they re-entered the drawing-room the older ladies were on their way to bed.

Effie, emboldened by the privileges of the evening, was for coaxing Owen to round it off with a game of forfeits or some such reckless climax; but Sophy, resuming her professional rôle, sounded the summons to bed. In her pupil's wake she made her round of good-nights; but when she proffered her hand to Anna, the latter ignoring the gesture held out both arms.

"Good-night, dear child," she said impulsively, and drew the girl to her kiss.

BOOK IV

XXIII

T HE NEXT DAY was Darrow's last at Givré and, foreseeing that the afternoon and evening would have to be given to the family, he had asked Anna to devote an early hour to the final consideration of their plans. He was to meet her in the brown sitting-room at ten, and they were to walk down to the river and talk over their future in the little pavilion abutting on the wall of the park.

It was just a week since his arrival at Givré, and Anna wished, before he left, to return to the place where they had sat on their first afternoon together. Her sensitiveness to the appeal of inanimate things, to the colour and texture of whatever wove itself into the substance of her emotion, made her want to hear Darrow's voice, and to feel his eyes on her, in the spot where bliss had first flowed into her heart.

That bliss, in the interval, had wound itself into every fold of her being. Passing, in the first days, from a high shy tenderness to the rush of a secret surrender, it had gradually widened and deepened, to flow on in redoubled beauty. She thought she now knew exactly how and why she loved Darrow, and she could see her whole sky reflected in the deep and tranquil current of her love.

Early the next day, in her sitting-room, she was glancing through the letters which it was Effie's morning privilege to carry up to her. Effie meanwhile circled inquisitively about the room, where there was always something new to engage her infant fancy; and Anna, looking up, saw her suddenly arrested before a photograph of Darrow which, the day before, had taken its place on the writing-table.

Anna held out her arms with a faint blush. "You do like him, don't you, dear?"

"Oh, most awfully, dearest," Effie, against her breast, leaned back to assure her with a limpid look. "And so do Granny and Owen—and I *do* think Sophy does too," she added, after a moment's earnest pondering.

"I hope so," Anna laughed. She checked the impulse to continue: "Has she talked to you about him, that you're so

sure?" She did not know what had made the question spring
to her lips, but she was glad she had closed them before pronouncing it. Nothing could have been more distasteful to her
than to clear up such obscurities by turning on them the tiny
flame of her daughter's observation. And what, after all, now
that Owen's happiness was secured, did it matter if there were
certain reserves in Darrow's approval of his marriage?

A knock on the door made Anna glance at the clock.
"There's Nurse to carry you off."

"It's Sophy's knock," the little girl answered, jumping
down to open the door; and Miss Viner in fact stood on the
threshold.

"Come in," Anna said with a smile, instantly remarking
how pale she looked.

"May Effie go out for a turn with Nurse?" the girl asked.
"I should like to speak to you a moment."

"Of course. This ought to be *your* holiday, as yesterday was
Effie's. Run off, dear," she added, stooping to kiss the little
girl.

When the door had closed she turned back to Sophy Viner
with a look that sought her confidence. "I'm so glad you
came, my dear. We've got so many things to talk about, just
you and I together."

The confused intercourse of the last days had, in fact, left
little time for any speech with Sophy but such as related to
her marriage and the means of overcoming Madame de Chantelle's opposition to it. Anna had exacted of Owen that no
one, not even Sophy Viner, should be given a hint of her own
projects till all contingent questions had been disposed of.
She had felt, from the outset, a secret reluctance to intrude
her securer happiness on the doubts and fears of the young
pair.

From the sofa-corner to which she had dropped back she
pointed to Darrow's chair. "Come and sit by me, dear. I
wanted to see you alone. There's so much to say that I hardly
know where to begin."

She leaned forward, her hands clasped on the arms of the
sofa, her eyes bent smilingly on Sophy's. As she did so, she
noticed that the girl's unusual pallor was partly due to the
slight veil of powder on her face. The discovery was distinctly

disagreeable. Anna had never before noticed, on Sophy's part, any recourse to cosmetics, and, much as she wished to think herself exempt from old-fashioned prejudices, she suddenly became aware that she did not like her daughter's governess to have a powdered face. Then she reflected that the girl who sat opposite her was no longer Effie's governess, but her own future daughter-in-law; and she wondered whether Miss Viner had chosen this odd way of celebrating her independence, and whether, as Mrs. Owen Leath, she would present to the world a bedizened countenance. This idea was scarcely less distasteful than the other, and for a moment Anna continued to consider her without speaking. Then, in a flash, the truth came to her: Miss Viner had powdered her face because Miss Viner had been crying.

Anna leaned forward impulsively. "My dear child, what's the matter?" She saw the girl's blood rush up under the white mask, and hastened on: "Please don't be afraid to tell me. I do so want you to feel that you can trust me as Owen does. And you know you mustn't mind if, just at first, Madame de Chantelle occasionally relapses."

She spoke eagerly, persuasively, almost on a note of pleading. She had, in truth, so many reasons for wanting Sophy to like her: her love for Owen, her solicitude for Effie, and her own sense of the girl's fine mettle. She had always felt a romantic and almost humble admiration for those members of her sex who, from force of will, or the constraint of circumstances, had plunged into the conflict from which fate had so persistently excluded her. There were even moments when she fancied herself vaguely to blame for her immunity, and felt that she ought somehow to have affronted the perils and hardships which refused to come to her. And now, as she sat looking at Sophy Viner, so small, so slight, so visibly defenceless and undone, she still felt, through all the superiority of her worldly advantages and her seeming maturity, the same odd sense of ignorance and inexperience. She could not have said what there was in the girl's manner and expression to give her this feeling, but she was reminded, as she looked at Sophy Viner, of the other girls she had known in her youth, the girls who seemed possessed of a secret she had missed. Yes, Sophy Viner had their look—almost the obscurely menacing look of Kitty Mayne . . . Anna, with an inward smile, brushed aside the image of this forgotten rival. But she had felt, deep down, a twinge of the old pain, and she was sorry that, even for the flash of a thought, Owen's betrothed should have reminded her of so different a woman . . .

She laid her hand on the girl's. "When his grandmother sees how happy Owen is she'll be quite happy herself. If it's only that, don't be distressed. Just trust to Owen—and the future."

Sophy Viner, with an almost imperceptible recoil of her whole slight person, had drawn her hand from under the palm enclosing it.

"That's what I wanted to talk to you about—the future."

"Of course! We've all so many plans to make—and to fit into each other's. Please let's begin with yours."

The girl paused a moment, her hands clasped on the arms of her chair, her lids dropped under Anna's gaze; then she said: "I should like to make no plans at all . . . just yet . . ."

"No plans?"

"No—I should like to go away . . . my friends the Far-lows would let me go to them . . ." Her voice grew firmer and she lifted her eyes to add: "I should like to leave today, if you don't mind."

Anna listened with a rising wonder.

"You want to leave Givré at once?" She gave the idea a moment's swift consideration. "You prefer to be with your friends till your marriage? I understand that—but surely you needn't rush off today? There are so many details to discuss; and before long, you know, I shall be going away too."

"Yes, I know." The girl was evidently trying to steady her voice. "But I should like to wait a few days—to have a little more time to myself."

Anna continued to consider her kindly. It was evident that she did not care to say why she wished to leave Givré so suddenly, but her disturbed face and shaken voice betrayed a more pressing motive than the natural desire to spend the weeks before her marriage under her old friends' roof. Since she had made no response to the allusion to Madame de Chantelle, Anna could but conjecture that she had had a passing disagreement with Owen; and if this were so, random interference might do more harm than good.

"My dear child, if you really want to go at once I sha'n't, of course, urge you to stay. I suppose you have spoken to Owen?"

"No. Not yet . . ."

Anna threw an astonished glance at her. "You mean to say you haven't told him?"

"I wanted to tell you first. I thought I ought to, on account of Effie." Her look cleared as she put forth this reason.

"Oh, Effie!—" Anna's smile brushed away the scruple: "Owen has a right to ask that you should consider him before you think of his sister . . . Of course you shall do just as you wish," she went on, after another thoughtful interval.

"Oh, thank you," Sophy Viner murmured and rose to her feet.

Anna rose also, vaguely seeking for some word that should break down the girl's resistance. "You'll tell Owen at once?" she finally asked.

Miss Viner, instead of replying, stood before her in manifest uncertainty, and as she did so there was a light tap on the door, and Owen Leath walked into the room.

Anna's first glance told her that his face was unclouded. He met her greeting with his happiest smile and turned to lift Sophy's hand to his lips. The perception that he was utterly unconscious of any cause for Miss Viner's agitation came to his step-mother with a sharp thrill of surprise.

"Darrow's looking for you," he said to her. "He asked me to remind you that you'd promised to go for a walk with him."

Anna glanced at the clock. "I'll go down presently." She waited and looked again at Sophy Viner, whose troubled eyes seemed to commit their message to her. "You'd better tell Owen, my dear."

Owen's look also turned on the girl. "Tell me what? Why, what's happened?"

Anna summoned a laugh to ease the vague tension of the moment. "Don't look so startled! Nothing, except that Sophy proposes to desert us for a while for the Farlows."

Owen's brow cleared. "I was afraid she'd run off before

long." He glanced at Anna. "Do please keep her here as long as you can!"

Sophy intervened: "Mrs. Leath's already given me leave to go."

"Already? To go when?"

"Today," said Sophy in a low tone, her eyes on Anna's.

"Today? Why on earth should you go today?" Owen dropped back a step or two, flushing and paling under his bewildered frown. His eyes seemed to search the girl more closely. "Something's happened." He too looked at his step-mother. "I suppose she must have told you what it is?"

Anna was struck by the suddenness and vehemence of his appeal. It was as though some smouldering apprehension had lain close under the surface of his security.

"She's told me nothing except that she wishes to be with her friends. It's quite natural that she should want to go to them."

Owen visibly controlled himself. "Of course—quite natural." He spoke to Sophy. "But why didn't you tell me so? Why did you come first to my step-mother?"

Anna intervened with her calm smile. "That seems to me quite natural, too. Sophy was considerate enough to tell me first because of Effie."

He weighed it. "Very well, then: that's quite natural, as you say. And of course she must do exactly as she pleases." He still kept his eyes on the girl. "Tomorrow," he abruptly announced, "I shall go up to Paris to see you."

"Oh, no—no!" she protested.

Owen turned back to Anna. "*Now* do you say that nothing's happened?"

Under the influence of his agitation Anna felt a vague tightening of the heart. She seemed to herself like some one in a dark room about whom unseen presences are groping.

"If it's anything that Sophy wishes to tell you, no doubt she'll do so. I'm going down now, and I'll leave you here to talk it over by yourselves."

As she moved to the door the girl caught up with her. "But there's nothing to tell: why should there be? I've explained that I simply want to be quiet." Her look seemed to detain Mrs. Leath.

Owen broke in: "Is that why I mayn't go up tomorrow?"

"Not tomorrow!"

"Then when may I?"

"Later . . . in a little while . . . a few days . . ."

"In how many days?"

"Owen!" his step-mother interposed; but he seemed no longer aware of her. "If you go away today, the day that our engagement's made known, it's only fair," he persisted, "that you should tell me when I am to see you."

Sophy's eyes wavered between the two and dropped down wearily. "It's you who are not fair—when I've said I wanted to be quiet."

"But why should my coming disturb you? I'm not asking now to come tomorrow. I only ask you not to leave without telling me when I'm to see you."

"Owen, I don't understand you!" his step-mother exclaimed.

"You don't understand my asking for some explanation, some assurance, when I'm left in this way, without a word, without a sign? All I ask her to tell me is when she'll see me."

Anna turned back to Sophy Viner, who stood straight and tremulous between the two.

"After all, my dear, he's not unreasonable!"

"I'll write—I'll write," the girl repeated.

"*What* will you write?" he pressed her vehemently.

"Owen," Anna exclaimed, "you *are* unreasonable!"

He turned from Sophy to his step-mother. "I only want her to say what she means: that she's going to write to break off our engagement. Isn't that what you're going away for?"

Anna felt the contagion of his excitement. She looked at Sophy, who stood motionless, her lips set, her whole face drawn to a silent fixity of resistance.

"You ought to speak, my dear—you ought to answer him."

"I only ask him to wait——"

"Yes," Owen, broke in, "and you won't say how long!"

Both instinctively addressed themselves to Anna, who stood, nearly as shaken as themselves, between the double shock of their struggle. She looked again from Sophy's inscrutable eyes to Owen's stormy features; then she said:

"What can I do, when there's clearly something between you that I don't know about?"

"Oh, if it *were* between us! Can't you see it's outside of us—outside of her, dragging at her, dragging her away from me?" Owen wheeled round again upon his step-mother.

Anna turned from him to the girl. "Is it true that you want to break your engagement? If you do, you ought to tell him now."

Owen burst into a laugh. "She doesn't dare to—she's afraid I'll guess the reason!"

A faint sound escaped from Sophy's lips, but she kept them close on whatever answer she had ready.

"If she doesn't wish to marry you, why should she be afraid to have you know the reason?"

"She's afraid to have *you* know it—not me!"

"To have *me* know it?"

He laughed again, and Anna, at his laugh, felt a sudden rush of indignation.

"Owen, you must explain what you mean!"

He looked at her hard before answering; then: "Ask Darrow!" he said.

"Owen—Owen!" Sophy Viner murmured.

XXIV

Anna stood looking from one to the other. It had become apparent to her in a flash that Owen's retort, though it startled Sophy, did not take her by surprise; and the discovery shot its light along dark distances of fear.

The immediate inference was that Owen had guessed the reason of Darrow's disapproval of his marriage, or that, at least, he suspected Sophy Viner of knowing and dreading it. This confirmation of her own obscure doubt sent a tremor of alarm through Anna. For a moment she felt like exclaiming: "All this is really no business of mine, and I refuse to have you mix me up in it—" but her secret fear held her fast.

Sophy Viner was the first to speak.

"I should like to go now," she said in a low voice, taking a few steps toward the door.

Her tone woke Anna to the sense of her own share in the situation. "I quite agree with you, my dear, that it's useless to carry on this discussion. But since Mr. Darrow's name has been brought into it, for reasons which I fail to guess, I want to tell you that you're both mistaken if you think he's not in sympathy with your marriage. If that's what Owen means to imply, the idea's a complete delusion."

She spoke the words deliberately and incisively, as if hoping that the sound of their utterance would stifle the whisper in her bosom.

Sophy's only answer was a vague murmur, and a movement that brought her nearer to the door; but before she could reach it Owen had placed himself in her way.

"I don't mean to imply what you think," he said, addressing his step-mother but keeping his eyes on the girl. "I don't say Darrow doesn't like our marriage; I say it's Sophy who's hated it since Darrow's been here!"

He brought out the charge in a tone of forced composure, but his lips were white and he grasped the door-knob to hide the tremor of his hand.

Anna's anger surged up with her fears. "You're absurd, Owen! I don't know why I listen to you. Why should Sophy dislike Mr. Darrow, and if she does, why should that have anything to do with her wishing to break her engagement?"

"I don't say she dislikes him! I don't say she likes him; I don't know what it is they say to each other when they're shut up together alone."

"Shut up together alone?" Anna stared. Owen seemed like a man in delirium; such an exhibition was degrading to them all. But he pushed on without seeing her look.

"Yes—the first evening she came, in the study; the next morning, early, in the park; yesterday, again, in the spring-house, when you were at the lodge with the doctor . . . I don't know what they say to each other, but they've taken every chance they could to say it . . . and to say it when they thought that no one saw them."

Anna longed to silence him, but no words came to her. It was as though all her confused apprehensions had suddenly taken definite shape. There was "something"—yes, there was "something" . . . Darrow's reticences and evasions had been more than a figment of her doubts.

The next instant brought a recoil of pride. She turned indignantly on her step-son.

"I don't half understand what you've been saying; but what you seem to hint is so preposterous, and so insulting both to Sophy and to me, that I see no reason why we should listen to you any longer."

Though her tone steadied Owen, she perceived at once that it would not deflect him from his purpose. He spoke less vehemently, but with all the more precision.

"How can it be preposterous, since it's true? Or insulting, since I don't know, any more than *you*, the meaning of what I've been seeing? If you'll be patient with me I'll try to put it quietly. What I mean is that Sophy has completely changed since she met Darrow here, and that, having noticed the change, I'm hardly to blame for having tried to find out its cause."

Anna made an effort to answer him with the same composure. "You're to blame, at any rate, for so recklessly assuming that you *have* found it out. You seem to forget that, till they met here, Sophy and Mr. Darrow hardly knew each other."

"If so, it's all the stranger that they've been so often closeted together!"

"Owen, Owen—" the girl sighed out.

He turned his haggard face to her. "Can I help it, if I've seen and known what I wasn't meant to? For God's sake give me a reason—any reason I can decently make out with! Is it my fault if, the day after you arrived, when I came back late through the garden, the curtains of the study hadn't been drawn, and I saw you there alone with Darrow?"

Anna laughed impatiently. "Really, Owen, if you make it a grievance that two people who are staying in the same house should be seen talking together——!"

"They were not talking. That's the point——"

"Not talking? How do you know? You could hardly hear them from the garden!"

"No; but I could see. *He* was sitting at my desk, with his face in his hands. *She* was standing in the window, looking away from him . . ."

He waited, as if for Sophy Viner's answer; but still she neither stirred nor spoke.

"That was the first time," he went on; "and the second was the next morning in the park. It was natural enough, their meeting there. Sophy had gone out with Effie, and Effie ran back to look for me. She told me she'd left Sophy and Darrow in the path that leads to the river, and presently we saw them ahead of us. They didn't see us at first, because they were standing looking at each other; and this time they were not speaking either. We came up close before they heard us, and all that time they never spoke, or stopped looking at each other. After that I began to wonder; and so I watched them."

"Oh, Owen!"

"Oh, I only had to wait. Yesterday, when I motored you and the doctor back from the lodge, I saw Sophy coming out of the spring-house. I supposed she'd taken shelter from the rain, and when you got out of the motor I strolled back down the avenue to meet her. But she'd disappeared—she must have taken a short cut and come into the house by the side door. I don't know why I went on to the spring-house; I suppose it was what you'd call spying. I went up the steps and found the room empty; but two chairs had been moved out from the wall and were standing near the table; and one of the Chinese screens that lie on it had dropped to the floor."

Anna sounded a faint note of irony. "Really? Sophy'd gone there for shelter, and she dropped a screen and moved a chair?"

"I said two chairs——"

"Two? What damning evidence—of I don't know what!"

"Simply of the fact that Darrow'd been there with her. As I looked out of the window I saw him close by, walking away. He must have turned the corner of the spring-house just as I got to the door."

There was another silence, during which Anna paused, not only to collect her own words but to wait for Sophy Viner's; then, as the girl made no sign, she turned to her.

"I've absolutely nothing to say to all this; but perhaps you'd like me to wait and hear your answer?"

Sophy raised her head with a quick flash of colour. "I've no answer either—except that Owen must be mad."

In the interval since she had last spoken she seemed to have regained her self-control, and her voice rang clear, with a cold edge of anger.

Anna looked at her step-son. He had grown extremely pale, and his hand fell from the door with a discouraged gesture. "That's all then? You won't give me any reason?"

"I didn't suppose it was necessary to give you or any one else a reason for talking with a friend of Mrs. Leath's under Mrs. Leath's own roof."

Owen hardly seemed to feel the retort: he kept his dogged stare on her face.

"I won't ask for one, then. I'll only ask you to give me your assurance that your talks with Darrow have had nothing to do with your suddenly deciding to leave Givré."

She hesitated, not so much with the air of weighing her answer as of questioning his right to exact any. "I give you my assurance; and now I should like to go," she said.

As she turned away, Anna intervened. "My dear, I think you ought to speak."

The girl drew herself up with a faint laugh. "To him—or to *you*?"

"To him."

She stiffened. "I've said all there is to say."

Anna drew back, her eyes on her step-son. He had left the

threshold and was advancing toward Sophy Viner with a motion of desperate appeal; but as he did so there was a knock on the door. A moment's silence fell on the three; then Anna said: "Come in!"

Darrow came into the room. Seeing the three together, he looked rapidly from one to the other; then he turned to Anna with a smile.

"I came up to see if you were ready; but please send me off if I'm not wanted."

His look, his voice, the simple sense of his presence, restored Anna's shaken balance. By Owen's side he looked so strong, so urbane, so experienced, that the lad's passionate charges dwindled to mere boyish vapourings. A moment ago she had dreaded Darrow's coming; now she was glad that he was there.

She turned to him with sudden decision. "Come in, please; I want you to hear what Owen has been saying."

She caught a murmur from Sophy Viner, but disregarded it. An illuminating impulse urged her on. She, habitually so aware of her own lack of penetration, her small skill in reading hidden motives and detecting secret signals, now felt herself mysteriously inspired. She addressed herself to Sophy Viner. "It's much better for you both that this absurd question should be cleared up now." Then, turning to Darrow, she continued: "For some reason that I don't pretend to guess, Owen has taken it into his head that you've influenced Miss Viner to break her engagement."

She spoke slowly and deliberately, because she wished to give time and to gain it; time for Darrow and Sophy to receive the full impact of what she was saying, and time to observe its full effect on them. She had said to herself: "If there's nothing between them, they'll look at each other; if there *is* something, they won't;" and as she ceased to speak she felt as if all her life were in her eyes.

Sophy, after a start of protest, remained motionless, her gaze on the ground. Darrow, his face grown grave, glanced slowly from Owen Leath to Anna. With his eyes on the latter he asked: "Has Miss Viner broken her engagement?"

A moment's silence followed his question; then the girl looked up and said: "Yes!"

Owen, as she spoke, uttered a smothered exclamation and walked out of the room. She continued to stand in the same place, without appearing to notice his departure, and without vouchsafing an additional word of explanation; then, before Anna could find a cry to detain her, she too turned and went out.

"For God's sake, what's happened?" Darrow asked; but Anna, with a drop of the heart, was saying to herself that he and Sophy Viner had not looked at each other.

XXV

Anna stood in the middle of the room, her eyes on the door. Darrow's questioning gaze was still on her, and she said to herself with a quick-drawn breath: "If only he doesn't come near me!"

It seemed to her that she had been suddenly endowed with the fatal gift of reading the secret sense of every seemingly spontaneous look and movement, and that in his least gesture of affection she would detect a cold design.

For a moment longer he continued to look at her enquiringly; then he turned away and took up his habitual stand by the mantel-piece. She drew a deep breath of relief.

"Won't you please explain?" he said.

"I can't explain: I don't know. I didn't even know—till she told you—that she really meant to break her engagement. All I know is that she came to me just now and said she wished to leave Givré today; and that Owen, when he heard of it— for she hadn't told him—at once accused her of going away with the secret intention of throwing him over."

"And you think it's a definite break?" She perceived, as she spoke, that his brow had cleared.

"How should I know? Perhaps you can tell me."

"I?" She fancied his face clouded again, but he did not move from his tranquil attitude.

"As *I* told you," she went on, "Owen has worked himself up to imagining that for some mysterious reason you've influenced Sophy against him."

Darrow still visibly wondered. "It must indeed be a mysterious reason! He knows how slightly I know Miss Viner. Why should he imagine anything so wildly improbable?"

"I don't know that either."

"But he must have hinted at some reason."

"No: he admits he doesn't know your reason. He simply says that Sophy's manner to him has changed since she came back to Givré and that he's seen you together several times— in the park, the spring-house, I don't know where—talking alone in a way that seemed confidential—almost secret; and he draws the preposterous conclusion that you've used your influence to turn her against him."

"My influence? What kind of influence?"

"He doesn't say."

Darrow again seemed to turn over the facts she gave him. His face remained grave, but without the least trace of discomposure. "And what does Miss Viner say?"

"She says it's perfectly natural that she should occasionally talk to my friends when she's under my roof—and refuses to give him any other explanation."

"That at least is perfectly natural!"

Anna felt her cheeks flush as she answered: "Yes—but there *is* something——"

"Something——?"

"Some reason for her sudden decision to break her engagement. I can understand Owen's feeling, sorry as I am for his way of showing it. The girl owes him some sort of explanation, and as long as she refuses to give it his imagination is sure to run wild."

"She would have given it, no doubt, if he'd asked it in a different tone."

"I don't defend Owen's tone—but she knew what it was before she accepted him. She knows he's excitable and undisciplined."

"Well, she's been disciplining him a little—probably the best thing that could happen. Why not let the matter rest there?"

"Leave Owen with the idea that you *have* been the cause of the break?"

He met the question with his easy smile. "Oh, as to that—leave him with any idea of me he chooses! But leave him, at any rate, free."

"Free?" she echoed in surprise.

"Simply let things be. You've surely done all you could for him and Miss Viner. If they don't hit it off it's their own affair. What possible motive can you have for trying to interfere now?"

Her gaze widened to a deeper wonder. "Why—naturally, what he says of you!"

"I don't care a straw what he says of me! In such a situation a boy in love will snatch at the most far-fetched reason rather than face the mortifying fact that the lady may simply be tired of him."

"You don't quite understand Owen. Things go deep with him, and last long. It took him a long time to recover from his other unlucky love affair. He's romantic and extravagant: he can't live on the interest of his feelings. He worships Sophy and she seemed to be fond of him. If she's changed it's been very sudden. And if they part like this, angrily and inarticulately, it will hurt him horribly—hurt his very soul. But that, as you say, is between the two. What concerns me is his associating you with their quarrel. Owen's like my own son— if you'd seen him when I first came here you'd know why. We were like two prisoners who talk to each other by tapping on the wall. He's never forgotten it, nor I. Whether he breaks with Sophy, or whether they make it up, I can't let him think you had anything to do with it."

She raised her eyes entreatingly to Darrow's, and read in them the forbearance of the man resigned to the discussion of non-existent problems.

"I'll do whatever you want me to," he said; "but I don't yet know what it is."

His smile seemed to charge her with inconsequence, and the prick to her pride made her continue: "After all, it's not so unnatural that Owen, knowing you and Sophy to be almost strangers, should wonder what you were saying to each other when he saw you talking together."

She felt a warning tremor as she spoke, as though some instinct deeper than reason surged up in defense of its treasure. But Darrow's face was unstirred save by the flit of his half-amused smile.

"Well, my dear—and couldn't you have told him?"

"I?" she faltered out through her blush.

"You seem to forget, one and all of you, the position you put me in when I came down here: your appeal to me to see Owen through, your assurance to him that I would, Madame de Chantelle's attempt to win me over; and most of all, my own sense of the fact you've just recalled to me: the importance, for both of us, that Owen should like me. It seemed to me that the first thing to do was to get as much light as I could on the whole situation; and the obvious way of doing it was to try to know Miss Viner better. Of course I've talked with her alone—I've talked with her as often as I could. I've tried my best to find out if you were right in encouraging Owen to marry her."

She listened with a growing sense of reassurance, struggling to separate the abstract sense of his words from the persuasion in which his eyes and voice enveloped them.

"I see—I do see," she murmured.

"You must see, also, that I could hardly say this to Owen without offending him still more, and perhaps increasing the breach between Miss Viner and himself. What sort of figure should I cut if I told him I'd been trying to find out if he'd made a proper choice? In any case, it's none of my business to offer an explanation of what she justly says doesn't need one. If she declines to speak, it's obviously on the ground that Owen's insinuations are absurd; and that surely pledges me to silence."

"Yes, yes! I see," Anna repeated. "But I don't want you to explain anything to Owen."

"You haven't yet told me what you do want."

She hesitated, conscious of the difficulty of justifying her request; then: "I want you to speak to Sophy," she said.

Darrow broke into an incredulous laugh. "Considering what my previous attempts have resulted in——!"

She raised her eyes quickly. "They haven't, at least, resulted in your liking her less, in your thinking less well of her than you've told me?"

She fancied he frowned a little. "I wonder why you go back to that?"

"I want to be sure—I owe it to Owen. Won't you tell me the exact impression she's produced on you?"

"I have told you—I like Miss Viner."

"Do you still believe she's in love with Owen?"

"There was nothing in our short talks to throw any particular light on that."

"You still believe, though, that there's no reason why he shouldn't marry her?"

Again he betrayed a restrained impatience. "How can I

answer that without knowing her reasons for breaking with him?"

"That's just what I want you to find out from her."

"And why in the world should she tell me?"

"Because, whatever grievance she has against Owen, she can certainly have none against me. She can't want to have Owen connect me in his mind with this wretched quarrel; and she must see that he will until he's convinced you've had no share in it."

Darrow's elbow dropped from the mantel-piece and he took a restless step or two across the room. Then he halted before her.

"Why can't you tell her this yourself?"

"Don't you see?"

He eyed her intently, and she pressed on: "You must have guessed that Owen's jealous of you."

"Jealous of me?" The blood flew up under his brown skin.

"Blind with it—what else would drive him to this folly? And I can't have her think me jealous too! I've said all I could, short of making her think so; and she's refused a word more to either of us. Our only chance now is that she should listen to you—that you should make her see the harm her silence may do."

Darrow uttered a protesting exclamation. "It's all too preposterous—what you suggest! I can't, at any rate, appeal to her on such a ground as that!"

Anna laid her hand on his arm. "Appeal to her on the ground that I'm almost Owen's mother, and that any estrangement between you and him would kill me. She knows what he is—she'll understand. Tell her to say anything, do anything, she wishes; but not to go away without speaking, not to leave *that* between us when she goes!"

She drew back a step and lifted her face to his, trying to look into his eyes more deeply than she had ever looked; but before she could discern what they expressed he had taken hold of her hands and bent his head to kiss them.

"You'll see her? You'll see her?" she entreated; and he answered: "I'll do anything in the world you want me to."

XXVI

DARROW WAITED alone in the sitting-room.

No place could have been more distasteful as the scene of the talk that lay before him; but he had acceded to Anna's suggestion that it would seem more natural for her to summon Sophy Viner than for him to go in search of her. As his troubled pacings carried him back and forth a relentless hand seemed to be tearing away all the tender fibres of association that bound him to the peaceful room. Here, in this very place, he had drunk his deepest draughts of happiness, had had his lips at the fountain-head of its overflowing rivers; but now that source was poisoned and he would taste no more of an untainted cup.

For a moment he felt an actual physical anguish; then his nerves hardened for the coming struggle. He had no notion of what awaited him; but after the first instinctive recoil he had seen in a flash the urgent need of another word with Sophy Viner. He had been insincere in letting Anna think that he had consented to speak because she asked it. In reality he had been feverishly casting about for the pretext she had given him; and for some reason this trivial hypocrisy weighed on him more than all his heavy burden of deceit.

At length he heard a step behind him and Sophy Viner entered. When she saw him she paused on the threshold and half drew back.

"I was told that Mrs. Leath had sent for me."

"Mrs. Leath *did* send for you. She'll be here presently; but I asked her to let me see you first."

He spoke very gently, and there was no insincerity in his gentleness. He was profoundly moved by the change in the girl's appearance. At sight of him she had forced a smile; but it lit up her wretchedness like a candle-flame held to a dead face.

She made no reply, and Darrow went on: "You must understand my wanting to speak to you, after what I was told just now."

She interposed, with a gesture of protest: "I'm not responsible for Owen's ravings!"

"Of course——". He broke off and they stood facing each

other. She lifted a hand and pushed back her loose lock with the gesture that was burnt into his memory; then she looked about her and dropped into the nearest chair.

"Well, you've got what you wanted," she said.

"What do you mean by what I wanted?"

"My engagement's broken—you heard me say so."

"Why do you say that's what I wanted? All I wished, from the beginning, was to advise you, to help you as best I could——"

"That's what you've done," she rejoined. "You've convinced me that it's best I shouldn't marry him."

Darrow broke into a despairing laugh. "At the very moment when you'd convinced me to the contrary!"

"Had I?" Her smile flickered up. "Well, I really believed it till you showed me . . . warned me . . ."

"Warned you?"

"That I'd be miserable if I married a man I didn't love."

"Don't you love him?"

She made no answer, and Darrow started up and walked away to the other end of the room. He stopped before the writing-table, where his photograph, well-dressed, handsome, self-sufficient—the portrait of a man of the world, confident of his ability to deal adequately with the most delicate situations—offered its huge fatuity to his gaze. He turned back to her. "It's rather hard on Owen, isn't it, that you should have waited until now to tell him?"

She reflected a moment before answering. "I told him as soon as I knew."

"Knew that you couldn't marry him?"

"Knew that I could never live here with him." She looked about the room, as though the very walls must speak for her.

For a moment Darrow continued to search her face perplexedly; then their eyes met in a long disastrous gaze.

"Yes——" she said, and stood up.

Below the window they heard Effie whistling for her dogs, and then, from the terrace, her mother calling her.

"There—*that* for instance," Sophy Viner said.

Darrow broke out: "It's I who ought to go!"

She kept her small pale smile. "What good would that do any of us—now?"

He covered his face with his hands. "Good God!" he groaned. "How could I tell?"

"You couldn't tell. We neither of us could." She seemed to turn the problem over critically. "After all, it might have been *you* instead of me!"

He took another distracted turn about the room and coming back to her sat down in a chair at her side. A mocking hand seemed to dash the words from his lips. There was nothing on earth that he could say to her that wasn't foolish or cruel or contemptible . . .

"My dear," he began at last, "oughtn't you, at any rate, to try?"

Her gaze grew grave. "Try to forget you?"

He flushed to the forehead. "I meant, try to give Owen more time; to give him a chance. He's madly in love with you; all the good that's in him is in your hands. His stepmother felt that from the first. And she thought—she believed——"

"She thought I could make him happy. Would she think so now?"

"Now . . . ? I don't say now. But later? Time modifies . . . rubs out . . . more quickly than you think . . . Go away, but let him hope . . . I'm going too—*we're* going—" he stumbled on the plural—"in a very few weeks: going for a long time, probably. What you're thinking of now may never happen. We may not all be here together again for years."

She heard him out in silence, her hands clasped on her knee, her eyes bent on them. "For me," she said, "you'll always be here."

"Don't say that—oh, don't! Things change . . . people change . . . You'll see!"

"You don't understand. I don't want anything to change. I don't want to forget—to rub out. At first I imagined I did; but that was a foolish mistake. As soon as I saw you again I knew it . . . It's not being here with you that I'm afraid of—in the sense you think. It's being here, or anywhere, with Owen." She stood up and bent her tragic smile on him. "I want to keep you all to myself."

The only words that came to him were futile denunciations of his folly; but the sense of their futility checked them on his lips. "Poor child—you poor child!" he heard himself vainly repeating.

Suddenly he felt the strong reaction of reality and its impetus brought him to his feet. "Whatever happens, I intend to go—to go for good," he exclaimed. "I want you to understand that. Oh, don't be afraid—I'll find a reason. But it's perfectly clear that I must go."

She uttered a protesting cry. "Go away? You? Don't you see that that would tell everything—drag everybody into the horror?"

He found no answer, and her voice dropped back to its calmer note. "What good would your going do? Do you suppose it would change anything for me?" She looked at him with a musing wistfulness. "I wonder what your feeling for me was? It seems queer that I've never really known—I suppose we *don't* know much about that kind of feeling. Is it like taking a drink when you're thirsty? . . . I used to feel as if all of me was in the palm of your hand . . ."

He bowed his humbled head, but she went on almost exultantly: "Don't for a minute think I'm sorry! It was worth every penny it cost. My mistake was in being ashamed, just at first, of its having cost such a lot. I tried to carry it off as a joke—to talk of it to myself as an 'adventure'. I'd always wanted adventures, and you'd given me one, and I tried to take your attitude about it, to 'play the game' and convince myself that I hadn't risked any more on it than you. Then, when I met you again, I suddenly saw that I *had* risked more, but that I'd won more, too—such worlds! I'd been trying all the while to put everything I could between us; now I want to sweep everything away. I'd been trying to forget how you looked; now I want to remember you always. I'd been trying not to hear your voice; now I never want to hear any other. I've made my choice—that's all: I've had you and I mean to keep you." Her face was shining like her eyes. "To keep you hidden away here," she ended, and put her hand upon her breast.

After she had left him, Darrow continued to sit motionless, staring back into their past. Hitherto it had lingered on the edge of his mind in a vague pink blur, like one of the little rose-leaf clouds that a setting sun drops from its disk. Now it was a huge looming darkness, through which his eyes vainly strained. The whole episode was still obscure to him, save where here and there, as they talked, some phrase or gesture or intonation of the girl's had lit up a little spot in the night.

She had said: "I wonder what your feeling for me was?" and he found himself wondering too . . . He remembered distinctly enough that he had not meant the perilous passion—even in its most transient form—to play a part in their relation. In that respect his attitude had been above reproach. She was an unusually original and attractive creature, to whom he had wanted to give a few days of harmless pleasuring, and who was alert and expert enough to understand his intention and spare him the boredom of hesitations and misinterpretations. That had been his first impression, and her subsequent demeanour had justified it. She had been, from the outset, just the frank and easy comrade he had expected to find her. Was it he, then, who, in the sequel, had grown impatient of the bounds he had set himself? Was it his wounded vanity that, seeking balm for its hurt, yearned to dip deeper into the healing pool of her compassion? In his confused memory of the situation he seemed not to have been guiltless of such yearnings . . . Yet for the first few days the experiment had been perfectly successful. Her enjoyment had been unclouded and his pleasure in it undisturbed. It was very gradually—he seemed to see—that a shade of lassitude had crept over their intercourse. Perhaps it was because, when her light chatter about people failed, he found she had no other fund to draw on, or perhaps simply because of the sweetness of her laugh, or of the charm of the gesture with which, one day in the woods of Marly, she had tossed off her hat and tilted back her head at the call of a cuckoo; or because, whenever he looked at her unexpectedly, he found that she was looking at him and did not want him to know it; or perhaps, in varying degrees, because of all these things, that there had come a moment when no word seemed to fly high enough or dive deep enough to utter the sense of well-being each gave to the other, and the natural substitute for speech had been a kiss.

The kiss, at all events, had come at the precise moment to

save their venture from disaster. They had reached the point when her amazing reminiscences had begun to flag, when her future had been exhaustively discussed, her theatrical prospects minutely studied, her quarrel with Mrs. Murrett retold with the last amplification of detail, and when, perhaps conscious of her exhausted resources and his dwindling interest, she had committed the fatal error of saying that she could see he was unhappy, and entreating him to tell her why . . .

From the brink of estranging confidences, and from the risk of unfavourable comparisons, his gesture had snatched her back to safety; and as soon as he had kissed her he felt that she would never bore him again. She was one of the elemental creatures whose emotion is all in their pulses, and who become inexpressive or sentimental when they try to turn sensation into speech. His caress had restored her to her natural place in the scheme of things, and Darrow felt as if he had clasped a tree and a nymph had bloomed from it . . .

The mere fact of not having to listen to her any longer added immensely to her charm. She continued, of course, to talk to him, but it didn't matter, because he no longer made any effort to follow her words, but let her voice run on as a musical undercurrent to his thoughts. She hadn't a drop of poetry in her, but she had some of the qualities that create it in others; and in moments of heat the imagination does not always feel the difference . . .

Lying beside her in the shade, Darrow felt her presence as a part of the charmed stillness of the summer woods, as the element of vague well-being that suffused his senses and lulled to sleep the ache of wounded pride. All he asked of her, as yet, was a touch on the hand or on the lips—and that she should let him go on lying there through the long warm hours, while a black-bird's song throbbed like a fountain, and the summer wind stirred in the trees, and close by, between the nearest branches and the brim of his tilted hat, a slight white figure gathered up all the floating threads of joy . . .

He recalled, too, having noticed, as he lay staring at a break in the tree-tops, a stream of mares'-tails coming up the sky. He had said to himself: "It will rain tomorrow," and the thought had made the air seem warmer and the sun more vivid on her hair . . . Perhaps if the mares'-tails had not come up the sky their adventure might have had no sequel. But the cloud brought rain, and next morning he looked out of his window into a cold grey blur. They had planned an all-day excursion down the Seine, to the two Andelys and Rouen, and now, with the long hours on their hands, they were both a little at a loss . . . There was the Louvre, of course, and the Luxembourg; but he had tried looking at pictures with her, she had first so persistently admired the worst things, and then so frankly lapsed into indifference, that he had no wish to repeat the experiment. So they went out, aimlessly, and took a cold wet walk, turning at length into the deserted arcades of the Palais Royal, and finally drifting into one of its equally deserted restaurants, where they lunched alone and somewhat dolefully, served by a wan old waiter with the look of a castaway who has given up watching for a sail . . . It was odd how the waiter's face came back to him . . .

Perhaps but for the rain it might never have happened; but what was the use of thinking of that now? He tried to turn his thoughts to more urgent issues; but, by a strange perversity of association, every detail of the day was forcing itself on his mind with an insistence from which there was no escape. Reluctantly he relived the long wet walk back to the hotel, after a tedious hour at a cinematograph show on the Boulevard. It was still raining when they withdrew from this stale spectacle, but she had obstinately refused to take a cab, had even, on the way, insisted on loitering under the dripping awnings of shop-windows and poking into draughty passages, and finally, when they had nearly reached their destination, had gone so far as to suggest that they should turn back to hunt up some show she had heard of in a theatre at the Batignolles. But at that he had somewhat irritably protested: he remembered that, for the first time, they were both rather irritable, and vaguely disposed to resist one another's suggestions. His feet were wet, and he was tired of walking, and sick of the smell of stuffy unaired theatres, and he had said he must really get back to write some letters—and so they had kept on to the hotel . . .

XXVII

Darrow had no idea how long he had sat there when he heard Anna's hand on the door. The effort of rising, and of composing his face to meet her, gave him a factitious sense of self-control. He said to himself: "I must decide on something——" and that lifted him a hair's breadth above the whirling waters.

She came in with a lighter step, and he instantly perceived that something unforeseen and reassuring had happened.

"She's been with me. She came and found me on the terrace. We've had a long talk and she's explained everything. I feel as if I'd never known her before!"

Her voice was so moved and tender that it checked his start of apprehension.

"She's explained——?"

"It's natural, isn't it, that she should have felt a little sore at the kind of inspection she's been subjected to? Oh, not from *you*—I don't mean that! But Madame de Chantelle's opposition—and her sending for Adelaide Painter! She told me frankly she didn't care to owe her husband to Adelaide Painter . . . She thinks now that her annoyance at feeling herself so talked over and scrutinized may have shown itself in her manner to Owen, and set him imagining the insane things he did . . . I understand all she must have felt, and I agree with her that it's best she should go away for a while. She's made me," Anna summed up, "feel as if I'd been dreadfully thick-skinned and obtuse!"

"*You?*"

"Yes. As if I'd treated her like the bric-à-brac that used to be sent down here 'on approval,' to see if it would look well with the other pieces." She added, with a sudden flush of enthusiasm: "I'm glad she's got it in her to make one feel like that!"

She seemed to wait for Darrow to agree with her, or to put some other question, and he finally found voice to ask: "Then you think it's not a final break?"

"I hope not—I've never hoped it more! I had a word with Owen, too, after I left her, and I think he understands that

545

he must let her go without insisting on any positive promise. She's excited . . . he must let her calm down . . ."

Again she waited, and Darrow said: "Surely you can make him see that."

"She'll help me to—she's to see him, of course, before she goes. She starts immediately, by the way, with Adelaide Painter, who is motoring over to Francheuil to catch the one o'clock express—and who, of course, knows nothing of all this, and is simply to be told that Sophy has been sent for by the Farlows."

Darrow mutely signed his comprehension, and she went on: "Owen is particularly anxious that neither Adelaide nor his grandmother should have the least inkling of what's happened. The need of shielding Sophy will help him to control himself. He's coming to his senses, poor boy; he's ashamed of his wild talk already. He asked me to tell you so; no doubt he'll tell you so himself."

Darrow made a movement of protest. "Oh, as to that—the thing's not worth another word."

"Or another thought, either?" She brightened. "Promise me you won't even think of it—promise me you won't be hard on him!"

He was finding it easier to smile back at her. "Why should you think it necessary to ask my indulgence for Owen?"

She hesitated a moment, her eyes wandering from him. Then they came back with a smile. "Perhaps because I need it for myself."

"For yourself?"

"I mean, because I understand better how one can torture one's self over unrealities."

As Darrow listened, the tension of his nerves began to relax. Her gaze, so grave and yet so sweet, was like a deep pool into which he could plunge and hide himself from the hard glare of his misery. As this ecstatic sense enveloped him he found it more and more difficult to follow her words and to frame an answer; but what did anything matter, except that her voice should go on, and the syllables fall like soft touches on his tortured brain?

"Don't you know," she continued, "the bliss of waking from a bad dream in one's own quiet room, and going slowly over all the horror without being afraid of it any more? That's what I'm doing now. And that's why I understand Owen . . ." She broke off, and he felt her touch on his arm. *"Because I'd dreamed the horror too!"*

He understood her then, and stammered: "You?"

"Forgive me! And let me tell you! . . . It will help you to understand Owen . . . There *were* little things . . . little signs . . . once I had begun to watch for them: your reluctance to speak about her . . . her reserve with you . . . a sort of constraint we'd never seen in her before . . ."

She laughed up at him, and with her hands in his she contrived to say: "*Now* you understand why——?"

"Oh, I understand; of course I understand; and I want you to laugh at me—with me! Because there were other things too . . . crazier things still . . . There was even—last night on the terrace—her pink cloak . . ."

"Her pink cloak?" Now he honestly wondered, and as she saw it she blushed.

"You've forgotten about the cloak? The pink cloak that Owen saw you with at the play in Paris? Yes . . . yes . . . I was mad enough for that! . . . It does me good to laugh about it now! But you ought to know that I'm going to be a jealous woman . . . a ridiculously jealous woman . . . you ought to be warned of it in time . . ."

He had dropped her hands, and she leaned close and lifted her arms to his neck with one of her rare gestures of surrender.

"I don't know why it is; but it makes me happier now to have been so foolish!"

Her lips were parted in a noiseless laugh and the tremor of her lashes made their shadow move on her cheek. He looked at her through a mist of pain and saw all her offered beauty held up like a cup to his lips; but as he stooped to it a darkness seemed to fall between them, her arms slipped from his shoulders and she drew away from him abruptly.

"But she *was* with you, then?" she exclaimed; and then, as he stared at her: "Oh, don't say no! Only go and look at your eyes!"

He stood speechless, and she pressed on: "Don't deny it— oh, don't deny it! What will be left for me to imagine if you do? Don't you see how every single thing cries it out? Owen sees it—he saw it again just now! When I told him she'd relented, and would see him, he said: 'Is that Darrow's doing too?' "

Darrow took the onslaught in silence. He might have spoken, have summoned up the usual phrases of banter and denial; he was not even certain that they might not, for the moment, have served their purpose if he could have uttered them without being seen. But he was as conscious of what had happened to his face as if he had obeyed Anna's bidding and looked at himself in the glass. He knew he could no more hide from her what was written there than he could efface from his soul the fiery record of what he had just lived through. There before him, staring him in the eyes, and reflecting itself in all his lineaments, was the overwhelming fact of Sophy Viner's passion and of the act by which she had attested it.

Anna was talking again, hurriedly, feverishly, and his soul was wrung by the anguish in her voice. "Do speak at last—you must speak! I don't want to ask you to harm the girl; but you must see that your silence is doing her more harm than your answering my questions could. You're leaving me only the worst things to think of her . . . she'd see that herself if she were here. What worse injury can you do her than to make me hate her—to make me feel she's plotted with you to deceive us?"

"Oh, not that!" Darrow heard his own voice before he was aware that he meant to speak. "Yes; I did see her in Paris," he went on after a pause; "but I was bound to respect her reason for not wanting it known."

Anna paled. "It *was* she at the theatre that night?"

"I was with her at the theatre one night."

"Why should she have asked you not to say so?"

"She didn't wish it known that I'd met her."

"Why shouldn't she have wished it known?"

"She had quarrelled with Mrs. Murrett and come over suddenly to Paris, and she didn't want the Farlows to hear of it. I came across her by accident, and she asked me not to speak of having seen her."

"Because of her quarrel? Because she was ashamed of her part in it?"

"Oh, no. There was nothing for her to be ashamed of. But the Farlows had found the place for her, and she didn't want them to know how suddenly she'd had to leave, and how badly Mrs. Murrett had behaved. She was in a terrible plight—the woman had even kept back her month's salary. She knew the Farlows would be awfully upset, and she wanted more time to prepare them."

Darrow heard himself speak as though the words had proceeded from other lips. His explanation sounded plausible enough, and he half-fancied Anna's look grew lighter. She waited a moment, as though to be sure he had no more to add; then she said: "But the Farlows *did* know; they told me all about it when they sent her to me."

He flushed as if she had laid a deliberate trap for him. "They may know *now*; they didn't then——"

"That's no reason for her continuing now to make a mystery of having met you."

"It's the only reason I can give you."

"Then I'll go and ask her for one myself." She turned and took a few steps toward the door.

"Anna!" He started to follow her, and then checked himself. "Don't do that!"

"Why not?"

"It's not like you . . . not generous . . ."

She stood before him straight and pale, but under her rigid face he saw the tumult of her doubt and misery.

"I don't want to be ungenerous; I don't want to pry into her secrets. But things can't be left like this. Wouldn't it be better for me to go to her? Surely she'll understand—she'll explain . . . It may be some mere trifle she's concealing: something that would horrify the Farlows, but that I shouldn't see any harm in . . ." She paused, her eyes searching his face. "A love affair, I suppose . . . that's it? You met her with some man at the theatre—and she was frightened and begged you to fib about it? Those poor young things that have to go about among us like machines—oh, if you knew how I pity them!"

"If you pity her, why not let her go?"

She stared. "Let her go—go for good, you mean? Is that the best you can say for her?"

"Let things take their course. After all, it's between herself and Owen."

"And you and me—and Effie, if Owen marries her, and I leave my child with them! Don't you see the impossibility of what you're asking? We're all bound together in this coil."

Darrow turned away with a groan. "Oh, let her go—let her go."

"Then there *is* something—something really bad? She *was* with some one when you met her? Some one with whom she was——" She broke off, and he saw her struggling with new thoughts. "If it's *that*, of course . . . Oh, don't you see," she desperately appealed to him, "that I must find out, and that it's too late now for you not to speak? Don't be afraid that I'll betray you . . . I'll never, never let a soul suspect. But I must know the truth, and surely it's best for her that I should find it out from you."

Darrow waited a moment; then he said slowly: "What you imagine's mere madness. She was at the theatre with me."

"With you?" He saw a tremor pass through her, but she controlled it instantly and faced him straight and motionless as a wounded creature in the moment before it feels its wound. "Why should you both have made a mystery of that?"

"I've told you the idea was not mine." He cast about. "She may have been afraid that Owen——"

"But that was not a reason for her asking you to tell me that you hardly knew her—that you hadn't even seen her for years." She broke off and the blood rose to her face and forehead. "Even if *she* had other reasons, there could be only one reason for your obeying her——"

Silence fell between them, a silence in which the room seemed to become suddenly resonant with voices. Darrow's gaze wandered to the window and he noticed that the gale of two days before had nearly stripped the tops of the lime-trees in the court. Anna had moved away and was resting her elbows against the mantel-piece, her head in her hands. As she stood there he took in with a new intensity of vision little details of her appearance that his eyes had often cherished: the branching blue veins in the backs of her hands, the warm shadow that her hair cast on her ear, and the colour of the hair itself, dull black with a tawny under-surface, like the wings of certain birds. He felt it to be useless to speak.

After a while she lifted her head and said: "I shall not see her again before she goes."

He made no answer, and turning to him she added: "That *is* why she's going, I suppose? Because she loves you and won't give you up?"

Darrow waited. The paltriness of conventional denial was so apparent to him that even if it could have delayed discovery he could no longer have resorted to it. Under all his other fears was the dread of dishonouring the hour.

"She *has* given me up," he said at last.

XXVIII

WHEN HE HAD gone out of the room Anna stood where
he had left her. "I must believe him! I must believe
him!" she said.

A moment before, at the moment when she had lifted her
arms to his neck, she had been wrapped in a sense of complete security. All the spirits of doubt had been exorcised, and
her love was once more the clear habitation in which every
thought and feeling could move in blissful freedom. And
then, as she raised her face to Darrow's and met his eyes, she
had seemed to look into the very ruins of his soul. That was
the only way she could express it. It was as though he and
she had been looking at two sides of the same thing, and the
side she had seen had been all light and life, and his a place
of graves . . .

She didn't now recall who had spoken first, or even, very
clearly, what had been said. It seemed to her only a moment
later that she had found herself standing at the other end of
the room—the room which had suddenly grown so small
that, even with its length between them, she felt as if he
touched her—crying out to him "It *is* because of you she's
going!" and reading the avowal in his face.

That was his secret, then, *their* secret: he had met the girl
in Paris and helped her in her straits—lent her money, Anna
vaguely conjectured—and she had fallen in love with him,
and on meeting him again had been suddenly overmastered
by her passion. Anna, dropping back into her sofa-corner, sat
staring these facts in the face.

The girl had been in a desperate plight—frightened, penniless, outraged by what had happened, and not knowing
(with a woman like Mrs. Murrett) what fresh injury might
impend; and Darrow, meeting her in this distracted hour, had
pitied, counselled, been kind to her, with the fatal, the inevitable result. There were the facts as Anna made them out:
that, at least, was their external aspect, was as much of them
as she had been suffered to see; and into the secret intricacies
they might cover she dared not yet project her thoughts.

"I must believe him . . . I must believe him . . ." She kept on repeating the words like a talisman. It was natural, after all, that he should have behaved as he had: defended the girl's piteous secret to the last. She too began to feel the contagion of his pity—the stir, in her breast, of feelings deeper and more native to her than the pains of jealousy. From the security of her blessedness she longed to lean over with compassionate hands . . . But Owen? What was Owen's part to be? She owed herself first to him—she was bound to protect him not only from all knowledge of the secret she had surprised, but also—and chiefly!—from its consequences. Yes: the girl must go—there could be no doubt of it—Darrow himself had seen it from the first; and at the thought she had a wild revulsion of relief, as though she had been trying to create in her heart the delusion of a generosity she could not feel . . .

The one fact on which she could stay her mind was that Sophy was leaving immediately; would be out of the house within an hour. Once she was gone, it would be easier to bring Owen to the point of understanding that the break was final; if necessary, to work upon the girl to make him see it. But that, Anna was sure, would not be necessary. It was clear that Sophy Viner was leaving Givré with no thought of ever seeing it again . . .

Suddenly, as she tried to put some order in her thoughts, she heard Owen's call at the door: "Mother!——" a name he seldom gave her. There was a new note in his voice: the note of a joyous impatience. It made her turn hastily to the glass to see what face she was about to show him; but before she had had time to compose it he was in the room and she was caught in a school-boy hug.

"It's all right! It's all right! And it's all your doing! I want to do the worst kind of penance—bell and candle and the rest. I've been through it with *her*, and now she hands me on to you, and you're to call me any names you please." He freed her with his happy laugh. "I'm to be stood in the corner till next week, and then I'm to go up to see her. And she says I owe it all to you!"

"To me?" It was the first phrase she found to clutch at as she tried to steady herself in the eddies of his joy.

"Yes: you were so patient, and so dear to her; and you saw

at once what a damned ass I'd been!" She tried a smile, and
it seemed to pass muster with him, for he sent it back in a
broad beam. "That's not so difficult to see? No, I admit it
doesn't take a microscope. But you were so wise and wonderful—you always are. I've been mad these last days, simply
mad—you and she might well have washed your hands of
me! And instead, it's all right—all right!"

She drew back a little, trying to keep the smile on her lips
and not let him get the least glimpse of what it hid. Now if
ever, indeed, it behoved her to be wise and wonderful!

"I'm so glad, dear; so glad. If only you'll always feel like
that about me . . ." She stopped, hardly knowing what she
said, and aghast at the idea that her own hands should have
retied the knot she imagined to be broken. But she saw he
had something more to say; something hard to get out, but
absolutely necessary to express. He caught her hands, pulled
her close, and, with his forehead drawn into its whimsical
smiling wrinkles, "Look here," he cried, "if Darrow wants to
call me a damned ass too you're not to stop him!"

It brought her back to a sharper sense of her central peril:
of the secret to be kept from him at whatever cost to her
racked nerves.

"Oh, you know, he doesn't always wait for orders!" On the
whole it sounded better than she'd feared.

"You mean he's called me one already?" He accepted the
fact with his gayest laugh. "Well, that saves a lot of trouble;
now we can pass to the order of the day——" he broke off
and glanced at the clock—"which is, you know, dear, that
she's starting in about an hour; she and Adelaide must already
be snatching a hasty sandwich. You'll come down to bid them
good-bye?"

"Yes—of course."

There had, in fact, grown upon her while he spoke the
urgency of seeing Sophy Viner again before she left. The
thought was deeply distasteful: Anna shrank from encounter-
ing the girl till she had cleared a way through her own perplexities. But it was obvious that since they had separated,
barely an hour earlier, the situation had taken a new shape.
Sophy Viner had apparently reconsidered her decision to
break amicably but definitely with Owen, and stood again in

their path, a menace and a mystery; and confused impulses of resistance stirred in Anna's mind.

She felt Owen's touch on her arm. "Are you coming?"

"Yes . . . yes . . . presently."

"What's the matter? You look so strange."

"What do you mean by strange?"

"I don't know: startled—surprised——" She read what her look must be by its sudden reflection in his face.

"Do I? No wonder! You've given us all an exciting morning."

He held to his point. "You're more excited now that there's no cause for it. What on earth has happened since I saw you?"

He looked about the room, as if seeking the clue to her agitation, and in her dread of what he might guess she answered: "What has happened is simply that I'm rather tired. Will you ask Sophy to come up and see me here?"

While she waited she tried to think what she should say when the girl appeared; but she had never been more conscious of her inability to deal with the oblique and the tortuous. She had lacked the hard teachings of experience, and an instinctive disdain for whatever was less clear and open than her own conscience had kept her from learning anything of the intricacies and contradictions of other hearts. She said to herself: "I must find out——" yet everything in her recoiled from the means by which she felt it must be done . . .

Sophy Viner appeared almost immediately, dressed for departure, her little bag on her arm. She was still pale to the point of haggardness, but with a light upon her that struck Anna with surprise. Or was it, perhaps, that she was looking at the girl with new eyes: seeing her, for the first time, not as Effie's governess, not as Owen's bride, but as the embodiment of that unknown peril lurking in the background of every woman's thoughts about her lover? Anna, at any rate, with a sudden sense of estrangement, noted in her graces and snares never before perceived. It was only the flash of a primitive instinct, but it lasted long enough to make her ashamed of the darknesses it lit up in her heart . . .

She signed to Sophy to sit down on the sofa beside her. "I asked you to come up to me because I wanted to say good-bye quietly," she explained, feeling her lips tremble, but trying to speak in a tone of friendly naturalness.

The girl's only answer was a faint smile of acquiescence, and Anna, disconcerted by her silence, went on: "You've decided, then, not to break your engagement?"

Sophy Viner raised her head with a look of surprise. Evidently the question, thus abruptly put, must have sounded strangely on the lips of so ardent a partisan as Mrs. Leath! "I thought that was what you wished," she said.

"What I wished?" Anna's heart shook against her side. "I wish, of course, whatever seems best for Owen . . . It's natural, you must understand, that that consideration should come first with me . . ."

Sophy was looking at her steadily. "I supposed it was the only one that counted with you."

The curtness of retort roused Anna's latent antagonism. "It is," she said, in a hard voice that startled her as she heard it. Had she ever spoken so to any one before? She felt frightened, as though her very nature had changed without her knowing it . . . Feeling the girl's astonished gaze still on her, she continued: "The suddenness of the change has naturally surprised me. When I left you it was understood that you were to reserve your decision——"

"Yes."

"And now——?" Anna waited for a reply that did not come. She did not understand the girl's attitude, the edge of irony in her short syllables, the plainly premeditated determination to lay the burden of proof on her interlocutor. Anna felt the sudden need to lift their intercourse above this mean level of defiance and distrust. She looked appealingly at Sophy.

"Isn't it best that we should speak quite frankly? It's this change on your part that perplexes me. You can hardly be surprised at that. It's true, I asked you not to break with Owen too abruptly—and I asked it, believe me, as much for your sake as for his: I wanted you to take time to think over the difficulty that seems to have arisen between you. The fact that you felt it required thinking over seemed to show you wouldn't take the final step lightly—wouldn't, I mean, accept of Owen more than you could give him. But your change of mind obliges me to ask the question I thought you would have asked yourself. Is there any reason why you shouldn't marry Owen?"

She stopped a little breathlessly, her eyes on Sophy Viner's burning face. "Any reason——? What do you mean by a reason?"

Anna continued to look at her gravely. "Do you love some one else?" she asked.

Sophy's first look was one of wonder and a faint relief; then she gave back the other's scrutiny in a glance of indescribable reproach. "Ah, you might have waited!" she exclaimed.

"Waited——?"

"Till I'd gone: till I was out of the house. You might have known . . . you might have guessed . . ." She turned her eyes again on Anna. "I only meant to let him hope a little longer, so that he shouldn't suspect anything; of course I can't marry him," she said.

Anna stood motionless, silenced by the shock of the avowal. She too was trembling, less with anger than with a confused compassion. But the feeling was so blent with others, less generous and more obscure, that she found no words to express it, and the two women faced each other without speaking.

"I'd better go," Sophy murmured at length with lowered head.

The words roused in Anna a latent impulse of compunction. The girl looked so young, so exposed and desolate! And what thoughts must she be hiding in her heart! It was impossible that they should part in such a spirit.

"I want you to know that no one said anything . . . It was I who . . ."

Sophy looked at her. "You mean that Mr. Darrow didn't tell you? Of course not: do you suppose I thought he did? You found it out, that's all—I knew you would. In your place I should have guessed it sooner."

The words were spoken simply, without irony or emphasis; but they went through Anna like a sword. Yes, the girl would have had divinations, promptings that she had not had! She felt half envious of such a sad precocity of wisdom.

"I'm so sorry . . . so sorry . . ." she murmured.

"Things happen that way. Now I'd better go. I'd like to say good-bye to Effie."

"Oh——" it broke in a cry from Effie's mother. "Not like this—you mustn't! I feel—you make me feel too horribly: as if I were driving you away . . ." The words had rushed up from the depths of her bewildered pity.

"No one is driving me away: I had to go," she heard the girl reply.

There was another silence, during which passionate impulses of magnanimity warred in Anna with her doubts and dreads. At length, her eyes on Sophy's face: "Yes, you must go now," she began; "but later on . . . after a while, when all this is over . . . if there's no reason why you shouldn't marry Owen——" she paused a moment on the words—"I shouldn't want you to think I stood between you . . ."

"You?" Sophy flushed again, and then grew pale. She seemed to try to speak, but no words came.

"Yes! It was not true when I said just now that I was thinking only of Owen. I'm sorry—oh, so sorry!—for you too. Your life—I know how hard it's been; and mine . . . mine's so full . . . Happy women understand best!" Anna drew near and touched the girl's hand; then she began again, pouring all her soul into the broken phrases: "It's terrible now . . . you see no future; but if, by and bye . . . you know best . . . but you're so young . . . and at your age things *do* pass. If there's no reason, no real reason, why you shouldn't marry Owen, I *want* him to hope, I'll help him to hope . . . if you say so . . ."

With the urgency of her pleading her clasp tightened on Sophy's hand, but it warmed to no responsive tremor: the girl seemed numb, and Anna was frightened by the stony silence of her look. "I suppose I'm not more than half a woman," she mused, "for I don't want my happiness to hurt her;" and aloud she repeated: "If only you'll tell me there's no reason——"

The girl did not speak; but suddenly, like a snapped branch, she bent, stooped down to the hand that clasped her, and laid her lips upon it in a stream of weeping. She cried silently, continuously, abundantly, as though Anna's touch had released the waters of some deep spring of pain; then, as Anna, moved and half afraid, leaned over her with a sound of pity, she stood up and turned away.

"You're going, then—for good—like this?" Anna moved toward her and stopped. Sophy stopped too, with eyes that shrank from her.

"Oh——" Anna cried, and hid her face.

The girl walked across the room and paused again in the doorway. From there she flung back: "I wanted it—I chose it. He was good to me—no one ever was so good!"

The door-handle turned, and Anna heard her go.

XXIX

H ER FIRST thought was: "He's going too in a few hours—
I needn't see him again before he leaves . . ." At that
moment the possibility of having to look in Darrow's face
and hear him speak seemed to her more unendurable than
anything else she could imagine. Then, on the next wave of
feeling, came the desire to confront him at once and wring
from him she knew not what: avowal, denial, justification,
anything that should open some channel of escape to the
flood of her pent-up anguish.

She had told Owen she was tired, and this seemed a sufficient reason for remaining upstairs when the motor came to
the door and Miss Painter and Sophy Viner were borne off
in it; sufficient also for sending word to Madame de Chantelle
that she would not come down till after luncheon. Having
despatched her maid with this message, she lay down on her
sofa and stared before her into darkness . . .

She had been unhappy before, and the vision of old miseries flocked like hungry ghosts about her fresh pain: she
recalled her youthful disappointment, the failure of her
marriage, the wasted years that followed; but those were negative sorrows, denials and postponements of life. She seemed
in no way related to their shadowy victim, she who was
stretched on this fiery rack of the irreparable. She had suffered before—yes, but lucidly, reflectively, elegiacally: now
she was suffering as a hurt animal must, blindly, furiously,
with the single fierce animal longing that the awful pain
should stop . . .

She heard her maid knock, and she hid her face and made
no answer. The knocking continued, and the discipline of
habit at length made her lift her head, compose her face and
hold out her hand to the note the woman brought her. It was
a word from Darrow—"May I see you?"—and she said at
once, in a voice that sounded thin and empty: "Ask Mr. Darrow to come up."

The maid enquired if she wished to have her hair smoothed
first, and she answered that it didn't matter; but when the
door had closed, the instinct of pride drew her to her feet and

she looked at herself in the glass above the mantelpiece and passed her hands over her hair. Her eyes were burning and her face looked tired and thinner; otherwise she could see no change in her appearance, and she wondered that at such a moment her body should seem as unrelated to the self that writhed within her as if it had been a statue or a picture.

The maid reopened the door to show in Darrow, and he paused a moment on the threshold, as if waiting for Anna to speak. He was extremely pale, but he looked neither ashamed nor uncertain, and she said to herself, with a perverse thrill of appreciation: "He's as proud as I am."

Aloud she asked: "You wanted to see me?"

"Naturally," he replied in a grave voice.

"Don't! It's useless. I know everything. Nothing you can say will help."

At the direct affirmation he turned even paler, and his eyes, which he kept resolutely fixed on her, confessed his misery.

"You allow me no voice in deciding that?"

"Deciding what?"

"That there's nothing more to be said?" He waited for her to answer, and then went on: "I don't even know what you mean by 'everything'."

"Oh, I don't know what more there is! I know enough. I implored her to deny it, and she couldn't . . . What can you and I have to say to each other?" Her voice broke into a sob. The animal anguish was upon her again—just a blind cry against her pain!

Darrow kept his head high and his eyes steady. "It must be as you wish; and yet it's not like you to be afraid."

"Afraid?"

"To talk things out—to face them."

"It's for *you* to face this—not me!"

"All I ask is to face it—but with you." Once more he paused. "Won't you tell me what Miss Viner told you?"

"Oh, she's generous—to the utmost!" The pain caught her like a physical throe. It suddenly came to her how the girl must have loved him to be so generous—what memories there must be between them!

"Oh, go, please go. It's too horrible! Why should I have to see you?" she stammered, lifting her hands to her eyes.

With her face hidden she waited to hear him move away, to hear the door open and close again, as, a few hours earlier, it had opened and closed on Sophy Viner. But Darrow made no sound or movement: he too was waiting. Anna felt a thrill of resentment: his presence was an outrage on her sorrow, a humiliation to her pride. It was strange that he should wait for her to tell him so!

"You want me to leave Givré?" he asked at length. She made no answer, and he went on: "Of course I'll do as you wish; but if I go now am I not to see you again?"

His voice was firm: his pride was answering her pride!

She faltered: "You must see it's useless——"

"I might remind you that you're dismissing me without a hearing——"

"Without a hearing? I've heard you both!"

——"but I won't," he continued, "remind you of that, or of anything or any one but Owen."

"Owen——?"

"Yes; if we could somehow spare him——"

She had dropped her hands and turned her startled eyes on him. It seemed to her an age since she had thought of Owen!

"You see, don't you," Darrow continued, "that if you send me away now——"

She interrupted: "Yes, I see——" and there was a long silence between them. At length she said, very low: "I don't want any one else to suffer as I'm suffering . . ."

"Owen knows I meant to leave tomorrow," Darrow went on. "Any sudden change of plan may make him think . . ."

Oh, she saw his inevitable logic: the horror of it was on every side of her! It had seemed possible to control her grief and face Darrow calmly while she was upheld by the belief that this was their last hour together, that after he had passed out of the room there would be no fear of seeing him again, no fear that his nearness, his look, his voice, and all the unseen influences that flowed from him, would dissolve her soul to weakness. But her courage failed at the idea of having to conspire with him to shield Owen, of keeping up with him, for Owen's sake, a feint of union and felicity. To live at Darrow's side in seeming intimacy and harmony for another twenty-four hours seemed harder than to live without him for all the rest of her days. Her strength failed her, and she threw herself down and buried her sobs in the cushions where she had so often hidden a face aglow with happiness.

"Anna——" His voice was close to her. "Let me talk to you quietly. It's not worthy of either of us to be afraid."

Words of endearment would have offended her; but her heart rose at the call to her courage.

"I've no defense to make," he went on. "The facts are miserable enough; but at least I want you to see them as they are. Above all, I want you to know the truth about Miss Viner——"

The name sent the blood to Anna's forehead. She raised her head and faced him. "Why should I know more of her than what she's told me? I never wish to hear her name again!"

"It's because you feel about her in that way that I ask you—in the name of common charity—to let me give you the facts as they are, and not as you've probably imagined them."

"I've told you I don't think uncharitably of her. I don't want to think of her at all!"

"That's why I tell you you're afraid."

"Afraid?"

"Yes. You've always said you wanted, above all, to look at life, at the human problem, as it is, without fear and without hypocrisy; and it's not always a pleasant thing to look at." He broke off, and then began again: "Don't think this a plea for myself! I don't want to say a word to lessen my offense. I don't want to talk of myself at all. Even if I did, I probably couldn't make you understand—I don't, myself, as I look back. Be just to me—it's your right; all I ask you is to be generous to Miss Viner . . ."

She stood up trembling. "You're free to be as generous to her as you please!"

"Yes: you've made it clear to me that I'm free. But there's nothing I can do for her that will help her half as much as your understanding her would."

"Nothing you can do for her? You can marry her!"

His face hardened. "You certainly couldn't wish her a worse fate!"

"It must have been what she expected . . . relied on . . ." He was silent, and she broke out: "Or what *is* she? What are you? It's too horrible! On your way here . . . to *me* . . ." She felt the tears in her throat and stopped.

"That was it," he said bluntly. She stared at him.

"I was on my way to you—after repeated delays and post-ponements of your own making. At the very last you turned me back with a mere word—and without explanation. I waited for a letter; and none came. I'm not saying this to justify myself. I'm simply trying to make you understand. I felt hurt and bitter and bewildered. I thought you meant to give me up. And suddenly, in my way, I found some one to be sorry for, to be of use to. That, I swear to you, was the way it began. The rest was a moment's folly . . . a flash of madness . . . as such things are. We've never seen each other since . . ."

Anna was looking at him coldly. "You sufficiently describe her in saying that!"

"Yes, if you measure her by conventional standards—which is what you always declare you never do."

"Conventional standards? A girl who——" She was checked by a sudden rush of almost physical repugnance. Suddenly she broke out: "I always thought her an adventuress!"

"Always?"

"I don't mean always . . . but after you came . . ."

"She's not an adventuress."

"You mean that she professes to act on the new theories? The stuff that awful women rave about on platforms?"

"Oh, I don't think she pretended to have a theory——"

"She hadn't even *that* excuse?"

"She had the excuse of her loneliness, her unhappiness—of miseries and humiliations that a woman like you can't even guess. She had nothing to look back to but indifference or unkindness—nothing to look forward to but anxiety. She saw I was sorry for her and it touched her. She made too much of it—she exaggerated it. I ought to have seen the danger, but I didn't. There's no possible excuse for what I did."

Anna listened to him in speechless misery. Every word he spoke threw back a disintegrating light on their own past. He had come to her with an open face and a clear conscience—come to her from this! If his security was the security of falsehood it was horrible; if it meant that he had forgotten, it was worse. She would have liked to stop her ears, to close her eyes, to shut out every sight and sound and suggestion of a world in which such things could be; and at the same time she was tormented by the desire to know more, to understand better, to feel herself less ignorant and inexpert in matters which made so much of the stuff of human experience. What did he mean by "a moment's folly, a flash of madness"? How did people enter on such adventures, how pass out of them without more visible traces of their havoc? Her imagination recoiled from the vision of a sudden debasing familiarity: it seemed to her that her thoughts would never again be pure . . .

"I swear to you," she heard Darrow saying, "it was simply that, and nothing more."

She wondered at his composure, his competence, at his knowing so exactly what to say. No doubt men often had to make such explanations: they had the formulas by heart . . . A leaden lassitude descended on her. She passed from flame and torment into a colourless cold world where everything surrounding her seemed equally indifferent and remote. For a moment she simply ceased to feel.

She became aware that Darrow was waiting for her to speak, and she made an effort to represent to herself the meaning of what he had just said; but her mind was as blank as a blurred mirror. Finally she brought out: "I don't think I understand what you've told me."

"No; you don't understand," he returned with sudden bitterness; and on his lips the charge of incomprehension seemed an offense to her.

"I don't want to—about such things!"

He answered almost harshly: "Don't be afraid . . . you never will . . ." and for an instant they faced each other like enemies. Then the tears swelled in her throat at his reproach.

"You mean I don't feel things—I'm too hard?"

"No: you're too high . . . too fine . . . such things are too far from you."

He paused, as if conscious of the futility of going on with

whatever he had meant to say, and again, for a short space, they confronted each other, no longer as enemies—so it seemed to her—but as beings of different language who had forgotten the few words they had learned of each other's speech.

Darrow broke the silence. "It's best, on all accounts, that I should stay till tomorrow; but I needn't intrude on you; we needn't meet again alone. I only want to be sure I know your wishes." He spoke the short sentences in a level voice, as though he were summing up the results of a business conference.

Anna looked at him vaguely. "My wishes?"

"As to Owen——"

At that she started. "They must never meet again!"

"It's not likely they will. What I meant was, that it depends on you to spare him . . ."

She answered steadily: "He shall never know," and after another interval Darrow said: "This is good-bye, then."

At the word she seemed to understand for the first time whither the flying moments had been leading them. Resentment and indignation died down, and all her consciousness resolved itself into the mere visual sense that he was there before her, near enough for her to lift her hand and touch him, and that in another instant the place where he stood would be empty.

She felt a mortal weakness, a craven impulse to cry out to him to stay, a longing to throw herself into his arms, and take refuge there from the unendurable anguish he had caused her. Then the vision called up another thought: "I shall never know what that girl has known . . ." and the recoil of pride flung her back on the sharp edges of her anguish.

"Good-bye," she said, in dread lest he should read her face; and she stood motionless, her head high, while he walked to the door and went out.

BOOK V

XXX

ANNA LEATH, three days later, sat in Miss Painter's draw-ing-room in the rue de Matignon.

Coming up precipitately that morning from the country, she had reached Paris at one o'clock and Miss Painter's land-ing some ten minutes later. Miss Painter's mouldy little man-servant, dissembling a napkin under his arm, had mildly attempted to oppose her entrance; but Anna, insisting, had gone straight to the dining-room and surprised her friend—who ate as furtively as certain animals—over a strange meal of cold mutton and lemonade. Ignoring the embarrassment she caused, she had set forth the object of her journey, and Miss Painter, always hatted and booted for action, had immediately hastened out, leaving her to the solitude of the bare fireless drawing-room with its eternal slip-covers and "bowed" shutters.

In this inhospitable obscurity Anna had sat alone for close upon two hours. Both obscurity and solitude were acceptable to her, and impatient as she was to hear the result of the errand on which she had despatched her hostess, she desired still more to be alone. During her long meditation in a white-swathed chair before the muffled hearth she had been able for the first time to clear a way through the darkness and confu-sion of her thoughts. The way did not go far, and her attempt to trace it was as weak and spasmodic as a convalescent's first efforts to pick up the thread of living. She seemed to herself like some one struggling to rise from a long sickness of which it would have been so much easier to die. At Givré she had fallen into a kind of torpor, a deadness of soul traversed by wild flashes of pain; but whether she suffered or whether she was numb, she seemed equally remote from her real living and doing self.

It was only the discovery—that very morning—of Owen's unannounced departure for Paris that had caught her out of her dream and forced her back to action. The dread of what this flight might imply, and of the consequences that might result from it, had roused her to the sense of her responsibility, and from the moment when she had resolved to follow her step-son, and had made her rapid preparations for pursuit, her mind had begun to work again, feverishly, fitfully, but still with something of its normal order. In the train she had been too agitated, too preoccupied with what might next await her, to give her thoughts to anything but the turning over of dread alternatives; but Miss Painter's imperviousness had steadied her, and while she waited for the sound of the latch-key she resolutely returned upon herself.

With respect to her outward course she could at least tell herself that she had held to her purpose. She had, as people said, "kept up" during the twenty-four hours preceding George Darrow's departure; had gone with a calm face about her usual business, and even contrived not too obviously to avoid him. Then, the next day before dawn, from behind the closed shutters where she had kept for half the night her dry-eyed vigil, she had heard him drive off to the train which brought its passengers to Paris in time for the Calais express.

The fact of his taking that train, of his travelling so straight and far away from her, gave to what had happened the implacable outline of reality. He was gone; he would not come back; and her life had ended just as she had dreamed it was beginning. She had no doubt, at first, as to the absolute inevitability of this conclusion. The man who had driven away from her house in the autumn dawn was not the man she had loved; he was a stranger with whom she had not a single thought in common. It was terrible, indeed, that he wore the face and spoke in the voice of her friend, and that, as long as he was under one roof with her, the mere way in which he moved and looked could bridge at a stroke the gulf between them. That, no doubt, was the fault of her exaggerated sensibility to outward things: she was frightened to see how it enslaved her. A day or two before she had supposed the sense of honour was her deepest sentiment: if she had smiled at the conventions of others it was because they were too trivial, not because they were too grave. There were certain dishonours with which she had never dreamed that any pact could be made: she had had an incorruptible passion for good faith and fairness.

She had supposed that, once Darrow was gone, once she

was safe from the danger of seeing and hearing him, this high devotion would sustain her. She had believed it would be possible to separate the image of the man she had thought him from that of the man he was. She had even foreseen the hour when she might raise a mournful shrine to the memory of the Darrow she had loved, without fear that his double's shadow would desecrate it. But now she had begun to understand that the two men were really one. The Darrow she worshipped was inseparable from the Darrow she abhorred; and the inevitable conclusion was that both must go, and she be left in the desert of a sorrow without memories . . .

But if the future was thus void, the present was all too full. Never had blow more complex repercussions; and to remember Owen was to cease to think of herself. What impulse, what apprehension, had sent him suddenly to Paris? And why had he thought it needful to conceal his going from her? When Sophy Viner had left, it had been with the understanding that he was to await her summons; and it seemed improbable that he would break his pledge, and seek her without leave, unless his lover's intuition had warned him of some fresh danger. Anna recalled how quickly he had read the alarm in her face when he had rushed back to her sitting-room with the news that Miss Viner had promised to see him again in Paris. To be so promptly roused, his suspicions must have been but half-asleep; and since then, no doubt, if she and Darrow had dissembled, so had he. To her proud directness it was degrading to think that they had been living together like enemies who spy upon each other's movements: she felt a desperate longing for the days which had seemed so dull and narrow, but in which she had walked with her head high and her eyes unguarded.

She had come up to Paris hardly knowing what peril she feared, and still less how she could avert it. If Owen meant to see Miss Viner—and what other object could he have?—they must already be together, and it was too late to interfere. It had indeed occurred to Anna that Paris might not be his objective point: that his real purpose in leaving Givré without her knowledge had been to follow Darrow to London and exact the truth of him. But even to her alarmed imagination this seemed improbable. She and Darrow, to the last, had kept up so complete a feint of harmony that, whatever Owen had surmised, he could scarcely have risked acting on his suspicions. If he still felt the need of an explanation, it was almost certainly of Sophy Viner that he would ask it; and it was in quest of Sophy Viner that Anna had despatched Miss Painter.

She had found a blessed refuge from her perplexities in the stolid Adelaide's unawareness. One could so absolutely count on Miss Painter's guessing no more than one chose, and yet acting astutely on such hints as one vouchsafed her! She was like a well-trained retriever whose interest in his prey ceases when he lays it at his mater's feet. Anna, on arriving, had explained that Owen's unannounced flight had made her fear some fresh misunderstanding between himself and Miss Viner. In the interests of peace she had thought it best to follow him; but she hastily added that she did not wish to see Sophy, but only, if possible, to learn from her where Owen was. With these brief instructions Miss Painter had started out; but she was a woman of many occupations, and had given her visitor to understand that before returning she should have to call on a friend who had just arrived from Boston, and afterward despatch to another exiled compatriot a supply of cranberries and brandied peaches from the American grocery in the Champs Elysées.

Gradually, as the moments passed, Anna began to feel the reaction which, in moments of extreme nervous tension, follows on any effort of the will. She seemed to have gone as far as her courage would carry her, and she shrank more and more from the thought of Miss Painter's return, since whatever information the latter brought would necessitate some fresh decision. What should she say to Owen if she found him? What could she say that should not betray the one thing she would give her life to hide from him? "Give her life"— how the phrase derided her! It was a gift she would not have bestowed on her worst enemy. She would not have had Sophy Viner live the hours she was living now . . .

She tried again to look steadily and calmly at the picture that the image of the girl evoked. She had an idea that she ought to accustom herself to its contemplation. If life was like that, why the sooner one got used to it the better . . . But no! Life was not like that. Her adventure was a hideous accident. She dreaded above all the temptation to generalise from her own case, to doubt the high things she had lived by and seek a cheap solace in belittling what fate had refused her. There *was* such love as she had dreamed, and she meant to go on believing in it, and cherishing the thought that she was worthy of it. What had happened to her was grotesque and mean and miserable; but she herself was none of these things, and never, never would she make of herself the mock that fate had made of her . . .

She could not, as yet, bear to think deliberately of Darrow; but she kept on repeating to herself "By and bye that will come too." Even now she was determined not to let his image be distorted by her suffering. As soon as she could, she would try to single out for remembrance the individual things she had liked in him before she had loved him altogether. No "spiritual exercise" devised by the discipline of piety could have been more torturing; but its very cruelty attracted her. She wanted to wear herself out with new pains . . .

XXXI

THE SOUND of Miss Painter's latch-key made her start. She was still a bundle of quivering fears to whom each coming moment seemed a menace.

There was a slight interval, and a sound of voices in the hall; then Miss Painter's vigorous hand was on the door.

Anna stood up as she came in. "You've found him?"

"I've found Sophy."

"And Owen?—has she seen him? Is he here?"

"*She's* here: in the hall. She wants to speak to you."

"Here—*now?*" Anna found no voice for more.

"She drove back with me," Miss Painter continued in the tone of impartial narrative. "The cabman was impertinent. I've got his number." She fumbled in a stout black reticule.

"Oh, I can't—" broke from Anna; but she collected herself, remembering that to betray her unwillingness to see the girl was to risk revealing much more.

"She thought you might be too tired to see her: she wouldn't come in till I'd found out."

Anna drew a quick breath. An instant's thought had told her that Sophy Viner would hardly have taken such a step unless something more important had happened. "Ask her to come, please," she said.

Miss Painter, from the threshold, turned back to announce her intention of going immediately to the police station to report the cabman's delinquency; then she passed out, and Sophy Viner entered.

The look in the girl's face showed that she had indeed come unwillingly; yet she seemed animated by an eager resoluteness that made Anna ashamed of her tremors. For a moment they looked at each other in silence, as if the thoughts between them were packed too thick for speech; then Anna said, in a voice from which she strove to take the edge of hardness: "You know where Owen is, Miss Painter tells me."

"Yes; that was my reason for asking you to see me." Sophy spoke simply, without constraint or hesitation.

"I thought he'd promised you—" Anna interposed.

"He did; but he broke his promise. That's what I thought I ought to tell you."

"Thank you." Anna went on tentatively: "He left Givré this morning without a word. I followed him because I was afraid . . ."

She broke off again and the girl took up her phrase. "You were afraid he'd guessed? He *has* . . ."

"What do you mean—guessed what?"

"That you know something he doesn't . . . something that made you glad to have me go."

"Oh—" Anna moaned. If she had wanted more pain she had it now. "He's told you this?" she faltered.

"He hasn't told me, because I haven't seen him. I kept him off—I made Mrs. Farlow get rid of him. But he's written me what he came to say; and that was it."

"Oh, poor Owen!" broke from Anna. Through all the intricacies of her suffering she felt the separate pang of his.

"And I want to ask you," the girl continued, "to let me see him; for of course," she added in the same strange voice of energy, "I wouldn't unless you consented."

"To see him?" Anna tried to gather together her startled thoughts. "What use would it be? What could you tell him?"

"I want to tell him the truth," said Sophy Viner.

The two women looked at each other, and a burning blush rose to Anna's forehead. "I don't understand," she faltered.

Sophy waited a moment; then she lowered her voice to say: "I don't want him to think worse of me than he need . . ."

"Worse?"

"Yes—to think such things as you're thinking now . . . I want him to know exactly what happened . . . then I want to bid him good-bye."

Anna tried to clear a way through her own wonder and confusion. She felt herself obscurely moved.

"Wouldn't it be worse for him——?"

"To hear the truth? It would be better, at any rate, for you and Mr. Darrow."

At the sound of the name Anna lifted her head quickly. "I've only my step-son to consider!"

The girl threw a startled look at her. "You don't mean—you're not going to give him up?"

Anna felt her lips harden. "I don't think it's of any use to talk of that."

"Oh, I know! It's my fault for not knowing how to say what I want you to hear. Your words are different; you know how to choose them. Mine offend you . . . and the dread of it makes me blunder. That's why, the other day, I couldn't say anything . . . couldn't make things clear to you. But now I *must*, even if you hate it!" She drew a step nearer, her slender figure swayed forward in a passion of entreaty. "Do listen to me! What you've said is dreadful. How can you speak of him in that voice? Don't you see that I went away so that he shouldn't have to lose you?"

Anna looked at her coldly. "Are you speaking of Mr. Darrow? I don't know why you think your going or staying can in any way affect our relations."

"You mean that you *have* given him up—because of me? Oh, how could you? You can't really love him!—And yet," the girl suddenly added, "you must, or you'd be more sorry for me!"

"I'm very sorry for you," Anna said, feeling as if the iron band about her heart pressed on it a little less inexorably.

"Then why won't you hear me? Why won't you try to understand? It's all so different from what you imagine!"

"I've never judged you."

"I'm not thinking of myself. He loves you!"

"I thought you'd come to speak of Owen."

Sophy Viner seemed not to hear her. "He's never loved any one else. Even those few days . . . I knew it all the while . . . he never cared for me."

"Please don't say any more!" Anna said.

"I know it must seem strange to you that I should say so much. I shock you, I offend you: you think me a creature without shame. So I am—but not in the sense you think! I'm not ashamed of having loved him; no; and I'm not ashamed of telling you so. It's that that justifies me—and him too . . . Oh, let me tell you how it happened! He was sorry for me: he saw I cared. I *knew* that was all he ever felt. I could see he was thinking of some one else. I knew it was only for a week . . . He never said a word to mislead me . . . I wanted to be happy just once—and I didn't dream of the harm I might be doing him!"

Anna could not speak. She hardly knew, as yet, what the girl's words conveyed to her, save the sense of their tragic fervour; but she was conscious of being in the presence of an intenser passion than she had ever felt.

"I am sorry for you." She paused. "But why do you say this to me?" After another interval she exclaimed: "You'd no right to let Owen love you."

"No; that was wrong. At least what's happened since has made it so. If things had been different I think I could have made Owen happy. You were all so good to me—I wanted so to stay with you! I suppose you'll say that makes it worse: my daring to dream I had the right . . . But all that doesn't matter now. I won't see Owen unless you're willing. I should have liked to tell him what I've tried to tell you; but you must know better; you feel things in a finer way. Only you'll have to help him if I can't. He cares a great deal . . . it's going to hurt him . . ."

Anna trembled. "Oh, I know! What can I do?"

"You can go straight back to Givré—now, at once! So that Owen shall never know you've followed him." Sophy's clasped hands reached out urgently. "And you can send for Mr. Darrow—bring him back. Owen must be convinced that he's mistaken, and nothing else will convince him. Afterward I'll find a pretext—oh, I promise you! But first he must see for himself that nothing's changed for you."

Anna stood motionless, subdued and dominated. The girl's ardour swept her like a wind.

"Oh, can't I move you? Some day you'll know!" Sophy pleaded, her eyes full of tears.

Anna saw them, and felt a fullness in her throat. Again the band about her heart seemed loosened. She wanted to find a word, but could not: all within her was too dark and violent. She gave the girl a speechless look.

"I do believe you," she said suddenly; then she turned and walked out of the room.

XXXII

S HE DROVE from Miss Painter's to her own apartment.
The maid-servant who had it in charge had been apprised of her coming, and had opened one or two of the
rooms, and prepared a fire in her bedroom. Anna shut herself
in, refusing the woman's ministrations. She felt cold and
faint, and after she had taken off her hat and cloak she knelt
down by the fire and stretched her hands to it.

In one respect, at least, it was clear to her that she would
do well to follow Sophy Viner's counsel. It had been an act
of folly to follow Owen, and her first business was to get back
to Givré before him. But the only train leaving that evening
was a slow one, which did not reach Francheuil till midnight,
and she knew that her taking it would excite Madame de
Chantelle's wonder and lead to interminable talk. She had
come up to Paris on the pretext of finding a new governess
for Effie, and the natural thing was to defer her return till the
next morning. She knew Owen well enough to be sure that
he would make another attempt to see Miss Viner, and failing
that, would write again and await her answer; so that there
was no likelihood of his reaching Givré till the following
evening.

Her sense of relief at not having to start out at once
showed her for the first time how tired she was. The *bonne*
had suggested a cup of tea, but the dread of having any one
about her had made Anna refuse, and she had eaten nothing
since morning but a sandwich bought at a buffet. She was
too tired to get up, but stretching out her arm she drew toward her the arm-chair which stood beside the hearth and
rested her head against its cushions. Gradually the warmth of
the fire stole into her veins and her heaviness of soul was
replaced by a dreamy buoyancy. She seemed to be seated on
the hearth in her sitting-room at Givré, and Darrow was beside her, in the chair against which she leaned. He put his
arms about her shoulders and drawing her head back looked
into her eyes. "Of all the ways you do your hair, that's the
way I like best," he said . . .

A log dropped, and she sat up with a start. There was a

warmth in her heart, and she was smiling. Then she looked about her, and saw where she was, and the glory fell. She hid her face and sobbed.

Presently she perceived that it was growing dark, and getting up stiffly she began to undo the things in her bag and spread them on the dressing-table. She shrank from lighting the lights, and groped her way about, trying to find what she needed. She seemed immeasurably far off from every one, and most of all from herself. It was as if her consciousness had been transmitted to some stranger whose thoughts and gestures were indifferent to her . . .

Suddenly she heard a shrill tinkle, and with a beating heart she stood still in the middle of the room. It was the telephone in her dressing-room—a call, no doubt, from Adelaide Painter. Or could Owen have learned she was in town? The thought alarmed her and she opened the door and stumbled across the unlit room to the instrument. She held it to her ear, and heard Darrow's voice pronounce her name.

"Will you let me see you? I've come back—I had to come. Miss Painter told me you were here."

She began to tremble, and feared that he would guess it from her voice. She did not know what she answered: she heard him say: "I can't hear." She called "Yes!" and laid the telephone down, and caught it up again—but he was gone. She wondered if her "Yes" had reached him.

She sat in her chair and listened. Why had she said that she would see him? What did she mean to say to him when he came? Now and then, as she sat there, the sense of his presence enveloped her as in her dream, and she shut her eyes and felt his arms about her. Then she woke to reality and shivered. A long time elapsed, and at length she said to herself: "He isn't coming."

The door-bell rang as she said it, and she stood up, cold and trembling. She thought: "Can he imagine there's any use in coming?" and moved forward to bid the servant say she could not see him.

The door opened and she saw him standing in the drawing-room. The room was cold and fireless, and a hard glare fell from the wall-lights on the shrouded furniture and the white slips covering the curtains. He looked pale and stern, with a frown of fatigue between his eyes; and she remembered that in three days he had travelled from Givré to London and back. It seemed incredible that all that had befallen her should have been compressed within the space of three days!

"Thank you," he said as she came in.

She answered: "It's better, I suppose——"

He came toward her and took her in his arms. She struggled a little, afraid of yielding, but he pressed her to him, not bending to her but holding her fast, as though he had found her after a long search: she heard his hurried breathing. It seemed to come from her own breast, so close he held her; and it was she who, at last, lifted up her face and drew down his.

She freed herself and went and sat on a sofa at the other end of the room. A mirror between the shrouded window-curtains showed her crumpled travelling dress and the white face under her disordered hair.

She found her voice, and asked him how he had been able to leave London. He answered that he had managed—he'd arranged it; and she saw he hardly heard what she was saying.

"I had to see you," he went on, and moved nearer, sitting down at her side.

"Yes; we must think of Owen——"

"Oh, Owen—!"

Her mind had flown back to Sophy Viner's plea that she should let Darrow return to Givré in order that Owen might be persuaded of the folly of his suspicions. The suggestion was absurd, of course. She could not ask Darrow to lend himself to such a fraud, even had she had the inhuman courage to play her part in it. She was suddenly overwhelmed by the futility of every attempt to reconstruct her ruined world. No, it was useless; and since it was useless, every moment with Darrow was pure pain . . .

"I've come to talk of myself, not of Owen," she heard him saying. "When you sent me away the other day I understood that it couldn't be otherwise—then. But it's not possible that you and I should part like that. If I'm to lose you, it must be for a better reason."

"A better reason?"

"Yes: a deeper one. One that means a fundamental disaccord between us. This one doesn't—in spite of everything it doesn't. That's what I want you to see, and have the courage to acknowledge."

"If I saw it I should have the courage!"

"Yes: courage was the wrong word. You have that. That's why I'm here."

"But I don't see it," she continued sadly. "So it's useless, isn't it?—and so cruel . . ." He was about to speak, but she went on: "I shall never understand it—never!"

He looked at her. "You will some day: you were made to feel everything——"

"I should have thought this was a case of not feeling——"

"On my part, you mean?" He faced her resolutely. "Yes, it was: to my shame . . . What I meant was that when you've lived a little longer you'll see what complex blunderers we all are: how we're struck blind sometimes, and mad sometimes— and then, when our sight and our senses come back, how we have to set to work, and build up, little by little, bit by bit, the precious things we'd smashed to atoms without knowing it. Life's just a perpetual piecing together of broken bits."

She looked up quickly. "That's what I feel: that you ought to——"

He stood up, interrupting her with a gesture. "Oh, don't— don't say what you're going to! Men don't give their lives away like that. If you won't have mine, it's at least my own, to do the best I can with."

"The best you can—that's what I mean! How can there be a 'best' for you that's made of some one else's worst?"

He sat down again with a groan. "I don't know! It seemed such a slight thing—all on the surface—and I've gone aground on it because it *was* on the surface. I see the horror of it just as you do. But I see, a little more clearly, the extent, and the limits, of my wrong. It's not as black as you imagine."

She lowered her voice to say: "I suppose I shall never understand; but she seems to love you . . ."

"There's my shame! That I didn't guess it, didn't fly from it. You say you'll never understand: but why shouldn't you? Is it anything to be proud of, to know so little of the strings that pull us? If you knew a little more, I could tell you how such things happen without offending you; and perhaps you'd listen without condemning me."

"I don't condemn you." She was dizzy with struggling impulses. She longed to cry out: "I *do* understand! I've understood ever since you've been here!" For she was aware, in her own bosom, of sensations so separate from her romantic thoughts of him that she saw her body and soul divided against themselves. She recalled having read somewhere that in ancient Rome the slaves were not allowed to wear a distinctive dress lest they should recognize each other and learn their numbers and their power. So, in herself, she discerned for the first time instincts and desires, which, mute and unmarked, had gone to and fro in the dim passages of her mind, and now hailed each other with a cry of mutiny.

"Oh, I don't know what to think!" she broke out. "You say you didn't know she loved you. But you know it now. Doesn't that show you how you can put the broken bits together?"

"Can you seriously think it would be doing so to marry one woman while I care for another?"

"Oh, I don't know . . . I don't know . . ." The sense of her weakness made her try to harden herself against his arguments.

"You do know! We've often talked of such things: of the monstrousness of useless sacrifices. If I'm to expiate, it's not in that way." He added abruptly: "It's in having to say this to you now . . ."

She found no answer.

Through the silent apartment they heard the sudden peal of the door-bell, and she rose to her feet. "Owen!" she instantly exclaimed.

"Is Owen in Paris?"

She explained in a rapid undertone what she had learned from Sophy Viner.

"Shall I leave you?" Darrow asked.

"Yes . . . no . . ." She moved to the dining-room door, with the half-formed purpose of making him pass out, and then turned back. "It may be Adelaide."

They heard the outer door open, and a moment later Owen walked into the room. He was pale, with excited eyes: as they fell on Darrow, Anna saw his start of wonder. He made a slight sign of recognition, and then went up to his step-mother with an air of exaggerated gaiety.

"You furtive person! I ran across the omniscient Adelaide and heard from her that you'd rushed up suddenly and se-cretly——" He stood between Anna and Darrow, strained, questioning, dangerously on edge.

"I came up to meet Mr. Darrow," Anna answered. "His leave's been prolonged—he's going back with me."

The words seemed to have uttered themselves without her will, yet she felt a great sense of freedom as she spoke them.

The hard tension of Owen's face changed to incredulous surprise. He looked at Darrow.

"The merest luck . . . a colleague whose wife was ill . . . I came straight back," she heard the latter tranquilly explain-ing. His self-command helped to steady her, and she smiled at Owen.

"We'll all go back together tomorrow morning," she said as she slipped her arm through his.

XXXIII

OWEN LEATH did not go back with his step-mother to Givré. In reply to her suggestion he announced his intention of staying on a day or two longer in Paris.

Anna left alone by the first train the next morning. Darrow was to follow in the afternoon. When Owen had left them the evening before, Darrow waited a moment for her to speak; then, as she said nothing, he asked her if she really wished him to return to Givré. She made a mute sign of assent, and he added: "For you know that, much as I'm ready to do for Owen, I can't do that for him—I can't go back to be sent away again."

"No—no!"

He came nearer, and looked at her, and she went to him. All her fears seemed to fall from her as he held her. It was a different feeling from any she had known before: confused and turbid, as if secret shames and rancours stirred in it, yet richer, deeper, more enslaving. She leaned her head back and shut her eyes beneath his kisses. She knew now that she could never give him up.

Nevertheless she asked him, the next morning, to let her go back alone to Givré. She wanted time to think. She was convinced that what had happened was inevitable, that she and Darrow belonged to each other, and that he was right in saying no past folly could ever put them asunder. If there was a shade of difference in her feeling for him it was that of an added intensity. She felt restless, insecure out of his sight: she had a sense of incompleteness, of passionate dependence, that was somehow at variance with her own conception of her character.

It was partly the consciousness of this change in herself that made her want to be alone. The solitude of her inner life had given her the habit of these hours of self-examination, and she needed them as she needed her morning plunge into cold water.

During the journey she tried to review what had happened in the light of her new decision and of her sudden relief from pain. She seemed to herself to have passed through some fiery initiation from which she had emerged seared and quivering, but clutching to her breast a magic talisman. Sophy Viner had cried out to her: "Some day you'll know!" and Darrow had used the same words. They meant, she supposed, that when she had explored the intricacies and darknesses of her own heart her judgment of others would be less absolute. Well, she knew now—knew weaknesses and strengths she had not dreamed of, and the deep discord and still deeper complicities between what thought in her and what blindly wanted . . .

Her mind turned anxiously to Owen. At least the blow that was to fall on him would not seem to have been inflicted by her hand. He would be left with the impression that his breach with Sophy Viner was due to one of the ordinary causes of such disruptions: though he must lose her, his memory of her would not be poisoned. Anna never for a moment permitted herself the delusion that she had renewed her promise to Darrow in order to spare her step-son this last refinement of misery. She knew she had been prompted by the irresistible impulse to hold fast to what was most precious to her, and that Owen's arrival on the scene had been the pretext for her decision, and not its cause; yet she felt herself fortified by the thought of what she had spared him. It was as though a star she had been used to follow had shed its familiar ray on ways unknown to her.

All through these meditations ran the undercurrent of an absolute trust in Sophy Viner. She thought of the girl with a mingling of antipathy and confidence. It was humiliating to her pride to recognize kindred impulses in a character which she would have liked to feel completely alien to her. But what indeed was the girl really like? She seemed to have no scruples and a thousand delicacies. She had given herself to Darrow, and concealed the episode from Owen Leath, with no more apparent sense of debasement than the vulgarest of adventuresses; yet she had instantly obeyed the voice of her heart when it bade her part from the one and serve the other.

Anna tried to picture what the girl's life must have been: what experiences, what initiations, had formed her. But her own training had been too different: there were veils she could not lift. She looked back at her married life, and its colourless uniformity took on an air of high restraint and order. Was it because she had been so incurious that it had worn that look to her? It struck her with amazement that she had never given a thought to her husband's past, or wondered what he did and where he went when he was away from her. If she had been asked what she supposed he thought about when they were apart, she would instantly have answered: his snuff-boxes. It had never occurred to her that he might have passions, interests, preoccupations of which she was absolutely ignorant. Yet he went up to Paris rather regularly: ostensibly to attend sales and exhibitions, or to confer with dealers and collectors. She tried to picture him, straight, trim, beautifully brushed and varnished, walking furtively down a quiet street, and looking about him before he slipped into a doorway. She understood now that she had been cold to him: what more likely than that he had sought compensations? All men were like that, she supposed—no doubt her simplicity had amused him.

In the act of transposing Fraser Leath into a Don Juan she was pulled up by the ironic perception that she was simply trying to justify Darrow. She wanted to think that all men were "like that" because Darrow was "like that": she wanted to justify her acceptance of the fact by persuading herself that only through such concessions could women like herself hope to keep what they could not give up. And suddenly she was filled with anger at her blindness, and then at her disastrous attempt to see. Why had she forced the truth out of Darrow? If only she had held her tongue nothing need ever have been known. Sophy Viner would have broken her engagement, Owen would have been sent around the world, and her own dream would have been unshattered. But she had probed, insisted, cross-examined, not rested till she had dragged the secret to the light. She was one of the luckless women who always have the wrong audacities, and who always know it . . .

Was it she, Anna Leath, who was picturing herself to herself in that way? She recoiled from her thoughts as if with a sense of demoniac possession, and there flashed through her the longing to return to her old state of fearless ignorance. If at that moment she could have kept Darrow from following her to Givré she would have done so . . .

But he came; and with the sight of him the turmoil fell and she felt herself reassured, rehabilitated. He arrived toward dusk, and she motored to Francheuil to meet him. She wanted to see him as soon as possible, for she had divined, through the new insight that was in her, that only his presence could restore her to a normal view of things. In the motor, as they left the town and turned into the high-road, he lifted her hand and kissed it, and she leaned against him, and felt the currents flow between them. She was grateful to him for not saying anything, and for not expecting her to speak. She said to herself: "He never makes a mistake—he always knows what to do"; and then she thought with a start that it was doubtless because he had so often been in such situations. The idea that his tact was a kind of professional expertness filled her with repugnance, and insensibly she drew away from him. He made no motion to bring her nearer, and she instantly thought that that was calculated too. She sat beside him in frozen misery, wondering whether, henceforth, she would measure in this way his every look and gesture. Neither of them spoke again till the motor turned under the dark arch of the avenue, and they saw the lights of Givré twinkling at its end. Then Darrow laid his hand on hers and said: "I know, dear—" and the hardness in her melted. "He's suffering as I am," she thought; and for a moment the baleful fact between them seemed to draw them closer instead of walling them up in their separate wretchedness.

It was wonderful to be once more re-entering the doors of Givré with him, and as the old house received them into its mellow silence she had again the sense of passing out of a dreadful dream into the reassurance of kindly and familiar things. It did not seem possible that these quiet rooms, so full of the slowly-distilled accumulations of a fastidious taste, should have been the scene of tragic dissensions. The memory of them seemed to be shut out into the night with the closing and barring of its doors.

At the tea-table in the oak-room they found Madame de Chantelle and Effie. The little girl, catching sight of Darrow, raced down the drawing-rooms to meet him, and returned in triumph on his shoulder. Anna looked at them with a smile. Effie, for all her graces, was chary of such favours, and her

mother knew that in according them to Darrow she had admitted him to the circle where Owen had hitherto ruled.

Over the tea-table Darrow gave Madame de Chantelle the
explanation of his sudden return from England. On reaching
London, he told her, he had found that the secretary he was
to have replaced was detained there by the illness of his wife.
The Ambassador, knowing Darrow's urgent reasons for wishing to be in France, had immediately proposed his going
back, and awaiting at Givré the summons to relieve his colleague; and he had jumped into the first train, without even
waiting to telegraph the news of his release. He spoke naturally, easily, in his usual quiet voice, taking his tea from Effie,
helping himself to the toast she handed, and stooping now
and then to stroke the dozing terrier. And suddenly, as Anna
listened to his explanation, she asked herself if it were true.

The question, of course, was absurd. There was no possible
reason why he should invent a false account of his return, and
every probability that the version he gave was the real one.
But he had looked and spoken in the same way when he had
answered her probing questions about Sophy Viner, and she
reflected with a chill of fear that she would never again know
if he were speaking the truth or not. She was sure he loved
her, and she did not fear his insincerity as much as her own
distrust of him. For a moment it seemed to her that this must
corrupt the very source of love; then she said to herself: "By
and bye, when I am altogether his, we shall be so near each
other that there will be no room for any doubts between us."
But the doubts were there now, one moment lulled to quies-
cence, the next more torturingly alert. When the nurse appeared to summon Effie, the little girl, after kissing her
grandmother, entrenched herself on Darrow's knee with the
imperious demand to be carried up to bed; and Anna, while
she laughingly protested, said to herself with a pang: "Can I
give her a father about whom I think such things?"

The thought of Effie, and of what she owed to Effie, had
been the fundamental reason for her delays and hesitations
when she and Darrow had come together again in England.
Her own feeling was so clear that but for that scruple she
would have put her hand in his at once. But till she had seen
him again she had never considered the possibility of re-

marriage, and when it suddenly confronted her it seemed, for the moment, to disorganize the life she had planned for herself and her child. She had not spoken of this to Darrow because it appeared to her a subject to be debated within her own conscience. The question, then, was not as to his fitness to become the guide and guardian of her child; nor did she fear that her love for him would deprive Effie of the least fraction of her tenderness, since she did not think of love as something measured and exhaustible but as a treasure perpetually renewed. What she questioned was her right to introduce into her life any interests and duties which might rob Effie of a part of her time, or lessen the closeness of their daily intercourse.

She had decided this question as it was inevitable that she should; but now another was before her. Assuredly, at her age, there was no possible reason why she should cloister herself to bring up her daughter; but there was every reason for not marrying a man in whom her own faith was not complete . . .

XXXIV

WHEN SHE WOKE the next morning she felt a great lightness of heart. She recalled her last awakening at Givré, three days before, when it had seemed as though all her life had gone down in darkness. Now Darrow was once more under the same roof with her, and once more his nearness sufficed to make the looming horror drop away. She could almost have smiled at her scruples of the night before: as she looked back on them they seemed to belong to the old ignorant timorous time when she had feared to look life in the face, and had been blind to the mysteries and contradictions of the human heart because her own had not been revealed to her. Darrow had said: "You were made to feel everything"; and to feel was surely better than to judge.

When she came downstairs he was already in the oak-room with Effie and Madame de Chantelle, and the sense of reassurance which his presence gave her was merged in the relief of not being able to speak of what was between them. But there it was, inevitably, and whenever they looked at each other they saw it. In her dread of giving it a more tangible shape she tried to devise means of keeping the little girl with her, and, when the latter had been called away by the nurse, found an excuse for following Madame de Chantelle upstairs to the purple sitting-room. But a confidential talk with Madame de Chantelle implied the detailed discussion of plans of which Anna could hardly yet bear to consider the vaguest outline: the date of her marriage, the relative advantages of sailing from London or Lisbon, the possibility of hiring a habitable house at their new post; and, when these problems were exhausted, the application of the same method to the subject of Owen's future.

His grandmother, having no suspicion of the real reason of Sophy Viner's departure, had thought it "extremely suitable" of the young girl to withdraw to the shelter of her old friends' roof in the hour of bridal preparation. This maidenly retreat had in fact impressed Madame de Chantelle so favourably that she was disposed for the first time to talk over Owen's projects; and as every human event translated itself for her into

terms of social and domestic detail, Anna had perforce to
travel the same round again. She felt a momentary relief when
Darrow presently joined them; but his coming served only to
draw the conversation back to the question of their own future, and Anna felt a new pang as she heard him calmly and
lucidly discussing it. Did such self-possession imply indifference or insincerity? In that problem her mind perpetually revolved; and she dreaded the one answer as much as the other.

She was resolved to keep on her course as though nothing
had happened: to marry Darrow and never let the consciousness of the past intrude itself between them; but she was beginning to feel that the only way of attaining to this state of
detachment from the irreparable was once for all to turn back
with him to its contemplation. As soon as this desire had germinated it became so strong in her that she regretted having
promised Effie to take her out for the afternoon. But she
could think of no pretext for disappointing the little girl, and
soon after luncheon the three set forth in the motor to show
Darrow a château famous in the annals of the region. During
their excursion Anna found it impossible to guess from his
demeanour if Effie's presence between them was as much of
a strain to his composure as to hers. He remained imperturbably good-humoured and appreciative while they went the
round of the monument, and she remarked only that when
he thought himself unnoticed his face grew grave and his answers came less promptly.

On the way back, two or three miles from Givré, she suddenly proposed that they should walk home through the forest which skirted that side of the park. Darrow acquiesced,
and they got out and sent Effie on in the motor. Their way
led through a bit of sober French woodland, flat as a faded
tapestry, but with gleams of live emerald lingering here and
there among its browns and ochres. The luminous grey air
gave vividness to its dying colours, and veiled the distant
glimpses of the landscape in soft uncertainty. In such a solitude Anna had fancied it would be easier to speak; but as she
walked beside Darrow over the deep soundless flooring of
brown moss the words on her lips took flight again. It
seemed impossible to break the spell of quiet joy which his
presence laid on her, and when he began to talk of the place

they had just visited she answered his questions and then waited for what he should say next . . . No, decidedly she could not speak; she no longer even knew what she had meant to say . . .

The same experience repeated itself several times that day and the next. When she and Darrow were apart she exhausted herself in appeal and interrogation, she formulated with a fervent lucidity every point in her imaginary argument. But as soon as she was alone with him something deeper than reason and subtler than shyness laid its benumbing touch upon her, and the desire to speak became merely a dim disquietude, through which his looks, his words, his touch, reached her as through a mist of bodily pain. Yet this inertia was torn by wild flashes of resistance, and when they were apart she began to prepare again what she meant to say to him.

She knew he could not be with her without being aware of this inner turmoil, and she hoped he would break the spell by some releasing word. But she presently understood that he recognized the futility of words, and was resolutely bent on holding her to her own purpose of behaving as if nothing had happened. Once more she inwardly accused him of insensibility, and her imagination was beset by tormenting visions of his past . . . Had such things happened to him before? If the episode had been an isolated accident—"a moment of folly and madness", as he had called it—she could understand, or at least begin to understand (for at a certain point her imagination always turned back); but if it were a mere link in a chain of similar experiments, the thought of it dishonoured her whole past . . .

Effie, in the interregnum between governesses, had been given leave to dine downstairs; and Anna, on the evening of Darrow's return, kept the little girl with her till long after the nurse had signalled from the drawing-room door. When at length she had been carried off, Anna proposed a game of cards, and after this diversion had drawn to its languid close she said good-night to Darrow and followed Madame de Chantelle upstairs. But Madame de Chantelle never sat up late, and the second evening, with the amiably implied intention of leaving Anna and Darrow to themselves, she took an earlier leave of them than usual.

Anna sat silent, listening to her small stiff steps as they minced down the hall and died out in the distance. Madame de Chantelle had broken her wooden embroidery frame, and Darrow, having offered to repair it, had drawn his chair up to a table that held a lamp. Anna watched him as he sat with bent head and knitted brows, trying to fit together the disjoined pieces. The sight of him, so tranquilly absorbed in this trifling business, seemed to give to the quiet room a perfume of intimacy, to fill it with a sense of sweet familiar habit; and it came over her again that she knew nothing of the inner thoughts of this man who was sitting by her as a husband might. The lamplight fell on his white forehead, on the healthy brown of his cheek, the backs of his thin sun-burnt hands. As she watched the hands her sense of them became as vivid as a touch, and she said to herself: "That other woman has sat and watched him as I am doing. She has known him as I have never known him . . . Perhaps he is thinking of that now. Or perhaps he has forgotten it all as completely as I have forgotten everything that happened to me before he came . . ."

He looked young, active, stored with strength and energy; not the man for vain repinings or long memories. She wondered what she had to hold or satisfy him. He loved her now; she had no doubt of that; but how could she hope to keep him? They were so nearly of an age that already she felt herself his senior. As yet the difference was not visible; outwardly at least they were matched; but ill-health or unhappiness would soon do away with this equality. She thought with a pang of bitterness: "He won't grow any older because he doesn't feel things; and because he doesn't, I *shall* . . ."

And when she ceased to please him, what then? Had he the tradition of faith to the spoken vow, or the deeper piety of the unspoken dedication? What was his theory, what his inner conviction in such matters? But what did she care for his convictions or his theories? No doubt he loved her now, and believed he would always go on loving her, and was persuaded that, if he ceased to, his loyalty would be proof against the change. What she wanted to know was not what he thought about it in advance, but what would impel or restrain him at the crucial hour. She put no faith in her own arts: she was too sure of having none! And if some beneficent enchanter had bestowed them on her, she knew now that she would have rejected the gift. She could hardly conceive of wanting the kind of love that was a state one could be cozened into . . .

Darrow, putting away the frame, walked across the room and sat down beside her; and she felt he had something special to say.

"They're sure to send for me in a day or two now," he began.

She made no answer, and he continued: "You'll tell me before I go what day I'm to come back and get you?"

It was the first time since his return to Givré that he had made any direct allusion to the date of their marriage; and instead of answering him she broke out: "There's something I've been wanting you to know. The other day in Paris I saw Miss Viner."

She saw him flush with the intensity of his surprise.

"You sent for her?"

"No; she heard from Adelaide that I was in Paris and she came. She came because she wanted to urge me to marry you. I thought you ought to know what she had done."

Darrow stood up. "I'm glad you've told me." He spoke with a visible effort at composure. Her eyes followed him as he moved away.

"Is that all?" he asked after an interval.

"It seems to me a great deal."

"It's what she'd already asked me." His voice showed her how deeply he was moved, and a throb of jealousy shot through her.

"Oh, it was for your sake, I know!" He made no answer, and she added: "She's been exceedingly generous . . . Why shouldn't we speak of it?"

She had lowered her head, but through her dropped lids she seemed to be watching the crowded scene of his face.

"I've not shrunk from speaking of it."

"Speaking of *her*, then, I mean. It seems to me that if I could talk to you about her I should know better——"

She broke off, confused, and he questioned: "What is it you want to know better?"

The colour rose to her forehead. How could she tell him what she scarcely dared own to herself? There was nothing she did not want to know, no fold or cranny of his secret that her awakened imagination did not strain to penetrate; but she could not expose Sophy Viner to the base fingerings of a retrospective jealousy, nor Darrow to the temptation of be-littling her in the effort to better his own case. The girl had been magnificent, and the only worthy return that Anna could make was to take Darrow from her without a question if she took him at all . . .

She lifted her eyes to his face. "I think I only wanted to speak her name. It's not right that we should seem so afraid of it. If I were really afraid of it I should have to give you up," she said.

He bent over her and caught her to him. "Ah, you can't give me up now!" he exclaimed.

She suffered him to hold her fast without speaking; but the old dread was between them again, and it was on her lips to cry out: "How can I help it, when I *am* so afraid?"

XXXV

T HE NEXT MORNING the dread was still there, and she understood that she must snatch herself out of the torpor of the will into which she had been gradually sinking, and tell Darrow that she could not be his wife.

The knowledge came to her in the watches of a sleepless night, when, through the tears of disenchanted passion, she stared back upon her past. There it lay before her, her sole romance, in all its paltry poverty, the cheapest of cheap adventures, the most pitiful of sentimental blunders. She looked about her room, the room where, for so many years, if her heart had been quiescent her thoughts had been alive, and pictured herself henceforth cowering before a throng of mean suspicions, of unavowed compromises and concessions. In that moment of self-searching she saw that Sophy Viner had chosen the better part, and that certain renunciations might enrich where possession would have left a desert.

Passionate reactions of instinct fought against these efforts of her will. Why should past or future coerce her, when the present was so securely hers? Why insanely surrender what the other would after all never have? Her sense of irony whispered that if she sent away Darrow it would not be to Sophy Viner, but to the first woman who crossed his path—as, in a similar hour, Sophy Viner herself had crossed it . . . But the mere fact that she could think such things of him sent her shuddering back to the opposite pole. She pictured herself gradually subdued to such a conception of life and love, she pictured Effie growing up under the influence of the woman she saw herself becoming—and she hid her eyes from the humiliation of the picture . . .

They were at luncheon when the summons that Darrow expected was brought to him. He handed the telegram to Anna, and she learned that his Ambassador, on the way to a German cure, was to be in Paris the next evening and wished to confer with him there before he went back to London. The idea that the decisive moment was at hand was so agitating to her that when luncheon was over she slipped away to the terrace and thence went down alone to the garden. The day was grey but mild, with the heaviness of decay in the air. She rambled on aimlessly, following under the denuded boughs the path she and Darrow had taken on their first walk to the river. She was sure he would not try to overtake her: sure he would guess why she wished to be alone. There were moments when it seemed to double her loneliness to be so certain of his reading her heart while she was so desperately ignorant of his . . .

She wandered on for more than an hour, and when she returned to the house she saw, as she entered the hall, that Darrow was seated at the desk in Owen's study. He heard her step, and looking up turned in his chair without rising. Their eyes met, and she saw that his were clear and smiling. He had a heap of papers at his elbow and was evidently engaged in some official correspondence. She wondered that he could address himself so composedly to his task, and then ironically reflected that such detachment was a sign of his superiority. She crossed the threshold and went toward him; but as she advanced she had a sudden vision of Owen, standing outside in the cold autumn dusk and watching Darrow and Sophy Viner as they faced each other across the lamplit desk . . . The evocation was so vivid that it caught her breath like a blow, and she sank down helplessly on the divan among the piled-up books. Distinctly, at the moment, she understood that the end had come. "When he speaks to me I will tell him!" she thought . . .

Darrow, laying aside his pen, looked at her for a moment in silence; then he stood up and shut the door.

"I must go to-morrow early," he said, sitting down beside her. His voice was grave, with a slight tinge of sadness. She said to herself: "He knows what I am feeling . . ." and now the thought made her feel less alone. The expression of his face was stern and yet tender: for the first time she understood what he had suffered.

She had no doubt as to the necessity of giving him up, but it was impossible to tell him so then. She stood up and said: "I'll leave you to your letters." He made no protest, but merely answered: "You'll come down presently for a walk?" and it occurred to her at once that she would walk down to the river with him, and give herself for the last time the tragic luxury of sitting at his side in the little pavilion. "Perhaps," she thought, "it will be easier to tell him there."

It did not, on the way home from their walk, become any easier to tell him; but her secret decision to do so before he left gave her a kind of factitious calm and laid a melancholy ecstasy upon the hour. Still skirting the subject that fanned their very faces with its flame, they clung persistently to other topics, and it seemed to Anna that their minds had never been nearer together than in this hour when their hearts were so separate. In the glow of interchanged love she had grown less conscious of that other glow of interchanged thought which had once illumined her mind. She had forgotten how Darrow had widened her world and lengthened out all her perspectives, and with a pang of double destitution she saw herself alone among her shrunken thoughts.

For the first time, then, she had a clear vision of what her life would be without him. She imagined herself trying to take up the daily round, and all that had lightened and animated it seemed equally lifeless and vain. She tried to think of herself as wholly absorbed in her daughter's development, like other mothers she had seen; but she supposed those mothers must have had stored memories of happiness to nourish them. She had had nothing, and all her starved youth still claimed its due.

When she went up to dress for dinner she said to herself: "I'll have my last evening with him, and then, before we say good night, I'll tell him."

This postponement did not seem unjustified. Darrow had shown her how he dreaded vain words, how resolved he was to avoid all fruitless discussion. He must have been intensely aware of what had been going on in her mind since his return, yet when she had attempted to reveal it to him he had turned from the revelation. She was therefore merely following the line he had traced in behaving, till the final moment came, as though there were nothing more to say . . .

That moment seemed at last to be at hand when, at her usual hour after dinner, Madame de Chantelle rose to go upstairs. She lingered a little to bid good-bye to Darrow, whom she was not likely to see in the morning; and her affable allusions to his prompt return sounded in Anna's ear like the note of destiny.

A cold rain had fallen all day, and for greater warmth and intimacy they had gone after dinner to the oak-room, shutting out the chilly vista of the farther drawing-rooms. The autumn wind, coming up from the river, cried about the house with a voice of loss and separation; and Anna and Darrow sat silent, as if they feared to break the hush that shut them in. The solitude, the fire-light, the harmony of soft hangings and old dim pictures, wove about them a spell of security through which Anna felt, far down in her heart, the muffled beat of an inextinguishable bliss. How could she have thought that this last moment would be the moment to speak to him, when it seemed to have gathered up into its flight all the scattered splendours of her dream?

XXXVI

D ARROW CONTINUED to stand by the door after it had closed. Anna felt that he was looking at her, and sat still, disdaining to seek refuge in any evasive word or movement. For the last time she wanted to let him take from her the fulness of what the sight of her could give.

He crossed over and sat down on the sofa. For a moment neither of them spoke; then he said: "To-night, dearest, I must have my answer."

She straightened herself under the shock of his seeming to take the very words from her lips.

"To-night?" was all that she could falter.

"I must be off by the early train. There won't be more than a moment in the morning."

He had taken her hand, and she said to herself that she must free it before she could go on with what she had to say. Then she rejected this concession to a weakness she was resolved to defy. To the end she would leave her hand in his hand, her eyes in his eyes: she would not, in their final hour together, be afraid of any part of her love for him.

"You'll tell me to-night, dear," he insisted gently; and his insistence gave her the strength to speak.

"There's something I must ask you," she broke out, perceiving, as she heard her words, that they were not in the least what she had meant to say.

He sat still, waiting, and she pressed on: "Do such things happen to men often?"

The quiet room seemed to resound with the long reverberations of her question. She looked away from him, and he released her and stood up.

"I don't know what happens to other men. Such a thing never happened to me . . ."

She turned her eyes back to his face. She felt like a traveller on a giddy path between a cliff and a precipice: there was nothing for it now but to go on.

"Had it . . . had it begun . . . before you met her in Paris?"

"No; a thousand times no! I've told you the facts as they were."

"All the facts?"

He turned abruptly. "What do you mean?"

Her throat was dry and the loud pulses drummed in her temples.

"I mean—about her . . . Perhaps you knew . . . knew things about her . . . beforehand."

She stopped. The room had grown profoundly still. A log dropped to the hearth and broke there in a hissing shower.

Darrow spoke in a clear voice. "I knew nothing, absolutely nothing," he said.

She had the answer to her inmost doubt—to her last shameful unavowed hope. She sat powerless under her woe.

He walked to the fireplace and pushed back the broken log with his foot. A flame shot out of it, and in the upward glare she saw his pale face, stern with misery

"Is that all?" he asked.

She made a slight sign with her head and he came slowly back to her. "Then is this to be good-bye?"

Again she signed a faint assent, and he made no effort to touch her or draw nearer. "You understand that I sha'n't come back?"

He was looking at her, and she tried to return his look, but her eyes were blind with tears, and in dread of his seeing them she got up and walked away. He did not follow her, and she stood with her back to him, staring at a bowl of carnations on a little table strewn with books. Her tears magnified everything she looked at, and the streaked petals of the carnations, their fringed edges and frail curled stamens, pressed upon her, huge and vivid. She noticed among the books a volume of verse he had sent her from England, and tried to remember whether it was before or after . . .

She felt that he was waiting for her to speak, and at last she turned to him. "I shall see you to-morrow before you go . . ."

He made no answer.

She moved toward the door and he held it open for her. She saw his hand on the door, and his seal ring in its setting of twisted silver; and the sense of the end of all things came to her.

They walked down the drawing-rooms, between the shadowy reflections of screens and cabinets, and mounted the stairs side by side. At the end of the gallery, a lamp brought out turbid gleams in the smoky battle-piece above it.

On the landing Darrow stopped; his room was the nearest to the stairs. "Good night," he said, holding out his hand.

As Anna gave him hers the springs of grief broke loose in her. She struggled with her sobs, and subdued them; but her breath came unevenly, and to hide her agitation she leaned on him and pressed her face against his arm.

"Don't—don't," he whispered, soothing her.

Her troubled breathing sounded loudly in the silence of the sleeping house. She pressed her lips tight, but could not stop the nervous pulsations in her throat, and he put an arm about her and, opening his door, drew her across the threshold of his room. The door shut behind her and she sat down on the lounge at the foot of the bed. The pulsations in her throat had ceased, but she knew they would begin again if she tried to speak.

Darrow walked away and leaned against the mantel-piece. The red-veiled lamp shone on his books and papers, on the arm-chair by the fire, and the scattered objects on his dressing-table. A log glimmered on the hearth, and the room was warm and faintly smoke-scented. It was the first time she had ever been in a room he lived in, among his personal possessions and the traces of his daily usage. Every object about her seemed to contain a particle of himself: the whole air breathed of him, steeping her in the sense of his intimate presence.

Suddenly she thought: "This is what Sophy Viner knew" . . . and with a torturing precision she pictured them alone in such a scene . . . Had he taken the girl to an hotel . . . where did people go in such cases? Wherever they were, the silence of night had been around them, and the things he used had been strewn about the room . . . Anna, ashamed of dwelling on the detested vision, stood up with a confused impulse of flight; then a wave of contrary feeling arrested her and she paused with lowered head.

Darrow had come forward as she rose, and she perceived that he was waiting for her to bid him good night. It was clear that no other possibility had even brushed his mind; and the fact, for some dim reason, humiliated her. "Why not . . . why not?" something whispered in her, as though his forbearance, his tacit recognition of her pride, were a slight on other qualities she wanted him to feel in her.

"In the morning, then?" she heard him say.

"Yes, in the morning," she repeated.

She continued to stand in the same place, looking vaguely about the room. For once before they parted—since part they must—she longed to be to him all that Sophy Viner had been; but she remained rooted to the floor, unable to find a word or imagine a gesture that should express her meaning. Exasperated by her helplessness, she thought: "Don't I feel things as other women do?"

Her eye fell on a note-case she had given him. It was worn at the corners with the friction of his pocket and distended with thickly packed papers. She wondered if he carried her letters in it, and she put her hand out and touched it.

All that he and she had ever felt or seen, their close encounters of word and look, and the closer contact of their silences, trembled through her at the touch. She remembered things he had said that had been like new skies above her head: ways he had that seemed a part of the air she breathed. The faint warmth of her girlish love came back to her, gathering heat as it passed through her thoughts; and her heart rocked like a boat on the surge of its long long memories. "It's because I love him in too many ways," she thought; and slowly she turned to the door.

She was aware that Darrow was still silently watching her, but he neither stirred nor spoke till she had reached the threshold. Then he met her there and caught her in his arms.

"Not to-night—don't tell me to-night!" he whispered; and she leaned away from him, closing her eyes for an instant, and then slowly opening them to the flood of light in his.

XXXVII

A NNA AND DARROW, the next day, sat alone in a compartment of the Paris train.

Anna, when they entered it, had put herself in the farthest corner and placed her bag on the adjoining seat. She had decided suddenly to accompany Darrow to Paris, had even persuaded him to wait for a later train in order that they might travel together. She had an intense longing to be with him, an almost morbid terror of losing sight of him for a moment: when he jumped out of the train and ran back along the platform to buy a newspaper for her she felt as though she should never see him again, and shivered with the cold misery of her last journey to Paris, when she had thought herself parted from him forever. Yet she wanted to keep him at a distance, on the other side of the compartment, and as the train moved out of the station she drew from her bag the letters she had thrust in it as she left the house, and began to glance over them so that her lowered lids should hide her eyes from him.

She was his now, his for life: there could never again be any question of sacrificing herself to Effie's welfare, or to any other abstract conception of duty. Effie of course would not suffer; Anna would pay for her bliss as a wife by redoubled devotion as a mother. Her scruples were not overcome; but for the time their voices were drowned in the tumultuous rumour of her happiness.

As she opened her letters she was conscious that Darrow's gaze was fixed on her, and gradually it drew her eyes upward, and she drank deep of the passionate tenderness in his. Then the blood rose to her face and she felt again the desire to shield herself. She turned back to her letters and her glance lit on an envelope inscribed in Owen's hand.

Her heart began to beat oppressively: she was in a mood when the simplest things seemed ominous. What could Owen have to say to her? Only the first page was covered, and it contained simply the announcement that, in the company of a young compatriot who was studying at the Beaux Arts, he had planned to leave for Spain the following evening.

"He hasn't seen her, then!" was Anna's instant thought;

and her feeling was a strange compound of humiliation and relief. The girl had kept her word, lived up to the line of conduct she had set herself; and Anna had failed in the same attempt. She did not reproach herself with her failure; but she would have been happier if there had been less discrepancy between her words to Sophy Viner and the act which had followed them. It irritated her obscurely that the girl should have been so much surer of her power to carry out her purpose . . .

Anna looked up and saw that Darrow's eyes were on the newspaper. He seemed calm and secure, almost indifferent to her presence. "Will it become a matter of course to him so soon?" she wondered with a twinge of jealousy. She sat motionless, her eyes fixed on him, trying to make him feel the attraction of her gaze as she felt his. It surprised and shamed her to detect a new element in her love for him: a sort of suspicious tyrannical tenderness that seemed to deprive it of all serenity. Finally he looked up, his smile enveloped her, and she felt herself his in every fibre, his so completely and inseparably that she saw the vanity of imagining any other fate for herself.

To give herself a countenance she held out Owen's letter. He took it and glanced down the page, his face grown grave. She waited nervously till he looked up.

"That's a good plan; the best thing that could happen," he said, a just perceptible shade of constraint in his tone.

"Oh, yes," she hastily assented. She was aware of a faint current of relief silently circulating between them. They were both glad that Owen was going, that for a while he would be out of their way; and it seemed to her horrible that so much of the stuff of their happiness should be made of such unavowed feelings . . .

"I shall see him this evening," she said, wishing Darrow to feel that she was not afraid of meeting her step-son.

"Yes, of course; perhaps he might dine with you."

The words struck her as strangely obtuse. Darrow was to meet his Ambassador at the station on the latter's arrival, and would in all probability have to spend the evening with him, and Anna knew he had been concerned at the thought of having to leave her alone. But how could he speak in that careless tone of her dining with Owen? She lowered her voice to say: "I'm afraid he's desperately unhappy."

He answered, with a tinge of impatience: "It's much the best thing that he should travel."

"Yes—but don't you feel . . ." She broke off. She knew how he disliked these idle returns on the irrevocable, and her fear of doing or saying what he disliked was tinged by a new instinct of subserviency against which her pride revolted. She thought to herself: "He will see the change, and grow indifferent to me as he did to *her* . . ." and for a moment it seemed to her that she was reliving the experience of Sophy Viner.

Darrow made no attempt to learn the end of her unfinished sentence. He handed back Owen's letter and returned to his newspaper; and when he looked up from it a few minutes later it was with a clear brow and a smile that irresistibly drew her back to happier thoughts.

The train was just entering a station, and a moment later their compartment was invaded by a common-place couple preoccupied with the bestowal of bulging packages. Anna, at their approach, felt the possessive pride of the woman in love when strangers are between herself and the man she loves. She asked Darrow to open the window, to place her bag in the net, to roll her rug into a cushion for her feet; and while he was thus busied with her she was conscious of a new devotion in his tone, in his way of bending over her and meeting her eyes. He went back to his seat, and they looked at each other like lovers smiling at a happy secret.

Anna, before going back to Givré, had suggested Owen's moving into her apartment, but he had preferred to remain at the hotel to which he had sent his luggage, and on arriving in Paris she decided to drive there at once. She was impatient to have the meeting over, and glad that Darrow was obliged to leave her at the station in order to look up a colleague at the Embassy. She dreaded his seeing Owen again, and yet dared not tell him so; and to ensure his remaining away she mentioned an urgent engagement with her dress-maker and a long list of commissions to be executed for Madame de Chantelle.

"I shall see you to-morrow morning," she said; but he

replied with a smile that he would certainly find time to come
to her for a moment on his way back from meeting the Ambassador; and when he had put her in a cab he leaned
through the window to press his lips to hers.

She blushed like a girl, thinking, half vexed, half happy:
"Yesterday he would not have done it . . ." and a dozen
scarcely definable differences in his look and manner seemed
all at once to be summed up in the boyish act. "After all,
I'm engaged to him," she reflected, and then smiled at the absurdity of the word. The next instant, with a pang of self-
reproach, she remembered Sophy Viner's cry: "I knew all the
while he didn't care . . ." "Poor thing, oh poor thing!" Anna
murmured . . .

At Owen's hotel she waited in a tremor while the porter
went in search of him. Word was presently brought back that
he was in his room and begged her to come up, and as she
crossed the hall she caught sight of his portmanteaux lying on
the floor, already labelled for departure.

Owen sat at a table writing, his back to the door; and when
he stood up the window was behind him, so that, in the rainy
afternoon light, his features were barely discernible.

"Dearest—so you're really off?" she said, hesitating a moment on the threshold.

He pushed a chair forward, and they sat down, each waiting for the other to speak. Finally she put some random question about his travelling-companion, a slow shy meditative
youth whom he had once or twice brought down to Givré.
She reflected that it was natural he should have given this
uncommunicative comrade the preference over his livelier acquaintances, and aloud she said: "I'm so glad Fred Rempson
can go with you."

Owen answered in the same tone, and for a few minutes
their talk dragged itself on over a dry waste of commonplaces. Anna noticed that, though ready enough to impart his
own plans, Owen studiously abstained from putting any
questions about hers. It was evident from his allusions that
he meant to be away for some time, and he presently asked
her if she would give instructions about packing and sending
after him some winter clothes he had left at Givré. This gave

her the opportunity to say that she expected to go back within a day or two and would attend to the matter as soon as she returned. She added: "I came up this morning with George, who is going on to London to-morrow," intending, by the use of Darrow's Christian name, to give Owen the chance to speak of her marriage. But he made no comment, and she continued to hear the name sounding on unfamiliarly between them.

The room was almost dark, and she finally stood up and glanced about for the light-switch, saying: "I can't see you, dear."

"Oh, don't—I hate the light!" Owen exclaimed, catching her by the wrist and pushing her back into her seat. He gave a nervous laugh and added: "I'm half-blind with neuralgia. I suppose it's this beastly rain."

"Yes; it will do you good to get down to Spain."

She asked if he had the remedies the doctor had given him for a previous attack, and on his replying that he didn't know what he'd done with the stuff, she sprang up, offering to go to the chemist's. It was a relief to have something to do for him, and she knew from his "Oh, thanks—would you?" that it was a relief to him to have a pretext for not detaining her. His natural impulse would have been to declare that he didn't want any drugs, and would be all right in no time; and his acquiescence showed her how profoundly he felt the useless-ness of their trying to prolong their talk. His face was now no more than a white blur in the dusk, but she felt its indis-tinctness as a veil drawn over aching intensities of expression. "He knows . . . he knows . . ." she said to herself, and won-dered whether the truth had been revealed to him by some corroborative fact or by the sheer force of divination.

He had risen also, and was clearly waiting for her to go, and she turned to the door, saying: "I'll be back in a moment."

"Oh, don't come up again, please!" He paused, embar-rassed. "I mean—I may not be here. I've got to go and pick up Rempson, and see about some final things with him."

She stopped on the threshold with a sinking heart. He meant this to be their leave-taking, then—and he had not even asked her when she was to be married, or spoken of seeing her again before she set out for the other side of the world.

"Owen!" she cried, and turned back.

He stood mutely before her in the dimness.

"You haven't told me how long you're to be gone."

"How long? Oh, you see . . . that's rather vague . . . I hate definite dates, you know . . ."

He paused and she saw he did not mean to help her out. She tried to say: "You'll be here for my wedding?" but could not bring the words to her lips. Instead she murmured: "In six weeks I shall be going too . . ." and he rejoined, as if he had expected the announcement and prepared his answer: "Oh, by that time, very likely . . ."

"At any rate, I won't say good-bye," she stammered, feeling the tears beneath her veil.

"No, no; rather not!" he declared; but he made no movement, and she went up and threw her arms about him. "You'll write me, won't you?"

"Of course, of course——"

Her hands slipped down into his, and for a minute they held each other dumbly in the darkness; then he gave a vague laugh and said: "It's really time to light up." He pressed the electric button with one hand while with the other he opened the door; and she passed out without daring to turn back, lest the light on his face should show her what she feared to see.

XXXVIII

A NNA DROVE to the chemist's for Owen's remedy. On the way she stopped her cab at a book-shop, and emerged from it laden with literature. She knew what would interest Owen, and what he was likely to have read, and she had made her choice among the newest publications with the promptness of a discriminating reader. But on the way back to the hotel she was overcome by the irony of adding this mental panacea to the other. There was something grotesque and almost mocking in the idea of offering a judicious selection of literature to a man setting out on such a journey. "He knows . . . he knows . . ." she kept on repeating; and giving the porter the parcel from the chemist's she drove away without leaving the books.

She went to her apartment, whither her maid had preceded her. There was a fire in the drawing-room and the tea-table stood ready by the hearth. The stormy rain beat against the uncurtained windows, and she thought of Owen, who would soon be driving through it to the station, alone with his bitter thoughts. She had been proud of the fact that he had always sought her help in difficult hours; and now, in the most difficult of all, she was the one being to whom he could not turn. Between them, henceforth, there would always be the wall of an insurmountable silence . . . She strained her aching thoughts to guess how the truth had come to him. Had he seen the girl, and had she told him? Instinctively, Anna rejected this conjecture. But what need was there of assuming an explicit statement, when every breath they had drawn for the last weeks had been charged with the immanent secret? As she looked back over the days since Darrow's first arrival at Givré she perceived that at no time had any one deliberately spoken, or anything been accidentally disclosed. The truth had come to light by the force of its irresistible pressure; and the perception gave her a startled sense of hidden powers, of a chaos of attractions and repulsions far beneath the ordered surfaces of intercourse. She looked back with melancholy derision on her old conception of life, as a kind of well-lit and well-policed suburb to dark places one need never know about. Here they were, these dark places, in her own bosom, and henceforth she would always have to traverse them to reach the beings she loved best!

She was still sitting beside the untouched tea-table when she heard Darrow's voice in the hall. She started up, saying to herself: "I must tell him that Owen knows . . ." but when the door opened and she saw his face, still lit by the same smile of boyish triumph, she felt anew the uselessness of speaking . . . Had he ever supposed that Owen would not know? Probably, from the height of his greater experience, he had seen long since that all that happened was inevitable; and the thought of it, at any rate, was clearly not weighing on him now.

He was already dressed for the evening, and as he came toward her he said: "The Ambassador's booked for an official dinner and I'm free after all. Where shall we dine?"

Anna had pictured herself sitting alone all the evening with her wretched thoughts, and the fact of having to put them out of her mind for the next few hours gave her an immediate sensation of relief. Already her pulses were dancing to the tune of Darrow's, and as they smiled at each other she thought: "Nothing can ever change the fact that I belong to him."

"Where shall we dine?" he repeated gaily, and she named a well-known restaurant for which she had once heard him express a preference. But as she did so she fancied she saw a shadow on his face, and instantly she said to herself: "It was *there* he went with her!"

"Oh, no, not there, after all!" she interrupted herself; and now she was sure his colour deepened.

"Where shall it be, then?"

She noticed that he did not ask the reason of her change, and this convinced her that she had guessed the truth, and that he knew she had guessed it. "He will always know what I am thinking, and he will never dare to ask me," she thought; and she saw between them the same insurmountable wall of silence as between herself and Owen, a wall of glass through which they could watch each other's faintest motions but which no sound could ever traverse . . .

They drove to a restaurant on the Boulevard, and there, in

their intimate corner of the serried scene, the sense of what was unspoken between them gradually ceased to oppress her. He looked so light-hearted and handsome, so ingenuously proud of her, so openly happy at being with her, that no other fact could seem real in his presence. He had learned that the Ambassador was to spend two days in Paris, and he had reason to hope that in consequence his own departure for London would be deferred. He was exhilarated by the prospect of being with Anna for a few hours longer, and she did not ask herself if his exhilaration were a sign of insensibility, for she was too conscious of his power of swaying her moods not to be secretly proud of affecting his.

They lingered for some time over the fruit and coffee, and when they rose to go Darrow suggested that, if she felt disposed for the play, they were not too late for the second part of the programme at one of the smaller theatres.

His mention of the hour recalled Owen to her thoughts. She saw his train rushing southward through the storm, and, in a corner of the swaying compartment, his face, white and indistinct as it had loomed on her in the rainy twilight. It was horrible to be thus perpetually paying for her happiness!

Darrow had called for a theatrical journal, and he presently looked up from it to say: "I hear the second play at the Athénée is amusing."

It was on Anna's lips to acquiesce; but as she was about to speak she wondered if it were not at the Athénée that Owen had seen Darrow with Sophy Viner. She was not sure he had even mentioned the theatre, but the mere possibility was enough to darken her sky. It was hateful to her to think of accompanying Darrow to places where the girl had been with him. She tried to reason away this scruple, she even reminded herself with a bitter irony that whenever she was in Darrow's arms she was where the girl had been before her—but she could not shake off her superstitious dread of being with him in any of the scenes of the Parisian episode.

She replied that she was too tired for the play, and they drove back to her apartment. At the foot of the stairs she half-turned to wish him good night, but he appeared not to notice her gesture and followed her up to her door.

"This is ever so much better than the theatre," he said as they entered the drawing-room.

She had crossed the room and was bending over the hearth to light the fire. She knew he was approaching her, and that in a moment he would have drawn the cloak from her shoulders and laid his lips on her neck, just below the gathered-up hair. These privileges were his and, however deferently and tenderly he claimed them, the joyous ease of his manner marked a difference and proclaimed a right.

"After the theatre they came home like this," she thought; and at the same instant she felt his hands on her shoulders and shrank back.

"Don't—oh, don't!" she cried, drawing her cloak about her. She saw from his astonished stare that her face must be quivering with pain.

"Anna! What on earth is the matter?"

"Owen knows!" she broke out, with a confused desire to justify herself.

Darrow's countenance changed. "Did he tell you so? What did he say?"

"Nothing! I knew it from the things he didn't say."

"You had a talk with him this afternoon?"

"Yes: for a few minutes. I could see he didn't want me to stay."

She had dropped into a chair, and sat there huddled, still holding her cloak about her shoulders.

Darrow did not dispute her assumption, and she noticed that he expressed no surprise. He sat down at a little distance from her, turning about in his fingers the cigar-case he had drawn out as they came in. At length he said: "Had he seen Miss Viner?"

She shrank from the sound of the name. "No . . . I don't think so . . . I'm sure he hadn't . . ."

They remained silent, looking away from one another. Finally Darrow stood up and took a few steps across the room. He came back and paused before her, his eyes on her face.

"I think you ought to tell me what you mean to do."

She raised her head and gave him back his look. "Nothing I do can help Owen!"

"No; but things can't go on like this." He paused, as if to measure his words. "I fill you with aversion," he exclaimed.

She started up, half-sobbing. "No—oh, no!"

"Poor child—you can't see your face!"

She lifted her hands as if to hide it, and turning away from him bowed her head upon the mantel-shelf. She felt that he was standing a little way behind her, but he made no attempt to touch her or come nearer.

"I know you've felt as I've felt," he said in a low voice— "that we belong to each other and that nothing can alter that. But other thoughts come, and you can't banish them. Whenever you see me you remember . . . you associate me with things you abhor . . . You've been generous—immeasurably. You've given me all the chances a woman could; but if it's only made you suffer, what's the use?"

She turned to him with a tear-stained face. "It hasn't only done that."

"Oh, no! I know . . . There've been moments . . ." He took her hand and raised it to his lips. "They'll be with me as long as I live. But I can't see you paying such a price for them. I'm not worth what I'm costing you."

She continued to gaze at him through tear-dilated eyes; and suddenly she flung out the question: "Wasn't it the Athénée you took her to that evening?"

"Anna—Anna!"

"Yes; I want to know now: to know everything. Perhaps that will make me forget. I ought to have made you tell me before. Wherever we go, I imagine you've been there with her . . . I see you together. I want to know how it began, where you went, why you left her . . . I can't go on in this darkness any longer!"

She did not know what had prompted her passionate outburst, but already she felt lighter, freer, as if at last the evil spell were broken. "I want to know everything," she repeated. "It's the only way to make me forget."

After she had ceased speaking Darrow remained where he was, his arms folded, his eyes lowered, immovable. She waited, her gaze on his face.

"Aren't you going to tell me?"

"No."

The blood rushed to her temples. "You won't? Why not?"

"If I did, do you suppose you'd forget *that*?"

"Oh—" she moaned, and turned away from him.

"You see it's impossible," he went on. "I've done a thing I loathe, and to atone for it you ask me to do another. What sort of satisfaction would that give you? It would put something irremediable between us."

She leaned her elbow against the mantel-shelf and hid her face in her hands. She had the sense that she was vainly throwing away her last hope of happiness, yet she could do nothing, think of nothing, to save it. The conjecture flashed through her: "Should I be at peace if I gave him up?" and she remembered the desolation of the days after she had sent him away, and understood that that hope was vain. The tears welled through her lids and ran slowly down between her fingers.

"Good-bye," she heard him say, and his footsteps turned to the door.

She tried to raise her head, but the weight of her despair bowed it down. She said to herself: "This is the end . . . he won't try to appeal to me again . . ." and she remained in a sort of tranced rigidity, perceiving without feeling the fateful lapse of the seconds. Then the cords that bound her seemed to snap, and she lifted her head and saw him going.

"Why, he's mine—he's mine! He's no one else's!" His face was turned to her and the look in his eyes swept away all her terrors. She no longer understood what had prompted her senseless outcry; and the mortal sweetness of loving him became again the one real fact in the world.

XXXIX

Anna, the next day, woke to a humiliated memory of the previous evening.

Darrow had been right in saying that their sacrifice would benefit no one; yet she seemed dimly to discern that there were obligations not to be tested by that standard. She owed it, at any rate, as much to his pride as to hers to abstain from the repetition of such scenes; and she had learned that it was beyond her power to do so while they were together. Yet when he had given her the chance to free herself, everything had vanished from her mind but the blind fear of losing him; and she saw that he and she were as profoundly and inextricably bound together as two trees with interwoven roots.

For a long time she brooded on her plight, vaguely conscious that the only escape from it must come from some external chance. And slowly the occasion shaped itself in her mind. It was Sophy Viner only who could save her—Sophy Viner only who could give her back her lost serenity. She would seek the girl out and tell her that she had given Darrow up; and that step once taken there would be no retracing it, and she would perforce have to go forward alone.

Any pretext for action was a kind of anodyne, and she despatched her maid to the Farlows' with a note asking if Miss Viner would receive her. There was a long delay before the maid returned, and when at last she appeared it was with a slip of paper on which an address was written, and a verbal message to the effect that Miss Viner had left some days previously, and was staying with her sister in a hotel near the Place de l'Etoile. The maid added that Mrs. Farlow, on the plea that Miss Viner's plans were uncertain, had at first made some difficulty about giving this information; and Anna guessed that the girl had left her friends' roof, and instructed them to withhold her address, with the object of avoiding Owen. "She's kept faith with herself and I haven't," Anna mused; and the thought was a fresh incentive to action.

Darrow had announced his intention of coming soon after luncheon, and the morning was already so far advanced that Anna, still mistrustful of her strength, decided to drive immediately to the address Mrs. Farlow had given. On the way there she tried to recall what she had heard of Sophy Viner's sister, but beyond the girl's enthusiastic report of the absent Laura's loveliness she could remember only certain vague allusions of Mrs. Farlow's to her artistic endowments and matrimonial vicissitudes. Darrow had mentioned her but once, and in the briefest terms, as having apparently very little concern for Sophy's welfare, and being, at any rate, too geographically remote to give her any practical support; and Anna wondered what chance had brought her to her sister's side at this conjunction. Mrs. Farlow had spoken of her as a celebrity (in what line Anna failed to recall); but Mrs. Farlow's celebrities were legion, and the name on the slip of paper—Mrs. McTarvie-Birch—did not seem to have any definite association with fame.

While Anna waited in the dingy vestibule of the *Hôtel Chicago* she had so distinct a vision of what she meant to say to Sophy Viner that the girl seemed already to be before her; and her heart dropped from all the height of its courage when the porter, after a long delay, returned with the announcement that Miss Viner was no longer in the hotel. Anna, doubtful if she understood, asked if he merely meant that the young lady was out at the moment; but he replied that she had gone away the day before. Beyond this he had no information to impart, and after a moment's hesitation Anna sent him back to enquire if Mrs. McTarvie-Birch would receive her. She reflected that Sophy had probably pledged her sister to the same secrecy as Mrs. Farlow, and that a personal appeal to Mrs. Birch might lead to less negative results.

There was another long interval of suspense before the porter reappeared with an affirmative answer; and a third while an exiguous and hesitating lift bore her up past a succession of shabby landings.

When the last was reached, and her guide had directed her down a winding passage that smelt of sea-going luggage, she found herself before a door through which a strong odour of tobacco reached her simultaneously with the sounds of a suppressed altercation. Her knock was followed by a silence, and after a minute or two the door was opened by a handsome young man whose ruffled hair and general air of creased disorder led her to conclude that he had just risen from a long-limbed sprawl on a sofa strewn with tumbled cushions. This sofa, and a grand piano bearing a basket of faded roses, a biscuit-tin and a devastated breakfast tray, almost filled the narrow sitting-room, in the remaining corner of which another man, short, swarthy and humble, sat examining the lining of his hat.

Anna paused in doubt; but on her naming Mrs. Birch the young man politely invited her to enter, at the same time casting an impatient glance at the mute spectator in the background.

The latter, raising his eyes, which were round and bulging, fixed them, not on the young man but on Anna, whom, for a moment, he scrutinized as searchingly as the interior of his hat. Under his gaze she had the sense of being minutely catalogued and valued; and the impression, when he finally rose and moved toward the door, of having been accepted as a better guarantee than he had had any reason to hope for. On the threshold his glance crossed that of the young man in an exchange of intelligence as full as it was rapid; and this brief scene left Anna so oddly enlightened that she felt no surprise when her companion, pushing an arm-chair forward, sociably asked her if she wouldn't have a cigarette. Her polite refusal provoked the remark that *he* would, if she'd no objection; and while he groped for matches in his loose pockets, and behind the photographs and letters crowding the narrow mantel-shelf, she ventured another enquiry for Mrs. Birch.

"Just a minute," he smiled; "I think the *masseur's* with her." He spoke in a smooth denationalized English, which, like the look in his long-lashed eyes and the promptness of his charming smile, suggested a long training in all the arts of expediency. Having finally discovered a match-box on the floor beside the sofa, he lit his cigarette and dropped back among the cushions; and on Anna's remarking that she was sorry to disturb Mrs. Birch he replied that that was all right, and that she always kept everybody waiting.

After this, through the haze of his perpetually renewed cigarettes, they continued to chat for some time of indifferent topics; but when at last Anna again suggested the possibility of her seeing Mrs. Birch he rose from his corner with a slight shrug, and murmuring: "She's perfectly hopeless," lounged off through an inner door.

Anna was still wondering when and in what conjunction of circumstances the much-married Laura had acquired a partner so conspicuous for his personal charms, when the young man returned to announce: "She says it's all right, if you don't mind seeing her in bed."

He drew aside to let Anna pass, and she found herself in a dim untidy scented room, with a pink curtain pinned across its single window, and a lady with a great deal of fair hair and uncovered neck smiling at her from a pink bed on which an immense powder-puff trailed.

"You don't mind, do you? He costs such a frightful lot that I can't afford to send him off," Mrs. Birch explained, extending a thickly-ringed hand to Anna, and leaving her in doubt as to whether the person alluded to were her *masseur* or her husband. Before a reply was possible there was a convulsive stir beneath the pink expanse, and something that resembled another powder-puff hurled itself at Anna with a volley of sounds like the popping of Lilliputian champagne corks. Mrs. Birch, flinging herself forward, gasped out: "If you'd just give him a caramel . . . there, in that box on the dressing-table . . . it's the only earthly thing to stop him . . ." and when Anna had proffered this sop to her assailant, and he had withdrawn with it beneath the bedspread, his mistress sank back with a laugh.

"Isn't he a beauty? The Prince gave him to me down at Nice the other day—but he's perfectly awful," she confessed, beaming intimately on her visitor. In the roseate penumbra of the bed-curtains she presented to Anna's startled gaze an odd chromo-like resemblance to Sophy Viner, or a suggestion, rather, of what Sophy Viner might, with the years and in spite of the powder-puff, become. Larger, blonder, heavier-featured, she yet had glances and movements that disturbingly suggested what was freshest and most engaging in the girl; and as she stretched her bare plump arm across the bed she seemed to be pulling back the veil from dingy distances of family history.

"Do sit down, if there's a place to sit on," she cordially advised; adding, as Anna took the edge of a chair hung with miscellaneous raiment: "My singing takes so much time that I don't get a chance to walk the fat off—that's the worst of being an artist."

Anna murmured an assent. "I hope it hasn't inconvenienced you to see me; I told Mr. Birch——"

"Mr. *who*?" the recumbent beauty asked; and then: "Oh, *Jimmy!*" she faintly laughed, as if more for her own enlightenment than Anna's.

The latter continued eagerly: "I understand from Mrs. Farlow that your sister was with you, and I ventured to come up because I wanted to ask you when I should have a chance of finding her."

Mrs. McTarvie-Birch threw back her head with a long stare. "Do you mean to say the idiot at the door didn't tell you? Sophy went away last night."

"Last night?" Anna echoed. A sudden terror had possessed her. Could it be that the girl had tricked them all and gone with Owen? The idea was incredible, yet it took such hold of her that she could hardly steady her lips to say: "The porter did tell me, but I thought perhaps he was mistaken. Mrs. Farlow seemed to think that I should find her here."

"It was all so sudden that I don't suppose she had time to let the Farlows know. She didn't get Mrs. Murrett's wire till yesterday, and she just pitched her things into a trunk and rushed——"

"Mrs. Murrett?"

"Why, yes. Sophy's gone to India with Mrs. Murrett; they're to meet at Brindisi," Sophy's sister said with a calm smile.

Anna sat motionless, gazing at the disordered room, the pink bed, the trivial face among the pillows.

Mrs. McTarvie-Birch pursued: "They had a fearful kick-up last spring—I daresay you knew about it—but I told Sophy she'd better lump it, as long as the old woman was willing to . . . As an artist, of course, it's perfectly impossible for me to have her with me . . ."

"Of course," Anna mechanically assented.

Through the confused pain of her thoughts she was hardly aware that Mrs. Birch's explanations were still continuing. "Naturally I didn't altogether approve of her going back to that beast of a woman. I said all I could . . . I told her she was a fool to chuck up such a place as yours. But Sophy's restless—always was—and she's taken it into her head she'd rather travel . . ."

Anna rose from her seat, groping for some formula of leave-taking. The pushing back of her chair roused the white dog's smouldering animosity, and he drowned his mistress's further confidences in another outburst of hysterics. Through the tumult Anna signed an inaudible farewell, and Mrs. Birch, having momentarily succeeded in suppressing her pet under a pillow, called out: "Do come again! I'd love to sing to you."

Anna murmured a word of thanks and turned to the door. As she opened it she heard her hostess crying after her: "Jimmy! Do you hear me? Jimmy *Brance!*" and then, there being no response from the person summoned: "*Do* tell him he must go and call the lift for you!"

THE END.

THE CUSTOM
OF THE COUNTRY

I

"Undine Spragg—how *can* you?" her mother wailed, raising a prematurely-wrinkled hand heavy with rings to defend the note which a languid "bell-boy" had just brought in.

But her defence was as feeble as her protest, and she continued to smile on her visitor while Miss Spragg, with a turn of her quick young fingers, possessed herself of the missive and withdrew to the window to read it.

"I guess it's meant for me," she merely threw over her shoulder at her mother.

"Did you *ever*, Mrs. Heeny?" Mrs. Spragg murmured with deprecating pride.

Mrs. Heeny, a stout professional-looking person in a waterproof, her rusty veil thrown back, and a shabby alligator bag at her feet, followed the mother's glance with good-humoured approval.

"I never met with a lovelier form," she agreed, answering the spirit rather than the letter of her hostess's enquiry.

Mrs. Spragg and her visitor were enthroned in two heavy gilt armchairs in one of the private drawing-rooms of the Hotel Stentorian. The Spragg rooms were known as one of the Looey suites, and the drawing-room walls, above their wainscoting of highly-varnished mahogany, were hung with salmon-pink damask and adorned with oval portraits of Marie Antoinette and the Princess de Lamballe. In the centre of the florid carpet a gilt table with a top of Mexican onyx sustained a palm in a gilt basket tied with a pink bow. But for this ornament, and a copy of "The Hound of the Baskervilles" which lay beside it, the room showed no traces of human use, and Mrs. Spragg herself wore as complete an air of detachment as if she had been a wax figure in a show-window. Her attire was fashionable enough to justify such a post, and her pale soft-cheeked face, with puffy eye-lids and drooping mouth, suggested a partially-melted wax figure which had run to double-chin.

Mrs. Heeny, in comparison, had a reassuring look of solidity and reality. The planting of her firm black bulk in its chair, and the grasp of her broad red hands on the gilt arms, bespoke an organized and self-reliant activity, accounted for by the fact that Mrs. Heeny was a "society" manicure and masseuse. Toward Mrs. Spragg and her daughter she filled the double rôle of manipulator and friend; and it was in the latter capacity that, her day's task ended, she had dropped in for a moment to "cheer up" the lonely ladies of the Stentorian.

The young girl whose "form" had won Mrs. Heeny's professional commendation suddenly shifted its lovely lines as she turned back from the window.

"Here—you can have it after all," she said, crumpling the note and tossing it with a contemptuous gesture into her mother's lap.

"Why—isn't it from Mr. Popple?" Mrs. Spragg exclaimed unguardedly.

"No—it isn't. What made you think I thought it was?" snapped her daughter; but the next instant she added, with an outbreak of childish disappointment: "It's only from Mr. Marvell's sister—at least she says she's his sister."

Mrs. Spragg, with a puzzled frown, groped for her eyeglass among the jet fringes of her tightly-girded front.

Mrs. Heeny's small blue eyes shot out sparks of curiosity. "Marvell—what Marvell is that?"

The girl explained languidly: "A little fellow—I think Mr. Popple said his name was Ralph"; while her mother continued: "Undine met them both last night at that party downstairs. And from something Mr. Popple said to her about going to one of the new plays, she thought——"

"How on earth do you know what I thought?" Undine flashed back, her grey eyes darting warnings at her mother under their straight black brows.

"Why, you *said* you thought——" Mrs. Spragg began reproachfully; but Mrs. Heeny, heedless of their bickerings, was pursuing her own train of thought.

"What Popple? Claud Walsingham Popple—the portrait painter?"

"Yes—I suppose so. He said he'd like to paint me. Mabel Lipscomb introduced him. I don't care if I never see him again," the girl said, bathed in angry pink.

"Do you know him, Mrs. Heeny?" Mrs. Spragg enquired.

"I should say I did. I manicured him for his first society portrait—a full-length of Mrs. Harmon B. Driscoll." Mrs. Heeny smiled indulgently on her hearers. "I know everybody. If they don't know *me* they ain't in it, and Claud Walsingham Popple's in it. But he ain't nearly *as* in it," she continued judicially, "as Ralph Marvell—the little fellow, as you call him."

Undine Spragg, at the word, swept round on the speaker with one of the quick turns that revealed her youthful flexibility. She was always doubling and twisting on herself, and every movement she made seemed to start at the nape of her neck, just below the lifted roll of reddish-gold hair, and flow without a break through her whole slim length to the tips of her fingers and the points of her slender restless feet.

"Why, do you know the Marvells? Are *they* stylish?" she asked.

Mrs. Heeny gave the discouraged gesture of a pedagogue who has vainly striven to implant the rudiments of knowledge in a rebellious mind.

"Why, Undine Spragg, I've told you all about them time and again! His mother was a Dagonet. They live with old Urban Dagonet down in Washington Square."

To Mrs. Spragg this conveyed even less than to her daughter. " 'way down there? Why do they live with somebody else? Haven't they got the means to have a home of their own?"

Undine's perceptions were more rapid, and she fixed her eyes searchingly on Mrs. Heeny.

"Do you mean to say Mr. Marvell's as swell as Mr. Popple?"

"*As swell?* Why, Claud Walsingham Popple ain't in the same class with him!"

The girl was upon her mother with a spring, snatching and smoothing out the crumpled note.

"Laura Fairford—is that the sister's name?"

"Mrs. Henley Fairford; yes. What does she write about?"

Undine's face lit up as if a shaft of sunset had struck it through the triple-curtained windows of the Stentorian.

"She says she wants me to dine with her next Wednesday.

Isn't it queer? Why does *she* want me? She's never seen me!"
Her tone implied that she had long been accustomed to being
" wanted" by those who had.

Mrs. Heeny laughed. "*He* saw you, didn't he?"

"Who? Ralph Marvell? Why, of course he did—Mr. Popple brought him to the party here last night."

"Well, there you are. . . When a young man in society
wants to meet a girl again, he gets his sister to ask her."

Undine stared at her incredulously. "How queer! But they
haven't all got sisters, have they? It must be fearfully poky for
the ones that haven't."

"They get their mothers—or their married friends," said
Mrs. Heeny omnisciently.

"Married gentlemen?" enquired Mrs. Spragg, slightly
shocked, but genuinely desirous of mastering her lesson.

"Mercy, no! Married ladies."

"But are there never any gentlemen present?" pursued Mrs.
Spragg, feeling that if this were the case Undine would certainly be disappointed.

"Present where? At their dinners? Of course—Mrs. Fairford gives the smartest little dinners in town. There was an
account of one she gave last week in this morning's *Town
Talk*: I guess it's right here among my clippings." Mrs.
Heeny, swooping down on her bag, drew from it a handful
of newspaper cuttings, which she spread on her ample lap and
proceeded to sort with a moistened forefinger. "Here," she
said, holding one of the slips at arm's length; and throwing
back her head she read, in a slow unpunctuated chant: " 'Mrs.
Henley Fairford gave another of her natty little dinners last
Wednesday as usual it was smart small and exclusive and there
was much gnashing of teeth among the left-outs as Madame
Olga Loukowska gave some of her new steppe dances after
dinner'——that's the French for new dance steps," Mrs.
Heeny concluded, thrusting the documents back into her bag.

"Do you know Mrs. Fairford too?" Undine asked eagerly;
while Mrs. Spragg, impressed, but anxious for facts, pursued:
"Does she reside on Fifth Avenue?"

"No, she has a little house in Thirty-eighth Street, down
beyond Park Avenue."

The ladies' faces drooped again, and the masseuse went on

promptly: "But they're glad enough to have her in the big houses!—Why, yes, I know her," she said, addressing herself to Undine. "I mass'd her for a sprained ankle a couple of years ago. She's got a lovely manner, but *no* conversation. Some of my patients converse exquisitely," Mrs. Heeny added with discrimination.

Undine was brooding over the note. "It *is* written to mother—Mrs. Abner E. Spragg—I never saw anything so funny! 'Will you *allow* your daughter to dine with me?' Allow! Is Mrs. Fairford peculiar?"

"No—you are," said Mrs. Heeny bluntly. "Don't you know it's the thing in the best society to pretend that girls can't do anything without their mothers' permission? You just remember that, Undine. You mustn't accept invitations from gentlemen without you say you've got to ask your mother first."

"Mercy! But how'll mother know what to say?"

"Why, she'll say what you tell her to, of course. You'd better tell her you want to dine with Mrs. Fairford," Mrs. Heeny added humorously, as she gathered her waterproof together and stooped for her bag.

"Have I got to write the note, then?" Mrs. Spragg asked with rising agitation.

Mrs. Heeny reflected. "Why, no. I guess Undine can write it as if it was from you. Mrs. Fairford don't know your writing."

This was an evident relief to Mrs. Spragg, and as Undine swept to her room with the note her mother sank back, murmuring plaintively: "Oh, don't go yet, Mrs. Heeny. I haven't seen a human being all day, and I can't seem to find anything to say to that French maid."

Mrs. Heeny looked at her hostess with friendly compassion. She was well aware that she was the only bright spot on Mrs. Spragg's horizon. Since the Spraggs, some two years previously, had moved from Apex City to New York, they had made little progress in establishing relations with their new environment; and when, about four months earlier, Mrs. Spragg's doctor had called in Mrs. Heeny to minister professionally to his patient, he had done more for her spirit than for her body. Mrs. Heeny had had such "cases" before: she knew the rich helpless family, stranded in lonely splendour in a sumptuous West Side hotel, with a father compelled to seek a semblance of social life at the hotel bar, and a mother deprived of even this contact with her kind, and reduced to illness by boredom and inactivity. Poor Mrs. Spragg had done her own washing in her youth, but since her rising fortunes had made this occupation unsuitable she had sunk into the relative inertia which the ladies of Apex City regarded as one of the prerogatives of affluence. At Apex, however, she had belonged to a social club, and, until they moved to the Mealey House, had been kept busy by the incessant struggle with domestic cares; whereas New York seemed to offer no field for any form of lady-like activity. She therefore took her exercise vicariously, with Mrs. Heeny's help; and Mrs. Heeny knew how to manipulate her imagination as well as her muscles. It was Mrs. Heeny who peopled the solitude of the long ghostly days with lively anecdotes of the Van Degens, the Driscolls, the Chauncey Ellings and the other social potentates whose least doings Mrs. Spragg and Undine had followed from afar in the Apex papers, and who had come to seem so much more remote since only the width of the Central Park divided mother and daughter from their Olympian portals.

Mrs. Spragg had no ambition for herself—she seemed to have transferred her whole personality to her child—but she was passionately resolved that Undine should have what she wanted, and she sometimes fancied that Mrs. Heeny, who crossed those sacred thresholds so familiarly, might some day gain admission for Undine.

"Well—I'll stay a little mite longer if you want; and supposing I was to rub up your nails while we're talking? It'll be more sociable," the masseuse suggested, lifting her bag to the table and covering its shiny onyx surface with bottles and polishers.

Mrs. Spragg consentingly slipped the rings from her small mottled hands. It was soothing to feel herself in Mrs. Heeny's grasp, and though she knew the attention would cost her three dollars she was secure in the sense that Abner wouldn't mind. It had been clear to Mrs. Spragg, ever since their rather precipitate departure from Apex City, that Abner was resolved not to mind—resolved at any cost to "see through" the New York adventure. It seemed likely now that the cost would be considerable. They had lived in New York for two years without any social benefit to their daughter; and it was of course for that purpose that they had come. If, at the time, there had been other and more pressing reasons, they were such as Mrs. Spragg and her husband never touched on, even in the gilded privacy of their bedroom at the Stentorian; and so completely had silence closed in on the subject that to Mrs. Spragg it had become non-existent: she really believed that, as Abner put it, they had left Apex because Undine was too big for the place.

She seemed as yet—poor child!—too small for New York: actually imperceptible to its heedless multitudes; and her mother trembled for the day when her invisibility should be borne in on her. Mrs. Spragg did not mind the long delay for herself—she had stores of lymphatic patience. But she had noticed lately that Undine was beginning to be nervous, and there was nothing that Undine's parents dreaded so much as her being nervous. Mrs. Spragg's maternal apprehensions unconsciously escaped in her next words.

"I do hope she'll quiet down now," she murmured, feeling quieter herself as her hand sank into Mrs. Heeny's roomy palm.

"Who's that? Undine?"

"Yes. She seemed so set on that Mr. Popple's coming round. From the way he acted last night she thought he'd be sure to come round this morning. She's so lonesome, poor child—I can't say as I blame her."

"Oh, he'll come round. Things don't happen as quick as that in New York," said Mrs. Heeny, driving her nail-polisher cheeringly.

Mrs. Spragg sighed again. "They don't appear to. They say New Yorkers are always in a hurry; but I can't say as they've hurried much to make our acquaintance."

Mrs. Heeny drew back to study the effect of her work. "You wait, Mrs. Spragg, you wait. If you go too fast you sometimes have to rip out the whole seam."

"Oh, that's so—that's *so!*" Mrs. Spragg exclaimed, with a tragic emphasis that made the masseuse glance up at her.

"Of course it's so. And it's more so in New York than any-where. The wrong set's like fly-paper: once you're in it you can pull and pull, but you'll never get out of it again."

Undine's mother heaved another and more helpless sigh. "I wish *you'd* tell Undine that, Mrs. Heeny."

"Oh, I guess Undine's all right. A girl like her can afford to wait. And if young Marvell's really taken with her she'll have the run of the place in no time."

This solacing thought enabled Mrs. Spragg to yield herself unreservedly to Mrs. Heeny's ministrations, which were pro-longed for a happy confidential hour; and she had just bidden the masseuse good-bye, and was restoring the rings to her fingers, when the door opened to admit her husband.

Mr. Spragg came in silently, setting his high hat down on the centre-table, and laying his overcoat across one of the gilt chairs. He was tallish, grey-bearded and somewhat stooping, with the slack figure of the sedentary man who would be stout if he were not dyspeptic; and his cautious grey eyes with pouch-like underlids had straight black brows like his daugh-ter's. His thin hair was worn a little too long over his coat collar, and a Masonic emblem dangled from the heavy gold chain which crossed his crumpled black waistcoat.

He stood still in the middle of the room, casting a slow pioneering glance about its gilded void; then he said gently: "Well, mother?"

Mrs. Spragg remained seated, but her eyes dwelt on him affectionately.

"Undine's been asked out to a dinner-party; and Mrs. Heeny says it's to one of the first families. It's the sister of one of the gentlemen that Mabel Lipscomb introduced her to last night."

There was a mild triumph in her tone, for it was owing to her insistence and Undine's that Mr. Spragg had been in-duced to give up the house they had bought in West End Avenue, and move with his family to the Stentorian. Undine had early decided that they could not hope to get on while they "kept house"—all the fashionable people she knew either boarded or lived in hotels. Mrs. Spragg was easily in-duced to take the same view, but Mr. Spragg had resisted, being at the moment unable either to sell his house or to let it as advantageously as he had hoped. After the move was made it seemed for a time as though he had been right, and the first social steps would be as difficult to make in a hotel as in one's own house; and Mrs. Spragg was therefore eager to have him know that Undine really owed her first invitation to a meeting under the roof of the Stentorian.

"You see we were right to come here, Abner," she added, and he absently rejoined: "I guess you two always manage to be right."

But his face remained unsmiling, and instead of seating himself and lighting his cigar, as he usually did before dinner, he took two or three aimless turns about the room, and then paused in front of his wife.

"What's the matter—anything wrong down town?" she asked, her eyes reflecting his anxiety.

Mrs. Spragg's knowledge of what went on "down town" was of the most elementary kind, but her husband's face was the barometer in which she had long been accustomed to read the leave to go on unrestrictedly, or the warning to pause and abstain till the coming storm should be weathered.

He shook his head. "N—no. Nothing worse than what I can see to, if you and Undine will go steady for a while." He paused and looked across the room at his daughter's door. "Where is she—out?"

"I guess she's in her room, going over her dresses with that French maid. I don't know as she's got anything fit to wear to that dinner," Mrs. Spragg added in a tentative murmur.

Mr. Spragg smiled at last. "Well—I guess she *will* have," he said prophetically.

He glanced again at his daughter's door, as if to make sure of its being shut; then, standing close before his wife, he lowered his voice to say: "I saw Elmer Moffatt down town to-day."

"Oh, Abner!" A wave of almost physical apprehension passed over Mrs. Spragg. Her jewelled hands trembled in her black brocade lap, and the pulpy curves of her face collapsed as if it were a pricked balloon.

"Oh, Abner," she moaned again, her eyes also on her daughter's door.

Mr. Spragg's black eyebrows gathered in an angry frown, but it was evident that his anger was not against his wife.

"What's the good of Oh Abner-ing? Elmer Moffatt's nothing to us—no more'n if we never laid eyes on him."

"No—I know it; but what's he doing here? Did you speak to him?" she faltered.

He slipped his thumbs into his waistcoat pockets. "No—I guess Elmer and I are pretty well talked out."

Mrs. Spragg took up her moan. "Don't you tell her you saw him, Abner."

"I'll do as you say; but she may meet him herself."

"Oh, I guess not—not in this new set she's going with! Don't tell her *anyhow*."

He turned away, feeling for one of the cigars which he always carried loose in his pocket; and his wife, rising, stole after him, and laid her hand on his arm.

"He can't do anything to her, can he?"

"Do anything to her?" He swung about furiously. "I'd like to see him touch her—that's all!"

II

Undine's white and gold bedroom, with sea-green panels and old rose carpet, looked along Seventy-second Street toward the leafless tree-tops of the Central Park.

She went to the window, and drawing back its many layers of lace gazed eastward down the long brown-stone perspective. Beyond the Park lay Fifth Avenue—and Fifth Avenue was where she wanted to be!

She turned back into the room, and going to her writing-table laid Mrs. Fairford's note before her, and began to study it minutely. She had read in the "Boudoir Chat" of one of the Sunday papers that the smartest women were using the new pigeon-blood note-paper with white ink; and rather against her mother's advice she had ordered a large supply, with her monogram in silver. It was a disappointment, therefore, to find that Mrs. Fairford wrote on the old-fashioned white sheet, without even a monogram—simply her address and telephone number. It gave Undine rather a poor opinion of Mrs. Fairford's social standing, and for a moment she thought with considerable satisfaction of answering the note on her pigeon-blood paper. Then she remembered Mrs. Heeny's emphatic commendation of Mrs. Fairford, and her pen wavered. What if white paper were really newer than pigeon-blood? It might be more stylish, anyhow. Well, she didn't care if Mrs. Fairford didn't like red paper—*she* did! And she wasn't going to truckle to any woman who lived in a small house down beyond Park Avenue. . .

Undine was fiercely independent and yet passionately imitative. She wanted to surprise every one by her dash and originality, but she could not help modelling herself on the last person she met, and the confusion of ideals thus produced caused her much perturbation when she had to choose between two courses. She hesitated a moment longer, and then took from the drawer a plain sheet with the hotel address.

It was amusing to write the note in her mother's name—she giggled as she formed the phrase "I shall be happy to permit my daughter to take dinner with you" ("take dinner" seemed more elegant than Mrs. Fairford's "dine")—but when she came to the signature she was met by a new difficulty. Mrs. Fairford had signed herself "Laura Fairford"—just as one school-girl would write to another. But could this be a proper model for Mrs. Spragg? Undine could not tolerate the thought of her mother's abasing herself to a denizen of regions beyond Park Avenue, and she resolutely formed the signature: "Sincerely, Mrs. Abner E. Spragg." Then uncertainty overcame her, and she re-wrote her note and copied Mrs. Fairford's formula: "Yours sincerely, Leota B. Spragg." But this struck her as an odd juxtaposition of formality and freedom, and she made a third attempt: "Yours with love, Leota B. Spragg." This, however, seemed excessive, as the ladies had never met; and after several other experiments she finally decided on a compromise, and ended the note: "Yours sincerely, Mrs. Leota B. Spragg." That might be conventional, Undine reflected, but it was certainly correct.

This point settled, she flung open her door, calling imperiously down the passage: "Céleste!" and adding, as the French maid appeared: "I want to look over all my dinner-dresses."

Considering the extent of Miss Spragg's wardrobe her dinner-dresses were not many. She had ordered a number the year before but, vexed at her lack of use for them, had tossed them over impatiently to the maid. Since then, indeed, she and Mrs. Spragg had succumbed to the abstract pleasure of buying two or three more, simply because they were too exquisite and Undine looked too lovely in them; but she had grown tired of these also—tired of seeing them hang unworn in her wardrobe, like so many derisive points of interrogation. And now, as Céleste spread them out on the bed, they seemed disgustingly common-place, and as familiar as if she had danced them to shreds. Nevertheless, she yielded to the maid's persuasions and tried them on.

The first and second did not gain by prolonged inspection: they looked old-fashioned already. "It's something about the sleeves," Undine grumbled as she threw them aside.

The third was certainly the prettiest; but then it was the one she had worn at the hotel dance the night before, and the impossibility of wearing it again within the week was too obvious for discussion. Yet she enjoyed looking at herself in it, for it reminded her of her sparkling passages with Claud

Walsingham Popple, and her quieter but more fruitful talk with his little friend—the young man she had hardly noticed.

"You can go, Céleste—I'll take off the dress myself," she said: and when Céleste had passed out, laden with discarded finery, Undine bolted her door, dragged the tall pier-glass forward and, rummaging in a drawer for fan and gloves, swept to a seat before the mirror with the air of a lady arriving at an evening party. Céleste, before leaving, had drawn down the blinds and turned on the electric light, and the white and gold room, with its blazing wall-brackets, formed a sufficiently brilliant background to carry out the illusion. So untempered a glare would have been destructive to all half-tones and subtleties of modelling; but Undine's beauty was as vivid, and almost as crude, as the brightness suffusing it. Her black brows, her reddish-tawny hair and the pure red and white of her complexion defied the searching decomposing radiance: she might have been some fabled creature whose home was in a beam of light.

Undine, as a child, had taken but a lukewarm interest in the diversions of her playmates. Even in the early days when she had lived with her parents in a ragged outskirt of Apex, and hung on the fence with Indiana Frusk, the freckled daughter of the plumber "across the way," she had cared little for dolls or skipping-ropes, and still less for the riotous games in which the loud Indiana played Atalanta to all the boyhood of the quarter. Already Undine's chief delight was to "dress up" in her mother's Sunday skirt and "play lady" before the wardrobe mirror. The taste had outlasted childhood, and she still practised the same secret pantomime, gliding in, settling her skirts, swaying her fan, moving her lips in soundless talk and laughter; but lately she had shrunk from everything that reminded her of her baffled social yearnings. Now, however, she could yield without afterthought to the joy of dramatizing her beauty. Within a few days she would be enacting the scene she was now mimicking; and it amused her to see in advance just what impression she would produce on Mrs. Fairford's guests.

For a while she carried on her chat with an imaginary circle of admirers, twisting this way and that, fanning, fidgeting, twitching at her draperies, as she did in real life when people were noticing her. Her incessant movements were not the result of shyness: she thought it the correct thing to be animated in society, and noise and restlessness were her only notion of vivacity. She therefore watched herself approvingly, admiring the light on her hair, the flash of teeth between her smiling lips, the pure shadows of her throat and shoulders as she passed from one attitude to another. Only one fact disturbed her: there was a hint of too much fulness in the curves of her neck and in the spring of her hips. She was tall enough to carry off a little extra weight, but excessive slimness was the fashion, and she shuddered at the thought that she might some day deviate from the perpendicular.

Presently she ceased to twist and sparkle at her image, and sinking into her chair gave herself up to retrospection. She was vexed, in looking back, to think how little notice she had taken of young Marvell, who turned out to be so much less negligible than his brilliant friend. She remembered thinking him rather shy, less accustomed to society; and though in his quiet deprecating way he had said one or two droll things he lacked Mr. Popple's masterly manner, his domineering yet caressing address. When Mr. Popple had fixed his black eyes on Undine, and murmured something "artistic" about the colour of her hair, she had thrilled to the depths of her being. Even now it seemed incredible that he should not turn out to be more distinguished than young Marvell: he seemed so much more in the key of the world she read about in the Sunday papers—the dazzling auriferous world of the Van Degens, the Driscolls and their peers.

She was roused by the sound in the hall of her mother's last words to Mrs. Heeny. Undine waited till their adieux were over; then, opening her door, she seized the astonished masseuse and dragged her into the room.

Mrs. Heeny gazed in admiration at the luminous apparition in whose hold she found herself.

"Mercy, Undine—you do look stunning! Are you trying on your dress for Mrs. Fairford's?"

"Yes—no—this is only an old thing." The girl's eyes glittered under their black brows. "Mrs. Heeny, you've got to tell me the truth—*are* they as swell as you said?"

"Who? The Fairfords and Marvells? If they ain't swell

enough for you, Undine Spragg, you'd better go right over to the court of England!"

Undine straightened herself. "I want the best. Are they as swell as the Driscolls and Van Degens?"

Mrs. Heeny sounded a scornful laugh. "Look at here, now, you unbelieving girl! As sure as I'm standing here before you, I've seen Mrs. Harmon B. Driscoll of Fifth Avenue laying in her pink velvet bed with Honiton lace sheets on it, and crying her eyes out because she couldn't get asked to one of Mrs. Paul Marvell's musicals. She'd never 'a dreamt of being asked to a dinner there! Not all of her money couldn't 'a bought her that—and she knows it!"

Undine stood for a moment with bright cheeks and parted lips; then she flung her soft arms about the masseuse.

"Oh, Mrs. Heeny—you're lovely to me!" she breathed, her lips on Mrs. Heeny's rusty veil; while the latter, freeing herself with a good-natured laugh, said as she turned away: "Go steady, Undine, and you'll get anywheres."

Go steady, Undine! Yes, that was the advice she needed. Sometimes, in her dark moods, she blamed her parents for not having given it to her. She was so young . . . and they had told her so little! As she looked back she shuddered at some of her escapes. Even since they had come to New York she had been on the verge of one or two perilous adventures, and there had been a moment during their first winter when she had actually engaged herself to the handsome Austrian riding-master who accompanied her in the Park. He had carelessly shown her a card-case with a coronet, and had confided in her that he had been forced to resign from a crack cavalry regiment for fighting a duel about a Countess; and as a result of these confidences she had pledged herself to him, and bestowed on him her pink pearl ring in exchange for one of twisted silver, which he said the Countess had given him on her deathbed with the request that he should never take it off till he met a woman more beautiful than herself.

Soon afterward, luckily, Undine had run across Mabel Lipscomb, whom she had known at a middle western boarding-school as Mabel Blitch. Miss Blitch occupied a position of distinction as the only New York girl at the school, and for a time there had been sharp rivalry for her favour between

Undine and Indiana Frusk, whose parents had somehow contrived—for one term—to obtain her admission to the same
establishment. In spite of Indiana's unscrupulous methods,
and of a certain violent way she had of capturing attention,
the victory remained with Undine, whom Mabel pronounced
more refined; and the discomfited Indiana, denouncing her
schoolmates as a "bunch of mushes," had disappeared forever
from the scene of her defeat.

Since then Mabel had returned to New York and married a
stock-broker; and Undine's first steps in social enlightenment
dated from the day when she had met Mrs. Harry Lipscomb,
and been again taken under her wing.

Harry Lipscomb had insisted on investigating the riding-
master's record, and had found that his real name was Aaronson, and that he had left Cracow under a charge of swindling servant-girls out of their savings; in the light of which
discoveries Undine noticed for the first time that his lips were
too red and that his hair was pommaded. That was one of
the episodes that sickened her as she looked back, and made
her resolve once more to trust less to her impulses—especially
in the matter of giving away rings. In the interval, however,
she felt she had learned a good deal, especially since, by
Mabel Lipscomb's advice, the Spraggs had moved to the
Stentorian, where that lady was herself established.

There was nothing of the monopolist about Mabel, and she
lost no time in making Undine free of the Stentorian group
and its affiliated branches: a society addicted to "days," and
linked together by membership in countless clubs, mundane,
cultural or "earnest." Mabel took Undine to the days, and
introduced her as a "guest" to the club-meetings, where she
was supported by the presence of many other guests—"my
friend Miss Stager, of Phalanx, Georgia," or (if the lady were
literary) simply "my friend Ora Prance Chettle of Nebraska—
you know what Mrs. Chettle stands for."

Some of these reunions took place in the lofty hotels
moored like a sonorously named fleet of battle-ships along the
upper reaches of the West Side: the Olympian, the Incandescent, the Ormolu; while others, perhaps the more exclusive,
were held in the equally lofty but more romantically styled
apartment-houses: the Parthenon, the Tintern Abbey or the

Lido. Undine's preference was for the worldly parties, at which games were played, and she returned home laden with prizes in Dutch silver; but she was duly impressed by the debating clubs, where ladies of local distinction addressed the company from an improvised platform, or the members argued on subjects of such imperishable interest as: "What is charm?" or "The Problem-Novel"—after which pink lemonade and rainbow sandwiches were consumed amid heated discussion of the "ethical aspect" of the question.

It was all very novel and interesting, and at first Undine envied Mabel Lipscomb for having made herself a place in such circles; but in time she began to despise her for being content to remain there. For it did not take Undine long to learn that introduction to Mabel's "set" had brought her no nearer to Fifth Avenue. Even in Apex, Undine's tender imagination had been nurtured on the feats and gestures of Fifth Avenue. She knew all of New York's golden aristocracy by name, and the lineaments of its most distinguished scions had been made familiar by passionate poring over the daily press. In Mabel's world she sought in vain for the originals, and only now and then caught a tantalizing glimpse of one of their familiars: as when Claud Walsingham Popple, engaged on the portrait of a lady whom the Lipscombs described as "the wife of a Steel Magnet," felt it his duty to attend one of his client's teas, where it became Mabel's privilege to make his acquaintance and to name to him her friend Miss Spragg.

Unsuspected social gradations were thus revealed to the attentive Undine, but she was beginning to think that her sad proficiency had been acquired in vain when her hopes were revived by the appearance of Mr. Popple and his friend at the Stentorian dance. She thought she had learned enough to be safe from any risk of repeating the hideous Aaronson mistake; yet she now saw she had blundered again in distinguishing Claud Walsingham Popple while she almost snubbed his more retiring companion. It was all very puzzling, and her perplexity had been farther increased by Mrs. Heeny's tale of the great Mrs. Harmon B. Driscoll's despair.

Hitherto Undine had imagined that the Driscoll and Van Degen clans and their allies held undisputed suzerainty over New York society. Mabel Lipscomb thought so too, and was given to bragging of her acquaintance with a Mrs. Spoff, who was merely a second cousin of Mrs. Harmon B. Driscoll's. Yet here was she, Undine Spragg of Apex, about to be introduced into an inner circle to which Driscolls and Van Degens had laid siege in vain! It was enough to make her feel a little dizzy with her triumph—to work her up into that state of perilous self-confidence in which all her worst follies had been committed.

She stood up and, going close to the glass, examined the reflection of her bright eyes and glowing cheeks. This time her fears were superfluous: there were to be no more mistakes and no more follies now! She was going to know the right people at last—she was going to get what she wanted!

As she stood there, smiling at her happy image, she heard her father's voice in the room beyond, and instantly began to tear off her dress, strip the long gloves from her arms and unpin the rose in her hair. Tossing the fallen finery aside, she slipped on a dressing-gown and opened the door into the drawing-room.

Mr. Spragg was standing near her mother, who sat in a drooping attitude, her head sunk on her breast, as she did when she had one of her "turns." He looked up abruptly as Undine entered.

"Father—has mother told you? Mrs. Fairford has asked me to dine. She's Mrs. Paul Marvell's daughter—Mrs. Marvell was a Dagonet—and they're sweller than anybody; they *won't know* the Driscolls and Van Degens!"

Mr. Spragg surveyed her with humorous fondness.

"That so? What do they want to know you for, I wonder?" he jeered.

"Can't imagine—unless they think I'll introduce *you*!" she jeered back in the same key, her arms around his stooping shoulders, her shining hair against his cheek.

"Well—and are you going to? Have you accepted?" he took up her joke as she held him pinioned; while Mrs. Spragg, behind them, stirred in her seat with a little moan.

Undine threw back her head, plunging her eyes in his, and pressing so close that to his tired elderly sight her face was a mere bright blur.

"I want to awfully," she declared, "but I haven't got a single thing to wear."

Mrs. Spragg, at this, moaned more audibly. "Undine, I wouldn't ask father to buy any more clothes right on top of those last bills."

"I ain't on top of those last bills yet—I'm way down under them," Mr. Spragg interrupted, raising his hands to imprison his daughter's slender wrists.

"Oh, well—if you want me to look like a scarecrow, and not get asked again, I've got a dress that'll do *perfectly*," Undine threatened, in a tone between banter and vexation.

Mr. Spragg held her away at arm's length, a smile drawing up the loose wrinkles about his eyes.

"Well, that kind of dress might come in mighty handy on *some* occasions; so I guess you'd better hold on to it for future use, and go and select another for this Fairford dinner," he said; and before he could finish he was in her arms again, and she was smothering his last word in little cries and kisses.

III

THOUGH SHE would not for the world have owned it to her parents, Undine was disappointed in the Fairford dinner.

The house, to begin with, was small and rather shabby. There was no gilding, no lavish diffusion of light: the room they sat in after dinner, with its green-shaded lamps making faint pools of brightness, and its rows of books from floor to ceiling, reminded Undine of the old circulating library at Apex, before the new marble building was put up. Then, instead of a gas-log, or a polished grate with electric bulbs behind ruby glass, there was an old-fashioned wood-fire, like pictures of "Back to the farm for Christmas"; and when the logs fell forward Mrs. Fairford or her brother had to jump up to push them in place, and the ashes scattered over the hearth untidily.

The dinner too was disappointing. Undine was too young to take note of culinary details, but she had expected to view the company through a bower of orchids and eat pretty-coloured *entrées* in ruffled papers. Instead, there was only a low centre-dish of ferns, and plain roasted and broiled meat that one could recognize—as if they'd been dyspeptics on a diet! With all the hints in the Sunday papers, she thought it dull of Mrs. Fairford not to have picked up something newer; and as the evening progressed she began to suspect that it wasn't a real "dinner party," and that they had just asked her in to share what they had when they were alone.

But a glance about the table convinced her that Mrs. Fairford could not have meant to treat her other guests so lightly. They were only eight in number, but one was no less a person than young Mrs. Peter Van Degen—the one who had been a Dagonet—and the consideration which this young lady, herself one of the choicest ornaments of the Society Column, displayed toward the rest of the company, convinced Undine that they must be more important than they looked. She liked Mrs. Fairford, a small incisive woman, with a big nose and good teeth revealed by frequent smiles. In her dowdy black and antiquated ornaments she was not what Undine would have called "stylish"; but she had a droll kind way which reminded the girl of her father's manner when he was not tired or worried about money. One of the other ladies, having white hair, did not long arrest Undine's attention; and the fourth, a girl like herself, who was introduced as Miss Harriet Ray, she dismissed at a glance as plain and wearing a last year's "model." The men, too, were less striking than she had hoped. She had not expected much of Mr. Fairford, since married men were intrinsically uninteresting, and his baldness and grey moustache seemed naturally to relegate him to the background; but she had looked for some brilliant youths of her own age—in her inmost heart she had looked for Mr. Popple. He was not there, however, and of the other men one, whom they called Mr. Bowen, was hopelessly elderly—she supposed he was the husband of the white-haired lady—and the other two, who seemed to be friends of young Marvell's, were both lacking in Claud Walsingham's dash.

Undine sat between Mr. Bowen and young Marvell, who struck her as very "sweet" (it was her word for friendliness), but even shyer than at the hotel dance. Yet she was not sure if he were shy, or if his quietness were only a new kind of self-possession which expressed itself negatively instead of aggressively. Small, well-knit, fair, he sat stroking his slight blond moustache and looking at her with kindly, almost tender eyes; but he left it to his sister and the others to draw her out and fit her into the pattern.

Mrs. Fairford talked so well that the girl wondered why Mrs. Heeny had found her lacking in conversation. But though Undine thought silent people awkward she was not easily impressed by verbal fluency. All the ladies in Apex City were more voluble than Mrs. Fairford, and had a larger vocabulary: the difference was that with Mrs. Fairford conversation seemed to be a concert and not a solo. She kept drawing in the others, giving each a turn, beating time for them with her smile, and somehow harmonizing and linking together what they said. She took particular pains to give Undine her due part in the performance; but the girl's expansive impulses were always balanced by odd reactions of mistrust, and to-night the latter prevailed. She meant to watch and listen without letting herself go, and she sat very straight and pink, answering promptly but briefly, with the nervous laugh that punctuated all her phrases—saying "I don't care if I do" when her host asked her to try some grapes, and "I wouldn't wonder" when she thought any one was trying to astonish her.

This state of lucidity enabled her to take note of all that was being said. The talk ran more on general questions, and less on people, than she was used to; but though the allusions to pictures and books escaped her, she caught and stored up every personal reference, and the pink in her cheeks deepened at a random mention of Mr. Popple.

"Yes—he's doing me," Mrs. Peter Van Degen was saying, in her slightly drawling voice. "He's doing everybody this year, you know——"

"As if that were a reason!" Undine heard Mrs. Fairford breathe to Mr. Bowen; who replied, at the same pitch: "It's a Van Degen reason, isn't it?"—to which Mrs. Fairford shrugged assentingly.

"That delightful Popple—he paints so exactly as he talks!" the white-haired lady took it up. "All his portraits seem to proclaim what a gentleman he is, and how he fascinates women! They're not pictures of Mrs. or Miss So-and-so, but simply of the impression Popple thinks he's made on them."

Mrs. Fairford smiled. "I've sometimes thought," she mused, "that Mr. Popple must be the only gentleman I know; at least he's the only man who has ever told me he was a gentleman—and Mr. Popple never fails to mention it."

Undine's ear was too well attuned to the national note of irony for her not to perceive that her companions were making sport of the painter. She winced at their banter as if it had been at her own expense, yet it gave her a dizzy sense of being at last in the very stronghold of fashion. Her attention was diverted by hearing Mrs. Van Degen, under cover of the general laugh, say in a low tone to young Marvell: "I thought you liked his things, or I wouldn't have had him paint me."

Something in her tone made all Undine's perceptions bristle, and she strained her ears for the answer.

"I think he'll do you capitally—you must let me come and see some day soon." Marvell's tone was always so light, so unemphasized, that she could not be sure of its being as indifferent as it sounded. She looked down at the fruit on her plate and shot a side-glance through her lashes at Mrs. Peter Van Degen.

Mrs. Van Degen was neither beautiful nor imposing: just a dark girlish-looking creature with plaintive eyes and a fidgety frequent laugh. But she was more elaborately dressed and jewelled than the other ladies, and her elegance and her restlessness made her seem less alien to Undine. She had turned on Marvell a gaze at once pleading and possessive; but whether betokening merely an inherited intimacy (Undine had noticed that they were all more or less cousins) or a more personal feeling, her observer was unable to decide; just as the tone of the young man's reply might have expressed the open avowal of good-fellowship or the disguise of a different sentiment. All was blurred and puzzling to the girl in this world of half-lights, half-tones, eliminations and abbreviations; and she felt a violent longing to brush away the cobwebs and assert herself as the dominant figure of the scene.

Yet in the drawing-room, with the ladies, where Mrs. Fairford came and sat by her, the spirit of caution once more prevailed. She wanted to be noticed but she dreaded to be patronized, and here again her hostess's graduations of tone were confusing. Mrs. Fairford made no tactless allusions to her being a newcomer in New York—there was nothing as bitter to the girl as that—but her questions as to what pictures had interested Undine at the various exhibitions of the moment, and which of the new books she had read, were almost as open to suspicion, since they had to be answered in the negative. Undine did not even know that there were any pictures to be seen, much less that "people" went to see them; and she had read no new book but "When The Kissing Had to Stop," of which Mrs. Fairford seemed not to have heard. On the theatre they were equally at odds, for while Undine had seen "Oolaloo" fourteen times, and was " wild" about Ned Norris in "The Soda-Water Fountain," she had not heard of the famous Berlin comedians who were performing Shakespeare at the German Theatre, and knew only by name the clever American actress who was trying to give "repertory" plays with a good stock company. The conversation was revived for a moment by her recalling that she had seen Sarah

Burnhard in a play she called "Leg-long," and another which she pronounced "Fade"; but even this did not carry them far, as she had forgotten what both plays were about and had found the actress a good deal older than she expected.

Matters were not improved by the return of the men from the smoking-room. Henley Fairford replaced his wife at Undine's side; and since it was unheard-of at Apex for a married man to force his society on a young girl, she inferred that the others didn't care to talk to her, and that her host and hostess were in league to take her off their hands. This discovery resulted in her holding her vivid head very high, and answering "I couldn't really say," or "Is that so?" to all Mr. Fairford's ventures; and as these were neither numerous nor striking it was a relief to both when the rising of the elderly lady gave the signal for departure.

In the hall, where young Marvell had managed to precede her, Undine found Mrs. Van Degen putting on her cloak. As she gathered it about her she laid her hand on Marvell's arm.

"Ralphie, dear, you'll come to the opera with me on Friday? We'll dine together first—Peter's got a club dinner." They exchanged what seemed a smile of intelligence, and Undine heard the young man accept. Then Mrs. Van Degen turned to her.

"Good-bye, Miss Spragg. I hope you'll come——"

"—to dine with me too?" That must be what she was going to say, and Undine's heart gave a bound.

"—to see me some afternoon," Mrs. Van Degen ended, going down the steps to her motor, at the door of which a much-furred footman waited with more furs on his arm.

Undine's face burned as she turned to receive her cloak. When she had drawn it on with haughty deliberation she found Marvell at her side, in hat and over-coat, and her heart gave a higher bound. He was going to "escort" her home, of course! This brilliant youth—she felt now that he *was* brilliant—who dined alone with married women, whom the "Van Degen set" called "Ralphie, dear," had really no eyes for any one but herself; and at the thought her lost self-complacency flowed back warm through her veins.

The street was coated with ice, and she had a delicious moment descending the steps on Marvell's arm, and holding it fast while they waited for her cab to come up; but when he had helped her in he closed the door and held his hand out over the lowered window.

"Good-bye," he said, smiling; and she could not help the break of pride in her voice, as she faltered out stupidly, from the depths of her disillusionment: "Oh—good-bye."

IV

"FATHER, you've got to take a box for me at the opera next Friday."

From the tone of her voice Undine's parents knew at once that she was "nervous."

They had counted a great deal on the Fairford dinner as a means of tranquillization, and it was a blow to detect signs of the opposite result when, late the next morning, their daughter came dawdling into the sodden splendour of the Stentorian breakfast-room.

The symptoms of Undine's nervousness were unmistakable to Mr. and Mrs. Spragg. They could read the approaching storm in the darkening of her eyes from limpid grey to slate-colour, and in the way her straight black brows met above them and the red curves of her lips narrowed to a parallel line below.

Mr. Spragg, having finished the last course of his heterogeneous meal, was adjusting his gold eye-glasses for a glance at the paper when Undine trailed down the sumptuous stuffy room, where coffee-fumes hung perpetually under the emblazoned ceiling and the spongy carpet might have absorbed a year's crumbs without a sweeping.

About them sat other pallid families, richly dressed, and silently eating their way through a bill-of-fare which seemed to have ransacked the globe for gastronomic incompatibilities; and in the middle of the room a knot of equally pallid waiters, engaged in languid conversation, turned their backs by common consent on the persons they were supposed to serve.

Undine, who rose too late to share the family breakfast, usually had her chocolate brought to her in bed by Céleste, after the manner described in the articles on "A Society Woman's Day" which were appearing in *Boudoir Chat*. Her mere appearance in the restaurant therefore prepared her parents for those symptoms of excessive tension which a nearer inspection confirmed, and Mr. Spragg folded his paper and hooked his glasses to his waistcoat with the air of a man who prefers to know the worst and have it over.

"An opera box!" faltered Mrs. Spragg, pushing aside the

bananas and cream with which she had been trying to tempt an appetite too languid for fried liver or crab mayonnaise.

"A parterre box," Undine corrected, ignoring the exclamation, and continuing to address herself to her father. "Friday's the stylish night, and that new tenor's going to sing again in 'Cavaleeria,' " she condescended to explain.

"That so?" Mr. Spragg thrust his hands into his waistcoat pockets, and began to tilt his chair till he remembered there was no wall to meet it. He regained his balance and said: "Wouldn't a couple of good orchestra seats do you?"

"No; they wouldn't," Undine answered with a darkening brow.

He looked at her humorously. "You invited the whole dinner-party, I suppose?"

"No—no one."

"Going all alone in a box?" She was disdainfully silent. "I don't s'pose you're thinking of taking mother and me?"

This was so obviously comic that they all laughed—even Mrs. Spragg—and Undine went on more mildly: "I want to do something for Mabel Lipscomb: make some return. She's always taking me 'round, and I've never done a thing for her—not a single thing."

This appeal to the national belief in the duty of reciprocal "treating" could not fail of its effect, and Mrs. Spragg murmured: "She never *has*, Abner,"——but Mr. Spragg's brow remained unrelenting.

"Do you know what a box costs?"

"No; but I s'pose you do," Undine returned with unconscious flippancy.

"I do. That's the trouble. *Why* won't seats do you?"

"Mabel could buy seats for herself."

"That's so," interpolated Mrs. Spragg—always the first to succumb to her daughter's arguments.

"Well, I guess I can't buy a box for her."

Undine's face gloomed more deeply. She sat silent, her chocolate thickening in the cup, while one hand, almost as much beringed as her mother's, drummed on the crumpled table-cloth.

"We might as well go straight back to Apex," she breathed at last between her teeth.

Mrs. Spragg cast a frightened glance at her husband. These struggles between two resolute wills always brought on her palpitations, and she wished she had her phial of digitalis with her.

"A parterre box costs a hundred and twenty-five dollars a night," said Mr. Spragg, transferring a tooth-pick to his waistcoat pocket.

"I only want it once."

He looked at her with a quizzical puckering of his crows'-feet. "You only want most things once, Undine."

It was an observation they had made in her earliest youth —Undine never wanted anything long, but she wanted it "right off." And until she got it the house was uninhabitable.

"I'd a good deal rather have a box for the season," she rejoined, and he saw the opening he had given her. She had two ways of getting things out of him against his principles; the tender wheedling way, and the harsh-lipped and cold— and he did not know which he dreaded most. As a child they had admired her assertiveness, had made Apex ring with their boasts of it; but it had long since cowed Mrs. Spragg, and it was beginning to frighten her husband.

"Fact is, Undie," he said, weakening, "I'm a little mite strapped just this month."

Her eyes grew absent-minded, as they always did when he alluded to business. *That* was man's province; and what did men go "down town" for but to bring back the spoils to their women? She rose abruptly, leaving her parents seated, and said, more to herself than the others: "Think I'll go for a ride."

"Oh, Undine!" fluttered Mrs. Spragg. She always had palpitations when Undine rode, and since the Aaronson episode her fears were not confined to what the horse might do.

"Why don't you take your mother out shopping a little?" Mr. Spragg suggested, conscious of the limitation of his resources.

Undine made no answer, but swept down the room, and out of the door ahead of her mother, with scorn and anger in every line of her arrogant young back. Mrs. Spragg tottered meekly after her, and Mr. Spragg lounged out into the marble hall to buy a cigar before taking the Subway to his office.

*   *   *

Undine went for a ride, not because she felt particularly disposed for the exercise, but because she wished to discipline her mother. She was almost sure she would get her opera box, but she did not see why she should have to struggle for her rights, and she was especially annoyed with Mrs. Spragg for seconding her so half-heartedly. If she and her mother did not hold together in such crises she would have twice the work to do.

Undine hated "scenes": she was essentially peace-loving, and would have preferred to live on terms of unbroken harmony with her parents. But she could not help it if they were unreasonable. Ever since she could remember there had been "fusses" about money; yet she and her mother had always got what they wanted, apparently without lasting detriment to the family fortunes. It was therefore natural to conclude that there were ample funds to draw upon, and that Mr. Spragg's occasional resistances were merely due to an imperfect understanding of what constituted the necessities of life.

When she returned from her ride Mrs. Spragg received her as if she had come back from the dead. It was absurd, of course; but Undine was inured to the absurdity of parents.

"Has father telephoned?" was her first brief question.

"No, he hasn't yet."

Undine's lips tightened, but she proceeded deliberately with the removal of her habit.

"You'd think I'd asked him to buy me the Opera House, the way he's acting over a single box," she muttered, flinging aside her smartly-fitting coat.

Mrs. Spragg received the flying garment and smoothed it out on the bed. Neither of the ladies could "bear" to have their maid about when they were at their toilet, and Mrs. Spragg had always performed these ancillary services for Undine.

"You know, Undie, father hasn't always got the money in his pocket, and the bills have been pretty heavy lately. Father was a rich man for Apex, but that's different from being rich in New York."

She stood before her daughter, looking down on her appealingly.

Undine, who had seated herself while she detached her

stock and waistcoat, raised her head with an impatient jerk. "Why on earth did we ever leave Apex, then?" she exclaimed.

Mrs. Spragg's eyes usually dropped before her daughter's inclement gaze; but on this occasion they held their own with a kind of awe-struck courage, till Undine's lids sank above her flushing cheeks.

She sprang up, tugging at the waistband of her habit, while Mrs. Spragg, relapsing from temerity to meekness, hovered about her with obstructive zeal.

"If you'd only just let go of my skirt, mother—I can unhook it twice as quick myself."

Mrs. Spragg drew back, understanding that her presence was no longer wanted. But on the threshold she paused, as if overruled by a stronger influence, and said, with a last look at her daughter: "You didn't meet anybody when you were out, did you, Undie?"

Undine's brows drew together: she was struggling with her long patent-leather boot.

"Meet anybody? Do you mean anybody I know? I don't *know* anybody—I never shall, if father can't afford to let me go round with people!"

The boot was off with a wrench, and she flung it violently across the old-rose carpet, while Mrs. Spragg, turning away to hide a look of inexpressible relief, slipped discreetly from the room.

The day wore on. Undine had meant to go down and tell Mabel Lipscomb about the Fairford dinner, but its aftertaste was flat on her lips. What would it lead to? Nothing, as far as she could see. Ralph Marvell had not even asked when he might call; and she was ashamed to confess to Mabel that he had not driven home with her.

Suddenly she decided that she would go and see the pictures of which Mrs. Fairford had spoken. Perhaps she might meet some of the people she had seen at dinner—from their talk one might have imagined that they spent their lives in picture-galleries.

The thought reanimated her, and she put on her handsomest furs, and a hat for which she had not yet dared present the bill to her father. It was the fashionable hour in Fifth

Avenue, but Undine knew none of the ladies who were bowing to each other from interlocked motors. She had to content herself with the gaze of admiration which she left in her wake along the pavement; but she was used to the homage of the streets and her vanity craved a choicer fare.

When she reached the art gallery which Mrs. Fairford had named she found it even more crowded than Fifth Avenue; and some of the ladies and gentlemen wedged before the pictures had the "look" which signified social consecration. As Undine made her way among them, she was aware of attracting almost as much notice as in the street, and she flung herself into rapt attitudes before the canvases, scribbling notes in the catalogue in imitation of a tall girl in sables, while ripples of self-consciousness played up and down her watchful back.

Presently her attention was drawn to a lady in black who was examining the pictures through a tortoise-shell eye-glass adorned with diamonds and hanging from a long pearl chain. Undine was instantly struck by the opportunities which this toy presented for graceful wrist movements and supercilious turns of the head. It seemed suddenly plebeian and promiscuous to look at the world with a naked eye, and all her floating desires were merged in the wish for a jewelled eye-glass and chain. So violent was this wish that, drawn on in the wake of the owner of the eye-glass, she found herself inadvertently bumping against a stout tight-coated young man whose impact knocked her catalogue from her hand.

As the young man picked the catalogue up and held it out to her she noticed that his bulging eyes and queer retreating face were suffused with a glow of admiration. He was so unpleasant-looking that she would have resented his homage had not his odd physiognomy called up some vaguely agreeable association of ideas. Where had she seen before this grotesque saurian head, with eye-lids as thick as lips and lips as thick as ear-lobes? It fled before her down a perspective of innumerable newspaper portraits, all, like the original before her, tightly coated, with a huge pearl transfixing a silken tie. . .

"Oh, thank you," she murmured, all gleams and graces, while he stood hat in hand, saying sociably: "The crowd's simply awful, isn't it?"

At the same moment the lady of the eye-glass drifted closer, and with a tap of her wand, and a careless "Peter, look at this," swept him to the other side of the gallery.

Undine's heart was beating excitedly, for as he turned away she had identified him. Peter Van Degen—who could he be but young Peter Van Degen, the son of the great banker, Thurber Van Degen, the husband of Ralph Marvell's cousin, the hero of "Sunday Supplements," the captor of Blue Ribbons at Horse-Shows, of Gold Cups at Motor Races, the owner of winning race-horses and "crack" sloops: the supreme exponent, in short, of those crowning arts that made all life seem stale and unprofitable outside the magic ring of the Society Column?

Undine smiled as she recalled the look with which his pale protruding eyes had rested on her—it almost consoled her for his wife's indifference!

When she reached home she found that she could not remember anything about the pictures she had seen. . .

There was no message from her father, and a reaction of disgust set in. Of what good were such encounters if they were to have no sequel? She would probably never meet Peter Van Degen again—or, if she *did* run across him in the same accidental way, she knew they could not continue their conversation without being "introduced." What was the use of being beautiful and attracting attention if one were perpetually doomed to relapse again into the obscure mass of the Uninvited?

Her gloom was not lightened by finding Ralph Marvell's card on the drawing-room table. She thought it unflattering and almost impolite of him to call without making an appointment: it seemed to show that he did not wish to continue their acquaintance. But as she tossed the card aside her mother said: "He was real sorry not to see you, Undine—he sat here nearly an hour."

Undine's attention was roused. "Sat here—all alone? Didn't you tell him I was out?"

"Yes—but he came up all the same. He asked for me."

"Asked for *you?*"

The social order seemed to be falling in ruins at Undine's

feet. A visitor who asked for a girl's mother!—she stared at Mrs. Spragg with cold incredulity. "What makes you think he did?"

"Why, they told me so. I telephoned down that you were out, and they said he'd asked for me." Mrs. Spragg let the fact speak for itself—it was too much out of the range of her experience to admit of even a hypothetical explanation.

Undine shrugged her shoulders. "It was a mistake, of course. Why on earth did you let him come up?"

"I thought maybe he had a message for you, Undie."

This plea struck her daughter as not without weight. "Well, did he?" she asked, drawing out her hat-pins and tossing down her hat on the onyx table.

"Why, no—he just conversed. He was lovely to me, but I couldn't make out what he was after," Mrs. Spragg was obliged to own.

Her daughter looked at her with a kind of chill commiseration. "You never *can*," she murmured, turning away.

She stretched herself out moodily on one of the pink and gold sofas, and lay there brooding, an unread novel on her knee. Mrs. Spragg timidly slipped a cushion under her daughter's head, and then dissembled herself behind the lace window-curtains and sat watching the lights spring out down the long street and spread their glittering net across the Park. It was one of Mrs. Spragg's chief occupations to watch the nightly lighting of New York.

Undine lay silent, her hands clasped behind her head. She was plunged in one of the moods of bitter retrospection when all her past seemed like a long struggle for something she could not have, from a trip to Europe to an opera-box; and when she felt sure that, as the past had been, so the future would be. And yet, as she had often told her parents, all she sought for was improvement: she honestly wanted the best.

Her first struggle—after she had ceased to scream for candy, or sulk for a new toy—had been to get away from Apex in summer. Her summers, as she looked back on them, seemed to typify all that was dreariest and most exasperating in her life. The earliest had been spent in the yellow "frame" cottage where she had hung on the fence, kicking her toes against the broken palings and exchanging moist chewing-gum and half-eaten apples with Indiana Frusk. Later on, she had returned from her boarding-school to the comparative gentility of summer vacations at the Mealey House, whither her parents, forsaking their squalid suburb, had moved in the first flush of their rising fortunes. The tessellated floors, the plush parlours and organ-like radiators of the Mealey House had, aside from their intrinsic elegance, the immense advantage of lifting the Spraggs high above the Frusks, and making it possible for Undine, when she met Indiana in the street or at school, to chill her advances by a careless allusion to the splendours of hotel life. But even in such a setting, and in spite of the social superiority it implied, the long months of the middle western summer, fly-blown, torrid, exhaling stale odours, soon became as insufferable as they had been in the little yellow house.

At school Undine met other girls whose parents took them to the Great Lakes for August; some even went to California, others—oh bliss ineffable!—went "east."

Pale and listless under the stifling boredom of the Mealey House routine, Undine secretly sucked lemons, nibbled slate-pencils and drank pints of bitter coffee to aggravate her look of ill-health; and when she learned that even Indiana Frusk was to go on a month's visit to Buffalo it needed no artificial aids to emphasize the ravages of envy. Her parents, alarmed by her appearance, were at last convinced of the necessity of change, and timidly, tentatively, they transferred themselves for a month to a staring hotel on a glaring lake.

There Undine enjoyed the satisfaction of sending ironic post-cards to Indiana, and discovering that she could more than hold her own against the youth and beauty of the other visitors. Then she made the acquaintance of a pretty woman from Richmond, whose husband, a mining engineer, had brought her west with him while he inspected the newly developed Eubaw mines; and the southern visitor's dismay, her repugnances, her recoil from the faces, the food, the amusements, the general bareness and stridency of the scene, were a terrible initiation to Undine. There was something still better beyond, then—more luxurious, more exciting, more worthy of her! She once said to herself, afterward, that it was always her fate to find out just too late about the "something beyond." But in this case it was not too late—and obstinately, inflexibly, she set herself to the task of forcing her parents to take her "east" the next summer.

Yielding to the inevitable, they suffered themselves to be impelled to a Virginia "resort," where Undine had her first glimpse of more romantic possibilities—leafy moonlight rides and drives, picnics in mountain glades, and an atmosphere of Christmas-chromo sentimentality that tempered her hard edges a little, and gave her glimpses of a more delicate kind of pleasure. But here again everything was spoiled by a peep through another door. Undine, after a first mustering of the other girls in the hotel, had, as usual, found herself easily first—till the arrival, from Washington, of Mr. and Mrs. Wincher and their daughter. Undine was much handsomer than Miss Wincher, but she saw at a glance that she did not know how to use her beauty as the other used her plainness. She was exasperated, too, by the discovery that Miss Wincher seemed not only unconscious of any possible rivalry between them, but actually unaware of her existence. Listless, long-faced, supercilious, the young lady from Washington sat apart reading novels or playing solitaire with her parents, as though the huge hotel's loud life of gossip and flirtation were invisible and inaudible to her. Undine never even succeeded in catching her eye: she always lowered it to her book when the Apex beauty trailed or rattled past her secluded corner. But one day an acquaintance of the Winchers' turned up—a lady from Boston, who had come to Virginia on a botanizing tour; and from scraps of Miss Wincher's conversation with the newcomer, Undine, straining her ears behind a column of the long veranda, obtained a new glimpse into the unimagined.

The Winchers, it appeared, found themselves at Potash Springs merely because a severe illness of Mrs. Wincher's had made it impossible, at the last moment, to move her farther from Washington. They had let their house on the North Shore, and as soon as they could leave "this dreadful hole" were going to Europe for the autumn. Miss Wincher simply didn't know how she got through the days; though no doubt it was as good as a rest-cure after the rush of the winter. Of course they would have preferred to hire a house, but the "hole," if one could believe it, didn't offer one; so they had simply shut themselves off as best they could from the "hotel crew"—had her friend, Miss Wincher parenthetically asked, happened to notice the Sunday young men? They were queerer even than the "belles" they came for—and had escaped the promiscuity of the dinner-hour by turning one of their rooms into a dining-room, and picnicking there—with the Persimmon House standards, one couldn't describe it in any other way! But luckily the awful place was doing mamma good, and now they had nearly served their term. . .

Undine turned sick as she listened. Only the evening before she had gone on a "buggy-ride" with a young gentleman from Deposit—a dentist's assistant—and had let him kiss her, and given him the flower from her hair. She loathed the thought of him now: she loathed all the people about her, and most of all the disdainful Miss Wincher. It enraged her to think that the Winchers classed her with the "hotel crew"—with the "belles" who awaited their Sunday young men. The place was forever blighted for her, and the next week she dragged her amazed but thankful parents back to Apex.

But Miss Wincher's depreciatory talk had opened ampler vistas, and the pioneer blood in Undine would not let her rest. She had heard the call of the Atlantic seaboard, and the next summer found the Spraggs at Skog Harbour, Maine. Even now Undine felt a shiver of boredom as she recalled it. That summer had been the worst of all. The bare wind-beaten inn, all shingles without and blueberry pie within, was "exclusive," parochial, Bostonian; and the Spraggs wore through the interminable weeks in blank unmitigated isolation. The incomprehensible part of it was that every other woman in the hotel was plain, dowdy or elderly—and most of them all three. If there had been any competition on ordinary lines Undine would have won, as Van Degen said, "hands down." But there wasn't—the other "guests" simply formed a cold impenetrable group who walked, boated, played golf, and discussed Christian Science and the Subliminal, unaware of the tremulous organism drifting helplessly against their rock-bound circle.

It was on the day the Spraggs left Skog Harbour that

Undine vowed to herself with set lips: "I'll never try anything again till I try New York." Now she had gained her point and tried New York, and so far, it seemed, with no better success. From small things to great, everything went against her. In such hours of self-searching she was ready enough to acknowledge her own mistakes, but they exasperated her less than the blunders of her parents. She was sure, for instance, that she was on what Mrs. Heeny called "the right tack" at last: yet just at the moment when her luck seemed about to turn she was to be thwarted by her father's stupid obstinacy about the opera-box. . .

She lay brooding over these things till long after Mrs. Spragg had gone away to dress for dinner, and it was nearly eight o'clock when she heard her father's dragging tread in the hall.

She kept her eyes fixed on her book while he entered the room and moved about behind her, laying aside his hat and overcoat; then his steps came close and a small parcel dropped on the pages of her book.

"Oh, father!" She sprang up, all alight, the novel on the floor, her fingers twitching for the tickets. But a substantial packet emerged, like nothing she had ever seen. She looked at it, hoping, fearing—she beamed blissful interrogation on her father while his sallow smile continued to tantalize her. Then she closed on him with a rush, smothering his words against her hair.

"It's for more than one night—why, it's for every other Friday! Oh, you darling, you darling!" she exulted.

Mr. Spragg, through the glittering meshes, feigned dismay. "That so? They must have given me the wrong—!" Then, convicted by her radiant eyes as she swung round on him: "I knew you only wanted it *once* for yourself, Undine; but I thought maybe, off nights, you'd like to send it to your friends."

Mrs. Spragg, who from her doorway had assisted with moist eyes at this closing pleasantry, came forward as Undine hurried away to dress.

"Abner—can you really manage it all right?"

He answered her with one of his awkward brief caresses. "Don't you fret about that, Leota. I'm bound to have her go round with these people she knows. I want her to be with them all she can."

A pause fell between them, while Mrs. Spragg looked anxiously into his fagged eyes.

"You seen Elmer again?"

"No. Once was enough," he returned, with a scowl like Undine's.

"Why—you *said* he couldn't come after her, Abner!"

"No more he can. But what if she was to get nervous and lonesome, and want to go after him?"

Mrs. Spragg shuddered away from the suggestion. "How'd he look? Just the same?" she whispered.

"No. Spruced up. That's what scared me."

It scared her too, to the point of blanching her habitually lifeless cheek. She continued to scrutinize her husband broodingly. "You look fairly sick, Abner. You better let me get you some of those stomach drops right off," she proposed.

But he parried this with his unfailing humour. "I guess I'm too sick to risk that." He passed his hand through her arm with the conjugal gesture familiar to Apex City. "Come along down to dinner, mother—I guess Undine won't mind if I don't rig up to-night."

V

S HE HAD looked down at them, enviously, from the balcony—she had looked up at them, reverentially, from
the stalls; but now at last she was on a line with them, among
them, she was part of the sacred semicircle whose privilege it
is, between the acts, to make the mere public forget that the
curtain has fallen.

As she swept to the left-hand seat of their crimson niche,
waving Mabel Lipscomb to the opposite corner with a gesture learned during her apprenticeship in the stalls, Undine
felt that quickening of the faculties that comes in the high
moments of life. Her consciousness seemed to take in at once
the whole bright curve of the auditorium, from the unbroken
lines of spectators below her to the culminating blaze of the
central chandelier; and she herself was the core of that vast
illumination, the sentient throbbing surface which gathered
all the shafts of light into a centre.

It was almost a relief when, a moment later, the lights sank,
the curtain rose, and the focus of illumination was shifted.
The music, the scenery, and the movement on the stage, were
like a rich mist tempering the radiance that shot on her from
every side, and giving her time to subside, draw breath, adjust
herself to this new clear medium which made her feel so
oddly brittle and transparent.

When the curtain fell on the first act she began to be aware
of a subtle change in the house. In all the boxes cross-currents
of movement had set in: groups were coalescing and breaking
up, fans waving and heads twinkling, black coats emerging
among white shoulders, late comers dropping their furs and
laces in the red penumbra of the background. Undine, for the
moment unconscious of herself, swept the house with her
opera-glass, searching for familiar faces. Some she knew without being able to name them—fixed figure-heads of the social
prow—others she recognized from their portraits in the
papers; but of the few from whom she could herself claim
recognition not one was visible, and as she pursued her
investigations the whole scene grew blank and featureless.

Almost all the boxes were full now, but one, just opposite,

tantalized her by its continued emptiness. How queer to have
an opera-box and not use it! What on earth could the people
be doing—what rarer delight could they be tasting? Undine
remembered that the numbers of the boxes and the names of
their owners were given on the back of the programme, and
after a rapid computation she turned to consult the list. Mon-
days and Fridays, Mrs. Peter Van Degen. That was it: the box
was empty because Mrs. Van Degen was dining alone with
Ralph Marvell! *"Peter will be at one of his club dinners."* Undine
had a sharp vision of the Van Degen dining-room—she pictured it as oak-carved and sumptuous with gilding—with a
small table in the centre, and rosy lights and flowers, and
Ralph Marvell, across the hot-house grapes and champagne,
leaning to take a light from his hostess's cigarette. Undine had
seen such scenes on the stage, she had come upon them in
the glowing pages of fiction, and it seemed to her that every
detail was before her now, from the glitter of jewels on Mrs.
Van Degen's bare shoulders to the way young Marvell stroked
his slight blond moustache while he smiled and listened.

Undine blushed with anger at her own simplicity in fancy-
ing that he had been "taken" by her—that she could ever
really count among these happy self-absorbed people! They
all had their friends, their ties, their delightful crowding
obligations: why should they make room for an intruder in a
circle so packed with the initiated?

As her imagination developed the details of the scene in the
Van Degen dining-room it became clear to her that fashionable society was horribly immoral and that she could never
really be happy in such a poisoned atmosphere. She remembered that an eminent divine was preaching a series of sermons against Social Corruption, and she determined to go
and hear him on the following Sunday.

This train of thought was interrupted by the feeling that
she was being intently observed from the neighbouring box.
She turned around with a feint of speaking to Mrs. Lipscomb, and met the bulging stare of Peter Van Degen. He
was standing behind the lady of the eye-glass, who had replaced her tortoise-shell implement by one of closely-set bril-
liants, which, at a word from her companion, she critically
bent on Undine.

"No—I don't remember," she said; and the girl reddened, divining herself unidentified after this protracted scrutiny.

But there was no doubt as to young Van Degen's remembering her. She was even conscious that he was trying to provoke in her some reciprocal sign of recognition; and the attempt drove her to the haughty study of her programme.

"Why, there's Mr. Popple over there!" exclaimed Mabel Lipscomb, making large signs across the house with fan and play-bill.

Undine had already become aware that Mabel, planted, blond and brimming, too near the edge of the box, was somehow out of scale and out of drawing; and the freedom of her demonstrations increased the effect of disproportion. No one else was wagging and waving in that way: a gestureless mute telegraphy seemed to pass between the other boxes. Still, Undine could not help following Mrs. Lipscomb's glance, and there in fact was Claud Popple, taller and more dominant than ever, and bending easily over what she felt must be the back of a brilliant woman.

He replied by a discreet salute to Mrs. Lipscomb's intemperate motions, and Undine saw the brilliant woman's opera-glass turn in their direction, and said to herself that in a moment Mr. Popple would be "round." But the entr'acte wore on, and no one turned the handle of their door, or disturbed the peaceful somnolence of Harry Lipscomb, who, not being (as he put it) "onto" grand opera, had abandoned the struggle and withdrawn to the seclusion of the inner box. Undine jealously watched Mr. Popple's progress from box to box, from brilliant woman to brilliant woman; but just as it seemed about to carry him to their door he reappeared at his original post across the house.

"Undie, do look—there's Mr. Marvell!" Mabel began again, with another conspicuous outbreak of signalling; and this time Undine flushed to the nape as Mrs. Peter Van Degen appeared in the opposite box with Ralph Marvell behind her. The two seemed to be alone in the box—as they had doubtless been alone all the evening!—and Undine furtively turned to see if Mr. Van Degen shared her disapproval. But Mr. Van Degen had disappeared, and Undine, leaning forward, nervously touched Mabel's arm.

"What's the matter, Undine? Don't you see Mr. Marvell over there? Is that his sister he's with?"

"No.—I wouldn't beckon like that," Undine whispered between her teeth.

"Why not? Don't you want him to know you're here?"

"Yes—but the other people are not beckoning."

Mabel looked about unabashed. "Perhaps they've all found each other. Shall I send Harry over to tell him?" she shouted above the blare of the wind instruments.

"*No!*" gasped Undine as the curtain rose.

She was no longer capable of following the action on the stage. Two presences possessed her imagination: that of Ralph Marvell, small, unattainable, remote, and that of Mabel Lipscomb, near-by, immense and irrepressible.

It had become clear to Undine that Mabel Lipscomb was ridiculous. That was the reason why Popple did not come to the box. No one would care to be seen talking to her while Mabel was at her side: Mabel, monumental and moulded while the fashionable were flexible and diaphanous, Mabel strident and explicit while they were subdued and allusive. At the Stentorian she was the centre of her group—here she revealed herself as unknown and unknowing. Why, she didn't even know that Mrs. Peter Van Degen was not Ralph Marvell's sister! And she had a way of trumpeting out her ignorances that jarred on Undine's subtler methods. It was precisely at this point that there dawned on Undine what was to be one of the guiding principles of her career: *"It's better to watch than to ask questions."*

The curtain fell again, and Undine's eyes flew back to the Van Degen box. Several men were entering it together, and a moment later she saw Ralph Marvell rise from his seat and pass out. Half-unconsciously she placed herself in such a way as to have an eye on the door of the box. But its handle remained unturned, and Harry Lipscomb, leaning back on the sofa, his head against the opera cloaks, continued to breathe stertorously through his open mouth and stretched his legs a little farther across the threshold. . .

The entr'acte was nearly over when the door opened and two gentlemen stumbled over Mr. Lipscomb's legs. The foremost was Claud Walsingham Popple; and above his shoulder shone the batrachian countenance of Peter Van Degen. A brief murmur from Mr. Popple made his companion known to the two ladies, and Mr. Van Degen promptly seated himself behind Undine, relegating the painter to Mrs. Lipscomb's elbow.

"Queer go—I happened to see your friend there waving to old Popp across the house. So I bolted over and collared him: told him he'd got to introduce me before he was a minute older. I tried to find out who you were the other day at the Motor Show—no, where was it? Oh, those pictures at Goldmark's. What d'you think of 'em, by the way? You ought to be painted yourself—no, I mean it, you know—you ought to get old Popp to do you. He'd do your hair ripplingly. You must let me come and talk to you about it. . . About the picture or your hair? Well, your hair if you don't mind. Where'd you say you were staying? Oh, you *live* here, do you? I say, that's first rate!"

Undine sat well forward, curving toward him a little, as she had seen the other women do, but holding back sufficiently to let it be visible to the house that she was conversing with no less a person than Mr. Peter Van Degen. Mr. Popple's talk was certainly more brilliant and purposeful, and she saw him cast longing glances at her from behind Mrs. Lipscomb's shoulder; but she remembered how lightly he had been treated at the Fairford dinner, and she wanted!—oh, how she wanted!—to have Ralph Marvell see her talking to Van Degen.

She poured out her heart to him, improvising an opinion on the pictures and an opinion on the music, falling in gaily with his suggestion of a jolly little dinner some night soon, at the Café Martin, and strengthening her position, as she thought, by an easy allusion to her acquaintance with Mrs. Van Degen. But at the word her companion's eye clouded, and a shade of constraint dimmed his enterprising smile.

"My wife—? Oh, *she* doesn't go to restaurants—she moves on too high a plane. But we'll get old Popp, and Mrs. ——, Mrs. ——, what'd you say your fat friend's name was? Just a select little crowd of four—and some kind of a cheerful show afterward. . . Jove! There's the curtain, and I must skip."

As the door closed on him Undine's cheeks burned with

resentment. If Mrs. Van Degen didn't go to restaurants, why had he supposed that *she* would? and to have to drag Mabel in her wake! The leaden sense of failure overcame her again. Here was the evening nearly over, and what had it led to? Looking up from the stalls, she had fancied that to sit in a box was to be in society—now she saw it might but emphasize one's exclusion. And she was burdened with the box for the rest of the season! It was really stupid of her father to have exceeded his instructions: why had he not done as she told him? . . . Undine felt helpless and tired . . . hateful memories of Apex crowded back on her. Was it going to be as dreary here as there?

She felt Lipscomb's loud whisper in her back: "Say, you girls, I guess I'll cut this and come back for you when the show busts up." They heard him shuffle out of the box, and Mabel settled back to undisturbed enjoyment of the stage.

When the last entr'acte began Undine stood up, resolved to stay no longer. Mabel, lost in the study of the audience, had not noticed her movement, and as she passed alone into the back of the box the door opened and Ralph Marvell came in.

Undine stood with one arm listlessly raised to detach her cloak from the wall. Her attitude showed the long slimness of her figure and the fresh curve of the throat below her bent-back head. Her face was paler and softer than usual, and the eyes she rested on Marvell's face looked deep and starry under their fixed brows.

"Oh—you're not going?" he exclaimed.

"I thought you weren't coming," she answered simply.

"I waited till now on purpose to dodge your other visitors."

She laughed with pleasure. "Oh, we hadn't so many!"

Some intuition had already told her that frankness was the tone to take with him. They sat down together on the red damask sofa, against the hanging cloaks. As Undine leaned back her hair caught in the spangles of the wrap behind her, and she had to sit motionless while the young man freed the captive mesh. Then they settled themselves again, laughing a little at the incident.

A glance had made the situation clear to Mrs. Lipscomb,

and they saw her return to her rapt inspection of the boxes. In their mirror-hung recess the light was subdued to a rosy dimness and the hum of the audience came to them through half-drawn silken curtains. Undine noticed the delicacy and finish of her companion's features as his head detached itself against the red silk walls. The hand with which he stroked his small moustache was finely-finished too, but sinewy and not effeminate. She had always associated finish and refinement entirely with her own sex, but she began to think they might be even more agreeable in a man. Marvell's eyes were grey, like her own, with chestnut eyebrows and darker lashes; and his skin was as clear as a woman's, but pleasantly reddish, like his hands.

As he sat talking in a low tone, questioning her about the music, asking her what she had been doing since he had last seen her, she was aware that he looked at her less than usual, and she also glanced away; but when she turned her eyes suddenly they always met his gaze.

His talk remained impersonal. She was a little disappointed that he did not compliment her on her dress or her hair— Undine was accustomed to hearing a great deal about her hair, and the episode of the spangles had opened the way to a graceful allusion—but the instinct of sex told her that, under his quiet words, he was throbbing with the sense of her proximity. And his self-restraint sobered her, made her refrain from the flashing and fidgeting which were the only way she knew of taking part in the immemorial love-dance. She talked simply and frankly of herself, of her parents, of how few people they knew in New York, and of how, at times, she was almost sorry she had persuaded them to give up Apex.

"You see, they did it entirely on my account; they're awfully lonesome here; and I don't believe I shall ever learn New York ways either," she confessed, turning on him the eyes of youth and truthfulness. "Of course I know a few people; but they're not—not the way I expected New York people to be." She risked what seemed an involuntary glance at Mabel. "I've seen girls here to-night that I just *long* to know—they look so lovely and refined—but I don't suppose I ever shall. New York's not very friendly to strange girls, is it? I suppose you've got so many of your own already—and they're all so fascinating you don't care!" As she spoke she let her eyes rest on his, half-laughing, half-wistful, and then dropped her lashes while the pink stole slowly up to them.

When he left her he asked if he might hope to find her at home the next day.

The night was fine, and Marvell, having put his cousin into her motor, started to walk home to Washington Square. At the corner he was joined by Mr. Popple.

"Hallo, Ralph, old man—did you run across our auburn beauty of the Stentorian? Who'd have thought old Harry Lipscomb'd have put us onto anything as good as that? Peter Van Degen was fairly taken off his feet—pulled me out of Mrs. Monty Thurber's box and dragged me 'round by the collar to introduce him. Planning a dinner at Martin's already. Gad, young Peter must have what he wants *when* he wants it! I put in a word for you—told him you and I ought to be let in on the ground floor. Funny the luck some girls have about getting started. I believe this one'll take if she can manage to shake the Lipscombs. I think I'll ask to paint her; might be a good thing for the spring show. She'd show up splendidly as a *pendant* to my Mrs. Van Degen—Blonde and Brunette. . . Night and Morning. . . Of course I prefer Mrs. Van Degen's type—personally, I *must* have breeding—but as a mere bit of flesh and blood . . . hallo, ain't you coming into the club?"

Marvell was not coming into the club, and he drew a long breath of relief as his companion left him.

Was it possible that he had ever thought leniently of the egregious Popple? The tone of social omniscience which he had once found so comic was now as offensive to him as a coarse physical touch. And the worst of it was that Popple, with the slight exaggeration of a caricature, really expressed the ideals of the world he frequented. As he spoke of Miss Spragg, so others at any rate would think of her: almost every one in Ralph's set would agree that it was luck for a girl from Apex to be started by Peter Van Degen at a Café Martin dinner. . .

Ralph Marvell, mounting his grandfather's door-step, looked up at the symmetrical old red house-front, with its frugal marble ornament, as he might have looked into a familiar human face.

"They're right,—after all, in some ways they're right," he murmured, slipping his key into the door.

"They" were his mother and old Mr. Urban Dagonet, both, from Ralph's earliest memories, so closely identified with the old house in Washington Square that they might have passed for its inner consciousness as it might have stood for their outward form; and the question as to which the house now seemed to affirm their intrinsic rightness was that of the social disintegration expressed by widely-different architectural physiognomies at the other end of Fifth Avenue.

As Ralph pushed the bolts behind him, and passed into the hall, with its dark mahogany doors and the quiet "Dutch interior" effect of its black and white marble paving, he said to himself that what Popple called society was really just like the houses it lived in: a muddle of misapplied ornament over a thin steel shell of utility. The steel shell was built up in Wall Street, the social trimmings were hastily added in Fifth Avenue; and the union between them was as monstrous and factitious, as unlike the gradual homogeneous growth which flowers into what other countries know as society, as that between the Blois gargoyles on Peter Van Degen's roof and the skeleton walls supporting them.

That was what "they" had always said; what, at least, the Dagonet attitude, the Dagonet view of life, the very lines of the furniture in the old Dagonet house expressed.

Ralph sometimes called his mother and grandfather the Aborigines, and likened them to those vanishing denizens of the American continent doomed to rapid extinction with the advance of the invading race. He was fond of describing Washington Square as the "Reservation," and of prophesying that before long its inhabitants would be exhibited at ethnological shows, pathetically engaged in the exercise of their primitive industries.

Small, cautious, middle-class, had been the ideals of aboriginal New York; but it suddenly struck the young man that they were singularly coherent and respectable as contrasted with the chaos of indiscriminate appetites which made up its modern tendencies. He too had wanted to be "modern," had

revolted, half-humorously, against the restrictions and exclusions of the old code; and it must have been by one of the
ironic reversions of heredity that, at this precise point, he began to see what there was to be said on the other side— *his*
side, as he now felt it to be.

VI

UPSTAIRS, in his brown firelit room, he threw himself into an armchair, and remembered. . .

Harvard first—then Oxford; then a year of wandering and rich initiation. Returning to New York, he had read law, and now had his desk in the office of the respectable firm in whose charge the Dagonet estate had mouldered for several generations. But his profession was the least real thing in his life. The realities lay about him now: the books jamming his old college bookcases and overflowing on chairs and tables; sketches too—he could do charming things, if only he had known how to finish them!—and, on the writing-table at his elbow, scattered sheets of prose and verse; charming things also, but, like the sketches, unfinished.

Nothing in the Dagonet and Marvell tradition was opposed to this desultory dabbling with life. For four or five generations it had been the rule of both houses that a young fellow should go to Columbia or Harvard, read law, and then lapse into more or less cultivated inaction. The only essential was that he should live "like a gentleman"—that is, with a tranquil disdain for mere money-getting, a passive openness to the finer sensations, one or two fixed principles as to the quality of wine, and an archaic probity that had not yet learned to distinguish between private and "business" honour.

No equipment could more thoroughly have unfitted the modern youth for getting on: it hardly needed the scribbled pages on the desk to complete the hopelessness of Ralph Marvell's case. He had accepted the fact with a humorous fatalism. Material resources were limited on both sides of the house, but there would always be enough for his frugal wants—enough to buy books (not "editions"), and pay now and then for a holiday dash to the great centres of art and ideas. And meanwhile there was the world of wonders within him. As a boy at the sea-side, Ralph, between tides, had once come on a cave—a secret inaccessible place with glaucous lights, mysterious murmurs, and a single shaft of communication with the sky. He had kept his find from the other boys, not churlishly, for he was always an outspoken lad, but because he felt there were things about the cave that the others, good fellows as they all were, couldn't be expected to understand, and that, anyhow, it would never be quite his cave again after he had let his thick-set freckled cousins play smuggler and pirate in it.

And so with his inner world. Though so coloured by outer impressions, it wove a secret curtain about him, and he came and went in it with the same joy of furtive possession. One day, of course, some one would discover it and reign there with him—no, reign over it and him. Once or twice already a light foot had reached the threshold. His cousin Clare Dagonet, for instance: there had been a summer when her voice had sounded far down the windings . . . but he had run over to Spain for the autumn, and when he came back she was engaged to Peter Van Degen, and for a while it looked black in the cave. That was long ago, as time is reckoned under thirty; and for three years now he had felt for her only a half-contemptuous pity. To have stood at the mouth of his cave, and have turned from it to the Van Degen lair——!

Poor Clare repented, indeed—she wanted it clearly understood—but she repented in the Van Degen diamonds, and the Van Degen motor bore her broken heart from opera to ball. She had been subdued to what she worked in, and she could never again find her way to the enchanted cave. . . Ralph, since then, had reached the point of deciding that he would never marry; reached it not suddenly or dramatically, but with such sober advisedness as is urged on those about to take the opposite step. What he most wanted, now that the first flutter of being was over, was to learn and to do—to know what the great people had thought, think about their thinking, and then launch his own boat: write some good verse if possible; if not, then critical prose. A dramatic poem lay among the stuff at his elbow; but the prose critic was at his elbow too, and not to be satisfied about the poem; and poet and critic passed the nights in hot if unproductive debate. On the whole, it seemed likely that the critic would win the day, and the essay on "The Rhythmical Structures of Walt Whitman" take shape before "The Banished God." Yet if the light in the cave was less supernaturally blue, the chant of its tides less laden with unimaginable music, it was still a thronged and echoing place when Undine Spragg appeared on its threshold. . .

His mother and sister of course wanted him to marry. They had the usual theory that he was "made" for conjugal bliss: women always thought that of a fellow who didn't get drunk and have low tastes. Ralph smiled at the idea as he sat crouched among his secret treasures. Marry—but whom, in the name of light and freedom? The daughters of his own race sold themselves to the Invaders; the daughters of the Invaders bought their husbands as they bought an opera-box. It ought all to have been transacted on the Stock Exchange. His mother, he knew, had no such ambitions for him: she would have liked him to fancy a "nice girl" like Harriet Ray. Harriet Ray was neither vulgar nor ambitious. She regarded Washington Square as the birthplace of Society, knew by heart all the cousinships of early New York, hated motor-cars, could not make herself understood on the telephone, and was determined, if she married, never to receive a divorced woman. As Mrs. Marvell often said, such girls as Harriet were growing rare. Ralph was not sure about this. He was inclined to think that, certain modifications allowed for, there would always be plenty of Harriet Rays for unworldly mothers to commend to their sons; and he had no desire to diminish their number by removing one from the ranks of the marriageable. He had no desire to marry at all—that had been the whole truth of it till he met Undine Spragg. And now——? He lit a cigar, and began to recall his hour's conversation with Mrs. Spragg.

Ralph had never taken his mother's social faiths very seriously. Surveying the march of civilization from a loftier angle, he had early mingled with the Invaders, and curiously observed their rites and customs. But most of those he had met had already been modified by contact with the indigenous: they spoke the same language as his, though on their lips it had often so different a meaning. Ralph had never seen them actually in the making, before they had acquired the speech of the conquered race. But Mrs. Spragg still used the dialect of her people, and before the end of the visit Ralph had ceased to regret that her daughter was out. He felt obscurely that in the girl's presence—frank and simple as he thought her—he should have learned less of life in early Apex.

Mrs. Spragg, once reconciled—or at least resigned—to the mysterious necessity of having to "entertain" a friend of Undine's, had yielded to the first touch on the weak springs of her garrulity. She had not seen Mrs. Heeny for two days, and this friendly young man with the gentle manner was almost as easy to talk to as the masseuse. And then she could tell him things that Mrs. Heeny already knew, and Mrs. Spragg liked to repeat her stories. To do so gave her almost her sole sense of permanence among the shifting scenes of life. So that, after she had lengthily deplored the untoward accident of Undine's absence, and her visitor, with a smile, and echoes of *divers et ondoyant* in his brain, had repeated her daughter's name after her, saying: "It's a wonderful find—how could you tell it would be such a fit?"—it came to her quite easily to answer: "Why, we called her after a hair-waver father put on the market the week she was born——" and then to explain, as he remained struck and silent: "It's from *un*doolay, you know, the French for crimping; father always thought the name made it take. He was quite a scholar, and had the greatest knack for finding names. I remember the time he invented his Goliath Glue he sat up all night over the Bible to get the name. . . No, father didn't start *in* as a druggist," she went on, expanding with the signs of Marvell's interest; "he was educated for an undertaker, and built up a first-class business; but he was always a beautiful speaker, and after a while he sorter drifted into the ministry. Of course it didn't pay him anything like as well, so finally he opened a drugstore, and he did first-rate at that too, though his heart was always in the pulpit. But after he made such a success with his hair-waver he got speculating in land out at Apex, and somehow everything went—though Mr. Spragg did all he *could*——." Mrs. Spragg, when she found herself embarked on a long sentence, always ballasted it by italicizing the last word.

Her husband, she continued, could not, at the time, do much for his father-in-law. Mr. Spragg had come to Apex as a poor boy, and their early married life had been a protracted struggle, darkened by domestic affliction. Two of their three children had died of typhoid in the epidemic which devastated Apex before the new water-works were built; and this calamity, by causing Mr. Spragg to resolve that thereafter Apex should drink pure water, had led directly to the founding of his fortunes.

"He had taken over some of poor father's land for a bad debt, and when he got up the Pure Water move the company voted to buy the land and build the new reservoir up there: and after that we began to be better off, and it *did* seem as if it had come out so to comfort us some about the children."

Mr. Spragg, thereafter, had begun to be a power in Apex, and fat years had followed on the lean. Ralph Marvell was too little versed in affairs to read between the lines of Mrs. Spragg's untutored narrative, and he understood no more than she the occult connection between Mr. Spragg's domestic misfortunes and his business triumph. Mr. Spragg had "helped out" his ruined father-in-law, and had vowed on his children's graves that no Apex child should ever again drink poisoned water—and out of those two disinterested impulses, by some impressive law of compensation, material prosperity had come. What Ralph understood and appreciated was Mrs. Spragg's unaffected frankness in talking of her early life. Here was no retrospective pretense of an opulent past, such as the other Invaders were given to parading before the bland but undeceived subject race. The Spraggs had been "plain people" and had not yet learned to be ashamed of it. The fact drew them much closer to the Dagonet ideals than any sham elegance in the past tense. Ralph felt that his mother, who shuddered away from Mrs. Harmon B. Driscoll, would understand and esteem Mrs. Spragg.

But how long would their virgin innocence last? Popple's vulgar hands were on it already—Popple's and the unspeakable Van Degen's! Once they and theirs had begun the process of initiating Undine, there was no knowing—or rather there was too easy knowing—how it would end! It was incredible that she too should be destined to swell the ranks of the cheaply fashionable; yet were not her very freshness, her malleability, the mark of her fate? She was still at the age when the flexible soul offers itself to the first grasp. That the grasp should chance to be Van Degen's—that was what made Ralph's temples buzz, and swept away all his plans for his own future like a beaver's dam in a spring flood. To save her from Van Degen and Van Degenism: was that really to be his mission—the "call" for which his life had obscurely waited? It was not in the least what he had meant to do with the fugitive flash of consciousness he called self; but all that he had purposed for that transitory being sank into insignificance under the pressure of Undine's claims.

Ralph Marvell's notion of women had been formed on the experiences common to good-looking young men of his kind. Women were drawn to him as much by his winning appealing quality, by the sense of a youthful warmth behind his light ironic exterior, as by his charms of face and mind. Except during Clare Dagonet's brief reign the depths in him had not been stirred; but in taking what each sentimental episode had to give he had preserved, through all his minor adventures, his faith in the great adventure to come. It was this faith that made him so easy a victim when love had at last appeared clad in the attributes of romance: the imaginative man's indestructible dream of a rounded passion.

The clearness with which he judged the girl and himself seemed the surest proof that his feeling was more than a surface thrill. He was not blind to her crudity and her limitations, but they were a part of her grace and her persuasion. *Diverse et ondoyante*—so he had seen her from the first. But was not that merely the sign of a quicker response to the world's manifold appeal? There was Harriet Ray, sealed up tight in the vacuum of inherited opinion, where not a breath of fresh sensation could get at her: there could be no call to rescue young ladies so secured from the perils of reality! Undine had no such traditional safeguards—Ralph guessed Mrs. Spragg's opinions to be as fluid as her daughter's—and the girl's very sensitiveness to new impressions, combined with her obvious lack of any sense of relative values, would make her an easy prey to the powers of folly. He seemed to see her—as he sat there, pressing his fists into his temples—he seemed to see her like a lovely rock-bound Andromeda, with the devouring monster Society careering up to make a mouthful of her; and himself whirling down on his winged horse—just Pegasus turned Rosinante for the nonce—to cut her bonds, snatch her up, and whirl her back into the blue. . .

VII

S OME TWO MONTHS later than the date of young Marvell's
midnight vigil, Mrs. Heeny, seated on a low chair at
Undine's knee, gave the girl's left hand an approving pat as
she laid aside her lapful of polishers.

"There! I guess you can put your ring on again," she said
with a laugh of jovial significance; and Undine, echoing the
laugh in a murmur of complacency, slipped on the fourth finger of her recovered hand a band of sapphires in an intricate
setting.

Mrs. Heeny took up the hand again. "Them's old stones,
Undine—they've got a different look," she said, examining
the ring while she rubbed her cushioned palm over the girl's
brilliant finger-tips. "And the setting's quaint—I wouldn't
wonder but what it was one of old Gran'ma Dagonet's."

Mrs. Spragg, hovering near in fond beatitude, looked up
quickly.

"Why, don't you s'pose he *bought* it for her, Mrs. Heeny?
It came in a Tiff'ny box."

The manicure laughed again. "Of course he's had Tiff'ny
rub it up. Ain't you ever heard of ancestral jewels, Mrs.
Spragg? In the Eu-ropean aristocracy they never go out and
buy engagement rings; and Undine's marrying into our aristocracy."

Mrs. Spragg looked relieved. "Oh, I thought maybe they
were trying to scrimp on the ring——"

Mrs. Heeny, shrugging away this explanation, rose from
her seat and rolled back her shiny black sleeves.

"Look at here, Undine, if you really want me to do your
hair it's time we got to work."

The girl swung about in her seat so that she faced the
mirror on the dressing-table. Her shoulders shone through
transparencies of lace and muslin which slipped back as
she lifted her arms to draw the tortoise-shell pins from her
hair.

"Of course you've got to do it—I want to look perfectly
lovely!"

"Well—I dunno's my hand's in nowadays," said Mrs.

Heeny in a tone that belied the doubt she cast on her own ability.

"Oh, you're an *artist*, Mrs. Heeny—and I just couldn't have had that French maid 'round to-night," sighed Mrs. Spragg, sinking into a chair near the dressing-table.

Undine, with a backward toss of her head, scattered her loose locks about her. As they spread and sparkled under Mrs. Heeny's touch, Mrs. Spragg leaned back, drinking in through half-closed lids her daughter's loveliness. Some new quality seemed added to Undine's beauty: it had a milder bloom, a kind of melting grace, which might have been lent to it by the moisture in her mother's eyes.

"So you're to see the old gentleman for the first time at this dinner?" Mrs. Heeny pursued, sweeping the live strands up into a loosely woven crown.

"Yes. I'm frightened to death!" Undine, laughing confidently, took up a hand-glass and scrutinized the small brown mole above the curve of her upper lip.

"I guess she'll know how to talk to him," Mrs. Spragg averred with a kind of quavering triumph.

"She'll know how to *look* at him, anyhow," said Mrs. Heeny; and Undine smiled at her own image.

"I hope he won't think I'm too awful!"

Mrs. Heeny laughed. "Did you read the description of yourself in the *Radiator* this morning? I wish't I'd 'a had time to cut it out. I guess I'll have to start a separate bag for *your* clippings soon."

Undine stretched her arms luxuriously above her head and gazed through lowered lids at the foreshortened reflection of her face.

"Mercy! Don't jerk about like that. Am I to put in this rose?—There—you *are* lovely!" Mrs. Heeny sighed, as the pink petals sank into the hair above the girl's forehead.

Undine pushed her chair back, and sat supporting her chin on her clasped hands while she studied the result of Mrs. Heeny's manipulations.

"Yes—that's the way Mrs. Peter Van Degen's flower was put in the other night; only hers was a camellia.—Do you think I'd look better with a camellia?"

"I guess if Mrs. Van Degen looked like a rose she'd 'a worn

a rose," Mrs. Heeny rejoined poetically. "Sit still a minute longer," she added. "Your hair's so heavy I'd feel easier if I was to put in another pin."

Undine remained motionless, and the manicure, suddenly laying both hands on the girl's shoulders, and bending over to peer at her reflection, said playfully: "Ever been engaged before, Undine?"

A blush rose to the face in the mirror, spreading from chin to brow, and running rosily over the white shoulders from which their covering had slipped down.

"My! If he could see you now!" Mrs. Heeny jested.

Mrs. Spragg, rising noiselessly, glided across the room and became lost in a minute examination of the dress laid out on the bed.

With a supple twist Undine slipped from Mrs. Heeny's hold.

"Engaged? Mercy, yes! Didn't you know? To the Prince of Wales. I broke it off because I wouldn't live in the Tower."

Mrs. Spragg, lifting the dress cautiously over her arm, advanced with a reassured smile.

"I s'pose Undie'll go to Europe now," she said to Mrs. Heeny.

"I guess Undie *will*!" the young lady herself declared. "We're going to sail right afterward.—Here, mother, do be careful of my hair!" She ducked gracefully to slip into the lacy fabric which her mother held above her head.

As she rose Venus-like above its folds there was a tap on the door, immediately followed by its tentative opening.

"Mabel!" Undine muttered, her brows lowering like her father's; and Mrs. Spragg, wheeling about to screen her daughter, addressed herself protestingly to the half-open door.

"Who's there? Oh, that *you*, Mrs. Lipscomb? Well, I don't know as you *can*—Undie isn't half dressed yet——"

"Just like her—always pushing in!" Undine murmured as she slipped her arms into their transparent sleeves.

"Oh, that don't matter—I'll help dress her!" Mrs. Lipscomb's large blond person surged across the threshold. "Seems to me I ought to lend a hand to-night, considering I was the one that introduced them!"

Undine forced a smile, but Mrs. Spragg, her soft wrinkles

deepening with resentment, muttered to Mrs. Heeny, as she bent down to shake out the girl's train: "I guess my daughter's only got to show herself——"

The first meeting with old Mr. Dagonet was less formidable than Undine had expected. She had been once before to the house in Washington Square, when, with her mother, she had returned Mrs. Marvell's ceremonial visit; but on that occasion Ralph's grandfather had not been present. All the rites connected with her engagement were new and mysterious to Undine, and none more so than the unaccountable necessity of "dragging"—as she phrased it—Mrs. Spragg into the affair. It was an accepted article of the Apex creed that parental detachment should be completest at the moment when the filial fate was decided; and to find that New York reversed this rule was as puzzling to Undine as to her mother. Mrs. Spragg was so unprepared for the part she was to play that on the occasion of her visit to Mrs. Marvell her helplessness had infected Undine, and their half-hour in the sober faded drawing-room remained among the girl's most unsatisfactory memories.

She re-entered it alone with more assurance. Her confidence in her beauty had hitherto carried her through every ordeal; and it was fortified now by the feeling of power that came with the sense of being loved. If they would only leave her mother out she was sure, in her own phrase, of being able to "run the thing", and Mrs. Spragg had providentially been left out of the Dagonet dinner.

It was to consist, it appeared, only of the small family group Undine had already met; and, seated at old Mr. Dagonet's right, in the high dark dining-room with mahogany doors and dim portraits of "Signers" and their females, she felt a conscious joy in her ascendancy. Old Mr. Dagonet—small, frail and softly sardonic—appeared to fall at once under her spell. If she felt, beneath his amenity, a kind of delicate dangerousness, like that of some fine surgical instrument, she ignored it as unimportant; for she had as yet no clear perception of forces that did not directly affect her.

Mrs. Marvell, low-voiced, faded, yet impressive, was less responsive to her arts, and Undine divined in her the head of the opposition to Ralph's marriage. Mrs. Heeny had reported that Mrs. Marvell had other views for her son; and this was confirmed by such echoes of the short sharp struggle as reached the throbbing listeners at the Stentorian. But the conflict over, the air had immediately cleared, showing the enemy in the act of unconditional surrender. It surprised Undine that there had been no reprisals, no return on the points conceded. That was not her idea of warfare, and she could ascribe the completeness of the victory only to the effect of her charms.

Mrs. Marvell's manner did not express entire subjugation; yet she seemed anxious to dispel any doubts of her good faith, and if she left the burden of the talk to her lively daughter it might have been because she felt more capable of showing indulgence by her silence than in her speech.

As for Mrs. Fairford, she had never seemed more brilliantly bent on fusing the various elements under her hand. Undine had already discovered that she adored her brother, and had guessed that this would make her either a strong ally or a determined enemy. The latter alternative, however, did not alarm the girl. She thought Mrs. Fairford "bright," and wanted to be liked by her; and she was in the state of dizzy self-assurance when it seemed easy to win any sympathy she chose to seek.

For the only other guests—Mrs. Fairford's husband, and the elderly Charles Bowen who seemed to be her special friend—Undine had no attention to spare: they remained on a plane with the dim pictures hanging at her back. She had expected a larger party; but she was relieved, on the whole, that it was small enough to permit of her dominating it. Not that she wished to do so by any loudness of assertion. Her quickness in noting external differences had already taught her to modulate and lower her voice, and to replace "The i-dea!" and "I wouldn't wonder" by more polished locutions; and she had not been ten minutes at table before she found that to seem very much in love, and a little confused and subdued by the newness and intensity of the sentiment, was, to the Dagonet mind, the becoming attitude for a young lady in her situation. The part was not hard to play, for she *was* in love, of course. It was pleasant, when she looked across the table, to meet Ralph's grey eyes, with that new look in them, and to feel that she had kindled it; but it was only part of her larger pleasure in the general homage to her beauty, in the sensations of interest and curiosity excited by everything about her, from the family portraits overhead to the old Dagonet silver on the table—which were to be hers too, after all!

The talk, as at Mrs. Fairford's, confused her by its lack of the personal allusion, its tendency to turn to books, pictures and politics. "Politics," to Undine, had always been like a kind of back-kitchen to business—the place where the refuse was thrown and the doubtful messes were brewed. As a drawing-room topic, and one to provoke disinterested sentiments, it had the hollowness of Fourth of July orations, and her mind wandered in spite of the desire to appear informed and competent.

Old Mr. Dagonet, with his reedy staccato voice, that gave polish and relief to every syllable, tried to come to her aid by questioning her affably about her family and the friends she had made in New York. But the caryatid-parent, who exists simply as a filial prop, is not a fruitful theme, and Undine, called on for the first time to view her own progenitors as a subject of conversation, was struck by their lack of points. She had never paused to consider what her father and mother were "interested" in, and, challenged to specify, could have named—with sincerity—only herself. On the subject of her New York friends it was not much easier to enlarge; for so far her circle had grown less rapidly than she expected. She had fancied Ralph's wooing would at once admit her to all his social privileges; but he had shown a puzzling reluctance to introduce her to the Van Degen set, where he came and went with such familiarity; and the persons he seemed anxious to have her know—a few frumpy "clever women" of his sister's age, and one or two brisk old ladies in shabby houses with mahogany furniture and Stuart portraits—did not offer the opportunities she sought.

"Oh, I don't know many people yet—I tell Ralph he's got to hurry up and take me round," she said to Mr. Dagonet, with a side-sparkle for Ralph, whose gaze, between the flowers and lights, she was aware of perpetually drawing.

"My daughter will take you—you must know his mother's friends," the old gentleman rejoined while Mrs. Marvell smiled noncommittally.

"But you have a great friend of your own—the lady who takes you into society," Mr. Dagonet pursued; and Undine had the sense that the irrepressible Mabel was again "pushing in."

"Oh, yes—Mabel Lipscomb. We were school-mates," she said indifferently.

"Lipscomb? Lipscomb? What is Mr. Lipscomb's occupation?"

"He's a broker," said Undine, glad to be able to place her friend's husband in so handsome a light. The subtleties of a professional classification unknown to Apex had already taught her that in New York it is more distinguished to be a broker than a dentist; and she was surprised at Mr. Dagonet's lack of enthusiasm.

"Ah? A broker?" He said it almost as Popple might have said "A *dentist*?" and Undine found herself astray in a new labyrinth of social distinctions. She felt a sudden contempt for Harry Lipscomb, who had already struck her as too loud, and irrelevantly comic. "I guess Mabel'll get a divorce pretty soon," she added, desiring, for personal reasons, to present Mrs. Lipscomb as favourably as possible.

Mr. Dagonet's handsome eye-brows drew together. "A divorce? H'm—that's bad. Has he been misbehaving himself?"

Undine looked innocently surprised. "Oh, I guess not. They like each other well enough. But he's been a disappointment to her. He isn't in the right set, and I think Mabel realizes she'll never really get anywhere till she gets rid of him."

These words, uttered in the high fluting tone that she rose to when sure of her subject, fell on a pause which prolonged and deepened itself to receive them, while every face at the table, Ralph Marvell's excepted, reflected in varying degree Mr. Dagonet's pained astonishment.

"But, my dear young lady—what would your friend's own situation be if, as you put it, she 'got rid' of her husband on so trivial a pretext?"

Undine, surprised at his dullness, tried to explain. "Oh, that wouldn't be the reason *given*, of course. Any lawyer could fix it up for them. Don't they generally call it desertion?"

There was another, more palpitating, silence, broken by a laugh from Ralph.

"*Ralph!*" his mother breathed; then, turning to Undine, she said with a constrained smile: "I believe in certain parts of the country such—unfortunate arrangements—are beginning to be tolerated. But in New York, in spite of our growing indifference, a divorced woman is still—thank heaven!—at a decided disadvantage."

Undine's eyes opened wide. Here at last was a topic that really interested her, and one that gave another amazing glimpse into the camera obscura of New York society. "Do you mean to say Mabel would be worse off, then? Couldn't she even go round as much as she does now?"

Mrs. Marvell met this gravely. "It would depend, I should say, on the kind of people she wished to see."

"Oh, the very best, of course! That would be her only object."

Ralph interposed with another laugh. "You see, Undine, you'd better think twice before you divorce me!"

"*Ralph!*" his mother again breathed; but the girl, flushed and sparkling, flung back: "Oh, it all depends on *you*! Out in Apex, if a girl marries a man who don't come up to what she expected, people consider it's to her credit to want to change. *You'd* better think twice of that!"

"If I were only sure of knowing what you expect!" he caught up her joke, tossing it back at her across the fascinated silence of their listeners.

"Why, *everything!*" she announced—and Mr. Dagonet, turning, laid an intricately-veined old hand on hers, and said, with a change of tone that relaxed the tension of the listeners: "My child, if you look like that you'll get it."

VIII

I<small>T WAS DOUBTLESS</small> owing to Mrs. Fairford's foresight that such possibilities of tension were curtailed, after dinner, by her carrying off Ralph and his betrothed to the theatre.

Mr. Dagonet, it was understood, always went to bed after an hour's whist with his daughter; and the silent Mr. Fairford gave his evenings to bridge at his club. The party, therefore, consisted only of Undine and Ralph, with Mrs. Fairford and her attendant friend. Undine vaguely wondered why the grave and grey-haired Mr. Bowen formed so invariable a part of that lady's train; but she concluded that it was the New York custom for married ladies to have gentlemen " 'round" (as girls had in Apex), and that Mr. Bowen was the sole survivor of Laura Fairford's earlier triumphs.

She had, however, little time to give to such conjectures, for the performance they were attending—the début of a fashionable London actress—had attracted a large audience in which Undine immediately recognized a number of familiar faces. Her engagement had been announced only the day before, and she had the delicious sense of being "in all the papers," and of focussing countless glances of interest and curiosity as she swept through the theatre in Mrs. Fairford's wake. Their stalls were near the stage, and progress thither was slow enough to permit of prolonged enjoyment of this sensation. Before passing to her place she paused for Ralph to remove her cloak, and as he lifted it from her shoulders she heard a lady say behind her: "There she is—the one in white, with the lovely back——" and a man answer: "Gad! Where did he find anything as good as that?"

Anonymous approval was sweet enough; but she was to taste a moment more exquisite when, in the proscenium box across the house, she saw Clare Van Degen seated beside the prim figure of Miss Harriet Ray. "They're here to see me with him—they hate it, but they couldn't keep away!" She turned and lifted a smile of possessorship to Ralph.

Mrs. Fairford seemed also struck by the presence of the two ladies, and Undine heard her whisper to Mr. Bowen: "Do you see Clare over there—and Harriet with her? Harriet *would come*—I call it Spartan! And so like Clare to ask her!"

Her companion laughed. "It's one of the deepest instincts in human nature. The murdered are as much given as the murderer to haunting the scene of the crime."

Doubtless guessing Ralph's desire to have Undine to himself, Mrs. Fairford had sent the girl in first; and Undine, as she seated herself, was aware that the occupant of the next stall half turned to her, as with a vague gesture of recognition. But just then the curtain rose, and she became absorbed in the development of the drama, especially as it tended to display the remarkable toilets which succeeded each other on the person of its leading lady. Undine, seated at Ralph Marvell's side, and feeling the thrill of his proximity as a subtler element in the general interest she was exciting, was at last repaid for the disappointment of her evening at the opera. It was characteristic of her that she remembered her failures as keenly as her triumphs, and that the passionate desire to obliterate, to "get even" with them, was always among the latent incentives of her conduct. Now at last she was having what she wanted—she was in conscious possession of the "real thing"; and through her other, more diffused, sensations Ralph's adoration gave her such a last refinement of pleasure as might have come to some warrior Queen borne in triumph by captive princes, and reading in the eyes of one the passion he dared not speak.

When the curtain fell this vague enjoyment was heightened by various acts of recognition. All the people she wanted to "go with," as they said in Apex, seemed to be about her in the stalls and boxes; and her eyes continued to revert with special satisfaction to the incongruous group formed by Mrs. Peter Van Degen and Miss Ray. The sight made it irresistible to whisper to Ralph: "You ought to go round and talk to your cousin. Have you told her we're engaged?"

"Clare? of course. She's going to call on you to-morrow."

"Oh, she needn't put herself out—she's never been yet," said Undine loftily.

He made no rejoinder, but presently asked: "Who's that you're waving to?"

"Mr. Popple. He's coming round to see us. You know he wants to paint me." Undine fluttered and beamed as the bril-

liant Popple made his way across the stalls to the seat which
her neighbour had momentarily left.

"First-rate chap next to you—whoever he is—to give me
this chance," the artist declared. "Ha, Ralph, my boy, how
did you pull it off? That's what we're all of us wondering."
He leaned over to give Marvell's hand the ironic grasp of
celibacy. "Well, you've left us lamenting: he has, you know,
Miss Spragg. But I've got one pull over the others—I can
paint you! He can't forbid that, can he? Not before marriage,
anyhow!"

Undine divided her shining glances between the two. "I
guess he isn't going to treat me any different afterward," she
proclaimed with joyous defiance.

"Ah, well, there's no telling, you know. Hadn't we better
begin at once? Seriously, I want awfully to get you into the
spring show."

"Oh, really? That would be too lovely!"

"*You* would be, certainly—the way I mean to do you. But
I see Ralph getting glum. Cheer up, my dear fellow; I daresay
you'll be invited to some of the sittings—that's for Miss
Spragg to say.—Ah, here comes your neighbour back, confound him— You'll let me know when we can begin?"

As Popple moved away Undine turned eagerly to Marvell.
"Do you suppose there's time? I'd love to have him to do
me!"

Ralph smiled. "My poor child—he *would* 'do' you, with a
vengeance. Infernal cheek, his asking you to sit——"

She stared. "But why? He's painted your cousin, and all the
smart women."

"Oh, if a 'smart' portrait's all you want!"

"I want what the others want," she answered, frowning and
pouting a little.

She was already beginning to resent in Ralph the slightest
sign of resistance to her pleasure; and her resentment took
the form—a familiar one in Apex courtships—of turning on
him, in the next entr'acte, a deliberately averted shoulder. The
result of this was to bring her, for the first time, in more
direct relation to her other neighbour. As she turned he
turned too, showing her, above a shining shirt-front fastened
with a large imitation pearl, a ruddy plump snub face without

an angle in it, which yet looked sharper than a razor. Undine's eyes met his with a startled look, and for a long moment they remained suspended on each other's stare.

Undine at length shrank back with an unrecognizing face; but her movement made her opera-glass slip to the floor, and her neighbour bent down and picked it up.

"Well—don't you know me yet?" he said with a slight smile, as he restored the glass to her.

She had grown white to the lips, and when she tried to speak the effort produced only a faint click in her throat. She felt that the change in her appearance must be visible, and the dread of letting Marvell see it made her continue to turn her ravaged face to her other neighbour. The round black eyes set prominently in the latter's round glossy countenance had expressed at first only an impersonal and slightly ironic interest; but a look of surprise grew in them as Undine's silence continued.

"What's the matter? Don't you want me to speak to you?"

She became aware that Marvell, as if unconscious of her slight show of displeasure, had left his seat, and was making his way toward the aisle; and this assertion of independence, which a moment before she would so deeply have resented, now gave her a feeling of intense relief.

"No—don't speak to me, please. I'll tell you another time—I'll write." Her neighbour continued to gaze at her, forming his lips into a noiseless whistle under his small dark moustache.

"Well, I— That's about the stiffest," he murmured; and as she made no answer he added: "Afraid I'll ask to be introduced to your friend?"

She made a faint movement of entreaty. "I can't explain. I promise to see you; but I *ask* you not to talk to me now."

He unfolded his programme, and went on speaking in a low tone while he affected to study it. "Anything to oblige, of course. That's always been my motto. But *is* it a bargain—fair and square? You'll see me?"

She receded farther from him. "I promise. I—I *want* to," she faltered.

"All right, then. Call me up in the morning at the Driscoll Building. Seven-O-nine—got it?"

She nodded, and he added in a still lower tone: "I suppose I can congratulate you, anyhow?" and then, without waiting for her reply, turned to study Mrs. Van Degen's box through his opera-glass.

Clare, as if aware of the scrutiny fixed on her from below, leaned back and threw a question over her shoulder to Ralph Marvell, who had just seated himself behind her.

"Who's the funny man with the red face talking to Miss Spragg?"

Ralph bent forward. "The man next to her? Never saw him before. But I think you're mistaken: she's not speaking to him."

"She *was*— Wasn't she, Harriet?"

Miss Ray pinched her lips together without speaking, and Mrs. Van Degen paused for the fraction of a second. "Perhaps he's an Apex friend," she then suggested.

"Very likely. Only I think she'd have introduced him if he had been."

His cousin faintly shrugged. "Shall you encourage that?"

Peter Van Degen, who had strayed into his wife's box for a moment, caught the colloquy, and lifted his opera-glass.

"The fellow next to Miss Spragg? (By George, Ralph, she's ripping to-night!) Wait a minute—I know his face. Saw him in old Harmon Driscoll's office the day of the Eubaw Mine meeting. This chap's his secretary, or something. Driscoll called him in to give some facts to the directors, and he seemed a mighty wide-awake customer."

Clare Van Degen turned gaily to her cousin. "If he has anything to do with the Driscolls you'd better cultivate him! That's the kind of acquaintance the Dagonets have always needed. I married to set them an example!"

Ralph rose with a laugh. "You're right. I'll hurry back and make his acquaintance." He held out his hand to his cousin, avoiding her disappointed eyes.

Undine, on entering her bedroom late that evening, was startled by the presence of a muffled figure which revealed itself, through the dimness, as the ungirded midnight outline of Mrs. Spragg.

"*Mother?* What on earth——?" the girl exclaimed, as Mrs.

Spragg pressed the electric button and flooded the room with light. The idea of a mother's sitting up for her daughter was so foreign to Apex customs that it roused only mistrust and irritation in the object of the demonstration.

Mrs. Spragg came forward deprecatingly to lift the cloak from her daughter's shoulders.

"I just *had* to, Undie—I told father I *had* to. I wanted to hear all about it."

Undine shrugged away from her. "Mercy! At this hour? You'll be as white as a sheet to-morrow, sitting up all night like this."

She moved toward the toilet-table, and began to demolish with feverish hands the structure which Mrs. Heeny, a few hours earlier, had so lovingly raised. But the rose caught in a mesh of hair, and Mrs. Spragg, venturing timidly to release it, had a full view of her daughter's face in the glass.

"Why, Undie, *you're* as white as a sheet now! You look fairly sick. What's the matter, daughter?"

The girl broke away from her.

"Oh, can't you leave me alone, mother? There—do I look white *now*?" she cried, the blood flaming into her pale cheeks; and as Mrs. Spragg shrank back, she added more mildly, in the tone of a parent rebuking a persistent child: "It's enough to *make* anybody sick to be stared at that way!"

Mrs. Spragg overflowed with compunction. "I'm so sorry, Undie. I guess it was just seeing you in this glare of light."

"Yes—the light's awful; do turn some off," ordered Undine, for whom, ordinarily, no radiance was too strong; and Mrs. Spragg, grateful to have commands laid upon her, hastened to obey.

Undine, after this, submitted in brooding silence to having her dress unlaced, and her slippers and dressing-gown brought to her. Mrs. Spragg visibly yearned to say more, but she restrained the impulse lest it should provoke her dismissal.

"Won't you take just a sup of milk before you go to bed?" she suggested at length, as Undine sank into an armchair. "I've got some for you right here in the parlour."

Without looking up the girl answered: "No. I don't want anything. Do go to bed."

Her mother seemed to be struggling between the life-long instinct of obedience and a swift unformulated fear. "I'm going, Undie." She wavered. "Didn't they receive you right, daughter?" she asked with sudden resolution.

"What nonsense! How *should* they receive me? Everybody was lovely to me." Undine rose to her feet and went on with her undressing, tossing her clothes on the floor and shaking her hair over her bare shoulders.

Mrs. Spragg stooped to gather up the scattered garments as they fell, folding them with a wistful caressing touch, and laying them on the lounge, without daring to raise her eyes to her daughter. It was not till she heard Undine throw herself on the bed that she went toward her and drew the coverlet up with deprecating hands.

"Oh, do put the light out—I'm dead tired," the girl grumbled, pressing her face into the pillow.

Mrs. Spragg turned away obediently; then, gathering all her scattered impulses into a passionate act of courage, she moved back to the bedside.

"Undie—you didn't see anybody—I mean at the theatre? *Anybody you didn't want to see?*"

Undine, at the question, raised her head and started upright against the tossed pillows, her white exasperated face close to her mother's twitching features. The two women examined each other a moment, fear and anger in their crossed glances; then Undine answered: "No, nobody. Good-night."

IX

U NDINE, late the next day, waited alone under the leafless trellising of a wistaria arbour on the west side of the Central Park. She had put on her plainest dress, and wound a closely patterned veil over her least vivid hat; but even thus toned down to the situation she was conscious of blazing out from it inconveniently.

The habit of meeting young men in sequestered spots was not unknown to her: the novelty was in feeling any embarrassment about it. Even now she was disturbed not so much by the unlikely chance of an accidental encounter with Ralph Marvell as by the remembrance of similar meetings, far from accidental, with the romantic Aaronson. Could it be that the hand now adorned with Ralph's engagement ring had once, in this very spot, surrendered itself to the riding-master's pressure? At the thought a wave of physical disgust passed over her, blotting out another memory as distasteful but more remote.

It was revived by the appearance of a ruddy middle-sized young man, his stoutish figure tightly buttoned into a square-shouldered over-coat, who presently approached along the path that led to the arbour. Silhouetted against the slope of the asphalt, the new-comer revealed an outline thick yet compact, with a round head set on a neck in which, at the first chance, prosperity would be likely to develop a red crease. His face, with its rounded surfaces, and the sanguine innocence of a complexion belied by prematurely astute black eyes, had a look of jovial cunning which Undine had formerly thought "smart" but which now struck her as merely vulgar. She felt that in the Marvell set Elmer Moffatt would have been stamped as "not a gentleman." Nevertheless something in his look seemed to promise the capacity to develop into any character he might care to assume; though it did not seem probable that, for the present, that of a gentleman would be among them. He had always had a brisk swaggering step, and the faintly impudent tilt of the head that she had once thought "dashing"; but whereas this look had formerly denoted a somewhat desperate defiance of the world and its judgments it now suggested an almost assured relation to these powers; and Undine's heart sank at the thought of what the change implied.

As he drew nearer, the young man's air of assurance was replaced by an expression of mildly humorous surprise.

"Well—this is white of you, Undine!" he said, taking her lifeless fingers into his dapperly gloved hand.

Through her veil she formed the words: "I said I'd come."

He laughed. "That's so. And you see I believed you. Though I might not have——"

"I don't see the use of beginning like this," she interrupted nervously.

"That's so too. Suppose we walk along a little ways? It's rather chilly standing round."

He turned down the path that descended toward the Ramble and the girl moved on beside him with her long flowing steps.

When they had reached the comparative shelter of the interlacing trees Moffatt paused again to say: "If we're going to talk I'd like to see you, Undine;" and after a first moment of reluctance she submissively threw back her veil.

He let his eyes rest on her in silence; then he said judicially: "You've filled out some; but you're paler." After another appreciative scrutiny he added: "There's mighty few women as well worth looking at, and I'm obliged to you for letting me have the chance again."

Undine's brows drew together, but she softened her frown to a quivering smile.

"I'm glad to see you too, Elmer—I am, *really!*"

He returned her smile while his glance continued to study her humorously. "You didn't betray the fact last night, Miss Spragg."

"I was so taken aback. I thought you were out in Alaska somewhere."

The young man shaped his lips into the mute whistle by which he habitually vented his surprise. "You *did*? Didn't Abner E. Spragg tell you he'd seen me down town?"

Undine gave him a startled glance. "Father? Why, have you seen him? He never said a word about it!"

Her companion's whistle became audible. "He's running

yet!" he said gaily. "I wish I could scare some people as easy as I can your father."

The girl hesitated. "I never felt toward you the way father did," she hazarded at length; and he gave her another long look in return.

"Well, if they'd left you alone I don't believe you'd ever have acted mean to me," was the conclusion he drew from it.

"I didn't mean to, Elmer. . . . I give you my word—but I was so young . . . I didn't know anything. . ."

His eyes had a twinkle of reminiscent pleasantry. "No—I don't suppose it *would* teach a girl much to be engaged two years to a stiff like Millard Binch; and that was about all that had happened to you before I came along."

Undine flushed to the forehead. "Oh, Elmer—I was only a child when I was engaged to Millard——"

"That's a fact. And you went on being one a good while afterward. *The Apex Eagle* always head-lined you 'The child-bride'——"

"I can't see what's the use—now——."

"That ruled out of court too? See here, Undine—what *can* we talk about? I understood that was what we were here for."

"Of course." She made an effort at recovery. "I only meant to say—what's the use of raking up things that are over?"

"Rake up? That's the idea, is it? Was that why you tried to cut me last night?"

"I—oh, Elmer! I didn't mean to; only, you see, I'm engaged."

"Oh, I saw that fast enough. I'd have seen it even if I didn't read the papers." He gave a short laugh. "He was feeling pretty good, sitting there alongside of you, wasn't he? I don't wonder he was. I remember. But I don't see that that was a reason for cold-shouldering me. I'm a respectable member of society now—I'm one of Harmon B. Driscoll's private secretaries." He brought out the fact with mock solemnity.

But to Undine, though undoubtedly impressive, the statement did not immediately present itself as a subject for pleasantry.

"Elmer Moffatt—you *are*?"

He laughed again. "Guess you'd have remembered me last night if you'd known it."

She was following her own train of thought with a look of pale intensity. "You're *living* in New York, then—you're going to live here right along?"

"Well, it looks that way; as long as I can hang on to this job. Great men always gravitate to the metropolis. And I gravitated here just as Uncle Harmon B. was looking round for somebody who could give him an inside tip on the Eubaw mine deal—you know the Driscolls are pretty deep in Eubaw. I happened to go out there after our little unpleasantness at Apex, and it was just the time the deal went through. So in one way your folks did me a good turn when they made Apex too hot for me: funny to think of, ain't it?"

Undine, recovering herself, held out her hand impulsively.

"I'm real glad of it—I mean I'm real glad you've had such a stroke of luck!"

"Much obliged," he returned. "By the way, you might mention the fact to Abner E. Spragg next time you run across him."

"Father'll be real glad too, Elmer." She hesitated, and then went on: "You must see now that it was natural father and mother should have felt the way they did——"

"Oh, the only thing that struck me as unnatural was their making you feel so too. But I'm free to admit I wasn't a promising case in those days." His glance played over her for a moment. "Say, Undine—it was good while it lasted, though, wasn't it?"

She shrank back with a burning face and eyes of misery.

"Why, what's the matter? That ruled out too? Oh, all right. Look at here, Undine, suppose you let me know what you *are* here to talk about, anyhow."

She cast a helpless glance down the windings of the wooded glen in which they had halted.

"Just to ask you—to beg you—not to say anything of this kind again— *ever*——"

"Anything about you and me?"

She nodded mutely.

"Why, what's wrong? Anybody been saying anything against me?"

"Oh, no. It's not that!"

"What on earth *is* it, then—except that you're ashamed of

me, one way or another?" She made no answer, and he stood digging the tip of his walking-stick into a fissure of the asphalt. At length he went on in a tone that showed a first faint trace of irritation: "I don't want to break into your gilt-edged crowd, if it's that you're scared of."

His tone seemed to increase her distress. "No, no—you don't understand. All I want is that nothing shall be known."

"Yes; but *why*? It was all straight enough, if you come to that."

"It doesn't matter . . . whether it was straight . . . or . . . not. . ." He interpolated a whistle which made her add: "What I mean is that out here in the East they don't even like it if a girl's been *engaged* before."

This last strain on his credulity wrung a laugh from Moffatt. "Gee! How'd they expect her fair young life to pass? Playing 'Holy City' on the melodeon, and knitting tidies for church fairs?"

"Girls are looked after here. It's all different. Their mothers go round with them."

This increased her companion's hilarity and he glanced about him with a pretense of compunction. "Excuse *me*! I ought to have remembered. Where's your chaperon, Miss Spragg?" He crooked his arm with mock ceremony. "Allow me to escort you to the bew-fay. You see I'm onto the New York style myself."

A sigh of discouragement escaped her. "Elmer—if you really believe I never wanted to act mean to you, don't you act mean to me now!"

"Act mean?" He grew serious again and moved nearer to her. "What is it you want, Undine? Why can't you say it right out?"

"What I told you. I don't want Ralph Marvell—or any of them—to know anything. If any of his folks found out, they'd never let him marry me—never! And he wouldn't want to: he'd be so horrified. And it would *kill* me, Elmer—it would just kill me!"

She pressed close to him, forgetful of her new reserves and repugnances, and impelled by the passionate absorbing desire to wring from him some definite pledge of safety.

"Oh, Elmer, if you ever liked me, help me now, and I'll help you if I get the chance!"

He had recovered his coolness as hers forsook her, and stood his ground steadily, though her entreating hands, her glowing face, were near enough to have shaken less sturdy nerves.

"That so, Puss? You just ask me to pass the sponge over Elmer Moffatt of Apex City? Cut the gentleman when we meet? That the size of it?"

"Oh, Elmer, it's my first chance—I can't lose it!" she broke out, sobbing.

"Nonsense, child! Of course you shan't. Here, look up, Undine—why, I never saw you cry before. Don't you be afraid of me—*I* ain't going to interrupt the wedding march." He began to whistle a bar of Lohengrin. "I only just want one little promise in return."

She threw a startled look at him and he added reassuringly: "Oh, don't mistake me. I don't want to butt into your set—not for social purposes, anyhow; but if ever it should come handy to know any of 'em in a business way, would you fix it up for me— *after you're married?*"

Their eyes met, and she remained silent for a tremulous moment or two; then she held out her hand. "Afterward—yes. I promise. And *you* promise, Elmer?"

"Oh, to have and to hold!" he sang out, swinging about to follow her as she hurriedly began to retrace her steps.

The March twilight had fallen, and the Stentorian façade was all aglow, when Undine regained its monumental threshold. She slipped through the marble vestibule and soared skyward in the mirror-lined lift, hardly conscious of the direction she was taking. What she wanted was solitude, and the time to put some order into her thoughts; and she hoped to steal into her room without meeting her mother. Through her thick veil the clusters of lights in the Spragg drawing-room dilated and flowed together in a yellow blur, from which, as she entered, a figure detached itself; and with a start of annoyance she saw Ralph Marvell rise from the perusal of the "fiction number" of a magazine which had replaced "The Hound of the Baskervilles" on the onyx table.

"Yes; you told me not to come—and here I am." He lifted

her hand to his lips as his eyes tried to find hers through the veil.

She drew back with a nervous gesture. "I told you I'd be awfully late."

"I know—trying on! And you're horribly tired, and wishing with all your might I wasn't here."

"I'm not so sure I'm not!" she rejoined, trying to hide her vexation in a smile.

"What a tragic little voice! You really *are* done up. I couldn't help dropping in for a minute; but of course if you say so I'll be off." She was removing her long gloves, and he took her hands and drew her close. "Only take off your veil, and let me see you."

A quiver of resistance ran through her: he felt it and dropped her hands.

"Please don't tease. I never could bear it," she stammered, drawing away.

"Till to-morrow, then; that is, if the dress-makers permit."

She forced a laugh. "If I showed myself now you might not come back to-morrow. I look perfectly hideous—it was so hot and they kept me so long."

"All to make yourself more beautiful for a man who's blind with your beauty already?"

The words made her smile, and moving nearer she bent her head and stood still while he undid her veil. As he put it back their lips met, and his look of passionate tenderness was incense to her.

But the next moment his expression passed from worship to concern. "Dear! Why, what's the matter? You've been crying!"

She put both hands to her hat in the instinctive effort to hide her face. His persistence was as irritating as her mother's.

"I told you it was frightfully hot—and all my things were horrid; and it made me so cross and nervous!" She turned to the looking-glass with a feint of smoothing her hair.

Marvell laid his hand on her arm. "I can't bear to see you so done up. Why can't we be married to-morrow, and escape all these ridiculous preparations? I shall hate your fine clothes if they're going to make you so miserable."

She dropped her hands, and swept about on him, her face lit up by a new idea. He was extraordinarily handsome and appealing, and her heart began to beat faster.

"I hate it all too! I wish we *could* be married right away!"

Marvell caught her to him joyously. "Dearest—dearest! Don't, if you don't mean it! The thought's too glorious!"

Undine lingered in his arms, not with any intent of tenderness, but as if too deeply lost in a new train of thought to be conscious of his hold.

"I suppose most of the things *could* be got ready sooner— if I said they *must*," she brooded, with a fixed gaze that travelled past him. "And the rest—why shouldn't the rest be sent over to Europe after us? I want to go straight off with you, away from everything—ever so far away, where there'll be nobody but you and me alone!" She had a flash of illumination which made her turn her lips to his.

"Oh, my darling—my darling!" Marvell whispered.

X

M R. AND MRS. SPRAGG were both given to such long periods of ruminating apathy that the student of inheritance might have wondered whence Undine derived her overflowing activity. The answer would have been obtained by observing her father's business life. From the moment he set foot in Wall Street Mr. Spragg became another man. Physically the change revealed itself only by the subtlest signs. As he steered his way to his office through the jostling crowd of William Street his relaxed muscles did not grow more taut or his lounging gait less desultory. His shoulders were hollowed by the usual droop, and his rusty black waistcoat showed the same creased concavity at the waist, the same flabby prominence below. It was only in his face that the difference was perceptible, though even here it rather lurked behind the features than openly modified them: showing itself now and then in the cautious glint of half-closed eyes, the forward thrust of black brows, or a tightening of the lax lines of the mouth—as the gleam of a night-watchman's light might flash across the darkness of a shuttered house-front.

The shutters were more tightly barred than usual, when, on a morning some two weeks later than the date of the incidents last recorded, Mr. Spragg approached the steel and concrete tower in which his office occupied a lofty pigeon-hole. Events had moved rapidly and somewhat surprisingly in the interval, and Mr. Spragg had already accustomed himself to the fact that his daughter was to be married within the week, instead of awaiting the traditional post-Lenten date. Conventionally the change meant little to him; but on the practical side it presented unforeseen difficulties. Mr. Spragg had learned within the last weeks that a New York marriage involved material obligations unknown to Apex. Marvell, indeed, had been loftily careless of such questions; but his grandfather, on the announcement of the engagement, had called on Mr. Spragg and put before him, with polished precision, the young man's financial situation.

Mr. Spragg, at the moment, had been inclined to deal with his visitor in a spirit of indulgent irony. As he leaned back in his revolving chair, with feet adroitly balanced against a tilted scrap basket, his air of relaxed power made Mr. Dagonet's venerable elegance seem as harmless as that of an ivory jack-straw—and his first replies to his visitor were made with the mildness of a kindly giant.

"Ralph don't make a living out of the law, you say? No, it didn't strike me he'd be likely to, from the talks I've had with him. Fact is, the law's a business that wants——" Mr. Spragg broke off, checked by a protest from Mr. Dagonet. "Oh, a *profession*, you call it? It ain't a business?" His smile grew more indulgent as this novel distinction dawned on him. "Why, I guess that's the whole trouble with Ralph. Nobody expects to make money in a *profession*; and if you've taught him to regard the law that way, he'd better go right into cooking-stoves and done with it."

Mr. Dagonet, within a narrower range, had his own play of humour; and it met Mr. Spragg's with a leap. "It's because I knew he would manage to make cooking-stoves as unre-munerative as a profession that I saved him from so glaring a failure by putting him into the law."

The retort drew a grunt of amusement from Mr. Spragg; and the eyes of the two men met in unexpected understanding.

"That so? What *can* he do, then?" the future father-in-law enquired.

"He can write poetry—at least he tells me he can." Mr. Dagonet hesitated, as if aware of the inadequacy of the alter-native, and then added: "And he can count on three thousand a year from me."

Mr. Spragg tilted himself farther back without disturbing his subtly-calculated relation to the scrap basket.

"Does it cost anything like that to print his poetry?"

Mr. Dagonet smiled again: he was clearly enjoying his visit. "Dear, no—he doesn't go in for 'luxe' editions. And now and then he gets ten dollars from a magazine."

Mr. Spragg mused. "Wasn't he ever *taught* to work?"

"No; I really couldn't have afforded that."

"I see. Then they've got to live on two hundred and fifty dollars a month."

Mr. Dagonet remained pleasantly unmoved. "Does it cost anything like that to buy your daughter's dresses?"

A subterranean chuckle agitated the lower folds of Mr. Spragg's waistcoat.

"I might put him in the way of something—I guess he's smart enough."

Mr. Dagonet made a gesture of friendly warning. "It will pay us both in the end to keep him out of business," he said, rising as if to show that his mission was accomplished.

The results of this friendly conference had been more serious than Mr. Spragg could have foreseen—and the victory remained with his antagonist. It had not entered into Mr. Spragg's calculations that he would have to give his daughter any fixed income on her marriage. He meant that she should have the "handsomest" wedding the New York press had ever celebrated, and her mother's fancy was already afloat on a sea of luxuries—a motor, a Fifth Avenue house, and a tiara that should out-blaze Mrs. Van Degen's; but these were movable benefits, to be conferred whenever Mr. Spragg happened to be "on the right side" of the market. It was a different matter to be called on, at such short notice, to bridge the gap between young Marvell's allowance and Undine's requirements; and her father's immediate conclusion was that the engagement had better be broken off. Such scissions were almost painless in Apex, and he had fancied it would be easy, by an appeal to the girl's pride, to make her see that she owed it to herself to do better.

"You'd better wait awhile and look round again," was the way he had put it to her at the opening of the talk of which, even now, he could not recall the close without a tremor.

Undine, when she took his meaning, had been terrible. Everything had gone down before her, as towns and villages went down before one of the tornadoes of her native state. Wait awhile? Look round? Did he suppose she was marrying for *money*? Didn't he see it was all a question, now and here, of the kind of people she wanted to "go with"? Did he want to throw her straight back into the Lipscomb set, to have her marry a dentist and live in a West Side flat? Why hadn't they stayed in Apex, if that was all he thought she was fit for? She might as well have married Millard Binch, instead of handing him over to Indiana Frusk! Couldn't her father understand that nice girls, in New York, didn't regard getting married like going on a buggy-ride? It was enough to ruin a girl's chances if she broke her engagement to a man in Ralph Marvell's set. All kinds of spiteful things would be said about her, and she would never be able to go with the right people again. They had better go back to Apex right off—it was they and not *she* who had wanted to leave Apex, anyhow—she could call her mother to witness it. She had always, when it came to that, done what her father and mother wanted, but she'd given up trying to make out what they were after, unless it was to make her miserable; and if that was it, hadn't they had enough of it by this time? She had, anyhow. But after this she meant to lead her own life; and they needn't ask her where she was going, or what she meant to do, because this time she'd die before she told them—and they'd made life so hateful to her that she only wished she was dead already.

Mr. Spragg heard her out in silence, pulling at his beard with one sallow wrinkled hand, while the other dragged down the armhole of his waistcoat. Suddenly he looked up and said: "Ain't you in love with the fellow, Undie?"

The girl glared back at him, her splendid brows beetling like an Amazon's. "Do you think I'd care a cent for all the rest of it if I wasn't?"

"Well, if you are, you and he won't mind beginning in a small way."

Her look poured contempt on his ignorance. "Do you s'pose I'd drag him down?" With a magnificent gesture she tore Marvell's ring from her finger. "I'll send this back this minute. I'll tell him I thought he was a rich man, and now I see I'm mistaken——" She burst into shattering sobs, rocking her beautiful body back and forward in all the abandonment of young grief; and her father stood over her, stroking her shoulder and saying helplessly: "I'll see what I can do, Undine——"

All his life, and at ever-diminishing intervals, Mr. Spragg had been called on by his womenkind to "see what he could do"; and the seeing had almost always resulted as they wished. Undine did not have to send back her ring, and in her state of trance-like happiness she hardly asked by what

means her path had been smoothed, but merely accepted her
mother's assurance that "father had fixed everything all right."

Mr. Spragg accepted the situation also. A son-in-law who
expected to be pensioned like a Grand Army veteran was a
phenomenon new to his experience; but if that was what Undine wanted she should have it. Only two days later, however,
he was met by a new demand—the young people had decided to be married "right off," instead of waiting till June.
This change of plan was made known to Mr. Spragg at a
moment when he was peculiarly unprepared for the financial
readjustment it necessitated. He had always declared himself
able to cope with any crisis if Undine and her mother would
"go steady"; but he now warned them of his inability to keep
up with the new pace they had set.

Undine, not deigning to return to the charge, had commissioned her mother to speak for her; and Mr. Spragg was surprised to meet in his wife a firmness as inflexible as his
daughter's.

"I can't do it, Loot—can't put my hand on the cash," he
had protested; but Mrs. Spragg fought him inch by inch, her
back to the wall—flinging out at last, as he pressed her
closer: "Well, if you want to know, she's seen Elmer."

The bolt reached its mark, and her husband turned an agitated face on her.

"Elmer? What on earth—he didn't come *here*?"

"No; but he sat next to her the other night at the theatre,
and she's wild with us for not having warned her."

Mr. Spragg's scowl drew his projecting brows together.
"Warned her of what? What's Elmer to her? Why's she afraid
of Elmer Moffatt?"

"She's afraid of his talking."

"Talking? What on earth can he say that'll hurt *her*?"

"Oh, I don't know," Mrs. Spragg wailed. "She's so nervous
I can hardly get a word out of her."

Mr. Spragg's whitening face showed the touch of a new
fear. "Is she afraid he'll get round her again—make up to her?
Is that what she means by 'talking'?"

"I don't know, I don't know. I only know she *is* afraid—
she's afraid as death of him."

For a long interval they sat silently looking at each other

while their heavy eyes exchanged conjectures: then Mr. Spragg rose from his chair, saying, as he took up his hat: "Don't you fret, Leota; I'll see what I can do."

He had been "seeing" now for an arduous fortnight; and the strain on his vision had resulted in a state of tension such as he had not undergone since the epic days of the Pure Water Move at Apex. It was not his habit to impart his fears to Mrs. Spragg and Undine, and they continued the bridal preparations, secure in their invariable experience that, once "father" had been convinced of the impossibility of evading their demands, he might be trusted to satisfy them by means with which his womenkind need not concern themselves. Mr. Spragg, as he approached his office on the morning in question, felt reasonably sure of fulfilling these expectations; but he reflected that a few more such victories would mean disaster.

He entered the vast marble vestibule of the Ararat Trust Building and walked toward the express elevator that was to carry him up to his office. At the door of the elevator a man turned to him, and he recognized Elmer Moffatt, who put out his hand with an easy gesture.

Mr. Spragg did not ignore the gesture: he did not even withhold his hand. In his code the cut, as a conscious sign of disapproval, did not exist. In the south, if you had a grudge against a man you tried to shoot him; in the west, you tried to do him in a mean turn in business; but in neither region was the cut among the social weapons of offense. Mr. Spragg, therefore, seeing Moffatt in his path, extended a lifeless hand while he faced the young man scowlingly. Moffatt met the hand and the scowl with equal coolness.

"Going up to your office? I was on my way there."

The elevator door rolled back, and Mr. Spragg, entering it, found his companion at his side. They remained silent during the ascent to Mr. Spragg's threshold; but there the latter turned to enquire ironically of Moffatt: "Anything left to say?"

Moffatt smiled. "Nothing *left*—no; I'm carrying a whole new line of goods."

Mr. Spragg pondered the reply; then he opened the door

and suffered Moffatt to follow him in. Behind an inner glazed enclosure, with its one window dimmed by a sooty perspective barred with chimneys, he seated himself at a dusty littered desk, and groped instinctively for the support of the scrap basket. Moffatt, uninvited, dropped into the nearest chair, and Mr. Spragg said, after another silence: "I'm pretty busy this morning."

"I know you are: that's why I'm here," Moffatt serenely answered. He leaned back, crossing his legs, and twisting his small stiff moustache with a plump hand adorned by a cameo.

"Fact is," he went on, "this is a coals-of-fire call. You think I owe you a grudge, and I'm going to show you I'm not that kind. I'm going to put you onto a good thing—oh, not because I'm so fond of you; just because it happens to hit my sense of a joke."

While Moffatt talked Mr. Spragg took up the pile of letters on his desk and sat shuffling them like a pack of cards. He dealt them deliberately to two imaginary players; then he pushed them aside and drew out his watch.

"All right—I carry one too," said the young man easily. "But you'll find it's time gained to hear what I've got to say."

Mr. Spragg considered the vista of chimneys without speaking, and Moffatt continued: "I don't suppose you care to hear the story of my life, so I won't refer you to the back numbers. You used to say out in Apex that I spent too much time loafing round the bar of the Mealey House; that was one of the things you had against me. Well, maybe I did—but it taught me to talk, and to listen to the other fellows too. Just at present I'm one of Harmon B. Driscoll's private secretaries, and some of that Mealey House loafing has come in more useful than any job I ever put my hand to. The old man happened to hear I knew something about the inside of the Eubaw deal, and took me on to have the information where he could get at it. I've given him good talk for his money; but I've done some listening too. Eubaw ain't the only commodity the Driscolls deal in."

Mr. Spragg restored his watch to his pocket and shifted his drowsy gaze from the window to his visitor's face.

"Yes," said Moffatt, as if in reply to the movement, "the

Driscolls are getting busy out in Apex. Now they've got all the street railroads in their pocket they want the water-supply too—but you know that as well as I do. Fact is, they've got to have it; and there's where you and I come in."

Mr. Spragg thrust his hands in his waistcoat arm-holes and turned his eyes back to the window.

"I'm out of that long ago," he said indifferently.

"Sure," Moffatt acquiesced; "but you know what went on when you were in it."

"Well?" said Mr. Spragg, shifting one hand to the Masonic emblem on his watch-chain.

"Well, Representative James J. Rolliver, who was in it with you, ain't out of it yet. He's the man the Driscolls are up against. What d'you know about him?"

Mr. Spragg twirled the emblem thoughtfully. "Driscoll tell you to come here?"

Moffatt laughed. "No, *sir*—not by a good many miles."

Mr. Spragg removed his feet from the scrap basket and straightened himself in his chair.

"Well—I didn't either; good morning, Mr. Moffatt."

The young man stared a moment, a humorous glint in his small black eyes; but he made no motion to leave his seat.

"Undine's to be married next week, isn't she?" he asked in a conversational tone.

Mr. Spragg's face blackened and he swung about in his revolving chair.

"You go to——"

Moffatt raised a deprecating hand. "Oh, you needn't warn me off. I don't want to be invited to the wedding. And I don't want to forbid the banns."

There was a derisive sound in Mr. Spragg's throat.

"But I *do* want to get out of Driscoll's office," Moffatt imperturbably continued. "There's no future there for a fellow like me. I see things big. That's the reason Apex was too tight a fit for me. It's only the little fellows that succeed in little places. New York's my size—without a single alteration. I could prove it to you to-morrow if I could put my hand on fifty thousand dollars."

Mr. Spragg did not repeat his gesture of dismissal: he was

once more listening guardedly but intently. Moffatt saw it and continued.

"And I could put my hand on double that sum—yes, sir, *double*—if you'd just step round with me to old Driscoll's office before five P. M. See the connection, Mr. Spragg?"

The older man remained silent while his visitor hummed a bar or two of "In the Gloaming"; then he said: "You want me to tell Driscoll what I know about James J. Rolliver?"

"I want you to tell the truth—I want you to stand for political purity in your native state. A man of your prominence owes it to the community, sir," cried Moffatt.

Mr. Spragg was still tormenting his Masonic emblem.

"Rolliver and I always stood together," he said at last, with a tinge of reluctance.

"Well, how much have you made out of it? Ain't he always been ahead of the game?"

"I can't do it—I can't do it," said Mr. Spragg, bringing his clenched hand down on the desk, as if addressing an invisible throng of assailants.

Moffatt rose without any evidence of disappointment in his ruddy countenance. "Well, so long," he said, moving toward the door. Near the threshold he paused to add carelessly: "Excuse my referring to a personal matter—but I understand Miss Spragg's wedding takes place next Monday."

Mr. Spragg was silent.

"How's that?" Moffatt continued unabashed. "I saw in the papers the date was set for the end of June."

Mr. Spragg rose heavily from his seat. "I presume my daughter has her reasons," he said, moving toward the door in Moffatt's wake.

"I guess she has—same as I have for wanting you to step round with me to old Driscoll's. If Undine's reasons are as good as mine——"

"Stop right here, Elmer Moffatt!" the older man broke out with lifted hand.

Moffatt made a burlesque feint of evading a blow; then his face grew serious, and he moved close to Mr. Spragg, whose arm had fallen to his side.

"See here, I know Undine's reasons. I've had a talk with

her—didn't she tell you? *She* don't beat about the bush the way you do. She told me straight out what was bothering her. She wants the Marvells to think she's right out of Kindergarten. 'No goods sent out on approval from this counter.' And I see her point—*I* don't mean to publish my meemo'rs. Only a deal's a deal." He paused a moment, twisting his fingers about the heavy gold watch-chain that crossed his waistcoat. "Tell you what, Mr. Spragg, I don't bear malice—not against Undine, anyway—and if I could have afforded it I'd have been glad enough to oblige her and forget old times. But you didn't hesitate to kick me when I was down and it's taken me a day or two to get on my legs again after that kicking. I see my way now to get there and keep there; and there's a kinder poetic justice in your being the man to help me up. If I can get hold of fifty thousand dollars within a day or so I don't care who's got the start of me. I've got a dead sure thing in sight, and you're the only man that can get it for me. Now do you see where we're coming out?"

Mr. Spragg, during this discourse, had remained motionless, his hands in his pockets, his jaws moving mechanically, as though he mumbled a tooth-pick under his beard. His sallow cheek had turned a shade paler, and his brows hung threateningly over his half-closed eyes. But there was no threat—there was scarcely more than a note of dull curiosity—in the voice with which he said: "You mean to talk?"

Moffatt's rosy face grew as hard as a steel safe. "I mean *you* to talk—to old Driscoll." He paused, and then added: "It's a hundred thousand down, between us."

Mr. Spragg once more consulted his watch. "I'll see you again," he said with an effort.

Moffatt struck one fist against the other. "No, *sir*—you won't! You'll only hear from me—through the Marvell family. Your news ain't worth a dollar to Driscoll if he don't get it to-day."

He was checked by the sound of steps in the outer office, and Mr. Spragg's stenographer appeared in the doorway.

"It's Mr. Marvell," she announced; and Ralph Marvell, glowing with haste and happiness, stood between the two men, holding out his hand to Mr. Spragg.

"Am I awfully in the way, sir? Turn me out if I am—but

first let me just say a word about this necklace I've ordered for Un——"

He broke off, made aware by Mr. Spragg's glance of the presence of Elmer Moffatt, who, with unwonted discretion, had dropped back into the shadow of the door.

Marvell turned on Moffatt a bright gaze full of the instinctive hospitality of youth; but Moffatt looked straight past him at Mr. Spragg.

The latter, as if in response to an imperceptible signal, mechanically pronounced his visitor's name; and the two young men moved toward each other.

"I beg your pardon most awfully—am I breaking up an important conference?" Ralph asked as he shook hands.

"Why, no—I guess we're pretty nearly through. I'll step outside and woo the blonde while you're talking," Moffatt rejoined in the same key.

"Thanks so much—I shan't take two seconds." Ralph broke off to scrutinize him. "But haven't we met before? It seems to me I've seen you—just lately——"

Moffatt seemed about to answer, but his reply was checked by an abrupt movement on the part of Mr. Spragg. There was a perceptible pause, during which Moffatt's bright black glance rested questioningly on Ralph; then he looked again at the older man, and their eyes held each other for a silent moment.

"Why, no—not as I'm aware of, Mr. Marvell," Moffatt said, addressing himself amicably to Ralph. "Better late than never, though—and I hope to have the pleasure soon again."

He divided a nod between the two men, and passed into the outer office, where they heard him addressing the stenographer in a strain of exaggerated gallantry.

BOOK II

XI

THE JULY SUN enclosed in a ring of fire the ilex grove of a villa in the hills near Siena.

Below, by the roadside, the long yellow house seemed to waver and palpitate in the glare; but steep by steep, behind it, the cool ilex-dusk mounted to the ledge where Ralph Marvell, stretched on his back in the grass, lay gazing up at a black reticulation of branches between which bits of sky gleamed with the hardness and brilliancy of blue enamel.

Up there too the air was thick with heat; but compared with the white fire below it was a dim and tempered warmth, like that of the churches in which he and Undine sometimes took refuge at the height of the torrid days.

Ralph loved the heavy Italian summer, as he had loved the light spring days leading up to it: the long line of dancing days that had drawn them on and on ever since they had left their ship at Naples four months earlier. Four months of beauty, changeful, inexhaustible, weaving itself about him in shapes of softness and strength; and beside him, hand in hand with him, embodying that spirit of shifting magic, the radiant creature through whose eyes he saw it. This was what their hastened marriage had blessed them with, giving them leisure, before summer came, to penetrate to remote folds of the southern mountains, to linger in the shade of Sicilian orange-groves, and finally, travelling by slow stages to the Adriatic, to reach the central hill-country where even in July they might hope for a breathable air.

To Ralph the Sienese air was not only breathable but intoxicating. The sun, treading the earth like a vintager, drew from it heady fragrances, crushed out of it new colours. All the values of the temperate landscape were reversed: the noon high-lights were white, but the shadows had unimagined colour. On the blackness of cork and ilex and cypress lay the green and purple lustres, the coppery iridescences, of old bronze; and night after night the skies were wine-blue and bubbling with stars. Ralph said to himself that no one who had not seen Italy thus prostrate beneath the sun knew what secret treasures she could yield.

As he lay there, fragments of past states of emotion, fugitive felicities of thought and sensation, rose and floated on the surface of his thoughts. It was one of those moments when the accumulated impressions of life converge on heart and brain, elucidating, enlacing each other, in a mysterious confusion of beauty. He had had glimpses of such a state before, of such mergings of the personal with the general life that one felt one's self a mere wave on the wild stream of being, yet thrilled with a sharper sense of individuality than can be known within the mere bounds of the actual. But now he knew the sensation in its fulness, and with it came the releasing power of language. Words were flashing like brilliant birds through the boughs overhead; he had but to wave his magic wand to have them flutter down to him. Only they were so beautiful up there, weaving their fantastic flights against the blue, that it was pleasanter, for the moment, to watch them and let the wand lie.

He stared up at the pattern they made till his eyes ached with excess of light; then he changed his position and looked at his wife.

Undine, near by, leaned against a gnarled tree with the slightly constrained air of a person unused to sylvan abandonments. Her beautiful back could not adapt itself to the irregularities of the tree-trunk, and she moved a little now and then in the effort to find an easier position. But her expression was serene, and Ralph, looking up at her through drowsy lids, thought her face had never been more exquisite.

"You look as cool as a wave," he said, reaching out for the hand on her knee. She let him have it, and he drew it closer, scrutinizing it as if it had been a bit of precious porcelain or ivory. It was small and soft, a mere featherweight, a puff-ball of a hand—not quick and thrilling, not a speaking hand, but one to be fondled and dressed in rings, and to leave a rosy blur in the brain. The fingers were short and tapering, dimpled at the base, with nails as smooth as rose-leaves. Ralph lifted them one by one, like a child playing with piano-keys, but they were inelastic and did not spring back far—only far enough to show the dimples.

He turned the hand over and traced the course of its blue veins from the wrist to the rounding of the palm below the fingers; then he put a kiss in the warm hollow between. The upper world had vanished: his universe had shrunk to the palm of a hand. But there was no sense of diminution. In the mystic depths whence his passion sprang, earthly dimensions were ignored and the curve of beauty was boundless enough to hold whatever the imagination could pour into it. Ralph had never felt more convinced of his power to write a great poem; but now it was Undine's hand which held the magic wand of expression.

She stirred again uneasily, answering his last words with a faint accent of reproach.

"I don't *feel* cool. You said there'd be a breeze up here."

He laughed.

"You poor darling! Wasn't it ever as hot as this in Apex?"

She withdrew her hand with a slight grimace.

"Yes—but I didn't marry you to go back to Apex!"

Ralph laughed again; then he lifted himself on his elbow and regained the hand. "I wonder what you *did* marry me for?"

"Mercy! It's too hot for conundrums." She spoke without impatience, but with a lassitude less joyous than his.

He roused himself. "Do you really mind the heat so much? We'll go, if you do."

She sat up eagerly. "Go to Switzerland, you mean?"

"Well, I hadn't taken quite as long a leap. I only meant we might drive back to Siena."

She relapsed listlessly against her tree-trunk. "Oh, Siena's hotter than this."

"We could go and sit in the cathedral—it's always cool there at sunset."

"We've sat in the cathedral at sunset every day for a week."

"Well, what do you say to stopping at Lecceto on the way? I haven't shown you Lecceto yet; and the drive back by moonlight would be glorious."

This woke her to a slight show of interest. "It might be nice—but where could we get anything to eat?"

Ralph laughed again. "I don't believe we could. You're too practical."

"Well, somebody's got to be. And the food in the hotel is too disgusting if we're not on time."

"I admit that the best of it has usually been appropriated by the extremely good-looking cavalry-officer who's so keen to know you."

Undine's face brightened. "You know he's not a Count; he's a Marquis. His name's Roviano; his palace in Rome is in the guide-books, and he speaks English beautifully. Céleste found out about him from the head-waiter," she said, with the security of one who treats of recognized values.

Marvell, sitting upright, reached lazily across the grass for his hat. "Then there's all the more reason for rushing back to defend our share." He spoke in the bantering tone which had become the habitual expression of his tenderness; but his eyes softened as they absorbed in a last glance the glimmering submarine light of the ancient grove, through which Undine's figure wavered nereid-like above him.

"You never looked your name more than you do now," he said, kneeling at her side and putting his arm about her. She smiled back a little vaguely, as if not seizing his allusion, and being content to let it drop into the store of unexplained references which had once stimulated her curiosity but now merely gave her leisure to think of other things. But her smile was no less lovely for its vagueness, and indeed, to Ralph, the loveliness was enhanced by the latent doubt. He remembered afterward that at that moment the cup of life seemed to brim over.

"Come, dear—here or there—it's all divine!"

In the carriage, however, she remained insensible to the soft spell of the evening, noticing only the heat and dust, and saying, as they passed under the wooded cliff of Lecceto, that they might as well have stopped there after all, since with such a headache as she felt coming on she didn't care if she dined or not.

Ralph looked up yearningly at the long walls overhead; but Undine's mood was hardly favourable to communion with such scenes, and he made no attempt to stop the carriage. Instead he presently said: "If you're tired of Italy, we've got the world to choose from."

She did not speak for a moment; then she said: "It's the heat I'm tired of. Don't people generally come here earlier?"

"Yes. That's why I chose the summer: so that we could have it all to ourselves."

She tried to put a note of reasonableness into her voice. "If you'd told me we were going everywhere at the wrong time, of course I could have arranged about my clothes."

"You poor darling! Let us, by all means, go to the place where the clothes will be right: they're too beautiful to be left out of our scheme of life."

Her lips hardened. "I know you don't care how I look. But you didn't give me time to order anything before we were married, and I've got nothing but my last winter's things to wear."

Ralph smiled. Even his subjugated mind perceived the inconsistency of Undine's taxing him with having hastened their marriage; but her variations on the eternal feminine still enchanted him.

"We'll go wherever you please—you make every place the one place," he said, as if he were humouring an irresistible child.

"To Switzerland, then? Céleste says St. Moritz is too heavenly," exclaimed Undine, who gathered her ideas of Europe chiefly from the conversation of her experienced attendant.

"One can be cool short of the Engadine. Why not go south again—say to Capri?"

"Capri? Is that the island we saw from Naples, where the artists go?" She drew her brows together. "It would be simply awful getting there in this heat."

"Well, then, I know a little place in Switzerland where one can still get away from the crowd, and we can sit and look at a green water-fall while I lie in wait for adjectives."

Mr. Spragg's astonishment on learning that his son-in-law contemplated maintaining a household on the earnings of his Muse was still matter for pleasantry between the pair; and one of the humours of their first weeks together had consisted in picturing themselves as a primeval couple setting forth across a virgin continent and subsisting on the adjectives which Ralph was to trap for his epic. On this occasion, however, his wife did not take up the joke, and he remained silent while their carriage climbed the long dusty hill to the Fonte-branda gate. He had seen her face droop as he suggested the possibility of an escape from the crowds in Switzerland, and it came to him, with the sharpness of a knife-thrust, that a crowd was what she wanted—that she was sick to death of being alone with him.

He sat motionless, staring ahead at the red-brown walls and towers on the steep above them. After all there was nothing sudden in his discovery. For weeks it had hung on the edge of consciousness, but he had turned from it with the heart's instinctive clinging to the unrealities by which it lives. Even now a hundred qualifying reasons rushed to his aid. They told him it was not of himself that Undine had wearied, but only of their present way of life. He had said a moment before, without conscious exaggeration, that her presence made any place the one place; yet how willingly would he have consented to share in such a life as she was leading before their marriage? And he had to acknowledge their months of desultory wandering from one remote Italian hill-top to another must have seemed as purposeless to her as balls and dinners would have been to him. An imagination like his, peopled with such varied images and associations, fed by so many currents from the long stream of human experience, could hardly picture the bareness of the small half-lit place in which his wife's spirit fluttered. Her mind was as destitute of beauty and mystery as the prairie school-house in which she had been educated; and her ideals seemed to Ralph as pathetic as the ornaments made of corks and cigar-bands with which her infant hands had been taught to adorn it. He was beginning to understand this, and learning to adapt himself to the narrow compass of her experience. The task of opening new windows in her mind was inspiring enough to give him infinite patience; and he would not yet own to himself that her pliancy and variety were imitative rather than spontaneous.

Meanwhile he had no desire to sacrifice her wishes to his, and it distressed him that he dared not confess his real reason for avoiding the Engadine. The truth was that their funds were shrinking faster than he had expected. Mr. Spragg, after bluntly opposing their hastened marriage on the ground that he was not prepared, at such short notice, to make the necessary provision for his daughter, had shortly afterward (probably, as Undine observed to Ralph, in consequence of a lucky "turn" in the Street) met their wishes with all possible liberality, bestowing on them a wedding in conformity with Mrs. Spragg's ideals and up to the highest standard of Mrs. Heeny's clippings, and pledging himself to provide Undine with an income adequate to so brilliant a beginning. It was understood that Ralph, on their return, should renounce the law for some more paying business; but this seemed the smallest of sacrifices to make for the privilege of calling Undine his wife; and besides, he still secretly hoped that, in the interval, his real vocation might declare itself in some work which would justify his adopting the life of letters.

He had assumed that Undine's allowance, with the addition of his own small income, would be enough to satisfy their needs. His own were few, and had always been within his means; but his wife's daily requirements, combined with her intermittent outbreaks of extravagance, had thrown out all his calculations, and they were already seriously exceeding their income.

If any one had prophesied before his marriage that he would find it difficult to tell this to Undine he would have smiled at the suggestion; and during their first days together it had seemed as though pecuniary questions were the last likely to be raised between them. But his marital education had since made strides, and he now knew that a disregard for money may imply not the willingness to get on without it but merely a blind confidence that it will somehow be provided. If Undine, like the lilies of the field, took no care, it was not because her wants were as few but because she assumed that care would be taken for her by those whose privilege it was to enable her to unite floral insouciance with Sheban elegance.

She had met Ralph's first note of warning with the assurance that she "didn't mean to worry"; and her tone implied that it was his business to do so for her. He certainly wanted to guard her from this as from all other cares; he wanted also, and still more passionately after the topic had once or twice recurred between them, to guard himself from the risk of judging where he still adored. These restraints to frankness kept him silent during the remainder of the drive, and when, after dinner, Undine again complained of her headache, he let her go up to her room and wandered out into the dimly lit streets to renewed communion with his problems.

They hung on him insistently as darkness fell, and Siena grew vocal with that shrill diversity of sounds that breaks, on summer nights, from every cleft of the masonry in old Italian towns. Then the moon rose, unfolding depth by depth the lines of the antique land; and Ralph, leaning against an old brick parapet, and watching each silver-blue remoteness disclose itself between the dark masses of the middle distance, felt his spirit enlarged and pacified. For the first time, as his senses thrilled to the deep touch of beauty, he asked himself if out of these floating and fugitive vibrations he might not build something concrete and stable, if even such dull common cares as now oppressed him might not become the motive power of creation. If he could only, on the spot, do something with all the accumulated spoils of the last months—something that should both put money into his pocket and harmony into the rich confusion of his spirit! "I'll write—I'll write: that must be what the whole thing means," he said to himself, with a vague clutch at some solution which should keep him a little longer hanging half-way down the steep of disenchantment.

He would have stayed on, heedless of time, to trace the ramifications of his idea in the complex beauty of the scene, but for the longing to share his mood with Undine. For the last few months every thought and sensation had been instantly transmuted into such emotional impulses and, though the currents of communication between himself and Undine were neither deep nor numerous, each fresh rush of feeling seemed strong enough to clear a way to her heart. He hurried back, almost breathlessly, to the inn; but even as he knocked at her door the subtle emanation of other influences seemed to arrest and chill him.

She had put out the lamp, and sat by the window in the moonlight, her head propped on a listless hand. As Marvell entered she turned; then, without speaking, she looked away again.

He was used to this mute reception, and had learned that it had no personal motive, but was the result of an extremely simplified social code. Mr. and Mrs. Spragg seldom spoke to each other when they met, and words of greeting seemed almost unknown to their domestic vocabulary. Marvell, at first, had fancied that his own warmth would call forth a response from his wife, who had been so quick to learn the forms of worldly intercourse; but he soon saw that she regarded intimacy as a pretext for escaping from such forms into a total absence of expression.

To-night, however, he felt another meaning in her silence, and perceived that she intended him to feel it. He met it by silence, but of a different kind; letting his nearness speak for him as he knelt beside her and laid his cheek against hers. She seemed hardly aware of the gesture; but to that he was also used. She had never shown any repugnance to his tenderness, but such response as it evoked was remote and Ariel-like, suggesting, from the first, not so much of the recoil of ignorance as the coolness of the element from which she took her name.

As he pressed her to him she seemed to grow less impassive and he felt her resign herself like a tired child. He held his breath, not daring to break the spell.

At length he whispered: "I've just seen such a wonderful thing—I wish you'd been with me!"

"What sort of a thing?" She turned her head with a faint show of interest.

"A—I don't know—a vision. . . It came to me out there just now with the moonrise."

"A vision?" Her interest flagged. "I never cared much about spirits. Mother used to try to drag me to séances—but they always made me sleepy."

Ralph laughed. "I don't mean a dead spirit but a living one! I saw the vision of a book I mean to do. It came to me suddenly, magnificently, swooped down on me as that big white moon swooped down on the black landscape, tore at me like a great white eagle—like the bird of Jove! After all, imagination *was* the eagle that devoured Prometheus!"

She drew away abruptly, and the bright moonlight showed him the apprehension in her face. "You're not going to write a book *here*?"

He stood up and wandered away a step or two; then he turned and came back. "Of course not here. Wherever you want. The main point is that it's come to me—no, that it's come *back* to me! For it's all these months together, it's all our happiness—it's the meaning of life that I've found, and it's you, dearest, you who've given it to me!"

He dropped down beside her again; but she disengaged herself and he heard a little sob in her throat.

"Undine—what's the matter?"

"Nothing. . . I don't know. . . I suppose I'm homesick. . ."

"Homesick? You poor darling! You're tired of travelling? What is it?"

"I don't know. . . I don't like Europe . . . it's not what I expected, and I think it's all too dreadfully dreary!" The words broke from her in a long wail of rebellion.

Marvell gazed at her perplexedly. It seemed strange that such unguessed thoughts should have been stirring in the heart pressed to his. "It's less interesting than you expected—or less amusing? Is that it?"

"It's dirty and ugly—all the towns we've been to are disgustingly dirty. I loathe the smells and the beggars. I'm sick and tired of the stuffy rooms in the hotels. I thought it would all be so splendid—but New York's ever so much nicer!"

"Not New York in July?"

"I don't care—there are the roof-gardens, anyway; and there are always people round. All these places seem as if they were dead. It's all like some awful cemetery."

A sense of compunction checked Marvell's laughter. "Don't cry, dear—don't! I see, I understand. You're lonely and the heat has tired you out. It *is* dull here; awfully dull; I've been stupid not to feel it. But we'll start at once—we'll get out of it."

She brightened instantly. "We'll go up to Switzerland?"

"We'll go up to Switzerland." He had a fleeting glimpse of the quiet place with the green water-fall, where he might have made tryst with his vision; then he turned his mind from it and said: "We'll go just where you want. How soon can you be ready to start?"

"Oh, to-morrow—the first thing to-morrow! I'll make Céleste get out of bed now and pack. Can we go right through to St. Moritz? I'd rather sleep in the train than in another of these awful places."

She was on her feet in a flash, her face alight, her hair waving and floating about her as though it rose on her happy heart-beats.

"Oh, Ralph, it's *sweet* of you, and I love you!" she cried out, letting him take her to his breast.

XII

IN THE QUIET PLACE with the green water-fall Ralph's vision might have kept faith with him; but how could he
hope to surprise it in the midsummer crowds of St. Moritz?

Undine, at any rate, had found there what she wanted; and
when he was at her side, and her radiant smile included him,
every other question was in abeyance. But there were hours
of solitary striding over bare grassy slopes, face to face with
the ironic interrogation of sky and mountains, when his anxieties came back, more persistent and importunate. Sometimes they took the form of merely material difficulties. How,
for instance, was he to meet the cost of their ruinous suite at
the Engadine Palace while he awaited Mr. Spragg's next remittance? And once the hotel bills were paid, what would be
left for the journey back to Paris, the looming expenses there,
the price of the passage to America? These questions would
fling him back on the thought of his projected book, which
was, after all, to be what the masterpieces of literature had
mostly been—a pot-boiler. Well! Why not? Did not the wor-
shipper always heap the rarest essences on the altar of his divinity? Ralph still rejoiced in the thought of giving back to
Undine something of the beauty of their first months together. But even on his solitary walks the vision eluded him;
and he could spare so few hours to its pursuit!

Undine's days were crowded, and it was still a matter of
course that where she went he should follow. He had risen
visibly in her opinion since they had been absorbed into the
life of the big hotels, and she had seen that his command of
foreign tongues put him at an advantage even in circles where
English was generally spoken if not understood. Undine herself, hampered by her lack of languages, was soon drawn into
the group of compatriots who struck the social pitch of their
hotel. Their types were familiar enough to Ralph, who had
taken their measure in former wanderings, and come across
their duplicates in every scene of continental idleness. Foremost among them was Mrs. Harvey Shallum, a showy Pari-
sianized figure, with a small wax-featured husband whose
ultra-fashionable clothes seemed a tribute to his wife's impor-

tance rather than the mark of his personal taste. Mr. Shallum, in fact, could not be said to have any personal bent. Though he conversed with a colourless fluency in the principal European tongues, he seldom exercised his gift except in intercourse with hotel-managers and head-waiters; and his long silences were broken only by resigned allusions to the enormities he had suffered at the hands of this gifted but unscrupulous class.

Mrs. Shallum, though in command of but a few verbs, all of which, on her lips, became irregular, managed to express a polyglot personality as vivid as her husband's was effaced. Her only idea of intercourse with her kind was to organize it into bands and subject it to frequent displacements; and society smiled at her for these exertions like an infant vigorously rocked. She saw at once Undine's value as a factor in her scheme, and the two formed an alliance on which Ralph refrained from shedding the cold light of depreciation. It was a point of honour with him not to seem to disdain any of Undine's amusements: the noisy interminable picnics, the hot promiscuous balls, the concerts, bridge-parties and theatricals which helped to disguise the difference between the high Alps and Paris or New York. He told himself that there is always a Narcissus-element in youth, and that what Undine really enjoyed was the image of her own charm mirrored in the general admiration. With her quick perceptions and adaptabilities she would soon learn to care more about the quality of the reflecting surface; and meanwhile no criticism of his should mar her pleasure.

The appearance at their hotel of the cavalry-officer from Siena was a not wholly agreeable surprise; but even after the handsome Marquis had been introduced to Undine, and had whirled her through an evening's dances, Ralph was not seriously disturbed. Husband and wife had grown closer to each other since they had come to St. Moritz, and in the brief moments she could give him Undine was now always gay and approachable. Her fitful humours had vanished, and she showed qualities of comradeship that seemed the promise of a deeper understanding. But this very hope made him more subject to her moods, more fearful of disturbing the harmony between them. Least of all could he broach the subject of money: he had too keen a memory of the way her lips could narrow, and her eyes turn from him as if he were a stranger.

It was a different matter that one day brought the look he feared to her face. She had announced her intention of going on an excursion with Mrs. Shallum and three or four of the young men who formed the nucleus of their shifting circle, and for the first time she did not ask Ralph if he were coming; but he felt no resentment at being left out. He was tired of these noisy assaults on the high solitudes, and the prospect of a quiet afternoon turned his thoughts to his book. Now if ever there seemed a chance of recapturing the moonlight vision. . .

From his balcony he looked down on the assembling party. Mrs. Shallum was already screaming bilingually at various windows in the long façade; and Undine presently came out of the hotel with the Marchese Roviano and two young English diplomatists. Slim and tall in her trim mountain garb, she made the ornate Mrs. Shallum look like a piece of ambulant upholstery. The high air brightened her cheeks and struck new lights from her hair, and Ralph had never seen her so touched with morning freshness. The party was not yet complete, and he felt a movement of annoyance when he recognized, in the last person to join it, a Russian lady of cosmopolitan notoriety whom he had run across in his unmarried days, and as to whom he had already warned Undine. Knowing what strange specimens from the depths slip through the wide meshes of the watering-place world, he had foreseen that a meeting with the Baroness Adelschein was inevitable; but he had not expected her to become one of his wife's intimate circle.

When the excursionists had started he turned back to his writing-table and tried to take up his work; but he could not fix his thoughts: they were far away, in pursuit of Undine. He had been but five months married, and it seemed, after all, rather soon for him to be dropped out of such excursions as unquestioningly as poor Harvey Shallum. He smiled away this first twinge of jealousy, but the irritation it left found a pretext in his displeasure at Undine's choice of companions. Mrs. Shallum grated on his taste, but she was as open to inspection as a shop-window, and he was sure that time would teach his wife the cheapness of what she had to show. Roviano and the Englishmen were well enough too: frankly bent on amusement, but pleasant and well-bred. But they would naturally take their tone from the women they were with; and Madame Adelschein's tone was notorious. He knew also that Undine's faculty of self-defense was weakened by the instinct of adapting herself to whatever company she was in, of copying "the others" in speech and gesture as closely as she reflected them in dress; and he was disturbed by the thought of what her ignorance might expose her to.

She came back late, flushed with her long walk, her face all sparkle and mystery, as he had seen it in the first days of their courtship; and the look somehow revived his irritated sense of having been intentionally left out of the party.

"You've been gone forever. Was it the Adelschein who made you go such lengths?" he asked her, trying to keep to his usual joking tone.

Undine, as she dropped down on the sofa and unpinned her hat, shed on him the light of her guileless gaze.

"I don't know: everybody was amusing. The Marquis is awfully bright."

"I'd no idea you or Bertha Shallum knew Madame Adelschein well enough to take her off with you in that way."

Undine sat absently smoothing the tuft of glossy cock's-feathers in her hat.

"I don't see that you've got to know people particularly well to go for a walk with them. The Baroness is awfully bright too."

She always gave her acquaintances their titles, seeming not, in this respect, to have noticed that a simpler form prevailed.

"I don't dispute the interest of what she says; but I've told you what decent people think of what she does," Ralph retorted, exasperated by what seemed a wilful pretense of ignorance.

She continued to scrutinize him with her clear eyes, in which there was no shadow of offense.

"You mean they don't want to go round with her? You're mistaken: it's not true. She goes round with everybody. She dined last night with the Grand Duchess; Roviano told me so."

This was not calculated to make Ralph take a more tolerant view of the question.

"Does he also tell you what's said of her?"

"What's said of her?" Undine's limpid glance rebuked him. "Do you mean that disgusting scandal you told me about? Do you suppose I'd let him talk to me about such things? I meant you're mistaken about her social position. He says she goes everywhere."

Ralph laughed impatiently. "No doubt Roviano's an authority; but it doesn't happen to be his business to choose your friends for you."

Undine echoed his laugh. "Well, I guess I don't need anybody to do that: I can do it myself," she said, with the good-humoured curtness that was the habitual note of intercourse with the Spraggs.

Ralph sat down beside her and laid a caressing touch on her shoulder. "No, you can't, you foolish child. You know nothing of this society you're in; of its antecedents, its rules, its conventions; and it's my affair to look after you, and warn you when you're on the wrong track."

"Mercy, what a solemn speech!" She shrugged away his hand without ill-temper. "I don't believe an American woman needs to know such a lot about their old rules. They can see I mean to follow my own, and if they don't like it they needn't go with me."

"Oh, they'll go with you fast enough, as you call it. They'll be too charmed to. The question is how far they'll make you go with *them*, and where they'll finally land you."

She tossed her head back with the movement she had learned in "speaking" school-pieces about freedom and the British tyrant.

"No one's ever yet gone any farther with me than I wanted!" she declared. She was really exquisitely simple.

"I'm not sure Roviano hasn't, in vouching for Madame Adelschein. But he probably thinks you know about her. To him this isn't 'society' any more than the people in an omnibus are. Society, to everybody here, means the sanction of their own special group and of the corresponding groups elsewhere. The Adelschein goes about in a place like this because it's nobody's business to stop her; but the women who tolerate her here would drop her like a shot if she set foot on their own ground."

The thoughtful air with which Undine heard him out made him fancy this argument had carried; and as he ended she threw him a bright look.

"Well, that's easy enough: I can drop her if she comes to New York."

Ralph sat silent for a moment—then he turned away and began to gather up his scattered pages.

Undine, in the ensuing days, was no less often with Madame Adelschein, and Ralph suspected a challenge in her open frequentation of the lady. But if challenge there were, he let it lie. Whether his wife saw more or less of Madame Adelschein seemed no longer of much consequence: she had so amply shown him her ability to protect herself. The pang lay in the completeness of the proof—in the perfect functioning of her instinct of self-preservation. For the first time he was face to face with his hovering dread: he was judging where he still adored.

Before long more pressing cares absorbed him. He had already begun to watch the post for his father-in-law's monthly remittance, without precisely knowing how, even with its aid, he was to bridge the gulf of expense between St. Moritz and New York. The non-arrival of Mr. Spragg's cheque was productive of graver fears, and these were abruptly confirmed when, coming in one afternoon, he found Undine crying over a letter from her mother.

Her distress made him fear that Mr. Spragg was ill, and he drew her to him soothingly; but she broke away with an impatient movement.

"Oh, they're all well enough—but father's lost a lot of money. He's been speculating, and he can't send us anything for at least three months."

Ralph murmured reassuringly: "As long as there's no one ill!"—but in reality he was following her despairing gaze down the long perspective of their barren quarter.

"Three months! Three months!"

Undine dried her eyes, and sat with set lips and tapping foot while he read her mother's letter.

"Your poor father! It's a hard knock for him. I'm sorry," he said as he handed it back.

For a moment she did not seem to hear; then she said between her teeth: "It's hard for *us*. I suppose now we'll have to go straight home."

He looked at her with wonder. "If that were all! In any case I should have to be back in a few weeks."

"But we needn't have left here in August! It's the first place in Europe that I've liked, and it's just my luck to be dragged away from it!"

"I'm so awfully sorry, dearest. It's my fault for persuading you to marry a pauper."

"It's father's fault. Why on earth did he go and speculate? There's no use his saying he's sorry now!" She sat brooding for a moment and then suddenly took Ralph's hand. "Couldn't your people do something—help us out just this once, I mean?"

He flushed to the forehead: it seemed inconceivable that she should make such a suggestion.

"I couldn't ask them—it's not possible. My grandfather does as much as he can for me, and my mother has nothing but what he gives her."

Undine seemed unconscious of his embarrassment. "He doesn't give us nearly as much as father does," she said; and, as Ralph remained silent, she went on: "Couldn't you ask your sister, then? I must have some clothes to go home in."

His heart contracted as he looked at her. What sinister change came over her when her will was crossed? She seemed to grow inaccessible, implacable—her eyes were like the eyes of an enemy.

"I don't know—I'll see," he said, rising and moving away from her. At that moment the touch of her hand was repugnant. Yes—he might ask Laura, no doubt: and whatever she had would be his. But the necessity was bitter to him, and Undine's unconsciousness of the fact hurt him more than her indifference to her father's misfortune.

What hurt him most was the curious fact that, for all her light irresponsibility, it was always she who made the practical suggestion, hit the nail of expediency on the head. No sentimental scruple made the blow waver or deflected her resolute aim. She had thought at once of Laura, and Laura was his only, his inevitable, resource. His anxious mind pictured his sister's wonder, and made him wince under the sting of Henley Fairford's irony: Fairford, who at the time of the marriage had sat silent and pulled his moustache while every one else argued and objected, yet under whose silence Ralph had felt a deeper protest than under all the reasoning of the others. It was no comfort to reflect that Fairford would probably continue to say nothing! But necessity made light of these twinges, and Ralph set his teeth and cabled.

Undine's chief surprise seemed to be that Laura's response, though immediate and generous, did not enable them to stay on at St. Moritz. But she apparently read in her husband's look the uselessness of such a hope, for, with one of the sudden changes of mood that still disarmed him, she accepted the need of departure, and took leave philosophically of the Shallums and their band. After all, Paris was ahead, and in September one would have a chance to see the new models and surprise the secret councils of the dress-makers.

Ralph was astonished at the tenacity with which she held to her purpose. He tried, when they reached Paris, to make her feel the necessity of starting at once for home; but she complained of fatigue and of feeling vaguely unwell, and he had to yield to her desire for rest. The word, however, was to strike him as strangely misapplied, for from the day of their arrival she was in a state of perpetual activity. She seemed to have mastered her Paris by divination, and between the bounds of the Boulevards and the Place Vendôme she moved at once with supernatural ease.

"Of course," she explained to him, "I understand how little we've got to spend; but I left New York without a rag, and it was you who made me countermand my trousseau, instead of having it sent after us. I wish now I hadn't listened to you—father'd have had to pay for *that* before he lost his money. As it is, it will be cheaper in the end for me to pick up a few things here. The advantage of going to the French dressmakers is that they'll wait twice as long for their money as the people at home. And they're all crazy to dress me—Bertha Shallum will tell you so: she says no one ever had such a chance! That's why I was willing to come to this stuffy little hotel—I wanted to save every scrap I could to get a few decent things. And over here they're accustomed to being bargained with—you ought to see how I've beaten them down! Have you any idea what a dinner-dress costs in New York——?"

So it went on, obtusely and persistently, whenever he tried to sound the note of prudence. But on other themes she was more than usually responsive. Paris enchanted her, and they had delightful hours at the theatres—the "little" ones—amusing dinners at fashionable restaurants, and reckless evenings in haunts where she thrilled with simple glee at the thought of what she must so obviously be "taken for." All these familiar diversions regained, for Ralph, a fresh zest in her company. Her innocence, her high spirits, her astounding comments and credulities, renovated the old Parisian adventure and flung a veil of romance over its hackneyed scenes. Beheld through such a medium the future looked less near and implacable, and Ralph, when he had received a reassuring letter from his sister, let his conscience sleep and slipped forth on the high tide of pleasure. After all, in New York amusements would be fewer, and their life, for a time, perhaps more quiet. Moreover, Ralph's dim glimpses of Mr. Spragg's past suggested that the latter was likely to be on his feet again at any moment, and atoning by redoubled prodigalities for his temporary straits; and beyond all these possibilities there was the book to be written—the book on which Ralph was sure he should get a real hold as soon as they settled down in New York.

Meanwhile the daily cost of living, and the bills that could not be deferred, were eating deep into Laura's subsidy. Ralph's anxieties returned, and his plight was brought home to him with a shock when, on going one day to engage passages, he learned that the prices were that of the "rush season," and one of the conditions immediate payment. At other times, he was told the rules were easier; but in September and October no exception could be made.

As he walked away with this fresh weight on his mind he caught sight of the strolling figure of Peter Van Degen—Peter lounging and luxuriating among the seductions of the Boulevard with the disgusting ease of a man whose wants are all measured by money, and who always has enough to gratify them.

His present sense of these advantages revealed itself in the affability of his greeting to Ralph, and in his off-hand request that the latter should "look up Clare," who had come over with him to get her winter finery.

"She's motoring to Italy next week with some of her long-haired friends—but I'm off for the other side; going back on the *Sorceress*. She's just been overhauled at Greenock, and we ought to have a good spin over. Better come along with me, old man."

The *Sorceress* was Van Degen's steam-yacht, most huge and complicated of her kind: it was his habit, after his semi-annual flights to Paris and London, to take a joyous company back on her and let Clare return by steamer. The character of these parties made the invitation almost an offense to Ralph; but reflecting that it was probably a phrase distributed to every acquaintance when Van Degen was in a rosy mood, he merely answered: "Much obliged, my dear fellow; but Undine and I are sailing immediately."

Peter's glassy eye grew livelier. "Ah, to be sure—you're not over the honeymoon yet. How's the bride? Stunning as ever? My regards to her, please. I suppose she's too deep in dress-making to be called on?—but don't you forget to look up Clare!" He hurried on in pursuit of a flitting petticoat and Ralph continued his walk home.

He prolonged it a little in order to put off telling Undine of his plight; for he could devise only one way of meeting the cost of the voyage, and that was to take it at once, and thus curtail their Parisian expenses. But he knew how unwelcome this plan would be, and he shrank the more from seeing Undine's face harden since, of late, he had so basked in its brightness.

When at last he entered the little *salon* she called "stuffy" he found her in conference with a blond-bearded gentleman who wore the red ribbon in his lapel, and who, on Ralph's appearance—and at a sign, as it appeared, from Mrs. Marvell—swept into his note-case some small objects that had lain on the table, and bowed himself out with a "Madame—Monsieur" worthy of the highest traditions.

Ralph looked after him with amusement. "Who's your friend—an Ambassador or a tailor?"

Undine was rapidly slipping on her rings, which, as he now saw, had also been scattered over the table.

"Oh, it was only that jeweller I told you about—the one Bertha Shallum goes to."

"A jeweller? Good heavens, my poor girl! You're buying jewels?" The extravagance of the idea struck a laugh from him.

Undine's face did not harden: it took on, instead, an almost deprecating look. "Of course not—how silly you are! I only wanted a few old things reset. But I won't if you'd rather not."

She came to him and sat down at his side, laying her hand on his arm. He took the hand up and looked at the deep gleam of the sapphires in the old family ring he had given her.

"You won't have that reset?" he said, smiling and twisting the ring about on her finger; then he went on with his thankless explanation. "It's not that I don't want you to do this or that; it's simply that, for the moment, we're rather strapped. I've just been to see the steamer people, and our passages will cost a good deal more than I thought."

He mentioned the sum and the fact that he must give an answer the next day. Would she consent to sail that very Saturday? Or should they go a fortnight later, in a slow boat from Plymouth?

Undine frowned on both alternatives. She was an indifferent sailor and shrank from the possible "nastiness" of the cheaper boat. She wanted to get the voyage over as quickly and luxuriously as possible—Bertha Shallum had told her that in a "deck-suite" no one need be sea-sick—but she wanted still more to have another week or two of Paris; and it was always hard to make her see why circumstances could not be bent to her wishes.

"This week? But how on earth can I be ready? Besides, we're dining at Enghien with the Shallums on Saturday, and motoring to Chantilly with the Jim Driscolls on Sunday. I can't imagine how you thought we could go this week!"

But she still opposed the cheap steamer, and after they had

carried the question on to Voisin's, and there unprofitably discussed it through a long luncheon, it seemed no nearer a solution.

"Well, think it over—let me know this evening," Ralph said, proportioning the waiter's fee to a bill burdened by Undine's reckless choice of *primeurs*.

His wife was to join the newly-arrived Mrs. Shallum in a round of the rue de la Paix; and he had seized the opportunity of slipping off to a classical performance at the Français. On their arrival in Paris he had taken Undine to one of these entertainments, but it left her too weary and puzzled for him to renew the attempt, and he had not found time to go back without her. He was glad now to shed his cares in such an atmosphere. The play was of the greatest, the interpretation that of the vanishing grand manner which lived in his first memories of the Parisian stage, and his surrender to such influences as complete as in his early days. Caught up in the fiery chariot of art, he felt once more the tug of its coursers in his muscles, and the rush of their flight still throbbed in him when he walked back late to the hotel.

XIII

H E HAD EXPECTED to find Undine still out; but on the stairs he crossed Mrs. Shallum, who threw at him from under an immense hat-brim: "Yes, she's in, but you'd better come and have tea with me at the Luxe. I don't think husbands are wanted!"

Ralph laughingly rejoined that that was just the moment for them to appear; and Mrs. Shallum swept on, crying back: "All the same, I'll wait for you!"

In the sitting-room Ralph found Undine seated behind a tea-table on the other side of which, in an attitude of easy intimacy, Peter Van Degen stretched his lounging length.

He did not move on Ralph's appearance, no doubt thinking their kinship close enough to make his nod and "Hullo!" a sufficient greeting. Peter in intimacy was given to miscalculations of the sort, and Ralph's first movement was to glance at Undine and see how it affected her. But her eyes gave out the vivid rays that noise and banter always struck from them; her face, at such moments, was like a theatre with all the lustres blazing. That the illumination should have been kindled by his cousin's husband was not precisely agreeable to Marvell, who thought Peter a bore in society and an insufferable nuisance on closer terms. But he was becoming blunted to Undine's lack of discrimination; and his own treatment of Van Degen was always tempered by his sympathy for Clare.

He therefore listened with apparent good-humour to Peter's suggestion of an evening at a *petit théâtre* with the Harvey Shallums, and joined in the laugh with which Undine declared: "Oh, Ralph won't go—he only likes the theatres where they walk around in bath-towels and talk poetry.— Isn't that what you've just been seeing?" she added, with a turn of the neck that shed her brightness on him.

"What? One of those five-barrelled shows at the Français? Great Scott, Ralph—no wonder your wife's pining for the Folies Bergère!"

"She needn't, my dear fellow. We never interfere with each other's vices."

Peter, unsolicited, was comfortably lighting a cigarette.

"Ah, there's the secret of domestic happiness. Marry some-body who likes all the things you don't, and make love to somebody who likes all the things you do."

Undine laughed appreciatively. "Only it dooms poor Ralph to such awful frumps. Can't you see the sort of woman who'd love his sort of play?"

"Oh, I can see her fast enough—my wife loves 'em," said their visitor, rising with a grin; while Ralph threw out: "So don't waste your pity on me!" and Undine's laugh had the slight note of asperity that the mention of Clare always elicited.

"To-morrow night, then, at Paillard's," Van Degen con-cluded. "And about the other business—that's a go too? I leave it to you to settle the date."

The nod and laugh they exchanged seemed to hint at depths of collusion from which Ralph was pointedly ex-cluded; and he wondered how large a programme of pleasure they had already had time to sketch out. He disliked the idea of Undine's being too frequently seen with Van Degen, whose Parisian reputation was not fortified by the connections that propped it up in New York; but he did not want to interfere with her pleasure, and he was still wondering what to say when, as the door closed, she turned to him gaily.

"I'm so glad you've come! I've got some news for you." She laid a light touch on his arm.

Touch and tone were enough to disperse his anxieties, and he answered that he was in luck to find her already in when he had supposed her engaged, over a Nouveau Luxe tea-table, in repairing the afternoon's ravages.

"Oh, I didn't shop much—I didn't stay out long." She raised a kindling face to him. "And what do you think I've been doing? While you were sitting in your stuffy old theatre, worrying about the money I was spending (oh, you needn't fib—I know you were!) I was saving you hundreds and thou-sands. I've saved you the price of our passage!"

Ralph laughed in pure enjoyment of her beauty. When she shone on him like that what did it matter what nonsense she talked?

"You wonderful woman—how did you do it? By counter-manding a tiara?"

"You know I'm not such a fool as you pretend!" She held him at arm's length with a nod of joyous mystery. "You'll simply never guess! I've made Peter Van Degen ask us to go home on the *Sorceress*. What do you say to that?"

She flashed it out on a laugh of triumph, without appearing to have a doubt of the effect the announcement would produce.

Ralph stared at her. "The *Sorceress*? You *made* him?"

"Well, I managed it, I worked him round to it! He's crazy about the idea now—but I don't think he'd thought of it before he came."

"I should say not!" Ralph ejaculated. "He never would have had the cheek to think of it."

"Well, I've made him, anyhow! Did you ever know such luck?"

"Such luck?" He groaned at her obstinate innocence. "Do you suppose I'll let you cross the ocean on the *Sorceress*?"

She shrugged impatiently. "You say that because your cousin doesn't go on her."

"If she doesn't, it's because it's no place for decent women."

"It's Clare's fault if it isn't. Everybody knows she's crazy about you, and she makes him feel it. That's why he takes up with other women."

Her anger reddened her cheeks and dropped her brows like a black bar above her glowing eyes. Even in his recoil from what she said Ralph felt the tempestuous heat of her beauty. But for the first time his latent resentments rose in him, and he gave her back wrath for wrath.

"Is that the precious stuff he tells you?"

"Do you suppose I had to wait for him to tell me? Everybody knows it—everybody in New York knew she was wild when you married. That's why she's always been so nasty to me. If you won't go on the *Sorceress* they'll all say it's because she was jealous of me and wouldn't let you."

Ralph's indignation had already flickered down to disgust. Undine was no longer beautiful—she seemed to have the face of her thoughts. He stood up with an impatient laugh.

"Is that another of his arguments? I don't wonder they're convincing——" But as quickly as it had come the sneer dropped, yielding to a wave of pity, the vague impulse to silence and protect her. How could he have given way to the provocation of her weakness, when his business was to defend her from it and lift her above it? He recalled his old dreams of saving her from Van Degenism—it was not thus that he had imagined the rescue.

"Don't let's pay Peter the compliment of squabbling over him," he said, turning away to pour himself a cup of tea.

When he had filled his cup he sat down beside Undine, with a smile. "No doubt he was joking—and thought you were; but if you really made him believe we might go with him you'd better drop him a line."

Undine's brow still gloomed. "You refuse, then?"

"Refuse? I don't need to! Do you want to succeed to half the chorus-world of New York?"

"They won't be on board with us, I suppose!"

"The echoes of their conversation will. It's the only language Peter knows."

"He told me he longed for the influence of a good woman——" She checked herself, reddening at Ralph's laugh.

"Well, tell him to apply again when he's been under it a month or two. Meanwhile we'll stick to the liners."

Ralph was beginning to learn that the only road to her reason lay through her vanity, and he fancied that if she could be made to see Van Degen as an object of ridicule she might give up the idea of the *Sorceress* of her own accord. But her will hardened slowly under his joking opposition, and she became no less formidable as she grew more calm. He was used to women who, in such cases, yielded as a matter of course to masculine judgments: if one pronounced a man "not decent" the question was closed. But it was Undine's habit to ascribe all interference with her plans to personal motives, and he could see that she attributed his opposition to the furtive machinations of poor Clare. It was odious to him to prolong the discussion, for the accent of recrimination was the one he most dreaded on her lips. But the moment came when he had to take the brunt of it, averting his thoughts as best he might from the glimpse it gave of a world of mean familiarities, of reprisals drawn from the vulgarest of vocabularies. Certain

retorts sped through the air like the flight of household utensils, certain charges rang out like accusations of tampering
with the groceries. He stiffened himself against such comparisons, but they stuck in his imagination and left him thankful
when Undine's anger yielded to a burst of tears. He had held
his own and gained his point. The trip on the *Sorceress* was
given up, and a note of withdrawal despatched to Van Degen;
but at the same time Ralph cabled his sister to ask if she could
increase her loan. For he had conquered only at the cost of a
concession: Undine was to stay in Paris till October, and they
were to sail on a fast steamer, in a deck-suite, like the Harvey
Shallums.

Undine's ill-humour was soon dispelled by any new distrac-
tion, and she gave herself to the untroubled enjoyment of
Paris. The Shallums were the centre of a like-minded group,
and in the hours the ladies could spare from their dress-
makers the restaurants shook with their hilarity and the suburbs with the shriek of their motors. Van Degen, who had
postponed his sailing, was a frequent sharer in these amusements; but Ralph counted on New York influences to detach
him from Undine's train. He was learning to influence her
through her social instincts where he had once tried to appeal
to other sensibilities.

His worst moment came when he went to see Clare Van
Degen, who, on the eve of departure, had begged him to
come to her hotel. He found her less restless and rattling than
usual, with a look in her eyes that reminded him of the days
when she had haunted his thoughts. The visit passed off without vain returns to the past; but as he was leaving she surprised him by saying: "Don't let Peter make a goose of your
wife."

Ralph reddened, but laughed.

"Oh, Undine's wonderfully able to defend herself, even
against such seductions as Peter's."

Mrs. Van Degen looked down with a smile at the bracelets
on her thin brown wrist. "His personal seductions—yes. But
as an inventor of amusements he's inexhaustible; and Undine
likes to be amused."

Ralph made no reply but showed no annoyance. He simply

took her hand and kissed it as he said good-bye; and she turned from him without audible farewell.

As the day of departure approached, Undine's absorption in her dresses almost precluded the thought of amusement. Early and late she was closeted with fitters and packers—even the competent Céleste not being trusted to handle the treasures now pouring in—and Ralph cursed his weakness in not restraining her, and then fled for solace to museums and galleries.

He could not rouse in her any scruple about incurring fresh debts, yet he knew she was no longer unaware of the value of money. She had learned to bargain, pare down prices, evade fees, brow-beat the small tradespeople and wheedle concessions from the great—not, as Ralph perceived, from any effort to restrain her expenses, but only to prolong and intensify the pleasure of spending. Pained by the trait, he tried to laugh her out of it. He told her once that she had a miserly hand—showing her, in proof, that, for all their softness, the fingers would not bend back, or the pink palm open. But she retorted a little sharply that it was no wonder, since she'd heard nothing talked of since their marriage but economy; and this left him without any answer. So the purveyors continued to mount to their apartment, and Ralph, in the course of his frequent flights from it, found himself always dodging the corners of black glazed boxes and swaying pyramids of pasteboard; always lifting his hat to sidling milliners' girls, or effacing himself before slender *vendeuses* floating by in a mist of opopanax. He felt incompetent to pronounce on the needs to which these visitors ministered; but the reappearance among them of the blond-bearded jeweller gave him ground for fresh fears. Undine had assured him that she had given up the idea of having her ornaments reset, and there had been ample time for their return; but on his questioning her she explained that there had been delays and "bothers" and put him in the wrong by asking ironically if he supposed she was buying things "for pleasure" when she knew as well as he that there wasn't any money to pay for them.

But his thoughts were not all dark. Undine's moods still infected him, and when she was happy he felt an answering lightness. Even when her amusements were too primitive to be shared he could enjoy their reflection in her face. Only, as he looked back, he was struck by the evanescence, the lack of substance, in their moments of sympathy, and by the permanent marks left by each breach between them. Yet he still fancied that some day the balance might be reversed, and that as she acquired a finer sense of values the depths in her would find a voice.

Something of this was in his mind when, the afternoon before their departure, he came home to help her with their last arrangements. She had begged him, for the day, to leave her alone in their cramped *salon*, into which belated bundles were still pouring; and it was nearly dark when he returned. The evening before she had seemed pale and nervous, and at the last moment had excused herself from dining with the Shallums at a suburban restaurant. It was so unlike her to miss any opportunity of the kind that Ralph had felt a little anxious. But with the arrival of the packers she was afoot and in command again, and he withdrew submissively, as Mr. Spragg, in the early Apex days, might have fled from the spring storm of "house-cleaning."

When he entered the sitting-room, he found it still in disorder. Every chair was hidden under scattered dresses, tissue-paper surged from the yawning trunks and, prone among her heaped-up finery, Undine lay with closed eyes on the sofa.

She raised her head as he entered, and then turned listlessly away.

"My poor girl, what's the matter? Haven't they finished yet?"

Instead of answering she pressed her face into the cushion and began to sob. The violence of her weeping shook her hair down on her shoulders, and her hands, clenching the arm of the sofa, pressed it away from her as if any contact were insufferable.

Ralph bent over her in alarm. "Why, what's wrong, dear? What's happened?"

Her fatigue of the previous evening came back to him—a puzzled hunted look in her eyes; and with the memory a vague wonder revived. He had fancied himself fairly disencumbered of the stock formulas about the hallowing effects of motherhood, and there were many reasons for not welcoming the news he suspected she had to give; but the woman a man loves is always a special case, and everything was different that befell Undine. If this was what had befallen her it was wonderful and divine: for the moment that was all he felt.

"Dear, tell me what's the matter," he pleaded.

She sobbed on unheedingly and he waited for her agitation to subside. He shrank from the phrases considered appropriate to the situation, but he wanted to hold her close and give her the depth of his heart in a long kiss.

Suddenly she sat upright and turned a desperate face on him. "Why on earth are you staring at me like that? Anybody can see what's the matter!"

He winced at her tone, but managed to get one of her hands in his; and they stayed thus in silence, eye to eye.

"Are you as sorry as all that?" he began at length, conscious of the flatness of his voice.

"Sorry—sorry? I'm—I'm——" She snatched her hand away, and went on weeping.

"But, Undine—dearest—bye and bye you'll feel differently—I know you will!"

"Differently? Differently? When? In a year? It *takes* a year—a whole year out of life! What do I care how I shall feel in a year?"

The chill of her tone struck in. This was more than a revolt of the nerves: it was a settled, a reasoned resentment. Ralph found himself groping for extenuations, evasions—anything to put a little warmth into her!

"Who knows? Perhaps, after all, it's a mistake."

There was no answering light in her face. She turned her head from him wearily.

"Don't you think, dear, you may be mistaken?"

"Mistaken? How on earth can I be mistaken?"

Even in that moment of confusion he was struck by the cold competence of her tone, and wondered how she could be so sure.

"You mean you've asked—you've consulted——?"

The irony of it took him by the throat. They were the very words he might have spoken in some miserable secret colloquy—the words he was speaking to his wife!

She repeated dully: "I know I'm not mistaken."

There was another long silence. Undine lay still, her eyes shut, drumming on the arm of the sofa with a restless hand. The other lay cold in Ralph's clasp, and through it there gradually stole to him the benumbing influence of the thoughts she was thinking: the sense of the approach of illness, anxiety, and expense, and of the general unnecessary disorganization of their lives.

"That's all you feel, then?" he asked at length a little bitterly, as if to disguise from himself the hateful fact that he felt it too. He stood up and moved away. "That's all?" he repeated.

"Why, what else do you expect me to feel? I feel horribly ill, if that's what you want." He saw the sobs trembling up through her again.

"Poor dear—poor girl. . . I'm so sorry—so dreadfully sorry!"

The senseless reiteration seemed to exasperate her. He knew it by the quiver that ran through her like the premonitory ripple on smooth water before the coming of the wind. She turned about on him and jumped to her feet.

"Sorry—you're sorry? *You're* sorry? Why, what earthly difference will it make to *you*?" She drew back a few steps and lifted her slender arms from her sides. "Look at me—see how I look—how I'm going to look! *You* won't hate yourself more and more every morning when you get up and see yourself in the glass! *Your* life's going on just as usual! But what's mine going to be for months and months? And just as I'd been to all this bother—fagging myself to death about all these things——" her tragic gesture swept the disordered room—"just as I thought I was going home to enjoy myself, and look nice, and see people again, and have a little pleasure after all our worries——" She dropped back on the sofa with another burst of tears. "For all the good this rubbish will do me now! I loathe the very sight of it!" she sobbed with her face in her hands.

XIV

IT WAS ONE of the distinctions of Mr. Claud Walsingham Popple that his studio was never too much encumbered with the attributes of his art to permit the installing, in one of its cushioned corners, of an elaborately furnished tea-table flanked by the most varied seductions in sandwiches and pastry.

Mr. Popple, like all great men, had at first had his ups and downs; but his reputation had been permanently established by the verdict of a wealthy patron who, returning from an excursion into other fields of portraiture, had given it as the final fruit of his experience that Popple was the only man who could "do pearls." To sitters for whom this was of the first consequence it was another of the artist's merits that he always subordinated art to elegance, in life as well as in his portraits. The "messy" element of production was no more visible in his expensively screened and tapestried studio than its results were perceptible in his painting; and it was often said, in praise of his work, that he was the only artist who kept his studio tidy enough for a lady to sit to him in a new dress.

Mr. Popple, in fact, held that the personality of the artist should at all times be dissembled behind that of the man. It was his opinion that the essence of good-breeding lay in tossing off a picture as easily as you lit a cigarette. Ralph Marvell had once said of him that when he began a portrait he always turned back his cuffs and said: "Ladies and gentlemen, you can see there's absolutely nothing here;" and Mrs. Fairford supplemented the description by defining his painting as "chafing-dish" art.

On a certain late afternoon of December, some four years after Mr. Popple's first meeting with Miss Undine Spragg of Apex, even the symbolic chafing-dish was nowhere visible in his studio; the only evidence of its recent activity being the full-length portrait of Mrs. Ralph Marvell, who, from her lofty easel and her heavily garlanded frame, faced the doorway with the air of having been invited to "receive" for Mr. Popple.

The artist himself, becomingly clad in mouse-coloured vel-
veteen, had just turned away from the picture to hover above
the tea-cups; but his place had been taken by the considerably
broader bulk of Mr. Peter Van Degen, who, tightly moulded
into a coat of the latest cut, stood before the portrait in the
attitude of a first arrival.

"Yes, it's good—it's damn good, Popp; you've hit the hair
off ripplingly; but the pearls ain't big enough," he pronounced.

A slight laugh sounded from the raised dais behind the
easel.

"Of course they're not! But it's not *his* fault, poor man; *he*
didn't give them to me!" As she spoke Mrs. Ralph Marvell
rose from a monumental gilt arm-chair of pseudo-Venetian
design and swept her long draperies to Van Degen's side.

"He might, then—for the privilege of painting you!" the
latter rejoined, transferring his bulging stare from the coun-
terfeit to the original. His eyes rested on Mrs. Marvell's in
what seemed a quick exchange of understanding; then they
passed on to a critical inspection of her person. She was
dressed for the sitting in something faint and shining, above
which the long curves of her neck looked dead white in the
cold light of the studio; and her hair, all a shadowless rosy
gold, was starred with a hard glitter of diamonds.

"The privilege of painting me? Mercy, *I* have to pay for
being painted! He'll tell you he's giving me the picture—but
what do you suppose this cost?" She laid a finger-tip on her
shimmering dress.

Van Degen's eye rested on her with cold enjoyment. "Does
the price come higher than the dress?"

She ignored the allusion. "Of course what they charge for
is the cut——"

"What they cut away? That's what they ought to charge
for, ain't it, Popp?"

Undine took this with cool disdain, but Mr. Popple's sensibilities were offended.

"My dear Peter—really—the artist, you understand, sees
all this as a pure question of colour, of pattern; and it's a
point of honour with the *man* to steel himself against the
personal seduction."

Mr. Van Degen received this protest with a sound of almost vulgar derision, but Undine thrilled agreeably under the glance which her portrayer cast on her. She was flattered by Van Degen's notice, and thought his impertinence witty; but she glowed inwardly at Mr. Popple's eloquence. After more than three years of social experience she still thought he "spoke beautifully," like the hero of a novel, and she ascribed to jealousy the lack of seriousness with which her husband's friends regarded him. His conversation struck her as intellectual, and his eagerness to have her share his thoughts was in flattering contrast to Ralph's growing tendency to keep his to himself. Popple's homage seemed the subtlest proof of what Ralph could have made of her if he had "really understood" her. It was but another step to ascribe all her past mistakes to the lack of such understanding; and the satisfaction derived from this thought had once impelled her to tell the artist that he alone knew how to rouse her "higher self." He had assured her that the memory of her words would thereafter hallow his life; and as he hinted that it had been stained by the darkest errors she was moved at the thought of the purifying influence she exerted.

Thus it was that a man should talk to a true woman—but how few whom she had known possessed the secret! Ralph, in the first months of their marriage, had been eloquent too, had even gone the length of quoting poetry; but he disconcerted her by his baffling twists and strange allusions (she always scented ridicule in the unknown), and the poets he quoted were esoteric and abstruse. Mr. Popple's rhetoric was drawn from more familiar sources, and abounded in favourite phrases and in moving reminiscences of the Fifth Reader. He was moreover as literary as he was artistic; possessing an unequalled acquaintance with contemporary fiction, and dipping even into the lighter type of memoirs, in which the old acquaintances of history are served up in the disguise of "A Royal Sorceress" or "Passion in a Palace." The mastery with which Mr. Popple discussed the novel of the day, especially in relation to the sensibilities of its hero and heroine, gave Undine a sense of intellectual activity which contrasted strikingly with Marvell's flippant estimate of such works. "Passion," the artist implied, would have been the dominant note of his life, had it not been held in check by a sentiment of exalted chivalry, and by the sense that a nature of such emotional intensity as his must always be "ridden on the curb."

Van Degen was helping himself from the tray of iced cocktails which stood near the tea-table, and Popple, turning to Undine, took up the thread of his discourse. But why, he asked, why allude before others to feelings so few could understand? The average man—lucky devil!—(with a compassionate glance at Van Degen's back) the average man knew nothing of the fierce conflict between the lower and higher natures; and even the woman whose eyes had kindled it—how much did *she* guess of its violence? Did she know—Popple recklessly asked—how often the artist was forgotten in the man—how often the man would take the bit between his teeth, were it not that the look in her eyes recalled some sacred memory, some lesson learned perhaps beside his mother's knee?

"I say, Popp—was that where you learned to mix this drink? Because it does the old lady credit," Van Degen called out, smacking his lips; while the artist, dashing a nervous hand through his hair, muttered: "Hang it, Peter—is *nothing* sacred to you?"

It pleased Undine to feel herself capable of inspiring such emotions. She would have been fatigued by the necessity of maintaining her own talk on Popple's level, but she liked to listen to him, and especially to have others overhear what he said to her.

Her feeling for Van Degen was different. There was more similarity of tastes between them, though his manner flattered her vanity less than Popple's. She felt the strength of Van Degen's contempt for everything he did not understand or could not buy: that was the only kind of "exclusiveness" that impressed her. And he was still to her, as in her inexperienced days, the master of the mundane science she had once imagined that Ralph Marvell possessed. During the three years since her marriage she had learned to make distinctions unknown to her girlish categories. She had found out that she had given herself to the exclusive and the dowdy when the future belonged to the showy and the promiscuous; that she was in the case of those who have cast in their lot with a fallen cause, or—to use an analogy more within her range—who have hired an opera box on the wrong night. It was all confusing and exasperating. Apex ideals had been based on the myth of "old families" ruling New York from a throne of Revolutionary tradition, with the new millionaires paying them feudal allegiance. But experience had long since proved the delusiveness of the simile. Mrs. Marvell's classification of the world into the visited and the unvisited was as obsolete as a mediæval cosmogony. Some of those whom Washington Square left unvisited were the centre of social systems far outside its ken, and as indifferent to its opinions as the constellations to the reckonings of the astronomers; and all these systems joyously revolved about their central sun of gold.

There were moments after Undine's return to New York when she was tempted to class her marriage with the hateful early mistakes from the memories of which she had hoped it would free her. Since it was never her habit to accuse herself of such mistakes it was inevitable that she should gradually come to lay the blame on Ralph. She found a poignant pleasure, at this stage of her career, in the question: "What does a young girl know of life?" And the poignancy was deepened by the fact that each of the friends to whom she put the question seemed convinced that—had the privilege been his—he would have known how to spare her the disenchantment it implied.

The conviction of having blundered was never more present to her than when, on this particular afternoon, the guests invited by Mr. Popple to view her portrait began to assemble before it.

Some of the principal figures of Undine's group had rallied for the occasion, and almost all were in exasperating enjoyment of the privileges for which she pined. There was young Jim Driscoll, heir-apparent of the house, with his short stout mistrustful wife, who hated society, but went everywhere lest it might be thought she had been left out; the "beautiful Mrs. Beringer," a lovely aimless being, who kept (as Laura Fairford said) a home for stray opinions, and could never quite tell them apart; little Dicky Bowles, whom every one invited because he was understood to "say things" if one didn't; the Harvey Shallums, fresh from Paris, and dragging in their wake a bewildered nobleman vaguely designated as "the Count," who offered cautious conversational openings, like an explorer trying beads on savages; and, behind these more salient types, the usual filling in of those who are seen everywhere because they have learned to catch the social eye. Such a company was one to flatter the artist as much as his sitter, so completely did it represent that unanimity of opinion which constitutes social strength. Not one of the number was troubled by any personal theory of art: all they asked of a portrait was that the costume should be sufficiently "life-like," and the face not too much so; and a long experience in idealizing flesh and realizing dress-fabrics had enabled Mr. Popple to meet both demands.

"Hang it," Peter Van Degen pronounced, standing before the easel in an attitude of inspired interpretation, "the great thing in a man's portrait is to catch the likeness—we all know that; but with a woman's it's different—a woman's picture has got to be pleasing. Who wants it about if it isn't? Those big chaps who blow about what they call realism—how do *their* portraits look in a drawing-room? Do you suppose they ever ask themselves that? *They* don't care—they're not going to live with the things! And what do they know of drawing-rooms, anyhow? Lots of them haven't even got a dress-suit. There's where old Popp has the pull over 'em—*he* knows how we live and what we want."

This was received by the artist with a deprecating murmur, and by his public with warm expressions of approval.

"Happily in this case," Popple began ("as in that of so many of my sitters," he hastily put in), "there has been no need to idealize—nature herself has outdone the artist's dream."

Undine, radiantly challenging comparison with her portrait, glanced up at it with a smile of conscious merit, which deepened as young Jim Driscoll declared: "By Jove, Mamie, you must be done exactly like that for the new music-room."

His wife turned a cautious eye upon the picture.

"How big is it? For our house it would have to be a good deal bigger," she objected; and Popple, fired by the thought of such a dimensional opportunity, rejoined that it would be the chance of all others to "work in" a marble portico and a court-train: he had just done Mrs. Lycurgus Ambler in a court-train and feathers, and as *that* was for Buffalo of course the pictures needn't clash.

"Well, it would have to be a good deal bigger than Mrs. Ambler's," Mrs. Driscoll insisted; and on Popple's suggestion that in that case he might "work in" Driscoll, in court-dress also—("You've been presented? Well, you *will* be,—you'll *have* to, if I do the picture—which will make a lovely memento")—Van Degen turned aside to murmur to Undine: "Pure bluff, you know—Jim couldn't pay for a photograph. Old Driscoll's high and dry since the Ararat investigation."

She threw him a puzzled glance, having no time, in her crowded existence, to follow the perturbations of Wall Street save as they affected the hospitality of Fifth Avenue.

"You mean they've lost their money? Won't they give their fancy ball, then?"

Van Degen shrugged. "Nobody knows how it's coming out. That queer chap Elmer Moffatt threatens to give old Driscoll a fancy ball—says he's going to dress him in stripes! It seems he knows too much about the Apex street-railways."

Undine paled a little. Though she had already tried on her costume for the Driscoll ball her disappointment at Van Degen's announcement was effaced by the mention of Moffatt's name. She had not had the curiosity to follow the reports of the "Ararat Trust Investigation," but once or twice lately, in the snatches of smoking-room talk, she had been surprised by a vague allusion to Elmer Moffatt, as to an erratic financial influence, half ridiculed, yet already half redoubtable. Was it possible that the redoubtable element had prevailed? That the time had come when Elmer Moffatt—the Elmer Moffatt of Apex!—could, even for a moment, cause consternation in the Driscoll camp? He had always said he "saw things big"; but no one had ever believed he was destined to carry them out on the same scale. Yet apparently in those idle Apex days, while he seemed to be "loafing and fooling," as her father called it, he had really been sharpening his weapons of aggression; there had been something, after all, in the effect of loose-drifting power she had always felt in him. Her heart beat faster, and she longed to question Van Degen; but she was afraid of betraying herself, and turned back to the group about the picture.

Mrs. Driscoll was still presenting objections in a tone of small mild obstinacy. "Oh, it's a *likeness*, of course—I can see that; but there's one thing I must say, Mr. Popple. It looks like a last year's dress."

The attention of the ladies instantly rallied to the picture, and the artist paled at the challenge.

"It doesn't look like a last year's face, anyhow—that's what makes them all wild," Van Degen murmured.

Undine gave him back a quick smile. She had already forgotten about Moffatt. Any triumph in which she shared left a glow in her veins, and the success of the picture obscured all other impressions. She saw herself throning in a central panel at the spring exhibition, with the crowd pushing about the picture, repeating her name; and she decided to stop on the way home and telephone her press-agent to do a paragraph about Popple's tea.

But in the hall, as she drew on her cloak, her thoughts reverted to the Driscoll fancy ball. What a blow if it were given up after she had taken so much trouble about her dress! She was to go as the Empress Josephine, after the Prudhon portrait in the Louvre. The dress was already fitted and partly embroidered, and she foresaw the difficulty of persuading the dress-maker to take it back.

"Why so pale and sad, fair cousin? What's up?" Van Degen asked, as they emerged from the lift in which they had descended alone from the studio.

"I don't know—I'm tired of posing. And it was so frightfully hot."

"Yes. Popple always keeps his place at low-neck temperature, as if the portraits might catch cold." Van Degen glanced at his watch. "Where are you off to?"

"West End Avenue, of course—if I can find a cab to take me there."

It was not the least of Undine's grievances that she was still living in the house which represented Mr. Spragg's first real-estate venture in New York. It had been understood, at the time of her marriage, that the young couple were to be established within the sacred precincts of fashion; but on their return from the honeymoon the still untenanted house in West End Avenue had been placed at their disposal, and in view of Mr. Spragg's financial embarrassment even Undine had seen the folly of refusing it. That first winter, moreover, she had not regretted her exile; while she awaited her boy's birth she was glad to be out of sight of Fifth Avenue, and to take her hateful compulsory exercise where no familiar eye could fall on her. And the next year of course her father would give them a better house.

But the next year rents had risen in the Fifth Avenue quarter, and meanwhile little Paul Marvell, from his beautiful pink cradle, was already interfering with his mother's plans. Ralph, alarmed by the fresh rush of expenses, sided with his father-in-law in urging Undine to resign herself to West End Avenue; and thus after three years she was still submitting to the incessant pin-pricks inflicted by the incongruity between her social and geographical situation—the need of having to give a west side address to her tradesmen, and the deeper irritation of hearing her friends say: "Do let me give you a lift home, dear—Oh, I'd forgotten! I'm afraid I haven't the time to go so far——"

It was bad enough to have no motor of her own, to be avowedly dependent on "lifts," openly and unconcealably in quest of them, and perpetually plotting to provoke their offer (she did so hate to be seen in a cab!); but to miss them, as often as not, because of the remoteness of her destination, emphasized the hateful sense of being "out of things."

Van Degen looked out at the long snow-piled street, down which the lamps were beginning to put their dreary yellow splashes.

"Of course you won't get a cab on a night like this. If you don't mind the open car, you'd better jump in with me. I'll run you out to the High Bridge and give you a breath of air before dinner."

The offer was tempting, for Undine's triumph in the studio had left her tired and nervous—she was beginning to learn that success may be as fatiguing as failure. Moreover, she was going to a big dinner that evening, and the fresh air would give her the eyes and complexion she needed; but in the back of her mind there lingered the vague sense of a forgotten engagement. As she tried to recall it she felt Van Degen raising the fur collar about her chin.

"Got anything you can put over your head? Will that lace thing do? Come along, then." He pushed her through the swinging doors, and added with a laugh, as they reached the street: "You're not afraid of being seen with me, are you? It's all right at this hour—Ralph's still swinging on a strap in the elevated."

The winter twilight was deliciously cold, and as they swept through Central Park, and gathered impetus for their northward flight along the darkening Boulevard, Undine felt the rush of physical joy that drowns scruples and silences memory. Her scruples, indeed, were not serious; but Ralph disliked her being too much with Van Degen, and it was her way to get what she wanted with as little "fuss" as possible. Moreover, she knew it was a mistake to make herself too accessible to a man of Peter's sort: her impatience to enjoy was curbed by an instinct for holding off and biding her time that resembled the patient skill with which her father had conducted the sale of his "bad" real estate in the Pure Water Move days. But now and then youth had its way—she could not always resist the present pleasure. And it was amusing, too, to be "talked about" with Peter Van Degen, who was noted for not caring for "nice women." She enjoyed the thought of triumphing over meretricious charms: it ennobled her in her own eyes to influence such a man for good.

Nevertheless, as the motor flew on through the icy twilight, her present cares flew with it. She could not shake off the thought of the useless fancy dress which symbolized the other crowding expenses she had not dared confess to Ralph. Van Degen heard her sigh, and bent down, lowering the speed of the motor.

"What's the matter? Isn't everything all right?"

His tone made her suddenly feel that she could confide in him, and though she began by murmuring that it was nothing she did so with the conscious purpose of being persuaded to confess. And his extraordinary "niceness" seemed to justify her and to prove that she had been right in trusting her instinct rather than in following the counsels of prudence. Heretofore, in their talks, she had never gone beyond the vaguest hint of material "bothers"—as to which dissimulation seemed vain while one lived in West End Avenue! But now that the avowal of a definite worry had been wrung from her she felt the injustice of the view generally taken of poor Peter. For he had been neither too enterprising nor too cautious (though people said of him that he "didn't care to part"); he had just laughed away, in bluff brotherly fashion, the gnawing thought of the fancy dress, had assured her he'd give a ball himself rather than miss seeing her wear it, and had added: "Oh, hang waiting for the bill—won't a couple of thou' make it all right?" in a tone that showed what a small matter money was to any one who took the larger view of life.

The whole incident passed off so quickly and easily that within a few minutes she had settled down—with a nod for his "Everything jolly again now?"—to untroubled enjoyment of the hour. Peace of mind, she said to herself, was all she needed to make her happy—and that was just what Ralph had never given her! At the thought his face seemed to rise before her, with the sharp lines of care between the eyes: it was almost like a part of his "nagging" that he should thrust himself in at such a moment! She tried to shut her eyes to the face; but a moment later it was replaced by another, a small odd likeness of itself; and with a cry of compunction she started up from her furs.

"Mercy! It's the boy's birthday—I was to take him to his grandmother's. She was to have a cake for him, and Ralph was to come up town. I *knew* there was something I'd forgotten!"

XV

IN THE DAGONET drawing-room the lamps had long been lit, and Mrs. Fairford, after a last impatient turn, had put aside the curtains of worn damask to strain her eyes into the darkening square. She came back to the hearth, where Charles Bowen stood leaning between the prim caryatides of the white marble chimney-piece.

"No sign of her. She's simply forgotten."

Bowen looked at his watch, and turned to compare it with the high-waisted Empire clock.

"Six o'clock. Why not telephone again? There must be some mistake. Perhaps she knew Ralph would be late."

Laura laughed. "I haven't noticed that she follows Ralph's movements so closely. When I telephoned just now the servant said she'd been out since two. The nurse waited till half-past four, not liking to come without orders; and now it's too late for Paul to come."

She wandered away toward the farther end of the room, where, through half-open doors, a shining surface of mahogany reflected a flower-wreathed cake in which two candles dwindled.

"Put them out, please," she said to some one in the background; then she shut the doors and turned back to Bowen.

"It's all so unlucky—my grandfather giving up his drive, and mother backing out of her hospital meeting, and having all the committee down on her. And Henley: I'd even coaxed Henley away from his bridge! He escaped again just before you came. Undine promised she'd have the boy here at four. It's not as if it had never happened before. She's always breaking her engagements."

"She has so many that it's inevitable some should get broken."

"Ah, if she'd only choose! Now that Ralph has had to go into business, and is kept in his office so late, it's cruel of her to drag him out every night. He told us the other day they hadn't dined at home for a month. Undine doesn't seem to notice how hard he works."

Bowen gazed meditatively at the crumbling fire. "No—why should she?"

"Why *should* she? Really, Charles——!"

"Why should she, when she knows nothing about it?"

"She may know nothing about his business; but she must know it's her extravagance that's forced him into it." Mrs. Fairford looked at Bowen reproachfully. "You talk as if you were on her side!"

"Are there sides already? If so, I want to look down on them impartially from the heights of pure speculation. I want to get a general view of the whole problem of American marriages."

Mrs. Fairford dropped into her arm-chair with a sigh. "If that's what you want you must make haste! Most of them don't last long enough to be classified."

"I grant you it takes an active mind. But the weak point is so frequently the same that after a time one knows where to look for it."

"What do you call the weak point?"

He paused. "The fact that the average American looks down on his wife."

Mrs. Fairford was up with a spring. "If that's where paradox lands you!"

Bowen mildly stood his ground. "Well—doesn't he prove it? How much does he let her share in the real business of life? How much does he rely on her judgment and help in the conduct of serious affairs? Take Ralph, for instance—you say his wife's extravagance forces him to work too hard; but that's not what's wrong. It's normal for a man to work hard for a woman—what's abnormal is his not caring to tell her anything about it."

"To tell Undine? She'd be bored to death if he did!"

"Just so; she'd even feel aggrieved. But why? Because it's against the custom of the country. And whose fault is that? The man's again—I don't mean Ralph, I mean the genus he belongs to: homo sapiens, Americanus. Why haven't we taught our women to take an interest in our work? Simply because we don't take enough interest in *them*."

Mrs. Fairford, sinking back into her chair, sat gazing at the vertiginous depths above which his thought seemed to dangle her.

"*You* don't? The American man doesn't—the most slaving, self-effacing, self-sacrificing——?"

"Yes; and the most indifferent: there's the point. The 'slaving's' no argument against the indifference. To slave for women is part of the old American tradition; lots of people give their lives for dogmas they've ceased to believe in. Then again, in this country the passion for making money has preceded the knowing how to spend it, and the American man lavishes his fortune on his wife because he doesn't know what else to do with it."

"Then you call it a mere want of imagination for a man to spend his money on his wife?"

"Not necessarily—but it's a want of imagination to fancy it's all he owes her. Look about you and you'll see what I mean. Why does the European woman interest herself so much more in what the men are doing? Because she's so important to them that they make it worth her while! She's not a parenthesis, as she is here—she's in the very middle of the picture. I'm not implying that Ralph isn't interested in his wife—he's a passionate, a pathetic exception. But even he has to conform to an environment where all the romantic values are reversed. Where does the real life of most American men lie? In some woman's drawing-room or in their offices? The answer's obvious, isn't it? The emotional centre of gravity's not the same in the two hemispheres. In the effete societies it's love, in our new one it's business. In America the real *crime passionnel* is a 'big steal'—there's more excitement in wrecking railways than homes."

Bowen paused to light another cigarette, and then took up his theme. "Isn't that the key to our easy divorces? If we cared for women in the old barbarous possessive way do you suppose we'd give them up as readily as we do? The real paradox is the fact that the men who make, materially, the biggest sacrifices for their women, should do least for them ideally and romantically. And what's the result—how do the women avenge themselves? All my sympathy's with them, poor deluded dears, when I see their fallacious little attempts to trick out the leavings tossed them by the preoccupied male—the money and the motors and the clothes—and pretend to themselves and each other that *that's* what really constitues life! Oh, I know what you're going to say—it's less and less of a pretense with them, I grant you; they're more and more succumbing to the force of the suggestion; but here and there I fancy there's one who still sees through the humbug, and knows that money and motors and clothes are simply the big bribe she's paid for keeping out of some man's way!"

Mrs. Fairford presented an amazed silence to the rush of this tirade; but when she rallied it was to murmur: "And is Undine one of the exceptions?"

Her companion took the shot with a smile. "No—she's a monstrously perfect result of the system: the completest proof of its triumph. It's Ralph who's the victim and the exception."

"Ah, poor Ralph!" Mrs. Fairford raised her head quickly. "I hear him now. I suppose," she added in an undertone, " we can't give him your explanation for his wife's having forgotten to come?"

Bowen echoed her sigh, and then seemed to toss it from him with his cigarette-end; but he stood in silence while the door opened and Ralph Marvell entered.

"Well, Laura! Hallo, Charles—have you been celebrating too?" Ralph turned to his sister. "It's outrageous of me to be so late, and I daren't look my son in the face! But I stayed down town to make provision for his future birthdays." He returned Mrs. Fairford's kiss. "Don't tell me the party's over, and the guest of honour gone to bed?"

As he stood before them, laughing and a little flushed, the strain of long fatigue sounding through his gaiety and looking out of his anxious eyes, Mrs. Fairford threw a glance at Bowen and then turned away to ring the bell.

"Sit down, Ralph—you look tired. I'll give you some tea."

He dropped into an arm-chair. "I did have rather a rush to get here—but hadn't I better join the revellers? Where are they?"

He walked to the end of the room and threw open the dining-room doors. "Hallo—where have they all gone to? What a jolly cake!" He went up to it. "Why, it's never even been cut!"

Mrs. Fairford called after him: "Come and have your tea first."

"No, no—tea afterward, thanks. Are they all upstairs with my grandfather? I must make my peace with Undine——"

His sister put her arm through his, and drew him back to the fire.

"Undine didn't come."

"Didn't come? Who brought the boy, then?"

"He didn't come either. That's why the cake's not cut."

Ralph frowned. "What's the mystery? Is he ill, or what's happened?"

"Nothing's happened—Paul's all right. Apparently Undine forgot. She never went home for him, and the nurse waited till it was too late to come."

She saw his eyes darken; but he merely gave a slight laugh and drew out his cigarette case. "Poor little Paul—poor chap!" He moved toward the fire. "Yes, please—some tea."

He dropped back into his chair with a look of weariness, as if some strong stimulant had suddenly ceased to take effect on him; but before the tea-table was brought back he had glanced at his watch and was on his feet again.

"But this won't do. I must rush home and see the poor chap before dinner. And my mother—and my grandfather? I want to say a word to them—I must make Paul's excuses!"

"Grandfather's taking his nap. And mother had to rush out for a postponed committee meeting—she left as soon as we heard Paul wasn't coming."

"Ah, I see." He sat down again. "Yes, make the tea strong, please. I've had a beastly fagging sort of day."

He leaned back with half-closed eyes, his untouched cup in his hand. Bowen took leave, and Laura sat silent, watching her brother under lowered lids while she feigned to be busy with the kettle. Ralph presently emptied his cup and put it aside; then, sinking into his former attitude, he clasped his hands behind his head and lay staring apathetically into the fire. But suddenly he came to life and started up. A motor-horn had sounded outside, and there was a noise of wheels at the door.

"There's Undine! I wonder what could have kept her." He

jumped up and walked to the door; but it was Clare Van Degen who came in.

At sight of him she gave a little murmur of pleasure. "What luck to find you! No, not luck—I came because I knew you'd be here. He never comes near me, Laura: I have to hunt him down to get a glimpse of him!"

Slender and shadowy in her long furs, she bent to kiss Mrs. Fairford and then turned back to Ralph. "Yes, I knew I'd catch you here. I knew it was the boy's birthday, and I've brought him a present: a vulgar expensive Van Degen offering. I've not enough imagination left to find the right thing, the thing it takes feeling and not money to buy. When I look for a present nowadays I never say to the shopman: 'I want this or that'—I simply say: 'Give me something that costs so much.'" She drew a parcel from her muff. "Where's the victim of my vulgarity? Let me crush him under the weight of my gold."

Mrs. Fairford sighed out "Clare—Clare!" and Ralph smiled at his cousin.

"I'm sorry; but you'll have to depute me to present it. The birthday's over; you're too late."

She looked surprised. "Why, I've just left Mamie Driscoll, and she told me Undine was still at Popple's studio a few minutes ago: Popple's giving a tea to show the picture."

"Popple's giving a tea?" Ralph struck an attitude of mock consternation. "Ah, in that case——! In Popple's society who wouldn't forget the flight of time?"

He had recovered his usual easy tone, and Laura saw that Mrs. Van Degen's words had dispelled his preoccupation. He turned to his cousin. "Will you trust me with your present for the boy?"

Clare gave him the parcel. "I'm sorry not to give it myself. I said what I did because I knew what you and Laura were thinking—but it's really a battered old Dagonet bowl that came down to me from our revered great-grandmother."

"What—the heirloom you used to eat your porridge out of?" Ralph detained her hand to put a kiss on it. "That's dear of you!"

She threw him one of her strange glances. "Why not say: 'That's like you?' But you don't remember what I'm like."

She turned away to glance at the clock. "It's late, and I must be off. I'm going to a big dinner at the Chauncey Ellings'— but you must be going there too, Ralph? You'd better let me drive you home."

In the motor Ralph leaned back in silence, while the rug was drawn over their knees, and Clare restlessly fingered the row of gold-topped objects in the rack at her elbow. It was restful to be swept through the crowded streets in this smooth fashion, and Clare's presence at his side gave him a vague sense of ease.

For a long time now feminine nearness had come to mean to him, not this relief from tension, but the ever-renewed dread of small daily deceptions, evasions, subterfuges. The change had come gradually, marked by one disillusionment after another; but there had been one moment that formed the point beyond which there was no returning. It was the moment, a month or two before his boy's birth, when, glancing over a batch of belated Paris bills, he had come on one from the jeweller he had once found in private conference with Undine. The bill was not large, but two of its items stood out sharply. "Resetting pearl and diamond pendant. Resetting sapphire and diamond ring." The pearl and diamond pendant was his mother's wedding present; the ring was the one he had given Undine on their engagement. That they were both family relics, kept unchanged through several generations, scarcely mattered to him at the time: he felt only the stab of his wife's deception. She had assured him in Paris that she had not had her jewels reset. He had noticed, soon after their return to New York, that she had left off her engagement-ring; but the others were soon discarded also, and in answer to his question she had told him that, in her ailing state, rings "worried" her. Now he saw she had deceived him, and, forgetting everything else, he went to her, bill in hand. Her tears and distress filled him with immediate contrition. Was this a time to torment her about trifles? His anger seemed to cause her actual physical fear, and at the sight he abased himself in entreaties for forgiveness. When the scene ended she had pardoned him, and the reset ring was on her finger. . .

Soon afterward, the birth of the boy seemed to wipe out

these humiliating memories; yet Marvell found in time that they were not effaced, but only momentarily crowded out of sight. In reality, the incident had a meaning out of proportion to its apparent seriousness, for it put in his hand a clue to a new side of his wife's character. He no longer minded her having lied about the jeweller; what pained him was that she had been unconscious of the wound she inflicted in destroying the identity of the jewels. He saw that, even after their explanation, she still supposed he was angry only because she had deceived him; and the discovery that she was completely unconscious of states of feeling on which so much of his inner life depended marked a new stage in their relation.

He was not thinking of all this as he sat beside Clare Van Degen; but it was part of the chronic disquietude which made him more alive to his cousin's sympathy, her shy unspoken understanding. After all, he and she were of the same blood and had the same traditions. She was light and frivolous, without strength of will or depth of purpose; but she had the frankness of her foibles, and she would never have lied to him or traded on his tenderness.

Clare's nervousness gradually subsided, and she lapsed into a low-voiced mood which seemed like an answer to his secret thought. But she did not sound the personal note, and they chatted quietly of commonplace things: of the dinner-dance at which they were presently to meet, of the costume she had chosen for the Driscoll fancy-ball, the recurring rumours of old Driscoll's financial embarrassment, and the mysterious personality of Elmer Moffatt, on whose movements Wall Street was beginning to fix a fascinated eye. When Ralph, the year after his marriage, had renounced his profession to go into partnership with a firm of real-estate agents, he had come in contact for the first time with the drama of "business," and whenever he could turn his attention from his own tasks he found a certain interest in watching the fierce interplay of its forces. In the down-town world he had heard things of Moffatt that seemed to single him out from the common herd of money-makers: anecdotes of his coolness, his lazy good-temper, the humorous detachment he preserved in the heat of conflicting interests; and his figure was enlarged by the mystery that hung about it—the fact that no one seemed to know whence he came, or how he had acquired the information which, for the moment, was making him so formidable.

"I should like to see him," Ralph said; "he must be a good specimen of the one of the few picturesque types we've got."

"Yes—it might be amusing to fish him out; but the most picturesque types in Wall Street are generally the tamest in a drawing-room." Clare considered. "But doesn't Undine know him? I seem to remember seeing them together."

"Undine and Moffatt? Then *you* know him—you've met him?"

"Not actually met him—but he's been pointed out to me. It must have been some years ago. Yes—it was one night at the theatre, just after you announced your engagement." He fancied her voice trembled slightly, as though she thought he might notice her way of dating her memories. "You came into our box," she went on, "and I asked you the name of the red-faced man who was sitting in the stall next to Undine. You didn't know, but some one told us it was Moffatt."

Marvell was more struck by her tone than by what she was saying. "If Undine knows him it's odd she's never mentioned it," he answered indifferently.

The motor stopped at his door and Clare, as she held out her hand, turned a first full look on him.

"Why do you never come to see me? I miss you more than ever," she said.

He pressed her hand without answering, but after the motor had rolled away he stood for a while on the pavement, looking after it.

When he entered the house the hall was still dark and the small over-furnished drawing-room empty. The parlour-maid told him that Mrs. Marvell had not yet come in, and he went upstairs to the nursery. But on the threshold the nurse met him with the whispered request not to make a noise, as it had been hard to quiet the boy after the afternoon's disappointment, and she had just succeeded in putting him to sleep.

Ralph went down to his own room and threw himself in the old college arm-chair in which, four years previously, he had sat the night out, dreaming of Undine. He had no study of his own, and he had crowded into his narrow bed-room his prints and bookshelves, and the other relics of his youth.

As he sat among them now the memory of that other night swept over him—the night when he had heard the "call"! Fool as he had been not to recognize its meaning then, he knew himself triply mocked in being, even now, at its mercy. The flame of love that had played about his passion for his wife had died down to its embers; all the transfiguring hopes and illusions were gone, but they had left an unquenchable ache for her nearness, her smile, her touch. His life had come to be nothing but a long effort to win these mercies by one concession after another: the sacrifice of his literary projects, the exchange of his profession for an uncongenial business, and the incessant struggle to make enough money to satisfy her increasing exactions. That was where the "call" had led him. . .

The clock struck eight, but it was useless to begin to dress till Undine came in, and he stretched himself out in his chair, reached for a pipe and took up the evening paper. His passing annoyance had died out; he was usually too tired after his day's work for such feelings to keep their edge long. But he was curious—disinterestedly curious—to know what pretext Undine would invent for being so late, and what excuse she would have found for forgetting the little boy's birthday.

He read on till half-past eight; then he stood up and sauntered to the window. The avenue below it was deserted; not a carriage or motor turned the corner around which he expected Undine to appear, and he looked idly in the opposite direction. There too the perspective was nearly empty, so empty that he singled out, a dozen blocks away, the blazing lamps of a large touring-car that was bearing furiously down the avenue from Morningside. As it drew nearer its speed slackened, and he saw it hug the curb and stop at his door. By the light of the street lamp he recognized his wife as she sprang out and detected a familiar silhouette in her companion's fur-coated figure. Then the motor flew on and Undine ran up the steps.

Ralph went out on the landing. He saw her coming up quickly, as if to reach her room unperceived; but when she caught sight of him she stopped, her head thrown back and the light falling on her blown hair and glowing face.

"Well?" she said, smiling up at him.

"They waited for you all the afternoon in Washington Square—the boy never had his birthday," he answered.

Her colour deepened, but she instantly rejoined: "Why, what happened? Why didn't the nurse take him?"

"You said you were coming to fetch him, so she waited."

"But I telephoned——"

He said to himself: "Is *that* the lie?" and answered: "Where from?"

"Why, the studio, of course——" She flung her cloak open, as if to attest her veracity. "The sitting lasted longer than usual—there was something about the dress he couldn't get——"

"But I thought he was giving a tea."

"He had tea afterward; he always does. And he asked some people in to see my portrait. That detained me too. I didn't know they were coming, and when they turned up I couldn't rush away. It would have looked as if I didn't like the picture." She paused and they gave each other a searching simultaneous glance. "Who told you it was a tea?" she asked.

"Clare Van Degen. I saw her at my mother's."

"So you weren't unconsoled after all——!"

"The nurse didn't get any message. My people were awfully disappointed; and the poor boy has cried his eyes out."

"Dear me! What a fuss! But I might have known my message wouldn't be delivered. Everything always happens to put me in the wrong with your family."

With a little air of injured pride she started to go to her room; but he put out a hand to detain her.

"You've just come from the studio?"

"Yes. It is awfully late? I must go and dress. We're dining with the Ellings, you know."

"I know. . . How did you come? In a cab?"

She faced him limpidly. "No; I couldn't find one that would bring me—so Peter gave me a lift, like an angel. I'm blown to bits. He had his open car."

Her colour was still high, and Ralph noticed that her lower lip twitched a little. He had led her to the point they had reached solely to be able to say: "If you're straight from the studio, how was it that I saw you coming down from Morningside?"

Unless he asked her that there would be no point in his cross-questioning, and he would have sacrificed his pride without a purpose. But suddenly, as they stood there face to face, almost touching, she became something immeasurably alien and far off, and the question died on his lips.

"Is that all?" she asked with a slight smile.

"Yes; you'd better go and dress," he said, and turned back to his room.

XVI

THE TURNINGS of life seldom show a sign-post; or rather, though the sign is always there, it is usually placed some distance back, like the notices that give warning of a bad hill or a level railway-crossing.

Ralph Marvell, pondering upon this, reflected that for him the sign had been set, more than three years earlier, in an Italian ilex-grove. That day his life had brimmed over—so he had put it at the time. He saw now that it had brimmed over indeed: brimmed to the extent of leaving the cup empty, or at least of uncovering the dregs beneath the nectar. He knew now that he should never hereafter look at his wife's hand without remembering something he had read in it that day. Its surface-language had been sweet enough, but under the rosy lines he had seen the warning letters.

Since then he had been walking with a ghost: the miserable ghost of his illusion. Only he had somehow vivified, coloured, substantiated it, by the force of his own great need— as a man might breathe a semblance of life into a dear drowned body that he cannot give up for dead. All this came to him with aching distinctness the morning after his talk with his wife on the stairs. He had accused himself, in midnight retrospect, of having failed to press home his conclusion because he dared not face the truth. But he knew this was not the case. It was not the truth he feared, it was another lie. If he had foreseen a chance of her saying: "Yes, I was with Peter Van Degen, and for the reason you think," he would have put it to the touch, stood up to the blow like a man; but he knew she would never say that. She would go on eluding and doubling, watching him as he watched her; and at that game she was sure to beat him in the end.

On their way home from the Elling dinner this certainty had become so insufferable that it nearly escaped him in the cry: "You needn't watch me—I shall never again watch you!" But he had held his peace, knowing she would not understand. How little, indeed, she ever understood, had been made clear to him when, the same night, he had followed her upstairs through the sleeping house. She had gone on ahead while he stayed below to lock doors and put out lights, and he had supposed her to be already in her room when he reached the upper landing; but she stood there waiting, in the spot where he had waited for her a few hours earlier. She had shone her vividest at dinner, with the revolving brilliancy that collective approval always struck from her; and the glow of it still hung on her as she paused there in the dimness, her shining cloak dropped from her white shoulders.

"Ralphie——" she began, a soft hand on his arm.

He stopped, and she pulled him about so that their faces were close, and he saw her lips curving for a kiss. Every line of her face sought him, from the sweep of the narrowed eyelids to the dimples that played away from her smile. His eye received the picture with distinctness; but for the first time it did not pass into his veins. It was as if he had been struck with a subtle blindness that permitted images to give their colour to the eye but communicated nothing to the brain.

"Good-night," he said, as he passed on.

When a man felt in that way about a woman he was surely in a position to deal with his case impartially. This came to Ralph as the joyless solace of the morning. At last the bandage was off and he could see. And what did he see? Only the uselessness of driving his wife to subterfuges that were no longer necessary. Was Van Degen her lover? Probably not— the suspicion died as it rose. She would not take more risks than she could help, and it was admiration, not love, that she wanted. She wanted to enjoy herself, and her conception of enjoyment was publicity, promiscuity—the band, the banners, the crowd, the close contact of covetous impulses, and the sense of walking among them in cool security. Any personal entanglement might mean "bother," and bother was the thing she most abhorred. Probably, as the queer formula went, his "honour" was safe: he could count on the letter of her fidelity. At the moment the conviction meant no more to him than if he had been assured of the honesty of the first stranger he met in the street. A stranger—that was what she had always been to him. So malleable outwardly, she had remained insensible to the touch of the heart.

These thoughts accompanied him on his way to business the next morning. Then, as the routine took him back, the feeling of strangeness diminished. There he was again at his daily task—nothing tangible was altered. He was there for the same purpose as yesterday: to make money for his wife and child. The woman he had turned from on the stairs a few hours earlier was still his wife and the mother of Paul Marvell. She was an inherent part of his life; the inner disruption had not resulted in any outward upheaval. And with the sense of inevitableness there came a sudden wave of pity. Poor Undine! She was what the gods had made her—a creature of skin-deep reactions, a mote in the beam of pleasure. He had no desire to "preach down" such heart as she had—he felt only a stronger wish to reach it, teach it, move it to something of the pity that filled his own. They were fellow-victims in the *noyade* of marriage, but if they ceased to struggle perhaps the drowning would be easier for both. . . Meanwhile the first of the month was at hand, with its usual batch of bills; and there was no time to think of any struggle less pressing than that connected with paying them. . .

Undine had been surprised, and a little disconcerted, at her husband's acceptance of the birthday incident. Since the resetting of her bridal ornaments the relations between Washington Square and West End Avenue had been more and more strained; and the silent disapproval of the Marvell ladies was more irritating to her than open recrimination. She knew how keenly Ralph must feel her last slight to his family, and she had been frightened when she guessed that he had seen her returning with Van Degen. He must have been watching from the window, since, credulous as he always was, he evidently had a reason for not believing her when she told him she had come from the studio. There was therefore something both puzzling and disturbing in his silence; and she made up her mind that it must be either explained or cajoled away.

These thoughts were with her as she dressed; but at the Ellings' they fled like ghosts before light and laughter. She had never been more open to the suggestions of immediate enjoyment. At last she had reached the envied situation of the pretty woman with whom society must reckon, and if she had only had the means to live up to her opportunities she would have been perfectly content with life, with herself and her husband. She still thought Ralph "sweet" when she was not bored by his good advice or exasperated by his inability to pay her bills. The question of money was what chiefly stood between them; and now that this was momentarily disposed of by Van Degen's offer she looked at Ralph more kindly—she even felt a return of her first impersonal affection for him. Everybody could see that Clare Van Degen was "gone" on him, and Undine always liked to know that what belonged to her was coveted by others.

Her reassurance had been fortified by the news she had heard at the Elling dinner—the published fact of Harmon B. Driscoll's unexpected victory. The Ararat investigation had been mysteriously stopped—quashed, in the language of the law—and Elmer Moffatt "turned down," as Van Degen (who sat next to her) expressed it.

"I don't believe we'll ever hear of that gentleman again," he said contemptuously; and their eyes crossed gaily as she exclaimed: "Then they'll give the fancy ball after all?"

"I should have given you one anyhow—shouldn't you have liked that as well?"

"Oh, you can give me one too!" she returned; and he bent closer to say: "By Jove, I will—and anything else you want."

But on the way home her fears revived. Ralph's indifference struck her as unnatural. He had not returned to the subject of Paul's disappointment, had not even asked her to write a word of excuse to his mother. Van Degen's way of looking at her at dinner—he was incapable of graduating his glances—had made it plain that the favour she had accepted would necessitate her being more conspicuously in his company (though she was still resolved that it should be on just such terms as she chose); and it would be extremely troublesome if, at this juncture, Ralph should suddenly turn suspicious and secretive.

Undine, hitherto, had found more benefits than drawbacks in her marriage; but now the tie began to gall. It was hard to be criticized for every grasp at opportunity by a man so avowedly unable to do the reaching for her! Ralph had gone into business to make more money for her; but it was plain that the "more" would never be much, and that he would not achieve the quick rise to affluence which was man's natural

tribute to woman's merits. Undine felt herself trapped, deceived; and it was intolerable that the agent of her disillusionment should presume to be the critic of her conduct.

Her annoyance, however, died out with her fears. Ralph,
the morning after the Elling dinner, went his way as usual,
and after nerving herself for the explosion which did not
come she set down his indifference to the dulling effect of
"business." No wonder poor women whose husbands were
always "down-town" had to look elsewhere for sympathy!
Van Degen's cheque helped to calm her, and the weeks
whirled on toward the Driscoll ball.

The ball was as brilliant as she had hoped, and her own
part in it as thrilling as a page from one of the "society novels" with which she had cheated the monotony of Apex days.
She had no time for reading now: every hour was packed
with what she would have called life, and the intensity of her
sensations culminated on that triumphant evening. What
could be more delightful than to feel that, while all the
women envied her dress, the men did not so much as look at
it? Their admiration was all for herself, and her beauty deepened under it as flowers take a warmer colour in the rays of
sunset. Only Van Degen's glance weighed on her a little too
heavily. Was it possible that he might become a "bother" less
negligible than those he had relieved her of? Undine was not
greatly alarmed—she still had full faith in her powers of self-
defense; but she disliked to feel the least crease in the smooth
surface of existence. She had always been what her parents
called "sensitive."

As the winter passed, material cares once more assailed her.
In the thrill of liberation produced by Van Degen's gift she
had been imprudent—had launched into fresh expenses. Not
that she accused herself of extravagance: she had done nothing not really necessary. The drawing-room, for instance,
cried out to be "done over," and Popple, who was an authority on decoration, had shown her, with a few strokes of his
pencil, how easily it might be transformed into a French "period" room, all curves and cupids: just the setting for a pretty
woman and his portrait of her. But Undine, still hopeful of
leaving West End Avenue, had heroically resisted the suggestion, and contented herself with the renewal of the curtains

and carpet, and the purchase of some fragile gilt chairs which, as she told Ralph, would be "so much to the good" when they moved—the explanation, as she made it, seemed an additional evidence of her thrift.

Partly as a result of these exertions she had a "nervous breakdown" toward the middle of the winter, and her physician having ordered massage and a daily drive it became necessary to secure Mrs. Heeny's attendance and to engage a motor by the month. Other unforeseen expenses—the bills, that, at such times, seem to run up without visible impulsion—were added to by a severe illness of little Paul's: a long costly illness, with three nurses and frequent consultations. During these days Ralph's anxiety drove him to what seemed to Undine foolish excesses of expenditure and when the boy began to get better the doctors advised country air. Ralph at once hired a small house at Tuxedo and Undine of course accompanied her son to the country; but she spent only the Sundays with him, running up to town during the week to be with her husband, as she explained. This necessitated the keeping up of two households, and even for so short a time the strain on Ralph's purse was severe. So it came about that the bill for the fancy-dress was still unpaid, and Undine left to wonder distractedly what had become of Van Degen's money. That Van Degen seemed also to wonder was becoming unpleasantly apparent: his cheque had evidently not brought in the return he expected, and he put his grievance to her frankly one day when he motored down to lunch at Tuxedo.

They were sitting, after luncheon, in the low-ceilinged drawing-room to which Undine had adapted her usual background of cushions, bric-a-brac and flowers—since one must make one's setting "home-like," however little one's habits happened to correspond with that particular effect. Undine, conscious of the intimate charm of her *mise-en-scène*, and of the recovered freshness and bloom which put her in harmony with it, had never been more sure of her power to keep her friend in the desired state of adoring submission. But Peter, as he grew more adoring, became less submissive; and there came a moment when she needed all her wits to save the situation. It was easy enough to rebuff him, the easier as his physical proximity always roused in her a vague instinct of resistance; but it was hard so to temper the rebuff with promise that the game of suspense should still delude him. He put it to her at last, standing squarely before her, his batrachian sallowness unpleasantly flushed, and primitive man looking out of the eyes from which a frock-coated gentleman usually pined at her.

"Look here—the installment plan's all right; but ain't you a bit behind even on that?" (She had brusquely eluded a nearer approach.) "Anyhow, I think I'd rather let the interest accumulate for a while. This is good-bye till I get back from Europe."

The announcement took her by surprise. "Europe? Why, when are you sailing?"

"On the first of April: good day for a fool to acknowledge his folly. I'm beaten, and I'm running away."

She sat looking down, her hand absently occupied with the twist of pearls he had given her. In a flash she saw the peril of this departure. Once off on the *Sorceress*, he was lost to her—the power of old associations would prevail. Yet if she were as "nice" to him as he asked—"nice" enough to keep him—the end might not be much more to her advantage. Hitherto she had let herself drift on the current of their adventure, but she now saw what port she had half-unconsciously been trying for. If she had striven so hard to hold him, had "played" him with such patience and such skill, it was for something more than her passing amusement and convenience: for a purpose the more tenaciously cherished that she had not dared name it to herself. In the light of this discovery she saw the need of feigning complete indifference.

"Ah, you happy man! It's good-bye indeed, then," she threw back at him, lifting a plaintive smile to his frown.

"Oh, you'll turn up in Paris later, I suppose—to get your things for Newport."

"Paris? Newport? They're not on my map! When Ralph can get away we shall go to the Adirondacks for the boy. I hope I shan't need Paris clothes there! It doesn't matter, at any rate," she ended, laughing, "because nobody I care about will see me."

Van Degen echoed her laugh. "Oh, come—that's rough on Ralph!"

She looked down with a slight increase of colour. "I oughtn't to have said it, ought I? But the fact is I'm unhappy—and a little hurt——"

"Unhappy? Hurt?" He was at her side again. "Why, what's wrong?"

She lifted her eyes with a grave look. "I thought you'd be sorrier to leave me."

"Oh, it won't be for long—it needn't be, you know." He was perceptibly softening. "It's damnable, the way you're tied down. Fancy rotting all summer in the Adirondacks! Why do you stand it? You oughtn't to be bound for life by a girl's mistake."

The lashes trembled slightly on her cheek. "Aren't we all bound by our mistakes—we women? Don't let us talk of such things! Ralph would never let me go abroad without him." She paused, and then, with a quick upward sweep of the lids: "After all, it's better it should be good-bye—since I'm paying for another mistake in being so unhappy at your going."

"Another mistake? Why do you call it that?"

"Because I've misunderstood you—or you me." She continued to smile at him wistfully. "And some things are best mended by a break."

He met her smile with a loud sigh—she could feel him in the meshes again. "*Is* it to be a break between us?"

"Haven't you just said so? Anyhow, it might as well be, since we shan't be in the same place again for months."

The frock-coated gentleman once more languished from his eyes: she thought she trembled on the edge of victory. "Hang it," he broke out, "you ought to have a change—you're looking awfully pulled down. Why can't you coax your mother to run over to Paris with you? Ralph couldn't object to that."

She shook her head. "I don't believe she could afford it, even if I could persuade her to leave father. You know father hasn't done very well lately: I shouldn't like to ask him for the money."

"You're so confoundedly proud!" He was edging nearer. "It would all be so easy if you'd only be a little fond of me. . ."

She froze to her sofa-end. "We women can't repair our mistakes. Don't make me more miserable by reminding me of mine."

"Oh, nonsense! There's nothing cash won't do. Why won't you let me straighten things out for you?"

Her colour rose again, and she looked him quickly and consciously in the eye. It was time to play her last card. "You seem to forget that I am—married," she said.

Van Degen was silent—for a moment she thought he was swaying to her in the flush of surrender. But he remained doggedly seated, meeting her look with an odd clearing of his heated gaze, as if a shrewd businessman had suddenly replaced the pining gentleman at the window.

"Hang it—so am I!" he rejoined; and Undine saw that in the last issue he was still the stronger of the two.

XVII

NOTHING was bitterer to her than to confess to herself the failure of her power; but her last talk with Van Degen had taught her a lesson almost worth the abasement. She saw the mistake she had made in taking money from him, and understood that if she drifted into repeating that mistake her future would be irretrievably compromised. What she wanted was not a hand-to-mouth existence of precarious intrigue: to one with her gifts the privileges of life should come openly. Already in her short experience she had seen enough of the women who sacrifice future security for immediate success, and she meant to lay solid foundations before she began to build up the light superstructure of enjoyment.

Nevertheless it was galling to see Van Degen leave, and to know that for the time he had broken away from her. Over a nature so insensible to the spells of memory, the visible and tangible would always prevail. If she could have been with him again in Paris, where, in the shining spring days, every sight and sound ministered to such influences, she was sure she could have regained her hold. And the sense of frustration was intensified by the fact that every one she knew was to be there: her potential rivals were crowding the east-bound steamers. New York was a desert, and Ralph's seeming unconsciousness of the fact increased her resentment. She had had but one chance at Europe since her marriage, and that had been wasted through her husband's unaccountable perversity. She knew now with what packed hours of Paris and London they had paid for their empty weeks in Italy.

Meanwhile the long months of the New York spring stretched out before her in all their social vacancy to the measureless blank of a summer in the Adirondacks. In her girlhood she had plumbed the dim depths of such summers; but then she had been sustained by the hope of bringing some capture to the surface. Now she knew better: there were no "finds" for her in that direction. The people she wanted would be at Newport or in Europe, and she was too resolutely bent on a definite object, too sternly animated by her father's business instinct, to turn aside in quest of casual distractions.

The chief difficulty in the way of her attaining any distant end had always been her reluctance to plod through the intervening stretches of dulness and privation. She had begun to see this, but she could not always master the weakness: never had she stood in greater need of Mrs. Heeny's "Go slow, Undine!" Her imagination was incapable of long flights. She could not cheat her impatience with the mirage of far-off satisfactions, and for the moment present and future seemed equally void. But her desire to go to Europe and to rejoin the little New York world that was reforming itself in London and Paris was fortified by reasons which seemed urgent enough to justify an appeal to her father.

She went down to his office to plead her case, fearing Mrs. Spragg's intervention. For some time past Mr. Spragg had been rather continuously overworked, and the strain was beginning to tell on him. He had never quite regained, in New York, the financial security of his Apex days. Since he had changed his base of operations his affairs had followed an uncertain course, and Undine suspected that his breach with his old political ally, the Representative Rolliver who had seen him through the muddiest reaches of the Pure Water Move, was not unconnected with his failure to get a footing in Wall Street. But all this was vague and shadowy to her. Even had "business" been less of a mystery, she was too much absorbed in her own affairs to project herself into her father's case; and she thought she was sacrificing enough to delicacy of feeling in sparing him the "bother" of Mrs. Spragg's opposition.

When she came to him with a grievance he always heard her out with the same mild patience; but the long habit of "managing" him had made her, in his own language, "discount" this tolerance, and when she ceased to speak her heart throbbed with suspense as he leaned back, twirling an invisible toothpick under his sallow moustache. Presently he raised a hand to stroke the limp beard in which the moustache was merged; then he groped for the Masonic emblem that had lost itself in one of the folds of his depleted waistcoat.

He seemed to fish his answer from the same rusty depths,

for as his fingers closed about the trinket he said: "Yes, the heated term *is* trying in New York. That's why the Fresh Air Fund pulled my last dollar out of me last week."

Undine frowned: there was nothing more irritating, in these encounters with her father, than his habit of opening the discussion with a joke.

"I wish you'd understand that I'm serious, father. I've never been strong since the baby was born, and I need a change. But it's not only that: there are other reasons for my wanting to go."

Mr. Spragg still held to his mild tone of banter. "I never knew you short on reasons, Undie. Trouble is you don't always know other people's when you see 'em."

His daughter's lips tightened. "I know your reasons when I see them, father: I've heard them often enough. But you can't know mine because I haven't told you—not the real ones."

"Jehoshaphat! I thought they were all real as long as you had a use for them."

Experience had taught her that such protracted trifling usually concealed an exceptional vigour of resistance, and the suspense strengthened her determination.

"My reasons are all real enough," she answered; "but there's one more serious than the others."

Mr. Spragg's brows began to jut. "More bills?"

"No." She stretched out her hand and began to finger the dusty objects on his desk. "I'm unhappy at home."

"Unhappy——!" His start overturned the gorged waste-paper basket and shot a shower of paper across the rug. He stooped to put the basket back; then he turned his slow fagged eyes on his daughter. "Why, he worships the ground you walk on, Undie."

"That's not always a reason, for a woman——" It was the answer she would have given to Popple or Van Degen, but she saw in an instant the mistake of thinking it would impress her father. In the atmosphere of sentimental casuistry to which she had become accustomed, she had forgotten that Mr. Spragg's private rule of conduct was as simple as his business morality was complicated.

He glowered at her under thrust-out brows. "It isn't a

reason, isn't it? I can seem to remember the time when you used to think it was equal to a whole carload of white-wash."

She blushed a bright red, and her own brows were levelled at his above her stormy steel-grey eyes. The sense of her blunder made her angrier with him, and more ruthless.

"I can't expect you to understand—you never *have*, you or mother, when it came to my feelings. I suppose some people are born sensitive—I can't imagine anybody'd *choose* to be so. Because I've been too proud to complain you've taken it for granted that I was perfectly happy. But my marriage was a mistake from the beginning; and Ralph feels just as I do about it. His people hate me, they've always hated me; and he looks at everything as they do. They've never forgiven me for his having had to go into business—with their aristocratic ideas they look down on a man who works for his living. Of course it's all right for *you* to do it, because you're not a Marvell or a Dagonet; but they think Ralph ought to just lie back and let you support the baby and me."

This time she had found the right note: she knew it by the tightening of her father's slack muscles and the sudden straightening of his back.

"By George, he pretty near does!" he exclaimed, bringing down his fist on the desk. "They haven't been taking it out of you about that, have they?"

"They don't fight fair enough to say so. They just egg him on to turn against me. They only consented to his marrying me because they thought you were so crazy about the match you'd give us everything, and he'd have nothing to do but sit at home and write books."

Mr. Spragg emitted a derisive groan. "From what I hear of the amount of business he's doing I guess he could keep the Poet's Corner going right along. I suppose the old man was right—he hasn't got it in him to make money."

"Of course not; he wasn't brought up to it, and in his heart of hearts he's ashamed of having to do it. He told me it was killing a little more of him every day."

"Do they back him up in that kind of talk?"

"They back him up in everything. Their ideas are all different from ours. They look down on us—can't you see that?

Can't you guess how they treat me from the way they've acted to you and mother?"

He met this with a puzzled stare. "The way they've acted to me and mother? Why, we never so much as set eyes on them."

"That's just what I mean! I don't believe they've even called on mother this year, have they? Last year they just left their cards without asking. And why do you suppose they never invite you to dine? In their set lots of people older than you and mother dine out every night of the winter—society's full of them. The Marvells are ashamed to have you meet their friends: that's the reason. They're ashamed to have it known that Ralph married an Apex girl, and that you and mother haven't always had your own servants and carriages; and Ralph's ashamed of it too, now he's got over being crazy about me. If he was free I believe he'd turn round to-morrow and marry that Ray girl his mother's saving up for him."

Mr. Spragg listened with a heavy brow and pushed-out lip. His daughter's outburst seemed at last to have roused him to a faint resentment. After she had ceased to speak he remained silent, twisting an inky penhandle between his fingers; then he said: "I guess mother and I can worry along without having Ralph's relatives drop in; but I'd like to make it clear to them that if you came from Apex your income came from there too. I presume they'd be sorry if Ralph was left to support you on *his*."

She saw that she had scored in the first part of the argument, but every watchful nerve reminded her that the hardest stage was still ahead.

"Oh, they're willing enough he should take your money—that's only natural, they think."

A chuckle sounded deep down under Mr. Spragg's loose collar. "There seems to be practical unanimity on that point," he observed. "But I don't see," he continued, jerking round his bushy brows on her, "how going to Europe is going to help you out."

Undine leaned close enough for her lowered voice to reach him. "Can't you understand that, knowing how they all feel about me—and how Ralph feels—I'd give almost anything to get away?"

Her father looked at her compassionately. "I guess most of

us feel that once in a way when we're young, Undine. Later on you'll see going away ain't much use when you've got to turn round and come back."

She nodded at him with close-pressed lips, like a child in possession of some solemn secret.

"That's just it—that's the reason I'm so wild to go; because it *might* mean I wouldn't ever have to come back."

"Not come back? What on earth are you talking about?"

"It might mean that I could get free—begin over again. . ."

He had pushed his seat back with a sudden jerk and cut her short by striking his palm on the arm of the chair.

"For the Lord's sake, Undine—do you know what you're saying?"

"Oh, yes, I know." She gave him back a confident smile. "If I can get away soon—go straight over to Paris . . . there's some one there who'd do anything . . . who *could* do anything . . . if I was free . . ."

Mr. Spragg's hands continued to grasp his chair-arms. "Good God, Undine Marvell—are you sitting there in your sane senses and talking to me of what you could do if you were *free*?"

Their glances met in an interval of speechless communion; but Undine did not shrink from her father's eyes and when she lowered her own it seemed to be only because there was nothing left for them to say.

"I know just what I could do if I were free. I could marry the right man," she answered boldly.

He met her with a murmur of helpless irony. "The right man? The right man? Haven't you had enough of trying for him yet?"

As he spoke the door behind them opened, and Mr. Spragg looked up abruptly.

The stenographer stood on the threshold, and above her shoulder Undine perceived the ingratiating grin of Elmer Moffatt.

" 'A little farther lend thy guiding hand'—but I guess I can go the rest of the way alone," he said, insinuating himself through the doorway with an airy gesture of dismissal; then he turned to Mr. Spragg and Undine.

"I agree entirely with Mrs. Marvell—and I'm happy to have the opportunity of telling her so," he proclaimed, holding his hand out gallantly.

Undine stood up with a laugh. "It sounded like old times, I suppose—you thought father and I were quarrelling? But we never quarrel any more: he always agrees with me." She smiled at Mr. Spragg and turned her shining eyes on Moffatt.

"I wish that treaty had been signed a few years sooner!" the latter rejoined in his usual tone of humorous familiarity.

Undine had not met him since her marriage, and of late the adverse turn of his fortunes had carried him quite beyond her thoughts. But his actual presence was always stimulating, and even through her self-absorption she was struck by his air of almost defiant prosperity. He did not look like a man who has been beaten; or rather he looked like a man who does not know when he is beaten; and his eye had the gleam of mocking confidence that had carried him unabashed through his lowest hours at Apex.

"I presume you're here to see me on business?" Mr. Spragg enquired, rising from his chair with a glance that seemed to ask his daughter's silence.

"Why, yes, Senator," rejoined Moffatt, who was given, in playful moments, to the bestowal of titles high-sounding. "At least I'm here to ask you a little question that may lead to business."

Mr. Spragg crossed the office and held open the door. "Step this way, please," he said, guiding Moffatt out before him, though the latter hung back to exclaim: "No family secrets, Mrs. Marvell—anybody can turn the fierce white light on *me*!"

With the closing of the door Undine's thoughts turned back to her own preoccupations. It had not struck her as incongruous that Moffatt should have business dealings with her father: she was even a little surprised that Mr. Spragg should still treat him so coldly. But she had no time to give to such considerations. Her own difficulties were too importunately present to her. She moved restlessly about the office, listening to the rise and fall of the two voices on the other side of the partition without once wondering what they were discussing.

What should she say to her father when he came back—
what argument was most likely to prevail with him? If he
really had no money to give her she was imprisoned fast—
Van Degen was lost to her, and the old life must go on interminably. . . In her nervous pacings she paused before the
blotched looking-glass that hung in a corner of the office under a steel engraving of Daniel Webster. Even that defective
surface could not disfigure her, and she drew fresh hope from
the sight of her beauty. Her few weeks of ill-health had given
her cheeks a subtler curve and deepened the shadows beneath
her eyes, and she was handsomer than before her marriage.
No, Van Degen was not lost to her even! From narrowed lids
to parted lips her face was swept by a smile like refracted
sunlight. He was not lost to her while she could smile like
that! Besides, even if her father had no money, there were
always mysterious ways of "raising" it—in the old Apex days
he had often boasted of such feats. As the hope rose her eyes
widened trustfully, and this time the smile that flowed up to
them was as limpid as a child's. That was the way her father
liked her to look at him. . .

The door opened, and she heard Mr. Spragg say behind
her: "No, sir, I won't—that's final."

He came in alone, with a brooding face, and lowered himself heavily into his chair. It was plain that the talk between
the two men had had an abrupt ending. Undine looked at her
father with a passing flicker of curiosity. Certainly it was an
odd coincidence that Moffatt should have called while she
was there. . .

"What did he want?" she asked, glancing back toward the
door.

Mr. Spragg mumbled his invisible toothpick. "Oh, just another of his wild-cat schemes—some real-estate deal he's in."

"Why did he come to *you* about it?"

He looked away from her, fumbling among the letters on
the desk. "Guess he'd tried everybody else first. He'd go and
ring the devil's front-door bell if he thought he could get anything out of him."

"I suppose he did himself a lot of harm by testifying in the
Ararat investigation?"

"Yes, *sir*—he's down and out this time."

He uttered the words with a certain satisfaction. His daughter did not answer, and they sat silent, facing each other across the littered desk. Under their brief talk about Elmer Moffatt currents of rapid intelligence seemed to be flowing between them. Suddenly Undine leaned over the desk, her eyes widening trustfully, and the limpid smile flowing up to them.

"Father, I did what you wanted that one time, anyhow—won't you listen to me and help me out now?"

XVIII

U NDINE STOOD alone on the landing outside her father's office.

Only once before had she failed to gain her end with him—and there was a peculiar irony in the fact that Moffatt's intrusion should have brought before her the providential result of her previous failure. Not that she confessed to any real resemblance between the two situations. In the present case she knew well enough what she wanted, and how to get it. But the analogy had served her father's purpose, and Moffatt's unlucky entrance had visibly strengthened his resistance.

The worst of it was that the obstacles in the way were real enough. Mr. Spragg had not put her off with vague asseverations—somewhat against her will he had forced his proofs on her, showing her how much above his promised allowance he had contributed in the last three years to the support of her household. Since she could not accuse herself of extravagance—having still full faith in her gift of "managing"—she could only conclude that it was impossible to live on what her father and Ralph could provide; and this seemed a practical reason for desiring her freedom. If she and Ralph parted he would of course return to his family, and Mr. Spragg would no longer be burdened with a helpless son-in-law. But even this argument did not move him. Undine, as soon as she had risked Van Degen's name, found herself face to face with a code of domestic conduct as rigid as its exponent's business principles were elastic. Mr. Spragg did not regard divorce as intrinsically wrong or even inexpedient; and of its social disadvantages he had never even heard. Lots of women did it, as Undine said; and if their reasons were adequate they were justified. If Ralph Marvell had been a drunkard or "unfaithful" Mr. Spragg would have approved Undine's desire to divorce him; but that it should be prompted by her inclination for another man—and a man with a wife of his own—was as shocking to him as it would have been to the most uncompromising of the Dagonets and Marvells. Such things happened, as Mr. Spragg knew, but they should not happen to any woman of his name while he had the power to prevent it; and Undine recognized that for the moment he had that power.

As she emerged from the elevator she was surprised to see Moffatt in the vestibule. His presence was an irritating reminder of her failure, and she walked past him with a rapid bow; but he overtook her.

"Mrs. Marvell—I've been waiting to say a word to you."

If it had been any one else she would have passed on; but Moffatt's voice had always a detaining power. Even now that she knew him to be defeated and negligible the power asserted itself, and she paused to say: "I'm afraid I can't stop—I'm late for an engagement."

"I shan't make you much later; but if you'd rather have me call round at your house——"

"Oh, I'm so seldom in." She turned a wondering look on him. "What is it you wanted to say?"

"Just two words. I've got an office in this building and the shortest way would be to come up there for a minute." As her look grew distant he added: "I think what I've got to say is worth the trip."

His face was serious, without underlying irony: the face he wore when he wanted to be trusted.

"Very well," she said, turning back.

Undine, glancing at her watch as she came out of Moffatt's office, saw that he had been true to his promise of not keeping her more than ten minutes. The fact was characteristic. Under all his incalculableness there had always been a hard foundation of reliability: it seemed to be a matter of choice with him whether he let one feel that solid bottom or not. And in specific matters the same quality showed itself in an accuracy of statement, a precision of conduct, that contrasted curiously with his usual hyperbolic banter and his loose lounging manner. No one could be more elusive yet no one could be firmer to the touch.

Her face had cleared and she moved more lightly as she left the building. Moffatt's communication had not been completely clear to her, but she understood the outline of the plan he had laid before her, and was satisfied with the bargain they had struck. He had begun by reminding her of her promise to introduce him to any friend of hers who might be useful in the way of business. Over three years had passed since they had made the pact, and Moffatt had kept loyally to his side of it. With the lapse of time the whole matter had become less important to her, but she wanted to prove her good faith, and when he reminded her of her promise she at once admitted it.

"Well, then—I want you to introduce me to your husband."

Undine was surprised; but beneath her surprise she felt a quick sense of relief. Ralph was easier to manage than so many of her friends—and it was a mark of his present indifference to acquiesce in anything she suggested.

"My husband? Why, what can he do for you?"

Moffatt explained at once, in the fewest words, as his way was when it came to business. He was interested in a big "deal" which involved the purchase of a piece of real estate held by a number of wrangling heirs. The real-estate broker with whom Ralph Marvell was associated represented these heirs, but Moffatt had his reasons for not approaching him directly. And he didn't want to go to Marvell with a "business proposition"—it would be better to be thrown with him socially, as if by accident. It was with that object that Moffatt had just appealed to Mr. Spragg, but Mr. Spragg, as usual, had "turned him down," without even consenting to look into the case.

"He'd rather have you miss a good thing than have it come to you through me. I don't know what on earth he thinks it's in my power to do to you—or ever was, for that matter," he added. "Anyhow," he went on to explain, "the power's all on your side now; and I'll show you how little the doing will hurt you as soon as I can have a quiet chat with your husband." He branched off again into technicalities, nebulous projections of capital and interest, taxes and rents, from which she finally extracted, and clung to, the central fact that if the "deal went through" it would mean a commission of forty thousand dollars to Marvell's firm, of which something over a fourth would come to Ralph.

"By Jove, that's an amazing fellow!" Ralph Marvell exclaimed, turning back into the drawing-room, a few evenings later, at the conclusion of one of their little dinners.

Undine looked up from her seat by the fire. She had had the inspired thought of inviting Moffatt to meet Clare Van Degen, Mrs. Fairford and Charles Bowen. It had occurred to her that the simplest way of explaining Moffatt was to tell Ralph that she had unexpectedly discovered an old Apex acquaintance in the protagonist of the great Ararat Trust fight. Moffatt's defeat had not wholly divested him of interest. As a factor in affairs he no longer inspired apprehension, but as the man who had dared to defy Harmon B. Driscoll he was a conspicuous and, to some minds, almost an heroic figure.

Undine remembered that Clare and Mrs. Fairford had once expressed a wish to see this braver of the Olympians, and her suggestion that he should be asked to meet them gave Ralph evident pleasure. It was long since she had made any conciliatory sign to his family.

Moffatt's social gifts were hardly of a kind to please the two ladies: he would have shone more brightly in Peter Van Degen's set than in his wife's. But neither Clare nor Mrs. Fairford had expected a man of conventional cut, and Moffatt's loud easiness was obviously less disturbing to them than to their hostess. Undine felt only his crudeness, and the tacit criticism passed on it by the mere presence of such men as her husband and Bowen; but Mrs. Fairford seemed to enjoy provoking him to fresh excesses of slang and hyperbole. Gradually she drew him into talking of the Driscoll campaign, and he became recklessly explicit. He seemed to have nothing to hold back: all the details of the prodigious exploit poured from him with Homeric volume. Then he broke off abruptly, thrusting his hands into his trouser-pockets and shaping his red lips to a whistle which he checked as his glance met Undine's. To conceal his embarrassment he leaned back in his chair, looked about the table with complacency, and said "I don't mind if I do" to the servant who approached to re-fill his champagne glass.

The men sat long over their cigars; but after an interval Undine called Charles Bowen into the drawing-room to settle some question in dispute between Clare and Mrs. Fairford, and thus gave Moffatt a chance to be alone with her husband.

Now that their guests had gone she was throbbing with anxiety to know what had passed between the two; but when Ralph rejoined her in the drawing-room she continued to keep her eyes on the fire and twirl her fan listlessly.

"That's an amazing chap," Ralph repeated, looking down at her. "Where was it you ran across him—out at Apex?"

As he leaned against the chimney-piece, lighting his cigarette, it struck Undine that he looked less fagged and lifeless than usual, and she felt more and more sure that something important had happened during the moment of isolation she had contrived.

She opened and shut her fan reflectively. "Yes—years ago; father had some business with him and brought him home to dinner one day."

"And you've never seen him since?"

She waited, as if trying to piece her recollections together. "I suppose I must have; but all that seems so long ago," she said sighing. She had been given, of late, to such plaintive glances toward her happy girlhood; but Ralph seemed not to notice the allusion.

"Do you know," he exclaimed after a moment, "I don't believe the fellow's beaten yet."

She looked up quickly. "Don't you?"

"No; and I could see that Bowen didn't either. He strikes me as the kind of man who develops slowly, needs a big field, and perhaps makes some big mistakes, but gets where he wants to in the end. Jove, I wish I could put him in a book! There's something epic about him—a kind of epic effrontery."

Undine's pulses beat faster as she listened. Was it not what Moffatt had always said of himself—that all he needed was time and elbow-room? How odd that Ralph, who seemed so dreamy and unobservant, should instantly have reached the same conclusion! But what she wanted to know was the practical result of their meeting.

"What did you and he talk about when you were smoking?"

"Oh, he got on the Driscoll fight again—gave us some extraordinary details. The man's a thundering brute, but he's full of observation and humour. Then, after Bowen joined you, he told me about a new deal he's gone into—rather a promising scheme, but on the same Titanic scale. It's just possible, by the way, that we may be able to do something for him: part of the property he's after is held in our office." He paused, knowing Undine's indifference to business matters; but the face she turned to him was alive with interest.

"You mean you might sell the property to him?"

"Well, if the thing comes off. There would be a big commission if we did." He glanced down on her half ironically. "You'd like that, wouldn't you?"

She answered with a shade of reproach: "Why do you say that? I haven't complained."

"Oh, no; but I know I've been a disappointment as a money-maker."

She leaned back in her chair, closing her eyes as if in utter weariness and indifference, and in a moment she felt him bending over her. "What's the matter? Don't you feel well?"

"I'm a little tired. It's nothing." She pulled her hand away and burst into tears.

Ralph knelt down by her chair and put his arm about her. It was the first time he had touched her since the night of the boy's birthday, and the sense of her softness woke a momentary warmth in his veins.

"What is it, dear? What is it?"

Without turning her head she sobbed out: "You seem to think I'm too selfish and odious—that I'm just pretending to be ill."

"No, no," he assured her, smoothing back her hair. But she continued to sob on in a gradual crescendo of despair, till the vehemence of her weeping began to frighten him, and he drew her to her feet and tried to persuade her to let herself be led upstairs. She yielded to his arm, sobbing in short exhausted gasps, and leaning her whole weight on him as he guided her along the passage to her bedroom. On the lounge to which he lowered her she lay white and still, tears trickling through her lashes and her handkerchief pressed against her lips. He recognized the symptoms with a sinking heart: she was on the verge of a nervous attack such as she had had in the winter, and he foresaw with dismay the disastrous train of consequences, the doctors' and nurses' bills, and all the attendant confusion and expense. If only Moffatt's project might be realized—if for once he could feel a round sum in his pocket, and be freed from the perpetual daily strain!

The next morning Undine, though calmer, was too weak to leave her bed, and her doctor prescribed rest and absence of worry—later, perhaps, a change of scene. He explained to Ralph that nothing was so wearing to a high-strung nature as monotony, and that if Mrs. Marvell were contemplating a Newport season it was necessary that she should be fortified to meet it. In such cases he often recommended a dash to Paris or London, just to tone up the nervous system.

Undine regained her strength slowly, and as the days dragged on the suggestion of the European trip recurred with increasing frequency. But it came always from her medical adviser: she herself had grown strangely passive and indifferent. She continued to remain upstairs on her lounge, seeing no one but Mrs. Heeny, whose daily ministrations had once more been prescribed, and asking only that the noise of Paul's play should be kept from her. His scamperings overhead disturbed her sleep, and his bed was moved into the day nursery, above his father's room. The child's early romping did not trouble Ralph, since he himself was always awake before daylight. The days were not long enough to hold his cares, and they came and stood by him through the silent hours, when there was no other sound to drown their voices.

Ralph had not made a success of his business. The real-estate brokers who had taken him into partnership had done so only with the hope of profiting by his social connections; and in this respect the alliance had been a failure. It was in such directions that he most lacked facility, and so far he had been of use to his partners only as an office-drudge. He was resigned to the continuance of such drudgery, though all his powers cried out against it; but even for the routine of business his aptitude was small, and he began to feel that he was not considered an addition to the firm. The difficulty of finding another opening made him fear a break; and his thoughts turned hopefully to Elmer Moffatt's hint of a "deal." The success of the negotiation might bring advantages beyond the immediate pecuniary profit; and that, at the present juncture, was important enough in itself.

Moffatt reappeared two days after the dinner, presenting himself in West End Avenue in the late afternoon with the explanation that the business in hand necessitated discretion, and that he preferred not to be seen in Ralph's office. It was a question of negotiating with the utmost privacy for the purchase of a small strip of land between two large plots already acquired by purchasers cautiously designated by Moffatt as his "parties." How far he "stood in" with the parties he left it to Ralph to conjecture; but it was plain that he had a large stake in the transaction, and that it offered him his first chance of recovering himself since Driscoll had "thrown" him. The owners of the coveted plot did not seem anxious to sell, and there were personal reasons for Moffatt's not approaching them through Ralph's partners, who were the regular agents of the estate: so that Ralph's acquaintance with the conditions, combined with his detachments from the case, marked him out as a useful intermediary.

Their first talk left Ralph with a dazzled sense of Moffatt's strength and keenness, but with a vague doubt as to the "straightness" of the proposed transaction. Ralph had never seen his way clearly in that dim underworld of affairs where men of the Moffatt and Driscoll type moved like shadowy destructive monsters beneath the darting small fry of the surface. He knew that "business" has created its own special morality; and his musings on man's relation to his self-imposed laws had shown him how little human conduct is generally troubled about its own sanctions. He had a vivid sense of the things a man of his kind didn't do; but his inability to get a mental grasp on large financial problems made it hard to apply to them so simple a measure as this inherited standard. He only knew, as Moffatt's plan developed, that it seemed all right while he talked of it with its originator, but vaguely wrong when he thought it over afterward. It occurred to him to consult his grandfather; and if he renounced the idea for the obvious reason that Mr. Dagonet's ignorance of business was as fathomless as his own, this was not his sole motive. Finally it occurred to him to put the case hypothetically to Mr. Spragg. As far as Ralph knew, his father-in-law's business record was unblemished; yet one felt in him an elasticity of adjustment not allowed for in the Dagonet code.

Mr. Spragg listened thoughtfully to Ralph's statement of the case, growling out here and there a tentative correction, and turning his cigar between his lips as he seemed to turn the problem over in the loose grasp of his mind.

"Well, what's the trouble with it?" he asked at length, stretching his big square-toed shoes against the grate of his son-in-law's dining-room, where, in the after-dinner privacy of a family evening, Ralph had seized the occasion to consult him.

"The trouble?" Ralph considered. "Why, that's just what I should like you to explain to me."

Mr. Spragg threw back his head and stared at the garlanded French clock on the chimney-piece. Mrs. Spragg was sitting upstairs in her daughter's bedroom, and the silence of the house seemed to hang about the two men like a listening presence.

"Well, I dunno but what I agree with the doctor who said there warn't any diseases, but only sick people. Every case is different, I guess." Mr. Spragg, munching his cigar, turned a ruminating glance on Ralph. "Seems to me it all boils down to one thing. Was this fellow we're supposing about under any obligation to the other party—the one he was trying to buy the property from?"

Ralph hesitated. "Only the obligation recognized between decent men to deal with each other decently."

Mr. Spragg listened to this with the suffering air of a teacher compelled to simplify upon his simplest questions.

"Any personal obligation, I meant. Had the other fellow done him a good turn any time?"

"No—I don't imagine them to have had any previous relations at all."

His father-in-law stared. "Where's your trouble, then?" He sat for a moment frowning at the embers. "Even when it's the other way round it ain't always so easy to decide how far that kind of thing's binding . . . and they say shipwrecked fellows'll make a meal of a friend as quick as they would of a total stranger." He drew himself together with a shake of his shoulders and pulled back his feet from the grate. "But I don't see the conundrum in your case. I guess it's up to both parties to take care of their own skins."

He rose from his chair and wandered upstairs to Undine.

That was the Wall Street code: it all "boiled down" to the personal obligation, to the salt eaten in the enemy's tent. Ralph's fancy wandered off on a long trail of speculation from which he was pulled back with a jerk by the need of immediate action. Moffatt's "deal" could not wait: quick decisions were essential to effective action, and brooding over ethical shades of difference might work more ill than good in a world committed to swift adjustments. The arrival of several unforeseen bills confirmed this view, and once Ralph had adopted it he began to take a detached interest in the affair.

In Paris, in his younger days, he had once attended a lesson in acting given at the Conservatoire by one of the great lights of the theatre, and had seen an apparently uncomplicated rôle of the classic repertory, familiar to him through repeated performances, taken to pieces before his eyes, dissolved into its component elements, and built up again with a minuteness of elucidation and a range of reference that made him feel as though he had been let into the secret of some age-long natural process. As he listened to Moffatt the remembrance of that lesson came back to him. At the outset the "deal," and his own share in it, had seemed simple enough: he would have put on his hat and gone out on the spot in the full assurance of being able to transact the affair. But as Moffatt talked he began to feel as blank and blundering as the class of dramatic students before whom the great actor had analyzed his part. The affair was in fact difficult and complex, and Moffatt saw at once just where the difficulties lay and how the personal idiosyncrasies of "the parties" affected them. Such insight fascinated Ralph, and he strayed off into wondering why it did not qualify every financier to be a novelist, and what intrinsic barrier divided the two arts.

Both men had strong incentives for hastening the affair; and within a fortnight after Moffatt's first advance Ralph was able to tell him that his offer was accepted. Over and above his personal satisfaction he felt the thrill of the agent whom some powerful negotiator has charged with a delicate mission: he might have been an eager young Jesuit carrying compromising papers to his superior. It had been stimulating to

work with Moffatt, and to study at close range the large powerful instrument of his intelligence.

As he came out of Moffatt's office at the conclusion of this
visit Ralph met Mr. Spragg descending from his eyrie. He
stopped short with a backward glance at Moffatt's door.

"Hallo—what were you doing in there with those cut-
throats?"

Ralph judged discretion to be essential. "Oh, just a little
business for the firm."

Mr. Spragg said no more, but resorted to the soothing la-
bial motion of revolving his phantom toothpick.

"How's Undie getting along?" he merely asked, as he and
his son-in-law descended together in the elevator.

"She doesn't seem to feel much stronger. The doctor wants
her to run over to Europe for a few weeks. She thinks of
joining her friends the Shallums in Paris."

Mr. Spragg was again silent, but he left the building at
Ralph's side, and the two walked along together toward Wall
Street.

Presently the older man asked: "How did you get ac-
quainted with Moffatt?"

"Why, by chance—Undine ran across him somewhere and
asked him to dine the other night."

"Undine asked him to dine?"

"Yes: she told me you used to know him out at Apex."

Mr. Spragg appeared to search his memory for confirmation of the fact. "I believe he used to be round there at one
time. I've never heard any good of him yet." He paused at a
crossing and looked probingly at his son-in-law. "Is she terribly set on this trip to Europe?"

Ralph smiled. "You know how it is when she takes a fancy
to do anything——"

Mr. Spragg, by a slight lift of his brooding brows, seemed
to convey a deep if unspoken response.

"Well, I'd let her do it this time—I'd let her do it," he said
as he turned down the steps of the Subway.

Ralph was surprised, for he had gathered from some frightened references of Mrs. Spragg's that Undine's parents had
wind of her European plan and were strongly opposed to it.
He concluded that Mr. Spragg had long since measured the

extent of profitable resistance, and knew just when it became vain to hold out against his daughter or advise others to do so.

Ralph, for his own part, had no inclination to resist. As he left Moffatt's office his inmost feeling was one of relief. He had reached the point of recognizing that it was best for both that his wife should go. When she returned perhaps their lives would readjust themselves—but for the moment he longed for some kind of benumbing influence, something that should give relief to the dull daily ache of feeling her so near and yet so inaccessible. Certainly there were more urgent uses for their brilliant wind-fall: heavy arrears of household debts had to be met, and the summer would bring its own burden. But perhaps another stroke of luck might befall him: he was getting to have the drifting dependence on "luck" of the man conscious of his inability to direct his life. And meanwhile it seemed easier to let Undine have what she wanted.

Undine, on the whole, behaved with discretion. She received the good news languidly and showed no unseemly haste to profit by it. But it was as hard to hide the light in her eyes as to dissemble the fact that she had not only thought out every detail of the trip in advance, but had decided exactly how her husband and son were to be disposed of in her absence. Her suggestion that Ralph should take Paul to his grandparents, and that the West End Avenue house should be let for the summer, was too practical not to be acted on; and Ralph found she had already put her hand on the Harry Lipscombs, who, after three years of neglect, were to be dragged back to favour and made to feel, as the first step in their reinstatement, the necessity of hiring for the summer months a cool airy house on the West Side. On her return from Europe, Undine explained, she would of course go straight to Ralph and the boy in the Adirondacks; and it seemed a foolish extravagance to let the house stand empty when the Lipscombs were so eager to take it.

As the day of departure approached it became harder for her to temper her beams; but her pleasure showed itself so amiably that Ralph began to think she might, after all, miss the boy and himself more than she imagined. She was tenderly preoccupied with Paul's welfare, and, to prepare for his translation to his grandparents' she gave the household in Washington Square more of her time than she had accorded it since her marriage. She explained that she wanted Paul to grow used to his new surroundings; and with that object she took him frequently to his grandmother's, and won her way into old Mr. Dagonet's sympathies by her devotion to the child and her pretty way of joining in his games.

Undine was not consciously acting a part: this new phase was as natural to her as the other. In the joy of her gratified desires she wanted to make everybody about her happy. If only everyone would do as she wished she would never be unreasonable. She much preferred to see smiling faces about her, and her dread of the reproachful and dissatisfied countenance gave the measure of what she would do to avoid it.

These thoughts were in her mind when, a day or two before sailing, she came out of the Washington Square house with her boy. It was a late spring afternoon, and she and Paul had lingered on till long past the hour sacred to his grandfather's nap. Now, as she came out into the square she saw that, however well Mr. Dagonet had borne their protracted romp, it had left his playmate flushed and sleepy; and she lifted Paul in her arms to carry him to the nearest cab-stand.

As she raised herself she saw a thick-set figure approaching her across the square; and a moment later she was shaking hands with Elmer Moffatt. In the bright spring air he looked seasonably glossy and prosperous; and she noticed that he wore a bunch of violets in his buttonhole. His small black eyes twinkled with approval as they rested on her, and Undine reflected that, with Paul's arms about her neck, and his little flushed face against her own, she must present a not unpleasing image of young motherhood.

"That the heir apparent?" Moffatt asked; adding "Happy to make your acquaintance, sir," as the boy, at Undine's bidding, held out a fist sticky with sugar-plums.

"He's been spending the afternoon with his grandfather, and they played so hard that he's sleepy," she explained. Little Paul, at that stage in his career, had a peculiar grace of wide-gazing deep-lashed eyes and arched cherubic lips, and Undine saw that Moffatt was not insensible to the picture she and her son composed. She did not dislike his admiration, for she no longer felt any shrinking from him—she would even have been glad to thank him for the service he had done her husband if she had known how to allude to it without awkwardness. Moffatt seemed equally pleased at the meeting, and they looked at each other almost intimately over Paul's tumbled curls.

"He's a mighty fine fellow and no mistake—but isn't he rather an armful for you?" Moffatt asked, his eyes lingering with real kindliness on the child's face.

"Oh, we haven't far to go. I'll pick up a cab at the corner."

"Well, let me carry him that far anyhow," said Moffatt.

Undine was glad to be relieved of her burden, for she was unused to the child's weight, and disliked to feel that her skirt was dragging on the pavement. "Go to the gentleman, Pauly—he'll carry you better than mother," she said.

The little boy's first movement was one of recoil from the ruddy sharp-eyed countenance that was so unlike his father's delicate face; but he was an obedient child, and after a moment's hesitation he wound his arms trustfully about the red gentleman's neck.

"That's a good fellow—sit tight and I'll give you a ride," Moffatt cried, hoisting the boy to his shoulder.

Paul was not used to being perched at such a height, and his nature was hospitable to new impressions. "Oh, I like it up here—you're higher than father!" he exclaimed; and Moffatt hugged him with a laugh.

"It must feel mighty good to come uptown to a fellow like you in the evenings," he said, addressing the child but looking at Undine, who also laughed a little.

"Oh, they're a dreadful nuisance, you know; but Paul's a very good boy."

"I wonder if he knows what a friend I've been to him lately," Moffatt went on, as they turned into Fifth Avenue.

Undine smiled: she was glad he should have given her an opening.

"He shall be told as soon as he's old enough to thank you. I'm so glad you came to Ralph about that business."

"Oh, I gave him a leg up, and I guess he's given me one too. Queer the way things come round—he's fairly put me in the way of a fresh start."

Their eyes met in a silence which Undine was the first to break. "It's been awfully nice of you to do what you've done—right along. And this last thing has made a lot of difference to us."

"Well, I'm glad you feel that way. I never wanted to be anything but 'nice,' as you call it." Moffatt paused a moment and then added: "If you're less scared of me than your father is I'd be glad to call round and see you once in a while."

The quick blood rushed to her cheeks. There was nothing challenging, demanding in his tone—she guessed at once that if he made the request it was simply for the pleasure of being with her, and she liked the magnanimity implied. Nevertheless she was not sorry to have to answer: "Of course I'll always be glad to see you—only, as it happens, I'm just sailing for Europe."

"For Europe?" The word brought Moffatt to a stand so abruptly that little Paul lurched on his shoulder.

"For Europe?" he repeated. "Why, I thought you said the other evening you expected to stay on in town till July. Didn't you think of going to the Adirondacks?"

Flattered by his evident disappointment, she became high and careless in her triumph. "Oh, yes,—but that's all changed. Ralph and the boy are going; but I sail on Saturday to join some friends in Paris—and later I may do some motoring in Switzerland and Italy."

She laughed a little in the mere enjoyment of putting her plans into words and Moffatt laughed too, but with an edge of sarcasm.

"I see—I see: everything's changed, as you say, and your husband can blow you off to the trip. Well, I hope you'll have a first-class time."

Their glances crossed again, and something in his cool scrutiny impelled Undine to say, with a burst of candour: "If I do, you know, I shall owe it all to you!"

"Well, I always told you I meant to act white by you," he answered.

They walked on in silence, and presently he began again in his usual joking strain: "See what one of the Apex girls has been up to?"

Apex was too remote for her to understand the reference,

and he went on: "Why, Millard Binch's wife—Indiana Frusk that was. Didn't you see in the papers that Indiana'd fixed it up with James J. Rolliver to marry her? They say it was easy enough squaring Millard Binch—you'd know it *would* be— but it cost Rolliver near a million to mislay Mrs. R. and the children. Well, Indiana's pulled it off, anyhow; she always *was* a bright girl. But she never came up to you."

"Oh——" she stammered with a laugh, astonished and agitated by his news. Indiana Frusk and Rolliver! It showed how easily the thing could be done. If only her father had listened to her! If a girl like Indiana Frusk could gain her end so easily, what might not Undine have accomplished? She knew Moffatt was right in saying that Indiana had never come up to her. . . She wondered how the marriage would strike Van Degen. . .

She signalled to a cab and they walked toward it without speaking. Undine was recalling with intensity that one of Indiana's shoulders was higher than the other, and that people in Apex had thought her lucky to catch Millard Binch, the druggist's clerk, when Undine herself had cast him off after a lingering engagement. And now Indiana Frusk was to be Mrs. James J. Rolliver!

Undine got into the cab and bent forward to take little Paul.

Moffatt lowered his charge with exaggerated care, and a "Steady there, steady," that made the child laugh; then, stooping over, he put a kiss on Paul's lips before handing him over to his mother.

XIX

The PARISIAN DIAMOND COMPANY—Anglo-American branch."

Charles Bowen, seated, one rainy evening of the Paris season, in a corner of the great Nouveau Luxe restaurant, was lazily trying to resolve his impressions of the scene into the phrases of a letter to his old friend Mrs. Henley Fairford.

The long habit of unwritten communion with this lady—in no way conditioned by the short rare letters they actually exchanged—usually caused his notations, in absence, to fall into such terms when the subject was of a kind to strike an answering flash from her. And who but Mrs. Fairford would see, from his own precise angle, the fantastic improbability, the layers on layers of unsubstantialness, on which the seemingly solid scene before him rested?

The dining-room of the Nouveau Luxe was at its fullest, and, having contracted on the garden side through stress of weather, had even overflowed to the farther end of the long hall beyond; so that Bowen, from his corner, surveyed a seemingly endless perspective of plumed and jewelled heads, of shoulders bare or black-coated, encircling the close-packed tables. He had come half an hour before the time he had named to his expected guest, so that he might have the undisturbed amusement of watching the picture compose itself again before his eyes. During some forty years' perpetual exercise of his perceptions he had never come across anything that gave them the special titillation produced by the sight of the dinner-hour at the Nouveau Luxe: the same sense of putting his hand on human nature's passion for the factitious, its incorrigible habit of imitating the imitation.

As he sat watching the familiar faces swept toward him on the rising tide of arrival—for it was one of the joys of the scene that the type was always the same even when the individual was not—he hailed with renewed appreciation this costly expression of a social ideal. The dining-room at the Nouveau Luxe represented, on such a spring evening, what unbounded material power had devised for the delusion of its leisure: a phantom "society," with all the rules, smirks,

gestures of its model, but evoked out of promiscuity and incoherence while the other had been the product of continuity
and choice. And the instinct which had driven a new class of
world-compellers to bind themselves to slavish imitation of
the superseded, and their prompt and reverent faith in the
reality of the sham they had created, seemed to Bowen the
most satisfying proof of human permanence.

With this thought in his mind he looked up to greet his
guest. The Comte Raymond de Chelles, straight, slim and
gravely smiling, came toward him with frequent pauses of sal-
utation at the crowded tables; saying, as he seated himself and
turned his pleasant eyes on the scene: "*Il n'y a pas à dire*, my
dear Bowen, it's charming and sympathetic and original—we
owe America a debt of gratitude for inventing it!"

Bowen felt a last touch of satisfaction: they were the very
words to complete his thought.

"My dear fellow, it's really you and your kind who are responsible. It's the direct creation of feudalism, like all the
great social upheavals!"

Raymond de Chelles stroked his handsome brown moustache. "I should have said, on the contrary, that one enjoyed
it for the contrast. It's such a refreshing change from our institutions—which are, nevertheless, the necessary foundations
of society. But just as one may have an infinite admiration for
one's wife, and yet occasionally——" he waved a light hand
toward the spectacle. "This, in the social order, is the diversion, the permitted diversion, that your original race has devised: a kind of superior Bohemia, where one may be
respectable without being bored."

Bowen laughed. "You've put it in a nutshell: the ideal of
the American woman is to be respectable without being
bored; and from that point of view this world they've invented has more originality than I gave it credit for."

Chelles thoughtfully unfolded his napkin. "My impression's
a superficial one, of course—for as to what goes on underneath—!" He looked across the room. "If I married I
shouldn't care to have my wife come here too often."

Bowen laughed again. "She'd be as safe as in a bank!
Nothing ever goes on! Nothing that ever happens here is
real."

"*Ah, quant à cela*——" the Frenchman murmured, inserting a fork into his melon.

Bowen looked at him with enjoyment—he was such a precious foot-note to the page! The two men, accidentally thrown together some years previously during a trip up the Nile, always met again with pleasure when Bowen returned to France. Raymond de Chelles, who came of a family of moderate fortune, lived for the greater part of the year on his father's estates in Burgundy; but he came up every spring to the *entresol* of the old Marquis's hôtel for a two months' study of human nature, applying to the pursuit the discriminating taste and transient ardour that give the finest bloom to pleasure. Bowen liked him as a companion and admired him as a charming specimen of the Frenchman of his class, embodying in his lean, fatigued and finished person that happy mean of simplicity and intelligence of which no other race has found the secret. If Raymond de Chelles had been English he would have been a mere fox-hunting animal, with appetites but without tastes; but in his lighter Gallic clay the wholesome territorial savour, the inherited passion for sport and agriculture, were blent with an openness to finer sensations, a sense of the come-and-go of ideas, under which one felt the tight hold of two or three inherited notions, religious, political, and domestic, in total contradiction to his surface attitude. That the inherited notions would in the end prevail, everything in his appearance declared, from the distinguished slant of his nose to the narrow forehead under his thinning hair; he was the kind of man who would inevitably "revert" when he married. But meanwhile the surface he presented to the play of life was broad enough to take in the fantastic spectacle of the Nouveau Luxe; and to see its gestures reflected in a Latin consciousness was an endless entertainment to Bowen.

The tone of his guest's last words made him take them up. "But is the lady you allude to more than a hypothesis? Surely you're not thinking of getting married?"

Chelles raised his eye-brows ironically. "When hasn't one to think of it, in my situation? One hears of nothing else at home—one knows that, like death, it has to come." His glance, which was still mustering the room, came to a sudden pause and kindled.

"Who's the lady over there—fair-haired, in white—the one who's just come in with the red-faced man? They seem to be with a party of your compatriots."

Bowen followed his glance to a neighbouring table, where, at the moment, Undine Marvell was seating herself at Peter Van Degen's side, in the company of the Harvey Shallums, the beautiful Mrs. Beringer and a dozen other New York figures.

She was so placed that as she took her seat she recognized Bowen and sent him a smile across the tables. She was more simply dressed than usual, and the pink lights, warming her cheeks and striking gleams from her hair, gave her face a dewy freshness that was new to Bowen. He had always thought her beauty too obvious, too bathed in the bright publicity of the American air; but to-night she seemed to have been brushed by the wing of poetry, and its shadow lingered in her eyes.

Chelles' gaze made it evident that he had received the same impression.

"One is sometimes inclined to deny your compatriots actual beauty—to charge them with producing the effect without having the features; but in this case—you say you know the lady?"

"Yes: she's the wife of an old friend."

"The wife? She's married? There, again, it's so puzzling! Your young girls look so experienced, and your married women sometimes so—unmarried."

"Well, they often are—in these days of divorce!"

The other's interest quickened. "Your friend's divorced?"

"Oh, no; heaven forbid! Mrs. Marvell hasn't been long married; and it was a love-match of the good old kind."

"Ah—and the husband? Which is he?"

"He's not here—he's in New York."

"Feverishly adding to a fortune already monstrous?"

"No; not precisely monstrous. The Marvells are not well off," said Bowen, amused by his friend's interrogations.

"And he allows an exquisite being like that to come to Paris without him—and in company with the red-faced gentleman who seems so alive to his advantages?"

"We don't 'allow' our women this or that; I don't think we set much store by the compulsory virtues."

His companion received this with amusement. "If you're as detached as that, why does the obsolete institution of marriage survive with you?"

"Oh, it still has its uses. One couldn't be divorced without it."

Chelles laughed again; but his straying eye still followed the same direction, and Bowen noticed that the fact was not unremarked by the object of his contemplation. Undine's party was one of the liveliest in the room: the American laugh rose above the din of the orchestra as the American toilets dominated the less daring effects at the other tables. Undine, on entering, had seemed to be in the same mood as her companions; but Bowen saw that, as she became conscious of his friend's observation, she isolated herself in a kind of soft abstraction; and he admired the adaptability which enabled her to draw from such surroundings the contrasting graces of reserve.

They had greeted each other with all the outer signs of cordiality, but Bowen fancied she would not care to have him speak to her. She was evidently dining with Van Degen, and Van Degen's proximity was the last fact she would wish to have transmitted to the critics in Washington Square. Bowen was therefore surprised when, as he rose to leave the restaurant, he heard himself hailed by Peter.

"Hallo—hold on! When did you come over? Mrs. Marvell's dying for the last news about the old homestead."

Undine's smile confirmed the appeal. She wanted to know how lately Bowen had left New York, and pressed him to tell her when he had last seen her boy, how he was looking, and whether Ralph had been persuaded to go down to Clare's on Saturdays and get a little riding and tennis? And dear Laura—was she well too, and was Paul with her, or still with his grandmother? They were all dreadfully bad correspondents, and so was she, Undine laughingly admitted; and when Ralph had last written her these questions had still been undecided.

As she smiled up at Bowen he saw her glance stray to the spot where his companion hovered; and when the diners rose to move toward the garden for coffee she said, with a sweet note and a detaining smile: "Do come with us—I haven't half finished."

Van Degen echoed the request, and Bowen, amused by Undine's arts, was presently introducing Chelles, and joining with him in the party's transit to the terrace.

The rain had ceased, and under the clear evening sky the restaurant garden opened green depths that skilfully hid its narrow boundaries. Van Degen's company was large enough to surround two of the tables on the terrace, and Bowen noted the skill with which Undine, leaving him to Mrs. Shallum's care, contrived to draw Raymond de Chelles to the other table. Still more noticeable was the effect of this stratagem on Van Degen, who also found himself relegated to Mrs. Shallum's group. Poor Peter's state was betrayed by the irascibility which wreaked itself on a jostling waiter, and found cause for loud remonstrance in the coldness of the coffee and the badness of the cigars; and Bowen, with something more than the curiosity of the looker-on, wondered whether this were the real clue to Undine's conduct. He had always smiled at Mrs. Fairford's fears for Ralph's domestic peace. He thought Undine too clear-headed to forfeit the advantages of her marriage; but it now struck him that she might have had a glimpse of larger opportunities. Bowen, at the thought, felt the pang of the sociologist over the individual havoc wrought by every social readjustment: it had so long been clear to him that poor Ralph was a survival, and destined, as such, to go down in any conflict with the rising forces.

XX

Some six weeks later, Undine Marvell stood at the window smiling down on her recovered Paris.

Her hotel sitting-room had, as usual, been flowered, cushioned and lamp-shaded into a delusive semblance of stability; and she had really felt, for the last few weeks, that the life she was leading there must be going to last—it seemed so perfect an answer to all her wants!

As she looked out at the thronged street, on which the summer light lay like a blush of pleasure, she felt herself naturally akin to all the bright and careless freedom of the scene. She had been away from Paris for two days, and the spectacle before her seemed more rich and suggestive after her brief absence from it. Her senses luxuriated in all its material details: the thronging motors, the brilliant shops, the novelty and daring of the women's dresses, the piled-up colours of the ambulant flower-carts, the appetizing expanse of the fruiterers' windows, even the chromatic effects of the *petits fours* behind the plate-glass of the pastry-cooks: all the surface-sparkle and variety of the inexhaustible streets of Paris.

The scene before her typified to Undine her first real taste of life. How meagre and starved the past appeared in comparison with this abundant present! The noise, the crowd, the promiscuity beneath her eyes symbolized the glare and movement of her life. Every moment of her days was packed with excitement and exhilaration. Everything amused her: the long hours of bargaining and debate with dress-makers and jewellers, the crowded lunches at fashionable restaurants, the perfunctory dash through a picture-show or the lingering visit to the last new milliner; the afternoon motor-rush to some leafy suburb, where tea and music and sunset were hastily absorbed on a crowded terrace above the Seine; the whirl home through the Bois to dress for dinner and start again on the round of evening diversions; the dinner at the Nouveau Luxe or the Café de Paris, and the little play at the Capucines or the Variétés, followed, because the night was "too lovely," and it was a shame to waste it, by a breathless flight back to the Bois, with supper in one of its lamp-hung restaurants, or, if the weather forbade, a tumultuous progress through the midnight haunts where "ladies" were not supposed to show themselves, and might consequently taste the thrill of being occasionally taken for their opposites.

As the varied vision unrolled itself, Undine contrasted it with the pale monotony of her previous summers. The one she most resented was the first after her marriage, the European summer out of whose joys she had been cheated by her own ignorance and Ralph's perversity. They had been free then, there had been no child to hamper their movements, their money anxieties had hardly begun, the face of life had been fresh and radiant, and she had been doomed to waste such opportunities on a succession of ill-smelling Italian towns. She still felt it to be her deepest grievance against her husband; and now that, after four years of petty household worries, another chance of escape had come, he already wanted to drag her back to bondage!

This fit of retrospection had been provoked by two letters which had come that morning. One was from Ralph, who began by reminding her that he had not heard from her for weeks, and went on to point out, in his usual tone of good-humoured remonstrance, that since her departure the drain on her letter of credit had been deep and constant. "I wanted you," he wrote, "to get all the fun you could out of the money I made last spring; but I didn't think you'd get through it quite so fast. Try to come home without leaving too many bills behind you. Your illness and Paul's cost more than I expected, and Lipscomb has had a bad knock in Wall Street, and hasn't yet paid his first quarter. . ."

Always the same monotonous refrain! Was it her fault that she and the boy had been ill? Or that Harry Lipscomb had been "on the wrong side" of Wall Street? Ralph seemed to have money on the brain: his business life had certainly deteriorated him. And, since he hadn't made a success of it after all, why shouldn't he turn back to literature and try to write his novel? Undine, the previous winter, had been dazzled by the figures which a well-known magazine editor whom she had met at dinner had named as within reach of the successful novelist. She perceived for the first time that literature was becoming fashionable, and instantly decided that it would be

amusing and original if she and Ralph should owe their prosperity to his talent. She already saw herself, as the wife of a
celebrated author, wearing "artistic" dresses and doing the
drawing-room over with Gothic tapestries and dim lights in
altar candle-sticks. But when she suggested Ralph's taking up
his novel he answered with a laugh that his brains were sold
to the firm—that when he came back at night the tank was
empty. . . And now he wanted her to sail for home in a
week!

The other letter excited a deeper resentment. It was an appeal from Laura Fairford to return and look after Ralph. He
was overworked and out of spirits, she wrote, and his mother
and sister, reluctant as they were to interfere, felt they ought
to urge Undine to come back to him. Details followed, unwelcome and officious. What right had Laura Fairford to
preach to her of wifely obligations? No doubt Charles Bowen
had sent home a highly-coloured report—and there was
really a certain irony in Mrs. Fairford's criticizing her sister-
in-law's conduct on information obtained from such a source!

Undine turned from the window and threw herself down
on her deeply cushioned sofa. She was feeling the pleasant
fatigue consequent on her trip to the country, whither she
and Mrs. Shallum had gone with Raymond de Chelles to
spend a night at the old Marquis's château. When her travelling companions, an hour earlier, had left her at her door, she
had half-promised to rejoin them for a late dinner in the Bois;
and as she leaned back among the cushions disturbing
thoughts were banished by the urgent necessity of deciding
what dress she should wear.

These bright weeks of the Parisian spring had given her a
first real glimpse into the art of living. From the experts who
had taught her to subdue the curves of her figure and soften
her bright free stare with dusky pencillings, to the skilled
purveyors of countless forms of pleasure—the theatres and
restaurants, the green and blossoming suburbs, the whole
shining shifting spectacle of nights and days—every sight and
sound and word had combined to charm her perceptions and
refine her taste. And her growing friendship with Raymond
de Chelles had been the most potent of these influences.

Chelles, at once immensely "taken," had not only shown

his eagerness to share in the helter-skelter motions of Undine's party, but had given her glimpses of another, still more brilliant existence, that life of the inaccessible "Faubourg" of which the first tantalizing hints had but lately reached her. Hitherto she had assumed that Paris existed for the stranger, that its native life was merely an obscure foundation for the dazzling superstructure of hotels and restaurants in which her compatriots disported themselves. But lately she had begun to hear about other American women, the women who had married into the French aristocracy, and who led, in the high-walled houses beyond the Seine which she had once thought so dull and dingy, a life that made her own seem as undistinguished as the social existence of the Mealey House. Perhaps what most exasperated her was the discovery, in this impenetrable group, of the Miss Wincher who had poisoned her far-off summer at Potash Springs. To recognize her old enemy in the Marquise de Trézac who so frequently figured in the Parisian chronicle was the more irritating to Undine because her intervening social experiences had caused her to look back on Nettie Wincher as a frumpy girl who wouldn't have "had a show" in New York.

Once more all the accepted values were reversed, and it turned out that Miss Wincher had been in possession of some key to success on which Undine had not yet put her hand. To know that others were indifferent to what she had thought important was to cheapen all present pleasure and turn the whole force of her desires in a new direction. What she wanted for the moment was to linger on in Paris, prolonging her flirtation with Chelles, and profiting by it to detach herself from her compatriots and enter doors closed to their approach. And Chelles himself attracted her: she thought him as "sweet" as she had once thought Ralph, whose fastidiousness and refinement were blent in him with a delightful foreign vivacity. His chief value, however, lay in his power of exciting Van Degen's jealousy. She knew enough of French customs to be aware that such devotion as Chelles' was not likely to have much practical bearing on her future; but Peter had an alarming way of lapsing into security, and as a spur to his ardour she knew the value of other men's attentions.

It had become Undine's fixed purpose to bring Van Degen

to a definite expression of his intentions. The case of Indiana
Frusk, whose brilliant marriage the journals of two continents
had recently chronicled with unprecedented richness of detail,
had made less impression on him than she hoped. He treated
it as a comic episode without special bearing on their case,
and once, when Undine cited Rolliver's expensive fight for
freedom as an instance of the power of love over the most
invulnerable natures, had answered carelessly: "Oh, his first
wife was a laundress, I believe."

But all about them couples were unpairing and pairing
again with an ease and rapidity that encouraged Undine to
bide her time. It was simply a question of making Van Degen
want her enough, and of not being obliged to abandon the
game before he wanted her as much as she meant he should.
This was precisely what would happen if she were compelled
to leave Paris now. Already the event had shown how right
she had been to come abroad: the attention she attracted in
Paris had reawakened Van Degen's fancy, and her hold over
him was stronger than when they had parted in America. But
the next step must be taken with coolness and circumspec-
tion; and she must not throw away what she had gained by
going away at a stage when he was surer of her than she of
him.

She was still intensely considering these questions when the
door behind her opened and he came in.

She looked up with a frown and he gave a deprecating
laugh. "Didn't I knock? Don't look so savage! They told
me downstairs you'd got back, and I just bolted in without
thinking."

He had widened and purpled since their first encounter,
five years earlier, but his features had not matured. His face
was still the face of a covetous bullying boy, with a large appetite for primitive satisfactions and a sturdy belief in his intrinsic right to them. It was all the more satisfying to
Undine's vanity to see his look change at her tone from command to conciliation, and from conciliation to the entreaty of
a capriciously-treated animal.

"What a ridiculous hour for a visit!" she exclaimed, ignoring his excuse.

"Well, if you disappear like that, without a word——"

"I told my maid to telephone you I was going away."

"You couldn't make time to do it yourself, I suppose?"

"We rushed off suddenly; I'd hardly time to get to the station."

"You rushed off where, may I ask?" Van Degen still lowered down on her.

"Oh, didn't I tell you? I've been down staying at Chelles' château in Burgundy." Her face lit up and she raised herself eagerly on her elbow.

"It's the most wonderful old house you ever saw: a real castle, with towers, and water all round it, and a funny kind of bridge they pull up. Chelles said he wanted me to see just how they lived at home, and I did; I saw everything: the tapestries that Louis Quinze gave them, and the family portraits, and the chapel, where their own priest says mass, and they sit by themselves in a balcony with crowns all over it. The priest was a lovely old man—he said he'd give anything to convert me. Do you know, I think there's something very beautiful about the Roman Catholic religion? I've often felt I might have been happier if I'd had some religious influence in my life."

She sighed a little, and turned her head away. She flattered herself that she had learned to strike the right note with Van Degen. At this crucial stage he needed a taste of his own methods, a glimpse of the fact that there were women in the world who could get on without him.

He continued to gaze down at her sulkily. "Were the old people there? You never told me you knew his mother."

"I don't. They weren't there. But it didn't make a bit of difference, because Raymond sent down a cook from the Luxe."

"Oh, Lord," Van Degen groaned, dropping down on the end of the sofa. "Was the cook got down to chaperon you?"

Undine laughed. "You talk like Ralph! I had Bertha with me."

"Bertha!" His tone of contempt surprised her. She had supposed that Mrs. Shallum's presence had made the visit perfectly correct.

"You went without knowing his parents, and without their

inviting you? Don't you know what that sort of thing means out here? Chelles did it to brag about you at his club. He wants to compromise you—that's his game!"

"Do you suppose he does?" A flicker of a smile crossed her lips. "I'm so unconventional: when I like a man I never stop to think about such things. But I ought to, of course—you're quite right." She looked at Van Degen thoughtfully. "At any rate, he's not a married man."

Van Degen had got to his feet again and was standing accusingly before her; but as she spoke the blood rose to his neck and ears.

"What difference does that make?"

"It might make a good deal. I see," she added, "how careful I ought to be about going round with you."

"With *me*?" His face fell at the retort; then he broke into a laugh. He adored Undine's "smartness," which was of precisely the same quality as his own. "Oh, that's another thing: you can always trust me to look after you!"

"With your reputation? Much obliged!"

Van Degen smiled. She knew he liked such allusions, and was pleased that she thought him compromising.

"Oh, I'm as good as gold. You've made a new man of me!"

"Have I?" She considered him in silence for a moment. "I wonder what you've done to me but make a discontented woman of me—discontented with everything I had before I knew you?"

The change of tone was thrilling to him. He forgot her mockery, forgot his rival, and sat down at her side, almost in possession of her waist. "Look here," he asked, "where are we going to dine to-night?"

His nearness was not agreeable to Undine, but she liked his free way, his contempt for verbal preliminaries. Ralph's reserves and delicacies, his perpetual desire that he and she should be attuned to the same key, had always vaguely bored her; whereas in Van Degen's manner she felt a hint of the masterful way that had once subdued her in Elmer Moffatt. But she drew back, releasing herself.

"To-night? I can't—I'm engaged."

"I know you are: engaged to *me*! You promised last Sunday you'd dine with me out of town to-night."

"How can I remember what I promised last Sunday? Besides, after what you've said, I see I oughtn't to."

"What do you mean by what I've said?"

"Why, that I'm imprudent; that people are talking——"

He stood up with an angry laugh. "I suppose you're dining with Chelles. Is that it?"

"Is that the way you cross-examine Clare?"

"I don't care a hang what Clare does—I never have."

"That must—in some ways—be rather convenient for her!"

"Glad you think so. *Are* you dining with him?"

She slowly turned the wedding-ring upon her finger. "You know I'm *not* married to you—yet!"

He took a random turn through the room; then he came back and planted himself wrathfully before her. "Can't you see the man's doing his best to make a fool of you?"

She kept her amused gaze on him. "Does it strike you that it's such an awfully easy thing to do?"

The edges of his ears were purple. "I sometimes think it's easier for these damned little dancing-masters than for one of us."

Undine was still smiling up at him; but suddenly her face grew grave. "What does it matter what I do or don't do, when Ralph has ordered me home next week?"

"Ordered you home?" His face changed. "Well, you're not going, are you?"

"What's the use of saying such things?" She gave a disenchanted laugh. "I'm a poor man's wife, and can't do the things my friends do. It's not because Ralph loves me that he wants me back—it's simply because he can't afford to let me stay!"

Van Degen's perturbation was increasing. "But you mustn't go—it's preposterous! Why should a woman like you be sacrificed when a lot of dreary frumps have everything they want? Besides, you can't chuck me like this! Why, we're all to motor down to Aix next week, and perhaps take a dip into Italy——"

"*Oh, Italy*——" she murmured on a note of yearning.

He was closer now, and had her hands. "You'd love that, wouldn't you? As far as Venice, anyhow; and then in August there's Trouville—you've never tried Trouville? There's an awfully jolly crowd there—and the motoring's ripping in Normandy. If you say so I'll take a villa there instead of going back to Newport. And I'll put the *Sorceress* in commission, and you can make up parties and run off whenever you like, to Scotland or Norway——" He hung above her. "Don't dine with Chelles to-night! Come with me, and we'll talk things over; and next week we'll run down to Trouville to choose the villa."

Undine's heart was beating fast, but she felt within her a strange lucid force of resistance. Because of that sense of security she left her hands in Van Degen's. So Mr. Spragg might have felt at the tensest hour of the Pure Water move. She leaned forward, holding her suitor off by the pressure of her bent-back palms.

"Kiss me good-bye, Peter; I sail on Wednesday," she said.

It was the first time she had permitted him a kiss, and as his face darkened down on her she felt a moment's recoil. But her physical reactions were never very acute: she always vaguely wondered why people made "such a fuss," were so violently for or against such demonstrations. A cool spirit within her seemed to watch over and regulate her sensations, and leave her capable of measuring the intensity of those she provoked.

She turned to look at the clock. "You must go now—I shall be hours late for dinner."

"Go—after that?" He held her fast. "Kiss me again," he commanded.

It was wonderful how cool she felt—how easily she could slip out of his grasp! Any man could be managed like a child if he were really in love with one. . .

"Don't be a goose, Peter; do you suppose I'd have kissed you if——"

"If what—what—what?" he mimicked her ecstatically, not listening.

She saw that if she wished to make him hear her she must put more distance between them, and she rose and moved across the room. From the fireplace she turned to add—"if we hadn't been saying good-bye?"

"Good-bye—now? What's the use of talking like that?" He

jumped up and followed her. "Look here, Undine—I'll do any-thing on earth you want; only don't talk of going! If you'll only stay I'll make it all as straight and square as you please. I'll get Bertha Shallum to stop over with you for the summer; I'll take a house at Trouville and make my wife come out there. Hang it, she *shall*, if you say so! Only be a little good to me!"

Still she stood before him without speaking, aware that her implacable brows and narrowed lips would hold him off as long as she chose.

"What's the matter, Undine? Why don't you answer? You know you can't go back to that deadly dry-rot!"

She swept about on him with indignant eyes. "I can't go on with my present life either. It's hateful—as hateful as the other. If I don't go home I've got to decide on something different."

"What do you mean by 'something different'?" She was silent, and he insisted: "Are you really thinking of marrying Chelles?"

She started as if he had surprised a secret. "I'll never forgive you if you speak of it——"

"Good Lord! Good Lord!" he groaned.

She remained motionless, with lowered lids, and he went up to her and pulled her about so that she faced him. "Un-dine, honour bright—do you think he'll marry you?"

She looked at him with a sudden hardness in her eyes. "I really can't discuss such things with you."

"Oh, for the Lord's sake don't take that tone! I don't half know what I'm saying . . . but you mustn't throw yourself away a second time. I'll do anything you want—I swear I will!"

A knock on the door sent them apart, and a servant entered with a telegram.

Undine turned away to the window with the narrow blue slip. She was glad of the interruption: the sense of what she had at stake made her want to pause a moment and to draw breath.

The message was a long cable signed with Laura Fairford's name. It told her that Ralph had been taken suddenly ill with pneumonia, that his condition was serious and that the doc-tors advised his wife's immediate return.

Undine had to read the words over two or three times to get them into her crowded mind; and even after she had done so she needed more time to see their bearing on her own situation. If the message had concerned her boy her brain would have acted more quickly. She had never troubled herself over the possibility of Paul's falling ill in her absence, but she understood now that if the cable had been about him she would have rushed to the earliest steamer. With Ralph it was different. Ralph was always perfectly well—she could not picture him as being suddenly at death's door and in need of her. Probably his mother and sister had had a panic: they were always full of sentimental terrors. The next moment an angry suspicion flashed across her: what if the cable were a device of the Marvell women to bring her back? Perhaps it had been sent with Ralph's connivance! No doubt Bowen had written home about her—Washington Square had received some monstrous report of her doings! . . . Yes, the cable was clearly an echo of Laura's letter—mother and daughter had cooked it up to spoil her pleasure. Once the thought had occurred to her it struck root in her mind and began to throw out giant branches.

Van Degen followed her to the window, his face still flushed and working. "What's the matter?" he asked, as she continued to stare silently at the telegram.

She crumpled the strip of paper in her hand. If only she had been alone, had had a chance to think out her answers!

"What on earth's the matter?" he repeated.

"Oh, nothing—nothing."

"Nothing? When you're as white as a sheet?"

"Am I?" She gave a slight laugh. "It's only a cable from home."

"Ralph?"

She hesitated. "No. Laura."

"What the devil is *she* cabling you about?"

"She says Ralph wants me."

"Now—at once?"

"At once."

Van Degen laughed impatiently. "Why don't he tell you so himself? What business is it of Laura Fairford's?"

Undine's gesture implied a "What indeed?"

"Is that all she says?"

She hesitated again. "Yes—that's all." As she spoke she tossed the telegram into the basket beneath the writing-table. "As if I didn't *have* to go anyhow?" she exclaimed.

With an aching clearness of vision she saw what lay before her—the hurried preparations, the long tedious voyage on a steamer chosen at haphazard, the arrival in the deadly July heat, and the relapse into all the insufferable daily fag of nursery and kitchen—she saw it and her imagination recoiled.

Van Degen's eyes still hung on her: she guessed that he was intensely engaged in trying to follow what was passing through her mind. Presently he came up to her again, no longer perilous and importunate, but awkwardly tender, ridiculously moved by her distress.

"Undine, listen: won't you let me make it all right for you to stay?"

Her heart began to beat more quickly, and she let him come close, meeting his eyes coldly but without anger.

"What do you call 'making it all right'? Paying my bills? Don't you see that's what I hate, and will never let myself be dragged into again?" She laid her hand on his arm. "The time has come when I must be sensible, Peter; that's why we must say good-bye."

"Do you mean to tell me you're going back to Ralph?"

She paused a moment; then she murmured between her lips: "I shall never go back to him."

"Then you *do* mean to marry Chelles?"

"I've told you we must say good-bye. I've got to look out for my future."

He stood before her, irresolute, tormented, his lazy mind and impatient senses labouring with a problem beyond their power. "Ain't I here to look out for your future?" he said at last.

"No one shall look out for it in the way you mean. I'd rather never see you again——"

He gave her a baffled stare. "Oh, damn it—if that's the way you feel!" He turned and flung away toward the door.

She stood motionless where he left her, every nerve strung to the highest pitch of watchfulness. As she stood there, the scene about her stamped itself on her brain with the sharpest precision. She was aware of the fading of the summer light outside, of the movements of her maid, who was laying out her dinner-dress in the room beyond, and of the fact that the tea-roses on her writing-table, shaken by Van Degen's tread, were dropping their petals over Ralph's letter, and down on the crumpled telegram which she could see through the trellised sides of the scrap-basket.

In another moment Van Degen would be gone. Worse yet, while he wavered in the doorway the Shallums and Chelles, after vainly awaiting her, might dash back from the Bois and break in on them. These and other chances rose before her, urging her to action; but she held fast, immovable, unwavering, a proud yet plaintive image of renunciation.

Van Degen's hand was on the door. He half-opened it and then turned back.

"That's all you've got to say, then?"

"That's all."

He jerked the door open and passed out. She saw him stop in the ante-room to pick up his hat and stick, his heavy figure silhouetted against the glare of the wall-lights. A ray of the same light fell on her where she stood in the unlit sitting-room, and her reflection bloomed out like a flower from the mirror that faced her. She looked at the image and waited.

Van Degen put his hat on his head and slowly opened the door into the outer hall. Then he turned abruptly, his bulk eclipsing her reflection as he plunged back into the room and came up to her.

"I'll do anything you say, Undine; I'll do anything in God's world to keep you!"

She turned her eyes from the mirror and let them rest on his face, which looked as small and withered as an old man's, with a lower lip that trembled queerly. . .

BOOK III

XXI

THE SPRING in New York proceeded through more than its usual extremes of temperature to the threshold of a sultry June.

Ralph Marvell, wearily bent to his task, felt the fantastic humours of the weather as only one more incoherence in the general chaos of his case. It was strange enough, after four years of marriage, to find himself again in his old brown room in Washington Square. It was hardly there that he had expected Pegasus to land him; and, like a man returning to the scenes of his childhood, he found everything on a much smaller scale than he had imagined. Had the Dagonet boundaries really narrowed, or had the breach in the walls of his own life let in a wider vision?

Certainly there had come to be other differences between his present and his former self than that embodied in the presence of his little boy in the next room. Paul, in fact, was now the chief link between Ralph and his past. Concerning his son he still felt and thought, in a general way, in the terms of the Dagonet tradition; he still wanted to implant in Paul some of the reserves and discriminations which divided that tradition from the new spirit of limitless concession. But for himself it was different. Since his transaction with Moffatt he had had the sense of living under a new dispensation. He was not sure that it was any worse than the other; but then he was no longer very sure about anything. Perhaps this growing indifference was merely the reaction from a long nervous strain: that his mother and sister thought it so was shown by the way in which they mutely watched and hovered. Their discretion was like the hushed tread about a sick-bed. They permitted themselves no criticism of Undine; he was asked no awkward questions, subjected to no ill-timed sympathy. They simply took him back, on his own terms, into the life he had left them to; and their silence had none of those subtle implications of disapproval which may be so much more wounding than speech.

For a while he received a weekly letter from Undine. Vague

and disappointing though they were, these missives helped
him through the days; but he looked forward to them rather
as a pretext for replies than for their actual contents. Undine
was never at a loss for the spoken word: Ralph had often
wondered at her verbal range and her fluent use of terms outside the current vocabulary. She had certainly not picked
these up in books, since she never opened one: they seemed
rather like some odd transmission of her preaching grand-
parent's oratory. But in her brief and colourless letters she
repeated the same bald statements in the same few terms. She
was well, she had been "round" with Bertha Shallum, she had
dined with the Jim Driscolls or May Beringer or Dicky
Bowles, the weather was too lovely or too awful; such was
the gist of her news. On the last page she hoped Paul was
well and sent him a kiss; but she never made a suggestion
concerning his care or asked a question about his pursuits.
One could only infer that, knowing in what good hands he
was, she judged such solicitude superfluous; and it was thus
that Ralph put the matter to his mother.

"Of course she's not worrying about the boy—why should
she? She knows that with you and Laura he's as happy as a
king."

To which Mrs. Marvell would answer gravely: "When you
write, be sure to say I shan't put on his thinner flannels as
long as this east wind lasts."

As for her husband's welfare, Undine's sole allusion to it
consisted in the invariable expression of the hope that he was
getting along all right: the phrase was always the same, and
Ralph learned to know just how far down the third page to
look for it. In a postscript she sometimes asked him to tell
her mother about a new way of doing hair or cutting a skirt;
and this was usually the most eloquent passage of the letter.

What satisfaction he extracted from these communications
he would have found it hard to say; yet when they did not
come he missed them hardly less than if they had given him
all he craved. Sometimes the mere act of holding the blue or
mauve sheet and breathing its scent was like holding his wife's
hand and being enveloped in her fresh young fragrance: the
sentimental disappointment vanished in the penetrating physical sensation. In other moods it was enough to trace the

letters of the first line and the last for the desert of perfunctory phrases between the two to vanish, leaving him only the vision of their interlaced names, as of a mystic bond which her own hand had tied. Or else he saw her, closely, palpably before him, as she sat at her writing-table, frowning and a little flushed, her bent nape showing the light on her hair, her short lip pulled up by the effort of composition; and this picture had the violent reality of dream-images on the verge of waking. At other times, as he read her letter, he felt simply that at least in the moment of writing it she had been with him. But in one of the last she had said (to excuse a bad blot and an incoherent sentence): "Everybody's talking to me at once, and I don't know what I'm writing." That letter he had thrown into the fire. . .

After the first few weeks, the letters came less and less regularly: at the end of two months they ceased. Ralph had got into the habit of watching for them on the days when a foreign post was due, and as the weeks went by without a sign he began to invent excuses for leaving the office earlier and hurrying back to Washington Square to search the letter-box for a big tinted envelope with a straggling blotted superscription. Undine's departure had given him a momentary sense of liberation: at that stage in their relations any change would have brought relief. But now that she was gone he knew she could never really go. Though his feeling for her had changed, it still ruled his life. If he saw her in her weakness he felt her in her power: the power of youth and physical radiance that clung to his disenchanted memories as the scent she used clung to her letters. Looking back at their four years of marriage he began to ask himself if he had done all he could to draw her half-formed spirit from its sleep. Had he not expected too much at first, and grown too indifferent in the sequel? After all, she was still in the toy age; and perhaps the very extravagance of his love had retarded her growth, helped to imprison her in a little circle of frivolous illusions. But the last months had made a man of him, and when she came back he would know how to lift her to the height of his experience.

So he would reason, day by day, as he hastened back to Washington Square; but when he opened the door, and his

first glance at the hall table showed him there was no letter
there, his illusions shrivelled down to their weak roots. She
had not written: she did not mean to write. He and the boy
were no longer a part of her life. When she came back everything would be as it had been before, with the dreary difference that she had tasted new pleasures and that their absence
would take the savour from all he had to give her. Then the
coming of another foreign mail would lift his hopes, and as
he hurried home he would imagine new reasons for expecting
a letter. . .

Week after week he swung between the extremes of hope
and dejection, and at last, when the strain had become unbearable, he cabled her. The answer ran: "Very well best love
writing"; but the promised letter never came. . .

He went on steadily with his work: he even passed through
a phase of exaggerated energy. But his baffled youth fought
in him for air. Was this to be the end? Was he to wear his life
out in useless drudgery? The plain prose of it, of course, was
that the economic situation remained unchanged by the sentimental catastrophe and that he must go on working for his
wife and child. But at any rate, as it was mainly for Paul that
he would henceforth work, it should be on his own terms and
according to his inherited notions of "straightness." He
would never again engage in any transaction resembling his
compact with Moffatt. Even now he was not sure there had
been anything crooked in that; but the fact of his having instinctively referred the point to Mr. Spragg rather than to his
grandfather implied a presumption against it.

His partners were quick to profit by his sudden spurt of
energy, and his work grew no lighter. He was not only the
youngest and most recent member of the firm, but the one
who had so far added least to the volume of its business. His
hours were the longest, his absences, as summer approached,
the least frequent and the most grudgingly accorded. No
doubt his associates knew that he was pressed for money and
could not risk a break. They " worked" him, and he was aware
of it, and submitted because he dared not lose his job. But
the long hours of mechanical drudgery were telling on his
active body and undisciplined nerves. He had begun too late
to subject himself to the persistent mortification of spirit and

flesh which is a condition of the average business life; and after the long dull days in the office the evenings at his grandfather's whist-table did not give him the counter-stimulus he needed.

Almost every one had gone out of town; but now and then Miss Ray came to dine, and Ralph, seated beneath the family portraits and opposite the desiccated Harriet, who had already faded to the semblance of one of her own great-aunts, listened languidly to the kind of talk that the originals might have exchanged about the same table when New York gentility centred in the Battery and the Bowling Green. Mr. Dagonet was always pleasant to see and hear, but his sarcasms were growing faint and recondite: they had as little bearing on life as the humours of a Restoration comedy. As for Mrs. Marvell and Miss Ray, they seemed to the young man even more spectrally remote: hardly anything that mattered to him existed for them, and their prejudices reminded him of signposts warning off trespassers who have long since ceased to intrude.

Now and then he dined at his club and went on to the theatre with some young men of his own age; but he left them afterward, half vexed with himself for not being in the humour to prolong the adventure. There were moments when he would have liked to affirm his freedom in however commonplace a way: moments when the vulgarest way would have seemed the most satisfying. But he always ended by walking home alone and tip-toeing upstairs through the sleeping house lest he should wake his boy. . .

On Saturday afternoons, when the business world was hurrying to the country for golf and tennis, he stayed in town and took Paul to see the Spraggs. Several times since his wife's departure he had tried to bring about closer relations between his own family and Undine's; and the ladies of Washington Square, in their eagerness to meet his wishes, had made various friendly advances to Mrs. Spragg. But they were met by a mute resistance which made Ralph suspect that Undine's strictures on his family had taken root in her mother's brooding mind; and he gave up the struggle to bring together what had been so effectually put asunder.

If he regretted his lack of success it was chiefly because he was so sorry for the Spraggs. Soon after Undine's marriage they had abandoned their polychrome suite at the Stentorian, and since then their peregrinations had carried them through half the hotels of the metropolis. Undine, who had early discovered her mistake in thinking hotel life fashionable, had tried to persuade her parents to take a house of their own; but though they refrained from taxing her with inconsistency they did not act on her suggestion. Mrs. Spragg seemed to shrink from the thought of "going back to house-keeping," and Ralph suspected that she depended on the transit from hotel to hotel as the one element of variety in her life. As for Mr. Spragg, it was impossible to imagine any one in whom the domestic sentiments were more completely unlocalized and disconnected from any fixed habits; and he was probably aware of his changes of abode chiefly as they obliged him to ascend from the Subway, or descend from the "Elevated," a few blocks higher up or lower down.

Neither husband nor wife complained to Ralph of their frequent displacements, or assigned to them any cause save the vague one of "guessing they could do better"; but Ralph noticed that the decreasing luxury of their life synchronized with Undine's growing demands for money. During the last few months they had transferred themselves to the "Malibran," a tall narrow structure resembling a grain-elevator divided into cells, where linoleum and lincrusta simulated the stucco and marble of the Stentorian, and fagged business men and their families consumed the watery stews dispensed by "coloured help" in the grey twilight of a basement dining-room.

Mrs. Spragg had no sitting-room, and Paul and his father had to be received in one of the long public parlours, between ladies seated at rickety desks in the throes of correspondence and groups of listlessly conversing residents and callers.

The Spraggs were intensely proud of their grandson, and Ralph perceived that they would have liked to see Paul charging uproariously from group to group and thrusting his bright curls and cherubic smile upon the general attention. The fact that the boy preferred to stand between his grandfather's knees and play with Mr. Spragg's Masonic emblem, or dangle his legs from the arm of Mrs. Spragg's chair, seemed to his grandparents evidence of ill-health or undue repression, and he was subjected by Mrs. Spragg to searching enquiries as to how his food set, and whether he didn't think his Popper was too strict with him. A more embarrassing problem was raised by the "surprise" (in the shape of peanut candy or chocolate creams) which he was invited to hunt for in Gran'ma's pockets, and which Ralph had to confiscate on the way home lest the dietary rules of Washington Square should be too visibly infringed.

Sometimes Ralph found Mrs. Heeny, ruddy and jovial, seated in the arm-chair opposite Mrs. Spragg, and regaling her with selections from a new batch of clippings. During Undine's illness of the previous winter Mrs. Heeny had become a familiar figure to Paul, who had learned to expect almost as much from her bag as from his grandmother's pockets; so that the intemperate Saturdays at the Malibran were usually followed by languid and abstemious Sundays in Washington Square.

Mrs. Heeny, being unaware of this sequel to her bounties, formed the habit of appearing regularly on Saturdays, and while she chatted with his grandmother the little boy was encouraged to scatter the grimy carpet with face-creams and bunches of clippings in his thrilling quest for the sweets at the bottom of her bag.

"I declare, if he ain't in just as much of a hurry f'r everything as his mother!" she exclaimed one day in her rich rolling voice; and stooping to pick up a long strip of newspaper which Paul had flung aside she added, as she smoothed it out: "I guess 'f he was a little mite older he'd be better pleased with this 'n with the candy. It's the very thing I was trying to find for you the other day, Mrs. Spragg," she went on, holding the bit of paper at arm's length; and she began to read out, with a loudness proportioned to the distance between her eyes and the text:

"With two such sprinters as 'Pete' Van Degen and Dicky Bowles to set the pace, it's no wonder the New York set in Paris has struck a livelier gait than ever this spring. It's a high-pressure season and no mistake, and no one lags behind less than the fascinating Mrs. Ralph Marvell, who is to be seen daily and nightly in all the smartest restaurants and naughtiest theatres, with so many devoted swains in attendance that the

rival beauties of both worlds are said to be making catty comments. But then Mrs. Marvell's gowns are almost as good as
her looks—and how can you expect the other women to
stand for such a monopoly?"

To escape the strain of these visits, Ralph once or twice
tried the experiment of leaving Paul with his grand-parents
and calling for him in the late afternoon; but one day, on re-
entering the Malibran, he was met by a small abashed figure
clad in a kaleidoscopic tartan and a green velvet cap with a
silver thistle. After this experience of the "surprises" of which
Gran'ma was capable when she had a chance to take Paul
shopping Ralph did not again venture to leave his son, and
their subsequent Saturdays were passed together in the sultry
gloom of the Malibran.

Conversation with the Spraggs was almost impossible.
Ralph could talk with his father-in-law in his office, but in
the hotel parlour Mr. Spragg sat in a ruminating silence broken only by the emission of an occasional "Well—well" addressed to his grandson. As for Mrs. Spragg, her son-in-law
could not remember having had a sustained conversation with
her since the distant day when he had first called at the Stentorian, and had been "entertained," in Undine's absence, by
her astonished mother. The shock of that encounter had
moved Mrs. Spragg to eloquence; but Ralph's entrance into
the family, without making him seem less of a stranger, appeared once for all to have relieved her of the obligation of
finding something to say to him.

The one question she invariably asked: "You heard from
Undie?" had been relatively easy to answer while his wife's
infrequent letters continued to arrive; but a Saturday came
when he felt the blood rise to his temples as, for the fourth
consecutive week, he stammered out, under the snapping eyes
of Mrs. Heeny: "No, not by this post either—I begin to
think I must have lost a letter"; and it was then that Mr.
Spragg, who had sat silently looking up at the ceiling, cut
short his wife's exclamation by an enquiry about real estate in
the Bronx. After that, Ralph noticed, Mrs. Spragg never
again renewed her question; and he understood that his
father-in-law had guessed his embarrassment and wished to
spare it.

Ralph had never thought of looking for any delicacy of feeling under Mr. Spragg's large lazy irony, and the incident drew the two men nearer together. Mrs. Spragg, for her part, was certainly not delicate; but she was simple and without malice, and Ralph liked her for her silent acceptance of her diminished state. Sometimes, as he sat between the lonely primitive old couple, he wondered from what source Undine's voracious ambitions had been drawn: all she cared for, and attached importance to, was as remote from her parents' conception of life as her impatient greed from their passive stoicism.

One hot afternoon toward the end of June Ralph suddenly wondered if Clare Van Degen were still in town. She had dined in Washington Square some ten days earlier, and he remembered her saying that she had sent the children down to Long Island, but that she herself meant to stay on in town till the heat grew unbearable. She hated her big showy place on Long Island, she was tired of the spring trip to London and Paris, where one met at every turn the faces one had grown sick of seeing all winter, and she declared that in the early summer New York was the only place in which one could escape from New Yorkers. . . She put the case amusingly, and it was like her to take up any attitude that went against the habits of her set; but she lived at the mercy of her moods, and one could never tell how long any one of them would rule her.

As he sat in his office, with the noise and glare of the endless afternoon rising up in hot waves from the street, there wandered into Ralph's mind a vision of her shady drawing-room. All day it hung before him like the mirage of a spring before a dusty traveller: he felt a positive thirst for her presence, for the sound of her voice, the wide spaces and luxurious silences surrounding her.

It was perhaps because, on that particular day, a spiral pain was twisting around in the back of his head, and digging in a little deeper with each twist, and because the figures on the balance sheet before him were hopping about like black imps in an infernal forward-and-back, that the picture hung there so persistently. It was a long time since he had wanted anything as much as, at that particular moment, he wanted to be with Clare and hear her voice; and as soon as he had ground out the day's measure of work he rang up the Van Degen palace and learned that she was still in town.

The lowered awnings of her inner drawing-room cast a luminous shadow on old cabinets and consoles, and on the pale flowers scattered here and there in vases of bronze and porcelain. Clare's taste was as capricious as her moods, and the rest of the house was not in harmony with this room. There was, in particular, another drawing-room, which she now described as Peter's creation, but which Ralph knew to be partly hers: a heavily decorated apartment, where Popple's portrait of her throned over a waste of gilt furniture. It was characteristic that to-day she had had Ralph shown in by another way; and that, as she had spared him the polyphonic drawing-room, so she had skilfully adapted her own appearance to her soberer background. She sat near the window, reading, in a clear cool dress: and at his entrance she merely slipped a finger between the pages and looked up at him.

Her way of receiving him made him feel that her restlessness and stridency were as unlike her genuine self as the gilded drawing-room, and that this quiet creature was the only real Clare, the Clare who had once been so nearly his, and who seemed to want him to know that she had never wholly been any one else's.

"Why didn't you let me know you were still in town?" he asked, as he sat down in the sofa-corner near her chair.

Her dark smile deepened. "I hoped you'd come and see."

"One never knows, with you."

He was looking about the room with a kind of confused pleasure in its pale shadows and spots of dark rich colour. The old lacquer screen behind Clare's head looked like a lustreless black pool with gold leaves floating on it; and another piece, a little table at her elbow, had the brown bloom and the pear-like curves of an old violin.

"I like to be here," Ralph said.

She did not make the mistake of asking: "Then why do you never come?" Instead, she turned away, and drew an inner curtain across the window to shut out the sunlight which was beginning to slant in under the awning.

The mere fact of her not answering, and the final touch of well-being which her gesture gave, reminded him of other summer days they had spent together, long rambling boy-and-girl days in the hot woods and sunny fields, when they had never thought of talking to each other unless there was something they particularly wanted to say. His tired fancy strayed off for a second to the thought of what it would have been like to come back, at the end of the day, to such a sweet community of silence; but his mind was too crowded with importunate facts for any lasting view of visionary distances. The thought faded, and he merely felt how restful it was to have her near. . .

"I'm glad you stayed in town: you must let me come again," he said.

"I suppose you can't always get away," she answered; and she began to listen, with grave intelligent eyes, to his description of his tedious days.

With her eyes on him he felt the exquisite relief of talking about himself as he had not dared to talk to any one since his marriage. He would not for the world have confessed his discouragement, his consciousness of incapacity; to Undine and in Washington Square any hint of failure would have been taken as a criticism of what his wife demanded of him. Only to Clare Van Degen could he cry out his present despondency and his loathing of the interminable task ahead.

"A man doesn't know till he tries it how killing uncongenial work is, and how it destroys the power of doing what one's fit for, even if there's time for both. But there's Paul to be looked out for, and I daren't chuck my job—I'm in mortal terror of its chucking me. . ."

Little by little he slipped into a detailed recital of all his lesser worries, the most recent of which was his experience with the Lipscombs, who, after a two months' tenancy of the West End Avenue house, had decamped without paying their rent.

Clare laughed contemptuously. "Yes—I heard he'd come to grief and been suspended from the Stock Exchange, and I see in the papers that his wife's retort has been to sue for a divorce."

Ralph knew that, like all their clan, his cousin regarded a

divorce-suit as a vulgar and unnecessary way of taking the public into one's confidence. His mind flashed back to the family feast in Washington Square in celebration of his engagement. He recalled his grandfather's chance allusion to Mrs. Lipscomb, and Undine's answer, fluted out on her highest note: "Oh, I guess she'll get a divorce pretty soon. He's been a disappointment to her."

Ralph could still hear the horrified murmur with which his mother had rebuked his laugh. For he had laughed—had thought Undine's speech fresh and natural! Now he felt the ironic rebound of her words. Heaven knew he had been a disappointment to her; and what was there in her own feeling, or in her inherited prejudices, to prevent her seeking the same redress as Mabel Lipscomb? He wondered if the same thought were in his cousin's mind. . .

They began to talk of other things: books, pictures, plays; and one by one the closed doors opened and light was let into dusty shuttered places. Clare's mind was neither keen nor deep: Ralph, in the past, had often smiled at her rash ardours and vague intensities. But she had his own range of allusions, and a great gift of momentary understanding; and he had so long beaten his thoughts out against a blank wall of incomprehension that her sympathy seemed full of insight.

She began by a question about his writing, but the subject was distasteful to him, and he turned the talk to a new book in which he had been interested. She knew enough of it to slip in the right word here and there; and thence they wandered on to kindred topics. Under the warmth of her attention his torpid ideas awoke again, and his eyes took their fill of pleasure as she leaned forward, her thin brown hands clasped on her knees and her eager face reflecting all his feelings.

There was a moment when the two currents of sensation were merged in one, and he began to feel confusedly that he was young and she was kind, and that there was nothing he would like better than to go on sitting there, not much caring what she said or how he answered, if only she would let him look at her and give him one of her thin brown hands to hold. Then the corkscrew in the back of his head dug into him again with a deeper thrust, and she seemed suddenly to recede to a great distance and be divided from him by a fog of pain. The fog lifted after a minute, but it left him queerly remote from her, from the cool room with its scents and shadows, and from all the objects which, a moment before, had so sharply impinged upon his senses. It was as though he looked at it all through a rain-blurred pane, against which his hand would strike if he held it out to her. . .

That impression passed also, and he found himself thinking how tired he was and how little anything mattered. He recalled the unfinished piece of work on his desk, and for a moment had the odd illusion that it was there before him. . .

She exclaimed: "But are you going?" and her exclamation made him aware that he had left his seat and was standing in front of her. . . He fancied there was some kind of appeal in her brown eyes; but she was so dim and far off that he couldn't be sure of what she wanted, and the next moment he found himself shaking hands with her, and heard her saying something kind and cold about its having been so nice to see him. . .

Half way up the stairs little Paul, shining and rosy from supper, lurked in ambush for his evening game. Ralph was fond of stooping down to let the boy climb up his outstretched arms to his shoulders, but to-day, as he did so, Paul's hug seemed to crush him in a vice, and the shout of welcome that accompanied it racked his ears like an explosion of steam-whistles. The queer distance between himself and the rest of the world was annihilated again: everything stared and glared and clutched him. He tried to turn away his face from the child's hot kisses; and as he did so he caught sight of a mauve envelope among the hats and sticks on the hall table.

Instantly he passed Paul over to his nurse, stammered out a word about being tired, and sprang up the long flights to his study. The pain in his head had stopped, but his hands trembled as he tore open the envelope. Within it was a second letter bearing a French stamp and addressed to himself. It looked like a business communication and had apparently been sent to Undine's hotel in Paris and forwarded to him by her hand. "Another bill!" he reflected grimly, as he threw it aside and felt in the outer envelope for her letter. There was nothing there, and after a first sharp pang of disappointment he picked up the enclosure and opened it.

Inside was a lithographed circular, headed "Confidential" and bearing the Paris address of a firm of private detectives who undertook, in conditions of attested and inviolable discretion, to investigate "delicate" situations, look up doubtful antecedents, and furnish reliable evidence of misconduct—all on the most reasonable terms.

For a long time Ralph sat and stared at this document; then he began to laugh and tossed it into the scrap-basket. After that, with a groan, he dropped his head against the edge of his writing table.

XXII

WHEN HE WOKE, the first thing he remembered was the fact of having cried.

He could not think how he had come to be such a fool. He hoped to heaven no one had seen him. He supposed he must have been worrying about the unfinished piece of work at the office: where was it, by the way, he wondered? Why—where he had left it the day before, of course! What a ridiculous thing to worry about—but it seemed to follow him about like a dog. . .

He said to himself that he must get up presently and go down to the office. Presently—when he could open his eyes. Just now there was a dead weight on them; he tried one after another in vain. The effort set him weakly trembling, and he wanted to cry again. Nonsense! He must get out of bed.

He stretched his arms out, trying to reach something to pull himself up by; but everything slipped away and evaded him. It was like trying to catch at bright short waves. Then suddenly his fingers clasped themselves about something firm and warm. A hand: a hand that gave back his pressure! The relief was inexpressible. He lay still and let the hand hold him, while mentally he went through the motions of getting up and beginning to dress. So indistinct were the boundaries between thought and action that he really felt himself moving about the room, in a queer disembodied way, as one treads the air in sleep. Then he felt the bed-clothes over him and the pillows under his head.

"I *must* get up," he said, and pulled at the hand.

It pressed him down again: down into a dim deep pool of sleep. He lay there for a long time, in a silent blackness far below light and sound; then he gradually floated to the surface with the buoyancy of a dead body. But his body had never been more alive. Jagged strokes of pain tore through it, hands dragged at it with nails that bit like teeth. They wound thongs about him, bound him, tied weights to him, tried to pull him down with them; but still he floated, floated, danced on the fiery waves of pain, with barbed light pouring down on him from an arrowy sky.

Charmed intervals of rest, blue sailings on melodious seas, alternated with the anguish. He became a leaf on the air, a feather on a current, a straw on the tide, the spray of the wave spinning itself to sunshine as the wave toppled over into gulfs of blue. . .

He woke on a stony beach, his legs and arms still lashed to his sides and the thongs cutting into him; but the fierce sky was hidden, and hidden by his own languid lids. He felt the ecstasy of decreasing pain, and courage came to him to open his eyes and look about him. . .

The beach was his own bed; the tempered light lay on familiar things, and some one was moving about in a shadowy way between bed and window. He was thirsty, and some one gave him a drink. His pillow burned, and some one turned the cool side out. His brain was clear enough now for him to understand that he was ill, and to want to talk about it; but his tongue hung in his throat like a clapper in a bell. He must wait till the rope was pulled. . .

So time and life stole back on him, and his thoughts laboured weakly with dim fears. Slowly he cleared a way through them, adjusted himself to his strange state, and found out that he was in his own room, in his grandfather's house, that alternating with the white-capped faces about him were those of his mother and sister, and that in a few days— if he took his beef-tea and didn't fret—Paul would be brought up from Long Island, whither, on account of the great heat, he had been carried off by Clare Van Degen.

No one named Undine to him, and he did not speak of her. But one day, as he lay in bed in the summer twilight, he had a vision of a moment, a long way behind him—at the beginning of his illness, it must have been—when he had called out for her in his anguish, and some one had said: "She's coming: she'll be here next week."

Could it be that next week was not yet here? He supposed that illness robbed one of all sense of time, and he lay still, as if in ambush, watching his scattered memories come out one by one and join themselves together. If he watched long enough he was sure he should recognize one that fitted into his picture of the day when he had asked for Undine. And at length a face came out of the twilight: a freckled face, benevolently bent over him under a starched cap. He had not seen the face for a long time, but suddenly it took shape and fitted itself into the picture. . .

Laura Fairford sat near by, a book on her knee. At the sound of his voice she looked up.

"What was the name of the first nurse?"

"The first——?"

"The one that went away."

"Oh—Miss Hicks, you mean?"

"How long is it since she went?"

"It must be three weeks. She had another case."

He thought this over carefully; then he spoke again. "Call Undine."

She made no answer, and he repeated irritably: "Why don't you call her? I want to speak to her."

Mrs. Fairford laid down her book and came to him.

"She's not here—just now."

He dealt with this also, laboriously. "You mean she's out—she's not in the house?"

"I mean she hasn't come yet."

As she spoke Ralph felt a sudden strength and hardness in his brain and body. Everything in him became as clear as noon.

"But it was before Miss Hicks left that you told me you'd sent for her, and that she'd be here the following week. And you say Miss Hicks has been gone three weeks."

This was what he had worked out in his head, and what he meant to say to his sister; but something seemed to snap shut in his throat, and he closed his eyes without speaking.

Even when Mr. Spragg came to see him he said nothing. They talked about his illness, about the hot weather, about the rumours that Harmon B. Driscoll was again threatened with indictment; and then Mr. Spragg pulled himself out of his chair and said: "I presume you'll call round at the office before you leave the city."

"Oh, yes: as soon as I'm up," Ralph answered. They understood each other.

Clare had urged him to come down to Long Island and complete his convalescence there, but he preferred to stay in Washington Square till he should be strong enough for the

journey to the Adirondacks, whither Laura had already preceded him with Paul. He did not want to see any one but his
mother and grandfather till his legs could carry him to Mr.
Spragg's office.

It was an oppressive day in mid-August, with a yellow mist
of heat in the sky, when at last he entered the big office-
building. Swirls of dust lay on the mosaic floor, and a stale
smell of decayed fruit and salt air and steaming asphalt filled
the place like a fog. As he shot up in the elevator some one
slapped him on the back, and turning he saw Elmer Moffatt
at his side, smooth and rubicund under a new straw hat.

Moffatt was loudly glad to see him. "I haven't laid eyes on
you for months. At the old stand still?"

"So am I," he added, as Ralph assented. "Hope to see you
there again some day. Don't forget it's *my* turn this time:
glad if I can be any use to you. So long." Ralph's weak bones
ached under his handshake.

"How's Mrs. Marvell?" he turned back from his landing to
call out; and Ralph answered: "Thanks; she's very well."

Mr. Spragg sat alone in his murky inner office, the fly-
blown engraving of Daniel Webster above his head and the
congested scrap-basket beneath his feet. He looked fagged
and sallow, like the day.

Ralph sat down on the other side of the desk. For a moment his throat contracted as it had when he had tried to
question his sister; then he asked: "Where's Undine?"

Mr. Spragg glanced at the calendar that hung from a
hat-peg on the door. Then he released the Masonic emblem
from his grasp, drew out his watch and consulted it
critically.

"If the train's on time I presume she's somewhere between
Chicago and Omaha round about now."

Ralph stared at him, wondering if the heat had gone to his
head.

"I don't understand."

"The Twentieth Century's generally considered the best
route to Dakota," explained Mr. Spragg, who pronounced
the word *rowt*.

"Do you mean to say Undine's in the United States?"

Mr. Spragg's lower lip groped for the phantom tooth-pick.

"Why, let me see: hasn't Dakota been a state a year or two now?"

"Oh, God——" Ralph cried, pushing his chair back violently and striding across the narrow room.

As he turned, Mr. Spragg stood up and advanced a few steps. He had given up the quest for the tooth-pick, and his drawn-in lips were no more than a narrow depression in his beard. He stood before Ralph, absently shaking the loose change in his trouser-pockets.

Ralph felt the same hardness and lucidity that had come to him when he had heard his sister's answer.

"She's gone, you mean? Left me? With another man?"

Mr. Spragg drew himself up with a kind of slouching majesty. "My daughter is not that style. I understand Undine thinks there have been mistakes on both sides. She considers the tie was formed too hastily. I believe desertion is the usual plea in such cases."

Ralph stared about him, hardly listening. He did not resent his father-in-law's tone. In a dim way he guessed that Mr. Spragg was suffering hardly less than himself. But nothing was clear to him save the monstrous fact suddenly upheaved in his path. His wife had left him, and the plan for her evasion had been made and executed while he lay helpless: she had seized the opportunity of his illness to keep him in ignorance of her design. The humour of it suddenly struck him and he laughed.

"Do you mean to tell me that Undine's divorcing *me?*"

"I presume that's her plan," Mr. Spragg admitted.

"For desertion?" Ralph pursued, still laughing.

His father-in-law hesitated a moment; then he answered: "You've always done all you could for my daughter. There wasn't any other plea she could think of. She presumed this would be the most agreeable to your family."

"It was good of her to think of that!"

Mr. Spragg's only comment was a sigh.

"Does she imagine I won't fight it?" Ralph broke out with sudden passion.

His father-in-law looked at him thoughtfully. "I presume you realize it ain't easy to change Undine, once she's set on a thing."

"Perhaps not. But if she really means to apply for a divorce I can make it a little less easy for her to get."

"That's so," Mr. Spragg conceded. He turned back to his revolving chair, and seating himself in it began to drum on the desk with cigar-stained fingers.

"And by God, I will!" Ralph thundered. Anger was the only emotion in him now. He had been fooled, cheated, made a mock of; but the score was not settled yet. He turned back and stood before Mr. Spragg.

"I suppose she's gone with Van Degen?"

"My daughter's gone alone, sir. I saw her off at the station. I understood she was to join a lady friend."

At every point Ralph felt his hold slip off the surface of his father-in-law's impervious fatalism.

"Does she suppose Van Degen's going to marry her?"

"Undine didn't mention her future plans to me." After a moment Mr. Spragg appended: "If she had, I should have declined to discuss them with her."

Ralph looked at him curiously, perceiving that he intended in this negative way to imply his disapproval of his daughter's course.

"I shall fight it—I shall fight it!" the young man cried again. "You may tell her I shall fight it to the end!"

Mr. Spragg pressed the nib of his pen against the dust-coated inkstand. "I suppose you would have to engage a lawyer. She'll know it that way," he remarked.

"She'll know it—you may count on that!"

Ralph had begun to laugh again. Suddenly he heard his own laugh and it pulled him up. What was he laughing about? What was he talking about? The thing was to act—to hold his tongue and act. There was no use uttering windy threats to this broken-spirited old man. A fury of action burned in Ralph, pouring light into his mind and strength into his muscles. He caught up his hat and turned to the door.

As he opened it Mr. Spragg rose again and came forward with his slow shambling step. He laid his hand on Ralph's arm.

"I'd 'a' given anything—anything short of my girl herself—not to have this happen to you, Ralph Marvell."

"Thank you, sir," said Ralph.

They looked at each other for a moment; then Mr. Spragg added: "But it *has* happened, you know. Bear that in mind. Nothing you can do will change it. Time and again, I've found that a good thing to remember."

XXIII

IN THE ADIRONDACKS Ralph Marvell sat day after day on
the balcony of his little house above the lake, staring at the
great white cloud-reflections in the water and at the dark line
of trees that closed them in. Now and then he got into the
canoe and paddled himself through a winding chain of ponds
to some lonely clearing in the forest; and there he lay on his
back in the pine-needles and watched the great clouds form
and dissolve themselves above his head.

All his past life seemed to be symbolized by the building-
up and breaking-down of those fluctuating shapes, which incalculable wind-currents perpetually shifted and remodelled
or swept from the zenith like a pinch of dust.

His sister told him that he looked well—better than he had
in years; and there were moments when his listlessness, his
stony insensibility to the small pricks and frictions of daily
life, might have passed for the serenity of recovered health.

There was no one with whom he could speak of Undine.
His family had thrown over the whole subject a pall of silence
which even Laura Fairford shrank from raising. As for his
mother, Ralph had seen at once that the idea of talking over
the situation was positively frightening to her. There was no
provision for such emergencies in the moral order of Washington Square. The affair was a "scandal," and it was not in
the Dagonet tradition to acknowledge the existence of scandals. Ralph recalled a dim memory of his childhood, the tale
of a misguided friend of his mother's who had left her husband for a more congenial companion, and who, years later,
returning ill and friendless to New York, had appealed for
sympathy to Mrs. Marvell. The latter had not refused to give
it; but she had put on her black cashmere and two veils when
she went to see her unhappy friend, and had never mentioned
these errands of mercy to her husband.

Ralph suspected that the constraint shown by his mother
and sister was partly due to their having but a dim and confused view of what had happened. In their vocabulary the
word "divorce" was wrapped in such a dark veil of innuendo
as no ladylike hand would care to lift. They had not reached

the point of differentiating divorces, but classed them indistinctively as disgraceful incidents, in which the woman was always to blame, but the man, though her innocent victim, was yet inevitably contaminated. The time involved in the "proceedings" was viewed as a penitential season during which it behoved the family of the persons concerned to behave as if they were dead; yet any open allusion to the reason for adopting such an attitude would have been regarded as the height of indelicacy.

Mr. Dagonet's notion of the case was almost as remote from reality. All he asked was that his grandson should "thrash" somebody, and he could not be made to understand that the modern drama of divorce is sometimes cast without a Lovelace.

"You might as well tell me there was nobody but Adam in the garden when Eve picked the apple. You say your wife was discontented? No woman ever knows she's discontented till some man tells her so. My God! I've seen smash-ups before now; but I never yet saw a marriage dissolved like a business partnership. Divorce without a lover? Why, it's—it's as unnatural as getting drunk on lemonade."

After this first explosion Mr. Dagonet also became silent; and Ralph perceived that what annoyed him most was the fact of the "scandal's" not being one in any gentlemanly sense of the word. It was like some nasty business mess, about which Mr. Dagonet couldn't pretend to have an opinion, since such things didn't happen to men of his kind. That such a thing should have happened to his only grandson was probably the bitterest experience of his pleasantly uneventful life; and it added a touch of irony to Ralph's unhappiness to know how little, in the whole affair, he was cutting the figure Mr. Dagonet expected him to cut.

At first he had chafed under the taciturnity surrounding him: had passionately longed to cry out his humiliation, his rebellion, his despair. Then he began to feel the tonic effect of silence; and the next stage was reached when it became clear to him that there was nothing to say. There were thoughts and thoughts: they bubbled up perpetually from the black springs of his hidden misery, they stole on him in the darkness of night, they blotted out the light of day; but when it came to putting them into words and applying them to the external facts of the case, they seemed totally unrelated to it. One more white and sun-touched glory had gone from his sky; but there seemed no way of connecting that with such practical issues as his being called on to decide whether Paul was to be put in knickerbockers or trousers, and whether he should go back to Washington Square for the winter or hire a small house for himself and his son.

The latter question was ultimately decided by his remaining under his grandfather's roof. November found him back in the office again, in fairly good health, with an outer skin of indifference slowly forming over his lacerated soul. There had been a hard minute to live through when he came back to his old brown room in Washington Square. The walls and tables were covered with photographs of Undine: effigies of all shapes and sizes, expressing every possible sentiment dear to the photographic tradition. Ralph had gathered them all up when he had moved from West End Avenue after Undine's departure for Europe, and they throned over his other possessions as her image had throned over his future the night he had sat in that very room and dreamed of soaring up with her into the blue. . .

It was impossible to go on living with her photographs about him; and one evening, going up to his room after dinner, he began to unhang them from the walls, and to gather them up from book-shelves and mantel-piece and tables. Then he looked about for some place in which to hide them. There were drawers under his book-cases; but they were full of old discarded things, and even if he emptied the drawers, the photographs, in their heavy frames, were almost all too large to fit into them. He turned next to the top shelf of his cupboard; but here the nurse had stored Paul's old toys, his sandpails, shovels and croquet-box. Every corner was packed with the vain impedimenta of living, and the mere thought of clearing a space in the chaos was too great an effort.

He began to replace the pictures one by one; and the last was still in his hand when he heard his sister's voice outside. He hurriedly put the portrait back in its usual place on his writing-table, and Mrs. Fairford, who had been dining in Washington Square, and had come up to bid him good night, flung her arms about him in a quick embrace and went down to her carriage.

The next afternoon, when he came home from the office, he did not at first see any change in his room; but when he had lit his pipe and thrown himself into his arm-chair he noticed that the photograph of his wife's picture by Popple no longer faced him from the mantel-piece. He turned to his writing-table, but her image had vanished from there too; then his eye, making the circuit of the walls, perceived that they also had been stripped. Not a single photograph of Undine was left; yet so adroitly had the work of elimination been done, so ingeniously the remaining objects readjusted, that the change attracted no attention.

Ralph was angry, sore, ashamed. He felt as if Laura, whose hand he instantly detected, had taken a cruel pleasure in her work, and for an instant he hated her for it. Then a sense of relief stole over him. He was glad he could look about him without meeting Undine's eyes, and he understood that what had been done to his room he must do to his memory and his imagination: he must so readjust his mind that, whichever way he turned his thoughts, her face should no longer confront him. But that was a task that Laura could not perform for him, a task to be accomplished only by the hard continuous tension of his will.

With the setting in of the mood of silence all desire to fight his wife's suit died out. The idea of touching publicly on anything that had passed between himself and Undine had become unthinkable. Insensibly he had been subdued to the point of view about him, and the idea of calling on the law to repair his shattered happiness struck him as even more grotesque than it was degrading. Nevertheless, some contradictory impulse of his divided spirit made him resent, on the part of his mother and sister, a too-ready acceptance of his attitude. There were moments when their tacit assumption that his wife was banished and forgotten irritated him like the hushed tread of sympathizers about the bed of an invalid who will not admit that he suffers.

His irritation was aggravated by the discovery that Mrs. Marvell and Laura had already begun to treat Paul as if he were an orphan. One day, coming unnoticed into the nursery,

Ralph heard the boy ask when his mother was coming back; and Mrs. Fairford, who was with him, answered: "She's not coming back, dearest; and you're not to speak of her to father."

Ralph, when the boy was out of hearing, rebuked his sister for her answer. "I don't want you to talk of his mother as if she were dead. I don't want you to forbid Paul to speak of her."

Laura, though usually so yielding, defended herself. "What's the use of encouraging him to speak of her when he's never to see her? The sooner he forgets her the better."

Ralph pondered. "Later—if she asks to see him—I shan't refuse."

Mrs. Fairford pressed her lips together to check the answer: "She never will!"

Ralph heard it, nevertheless, and let it pass. Nothing gave him so profound a sense of estrangement from his former life as the conviction that his sister was probably right. He did not really believe that Undine would ever ask to see her boy; but if she did he was determined not to refuse her request.

Time wore on, the Christmas holidays came and went, and the winter continued to grind out the weary measure of its days. Toward the end of January Ralph received a registered letter, addressed to him at his office, and bearing in the corner of the envelope the names of a firm of Sioux Falls attorneys. He instantly divined that it contained the legal notification of his wife's application for divorce, and as he wrote his name in the postman's book he smiled grimly at the thought that the stroke of his pen was doubtless signing her release. He opened the letter, found it to be what he had expected, and locked it away in his desk without mentioning the matter to any one.

He supposed that with the putting away of this document he was thrusting the whole subject out of sight; but not more than a fortnight later, as he sat in the Subway on his way down-town, his eye was caught by his own name on the first page of the heavily head-lined paper which the unshaved occupant of the next seat held between grimy fists. The blood rushed to Ralph's forehead as he looked over the man's arm and read: "Society Leader Gets Decree," and beneath it the subordinate clause: "Says Husband Too Absorbed In Business To Make Home Happy." For weeks afterward, wherever he went, he felt that blush upon his forehead. For the first time in his life the coarse fingering of public curiosity had touched the secret places of his soul, and nothing that had gone before seemed as humiliating as this trivial comment on his tragedy. The paragraph continued on its way through the press, and whenever he took up a newspaper he seemed to come upon it, slightly modified, variously developed, but always reverting with a kind of unctuous irony to his financial preoccupations and his wife's consequent loneliness. The phrase was even taken up by the paragraph writer, called forth excited letters from similarly situated victims, was commented on in humorous editorials and served as a text for pulpit denunciations of the growing craze for wealth; and finally, at his dentist's, Ralph came across it in a Family Weekly, as one of the "Heart problems" propounded to subscribers, with a Gramophone, a Straight-front Corset and a Vanity-box among the prizes offered for its solution.

XXIV

IF YOU'D ONLY had the sense to come straight to me, Undine Spragg! There isn't a tip I couldn't have given you—not one!"

This speech, in which a faintly contemptuous compassion for her friend's case was blent with the frankest pride in her own, probably represented the nearest approach to "tact" that Mrs. James J. Rolliver had yet acquired. Undine was impartial enough to note in it a distinct advance on the youthful methods of Indiana Frusk; yet it required a good deal of self-control to take the words to herself with a smile, while they seemed to be laying a visible scarlet welt across the pale face she kept valiantly turned to her friend. The fact that she must permit herself to be pitied by Indiana Frusk gave her the uttermost measure of the depth to which her fortunes had fallen.

This abasement was inflicted on her in the staring gold apartment of the Hôtel Nouveau Luxe in which the Rollivers had established themselves on their recent arrival in Paris. The vast drawing-room, adorned only by two high-shouldered gilt baskets of orchids drooping on their wires, reminded Undine of the "Looey suite" in which the opening scenes of her own history had been enacted; and the resemblance and the difference were emphasized by the fact that the image of her past self was not inaccurately repeated in the triumphant presence of Indiana Rolliver.

"There isn't a tip I couldn't have given you—not one!" Mrs. Rolliver reproachfully repeated; and all Undine's superiorities and discriminations seemed to shrivel up in the crude blaze of the other's solid achievement.

There was little comfort in noting, for one's private delectation, that Indiana spoke of her husband as "Mr. Rolliver," that she twanged a piercing *r*, that one of her shoulders was still higher than the other, and that her striking dress was totally unsuited to the hour, the place and the occasion. She still did and was all that Undine had so sedulously learned not to be and to do; but to dwell on these obstacles to her success was but to be more deeply impressed by the fact that she had nevertheless succeeded.

Not much more than a year had elapsed since Undine Marvell, sitting in the drawing-room of another Parisian hotel, had heard the immense orchestral murmur of Paris rise through the open windows like the ascending movement of her own hopes. The immense murmur still sounded on, deafening and implacable as some elemental force; and the discord in her fate no more disturbed it than the motor wheels rolling by under the windows were disturbed by the particles of dust that they ground to finer powder as they passed.

"I could have told you one thing right off," Mrs. Rolliver went on with her ringing energy. "And that is, to get your divorce first thing. A divorce is always a good thing to have: you never can tell when you may want it. You ought to have attended to that before you even *began* with Peter Van Degen."

Undine listened, irresistibly impressed. "Did *you?*" she asked; but Mrs. Rolliver, at this, grew suddenly veiled and sibylline. She wound her big bejewelled hand through her pearls—there were ropes and ropes of them—and leaned back, modestly sinking her lids.

"I'm here, anyhow," she rejoined, with *"Circumspice!"* in look and tone.

Undine, obedient to the challenge, continued to gaze at the pearls. They were real; there was no doubt about that. And so was Indiana's marriage—if she kept out of certain states.

"Don't you see," Mrs. Rolliver continued, "that having to leave him when you did, and rush off to Dakota for six months, was—was giving him too much time to think; and giving it at the wrong time, too?"

"Oh, I see. But what could I do? I'm not an immoral woman."

"Of course not, dearest. You were merely thoughtless—that's what I meant by saying you ought to have had your divorce ready."

A flicker of self-esteem caused Undine to protest. "It wouldn't have made any difference. His wife would never have given him up."

"She's so crazy about him?"

"No: she hates him so. And she hates me too, because she's in love with my husband."

Indiana bounced out of her lounging attitude and struck her hands together with a rattle of rings.

"In love with your husband? What's the matter, then? Why on earth didn't the four of you fix it up together?"

"You don't understand." (It was an undoubted relief to be able, at last, to say that to Indiana!) "Clare Van Degen thinks divorce wrong—or rather awfully vulgar."

"*Vulgar?*" Indiana flamed. "If that isn't just too much! A woman who's in love with another woman's husband? What does she think refined, I'd like to know? Having a lover, I suppose—like the women in these nasty French plays? I've told Mr. Rolliver I won't go to the theatre with him again in Paris—it's too utterly low. And the swell society's just as bad: it's simply rotten. Thank goodness I was brought up in a place where there's some sense of decency left!" She looked compassionately at Undine. "It was New York that demoralized you—and I don't blame you for it. Out at Apex you'd have acted different. You never *never* would have given way to your feelings before you'd got your divorce."

A slow blush rose to Undine's forehead.

"He seemed so unhappy——" she murmured.

"Oh, I *know!*" said Indiana in a tone of cold competence. She gave Undine an impatient glance. "What was the understanding between you, when you left Europe last August to go out to Dakota?"

"Peter was to go to Reno in the autumn—so that it wouldn't look too much as if we were acting together. I was to come to Chicago to see him on his way out there."

"And he never came?"

"No."

"And he stopped writing?"

"Oh, he never writes."

Indiana heaved a deep sigh of intelligence. "There's one perfectly clear rule: never let out of your sight a man who doesn't write."

"I know. That's why I stayed with him—those few weeks last summer. . ."

Indiana sat thinking, her fine shallow eyes fixed unblinkingly on her friend's embarrassed face.

"I suppose there isn't anybody else——?"

"Anybody——?"

"Well—now you've got your divorce: anybody else it would come in handy for?"

This was harder to bear than anything that had gone before: Undine could not have borne it if she had not had a purpose. "Mr. Van Degen owes it to me——" she began with an air of wounded dignity.

"Yes, yes: I know. But that's just talk. If there *is* anybody else——"

"I can't imagine what you think of me, Indiana!"

Indiana, without appearing to resent this challenge, again lost herself in meditation.

"Well, I'll tell him he's just *got* to see you," she finally emerged from it to say.

Undine gave a quick upward look: this was what she had been waiting for ever since she had read, a few days earlier, in the columns of her morning journal, that Mr. Peter Van Degen and Mr. and Mrs. James J. Rolliver had been fellow-passengers on board the *Semantic*. But she did not betray her expectations by as much as the tremor of an eye-lash. She knew her friend well enough to pour out to her the expected tribute of surprise.

"Why, do you mean to say you know him, Indiana?"

"Mercy, yes! He's round here all the time. He crossed on the steamer with us, and Mr. Rolliver's taken a fancy to him," Indiana explained, in the tone of the absorbed bride to whom her husband's preferences are the sole criterion.

Undine turned a tear-suffused gaze on her. "Oh, Indiana, if I could only see him again I know it would be all right! He's awfully, awfully fond of me; but his family have influenced him against me——"

"I know what *that* is!" Mrs. Rolliver interjected.

"But perhaps," Undine continued, "it would be better if I could meet him first without his knowing beforehand—without your telling him. . . I love him too much to reproach him!" she added nobly.

Indiana pondered: it was clear that, though the nobility of

the sentiment impressed her, she was disinclined to renounce the idea of taking a more active part in her friend's rehabilitation. But Undine went on: "Of course you've found out by this time that he's just a big spoiled baby. Afterward—when I've seen him—if you'd talk to him; or if you'd only just let him *be* with you, and see how perfectly happy you and Mr. Rolliver are!"

Indiana seized on this at once. "You mean that what he wants is the influence of a home like ours? Yes, yes, I understand. I tell you what I'll do: I'll just ask him round to dine, and let you know the day, without telling him beforehand that you're coming."

"Oh, Indiana!" Undine held her in a close embrace, and then drew away to say: "I'm so glad I found you. You must go round with me everywhere. There are lots of people here I want you to know."

Mrs. Rolliver's expression changed from vague sympathy to concentrated interest. "I suppose it's awfully gay here? Do you go round a great deal with the American set?"

Undine hesitated for a fraction of a moment. "There are a few of them who are rather jolly. But I particularly want you to meet my friend the Marquis Roviano—he's from Rome; and a lovely Austrian woman, Baroness Adelschein."

Her friend's face was brushed by a shade of distrust. "I don't know as I care much about meeting foreigners," she said indifferently.

Undine smiled: it was agreeable at last to be able to give Indiana a "point" as valuable as any of hers on divorce.

"Oh, some of them are awfully attractive; and *they'll* make you meet the Americans."

Indiana caught this on the bound: one began to see why she had got on in spite of everything.

"Of course I'd love to know your friends," she said, kissing Undine; who answered, giving back the kiss: "You know there's nothing on earth I wouldn't do for you."

Indiana drew back to look at her with a comic grimace under which a shade of anxiety was visible. "Well, that's a pretty large order. But there's just one thing you *can* do, dearest: please to let Mr. Rolliver alone!"

"Mr. Rolliver, my dear?" Undine's laugh showed that she

took this for unmixed comedy. "That's a nice way to remind me that you're heaps and heaps better-looking than I am!"

Indiana gave her an acute glance. "Millard Binch didn't think so—not even at the very end."

"Oh, poor Millard!" The women's smiles mingled easily over the common reminiscence, and once again, on the threshold, Undine enfolded her friend.

In the light of the autumn afternoon she paused a moment at the door of the Nouveau Luxe, and looked aimlessly forth at the brave spectacle in which she seemed no longer to have a stake.

Many of her old friends had already returned to Paris: the Harvey Shallums, May Beringer, Dicky Bowles and other westward-bound nomads lingering on for a glimpse of the autumn theatres and fashions before hurrying back to inaugurate the New York season. A year ago Undine would have had no difficulty in introducing Indiana Rolliver to this group—a group above which her own aspirations already beat an impatient wing. Now her place in it had become too precarious for her to force an entrance for her protectress. Her New York friends were at no pains to conceal from her that in their opinion her divorce had been a blunder. Their logic was that of Apex reversed. Since she had not been "sure" of Van Degen, why in the world, they asked, had she thrown away a position she *was* sure of? Mrs. Harvey Shallum, in particular, had not scrupled to put the question squarely. "Chelles was awfully taken—he would have introduced you everywhere. I thought you were wild to know smart French people; I thought Harvey and I weren't good enough for you any longer. And now you've done your best to spoil everything! Of course I feel for you tremendously— that's the reason why I'm talking so frankly. You must be horribly depressed. Come and dine to-night—or no, if you don't mind I'd rather you chose another evening. I'd forgotten that I'd asked the Jim Driscolls, and it might be uncomfortable—for *you* . . ."

In another world she was still welcome, at first perhaps even more so than before: the world, namely, to which she had proposed to present Indiana Rolliver. Roviano, Madame Adelschein, and a few of the freer spirits of her old St. Moritz band, reappearing in Paris with the close of the watering-place season, had quickly discovered her and shown a keen interest in her liberation. It appeared in some mysterious way to make her more available for their purpose, and she found that, in the character of the last American divorcée, she was even regarded as eligible to the small and intimate inner circle of their loosely-knit association. At first she could not make out what had entitled her to this privilege, and increasing enlightenment produced a revolt of the Apex puritanism which, despite some odd accommodations and compliances, still carried its head so high in her.

Undine had been perfectly sincere in telling Indiana Rolliver that she was not "an immoral woman." The pleasures for which her sex took such risks had never attracted her, and she did not even crave the excitement of having it thought that they did. She wanted, passionately and persistently, two things which she believed should subsist together in any well-ordered life: amusement and respectability; and despite her surface-sophistication her notion of amusement was hardly less innocent than when she had hung on the plumber's fence with Indiana Frusk.

It gave her, therefore, no satisfaction to find herself included among Madame Adelschein's intimates. It embarrassed her to feel that she was expected to be "queer" and "different," to respond to pass-words and talk in innuendo, to associate with the equivocal and the subterranean and affect to despise the ingenuous daylight joys which really satisfied her soul. But the business shrewdness which was never quite dormant in her suggested that this was not the moment for such scruples. She must make the best of what she could get and wait her chance of getting something better; and meanwhile the most practical use to which she could put her shady friends was to flash their authentic nobility in the dazzled eyes of Mrs. Rolliver.

With this object in view she made haste, in a fashionable tea-room of the rue de Rivoli, to group about Indiana the most titled members of the band; and the felicity of the occasion would have been unmarred had she not suddenly caught sight of Raymond de Chelles sitting on the other side of the room.

She had not seen Chelles since her return to Paris. It had seemed preferable to leave their meeting to chance, and the present chance might have served as well as another but for the fact that among his companions were two or three of the most eminent ladies of the proud quarter beyond the Seine. It was what Undine, in moments of discouragement, characterized as "her luck" that one of these should be the hated Miss Wincher of Potash Springs, who had now become the Marquise de Trézac. Undine knew that Chelles and his compatriots, however scandalized at her European companions, would be completely indifferent to Mrs. Rolliver's appearance; but one gesture of Madame de Trézac's eye-glass would wave Indiana to her place and thus brand the whole party as " wrong."

All this passed through Undine's mind in the very moment of her noting the change of expression with which Chelles had signalled his recognition. If their encounter could have occurred in happier conditions it might have had far-reaching results. As it was, the crowded state of the tea-room, and the distance between their tables, sufficiently excused his restricting his greeting to an eager bow; and Undine went home heavy-hearted from this first attempt to reconstruct her past.

Her spirits were not lightened by the developments of the next few days. She kept herself well in the foreground of Indiana's life, and cultivated toward the rarely-visible Rolliver a manner in which impersonal admiration for the statesman was tempered with the politest indifference to the man. Indiana seemed to do justice to her efforts and to be reassured by the result; but still there came no hint of a reward. For a time Undine restrained the question on her lips; but one afternoon, when she had inducted Indiana into the deepest mysteries of Parisian complexion-making, the importance of the service and the confidential mood it engendered seemed to warrant a discreet allusion to their bargain.

Indiana leaned back among her cushions with an embarrassed laugh.

"Oh, my dear, I've been meaning to tell you—it's off, I'm afraid. The dinner is, I mean. You see, Mr. Van Degen has seen you 'round with me, and the very minute I asked him to come and dine he guessed——"

"He guessed—and he wouldn't?"

"Well, no. He wouldn't. I hate to tell you."

"Oh——" Undine threw off a vague laugh. "Since you're intimate enough for him to tell you *that* he must have told you more—told you something to justify his behaviour. He couldn't—even Peter Van Degen couldn't—just simply have said to you: 'I won't see her.' "

Mrs. Rolliver hesitated, visibly troubled to the point of regretting her intervention.

"He *did* say more?" Undine insisted. "He gave you a reason?"

"He said you'd know."

"Oh, how base—how base!" Undine was trembling with one of her little-girl rages, the storms of destructive fury before which Mr. and Mrs. Spragg had cowered when she was a charming golden-curled cherub. But life had administered some of the discipline which her parents had spared her, and she pulled herself together with a gasp of pain. "Of course he's been turned against me. His wife has the whole of New York behind her, and I've no one; but I know it would be all right if I could only see him."

Her friend made no answer, and Undine pursued, with an irrepressible outbreak of her old vehemence: "Indiana Rolliver, if you won't do it for me I'll go straight off to his hotel this very minute. I'll wait there in the hall till he sees me!"

Indiana lifted a protesting hand. "Don't, Undine—not that!"

"Why not?"

"Well—I wouldn't, that's all."

"You wouldn't? Why wouldn't you? You must have a reason." Undine faced her with levelled brows. "Without a reason you can't have changed so utterly since our last talk. You were positive enough then that I had a right to make him see me."

Somewhat to her surprise, Indiana made no effort to elude the challenge. "Yes, I did think so then. But I know now that it wouldn't do you the least bit of good."

"Have they turned him so completely against me? I don't care if they have! I know him—I can get him back."

"That's the trouble." Indiana shed on her a gaze of cold compassion. "It's not that any one has turned him against you. It's worse than that——"

"What can be?"

"You'll hate me if I tell you."

"Then you'd better make him tell me himself!"

"I can't. I tried to. The trouble is that it was *you*—something you did, I mean. Something he found out about you——"

Undine, to restrain a spring of anger, had to clutch both arms of her chair. "About me? How fearfully false! Why, I've never even *looked* at anybody——!"

"It's nothing of that kind." Indiana's mournful head-shake seemed to deplore, in Undine, an unsuspected moral obtuseness. "It's the way you acted to your own husband."

"I—my—to Ralph? *He* reproaches me for that? Peter Van Degen does?"

"Well, for one particular thing. He says that the very day you went off with him last year you got a cable from New York telling you to come back at once to Mr. Marvell, who was desperately ill."

"How on earth did he know?" The cry escaped Undine before she could repress it.

"It's true, then?" Indiana exclaimed. "Oh, Undine——"

Undine sat speechless and motionless, the anger frozen to terror on her lips.

Mrs. Rolliver turned on her the reproachful gaze of the deceived benefactress. "I didn't believe it when he told me; I'd never have thought it of you. Before you'd even applied for your divorce!"

Undine made no attempt to deny the charge or to defend herself. For a moment she was lost in the pursuit of an unseizable clue—the explanation of this monstrous last perversity of fate. Suddenly she rose to her feet with a set face.

"The Marvells must have told him—the beasts!" It relieved her to be able to cry it out.

"It was your husband's sister—what did you say her name was? When you didn't answer her cable, she cabled Mr. Van

Degen to find out where you were and tell you to come straight back."

Undine stared. "He never did!"

"No."

"Doesn't that show you the story's all trumped up?"

Indiana shook her head. "He said nothing to you about it because he was with you when you received the first cable, and you told him it was from your sister-in-law, just worrying you as usual to go home; and when he asked if there was anything else in it you said there wasn't another thing."

Undine, intently following her, caught at this with a spring. "Then he knew it all along—he admits that? And it made no earthly difference to him at the time?" She turned almost victoriously on her friend. "Did he happen to explain *that*, I wonder?"

"Yes." Indiana's longanimity grew almost solemn. "It came over him gradually, he said. One day when he wasn't feeling very well he thought to himself: 'Would she act like that to *me* if I was dying?' And after that he never felt the same to you." Indiana lowered her empurpled lids. "Men have their feelings too—even when they're carried away by passion." After a pause she added: "I don't know as I can blame him, Undine. You see, you were his ideal."

XXV

U NDINE MARVELL, for the next few months, tasted all the accumulated bitterness of failure.

After January the drifting hordes of her compatriots had scattered to the four quarters of the globe, leaving Paris to resume, under its low grey sky, its compacter winter personality. Noting, from her more and more deserted corner, each least sign of the social revival, Undine felt herself as stranded and baffled as after the ineffectual summers of her girlhood. She was not without possible alternatives; but the sense of what she had lost took the savour from all that was left. She might have attached herself to some migratory group winged for Italy or Egypt; but the prospect of travel did not in itself appeal to her, and she was doubtful of its social benefit. She lacked the adventurous curiosity which seeks its occasion in the unknown; and though she could work doggedly for a given object the obstacles to be overcome had to be as distinct as the prize.

Her one desire was to get back an equivalent of the precise value she had lost in ceasing to be Ralph Marvell's wife. Her new visiting-card, bearing her Christian name in place of her husband's, was like the coin of a debased currency testifying to her diminished trading capacity. Her restricted means, her vacant days, all the minor irritations of her life, were as nothing compared to this sense of a lost advantage. Even in the narrowed field of a Parisian winter she might have made herself a place in some more or less extra-social world; but her experiments in this line gave her no pleasure proportioned to the possible derogation. She feared to be associated with "the wrong people," and scented a shade of disrespect in every amicable advance. The more pressing attentions of one or two men she had formerly known filled her with a glow of outraged pride, and for the first time in her life she felt that even solitude might be preferable to certain kinds of society.

Since ill health was the most plausible pretext for seclusion, it was almost a relief to find that she was really growing "nervous" and sleeping badly. The doctor she summoned advised her trying a small quiet place on the Riviera, not too near the

sea; and thither, in the early days of December, she transported herself with her maid and an omnibus-load of luggage.

The place disconcerted her by being really small and quiet,
and for a few days she struggled against the desire for flight.
She had never before known a world as colourless and negative as that of the large white hotel where everybody went to
bed at nine, and donkey-rides over stony hills were the only
alternative to slow drives along dusty roads. Many of the
dwellers in this temple of repose found even these exercises
too stimulating, and preferred to sit for hours under the
palms in the garden, playing Patience, embroidering, or reading odd volumes of Tauchnitz. Undine, driven by despair to
an inspection of the hotel book-shelves, discovered that
scarcely any work they contained was complete; but this did
not seem to trouble the readers, who continued to feed their
leisure with mutilated fiction, from which they occasionally
raised their eyes to glance mistrustfully at the new arrival
sweeping the garden gravel with her frivolous draperies. The
inmates of the hotel were of different nationalities, but their
racial differences were levelled by the stamp of a common mediocrity. All differences of tongue, of custom, of physiognomy, disappeared in this deep community of insignificance,
which was like some secret bond, with the manifold signs and
pass-words of its ignorances and its imperceptions. It was not
the heterogeneous mediocrity of the American summer hotel,
where the lack of any standard is the nearest approach to a
tie, but an organized codified dulness, in conscious possession
of its rights, and strong in the voluntary ignorance of any
others.

It took Undine a long time to accustom herself to such an
atmosphere, and meanwhile she fretted, fumed and flaunted,
or abandoned herself to long periods of fruitless brooding.
Sometimes a flame of anger shot up in her, dismally illuminating the path she had travelled and the blank wall to which
it led. At other moments past and present were enveloped in
a dull fog of rancour which distorted and faded even the image she presented to her morning mirror. There were days
when every young face she saw left in her a taste of poison.
But when she compared herself with the specimens of her sex
who plied their languid industries under the palms, or looked

away as she passed them in hall or staircase, her spirits rose, and she rang for her maid and dressed herself in her newest and vividest. These were unprofitable triumphs, however. She never made one of her attacks on the organized disapproval of the community without feeling she had lost ground by it; and the next day she would lie in bed and send down capricious orders for food, which her maid would presently remove untouched, with instructions to transmit her complaints to the landlord.

Sometimes the events of the past year, ceaselessly revolving through her brain, became no longer a subject for criticism or justification but simply a series of pictures monotonously unrolled. Hour by hour, in such moods, she re-lived the incidents of her flight with Peter Van Degen: the part of her career that, since it had proved a failure, seemed least like herself and most difficult to justify. She had gone away with him, and had lived with him for two months: she, Undine Marvell, to whom respectability was the breath of life, to whom such follies had always been unintelligible and therefore inexcusable.—She had done this incredible thing, and she had done it from a motive that seemed, at the time, as clear, as logical, as free from the distorting mists of sentimentality, as any of her father's financial enterprises. It had been a bold move, but it had been as carefully calculated as the happiest Wall Street "stroke." She had gone away with Peter because, after the decisive scene in which she had put her power to the test, to yield to him seemed the surest means of victory. Even to her practical intelligence it was clear that an immediate dash to Dakota might look too calculated; and she had preserved her self-respect by telling herself that she was really his wife, and in no way to blame if the law delayed to ratify the bond.

She was still persuaded of the justness of her reasoning; but she now saw that it had left certain risks out of account. Her life with Van Degen had taught her many things. The two had wandered from place to place, spending a great deal of money, always more and more money; for the first time in her life she had been able to buy everything she wanted. For a while this had kept her amused and busy; but presently she began to perceive that her companion's view of their relation was not the same as hers. She saw that he had always meant it to be an unavowed tie, screened by Mrs. Shallum's companionship and Clare's careless tolerance; and that on those terms he would have been ready to shed on their adventure the brightest blaze of notoriety. But since Undine had insisted on being carried off like a sentimental school-girl he meant to shroud the affair in mystery, and was as zealous in concealing their relation as she was bent on proclaiming it. In the "powerful" novels which Popple was fond of lending her she had met with increasing frequency the type of heroine who scorns to love clandestinely, and proclaims the sanctity of passion and the moral duty of obeying its call. Undine had been struck by these arguments as justifying and even ennobling her course, and had let Peter understand that she had been actuated by the highest motives in openly associating her life with his; but he had opposed a placid insensibility to these allusions, and had persisted in treating her as though their journey were the kind of escapade that a man of the world is bound to hide. She had expected him to take her to all the showy places where couples like themselves are relieved from a too sustained contemplation of nature by the distractions of the restaurant and the gaming-table; but he had carried her from one obscure corner of Europe to another, shunning fashionable hotels and crowded watering-places, and displaying an ingenuity in the discovery of the unvisited and the out-of-season that gave their journey an odd resemblance to her melancholy wedding-tour.

She had never for a moment ceased to remember that the Dakota divorce-court was the objective point of this later honeymoon, and her allusions to the fact were as frequent as prudence permitted. Peter seemed in no way disturbed by them. He responded with expressions of increasing tenderness, or the purchase of another piece of jewelry; and though Undine could not remember his ever voluntarily bringing up the subject of their marriage he did not shrink from her recurring mention of it. He seemed merely too steeped in present well-being to think of the future; and she ascribed this to the fact that his faculty of enjoyment could not project itself beyond the moment. Her business was to make each of their days so agreeable that when the last came he should be conscious of a void to be bridged over as rapidly as possible; and when she thought this point had been reached she packed her trunks and started for Dakota.

The next picture to follow was that of the dull months in the western divorce-town, where, to escape loneliness and avoid comment, she had cast in her lot with Mabel Lipscomb, who had lately arrived there on the same errand.

Undine, at the outset, had been sorry for the friend whose new venture seemed likely to result so much less brilliantly than her own; but compassion had been replaced by irritation as Mabel's unpruned vulgarities, her enormous encroaching satisfaction with herself and her surroundings, began to pervade every corner of their provisional household. Undine, during the first months of her exile, had been sustained by the fullest confidence in her future. When she had parted from Van Degen she had felt sure he meant to marry her, and the fact that Mrs. Lipscomb was fortified by no similar hope made her easier to bear with. Undine was almost ashamed that the unwooed Mabel should be the witness of her own felicity, and planned to send her off on a trip to Denver when Peter should announce his arrival; but the weeks passed, and Peter did not come. Mabel, on the whole, behaved well in this contingency. Undine, in her first exultation, had confided all her hopes and plans to her friend, but Mabel took no undue advantage of the confidence. She was even tactful in her loud fond clumsy way, with a tact that insistently boomed and buzzed about its victim's head. But one day she mentioned that she had asked to dinner a gentleman from Little Rock who had come to Dakota with the same object as themselves, and whose acquaintance she had made through her lawyer.

The gentleman from Little Rock came to dine, and within a week Undine understood that Mabel's future was assured. If Van Degen had been at hand Undine would have smiled with him at poor Mabel's infatuation and her suitor's crudeness. But Van Degen was not there. He made no sign, he sent no excuse; he simply continued to absent himself; and it was Undine who, in due course, had to make way for Mrs.

Lipscomb's caller, and sit upstairs with a novel while the drawing-room below was given up to the enacting of an actual love-story.

Even then, even to the end, Undine had to admit that Mabel had behaved "beautifully." But it is comparatively easy to behave beautifully when one is getting what one wants, and when some one else, who has not always been altogether kind, is not. The net result of Mrs. Lipscomb's magnanimity was that when, on the day of parting, she drew Undine to her bosom with the hand on which her new engagement-ring blazed, Undine hated her as she hated everything else connected with her vain exile in the wilderness.

XXVI

THE NEXT PHASE in the unrolling vision was the episode of her return to New York. She had gone to the Malibran, to her parents—for it was a moment in her career when she clung passionately to the conformities, and when the fact of being able to say: "I'm here with my father and mother" was worth paying for even in the discomfort of that grim abode. Nevertheless, it was another thorn in her pride that her parents could not—for the meanest of material reasons—transfer themselves at her coming to one of the big Fifth Avenue hotels. When she had suggested it Mr. Spragg had briefly replied that, owing to the heavy expenses of her divorce suit, he couldn't for the moment afford anything better; and this announcement cast a deeper gloom over the future.

It was not an occasion for being "nervous," however; she had learned too many hard facts in the last few months to think of having recourse to her youthful methods. And something told her that if she made the attempt it would be useless. Her father and mother seemed much older, seemed tired and defeated, like herself.

Parents and daughter bore their common failure in a common silence, broken only by Mrs. Spragg's occasional tentative allusions to her grandson. But her anecdotes of Paul left a deeper silence behind them. Undine did not want to talk of her boy. She could forget him when, as she put it, things were "going her way," but in moments of discouragement the thought of him was an added bitterness, subtly different from her other bitter thoughts, and harder to quiet. It had not occurred to her to try to gain possession of the child. She was vaguely aware that the courts had given her his custody; but she had never seriously thought of asserting this claim. Her parents' diminished means and her own uncertain future made her regard the care of Paul as an additional burden, and she quieted her scruples by thinking of him as "better off" with Ralph's family, and of herself as rather touchingly disinterested in putting his welfare before her own. Poor Mrs. Spragg was pining for him, but Undine rejected her artless suggestion that Mrs. Heeny should be sent to "bring him round." "I wouldn't ask them a favour for the world—they're just waiting for a chance to be hateful to me," she scornfully declared; but it pained her that her boy should be so near, yet inaccessible, and for the first time she was visited by unwonted questionings as to her share in the misfortunes that had befallen her. She had voluntarily stepped out of her social frame, and the only person on whom she could with any satisfaction have laid the blame was the person to whom her mind now turned with a belated tenderness. It was thus, in fact, that she thought of Ralph. His pride, his reserve, all the secret expressions of his devotion, the tones of his voice, his quiet manner, even his disconcerting irony: these seemed, in contrast to what she had since known, the qualities essential to her happiness. She could console herself only by regarding it as part of her sad lot that poverty, and the relentless animosity of his family, should have put an end to so perfect a union: she gradually began to look on herself and Ralph as the victims of dark machinations, and when she mentioned him she spoke forgivingly, and implied that "everything might have been different" if "people" had not "come between" them.

She had arrived in New York in midseason, and the dread of seeing familiar faces kept her shut up in her room at the Malibran, reading novels and brooding over possibilities of escape. She tried to avoid the daily papers, but they formed the staple diet of her parents, and now and then she could not help taking one up and turning to the "Society Column." Its perusal produced the impression that the season must be the gayest New York had ever known. The Harmon B. Driscolls, young Jim and his wife, the Thurber Van Degens, the Chauncey Ellings, and all the other Fifth Avenue potentates, seemed to have their doors perpetually open to a stream of feasters among whom the familiar presences of Grace Beringer, Bertha Shallum, Dicky Bowles and Claud Walsingham Popple came and went with the irritating sameness of the figures in a stage-procession.

Among them also Peter Van Degen presently appeared. He had been on a tour around the world, and Undine could not look at a newspaper without seeing some allusion to his progress. After his return she noticed that his name was usually coupled with his wife's: he and Clare seemed to be celebrating his home-coming in a series of festivities, and Undine guessed that he had reasons for wishing to keep before the world the evidences of his conjugal accord.

Mrs. Heeny's clippings supplied her with such items as her own reading missed; and one day the masseuse appeared with a long article from the leading journal of Little Rock, describing the brilliant nuptials of Mabel Lipscomb—now Mrs. Homer Branney—and her departure for "the Coast" in the bridegroom's private car. This put the last touch to Undine's irritation, and the next morning she got up earlier than usual, put on her most effective dress, went for a quick walk around the Park, and told her father when she came in that she wanted him to take her to the opera that evening.

Mr. Spragg stared and frowned. "You mean you want me to go round and hire a box for you?"

"Oh, no." Undine coloured at the infelicitous allusion: besides, she knew now that the smart people who were "musical" went in stalls.

"I only want two good seats. I don't see why I should stay shut up. I want you to go with me," she added.

Her father received the latter part of the request without comment: he seemed to have gone beyond surprise. But he appeared that evening at dinner in a creased and loosely fitting dress-suit which he had probably not put on since the last time he had dined with his son-in-law, and he and Undine drove off together, leaving Mrs. Spragg to gaze after them with the pale stare of Hecuba.

Their stalls were in the middle of the house, and around them swept the great curve of boxes at which Undine had so often looked up in the remote Stentorian days. Then all had been one indistinguishable glitter, now the scene was full of familiar details: the house was thronged with people she knew, and every box seemed to contain a parcel of her past. At first she had shrunk from recognition; but gradually, as she perceived that no one noticed her, that she was merely part of the invisible crowd out of range of the exploring opera glasses, she felt a defiant desire to make herself seen. When the performance was over her father wanted to leave the house by the door at which they had entered, but she guided him toward the stockholders' entrance, and pressed her way among the furred and jewelled ladies waiting for their motors. "Oh, it's the wrong door—never mind, we'll walk to the corner and get a cab," she exclaimed, speaking loudly enough to be overheard. Two or three heads turned, and she met Dicky Bowles's glance, and returned his laughing bow. The woman talking to him looked around, coloured slightly, and made a barely perceptible motion of her head. Just beyond her, Mrs. Chauncey Elling, plumed and purple, stared, parted her lips, and turned to say something important to young Jim Driscoll, who looked up involuntarily and then squared his shoulders and gazed fixedly at a distant point, as people do at a funeral. Behind them Undine caught sight of Clare Van Degen; she stood alone, and her face was pale and listless. "Shall I go up and speak to her?" Undine wondered. Some intuition told her that, alone of all the women present, Clare might have greeted her kindly; but she hung back, and Mrs. Harmon Driscoll surged by on Popple's arm. Popple crimsoned, coughed, and signalled despotically to Mrs. Driscoll's footman. Over his shoulder Undine received a bow from Charles Bowen, and behind Bowen she saw two or three other men she knew, and read in their faces surprise, curiosity, and the wish to show their pleasure at seeing her. But she grasped her father's arm and drew him out among the entangled motors and vociferating policemen.

Neither she nor Mr. Spragg spoke a word on the way home; but when they reached the Malibran her father followed her up to her room. She had dropped her cloak and stood before the wardrobe mirror studying her reflection when he came up behind her and she saw that he was looking at it too.

"Where did that necklace come from?"

Undine's neck grew pink under the shining circlet. It was the first time since her return to New York that she had put on a low dress and thus uncovered the string of pearls she always wore. She made no answer, and Mr. Spragg continued: "Did your husband give them to you?"

"*Ralph!*" She could not restrain a laugh.

"Who did, then?"

Undine remained silent. She really had not thought about

the pearls, except in so far as she consciously enjoyed the pleasure of possessing them; and her father, habitually so unobservant, had seemed the last person likely to raise the awkward question of their origin.

"Why——" she began, without knowing what she meant to say.

"I guess you better send 'em back to the party they belong to," Mr. Spragg continued, in a voice she did not know.

"They belong to me!" she flamed up.

He looked at her as if she had grown suddenly small and insignificant. "You better send 'em back to Peter Van Degen the first thing to-morrow morning," he said as he went out of the room.

As far as Undine could remember, it was the first time in her life that he had ever ordered her to do anything; and when the door closed on him she had the distinct sense that the question had closed with it, and that she would have to obey. She took the pearls off and threw them from her angrily. The humiliation her father had inflicted on her was merged with the humiliation to which she had subjected herself in going to the opera, and she had never before hated her life as she hated it then.

All night she lay sleepless, wondering miserably what to do; and out of her hatred of her life, and her hatred of Peter Van Degen, there gradually grew a loathing of Van Degen's pearls. How could she have kept them, how have continued to wear them about her neck? Only her absorption in other cares could have kept her from feeling the humiliation of carrying about with her the price of her shame. Her novel-reading had filled her mind with the vocabulary of outraged virtue, and with pathetic allusions to woman's frailty, and while she pitied herself she thought her father heroic. She was proud to think that she had such a man to defend her, and rejoiced that it was in her power to express her scorn of Van Degen by sending back his jewels.

But her righteous ardour gradually cooled, and she was left once more to face the dreary problem of the future. Her evening at the opera had shown her the impossibility of remaining in New York. She had neither the skill nor the power to fight the forces of indifference leagued against her: she must get away at once, and try to make a fresh start. But, as usual, the lack of money hampered her. Mr. Spragg could no longer afford to make her the allowance she had intermittently received from him during the first years of her marriage, and since she was now without child or household she could hardly make it a grievance that he had reduced her income. But what he allowed her, even with the addition of her alimony, was absurdly insufficient. Not that she looked far ahead; she had always felt herself predestined to ease and luxury, and the possibility of a future adapted to her present budget did not occur to her. But she desperately wanted enough money to carry her without anxiety through the coming year.

When her breakfast tray was brought in she sent it away untouched and continued to lie in her darkened room. She knew that when she got up she must send back the pearls; but there was no longer any satisfaction in the thought, and she lay listlessly wondering how she could best transmit them to Van Degen.

As she lay there she heard Mrs. Heeny's voice in the passage. Hitherto she had avoided the masseuse, as she did every one else associated with her past. Mrs. Heeny had behaved with extreme discretion, refraining from all direct allusions to Undine's misadventure; but her silence was obviously the criticism of a superior mind. Once again Undine had disregarded her injunction to "go slow," with results that justified the warning. Mrs. Heeny's very reserve, however, now marked her as a safe adviser; and Undine sprang up and called her in.

"My sakes, Undine! You look's if you'd been setting up all night with a remains!" the masseuse exclaimed in her round rich tones.

Undine, without answering, caught up the pearls and thrust them into Mrs. Heeny's hands.

"Good land alive!" The masseuse dropped into a chair and let the twist slip through her fat flexible fingers. "Well, you got a fortune right round your neck whenever you wear them, Undine Spragg."

Undine murmured something indistinguishable. "I want you to take them——" she began.

"Take 'em? Where to?"

"Why, to——" She was checked by the wondering simplicity of Mrs. Heeny's stare. The masseuse must know where the pearls had come from, yet it had evidently not occurred to her that Mrs. Marvell was about to ask her to return them to their donor. In the light of Mrs. Heeny's unclouded gaze the whole episode took on a different aspect, and Undine began to be vaguely astonished at her immediate submission to her father's will. The pearls were hers, after all!

"To be re-strung?" Mrs. Heeny placidly suggested. "Why, you'd oughter to have it done right here before your eyes, with pearls that are worth what these are."

As Undine listened, a new thought shaped itself. She could not continue to wear the pearls: the idea had become intolerable. But for the first time she saw what they might be converted into, and what they might rescue her from; and suddenly she brought out: "Do you suppose I could get anything for them?"

"Get anything? Why, what——"

"Anything like what they're worth, I mean. They cost a lot of money: they came from the biggest place in Paris." Under Mrs. Heeny's simplifying eye it was comparatively easy to make these explanations. "I want you to try and sell them for me—I want you to do the best you can with them. I can't do it myself—but you must swear you'll never tell a soul," she pressed on breathlessly.

"Why, you poor child—it ain't the first time," said Mrs. Heeny, coiling the pearls in her big palm. "It's a pity too: they're such beauties. But you'll get others," she added, as the necklace vanished into her bag.

A few days later there appeared from the same receptacle a bundle of banknotes considerable enough to quiet Undine's last scruples. She no longer understood why she had hesitated. Why should she have thought it necessary to give back the pearls to Van Degen? His obligation to her represented far more than the relatively small sum she had been able to realize on the necklace. She hid the money in her dress, and when Mrs. Heeny had gone on to Mrs. Spragg's room she drew the packet out, and counting the bills over, murmured to herself: "Now I can get away!"

Her one thought was to return to Europe; but she did not

want to go alone. The vision of her solitary figure adrift in
the spring mob of trans-Atlantic pleasure-seekers depressed
and mortified her. She would be sure to run across acquaintances, and they would infer that she was in quest of a new
opportunity, a fresh start, and would suspect her of trying to
use them for the purpose. The thought was repugnant to her
newly awakened pride, and she decided that if she went to
Europe her father and mother must go with her. The project
was a bold one, and when she broached it she had to run the
whole gamut of Mr. Spragg's irony. He wanted to know
what she expected to do with him when she got him there;
whether she meant to introduce him to "all those old Kings,"
how she thought he and her mother would look in court
dress, and how she supposed he was going to get on without
his New York paper. But Undine had been aware of having
what he himself would have called "a pull" over her father
since, the day after their visit to the opera, he had taken her
aside to ask: "You sent back those pearls?" and she had answered coldly: "Mrs. Heeny's taken them."

After a moment of half-bewildered resistance her parents,
perhaps secretly flattered by this first expression of her need
for them, had yielded to her entreaty, packed their trunks,
and stoically set out for the unknown. Neither Mr. Spragg
nor his wife had ever before been out of their country; and
Undine had not understood, till they stood beside her
tongue-tied and helpless on the dock at Cherbourg, the task
she had undertaken in uprooting them. Mr. Spragg had never
been physically active, but on foreign shores he was seized by
a strange restlessness, and a helpless dependence on his
daughter. Mrs. Spragg's long habit of apathy was overcome
by her dread of being left alone when her husband and Undine went out, and she delayed and impeded their expeditions
by insisting on accompanying them; so that, much as Undine
disliked sight-seeing, there seemed no alternative between
"going round" with her parents and shutting herself up with
them in the crowded hotels to which she successively transported them.

The hotels were the only European institutions that really
interested Mr. Spragg. He considered them manifestly inferior to those at home; but he was haunted by a statistical

curiosity as to their size, their number, their cost and their capacity for housing and feeding the incalculable hordes of his countrymen. He went through galleries, churches and museums in a stolid silence like his daughter's; but in the hotels he never ceased to enquire and investigate, questioning every one who could speak English, comparing bills, collecting prospectuses and computing the cost of construction and the probable return on the investment. He regarded the non-existence of the cold-storage system as one more proof of European inferiority, and no longer wondered, in the absence of the room-to-room telephone, that foreigners hadn't yet mastered the first principles of time-saving.

After a few weeks it became evident to both parents and daughter that their unnatural association could not continue much longer. Mrs. Spragg's shrinking from everything new and unfamiliar had developed into a kind of settled terror, and Mr. Spragg had begun to be depressed by the incredible number of the hotels and their simply incalculable housing capacity.

"It ain't that they're any great shakes in themselves, any one of 'em; but there's such a darned lot of 'em: they're as thick as mosquitoes, every place you go." And he began to reckon up, on slips of paper, on the backs of bills and the margins of old newspapers, the number of travellers who could be simultaneously lodged, bathed and boarded on the continent of Europe. "Five hundred bedrooms—three hundred bath-rooms—no; three hundred and fifty bath-rooms, that one has: that makes, supposing two-thirds of 'em double up—do you s'pose as many as that do, Undie? That porter at Lucerne told me the Germans slept three in a room—well, call it eight hundred people; and three meals a day per head; no, four meals, with that afternoon tea they take; and the last place we were at—'way up on that mountain there—why, there were seventy-five hotels in that one spot alone, and all jam full— well, it beats me to know where all the people come from. . ."

He had gone on in this fashion for what seemed to his daughter an endless length of days; and then suddenly he had roused himself to say: "See here, Undie, I got to go back and make the money to pay for all this."

There had been no question on the part of any of the three of Undine's returning with them; and after she had conveyed them to their steamer, and seen their vaguely relieved faces merged in the handkerchief-waving throng along the taffrail, she had returned alone to Paris and made her unsuccessful attempt to enlist the aid of Indiana Rolliver.

XXVII

SHE WAS STILL brooding over this last failure when one afternoon, as she loitered on the hotel terrace, she was approached by a young woman whom she had seen sitting near the wheeled chair of an old lady wearing a crumpled black bonnet under a funny fringed parasol with a jointed handle.

The young woman, who was small, slight and brown, was dressed with a disregard of the fashion which contrasted oddly with the mauve powder on her face and the traces of artificial colour in her dark untidy hair. She looked as if she might have several different personalities, and as if the one of the moment had been hanging up a long time in her wardrobe and been hurriedly taken down as probably good enough for the present occasion.

With her hands in her jacket pockets, and an agreeable smile on her boyish face, she strolled up to Undine and asked, in a pretty variety of Parisian English, if she had the pleasure of speaking to Mrs. Marvell.

On Undine's assenting, the smile grew more alert and the lady continued: "I think you know my friend Sacha Adelschein?"

No question could have been less welcome to Undine. If there was one point on which she was doggedly and puritanically resolved, it was that no extremes of social adversity should ever again draw her into the group of people among whom Madame Adelschein too conspicuously figured. Since her unsuccessful attempt to win over Indiana by introducing her to that group, Undine had been righteously resolved to remain aloof from it; and she was drawing herself up to her loftiest height of disapproval when the stranger, as if unconscious of it, went on: "Sacha speaks of you so often—she admires you so much.—I think you know also my cousin Chelles," she added, looking into Undine's eyes. "I am the Princess Estradina. I've come here with my mother for the air."

The murmur of negation died on Undine's lips. She found herself grappling with a new social riddle, and such surprises were always stimulating. The name of the untidy-looking young woman she had been about to repel was one of the most eminent in the impregnable quarter beyond the Seine. No one figured more largely in the Parisian chronicle than the Princess Estradina, and no name more impressively headed the list at every marriage, funeral and philanthropic entertainment of the Faubourg Saint Germain than that of her mother, the Duchesse de Dordogne, who must be no other than the old woman sitting in the Bath-chair with the crumpled bonnet and the ridiculous sunshade.

But it was not the appearance of the two ladies that surprised Undine. She knew that social gold does not always glitter, and that the lady she had heard spoken of as Lili Estradina was notoriously careless of the conventions; but that she should boast of her intimacy with Madame Adelschein, and use it as a pretext for naming herself, overthrew all Undine's hierarchies.

"Yes—it's hideously dull here, and I'm dying of it. Do come over and speak to my mother. She's dying of it too; but don't tell her so, because she hasn't found it out. There were so many things our mothers never found out," the Princess rambled on, with her half-mocking half-intimate smile; and in another moment Undine, thrilled at having Mrs. Spragg thus coupled with a Duchess, found herself seated between mother and daughter, and responding by a radiant blush to the elder lady's amiable opening: "You know my nephew Raymond—he's your great admirer."

How had it happened, whither would it lead, how long could it last? The questions raced through Undine's brain as she sat listening to her new friends—they seemed already too friendly to be called acquaintances!—replying to their enquiries, and trying to think far enough ahead to guess what they would expect her to say, and what tone it would be well to take. She was used to such feats of mental agility, and it was instinctive with her to become, for the moment, the person she thought her interlocutors expected her to be; but she had never had quite so new a part to play at such short notice. She took her cue, however, from the fact that the Princess Estradina, in her mother's presence, made no farther allusion to her dear friend Sacha, and seemed some-

how, though she continued to chat on in the same easy
strain, to look differently and throw out different implications. All these shades of demeanour were immediately perceptible to Undine, who tried to adapt herself to them by
combining in her manner a mixture of Apex dash and New
York dignity; and the result was so successful that when she
rose to go the Princess, with a hand on her arm, said almost
wistfully: "You're staying on too? Then do take pity on us!
We might go on some trips together; and in the evenings we
could make a bridge."

A new life began for Undine. The Princess, chained to her
mother's side, and frankly restive under her filial duty, clung
to her new acquaintance with a persistence too flattering to
be analyzed. "My dear, I was on the brink of suicide when I
saw your name in the visitors' list," she explained; and Undine felt like answering that she had nearly reached the same
pass when the Princess's thin little hand had been held out to
her. For the moment she was dizzy with the effect of that
random gesture. Here she was, at the lowest ebb of her fortunes, miraculously rehabilitated, reinstated, and restored to
the old victorious sense of her youth and her power! Her sole
graces, her unaided personality, had worked the miracle; how
should she not trust in them hereafter?

Aside from her feeling of concrete attainment, Undine was
deeply interested in her new friends. The Princess and her
mother, in their different ways, were different from any one
else she had known. The Princess, who might have been of
any age between twenty and forty, had a small triangular face
with caressing impudent eyes, a smile like a silent whistle and
the gait of a baker's boy balancing his basket. She wore either
baggy shabby clothes like a man's, or rich draperies that
looked as if they had been rained on; and she seemed equally
at ease in either style of dress, and carelessly unconscious of
both. She was extremely familiar and unblushingly inquisi-
tive, but she never gave Undine the time to ask her any questions or the opportunity to venture on any freedom with her.
Nevertheless she did not scruple to talk of her sentimental
experiences, and seemed surprised, and rather disappointed,
that Undine had so few to relate in return. She playfully
accused her beautiful new friend of being *cachottière*, and at

the sight of Undine's blush cried out: "Ah, you funny Americans! Why do you all behave as if love were a secret infirmity?"

The old Duchess was even more impressive, because she fitted better into Undine's preconceived picture of the Faubourg Saint Germain, and was more like the people with whom she pictured the former Nettie Wincher as living in privileged intimacy. The Duchess was, indeed, more amiable and accessible than Undine's conception of a Duchess, and displayed a curiosity as great as her daughter's, and much more puerile, concerning her new friend's history and habits. But through her mild prattle, and in spite of her limited perceptions, Undine felt in her the same clear impenetrable barrier that she ran against occasionally in the Princess; and she was beginning to understand that this barrier represented a number of things about which she herself had yet to learn. She would not have known this a few years earlier, nor would she have seen in the Duchess anything but the ruin of an ugly woman, dressed in clothes that Mrs. Spragg wouldn't have touched. The Duchess certainly looked like a ruin; but Undine now saw that she looked like the ruin of a castle.

The Princess, who was unofficially separated from her husband, had with her her two little girls. She seemed extremely attached to both—though avowing for the younger a preference she frankly ascribed to the interesting accident of its parentage—and she could not understand that Undine, as to whose domestic difficulties she minutely informed herself, should have consented to leave her child to strangers. "For, to one's child, every one but one's self is a stranger; and whatever your *égarements*——" she began, breaking off with a stare when Undine interrupted her to explain that the courts had ascribed all the wrongs in the case to her husband. "But then—but then——" murmured the Princess, turning away from the subject as if checked by too deep an abyss of difference.

The incident had embarrassed Undine, and though she tried to justify herself by allusions to her boy's dependence on his father's family, and to the duty of not standing in his way, she saw that she made no impression. "Whatever one's errors, one's child belongs to one," her hearer continued to repeat; and Undine, who was frequently scandalized by the Princess's conversation, now found herself in the odd position of having to set a watch upon her own in order not to scandalize the Princess.

Each day, nevertheless, strengthened her hold on her new friends. After her first flush of triumph she began indeed to suspect that she had been a slight disappointment to the Princess, had not completely justified the hopes raised by the doubtful honour of being one of Sacha Adelschein's intimates. Undine guessed that the Princess had expected to find her more amusing, "queerer," more startling in speech and conduct. Though by instinct she was none of these things, she was eager to go as far as was expected; but she felt that her audacities were on lines too normal to be interesting, and that the Princess thought her rather school-girlish and old-fashioned. Still, they had in common their youth, their boredom, their high spirits and their hunger for amusement; and Undine was making the most of these ties when one day, coming back from a trip to Monte-Carlo with the Princess, she was brought up short by the sight of a lady—evidently a new arrival—who was seated in an attitude of respectful intimacy beside the old Duchess's chair. Undine, advancing unheard over the fine gravel of the garden path, recognized at a glance the Marquise de Trézac's drooping nose and disdainful back, and at the same moment heard her say: "—And her husband?"

"Her husband? But she's an American—she's divorced," the Duchess replied, as if she were merely stating the same fact in two different ways; and Undine stopped short with a pang of apprehension.

The Princess came up behind her. "Who's the solemn person with Mamma? Ah, that old bore of a Trézac!" She dropped her long eye-glass with a laugh. "Well, she'll be useful—she'll stick to Mamma like a leech, and we shall get away oftener. Come, let's go and be charming to her."

She approached Madame de Trézac effusively, and after an interchange of exclamations Undine heard her say: "You know my friend Mrs. Marvell? No? How odd! Where do you manage to hide yourself, *chère Madame*? Undine, here's a compatriot who hasn't the pleasure——"

"I'm such a hermit, dear Mrs. Marvell—the Princess shows me what I miss," the Marquise de Trézac murmured, rising to give her hand to Undine, and speaking in a voice so different from that of the supercilious Miss Wincher that only her facial angle and the droop of her nose linked her to the hated vision of Potash Springs.

Undine felt herself dancing on a flood-tide of security. For the first time the memory of Potash Springs became a thing to smile at, and with the Princess's arm through hers she shone back triumphantly on Madame de Trézac, who seemed to have grown suddenly obsequious and insignificant, as though the waving of the Princess's wand had stripped her of all her false advantages.

But upstairs, in her own room, Undine's courage fell. Madame de Trézac had been civil, effusive even, because for the moment she had been taken off her guard by finding Mrs. Marvell on terms of intimacy with the Princess Estradina and her mother. But the force of facts would reassert itself. Far from continuing to see Undine through her French friends' eyes she would probably invite them to view her compatriot through the searching lens of her own ampler information. "The old hypocrite—she'll tell them everything," Undine murmured, wincing at the recollection of the dentist's assistant from Deposit, and staring miserably at her reflection in the dressing-table mirror. Of what use were youth and grace and good looks, if one drop of poison distilled from the envy of a narrow-minded woman was enough to paralyze them? Of course Madame de Trézac knew and remembered, and, secure in her own impregnable position, would never rest till she had driven out the intruder.

XXVIII

W^HAT DO YOU say to Nice to-morrow, dearest?" the Princess suggested a few evenings later, as she followed Undine upstairs after a languid evening at bridge with the Duchess and Madame de Trézac.

Half-way down the passage she stopped to open a door and, putting her finger to her lip, signed to Undine to enter. In the taper-lit dimness stood two small white beds, each surmounted by a crucifix and a palm-branch, and each containing a small brown sleeping child with a mop of hair and a curiously finished little face. As the Princess stood gazing on their innocent slumbers she seemed for a moment like a third little girl, scarcely bigger and browner than the others; and the smile with which she watched them was as clear as theirs.

"Ah, si seulement je pouvais choisir leurs amants!" she sighed as she turned away.

"—Nice to-morrow," she repeated, as she and Undine walked on to their rooms with linked arms. "We may as well make hay while the Trézac shines. She bores Mamma frightfully, but Mamma won't admit it because they belong to the same *œuvres*. Shall it be the eleven train, dear? We can lunch at the *Royal* and look in the shops—we may meet somebody amusing. Anyhow, it's better than staying here!"

Undine was sure the trip to Nice would be delightful. Their previous expeditions had shown her the Princess's faculty for organizing such adventures. At Monte-Carlo, a few days before, they had run across two or three amusing but unassorted people, and the Princess, having fused them in a jolly lunch, had followed it up by a bout at baccarat, and, finally hunting down an eminent composer who had just arrived to rehearse a new production, had insisted on his asking the party to tea, and treating them to fragments of his opera.

A few days earlier, Undine's hope of renewing such pleasures would have been clouded by the dread of leaving Madame de Trézac alone with the Duchess. But she had no longer any fear of Madame de Trézac. She had discovered that her old rival of Potash Springs was in actual dread of her disfavour, and nervously anxious to conciliate her, and the discovery gave her such a sense of the heights she had scaled, and the security of her footing, that all her troubled past began to seem like the result of some providential "design," and vague impulses of piety stirred in her as she and the Princess whirled toward Nice through the blue and gold glitter of the morning.

They wandered about the lively streets, they gazed into the beguiling shops, the Princess tried on hats and Undine bought them, and they lunched at the *Royal* on all sorts of succulent dishes prepared under the head-waiter's special supervision. But as they were savouring their "double" coffee and liqueurs, and Undine was wondering what her companion would devise for the afternoon, the Princess clapped her hands together and cried out: "Dearest, I'd forgotten! I must desert you."

She explained that she'd promised the Duchess to look up a friend who was ill—a poor wretch who'd been sent to Cimiez for her lungs—and that she must rush off at once, and would be back as soon as possible—well, if not in an hour, then in two at latest. She was full of compunction, but she knew Undine would forgive her, and find something amusing to fill up the time: she advised her to go back and buy the black hat with the osprey, and try on the crêpe de Chine they'd thought so smart: for any one as good-looking as herself the woman would probably alter it for nothing; and they could meet again at the Palace Tea-Rooms at four.

She whirled away in a cloud of explanations, and Undine, left alone, sat down on the Promenade des Anglais. She did not believe a word the Princess had said. She had seen in a flash why she was being left, and why the plan had not been divulged to her beforehand; and she quivered with resentment and humiliation. "That's what she's wanted me for . . . that's why she made up to me. She's trying it to-day, and after this it'll happen regularly . . . she'll drag me over here every day or two . . . at least she thinks she will!"

A sincere disgust was Undine's uppermost sensation. She was as much ashamed as Mrs. Spragg might have been at finding herself used to screen a clandestine adventure.

"I'll let her see. . . I'll make her understand," she repeated angrily; and for a moment she was half-disposed to drive to the station and take the first train back. But the sense of her precarious situation withheld her; and presently, with bitterness in her heart, she got up and began to stroll toward the shops.

To show that she was not a dupe, she arrived at the designated meeting-place nearly an hour later than the time appointed; but when she entered the Tea-Rooms the Princess was nowhere to be seen. The rooms were crowded, and Undine was guided toward a small inner apartment where isolated couples were absorbing refreshments in an atmosphere of intimacy that made it seem incongruous to be alone. She glanced about for a face she knew, but none was visible, and she was just giving up the search when she beheld Elmer Moffatt shouldering his way through the crowd.

The sight was so surprising that she sat gazing with unconscious fixity at the round black head and glossy reddish face which kept appearing and disappearing through the intervening jungle of aigrettes. It was long since she had either heard of Moffatt or thought about him, and now, in her loneliness and exasperation, she took comfort in the sight of his confident capable face, and felt a longing to hear his voice and unbosom her woes to him. She had half risen to attract his attention when she saw him turn back and make way for a companion, who was cautiously steering her huge feathered hat between the tea-tables. The woman was of the vulgarest type; everything about her was cheap and gaudy. But Moffatt was obviously elated: he stood aside with a flourish to usher her in, and as he followed he shot out a pink shirt-cuff with jewelled links, and gave his moustache a gallant twist. Undine felt an unreasoning irritation: she was vexed with him both for not being alone and for being so vulgarly accompanied. As the couple seated themselves she caught Moffatt's glance and saw him redden to the edge of his white forehead; but he elaborately avoided her eye—he evidently wanted her to see him do it—and proceeded to minister to his companion's wants with an air of experienced gallantry.

The incident, trifling as it was, filled up the measure of Undine's bitterness. She thought Moffatt pitiably ridiculous, and she hated him for showing himself in such a light at that particular moment. Her mind turned back to her own grievance, and she was just saying to herself that nothing on earth should prevent her letting the Princess know what she thought of her, when the lady in question at last appeared. She came hurriedly forward and behind her Undine perceived the figure of a slight quietly dressed man, as to whom her immediate impression was that he made every one else in the room look as common as Moffatt. An instant later the colour had flown to her face and her hand was in Raymond de Chelles', while the Princess, murmuring: "Cimiez's such a long way off; but you *will* forgive me?" looked into her eyes with a smile that added: "See how I pay for what I get!"

Her first glance showed Undine how glad Raymond de Chelles was to see her. Since their last meeting his admiration for her seemed not only to have increased but to have acquired a different character. Undine, at an earlier stage in her career, might not have known exactly what the difference signified; but it was as clear to her now as if the Princess had said—what her beaming eyes seemed, in fact, to convey— "I'm only too glad to do my cousin the same kind of turn you're doing me."

But Undine's increased experience, if it had made her more vigilant, had also given her a clearer measure of her power. She saw at once that Chelles, in seeking to meet her again, was not in quest of a mere passing adventure. He was evidently deeply drawn to her, and her present situation, if it made it natural to regard her as more accessible, had not altered the nature of his feeling. She saw and weighed all this in the first five minutes during which, over tea and muffins, the Princess descanted on her luck in happening to run across her cousin, and Chelles, his enchanted eyes on Undine, expressed his sense of his good fortune. He was staying, it appeared, with friends at Beaulieu, and had run over to Nice that afternoon by the merest chance: he added that, having just learned of his aunt's presence in the neighbourhood, he had already planned to present his homage to her.

"Oh, don't come to us—we're too dull!" the Princess exclaimed. "Let us run over occasionally and call on you: we're dying for a pretext, aren't we?" she added, smiling at Undine.

The latter smiled back vaguely, and looked across the room.

Moffatt, looking flushed and foolish, was just pushing back his chair. To carry off his embarrassment he put on an additional touch of importance; and as he swaggered out behind his companion, Undine said to herself, with a shiver: "If he'd been alone they would have found me taking tea with him."

Undine, during the ensuing weeks, returned several times to Nice with the Princess; but, to the latter's surprise, she absolutely refused to have Raymond de Chelles included in their luncheon-parties, or even apprised in advance of their expeditions.

The Princess, always impatient of unnecessary dissimulation, had not attempted to keep up the feint of the interesting invalid at Cimiez. She confessed to Undine that she was drawn to Nice by the presence there of the person without whom, for the moment, she found life intolerable, and whom she could not well receive under the same roof with her little girls and her mother. She appealed to Undine's sisterly heart to feel for her in her difficulty, and implied that—as her conduct had already proved—she would always be ready to render her friend a like service.

It was at this point that Undine checked her by a decided word. "I understand your position, and I'm very sorry for you, of course," she began (the Princess stared at the "sorry"). "Your secret's perfectly safe with me, and I'll do anything I can for you . . . but if I go to Nice with you again you must promise not to ask your cousin to meet us."

The Princess's face expressed the most genuine astonishment. "Oh, my dear, do forgive me if I've been stupid! He admires you so tremendously; and I thought——"

"You'll do as I ask, please—won't you?" Undine went on, ignoring the interruption and looking straight at her under level brows; and the Princess, with a shrug, merely murmured: "What a pity! I fancied you liked him."

XXIX

THE EARLY SPRING found Undine once more in Paris. She had every reason to be satisfied with the result of the course she had pursued since she had pronounced her ultimatum on the subject of Raymond de Chelles. She had continued to remain on the best of terms with the Princess, to rise in the estimation of the old Duchess, and to measure the rapidity of her ascent in the upward gaze of Madame de Trézac; and she had given Chelles to understand that, if he wished to renew their acquaintance, he must do so in the shelter of his venerable aunt's protection.

To the Princess she was careful to make her attitude equally clear. "I like your cousin very much—he's delightful, and if I'm in Paris this spring I hope I shall see a great deal of him. But I know how easy it is for a woman in my position to get talked about—and I have my little boy to consider."

Nevertheless, whenever Chelles came over from Beaulieu to spend a day with his aunt and cousin—an excursion he not infrequently repeated—Undine was at no pains to conceal her pleasure. Nor was there anything calculated in her attitude. Chelles seemed to her more charming than ever, and the warmth of his wooing was in flattering contrast to the cool reserve of his manners. At last she felt herself alive and young again, and it became a joy to look in her glass and to try on her new hats and dresses. . .

The only menace ahead was the usual one of the want of money. While she had travelled with her parents she had been at relatively small expense, and since their return to America Mr. Spragg had sent her allowance regularly; yet almost all the money she had received for the pearls was already gone, and she knew her Paris season would be far more expensive than the quiet weeks on the Riviera.

Meanwhile the sense of reviving popularity, and the charm of Chelles' devotion, had almost effaced the ugly memories of failure, and refurbished that image of herself in other minds which was her only notion of self-seeing. Under the guidance of Madame de Trézac she had found a prettily furnished apartment in a not too inaccessible quarter, and in its light bright drawing-room she sat one June afternoon listening, with all the forbearance of which she was capable, to the counsels of her newly-acquired guide.

"Everything but marriage——" Madame de Trézac was repeating, her long head slightly tilted, her features wearing the rapt look of an adept reciting a hallowed formula.

Raymond de Chelles had not been mentioned by either of the ladies, and the former Miss Wincher was merely imparting to her young friend one of the fundamental dogmas of her social creed; but Undine was conscious that the air between them vibrated with an unspoken name. She made no immediate answer, but her glance, passing by Madame de Trézac's dull countenance, sought her own reflection in the mirror behind her visitor's chair. A beam of spring sunlight touched the living masses of her hair and made the face beneath as radiant as a girl's. Undine smiled faintly at the promise her own eyes gave her, and then turned them back to her friend. "What can such women know about anything?" she thought compassionately.

"There's everything against it," Madame de Trézac continued in a tone of patient exposition. She seemed to be doing her best to make the matter clear. "In the first place, between people in society a religious marriage is necessary; and, since the Church doesn't recognize divorce, that's obviously out of the question. In France, a man of position who goes through the form of civil marriage with a divorced woman is simply ruining himself and her. They might much better—from her point of view as well as his—be 'friends,' as it's called over here: such arrangements are understood and allowed for. But when a Frenchman marries he wants to marry as his people always have. He knows there are traditions he can't fight against—and in his heart he's glad there are."

"Oh, I know: they've so much religious feeling. I admire that in them: their religion's so beautiful." Undine looked thoughtfully at her visitor. "I suppose even money—a great deal of money—wouldn't make the least bit of difference?"

"None whatever, except to make matters worse," Madame de Trézac decisively rejoined. She returned Undine's look with something of Miss Wincher's contemptuous authority. "But," she added, softening to a smile, "between ourselves—

I can say it, since we're neither of us children—a woman with tact, who's not in a position to remarry, will find society extremely indulgent . . . provided, of course, she keeps up appearances. . ."

Undine turned to her with the frown of a startled Diana. "We don't look at things that way out at Apex," she said coldly; and the blood rose in Madame de Trézac's sallow cheek.

"Oh, my dear, it's so refreshing to hear you talk like that! Personally, of course, I've never quite got used to the French view——"

"I hope no American woman ever does," said Undine.

She had been in Paris for about two months when this conversation took place, and in spite of her reviving self-confidence she was beginning to recognize the strength of the forces opposed to her. It had taken a long time to convince her that even money could not prevail against them; and, in the intervals of expressing her admiration for the Catholic creed, she now had violent reactions of militant Protestantism, during which she talked of the tyranny of Rome and recalled school stories of immoral Popes and persecuting Jesuits.

Meanwhile her demeanour to Chelles was that of the incorruptible but fearless American woman, who cannot even conceive of love outside of marriage, but is ready to give her devoted friendship to the man on whom, in happier circumstances, she might have bestowed her hand. This attitude was provocative of many scenes, during which her suitor's unfailing powers of expression—his gift of looking and saying all the desperate and devoted things a pretty woman likes to think she inspires—gave Undine the thrilling sense of breathing the very air of French fiction. But she was aware that too prolonged tension of these cords usually ends in their snapping, and that Chelles' patience was probably in inverse ratio to his ardour.

When Madame de Trézac had left her these thoughts remained in her mind. She understood exactly what each of her new friends wanted of her. The Princess, who was fond of her cousin, and had the French sense of family solidarity, would have liked to see Chelles happy in what seemed to her the only imaginable way. Madame de Trézac would have liked to do what she could to second the Princess's efforts in this or any other line; and even the old Duchess—though piously desirous of seeing her favourite nephew married—would have thought it not only natural but inevitable that, while awaiting that happy event, he should try to induce an amiable young woman to mitigate the drawbacks of celibacy. Meanwhile, they might one and all weary of her if Chelles did; and a persistent rejection of his suit would probably imperil her scarcely-gained footing among his friends. All this was clear to her, yet it did not shake her resolve. She was determined to give up Chelles unless he was willing to marry her; and the thought of her renunciation moved her to a kind of wistful melancholy.

In this mood her mind reverted to a letter she had just received from her mother. Mrs. Spragg wrote more fully than usual, and the unwonted flow of her pen had been occasioned by an event for which she had long yearned. For months she had pined for a sight of her grandson, had tried to screw up her courage to write and ask permission to visit him, and, finally breaking through her sedentary habits, had begun to haunt the neighbourhood of Washington Square, with the result that one afternoon she had had the luck to meet the little boy coming out of the house with his nurse. She had spoken to him, and he had remembered her and called her "Granny"; and the next day she had received a note from Mrs. Fairford saying that Ralph would be glad to send Paul to see her. Mrs. Spragg enlarged on the delights of the visit and the growing beauty and cleverness of her grandson. She described to Undine exactly how Paul was dressed, how he looked and what he said, and told her how he had examined everything in the room, and, finally coming upon his mother's photograph, had asked who the lady was; and, on being told, had wanted to know if she was a very long way off, and when Granny thought she would come back.

As Undine re-read her mother's pages, she felt an unusual tightness in her throat and two tears rose to her eyes. It was dreadful that her little boy should be growing up far away from her, perhaps dressed in clothes she would have hated; and wicked and unnatural that when he saw her picture he should have to be told who she was. "If I could only meet some good man who would give me a home and be a father to him," she thought—and the tears overflowed and ran down.

Even as they fell, the door was thrown open, to admit Raymond de Chelles, and the consciousness of the moisture still glistening on her cheeks perhaps strengthened her resolve to resist him, and thus made her more imperiously to be desired. Certain it is that on that day her suitor first alluded to a possibility which Madame de Trézac had prudently refrained from suggesting, and there fell upon Undine's attentive ears the magic phrase "annulment of marriage."

Her alert intelligence immediately set to work in this new direction; but almost at the same moment she became aware of a subtle change of tone in the Princess and her mother, a change reflected in the corresponding decline of Madame de Trézac's cordiality. Undine, since her arrival in Paris, had necessarily been less in the Princess's company, but when they met she had found her as friendly as ever. It was manifestly not a failing of the Princess's to forget past favours, and though increasingly absorbed by the demands of town life she treated her new friend with the same affectionate frankness, and Undine was given frequent opportunities to enlarge her Parisian acquaintance, not only in the Princess's intimate circle but in the majestic drawing-rooms of the Hôtel de Dordogne. Now, however, there was a perceptible decline in these signs of hospitality, and Undine, on calling one day on the Duchess, noticed that her appearance sent a visible flutter of discomfort through the circle about her hostess's chair. Two or three of the ladies present looked away from the new-comer and at each other, and several of them seemed spontaneously to encircle without approaching her, while another—grey-haired, elderly and slightly frightened—with an *"Adieu, ma bonne tante"* to the Duchess, was hastily aided in her retreat down the long line of old gilded rooms.

The incident was too mute and rapid to have been noticeable had it not been followed by the Duchess's resuming her conversation with the ladies nearest her as though Undine had just gone out of the room instead of entering it. The sense of having been thus rendered invisible filled Undine with a vehement desire to make herself seen, and an equally strong sense that all attempts to do so would be vain; and when, a few minutes later, she issued from the portals of the Hôtel de Dordogne it was with the fixed resolve not to enter them again till she had had an explanation with the Princess.

She was spared the trouble of seeking one by the arrival, early the next morning, of Madame de Trézac, who, entering almost with the breakfast tray, mysteriously asked to be allowed to communicate something of importance.

"You'll understand, I know, the Princess's not coming herself——" Madame de Trézac began, sitting up very straight on the edge of the arm-chair over which Undine's lace dressing-gown hung.

"If there's anything she wants to say to me, I don't," Undine answered, leaning back among her rosy pillows, and reflecting compassionately that the face opposite her was just the colour of the *café au lait* she was pouring out.

"There are things that are . . . that might seem too pointed . . . if one said them one's self," Madame de Trézac continued. "Our dear Lili's so good-natured . . . she so hates to do anything unfriendly; but she naturally thinks first of her mother. . ."

"Her mother? What's the matter with her mother?"

"I told her I knew you didn't understand. I was sure you'd take it in good part. . ."

Undine raised herself on her elbow. "What did Lili tell you to tell me?"

"Oh, not to *tell* you . . . simply to ask if, just for the present, you'd mind avoiding the Duchess's Thursdays . . . calling on any other day, that is."

"Any other day? She's not at home on any other. Do you mean she doesn't want me to call?"

"Well—not while the Marquise de Chelles is in Paris. She's the Duchess's favourite niece—and of course they all hang together. That kind of family feeling is something you naturally don't——"

Undine had a sudden glimpse of hidden intricacies.

"That was Raymond de Chelles' mother I saw there yesterday? The one they hurried out when I came in?"

"It seems she was very much upset. She somehow heard your name."

"Why shouldn't she have heard my name? And why in the world should it upset her?"

Madame de Trézac heaved a hesitating sigh. "Isn't it better to be frank? She thinks she has reason to feel badly—they all do."

"To feel badly? Because her son wants to marry me?"

"Of course they know that's impossible." Madame de Trézac smiled compassionately. "But they're afraid of your spoiling his other chances."

Undine paused a moment before answering. "It won't be impossible when my marriage is annulled," she said.

The effect of this statement was less electrifying than she had hoped. Her visitor simply broke into a laugh. "My dear child! Your marriage annulled? Who can have put such a mad idea into your head?"

Undine's gaze followed the pattern she was tracing with a lustrous nail on her embroidered bedspread. "Raymond himself," she let fall.

This time there was no mistaking the effect she produced. Madame de Trézac, with a murmured "Oh," sat gazing before her as if she had lost the thread of her argument; and it was only after a considerable interval that she recovered it sufficiently to exclaim: "They'll never hear of it—absolutely never!"

"But they can't prevent it, can they?"

"They can prevent its being of any use to you."

"I see," Undine pensively assented.

She knew the tone she had taken was virtually a declaration of war; but she was in a mood when the act of defiance, apart from its strategic value, was a satisfaction in itself. Moreover, if she could not gain her end without a fight it was better that the battle should be engaged while Raymond's ardour was at its height. To provoke immediate hostilities she sent for him the same afternoon, and related, quietly and without comment, the incident of her visit to the Duchess, and the mission with which Madame de Trézac had been charged. In the circumstances, she went on to explain, it was manifestly impossible that she should continue to receive his visits; and she met his wrathful comments on his relatives by the gently but firmly expressed resolve not to be the cause of any disagreement between himself and his family.

XXX

A FEW DAYS after her decisive conversation with Raymond de Chelles, Undine, emerging from the doors of the Nouveau Luxe, where she had been to call on the newly-arrived Mrs. Homer Branney, once more found herself face to face with Elmer Moffatt.

This time there was no mistaking his eagerness to be recognized. He stopped short as they met, and she read such pleasure in his eyes that she too stopped, holding out her hand.

"I'm glad you're going to speak to me," she said, and Moffatt reddened at the allusion.

"Well, I very nearly didn't. I didn't know you. You look about as old as you did when I first landed at Apex—remember?"

He turned back and began to walk at her side in the direction of the Champs Elysées.

"Say—this is all right!" he exclaimed; and she saw that his glance had left her and was ranging across the wide silvery square ahead of them to the congregated domes and spires beyond the river.

"Do you like Paris?" she asked, wondering what theatres he had been to.

"It beats everything." He seemed to be breathing in deeply the impression of fountains, sculpture, leafy avenues and long-drawn architectural distances fading into the afternoon haze.

"I suppose you've been to that old church over there?" he went on, his gold-topped stick pointing toward the towers of Notre Dame.

"Oh, of course; when I used to sightsee. Have you never been to Paris before?"

"No, this is my first look-round. I came across in March."

"In March?" she echoed inattentively. It never occurred to her that other people's lives went on when they were out of her range of vision, and she tried in vain to remember what she had last heard of Moffatt. "Wasn't that a bad time to leave Wall Street?"

"Well, so-so. Fact is, I was played out: needed a change."

Nothing in his robust mien confirmed the statement, and he did not seem inclined to develop it. "I presume you're settled here now?" he went on. "I saw by the papers——"

"Yes," she interrupted; adding, after a moment: "It was all a mistake from the first."

"Well, I never thought he was your form," said Moffatt.

His eyes had come back to her, and the look in them struck her as something she might use to her advantage; but the next moment he had glanced away with a furrowed brow, and she felt she had not wholly fixed his attention.

"I live at the other end of Paris. Why not come back and have tea with me?" she suggested, half moved by a desire to know more of his affairs, and half by the thought that a talk with him might help to shed some light on hers.

In the open taxi-cab he seemed to recover his sense of well-being, and leaned back, his hands on the knob of his stick, with the air of a man pleasantly aware of his privileges. "This Paris is a thundering good place," he repeated once or twice as they rolled on through the crush and glitter of the afternoon; and when they had descended at Undine's door, and he stood in her drawing-room, and looked out on the horse-chestnut trees rounding their green domes under the balcony, his satisfaction culminated in the comment: "I guess this lays out West End Avenue!"

His eyes met Undine's with their old twinkle, and their expression encouraged her to murmur: "Of course there are times when I'm very lonely."

She sat down behind the tea-table, and he stood at a little distance, watching her pull off her gloves with a queer comic twitch of his elastic mouth. "Well, I guess it's only when you want to be," he said, grasping a lyre-backed chair by its gilt cords, and sitting down astride of it, his light grey trousers stretching too tightly over his plump thighs. Undine was perfectly aware that he was a vulgar over-dressed man, with a red crease of fat above his collar and an impudent swaggering eye; yet she liked to see him there, and was conscious that he stirred the fibres of a self she had forgotten but had not ceased to understand.

She had fancied her avowal of loneliness might call forth some sentimental phrase; but though Moffatt was clearly pleased to be with her she saw that she was not the centre of his thoughts, and the discovery irritated her.

"I don't suppose *you've* known what it is to be lonely since you've been in Europe?" she continued as she held out his tea-cup.

"Oh," he said jocosely, "I don't always go round with a guide"; and she rejoined on the same note: "Then perhaps I shall see something of you."

"Why, there's nothing would suit me better; but the fact is, I'm probably sailing next week."

"Oh, are you? I'm sorry." There was nothing feigned in her regret.

"Anything I can do for you across the pond?"

She hesitated. "There's something you can do for me right off."

He looked at her more attentively, as if his practised eye had passed through the surface of her beauty to what might be going on behind it. "Do you want my blessing again?" he asked with sudden irony.

Undine opened her eyes with a trustful look. "Yes—I do."

"Well—I'll be damned!" said Moffatt gaily.

"You've always been so awfully nice," she began; and he leaned back, grasping both sides of the chair-back, and shaking it a little with his laugh.

He kept the same attitude while she proceeded to unfold her case, listening to her with the air of sober concentration that his frivolous face took on at any serious demand on his attention. When she had ended he kept the same look during an interval of silent pondering. "Is it the fellow who was over at Nice with you that day?"

She looked at him with surprise. "How did you know?"

"Why, I liked his looks," said Moffatt simply.

He got up and strolled toward the window. On the way he stopped before a table covered with showy trifles, and after looking at them for a moment singled out a dim old brown and golden book which Chelles had given her. He examined it lingeringly, as though it touched the spring of some choked-up sensibility for which he had no language. "Say——" he began: it was the usual prelude to his enthusiasms; but he laid the book down and turned back.

"Then you think if you had the cash you could fix it up all right with the Pope?"

Her heart began to beat. She remembered that he had once put a job in Ralph's way, and had let her understand that he had done it partly for her sake.

"Well," he continued, relapsing into hyperbole, "I wish I could send the old gentleman my cheque to-morrow morning: but the fact is I'm high and dry." He looked at her with a sudden odd intensity. "If I *wasn't*, I dunno but what——" The phrase was lost in his familiar whistle. "That's an awfully fetching way you do your hair," he said.

It was a disappointment to Undine to hear that his affairs were not prospering, for she knew that in his world "pull" and solvency were closely related, and that such support as she had hoped he might give her would be contingent on his own situation. But she had again a fleeting sense of his mysterious power of accomplishing things in the teeth of adversity; and she answered: "What I want is your advice."

He turned away and wandered across the room, his hands in his pockets. On her ornate writing desk he saw a photograph of Paul, bright-curled and sturdy-legged, in a manly reefer, and bent over it with a murmur of approval. "Say— what a fellow! Got him with you?"

Undine coloured. "No——" she began; and seeing his look of surprise, she embarked on her usual explanation. "I can't tell you how I miss him," she ended, with a ring of truth that carried conviction to her own ears if not to Moffatt's.

"Why don't you get him back, then?"

"Why, I——"

Moffatt had picked up the frame and was looking at the photograph more closely. "Pants!" he chuckled. "I declare!"

He turned back to Undine. "Who *does* he belong to, any-how?"

"Belong to?"

"Who got him when you were divorced? Did you?"

"Oh, I got everything," she said, her instinct of self-defense on the alert.

"So I thought." He stood before her, stoutly planted on his short legs, and speaking with an aggressive energy. "Well, I know what I'd do if he was mine."

"If he was yours?"

"And you tried to get him away from me. Fight you to a finish! If it cost me down to my last dollar I would."

The conversation seemed to be wandering from the point, and she answered, with a touch of impatience: "It wouldn't cost you anything like that. I haven't got a dollar to fight back with."

"Well, you ain't got to fight. Your decree gave him to you, didn't it? Why don't you send right over and get him? That's what I'd do if I was you."

Undine looked up. "But I'm awfully poor; I can't afford to have him here."

"You couldn't, up to now; but now you're going to get married. You're going to be able to give him a home and a father's care—and the foreign languages. That's what I'd say if I was you. . . His father takes considerable stock in him, don't he?"

She coloured, a denial on her lips; but she could not shape it. "We're both awfully fond of him, of course. . . His fa-ther'd never give him up!"

"Just so." Moffatt's face had grown as sharp as glass. "You've got the Marvells running. All you've got to do's to sit tight and wait for their cheque." He dropped back to his equestrian seat on the lyre-backed chair.

Undine stood up and moved uneasily toward the window. She seemed to see her little boy as though he were in the room with her; she did not understand how she could have lived so long without him. . . She stood for a long time without speaking, feeling behind her the concentrated irony of Moffatt's gaze.

"You couldn't lend me the money—manage to borrow it for me, I mean?" she finally turned back to ask.

He laughed. "If I could manage to borrow any money at this particular minute—well, I'd have to lend every dollar of it to Elmer Moffatt, Esquire. I'm stone-broke, if you want to know. And wanted for an Investigation too. That's why I'm over here improving my mind."

"Why, I thought you were going home next week?"

He grinned. "I am, because I've found out there's a party wants me to stay away worse than the courts want me back.

Making the trip just for my private satisfaction—there won't be any money in it, I'm afraid."

Leaden disappointment descended on Undine. She had felt almost sure of Moffatt's helping her, and for an instant she wondered if some long-smouldering jealousy had flamed up under its cold cinders. But another look at his face denied her this solace; and his evident indifference was the last blow to her pride. The twinge it gave her prompted her to ask: "Don't you ever mean to get married?"

Moffatt gave her a quick look. "Why, I shouldn't wonder—one of these days. Millionaires always collect something; but I've got to collect my millions first."

He spoke coolly and half-humorously, and before he had ended she had lost all interest in his reply. He seemed aware of the fact, for he stood up and held out his hand.

"Well, so long, Mrs. Marvell. It's been uncommonly pleasant to see you; and you'd better think over what I've said."

She laid her hand sadly in his. "You've never had a child," she replied.

BOOK IV

XXXI

NEARLY TWO YEARS had passed since Ralph Marvell, waking from his long sleep in the hot summer light of Washington Square, had found that the face of life was changed for him.

In the interval he had gradually adapted himself to the new order of things; but the months of adaptation had been a time of such darkness and confusion that, from the vantage-ground of his recovered lucidity, he could not yet distinguish the stages by which he had worked his way out; and even now his footing was not secure.

His first effort had been to readjust his values—to take an inventory of them, and reclassify them, so that one at least might be made to appear as important as those he had lost; otherwise there could be no reason why he should go on living. He applied himself doggedly to this attempt; but whenever he thought he had found a reason that his mind could rest in, it gave way under him, and the old struggle for a foothold began again. His two objects in life were his boy and his book. The boy was incomparably the stronger argument, yet the less serviceable in filling the void. Ralph felt his son all the while, and all through his other feelings; but he could not think about him actively and continuously, could not forever exercise his eager empty dissatisfied mind on the relatively simple problem of clothing, educating and amusing a little boy of six. Yet Paul's existence was the all-sufficient reason for his own; and he turned again, with a kind of cold fervour, to his abandoned literary dream. Material needs obliged him to go on with his regular business; but, the day's work over, he was possessed of a leisure as bare and as blank as an unfurnished house, yet that was at least his own to furnish as he pleased.

Meanwhile he was beginning to show a presentable face to the world, and to be once more treated like a man in whose case no one is particularly interested. His men friends ceased to say: "Hallo, old chap, I never saw you looking fitter!" and elderly ladies no longer told him they were sure he kept too much to himself, and urged him to drop in any afternoon for a quiet talk. People left him to his sorrow as a man is left to an incurable habit, an unfortunate tie: they ignored it, or looked over its head if they happened to catch a glimpse of it at his elbow.

These glimpses were given to them more and more rarely. The smothered springs of life were bubbling up in Ralph, and there were days when he was glad to wake and see the sun in his window, and when he began to plan his book, and to fancy that the planning really interested him. He could even maintain the delusion for several days—for intervals each time appreciably longer—before it shrivelled up again in a scorching blast of disenchantment. The worst of it was that he could never tell when these hot gusts of anguish would overtake him. They came sometimes just when he felt most secure, when he was saying to himself: "After all, things are really worth while——" sometimes even when he was sitting with Clare Van Degen, listening to her voice, watching her hands, and turning over in his mind the opening chapters of his book.

"You ought to write"; they had one and all said it to him from the first; and he fancied he might have begun sooner if he had not been urged on by their watchful fondness. Everybody wanted him to write—everybody had decided that he ought to, that he would, that he must be persuaded to; and the incessant imperceptible pressure of encouragement—the assumption of those about him that because it would be good for him to write he must naturally be able to—acted on his restive nerves as a stronger deterrent than disapproval.

Even Clare had fallen into the same mistake; and one day, as he sat talking with her on the verandah of Laura Fairford's house on the Sound—where they now most frequently met—Ralph had half-impatiently rejoined: "Oh, if you think it's literature I need——!"

Instantly he had seen her face change, and the speaking hands tremble on her knee. But she achieved the feat of not answering him, or turning her steady eyes from the dancing mid-summer water at the foot of Laura's lawn. Ralph leaned a little nearer, and for an instant his hand imagined the flutter of hers. But instead of clasping it he drew back, and rising

from his chair wandered away to the other end of the verandah. . . No, he didn't feel as Clare felt. If he loved her—as
he sometimes thought he did—it was not in the same way.
He had a great tenderness for her, he was more nearly happy
with her than with any one else; he liked to sit and talk with
her, and watch her face and her hands, and he wished there
were some way—some different way—of letting her know
it; but he could not conceive that tenderness and desire could
ever again be one for him: such a notion as that seemed part
of the monstrous sentimental muddle on which his life had
gone aground.

"I shall write—of course I shall write some day," he said,
turning back to his seat. "I've had a novel in the back of my
head for years; and now's the time to pull it out."

He hardly knew what he was saying; but before the end of
the sentence he saw that Clare had understood what he meant
to convey, and henceforth he felt committed to letting her
talk to him as much as she pleased about his book. He himself, in consequence, took to thinking about it more consec-
utively; and just as his friends ceased to urge him to write, he
sat down in earnest to begin.

The vision that had come to him had no likeness to any of
his earlier imaginings. Two or three subjects had haunted
him, pleading for expression, during the first years of his marriage; but these now seemed either too lyrical or too tragic.
He no longer saw life on the heroic scale: he wanted to do
something in which men should look no bigger than the insects they were. He contrived in the course of time to reduce
one of his old subjects to these dimensions, and after nights
of brooding he made a dash at it, and wrote an opening chapter that struck him as not too bad. In the exhilaration of this
first attempt he spent some pleasant evenings revising and
polishing his work; and gradually a feeling of authority and
importance developed in him. In the morning, when he
woke, instead of his habitual sense of lassitude, he felt an eagerness to be up and doing, and a conviction that his individual task was a necessary part of the world's machinery. He
kept his secret with the beginner's deadly fear of losing his
hold on his half-real creations if he let in any outer light on
them; but he went about with a more assured step, shrank

less from meeting his friends, and even began to dine out again, and to laugh at some of the jokes he heard.

Laura Fairford, to get Paul away from town, had gone early to the country; and Ralph, who went down to her every Saturday, usually found Clare Van Degen there. Since his divorce he had never entered his cousin's pinnacled palace; and Clare had never asked him why he stayed away. This mutual silence had been their sole allusion to Van Degen's share in the catastrophe, though Ralph had spoken frankly of its other aspects. They talked, however, most often of impersonal subjects—books, pictures, plays, or whatever the world that interested them was doing—and she showed no desire to draw him back to his own affairs. She was again staying late in town—to have a pretext, as he guessed, for coming down on Sundays to the Fairfords'—and they often made the trip together in her motor; but he had not yet spoken to her of having begun his book. One May evening, however, as they sat alone in the verandah, he suddenly told her that he was writing. As he spoke his heart beat like a boy's; but once the words were out they gave him a feeling of self-confidence, and he began to sketch his plan, and then to go into its details. Clare listened devoutly, her eyes burning on him through the dusk like the stars deepening above the garden; and when she got up to go in he followed her with a new sense of reassurance.

The dinner that evening was unusually pleasant. Charles Bowen, just back from his usual spring travels, had come straight down to his friends from the steamer; and the fund of impressions he brought with him gave Ralph a desire to be up and wandering. And why not—when the book was done? He smiled across the table at Clare.

"Next summer you'll have to charter a yacht, and take us all off to the Ægean. We can't have Charles condescending to us about the out-of-the-way places he's been seeing."

Was it really he who was speaking, and his cousin who was sending him back her dusky smile? Well—why not, again? The seasons renewed themselves, and he too was putting out a new growth. "My book—my book—my book," kept repeating itself under all his thoughts, as Undine's name had once perpetually murmured there. That night as he went up to bed he said to himself that he was actually ceasing to think about his wife. . .

As he passed Laura's door she called him in, and put her arms about him.

"You look so well, dear!"

"But why shouldn't I?" he answered gaily, as if ridiculing the fancy that he had ever looked otherwise. Paul was sleeping behind the next door, and the sense of the boy's nearness gave him a warmer glow. His little world was rounding itself out again, and once more he felt safe and at peace in its circle.

His sister looked as if she had something more to say; but she merely kissed him good night, and he went up whistling to his room.

The next morning he was to take a walk with Clare, and while he lounged about the drawing-room, waiting for her to come down, a servant came in with the Sunday papers. Ralph picked one up, and was absently unfolding it when his eye fell on his own name: a sight he had been spared since the last echoes of his divorce had subsided. His impulse was to fling the paper down, to hurl it as far from him as he could; but a grim fascination tightened his hold and drew his eyes back to the hated head-line.

NEW YORK BEAUTY WEDS FRENCH NOBLEMAN

Mrs. Undine Marvell Confident Pope Will Annul Previous Marriage

MRS. MARVELL TALKS ABOUT HER CASE

There it was before him in all its long-drawn horror—an "interview"—an "interview" of Undine's about her coming marriage! Ah, she talked about her case indeed! Her confidences filled the greater part of a column, and the only detail she seemed to have omitted was the name of her future husband, who was referred to by herself as "my fiancé" and by the interviewer as "the Count" or "a prominent scion of the French nobility."

Ralph heard Laura's step behind him. He threw the paper aside and their eyes met.

"Is this what you wanted to tell me last night?"

"Last night?—Is it in the papers?"

"Who told you? Bowen? What else has he heard?"

"Oh, Ralph, what does it matter—what can it matter?"

"Who's the man? Did he tell you that?" Ralph insisted. He saw her growing agitation. "Why can't you answer? Is it any one I know?"

"He was told in Paris it was his friend Raymond de Chelles."

Ralph laughed, and his laugh sounded in his own ears like an echo of the dreary mirth with which he had filled Mr. Spragg's office the day he had learned that Undine intended to divorce him. But now his wrath was seasoned with a wholesome irony. The fact of his wife's having reached another stage in her ascent fell into its place as a part of the huge human buffoonery.

"Besides," Laura went on, "it's all perfect nonsense, of course. How in the world can she have her marriage annulled?"

Ralph pondered: this put the matter in another light. "With a great deal of money I suppose she might."

"Well, she certainly won't get that from Chelles. He's far from rich, Charles tells me." Laura waited, watching him, before she risked: "That's what convinces me she wouldn't have him if she could."

Ralph shrugged. "There may be other inducements. But she won't be able to manage it." He heard himself speaking quite collectedly. Had Undine at last lost her power of wounding him?

Clare came in, dressed for their walk, and under Laura's anxious eyes he picked up the newspaper and held it out with a careless: "Look at this!"

His cousin's glance flew down the column, and he saw the tremor of her lashes as she read. Then she lifted her head. "But you'll be free!" Her face was as vivid as a flower.

"Free? I'm free now, as far as that goes!"

"Oh, but it will go so much farther when she has another name—when she's a different person altogether! Then you'll really have Paul to yourself."

"Paul?" Laura intervened with a nervous laugh. "But there's never been the least doubt about his having Paul!"

They heard the boy's laughter on the lawn, and she went out to join him. Ralph was still looking at his cousin.

"You're glad, then?" came from him involuntarily; and she startled him by bursting into tears. He bent over and kissed her on the cheek.

XXXII

RALPH, as the days passed, felt that Clare was right: if Undine married again he would possess himself more completely, be more definitely rid of his past. And he did not doubt that she would gain her end: he knew her violent desires and her cold tenacity. If she had failed to capture Van Degen it was probably because she lacked experience of that particular type of man, of his huge immediate wants and feeble vacillating purposes; most of all, because she had not yet measured the strength of the social considerations that restrained him. It was a mistake she was not likely to repeat, and her failure had probably been a useful preliminary to success. It was a long time since Ralph had allowed himself to think of her, and as he did so the overwhelming fact of her beauty became present to him again, no longer as an element of his being but as a power dispassionately estimated. He said to himself: "Any man who can feel at all will feel it as I did"; and the conviction grew in him that Raymond de Chelles, of whom he had formed an idea through Bowen's talk, was not the man to give her up, even if she failed to obtain the release his religion exacted.

Meanwhile Ralph was gradually beginning to feel himself freer and lighter. Undine's act, by cutting the last link between them, seemed to have given him back to himself; and the mere fact that he could consider his case in all its bearings, impartially and ironically, showed him the distance he had travelled, the extent to which he had renewed himself. He had been moved, too, by Clare's cry of joy at his release. Though the nature of his feeling for her had not changed he was aware of a new quality in their friendship. When he went back to his book again his sense of power had lost its asperity, and the spectacle of life seemed less like a witless dangling of limp dolls. He was well on in his second chapter now.

This lightness of mood was still on him when, returning one afternoon to Washington Square, full of projects for a long evening's work, he found his mother awaiting him with a strange face. He followed her into the drawing-room, and she explained that there had been a telephone message she didn't understand—something perfectly crazy about Paul—of course it was all a mistake. . .

Ralph's first thought was of an accident, and his heart contracted. "Did Laura telephone?"

"No, no; not Laura. It seemed to be a message from Mrs. Spragg: something about sending some one here to fetch him—a queer name like Heeny—to fetch him to a steamer on Saturday. I was to be sure to have his things packed . . . but of course it's a misunderstanding. . ." She gave an uncertain laugh, and looked up at Ralph as though entreating him to return the reassurance she had given him.

"Of course, of course," he echoed.

He made his mother repeat her statement; but the unforeseen always flurried her, and she was confused and inaccurate. She didn't actually know who had telephoned: the voice hadn't sounded like Mrs. Spragg's. . . A woman's voice; yes—oh, not a lady's! And there was certainly something about a steamer . . . but he knew how the telephone bewildered her . . . and she was sure she was getting a little deaf. Hadn't he better call up the Malibran? Of course it was all a mistake—but . . . well, perhaps he *had* better go there himself. . .

As he reached the front door a letter clinked in the box, and he saw his name on an ordinary looking business envelope. He turned the door-handle, paused again, and stopped to take out the letter. It bore the address of the firm of lawyers who had represented Undine in the divorce proceedings and as he tore open the envelope Paul's name started out at him.

Mrs. Marvell had followed him into the hall, and her cry broke the silence. "Ralph—Ralph—is it anything she's done?"

"Nothing—it's nothing." He stared at her. "What's the day of the week?"

"Wednesday. Why, what——?" She suddenly seemed to understand. "She's not going to take him away from us?"

Ralph dropped into a chair, crumpling the letter in his hand. He had been in a dream, poor fool that he was—a dream about his child! He sat gazing at the type-written phrases that spun themselves out before him. "My client's circumstances now happily permitting . . . at last in a position to offer her son a home . . . long separation . . . a mother's feelings . . . every social and educational advantage" . . . and then, at the end, the poisoned dart that struck him speechless: "The courts having awarded her the sole custody. . ."

The sole custody! But that meant that Paul was hers, hers only, hers for always: that his father had no more claim on him than any casual stranger in the street! And he, Ralph Marvell, a sane man, young, able-bodied, in full possession of his wits, had assisted at the perpetration of this abominable wrong, had passively forfeited his right to the flesh of his body, the blood of his being! But it couldn't be—of course it couldn't be. The preposterousness of it proved that it wasn't true. There was a mistake somewhere; a mistake his own lawyer would instantly rectify. If a hammer hadn't been drumming in his head he could have recalled the terms of the decree—but for the moment all the details of the agonizing episode were lost in a blur of uncertainty.

To escape his mother's silent anguish of interrogation he stood up and said: "I'll see Mr. Spragg—of course it's a mistake." But as he spoke he retravelled the hateful months during the divorce proceedings, remembering his incomprehensible lassitude, his acquiescence in his family's determination to ignore the whole episode, and his gradual lapse into the same state of apathy. He recalled all the old family catch-words, the full and elaborate vocabulary of evasion: "delicacy," "pride," "personal dignity," "preferring not to know about such things"; Mrs. Marvell's: "All I ask is that you won't mention the subject to your grandfather," Mr. Dagonet's: "Spare your mother, Ralph, whatever happens," and even Laura's terrified: "Of course, for Paul's sake, there must be no scandal."

For Paul's sake! And it was because, for Paul's sake, there must be no scandal, that he, Paul's father, had tamely abstained from defending his rights and contesting his wife's charges, and had thus handed the child over to her keeping!

As his cab whirled him up Fifth Avenue, Ralph's whole body throbbed with rage against the influences that had reduced him to such weakness. Then, gradually, he saw that the weakness was innate in him. He had been eloquent enough, in his free youth, against the conventions of his class; yet when the moment came to show his contempt for them they had mysteriously mastered him, deflecting his course like some hidden hereditary failing. As he looked back it seemed as though even his great disaster had been conventionalized and sentimentalized by this inherited attitude: that the thoughts he had thought about it were only those of generations of Dagonets, and that there had been nothing real and his own in his life but the foolish passion he had been trying so hard to think out of existence.

Halfway to the Malibran he changed his direction, and drove to the house of the lawyer he had consulted at the time of his divorce. The lawyer had not yet come up town, and Ralph had a half hour of bitter meditation before the sound of a latch-key brought him to his feet. The visit did not last long. His host, after an affable greeting, listened without surprise to what he had to say, and when he had ended reminded him with somewhat ironic precision that, at the time of the divorce, he had asked for neither advice nor information—had simply declared that he wanted to "turn his back on the whole business" (Ralph recognized the phrase as one of his grandfather's), and, on hearing that in that case he had only to abstain from action, and was in no need of legal services, had gone away without farther enquiries.

"You led me to infer you had your reasons——" the slighted counsellor concluded; and, in reply to Ralph's breathless question, he subjoined, "Why, you see, the case is closed, and I don't exactly know on what ground you can re-open it—unless, of course, you can bring evidence showing that the irregularity of the mother's life is such . . ."

"She's going to marry again," Ralph threw in.

"Indeed? Well, that in itself can hardly be described as irregular. In fact, in certain circumstances it might be construed as an advantage to the child."

"Then I'm powerless?"

"Why—unless there's an ulterior motive—through which pressure might be brought to bear."

"You mean that the first thing to do is to find out what she's up to?"

"Precisely. Of course, if it should prove to be a genuine case of maternal feeling, I won't conceal from you that the outlook's bad. At most, you could probably arrange to see your boy at stated intervals."

To see his boy at stated intervals! Ralph wondered how a sane man could sit there, looking responsible and efficient, and talk such rubbish. . . As he got up to go the lawyer detained him to add: "Of course there's no immediate cause for alarm. It will take time to enforce the provision of the Dakota decree in New York, and till it's done your son can't be taken from you. But there's sure to be a lot of nasty talk in the papers; and you're bound to lose in the end."

Ralph thanked him and left.

He sped northward to the Malibran, where he learned that Mr. and Mrs. Spragg were at dinner. He sent his name down to the subterranean restaurant, and Mr. Spragg presently appeared between the limp portières of the "Adam" writing-room. He had grown older and heavier, as if illness instead of health had put more flesh on his bones, and there were greyish tints in the hollows of his face.

"What's this about Paul?" Ralph exclaimed. "My mother's had a message we can't make out."

Mr. Spragg sat down, with the effect of immersing his spinal column in the depths of the arm-chair he selected. He crossed his legs, and swung one foot to and fro in its high wrinkled boot with elastic sides.

"Didn't you get a letter?" he asked.

"From my—from Undine's lawyers? Yes." Ralph held it out. "It's queer reading. She hasn't hitherto been very keen to have Paul with her."

Mr. Spragg, adjusting his glasses, read the letter slowly, restored it to the envelope and gave it back. "My daughter has intimated that she wishes these gentlemen to act for her. I haven't received any additional instructions from her," he said, with none of the curtness of tone that his stiff legal vocabulary implied.

"But the first communication I received was from you—at least from Mrs. Spragg."

Mr. Spragg drew his beard through his hand. "The ladies are apt to be a trifle hasty. I believe Mrs. Spragg had a letter yesterday instructing her to select a reliable escort for Paul; and I suppose she thought——"

"Oh, this is all too preposterous!" Ralph burst out, springing from his seat. "You don't for a moment imagine, do you—any of you—that I'm going to deliver up my son like a bale of goods in answer to any instructions in God's world?—Oh, yes, I know—I let him go—I abandoned my right to him . . . but I didn't know what I was doing. . . I was sick with grief and misery. My people were awfully broken up over the whole business, and I wanted to spare them. I wanted, above all, to spare my boy when he grew up. If I'd contested the case you know what the result would have been. I let it go by default—I made no conditions—all I wanted was to keep Paul, and never to let him hear a word against his mother!"

Mr. Spragg received this passionate appeal in a silence that implied not so much disdain or indifference, as the total inability to deal verbally with emotional crises. At length, he said, a slight unsteadiness in his usually calm tones: "I presume at the time it was optional with you to demand Paul's custody."

"Oh, yes—it was optional," Ralph sneered.

Mr. Spragg looked at him compassionately. "I'm sorry you didn't do it," he said.

XXXIII

THE UPSHOT of Ralph's visit was that Mr. Spragg, after considerable deliberation, agreed, pending farther negotiations between the opposing lawyers, to undertake that no attempt should be made to remove Paul from his father's custody. Nevertheless, he seemed to think it quite natural that Undine, on the point of making a marriage which would put it in her power to give her child a suitable home, should assert her claim on him. It was more disconcerting to Ralph to learn that Mrs. Spragg, for once departing from her attitude of passive impartiality, had eagerly abetted her daughter's move; he had somehow felt that Undine's desertion of the child had established a kind of mute understanding between himself and his mother-in-law.

"I thought Mrs. Spragg would know there's no earthly use trying to take Paul from me," he said with a desperate awkwardness of entreaty, and Mr. Spragg startled him by replying: "I presume his grandma thinks he'll belong to her more if we keep him in the family."

Ralph, abruptly awakened from his dream of recovered peace, found himself confronted on every side by indifference or hostility: it was as though the June fields in which his boy was playing had suddenly opened to engulph him. Mrs. Marvell's fears and tremors were almost harder to bear than the Spraggs' antagonism; and for the next few days Ralph wandered about miserably, dreading some fresh communication from Undine's lawyers, yet racked by the strain of hearing nothing more from them. Mr. Spragg had agreed to cable his daughter asking her to await a letter before enforcing her demands; but on the fourth day after Ralph's visit to the Malibran a telephone message summoned him to his father-in-law's office.

Half an hour later their talk was over and he stood once more on the landing outside Mr. Spragg's door. Undine's answer had come and Paul's fate was sealed. His mother refused to give him up, refused to await the arrival of her lawyer's letter, and reiterated, in more peremptory language, her demand that the child should be sent immediately to Paris in Mrs. Heeny's care.

Mr. Spragg, in face of Ralph's entreaties, remained pacific but remote. It was evident that, though he had no wish to quarrel with Ralph, he saw no reason for resisting Undine. "I guess she's got the law on her side," he said; and in response to Ralph's passionate remonstrances he added fatalistically: "I presume you'll have to leave the matter to my daughter."

Ralph had gone to the office resolved to control his temper and keep on the watch for any shred of information he might glean; but it soon became clear that Mr. Spragg knew as little as himself of Undine's projects, or of the stage her plans had reached. All she had apparently vouchsafed her parent was the statement that she intended to re-marry, and the command to send Paul over; and Ralph reflected that his own betrothal to her had probably been announced to Mr. Spragg in the same curt fashion.

The thought brought back an overwhelming sense of the past. One by one the details of that incredible moment revived, and he felt in his veins the glow of rapture with which he had first approached the dingy threshold he was now leaving. There came back to him with peculiar vividness the memory of his rushing up to Mr. Spragg's office to consult him about a necklace for Undine. Ralph recalled the incident because his eager appeal for advice had been received by Mr. Spragg with the very phrase he had just used: "I presume you'll have to leave the matter to my daughter."

Ralph saw him slouching in his chair, swung sideways from the untidy desk, his legs stretched out, his hands in his pockets, his jaws engaged on the phantom tooth-pick; and, in a corner of the office, the figure of a middle-sized red-faced young man who seemed to have been interrupted in the act of saying something disagreeable.

"Why, it must have been then that I first saw Moffatt," Ralph reflected; and the thought suggested the memory of other, subsequent meetings in the same building, and of frequent ascents to Moffatt's office during the ardent weeks of their mysterious and remunerative "deal."

Ralph wondered if Moffatt's office were still in the Ararat; and on the way out he paused before the black tablet affixed to the wall of the vestibule and sought and found the name in its familiar place.

The next moment he was again absorbed in his own cares. Now that he had learned the imminence of Paul's danger, and the futility of pleading for delay, a thousand fantastic projects were contending in his head. To get the boy away—that seemed the first thing to do: to put him out of reach, and then invoke the law, get the case re-opened, and carry the fight from court to court till his rights should be recognized. It would cost a lot of money—well, the money would have to be found. The first step was to secure the boy's temporary safety; after that, the question of ways and means would have to be considered. . . . Had there ever been a time, Ralph wondered, when that question hadn't been at the root of all the others?

He had promised to let Clare Van Degen know the result of his visit, and half an hour later he was in her drawing-room. It was the first time he had entered it since his divorce; but Van Degen was tarpon-fishing in California—and besides, he had to see Clare. His one relief was in talking to her, in feverishly turning over with her every possibility of delay and obstruction; and he marvelled at the intelligence and energy she brought to the discussion of these questions. It was as if she had never before felt strongly enough about anything to put her heart or her brains into it; but now everything in her was at work for him.

She listened intently to what he told her; then she said: "You tell me it will cost a great deal; but why take it to the courts at all? Why not give the money to Undine instead of to your lawyers?"

Ralph looked at her in surprise, and she continued: "Why do you suppose she's suddenly made up her mind she must have Paul?"

"That's comprehensible enough to any one who knows her. She wants him because he'll give her the appearance of respectability. Having him with her will prove, as no mere assertions can, that all the rights are on her side and the 'wrongs' on mine."

Clare considered. "Yes; that's the obvious answer. But shall I tell you what I think, my dear? You and I are both completely out-of-date. I don't believe Undine cares a straw for 'the appearance of respectability.' What she wants is the money for her annulment."

Ralph uttered an incredulous exclamation. "But don't you see?" she hurried on. "It's her only hope—her last chance. She's much too clever to burden herself with the child merely to annoy you. What she wants is to make you buy him back from her." She stood up and came to him with outstretched hands. "Perhaps I can be of use to you at last!"

"You?" He summoned up a haggard smile. "As if you weren't always—letting me load you with all my bothers!"

"Oh, if only I've hit on the way out of this one! Then there wouldn't be any others left!" Her eyes followed him intently as he turned away to the window and stood staring down at the sultry prospect of Fifth Avenue. As he turned over her conjecture its probability became more and more apparent. It put into logical relation all the incoherencies of Undine's recent conduct, completed and defined her anew as if a sharp line had been drawn about her fading image.

"If it's that, I shall soon know," he said, turning back into the room. His course had instantly become plain. He had only to resist and Undine would have to show her hand. Simultaneously with this thought there sprang up in his mind the remembrance of the autumn afternoon in Paris when he had come home and found her, among her half-packed finery, desperately bewailing her coming motherhood.

Clare's touch was on his arm. "If I'm right—you *will* let me help?"

He laid his hands on hers without speaking, and she went on:

"It will take a lot of money: all these law-suits do. Besides, she'd be ashamed to sell him cheap. You must be ready to give her anything she wants. And I've got a lot saved up—money of my own, I mean. . ."

"Your own?" As he looked at her the rare blush rose under her brown skin.

"My very own. Why shouldn't you believe me? I've been hoarding up my scrap of an income for years, thinking that some day I'd find I couldn't stand this any longer. . ." Her gesture embraced their sumptuous setting. "But now I know

I shall never budge. There are the children; and besides, things are easier for me since——" she paused, embarrassed.

"Yes, yes; I know." He felt like completing her phrase: "Since my wife has furnished you with the means of putting pressure on your husband——" but he simply repeated: "I know."

"And you *will* let me help?"

"Oh, we must get at the facts first." He caught her hands in his with sudden energy. "As you say, when Paul's safe there won't be another bother left!"

XXXIV

THE MEANS of raising the requisite amount of money became, during the next few weeks, the anxious theme of all Ralph's thoughts. His lawyers' enquiries soon brought the confirmation of Clare's surmise, and it became clear that—for reasons swathed in all the ingenuities of legal verbiage—Undine might, in return for a substantial consideration, be prevailed on to admit that it was for her son's advantage to remain with his father.

The day this admission was communicated to Ralph his first impulse was to carry the news to his cousin. His mood was one of pure exaltation; he seemed to be hugging his boy to him as he walked. Paul and he were to belong to each other forever: no mysterious threat of separation could ever menace them again! He had the blissful sense of relief that the child himself might have had on waking out of a frightened dream and finding the jolly daylight in his room.

Clare at once renewed her entreaty to be allowed to aid in ransoming her little cousin, but Ralph tried to put her off by explaining that he meant to "look about."

"Look where? In the Dagonet coffers? Oh, Ralph, what's the use of pretending? Tell me what you've got to give her." It was amazing how his cousin suddenly dominated him. But as yet he couldn't go into the details of the bargain. That the reckoning between himself and Undine should be settled in dollars and cents seemed the last bitterest satire on his dreams: he felt himself miserably diminished by the smallness of what had filled his world.

Nevertheless, the looking about had to be done; and a day came when he found himself once more at the door of Elmer Moffatt's office. His thoughts had been drawn back to Moffatt by the insistence with which the latter's name had lately been put forward by the press in connection with a revival of the Ararat investigation. Moffatt, it appeared, had been regarded as one of the most valuable witnesses for the State; his return from Europe had been anxiously awaited, his unreadiness to testify caustically criticized; then at last he had arrived, had gone on to Washington—and had apparently had nothing to tell.

Ralph was too deep in his own troubles to waste any wonder over this anticlimax; but the frequent appearance of Moffatt's name in the morning papers acted as an unconscious suggestion. Besides, to whom else could he look for help? The sum his wife demanded could be acquired only by "a quick turn," and the fact that Ralph had once rendered the same kind of service to Moffatt made it natural to appeal to him now. The market, moreover, happened to be booming, and it seemed not unlikely that so experienced a speculator might have a "good thing" up his sleeve.

Moffatt's office had been transformed since Ralph's last visit. Paint, varnish and brass railings gave an air of opulence to the outer precincts, and the inner room, with its mahogany bookcases containing morocco-bound "sets" and its wide blue leather arm-chairs, lacked only a palm or two to resemble the lounge of a fashionable hotel. Moffatt himself, as he came forward, gave Ralph the impression of having been done over by the same hand: he was smoother, broader, more supremely tailored, and his whole person exhaled the faintest whiff of an expensive scent.

He installed his visitor in one of the blue arm-chairs, and sitting opposite, an elbow on his impressive "Washington" desk, listened attentively while Ralph made his request.

"You want to be put onto something good in a damned hurry?" Moffatt twisted his moustache between two plump square-tipped fingers with a little black growth on their lower joints. "I don't suppose," he remarked, "there's a sane man between here and San Francisco who isn't consumed by that yearning."

Having permitted himself this pleasantry he passed on to business. "Yes—it's a first-rate time to buy: no doubt of that. But you say you want to make a quick turn-over? Heard of a soft thing that won't wait, I presume? That's apt to be the way with soft things—all kinds of 'em. There's always other fellows after them." Moffatt's smile was playful. "Well, I'd go considerably out of my way to do you a good turn, because you did me one when I needed it mighty bad. 'In youth you sheltered me.' Yes, sir, that's the kind I am." He stood up, sauntered to the other side of the room, and took a small object from the top of the bookcase.

"Fond of these pink crystals?" He held the oriental toy against the light. "Oh, I ain't a judge—but now and then I like to pick up a pretty thing." Ralph noticed that his eyes caressed it.

"Well—now let's talk. You say you've got to have the funds for your—your investment within three weeks. That's quick work. And you want a hundred thousand. Can you put up fifty?"

Ralph had been prepared for the question, but when it came he felt a moment's tremor. He knew he could count on half the amount from his grandfather; could possibly ask Fairford for a small additional loan—but what of the rest? Well, there was Clare. He had always known there would be no other way. And after all, the money was Clare's—it was Dagonet money. At least she said it was. All the misery of his predicament was distilled into the short silence that preceded his answer: "Yes—I think so."

"Well, I guess I can double it for you." Moffatt spoke with an air of Olympian modesty. "Anyhow, I'll try. Only don't tell the other girls!"

He proceeded to develop his plan to ears which Ralph tried to make alert and attentive, but in which perpetually, through the intricate concert of facts and figures, there broke the shout of a small boy racing across a suburban lawn. "When I pick him up to-night he'll be mine for good!" Ralph thought as Moffatt summed up: "There's the whole scheme in a nut-shell; but you'd better think it over. I don't want to let you in for anything you ain't quite sure about."

"Oh, if you're sure——" Ralph was already calculating the time it would take to dash up to Clare Van Degen's on his way to catch the train for the Fairfords'.

His impatience made it hard to pay due regard to Moffatt's parting civilities. "Glad to have seen you," he heard the latter assuring him with a final hand-grasp. "Wish you'd dine with me some evening at my club"; and, as Ralph murmured a vague acceptance: "How's that boy of yours, by the way?" Moffatt continued. "He was a stunning chap last time I saw him.—Excuse me if I've put my foot in it; but I understood you kept him with you . . . ? Yes: that's what I thought. . . Well, so long."

Clare's inner sitting-room was empty; but the servant, presently returning, led Ralph into the gilded and tapestried wilderness where she occasionally chose to receive her visitors. There, under Popple's effigy of herself, she sat, small and alone, on a monumental sofa behind a tea-table laden with gold plate; while from his lofty frame, on the opposite wall Van Degen, portrayed by a "powerful" artist, cast on her the satisfied eye of proprietorship.

Ralph, swept forward on the blast of his excitement, felt as in a dream the frivolous perversity of her receiving him in such a setting instead of in their usual quiet corner; but there was no room in his mind for anything but the cry that broke from him: "I believe I've done it!"

He sat down and explained to her by what means, trying, as best he could, to restate the particulars of Moffatt's deal; and her manifest ignorance of business methods had the effect of making his vagueness appear less vague.

"Anyhow, he seems to be sure it's a safe thing. I understand he's in with Rolliver now, and Rolliver practically controls Apex. This is some kind of a scheme to buy up all the works of public utility at Apex. They're practically sure of their charter, and Moffatt tells me I can count on doubling my investment within a few weeks. Of course I'll go into the details if you like——"

"Oh, no; you've made it all so clear to me!" She really made him feel he had. "And besides, what on earth does it matter? The great thing is that it's done." She lifted her sparkling eyes. "And now—my share—you haven't told me. . ."

He explained that Mr. Dagonet, to whom he had already named the amount demanded, had at once promised him twenty-five thousand dollars, to be eventually deducted from his share of the estate. His mother had something put by that she insisted on contributing; and Henley Fairford, of his own accord, had come forward with ten thousand: it was awfully decent of Henley. . .

"Even Henley!" Clare sighed. "Then I'm the only one left out?"

Ralph felt the colour in his face. "Well, you see, I shall need as much as fifty——"

Her hands flew together joyfully. "But then you've got to let me help! Oh, I'm so glad—so glad! I've twenty thousand waiting."

He looked about the room, checked anew by all its oppressive implications. "You're a darling . . . but I couldn't take it."

"I've told you it's mine, every penny of it!"

"Yes; but supposing things went wrong?"

"Nothing *can*—if you'll only take it. . ."

"I may lose it——"

"*I* sha'n't, if I've given it to you!" Her look followed his about the room and then came back to him. "Can't you imagine all it will make up for?"

The rapture of the cry caught him up with it. Ah, yes, he could imagine it all! He stooped his head above her hands. "I accept," he said; and they stood and looked at each other like radiant children.

She followed him to the door, and as he turned to leave he broke into a laugh. "It's queer, though, its happening in this room!"

She was close beside him, her hand on the heavy tapestry curtaining the door; and her glance shot past him to her husband's portrait. Ralph caught the look, and a flood of old tendernesses and hates welled up in him. He drew her under the portrait and kissed her vehemently.

XXXV

WITHIN FORTY-EIGHT HOURS Ralph's money was in Moffatt's hands, and the interval of suspense had begun. The transaction over, he felt the deceptive buoyancy that follows on periods of painful indecision. It seemed to him that now at last life had freed him from all trammelling delusions, leaving him only the best thing in its gift—his boy.

The things he meant Paul to do and to be filled his fancy with happy pictures. The child was growing more and more interesting—throwing out countless tendrils of feeling and perception that delighted Ralph but preoccupied the watchful Laura.

"He's going to be exactly like you, Ralph——" she paused and then risked it: "For his own sake, I wish there were just a drop or two of Spragg in him."

Ralph laughed, understanding her. "Oh, the plodding citizen I've become will keep him from taking after the lyric idiot who begot him. Paul and I, between us, are going to turn out something first-rate."

His book too was spreading and throwing out tendrils, and he worked at it in the white heat of energy which his factitious exhilaration produced. For a few weeks everything he did and said seemed as easy and unconditioned as the actions in a dream.

Clare Van Degen, in the light of this mood, became again the comrade of his boyhood. He did not see her often, for she had gone down to the country with her children, but they communicated daily by letter or telephone, and now and then she came over to the Fairfords' for a night. There they renewed the long rambles of their youth, and once more the summer fields and woods seemed full of magic presences. Clare was no more intelligent, she followed him no farther in his flights; but some of the qualities that had become most precious to him were as native to her as its perfume to a flower. So, through the long June afternoons, they ranged together over many themes; and if her answers sometimes missed the mark it did not matter, because her silences never did.

Meanwhile Ralph, from various sources, continued to pick up a good deal of more or less contradictory information about Elmer Moffatt. It seemed to be generally understood that Moffatt had come back from Europe with the intention of testifying in the Ararat investigation, and that his former patron, the great Harmon B. Driscoll, had managed to silence him; and it was implied that the price of this silence, which was set at a considerable figure, had been turned to account in a series of speculations likely to lift Moffatt to permanent eminence among the rulers of Wall Street. The stories as to his latest achievement, and the theories as to the man himself, varied with the visual angle of each reporter: and whenever any attempt was made to focus his hard sharp personality some guardian divinity seemed to throw a veil of mystery over him. His detractors, however, were the first to own that there was "something about him"; it was felt that he had passed beyond the meteoric stage, and the business world was unanimous in recognizing that he had "come to stay." A dawning sense of his stability was even beginning to make itself felt in Fifth Avenue. It was said that he had bought a house in Seventy-second Street, then that he meant to build near the Park; one or two people (always "taken by a friend") had been to his flat in the Pactolus, to see his Chinese porcelains and Persian rugs; now and then he had a few important men to dine at a Fifth Avenue restaurant; his name began to appear in philanthropic reports and on municipal committees (there were even rumours of its having been put up at a well-known club); and the rector of a wealthy parish, who was raising funds for a chantry, was known to have met him at dinner and to have stated afterward that "the man was not wholly a materialist."

All these converging proofs of Moffatt's solidity strengthened Ralph's faith in his venture. He remembered with what astuteness and authority Moffatt had conducted their real estate transaction—how far off and unreal it all seemed!—and awaited events with the passive faith of a sufferer in the hands of a skilful surgeon.

The days moved on toward the end of June, and each morning Ralph opened his newspaper with a keener thrill of expectation. Any day now he might read of the granting of the Apex charter: Moffatt had assured him it would "go through" before the close of the month. But the announcement did not appear, and after what seemed to Ralph a decent lapse of time he telephoned to ask for news. Moffatt was away, and when he came back a few days later he answered Ralph's enquiries evasively, with an edge of irritation in his voice. The same day Ralph received a letter from his lawyer, who had been reminded by Mrs. Marvell's representatives that the latest date agreed on for the execution of the financial agreement was the end of the following week.

Ralph, alarmed, betook himself at once to the Ararat, and his first glimpse of Moffatt's round common face and fastidiously dressed person gave him an immediate sense of reassurance. He felt that under the circle of baldness on top of that carefully brushed head lay the solution of every monetary problem that could beset the soul of man. Moffatt's voice had recovered its usual cordial note, and the warmth of his welcome dispelled Ralph's last apprehension.

"Why, yes, everything's going along first-rate. They thought they'd hung us up last week—but they haven't. There may be another week's delay; but we ought to be opening a bottle of wine on it by the Fourth."

An office-boy came in with a name on a slip of paper, and Moffatt looked at his watch and held out a hearty hand. "Glad you came. Of course I'll keep you posted. . . No, this way. . . Look in again . . ." and he steered Ralph out by another door.

July came, and passed into its second week. Ralph's lawyer had obtained a postponement from the other side, but Undine's representatives had given him to understand that the transaction must be closed before the first of August. Ralph telephoned once or twice to Moffatt, receiving genially-worded assurances that everything was "going their way"; but he felt a certain embarrassment in returning again to the office, and let himself drift through the days in a state of hungry apprehension. Finally one afternoon Henley Fairford, coming back from town (which Ralph had left in the morning to join his boy over Sunday), brought word that the Apex consolidation scheme had failed to get its charter. It was useless to attempt to reach Moffatt on Sunday, and Ralph wore on as he could through the succeeding twenty-four hours. Clare Van Degen had come down to stay with her youngest boy, and in the afternoon she and Ralph took the two children for a sail. A light breeze brightened the waters of the Sound, and they ran down the shore before it and then tacked out toward the sunset, coming back at last, under a failing breeze, as the summer sky passed from blue to a translucid green and then into the accumulating greys of twilight.

As they left the landing and walked up behind the children across the darkening lawn, a sense of security descended again on Ralph. He could not believe that such a scene and such a mood could be the disguise of any impending evil, and all his doubts and anxieties fell away from him.

The next morning, he and Clare travelled up to town together, and at the station he put her in the motor which was to take her to Long Island, and hastened down to Moffatt's office. When he arrived he was told that Moffatt was "engaged," and he had to wait for nearly half an hour in the outer office, where, to the steady click of the type-writer and the spasmodic buzzing of the telephone, his thoughts again began their restless circlings. Finally the inner door opened, and he found himself in the sanctuary. Moffatt was seated behind his desk, examining another little crystal vase somewhat like the one he had shown Ralph a few weeks earlier. As his visitor entered, he held it up against the light, revealing on its dewy sides an incised design as frail as the shadow of grass-blades on water.

"Ain't she a peach?" He put the toy down and reached across the desk to shake hands. "Well, well," he went on, leaning back in his chair, and pushing out his lower lip in a half-comic pout, "they've got us in the neck this time and no mistake. Seen this morning's *Radiator*? I don't know how the thing leaked out—but the reformers somehow got a smell of the scheme, and whenever they get swishing round something's bound to get spilt."

He talked gaily, genially, in his roundest tones and with his easiest gestures; never had he conveyed a completer sense of unhurried power; but Ralph noticed for the first time the crow's-feet about his eyes, and the sharpness of the contrast between the white of his forehead and the redness of the fold of neck above his collar.

"Do you mean to say it's not going through?"

"Not this time, anyhow. We're high and dry."

Something seemed to snap in Ralph's head, and he sat down in the nearest chair. "Has the common stock dropped a lot?"

"Well, you've got to lean over to see it." Moffatt pressed his finger-tips together and added thoughtfully: "But it's *there* all right. We're bound to get our charter in the end."

"What do you call the end?"

"Oh, before the Day of Judgment, sure: next year, I guess."

"Next year?" Ralph flushed. "What earthly good will that do me?"

"I don't say it's as pleasant as driving your best girl home by moonlight. But that's how it is. And the stuff's safe enough any way—I've told you that right along."

"But you've told me all along I could count on a rise before August. You knew I had to have the money now."

"I knew you *wanted* to have the money now; and so did I, and several of my friends. I put you onto it because it was the only thing in sight likely to give you the return you wanted."

"You ought at least to have warned me of the risk!"

"Risk? I don't call it much of a risk to lie back in your chair and wait another few months for fifty thousand to drop into your lap. I tell you the thing's as safe as a bank."

"How do I know it is? You've misled me about it from the first."

Moffatt's face grew dark red to the forehead: for the first time in their acquaintance Ralph saw him on the verge of anger.

"Well, if you get stuck so do I. I'm in it a good deal deeper than you. That's about the best guarantee I can give; unless you won't take my word for that either." To control himself Moffatt spoke with extreme deliberation, separating his syllables like a machine cutting something into even lengths.

Ralph listened through a cloud of confusion; but he saw the madness of offending Moffatt, and tried to take a more conciliatory tone. "Of course I take your word for it. But I can't—I simply can't afford to lose. . ."

"You ain't going to lose: I don't believe you'll even have to put up any margin. It's *there* safe enough, I tell you. . ."

"Yes, yes; I understand. I'm sure you wouldn't have advised me——" Ralph's tongue seemed swollen, and he had difficulty in bringing out the words. "Only, you see—I can't wait; it's not possible; and I want to know if there isn't a way——"

Moffatt looked at him with a sort of resigned compassion, as a doctor looks at a despairing mother who will not understand what he has tried to imply without uttering the word she dreads. Ralph understood the look, but hurried on.

"You'll think I'm mad, or an ass, to talk like this; but the fact is, I must have the money." He waited and drew a hard breath. "I must have it: that's all. Perhaps I'd better tell you——"

Moffatt, who had risen, as if assuming that the interview was over, sat down again and turned an attentive look on him. "Go ahead," he said, more humanly than he had hitherto spoken.

"My boy . . . you spoke of him the other day . . . I'm awfully fond of him——" Ralph broke off, deterred by the impossibility of confiding his feeling for Paul to this coarse-grained man with whom he hadn't a sentiment in common.

Moffatt was still looking at him. "I should say you would be! He's as smart a little chap as I ever saw; and I guess he's the kind that gets better every day."

Ralph had collected himself, and went on with sudden resolution: "Well, you see—when my wife and I separated, I never dreamed she'd want the boy: the question never came up. If it had, of course—but she'd left him with me when she went away two years before, and at the time of the divorce I was a fool. . . I didn't take the proper steps. . ."

"You mean she's got sole custody?"

Ralph made a sign of assent, and Moffatt pondered. "That's bad—bad."

"And now I understand she's going to marry again—and of course I can't give up my son."

"She wants you to, eh?"

Ralph again assented.

Moffatt swung his chair about and leaned back in it, stretching out his plump legs and contemplating the tips of his varnished boots. He hummed a low tune behind inscrutable lips.

"That's what you want the money for?" he finally raised his head to ask.

The word came out of the depths of Ralph's anguish: "Yes."

"And why you want it in such a hurry. I see." Moffatt reverted to the study of his boots. "It's a lot of money."

"Yes. That's the difficulty. And I . . . she . . ."

Ralph's tongue was again too thick for his mouth. "I'm afraid she won't wait . . . or take less. . ."

Moffatt, abandoning the boots, was scrutinizing him through half-shut lids. "No," he said slowly, "I don't believe Undine Spragg'll take a single cent less."

Ralph felt himself whiten. Was it insolence or ignorance that had prompted Moffatt's speech? Nothing in his voice or face showed the sense of any shades of expression or of feeling: he seemed to apply to everything the measure of the same crude flippancy. But such considerations could not curb Ralph now. He said to himself "Keep your temper—keep your temper——" and his anger suddenly boiled over.

"Look here, Moffatt," he said, getting to his feet, "the fact that I've been divorced from Mrs. Marvell doesn't authorize any one to take that tone to me in speaking of her."

Moffatt met the challenge with a calm stare under which there were dawning signs of surprise and interest. "That so? Well, if that's the case I presume I ought to feel the same way: I've been divorced from her myself."

For an instant the words conveyed no meaning to Ralph; then they surged up into his brain and flung him forward with half-raised arm. But he felt the grotesqueness of the gesture and his arm dropped back to his side. A series of unimportant and irrelevant things raced through his mind; then obscurity settled down on it. "*This* man . . . *this* man . . ." was the one fiery point in his darkened consciousness. . .

"What on earth are you talking about?" he brought out.

"Why, facts," said Moffatt, in a cool half-humorous voice.

"You didn't know? I understood from Mrs. Marvell your folks had a prejudice against divorce, so I suppose she kept quiet about that early episode. The truth is," he continued amicably, "I wouldn't have alluded to it now if you hadn't taken rather a high tone with me about our little venture; but now it's out I guess you may as well hear the whole story. It's mighty wholesome for a man to have a round now and then with a few facts. Shall I go on?"

Ralph had stood listening without a sign, but as Moffatt ended he made a slight motion of acquiescence. He did not otherwise change his attitude, except to grasp with one hand the back of the chair that Moffatt pushed toward him.

"Rather stand? . . ." Moffatt himself dropped back into his seat and took the pose of easy narrative. "Well, it was this way. Undine Spragg and I were made one at Opake, Nebraska, just nine years ago last month. My! She was a beauty then. Nothing much had happened to her before but being engaged for a year or two to a soft called Millard Binch; the same she passed on to Indiana Rolliver; and— well, I guess she liked the change. We didn't have what you'd called a society wedding: no best man or bridesmaids or Voice that Breathed o'er Eden. Fact is, Pa and Ma didn't know about it till it was over. But it was a marriage fast enough, as they found out when they tried to undo it. Trouble was, they caught on too soon; we only had a fortnight. Then they hauled Undine back to Apex, and—well, I hadn't the cash or the pull to fight 'em. Uncle Abner was a pretty big man out there then; and he had James J. Rolliver behind him. I always know when I'm licked; and I was licked that time. So we unlooped the loop, and they fixed it up for me to make a trip to Alaska. Let me see—that was the year before they moved over to New York. Next time I saw Undine I sat alongside of her at the theatre the day your engagement was announced."

He still kept to his half-humorous minor key, as though he were in the first stages of an after-dinner speech; but as he went on his bodily presence, which hitherto had seemed to Ralph the mere average garment of vulgarity, began to loom, huge and portentous as some monster released from a magician's bottle. His redness, his glossiness, his baldness, and the carefully brushed ring of hair encircling it; the square line of his shoulders, the too careful fit of his clothes, the prominent lustre of his scarf-pin, the growth of short black hair on his manicured hands, even the tiny cracks and crows'-feet beginning to show in the hard close surface of his complexion: all these solid witnesses to his reality and his proximity pressed on Ralph with the mounting pang of physical nausea.

"*This* man . . . *this* man . . ." he couldn't get beyond the thought: whichever way he turned his haggard thought, there was Moffatt bodily blocking the perspective. . . Ralph's eyes roamed toward the crystal toy that stood on the desk beside Moffatt's hand. Faugh! That such a hand should have touched it!

Suddenly he heard himself speaking. "Before my marriage—did you know they hadn't told me?"

"Why, I understood as much. . ."

Ralph pushed on: "You knew it the day I met you in Mr. Spragg's office?"

Moffatt considered a moment, as if the incident had escaped him. "Did we meet there?" He seemed benevolently ready for enlightenment. But Ralph had been assailed by another memory; he recalled that Moffatt had dined one night in his house, that he and the man who now faced him had sat at the same table, their wife between them. . .

He was seized with another dumb gust of fury; but it died out and left him face to face with the uselessness, the irrelevance of all the old attitudes of appropriation and defiance. He seemed to be stumbling about in his inherited prejudices like a modern man in mediæval armour. . . Moffatt still sat at his desk, unmoved and apparently uncomprehending. "He doesn't even know what I'm feeling," flashed through Ralph; and the whole archaic structure of his rites and sanctions tumbled down about him.

Through the noise of the crash he heard Moffatt's voice going on without perceptible change of tone: "About that other matter now . . . you can't feel any meaner about it than I do, I can tell you that . . . but all we've got to do is to sit tight. . ."

Ralph turned from the voice, and found himself outside on the landing, and then in the street below.

XXXVI

H
E STOOD at the corner of Wall Street, looking up and down its hot summer perspective. He noticed the swirls of dust in the cracks of the pavement, the rubbish in the gutters, the ceaseless stream of perspiring faces that poured by under tilted hats.

He found himself, next, slipping northward between the glazed walls of the Subway, another languid crowd in the seats about him and the nasal yelp of the stations ringing through the car like some repeated ritual wail. The blindness within him seemed to have intensified his physical perceptions, his sensitiveness to the heat, the noise, the smells of the dishevelled midsummer city; but combined with the acuter perception of these offenses was a complete indifference to them, as though he were some vivisected animal deprived of the power of discrimination.

Now he had turned into Waverly Place, and was walking westward toward Washington Square. At the corner he pulled himself up, saying half-aloud: "The office—I ought to be at the office." He drew out his watch and stared at it blankly. What the devil had he taken it out for? He had to go through a laborious process of readjustment to find out what it had to say. . . Twelve o'clock. . . Should he turn back to the office? It seemed easier to cross the square, go up the steps of the old house and slip his key into the door. . .

The house was empty. His mother, a few days previously, had departed with Mr. Dagonet for their usual two months on the Maine coast, where Ralph was to join them with his boy. . . The blinds were all drawn down, and the freshness and silence of the marble-paved hall laid soothing hands on him. . . He said to himself: "I'll jump into a cab presently, and go and lunch at the club——" He laid down his hat and stick and climbed the carpetless stairs to his room. When he entered it he had the shock of feeling himself in a strange place: it did not seem like anything he had ever seen before. Then, one by one, all the old stale usual things in it confronted him, and he longed with a sick intensity to be in a place that was really strange.

933

"How on earth can I go on living here?" he wondered.

A careless servant had left the outer shutters open, and the sun was beating on the window-panes. Ralph pushed open the windows, shut the shutters, and wandered toward his arm-chair. Beads of perspiration stood on his forehead: the temperature of the room reminded him of the heat under the ilexes of the Sienese villa where he and Undine had sat through a long July afternoon. He saw her before him, leaning against the tree-trunk in her white dress, limpid and inscrutable. . . "We were made one at Opake, Nebraska. . ." Had she been thinking of it that afternoon at Siena, he wondered? Did she ever think of it at all? . . . It was she who had asked Moffatt to dine. She had said: "Father brought him home one day at Apex. . . I don't remember ever having seen him since"—and the man she spoke of had had her in his arms . . . and perhaps it was really all she remembered!

She had lied to him—lied to him from the first . . . there hadn't been a moment when she hadn't lied to him, deliberately, ingeniously and inventively. As he thought of it, there came to him, for the first time in months, that overwhelming sense of her physical nearness which had once so haunted and tortured him. Her freshness, her fragrance, the luminous haze of her youth, filled the room with a mocking glory; and he dropped his head on his hands to shut it out. . .

The vision was swept away by another wave of hurrying thoughts. He felt it was intensely important that he should keep the thread of every one of them, that they all represented things to be said or done, or guarded against; and his mind, with the unwondering versatility and tireless haste of the dreamer's brain, seemed to be pursuing them all simultaneously. Then they became as unreal and meaningless as the red specks dancing behind the lids against which he had pressed his fists clenched, and he had the feeling that if he opened his eyes they would vanish, and the familiar daylight look in on him. . .

A knock disturbed him. The old parlour-maid who was always left in charge of the house had come up to ask if he wasn't well, and if there was anything she could do for him. He told her no . . . he was perfectly well . . . or, rather, no, he wasn't . . . he supposed it must be the heat; and he began to scold her for having forgotten to close the shutters.

It wasn't her fault, it appeared, but Eliza's: her tone implied that he knew what one had to expect of Eliza . . . and wouldn't he go down to the nice cool shady dining-room, and let her make him an iced drink and a few sandwiches?

"I've always told Mrs. Marvell I couldn't turn my back for a second but what Eliza'd find a way to make trouble," the old woman continued, evidently glad of the chance to air a perennial grievance. "It's not only the things she *forgets* to do," she added significantly; and it dawned on Ralph that she was making an appeal to him, expecting him to take sides with her in the chronic conflict between herself and Eliza. He said to himself that perhaps she was right . . . that perhaps there was something he ought to do . . . that his mother was old, and didn't always see things; and for a while his mind revolved this problem with feverish intensity. . .

"Then you'll come down, sir?"

"Yes."

The door closed, and he heard her heavy heels along the passage.

"But the money—where's the money to come from?" The question sprang out from some denser fold of the fog in his brain. The money—how on earth was he to pay it back? How could he have wasted his time in thinking of anything else while that central difficulty existed?

"But I can't . . . I can't . . . it's gone . . . and even if it weren't . . ." He dropped back in his chair and took his head between his hands. He had forgotten what he wanted the money for. He made a great effort to regain hold of the idea, but all the whirring, shuttling, flying had abruptly ceased in his brain, and he sat with his eyes shut, staring straight into darkness. . .

The clock struck, and he remembered that he had said he would go down to the dining-room. "If I don't she'll come up——" He raised his head and sat listening for the sound of the old woman's step: it seemed to him perfectly intolerable that any one should cross the threshold of the room again.

"Why can't they leave me alone?" he groaned. . . At

length through the silence of the empty house, he fancied he heard a door opening and closing far below; and he said to himself: "She's coming."

He got to his feet and went to the door. He didn't feel anything now except the insane dread of hearing the woman's steps come nearer. He bolted the door and stood looking about the room. For a moment he was conscious of seeing it in every detail with a distinctness he had never before known; then everything in it vanished but the single narrow panel of a drawer under one of the bookcases. He went up to the drawer, knelt down and slipped his hand into it.

As he raised himself he listened again, and this time he distinctly heard the old servant's steps on the stairs. He passed his left hand over the side of his head, and down the curve of the skull behind the ear. He said to himself: "My wife . . . this will make it all right for her . . ." and a last flash of irony twitched through him. Then he felt again, more deliberately, for the spot he wanted, and put the muzzle of his revolver against it.

BOOK V

XXXVII

IN A DRAWING-ROOM hung with portraits of high-nosed personages in perukes and orders, a circle of ladies and gentlemen, looking not unlike every-day versions of the official figures above their heads, sat examining with friendly interest a little boy in mourning.

The boy was slim, fair and shy, and his small black figure, islanded in the middle of the wide lustrous floor, looked curiously lonely and remote. This effect of remoteness seemed to strike his mother as something intentional, and almost naughty, for after having launched him from the door, and waited to judge of the impression he produced, she came forward and, giving him a slight push, said impatiently: "Paul! Why don't you go and kiss your new granny?"

The boy, without turning to her, or moving, sent his blue glance gravely about the circle. "Does she want me to?" he asked, in a tone of evident apprehension; and on his mother's answering: "Of course, you silly!" he added earnestly: "How many more do you think there'll be?"

Undine blushed to the ripples of her brilliant hair. "I never knew such a child! They've turned him into a perfect little savage!"

Raymond de Chelles advanced from behind his mother's chair.

"He won't be a savage long with me," he said, stooping down so that his fatigued finely-drawn face was close to Paul's. Their eyes met and the boy smiled. "Come along, old chap," Chelles continued in English, drawing the little boy after him.

"*Il est bien beau,*" the Marquise de Chelles observed, her eyes turning from Paul's grave face to her daughter-in-law's vivid countenance.

"Do be nice, darling! Say, '*bonjour, Madame,*'" Undine urged.

An odd mingling of emotions stirred in her while she stood watching Paul make the round of the family group under her husband's guidance. It was "lovely" to have the child back, and to find him, after their three years' separation, grown into so endearing a figure: her first glimpse of him when, in Mrs. Heeny's arms, he had emerged that morning from the steamer train, had shown what an acquisition he would be. If she had had any lingering doubts on the point, the impression produced on her husband would have dispelled them. Chelles had been instantly charmed, and Paul, in a shy confused way, was already responding to his advances. The Count and Countess Raymond had returned but a few weeks before from their protracted wedding journey, and were staying—as they were apparently to do whenever they came to Paris—with the old Marquis, Raymond's father, who had amicably proposed that little Paul Marvell should also share the hospitality of the Hôtel de Chelles. Undine, at first, was somewhat dismayed to find that she was expected to fit the boy and his nurse into a corner of her contracted *entresol*. But the possibility of a mother's not finding room for her son, however cramped her own quarters, seemed not to have occurred to her new relations, and the preparing of her dressing-room and boudoir for Paul's occupancy was carried on by the household with a zeal which obliged her to dissemble her lukewarmness.

Undine had supposed that on her marriage one of the great suites of the Hôtel de Chelles would be emptied of its tenants and put at her husband's disposal; but she had since learned that, even had such a plan occurred to her parents-in-law, considerations of economy would have hindered it. The old Marquis and his wife, who were content, when they came up from Burgundy in the spring, with a modest set of rooms looking out on the court of their ancestral residence, expected their son and his wife to fit themselves into the still smaller apartment which had served as Raymond's bachelor lodging. The rest of the fine old mouldering house—the tall-windowed *premier* on the garden, and the whole of the floor above—had been let for years to old-fashioned tenants who would have been more surprised than their landlord had he suddenly proposed to dispossess them. Undine, at first, had regarded these arrangements as merely provisional. She was persuaded that, under her influence, Raymond would soon convert his parents to more modern ideas, and meanwhile she was still in the flush of a completer well-being than she had ever known, and disposed, for the moment, to make light of any inconveniences connected with it. The three months since her marriage had been more nearly like what she had dreamed of than any of her previous experiments in happiness. At last she had what she wanted, and for the first time the glow of triumph was warmed by a deeper feeling. Her husband was really charming (it was odd how he reminded her of Ralph!), and after her bitter two years of loneliness and humiliation it was delicious to find herself once more adored and protected.

The very fact that Raymond was more jealous of her than Ralph had ever been—or at any rate less reluctant to show it—gave her a keener sense of recovered power. None of the men who had been in love with her before had been so frankly possessive, or so eager for reciprocal assurances of constancy. She knew that Ralph had suffered deeply from her intimacy with Van Degen, but he had betrayed his feeling only by a more studied detachment; and Van Degen, from the first, had been contemptuously indifferent to what she did or felt when she was out of his sight. As to her earlier experiences, she had frankly forgotten them: her sentimental memories went back no farther than the beginning of her New York career.

Raymond seemed to attach more importance to love, in all its manifestations, than was usual or convenient in a husband; and she gradually began to be aware that her domination over him involved a corresponding loss of independence. Since their return to Paris she had found that she was expected to give a circumstantial report of every hour she spent away from him. She had nothing to hide, and no designs against his peace of mind except those connected with her frequent and costly sessions at the dress-makers'; but she had never before been called upon to account to any one for the use of her time, and after the first amused surprise at Raymond's always wanting to know where she had been and whom she had seen she began to be oppressed by so exacting a devotion. Her parents, from her tenderest youth, had tacitly recognized her inalienable right to "go around," and Ralph—though from motives which she divined to be different—had shown the same respect for her freedom. It was therefore disconcerting to find that Raymond expected her to choose her friends, and even her acquaintances, in conformity not only with his personal tastes but with a definite and complicated code of family prejudices and traditions; and she was especially surprised to discover that he viewed with disapproval her intimacy with the Princess Estradina.

"My cousin's extremely amusing, of course, but utterly mad and very *mal entourée*. Most of the people she has about her ought to be in prison or Bedlam: especially that unspeakable Madame Adelschein, who's a candidate for both. My aunt's an angel, but she's been weak enough to let Lili turn the Hôtel de Dordogne into an annex of Montmartre. Of course you'll have to show yourself there now and then: in these days families like ours must hold together. But go to the *réunions de famille* rather than to Lili's intimate parties; go with me, or with my mother; don't let yourself be seen there alone. You're too young and good-looking to be mixed up with that crew. A woman's classed—or rather unclassed—by being known as one of Lili's set."

Agreeable as it was to Undine that an appeal to her discretion should be based on the ground of her youth and good-looks, she was dismayed to find herself cut off from the very circle she had meant them to establish her in. Before she had become Raymond's wife there had been a moment of sharp tension in her relations with the Princess Estradina and the old Duchess. They had done their best to prevent her marrying their cousin, and had gone so far as openly to accuse her of being the cause of a breach between themselves and his parents. But Ralph Marvell's death had brought about a sudden change in her situation. She was now no longer a divorced woman struggling to obtain ecclesiastical sanction for her remarriage, but a widow whose conspicuous beauty and independent situation made her the object of lawful aspirations. The first person to seize on this distinction and make the most of it was her old enemy the Marquise de Trézac. The latter, who had been loudly charged by the house of Chelles with furthering her beautiful compatriot's designs, had instantly seen a chance of vindicating herself by taking the widowed Mrs. Marvell under her wing and favouring the attentions of other suitors. These were not lacking, and the

expected result had followed. Raymond de Chelles, more than
ever infatuated as attainment became less certain, had claimed
a definite promise from Undine, and his family, discouraged
by his persistent bachelorhood, and their failure to fix his attention on any of the amiable maidens obviously designed to
continue the race, had ended by withdrawing their opposition
and discovering in Mrs. Marvell the moral and financial merits necessary to justify their change of front.

"A good match? If she isn't, I should like to know what
the Chelles call one!" Madame de Trézac went about indefat-
igably proclaiming. "Related to the best people in New
York—well, by marriage, that is; and her husband left much
more money than was expected. It goes to the boy, of course;
but as the boy is with his mother she naturally enjoys the
income. And her father's a rich man—much richer than is
generally known; I mean what *we* call rich in America, you
understand!"

Madame de Trézac had lately discovered that the proper
attitude for the American married abroad was that of a militant patriotism; and she flaunted Undine Marvell in the face
of the Faubourg like a particularly showy specimen of her
national banner. The success of the experiment emboldened
her to throw off the most sacred observances of her past. She
took up Madame Adelschein, she entertained the James J.
Rollivers, she resuscitated Creole dishes, she patronized negro
melodists, she abandoned her weekly teas for impromptu afternoon dances, and the prim drawing-room in which dowagers had droned echoed with a cosmopolitan hubbub.

Even when the period of tension was over, and Undine had
been officially received into the family of her betrothed, Madame de Trézac did not at once surrender. She laughingly
professed to have had enough of the proprieties, and declared
herself bored by the social rites she had hitherto so piously
performed. "You'll always find a corner of home here, dearest,
when you get tired of their ceremonies and solemnities," she
said as she embraced the bride after the wedding breakfast;
and Undine hoped that the devoted Nettie would in fact provide a refuge from the extreme domesticity of her new state.
But since her return to Paris, and her taking up her domicile
in the Hôtel de Chelles, she had found Madame de Trézac

less and less disposed to abet her in any assertion of independence.

"My dear, a woman must adopt her husband's nationality whether she wants to or not. It's the law, and it's the custom besides. If you wanted to amuse yourself with your Nouveau Luxe friends you oughtn't to have married Raymond—but of course I say that only in joke. As if any woman would have hesitated who'd had your chance! Take my advice—keep out of Lili's set just at first. Later . . . well, perhaps Raymond won't be so particular; but meanwhile you'd make a great mistake to go against his people——" and Madame de Trézac, with a *"Chère Madame,"* swept forward from her teatable to receive the first of the returning dowagers.

It was about this time that Mrs. Heeny arrived with Paul; and for a while Undine was pleasantly absorbed in her boy. She kept Mrs. Heeny in Paris for a fortnight, and between her more pressing occupations it amused her to listen to the *masseuse's* New York gossip and her comments on the social organization of the old world. It was Mrs. Heeny's first visit to Europe, and she confessed to Undine that she had always wanted to "see something of the aristocracy"—using the phrase as a naturalist might, with no hint of personal pretensions. Mrs. Heeny's democratic ease was combined with the strictest professional discretion, and it would never have occurred to her to regard herself, or to wish others to regard her, as anything but a manipulator of muscles; but in that character she felt herself entitled to admission to the highest circles.

"They certainly do things with style over here—but it's kinder one-horse after New York, ain't it? Is this what they call their season? Why, you dined home two nights last week. They ought to come over to New York and see!" And she poured into Undine's half-envious ear a list of the entertainments which had illuminated the last weeks of the New York winter. "I suppose you'll begin to give parties as soon as ever you get into a house of your own. You're not going to have one? Oh, well, then you'll give a lot of big week-ends at your place down in the Shatter-country—that's where the swells all go to in the summer time, ain't it? But I dunno what your ma would say if she knew you were going to live on with *his* folks after you're done honey-mooning. Why, we read in the papers you were going to live in some grand hotel or other—oh, they call their houses *hotels*, do they? That's funny: I suppose it's because they let out part of 'em. Well, you look handsomer than ever, Undine; I'll take *that* back to your mother, anyhow. And he's dead in love, I can see that; reminds me of the way——" but she broke off suddenly, as if something in Undine's look had silenced her.

Even to herself, Undine did not like to call up the image of Ralph Marvell; and any mention of his name gave her a vague sense of distress. His death had released her, had given her what she wanted; yet she could honestly say to herself that she had not wanted him to die—at least not to die like that. . . People said at the time that it was the hot weather—his own family had said so: he had never quite got over his attack of pneumonia, and the sudden rise of temperature—one of the fierce "heat-waves" that devastate New York in summer—had probably affected his brain: the doctors said such cases were not uncommon. . . She had worn black for a few weeks—not quite mourning, but something decently regretful (the dress-makers were beginning to provide a special garb for such cases); and even since her remarriage, and the lapse of a year, she continued to wish that she could have got what she wanted without having had to pay that particular price for it.

This feeling was intensified by an incident—in itself far from unwelcome—which had occurred about three months after Ralph's death. Her lawyers had written to say that the sum of a hundred thousand dollars had been paid over to Marvell's estate by the Apex Consolidation Company; and as Marvell had left a will bequeathing everything he possessed to his son, this unexpected windfall handsomely increased Paul's patrimony. Undine had never relinquished her claim on her child; she had merely, by the advice of her lawyers, waived the assertion of her right for a few months after Marvell's death, with the express stipulation that her doing so was only a temporary concession to the feelings of her husband's family; and she had held out against all attempts to induce her to surrender Paul permanently. Before her marriage she had somewhat conspicuously adopted her husband's creed, and the Dagonets, picturing Paul as the prey of the Jesuits, had made the mistake of appealing to the courts for his custody. This had confirmed Undine's resistance, and her determination to keep the child. The case had been decided in her favour, and she had thereupon demanded, and obtained, an allowance of five thousand dollars, to be devoted to the bringing up and education of her son. This sum, added to what Mr. Spragg had agreed to give her, made up an income which had appreciably bettered her position, and justified Madame de Trézac's discreet allusions to her wealth. Nevertheless, it was one of the facts about which she least liked to think when any chance allusion evoked Ralph's image. The money was hers, of course; she had a right to it, and she was an ardent believer in "rights." But she wished she could have got it in some other way—she hated the thought of it as one more instance of the perverseness with which things she was entitled to always came to her as if they had been stolen.

The approach of summer, and the culmination of the Paris season, swept aside such thoughts. The Countess Raymond de Chelles, contrasting her situation with that of Mrs. Undine Marvell, and the fulness and animation of her new life with the vacant dissatisfied days which had followed on her return from Dakota, forgot the smallness of her apartment, the inconvenient proximity of Paul and his nurse, the interminable round of visits with her mother-in-law, and the long dinners in the solemn hôtels of all the family connection. The world was radiant, the lights were lit, the music playing; she was still young, and better-looking than ever, with a Countess's coronet, a famous château and a handsome and popular husband who adored her. And then suddenly the lights went out and the music stopped when one day Raymond, putting his arm about her, said in his tenderest tones: "And now, my dear, the world's had you long enough and it's my turn. What do you say to going down to Saint Désert?"

XXXVIII

IN A WINDOW of the long gallery of the château de Saint
Désert the new Marquise de Chelles stood looking down
the poplar avenue into the November rain. It had been raining heavily and persistently for a longer time than she could
remember. Day after day the hills beyond the park had been
curtained by motionless clouds, the gutters of the long steep
roofs had gurgled with a perpetual overflow, the opaque surface of the moat been peppered by a continuous pelting of
big drops. The water lay in glassy stretches under the trees
and along the sodden edges of the garden-paths, it rose in a
white mist from the fields beyond, it exuded in a chill moisture from the brick flooring of the passages and from the
walls of the rooms on the lower floor. Everything in the great
empty house smelt of dampness: the stuffing of the chairs, the
threadbare folds of the faded curtains, the splendid tapestries,
that were fading too, on the walls of the room in which
Undine stood, and the wide bands of crape which her husband had insisted on her keeping on her black dresses till the
last hour of her mourning for the old Marquis.

The summer had been more than usually inclement, and
since her first coming to the country Undine had lived
through many periods of rainy weather; but none which had
gone before had so completely epitomized, so summed up in
one vast monotonous blur, the image of her long months at
Saint Désert.

When, the year before, she had reluctantly suffered herself
to be torn from the joys of Paris, she had been sustained by
the belief that her exile would not be of long duration. Once
Paris was out of sight, she had even found a certain lazy
charm in the long warm days at Saint Désert. Her parents-in-
law had remained in town, and she enjoyed being alone with
her husband, exploring and appraising the treasures of the
great half-abandoned house, and watching her boy scamper
over the June meadows or trot about the gardens on the
poney his stepfather had given him. Paul, after Mrs. Heeny's
departure, had grown fretful and restive, and Undine had
found it more and more difficult to fit his small exacting

personality into her cramped rooms and crowded life. He irritated her by pining for his Aunt Laura, his Marvell granny,
and old Mr. Dagonet's funny stories about gods and fairies;
and his wistful allusions to his games with Clare's children
sounded like a lesson he might have been drilled in to make
her feel how little he belonged to her. But once released from
Paris, and blessed with rabbits, a poney and the freedom of
the fields, he became again all that a charming child should
be, and for a time it amused her to share in his romps and
rambles. Raymond seemed enchanted at the picture they
made, and the quiet weeks of fresh air and outdoor activity
gave her back a bloom that reflected itself in her tranquillized
mood. She was the more resigned to this interlude because
she was so sure of its not lasting. Before they left Paris a doctor had been found to say that Paul—who was certainly looking pale and pulled-down—was in urgent need of sea air, and
Undine had nearly convinced her husband of the expediency
of hiring a châlet at Deauville for July and August, when this
plan, and with it every other prospect of escape, was dashed
by the sudden death of the old Marquis.

Undine, at first, had supposed that the resulting change
could not be other than favourable. She had been on too formal terms with her father-in-law—a remote and ceremonious
old gentleman to whom her own personality was evidently an
insoluble enigma—to feel more than the merest conventional
pang at his death; and it was certainly "more fun" to be a
marchioness than a countess, and to know that one's husband
was the head of the house. Besides, now they would have the
château to themselves—or at least the old Marquise, when
she came, would be there as a guest and not a ruler—
and visions of smart house-parties and big shoots lit up the
first weeks of Undine's enforced seclusion. Then, by degrees,
the inexorable conditions of French mourning closed in on
her. Immediately after the long-drawn funeral observances the
bereaved family—mother, daughters, sons and sons-in-law—
came down to seclude themselves at Saint Désert; and Undine, through the slow hot crape-smelling months, lived encircled by shrouded images of woe in which the only live
points were the eyes constantly fixed on her least movements.
The hope of escaping to the seaside with Paul vanished in the

pained stare with which her mother-in-law received the suggestion. Undine learned the next day that it had cost the old Marquise a sleepless night, and might have had more distressing results had it not been explained as a harmless instance of transatlantic oddness. Raymond entreated his wife to atone for her involuntary *légèreté* by submitting with a good grace to the usages of her adopted country; and he seemed to regard the remaining months of the summer as hardly long enough for this act of expiation. As Undine looked back on them, they appeared to have been composed of an interminable succession of identical days, in which attendance at early mass (in the coroneted gallery she had once so glowingly depicted to Van Degen) was followed by a great deal of conversational sitting about, a great deal of excellent eating, an occasional drive to the nearest town behind a pair of heavy draft horses, and long evenings in a lamp-heated drawing-room with all the windows shut, and the stout curé making an asthmatic fourth at the Marquise's card-table.

Still, even these conditions were not permanent, and the discipline of the last years had trained Undine to wait and dissemble. The summer over, it was decided—after a protracted family conclave—that the state of the old Marquise's health made it advisable for her to spend the winter with the married daughter who lived near Pau. The other members of the family returned to their respective estates, and Undine once more found herself alone with her husband. But she knew by this time that there was to be no thought of Paris that winter, or even the next spring. Worse still, she was presently to discover that Raymond's accession of rank brought with it no financial advantages. Having but the vaguest notion of French testamentary law, she was dismayed to learn that the compulsory division of property made it impossible for a father to benefit his eldest son at the expense of the others. Raymond was therefore little richer than before, and with the debts of honour of a troublesome younger brother to settle, and Saint Désert to keep up, his available income was actually reduced. He held out, indeed, the hope of eventual improvement, since the old Marquis had managed his estates with a lofty contempt for modern methods, and the application of new principles of agriculture and forestry were

certain to yield profitable results. But for a year or two, at any
rate, this very change of treatment would necessitate the owner's continual supervision, and would not in the meanwhile
produce any increase of income.

To *faire valoir* the family acres had always, it appeared, been
Raymond's deepest-seated purpose, and all his frivolities
dropped from him with the prospect of putting his hand to
the plough. He was not, indeed, inhuman enough to condemn his wife to perpetual exile. He meant, he assured her,
that she should have her annual spring visit to Paris—but he
stared in dismay at her suggestion that they should take possession of the coveted *premier* of the Hôtel de Chelles. He
was gallant enough to express the wish that it were in his
power to house her on such a scale; but he could not conceal
his surprise that she had ever seriously expected it. She was
beginning to see that he felt her constitutional inability to
understand anything about money as the deepest difference
between them. It was a proficiency no one had ever expected
her to acquire, and the lack of which she had even been encouraged to regard as a grace and to use as a pretext. During
the interval between her divorce and her remarriage she had
learned what things cost, but not how to do without them;
and money still seemed to her like some mysterious and uncertain stream which occasionally vanished underground but
was sure to bubble up again at one's feet. Now, however, she
found herself in a world where it represented not the means
of individual gratification but the substance binding together
whole groups of interests, and where the uses to which it
might be put in twenty years were considered before the reasons for spending it on the spot. At first she was sure she
could laugh Raymond out of his prudence or coax him round
to her point of view. She did not understand how a man so
romantically in love could be so unpersuadable on certain
points. Hitherto she had had to contend with personal
moods, now she was arguing against a policy; and she was
gradually to learn that it was as natural to Raymond de
Chelles to adore her and resist her as it had been to Ralph
Marvell to adore her and let her have her way.

At first, indeed, he appealed to her good sense, using arguments evidently drawn from accumulations of hereditary

experience. But his economic plea was as unintelligible to her as the silly problems about pen-knives and apples in the "Mental Arithmetic" of her infancy; and when he struck a tenderer note and spoke of the duty of providing for the son he hoped for, she put her arms about him to whisper: "But then I oughtn't to be worried. . ."

After that, she noticed, though he was as charming as ever, he behaved as if the case were closed. He had apparently decided that his arguments were unintelligible to her, and under all his ardour she felt the difference made by the discovery. It did not make him less kind, but it evidently made her less important; and she had the half-frightened sense that the day she ceased to please him she would cease to exist for him. That day was a long way off, of course, but the chill of it had brushed her face; and she was no longer heedless of such signs. She resolved to cultivate all the arts of patience and compliance, and habit might have helped them to take root if they had not been nipped by a new cataclysm.

It was barely a week ago that her husband had been called to Paris to straighten out a fresh tangle in the affairs of the troublesome brother whose difficulties were apparently a part of the family tradition. Raymond's letters had been hurried, his telegrams brief and contradictory, and now, as Undine stood watching for the brougham that was to bring him from the station, she had the sense that with his arrival all her vague fears would be confirmed. There would be more money to pay out, of course—since the funds that could not be found for her just needs were apparently always forthcoming to settle Hubert's scandalous prodigalities—and that meant a longer perspective of solitude at Saint Désert, and a fresh pretext for postponing the hospitalities that were to follow on their period of mourning.

The brougham—a vehicle as massive and lumbering as the pair that drew it—presently rolled into the court, and Raymond's sable figure (she had never before seen a man travel in such black clothes) sprang up the steps to the door. Whenever Undine saw him after an absence she had a curious sense of his coming back from unknown distances and not belonging to her or to any state of things she understood. Then habit reasserted itself, and she began to think of him again with a querulous familiarity. But she had learned to hide her feelings, and as he came in she put up her face for a kiss.

"Yes—everything's settled——" his embrace expressed the satisfaction of the man returning from an accomplished task to the joys of his fireside.

"Settled?" Her face kindled. "Without your having to pay?"

He looked at her with a shrug. "Of course I've had to pay. Did you suppose Hubert's creditors would be put off with vanilla éclairs?"

"Oh, if *that's* what you mean—if Hubert has only to wire you at any time to be sure of his affairs being settled——!"

She saw his lips narrow and a line come out between his eyes. "Wouldn't it be a happy thought to tell them to bring tea?" he suggested.

"In the library, then. It's so cold here—and the tapestries smell so of rain."

He paused a moment to scrutinize the long walls, on which the fabulous blues and pinks of the great Boucher series looked as livid as withered roses. "I suppose they ought to be taken down and aired," he said.

She thought: "In *this* air—much good it would do them!" But she had already repented her outbreak about Hubert, and she followed her husband into the library with the resolve not to let him see her annoyance. Compared with the long grey gallery the library, with its brown walls of books, looked warm and home-like, and Raymond seemed to feel the influence of the softer atmosphere. He turned to his wife and put his arm about her.

"I know it's been a trial to you, dearest; but this is the last time I shall have to pull the poor boy out."

In spite of herself she laughed incredulously: Hubert's "last times" were a household word.

But when tea had been brought, and they were alone over the fire, Raymond unfolded the amazing sequel. Hubert had found an heiress, Hubert was to be married, and henceforth the business of paying his debts (which might be counted on to recur as inevitably as the changes of the seasons) would devolve on his American bride—the charming Miss Looty Arlington, whom Raymond had remained over in Paris to meet.

"An American? He's marrying an American?" Undine wavered between wrath and satisfaction. She felt a flash of resentment at any other intruder's venturing upon her territory—("Looty Arlington? Who is she? What a name!")—but it was quickly superseded by the relief of knowing that henceforth, as Raymond said, Hubert's debts would be some one else's business. Then a third consideration prevailed. "But if he's engaged to a rich girl, why on earth do *we* have to pull him out?"

Her husband explained that no other course was possible. Though General Arlington was immensely wealthy, ("her father's a general—a General Manager, whatever that may be,") he had exacted what he called "a clean slate" from his future son-in-law, and Hubert's creditors (the boy was such a donkey!) had in their possession certain papers that made it possible for them to press for immediate payment.

"Your compatriots' views on such matters are so rigid—and it's all to their credit—that the marriage would have fallen through at once if the least hint of Hubert's mess had got out—and then we should have had him on our hands for life."

Yes—from that point of view it was doubtless best to pay up; but Undine obscurely wished that their doing so had not incidentally helped an unknown compatriot to what the American papers were no doubt already announcing as "another brilliant foreign alliance."

"Where on earth did your brother pick up anybody respectable? Do you know where her people come from? I suppose she's perfectly awful," she broke out with a sudden escape of irritation.

"I believe Hubert made her acquaintance at a skating rink. They come from some new state—the general apologized for its not yet being on the map, but seemed surprised I hadn't heard of it. He said it was already known as one of 'the divorce states,' and the principal city had, in consequence, a very agreeable society. *La petite n'est vraiment pas trop mal.*"

"I daresay not! We're all good-looking. But she must be horribly common."

Raymond seemed sincerely unable to formulate a judgment. "My dear, you have your own customs. . ."

"Oh, I know we're all alike to you!" It was one of her grievances that he never attempted to discriminate between Americans. "You see no difference between me and a girl one gets engaged to at a skating rink!"

He evaded the challenge by rejoining: "Miss Arlington's burning to know you. She says she's heard a great deal about you, and Hubert wants to bring her down next week. I think we'd better do what we can."

"Of course." But Undine was still absorbed in the economic aspect of the case. "If they're as rich as you say, I suppose Hubert means to pay you back by and bye?"

"Naturally. It's all arranged. He's given me a paper." He drew her hands into his. "You see we've every reason to be kind to Miss Arlington."

"Oh, I'll be as kind as you like!" She brightened at the prospect of repayment. Yes, they would ask the girl down. . . She leaned a little nearer to her husband. "But then after a while we shall be a good deal better off—especially, as you say, with no more of Hubert's debts to worry us." And leaning back far enough to give her upward smile, she renewed her plea for the *premier* in the Hôtel de Chelles: "Because, really, you know, as the head of the house you ought to——"

"Ah, my dear, as the head of the house I've so many obligations; and one of them is not to miss a good stroke of business when it comes my way."

Her hands slipped from his shoulders and she drew back. "What do you mean by a good stroke of business?"

"Why, an incredible piece of luck—it's what kept me on so long in Paris. Miss Arlington's father was looking for an apartment for the young couple, and I've let him the *premier* for twelve years on the understanding that he puts electric light and heating into the whole hôtel. It's a wonderful chance, for of course we all benefit by it as much as Hubert."

"A wonderful chance . . . benefit by it as much as Hubert!" He seemed to be speaking a strange language in which familiar-sounding syllables meant something totally unknown. Did he really think she was going to coop herself up again in their cramped quarters while Hubert and his skating-rink bride luxuriated overhead in the coveted *premier*? All the resentments that had been accumulating in her during the long baffled months since her marriage broke into speech. "It's extraordinary of you to do such a thing without consulting me!"

"Without consulting you? But, my dear child, you've always professed the most complete indifference to business matters—you've frequently begged me not to bore you with them. You may be sure I've acted on the best advice; and my mother, whose head is as good as a man's, thinks I've made a remarkably good arrangement."

"I daresay—but I'm not always thinking about money, as you are."

As she spoke she had an ominous sense of impending peril; but she was too angry to avoid even the risks she saw. To her surprise Raymond put his arm about her with a smile. "There are many reasons why I have to think about money. One is that *you* don't; and another is that I must look out for the future of our son."

Undine flushed to the forehead. She had grown accustomed to such allusions and the thought of having a child no longer filled her with the resentful terror she had felt before Paul's birth. She had been insensibly influenced by a different point of view, perhaps also by a difference in her own feeling; and the vision of herself as the mother of the future Marquis de Chelles was softened to happiness by the thought of giving Raymond a son. But all these lightly-rooted sentiments went down in the rush of her resentment, and she freed herself with a petulant movement. "Oh, my dear, you'd better leave it to your brother to perpetuate the race. There'll be more room for nurseries in their apartment!"

She waited a moment, quivering with the expectation of her husband's answer; then, as none came except the silent darkening of his face, she walked to the door and turned round to fling back: "Of course you can do what you like with your own house, and make any arrangements that suit your family, without consulting me; but you needn't think I'm ever going back to live in that stuffy little hole, with Hubert and his wife splurging round on top of our heads!"

"Ah——" said Raymond de Chelles in a low voice.

XXXIX

UNDINE did not fulfil her threat. The month of May saw her back in the rooms she had declared she would never set foot in, and after her long sojourn among the echoing vistas of Saint Désert the exiguity of her Paris quarters seemed like cosiness.

In the interval many things had happened. Hubert, permitted by his anxious relatives to anticipate the term of the family mourning, had been showily and expensively united to his heiress; the Hôtel de Chelles had been piped, heated and illuminated in accordance with the bride's requirements; and the young couple, not content with these utilitarian changes had moved doors, opened windows, torn down partitions, and given over the great trophied and pilastered dining-room to a decorative painter with a new theory of the human anatomy. Undine had silently assisted at this spectacle, and at the sight of the old Marquise's abject acquiescence; she had seen the Duchesse de Dordogne and the Princesse Estradina go past her door to visit Hubert's *premier* and marvel at the American bath-tubs and the Annamite bric-a-brac; and she had been present, with her husband, at the banquet at which Hubert had revealed to the astonished Faubourg the prehistoric episodes depicted on his dining-room walls. She had accepted all these necessities with the stoicism which the last months had developed in her; for more and more, as the days passed, she felt herself in the grasp of circumstances stronger than any effort she could oppose to them. The very absence of external pressure, of any tactless assertion of authority on her husband's part, intensified the sense of her helplessness. He simply left it to her to infer that, important as she might be to him in certain ways, there were others in which she did not weigh a feather.

Their outward relations had not changed since her outburst on the subject of Hubert's marriage. That incident had left her half-ashamed, half-frightened at her behavior, and she had tried to atone for it by the indirect arts that were her nearest approach to acknowledging herself in the wrong. Raymond met her advances with a good grace, and they lived through the rest of the winter on terms of apparent understanding. When the spring approached it was he who suggested that, since his mother had consented to Hubert's marrying before the year of mourning was over, there was really no reason why they should not go up to Paris as usual; and she was surprised at the readiness with which he prepared to accompany her.

A year earlier she would have regarded this as another proof of her power; but she now drew her inferences less quickly. Raymond was as "lovely" to her as ever; but more than once, during their months in the country, she had had a startled sense of not giving him all he expected of her. She had admired him, before their marriage, as a model of social distinction; during the honeymoon he had been the most ardent of lovers; and with their settling down at Saint Désert she had prepared to resign herself to the society of a country gentleman absorbed in sport and agriculture. But Raymond, to her surprise, had again developed a disturbing resemblance to his predecessor. During the long winter afternoons, after he had gone over his accounts with the bailiff, or written his business letters, he took to dabbling with a paint-box, or picking out new scores at the piano; after dinner, when they went to the library, he seemed to expect to read aloud to her from the reviews and papers he was always receiving; and when he had discovered her inability to fix her attention he fell into the way of absorbing himself in one of the old brown books with which the room was lined. At first he tried—as Ralph had done—to tell her about what he was reading or what was happening in the world; but her sense of inadequacy made her slip away to other subjects, and little by little their talk died down to monosyllables.

Was it possible that, in spite of his books, the evenings seemed as long to Raymond as to her, and that he had suggested going back to Paris because he was bored at Saint Désert? Bored as she was herself, she resented his not finding her company all-sufficient, and was mortified by the discovery that there were regions of his life she could not enter.

But once back in Paris she had less time for introspection, and Raymond less for books. They resumed their dispersed and busy life, and in spite of Hubert's ostentatious vicinity,

of the perpetual lack of money, and of Paul's innocent en-
croachments on her freedom, Undine, once more in her element, ceased to brood upon her grievances. She enjoyed
going about with her husband, whose presence at her side
was distinctly ornamental. He seemed to have grown suddenly younger and more animated, and when she saw other
women looking at him she remembered how distinguished he
was. It amused her to have him in her train, and driving
about with him to dinners and dances, waiting for him on
flower-decked landings, or pushing at his side through blazing theatre-lobbies, answered to her inmost ideal of domestic
intimacy.

He seemed disposed to allow her more liberty than before,
and it was only now and then that he let drop a brief reminder of the conditions on which it was accorded. She was
to keep certain people at a distance, she was not to cheapen
herself by being seen at vulgar restaurants and tea-rooms, she
was to join with him in fulfilling certain family obligations
(going to a good many dull dinners among the number); but
in other respects she was free to fill her days as she pleased.

"Not that it leaves me much time," she admitted to
Madame de Trézac; "what with going to see his mother every
day, and never missing one of his sisters' *jours*, and showing
myself at the Hôtel de Dordogne whenever the Duchess gives
a pay-up party to the stuffy people Lili Estradina won't be
bothered with, there are days when I never lay eyes on Paul,
and barely have time to be waved and manicured; but, apart
from that, Raymond's really much nicer and less fussy than
he was."

Undine, as she grew older, had developed her mother's
craving for a confidante, and Madame de Trézac had succeeded in that capacity to Mabel Lipscomb and Bertha
Shallum.

"Less fussy?" Madame de Trézac's long nose lengthened
thoughtfully. "H'm—are you sure that's a good sign?"

Undine stared and laughed. "Oh, my dear, you're so
quaint! Why, nobody's jealous any more."

"No; that's the worst of it." Madame de Trézac pondered.
"It's a thousand pities you haven't got a son."

"Yes; I wish we had." Undine stood up, impatient to end

the conversation. Since she had learned that her continued childlessness was regarded by every one about her as not only unfortunate but somehow vaguely derogatory to her, she had genuinely begun to regret it; and any allusion to the subject disturbed her.

"Especially," Madame de Trézac continued, "as Hubert's wife——"

"Oh, if *that's* all they want, it's a pity Raymond didn't marry Hubert's wife," Undine flung back; and on the stairs she murmured to herself: "Nettie has been talking to my mother-in-law."

But this explanation did not quiet her, and that evening, as she and Raymond drove back together from a party, she felt a sudden impulse to speak. Sitting close to him in the darkness of the carriage, it ought to have been easy for her to find the needed word; but the barrier of his indifference hung between them, and street after street slipped by, and the spangled blackness of the river unrolled itself beneath their wheels, before she leaned over to touch his hand.

"What is it, my dear?"

She had not yet found the word, and already his tone told her she was too late. A year ago, if she had slipped her hand in his, she would not have had that answer.

"Your mother blames me for our not having a child. Everybody thinks it's my fault."

He paused before answering, and she sat watching his shadowy profile against the passing lamps.

"My mother's ideas are old-fashioned; and I don't know that it's anybody's business but yours and mine."

"Yes, but——"

"Here we are." The brougham was turning under the archway of the hotel, and the light of Hubert's tall windows fell across the dusky court. Raymond helped her out, and they mounted to their door by the stairs which Hubert had recarpeted in velvet, with a marble nymph lurking in the azaleas on the landing.

In the antechamber Raymond paused to take her cloak from her shoulders, and his eyes rested on her with a faint smile of approval.

"You never looked better; your dress is extremely becoming. Good-night, my dear," he said, kissing her hand as he turned away.

Undine kept this incident to herself: her wounded pride made her shrink from confessing it even to Madame de Trézac. She was sure Raymond would "come back"; Ralph always had, to the last. During their remaining weeks in Paris she reassured herself with the thought that once they were back at Saint Désert she would easily regain her lost hold; and when Raymond suggested their leaving Paris she acquiesced without a protest. But at Saint Désert she seemed no nearer to him than in Paris. He continued to treat her with unvarying amiability, but he seemed wholly absorbed in the management of the estate, in his books, his sketching and his music. He had begun to interest himself in politics and had been urged to stand for his department. This necessitated frequent displacements: trips to Beaune or Dijon and occasional absences in Paris. Undine, when he was away, was not left alone, for the dowager Marquise had established herself at Saint Désert for the summer, and relays of brothers and sisters-in-law, aunts, cousins and ecclesiastical friends and connections succeeded each other under its capacious roof. Only Hubert and his wife were absent. They had taken a villa at Deauville, and in the morning papers Undine followed the chronicle of Hubert's polo scores and of the Countess Hubert's racing toilets.

The days crawled on with a benumbing sameness. The old Marquise and the other ladies of the party sat on the terrace with their needle-work, the curé or one of the visiting uncles read aloud the *Journal des Débats* and prognosticated dark things of the Republic, Paul scoured the park and despoiled the kitchen-garden with the other children of the family, the inhabitants of the adjacent châteaux drove over to call, and occasionally the ponderous pair were harnessed to a landau as lumbering as the brougham, and the ladies of Saint Désert measured the dusty kilometres between themselves and their neighbours.

It was the first time that Undine had seriously paused to consider the conditions of her new life, and as the days passed she began to understand that so they would continue to succeed each other till the end. Every one about her took it for granted that as long as she lived she would spend ten months of every year at Saint Désert and the remaining two in Paris. Of course, if health required it, she might go to *les eaux* with her husband; but the old Marquise was very doubtful as to the benefit of a course of waters, and her uncle the Duke and her cousin the Canon shared her view. In the case of young married women, especially, the unwholesome excitement of the modern watering-place was more than likely to do away with the possible benefit of the treatment. As to travel—had not Raymond and his wife been to Egypt and Asia Minor on their wedding-journey? Such reckless enterprise was unheard of in the annals of the house! Had they not spent days and days in the saddle, and slept in tents among the Arabs? (Who could tell, indeed, whether these imprudences were not the cause of the disappointment which it had pleased heaven to inflict on the young couple?) No one in the family had ever taken so long a wedding-journey. One bride had gone to England (even that was considered extreme), and another—the artistic daughter—had spent a week in Venice; which certainly showed that they were not behind the times, and had no old-fashioned prejudices. Since wedding-journeys were the fashion, they had taken them; but who had ever heard of travelling afterward? What could be the possible object of leaving one's family, one's habits, one's friends? It was natural that the Americans, who had no homes, who were born and died in hotels, should have contracted nomadic habits; but the new Marquise de Chelles was no longer an American, and she had Saint Désert and the Hôtel de Chelles to live in, as generations of ladies of her name had done before her.

Thus Undine beheld her future laid out for her, not directly and in blunt words, but obliquely and affably, in the allusions, the assumptions, the insinuations of the amiable women among whom her days were spent. Their interminable conversations were carried on to the click of knitting-needles and the rise and fall of industrious fingers above embroidery-frames; and as Undine sat staring at the lustrous nails of her idle hands she felt that her inability to occupy them was regarded as one of the chief causes of her restlessness. The innumerable rooms of Saint Désert were furnished with the embroidered hangings and tapestry chairs produced by generations of diligent châtelaines, and the untiring needles of the old Marquise, her daughters and dependents were still steadily increasing the provision.

It struck Undine as curious that they should be willing to go on making chair-coverings and bed-curtains for a house that didn't really belong to them, and that she had a right to pull about and rearrange as she chose; but then that was only a part of their whole incomprehensible way of regarding themselves (in spite of their acute personal and parochial absorptions) as minor members of a powerful and indivisible whole, the huge voracious fetish they called The Family.

Notwithstanding their very definite theories as to what Americans were and were not, they were evidently bewildered at finding no corresponding sense of solidarity in Undine; and little Paul's rootlessness, his lack of all local and linear ties, made them (for all the charm he exercised) regard him with something of the shyness of pious Christians toward an elfin child. But though mother and child gave them a sense of insuperable strangeness, it plainly never occurred to them that both would not be gradually subdued to the customs of Saint Désert. Dynasties had fallen, institutions changed, manners and morals, alas, deplorably declined; but as far back as memory went, the ladies of the line of Chelles had always sat at their needle-work on the terrace of Saint Désert, while the men of the house lamented the corruption of the government and the curé ascribed the unhappy state of the country to the decline of religious feeling and the rise in the cost of living. It was inevitable that, in the course of time, the new Marquise should come to understand the fundamental necessity of these things being as they were; and meanwhile the forbearance of her husband's family exercised itself, with the smiling discretion of their race, through the long succession of uneventful days.

Once, in September, this routine was broken in upon by the unannounced descent of a flock of motors bearing the Princess Estradina and a chosen band from one watering-place to another. Raymond was away at the time, but family loyalty constrained the old Marquise to welcome her kinswoman and the latter's friends; and Undine once more found herself immersed in the world from which her marriage had removed her.

The Princess, at first, seemed totally to have forgotten their former intimacy, and Undine was made to feel that in a life so variously agitated the episode could hardly have left a trace. But the night before her departure the incalculable Lili, with one of her sudden changes of humour, drew her former friend into her bedroom and plunged into an exchange of confidences. She naturally unfolded her own history first, and it was so packed with incident that the courtyard clock had struck two before she turned her attention to Undine.

"My dear, you're handsomer than ever; only perhaps a shade too stout. Domestic bliss, I suppose? Take care! You need an emotion, a drama. . . You Americans are really extraordinary. You appear to live on change and excitement; and then suddenly a man comes along and claps a ring on your finger, and you never look through it to see what's going on outside. Aren't you ever the least bit bored? Why do I never see anything of you any more? I suppose it's the fault of my venerable aunt—she's never forgiven me for having a better time than her daughters. How can I help it if I don't look like the curé's umbrella? I daresay she owes you the same grudge. But why do you let her coop you up here? It's a thousand pities you haven't had a child. They'd all treat you differently if you had."

It was the same perpetually reiterated condolence; and Undine flushed with anger as she listened. Why indeed had she let herself be cooped up? She could not have answered the Princess's question: she merely felt the impossibility of breaking through the mysterious web of traditions, conventions, prohibitions that enclosed her in their impenetrable net-work. But her vanity suggested the obvious pretext, and she murmured with a laugh: "I didn't know Raymond was going to be so jealous——"

The Princess stared. "Is it Raymond who keeps you shut up here? And what about his trips to Dijon? And what do you suppose he does with himself when he runs up to Paris? Politics?" She shrugged ironically. "Politics don't occupy a man after midnight. Raymond jealous of you? *Ah, merci!* My dear, it's what I always say when people talk to me about fast Americans: you're the only innocent women left in the world. . ."

XL

AFTER THE Princess Estradina's departure, the days at Saint Désert succeeded each other indistinguishably; and more and more, as they passed, Undine felt herself drawn into the slow strong current already fed by so many tributary lives. Some spell she could not have named seemed to emanate from the old house which had so long been the custodian of an unbroken tradition: things had happened there in the same way for so many generations that to try to alter them seemed as vain as to contend with the elements.

Winter came and went, and once more the calendar marked the first days of spring; but though the horse-chestnuts of the Champs Elysées were budding snow still lingered in the grass drives of Saint Désert and along the ridges of the hills beyond the park. Sometimes, as Undine looked out of the windows of the Boucher gallery, she felt as if her eyes had never rested on any other scene. Even her occasional brief trips to Paris left no lasting trace: the life of the vivid streets faded to a shadow as soon as the black and white horizon of Saint Désert closed in on her again.

Though the afternoons were still cold she had lately taken to sitting in the gallery. The smiling scenes on its walls and the tall screens which broke its length made it more habitable than the drawing-rooms beyond; but her chief reason for preferring it was the satisfaction she found in having fires lit in both the monumental chimneys that faced each other down its long perspective. This satisfaction had its source in the old Marquise's disapproval. Never before in the history of Saint Désert had the consumption of fire-wood exceeded a certain carefully-calculated measure; but since Undine had been in authority this allowance had been doubled. If any one had told her, a year earlier, that one of the chief distractions of her new life would be to invent ways of annoying her mother-in-law, she would have laughed at the idea of wasting her time on such trifles. But she found herself with a great deal of time to waste, and with a fierce desire to spend it in upsetting the immemorial customs of Saint Désert. Her husband had mastered her in essentials, but she had discovered in-

numerable small ways of irritating and hurting him, and one—
and not the least effectual—was to do anything that went
counter to his mother's prejudices. It was not that he always
shared her views, or was a particularly subservient son; but it
seemed to be one of his fundamental principles that a man
should respect his mother's wishes, and see to it that his
household respected them. All Frenchmen of his class appeared to share this view, and to regard it as beyond discussion: it was based on something so much more immutable
than personal feeling that one might even hate one's mother
and yet insist that her ideas as to the consumption of fire-
wood should be regarded.

The old Marquise, during the cold weather, always sat in
her bedroom; and there, between the tapestried four-poster
and the fireplace, the family grouped itself around the
ground-glass of her single carcel lamp. In the evening, if there
were visitors, a fire was lit in the library; otherwise the family
again sat about the Marquise's lamp till the footman came in
at ten with tisane and *biscuits de Reims*; after which every one
bade the dowager good night and scattered down the corridors to chill distances marked by tapers floating in cups of
oil.

Since Undine's coming the library fire had never been allowed to go out; and of late, after experimenting with the
two drawing-rooms and the so-called "study" where Raymond kept his guns and saw the bailiff, she had selected the
gallery as the most suitable place for the new and unfamiliar
ceremony of afternoon tea. Afternoon refreshments had never
before been served at Saint Désert except when company was
expected; when they had invariably consisted in a decanter of
sweet port and a plate of small dry cakes—the kind that kept.
That the complicated rites of the tea-urn, with its offering-up
of perishable delicacies, should be enacted for the sole enjoyment of the family, was a thing so unheard of that for a while
Undine found sufficient amusement in elaborating the ceremonial, and in making the ancestral plate groan under more
varied viands; and when this palled she devised the plan of
performing the office in the gallery and lighting sacrificial fires
in both chimneys.

She had said to Raymond, at first: "It's ridiculous that your mother should sit in her bedroom all day. She says she does it to save fires; but if we have a fire downstairs why can't she let hers go out, and come down? I don't see why I should spend my life in your mother's bedroom."

Raymond made no answer, and the Marquise did, in fact, let her fire go out. But she did not come down—she simply continued to sit upstairs without a fire.

At first this also amused Undine; then the tacit criticism implied began to irritate her. She hoped Raymond would speak of his mother's attitude: she had her answer ready if he did! But he made no comment, he took no notice; her impulses of retaliation spent themselves against the blank surface of his indifference. He was as amiable, as considerate as ever; as ready, within reason, to accede to her wishes and gratify her whims. Once or twice, when she suggested running up to Paris to take Paul to the dentist, or to look for a servant, he agreed to the necessity and went up with her. But instead of going to an hotel they went to their apartment, where carpets were up and curtains down, and a care-taker prepared primitive food at uncertain hours; and Undine's first glimpse of Hubert's illuminated windows deepened her rancour and her sense of helplessness.

As Madame de Trézac had predicted, Raymond's vigilance gradually relaxed, and during their excursions to the capital Undine came and went as she pleased. But her visits were too short to permit of her falling in with the social pace, and when she showed herself among her friends she felt countrified and out-of-place, as if even her clothes had come from Saint Désert. Nevertheless her dresses were more than ever her chief preoccupation: in Paris she spent hours at the dressmaker's, and in the country the arrival of a box of new gowns was the chief event of the vacant days. But there was more bitterness than joy in the unpacking, and the dresses hung in her wardrobe like so many unfulfilled promises of pleasure, reminding her of the days at the Stentorian when she had reviewed other finery with the same cheated eyes. In spite of this, she multiplied her orders, writing up to the dress-makers for patterns, and to the milliners for boxes of hats which she tried on, and kept for days, without being able to make a choice. Now and then she even sent her maid up to Paris to bring back great assortments of veils, gloves, flowers and laces; and after periods of painful indecision she ended by keeping the greater number, lest those she sent back should turn out to be the ones that were worn in Paris. She knew she was spending too much money, and she had lost her youthful faith in providential solutions; but she had always had the habit of going out to buy something when she was bored, and never had she been in greater need of such solace.

The dulness of her life seemed to have passed into her blood: her complexion was less animated, her hair less shining. The change in her looks alarmed her, and she scanned the fashion-papers for new scents and powders, and experimented in facial bandaging, electric massage and other processes of renovation. Odd atavisms woke in her, and she began to pore over patent medicine advertisements, to send stamped envelopes to beauty doctors and professors of physical development, and to brood on the advantage of consulting faith-healers, mind-readers and their kindred adepts. She even wrote to her mother for the receipts of some of her grandfather's forgotten nostrums, and modified her daily life, and her hours of sleeping, eating and exercise, in accordance with each new experiment.

Her constitutional restlessness lapsed into an apathy like Mrs. Spragg's, and the least demand on her activity irritated her. But she was beset by endless annoyances: bickerings with discontented maids, the difficulty of finding a tutor for Paul, and the problem of keeping him amused and occupied without having him too much on her hands. A great liking had sprung up between Raymond and the little boy, and during the summer Paul was perpetually at his step-father's side in the stables and the park. But with the coming of winter Raymond was oftener away, and Paul developed a persistent cold that kept him frequently indoors. The confinement made him fretful and exacting, and the old Marquise ascribed the change in his behavior to the deplorable influence of his tutor, a "laic" recommended by one of Raymond's old professors. Raymond himself would have preferred an abbé: it was in the tradition of the house, and though Paul was not of the house it seemed fitting that he should conform to its ways. Moreover, when the married sisters came to stay they objected to having their children exposed to the tutor's influence, and even implied that Paul's society might be contaminating. But Undine, though she had so readily embraced her husband's faith, stubbornly resisted the suggestion that she should hand over her son to the Church. The tutor therefore remained; but the friction caused by his presence was so irritating to Undine that she began to consider the alternative of sending Paul to school. He was still small and tender for the experiment; but she persuaded herself that what he needed was "hardening," and having heard of a school where fashionable infancy was subjected to this process, she entered into correspondence with the master. His first letter convinced her that his establishment was just the place for Paul; but the second contained the price-list, and after comparing it with the tutor's keep and salary she wrote to say that she feared her little boy was too young to be sent away from home.

Her husband, for some time past, had ceased to make any comment on her expenditure. She knew he thought her too extravagant, and felt sure he was minutely aware of what she spent; for Saint Désert projected on economic details a light as different as might be from the haze that veiled them in West End Avenue. She therefore concluded that Raymond's silence was intentional, and ascribed it to his having shortcomings of his own to conceal. The Princess Estradina's pleasantry had reached its mark. Undine did not believe that her husband was seriously in love with another woman—she could not conceive that any one could tire of her of whom she had not first tired—but she was humiliated by his indifference, and it was easier to ascribe it to the arts of a rival than to any deficiency in herself. It exasperated her to think that he might have consolations for the outward monotony of his life, and she resolved that when they returned to Paris he should see that she was not without similar opportunities.

March, meanwhile, was verging on April, and still he did not speak of leaving. Undine had learned that he expected to have such decisions left to him, and she hid her impatience lest her showing it should incline him to delay. But one day, as she sat at tea in the gallery, he came in in his riding-clothes and said: "I've been over to the other side of the mountain.

The February rains have weakened the dam of the Alette, and the vineyards will be in danger if we don't rebuild at once."

She suppressed a yawn, thinking, as she did so, how dull he always looked when he talked of agriculture. It made him seem years older, and she reflected with a shiver that listening to him probably gave her the same look.

He went on, as she handed him his tea: "I'm sorry it should happen just now. I'm afraid I shall have to ask you to give up your spring in Paris."

"Oh, no—no!" she broke out. A throng of half-subdued grievances choked in her: she wanted to burst into sobs like a child.

"I know it's a disappointment. But our expenses have been unusually heavy this year."

"It seems to me they always are. I don't see why we should give up Paris because you've got to make repairs to a dam. Isn't Hubert ever going to pay back that money?"

He looked at her with a mild surprise. "But surely you understood at the time that it won't be possible till his wife inherits?"

"Till General Arlington dies, you mean? He doesn't look much older than you!"

"You may remember that I showed you Hubert's note. He has paid the interest quite regularly."

"That's kind of him!" She stood up, flaming with rebellion. "You can do as you please; but I mean to go to Paris."

"My mother is not going. I didn't intend to open our apartment."

"I understand. But I shall open it—that's all!"

He had risen too, and she saw his face whiten. "I prefer that you shouldn't go without me."

"Then I shall go and stay at the Nouveau Luxe with my American friends."

"That never!"

"Why not?"

"I consider it unsuitable."

"Your considering it so doesn't prove it."

They stood facing each other, quivering with an equal anger; then he controlled himself and said in a more conciliatory tone: "You never seem to see that there are necessities——"

"Oh, neither do you—that's the trouble. You can't keep me shut up here all my life, and interfere with everything I want to do, just by saying it's unsuitable."

"I've never interfered with your spending your money as you please."

It was her turn to stare, sincerely wondering. "Mercy, I should hope not, when you've always grudged me every penny of yours!"

"You know it's not because I grudge it. I would gladly take you to Paris if I had the money."

"You can always find the money to spend on this place. Why don't you sell it if it's so fearfully expensive?"

"Sell it? Sell Saint Désert?"

The suggestion seemed to strike him as something monstrously, almost fiendishly significant: as if her random word had at last thrust into his hand the clue to their whole unhappy difference. Without understanding this, she guessed it from the change in his face: it was as if a deadly solvent had suddenly decomposed its familiar lines.

"Well, why not?" His horror spurred her on. "You might sell some of the things in it anyhow. In America we're not ashamed to sell what we can't afford to keep." Her eyes fell on the storied hangings at his back. "Why, there's a fortune in this one room: you could get anything you chose for those tapestries. And you stand here and tell me you're a pauper!"

His glance followed hers to the tapestries, and then returned to her face. "Ah, you don't understand," he said.

"I understand that you care for all this old stuff more than you do for me, and that you'd rather see me unhappy and miserable than touch one of your great-grandfather's armchairs."

The colour came slowly back to his face, but it hardened into lines she had never seen. He looked at her as though the place where she stood were empty. "You don't understand," he said again.

XLI

T HE INCIDENT left Undine with the baffled feeling of not
being able to count on any of her old weapons of aggression. In all her struggles for authority her sense of the right-
fulness of her cause had been measured by her power of
making people do as she pleased. Raymond's firmness shook
her faith in her own claims, and a blind desire to wound and
destroy replaced her usual business-like intentness on gaining
her end. But her ironies were as ineffectual as her arguments,
and his imperviousness was the more exasperating because
she divined that some of the things she said would have hurt
him if any one else had said them: it was the fact of their
coming from her that made them innocuous. Even when, at
the close of their talk, she had burst out: "If you grudge me
everything I care about we'd better separate," he had merely
answered with a shrug: "It's one of the things we don't
do——" and the answer had been like the slamming of an
iron door in her face.

An interval of silent brooding had resulted in a reaction of
rebellion. She dared not carry out her threat of joining her
compatriots at the Nouveau Luxe: she had too clear a memory of the results of her former revolt. But neither could she
submit to her present fate without attempting to make Raymond understand his selfish folly. She had failed to prove it
by argument, but she had an inherited faith in the value of
practical demonstration. If he could be made to see how easily he could give her what she wanted perhaps he might come
round to her view.

With this idea in mind, she had gone up to Paris for
twenty-four hours, on the pretext of finding a new nurse for
Paul; and the steps then taken had enabled her, on the first
occasion, to set her plan in motion. The occasion was furnished by Raymond's next trip to Beaune. He went off early
one morning, leaving word that he should not be back till
night; and on the afternoon of the same day she stood at her
usual post in the gallery, scanning the long perspective of the
poplar avenue.

She had not stood there long before a black speck at the

end of the avenue expanded into a motor that was presently throbbing at the entrance. Undine, at its approach, turned from the window, and as she moved down the gallery her glance rested on the great tapestries, with their ineffable minglings of blue and rose, as complacently as though they had been mirrors reflecting her own image.

She was still looking at them when the door opened and a servant ushered in a small swarthy man who, in spite of his conspicuously London-made clothes, had an odd exotic air, as if he had worn rings in his ears or left a bale of spices at the door.

He bowed to Undine, cast a rapid eye up and down the room, and then, with his back to the windows, stood intensely contemplating the wall that faced them.

Undine's heart was beating excitedly. She knew the old Marquise was taking her afternoon nap in her room, yet each sound in the silent house seemed to be that of her heels on the stairs.

"Ah——" said the visitor.

He had begun to pace slowly down the gallery, keeping his face to the tapestries, like an actor playing to the footlights.

"*Ah*——" he said again.

To ease the tension of her nerves Undine began: "They were given by Louis the Fifteenth to the Marquis de Chelles who——"

"Their history has been published," the visitor briefly interposed; and she coloured at her blunder.

The swarthy stranger, fitting a pair of eye-glasses to a nose that was like an instrument of precision, had begun a closer and more detailed inspection of the tapestries. He seemed totally unmindful of her presence, and his air of lofty indifference was beginning to make her wish she had not sent for him. His manner in Paris had been so different!

Suddenly he turned and took off the glasses, which sprang back into a fold of his clothing like retracted feelers.

"Yes." He stood and looked at her without seeing her. "Very well. I have brought down a gentleman."

"A gentleman——?"

"The greatest American collector—he buys only the best.

He will not be long in Paris, and it was his only chance of coming down."

Undine drew herself up. "I don't understand—I never said the tapestries were for sale."

"Precisely. But this gentleman buys only things that are not for sale."

It sounded dazzling and she wavered. "I don't know—you were only to put a price on them——"

"Let me see him look at them first; then I'll put a price on them," he chuckled; and without waiting for her answer he went to the door and opened it. The gesture revealed the fur-coated back of a gentleman who stood at the opposite end of the hall examining the bust of a seventeenth century field-marshal.

The dealer addressed the back respectfully. "Mr. Moffatt!"

Moffatt, who appeared to be interested in the bust, glanced over his shoulder without moving. "See here——"

His glance took in Undine, widened to astonishment and passed into apostrophe. "Well, if this ain't the darnedest——!" He came forward and took her by both hands. "Why, what on earth are you doing down here?"

She laughed and blushed, in a tremor at the odd turn of the adventure. "I live here. Didn't you know?"

"Not a word—never thought of asking the party's name." He turned jovially to the bowing dealer. "Say—I told you those tapestries 'd have to be out and outers to make up for the trip; but now I see I was mistaken."

Undine looked at him curiously. His physical appearance was unchanged: he was as compact and ruddy as ever, with the same astute eyes under the same guileless brow; but his self-confidence had become less aggressive, and she had never seen him so gallantly at ease.

"I didn't know you'd become a great collector."

"The greatest! Didn't he tell you so? I thought that was why I was allowed to come."

She hesitated. "Of course, you know, the tapestries are not for sale——"

"That so? I thought that was only his dodge to get me down. Well, I'm glad they ain't: it'll give us more time to talk."

Watch in hand, the dealer intervened. "If, nevertheless, you would first take a glance. Our train——"

"It ain't mine!" Moffatt interrupted; "at least not if there's a later one."

Undine's presence of mind had returned. "Of course there is," she said gaily. She led the way back into the gallery, half hoping the dealer would allege a pressing reason for departure. She was excited and amused at Moffatt's unexpected appearance, but humiliated that he should suspect her of being in financial straits. She never wanted to see Moffatt except when she was happy and triumphant.

The dealer had followed the other two into the gallery, and there was a moment's pause while they all stood silently before the tapestries. "By George!" Moffatt finally brought out.

"They're historical, you know: the King gave them to Raymond's great-great-grandfather. The other day when I was in Paris," Undine hurried on, "I asked Mr. Fleischhauer to come down some time and tell us what they're worth . . . and he seems to have misunderstood . . . to have thought we meant to sell them." She addressed herself more pointedly to the dealer. "I'm sorry you've had the trip for nothing."

Mr. Fleischhauer inclined himself eloquently. "It is not nothing to have seen such beauty."

Moffatt gave him a humorous look. "I'd hate to see Mr. Fleischhauer miss his train——"

"I shall not miss it: I miss nothing," said Mr. Fleischhauer. He bowed to Undine and backed toward the door.

"See here," Moffatt called to him as he reached the threshold, "you let the motor take you to the station, and charge up this trip to me."

When the door closed he turned to Undine with a laugh. "Well, this beats the band. I thought of course you were living up in Paris."

Again she felt a twinge of embarrassment. "Oh, French people—I mean my husband's kind—always spend a part of the year on their estates."

"But not this part, do they? Why, everything's humming up there now. I was dining at the Nouveau Luxe last night with the Driscolls and Shallums and Mrs. Rolliver, and all your old crowd were there whooping things up."

The Driscolls and Shallums and Mrs. Rolliver! How carelessly he reeled off their names! One could see from his tone
that he was one of them and wanted her to know it. And
nothing could have given her a completer sense of his
achievement—of the number of millions he must be worth.
It must have come about very recently, yet he was already at
ease in his new honours—he had the metropolitan tone.
While she examined him with these thoughts in her mind she
was aware of his giving her as close a scrutiny. "But I suppose
you've got your own crowd now," he continued; "you always
were a lap ahead of me." He sent his glance down the lordly
length of the room. "It's sorter funny to see you in this kind
of place; but you look it—you always *do* look it!"

She laughed. "So do you—I was just thinking it!" Their
eyes met. "I suppose you must be awfully rich."

He laughed too, holding her eyes. "Oh, out of sight! The
Consolidation set me on my feet. I own pretty near the whole
of Apex. I came down to buy these tapestries for my private
car."

The familiar accent of hyperbole exhilarated her. "I don't
suppose I could stop you if you really wanted them!"

"Nobody can stop me now if I want anything."

They were looking at each other with challenge and complicity in their eyes. His voice, his look, all the loud confident
vigorous things he embodied and expressed, set her blood
beating with curiosity. "I didn't know you and Rolliver were
friends," she said.

"Oh *Jim*——" his accent verged on the protective. "Old
Jim's all right. He's in Congress now. I've got to have somebody up in Washington." He had thrust his hands in his
pockets, and with his head thrown back and his lips shaped
to the familiar noiseless whistle, was looking slowly and dis-
cerningly about him.

Presently his eyes reverted to her face. "So this is what I
helped you to get," he said. "I've always meant to run over
some day and take a look. What is it they call you—a
Marquise?"

She paled a little, and then flushed again. "What made you
do it?" she broke out abruptly. "I've often wondered."

He laughed. "What—lend you a hand? Why, my business

instinct, I suppose. I saw you were in a tight place that time I ran across you in Paris—and I hadn't any grudge against you. Fact is, I've never had the time to nurse old scores, and if you neglect 'em they die off like gold-fish." He was still composedly regarding her. "It's funny to think of your having settled down to this kind of life; I hope you've got what you wanted. This is a great place you live in."

"Yes; but I see a little too much of it. We live here most of the year." She had meant to give him the illusion of success, but some underlying community of instinct drew the confession from her lips.

"That so? Why on earth don't you cut it and come up to Paris?"

"Oh, Raymond's absorbed in the estates—and we haven't got the money. This place eats it all up."

"Well, that sounds aristocratic; but ain't it rather out of date? When the swells are hard-up nowadays they generally chip off an heirloom." He wheeled round again to the tapestries. "There are a good many Paris seasons hanging right here on this wall."

"Yes—I know." She tried to check herself, to summon up a glittering equivocation; but his face, his voice, the very words he used, were like so many hammer-strokes demolishing the unrealities that imprisoned her. Here was some one who spoke her language, who knew her meanings, who understood instinctively all the deep-seated wants for which her acquired vocabulary had no terms; and as she talked she once more seemed to herself intelligent, eloquent and interesting.

"Of course it's frightfully lonely down here," she began; and through the opening made by the admission the whole flood of her grievances poured forth. She tried to let him see that she had not sacrificed herself for nothing; she touched on the superiorities of her situation, she gilded the circumstances of which she called herself the victim, and let titles, offices and attributes shed their utmost lustre on her tale; but what she had to boast of seemed small and tinkling compared with the evidences of his power.

"Well, it's a downright shame you don't go round more," he kept saying; and she felt ashamed of her tame acceptance of her fate.

When she had told her story she asked for his; and for the first time she listened to it with interest. He had what he wanted at last. The Apex Consolidation scheme, after a long interval of suspense, had obtained its charter and shot out huge ramifications. Rolliver had "stood in" with him at the critical moment, and between them they had "chucked out" old Harmon B. Driscoll bag and baggage, and got the whole town in their control. Absorbed in his theme, and forgetting her inability to follow him, Moffatt launched out on an epic recital of plot and counterplot, and she hung, a new Desdemona, on his conflict with the new anthropophagi. It was of no consequence that the details and the technicalities escaped her: she knew their meaningless syllables stood for success, and what that meant was as clear as day to her. Every Wall Street term had its equivalent in the language of Fifth Avenue, and while he talked of building up railways she was building up palaces, and picturing all the multiple lives he would lead in them. To have things had always seemed to her the first essential of existence, and as she listened to him the vision of the things he could have unrolled itself before her like the long triumph of an Asiatic conqueror.

"And what are you going to do next?" she asked, almost breathlessly, when he had ended.

"Oh, there's always a lot to do next. Business never goes to sleep."

"Yes; but I mean besides business."

"Why—everything I can, I guess." He leaned back in his chair with an air of placid power, as if he were so sure of getting what he wanted that there was no longer any use in hurrying, huge as his vistas had become.

She continued to question him, and he began to talk of his growing passion for pictures and furniture, and of his desire to form a collection which should be a great representative assemblage of unmatched specimens. As he spoke she saw his expression change, and his eyes grow younger, almost boyish, with a concentrated look in them that reminded her of long-forgotten things.

"I mean to have the best, you know; not just to get ahead of the other fellows, but because I know it when I see it. I guess that's the only good reason," he concluded; and he added, looking at her with a smile: "It was what you were always after, wasn't it?"

XLII

UNDINE HAD gained her point, and the *entresol* of the Hôtel de Chelles reopened its doors for the season.

Hubert and his wife, in expectation of the birth of an heir, had withdrawn to the sumptuous château which General Arlington had hired for them near Compiègne, and Undine was at least spared the sight of their bright windows and animated stairway. But she had to take her share of the felicitations which the whole far-reaching circle of friends and relations distributed to every member of Hubert's family on the approach of the happy event. Nor was this the hardest of her trials. Raymond had done what she asked—he had stood out against his mother's protests, set aside considerations of prudence, and consented to go up to Paris for two months; but he had done so on the understanding that during their stay they should exercise the most unremitting economy. As dinner-giving put the heaviest strain on their budget, all hospitality was suspended; and when Undine attempted to invite a few friends informally she was warned that she could not do so without causing the gravest offense to the many others genealogically entitled to the same attention.

Raymond's insistence on this rule was simply part of an elaborate and inveterate system of "relations" (the whole of French social life seemed to depend on the exact interpretation of that word), and Undine felt the uselessness of struggling against such mysterious inhibitions. He reminded her, however, that their inability to receive would give them all the more opportunity for going out, and he showed himself more socially disposed than in the past. But his concession did not result as she had hoped. They were asked out as much as ever, but they were asked to big dinners, to impersonal crushes, to the kind of entertainment it is a slight to be omitted from but no compliment to be included in. Nothing could have been more galling to Undine, and she frankly bewailed the fact to Madame de Trézac.

"Of course it's what was sure to come of being mewed up for months and months in the country. We're out of everything, and the people who are having a good time are simply too busy to remember us. We're only asked to the things that are made up from visiting-lists."

Madame de Trézac listened sympathetically, but did not suppress a candid answer.

"It's not altogether that, my dear; Raymond's not a man his friends forget. It's rather more, if you'll excuse my saying so, the fact of your being—you personally—in the wrong set."

"The wrong set? Why, I'm in *his* set—the one that thinks itself too good for all the others. That's what you've always told me when I've said it bored me."

"Well, that's what I mean——" Madame de Trézac took the plunge. "It's not a question of *your* being bored."

Undine coloured; but she could take the hardest thrusts where her personal interest was involved. "You mean that *I'm* the bore, then?"

"Well, you don't work hard enough—you don't keep up. It's not that they don't admire you—your looks, I mean; they think you beautiful; they're delighted to bring you out at their big dinners, with the Sèvres and the plate. But a woman has got to be something more than good-looking to have a chance to be intimate with them: she's got to know what's being said about things. I watched you the other night at the Duchess's, and half the time you hadn't an idea what they were talking about. I haven't always, either; but then I have to put up with the big dinners."

Undine winced under the criticism; but she had never lacked insight into the cause of her own failures, and she had already had premonitions of what Madame de Trézac so bluntly phrased. When Raymond ceased to be interested in her conversation she had concluded it was the way of husbands; but since then it had been slowly dawning on her that she produced the same effect on others. Her entrances were always triumphs; but they had no sequel. As soon as people began to talk they ceased to see her. Any sense of insufficiency exasperated her, and she had vague thoughts of cultivating herself, and went so far as to spend a morning in the Louvre and go to one or two lectures by a fashionable philosopher. But though she returned from these expeditions charged with opinions, their expression did not excite the interest she had hoped. Her views, if abundant, were confused, and the more she said the more nebulous they seemed to grow. She was disconcerted, moreover, by finding that everybody appeared to know about the things she thought she had discovered, and her comments clearly produced more bewilderment than interest.

Remembering the attention she had attracted on her first appearance in Raymond's world she concluded that she had "gone off" or grown dowdy, and instead of wasting more time in museums and lecture-halls she prolonged her hours at the dress-maker's and gave up the rest of the day to the scientific cultivation of her beauty.

"I suppose I've turned into a perfect frump down there in that wilderness," she lamented to Madame de Trézac, who replied inexorably: "Oh, no, you're as handsome as ever; but people here don't go on looking at each other forever as they do in London."

Meanwhile financial cares became more pressing. A dunning letter from one of her tradesmen fell into Raymond's hands, and the talk it led to ended in his making it clear to her that she must settle her personal debts without his aid. All the "scenes" about money which had disturbed her past had ended in some mysterious solution of her difficulty. Disagreeable as they were, she had always, vulgarly speaking, found they paid; but now it was she who was expected to pay. Raymond took his stand without ill-temper or apology: he simply argued from inveterate precedent. But it was impossible for Undine to understand a social organization which did not regard the indulging of woman as its first purpose, or to believe that any one taking another view was not moved by avarice or malice; and the discussion ended in mutual acrimony.

The morning afterward, Raymond came into her room with a letter in his hand.

"Is this your doing?" he asked. His look and voice expressed something she had never known before: the disciplined anger of a man trained to keep his emotions in fixed channels, but knowing how to fill them to the brim.

The letter was from Mr. Fleischhauer, who begged to

transmit to the Marquis de Chelles an offer for his Boucher tapestries from a client prepared to pay the large sum named on condition that it was accepted before his approaching departure for America.

"What does it mean?" Raymond continued, as she did not speak.

"How should I know? It's a lot of money," she stammered, shaken out of her self-possession. She had not expected so prompt a sequel to the dealer's visit, and she was vexed with him for writing to Raymond without consulting her. But she recognized Moffatt's high-handed way, and her fears faded in the great blaze of the sum he offered.

Her husband was still looking at her. "It was Fleischhauer who brought a man down to see the tapestries one day when I was away at Beaune?"

He had known, then—everything was known at Saint Désert!

She wavered a moment and then gave him back his look.

"Yes—it was Fleischhauer; and I sent for him."

"You sent for him?"

He spoke in a voice so veiled and repressed that he seemed to be consciously saving it for some premeditated outbreak. Undine felt its menace, but the thought of Moffatt sent a flame through her, and the words he would have spoken seemed to fly to her lips.

"Why shouldn't I? Something had to be done. We can't go on as we are. I've tried my best to economize—I've scraped and scrimped, and gone without heaps of things I've always had. I've moped for months and months at Saint Désert, and given up sending Paul to school because it was too expensive, and asking my friends to dine because we couldn't afford it. And you expect me to go on living like this for the rest of my life, when all you've got to do is to hold out your hand and have two million francs drop into it!"

Her husband stood looking at her coldly and curiously, as though she were some alien apparition his eyes had never before beheld.

"Ah, that's your answer—that's all you feel when you lay hands on things that are sacred to us!" He stopped a moment, and then let his voice break out with the volume she had felt it to be gathering. "And you're all alike," he exclaimed, "every one of you. You come among us from a country we don't know, and can't imagine, a country you care for so little that before you've been a day in ours you've forgotten the very house you were born in—if it wasn't torn down before you knew it! You come among us speaking our language and not knowing what we mean; wanting the things we want, and not knowing why we want them; aping our weaknesses, exaggerating our follies, ignoring or ridiculing all we care about—you come from hotels as big as towns, and from towns as flimsy as paper, where the streets haven't had time to be named, and the buildings are demolished before they're dry, and the people are as proud of changing as we are of holding to what we have—and we're fools enough to imagine that because you copy our ways and pick up our slang you understand anything about the things that make life decent and honourable for us!"

He stopped again, his white face and drawn nostrils giving him so much the look of an extremely distinguished actor in a fine part that, in spite of the vehemence of his emotion, his silence might have been the deliberate pause for a *réplique*. Undine kept him waiting long enough to give the effect of having lost her cue—then she brought out, with a little soft stare of incredulity: "Do you mean to say you're going to refuse such an offer?"

"Ah——!" He turned back from the door, and picking up the letter that lay on the table between them, tore it in pieces and tossed the pieces on the floor. "That's how I refuse it!"

The violence of his tone and gesture made her feel as though the fluttering strips were so many lashes laid across her face, and a rage that was half fear possessed her.

"How dare you speak to me like that? Nobody's ever dared to before. Is talking to a woman in that way one of the things you call decent and honourable? Now that I know what you feel about me I don't want to stay in your house another day. And I don't mean to—I mean to walk out of it this very hour!"

For a moment they stood face to face, the depths of their mutual incomprehension at last bared to each other's angry eyes; then Raymond, his glance travelling past her, pointed to the fragments of paper on the floor.

"If you're capable of that you're capable of anything!" he said as he went out of the room.

XLIII

SHE WATCHED HIM go in a kind of stupour, knowing that when they next met he would be as courteous and self-possessed as if nothing had happened, but that everything would nevertheless go on in the same way—in *his* way—and that there was no more hope of shaking his resolve or altering his point of view than there would have been of transporting the deep-rooted masonry of Saint Désert by means of the wheeled supports on which Apex architecture performed its easy transits.

One of her childish rages possessed her, sweeping away every feeling save the primitive impulse to hurt and destroy; but search as she would she could not find a crack in the strong armour of her husband's habits and prejudices. For a long time she continued to sit where he had left her, staring at the portraits on the walls as though they had joined hands to imprison her. Hitherto she had almost always felt herself a match for circumstances, but now the very dead were leagued to defeat her: people she had never seen and whose names she couldn't even remember seemed to be plotting and con-triving against her under the escutcheoned grave-stones of Saint Désert.

Her eyes turned to the old warm-toned furniture beneath the pictures, and to her own idle image in the mirror above the mantelpiece. Even in that one small room there were enough things of price to buy a release from her most press-ing cares; and the great house, in which the room was a mere cell, and the other greater house in Burgundy, held treasures to deplete even such a purse as Moffatt's. She liked to see such things about her—without any real sense of their mean-ing she felt them to be the appropriate setting of a pretty woman, to embody something of the rareness and distinction she had always considered she possessed; and she reflected that if she had still been Moffatt's wife he would have given her just such a setting, and the power to live in it as became her.

The thought sent her memory flying back to things she had turned it from for years. For the first time since their far-off weeks together she let herself relive the brief adventure. She had been drawn to Elmer Moffatt from the first—from the day when Ben Frusk, Indiana's brother, had brought him to a church picnic at Mulvey's Grove, and he had taken instant possession of Undine, sitting in the big "stage" beside her on the "ride" to the grove, supplanting Millard Binch (to whom she was still, though intermittently and incompletely, engaged), swinging her between the trees, rowing her on the lake, catching and kissing her in "forfeits," awarding her the first prize in the Beauty Show he hilariously organized and gallantly carried out, and finally (no one knew how) contriving to borrow a buggy and a fast colt from old Mulvey, and driving off with her at a two-forty gait while Millard and the others took their dust in the crawling stage.

No one in Apex knew where young Moffatt had come from, and he offered no information on the subject. He simply appeared one day behind the counter in Luckaback's Dollar Shoe-store, drifted thence to the office of Semple and Binch, the coal-merchants, reappeared as the stenographer of the Police Court, and finally edged his way into the power-house of the Apex Water-Works. He boarded with old Mrs. Flynn, down in North Fifth Street, on the edge of the red-light slum, he never went to church or attended lectures, or showed any desire to improve or refine himself; but he managed to get himself invited to all the picnics and lodge sociables, and at a supper of the Phi Upsilon Society, to which he had contrived to affiliate himself, he made the best speech that had been heard there since young Jim Rolliver's first flights. The brothers of Undine's friends all pronounced him "great," though he had fits of uncouthness that made the young women slower in admitting him to favour. But at the Mulvey's Grove picnic he suddenly seemed to dominate them all, and Undine, as she drove away with him, tasted the public triumph which was necessary to her personal enjoyment.

After that he became a leading figure in the youthful world of Apex, and no one was surprised when the Sons of Jonadab, (the local Temperance Society) invited him to deliver their Fourth of July oration. The ceremony took place, as usual, in the Baptist church, and Undine, all in white, with a red rose in her breast, sat just beneath the platform, with Indiana jealously glaring at her from a less privileged seat, and poor Millard's long neck craning over the row of prominent citizens behind the orator.

Elmer Moffatt had been magnificent, rolling out his alternating effects of humour and pathos, stirring his audience by moving references to the Blue and the Gray, convulsing them by a new version of Washington and the Cherry Tree (in which the infant patriot was depicted as having cut down the tree to check the deleterious spread of cherry bounce), dazzling them by his erudite allusions and apt quotations (he confessed to Undine that he had sat up half the night over Bartlett), and winding up with a peroration that drew tears from the Grand Army pensioners in the front row and caused the minister's wife to say that many a sermon from that platform had been less uplifting.

An ice-cream supper always followed the "exercises," and as repairs were being made in the church basement, which was the usual scene of the festivity, the minister had offered the use of his house. The long table ran through the doorway between parlour and study, and another was set in the passage outside, with one end under the stairs. The stair-rail was wreathed in fire-weed and early golden-rod, and Temperance texts in smilax decked the walls. When the first course had been despatched the young ladies, gallantly seconded by the younger of the "Sons," helped to ladle out and carry in the ice-cream, which stood in great pails on the larder floor, and to replenish the jugs of lemonade and coffee. Elmer Moffatt was indefatigable in performing these services, and when the minister's wife pressed him to sit down and take a mouthful himself he modestly declined the place reserved for him among the dignitaries of the evening, and withdrew with a few chosen spirits to the dim table-end beneath the stairs. Explosions of hilarity came from this corner with increasing frequency, and now and then tumultuous rappings and howls of "Song! Song!" followed by adjurations to "Cough it up" and "Let her go," drowned the conversational efforts at the other table.

At length the noise subsided, and the group was ceasing to attract attention when, toward the end of the evening, the upper table, drooping under the lengthy elucubrations of the

minister and the President of the Temperance Society, called
on the orator of the day for a few remarks. There was an
interval of scuffling and laughter beneath the stairs, and then
the minister's lifted hand enjoined silence and Elmer Moffatt
got to his feet.

"Step out where the ladies can hear you better, Mr. Moffatt!" the minister called. Moffatt did so, steadying himself
against the table and twisting his head about as if his collar
had grown too tight. But if his bearing was vacillating his
smile was unabashed, and there was no lack of confidence in
the glance he threw at Undine Spragg as he began: "Ladies
and Gentlemen, if there's one thing I like better than another
about getting drunk—and I like most everything about it except the next morning—it's the opportunity you've given me
of doing it right here, in the presence of this Society, which,
as I gather from its literature, knows more about the subject
than anybody else. Ladies and Gentlemen"—he straightened
himself, and the table-cloth slid toward him—"ever since you
honoured me with an invitation to address you from the temperance platform I've been assiduously studying that literature; and I've gathered from your own evidence—what I'd
strongly suspected before—that all your converted drunkards
had a hell of a good time before you got at 'em, and that . . .
and that a good many of 'em have gone on having it
since. . ."

At this point he broke off, swept the audience with his confident smile, and then, collapsing, tried to sit down on a chair
that didn't happen to be there, and disappeared among his
agitated supporters.

There was a night-mare moment during which Undine,
through the doorway, saw Ben Frusk and the others close
about the fallen orator to the crash of crockery and tumbling
chairs; then some one jumped up and shut the parlour door,
and a long-necked Sunday school teacher, who had been nervously waiting his chance, and had almost given it up, rose
from his feet and recited High Tide at Gettysburg amid hys-
terical applause.

The scandal was considerable, but Moffatt, though he vanished from the social horizon, managed to keep his place in
the power-house till he went off for a week and turned up

again without being able to give a satisfactory reason for his absence. After that he drifted from one job to another, now extolled for his "smartness" and business capacity, now dismissed in disgrace as an irresponsible loafer. His head was always full of immense nebulous schemes for the enlargement and development of any business he happened to be employed in. Sometimes his suggestions interested his employers, but proved unpractical and inapplicable; sometimes he wore out their patience or was thought to be a dangerous dreamer. Whenever he found there was no hope of his ideas being adopted he lost interest in his work, came late and left early, or disappeared for two or three days at a time without troubling himself to account for his absences. At last even those who had been cynical enough to smile over his disgrace at the temperance supper began to speak of him as a hopeless failure, and he lost the support of the feminine community when one Sunday morning, just as the Baptist and Methodist churches were releasing their congregations, he walked up Eubaw Avenue with a young woman less known to those sacred edifices than to the saloons of North Fifth Street.

Undine's estimate of people had always been based on their apparent power of getting what they wanted—provided it came under the category of things she understood wanting. Success was beauty and romance to her; yet it was at the moment when Elmer Moffatt's failure was most complete and flagrant that she suddenly felt the extent of his power. After the Eubaw Avenue scandal he had been asked not to return to the surveyor's office to which Ben Frusk had managed to get him admitted; and on the day of his dismissal he met Undine in Main Street, at the shopping hour, and, sauntering up cheerfully, invited her to take a walk with him. She was about to refuse when she saw Millard Binch's mother looking at her disapprovingly from the opposite street-corner.

"Oh, well, I will——" she said; and they walked the length of Main Street and out to the immature park in which it ended. She was in a mood of aimless discontent and unrest, tired of her engagement to Millard Binch, disappointed with Moffatt, half-ashamed of being seen with him, and yet not sorry to have it known that she was independent enough to choose her companions without regard to the Apex verdict.

"Well, I suppose you know I'm down and out," he began; and she responded virtuously: "You must have wanted to be, or you wouldn't have behaved the way you did last Sunday."

"Oh, shucks!" he sneered. "What do I care, in a one-horse place like this? If it hadn't been for you I'd have got a move on long ago."

She did not remember afterward what else he said: she recalled only the expression of a great sweeping scorn of Apex, into which her own disdain of it was absorbed like a drop in the sea, and the affirmation of a soaring self-confidence that seemed to lift her on wings. All her own attempts to get what she wanted had come to nothing; but she had always attributed her lack of success to the fact that she had had no one to second her. It was strange that Elmer Moffatt, a shiftless outcast from even the small world she despised, should give her, in the very moment of his downfall, the sense of being able to succeed where she had failed. It was a feeling she never had in his absence, but that his nearness always instantly revived; and he seemed nearer to her now than he had ever been. They wandered on to the edge of the vague park, and sat down on a bench behind the empty band-stand.

"I went with that girl on purpose, and you know it," he broke out abruptly. "It makes me too damned sick to see Millard Binch going around looking as if he'd patented you."

"You've got no right——" she interrupted; and suddenly she was in his arms, and feeling that no one had ever kissed her before. . .

The week that followed was a big bright blur—the wildest vividest moment of her life. And it was only eight days later that they were in the train together, Apex and all her plans and promises behind them, and a bigger and brighter blur ahead, into which they were plunging as the "Limited" plunged into the sunset. . .

Undine stood up, looking about her with vague eyes, as if she had come back from a long distance. Elmer Moffatt was still in Paris—he was in reach, within telephone-call. She stood hesitating a moment; then she went into her dressing-room, and turning over the pages of the telephone book, looked out the number of the Nouveau Luxe. . .

XLIV

UNDINE HAD been right in supposing that her husband would expect their life to go on as before. There was no appreciable change in the situation save that he was more often absent—finding abundant reasons, agricultural and political, for frequent trips to Saint Désert—and that, when in Paris, he no longer showed any curiosity concerning her occupations and engagements. They lived as much apart as if their cramped domicile had been a palace; and when Undine—as she now frequently did—joined the Shallums or Rollivers for a dinner at the Nouveau Luxe, or a party at a *petit théâtre*, she was not put to the trouble of prevaricating.

Her first impulse, after her scene with Raymond, had been to ring up Indiana Rolliver and invite herself to dine. It chanced that Indiana (who was now in full social progress, and had "run over" for a few weeks to get her dresses for Newport) had organized for the same evening a showy cosmopolitan banquet in which she was enchanted to include the Marquise de Chelles; and Undine, as she had hoped, found Elmer Moffatt of the party. When she drove up to the Nouveau Luxe she had not fixed on any plan of action; but once she had crossed its magic threshold her energies revived like plants in water. At last she was in her native air again, among associations she shared and conventions she understood; and all her self-confidence returned as the familiar accents uttered the accustomed things.

Save for an occasional perfunctory call, she had hitherto made no effort to see her compatriots, and she noticed that Mrs. Jim Driscoll and Bertha Shallum received her with a touch of constraint; but it vanished when they remarked the cordiality of Moffatt's greeting. Her seat was at his side, and her old sense of triumph returned as she perceived the importance his notice conferred, not only in the eyes of her own party but of the other diners. Moffatt was evidently a notable figure in all the worlds represented about the crowded tables, and Undine saw that many people who seemed personally unacquainted with him were recognizing and pointing him out. She was conscious of receiving a large share of the attention he attracted, and, bathed again in the bright air of publicity, she remembered the evening when Raymond de Chelles' first admiring glance had given her the same sense of triumph.

This inopportune memory did not trouble her: she was almost grateful to Raymond for giving her the touch of superiority her compatriots clearly felt in her. It was not merely her title and her "situation," but the experiences she had gained through them, that gave her this advantage over the loud vague company. She had learned things they did not guess: shades of conduct, turns of speech, tricks of attitude—and easy and free and enviable as she thought them, she would not for the world have been back among them at the cost of knowing no more than they.

Moffatt made no allusion to his visit to Saint Désert; but when the party had re-grouped itself about coffee and liqueurs on the terrace, he bent over to ask confidentially: "What about my tapestries?"

She replied in the same tone: "You oughtn't to have let Fleischhauer write that letter. My husband's furious."

He seemed honestly surprised. "Why? Didn't I offer him enough?"

"He's furious that any one should offer anything. I thought when he found out what they were worth he might be tempted; but he'd rather see me starve than part with one of his grand-father's snuff-boxes."

"Well, he knows now what the tapestries are worth. I offered more than Fleischhauer advised."

"Yes; but you were in too much of a hurry."

"I've got to be; I'm going back next week."

She felt her eyes cloud with disappointment. "Oh, why do you? I hoped you might stay on."

They looked at each other uncertainly a moment; then he dropped his voice to say: "Even if I did, I probably shouldn't see anything of you."

"Why not? Why won't you come and see me? I've always wanted to be friends."

He came the next day and found in her drawing-room two ladies whom she introduced as her sisters-in-law. The ladies lingered on for a long time, sipping their tea stiffly and exchanging low-voiced remarks while Undine talked with

Moffatt; and when they left, with small sidelong bows in his direction, Undine exclaimed: "Now you see how they all watch me!"

She began to go into the details of her married life, drawing on the experiences of the first months for instances that scarcely applied to her present liberated state. She could thus, without great exaggeration, picture herself as entrapped into a bondage hardly conceivable to Moffatt, and she saw him redden with excitement as he listened. "I call it darned low— darned low——" he broke in at intervals.

"Of course I go round more now," she concluded. "I mean to see my friends—I don't care what he says."

"What *can* he say?"

"Oh, he despises Americans—they all do."

"Well, I guess we can still sit up and take nourishment."

They laughed and slipped back to talking of earlier things. She urged him to put off his sailing—there were so many things they might do together: sight-seeing and excursions— and she could perhaps show him some of the private collections he hadn't seen, the ones it was hard to get admitted to. This instantly roused his attention, and after naming one or two collections he had already seen she hit on one he had found inaccessible and was particularly anxious to visit. "There's an Ingres there that's one of the things I came over to have a look at; but I was told there was no use trying."

"Oh, I can easily manage it: the Duke's Raymond's uncle." It gave her a peculiar satisfaction to say it: she felt as though she were taking a surreptitious revenge on her husband. "But he's down in the country this week," she continued, "and no one—not even the family—is allowed to see the pictures when he's away. Of course his Ingres are the finest in France."

She ran it off glibly, though a year ago she had never heard of the painter, and did not, even now, remember whether he was an Old Master or one of the very new ones whose names one hadn't had time to learn.

Moffatt put off sailing, saw the Duke's Ingres under her guidance, and accompanied her to various other private galleries inaccessible to strangers. She had lived in almost total ignorance of such opportunities, but now that she could use them to advantage she showed a surprising quickness in picking up "tips," ferreting out rare things and getting a sight of hidden treasures. She even acquired as much of the jargon as a pretty woman needs to produce the impression of being well-informed; and Moffatt's sailing was more than once postponed.

They saw each other almost daily, for she continued to come and go as she pleased, and Raymond showed neither surprise nor disapproval. When they were asked to family dinners she usually excused herself at the last moment on the plea of a headache and, calling up Indiana or Bertha Shallum, improvised a little party at the Nouveau Luxe; and on other occasions she accepted such invitations as she chose, without mentioning to her husband where she was going.

In this world of lavish pleasures she lost what little prudence the discipline of Saint Désert had inculcated. She could never be with people who had all the things she envied without being hypnotized into the belief that she had only to put her hand out to obtain them, and all the unassuaged rancours and hungers of her early days in West End Avenue came back with increased acuity. She knew her wants so much better now, and was so much more worthy of the things she wanted!

She had given up hoping that her father might make another hit in Wall Street. Mrs. Spragg's letters gave the impression that the days of big strokes were over for her husband, that he had gone down in the conflict with forces beyond his measure. If he had remained in Apex the tide of its new prosperity might have carried him to wealth; but New York's huge waves of success had submerged instead of floating him, and Rolliver's enmity was a hand perpetually stretched out to strike him lower. At most, Mr. Spragg's tenacity would keep him at the level he now held, and though he and his wife had still further simplified their way of living Undine understood that their self-denial would not increase her opportunities. She felt no compunction in continuing to accept an undiminished allowance: it was the hereditary habit of the parent animal to despoil himself for his progeny. But this conviction did not seem incompatible with a sentimental pity for her parents. Aside from all interested motives, she wished for their own sakes that they were better off. Their personal requirements were pathetically limited, but renewed prosperity would at least have procured them the happiness of giving her what she wanted.

Moffatt lingered on; but he began to speak more definitely of sailing, and Undine foresaw the day when, strong as her attraction was, stronger influences would snap it like a thread. She knew she interested and amused him, and that it flattered his vanity to be seen with her, and to hear that rumour coupled their names; but he gave her, more than any one she had ever known, the sense of being detached from his life, in control of it, and able, without weakness or uncertainty, to choose which of its calls he should obey. If the call were that of business—of any of the great perilous affairs he handled like a snake-charmer spinning the deadly reptiles about his head—she knew she would drop from his life like a loosened leaf.

These anxieties sharpened the intensity of her enjoyment, and made the contrast keener between her crowded sparkling hours and the vacant months at Saint Désert. Little as she understood of the qualities that made Moffatt what he was, the results were of the kind most palpable to her. He used life exactly as she would have used it in his place. Some of his enjoyments were beyond her range, but even these appealed to her because of the money that was required to gratify them. When she took him to see some inaccessible picture, or went with him to inspect the treasures of a famous dealer, she saw that the things he looked at moved him in a way she could not understand, and that the actual touching of rare textures—bronze or marble, or velvets flushed with the bloom of age—gave him sensations like those her own beauty had once roused in him. But the next moment he was laughing over some commonplace joke, or absorbed in a long cipher cable handed to him as they re-entered the Nouveau Luxe for tea, and his æsthetic emotions had been thrust back into their own compartment of the great steel strong-box of his mind.

Her new life went on without comment or interference from her husband, and she saw that he had accepted their altered relation, and intended merely to keep up an external semblance of harmony. To that semblance she knew he

attached intense importance: it was an article of his complicated social creed that a man of his class should appear to live
on good terms with his wife. For different reasons it was
scarcely less important to Undine: she had no wish to affront
again the social reprobation that had so nearly wrecked her.
But she could not keep up the life she was leading without
more money, a great deal more money; and the thought of
contracting her expenditure was no longer tolerable.

One afternoon, several weeks later, she came in to find a
tradesman's representative waiting with a bill. There was a
noisy scene in the anteroom before the man threateningly
withdrew—a scene witnessed by the servants, and overheard
by her mother-in-law, whom she found seated in the drawing-room when she entered.

The old Marquise's visits to her daughter-in-law were made
at long intervals but with ritual regularity; she called every
other Friday at five, and Undine had forgotten that she was
due that day. This did not make for greater cordiality between
them, and the altercation in the anteroom had been too loud
for concealment. The Marquise was on her feet when her
daughter-in-law came in, and instantly said with lowered
eyes: "It would perhaps be best for me to go."

"Oh, I don't care. You're welcome to tell Raymond you've
heard me insulted because I'm too poor to pay my bills—
he knows it well enough already!" The words broke from
Undine unguardedly, but once spoken they nourished her
defiance.

"I'm sure my son has frequently recommended greater
prudence——" the Marquise murmured.

"Yes! It's a pity he didn't recommend it to your other son
instead! All the money I was entitled to has gone to pay Hubert's debts."

"Raymond has told me that there are certain things you fail
to understand—I have no wish whatever to discuss them."
The Marquise had gone toward the door; with her hand on
it she paused to add: "I shall say nothing whatever of what
has happened."

Her icy magnanimity added the last touch to Undine's
wrath. They knew her extremity, one and all, and it did not
move them. At most, they would join in concealing it like a

blot on their honour. And the menace grew and mounted, and not a hand was stretched to help her. . .

Hardly a half-hour earlier Moffatt, with whom she had been visiting a "private view," had sent her home in his motor with the excuse that he must hurry back to the Nouveau Luxe to meet his stenographer and sign a batch of letters for the New York mail. It was therefore probable that he was still at home—that she should find him if she hastened there at once. An overwhelming desire to cry out her wrath and wretchedness brought her to her feet and sent her down to hail a passing cab. As it whirled her through the bright streets powdered with amber sunlight her brain throbbed with confused intentions. She did not think of Moffatt as a power she could use, but simply as some one who knew her and understood her grievance. It was essential to her at that moment to be told that she was right and that every one opposed to her was wrong.

At the hotel she asked his number and was carried up in the lift. On the landing she paused a moment, disconcerted— it had occurred to her that he might not be alone. But she walked on quickly, found the number and knocked. . . Moffatt opened the door, and she glanced beyond him and saw that the big bright sitting-room was empty.

"Hullo!" he exclaimed, surprised; and as he stood aside to let her enter she saw him draw out his watch and glance at it surreptitiously. He was expecting some one, or he had an engagement elsewhere—something claimed him from which she was excluded. The thought flushed her with sudden resolution. She knew now what she had come for—to keep him from every one else, to keep him for herself alone.

"Don't send me away!" she said, and laid her hand on his beseechingly.

XLV

SHE ADVANCED into the room and slowly looked about her. The big vulgar writing-table wreathed in bronze was heaped with letters and papers. Among them stood a lapis bowl in a Renaissance mounting of enamel and a vase of Phenician glass that was like a bit of rainbow caught in cobwebs. On a table against the window a little Greek marble lifted its pure lines. On every side some rare and sensitive object seemed to be shrinking back from the false colours and crude contours of the hotel furniture. There were no books in the room, but the florid console under the mirror was stacked with old numbers of *Town Talk* and the New York *Radiator*. Undine recalled the dingy hall-room that Moffatt had lodged in at Mrs. Flynn's, over Hober's livery stable, and her heart beat at the signs of his altered state. When her eyes came back to him their lids were moist.

"Don't send me away," she repeated. He looked at her and smiled. "What is it? What's the matter?"

"I don't know—but I had to come. To-day, when you spoke again of sailing, I felt as if I couldn't stand it." She lifted her eyes and looked in his profoundly.

He reddened a little under her gaze, but she could detect no softening or confusion in the shrewd steady glance he gave her back.

"Things going wrong again—is that the trouble?" he merely asked with a comforting inflexion.

"They always *are* wrong; it's all been an awful mistake. But I shouldn't care if you were here and I could see you sometimes. You're so *strong*: that's what I feel about you, Elmer. I was the only one to feel it that time they all turned against you out at Apex. . . Do you remember the afternoon I met you down on Main Street, and we walked out together to the Park? I knew then that you were stronger than any of them. . ."

She had never spoken more sincerely. For the moment all thought of self-interest was in abeyance, and she felt again, as she had felt that day, the instinctive yearning of her nature to be one with his. Something in her voice must have attested it, for she saw a change in his face.

"You're not the beauty you were," he said irrelevantly; "but you're a lot more fetching."

The oddly qualified praise made her laugh with mingled pleasure and annoyance.

"I suppose I must be dreadfully changed——"

"You're all right!—But I've got to go back home," he broke off abruptly. "I've put it off too long."

She paled and looked away, helpless in her sudden disappointment. "I knew you'd say that. . . And I shall just be left here. . ." She sat down on the sofa near which they had been standing, and two tears formed on her lashes and fell.

Moffatt sat down beside her, and both were silent. She had never seen him at a loss before. She made no attempt to draw nearer, or to use any of the arts of cajolery; but presently she said, without rising: "I saw you look at your watch when I came in. I suppose somebody else is waiting for you."

"It don't matter."

"Some other woman?"

"It don't matter."

"I've wondered so often—but of course I've got no right to ask." She stood up slowly, understanding that he meant to let her go.

"Just tell me one thing—did you never miss me?"

"Oh, damnably!" he brought out with sudden bitterness.

She came nearer, sinking her voice to a low whisper. "It's the only time I ever really cared—all through!"

He had risen too, and they stood intensely gazing at each other. Moffatt's face was fixed and grave, as she had seen it in hours she now found herself rapidly reliving.

"I believe you *did*," he said.

"Oh, Elmer—if I'd known—if I'd only known!"

He made no answer, and she turned away, touching with an unconscious hand the edge of the lapis bowl among his papers.

"Elmer, if you're going away it can't do any harm to tell me—is there anyone else?"

He gave a laugh that seemed to shake him free. "In that kind of way? Lord, no! Too busy!"

She came close again and laid a hand on his shoulder. "Then why not—why shouldn't we——?" She leaned her head back so that her gaze slanted up through her wet lashes. "I can do as I please—my husband does. They think so differently about marriage over here: it's just a business contract. As long as a woman doesn't make a show of herself no one cares." She put her other hand up, so that she held him facing her. "I've always felt, all through everything, that I belonged to you."

Moffatt left her hands on his shoulders, but did not lift his own to clasp them. For a moment she thought she had mistaken him, and a leaden sense of shame descended on her. Then he asked: "You say your husband goes with other women?"

Lili Estradina's taunt flashed through her and she seized on it. "People have told me so—his own relations have. I've never stooped to spy on him. . ."

"And the women in your set—I suppose it's taken for granted they all do the same?"

She laughed.

"Everything fixed up for them, same as it is for the husbands, eh? Nobody meddles or makes trouble if you know the ropes?"

"No, nobody . . . it's all quite easy. . ." She stopped, her faint smile checked, as his backward movement made her hands drop from his shoulders.

"And that's what you're proposing to me? That you and I should do like the rest of 'em?" His face had lost its comic roundness and grown harsh and dark, as it had when her father had taken her away from him at Opake. He turned on his heel, walked the length of the room and halted with his back to her in the embrasure of the window. There he paused a full minute, his hands in his pockets, staring out at the perpetual interweaving of motors in the luminous setting of the square. Then he turned and spoke from where he stood.

"Look here, Undine, if I'm to have you again I don't want to have you that way. That time out in Apex, when everybody in the place was against me, and I was down and out, you stood up to them and stuck by me. Remember that walk down Main Street? Don't I!—and the way the people glared and hurried by; and how you kept on alongside of me, talking and laughing, and looking your Sunday best. When Abner Spragg came out to Opake after us and pulled you back I was pretty sore at your deserting; but I came to see it was natural enough. You were only a spoilt girl, used to having everything you wanted; and I couldn't give you a thing then, and the folks you'd been taught to believe in all told you I never would. Well, I did look like a back number, and no blame to you for thinking so. I used to say it to myself over and over again, laying awake nights and totting up my mistakes . . . and then there were days when the wind set another way, and I knew I'd pull it off yet, and I thought you might have held on. . ." He stopped, his head a little lowered, his concentrated gaze on her flushed face. "Well, anyhow," he broke out, "you were my wife once, and you were my wife first—and if you want to come back you've got to come that way: not slink through the back way when there's no one watching, but walk in by the front door, with your head up, and your Main Street look."

Since the days when he had poured out to her his great fortune-building projects she had never heard him make so long a speech; and her heart, as she listened, beat with a new joy and terror. It seemed to her that the great moment of her life had come at last—the moment all her minor failures and successes had been building up with blind indefatigable hands.

"Elmer—Elmer——" she sobbed out.

She expected to find herself in his arms, shut in and shielded from all her troubles; but he stood his ground across the room, immovable.

"Is it yes?"

She faltered the word after him: "Yes——?"

"Are you going to marry me?"

She stared, bewildered. "Why, Elmer—marry you? You forget!"

"Forget what? That you don't want to give up what you've got?"

"How can I? Such things are not done out here. Why, I'm a Catholic; and the Catholic Church——" She broke off, reading the end in his face. "But later, perhaps . . . things might change. Oh, Elmer, if only you'd stay over here and let me see you sometimes!"

"Yes—the way your friends see each other. We're differently made out in Apex. When I want that sort of thing I go down to North Fifth Street for it."

She paled under the retort, but her heart beat high with it. What he asked was impossible—and she gloried in his asking it. Feeling her power, she tried to temporize. "At least if you stayed we could be friends—I shouldn't feel so terribly alone."

He laughed impatiently. "Don't talk magazine stuff to me, Undine Spragg. I guess we want each other the same way. Only our ideas are different. You've got all muddled, living out here among a lot of loafers who call it a career to run round after every petticoat. I've got my job out at home, and I belong where my job is."

"Are you going to be tied to business all your life?" Her smile was faintly depreciatory.

"I guess business is tied to *me*: Wall Street acts as if it couldn't get along without me." He gave his shoulders a shake and moved a few steps nearer. "See here, Undine— you're the one that don't understand. If I was to sell out to-morrow, and spend the rest of my life reading art magazines in a pink villa, I wouldn't do what you're asking me. And I've about as much idea of dropping business as you have of taking to district nursing. There are things a man doesn't do. I understand why your husband won't sell those tapestries— till he's got to. His ancestors are *his* business: Wall Street's mine."

He paused, and they silently faced each other. Undine made no attempt to approach him: she understood that if he yielded it would be only to recover his advantage and deepen her feeling of defeat. She put out her hand and took up the sunshade she had dropped on entering. "I suppose it's good-bye then," she said.

"You haven't got the nerve?"

"The nerve for what?"

"To come where you belong: with me."

She laughed a little and then sighed. She wished he would come nearer, or look at her differently: she felt, under his cool eye, no more compelling than a woman of wax in a show-case.

"How could I get a divorce? With my religion——"

"Why, you were born a Baptist, weren't you? That's where you used to attend church when I waited round the corner, Sunday mornings, with one of old Hober's buggies." They both laughed, and he went on: "If you'll come along home with me I'll see you get your divorce all right. Who cares what they do over here? You're an American, ain't you? What you want is the home-made article."

She listened, discouraged yet fascinated by his sturdy inaccessibility to all her arguments and objections. He knew what he wanted, saw his road before him, and acknowledged no obstacles. Her defense was drawn from reasons he did not understand, or based on difficulties that did not exist for him; and gradually she felt herself yielding to the steady pressure of his will. Yet the reasons he brushed away came back with redoubled tenacity whenever he paused long enough for her to picture the consequences of what he exacted.

"You don't know—you don't understand——" she kept repeating; but she knew that his ignorance was part of his terrible power, and that it was hopeless to try to make him feel the value of what he was asking her to give up.

"See here, Undine," he said slowly, as if he measured her resistance though he couldn't fathom it, "I guess it had better be yes or no right here. It ain't going to do either of us any good to drag this thing out. If you want to come back to me, come—if you don't, we'll shake hands on it now. I'm due in Apex for a directors' meeting on the twentieth, and as it is I'll have to cable for a special to get me out there. No, no, don't cry—it ain't that kind of a story . . . but I'll have a deck suite for you on the *Semantic* if you'll sail with me the day after to-morrow."

XLVI

I N THE GREAT high-ceilinged library of a private *hôtel* overlooking one of the new quarters of Paris, Paul Marvell
stood listlessly gazing out into the twilight.

The trees were budding symmetrically along the avenue below; and Paul, looking down, saw, between windows and
tree-tops, a pair of tall iron gates with gilt ornaments, the
marble curb of a semi-circular drive, and bands of spring
flowers set in turf. He was now a big boy of nearly nine, who
went to a fashionable private school, and he had come home
that day for the Easter holidays. He had not been back since
Christmas, and it was the first time he had seen the new *hôtel*
which his step-father had bought, and in which Mr. and Mrs.
Moffatt had hastily established themselves, a few weeks earlier, on their return from a flying trip to America. They were
always coming and going; during the two years since their
marriage they had been perpetually dashing over to New York
and back, or rushing down to Rome or up to the Engadine:
Paul never knew where they were except when a telegram announced that they were going somewhere else. He did not
even know that there was any method of communication between mothers and sons less laconic than that of the electric
wire; and once, when a boy at school asked him if his mother
often wrote, he had answered in all sincerity: "Oh yes—I got
a telegram last week."

He had been almost sure—as sure as he ever was of anything—that he should find her at home when he arrived; but
a message (for she hadn't had time to telegraph) apprised him
that she and Mr. Moffatt had run down to Deauville to look
at a house they thought of hiring for the summer; they were
taking an early train back, and would be at home for dinner—were in fact having a lot of people to dine.

It was just what he ought to have expected, and had been
used to ever since he could remember; and generally he didn't
mind much, especially since his mother had become Mrs.
Moffatt, and the father he had been most used to, and liked
best, had abruptly disappeared from his life. But the new *hôtel*
was big and strange, and his own room, in which there was

not a toy or a book, or one of his dear battered relics (none of the new servants—they were always new—could find his things, or think where they had been put), seemed the lone-liest spot in the whole house. He had gone up there after his solitary luncheon, served in the immense marble dining-room by a footman on the same scale, and had tried to occupy him-self with pasting post-cards into his album; but the newness and sumptuousness of the room embarrassed him—the white fur rugs and brocade chairs seemed maliciously on the watch for smears and ink-spots—and after a while he pushed the album aside and began to roam through the house.

He went to all the rooms in turn: his mother's first, the wonderful lacy bedroom, all pale silks and velvets, artful mir-rors and veiled lamps, and the boudoir as big as a drawing-room, with pictures he would have liked to know about, and tables and cabinets holding things he was afraid to touch. Mr. Moffatt's rooms came next. They were soberer and darker, but as big and splendid; and in the bedroom, on the brown wall, hung a single picture—the portrait of a boy in grey velvet—that interested Paul most of all. The boy's hand rested on the head of a big dog, and he looked infinitely no-ble and charming, and yet (in spite of the dog) so sad and lonely that he too might have come home that very day to a strange house in which none of his old things could be found.

From these rooms Paul wandered downstairs again. The library attracted him most: there were rows and rows of books, bound in dim browns and golds, and old faded reds as rich as velvet: they all looked as if they might have had stories in them as splendid as their bindings. But the book-cases were closed with gilt trellising, and when Paul reached up to open one, a servant told him that Mr. Moffatt's secre-tary kept them locked because the books were too valuable to be taken down. This seemed to make the library as strange as the rest of the house, and he passed on to the ballroom at the back. Through its closed doors he heard a sound of hammer-ing, and when he tried the door-handle a servant passing with a tray-full of glasses told him that "they" hadn't finished, and wouldn't let anybody in.

The mysterious pronoun somehow increased Paul's sense of isolation, and he went on to the drawing-rooms, steering his way prudently between the gold arm-chairs and shining tables, and wondering whether the wigged and corseleted heroes on the walls represented Mr. Moffatt's ancestors, and why, if they did, he looked so little like them. The dining-room beyond was more amusing, because busy servants were already laying the long table. It was too early for the florist, and the centre of the table was empty, but down the sides were gold baskets heaped with pulpy summer fruits—figs, strawberries and big blushing nectarines. Between them stood crystal decanters with red and yellow wine, and little dishes full of sweets; and against the walls were sideboards with great pieces of gold and silver, ewers and urns and branching candelabra, which sprinkled the green marble walls with star-like reflections.

After a while he grew tired of watching the coming and going of white-sleeved footmen, and of listening to the but-ler's vociferated orders, and strayed back into the library. The habit of solitude had given him a passion for the printed page, and if he could have found a book anywhere—any kind of a book—he would have forgotten the long hours and the empty house. But the tables in the library held only massive unused inkstands and immense immaculate blotters: not a sin-gle volume had slipped its golden prison.

His loneliness had grown overwhelming, and he suddenly thought of Mrs. Heeny's clippings. His mother, alarmed by an insidious gain in weight, had brought the masseuse back from New York with her, and Mrs. Heeny, with her old black bag and waterproof, was established in one of the grand bed-rooms lined with mirrors. She had been loud in her joy at seeing her little friend that morning, but four years had passed since their last parting, and her personality had grown remote to him. He saw too many people, and they too often disappeared and were replaced by others: his scattered affec-tions had ended by concentrating themselves on the charming image of the gentleman he called his French father; and since his French father had vanished no one else seemed to matter much to him.

"Oh, well," Mrs. Heeny had said, discerning the reluctance under his civil greeting, "I guess you're as strange here as I am, and we're both pretty strange to each other. You just go and look around, and see what a lovely home your Ma's got to live in; and when you get tired of that, come up here to me and I'll give you a look at my clippings."

The word woke a train of dormant associations, and Paul saw himself seated on a dingy carpet, between two familiar taciturn old presences, while he rummaged in the depths of a bag stuffed with strips of newspaper.

He found Mrs. Heeny sitting in a pink arm-chair, her bonnet perched on a pink-shaded electric lamp and her numerous implements spread out on an immense pink toilet-table. Vague as his recollection of her was, she gave him at once a sense of reassurance that nothing else in the house conveyed, and after he had examined all her scissors and pastes and nail-polishers he turned to the bag, which stood on the carpet at her feet as if she were waiting for a train.

"My, my!" she said, "do you want to get into that again? How you used to hunt in it for taffy, to be sure, when your Pa brought you up to Grandma Spragg's o' Saturdays! Well, I'm afraid there ain't any taffy in it now; but there's piles and piles of lovely new clippings you ain't seen."

"My Papa?" He paused, his hand among the strips of newspaper. "My Papa never saw my Grandma Spragg. He never went to America."

"Never went to America? Your Pa never——? Why, land alive!" Mrs. Heeny gasped, a blush empurpling her large warm face. "Why, Paul Marvell, don't you remember your own father, you that bear his name?" she exclaimed.

The boy blushed also, conscious that it must have been wrong to forget, and yet not seeing how he was to blame.

"That one died a long long time ago, didn't he? I was thinking of my French father," he explained.

"Oh, mercy," ejaculated Mrs. Heeny; and as if to cut the conversation short she stooped over, creaking like a ship, and thrust her plump strong hand into the bag.

"Here, now, just you look at these clippings—I guess you'll find a lot in them about your Ma.—Where do they come from? Why, out of the papers, of course," she added, in response to Paul's enquiry. "You'd oughter start a scrap-book yourself—you're plenty old enough. You could make a beauty just about your Ma, with her picture pasted in the front—and another about Mr. Moffatt and his collections. There's one I cut out the other day that says he's the greatest collector in America."

Paul listened, fascinated. He had the feeling that Mrs. Heeny's clippings, aside from their great intrinsic interest, might furnish him the clue to many things he didn't understand, and that nobody had ever had time to explain to him. His mother's marriages, for instance: he was sure there was a great deal to find out about them. But she always said: "I'll tell you all about it when I come back"—and when she came back it was invariably to rush off somewhere else. So he had remained without a key to her transitions, and had had to take for granted numberless things that seemed to have no parallel in the experience of the other boys he knew.

"Here—here it is," said Mrs. Heeny, adjusting the big tortoiseshell spectacles she had taken to wearing, and reading out in a slow chant that seemed to Paul to come out of some lost remoteness of his infancy.

" 'It is reported in London that the price paid by Mr. Elmer Moffatt for the celebrated Grey Boy is the largest sum ever given for a Vandyck. Since Mr. Moffatt began to buy extensively it is estimated in art circles that values have gone up at least seventy-five per cent.' "

But the price of the Grey Boy did not interest Paul, and he said a little impatiently: "I'd rather hear about my mother."

"To be sure you would! You wait now." Mrs. Heeny made another dive, and again began to spread her clippings on her lap like cards on a big black table.

"Here's one about her last portrait—no, here's a better one about her pearl necklace, the one Mr. Moffatt gave her last Christmas. 'The necklace, which was formerly the property of an Austrian Archduchess, is composed of five hundred perfectly matched pearls that took thirty years to collect. It is estimated among dealers in precious stones that since Mr. Moffatt began to buy the price of pearls has gone up over fifty per cent.' "

Even this did not fix Paul's attention. He wanted to hear about his mother and Mr. Moffatt, and not about their things; and he didn't quite know how to frame his question.

But Mrs. Heeny looked kindly at him and he tried. "Why is mother married to Mr. Moffatt now?"

"Why, you must know that much, Paul." Mrs. Heeny again looked warm and worried. "She's married to him because she got a divorce—that's why." And suddenly she had another inspiration. "Didn't she ever send you over any of those splendid clippings that came out the time they were married? Why, I declare, that's a shame; but I must have some of 'em right here."

She dived again, shuffled, sorted, and pulled out a long discoloured strip. "I've carried this round with me ever since, and so many's wanted to read it, it's all torn." She smoothed out the paper and began:

" 'Divorce and remarriage of Mrs. Undine Spragg–de Chelles. American Marquise renounces ancient French title to wed Railroad King. Quick work untying and tying. Boy and girl romance renewed.

" 'Reno, November 23d. The Marquise de Chelles, of Paris, France, formerly Mrs. Undine Spragg Marvell, of Apex City and New York, got a decree of divorce at a special session of the Court last night, and was remarried fifteen minutes later to Mr. Elmer Moffatt, the billionaire Railroad King, who was the Marquise's first husband.

" 'No case has ever been railroaded through the divorce courts of this State at a higher rate of speed: as Mr. Moffatt said last night, before he and his bride jumped onto their east-bound special, every record has been broken. It was just six months ago yesterday that the present Mrs. Moffatt came to Reno to look for her divorce. Owing to a delayed train, her counsel was late yesterday in receiving some necessary papers, and it was feared the decision would have to be held over; but Judge Toomey, who is a personal friend of Mr. Moffatt's, held a night session and rushed it through so that the happy couple could have the knot tied and board their special in time for Mrs. Moffatt to spend Thanksgiving in New York with her aged parents. The hearing began at seven ten p. m. and at eight o'clock the bridal couple were steaming out of the station.

" 'At the trial Mrs. Spragg–de Chelles, who wore copper velvet and sables, gave evidence as to the brutality of her

French husband, but she had to talk fast as time pressed, and Judge Toomey wrote the entry at top speed, and then jumped into a motor with the happy couple and drove to the Justice of the Peace, where he acted as best man to the bridegroom. The latter is said to be one of the six wealthiest men east of the Rockies. His gifts to the bride are a necklace and tiara of pigeon-blood rubies belonging to Queen Marie Antoinette, a million dollar cheque and a house in New York. The happy pair will pass the honeymoon in Mrs. Moffatt's new home, 5009 Fifth Avenue, which is an exact copy of the Pitti Palace, Florence. They plan to spend their springs in France.' "

Mrs. Heeny drew a long breath, folded the paper and took off her spectacles. "There," she said, with a benignant smile and a tap on Paul's cheek, "now you see how it all happened. . ."

Paul was not sure he did; but he made no answer. His mind was too full of troubled thoughts. In the dazzling description of his mother's latest nuptials one fact alone stood out for him—that she had said things that weren't true of his French father. Something he had half-guessed in her, and averted his frightened thoughts from, took his little heart in an iron grasp. She said things that weren't true. . . That was what he had always feared to find out. . . She had got up and said before a lot of people things that were awfully false about his dear French father. . .

The sound of a motor turning in at the gates made Mrs. Heeny exclaim "Here they are!" and a moment later Paul heard his mother calling to him. He got up reluctantly, and stood wavering till he felt Mrs. Heeny's astonished eye upon him. Then he heard Mr. Moffatt's jovial shout of "Paul Marvell, ahoy there!" and roused himself to run downstairs.

As he reached the landing he saw that the ballroom doors were open and all the lustres lit. His mother and Mr. Moffatt stood in the middle of the shining floor, looking up at the walls; and Paul's heart gave a wondering bound, for there, set in great gilt panels, were the tapestries that had always hung in the gallery at Saint Désert.

"Well, Senator, it feels good to shake your fist again!" his step-father said, taking him in a friendly grasp; and his mother, who looked handsomer and taller and more splen-

didly dressed than ever, exclaimed: "Mercy! how they've cut
his hair!" before she bent to kiss him.

"Oh, mother, mother!" he burst out, feeling, between his
mother's face and the others, hardly less familiar, on the
walls, that he was really at home again, and not in a strange
house.

"Gracious, how you squeeze!" she protested, loosening his
arms. "But you look splendidly—and how you've grown!"
She turned away from him and began to inspect the tapestries
critically. "Somehow they look smaller here," she said with a
tinge of disappointment.

Mr. Moffatt gave a slight laugh and walked slowly down
the room, as if to study its effect. As he turned back his wife
said: "I didn't think you'd ever get them."

He laughed again, more complacently. "Well, I don't know
as I ever should have, if General Arlington hadn't happened
to bust up."

They both smiled, and Paul, seeing his mother's softened
face, stole his hand in hers and began: "Mother, I took a prize
in composition——"

"Did you? You must tell me about it to-morrow. No, I
really must rush off now and dress—I haven't even placed the
dinner-cards." She freed her hand, and as she turned to go
Paul heard Mr. Moffatt say: "Can't you ever give him a minute's time, Undine?"

She made no answer, but sailed through the door with
her head high, as she did when anything annoyed her; and
Paul and his step-father stood alone in the illuminated ball-
room.

Mr. Moffatt smiled good-naturedly at the little boy and
then turned back to the contemplation of the hangings.

"I guess you know where those come from, don't you?" he
asked in a tone of satisfaction.

"Oh, yes," Paul answered eagerly, with a hope he dared not
utter that, since the tapestries were there, his French father
might be coming too.

"You're a smart boy to remember them. I don't suppose
you ever thought you'd see them here?"

"I don't know," said Paul, embarrassed.

"Well, I guess you wouldn't have if their owner hadn't been

in a pretty tight place. It was like drawing teeth for him to let them go."

Paul flushed up, and again the iron grasp was on his heart. He hadn't, hitherto, actually disliked Mr. Moffatt, who was always in a good humour, and seemed less busy and absent-minded than his mother; but at that instant he felt a rage of hate for him. He turned away and burst into tears.

"Why, hullo, old chap—why, what's up?" Mr. Moffatt was on his knees beside the boy, and the arms embracing him were firm and friendly. But Paul, for the life of him, couldn't answer: he could only sob and sob as the great surges of loneliness broke over him.

"Is it because your mother hadn't time for you? Well, she's like that, you know; and you and I have got to lump it," Mr. Moffatt continued, getting to his feet. He stood looking down at the boy with a queer smile. "If we two chaps stick together it won't be so bad—we can keep each other warm, don't you see? I like you first rate, you know; when you're big enough I mean to put you in my business. And it looks as if one of these days you'd be the richest boy in America. . ."

The lamps were lit, the vases full of flowers, the footmen assembled on the landing and in the vestibule below, when Undine descended to the drawing-room. As she passed the ballroom door she glanced in approvingly at the tapestries. They really looked better than she had been willing to admit: they made her ballroom the handsomest in Paris. But something had put her out on the way up from Deauville, and the simplest way of easing her nerves had been to affect indifference to the tapestries. Now she had quite recovered her good humour, and as she glanced down the list of guests she was awaiting she said to herself, with a sigh of satisfaction, that she was glad she had put on her rubies.

For the first time since her marriage to Moffatt she was about to receive in her house the people she most wished to see there. The beginnings had been a little difficult; their first attempt in New York was so unpromising that she feared they might not be able to live down the sensational details of their reunion, and had insisted on her husband's taking her back to

Paris. But her apprehensions were unfounded. It was only necessary to give people the time to pretend they had forgotten; and already they were all pretending beautifully. The French world had of course held out longest; it had strongholds she might never capture. But already seceders were beginning to show themselves, and her dinner-list that evening was graced with the names of an authentic Duke and a not too-damaged Countess. In addition, of course, she had the Shallums, the Chauncey Ellings, May Beringer, Dicky Bowles, Walsingham Popple, and the rest of the New York frequenters of the Nouveau Luxe; she had even, at the last minute, had the amusement of adding Peter Van Degen to their number. In the evening there were to be Spanish dancing and Russian singing; and Dicky Bowles had promised her a Grand Duke for her next dinner, if she could secure the new tenor who always refused to sing in private houses.

Even now, however, she was not always happy. She had everything she wanted, but she still felt, at times, that there were other things she might want if she knew about them. And there had been moments lately when she had had to confess to herself that Moffatt did not fit into the picture. At first she had been dazzled by his success and subdued by his authority. He had given her all she had ever wished for, and more than she had ever dreamed of having: he had made up to her for all her failures and blunders, and there were hours when she still felt his dominion and exulted in it. But there were others when she saw his defects and was irritated by them: when his loudness and redness, his misplaced joviality, his familiarity with the servants, his alternating swagger and ceremony with her friends, jarred on perceptions that had developed in her unawares. Now and then she caught herself thinking that his two predecessors—who were gradually becoming merged in her memory—would have said this or that differently, behaved otherwise in such and such a case. And the comparison was almost always to Moffatt's disadvantage.

This evening, however, she thought of him indulgently. She was pleased with his clever stroke in capturing the Saint Désert tapestries, which General Arlington's sudden bankruptcy, and a fresh gambling scandal of Hubert's, had compelled their owner to part with. She knew that Raymond de Chelles had told the dealers he would sell his tapestries to anyone but Mr. Elmer Moffatt, or a buyer acting for him; and it amused her to think that, thanks to Elmer's astuteness, they were under her roof after all, and that Raymond and all his clan were by this time aware of it. These facts disposed her favourably toward her husband, and deepened the sense of well-being with which—according to her invariable habit—she walked up to the mirror above the mantelpiece and studied the image it reflected.

She was still lost in this pleasing contemplation when her husband entered, looking stouter and redder than ever, in evening clothes that were a little too tight. His shirt front was as glossy as his baldness, and in his buttonhole he wore the red ribbon bestowed on him for waiving his claim to a Velasquez that was wanted for the Louvre. He carried a newspaper in his hand, and stood looking about the room with a complacent eye.

"Well, I guess this is all right," he said, and she answered briefly: "Don't forget you're to take down Madame de Follerive; and for goodness' sake don't call her 'Countess.'"

"Why, she is one, ain't she?" he returned good-humouredly.

"I wish you'd put that newspaper away," she continued; his habit of leaving old newspapers about the drawing-room annoyed her.

"Oh, that reminds me——" instead of obeying her he unfolded the paper. "I brought it in to show you something. Jim Driscoll's been appointed Ambassador to England."

"Jim Driscoll——!" She caught up the paper and stared at the paragraph he pointed to. Jim Driscoll—that pitiful nonentity, with his stout mistrustful commonplace wife! It seemed extraordinary that the government should have hunted up such insignificant people. And immediately she had a great vague vision of the splendours they were going to—all the banquets and ceremonies and precedences. . .

"I shouldn't say she'd want to, with so few jewels——" She dropped the paper and turned to her husband. "If you had a spark of ambition, that's the kind of thing you'd try for. You could have got it just as easily as not!"

He laughed and thrust his thumbs in his waistcoat arm-holes with the gesture she disliked. "As it happens, it's about the one thing I couldn't."

"You couldn't? Why not?"

"Because you're divorced. They won't have divorced Ambassadresses."

"They won't? Why not, I'd like to know?"

"Well, I guess the court ladies are afraid there'd be too many pretty women in the Embassies," he answered jocularly.

She burst into an angry laugh, and the blood flamed up into her face. "I never heard of anything so insulting!" she cried, as if the rule had been invented to humiliate her.

There was a noise of motors backing and advancing in the court, and she heard the first voices on the stairs. She turned to give herself a last look in the glass, saw the blaze of her rubies, the glitter of her hair, and remembered the brilliant names on her list.

But under all the dazzle a tiny black cloud remained. She had learned that there was something she could never get, something that neither beauty nor influence nor millions could ever buy for her. She could never be an Ambassador's wife; and as she advanced to welcome her first guests she said to herself that it was the one part she was really made for.

THE END

THE AGE OF INNOCENCE

I

O N A JANUARY EVENING of the early seventies, Christine Nilsson was singing in Faust at the Academy of Music in New York.

Though there was already talk of the erection, in remote metropolitan distances "above the Forties," of a new Opera House which should compete in costliness and splendour with those of the great European capitals, the world of fashion was still content to reassemble every winter in the shabby red and gold boxes of the sociable old Academy. Conservatives cherished it for being small and inconvenient, and thus keeping out the "new people" whom New York was beginning to dread and yet be drawn to; and the sentimental clung to it for its historic associations, and the musical for its excellent acoustics, always so problematic a quality in halls built for the hearing of music.

It was Madame Nilsson's first appearance that winter, and what the daily press had already learned to describe as "an exceptionally brilliant audience" had gathered to hear her, transported through the slippery, snowy streets in private broughams, in the spacious family landau, or in the humbler but more convenient "Brown *coupé*." To come to the Opera in a Brown *coupé* was almost as honourable a way of arriving as in one's own carriage; and departure by the same means had the immense advantage of enabling one (with a playful allusion to democratic principles) to scramble into the first Brown conveyance in the line, instead of waiting till the cold-and-gin congested nose of one's own coachman gleamed under the portico of the Academy. It was one of the great livery-stableman's most masterly intuitions to have discovered that Americans want to get away from amusement even more quickly than they want to get to it.

When Newland Archer opened the door at the back of the club box the curtain had just gone up on the garden scene. There was no reason why the young man should not have come earlier, for he had dined at seven, alone with his mother and sister, and had lingered afterward over a cigar in the

Gothic library with glazed black-walnut bookcases and finial-topped chairs which was the only room in the house where Mrs. Archer allowed smoking. But, in the first place, New York was a metropolis, and perfectly aware that in metropolises it was "not the thing" to arrive early at the opera; and what was or was not "the thing" played a part as important in Newland Archer's New York as the inscrutable totem terrors that had ruled the destinies of his forefathers thousands of years ago.

The second reason for his delay was a personal one. He had dawdled over his cigar because he was at heart a dilettante, and thinking over a pleasure to come often gave him a subtler satisfaction than its realisation. This was especially the case when the pleasure was a delicate one, as his pleasures mostly were; and on this occasion the moment he looked forward to was so rare and exquisite in quality that—well, if he had timed his arrival in accord with the prima donna's stage-manager he could not have entered the Academy at a more significant moment than just as she was singing: "He loves me—he loves me not—*he loves me!*" and sprinkling the falling daisy petals with notes as clear as dew.

She sang, of course, *"M'ama!"* and not "he loves me," since an unalterable and unquestioned law of the musical world required that the German text of French operas sung by Swedish artists should be translated into Italian for the clearer understanding of English-speaking audiences. This seemed as natural to Newland Archer as all the other conventions on which his life was moulded: such as the duty of using two silver-backed brushes with his monogram in blue enamel to part his hair, and of never appearing in society without a flower (preferably a gardenia) in his buttonhole.

"M'ama . . . non m'ama . . ." the prima donna sang, and *"M'ama!"*, with a final burst of love triumphant, as she pressed the dishevelled daisy to her lips and lifted her large eyes to the sophisticated countenance of the little brown Faust-Capoul, who was vainly trying, in a tight purple velvet doublet and plumed cap, to look as pure and true as his artless victim.

Newland Archer, leaning against the wall at the back of the club box, turned his eyes from the stage and scanned the opposite side of the house. Directly facing him was the box of old Mrs. Manson Mingott, whose monstrous obesity had long since made it impossible for her to attend the Opera, but who was always represented on fashionable nights by some of the younger members of the family. On this occasion, the front of the box was filled by her daughter-in-law, Mrs. Lovell Mingott, and her daughter, Mrs. Welland; and slightly withdrawn behind these brocaded matrons sat a young girl in white with eyes ecstatically fixed on the stage-lovers. As Madame Nilsson's "*M'ama!*" thrilled out above the silent house (the boxes always stopped talking during the Daisy Song) a warm pink mounted to the girl's cheek, mantled her brow to the roots of her fair braids, and suffused the young slope of her breast to the line where it met a modest tulle tucker fastened with a single gardenia. She dropped her eyes to the immense bouquet of lilies-of-the-valley on her knee, and Newland Archer saw her white-gloved finger-tips touch the flowers softly. He drew a breath of satisfied vanity and his eyes returned to the stage.

No expense had been spared on the setting, which was acknowledged to be very beautiful even by people who shared his acquaintance with the Opera houses of Paris and Vienna. The foreground, to the footlights, was covered with emerald green cloth. In the middle distance symmetrical mounds of woolly green moss bounded by croquet hoops formed the base of shrubs shaped like orange-trees but studded with large pink and red roses. Gigantic pansies, considerably larger than the roses, and closely resembling the floral pen-wipers made by female parishioners for fashionable clergymen, sprang from the moss beneath the rose-trees; and here and there a daisy grafted on a rose-branch flowered with a luxuriance prophetic of Mr. Luther Burbank's far-off prodigies.

In the centre of this enchanted garden Madame Nilsson, in white cashmere slashed with pale blue satin, a reticule dangling from a blue girdle, and large yellow braids carefully disposed on each side of her muslin chemisette, listened with downcast eyes to M. Capoul's impassioned wooing, and affected a guileless incomprehension of his designs whenever, by word or glance, he persuasively indicated the ground floor

window of the neat brick villa projecting obliquely from the
right wing.

"The darling!" thought Newland Archer, his glance flitting
back to the young girl with the lilies-of-the-valley. "She
doesn't even guess what it's all about." And he contemplated
her absorbed young face with a thrill of possessorship in
which pride in his own masculine initiation was mingled with
a tender reverence for her abysmal purity. "We'll read Faust
together . . . by the Italian lakes . . ." he thought, somewhat hazily confusing the scene of his projected honey-moon
with the masterpieces of literature which it would be his
manly privilege to reveal to his bride. It was only that afternoon that May Welland had let him guess that she "cared"
(New York's consecrated phrase of maiden avowal), and already his imagination, leaping ahead of the engagement ring,
the betrothal kiss and the march from Lohengrin, pictured
her at his side in some scene of old European witchery.

He did not in the least wish the future Mrs. Newland
Archer to be a simpleton. He meant her (thanks to his en-
lightening companionship) to develop a social tact and readiness of wit enabling her to hold her own with the most
popular married women of the "younger set," in which it was
the recognised custom to attract masculine homage while
playfully discouraging it. If he had probed to the bottom of
his vanity (as he sometimes nearly did) he would have found
there the wish that his wife should be as worldly-wise and as
eager to please as the married lady whose charms had held his
fancy through two mildly agitated years; without, of course,
any hint of the frailty which had so nearly marred that unhappy being's life, and had disarranged his own plans for a
whole winter.

How this miracle of fire and ice was to be created, and to
sustain itself in a harsh world, he had never taken the time to
think out; but he was content to hold his view without ana-
lysing it, since he knew it was that of all the carefully-brushed,
white-waistcoated, buttonhole-flowered gentlemen who succeeded each other in the club box, exchanged friendly greetings with him, and turned their opera-glasses critically on the
circle of ladies who were the product of the system. In matters intellectual and artistic Newland Archer felt himself dis-

tinctly the superior of these chosen specimens of old New York gentility; he had probably read more, thought more, and even seen a good deal more of the world, than any other man of the number. Singly they betrayed their inferiority; but grouped together they represented "New York," and the habit of masculine solidarity made him accept their doctrine on all the issues called moral. He instinctively felt that in this respect it would be troublesome—and also rather bad form—to strike out for himself.

"Well—upon my soul!" exclaimed Lawrence Lefferts, turning his opera-glass abruptly away from the stage. Lawrence Lefferts was, on the whole, the foremost authority on "form" in New York. He had probably devoted more time than any one else to the study of this intricate and fascinating question; but study alone could not account for his complete and easy competence. One had only to look at him, from the slant of his bald forehead and the curve of his beautiful fair moustache to the long patent-leather feet at the other end of his lean and elegant person, to feel that the knowledge of "form" must be congenital in any one who knew how to wear such good clothes so carelessly and carry such height with so much lounging grace. As a young admirer had once said of him: "If anybody can tell a fellow just when to wear a black tie with evening clothes and when not to, it's Larry Lefferts." And on the question of pumps versus patent-leather "Oxfords" his authority had never been disputed.

"My God!" he said; and silently handed his glass to old Sillerton Jackson.

Newland Archer, following Lefferts's glance, saw with surprise that his exclamation had been occasioned by the entry of a new figure into old Mrs. Mingott's box. It was that of a slim young woman, a little less tall than May Welland, with brown hair growing in close curls about her temples and held in place by a narrow band of diamonds. The suggestion of this headdress, which gave her what was then called a "Josephine look," was carried out in the cut of the dark blue velvet gown rather theatrically caught up under her bosom by a girdle with a large old-fashioned clasp. The wearer of this unusual dress, who seemed quite unconscious of the attention it was attracting, stood a moment in the centre of

the box, discussing with Mrs. Welland the propriety of taking the latter's place in the front right-hand corner; then she
yielded with a slight smile, and seated herself in line with
Mrs. Welland's sister-in-law, Mrs. Lovell Mingott, who was
installed in the opposite corner.

Mr. Sillerton Jackson had returned the opera-glass to Law-
rence Lefferts. The whole of the club turned instinctively,
waiting to hear what the old man had to say; for old Mr.
Jackson was as great an authority on "family" as Lawrence
Lefferts was on "form." He knew all the ramifications of New
York's cousinships; and could not only elucidate such complicated questions as that of the connection between the Mingotts (through the Thorleys) with the Dallases of South
Carolina, and that of the relationship of the elder branch of
Philadelphia Thorleys to the Albany Chiverses (on no account
to be confused with the Manson Chiverses of University
Place), but could also enumerate the leading characteristics of
each family: as, for instance, the fabulous stinginess of the
younger lines of Leffertses (the Long Island ones); or the
fatal tendency of the Rushworths to make foolish matches;
or the insanity recurring in every second generation of the
Albany Chiverses, with whom their New York cousins had
always refused to intermarry—with the disastrous exception
of poor Medora Manson, who, as everybody knew . . . but
then her mother was a Rushworth.

In addition to this forest of family trees, Mr. Sillerton Jackson carried between his narrow hollow temples, and under
his soft thatch of silver hair, a register of most of the scandals
and mysteries that had smouldered under the unruffled surface of New York society within the last fifty years. So far
indeed did his information extend, and so acutely retentive
was his memory, that he was supposed to be the only man
who could have told you who Julius Beaufort, the banker,
really was, and what had become of handsome Bob Spicer,
old Mrs. Manson Mingott's father, who had disappeared so
mysteriously (with a large sum of trust money) less than a
year after his marriage, on the very day that a beautiful
Spanish dancer who had been delighting thronged audiences
in the old Opera-house on the Battery had taken ship for
Cuba. But these mysteries, and many others, were closely

locked in Mr. Jackson's breast; for not only did his keen sense of honour forbid his repeating anything privately imparted, but he was fully aware that his reputation for discretion increased his opportunities of finding out what he wanted to know.

The club box, therefore, waited in visible suspense while Mr. Sillerton Jackson handed back Lawrence Lefferts's opera-glass. For a moment he silently scrutinised the attentive group out of his filmy blue eyes overhung by old veined lids; then he gave his moustache a thoughtful twist, and said simply: "I didn't think the Mingotts would have tried it on."

II

NEWLAND ARCHER, during this brief episode, had been thrown into a strange state of embarrassment.

It was annoying that the box which was thus attracting the undivided attention of masculine New York should be that in which his betrothed was seated between her mother and aunt; and for a moment he could not identify the lady in the Empire dress, nor imagine why her presence created such excitement among the initiated. Then light dawned on him, and with it came a momentary rush of indignation. No, indeed; no one would have thought the Mingotts would have tried it on!

But they had; they undoubtedly had; for the low-toned comments behind him left no doubt in Archer's mind that the young woman was May Welland's cousin, the cousin always referred to in the family as "poor Ellen Olenska." Archer knew that she had suddenly arrived from Europe a day or two previously; he had even heard from Miss Welland (not disapprovingly) that she had been to see poor Ellen, who was staying with old Mrs. Mingott. Archer entirely approved of family solidarity, and one of the qualities he most admired in the Mingotts was their resolute championship of the few black sheep that their blameless stock had produced. There was nothing mean or ungenerous in the young man's heart, and he was glad that his future wife should not be restrained by false prudery from being kind (in private) to her unhappy cousin; but to receive Countess Olenska in the family circle was a different thing from producing her in public, at the Opera of all places, and in the very box with the young girl whose engagement to him, Newland Archer, was to be announced within a few weeks. No, he felt as old Sillerton Jackson felt; he did not think the Mingotts would have tried it on!

He knew, of course, that whatever man dared (within Fifth Avenue's limits) that old Mrs. Manson Mingott, the Matriarch of the line, would dare. He had always admired the high and mighty old lady, who, in spite of having been only Catherine Spicer of Staten Island, with a father mysteriously discredited, and neither money nor position enough to make people forget it, had allied herself with the head of the wealthy Mingott line, married two of her daughters to "foreigners" (an Italian marquis and an English banker), and put the crowning touch to her audacities by building a large house of pale cream-coloured stone (when brown sandstone seemed as much the only wear as a frock-coat in the afternoon) in an inaccessible wilderness near the Central Park.

Old Mrs. Mingott's foreign daughters had become a legend. They never came back to see their mother, and the latter being, like many persons of active mind and dominating will, sedentary and corpulent in her habit, had philosophically remained at home. But the cream-coloured house (supposed to be modelled on the private hotels of the Parisian aristocracy) was there as a visible proof of her moral courage; and she throned in it, among pre-Revolutionary furniture and souvenirs of the Tuileries of Louis Napoleon (where she had shone in her middle age), as placidly as if there were nothing peculiar in living above Thirty-fourth Street, or in having French windows that opened like doors instead of sashes that pushed up.

Every one (including Mr. Sillerton Jackson) was agreed that old Catherine had never had beauty—a gift which, in the eyes of New York, justified every success, and excused a certain number of failings. Unkind people said that, like her Imperial namesake, she had won her way to success by strength of will and hardness of heart, and a kind of haughty effrontery that was somehow justified by the extreme decency and dignity of her private life. Mr. Manson Mingott had died when she was only twenty-eight, and had "tied up" the money with an additional caution born of the general distrust of the Spicers; but his bold young widow went her way fearlessly, mingled freely in foreign society, married her daughters in heaven knew what corrupt and fashionable circles, hobnobbed with Dukes and Ambassadors, associated familiarly with Papists, entertained Opera singers, and was the intimate friend of Mme. Taglioni; and all the while (as Sillerton Jackson was the first to proclaim) there had never been a breath on her reputation; the only respect, he always added, in which she differed from the earlier Catherine.

Mrs. Manson Mingott had long since succeeded in untying her husband's fortune, and had lived in affluence for half a century; but memories of her early straits had made her excessively thrifty, and though, when she bought a dress or a piece of furniture, she took care that it should be of the best, she could not bring herself to spend much on the transient pleasures of the table. Therefore, for totally different reasons, her food was as poor as Mrs. Archer's, and her wines did nothing to redeem it. Her relatives considered that the penury of her table discredited the Mingott name, which had always been associated with good living; but people continued to come to her in spite of the "made dishes" and flat champagne, and in reply to the remonstrances of her son Lovell (who tried to retrieve the family credit by having the best *chef* in New York) she used to say laughingly: "What's the use of two good cooks in one family, now that I've married the girls and can't eat sauces?"

Newland Archer, as he mused on these things, had once more turned his eyes toward the Mingott box. He saw that Mrs. Welland and her sister-in-law were facing their semicircle of critics with the Mingottian *aplomb* which old Catherine had inculcated in all her tribe, and that only May Welland betrayed, by a heightened colour (perhaps due to the knowledge that he was watching her) a sense of the gravity of the situation. As for the cause of the commotion, she sat gracefully in her corner of the box, her eyes fixed on the stage, and revealing, as she leaned forward, a little more shoulder and bosom than New York was accustomed to seeing, at least in ladies who had reasons for wishing to pass unnoticed.

Few things seemed to Newland Archer more awful than an offence against "Taste," that far-off divinity of whom "Form" was the mere visible representative and vicegerent. Madame Olenska's pale and serious face appealed to his fancy as suited to the occasion and to her unhappy situation; but the way her dress (which had no tucker) sloped away from her thin shoulders shocked and troubled him. He hated to think of May Welland's being exposed to the influence of a young woman so careless of the dictates of Taste.

"After all," he heard one of the younger men begin behind

him (everybody talked through the Mephistopheles-and-Martha scenes), "after all, just *what* happened?"

"Well—she left him; nobody attempts to deny that."

"He's an awful brute, isn't he?" continued the young enquirer, a candid Thorley, who was evidently preparing to enter the lists as the lady's champion.

"The very worst; I knew him at Nice," said Lawrence Lefferts with authority. "A half-paralysed white sneering fellow—rather handsome head, but eyes with a lot of lashes. Well, I'll tell you the sort: when he wasn't with women he was collecting china. Paying any price for both, I understand."

There was a general laugh, and the young champion said: "Well, then——?"

"Well, then; she bolted with his secretary."

"Oh, I see." The champion's face fell.

"It didn't last long, though: I heard of her a few months later living alone in Venice. I believe Lovell Mingott went out to get her. He said she was desperately unhappy. That's all right—but this parading her at the Opera's another thing."

"Perhaps," young Thorley hazarded, "she's too unhappy to be left at home."

This was greeted with an irreverent laugh, and the youth blushed deeply, and tried to look as if he had meant to insinuate what knowing people called a *"double entendre."*

"Well—it's queer to have brought Miss Welland, anyhow," some one said in a low tone, with a side-glance at Archer.

"Oh, that's part of the campaign: Granny's orders, no doubt," Lefferts laughed. "When the old lady does a thing she does it thoroughly."

The act was ending, and there was a general stir in the box. Suddenly Newland Archer felt himself impelled to decisive action. The desire to be the first man to enter Mrs. Mingott's box, to proclaim to the waiting world his engagement to May Welland, and to see her through whatever difficulties her cousin's anomalous situation might involve her in; this impulse had abruptly overruled all scruples and hesitations, and sent him hurrying through the red corridors to the farther side of the house.

As he entered the box his eyes met Miss Welland's, and he

saw that she had instantly understood his motive, though the family dignity which both considered so high a virtue would not permit her to tell him so. The persons of their world lived in an atmosphere of faint implications and pale delicacies, and the fact that he and she understood each other without a word seemed to the young man to bring them nearer than any explanation would have done. Her eyes said: "You see why Mamma brought me," and his answered: "I would not for the world have had you stay away."

"You know my niece Countess Olenska?" Mrs. Welland enquired as she shook hands with her future son-in-law. Archer bowed without extending his hand, as was the custom on being introduced to a lady; and Ellen Olenska bent her head slightly, keeping her own pale-gloved hands clasped on her huge fan of eagle feathers. Having greeted Mrs. Lovell Mingott, a large blonde lady in creaking satin, he sat down beside his betrothed, and said in a low tone: "I hope you've told Madame Olenska that we're engaged? I want everybody to know—I want you to let me announce it this evening at the ball."

Miss Welland's face grew rosy as the dawn, and she looked at him with radiant eyes. "If you can persuade Mamma," she said; "but why should we change what is already settled?" He made no answer but that which his eyes returned, and she added, still more confidently smiling: "Tell my cousin yourself: I give you leave. She says she used to play with you when you were children."

She made way for him by pushing back her chair, and promptly, and a little ostentatiously, with the desire that the whole house should see what he was doing, Archer seated himself at the Countess Olenska's side.

"We *did* use to play together, didn't we?" she asked, turning her grave eyes to his. "You were a horrid boy, and kissed me once behind a door; but it was your cousin Vandie Newland, who never looked at me, that I was in love with." Her glance swept the horse-shoe curve of boxes. "Ah, how this brings it all back to me—I see everybody here in knickerbockers and pantalettes," she said, with her trailing slightly foreign accent, her eyes returning to his face.

Agreeable as their expression was, the young man was

shocked that they should reflect so unseemly a picture of the august tribunal before which, at that very moment, her case was being tried. Nothing could be in worse taste than misplaced flippancy; and he answered somewhat stiffly: "Yes, you have been away a very long time."

"Oh, centuries and centuries; so long," she said, "that I'm sure I'm dead and buried, and this dear old place is heaven;" which, for reasons he could not define, struck Newland Archer as an even more disrespectful way of describing New York society.

III

IT INVARIABLY happened in the same way.

Mrs. Julius Beaufort, on the night of her annual ball, never failed to appear at the Opera; indeed, she always gave her ball on an Opera night in order to emphasise her complete superiority to household cares, and her possession of a staff of servants competent to organise every detail of the entertainment in her absence.

The Beauforts' house was one of the few in New York that possessed a ball-room (it antedated even Mrs. Manson Mingott's and the Headly Chiverses'); and at a time when it was beginning to be thought "provincial" to put a "crash" over the drawing-room floor and move the furniture upstairs, the possession of a ballroom that was used for no other purpose, and left for three-hundred-and-sixty-four days of the year to shuttered darkness, with its gilt chairs stacked in a corner and its chandelier in a bag; this undoubted superiority was felt to compensate for whatever was regrettable in the Beaufort past.

Mrs. Archer, who was fond of coining her social philosophy into axioms, had once said: "We all have our pet common people—" and though the phrase was a daring one, its truth was secretly admitted in many an exclusive bosom. But the Beauforts were not exactly common; some people said they were even worse. Mrs. Beaufort belonged indeed to one of America's most honoured families; she had been the lovely Regina Dallas (of the South Carolina branch), a penniless beauty introduced to New York society by her cousin, the imprudent Medora Manson, who was always doing the wrong thing from the right motive. When one was related to the Mansons and the Rushworths one had a *"droit de cité"* (as Mr. Sillerton Jackson, who had frequented the Tuileries, called it) in New York society; but did one not forfeit it in marrying Julius Beaufort?

The question was: who *was* Beaufort? He passed for an Englishman, was agreeable, handsome, ill-tempered, hospitable and witty. He had come to America with letters of recommendation from old Mrs. Manson Mingott's English son-in-law, the banker, and had speedily made himself an important position in the world of affairs; but his habits were dissipated, his tongue was bitter, his antecedents were mysterious; and when Medora Manson announced her cousin's engagement to him it was felt to be one more act of folly in poor Medora's long record of imprudences.

But folly is as often justified of her children as wisdom, and two years after young Mrs. Beaufort's marriage it was admitted that she had the most distinguished house in New York. No one knew exactly how the miracle was accomplished. She was indolent, passive, the caustic even called her dull; but dressed like an idol, hung with pearls, growing younger and blonder and more beautiful each year, she throned in Mr. Beaufort's heavy brown-stone palace, and drew all the world there without lifting her jewelled little finger. The knowing people said it was Beaufort himself who trained the servants, taught the *chef* new dishes, told the gardeners what hot-house flowers to grow for the dinner-table and the drawing-rooms, selected the guests, brewed the after-dinner punch and dictated the little notes his wife wrote to her friends. If he did, these domestic activities were privately performed, and he presented to the world the appearance of a careless and hospitable millionaire strolling into his own drawing-room with the detachment of an invited guest, and saying: "My wife's gloxinias are a marvel, aren't they? I believe she gets them out from Kew."

Mr. Beaufort's secret, people were agreed, was the way he carried things off. It was all very well to whisper that he had been "helped" to leave England by the international banking-house in which he had been employed; he carried off that rumour as easily as the rest—though New York's business conscience was no less sensitive than its moral standard—he carried everything before him, and all New York into his drawing-rooms, and for over twenty years now people had said they were "going to the Beauforts'" with the same tone of security as if they had said they were going to Mrs. Manson Mingott's, and with the added satisfaction of knowing they would get hot canvas-back ducks and vintage wines, instead of tepid Veuve Clicquot without a year and warmed-up croquettes from Philadelphia.

Mrs. Beaufort, then, had as usual appeared in her box just

before the Jewel Song; and when, again as usual, she rose at
the end of the third act, drew her opera cloak about her lovely
shoulders, and disappeared, New York knew that meant that
half an hour later the ball would begin.

The Beaufort house was one that New Yorkers were proud
to show to foreigners, especially on the night of the annual
ball. The Beauforts had been among the first people in New
York to own their own red velvet carpet and have it rolled
down the steps by their own footmen, under their own awning, instead of hiring it with the supper and the ball-room
chairs. They had also inaugurated the custom of letting the
ladies take their cloaks off in the hall, instead of shuffling up
to the hostess's bedroom and recurling their hair with the aid
of the gas-burner; Beaufort was understood to have said that
he supposed all his wife's friends had maids who saw to it
that they were properly *coiffées* when they left home.

Then the house had been boldly planned with a ball-room,
so that, instead of squeezing through a narrow passage to get
to it (as at the Chiverses') one marched solemnly down a vista
of enfiladed drawing-rooms (the sea-green, the crimson and
the *bouton d'or*), seeing from afar the many-candled lustres
reflected in the polished parquetry, and beyond that the
depths of a conservatory where camellias and tree-ferns
arched their costly foliage over seats of black and gold bamboo.

Newland Archer, as became a young man of his position,
strolled in somewhat late. He had left his overcoat with the
silk-stockinged footmen (the stockings were one of Beaufort's
few fatuities), had dawdled a while in the library hung with
Spanish leather and furnished with Buhl and malachite, where
a few men were chatting and putting on their dancing-gloves,
and had finally joined the line of guests whom Mrs. Beaufort
was receiving on the threshold of the crimson drawing-room.

Archer was distinctly nervous. He had not gone back to his
club after the Opera (as the young bloods usually did), but,
the night being fine, had walked for some distance up Fifth
Avenue before turning back in the direction of the Beauforts'
house. He was definitely afraid that the Mingotts might be
going too far; that, in fact, they might have Granny Mingott's orders to bring the Countess Olenska to the ball.

From the tone of the club box he had perceived how grave a mistake that would be; and, though he was more than ever determined to "see the thing through," he felt less chivalrously eager to champion his betrothed's cousin than before their brief talk at the Opera.

Wandering on to the *bouton d'or* drawing-room (where Beaufort had had the audacity to hang "Love Victorious," the much-discussed nude of Bouguereau) Archer found Mrs. Welland and her daughter standing near the ball-room door. Couples were already gliding over the floor beyond: the light of the wax candles fell on revolving tulle skirts, on girlish heads wreathed with modest blossoms, on the dashing aigrettes and ornaments of the young married women's *coiffures*, and on the glitter of highly glazed shirt-fronts and fresh glacé gloves.

Miss Welland, evidently about to join the dancers, hung on the threshold, her lilies-of-the-valley in her hand (she carried no other bouquet), her face a little pale, her eyes burning with a candid excitement. A group of young men and girls were gathered about her, and there was much hand-clasping, laughing and pleasantry on which Mrs. Welland, standing slightly apart, shed the beam of a qualified approval. It was evident that Miss Welland was in the act of announcing her engagement, while her mother affected the air of parental reluctance considered suitable to the occasion.

Archer paused a moment. It was at his express wish that the announcement had been made, and yet it was not thus that he would have wished to have his happiness known. To proclaim it in the heat and noise of a crowded ball-room was to rob it of the fine bloom of privacy which should belong to things nearest the heart. His joy was so deep that this blurring of the surface left its essence untouched; but he would have liked to keep the surface pure too. It was something of a satisfaction to find that May Welland shared this feeling. Her eyes fled to his beseechingly, and their look said: "Remember, we're doing this because it's right."

No appeal could have found a more immediate response in Archer's breast; but he wished that the necessity of their action had been represented by some ideal reason, and not simply by poor Ellen Olenska. The group about Miss Welland made way for him with significant smiles, and after taking his share of the felicitations he drew his betrothed into the middle of the ball-room floor and put his arm about her waist.

"Now we shan't have to talk," he said, smiling into her candid eyes, as they floated away on the soft waves of the Blue Danube.

She made no answer. Her lips trembled into a smile, but the eyes remained distant and serious, as if bent on some ineffable vision. "Dear," Archer whispered, pressing her to him: it was borne in on him that the first hours of being engaged, even if spent in a ball-room, had in them something grave and sacramental. What a new life it was going to be, with this whiteness, radiance, goodness at one's side!

The dance over, the two, as became an affianced couple, wandered into the conservatory; and sitting behind a tall screen of tree-ferns and camellias Newland pressed her gloved hand to his lips.

"You see I did as you asked me to," she said.

"Yes: I couldn't wait," he answered smiling. After a moment he added: "Only I wish it hadn't had to be at a ball."

"Yes, I know." She met his glance comprehendingly. "But after all—even here we're alone together, aren't we?"

"Oh, dearest—always!" Archer cried.

Evidently she was always going to understand; she was always going to say the right thing. The discovery made the cup of his bliss overflow, and he went on gaily: "The worst of it is that I want to kiss you and I can't." As he spoke he took a swift glance about the conservatory, assured himself of their momentary privacy, and catching her to him laid a fugitive pressure on her lips. To counteract the audacity of this proceeding he led her to a bamboo sofa in a less secluded part of the conservatory, and sitting down beside her broke a lily-of-the-valley from her bouquet. She sat silent, and the world lay like a sunlit valley at their feet.

"Did you tell my cousin Ellen?" she asked presently, as if she spoke through a dream.

He roused himself, and remembered that he had not done so. Some invincible repugnance to speak of such things to the strange foreign woman had checked the words on his lips.

"No—I hadn't the chance after all," he said, fibbing hastily.

"Ah." She looked disappointed, but gently resolved on gaining her point. "You must, then, for I didn't either; and I shouldn't like her to think—"

"Of course not. But aren't you, after all, the person to do it?"

She pondered on this. "If I'd done it at the right time, yes: but now that there's been a delay I think you must explain that I'd asked you to tell her at the Opera, before our speaking about it to everybody here. Otherwise she might think I had forgotten her. You see, she's one of the family, and she's been away so long that she's rather—sensitive."

Archer looked at her glowingly. "Dear and great angel! Of course I'll tell her." He glanced a trifle apprehensively toward the crowded ball-room. "But I haven't seen her yet. Has she come?"

"No; at the last minute she decided not to."

"At the last minute?" he echoed, betraying his surprise that she should ever have considered the alternative possible.

"Yes. She's awfully fond of dancing," the young girl answered simply. "But suddenly she made up her mind that her dress wasn't smart enough for a ball, though we thought it so lovely; and so my aunt had to take her home."

"Oh, well—" said Archer with happy indifference. Nothing about his betrothed pleased him more than her resolute determination to carry to its utmost limit that ritual of ignoring the "unpleasant" in which they had both been brought up.

"She knows as well as I do," he reflected, "the real reason of her cousin's staying away; but I shall never let her see by the least sign that I am conscious of there being a shadow of a shade on poor Ellen Olenska's reputation."

IV

IN THE COURSE of the next day the first of the usual betrothal visits were exchanged. The New York ritual was
precise and inflexible in such matters; and in conformity with
it Newland Archer first went with his mother and sister to
call on Mrs. Welland, after which he and Mrs. Welland and
May drove out to old Mrs. Manson Mingott's to receive that
venerable ancestress's blessing.

A visit to Mrs. Manson Mingott was always an amusing
episode to the young man. The house in itself was already an
historic document, though not, of course, as venerable as certain other old family houses in University Place and lower
Fifth Avenue. Those were of the purest 1830, with a grim harmony of cabbage-rose-garlanded carpets, rosewood consoles,
round-arched fire-places with black marble mantels, and immense glazed book-cases of mahogany; whereas old Mrs.
Mingott, who had built her house later, had bodily cast out
the massive furniture of her prime, and mingled with the
Mingott heirlooms the frivolous upholstery of the Second
Empire. It was her habit to sit in a window of her sitting-
room on the ground floor, as if watching calmly for life and
fashion to flow northward to her solitary doors. She seemed
in no hurry to have them come, for her patience was equalled
by her confidence. She was sure that presently the hoardings,
the quarries, the one-story saloons, the wooden green-houses
in ragged gardens, and the rocks from which goats surveyed
the scene, would vanish before the advance of residences as
stately as her own—perhaps (for she was an impartial
woman) even statelier; and that the cobblestones over which
the old clattering omnibuses bumped would be replaced by
smooth asphalt, such as people reported having seen in Paris.
Meanwhile, as every one she cared to see came to *her* (and
she could fill her rooms as easily as the Beauforts, and without
adding a single item to the *menu* of her suppers), she did not
suffer from her geographic isolation.

The immense accretion of flesh which had descended on
her in middle life like a flood of lava on a doomed city had
changed her from a plump active little woman with a neatly-

turned foot and ankle into something as vast and august as a natural phenomenon. She had accepted this submergence as philosophically as all her other trials, and now, in extreme old age, was rewarded by presenting to her mirror an almost un-wrinkled expanse of firm pink and white flesh, in the centre of which the traces of a small face survived as if awaiting ex-cavation. A flight of smooth double chins led down to the dizzy depths of a still-snowy bosom veiled in snowy muslins that were held in place by a miniature portrait of the late Mr. Mingott; and around and below, wave after wave of black silk surged away over the edges of a capacious armchair, with two tiny white hands poised like gulls on the surface of the billows.

The burden of Mrs. Manson Mingott's flesh had long since made it impossible for her to go up and down stairs, and with characteristic independence she had made her reception rooms upstairs and established herself (in flagrant violation of all the New York proprieties) on the ground floor of her house; so that, as you sat in her sitting-room window with her, you caught (through a door that was always open, and a looped-back yellow damask portière) the unexpected vista of a bedroom with a huge low bed upholstered like a sofa, and a toilet-table with frivolous lace flounces and a gilt-framed mirror.

Her visitors were startled and fascinated by the foreignness of this arrangement, which recalled scenes in French fiction, and architectural incentives to immorality such as the simple American had never dreamed of. That was how women with lovers lived in the wicked old societies, in apartments with all the rooms on one floor, and all the indecent propinquities that their novels described. It amused Newland Archer (who had secretly situated the love-scenes of "Monsieur de Camors" in Mrs. Mingott's bedroom) to picture her blameless life led in the stage-setting of adultery; but he said to himself, with considerable admiration, that if a lover had been what she wanted, the intrepid woman would have had him too.

To the general relief the Countess Olenska was not present in her grandmother's drawing-room during the visit of the betrothed couple. Mrs. Mingott said she had gone out; which, on a day of such glaring sunlight, and at the "shop-

ping hour," seemed in itself an indelicate thing for a compromised woman to do. But at any rate it spared them the
embarrassment of her presence, and the faint shadow that her
unhappy past might seem to shed on their radiant future. The
visit went off successfully, as was to have been expected. Old
Mrs. Mingott was delighted with the engagement, which,
being long foreseen by watchful relatives, had been carefully
passed upon in family council; and the engagement ring, a
large thick sapphire set in invisible claws, met with her unqualified admiration.

"It's the new setting: of course it shows the stone beautifully, but it looks a little bare to old-fashioned eyes," Mrs.
Welland had explained, with a conciliatory side-glance at her
future son-in-law.

"Old-fashioned eyes? I hope you don't mean mine, my
dear? I like all the novelties," said the ancestress, lifting the
stone to her small bright orbs, which no glasses had ever disfigured. "Very handsome," she added, returning the jewel;
"very liberal. In my time a cameo set in pearls was thought
sufficient. But it's the hand that sets off the ring, isn't it, my
dear Mr. Archer?" and she waved one of her tiny hands, with
small pointed nails and rolls of aged fat encircling the wrist
like ivory bracelets. "Mine was modelled in Rome by the
great Ferrigiani. You should have May's done: no doubt he'll
have it done, my child. Her hand is large—it's these modern
sports that spread the joints—but the skin is white.—And
when's the wedding to be?" she broke off, fixing her eyes on
Archer's face.

"Oh—" Mrs. Welland murmured, while the young man,
smiling at his betrothed, replied: "As soon as ever it can, if
only you'll back me up, Mrs. Mingott."

"We must give them time to get to know each other a little
better, mamma," Mrs. Welland interposed, with the proper
affectation of reluctance; to which the ancestress rejoined:
"Know each other? Fiddlesticks! Everybody in New York has
always known everybody. Let the young man have his way,
my dear; don't wait till the bubble's off the wine. Marry them
before Lent; I may catch pneumonia any winter now, and I
want to give the wedding-breakfast."

These successive statements were received with the proper

expressions of amusement, incredulity and gratitude; and the visit was breaking up in a vein of mild pleasantry when the door opened to admit the Countess Olenska, who entered in bonnet and mantle followed by the unexpected figure of Julius Beaufort.

There was a cousinly murmur of pleasure between the ladies, and Mrs. Mingott held out Ferrigiani's model to the banker. "Ha! Beaufort, this is a rare favour!" (She had an odd foreign way of addressing men by their surnames.)

"Thanks. I wish it might happen oftener," said the visitor in his easy arrogant way. "I'm generally so tied down; but I met the Countess Ellen in Madison Square, and she was good enough to let me walk home with her."

"Ah—I hope the house will be gayer, now that Ellen's here!" cried Mrs. Mingott with a glorious effrontery. "Sit down—sit down, Beaufort: push up the yellow armchair; now I've got you I want a good gossip. I hear your ball was magnificent; and I understand you invited Mrs. Lemuel Struthers? Well—I've a curiosity to see the woman myself."

She had forgotten her relatives, who were drifting out into the hall under Ellen Olenska's guidance. Old Mrs. Mingott had always professed a great admiration for Julius Beaufort, and there was a kind of kinship in their cool domineering way and their short-cuts through the conventions. Now she was eagerly curious to know what had decided the Beauforts to invite (for the first time) Mrs. Lemuel Struthers, the widow of Struthers's Shoe-polish, who had returned the previous year from a long initiatory sojourn in Europe to lay siege to the tight little citadel of New York. "Of course if you and Regina invite her the thing is settled. Well, we need new blood and new money—and I hear she's still very good-looking," the carnivorous old lady declared.

In the hall, while Mrs. Welland and May drew on their furs, Archer saw that the Countess Olenska was looking at him with a faintly questioning smile.

"Of course you know already—about May and me," he said, answering her look with a shy laugh. "She scolded me for not giving you the news last night at the Opera: I had her orders to tell you that we were engaged—but I couldn't, in that crowd."

The smile passed from Countess Olenska's eyes to her lips: she looked younger, more like the bold brown Ellen Mingott of his boyhood. "Of course I know; yes. And I'm so glad. But one doesn't tell such things first in a crowd." The ladies were on the threshold and she held out her hand.

"Good-bye; come and see me some day," she said, still looking at Archer.

In the carriage, on the way down Fifth Avenue, they talked pointedly of Mrs. Mingott, of her age, her spirit, and all her wonderful attributes. No one alluded to Ellen Olenska; but Archer knew that Mrs. Welland was thinking: "It's a mistake for Ellen to be seen, the very day after her arrival, parading up Fifth Avenue at the crowded hour with Julius Beaufort—" and the young man himself mentally added: "And she ought to know that a man who's just engaged doesn't spend his time calling on married women. But I daresay in the set she's lived in they do—they never do anything else." And, in spite of the cosmopolitan views on which he prided himself, he thanked heaven that he was a New Yorker, and about to ally himself with one of his own kind.

V

THE NEXT EVENING old Mr. Sillerton Jackson came to dine with the Archers.

Mrs. Archer was a shy woman and shrank from society; but she liked to be well-informed as to its doings. Her old friend Mr. Sillerton Jackson applied to the investigation of his friends' affairs the patience of a collector and the science of a naturalist; and his sister, Miss Sophy Jackson, who lived with him, and was entertained by all the people who could not secure her much-sought-after brother, brought home bits of minor gossip that filled out usefully the gaps in his picture.

Therefore, whenever anything happened that Mrs. Archer wanted to know about, she asked Mr. Jackson to dine; and as she honoured few people with her invitations, and as she and her daughter Janey were an excellent audience, Mr. Jackson usually came himself instead of sending his sister. If he could have dictated all the conditions, he would have chosen the evenings when Newland was out; not because the young man was uncongenial to him (the two got on capitally at their club) but because the old anecdotist sometimes felt, on Newland's part, a tendency to weigh his evidence that the ladies of the family never showed.

Mr. Jackson, if perfection had been attainable on earth, would also have asked that Mrs. Archer's food should be a little better. But then New York, as far back as the mind of man could travel, had been divided into the two great fundamental groups of the Mingotts and Mansons and all their clan, who cared about eating and clothes and money, and the Archer-Newland-van-der-Luyden tribe, who were devoted to travel, horticulture and the best fiction, and looked down on the grosser forms of pleasure.

You couldn't have everything, after all. If you dined with the Lovell Mingotts you got canvas-back and terrapin and vintage wines; at Adeline Archer's you could talk about Alpine scenery and "The Marble Faun"; and luckily the Archer Madeira had gone round the Cape. Therefore when a friendly summons came from Mrs. Archer, Mr. Jackson, who was a true eclectic, would usually say to his sister: "I've been a little gouty since my last dinner at the Lovell Mingotts'—it will do me good to diet at Adeline's."

Mrs. Archer, who had long been a widow, lived with her son and daughter in West Twenty-eighth Street. An upper floor was dedicated to Newland, and the two women squeezed themselves into narrower quarters below. In an unclouded harmony of tastes and interests they cultivated ferns in Wardian cases, made macramé lace and wool embroidery on linen, collected American revolutionary glazed ware, subscribed to "Good Words," and read Ouida's novels for the sake of the Italian atmosphere. (They preferred those about peasant life, because of the descriptions of scenery and the pleasanter sentiments, though in general they liked novels about people in society, whose motives and habits were more comprehensible, spoke severely of Dickens, who "had never drawn a gentleman," and considered Thackeray less at home in the great world than Bulwer—who, however, was beginning to be thought old-fashioned.)

Mrs. and Miss Archer were both great lovers of scenery. It was what they principally sought and admired on their occasional travels abroad; considering architecture and painting as subjects for men, and chiefly for learned persons who read Ruskin. Mrs. Archer had been born a Newland, and mother and daughter, who were as like as sisters, were both, as people said, "true Newlands"; tall, pale, and slightly round-shouldered, with long noses, sweet smiles and a kind of drooping distinction like that in certain faded Reynolds portraits. Their physical resemblance would have been complete if an elderly *embonpoint* had not stretched Mrs. Archer's black brocade, while Miss Archer's brown and purple poplins hung, as the years went on, more and more slackly on her virgin frame.

Mentally, the likeness between them, as Newland was aware, was less complete than their identical mannerisms often made it appear. The long habit of living together in mutually dependent intimacy had given them the same vocabulary, and the same habit of beginning their phrases "Mother thinks" or "Janey thinks," according as one or the other wished to advance an opinion of her own; but in reality, while Mrs. Archer's serene unimaginativeness rested easily in the accepted and familiar, Janey was subject to starts and aberrations of fancy welling up from springs of suppressed romance.

Mother and daughter adored each other and revered their son and brother; and Archer loved them with a tenderness made compunctious and uncritical by the sense of their exaggerated admiration, and by his secret satisfaction in it. After all, he thought it a good thing for a man to have his authority respected in his own house, even if his sense of humour sometimes made him question the force of his mandate.

On this occasion the young man was very sure that Mr. Jackson would rather have had him dine out; but he had his own reasons for not doing so.

Of course old Jackson wanted to talk about Ellen Olenska, and of course Mrs. Archer and Janey wanted to hear what he had to tell. All three would be slightly embarrassed by Newland's presence, now that his prospective relation to the Mingott clan had been made known; and the young man waited with an amused curiosity to see how they would turn the difficulty.

They began, obliquely, by talking about Mrs. Lemuel Struthers.

"It's a pity the Beauforts asked her," Mrs. Archer said gently. "But then Regina always does what he tells her; and *Beaufort*—"

"Certain *nuances* escape Beaufort," said Mr. Jackson, cautiously inspecting the broiled shad, and wondering for the thousandth time why Mrs. Archer's cook always burnt the roe to a cinder. (Newland, who had long shared his wonder, could always detect it in the older man's expression of melancholy disapproval.)

"Oh, necessarily; Beaufort is a vulgar man," said Mrs. Archer. "My grandfather Newland always used to say to my mother: 'Whatever you do, don't let that fellow Beaufort be introduced to the girls.' But at least he's had the advantage of associating with gentlemen; in England too, they say. It's all very mysterious—" She glanced at Janey and paused. She and Janey knew every fold of the Beaufort mystery, but in public Mrs. Archer continued to assume that the subject was not one for the unmarried.

"But this Mrs. Struthers," Mrs. Archer continued; "what did you say *she* was, Sillerton?"

"Out of a mine: or rather out of the saloon at the head of the pit. Then with Living Wax-Works, touring New England. After the police broke *that* up, they say she lived—" Mr. Jackson in his turn glanced at Janey, whose eyes began to bulge from under her prominent lids. There were still hiatuses for her in Mrs. Struthers's past.

"Then," Mr. Jackson continued (and Archer saw he was wondering why no one had told the butler never to slice cucumbers with a steel knife), "then Lemuel Struthers came along. They say his advertiser used the girl's head for the shoe-polish posters; her hair's intensely black, you know—the Egyptian style. Anyhow, he—eventually—married her." There were volumes of innuendo in the way the "eventually" was spaced, and each syllable given its due stress.

"Oh, well—at the pass we've come to nowadays, it doesn't matter," said Mrs. Archer indifferently. The ladies were not really interested in Mrs. Struthers just then; the subject of Ellen Olenska was too fresh and too absorbing to them. Indeed, Mrs. Struthers's name had been introduced by Mrs. Archer only that she might presently be able to say: "And Newland's new cousin—Countess Olenska? Was *she* at the ball too?"

There was a faint touch of sarcasm in the reference to her son, and Archer knew it and had expected it. Even Mrs. Archer, who was seldom unduly pleased with human events, had been altogether glad of her son's engagement. ("Especially after that silly business with Mrs. Rushworth," as she had remarked to Janey, alluding to what had once seemed to Newland a tragedy of which his soul would always bear the scar.) There was no better match in New York than May Welland, look at the question from whatever point you chose. Of course such a marriage was only what Newland was entitled to; but young men are so foolish and incalculable—and some women so ensnaring and unscrupulous—that it was nothing short of a miracle to see one's only son safe past the Siren Isle and in the haven of a blameless domesticity.

All this Mrs. Archer felt, and her son knew she felt; but he knew also that she had been perturbed by the premature announcement of his engagement, or rather by its cause; and it was for that reason—because on the whole he was a tender and indulgent master—that he had stayed at home that evening. "It's not that I don't approve of the Mingotts' *esprit de corps*; but why Newland's engagement should be mixed up with that Olenska woman's comings and goings I don't see," Mrs. Archer grumbled to Janey, the only witness of her slight lapses from perfect sweetness.

She had behaved beautifully—and in beautiful behaviour she was unsurpassed—during the call on Mrs. Welland; but Newland knew (and his betrothed doubtless guessed) that all through the visit she and Janey were nervously on the watch for Madame Olenska's possible intrusion; and when they left the house together she had permitted herself to say to her son: "I'm thankful that Augusta Welland received us alone."

These indications of inward disturbance moved Archer the more that he too felt that the Mingotts had gone a little too far. But, as it was against all the rules of their code that the mother and son should ever allude to what was uppermost in their thoughts, he simply replied: "Oh, well, there's always a phase of family parties to be gone through when one gets engaged, and the sooner it's over the better." At which his mother merely pursed her lips under the lace veil that hung down from her grey velvet bonnet trimmed with frosted grapes.

Her revenge, he felt—her lawful revenge—would be to "draw" Mr. Jackson that evening on the Countess Olenska; and, having publicly done his duty as a future member of the Mingott clan, the young man had no objection to hearing the lady discussed in private—except that the subject was already beginning to bore him.

Mr. Jackson had helped himself to a slice of the tepid *filet* which the mournful butler had handed him with a look as sceptical as his own, and had rejected the mushroom sauce after a scarcely perceptible sniff. He looked baffled and hungry, and Archer reflected that he would probably finish his meal on Ellen Olenska.

Mr. Jackson leaned back in his chair, and glanced up at the candlelit Archers, Newlands and van der Luydens hanging in dark frames on the dark walls.

"Ah, how your grandfather Archer loved a good dinner, my dear Newland!" he said, his eyes on the portrait of a plump full-chested young man in a stock and a blue coat, with a view of a white-columned country-house behind him. "Well—well—well . . . I wonder what he would have said to all these foreign marriages!"

Mrs. Archer ignored the allusion to the ancestral *cuisine* and Mr. Jackson continued with deliberation: "No, she was *not* at the ball."

"Ah—" Mrs. Archer murmured, in a tone that implied: "She had that decency."

"Perhaps the Beauforts don't know her," Janey suggested, with her artless malice.

Mr. Jackson gave a faint sip, as if he had been tasting invisible Madeira. "Mrs. Beaufort may not—but Beaufort certainly does, for she was seen walking up Fifth Avenue this afternoon with him by the whole of New York."

"Mercy—" moaned Mrs. Archer, evidently perceiving the uselessness of trying to ascribe the actions of foreigners to a sense of delicacy.

"I wonder if she wears a round hat or a bonnet in the afternoon," Janey speculated. "At the Opera I know she had on dark blue velvet, perfectly plain and flat—like a night-gown."

"Janey!" said her mother; and Miss Archer blushed and tried to look audacious.

"It was, at any rate, in better taste not to go to the ball," Mrs. Archer continued.

A spirit of perversity moved her son to rejoin: "I don't think it was a question of taste with her. May said she meant to go, and then decided that the dress in question wasn't smart enough."

Mrs. Archer smiled at this confirmation of her inference. "Poor Ellen," she simply remarked; adding compassionately: "We must always bear in mind what an eccentric bringing-up Medora Manson gave her. What can you expect of a girl who was allowed to wear black satin at her coming-out ball?"

"Ah—don't I remember her in it!" said Mr. Jackson; adding: "Poor girl!" in the tone of one who, while enjoying the memory, had fully understood at the time what the sight portended.

"It's odd," Janey remarked, "that she should have kept such an ugly name as Ellen. I should have changed it to Elaine." She glanced about the table to see the effect of this.

Her brother laughed. "Why Elaine?"

"I don't know; it sounds more—more Polish," said Janey, blushing.

"It sounds more conspicuous; and that can hardly be what she wishes," said Mrs. Archer distantly.

"Why not?" broke in her son, growing suddenly argumentative. "Why shouldn't she be conspicuous if she chooses? Why should she slink about as if it were she who had disgraced herself? She's 'poor Ellen' certainly, because she had the bad luck to make a wretched marriage; but I don't see that that's a reason for hiding her head as if she were the culprit."

"That, I suppose," said Mr. Jackson, speculatively, "is the line the Mingotts mean to take."

The young man reddened. "I didn't have to wait for their cue, if that's what you mean, sir. Madame Olenska has had an unhappy life: that doesn't make her an outcast."

"There are rumours," began Mr. Jackson, glancing at Janey.

"Oh, I know: the secretary," the young man took him up. "Nonsense, mother; Janey's grown-up. They say, don't they," he went on, "that the secretary helped her to get away from her brute of a husband, who kept her practically a prisoner? Well, what if he did? I hope there isn't a man among us who wouldn't have done the same in such a case."

Mr. Jackson glanced over his shoulder to say to the sad butler: "Perhaps . . . that sauce . . . just a little, after all—"; then, having helped himself, he remarked: "I'm told she's looking for a house. She means to live here."

"I hear she means to get a divorce," said Janey boldly.

"I hope she will!" Archer exclaimed.

The word had fallen like a bombshell in the pure and tranquil atmosphere of the Archer dining-room. Mrs. Archer raised her delicate eye-brows in the particular curve that signified: "The butler—" and the young man, himself mindful of the bad taste of discussing such intimate matters in public, hastily branched off into an account of his visit to old Mrs. Mingott.

After dinner, according to immemorial custom, Mrs. Archer and Janey trailed their long silk draperies up to the drawing-room, where, while the gentlemen smoked below stairs, they sat beside a Carcel lamp with an engraved globe, facing each other across a rosewood work-table with a green silk bag under it, and stitched at the two ends of a tapestry band of field-flowers destined to adorn an "occasional" chair in the drawing-room of young Mrs. Newland Archer.

While this rite was in progress in the drawing-room, Archer settled Mr. Jackson in an armchair near the fire in the Gothic library and handed him a cigar. Mr. Jackson sank into the armchair with satisfaction, lit his cigar with perfect confidence (it was Newland who bought them), and stretching his thin old ankles to the coals, said: "You say the secretary merely helped her to get away, my dear fellow? Well, he was still helping her a year later, then; for somebody met 'em living at Lausanne together."

Newland reddened. "Living together? Well, why not? Who had the right to make her life over if she hadn't? I'm sick of the hypocrisy that would bury alive a woman of her age if her husband prefers to live with harlots."

He stopped and turned away angrily to light his cigar. "Women ought to be free—as free as we are," he declared, making a discovery of which he was too irritated to measure the terrific consequences.

Mr. Sillerton Jackson stretched his ankles nearer the coals and emitted a sardonic whistle.

"Well," he said after a pause, "apparently Count Olenski takes your view; for I never heard of his having lifted a finger to get his wife back."

VI

THAT EVENING, after Mr. Jackson had taken himself away, and the ladies had retired to their chintz-curtained bedroom, Newland Archer mounted thoughtfully to his own study. A vigilant hand had, as usual, kept the fire alive and the lamp trimmed; and the room, with its rows and rows of books, its bronze and steel statuettes of "The Fencers" on the mantelpiece and its many photographs of famous pictures, looked singularly home-like and welcoming.

As he dropped into his armchair near the fire his eyes rested on a large photograph of May Welland, which the young girl had given him in the first days of their romance, and which had now displaced all the other portraits on the table. With a new sense of awe he looked at the frank forehead, serious eyes and gay innocent mouth of the young creature whose soul's custodian he was to be. That terrifying product of the social system he belonged to and believed in, the young girl who knew nothing and expected everything, looked back at him like a stranger through May Welland's familiar features; and once more it was borne in on him that marriage was not the safe anchorage he had been taught to think, but a voyage on uncharted seas.

The case of the Countess Olenska had stirred up old settled convictions and set them drifting dangerously through his mind. His own exclamation: "Women should be free—as free as we are," struck to the root of a problem that it was agreed in his world to regard as non-existent. "Nice" women, however wronged, would never claim the kind of freedom he meant, and generous-minded men like himself were therefore—in the heat of argument—the more chivalrously ready to concede it to them. Such verbal generosities were in fact only a humbugging disguise of the inexorable conventions that tied things together and bound people down to the old pattern. But here he was pledged to defend, on the part of his betrothed's cousin, conduct that, on his own wife's part, would justify him in calling down on her all the thunders of Church and State. Of course the dilemma was purely hypothetical; since he wasn't a blackguard Polish nobleman, it was absurd to speculate what his wife's rights would be if he *were*. But Newland Archer was too imaginative not to feel that, in his case and May's, the tie might gall for reasons far less gross and palpable. What could he and she really know of each other, since it was his duty, as a "decent" fellow, to conceal his past from her, and hers, as a marriageable girl, to have no past to conceal? What if, for some one of the subtler reasons that would tell with both of them, they should tire of each other, misunderstand or irritate each other? He reviewed his friends' marriages—the supposedly happy ones—and saw none that answered, even remotely, to the passionate and tender comradeship which he pictured as his permanent relation with May Welland. He perceived that such a picture presupposed, on her part, the experience, the versatility, the freedom of judgment, which she had been carefully trained not to possess; and with a shiver of foreboding he saw his marriage becoming what most of the other marriages about him were: a dull association of material and social interests held together by ignorance on the one side and hypocrisy on the other. Lawrence Lefferts occurred to him as the husband who had most completely realised this enviable ideal. As became the high-priest of form, he had formed a wife so completely to his own convenience that, in the most conspicuous moments of his frequent love-affairs with other men's wives, she went about in smiling unconsciousness, saying that "Lawrence was so frightfully strict"; and had been known to blush indignantly, and avert her gaze, when some one alluded in her presence to the fact that Julius Beaufort (as became a "foreigner" of doubtful origin) had what was known in New York as "another establishment."

Archer tried to console himself with the thought that he was not quite such an ass as Larry Lefferts, nor May such a simpleton as poor Gertrude; but the difference was after all one of intelligence and not of standards. In reality they all lived in a kind of hieroglyphic world, where the real thing was never said or done or even thought, but only represented by a set of arbitrary signs; as when Mrs. Welland, who knew exactly why Archer had pressed her to announce her daughter's engagement at the Beaufort ball (and had indeed expected him to do no less), yet felt obliged to simulate reluctance, and the air of having had her hand forced, quite as, in the books on Primitive Man that people of advanced culture were beginning to read, the savage bride is dragged with shrieks from her parents' tent.

The result, of course, was that the young girl who was the centre of this elaborate system of mystification remained the more inscrutable for her very frankness and assurance. She was frank, poor darling, because she had nothing to conceal, assured because she knew of nothing to be on her guard against; and with no better preparation than this, she was to be plunged overnight into what people evasively called "the facts of life."

The young man was sincerely but placidly in love. He delighted in the radiant good looks of his betrothed, in her health, her horsemanship, her grace and quickness at games, and the shy interest in books and ideas that she was beginning to develop under his guidance. (She had advanced far enough to join him in ridiculing the Idyls of the King, but not to feel the beauty of Ulysses and the Lotus Eaters.) She was straightforward, loyal and brave; she had a sense of humour (chiefly proved by her laughing at *his* jokes); and he suspected, in the depths of her innocently-gazing soul, a glow of feeling that it would be a joy to waken. But when he had gone the brief round of her he returned discouraged by the thought that all this frankness and innocence were only an artificial product. Untrained human nature was not frank and innocent; it was full of the twists and defences of an instinctive guile. And he felt himself oppressed by this creation of factitious purity, so cunningly manufactured by a conspiracy of mothers and aunts and grandmothers and long-dead ancestresses, because it was supposed to be what he wanted, what he had a right to, in order that he might exercise his lordly pleasure in smashing it like an image made of snow.

There was a certain triteness in these reflections: they were those habitual to young men on the approach of their wedding day. But they were generally accompanied by a sense of compunction and self-abasement of which Newland Archer felt no trace. He could not deplore (as Thackeray's heroes so often exasperated him by doing) that he had not a blank page to offer his bride in exchange for the unblemished one she was to give to him. He could not get away from the fact that if he had been brought up as she had they would have been no more fit to find their way about than the Babes in the Wood; nor could he, for all his anxious cogitations, see any honest reason (any, that is, unconnected with his own momentary pleasure, and the passion of masculine vanity) why his bride should not have been allowed the same freedom of experience as himself.

Such questions, at such an hour, were bound to drift through his mind; but he was conscious that their uncomfortable persistence and precision were due to the inopportune arrival of the Countess Olenska. Here he was, at the very moment of his betrothal—a moment for pure thoughts and cloudless hopes—pitchforked into a coil of scandal which raised all the special problems he would have preferred to let lie. "Hang Ellen Olenska!" he grumbled, as he covered his fire and began to undress. He could not really see why her fate should have the least bearing on his; yet he dimly felt that he had only just begun to measure the risks of the championship which his engagement had forced upon him.

A few days later the bolt fell.

The Lovell Mingotts had sent out cards for what was known as "a formal dinner" (that is, three extra footmen, two dishes for each course, and a Roman punch in the middle), and had headed their invitations with the words "To meet the Countess Olenska," in accordance with the hospitable American fashion, which treats strangers as if they were royalties, or at least as their ambassadors.

The guests had been selected with a boldness and discrimination in which the initiated recognised the firm hand of Catherine the Great. Associated with such immemorial standbys as the Selfridge Merrys, who were asked everywhere because they always had been, the Beauforts, on whom there was a claim of relationship, and Mr. Sillerton Jackson and his sister Sophy (who went wherever her brother told her to), were some of the most fashionable and yet most irreproachable of the dominant "young married" set; the Lawrence Leffertses, Mrs. Lefferts Rushworth (the lovely widow), the Harry Thorleys, the Reggie Chiverses and young Morris

Dagonet and his wife (who was a van der Luyden). The company indeed was perfectly assorted, since all the members belonged to the little inner group of people who, during the long New York season, disported themselves together daily and nightly with apparently undiminished zest.

Forty-eight hours later the unbelievable had happened; every one had refused the Mingotts' invitation except the Beauforts and old Mr. Jackson and his sister. The intended slight was emphasised by the fact that even the Reggie Chiverses, who were of the Mingott clan, were among those inflicting it; and by the uniform wording of the notes, in all of which the writers "regretted that they were unable to accept," without the mitigating plea of a "previous engagement" that ordinary courtesy prescribed.

New York society was, in those days, far too small, and too scant in its resources, for every one in it (including livery-stable-keepers, butlers and cooks) not to know exactly on which evenings people were free; and it was thus possible for the recipients of Mrs. Lovell Mingott's invitations to make cruelly clear their determination not to meet the Countess Olenska.

The blow was unexpected; but the Mingotts, as their way was, met it gallantly. Mrs. Lovell Mingott confided the case to Mrs. Welland, who confided it to Newland Archer; who, aflame at the outrage, appealed passionately and authoritatively to his mother; who, after a painful period of inward resistance and outward temporising, succumbed to his instances (as she always did), and immediately embracing his cause with an energy redoubled by her previous hesitations, put on her grey velvet bonnet and said: "I'll go and see Louisa van der Luyden."

The New York of Newland Archer's day was a small and slippery pyramid, in which, as yet, hardly a fissure had been made or a foothold gained. At its base was a firm foundation of what Mrs. Archer called "plain people"; an honourable but obscure majority of respectable families who (as in the case of the Spicers or the Leffertses or the Jacksons) had been raised above their level by marriage with one of the ruling clans. People, Mrs. Archer always said, were not as particular as they used to be; and with old Catherine Spicer ruling one end of

Fifth Avenue, and Julius Beaufort the other, you couldn't expect the old traditions to last much longer.

Firmly narrowing upward from this wealthy but inconspicuous substratum was the compact and dominant group which the Mingotts, Newlands, Chiverses and Mansons so actively represented. Most people imagined them to be the very apex of the pyramid; but they themselves (at least those of Mrs. Archer's generation) were aware that, in the eyes of the professional genealogist, only a still smaller number of families could lay claim to that eminence.

"Don't tell me," Mrs. Archer would say to her children, "all this modern newspaper rubbish about a New York aristocracy. If there is one, neither the Mingotts nor the Mansons belong to it; no, nor the Newlands or the Chiverses either. Our grandfathers and great-grandfathers were just respectable English or Dutch merchants, who came to the colonies to make their fortune, and stayed here because they did so well. One of your great-grandfathers signed the Declaration, and another was a general on Washington's staff, and received General Burgoyne's sword after the battle of Saratoga. These are things to be proud of, but they have nothing to do with rank or class. New York has always been a commercial community, and there are not more than three families in it who can claim an aristocratic origin in the real sense of the word."

Mrs. Archer and her son and daughter, like every one else in New York, knew who these privileged beings were: the Dagonets of Washington Square, who came of an old English county family allied with the Pitts and Foxes; the Lannings, who had intermarried with the descendants of Count de Grasse, and the van der Luydens, direct descendants of the first Dutch governor of Manhattan, and related by pre-revolutionary marriages to several members of the French and British aristocracy.

The Lannings survived only in the person of two very old but lively Miss Lannings, who lived cheerfully and reminiscently among family portraits and Chippendale; the Dagonets were a considerable clan, allied to the best names in Baltimore and Philadelphia; but the van der Luydens, who stood above all of them, had faded into a kind of super-terrestrial twilight, from which only two figures impressively emerged; those of Mr. and Mrs. Henry van der Luyden.

Mrs. Henry van der Luyden had been Louisa Dagonet, and her mother had been the granddaughter of Colonel du Lac, of an old Channel Island family, who had fought under Cornwallis and had settled in Maryland, after the war, with his bride, Lady Angelica Trevenna, fifth daughter of the Earl of St. Austrey. The tie between the Dagonets, the du Lacs of Maryland, and their aristocratic Cornish kinsfolk, the Trevennas, had always remained close and cordial. Mr. and Mrs. van der Luyden had more than once paid long visits to the present head of the house of Trevenna, the Duke of St. Austrey, at his country-seat in Cornwall and at St. Austrey in Gloucestershire; and his Grace had frequently announced his intention of some day returning their visit (without the Duchess, who feared the Atlantic).

Mr. and Mrs. van der Luyden divided their time between Trevenna, their place in Maryland, and Skuytercliff, the great estate on the Hudson which had been one of the colonial grants of the Dutch government to the famous first Governor, and of which Mr. van der Luyden was still "Patroon." Their large solemn house in Madison Avenue was seldom opened, and when they came to town they received in it only their most intimate friends.

"I wish you would go with me, Newland," his mother said, suddenly pausing at the door of the Brown *coupé*. "Louisa is fond of you; and of course it's on account of dear May that I'm taking this step—and also because, if we don't all stand together, there'll be no such thing as Society left."

VII

Mrs. henry van der luyden listened in silence to her cousin Mrs. Archer's narrative.

It was all very well to tell yourself in advance that Mrs. van der Luyden was always silent, and that, thought non-committal by nature and training, she was very kind to the people she really liked. Even personal experience of these facts was not always a protection from the chill that descended on one in the high-ceilinged white-walled Madison Avenue drawing-room, with the pale brocaded armchairs so obviously uncovered for the occasion, and the gauze still veiling the ormolu mantel ornaments and the beautiful old carved frame of Gainsborough's "Lady Angelica du Lac."

Mrs. van der Luyden's portrait by Huntington (in black velvet and Venetian point) faced that of her lovely ancestress. It was generally considered "as fine as a Cabanel," and, though twenty years had elapsed since its execution, was still "a perfect likeness." Indeed the Mrs. van der Luyden who sat beneath it listening to Mrs. Archer might have been the twin-sister of the fair and still youngish woman drooping against a gilt armchair before a green rep curtain. Mrs. van der Luyden still wore black velvet and Venetian point when she went into society—or rather (since she never dined out) when she threw open her own doors to receive it. Her fair hair, which had faded without turning grey, was still parted in flat over-lapping points on her forehead, and the straight nose that divided her pale blue eyes was only a little more pinched about the nostrils than when the portrait had been painted. She always, indeed, struck Newland Archer as having been rather gruesomely preserved in the airless atmosphere of a perfectly irreproachable existence, as bodies caught in glaciers keep for years a rosy life-in-death.

Like all his family, he esteemed and admired Mrs. van der Luyden; but he found her gentle bending sweetness less ap-proachable than the grimness of some of his mother's old aunts, fierce spinsters who said "No" on principle before they knew what they were going to be asked.

Mrs. van der Luyden's attitude said neither yes nor no, but

always appeared to incline to clemency till her thin lips, wavering into the shadow of a smile, made the almost invariable reply: "I shall first have to talk this over with my husband."

She and Mr. van der Luyden were so exactly alike that Archer often wondered how, after forty years of the closest conjugality, two such merged identities ever separated themselves enough for anything as controversial as a talking-over. But as neither had ever reached a decision without prefacing it by this mysterious conclave, Mrs. Archer and her son, having set forth their case, waited resignedly for the familiar phrase.

Mrs. van der Luyden, however, who had seldom surprised any one, now surprised them by reaching her long hand toward the bell-rope.

"I think," she said, "I should like Henry to hear what you have told me."

A footman appeared, to whom she gravely added: "If Mr. van der Luyden has finished reading the newspaper, please ask him to be kind enough to come."

She said "reading the newspaper" in the tone in which a Minister's wife might have said: "Presiding at a Cabinet meeting"—not from any arrogance of mind, but because the habit of a life-time, and the attitude of her friends and relations, had led her to consider Mr. van der Luyden's least gesture as having an almost sacerdotal importance.

Her promptness of action showed that she considered the case as pressing as Mrs. Archer; but, lest she should be thought to have committed herself in advance, she added, with the sweetest look: "Henry always enjoys seeing you, dear Adeline; and he will wish to congratulate Newland."

The double doors had solemnly reopened and between them appeared Mr. Henry van der Luyden, tall, spare and frock-coated, with faded fair hair, a straight nose like his wife's and the same look of frozen gentleness in eyes that were merely pale grey instead of pale blue.

Mr. van der Luyden greeted Mrs. Archer with cousinly affability, proffered to Newland low-voiced congratulations couched in the same language as his wife's, and seated himself in one of the brocade armchairs with the simplicity of a reigning sovereign.

"I had just finished reading the Times," he said, laying his long finger-tips together. "In town my mornings are so much occupied that I find it more convenient to read the newspapers after luncheon."

"Ah, there's a great deal to be said for that plan—indeed I think my uncle Egmont used to say he found it less agitating not to read the morning papers till after dinner," said Mrs. Archer responsively.

"Yes: my good father abhorred hurry. But now we live in a constant rush," said Mr. van der Luyden in measured tones, looking with pleasant deliberation about the large shrouded room which to Archer was so complete an image of its owners.

"But I hope you *had* finished your reading, Henry?" his wife interposed.

"Quite—quite," he reassured her.

"Then I should like Adeline to tell you—"

"Oh, it's really Newland's story," said his mother smiling; and proceeded to rehearse once more the monstrous tale of the affront inflicted on Mrs. Lovell Mingott.

"Of course," she ended, "Augusta Welland and Mary Mingott both felt that, especially in view of Newland's engagement, you and Henry *ought to know*."

"Ah—" said Mr. van der Luyden, drawing a deep breath.

There was a silence during which the tick of the monumental ormolu clock on the white marble mantelpiece grew as loud as the boom of a minute-gun. Archer contemplated with awe the two slender faded figures, seated side by side in a kind of viceregal rigidity, mouth-pieces of some remote ancestral authority which fate compelled them to wield, when they would so much rather have lived in simplicity and seclusion, digging invisible weeds out of the perfect lawns of Skuytercliff, and playing Patience together in the evenings.

Mr. van der Luyden was the first to speak.

"You really think this is due to some—some intentional interference of Lawrence Lefferts's?" he enquired, turning to Archer.

"I'm certain of it, sir. Larry has been going it rather harder than usual lately—if cousin Louisa won't mind my mentioning it—having rather a stiff affair with the postmaster's wife

in their village, or some one of that sort; and whenever poor
Gertrude Lefferts begins to suspect anything, and he's afraid
of trouble, he gets up a fuss of this kind, to show how awfully
moral he is, and talks at the top of his voice about the impertinence of inviting his wife to meet people he doesn't wish
her to know. He's simply using Madame Olenska as a light-
ning-rod; I've seen him try the same thing often before."

"The *Leffertses!*—" said Mrs. van der Luyden.

"The *Leffertses!*—" echoed Mrs. Archer. "What would
uncle Egmont have said of Lawrence Lefferts's pronouncing
on anybody's social position? It shows what Society has come
to."

"We'll hope it has not quite come to that," said Mr. van
der Luyden firmly.

"Ah, if only you and Louisa went out more!" sighed Mrs.
Archer.

But instantly she became aware of her mistake. The van der
Luydens were morbidly sensitive to any criticism of their secluded existence. They were the arbiters of fashion, the Court
of last Appeal, and they knew it, and bowed to their fate. But
being shy and retiring persons, with no natural inclination for
their part, they lived as much as possible in the sylvan solitude
of Skuytercliff, and when they came to town, declined all invitations on the plea of Mrs. van der Luyden's health.

Newland Archer came to his mother's rescue. "Everybody
in New York knows what you and cousin Louisa represent.
That's why Mrs. Mingott felt she ought not to allow this
slight on Countess Olenska to pass without consulting you."

Mrs. van der Luyden glanced at her husband, who glanced
back at her.

"It is the principle that I dislike," said Mr. van der Luyden.
"As long as a member of a well-known family is backed up
by that family it should be considered—final."

"It seems so to me," said his wife, as if she were producing
a new thought.

"I had no idea," Mr. van der Luyden continued, "that
things had come to such a pass." He paused, and looked at
his wife again. "It occurs to me, my dear, that the Countess
Olenska is already a sort of relation—through Medora
Manson's first husband. At any rate, she will be when New-

land marries." He turned toward the young man. "Have you read this morning's Times, Newland?"

"Why, yes, sir," said Archer, who usually tossed off half a dozen papers with his morning coffee.

Husband and wife looked at each other again. Their pale eyes clung together in prolonged and serious consultation; then a faint smile fluttered over Mrs. van der Luyden's face. She had evidently guessed and approved.

Mr. van der Luyden turned to Mrs. Archer. "If Louisa's health allowed her to dine out—I wish you would say to Mrs. Lovell Mingott—she and I would have been happy to—er—fill the places of the Lawrence Leffertses at her dinner." He paused to let the irony of this sink in. "As you know, this is impossible." Mrs. Archer sounded a sympathetic assent. "But Newland tells me he has read this morning's Times; therefore he has probably seen that Louisa's relative, the Duke of St. Austrey, arrives next week on the Russia. He is coming to enter his new sloop, the Guinevere, in next summer's International Cup Race; and also to have a little canvasback shooting at Trevenna." Mr. van der Luyden paused again, and continued with increasing benevolence: "Before taking him down to Maryland we are inviting a few friends to meet him here—only a little dinner—with a reception afterward. I am sure Louisa will be as glad as I am if Countess Olenska will let us include her among our guests." He got up, bent his long body with a stiff friendliness toward his cousin, and added: "I think I have Louisa's authority for saying that she will herself leave the invitation to dine when she drives out presently: with our cards—of course with our cards."

Mrs. Archer, who knew this to be a hint that the seventeen-hand chestnuts which were never kept waiting were at the door, rose with a hurried murmur of thanks. Mrs. van der Luyden beamed on her with the smile of Esther interceding with Ahasuerus; but her husband raised a protesting hand.

"There is nothing to thank me for, dear Adeline; nothing whatever. This kind of thing must not happen in New York; it shall not, as long as I can help it," he pronounced with sovereign gentleness as he steered his cousins to the door.

Two hours later, every one knew that the great C-spring

barouche in which Mrs. van der Luyden took the air at all seasons had been seen at old Mrs. Mingott's door, where a large square envelope was handed in; and that evening at the Opera Mr. Sillerton Jackson was able to state that the envelope contained a card inviting the Countess Olenska to the dinner which the van der Luydens were giving the following week for their cousin, the Duke of St. Austrey.

Some of the younger men in the club box exchanged a smile at this announcement, and glanced sideways at Lawrence Lefferts, who sat carelessly in the front of the box, pulling his long fair moustache, and who remarked with authority, as the soprano paused: "No one but Patti ought to attempt the Sonnambula."

VIII

I<small>T WAS GENERALLY</small> agreed in New York that the Countess Olenska had "lost her looks."

She had appeared there first, in Newland Archer's boyhood, as a brilliantly pretty little girl of nine or ten, of whom people said that she "ought to be painted." Her parents had been continental wanderers, and after a roaming babyhood she had lost them both, and been taken in charge by her aunt, Medora Manson, also a wanderer, who was herself returning to New York to "settle down."

Poor Medora, repeatedly widowed, was always coming home to settle down (each time in a less expensive house), and bringing with her a new husband or an adopted child; but after a few months she invariably parted from her husband or quarrelled with her ward, and, having got rid of her house at a loss, set out again on her wanderings. As her mother had been a Rushworth, and her last unhappy marriage had linked her to one of the crazy Chiverses, New York looked indulgently on her eccentricities; but when she returned with her little orphaned niece, whose parents had been popular in spite of their regrettable taste for travel, people thought it a pity that the pretty child should be in such hands.

Every one was disposed to be kind to little Ellen Mingott, though her dusky red cheeks and tight curls gave her an air of gaiety that seemed unsuitable in a child who should still have been in black for her parents. It was one of the misguided Medora's many peculiarities to flout the unalterable rules that regulated American mourning, and when she stepped from the steamer her family were scandalised to see that the crape veil she wore for her own brother was seven inches shorter than those of her sisters-in-law, while little Ellen was in crimson merino and amber beads, like a gipsy foundling.

But New York had so long resigned itself to Medora that only a few old ladies shook their heads over Ellen's gaudy clothes, while her other relations fell under the charm of her high colour and high spirits. She was a fearless and familiar little thing, who asked disconcerting questions, made precocious comments, and possessed outlandish arts, such as dancing a Spanish shawl dance and singing Neapolitan love-songs to a guitar. Under the direction of her aunt (whose real name was Mrs. Thorley Chivers, but who, having received a Papal title, had resumed her first husband's patronymic, and called herself the Marchioness Manson, because in Italy she could turn it into Manzoni) the little girl received an expensive but incoherent education, which included "drawing from the model," a thing never dreamed of before, and playing the piano in quintets with professional musicians.

Of course no good could come of this; and when, a few years later, poor Chivers finally died in a madhouse, his widow (draped in strange weeds) again pulled up stakes and departed with Ellen, who had grown into a tall bony girl with conspicuous eyes. For some time no more was heard of them; then news came of Ellen's marriage to an immensely rich Polish nobleman of legendary fame, whom she had met at a ball at the Tuileries, and who was said to have princely establishments in Paris, Nice and Florence, a yacht at Cowes, and many square miles of shooting in Transylvania. She disappeared in a kind of sulphurous apotheosis, and when a few years later Medora again came back to New York, subdued, impoverished, mourning a third husband, and in quest of a still smaller house, people wondered that her rich niece had not been able to do something for her. Then came the news that Ellen's own marriage had ended in disaster, and that she was herself returning home to seek rest and oblivion among her kinsfolk.

These things passed through Newland Archer's mind a week later as he watched the Countess Olenska enter the van der Luyden drawing-room on the evening of the momentous dinner. The occasion was a solemn one, and he wondered a little nervously how she would carry it off. She came rather late, one hand still ungloved, and fastening a bracelet about her wrist; yet she entered without any appearance of haste or embarrassment the drawing-room in which New York's most chosen company was somewhat awfully assembled.

In the middle of the room she paused, looking about her with a grave mouth and smiling eyes; and in that instant

Newland Archer rejected the general verdict on her looks. It was true that her early radiance was gone. The red cheeks had paled; she was thin, worn, a little older-looking than her age, which must have been nearly thirty. But there was about her the mysterious authority of beauty, a sureness in the carriage of the head, the movement of the eyes, which, without being in the least theatrical, struck his as highly trained and full of a conscious power. At the same time she was simpler in manner than most of the ladies present, and many people (as he heard afterward from Janey) were disappointed that her appearance was not more "stylish"—for stylishness was what New York most valued. It was, perhaps, Archer reflected, because her early vivacity had disappeared; because she was so quiet—quiet in her movements, her voice, and the tones of her low-pitched voice. New York had expected something a good deal more reasonant in a young woman with such a history.

The dinner was a somewhat formidable business. Dining with the van der Luydens was at best no light matter, and dining there with a Duke who was their cousin was almost a religious solemnity. It pleased Archer to think that only an old New Yorker could perceive the shade of difference (to New York) between being merely a Duke and being the van der Luydens' Duke. New York took stray noblemen calmly, and even (except in the Struthers set) with a certain distrustful *hauteur*; but when they presented such credentials as these they were received with an old-fashioned cordiality that they would have been greatly mistaken in ascribing solely to their standing in Debrett. It was for just such distinctions that the young man cherished his old New York even while he smiled at it.

The van der Luydens had done their best to emphasise the importance of the occasion. The du Lac Sèvres and the Trevenna George II plate were out; so was the van der Luyden "Lowestoft" (East India Company) and the Dagonet Crown Derby. Mrs. van der Luyden looked more than ever like a Cabanel, and Mrs. Archer, in her grandmother's seed-pearls and emeralds, reminded her son of an Isabey miniature. All the ladies had on their handsomest jewels, but it was characteristic of the house and the occasion that these were mostly in rather heavy old-fashioned settings; and old Miss Lanning, who had been persuaded to come, actually wore her mother's cameos and a Spanish blonde shawl.

The Countess Olenska was the only young woman at the dinner; yet, as Archer scanned the smooth plump elderly faces between their diamond necklaces and towering ostrich feathers, they struck him as curiously immature compared with hers. It frightened him to think what must have gone to the making of her eyes.

The Duke of St. Austrey, who sat at his hostess's right, was naturally the chief figure of the evening. But if the Countess Olenska was less conspicuous than had been hoped, the Duke was almost invisible. Being a well-bred man he had not (like another recent ducal visitor) come to the dinner in a shooting-jacket; but his evening clothes were so shabby and baggy, and he wore them with such an air of their being homespun, that (with his stooping way of sitting, and the vast beard spreading over his shirt-front) he hardly gave the appearance of being in dinner attire. He was short, round-shouldered, sunburnt, with a thick nose, small eyes and a sociable smile; but he seldom spoke, and when he did it was in such low tones that, despite the frequent silences of expectation about the table, his remarks were lost to all but his neighbours.

When the men joined the ladies after dinner the Duke went straight up to the Countess Olenska, and they sat down in a corner and plunged into animated talk. Neither seemed aware that the Duke should first have paid his respects to Mrs. Lovell Mingott and Mrs. Headly Chivers, and the Countess have conversed with that amiable hypochondriac, Mr. Urban Dagonet of Washington Square, who, in order to have the pleasure of meeting her, had broken through his fixed rule of not dining out between January and April. The two chatted together for nearly twenty minutes; then the Countess rose and, walking alone across the wide drawing-room, sat down at Newland Archer's side.

It was not the custom in New York drawing-rooms for a lady to get up and walk away from one gentleman in order to seek the company of another. Etiquette required that she should wait, immovable as an idol, while the men who wished to converse with her succeeded each other at her side.

But the Countess was apparently unaware of having broken any rule; she sat at perfect ease in a corner of the sofa beside Archer, and looked at him with the kindest eyes.

"I want you to talk to me about May," she said.

Instead of answering her he asked: "You knew the Duke before?"

"Oh, yes—we used to see him every winter at Nice. He's very fond of gambling—he used to come to the house a great deal." She said it in the simplest manner, as if she had said: "He's fond of wild-flowers"; and after a moment she added candidly: "I think he's the dullest man I ever met."

This pleased her companion so much that he forgot the slight shock her previous remark had caused him. It was undeniably exciting to meet a lady who found the van der Luydens' Duke dull, and dared to utter the opinion. He longed to question her, to hear more about the life of which her careless words had given him so illuminating a glimpse; but he feared to touch on distressing memories, and before he could think of anything to say she had strayed back to her original subject.

"May is a darling; I've seen no young girl in New York so handsome and so intelligent. Are you very much in love with her?"

Newland Archer reddened and laughed. "As much as a man can be."

She continued to consider him thoughtfully, as if not to miss any shade of meaning in what he said, "Do you think, then, there is a limit?"

"To being in love? If there is, I haven't found it!"

She glowed with sympathy. "Ah—it's really and truly a romance?"

"The most romantic of romances!"

"How delightful! And you found it all out for yourselves—it was not in the least arranged for you?"

Archer looked at her incredulously. "Have you forgotten," he asked with a smile, "that in our country we don't allow our marriages to be arranged for us?"

A dusky blush rose to her cheek, and he instantly regretted his words.

"Yes," she answered, "I'd forgotten. You must forgive me

if I sometimes make these mistakes. I don't always remember that everything here is good that was—that was bad where I've come from." She looked down at her Viennese fan of eagle feathers, and he saw that her lips trembled.

"I'm so sorry," he said impulsively; "but you *are* among friends here, you know."

"Yes—I know. Wherever I go I have that feeling. That's why I came home. I want to forget everything else, to become a complete American again, like the Mingotts and Wellands, and you and your delightful mother, and all the other good people here tonight. Ah, here's May arriving, and you will want to hurry away to her," she added, but without moving; and her eyes turned back from the door to rest on the young man's face.

The drawing-rooms were beginning to fill up with after-dinner guests, and following Madame Olenska's glance Archer saw May Welland entering with her mother. In her dress of white and silver, with a wreath of silver blossoms in her hair, the tall girl looked like a Diana just alight from the chase.

"Oh," said Archer, "I have so many rivals; you see she's already surrounded. There's the Duke being introduced."

"Then stay with me a little longer," Madame Olenska said in a low tone, just touching his knee with her plumed fan. It was the lightest touch, but it thrilled him like a caress.

"Yes, let me stay," he answered in the same tone, hardly knowing what he said; but just then Mr. van der Luyden came up, followed by old Mr. Urban Dagonet. The Countess greeted them with her grave smile, and Archer, feeling his host's admonitory glance on him, rose and surrendered his seat.

Madame Olenska held out her hand as if to bid him good-bye.

"Tomorrow, then, after five—I shall expect you," she said; and then turned back to make room for Mr. Dagonet.

"Tomorrow—" Archer heard himself repeating, though there had been no engagement, and during their talk she had given him no hint that she wished to see him again.

As he moved away he saw Lawrence Lefferts, tall and resplendent, leading his wife up to be introduced; and heard

Gertrude Lefferts say, as she beamed on the Countess with her large unperceiving smile: "But I think we used to go to dancing-school together when we were children—." Behind her, waiting their turn to name themselves to the Countess, Archer noticed a number of the recalcitrant couples who had declined to meet her at Mrs. Lovell Mingott's. As Mrs. Archer remarked: when the van der Luydens chose, they knew how to give a lesson. The wonder was that they chose so seldom.

The young man felt a touch on his arm and saw Mrs. van der Luyden looking down on him from the pure eminence of black velvet and the family diamonds. "It was good of you, dear Newland, to devote yourself so unselfishly to Madame Olenska. I told your cousin Henry he must really come to the rescue."

He was aware of smiling at her vaguely, and she added, as if condescending to his natural shyness: "I've never seen May looking lovelier. The Duke thinks her the handsomest girl in the room."

IX

T HE COUNTESS OLENSKA had said "after five"; and at half after the hour Newland Archer rang the bell of the peeling stucco house with a giant wisteria throttling its feeble cast-iron balcony, which she had hired, far down West Twenty-third Street, from the vagabond Medora.

It was certainly a strange quarter to have settled in. Small dress-makers, bird-stuffers and "people who wrote" were her nearest neighbours; and further down the dishevelled street Archer recognised a dilapidated wooden house, at the end of a paved path, in which a writer and journalist called Winsett, whom he used to come across now and then, had mentioned that he lived. Winsett did not invite people to his house; but he had once pointed it out to Archer in the course of a nocturnal stroll, and the latter had asked himself, with a little shiver, if the humanities were so meanly housed in other capitals.

Madame Olenska's own dwelling was redeemed from the same appearance only by a little more paint about the window-frames; and as Archer mustered its modest front he said to himself that the Polish Count must have robbed her of her fortune as well as of her illusions.

The young man had spent an unsatisfactory day. He had lunched with the Wellands, hoping afterward to carry off May for a walk in the Park. He wanted to have her to himself, to tell her how enchanting she had looked the night before, and how proud he was of her, and to press her to hasten their marriage. But Mrs. Welland had firmly reminded him that the round of family visits was not half over, and, when he hinted at advancing the date of the wedding, had raised reproachful eye-brows and sighed out: "Twelve dozen of everything—hand-embroidered—"

Packed in the family landau they rolled from one tribal doorstep to another, and Archer, when the afternoon's round was over, parted from his betrothed with the feeling that he had been shown off like a wild animal cunningly trapped. He supposed that his readings in anthropology caused him to take such a coarse view of what was after all a simple and natural demonstration of family feeling; but when he remembered that the Wellands did not expect the wedding to take place till the following autumn, and pictured what his life would be till then, a dampness fell upon his spirit.

"Tomorrow," Mrs. Welland called after him, "we'll do the Chiverses and the Dallases"; and he perceived that she was going through their two families alphabetically, and that they were only in the first quarter of the alphabet.

He had meant to tell May of the Countess Olenska's request—her command, rather—that he should call on her that afternoon; but in the brief moments when they were alone he had had more pressing things to say. Besides, it struck him as a little absurd to allude to the matter. He knew that May most particularly wanted him to be kind to her cousin; was it not that wish which had hastened the announcement of their engagement? It gave him an odd sensation to reflect that, but for the Countess's arrival, he might have been, if not still a free man, at least a man less irrevocably pledged. But May had willed it so, and he felt himself somehow relieved of further responsibility—and therefore at liberty, if he chose, to call on her cousin without telling her.

As he stood on Madame Olenska's threshold curiosity was his uppermost feeling. He was puzzled by the tone in which she had summoned him; he concluded that she was less simple than she seemed.

The door was opened by a swarthy foreign-looking maid, with a prominent bosom under a gay neckerchief, whom he vaguely fancied to be Sicilian. She welcomed him with all her white teeth, and answering his enquiries by a head-shake of incomprehension led him through the narrow hall into a low firelit drawing-room. The room was empty, and she left him, for an appreciable time, to wonder whether she had gone to find her mistress, or whether she had not understood what he was there for, and thought it might be to wind the clocks— of which he perceived that the only visible specimen had stopped. He knew that the southern races communicated with each other in the language of pantomime, and was mortified to find her shrugs and smiles so unintelligible. At length she returned with a lamp; and Archer, having meanwhile put together a phrase out of Dante and Petrarch, evoked the answer: *"La signora è fuori; ma verrà subito"*; which he took to mean: "She's out—but you'll soon see."

What he saw, meanwhile, with the help of the lamp, was the faded shadowy charm of a room unlike any room he had known. He knew that the Countess Olenska had brought some of her possessions with her—bits of wreckage, she called them—and these, he supposed, were represented by some small slender tables of dark wood, a delicate little Greek bronze on the chimney-piece, and a stretch of red damask nailed on the discoloured wallpaper behind a couple of Italian-looking pictures in old frames.

Newland Archer prided himself on his knowledge of Italian art. His boyhood had been saturated with Ruskin, and he had read all the latest books: John Addington Symonds, Vernon Lee's "Euphorion," the essays of P. G. Hamerton, and a wonderful new volume called "The Renaissance" by Walter Pater. He talked easily of Botticelli, and spoke of Fra Angelico with a faint condescension. But these pictures bewildered him, for they were like nothing that he was accustomed to look at (and therefore able to see) when he travelled in Italy; and perhaps, also, his powers of observation were impaired by the oddness of finding himself in this strange empty house, where apparently no one expected him. He was sorry that he had not told May Welland of Countess Olenska's request, and a little disturbed by the thought that his betrothed might come in to see her cousin. What would she think if she found him sitting there with the air of intimacy implied by waiting alone in the dusk at a lady's fireside?

But since he had come he meant to wait; and he sank into a chair and stretched his feet to the logs.

It was odd to have summoned him in that way, and then forgotten him; but Archer felt more curious than mortified. The atmosphere of the room was so different from any he had ever breathed that self-consciousness vanished in the sense of adventure. He had been before in drawing-rooms hung with red damask, with pictures "of the Italian school"; what struck him was the way in which Medora Manson's shabby hired house, with its blighted background of pampas grass and Rogers statuettes, had, by a turn of the hand, and the skilful use of a few properties, been transformed into

something intimate, "foreign," subtly suggestive of old romantic scenes and sentiments. He tried to analyse the trick, to
find a clue to it in the way the chairs and tables were grouped,
in the fact that only two Jacqueminot roses (of which nobody
ever bought less than a dozen) had been placed in the slender
vase at his elbow, and in the vague pervading perfume that
was not what one put on handkerchiefs, but rather like the
scent of some far-off bazaar, a smell made up of Turkish coffee and ambergris and dried roses.

His mind wandered away to the question of what May's
drawing-room would look like. He knew that Mr. Welland,
who was behaving "very handsomely," already had his eye on
a newly built house in East Thirty-ninth Street. The neighbourhood was thought remote, and the house was built in a
ghastly greenish-yellow stone that the younger architects were
beginning to employ as a protest against the brownstone of
which the uniform hue coated New York like a cold chocolate
sauce; but the plumbing was perfect. Archer would have liked
to travel, to put off the housing question; but, though the
Wellands approved of an extended European honeymoon
(perhaps even a winter in Egypt), they were firm as to the
need of a house for the returning couple. The young man felt
that his fate was sealed: for the rest of his life he would go
up every evening between the cast-iron railings of that greenish-yellow doorstep, and pass through a Pompeian vestibule
into a hall with a wainscoting of varnished yellow wood. But
beyond that his imagination could not travel. He knew the
drawing-room above had a bay window, but he could not
fancy how May would deal with it. She submitted cheerfully
to the purple satin and yellow tuftings of the Welland drawing-room, to its sham Buhl tables and gilt vitrines full of
modern Saxe. He saw no reason to suppose that she would
want anything different in her own house; and his only comfort was to reflect that she would probably let him arrange
his library as he pleased—which would be, of course, with
"sincere" Eastlake furniture, and the plain new book-cases
without glass doors.

The round-bosomed maid came in, drew the curtains,
pushed back a log, and said consolingly: *"Verrà—verrà."*
When she had gone Archer stood up and began to wander

about. Should he wait any longer? His position was becoming rather foolish. Perhaps he had misunderstood Madame Olenska—perhaps she had not invited him after all.

Down the cobblestones of the quiet street came the ring of a stepper's hoofs; they stopped before the house, and he caught the opening of a carriage door. Parting the curtains he looked out into the early dusk. A street-lamp faced him, and in its light he saw Julius Beaufort's compact English brougham, drawn by a big roan, and the banker descending from it, and helping out Madame Olenska.

Beaufort stood, hat in hand, saying something which his companion seemed to negative; then they shook hands, and he jumped into his carriage while she mounted the steps.

When she entered the room she showed no surprise at seeing Archer there; surprise seemed the emotion that she was least addicted to.

"How do you like my funny house?" she asked. "To me it's like heaven."

As she spoke she untied her little velvet bonnet and tossing it away with her long cloak stood looking at him with meditative eyes.

"You've arranged it delightfully," he rejoined, alive to the flatness of the words, but imprisoned in the conventional by his consuming desire to be simple and striking.

"Oh, it's a poor little place. My relations despise it. But at any rate it's less gloomy than the van der Luydens'."

The words gave him an electric shock, for few were the rebellious spirits who would have dared to call the stately home of the van der Luydens gloomy. Those privileged to enter it shivered there, and spoke of it as "handsome." But suddenly he was glad that she had given voice to the general shiver.

"It's delicious—what you've done here," he repeated.

"I like the little house," she admitted; "but I suppose what I like is the blessedness of its being here, in my own country and my own town; and then, of being alone in it." She spoke so low that he hardly heard the last phrase; but in his awkwardness he took it up.

"You like so much to be alone?"

"Yes; as long as my friends keep me from feeling lonely."

She sat down near the fire, said: "Nastasia will bring the tea presently," and signed to him to return to his armchair, adding: "I see you've already chosen your corner."

Leaning back, she folded her arms behind her head, and looked at the fire under drooping lids.

"This is the hour I like best—don't you?"

A proper sense of his dignity caused him to answer: "I was afraid you'd forgotten the hour. Beaufort must have been very engrossing."

She looked amused. "Why—have you waited long? Mr. Beaufort took me to see a number of houses—since it seems I'm not to be allowed to stay in this one." She appeared to dismiss both Beaufort and himself from her mind, and went on: "I've never been in a city where there seems to be such a feeling against living in *des quartiers excentriques*. What does it matter where one lives? I'm told this street is respectable."

"It's not fashionable."

"Fashionable! Do you all think so much of that? Why not make one's own fashions? But I suppose I've lived too independently; at any rate, I want to do what you all do—I want to feel cared for and safe."

He was touched, as he had been the evening before when she spoke of her need of guidance.

"That's what your friends want you to feel. New York's an awfully safe place," he added with a flash of sarcasm.

"Yes, isn't it? One feels that," she cried, missing the mockery. "Being here is like—like—being taken on a holiday when one has been a good little girl and done all one's lessons."

The analogy was well meant, but did not altogether please him. He did not mind being flippant about New York, but disliked to hear any one else take the same tone. He wondered if she did not begin to see what a powerful engine it was, and how nearly it had crushed her. The Lovell Mingotts' dinner, patched up *in extremis* out of all sorts of social odds and ends, ought to have taught her the narrowness of her escape; but either she had been all along unaware of having skirted disaster, or else she had lost sight of it in the triumph of the van der Luyden evening. Archer inclined to the former theory; he fancied that her New York was still completely un-differentiated, and the conjecture nettled him.

"Last night," he said, "New York laid itself out for you. The van der Luydens do nothing by halves."

"No: how kind they are! It was such a nice party. Every one seems to have such an esteem for them."

The terms were hardly adequate; she might have spoken in that way of a tea-party at the dear old Miss Lannings'.

"The van der Luydens," said Archer, feeling himself pompous as he spoke, "are the most powerful influence in New York society. Unfortunately—owing to her health—they receive very seldom."

She unclasped her hands from behind her head, and looked at him meditatively.

"Isn't that perhaps the reason?"

"The reason—?"

"For their great influence; that they make themselves so rare."

He coloured a little, stared at her—and suddenly felt the penetration of the remark. At a stroke she had pricked the van der Luydens and they collapsed. He laughed, and sacrificed them.

Nastasia brought the tea, with handleless Japanese cups and little covered dishes, placing the tray on a low table.

"But you'll explain these things to me—you'll tell me all I ought to know," Madame Olenska continued, leaning forward to hand him his cup.

"It's you who are telling me; opening my eyes to things I'd looked at so long that I'd ceased to see them."

She detached a small gold cigarette-case from one of her bracelets, held it out to him, and took a cigarette herself. On the chimney were long spills for lighting them.

"Ah, then we can both help each other. But I want help so much more. You must tell me just what to do."

It was on the tip of his tongue to reply: "Don't be seen driving about the streets with Beaufort—" but he was being too deeply drawn into the atmosphere of the room, which was her atmosphere, and to give advice of that sort would have been like telling some one who was bargaining for attar-of-roses in Samarkand that one should always be provided with arctics for a New York winter. New York seemed much farther off than Samarkand, and if they were indeed to help each other she was rendering what might prove the first of their mutual services by making him look at his native city objectively. Viewed thus, as through the wrong end of a telescope, it looked disconcertingly small and distant; but then from Samarkand it would.

A flame darted from the logs and she bent over the fire, stretching her thin hands so close to it that a faint halo shone about the oval nails. The light touched to russet the rings of dark hair escaping from her braids, and made her pale face paler.

"There are plenty of people to tell you what to do," Archer rejoined, obscurely envious of them.

"Oh—all my aunts? And my dear old Granny?" She considered the idea impartially. "They're all a little vexed with me for setting up for myself—poor Granny especially. She wanted to keep me with her; but I had to be free—" He was impressed by this light way of speaking of the formidable Catherine, and moved by the thought of what must have given Madame Olenska this thirst for even the loneliest kind of freedom. But the idea of Beaufort gnawed him.

"I think I understand how you feel," he said. "Still, your family can advise you; explain differences; show you the way."

She lifted her thin black eyebrows. "Is New York such a labyrinth? I thought it so straight up and down—like Fifth Avenue. And with all the cross streets numbered!" She seemed to guess his faint disapproval of this, and added, with the rare smile that enchanted her whole face: "If you knew how I like it for just *that*—the straight-up-and-downness, and the big honest labels on everything!"

He saw his chance. "Everything may be labelled—but everybody is not."

"Perhaps. I may simplify too much—but you'll warn me if I do." She turned from the fire to look at him. "There are only two people here who make me feel as if they understood what I mean and could explain things to me: you and Mr. Beaufort."

Archer winced at the joining of the names, and then, with

a quick readjustment, understood, sympathised and pitied. So close to the powers of evil she must have lived that she still breathed more freely in their air. But since she felt that he understood her also, his business would be to make her see Beaufort as he really was, with all he represented—and abhor it.

He answered gently: "I understand. But just at first don't let go of your old friends' hands: I mean the older women, your Granny Mingott, Mrs. Welland, Mrs. van der Luyden. They like and admire you—they want to help you."

She shook her head and sighed. "Oh, I know—I know! But on condition that they don't hear anything unpleasant. Aunt Welland put it in those very words when I tried. . . . Does no one want to know the truth here, Mr. Archer? The real loneliness is living among all these kind people who only ask one to pretend!" She lifted her hands to her face, and he saw her thin shoulders shaken by a sob.

"Madame Olenska!—Oh, don't, Ellen," he cried, starting up and bending over her. He drew down one of her hands, clasping and chafing it like a child's while he murmured reassuring words; but in a moment she freed herself, and looked up at him with wet lashes.

"Does no one cry here, either? I suppose there's no need to, in heaven," she said, straightening her loosened braids with a laugh, and bending over the tea-kettle. It was burnt into his consciousness that he had called her "Ellen"—called her so twice; and that she had not noticed it. Far down the inverted telescope he saw the faint white figure of May Welland—in New York.

Suddenly Nastasia put her head in to say something in her rich Italian.

Madame Olenska, again with a hand at her hair, uttered an exclamation of assent—a flashing *"Già—già"*—and the Duke of St. Austrey entered, piloting a tremendous black-wigged and red-plumed lady in overflowing furs.

"My dear Countess, I've brought an old friend of mine to see you—Mrs. Struthers. She wasn't asked to the party last night, and she wants to know you."

The Duke beamed on the group, and Madame Olenska advanced with a murmur of welcome toward the queer couple.

She seemed to have no idea how oddly matched they were, nor what a liberty the Duke had taken in bringing his companion—and to do him justice, as Archer perceived, the Duke seemed as unaware of it himself.

"Of course I want to know you, my dear," cried Mrs. Struthers in a round rolling voice that matched her bold feathers and her brazen wig. "I want to know everybody who's young and interesting and charming. And the Duke tells me you like music—didn't you, Duke? You're a pianist yourself, I believe? Well, do you want to hear Sarasate play tomorrow evening at my house? You know I've something going on every Sunday evening—it's the day when New York doesn't know what to do with itself, and so I say to it: 'Come and be amused.' And the Duke thought you'd be tempted by Sarasate. You'll find a number of your friends."

Madame Olenska's face grew brilliant with pleasure. "How kind! How good of the Duke to think of me!" She pushed a chair up to the tea-table and Mrs. Struthers sank into it delectably. "Of course I shall be too happy to come."

"That's all right, my dear. And bring your young gentleman with you." Mrs. Struthers extended a hail-fellow hand to Archer. "I can't put a name to you—but I'm sure I've met you—I've met everybody, here, or in Paris or London. Aren't you in diplomacy? All the diplomatists come to me. You like music too? Duke, you must be sure to bring him."

The Duke said "Rather" from the depths of his beard, and Archer withdrew with a stiffly circular bow that made him feel as full of spine as a self-conscious school-boy among careless and unnoticing elders.

He was not sorry for the *dénouement* of his visit: he only wished it had come sooner, and spared him a certain waste of emotion. As he went out into the wintry night, New York again became vast and imminent, and May Welland the loveliest woman in it. He turned into his florist's to send her the daily box of lilies-of-the-valley which, to his confusion, he found he had forgotten that morning.

As he wrote a word on his card and waited for an envelope he glanced about the embowered shop, and his eye lit on a cluster of yellow roses. He had never seen any as sun-golden before, and his first impulse was to send them to May instead of the lilies. But they did not look like her—there was something too rich, too strong, in their fiery beauty. In a sudden revulsion of mood, and almost without knowing what he did, he signed to the florist to lay the roses in another long box, and slipped his card into a second envelope, on which he wrote the name of the Countess Olenska; then, just as he was turning away, he drew the card out again, and left the empty envelope on the box.

"They'll go at once?" he enquired, pointing to the roses.

The florist assured him that they would.

X

THE NEXT DAY he persuaded May to escape for a walk in the Park after luncheon. As was the custom in old-fashioned Episcopalian New York, she usually accompanied her parents to church on Sunday afternoons; but Mrs. Welland condoned her truancy, having that very morning won her over to the necessity of a long engagement, with time to prepare a hand-embroidered trousseau containing the proper number of dozens.

The day was delectable. The bare vaulting of trees along the Mall was ceiled with lapis lazuli, and arched above snow that shone like splintered crystals. It was the weather to call out May's radiance, and she burned like a young maple in the frost. Archer was proud of the glances turned on her, and the simple joy of possessorship cleared away his underlying perplexities.

"It's so delicious—waking every morning to smell lilies-of-the-valley in one's room!" she said.

"Yesterday they came late. I hadn't time in the morning—"

"But your remembering each day to send them makes me love them so much more than if you'd given a standing order, and they came every morning on the minute, like one's music-teacher—as I know Gertrude Lefferts's did, for instance, when she and Lawrence were engaged."

"Ah—they would!" laughed Archer, amused at her keenness. He looked sideways at her fruit-like cheek and felt rich and secure enough to add: "When I sent your lilies yesterday afternoon I saw some rather gorgeous yellow roses and packed them off to Madame Olenska. Was that right?"

"How dear of you! Anything of that kind delights her. It's odd she didn't mention it: she lunched with us today, and spoke of Mr. Beaufort's having sent her wonderful orchids, and cousin Henry van der Luyden a whole hamper of carnations from Skuytercliff. She seems so surprised to receive flowers. Don't people send them in Europe? She thinks it such a pretty custom."

"Oh, well, no wonder mine were overshadowed by Beaufort's," said Archer irritably. Then he remembered that he had not put a card with the roses, and was vexed at having spoken of them. He wanted to say: "I called on your cousin yesterday," but hesitated. If Madame Olenska had not spoken of his visit it might seem awkward that he should. Yet not to do so gave the affair an air of mystery that he disliked. To shake off the question he began to talk of their own plans, their future, and Mrs. Welland's insistence on a long engagement.

"If you call it long! Isabel Chivers and Reggie were engaged for two years: Grace and Thorley for nearly a year and a half. Why aren't we very well off as we are?"

It was the traditional maidenly interrogation, and he felt ashamed of himself for finding it singularly childish. No doubt she simply echoed what was said for her; but she was nearing her twenty-second birthday, and he wondered at what age "nice" women began to speak for themselves.

"Never, if we won't let them, I suppose," he mused, and recalled his mad outburst to Mr. Sillerton Jackson: "Women ought to be as free as we are—"

It would presently be his task to take the bandage from this young woman's eyes, and bid her look forth on the world. But how many generations of the women who had gone to her making had descended bandaged to the family vault? He shivered a little, remembering some of the new ideas in his scientific books, and the much-cited instance of the Kentucky cave-fish, which had ceased to develop eyes because they had no use for them. What if, when he had bidden May Welland to open hers, they could only look out blankly at blankness?

"We might be much better off. We might be altogether together—we might travel."

Her face lit up. "That would be lovely," she owned: she would love to travel. But her mother would not understand their wanting to do things so differently.

"As if the mere 'differently' didn't account for it!" the wooer insisted.

"Newland! You're so original!" she exulted.

His heart sank, for he saw that he was saying all the things that young men in the same situation were expected to say, and that she was making the answers that instinct and tradition taught her to make—even to the point of calling him original.

"Original! We're all as like each other as those dolls cut out of the same folded paper. We're like patterns stencilled on a wall. Can't you and I strike out for ourselves, May?"

He had stopped and faced her in the excitement of their discussion, and her eyes rested on him with a bright unclouded admiration.

"Mercy—shall we elope?" she laughed.

"If you would—"

"You *do* love me, Newland! I'm so happy."

"But then—why not be happier?"

"We can't behave like people in novels, though, can we?"

"Why not—why not—why not?"

She looked a little bored by his insistence. She knew very well that they couldn't, but it was troublesome to have to produce a reason. "I'm not clever enough to argue with you. But that kind of thing is rather—vulgar, isn't it?" she suggested, relieved to have hit on a word that would assuredly extinguish the whole subject.

"Are you so much afraid, then, of being vulgar?"

She was evidently staggered by this. "Of course I should hate it—so would you," she rejoined, a trifle irritably.

He stood silent, beating his stick nervously against his boot-top; and feeling that she had indeed found the right way of closing the discussion, she went on light-heartedly: "Oh, did I tell you that I showed Ellen my ring? She thinks it the most beautiful setting she ever saw. There's nothing like it in the rue de la Paix, she said. I do love you, Newland, for being so artistic!"

The next afternoon, as Archer, before dinner, sat smoking sullenly in his study, Janey wandered in on him. He had failed to stop at his club on the way up from the office where he exercised the profession of the law in the leisurely manner common to well-to-do New Yorkers of his class. He was out of spirits and slightly out of temper, and a haunting horror of doing the same thing every day at the same hour besieged his brain.

"Sameness—sameness!" he muttered, the word running

through his head like a persecuting tune as he saw the familiar tall-hatted figures lounging behind the plate-glass; and because he usually dropped in at the club at that hour he had gone home instead. He knew not only what they were likely to be talking about, but the part each one would take in the discussion. The Duke of course would be their principal theme; though the appearance in Fifth Avenue of a golden-haired lady in a small canary-coloured brougham with a pair of black cobs (for which Beaufort was generally thought responsible) would also doubtless be thoroughly gone into. Such "women" (as they were called) were few in New York, those driving their own carriages still fewer, and the appearance of Miss Fanny Ring in Fifth Avenue at the fashionable hour had profoundly agitated society. Only the day before, her carriage had passed Mrs. Lovell Mingott's, and the latter had instantly rung the little bell at her elbow and ordered the coachman to drive her home. "What if it had happened to Mrs. van der Luyden?" people asked each other with a shudder. Archer could hear Lawrence Lefferts, at that very hour, holding forth on the disintegration of society.

He raised his head irritably when his sister Janey entered, and then quickly bent over his book (Swinburne's "Chastelard"—just out) as if he had not seen her. She glanced at the writing-table heaped with books, opened a volume of the "Contes Drôlatiques," made a wry face over the archaic French, and sighed: "What learned things you read!"

"Well—?" he asked, as she hovered Cassandra-like before him.

"Mother's very angry."

"Angry? With whom? About what?"

"Miss Sophy Jackson has just been here. She brought word that her brother would come in after dinner: she couldn't say very much, because he forbade her to: he wishes to give all the details himself. He's with cousin Louisa van der Luyden now."

"For heaven's sake, my dear girl, try a fresh start. It would take an omniscient Deity to know what you're talking about."

"It's not a time to be profane, Newland. . . . Mother feels badly enough about your not going to church . . ."

With a groan he plunged back into his book.

"*Newland!* Do listen. Your friend Madame Olenska was at Mrs. Lemuel Struthers's party last night: she went there with the Duke and Mr. Beaufort."

At the last clause of this announcement a senseless anger swelled the young man's breast. To smother it he laughed. "Well, what of it? I knew she meant to."

Janey paled and her eyes began to project. "You knew she meant to—and you didn't try to stop her? To warn her?"

"Stop her? Warn her?" He laughed again. "I'm not engaged to be married to the Countess Olenska!" The words had a fantastic sound in his own ears.

"You're marrying into her family."

"Oh, family—family!" he jeered.

"Newland—don't you care about Family?"

"Not a brass farthing."

"Nor about what cousin Louisa van der Luyden will think?"

"Not the half of one—if she thinks such old maid's rubbish."

"Mother is not an old maid," said his virgin sister with pinched lips.

He felt like shouting back: "Yes, she is, and so are the van der Luydens, and so we all are, when it comes to being so much as brushed by the wing-tip of Reality." But he saw her long gentle face puckering into tears, and felt ashamed of the useless pain he was inflicting.

"Hang Countess Olenska! Don't be a goose, Janey—I'm not her keeper."

"No; but you *did* ask the Wellands to announce your engagement sooner so that we might all back her up; and if it hadn't been for that cousin Louisa would never have invited her to the dinner for the Duke."

"Well—what harm was there in inviting her? She was the best-looking woman in the room; she made the dinner a little less funereal than the usual van der Luyden banquet."

"You know cousin Henry asked her to please you: he persuaded cousin Louisa. And now they're so upset that they're going back to Skuytercliff tomorrow. I think, Newland, you'd better come down. You don't seem to understand how mother feels."

In the drawing-room Newland found his mother. She raised a troubled brow from her needlework to ask: "Has Janey told you?"

"Yes." He tried to keep his tone as measured as her own. "But I can't take it very seriously."

"Not the fact of having offended cousin Louisa and cousin Henry?"

"The fact that they can be offended by such a trifle as Countess Olenska's going to the house of a woman they consider common."

"*Consider—!*"

"Well, who is; but who has good music, and amuses people on Sunday evenings, when the whole of New York is dying of inanition."

"Good music? All I know is, there was a woman who got up on a table and sang the things they sing at the places you go to in Paris. There was smoking and champagne."

"Well—that kind of thing happens in other places, and the world still goes on."

"I don't suppose, dear, you're really defending the French Sunday?"

"I've heard you often enough, mother, grumble at the English Sunday when we've been in London."

"New York is neither Paris nor London."

"Oh, no, it's not!" her son groaned.

"You mean, I suppose, that society here is not as brilliant? You're right, I daresay; but we belong here, and people should respect our ways when they come among us. Ellen Olenska especially: she came back to get away from the kind of life people lead in brilliant societies."

Newland made no answer, and after a moment his mother ventured: "I was going to put on my bonnet and ask you to take me to see cousin Louisa for a moment before dinner." He frowned, and she continued: "I thought you might explain to her what you've just said: that society abroad is different . . . that people are not as particular, and that Madame Olenska may not have realised how we feel about such things. It would be, you know, dear," she added with an innocent adroitness, "in Madame Olenska's interest if you did."

"Dearest mother, I really don't see how we're concerned in the matter. The Duke took Madame Olenska to Mrs. Struthers's—in fact he brought Mrs. Struthers to call on her. I was there when they came. If the van der Luydens want to quarrel with anybody, the real culprit is under their own roof."

"Quarrel? Newland, did you ever know of cousin Henry's quarrelling? Besides, the Duke's his guest; and a stranger too. Strangers don't discriminate: how should they? Countess Olenska is a New Yorker, and should have respected the feelings of New York."

"Well, then, if they must have a victim, you have my leave to throw Madame Olenska to them," cried her son, exasperated. "I don't see myself—or you either—offering ourselves up to expiate her crimes."

"Oh, of course you see only the Mingott side," his mother answered, in the sensitive tone that was her nearest approach to anger.

The sad butler drew back the drawing-room portières and announced: "Mr. Henry van der Luyden."

Mrs. Archer dropped her needle and pushed her chair back with an agitated hand.

"Another lamp," she cried to the retreating servant, while Janey bent over to straighten her mother's cap.

Mr. van der Luyden's figure loomed on the threshold, and Newland Archer went forward to greet his cousin.

"We were just talking about you, sir," he said.

Mr. van der Luyden seemed overwhelmed by the announcement. He drew off his glove to shake hands with the ladies, and smoothed his tall hat shyly, while Janey pushed an arm-chair forward, and Archer continued: "And the Countess Olenska."

Mrs. Archer paled.

"Ah—a charming woman. I have just been to see her," said Mr. van der Luyden, complacency restored to his brow. He sank into the chair, laid his hat and gloves on the floor beside him in the old-fashioned way, and went on: "She has a real gift for arranging flowers. I had sent her a few carnations from Skuytercliff, and I was astonished. Instead of massing them in big bunches as our head-gardener does, she had scattered them about loosely, here and there . . . I can't say how.

The Duke had told me: he said: 'Go and see how cleverly she's arranged her drawing-room.' And she has. I should really like to take Louisa to see her, if the neighbourhood were not so—unpleasant."

A dead silence greeted this unusual flow of words from Mr. van der Luyden. Mrs. Archer drew her embroidery out of the basket into which she had nervously tumbled it, and Newland, leaning against the chimney-place and twisting a humming-bird-feather screen in his hand, saw Janey's gaping countenance lit up by the coming of the second lamp.

"The fact is," Mr. van der Luyden continued, stroking his long grey leg with a bloodless hand weighed down by the Patroon's great signet-ring, "the fact is, I dropped in to thank her for the very pretty note she wrote me about my flowers; and also—but this is between ourselves, of course—to give her a friendly warning about allowing the Duke to carry her off to parties with him. I don't know if you've heard—"

Mrs. Archer produced an indulgent smile. "Has the Duke been carrying her off to parties?"

"You know what these English grandees are. They're all alike. Louisa and I are very fond of our cousin—but it's hopeless to expect people who are accustomed to the European courts to trouble themselves about our little republican distinctions. The Duke goes where he's amused." Mr. van der Luyden paused, but no one spoke. "Yes—it seems he took her with him last night to Mrs. Lemuel Struthers's. Sillerton Jackson has just been to us with the foolish story, and Louisa was rather troubled. So I thought the shortest way was to go straight to Countess Olenska and explain—by the merest hint, you know—how we feel in New York about certain things. I felt I might, without indelicacy, because the evening she dined with us she rather suggested . . . rather let me see that she would be grateful for guidance. And she *was*."

Mr. van der Luyden looked about the room with what would have been self-satisfaction on features less purged of the vulgar passions. On his face it became a mild benevolence which Mrs. Archer's countenance dutifully reflected.

"How kind you both are, dear Henry—always! Newland will particularly appreciate what you have done because of dear May and his new relations."

She shot an admonitory glance at her son, who said: "Immensely, sir. But I was sure you'd like Madame Olenska."

Mr. van der Luyden looked at him with extreme gentleness. "I never ask to my house, my dear Newland," he said, "any one whom I do not like. And so I have just told Sillerton Jackson." With a glance at the clock he rose and added: "But Louisa will be waiting. We are dining early, to take the Duke to the Opera."

After the portières had solemnly closed behind their visitor a silence fell upon the Archer family.

"Gracious—how romantic!" at last broke explosively from Janey. No one knew exactly what inspired her elliptic comments, and her relations had long since given up trying to interpret them.

Mrs. Archer shook her head with a sigh. "Provided it all turns out for the best," she said, in the tone of one who knows how surely it will not. "Newland, you must stay and see Sillerton Jackson when he comes this evening: I really shan't know what to say to him."

"Poor mother! But he won't come—" her son laughed, stooping to kiss away her frown.

XI

SOME TWO WEEKS LATER, Newland Archer, sitting in abstracted idleness in his private compartment of the office of Letterblair, Lamson and Low, attorneys at law, was summoned by the head of the firm.

Old Mr. Letterblair, the accredited legal adviser of three generations of New York gentility, throned behind his mahogany desk in evident perplexity. As he stroked his close-clipped white whiskers and ran his hand through the rumpled grey locks above his jutting brows, his disrespectful junior partner thought how much he looked like the Family Physician annoyed with a patient whose symptoms refuse to be classified.

"My dear sir—" he always addressed Archer as "sir"—"I have sent for you to go into a little matter; a matter which, for the moment, I prefer not to mention either to Mr. Skipworth or Mr. Redwood." The gentlemen he spoke of were the other senior partners of the firm; for, as was always the case with legal associations of old standing in New York, all the partners named on the office letter-head were long since dead; and Mr. Letterblair, for example, was, professionally speaking, his own grandson.

He leaned back in his chair with a furrowed brow. "For family reasons—" he continued.

Archer looked up.

"The Mingott family," said Mr. Letterblair with an explanatory smile and bow. "Mrs. Manson Mingott sent for me yesterday. Her grand-daughter the Countess Olenska wishes to sue her husband for divorce. Certain papers have been placed in my hands." He paused and drummed on his desk. "In view of your prospective alliance with the family I should like to consult you—to consider the case with you—before taking any farther steps."

Archer felt the blood in his temples. He had seen the Countess Olenska only once since his visit to her, and then at the Opera, in the Mingott box. During this interval she had become a less vivid and importunate image, receding from his foreground as May Welland resumed her rightful place in it.

He had not heard her divorce spoken of since Janey's first random allusion to it, and had dismissed the tale as unfounded gossip. Theoretically, the idea of divorce was almost as distasteful to him as to his mother; and he was annoyed that Mr. Letterblair (no doubt prompted by old Catherine Mingott) should be so evidently planning to draw him into the affair. After all, there were plenty of Mingott men for such jobs, and as yet he was not even a Mingott by marriage.

He waited for the senior partner to continue. Mr. Letterblair unlocked a drawer and drew out a packet. "If you will run your eye over these papers—"

Archer frowned. "I beg your pardon, sir; but just because of the prospective relationship, I should prefer your consulting Mr. Skipworth or Mr. Redwood."

Mr. Letterblair looked surprised and slightly offended. It was unusual for a junior to reject such an opening.

He bowed. "I respect your scruple, sir; but in this case I believe true delicacy requires you to do as I ask. Indeed, the suggestion is not mine but Mrs. Manson Mingott's and her son's. I have seen Lovell Mingott; and also Mr. Welland. They all named you."

Archer felt his temper rising. He had been somewhat languidly drifting with events for the last fortnight, and letting May's fair looks and radiant nature obliterate the rather importunate pressure of the Mingott claims. But this behest of old Mrs. Mingott's roused him to a sense of what the clan thought they had the right to exact from a prospective son-in-law; and he chafed at the rôle.

"Her uncles ought to deal with this," he said.

"They have. The matter has been gone into by the family. They are opposed to the Countess's idea; but she is firm, and insists on a legal opinion."

The young man was silent: he had not opened the packet in his hand.

"Does she want to marry again?"

"I believe it is suggested; but she denies it."

"Then—"

"Will you oblige me, Mr. Archer, by first looking through these papers? Afterward, when we have talked the case over, I will give you my opinion."

Archer withdrew reluctantly with the unwelcome documents. Since their last meeting he had half-unconsciously collaborated with events in ridding himself of the burden of Madame Olenska. His hour alone with her by the firelight had drawn them into a momentary intimacy on which the Duke of St. Austrey's intrusion with Mrs. Lemuel Struthers, and the Countess's joyous greeting of them, had rather providentially broken. Two days later Archer had assisted at the comedy of her reinstatement in the van der Luydens' favour, and had said to himself, with a touch of tartness, that a lady who knew how to thank all-powerful elderly gentlemen to such good purpose for a bunch of flowers did not need either the private consolations or the public championship of a young man of his small compass. To look at the matter in this light simplified his own case and surprisingly furbished up all the dim domestic virtues. He could not picture May Welland, in whatever conceivable emergency, hawking about her private difficulties and lavishing her confidences on strange men; and she had never seemed to him finer or fairer than in the week that followed. He had even yielded to her wish for a long engagement, since she had found the one disarming answer to his plea for haste.

"You know, when it comes to the point, your parents have always let you have your way ever since you were a little girl," he argued; and she had answered, with her clearest look: "Yes; and that's what makes it so hard to refuse the very last thing they'll ever ask of me as a little girl."

That was the old New York note; that was the kind of answer he would like always to be sure of his wife's making. If one had habitually breathed the New York air there were times when anything less crystalline seemed stifling.

The papers he had retired to read did not tell him much in fact; but they plunged him into an atmosphere in which he choked and spluttered. They consisted mainly of an exchange of letters between Count Olenski's solicitors and a French legal firm to whom the Countess had applied for the settlement of her financial situation. There was also a short letter from the Count to his wife: after reading it, Newland Archer rose, jammed the papers back into their envelope, and re-entered Mr. Letterblair's office.

"Here are the letters, sir. If you wish, I'll see Madame Olenska," he said in a constrained voice.

"Thank you—thank you, Mr. Archer. Come and dine with me tonight if you're free, and we'll go into the matter afterward: in case you wish to call on our client tomorrow."

Newland Archer walked straight home again that afternoon. It was a winter evening of transparent clearness, with an innocent young moon above the house-tops; and he wanted to fill his soul's lungs with the pure radiance, and not exchange a word with any one till he and Mr. Letterblair were closeted together after dinner. It was impossible to decide otherwise than he had done: he must see Madame Olenska himself rather than let her secrets be bared to other eyes. A great wave of compassion had swept away his indifference and impatience: she stood before him as an exposed and pitiful figure, to be saved at all costs from farther wounding herself in her mad plunges against fate.

He remembered what she had told him of Mrs. Welland's request to be spared whatever was "unpleasant" in her history, and winced at the thought that it was perhaps this attitude of mind which kept the New York air so pure. "Are we only Pharisees after all?" he wondered, puzzled by the effort to reconcile his instinctive disgust at human vileness with his equally instinctive pity for human frailty.

For the first time he perceived how elementary his own principles had always been. He passed for a young man who had not been afraid of risks, and he knew that his secret love-affair with poor silly Mrs. Thorley Rushworth had not been too secret to invest him with a becoming air of adventure. But Mrs. Rushworth was "that kind of woman"; foolish, vain, clandestine by nature, and far more attracted by the secrecy and peril of the affair than by such charms and qualities as he possessed. When the fact dawned on him it nearly broke his heart, but now it seemed the redeeming feature of the case. The affair, in short, had been of the kind that most of the young men of his age had been through, and emerged from with calm consciences and an undisturbed belief in the abysmal distinction between the women one loved and respected and those one enjoyed—and pitied. In this view they were sedulously abetted by their mothers, aunts and other elderly female relatives, who all shared Mrs. Archer's belief that when "such things happened" it was undoubtedly foolish of the man, but somehow always criminal of the woman. All the elderly ladies whom Archer knew regarded any woman who loved imprudently as necessarily unscrupulous and designing, and mere simple-minded man as powerless in her clutches. The only thing to do was to persuade him, as early as possible, to marry a nice girl, and then trust to her to look after him.

In the complicated old European communities, Archer began to guess, love-problems might be less simple and less easily classified. Rich and idle and ornamental societies must produce many more such situations; and there might even be one in which a woman naturally sensitive and aloof would yet, from the force of circumstances, from sheer defencelessness and loneliness, be drawn into a tie inexcusable by conventional standards.

On reaching home he wrote a line to the Countess Olenska, asking at what hour of the next day she could receive him, and despatched it by a messenger-boy, who returned presently with a word to the effect that she was going to Skuytercliff the next morning to stay over Sunday with the van der Luydens, but that he would find her alone that evening after dinner. The note was written on a rather untidy half-sheet, without date or address, but her hand was firm and free. He was amused at the idea of her week-ending in the stately solitude of Skuytercliff, but immediately afterward felt that there, of all places, she would most feel the chill of minds rigorously averted from the "unpleasant."

He was at Mr. Letterblair's punctually at seven, glad of the pretext for excusing himself soon after dinner. He had formed his own opinion from the papers entrusted to him, and did not especially want to go into the matter with his senior partner. Mr. Letterblair was a widower, and they dined alone, copiously and slowly, in a dark shabby room hung with yellowing prints of "The Death of Chatham" and "The Coronation of Napoleon." On the sideboard, between fluted

Sheraton knife-cases, stood a decanter of Haut Brion, and another of the old Lanning port (the gift of a client), which the wastrel Tom Lanning had sold off a year or two before his mysterious and discreditable death in San Francisco—an incident less publicly humiliating to the family than the sale of the cellar.

After a velvety oyster soup came shad and cucumbers, then a young broiled turkey with corn fritters, followed by a canvas-back with currant jelly and a celery mayonnaise. Mr. Letterblair, who lunched on a sandwich and tea, dined deliberately and deeply, and insisted on his guest's doing the same. Finally, when the closing rites had been accomplished, the cloth was removed, cigars were lit, and Mr. Letterblair, leaning back in his chair and pushing the port westward, said, spreading his back agreeably to the coal fire behind him: "The whole family are against a divorce. And I think rightly."

Archer instantly felt himself on the other side of the argument. "But why, sir? If there ever was a case—"

"Well—what's the use? *She's* here—he's there; the Atlantic's between them. She'll never get back a dollar more of her money than what he's voluntarily returned to her: their damned heathen marriage settlements take precious good care of that. As things go over there, Olenski's acted generously: he might have turned her out without a penny."

The young man knew this and was silent.

"I understand, though," Mr. Letterblair continued, "that she attaches no importance to the money. Therefore, as the family say, why not let well enough alone?"

Archer had gone to the house an hour earlier in full agreement with Mr. Letterblair's view; but put into words by this selfish, well-fed and supremely indifferent old man it suddenly became the Pharisaic voice of a society wholly absorbed in barricading itself against the unpleasant.

"I think that's for her to decide."

"H'm—have you considered the consequences if she decides for divorce?"

"You mean the threat in her husband's letter? What weight would that carry? It's no more than the vague charge of an angry blackguard."

"Yes; but it might make some unpleasant talk if he really defends the suit."

"Unpleasant—!" said Archer explosively.

Mr. Letterblair looked at him from under enquiring eyebrows, and the young man, aware of the uselessness of trying to explain what was in his mind, bowed acquiescently while his senior continued: "Divorce is always unpleasant."

"You agree with me?" Mr. Letterblair resumed, after a waiting silence.

"Naturally," said Archer.

"Well, then, I may count on you; the Mingotts may count on you; to use your influence against the idea?"

Archer hesitated. "I can't pledge myself till I've seen the Countess Olenska," he said at length.

"Mr. Archer, I don't understand you. Do you want to marry into a family with a scandalous divorce-suit hanging over it?"

"I don't think that has anything to do with the case."

Mr. Letterblair put down his glass of port and fixed on his young partner a cautious and apprehensive gaze.

Archer understood that he ran the risk of having his mandate withdrawn, and for some obscure reason he disliked the prospect. Now that the job had been thrust on him he did not propose to relinquish it; and, to guard against the possibility, he saw that he must reassure the unimaginative old man who was the legal conscience of the Mingotts.

"You may be sure, sir, that I shan't commit myself till I've reported to you; what I meant was that I'd rather not give an opinion till I've heard what Madame Olenska has to say."

Mr. Letterblair nodded approvingly at an excess of caution worthy of the best New York tradition, and the young man, glancing at his watch, pleaded an engagement and took leave.

XII

O LD-FASHIONED New York dined at seven, and the habit of after-dinner calls, though derided in Archer's set, still generally prevailed. As the young man strolled up Fifth Avenue from Waverley Place, the long thoroughfare was deserted but for a group of carriages standing before the Reggie Chiverses' (where there was a dinner for the Duke), and the occasional figure of an elderly gentleman in heavy overcoat and muffler ascending a brownstone doorstep and disappearing into a gas-lit hall. Thus, as Archer crossed Washington Square, he remarked that old Mr. du Lac was calling on his cousins the Dagonets, and turning down the corner of West Tenth Street he saw Mr. Skipworth, of his own firm, obviously bound on a visit to the Miss Lannings. A little farther up Fifth Avenue, Beaufort appeared on his doorstep, darkly projected against a blaze of light, descended to his private brougham, and rolled away to a mysterious and probably unmentionable destination. It was not an Opera night, and no one was giving a party, so that Beaufort's outing was undoubtedly of a clandestine nature. Archer connected it in his mind with a little house beyond Lexington Avenue in which beribboned window curtains and flower-boxes had recently appeared, and before whose newly painted door the canary-coloured brougham of Miss Fanny Ring was frequently seen to wait.

Beyond the small and slippery pyramid which composed Mrs. Archer's world lay the almost unmapped quarter inhabited by artists, musicians and "people who wrote." These scattered fragments of humanity had never shown any desire to be amalgamated with the social structure. In spite of odd ways they were said to be, for the most part, quite respectable; but they preferred to keep to themselves. Medora Manson, in her prosperous days, had inaugurated a "literary salon"; but it had soon died out owing to the reluctance of the literary to frequent it.

Others had made the same attempt, and there was a household of Blenkers—an intense and voluble mother, and three blowsy daughters who imitated her—where one met Edwin Booth and Patti and William Winter, and the new Shakespearian actor George Rignold, and some of the magazine editors and musical and literary critics.

Mrs. Archer and her group felt a certain timidity concerning these persons. They were odd, they were uncertain, they had things one didn't know about in the background of their lives and minds. Literature and art were deeply respected in the Archer set, and Mrs. Archer was always at pains to tell her children how much more agreeable and cultivated society had been when it included such figures as Washington Irving, Fitz-Greene Halleck and the poet of "The Culprit Fay." The most celebrated authors of that generation had been "gentlemen"; perhaps the unknown persons who succeeded them had gentlemanly sentiments, but their origin, their appearance, their hair, their intimacy with the stage and the Opera, made any old New York criterion inapplicable to them.

"When I was a girl," Mrs. Archer used to say, " we knew everybody between the Battery and Canal Street; and only the people one knew had carriages. It was perfectly easy to place any one then; now one can't tell, and I prefer not to try."

Only old Catherine Mingott, with her absence of moral prejudices and almost *parvenu* indifference to the subtler distinctions, might have bridged the abyss; but she had never opened a book or looked at a picture, and cared for music only because it reminded her of gala nights at the *Italiens*, in the days of her triumph at the Tuileries. Possibly Beaufort, who was her match in daring, would have succeeded in bringing about a fusion; but his grand house and silk-stockinged footmen were an obstacle to informal sociability. Moreover, he was as illiterate as old Mrs. Mingott, and considered "fellows who wrote" as the mere paid purveyors of rich men's pleasures; and no one rich enough to influence his opinion had ever questioned it.

Newland Archer had been aware of these things ever since he could remember, and had accepted them as part of the structure of his universe. He knew that there were societies where painters and poets and novelists and men of science, and even great actors, were as sought after as Dukes; he had often pictured to himself what it would have been to live in the intimacy of drawing-rooms dominated by the talk of Mérimée (whose "Lettres à une Inconnue" was one of his inseparables), of Thackeray, Browning or William Morris. But such things were inconceivable in New York, and unsettling to think of. Archer knew most of the "fellows who wrote," the musicians and the painters: he met them at the Century, or at the little musical and theatrical clubs that were beginning to come into existence. He enjoyed them there, and was bored with them at the Blenkers', where they were mingled with fervid and dowdy women who passed them about like captured curiosities; and even after his most exciting talks with Ned Winsett he always came away with the feeling that if his world was small, so was theirs, and that the only way to enlarge either was to reach a stage of manners where they would naturally merge.

He was reminded of this by trying to picture the society in which the Countess Olenska had lived and suffered, and also—perhaps—tasted mysterious joys. He remembered with what amusement she had told him that her grandmother Mingott and the Wellands objected to her living in a "Bohemian" quarter given over to "people who wrote." It was not the peril but the poverty that her family disliked; but that shade escaped her, and she supposed they considered literature compromising.

She herself had no fears of it, and the books scattered about her drawing-room (a part of the house in which books were usually supposed to be "out of place"), though chiefly works of fiction, had whetted Archer's interest with such new names as those of Paul Bourget, Huysmans, and the Goncourt brothers. Ruminating on these things as he approached her door, he was once more conscious of the curious way in which she reversed his values, and of the need of thinking himself into conditions incredibly different from any that he knew if he were to be of use in her present difficulty.

Nastasia opened the door, smiling mysteriously. On the bench in the hall lay a sable-lined overcoat, a folded opera hat of dull silk with a gold J. B. on the lining, and a white silk muffler: there was no mistaking the fact that these costly articles were the property of Julius Beaufort.

Archer was angry: so angry that he came near scribbling a word on his card and going away; then he remembered that in writing to Madame Olenska he had been kept by excess of discretion from saying that he wished to see her privately. He had therefore no one but himself to blame if she had opened her doors to other visitors; and he entered the drawing-room with the dogged determination to make Beaufort feel himself in the way, and to outstay him.

The banker stood leaning against the mantelshelf, which was draped with an old embroidery held in place by brass candelabra containing church candles of yellowish wax. He had thrust his chest out, supporting his shoulders against the mantel and resting his weight on one large patent-leather foot. As Archer entered he was smiling and looking down on his hostess, who sat on a sofa placed at right angles to the chimney. A table banked with flowers formed a screen behind it, and against the orchids and azaleas which the young man recognised as tributes from the Beaufort hot-houses, Madame Olenska sat half-reclined, her head propped on a hand and her wide sleeve leaving the arm bare to the elbow.

It was usual for ladies who received in the evenings to wear what were called "simple dinner dresses": a close-fitting armour of whale-boned silk, slightly open in the neck, with lace ruffles filling in the crack, and tight sleeves with a flounce uncovering just enough wrist to show an Etruscan gold bracelet or a velvet band. But Madame Olenska, heedless of tradition, was attired in a long robe of red velvet bordered about the chin and down the front with glossy black fur. Archer remembered, on his last visit to Paris, seeing a portrait by the new painter, Carolus Duran, whose pictures were the sensation of the Salon, in which the lady wore one of these bold sheath-like robes with her chin nestling in fur. There was something perverse and provocative in the notion of fur worn in the evening in a heated drawing-room, and in the combination of a muffled throat and bare arms; but the effect was undeniably pleasing.

"Lord love us—three whole days at Skuytercliff!" Beaufort was saying in his loud sneering voice as Archer entered. "You'd better take all your furs, and a hot-water-bottle."

"Why? Is the house so cold?" she asked, holding out her left hand to Archer in a way mysteriously suggesting that she expected him to kiss it.

"No; but the missus is," said Beaufort, nodding carelessly to the young man.

"But I thought her so kind. She came herself to invite me. Granny says I must certainly go."

"Granny would, of course. And *I* say it's a shame you're going to miss the little oyster supper I'd planned for you at Delmonico's next Sunday, with Campanini and Scalchi and a lot of jolly people."

She looked doubtfully from the banker to Archer.

"Ah—that does tempt me! Except the other evening at Mrs. Struthers's I've not met a single artist since I've been here."

"What kind of artists? I know one or two painters, very good fellows, that I could bring to see you if you'd allow me," said Archer boldly.

"Painters? Are there painters in New York?" asked Beaufort, in a tone implying that there could be none since he did not buy their pictures; and Madame Olenska said to Archer, with her grave smile: "That would be charming. But I was really thinking of dramatic artists, singers, actors, musicians. My husband's house was always full of them."

She said the words "my husband" as if no sinister associations were connected with them, and in a tone that seemed almost to sigh over the lost delights of her married life. Archer looked at her perplexedly, wondering if it were lightness or dissimulation that enabled her to touch so easily on the past at the very moment when she was risking her reputation in order to break with it.

"I do think," she went on, addressing both men, "that the *imprévu* adds to one's enjoyment. It's perhaps a mistake to see the same people every day."

"It's confoundedly dull, anyhow; New York is dying of dulness," Beaufort grumbled. "And when I try to liven it up for you, you go back on me. Come—think better of it! Sunday is your last chance, for Campanini leaves next week for Baltimore and Philadelphia; and I've a private room, and a Steinway, and they'll sing all night for me."

"How delicious! May I think it over, and write to you to-morrow morning?"

She spoke amiably, yet with the least hint of dismissal in

her voice. Beaufort evidently felt it, and being unused to dismissals, stood staring at her with an obstinate line between his eyes.

"Why not now?"

"It's too serious a question to decide at this late hour."

"Do you call it late?"

She returned his glance coolly. "Yes; because I have still to talk business with Mr. Archer for a little while."

"Ah," Beaufort snapped. There was no appeal from her tone, and with a slight shrug he recovered his composure, took her hand, which he kissed with a practised air, and calling out from the threshold: "I say, Newland, if you can persuade the Countess to stop in town of course you're included in the supper," left the room with his heavy important step.

For a moment Archer fancied that Mr. Letterblair must have told her of his coming; but the irrelevance of her next remark made him change his mind.

"You know painters, then? You live in their *milieu*?" she asked, her eyes full of interest.

"Oh, not exactly. I don't know that the arts have a *milieu* here, any of them; they're more like a very thinly settled outskirt."

"But you care for such things?"

"Immensely. When I'm in Paris or London I never miss an exhibition. I try to keep up."

She looked down at the tip of the little satin boot that peeped from her long draperies.

"I used to care immensely too: my life was full of such things. But now I want to try not to."

"You want to try not to?"

"Yes: I want to cast off all my old life, to become just like everybody else here."

Archer reddened. "You'll never be like everybody else," he said.

She raised her straight eyebrows a little. "Ah, don't say that. If you knew how I hate to be different!"

Her face had grown as sombre as a tragic mask. She leaned forward, clasping her knee in her thin hands, and looking away from him into remote dark distances.

"I want to get away from it all," she insisted.

He waited a moment and cleared his throat. "I know. Mr. Letterblair has told me."

"Ah?"

"That's the reason I've come. He asked me to—you see I'm in the firm."

She looked slightly surprised, and then her eyes brightened. "You mean you can manage it for me? I can talk to you instead of Mr. Letterblair? Oh, that will be so much easier!"

Her tone touched him, and his confidence grew with his self-satisfaction. He perceived that she had spoken of business to Beaufort simply to get rid of him; and to have routed Beaufort was something of a triumph.

"I am here to talk about it," he repeated.

She sat silent, her head still propped by the arm that rested on the back of the sofa. Her face looked pale and extinguished, as if dimmed by the rich red of her dress. She struck Archer, of a sudden, as a pathetic and even pitiful figure.

"Now we're coming to hard facts," he thought, conscious in himself of the same instinctive recoil that he had so often criticised in his mother and her contemporaries. How little practice he had had in dealing with unusual situations! Their very vocabulary was unfamiliar to him, and seemed to belong to fiction and the stage. In face of what was coming he felt as awkward and embarrassed as a boy.

After a pause Madame Olenska broke out with unexpected vehemence: "I want to be free; I want to wipe out all the past."

"I understand that."

Her face warmed. "Then you'll help me?"

"First—" he hesitated—"perhaps I ought to know a little more."

She seemed surprised. "You know about my husband—my life with him?"

He made a sign of assent.

"Well—then—what more is there? In this country are such things tolerated? I'm a Protestant—our church does not forbid divorce in such cases."

"Certainly not."

They were both silent again, and Archer felt the spectre of Count Olenski's letter grimacing hideously between them.

The letter filled only half a page, and was just what he had described it to be in speaking of it to Mr. Letterblair: the vague charge of an angry blackguard. But how much truth was behind it? Only Count Olenski's wife could tell.

"I've looked through the papers you gave to Mr. Letterblair," he said at length.

"Well—can there be anything more abominable?"

"No."

She changed her position slightly, screening her eyes with her lifted hand.

"Of course you know," Archer continued, "that if your husband chooses to fight the case—as he threatens to—"

"Yes—?"

"He can say things—things that might be unpl—might be disagreeable to you: say them publicly, so that they would get about, and harm you even if—"

"If—?"

"I mean: no matter how unfounded they were."

She paused for a long interval; so long that, not wishing to keep his eyes on her shaded face, he had time to imprint on his mind the exact shape of her other hand, the one on her knee, and every detail of the three rings on her fourth and fifth fingers; among which, he noticed, a wedding ring did not appear.

"What harm could such accusations, even if he made them publicly, do me here?"

It was on his lips to exclaim: "My poor child—far more harm than anywhere else!" Instead, he answered, in a voice that sounded in his ears like Mr. Letterblair's: "New York society is a very small world compared with the one you've lived in. And it's ruled, in spite of appearances, by a few people with—well, rather old-fashioned ideas."

She said nothing, and he continued: "Our ideas about marriage and divorce are particularly old-fashioned. Our legislation favours divorce—our social customs don't."

"Never?"

"Well—not if the woman, however injured, however irreproachable, has appearances in the least degree against her, has exposed herself by any unconventional action to—to offensive insinuations—"

She drooped her head a little lower, and he waited again, intensely hoping for a flash of indignation, or at least a brief cry of denial. None came.

A little travelling clock ticked purringly at her elbow, and a log broke in two and sent up a shower of sparks. The whole hushed and brooding room seemed to be waiting silently with Archer.

"Yes," she murmured at length, "that's what my family tell me."

He winced a little. "It's not unnatural—"

"*Our* family," she corrected herself; and Archer coloured. "For you'll be my cousin soon," she continued gently.

"I hope so."

"And you take their view?"

He stood up at this, wandered across the room, stared with void eyes at one of the pictures against the old red damask, and came back irresolutely to her side. How could he say: "Yes, if what your husband hints is true, or if you've no way of disproving it?"

"Sincerely—" she interjected, as he was about to speak.

He looked down into the fire. "Sincerely, then—what should you gain that would compensate for the possibility— the certainty—of a lot of beastly talk?"

"But my freedom—is that nothing?"

It flashed across him at that instant that the charge in the letter was true, and that she hoped to marry the partner of her guilt. How was he to tell her that, if she really cherished such a plan, the laws of the State were inexorably opposed to it? The mere suspicion that the thought was in her mind made him feel harshly and impatiently toward her. "But aren't you as free as air as it is?" he returned. "Who can touch you? Mr. Letterblair tells me the financial question has been settled—"

"Oh, yes," she said indifferently.

"Well, then: is it worth while to risk what may be infinitely disagreeable and painful? Think of the newspapers—their vileness! It's all stupid and narrow and unjust—but one can't make over society."

"No," she acquiesced; and her tone was so faint and desolate that he felt a sudden remorse for his own hard thoughts.

"The individual, in such cases, is nearly always sacrificed to what is supposed to be the collective interest: people cling to any convention that keeps the family together—protects the children, if there are any," he rambled on, pouring out all the stock phrases that rose to his lips in his intense desire to cover over the ugly reality which her silence seemed to have laid bare. Since she would not or could not say the one word that would have cleared the air, his wish was not to let her feel that he was trying to probe into her secret. Better keep on the surface, in the prudent old New York way, than risk uncovering a wound he could not heal.

"It's my business, you know," he went on, "to help you to see these things as the people who are fondest of you see them. The Mingotts, the Wellands, the van der Luydens, all your friends and relations: if I didn't show you honestly how they judge such questions, it wouldn't be fair of me, would it?" He spoke insistently, almost pleading with her in his eagerness to cover up that yawning silence.

She said slowly: "No; it wouldn't be fair."

The fire had crumbled down to greyness, and one of the lamps made a gurgling appeal for attention. Madame Olenska rose, wound it up and returned to the fire, but without resuming her seat.

Her remaining on her feet seemed to signify that there was nothing more for either of them to say, and Archer stood up also.

"Very well; I will do what you wish," she said abruptly. The blood rushed to his forehead; and, taken aback by the suddenness of her surrender, he caught her two hands awkwardly in his.

"I—I do want to help you," he said.

"You do help me. Good night, my cousin."

He bent and laid his lips on her hands, which were cold and lifeless. She drew them away, and he turned to the door, found his coat and hat under the faint gas-light of the hall, and plunged out into the winter night bursting with the belated eloquence of the inarticulate.

XIII

IT WAS a crowded night at Wallack's theatre.

The play was "The Shaughraun," with Dion Boucicault in the title rôle and Harry Montague and Ada Dyas as the lovers. The popularity of the admirable English company was at its height, and the Shaughraun always packed the house. In the galleries the enthusiasm was unreserved; in the stalls and boxes, people smiled a little at the hackneyed sentiments and clap-trap situations, and enjoyed the play as much as the galleries did.

There was one episode, in particular, that held the house from floor to ceiling. It was that in which Harry Montague, after a sad, almost monosyllabic scene of parting with Miss Dyas, bade her good-bye, and turned to go. The actress, who was standing near the mantelpiece and looking down into the fire, wore a gray cashmere dress without fashionable loopings or trimmings, moulded to her tall figure and flowing in long lines about her feet. Around her neck was a narrow black velvet ribbon with the ends falling down her back.

When her wooer turned from her she rested her arms against the mantel-shelf and bowed her face in her hands. On the threshold he paused to look at her; then he stole back, lifted one of the ends of velvet ribbon, kissed it, and left the room without her hearing him or changing her attitude. And on this silent parting the curtain fell.

It was always for the sake of that particular scene that Newland Archer went to see "The Shaughraun." He thought the adieux of Montague and Ada Dyas as fine as anything he had ever seen Croisette and Bressant do in Paris, or Madge Robertson and Kendal in London; in its reticence, its dumb sorrow, it moved him more than the most famous histrionic outpourings.

On the evening in question the little scene acquired an added poignancy by reminding him—he could not have said why—of his leave-taking from Madame Olenska after their confidential talk a week or ten days earlier.

It would have been as difficult to discover any resemblance between the two situations as between the appearance of the persons concerned. Newland Archer could not pretend to anything approaching the young English actor's romantic good looks, and Miss Dyas was a tall red-haired woman of monumental build whose pale and pleasantly ugly face was utterly unlike Ellen Olenska's vivid countenance. Nor were Archer and Madame Olenska two lovers parting in heart-broken silence; they were client and lawyer separating after a talk which had given the lawyer the worst possible impression of the client's case. Wherein, then, lay the resemblance that made the young man's heart beat with a kind of restrospective excitement? It seemed to be in Madame Olenska's mysterious faculty of suggesting tragic and moving possibilities outside the daily run of experience. She had hardly ever said a word to him to produce this impression, but it was a part of her, either a projection of her mysterious and outlandish background or of something inherently dramatic, passionate and unusual in herself. Archer had always been inclined to think that chance and circumstance played a small part in shaping people's lots compared with their innate tendency to have things happen to them. This tendency he had felt from the first in Madame Olenska. The quiet, almost passive young woman struck him as exactly the kind of person to whom things were bound to happen, no matter how much she shrank from them and went out of her way to avoid them. The exciting fact was her having lived in an atmosphere so thick with drama that her own tendency to provoke it had apparently passed unperceived. It was precisely the odd absence of surprise in her that gave him the sense of her having been plucked out of a very maelstrom: the things she took for granted gave the measure of those she had rebelled against.

Archer had left her with the conviction that Count Olenski's accusation was not unfounded. The mysterious person who figured in his wife's past as "the secretary" had probably not been unrewarded for his share in her escape. The conditions from which she had fled were intolerable, past speaking of, past believing: she was young, she was frightened, she was desperate—what more natural than that she should be grateful to her rescuer? The pity was that her gratitude put her, in the law's eyes and the world's, on a par with her abominable husband. Archer had made her understand this, as he was bound to do; he had also made her understand that simple-hearted kindly New York, on whose larger charity she had apparently counted, was precisely the place where she could least hope for indulgence.

To have to make this fact plain to her—and to witness her resigned acceptance of it—had been intolerably painful to him. He felt himself drawn to her by obscure feelings of jealousy and pity, as if her dumbly-confessed error had put him at his mercy, humbling yet endearing her. He was glad it was to him she had revealed her secret, rather than to the cold scrutiny of Mr. Letterblair, or the embarrassed gaze of her family. He immediately took it upon himself to assure them both that she had given up her idea of seeking a divorce, basing her decision on the fact that she had understood the uselessness of the proceeding; and with infinite relief they had all turned their eyes from the "unpleasantness" she had spared them.

"I was sure Newland would manage it," Mrs. Welland had said proudly of her future son-in-law; and old Mrs. Mingott, who had summoned him for a confidential interview, had congratulated him on his cleverness, and added impatiently: "Silly goose! I told her myself what nonsense it was. Wanting to pass herself off as Ellen Mingott and an old maid, when she has the luck to be a married woman and a Countess!"

These incidents had made the memory of his last talk with Madame Olenska so vivid to the young man that as the curtain fell on the parting of the two actors his eyes filled with tears, and he stood up to leave the theatre.

In doing so, he turned to the side of the house behind him, and saw the lady of whom he was thinking seated in a box with the Beauforts, Lawrence Lefferts and one or two other men. He had not spoken with her alone since their evening together, and had tried to avoid being with her in company; but now their eyes met, and as Mrs. Beaufort recognised him at the same time, and made her languid little gesture of invitation, it was impossible not to go into the box.

Beaufort and Lefferts made way for him, and after a few words with Mrs. Beaufort, who always preferred to look beautiful and not have to talk, Archer seated himself behind Madame Olenska. There was no one else in the box but

Mr. Sillerton Jackson, who was telling Mrs. Beaufort in a confidential undertone about Mrs. Lemuel Struthers's last Sunday reception (where some people reported that there had been dancing). Under cover of this circumstantial narrative, to which Mrs. Beaufort listened with her perfect smile, and her head at just the right angle to be seen in profile from the stalls, Madame Olenska turned and spoke in a low voice.

"Do you think," she asked, glancing toward the stage, "he will send her a bunch of yellow roses tomorrow morning?"

Archer reddened, and his heart gave a leap of surprise. He had called only twice on Madame Olenska, and each time he had sent her a box of yellow roses, and each time without a card. She had never before made any allusion to the flowers, and he supposed she had never thought of him as the sender. Now her sudden recognition of the gift, and her associating it with the tender leave-taking on the stage, filled him with an agitated pleasure.

"I was thinking of that too—I was going to leave the theatre in order to take the picture away with me," he said.

To his surprise her colour rose, reluctantly and duskily. She looked down at the mother-of-pearl opera-glass in her smoothly gloved hands, and said, after a pause: "What do you do while May is away?"

"I stick to my work," he answered, faintly annoyed by the question.

In obedience to a long-established habit, the Wellands had left the previous week for St. Augustine, where, out of regard for the supposed susceptibility of Mr. Welland's bronchial tubes, they always spent the latter part of the winter. Mr. Welland was a mild and silent man, with no opinions but with many habits. With these habits none might interfere; and one of them demanded that his wife and daughter should always go with him on his annual journey to the south. To preserve an unbroken domesticity was essential to his peace of mind; he would not have known where his hair-brushes were, or how to provide stamps for his letters, if Mrs. Welland had not been there to tell him.

As all the members of the family adored each other, and as Mr. Welland was the central object of their idolatry, it never occurred to his wife and May to let him go to St. Augustine alone; and his sons, who were both in the law, and could not leave New York during the winter, always joined him for Easter and travelled back with him.

It was impossible for Archer to discuss the necessity of May's accompanying her father. The reputation of the Mingotts' family physician was largely based on the attack of pneumonia which Mr. Welland had never had; and his insistence on St. Augustine was therefore inflexible. Originally, it had been intended that May's engagement should not be announced till her return from Florida, and the fact that it had been made known sooner could not be expected to alter Mr. Welland's plans. Archer would have liked to join the travellers and have a few weeks of sunshine and boating with his betrothed; but he too was bound by custom and conventions. Little arduous as his professional duties were, he would have been convicted of frivolity by the whole Mingott clan if he had suggested asking for a holiday in mid-winter; and he accepted May's departure with the resignation which he perceived would have to be one of the principal constituents of married life.

He was conscious that Madame Olenska was looking at him under lowered lids. "I have done what you wished—what you advised," she said abruptly.

"Ah—I'm glad," he returned, embarrassed by her broaching the subject at such a moment.

"I understand—that you were right," she went on a little breathlessly; "but sometimes life is difficult . . . perplexing . . ."

"I know."

"And I wanted to tell you that I *do* feel you were right; and that I'm grateful to you," she ended, lifting her opera-glass quickly to her eyes as the door of the box opened and Beaufort's resonant voice broke in on them.

Archer stood up, and left the box and the theatre.

Only the day before he had received a letter from May Welland in which, with characteristic candour, she had asked him to "be kind to Ellen" in their absence. "She likes you and admires you so much—and you know, though she doesn't show it, she's still very lonely and unhappy. I don't think Granny understands her, or uncle Lovell Mingott either; they really think she's much worldlier and fonder of society than she is. And I can quite see that New York must seem dull to her, though the family won't admit it. I think she's been used to lots of things we haven't got; wonderful music, and picture shows, and celebrities—artists and authors and all the clever people you admire. Granny can't understand her wanting anything but lots of dinners and clothes—but I can see that you're almost the only person in New York who can talk to her about what she really cares for."

His wise May—how he had loved her for that letter! But he had not meant to act on it; he was too busy, to begin with, and he did not care, as an engaged man, to play too conspicuously the part of Madame Olenska's champion. He had an idea that she knew how to take care of herself a good deal better than the ingenuous May imagined. She had Beaufort at her feet, Mr. van der Luyden hovering above her like a protecting deity, and any number of candidates (Lawrence Lefferts among them) waiting their opportunity in the middle distance. Yet he never saw her, or exchanged a word with her, without feeling that, after all, May's ingenuousness almost amounted to a gift of divination. Ellen Olenska was lonely and she was unhappy.

XIV

As HE CAME out into the lobby Archer ran across his friend
Ned Winsett, the only one among what Janey called his
"clever people" with whom he cared to probe into things a
little deeper than the average level of club and chop-house
banter.

He had caught sight, across the house, of Winsett's shabby
round-shouldered back, and had once noticed his eyes turned
toward the Beaufort box. The two men shook hands, and
Winsett proposed a bock at a little German restaurant around
the corner. Archer, who was not in the mood for the kind of
talk they were likely to get there, declined on the plea that he
had work to do at home; and Winsett said: "Oh, well so have
I for that matter, and I'll be the Industrious Apprentice too."

They strolled along together, and presently Winsett said:
"Look here, what I'm really after is the name of the dark lady
in that swell box of yours—with the Beauforts, wasn't she?
The one your friend Lefferts seems so smitten by."

Archer, he could not have said why, was slightly annoyed.
What the devil did Ned Winsett want with Ellen Olenska's
name? And above all, why did he couple it with Lefferts's? It
was unlike Winsett to manifest such curiosity; but after all,
Archer remembered, he was a journalist.

"It's not for an interview, I hope?" he laughed.

"Well—not for the press; just for myself," Winsett rejoined. "The fact is she's a neighbour of mine—queer quarter
for such a beauty to settle in—and she's been awfully kind to
my little boy, who fell down her area chasing his kitten, and
gave himself a nasty cut. She rushed in bareheaded, carrying
him in her arms, with his knee all beautifully bandaged, and
was so sympathetic and beautiful that my wife was too dazzled to ask her name."

A pleasant glow dilated Archer's heart. There was nothing
extraordinary in the tale: any woman would have done as
much for a neighbour's child. But it was just like Ellen, he
felt, to have rushed in bareheaded, carrying the boy in her
arms, and to have dazzled poor Mrs. Winsett into forgetting
to ask who she was.

"That is the Countess Olenska—a granddaughter of old Mrs. Mingott's."

"Whew—a Countess!" whistled Ned Winsett. "Well, I didn't know Countesses were so neighbourly. Mingotts ain't."

"They would be, if you'd let them."

"Ah, well—" It was their old interminable argument as to the obstinate unwillingness of the "clever people" to frequent the fashionable, and both men knew that there was no use in prolonging it.

"I wonder," Winsett broke off, "how a Countess happens to live in our slum?"

"Because she doesn't care a hang about where she lives—or about any of our little social sign-posts," said Archer, with a secret pride in his own picture of her.

"H'm—been in bigger places, I suppose," the other commented. "Well, here's my corner."

He slouched off across Broadway, and Archer stood looking after him and musing on his last words.

Ned Winsett had those flashes of penetration; they were the most interesting thing about him, and always made Archer wonder why they had allowed him to accept failure so stolidly at an age when most men are still struggling.

Archer had known that Winsett had a wife and child, but he had never seen them. The two men always met at the Century, or at some haunt of journalists and theatrical people, such as the restaurant where Winsett had proposed to go for a bock. He had given Archer to understand that his wife was an invalid; which might be true of the poor lady, or might merely mean that she was lacking in social gifts or in evening clothes, or in both. Winsett himself had a savage abhorrence of social observances: Archer, who dressed in the evening because he thought it cleaner and more comfortable to do so, and who had never stopped to consider that cleanliness and comfort are two of the costliest items in a modest budget, regarded Winsett's attitude as part of the boring "Bohemian" pose that always made fashionable people, who changed their clothes without talking about it, and were not forever harping on the number of servants one kept, seem so much simpler and less self-conscious than the others. Nevertheless, he was always stimulated by Winsett, and whenever he caught sight of the journalist's lean bearded face and melancholy eyes he would rout him out of his corner and carry him off for a long talk.

Winsett was not a journalist by choice. He was a pure man of letters, untimely born in a world that had no need of letters; but after publishing one volume of brief and exquisite literary appreciations, of which one hundred and twenty copies were sold, thirty given away, and the balance eventually destroyed by the publishers (as per contract) to make room for more marketable material, he had abandoned his real calling, and taken a sub-editorial job on a women's weekly, where fashion-plates and paper patterns alternated with New England love-stories and advertisements of temperance drinks.

On the subject of "Hearth-fires" (as the paper was called) he was inexhaustibly entertaining; but beneath his fun lurked the sterile bitterness of the still young man who has tried and given up. His conversation always made Archer take the measure of his own life, and feel how little it contained; but Winsett's, after all, contained still less, and though their common fund of intellectual interests and curiosities made their talks exhilarating, their exchange of views usually remained within the limits of a pensive dilettantism.

"The fact is, life isn't much a fit for either of us," Winsett had once said. "I'm down and out; nothing to be done about it. I've got only one ware to produce, and there's no market for it here, and won't be in my time. But you're free and you're well-off. Why don't *you* get into touch? There's only one way to do it: to go into politics."

Archer threw his head back and laughed. There one saw at a flash the unbridgeable difference between men like Winsett and the others—Archer's kind. Every one in polite circles knew that, in America, "a gentleman couldn't go into politics." But, since he could hardly put it in that way to Winsett, he answered evasively: "Look at the career of the honest man in American politics! They don't want us."

"Who's 'they'? Why don't you all get together and be 'they' yourselves?"

Archer's laugh lingered on his lips in a slightly condescending smile. It was useless to prolong the discussion: everybody knew the melancholy fate of the few gentlemen who had risked their clean linen in municipal or state politics in New York. The day was past when that sort of thing was possible: the country was in possession of the bosses and the emigrant, and decent people had to fall back on sport or culture.

"Culture! Yes—if we had it! But there are just a few little local patches, dying out here and there for lack of—well, hoeing and cross-fertilising: the last remnants of the old European tradition that your forebears brought with them. But you're in a pitiful little minority: you've got no centre, no competition, no audience. You're like the pictures on the walls of a deserted house: 'The Portrait of a Gentleman.' You'll never amount to anything, any of you, till you roll up your sleeves and get right down into the muck. That, or emigrate . . . God! If I could emigrate . . ."

Archer mentally shrugged his shoulders and turned the conversation back to books, where Winsett, if uncertain, was always interesting. Emigrate! As if a gentleman could abandon his own country! One could no more do that than one could roll up one's sleeves and go down into the muck. A gentleman simply stayed at home and abstained. But you couldn't make a man like Winsett see that; and that was why the New York of literary clubs and exotic restaurants, though a first shake made it seem more of a kaleidoscope, turned out, in the end, to be a smaller box, with a more monotonous pattern, than the assembled atoms of Fifth Avenue.

The next morning Archer scoured the town in vain for more yellow roses. In consequence of this search he arrived late at the office, perceived that his doing so made no difference whatever to any one, and was filled with sudden exasperation at the elaborate futility of his life. Why should he not be, at that moment, on the sands of St. Augustine with May Welland? No one was deceived by his pretense of professional activity. In old-fashioned legal firms like that of which Mr. Letterblair was the head, and which were mainly engaged in the management of large estates and "conservative" investments, there were always two or three young men, fairly well-off, and without professional ambition, who, for a certain number of hours of each day, sat at their desks accomplishing trivial tasks, or simply reading the newspapers. Though it was supposed to be proper for them to have an occupation, the crude fact of money-making was still regarded as derogatory, and the law, being a profession, was accounted a more gentlemanly pursuit than business. But none of these young men had much hope of really advancing in his profession, or any earnest desire to do so; and over many of them the green mould of the perfunctory was already perceptibly spreading.

It made Archer shiver to think that it might be spreading over him too. He had, to be sure, other tastes and interests; he spent his vacations in European travel, cultivated the "clever people" May spoke of, and generally tried to "keep up," as he had somewhat wistfully put it to Madame Olenska. But once he was married, what would become of this narrow margin of life in which his real experiences were lived? He had seen enough of other young men who had dreamed his dream, though perhaps less ardently, and who had gradually sunk into the placid and luxurious routine of their elders.

From the office he sent a note by messenger to Madame Olenska, asking if he might call that afternoon, and begging her to let him find a reply at his club; but at the club he found nothing, nor did he receive any letter the following day. This unexpected silence mortified him beyond reason, and though the next morning he saw a glorious cluster of yellow roses behind a florist's window-pane, he left it there. It was only on the third morning that he received a line by post from the Countess Olenska. To his surprise it was dated from Skuytercliff, whither the van der Luydens had promptly retreated after putting the Duke on board his steamer.

"I ran away," the writer began abruptly (without the usual preliminaries), "the day after I saw you at the play, and these kind friends have taken me in. I wanted to be quiet, and think things over. You were right in telling me how kind they were; I feel myself so safe here. I wish that you were with us." She ended with a conventional "Yours sincerely," and without any allusion to the date of her return.

The tone of the note surprised the young man. What was Madame Olenska running away from, and why did she feel the need to be safe? His first thought was of some dark menace from abroad; then he reflected that he did not know her epistolary style, and that it might run to picturesque exaggeration. Women always exaggerated; and moreover she was not wholly at her ease in English, which she often spoke as if she were translating from the French. "Je me suis évadée—" put in that way, the opening sentence immediately suggested that she might merely have wanted to escape from a boring round of engagements; which was very likely true, for he judged her to be capricious, and easily wearied of the pleasure of the moment.

It amused him to think of the van der Ludyens' having carried her off to Skuytercliff on a second visit, and this time for an indefinite period. The doors of Skuytercliff were rarely and grudgingly opened to visitors, and a chilly week-end was the most ever offered to the few thus privileged. But Archer had seen, on his last visit to Paris, the delicious play of Labiche, "Le Voyage de M. Perrichon," and he remembered M. Perrichon's dogged and undiscouraged attachment to the young man whom he had pulled out of the glacier. The van der Luydens had rescued Madame Olenska from a doom almost as icy; and though there were many other reasons for being attracted to her, Archer knew that beneath them all lay the gentle and obstinate determination to go on rescuing her.

He felt a distinct disappointment on learning that she was away; and almost immediately remembered that, only the day before, he had refused an invitation to spend the following Sunday with the Reggie Chiverses at their house on the Hudson, a few miles below Skuytercliff.

He had had his fill long ago of the noisy friendly parties at Highbank, with coasting, ice-boating, sleighing, long tramps in the snow, and a general flavour of mild flirting and milder practical jokes. He had just received a box of new books from his London book-seller, and had preferred the prospect of a quiet Sunday at home with his spoils. But he now went into the club writing-room, wrote a hurried telegram, and told the servant to send it immediately. He knew that Mrs. Reggie didn't object to her visitors' suddenly changing their minds, and that there was always a room to spare in her elastic house.

XV

NEWLAND ARCHER arrived at the Chiverses' on Friday evening, and on Saturday went conscientiously through all the rites appertaining to a week-end at Highbank.

In the morning he had a spin in the ice-boat with his hostess and a few of the hardier guests; in the afternoon he "went over the farm" with Reggie, and listened, in the elaborately appointed stables, to long and impressive disquisitions on the horse; after tea he talked in a corner of the firelit hall with a young lady who had professed herself broken-hearted when his engagement was announced, but was now eager to tell him of her own matrimonial hopes; and finally, about midnight, he assisted in putting a gold-fish in one visitor's bed, dressed up a burglar in the bath-room of a nervous aunt, and saw in the small hours by joining in a pillow-fight that ranged from the nurseries to the basement. But on Sunday after luncheon he borrowed a cutter, and drove over to Skuytercliff.

People had always been told that the house at Skuytercliff was an Italian villa. Those who had never been to Italy believed it; so did some who had. The house had been built by Mr. van der Luyden in his youth, on his return from the "grand tour," and in anticipation of his approaching marriage with Miss Louisa Dagonet. It was a large square wooden structure, with tongued and grooved walls painted pale green and white, a Corinthian portico, and fluted pilasters between the windows. From the high ground on which it stood a series of terraces bordered by balustrades and urns descended in the steel-engraving style to a small irregular lake with an asphalt edge overhung by rare weeping conifers. To the right and left, the famous weedless lawns studded with "specimen" trees (each of a different variety) rolled away to long ranges of grass crested with elaborate cast-iron ornaments; and below, in a hollow, lay the four-roomed stone house which the first Patroon had built on the land granted him in 1612.

Against the uniform sheet of snow and the greyish winter sky the Italian villa loomed up rather grimly; even in summer it kept its distance, and the boldest coleus bed had never ventured nearer than thirty feet from its awful front. Now, as Archer rang the bell, the long tinkle seemed to echo through a mausoleum; and the surprise of the butler who at length responded to the call was as great as though he had been summoned from his final sleep.

Happily Archer was of the family, and therefore, irregular though his arrival was, entitled to be informed that the Countess Olenska was out, having driven to afternoon service with Mrs. van der Luyden exactly three quarters of an hour earlier.

"Mr. van der Luyden," the butler continued, "is in, sir; but my impression is that he is either finishing his nap or else reading yesterday's Evening Post. I heard him say, sir, on his return from church this morning, that he intended to look through the Evening Post after luncheon; if you like, sir, I might go to the library door and listen—"

But Archer, thanking him, said that he would go and meet the ladies; and the butler, obviously relieved, closed the door on him majestically.

A groom took the cutter to the stables, and Archer struck through the park to the high-road. The village of Skuytercliff was only a mile and a half away, but he knew that Mrs. van der Luyden never walked, and that he must keep to the road to meet the carriage. Presently, however, coming down a foot-path that crossed the highway, he caught sight of a slight figure in a red cloak, with a big dog running ahead. He hurried forward, and Madame Olenska stopped short with a smile of welcome.

"Ah, you've come!" she said, and drew her hand from her muff.

The red cloak made her look gay and vivid, like the Ellen Mingott of old days; and he laughed as he took her hand, and answered: "I came to see what you were running away from."

Her face clouded over, but she answered: "Ah, well—you will see, presently."

The answer puzzled him. "Why—do you mean that you've been overtaken?"

She shrugged her shoulders, with a little movement like Nastasia's, and rejoined in a lighter tone: "Shall we walk on?

I'm so cold after the sermon. And what does it matter, now you're here to protect me?"

The blood rose to his temples and he caught a fold of her cloak. "Ellen—what is it? You must tell me."

"Oh, presently—let's run a race first: my feet are freezing to the ground," she cried; and gathering up the cloak she fled away across the snow, the dog leaping about her with challenging barks. For a moment Archer stood watching, his gaze delighted by the flash of the red meteor against the snow; then he started after her, and they met, panting and laughing, at a wicket that led into the park.

She looked up at him and smiled. "I knew you'd come!"

"That shows you wanted me to," he returned, with a disproportionate joy in their nonsense. The white glitter of the trees filled the air with its own mysterious brightness, and as they walked on over the snow the ground seemed to sing under their feet.

"Where did you come from?" Madame Olenska asked.

He told her, and added: "It was because I got your note."

After a pause she said, with a just perceptible chill in her voice: "May asked you to take care of me."

"I didn't need any asking."

"You mean—I'm so evidently helpless and defenceless? What a poor thing you must all think me! But women here seem not—seem never to feel the need: any more than the blessed in heaven."

He lowered his voice to ask: "What sort of a need?"

"Ah, don't ask me! I don't speak your language," she retorted petulantly.

The answer smote him like a blow, and he stood still in the path, looking down at her.

"What did I come for, if I don't speak yours?"

"Oh, my friend—!" She laid her hand lightly on his arm, and he pleaded earnestly: "Ellen—why won't you tell me what's happened?"

She shrugged again. "Does anything ever happen in heaven?"

He was silent, and they walked on a few yards without exchanging a word. Finally she said: "I will tell you—but where, where, where? One can't be alone for a minute in that great seminary of a house, with all the doors wide open, and always a servant bringing tea, or a log for the fire, or the newspaper! Is there nowhere in an American house where one may be by one's self? You're so shy, and yet you're so public. I always feel as if I were in the convent again—or on the stage, before a dreadfully polite audience that never applauds."

"Ah, you don't like us!" Archer exclaimed.

They were walking past the house of the old Patroon, with its squat walls and small square windows compactly grouped about a central chimney. The shutters stood wide, and through one of the newly-washed windows Archer caught the light of a fire.

"Why—the house is open!" he said.

She stood still. "No; only for today, at least. I wanted to see it, and Mr. van der Luyden had the fire lit and the windows opened, so that we might stop there on the way back from church this morning." She ran up the steps and tried the door. "It's still unlocked—what luck! Come in and we can have a quiet talk. Mrs. van der Luyden has driven over to see her old aunts at Rhinebeck and we shan't be missed at the house for another hour."

He followed her into the narrow passage. His spirits, which had dropped at her last words, rose with an irrational leap. The homely little house stood there, its panels and brasses shining in the firelight, as if magically created to receive them. A big bed of embers still gleamed in the kitchen chimney, under an iron pot hung from an ancient crane. Rush-bottomed arm-chairs faced each other across the tiled hearth, and rows of Delft plates stood on shelves against the walls. Archer stooped over and threw a log upon the embers.

Madame Olenska, dropping her cloak, sat down in one of the chairs. Archer leaned against the chimney and looked at her.

"You're laughing now; but when you wrote me you were unhappy," he said.

"Yes." She paused. "But I can't feel unhappy when you're here."

"I sha'n't be here long," he rejoined, his lips stiffening with the effort to say just so much and no more.

"No; I know. But I'm improvident: I live in the moment when I'm happy."

The words stole through him like a temptation, and to close his senses to it he moved away from the hearth and stood gazing out at the black tree-boles against the snow. But it was as if she too had shifted her place, and he still saw her, between himself and the trees, drooping over the fire with her indolent smile. Archer's heart was beating insubordinately. What if it were from him that she had been running away, and if she had waited to tell him so till they were here alone together in this secret room?

"Ellen, if I'm really a help to you—if you really wanted me to come—tell me what's wrong, tell me what it is you're running away from," he insisted.

He spoke without shifting his position, without even turning to look at her: if the thing was to happen, it was to happen in this way, with the whole width of the room between them, and his eyes still fixed on the outer snow.

For a long moment she was silent; and in that moment Archer imagined her, almost heard her, stealing up behind him to throw her light arms about his neck. While he waited, soul and body throbbing with the miracle to come, his eyes mechanically received the image of a heavily-coated man with his fur collar turned up who was advancing along the path to the house. The man was Julius Beaufort.

"Ah—!" Archer cried, bursting into a laugh.

Madame Olenska had sprung up and moved to his side, slipping her hand into his; but after a glance through the window her face paled and she shrank back.

"So that was it?" Archer said derisively.

"I didn't know he was here," Madame Olenska murmured. Her hand still clung to Archer's; but he drew away from her, and walking out into the passage threw open the door of the house.

"Hallo, Beaufort—this way! Madame Olenska was expecting you," he said.

During his journey back to New York the next morning, Archer relived with a fatiguing vividness his last moments at Skuytercliff.

Beaufort, though clearly annoyed at finding him with Madame Olenska, had, as usual, carried off the situation high-handedly. His way of ignoring people whose presence inconvenienced him actually gave them, if they were sensitive to it, a feeling of invisibility, of non-existence. Archer, as the three strolled back through the park, was aware of this odd sense of disembodiment; and humbling as it was to his vanity it gave him the ghostly advantage of observing unobserved.

Beaufort had entered the little house with his usual easy assurance; but he could not smile away the vertical line between his eyes. It was fairly clear that Madame Olenska had not known that he was coming, though her words to Archer had hinted at the possibility; at any rate, she had evidently not told him where she was going when she left New York, and her unexplained departure had exasperated him. The ostensible reason of his appearance was the discovery, the very night before, of a "perfect little house," not in the market, which was really just the thing for her, but would be snapped up instantly if she didn't take it; and he was loud in mock-reproaches for the dance she had led him in running away just as he had found it.

"If only this new dodge for talking along a wire had been a little bit nearer perfection I might have told you all this from town, and been toasting my toes before the club fire at this minute, instead of tramping after you through the snow," he grumbled, disguising a real irritation under the pretence of it; and at this opening Madame Olenska twisted the talk away to the fantastic possibility that they might one day actually converse with each other from street to street, or even—incredible dream!—from one town to another. This struck from all three allusions to Edgar Poe and Jules Verne, and such platitudes as naturally rise to the lips of the most intelligent when they are talking against time, and dealing with a new invention in which it would seem ingenuous to believe too soon; and the question of the telephone carried them safely back to the big house.

Mrs. van der Luyden had not yet returned; and Archer took his leave and walked off to fetch the cutter, while Beaufort followed the Countess Olenska indoors. It was probable that, little as the van der Luydens encouraged unannounced

visits, he could count on being asked to dine, and sent back
to the station to catch the nine o'clock train; but more than
that he would certainly not get, for it would be inconceivable
to his hosts that a gentleman travelling without luggage
should wish to spend the night, and distasteful to them to
propose it to a person with whom they were on terms of such
limited cordiality as Beaufort.

Beaufort knew all this, and must have foreseen it; and his
taking the long journey for so small a reward gave the measure of his impatience. He was undeniably in pursuit of the
Countess Olenska; and Beaufort had only one object in view
in his pursuit of pretty women. His dull and childless home
had long since palled on him; and in addition to more permanent consolations he was always in quest of amorous
adventures in his own set. This was the man from whom Madame Olenska was avowedly flying: the question was whether
she had fled because his importunities displeased her, or because she did not wholly trust herself to resist them; unless,
indeed, all her talk of flight had been a blind, and her departure no more than a manœuvre.

Archer did not really believe this. Little as he had actually
seen of Madame Olenska, he was beginning to think that he
could read her face, and if not her face, her voice; and both
had betrayed annoyance, and even dismay, at Beaufort's sudden appearance. But, after all, if this were the case, was it not
worse than if she had left New York for the express purpose
of meeting him? If she had done that, she ceased to be an
object of interest, she threw in her lot with the vulgarest of
dissemblers: a woman engaged in a love affair with Beaufort
"classed" herself irretrievably.

No, it was worse a thousand times if, judging Beaufort,
and probably despising him, she was yet drawn to him by all
that gave him an advantage over the other men about her: his
habit of two continents and two societies, his familiar association with artists and actors and people generally in the
world's eye, and his careless contempt for local prejudices.
Beaufort was vulgar, he was uneducated, he was purse-proud;
but the circumstances of his life, and a certain native shrewdness, made him better worth talking to than many men, morally and socially his betters, whose horizon was bounded by

the Battery and the Central Park. How should any one coming from a wider world not feel the difference and be attracted by it?

Madame Olenska, in a burst of irritation, had said to
Archer that he and she did not talk the same language; and
the young man knew that in some respects this was true. But
Beaufort understood every turn of her dialect, and spoke it
fluently: his view of life, his tone, his attitude, were merely a
coarser reflection of those revealed in Count Olenski's letter.
This might seem to be to his disadvantage with Count Olenski's wife; but Archer was too intelligent to think that a
young woman like Ellen Olenska would necessarily recoil
from everything that reminded her of her past. She might
believe herself wholly in revolt against it; but what had
charmed her in it would still charm her, even though it were
against her will.

Thus, with a painful impartiality, did the young man make
out the case for Beaufort, and for Beaufort's victim. A longing to enlighten her was strong in him; and there were moments when he imagined that all she asked was to be
enlightened.

That evening he unpacked his books from London. The
box was full of things he had been waiting for impatiently; a
new volume of Herbert Spencer, another collection of the
prolific Alphonse Daudet's brilliant tales, and a novel called
"Middlemarch," as to which there had lately been interesting
things said in the reviews. He had declined three dinner invitations in favour of this feast; but though he turned the
pages with the sensuous joy of the book-lover, he did not
know what he was reading, and one book after another
dropped from his hand. Suddenly, among them, he lit on a
small volume of verse which he had ordered because the name
had attracted him: "The House of Life." He took it up, and
found himself plunged in an atmosphere unlike any he had
ever breathed in books; so warm, so rich, and yet so ineffably
tender, that it gave a new and haunting beauty to the most
elementary of human passions. All through the night he pursued through those enchanted pages the vision of a woman
who had the face of Ellen Olenska; but when he woke the
next morning, and looked out at the brownstone houses

across the street, and thought of his desk in Mr. Letterblair's office, and the family pew in Grace Church, his hour in the park of Skuytercliff became as far outside the pale of probability as the visions of the night.

"Mercy, how pale you look, Newland!" Janey commented over the coffee-cups at breakfast; and his mother added: "Newland, dear, I've noticed lately that you've been coughing; I do hope you're not letting yourself be overworked?" For it was the conviction of both ladies that, under the iron despotism of his senior partners, the young man's life was spent in the most exhausting professional labours—and he had never thought it necessary to undeceive them.

The next two or three days dragged by heavily. The taste of the usual was like cinders in his mouth, and there were moments when he felt as if he were being buried alive under his future. He heard nothing of the Countess Olenska, or of the perfect little house, and though he met Beaufort at the club they merely nodded at each other across the whist-tables. It was not till the fourth evening that he found a note awaiting him on his return home. "Come late tomorrow: I must explain to you. Ellen." These were the only words it contained.

The young man, who was dining out, thrust the note into his pocket, smiling a little at the Frenchness of the "to you." After dinner he went to a play; and it was not until his return home, after midnight, that he drew Madame Olenska's missive out again and re-read it slowly a number of times. There were several ways of answering it, and he gave considerable thought to each one during the watches of an agitated night. That on which, when morning came, he finally decided was to pitch some clothes into a portmanteau and jump on board a boat that was leaving that very afternoon for St. Augustine.

XVI

WHEN ARCHER walked down the sandy main street of St. Augustine to the house which had been pointed out to him as Mr. Welland's, and saw May Welland standing under a magnolia with the sun in her hair, he wondered why he had waited so long to come.

Here was the truth, here was reality, here was the life that belonged to him; and he, who fancied himself so scornful of arbitrary restraints, had been afraid to break away from his desk because of what people might think of his stealing a holiday!

Her first exclamation was: "Newland—has anything happened?" and it occurred to him that it would have been more "feminine" if she had instantly read in his eyes why he had come. But when he answered: "Yes—I found I had to see you," her happy blushes took the chill from her surprise, and he saw how easily he would be forgiven, and how soon even Mr. Letterblair's mild disapproval would be smiled away by a tolerant family.

Early as it was, the main street was no place for any but formal greetings, and Archer longed to be alone with May, and to pour out all his tenderness and his impatience. It still lacked an hour to the late Welland breakfast-time, and instead of asking him to come in she proposed that they should walk out to an old orange-garden beyond the town. She had just been for a row on the river, and the sun that netted the little waves with gold seemed to have caught her in its meshes. Across the warm brown of her cheek her blown hair glittered like silver wire; and her eyes too looked lighter, almost pale in their youthful limpidity. As she walked beside Archer with her long swinging gait her face wore the vacant serenity of a young marble athlete.

To Archer's strained nerves the vision was as soothing as the sight of the blue sky and the lazy river. They sat down on a bench under the orange-trees and he put his arm about her and kissed her. It was like drinking at a cold spring with the sun on it; but his pressure may have been more vehement than he had intended, for the blood rose to her face and she drew back as if he had startled her.

"What is it?" he asked, smiling; and she looked at him with surprise, and answered: "Nothing."

A slight embarrassment fell on them, and her hand slipped out of his. It was the only time that he had kissed her on the lips except for their fugitive embrace in the Beaufort conservatory, and he saw that she was disturbed, and shaken out of her cool boyish composure.

"Tell me what you do all day," he said, crossing his arms under his tilted-back head, and pushing his hat forward to screen the sun-dazzle. To let her talk about familiar and simple things was the easiest way of carrying on his own independent train of thought; and he sat listening to her simple chronicle of swimming, sailing and riding, varied by an occasional dance at the primitive inn when a man-of-war came in. A few pleasant people from Philadelphia and Baltimore were picknicking at the inn, and the Selfridge Merrys had come down for three weeks because Kate Merry had had bronchitis. They were planning to lay out a lawn tennis court on the sands; but no one but Kate and May had racquets, and most of the people had not even heard of the game.

All this kept her very busy, and she had not had time to do more than look at the little vellum book that Archer had sent her the week before (the "Sonnets from the Portuguese"); but she was learning by heart "How they brought the Good News from Ghent to Aix," because it was one of the first things he had ever read to her; and it amused her to be able to tell him that Kate Merry had never even heard of a poet called Robert Browning.

Presently she started up, exclaiming that they would be late for breakfast; and they hurried back to the tumble-down house with its paintless porch and unpruned hedge of plumbago and pink geraniums where the Wellands were installed for the winter. Mr. Welland's sensitive domesticity shrank from the discomforts of the slovenly southern hotel, and at immense expense, and in face of almost insuperable difficulties, Mrs. Welland was obliged, year after year, to improvise an establishment partly made up of discontented New York servants and partly drawn from the local African supply.

"The doctors want my husband to feel that he is in his own home; otherwise he would be so wretched that the climate would not do him any good," she explained, winter after winter, to the sympathising Philadelphians and Baltimoreans; and Mr. Welland, beaming across a breakfast table miraculously supplied with the most varied delicacies, was presently saying to Archer: "You see, my dear fellow, we camp—we literally camp. I tell my wife and May that I want to teach them how to rough it."

Mr. and Mrs. Welland had been as much surprised as their daughter by the young man's sudden arrival; but it had occurred to him to explain that he had felt himself on the verge of a nasty cold, and this seemed to Mr. Welland an all-sufficient reason for abandoning any duty.

"You can't be too careful, especially toward spring," he said, heaping his plate with straw-coloured griddle-cakes and drowning them in golden syrup. "If I'd only been as prudent at your age May would have been dancing at the Assemblies now, instead of spending her winters in a wilderness with an old invalid."

"Oh, but I love it here, Papa; you know I do. If only Newland could stay I should like it a thousand times better than New York."

"Newland must stay till he has quite thrown off his cold," said Mrs. Welland indulgently; and the young man laughed, and said he supposed there was such a thing as one's profession.

He managed, however, after an exchange of telegrams with the firm, to make his cold last a week; and it shed an ironic light on the situation to know that Mr. Letterblair's indulgence was partly due to the satisfactory way in which his brilliant young junior partner had settled the troublesome matter of the Olenski divorce. Mr. Letterblair had let Mrs. Welland know that Mr. Archer had "rendered an invaluable service" to the whole family, and that old Mrs. Manson Mingott had been particularly pleased; and one day when May had gone for a drive with her father in the only vehicle the place produced Mrs. Welland took occasion to touch on a topic which she always avoided in her daughter's presence.

"I'm afraid Ellen's ideas are not at all like ours. She was

barely eighteen when Medora Manson took her back to Europe—you remember the excitement when she appeared in black at her coming-out ball? Another of Medora's fads—really this time it was almost prophetic! That must have been at least twelve years ago; and since then Ellen has never been to America. No wonder she is completely Europeanised."

"But European society is not given to divorce: Countess Olenska thought she would be conforming to American ideas in asking for her freedom." It was the first time that the young man had pronounced her name since he had left Skuytercliff, and he felt the colour rise to his cheek.

Mrs. Welland smiled compassionately. "That is just like the extraordinary things that foreigners invent about us. They think we dine at two o'clock and countenance divorce! That is why it seems to me so foolish to entertain them when they come to New York. They accept our hospitality, and then they go home and repeat the same stupid stories."

Archer made no comment on this, and Mrs. Welland continued: "But we do most thoroughly appreciate your persuading Ellen to give up the idea. Her grandmother and her uncle Lovell could do nothing with her; both of them have written that her changing her mind was entirely due to your influence—in fact she said so to her grandmother. She has an unbounded admiration for you. Poor Ellen—she was always a wayward child. I wonder what her fate will be?"

"What we've all contrived to make it," he felt like answering. "If you'd all of you rather she should be Beaufort's mistress than some decent fellow's wife you've certainly gone the right way about it."

He wondered what Mrs. Welland would have said if he had uttered the words instead of merely thinking them. He could picture the sudden decomposure of her firm placid features, to which a lifelong mastery over trifles had given an air of factitious authority. Traces still lingered on them of a fresh beauty like her daughter's; and he asked himself if May's face was doomed to thicken into the same middle-aged image of invincible innocence.

Ah, no, he did not want May to have that kind of innocence, the innocence that seals the mind against imagination and the heart against experience!

"I verily believe," Mrs. Welland continued, "that if the horrible business had come out in the newspapers it would have been my husband's death-blow. I don't know any of the details; I only ask not to, as I told poor Ellen when she tried to talk to me about it. Having an invalid to care for, I have to keep my mind bright and happy. But Mr. Welland was terribly upset; he had a slight temperature every morning while we were waiting to hear what had been decided. It was the horror of his girl's learning that such things were possible— but of course, dear Newland, you felt that too. We all knew that you were thinking of May."

"I'm always thinking of May," the young man rejoined, rising to cut short the conversation.

He had meant to seize the opportunity of his private talk with Mrs. Welland to urge her to advance the date of his marriage. But he could think of no arguments that would move her, and with a sense of relief he saw Mr. Welland and May driving up to the door.

His only hope was to plead again with May, and on the day before his departure he walked with her to the ruinous garden of the Spanish Mission. The background lent itself to allusions to European scenes; and May, who was looking her loveliest under a wide-brimmed hat that cast a shadow of mystery over her too-clear eyes, kindled into eagerness as he spoke of Granada and the Alhambra.

"We might be seeing it all this spring—even the Easter ceremonies at Seville," he urged, exaggerating his demands in the hope of a larger concession.

"Easter in Seville? And it will be Lent next week!" she laughed.

"Why shouldn't we be married in Lent?" he rejoined; but she looked so shocked that he saw his mistake.

"Of course I didn't mean that, dearest; but soon after Easter—so that we could sail at the end of April. I know I could arrange it at the office."

She smiled dreamily upon the possibility; but he perceived that to dream of it sufficed her. It was like hearing him read aloud out of his poetry books the beautiful things that could not possibly happen in real life.

"Oh, do go on, Newland; I do love your descriptions."

"But why should they be only descriptions? Why shouldn't we make them real?"

"We shall, dearest, of course; next year." Her voice lingered over it.

"Don't you want them to be real sooner? Can't I persuade you to break away now?"

She bowed her head, vanishing from him under her conniving hat-brim.

"Why should we dream away another year? Look at me, dear! Don't you understand how I want you for my wife?"

For a moment she remained motionless; then she raised on him eyes of such despairing clearness that he half-released her waist from his hold. But suddenly her look changed and deepened inscrutably. "I'm not sure if I *do* understand," she said. "Is it—is it because you're not certain of continuing to care for me?"

Archer sprang up from his seat. "My God—perhaps—I don't know," he broke out angrily.

May Welland rose also; as they faced each other she seemed to grow in womanly stature and dignity. Both were silent for a moment, as if dismayed by the unforeseen trend of their words: then she said in a low voice: "If that is it—is there some one else?"

"Some one else—between you and me?" He echoed her words slowly, as though they were only half-intelligible and he wanted time to repeat the question to himself. She seemed to catch the uncertainty of his voice, for she went on in a deepening tone: "Let us talk frankly, Newland. Sometimes I've felt a difference in you; especially since our engagement has been announced."

"Dear—what madness!" he recovered himself to exclaim.

She met his protest with a faint smile. "If it is, it won't hurt us to talk about it." She paused, and added, lifting her head with one of her noble movements: "Or even if it's true: why shouldn't we speak of it? You might so easily have made a mistake."

He lowered his head, staring at the black leaf-pattern on the sunny path at their feet. "Mistakes are always easy to make; but if I had made one of the kind you suggest, is it likely that I should be imploring you to hasten our marriage?"

She looked downward too, disturbing the pattern with the point of her sunshade while she struggled for expression. "Yes," she said at length. "You might want—once for all—to settle the question: it's one way."

Her quiet lucidity startled him, but did not mislead him into thinking her insensible. Under her hat-brim he saw the pallor of her profile, and a slight tremor of the nostril above her resolutely steadied lips.

"Well—?" he questioned, sitting down on the bench, and looking up at her with a frown that he tried to make playful.

She dropped back into her seat and went on: "You mustn't think that a girl knows as little as her parents imagine. One hears and one notices—one has one's feelings and ideas. And of course, long before you told me that you cared for me, I'd known that there was some one else you were interested in; every one was talking about it two years ago at Newport. And once I saw you sitting together on the verandah at a dance—and when she came back into the house her face was sad, and I felt sorry for her; I remembered it afterward, when we were engaged."

Her voice had sunk almost to a whisper, and she sat clasping and unclasping her hands about the handle of her sunshade. The young man laid his upon them with a gentle pressure; his heart dilated with an inexpressible relief.

"My dear child—was *that* it? If you only knew the truth!"

She raised her head quickly. "Then there is a truth I don't know?"

He kept his hand over hers. "I meant, the truth about the old story you speak of."

"But that's what I want to know, Newland—what I ought to know. I couldn't have my happiness made out of a wrong—an unfairness—to somebody else. And I want to believe that it would be the same with you. What sort of a life could we build on such foundations?"

Her face had taken on a look of such tragic courage that he felt like bowing himself down at her feet. "I've wanted to say this for a long time," she went on. "I've wanted to tell you that, when two people really love each other, I understand that there may be situations which make it right that they should—should go against public opinion. And if you feel yourself in any way pledged . . . pledged to the person we've spoken of . . . and if there is any way . . . any way in which you can fulfill your pledge . . . even by her getting a divorce . . . Newland, don't give her up because of me!"

His surprise at discovering that her fears had fastened upon an episode so remote and so completely of the past as his love affair with Mrs. Thorley Rushworth gave way to wonder at the generosity of her view. There was something superhuman in an attitude so recklessly unorthodox, and if other problems had not pressed on him he would have been lost in wonder at the prodigy of the Wellands' daughter urging him to marry his former mistress. But he was still dizzy with the glimpse of the precipice they had skirted, and full of a new awe at the mystery of young-girlhood.

For a moment he could not speak; then he said: "There is no pledge—no obligation whatever—of the kind you think. Such cases don't always—present themselves quite as simply as . . . But that's no matter . . . I love your generosity, because I feel as you do about those things . . . I feel that each case must be judged individually, on its own merits . . . irrespective of stupid conventionalities . . . I mean, each woman's right to her liberty—" He pulled himself up, startled by the turn his thoughts had taken, and went on, looking at her with a smile: "Since you understand so many things, dearest, can't you go a little farther, and understand the uselessness of our submitting to another form of the same foolish conventionalities? If there's no one and nothing between us, isn't that an argument for marrying quickly, rather than for more delay?"

She flushed with joy and lifted her face to his; as he bent to it he saw that her eyes were full of happy tears. But in another moment she seemed to have descended from her womanly eminence to helpless and timorous girlhood; and he understood that her courage and initiative were all for others, and that she had none for herself. It was evident that the effort of speaking had been much greater than her studied composure betrayed, and that at his first word of reassurance she had dropped back into the usual, as a too-adventurous child takes refuge in its mother's arms.

Archer had no heart to go on pleading with her; he was

too much disappointed at the vanishing of the new being who had cast that one deep look at him from her transparent eyes. May seemed to be aware of his disappointment, but without knowing how to alleviate it; and they stood up and walked silently home.

XVII

"YOUR COUSIN the Countess called on mother while you were away," Janey Archer announced to her brother on the evening of his return.

The young man, who was dining alone with his mother and sister, glanced up in surprise and saw Mrs. Archer's gaze demurely bent on her plate. Mrs. Archer did not regard her seclusion from the world as a reason for being forgotten by it; and Newland guessed that she was slightly annoyed that he should be suprised by Madame Olenska's visit.

"She had on a black velvet polonaise with jet buttons, and a tiny green monkey muff; I never saw her so stylishly dressed," Janey continued. "She came alone, early on Sunday afternoon; luckily the fire was lit in the drawing-room. She had one of those new card-cases. She said she wanted to know us because you'd been so good to her."

Newland laughed. "Madame Olenska always takes that tone about her friends. She's very happy at being among her own people again."

"Yes, so she told us," said Mrs. Archer. "I must say she seems thankful to be here."

"I hope you liked her, mother."

Mrs. Archer drew her lips together. "She certainly lays herself out to please, even when she is calling on an old lady."

"Mother doesn't think her simple," Janey interjected, her eyes screwed upon her brother's face.

"It's just my old-fashioned feeling; dear May is my ideal," said Mrs. Archer.

"Ah," said her son, "they're not alike."

Archer had left St. Augustine charged with many messages for old Mrs. Mingott; and a day or two after his return to town he called on her.

The old lady received him with unusual warmth; she was grateful to him for persuading the Countess Olenska to give up the idea of a divorce; and when he told her that he had deserted the office without leave, and rushed down to St.

Augustine simply because he wanted to see May, she gave an adipose chuckle and patted his knee with her puff-ball hand.

"Ah, ah—so you kicked over the traces, did you? And I suppose Augusta and Welland pulled long faces, and behaved as if the end of the world had come? But little May—she knew better, I'll be bound?"

"I hoped she did; but after all she wouldn't agree to what I'd gone down to ask for."

"Wouldn't she indeed? And what was that?"

"I wanted to get her to promise that we should be married in April. What's the use of our wasting another year?"

Mrs. Manson Mingott screwed up her little mouth into a grimace of mimic prudery and twinkled at him through malicious lids. "'Ask Mamma,' I suppose—the usual story. Ah, these Mingotts—all alike! Born in a rut, and you can't root 'em out of it. When I built this house you'd have thought I was moving to California! Nobody ever *had* built above Fortieth Street—no, says I, nor above the Battery either, before Christopher Columbus discovered America. No, no; not one of them wants to be different; they're as scared of it as the small-pox. Ah, my dear Mr. Archer, I thank my stars I'm nothing but a vulgar Spicer; but there's not one of my own children that takes after me but my little Ellen." She broke off, still twinkling at him, and asked, with the casual irrelevance of old age: "Now, why in the world didn't you marry my little Ellen?"

Archer laughed. "For one thing, she wasn't there to be married."

"No—to be sure; more's the pity. And now it's too late; her life is finished." She spoke with the cold-blooded complacency of the aged throwing earth into the grave of young hopes. The young man's heart grew chill, and he said hurriedly: "Can't I persuade you to use your influence with the Wellands, Mrs. Mingott? I wasn't made for long engagements."

Old Catherine beamed on him approvingly. "No; I can see that. You've got a quick eye. When you were a little boy I've no doubt you liked to be helped first." She threw back her head with a laugh that made her chins ripple like little waves.

"Ah, here's my Ellen now!" she exclaimed, as the portières parted behind her.

Madame Olenska came forward with a smile. Her face looked vivid and happy, and she held out her hand gaily to Archer while she stooped to her grandmother's kiss.

"I was just saying to him, my dear: 'Now, why didn't you marry my little Ellen?'"

Madame Olenska looked at Archer, still smiling. "And what did he answer?"

"Oh, my darling, I leave you to find that out! He's been down to Florida to see his sweetheart."

"Yes, I know." She still looked at him. "I went to see your mother, to ask where you'd gone. I sent a note that you never answered, and I was afraid you were ill."

He muttered something about leaving unexpectedly, in a great hurry, and having intended to write to her from St. Augustine.

"And of course once you were there you never thought of me again!" She continued to beam on him with a gaiety that might have been a studied assumption of indifference.

"If she still needs me, she's determined not to let me see it," he thought, stung by her manner. He wanted to thank her for having been to see his mother, but under the ancestress's malicious eye he felt himself tongue-tied and constrained.

"Look at him—in such hot haste to get married that he took French leave and rushed down to implore the silly girl on his knees! That's something like a lover—that's the way handsome Bob Spicer carried off my poor mother; and then got tired of her before I was weaned—though they only had to wait eight months for me! But there—you're not a Spicer, young man; luckily for you and for May. It's only my poor Ellen that has kept any of their wicked blood; the rest of them are all model Mingotts," cried the old lady scornfully.

Archer was aware that Madame Olenska, who had seated herself at her grandmother's side, was still thoughtfully scrutinising him. The gaiety had faded from her eyes, and she said with great gentleness: "Surely, Granny, we can persuade them between us to do as he wishes."

Archer rose to go, and as his hand met Madame Olenska's

he felt that she was waiting for him to make some allusion to her unanswered letter.

"When can I see you?" he asked, as she walked with him to the door of the room.

"Whenever you like; but it must be soon if you want to see the little house again. I am moving next week."

A pang shot through him at the memory of his lamplit hours in the low-studded drawing-room. Few as they had been, they were thick with memories.

"Tomorrow evening?"

She nodded. "Tomorrow; yes; but early. I'm going out."

The next day was a Sunday, and if she were "going out" on a Sunday evening it could, of course, be only to Mrs. Lemuel Struthers's. He felt a slight movement of annoyance, not so much at her going there (for he rather liked her going where she pleased in spite of the van der Luydens), but because it was the kind of house at which she was sure to meet Beaufort, where she must have known beforehand that she would meet him—and where she was probably going for that purpose.

"Very well; tomorrow evening," he repeated, inwardly resolved that he would not go early, and that by reaching her door late he would either prevent her from going to Mrs. Struthers's, or else arrive after she had started—which, all things considered, would no doubt be the simplest solution.

It was only half-past eight, after all, when he rang the bell under the wisteria; not as late as he had intended by half an hour—but a singular restlessness had driven him to her door. He reflected, however, that Mrs. Struthers's Sunday evenings were not like a ball, and that her guests, as if to minimise their delinquency, usually went early.

The one thing he had not counted on, in entering Madame Olenska's hall, was to find hats and overcoats there. Why had she bidden him to come early if she was having people to dine? On a closer inspection of the garments besides which Nastasia was laying his own, his resentment gave way to curiosity. The overcoats were in fact the very strangest he had ever seen under a polite roof; and it took but a glance to assure himself that neither of them belonged to Julius Beaufort. One was a shaggy yellow ulster of "reach-me-down" cut, the other a very old and rusty cloak with a cape—something like what the French called a "Macfarlane." This garment, which appeared to be made for a person of prodigious size, had evidently seen long and hard wear, and its greenish-black folds gave out a moist sawdusty smell suggestive of prolonged sessions against bar-room walls. On it lay a ragged grey scarf and an odd felt hat of semiclerical shape.

Archer raised his eyebrows enquiringly at Nastasia, who raised hers in return with a fatalistic "Già!" as she threw open the drawing-room door.

The young man saw at once that his hostess was not in the room; then, with surprise, he discovered another lady standing by the fire. This lady, who was long, lean and loosely put together, was clad in raiment intricately looped and fringed, with plaids and stripes and bands of plain colour disposed in a design to which the clue seemed missing. Her hair, which had tried to turn white and only succeeded in fading, was surmounted by a Spanish comb and black lace scarf, and silk mittens, visibly darned, covered her rheumatic hands.

Beside her, in a cloud of cigar-smoke, stood the owners of the two overcoats, both in morning clothes that they had evidently not taken off since morning. In one of the two, Archer, to his surprise, recognised Ned Winsett; the other and older, who was unknown to him, and whose gigantic frame declared him to be the wearer of the "Macfarlane," had a feebly leonine head with crumpled grey hair, and moved his arms with large pawing gestures, as though he were distributing lay blessings to a kneeling multitude.

These three persons stood together on the hearth-rug, their eyes fixed on an extraordinarily large bouquet of crimson roses, with a knot of purple pansies at their base, that lay on the sofa where Madame Olenska usually sat.

"What they must have cost at this season—though of course it's the sentiment one cares about!" the lady was saying in a sighing staccato as Archer came in.

The three turned with surprise at his appearance, and the lady, advancing, held out her hand.

"Dear Mr. Archer—almost my cousin Newland!" she said. "I am the Marchioness Manson."

Archer bowed, and she continued: "My Ellen has taken me in for a few days. I came from Cuba, where I have been spending the winter with Spanish friends—such delightful distinguished people: the highest nobility of old Castile—how I wish you could know them! But I was called away by our dear great friend here, Dr. Carver. You don't know Dr. Agathon Carver, founder of the Valley of Love Community?"

Dr. Carver inclined his leonine head, and the Marchioness continued: "Ah, New York—New York—how little the life of the spirit has reached it! But I see you do know Mr. Winsett."

"Oh, yes—*I* reached him some time ago; but not by that route," Winsett said with his dry smile.

The Marchioness shook her head reprovingly. "How do you know, Mr. Winsett? The spirit bloweth where it listeth."

"List—oh, list!" interjected Dr. Carver in a stentorian murmur.

"But do sit down, Mr. Archer. We four have been having a delightful little dinner together, and my child has gone up to dress. She expects you; she will be down in a moment. We were just admiring these marvellous flowers, which will surprise her when she reappears."

Winsett remained on his feet. "I'm afraid I must be off. Please tell Madame Olenska that we shall all feel lost when she abandons our street. This house has been an oasis."

"Ah, but she won't abandon *you*. Poetry and art are the breath of life to her. It *is* poetry you write, Mr. Winsett?"

"Well, no; but I sometimes read it," said Winsett, including the group in a general nod and slipping out of the room.

"A caustic spirit—*un peu sauvage*. But so witty; Dr. Carver, you *do* think him witty?"

"I never think of wit," said Dr. Carver severely.

"Ah—ah—you never think of wit! How merciless he is to us weak mortals, Mr. Archer! But he lives only in the life of the spirit; and tonight he is mentally preparing the lecture he is to deliver presently at Mrs. Blenker's. Dr. Carver, would there be time, before you start for the Blenkers' to explain to Mr. Archer your illuminating discovery of the Direct Contact? But no; I see it is nearly nine o'clock, and we have no right to detain you while so many are waiting for your message."

Dr. Carver looked slightly disappointed at this conclusion, but, having compared his ponderous gold time-piece with Madame Olenska's little travelling-clock, he reluctantly gathered up his mighty limbs for departure.

"I shall see you later, dear friend?" he suggested to the Marchioness, who replied with a smile: "As soon as Ellen's carriage comes I will join you; I do hope the lecture won't have begun."

Dr. Carver looked thoughtfully at Archer. "Perhaps, if this young gentleman is interested in my experiences, Mrs. Blenker might allow you to bring him with you?"

"Oh, dear friend, if it were possible—I am sure she would be too happy. But I fear my Ellen counts on Mr. Archer herself."

"That," said Dr. Carver, "is unfortunate—but here is my card." He handed it to Archer, who read on it, in Gothic characters:

> 𝕬𝖌𝖆𝖙𝖍𝖔𝖓 𝕮𝖆𝖗𝖛𝖊𝖗
>
> 𝕿𝖍𝖊 𝖁𝖆𝖑𝖑𝖊𝖞 𝖔𝖋 𝕷𝖔𝖛𝖊
>
> 𝕶𝖎𝖙𝖙𝖆𝖘𝖖𝖚𝖆𝖙𝖙𝖆𝖒𝖞, 𝕹. 𝖸.

Dr. Carver bowed himself out, and Mrs. Manson, with a sigh that might have been either of regret or relief, again waved Archer to a seat.

"Ellen will be down in a moment; and before she comes, I am so glad of this quiet moment with you."

Archer murmured his pleasure at their meeting, and the Marchioness continued, in her low sighing accents: "I know everything, dear Mr. Archer—my child has told me all you have done for her. Your wise advice: your courageous firmness—thank heaven it was not too late!"

The young man listened with considerable embarrassment. Was there any one, he wondered, to whom Madame Olenska had not proclaimed his intervention in her private affairs?

"Madame Olenska exaggerates; I simply gave her a legal opinion, as she asked me to."

"Ah, but in doing it—in doing it you were the unconscious instrument of—of—what word have we moderns for Providence, Mr. Archer?" cried the lady, tilting her head on one side and drooping her lids mysteriously. "Little did you know that at that very moment I was being appealed to: being approached, in fact—from the other side of the Atlantic!"

She glanced over her shoulder, as though fearful of being overheard, and then, drawing her chair nearer, and raising a tiny ivory fan to her lips, breathed behind it: "By the Count himself—my poor, mad, foolish Olenski; who asks only to take her back on her own terms."

"Good God!" Archer exclaimed, springing up.

"You are horrified? Yes, of course; I understand. I don't defend poor Stanislas, though he has always called me his best friend. He does not defend himself—he casts himself at her feet: in my person." She tapped her emaciated bosom. "I have his letter here."

"A letter?— Has Madame Olenska seen it?" Archer stammered, his brain whirling with the shock of the announcement.

The Marchioness Manson shook her head softly. "Time—time; I must have time. I know my Ellen—haughty, intractable; shall I say, just a shade unforgiving?"

"But, good heavens, to forgive is one thing; to go back into that hell—"

"Ah, yes," the Marchioness acquiesced. "So she describes it—my sensitive child! But on the material side, Mr. Archer, if one may stoop to consider such things; do you know what she is giving up? Those roses there on the sofa—acres like them, under glass and in the open, in his matchless terraced gardens at Nice! Jewels—historic pearls: the Sobieski emeralds—sables—but she cares nothing for all these! Art and beauty, those she does care for, she lives for, as I always have; and those also surrounded her. Pictures, priceless furniture, music, brilliant conversation—ah, that, my dear young man, if you'll excuse me, is what you've no conception of here! And she had it all; and the homage of the greatest. She tells me she is not thought handsome in New York—good heavens! Her portrait has been painted nine times; the greatest artists in Europe have begged for the privilege. Are these things nothing? And the remorse of an adoring husband?"

As the Marchioness Manson rose to her climax her face assumed an expression of ecstatic retrospection which would have moved Archer's mirth had he not been numb with amazement.

He would have laughed if any one had foretold to him that his first sight of poor Medora Manson would have been in the guise of a messenger of Satan; but he was in no mood for laughing now, and she seemed to him to come straight out of the hell from which Ellen Olenska had just escaped.

"She knows nothing yet—of all this?" he asked abruptly.

Mrs. Manson laid a purple finger on her lips. "Nothing directly—but does she suspect? Who can tell? The truth is, Mr. Archer, I have been waiting to see you. From the moment I heard of the firm stand you had taken, and of your influence over her, I hoped it might be possible to count on your support—to convince you . . ."

"That she ought to go back? I would rather see her dead!" cried the young man violently.

"Ah," the Marchioness murmured, without visible resentment. For a while she sat in her arm-chair, opening and shutting the absurd ivory fan between her mittened fingers; but suddenly she lifted her head and listened.

"Here she comes," she said in a rapid whisper; and then, pointing to the bouquet on the sofa: "Am I to understand that you prefer *that*, Mr. Archer? After all, marriage is marriage . . . and my niece is still a wife. . . ."

XVIII

"WHAT ARE you two plotting together, aunt Medora?" Madame Olenska cried as she came into the room.

She was dressed as if for a ball. Everything about her shimmered and glimmered softly, as if her dress had been woven out of candle-beams; and she carried her head high, like a pretty woman challenging a roomful of rivals.

"We were saying, my dear, that here was something beautiful to surprise you with," Mrs. Manson rejoined, rising to her feet and pointing archly to the flowers.

Madame Olenska stopped short and looked at the bouquet. Her colour did not change, but a sort of white radiance of anger ran over her like summer lightning. "Ah," she exclaimed, in a shrill voice that the young man had never heard, "who is ridiculous enough to send me a bouquet? Why a bouquet? And why tonight of all nights? I am not going to a ball; I am not a girl engaged to be married. But some people are always ridiculous."

She turned back to the door, opened it, and called out: "Nastasia!"

The ubiquitous handmaiden promptly appeared, and Archer heard Madame Olenska say, in an Italian that she seemed to pronounce with intentional deliberateness in order that he might follow it: "Here—throw this into the dustbin!" and then, as Nastasia stared protestingly: "But no—it's not the fault of the poor flowers. Tell the boy to carry them to the house three doors away, the house of Mr. Winsett, the dark gentleman who dined here. His wife is ill—they may give her pleasure . . . The boy is out, you say? Then, my dear one, run yourself; here, put my cloak over you and fly. I want the thing out of the house immediately! And, as you live, don't say they come from me!"

She flung her velvet opera cloak over the maid's shoulders and turned back into the drawing-room, shutting the door sharply. Her bosom was rising high under its lace, and for a moment Archer thought she was about to cry; but she burst into a laugh instead, and looking from the Marchioness to

Archer, asked abruptly: "And you two—have you made friends!"

"It's for Mr. Archer to say, darling; he has waited patiently while you were dressing."

"Yes—I gave you time enough: my hair wouldn't go," Madame Olenska said, raising her hand to the heaped-up curls of her *chignon*. "But that reminds me: I see Dr. Carver is gone, and you'll be late at the Blenkers'. Mr. Archer, will you put my aunt in the carriage?"

She followed the Marchioness into the hall, saw her fitted into a miscellaneous heap of overshoes, shawls and tippets, and called from the doorstep: "Mind, the carriage is to be back for me at ten!" Then she returned to the drawing-room, where Archer, on re-entering it, found her standing by the mantelpiece, examining herself in the mirror. It was not usual, in New York society, for a lady to address her parlour-maid as "my dear one," and send her out on an errand wrapped in her own opera-cloak; and Archer, through all his deeper feelings, tasted the pleasurable excitement of being in a world where action followed on emotion with such Olympian speed.

Madame Olenska did not move when he came up behind her, and for a second their eyes met in the mirror; then she turned, threw herself into her sofa-corner, and sighed out: "There's time for a cigarette."

He handed her the box and lit a spill for her; and as the flame flashed up into her face she glanced at him with laughing eyes and said: "What do you think of me in a temper?"

Archer paused a moment; then he answered with sudden resolution: "It makes me understand what your aunt has been saying about you."

"I knew she'd been talking about me. Well?"

"She said you were used to all kinds of things—splendours and amusements and excitements—that we could never hope to give you here."

Madame Olenska smiled faintly into the circle of smoke about her lips.

"Medora is incorrigibly romantic. It has made up to her for so many things!"

Archer hesitated again, and again took his risk. "Is your aunt's romanticism always consistent with accuracy?"

"You mean: does she speak the truth?" Her niece considered. "Well, I'll tell you: in almost everything she says, there's something true and something untrue. But why do you ask? What has she been telling you?"

He looked away into the fire, and then back at her shining presence. His heart tightened with the thought that this was their last evening by that fireside, and that in a moment the carriage would come to carry her away.

"She says—she pretends that Count Olenski has asked her to persuade you to go back to him."

Madame Olenska made no answer. She sat motionless, holding her cigarette in her half-lifted hand. The expression of her face had not changed; and Archer remembered that he had before noticed her apparent incapacity for surprise.

"You knew, then?" he broke out.

She was silent for so long that the ash dropped from her cigarette. She brushed it to the floor. "She has hinted about a letter: poor darling! Medora's hints—"

"Is it at your husband's request that she has arrived here suddenly?"

Madame Olenska seemed to consider this question also. "There again: one can't tell. She told me she had had a 'spiritual summons,' whatever that is, from Dr. Carver. I'm afraid she's going to marry Dr. Carver . . . poor Medora, there's always some one she wants to marry. But perhaps the people in Cuba just got tired of her! I think she was with them as a sort of paid companion. Really, I don't know why she came."

"But you do believe she has a letter from your husband?"

Again Madame Olenska brooded silently; then she said: "After all, it was to be expected."

The young man rose and went to lean against the fireplace. A sudden restlessness possessed him, and he was tongue-tied by the sense that their minutes were numbered, and that at any moment he might hear the wheels of the returning carriage.

"You know that your aunt believes you will go back?"

Madame Olenska raised her head quickly. A deep blush

rose to her face and spread over her neck and shoulders. She blushed seldom and painfully, as if it hurt her like a burn.

"Many cruel things have been believed of me," she said.

"Oh, Ellen—forgive me; I'm a fool and a brute!"

She smiled a little. "You are horribly nervous; you have your own troubles. I know you think the Wellands are unreasonable about your marriage, and of course I agree with you. In Europe people don't understand our long American engagements; I suppose they are not as calm as we are." She pronounced the "we" with a faint emphasis that gave it an ironic sound.

Archer felt the irony but did not dare to take it up. After all, she had perhaps purposely deflected the conversation from her own affairs, and after the pain his last words had evidently caused her he felt that all he could do was to follow her lead. But the sense of the waning hour made him desperate: he could not bear the thought that a barrier of words should drop between them again.

"Yes," he said abruptly; "I went south to ask May to marry me after Easter. There's no reason why we shouldn't be married then."

"And May adores you—and yet you couldn't convince her? I thought her too intelligent to be the slave of such absurd superstitions."

"She *is* too intelligent—she's not their slave."

Madame Olenska looked at him. "Well, then—I don't understand."

Archer reddened, and hurried on with a rush. "We had a frank talk—almost the first. She thinks my impatience a bad sign."

"Merciful heavens—a bad sign?"

"She thinks it means that I can't trust myself to go on caring for her. She thinks, in short, I want to marry her at once to get away from some one that I—care for more."

Madame Olenska examined this curiously. "But if she thinks that—why isn't she in a hurry too?"

"Because she's not like that: she's so much nobler. She insists all the more on the long engagement, to give me time—"

"Time to give her up for the other woman?"

"If I want to."

Madame Olenska leaned toward the fire and gazed into it with fixed eyes. Down the quiet street Archer heard the approaching trot of her horses.

"That *is* noble," she said, with a slight break in her voice.

"Yes. But it's ridiculous."

"Ridiculous? Because you don't care for any one else?"

"Because I don't mean to marry any one else."

"Ah." There was another long interval. At length she looked up at him and asked: "This other woman—does she love you?"

"Oh, there's no other woman; I mean, the person that May was thinking of is—was never—"

"Then, why, after all, are you in such haste?"

"There's your carriage," said Archer.

She half-rose and looked about her with absent eyes. Her fan and gloves lay on the sofa beside her and she picked them up mechanically.

"Yes; I suppose I must be going."

"You're going to Mrs. Struthers's?"

"Yes." She smiled and added: "I must go where I am invited, or I should be too lonely. Why not come with me?"

Archer felt that at any cost he must keep her beside him, must make her give him the rest of her evening. Ignoring her question, he continued to lean against the chimney-piece, his eyes fixed on the hand in which she held her gloves and fan, as if watching to see if he had the power to make her drop them.

"May guessed the truth," he said. "There is another woman—but not the one she thinks."

Ellen Olenska made no answer, and did not move. After a moment he sat down beside her, and, taking her hand, softly unclasped it, so that the gloves and fan fell on the sofa between them.

She started up, and freeing herself from him moved away to the other side of the hearth. "Ah, don't make love to me! Too many people have done that," she said, frowning.

Archer, changing colour, stood up also: it was the bitterest rebuke she could have given him. "I have never made love to you," he said, "and I never shall. But you are the woman I would have married if it had been possible for either of us."

"Possible for either of us?" She looked at him with unfeigned astonishment. "And you say that—when it's you who've made it impossible?"

He stared at her, groping in a blackness through which a single arrow of light tore its blinding way.

"*I've* made it impossible—?"

"You, you, *you!*" she cried, her lip trembling like a child's on the verge of tears. "Isn't it you who made me give up divorcing—give it up because you showed me how selfish and wicked it was, how one must sacrifice one's self to preserve the dignity of marriage . . . and to spare one's family the publicity, the scandal? And because my family was going to be your family—for May's sake and for yours—I did what you told me, what you proved to me that I ought to do. Ah," she broke out with a sudden laugh, "I've made no secret of having done it for you!"

She sank down on the sofa again, crouching among the festive ripples of her dress like a stricken masquerader; and the young man stood by the fireplace and continued to gaze at her without moving.

"Good God," he groaned. "When I thought—"

"You thought?"

"Ah, don't ask me what I thought!"

Still looking at her, he saw the same burning flush creep up her neck to her face. She sat upright, facing him with a rigid dignity.

"I do ask you."

"Well, then: there were things in that letter you asked me to read—"

"My husband's letter?"

"Yes."

"I had nothing to fear from that letter: absolutely nothing! All I feared was to bring notoriety, scandal, on the family—on you and May."

"Good God," he groaned again, bowing his face in his hands.

The silence that followed lay on them with the weight of things final and irrevocable. It seemed to Archer to be crushing him down like his own grave-stone; in all the wide future he saw nothing that would ever lift that load from his heart. He did not move from his place, or raise his head from his hands; his hidden eyeballs went on staring into utter darkness.

"At least I loved you—" he brought out.

On the other side of the hearth, from the sofa-corner where he supposed that she still crouched, he heard a faint stifled crying like a child's. He started up and came to her side.

"Ellen! What madness! Why are you crying? Nothing's done that can't be undone. I'm still free, and you're going to be." He had her in his arms, her face like a wet flower at his lips, and all their vain terrors shrivelling up like ghosts at sunrise. The one thing that astonished him now was that he should have stood for five minutes arguing with her across the width of the room, when just touching her made everything so simple.

She gave him back all his kiss, but after a moment he felt her stiffening in his arms, and she put him aside and stood up.

"Ah, my poor Newland—I suppose this had to be. But it doesn't in the least alter things," she said, looking down at him in her turn from the hearth.

"It alters the whole of life for me."

"No, no—it mustn't, it can't. You're engaged to May Welland; and I'm married."

He stood up too, flushed and resolute. "Nonsense! It's too late for that sort of thing. We've no right to lie to other people or to ourselves. We won't talk of your marriage; but do you see me marrying May after this?"

She stood silent, resting her thin elbows on the mantel-piece, her profile reflected in the glass behind her. One of the locks of her *chignon* had become loosened and hung on her neck; she looked haggard and almost old.

"I don't see you," she said at length, "putting that question to May. Do you?"

He gave a reckless shrug. "It's too late to do anything else."

"You say that because it's the easiest thing to say at this moment—not because it's true. In reality it's too late to do anything but what we'd both decided on."

"Ah, I don't understand you!"

She forced a pitiful smile that pinched her face instead of smoothing it. "You don't understand because you haven't yet guessed how you've changed things for me: oh, from the first—long before I knew all you'd done."

"All I'd done?"

"Yes. I was perfectly unconscious at first that people here were shy of me—that they thought I was a dreadful sort of person. It seems they had even refused to meet me at dinner. I found that out afterward; and how you'd made your mother go with you to the van der Luydens'; and how you'd insisted on announcing your engagement at the Beaufort ball, so that I might have two families to stand by me instead of one—"

At that he broke into a laugh.

"Just imagine," she said, "how stupid and unobservant I was! I knew nothing of all this till Granny blurted it out one day. New York simply meant peace and freedom to me: it was coming home. And I was so happy at being among my own people that every one I met seemed kind and good, and glad to see me. But from the very beginning," she continued, "I felt there was no one as kind as you; no one who gave me reasons that I understood for doing what at first seemed so hard and—unnecessary. The very good people didn't convince me; I felt they'd never been tempted. But you knew; you understood; you had felt the world outside tugging at one with all its golden hands—and yet you hated the things it asks of one; you hated happiness bought by disloyalty and cruelty and indifference. That was what I'd never known before—and it's better than anything I've known."

She spoke in a low even voice, without tears or visible agitation; and each word, as it dropped from her, fell into his breast like burning lead. He sat bowed over, his head between his hands, staring at the hearth-rug, and at the tip of the satin shoe that showed under her dress. Suddenly he knelt down and kissed the shoe.

She bent over him, laying her hands on his shoulders, and looking at him with eyes so deep that he remained motionless under her gaze.

"Ah, don't let us undo what you've done!" she cried. "I

can't go back now to that other way of thinking. I can't love you unless I give you up."

His arms were yearning up to her; but she drew away, and they remained facing each other, divided by the distance that her words had created. Then, abruptly, his anger overflowed.

"And Beaufort? Is he to replace me?"

As the words sprang out he was prepared for an answering flare of anger; and he would have welcomed it as fuel for his own. But Madame Olenska only grew a shade paler, and stood with her arms hanging down before her, and her head slightly bent, as her way was when she pondered a question.

"He's waiting for you now at Mrs. Struthers's; why don't you go to him?" Archer sneered.

She turned to ring the bell. "I shall not go out this evening; tell the carriage to go and fetch the Signora Marchesa," she said when the maid came.

After the door had closed again Archer continued to look at her with bitter eyes. "Why this sacrifice? Since you tell me that you're lonely I've no right to keep you from your friends."

She smiled a little under her wet lashes. "I shan't be lonely now. I *was* lonely; I *was* afraid. But the emptiness and the darkness are gone; when I turn back into myself now I'm like a child going at night into a room where there's always a light."

Her tone and her look still enveloped her in a soft inaccessibility, and Archer groaned out again: "I don't understand you!"

"Yet you understand May!"

He reddened under the retort, but kept his eyes on her. "May is ready to give me up."

"What! Three days after you've entreated her on your knees to hasten your marriage?"

"She's refused; that gives me the right—"

"Ah, you've taught me what an ugly word that is," she said.

He turned away with a sense of utter weariness. He felt as though he had been struggling for hours up the face of a steep precipice, and now, just as he had fought his way to the top, his hold had given way and he was pitching down headlong into darkness.

If he could have got her in his arms again he might have swept away her arguments; but she still held him at a distance by something inscrutably aloof in her look and attitude, and by his own awed sense of her sincerity. At length he began to plead again.

"If we do this now it will be worse afterward—worse for every one—"

"No—no—no!" she almost screamed, as if he frightened her.

At that moment the bell sent a long tinkle through the house. They had heard no carriage stopping at the door, and they stood motionless, looking at each other with startled eyes.

Outside, Nastasia's step crossed the hall, the outer door opened, and a moment later she came in carrying a telegram which she handed to the Countess Olenska.

"The lady was very happy at the flowers," Nastasia said, smoothing her apron. "She thought it was her *signor marito* who had sent them, and she cried a little and said it was a folly."

Her mistress smiled and took the yellow envelope. She tore it open and carried it to the lamp; then, when the door had closed again, she handed the telegram to Archer.

It was dated from St. Augustine, and addressed to the Countess Olenska. In it he read: "Granny's telegram successful. Papa and Mamma agree marriage after Easter. Am telegraphing Newland. Am too happy for words and love you dearly. Your grateful May."

Half an hour later, when Archer unlocked his own front-door, he found a similar envelope on the hall-table on top of his pile of notes and letters. The message inside the envelope was also from May Welland, and ran as follows: "Parents consent wedding Tuesday after Easter at twelve Grace Church eight bridesmaids please see Rector so happy love May."

Archer crumpled up the yellow sheet as if the gesture could annihilate the news it contained. Then he pulled out a small pocket-diary and turned over the pages with trembling fingers; but he did not find what he wanted, and cramming the telegram into his pocket he mounted the stairs.

A light was shining through the door of the little hall-room which served Janey as a dressing-room and boudoir, and her brother rapped impatiently on the panel. The door opened, and his sister stood before him in her immemorial purple flannel dressing-gown, with her hair "on pins." Her face looked pale and apprehensive.

"Newland! I hope there's no bad news in that telegram? I waited on purpose, in case—" (No item of his correspondence was safe from Janey.)

He took no notice of her question. "Look here—what day is Easter this year?"

She looked shocked at such unchristian ignorance. "Easter? Newland! Why, of course, the first week in April. Why?"

"The first week?" He turned again to the pages of his diary, calculating rapidly under his breath. "The first week, did you say?" He threw back his head with a long laugh.

"For mercy's sake what's the matter?"

"Nothing's the matter, except that I'm going to be married in a month."

Janey fell upon his neck and pressed him to her purple flannel breast. "Oh Newland, how wonderful! I'm so glad! But, dearest, why do you keep on laughing? Do hush, or you'll wake Mamma."

BOOK II

XIX

T HE DAY was fresh, with a lively spring wind full of dust. All the old ladies in both families had got out their faded sables and yellowing ermines, and the smell of camphor from the front pews almost smothered the faint spring scent of the lilies banking the altar.

Newland Archer, at a signal from the sexton, had come out of the vestry and placed himself with his best man on the chancel step of Grace Church.

The signal meant that the brougham bearing the bride and her father was in sight; but there was sure to be a considerable interval of adjustment and consultation in the lobby, where the bridesmaids were already hovering like a cluster of Easter blossoms. During this unavoidable lapse of time the bridegroom, in proof of his eagerness was expected to expose himself alone to the gaze of the assembled company; and Archer had gone through this formality as resignedly as through all the others which made of a nineteenth century New York wedding a rite that seemed to belong to the dawn of history. Everything was equally easy—or equally painful, as one chose to put it—in the path he was committed to tread, and he had obeyed the flurried injunctions of his best man as piously as other bridegrooms had obeyed his own, in the days when he had guided them through the same labyrinth.

So far he was reasonably sure of having fulfilled all his obligations. The bridesmaids' eight bouquets of white lilac and lilies-of-the-valley had been sent in due time, as well as the gold and sapphire sleeve-links of the eight ushers and the best man's cat's-eye scarf-pin; Archer had sat up half the night trying to vary the wording of his thanks for the last batch of presents from men friends and ex-lady-loves; the fees for the Bishop and the Rector were safely in the pocket of his best man; his own luggage was already at Mrs. Manson Mingott's, where the wedding-breakfast was to take place, and so were the travelling clothes into which he was to change; and a private compartment had been engaged in the train that was to carry the young couple to their unknown destination—concealment of the spot in which the bridal night was to be spent being one of the most sacred taboos of the prehistoric ritual.

"Got the ring all right?" whispered young van der Luyden Newland, who was inexperienced in the duties of a best man, and awed by the weight of his responsibility.

Archer made the gesture which he had seen so many bridegrooms make: with his ungloved right hand he felt in the pocket of his dark grey waistcoat, and assured himself that the little gold circlet (engraved inside: *Newland to May, April* ——, *187*—) was in its place; then, resuming his former attitude, his tall hat and pearl-grey gloves with black stitchings grasped in his left hand, he stood looking at the door of the church.

Overhead, Handel's March swelled pompously through the imitation stone vaulting, carrying on its waves the faded drift of the many weddings at which, with cheerful indifference, he had stood on the same chancel step watching other brides float up the nave toward other bridegrooms.

"How like a first night at the Opera!" he thought, recognising all the same faces in the same boxes (no, pews), and wondering if, when the Last Trump sounded, Mrs. Selfridge Merry would be there with the same towering ostrich feathers in her bonnet, and Mrs. Beaufort with the same diamond earrings and the same smile—and whether suitable proscenium seats were already prepared for them in another world.

After that there was still time to review, one by one, the familiar countenances in the first rows; the women's sharp with curiosity and excitement, the men's sulky with the obligation of having to put on their frock-coats before luncheon, and fight for food at the wedding-breakfast.

"Too bad the breakfast is at old Catherine's," the bridegroom could fancy Reggie Chivers saying. "But I'm told that Lovell Mingott insisted on its being cooked by his own *chef*, so it ought to be good if one can only get at it." And he could imagine Sillerton Jackson adding with authority: "My dear fellow, haven't you heard? It's to be served at small tables, in the new English fashion."

Archer's eyes lingered a moment on the left-hand pew, where his mother, who had entered the church on Mr. Henry van der Luyden's arm, sat weeping softly under her Chantilly veil, her hands in her grandmother's ermine muff.

"Poor Janey!" he thought, looking at his sister, "even by screwing her head around she can see only the people in the few front pews; and they're mostly dowdy Newlands and Dagonets."

On the hither side of the white ribbon dividing off the seats reserved for the families he saw Beaufort, tall and red-faced, scrutinising the women with his arrogant stare. Beside him sat his wife, all silvery chinchilla and violets; and on the far side of the ribbon, Lawrence Lefferts's sleekly brushed head seemed to mount guard over the invisible deity of "Good Form" who presided at the ceremony.

Archer wondered how many flaws Lefferts's keen eyes would discover in the ritual of his divinity; then he suddenly recalled that he too had once thought such questions important. The things that had filled his days seemed now like a nursery parody of life, or like the wrangles of mediæval schoolmen over metaphysical terms that nobody had ever understood. A stormy discussion as to whether the wedding presents should be "shown" had darkened the last hours before the wedding; and it seemed inconceivable to Archer that grown-up people should work themselves into a state of agitation over such trifles, and that the matter should have been decided (in the negative) by Mrs. Welland's saying, with indignant tears: "I should as soon turn the reporters loose in my house." Yet there was a time when Archer had had definite and rather aggressive opinions on all such problems, and when everything concerning the manners and customs of his little tribe had seemed to him fraught with world-wide significance.

"And all the while, I suppose," he thought, "real people were living somewhere, and real things happening to them . . ."

"There they come!" breathed the best man excitedly; but the bridegroom knew better.

The cautious opening of the door of the church meant only that Mr. Brown the livery-stable keeper (gowned in black in his intermittent character of sexton) was taking a preliminary survey of the scene before marshalling his forces. The door was softly shut again; then after another interval it swung majestically open, and a murmur ran through the church: "The family!"

Mrs. Welland came first, on the arm of her eldest son. Her large pink face was appropriately solemn, and her plum-coloured satin with pale blue side-panels, and blue ostrich plumes in a small satin bonnet, met with general approval; but before she had settled herself with a stately rustle in the pew opposite Mrs. Archer's the spectators were craning their necks to see who was coming after her. Wild rumours had been abroad the day before to the effect that Mrs. Manson Mingott, in spite of her physical disabilities, had resolved on being present at the ceremony; and the idea was so much in keeping with her sporting character that bets ran high at the clubs as to her being able to walk up the nave and squeeze into a seat. It was known that she had insisted on sending her own carpenter to look into the possibility of taking down the end panel of the front pew, and to measure the space between the seat and the front; but the result had been discouraging, and for one anxious day her family had watched her dallying with the plan of being wheeled up the nave in her enormous Bath chair and sitting enthroned in it at the foot of the chancel.

The idea of this monstrous exposure of her person was so painful to her relations that they could have covered with gold the ingenious person who suddenly discovered that the chair was too wide to pass between the iron uprights of the awning which extended from the church door to the curb-stone. The idea of doing away with this awning, and revealing the bride to the mob of dressmakers and newspaper reporters who stood outside fighting to get near the joints of the canvas, exceeded even old Catherine's courage, though for a moment she had weighed the possibility. "Why, they might take a photograph of my child *and put it in the papers!*" Mrs. Welland exclaimed when her mother's last plan was hinted to her; and from this unthinkable indecency the clan recoiled with a collective shudder. The ancestress had had to give in; but her concession was bought only by the promise that the wedding-breakfast should take place under her roof, though (as the Washington Square connection said) with the Wellands' house in easy reach it was hard to have to make a special price with Brown to drive one to the other end of nowhere.

Though all these transactions had been widely reported by the Jacksons a sporting minority still clung to the belief that old Catherine would appear in church, and there was a distinct lowering of the temperature when she was found to have been replaced by her daughter-in-law. Mrs. Lovell Mingott had the high colour and glassy stare induced in ladies of her age and habit by the effort of getting into a new dress; but once the disappointment occasioned by her mother-in-law's non-appearance had subsided, it was agreed that her black Chantilly over lilac satin, with a bonnet of Parma violets, formed the happiest contrast to Mrs. Welland's blue and plum-colour. Far different was the impression produced by the gaunt and mincing lady who followed on Mr. Mingott's arm, in a wild dishevelment of stripes and fringes and floating scarves; and as this last apparition glided into view Archer's heart contracted and stopped beating.

He had taken it for granted that the Marchioness Manson was still in Washington, where she had gone some four weeks previously with her niece, Madame Olenska. It was generally understood that their abrupt departure was due to Madame Olenska's desire to remove her aunt from the baleful eloquence of Dr. Agathon Carver, who had nearly succeeded in enlisting her as a recruit for the Valley of Love; and in the circumstances no one had expected either of the ladies to return for the wedding. For a moment Archer stood with his eyes fixed on Medora's fantastic figure, straining to see who came behind her; but the little procession was at an end, for all the lesser members of the family had taken their seats, and the eight tall ushers, gathering themselves together like birds or insects preparing for some migratory manœuvre, were already slipping through the side doors into the lobby.

"Newland—I say: *she's here!*" the best man whispered.

Archer roused himself with a start.

A long time had apparently passed since his heart had stopped beating, for the white and rosy procession was in fact half way up the nave, the Bishop, the Rector and two white-winged assistants were hovering about the flower-banked altar, and the first chords of the Spohr symphony were strewing their flower-like notes before the bride.

Archer opened his eyes (but could they really have been shut, as he imagined?), and felt his heart beginning to resume its usual task. The music, the scent of the lilies on the altar, the vision of the cloud of tulle and orange-blossoms floating nearer and nearer, the sight of Mrs. Archer's face suddenly convulsed with happy sobs, the low benedictory murmur of the Rector's voice, the ordered evolutions of the eight pink bridesmaids and the eight black ushers: all these sights, sounds and sensations, so familiar in themselves, so unutterably strange and meaningless in his new relation to them, were confusedly mingled in his brain.

"My God," he thought, "*have* I got the ring?"—and once more he went through the bridegroom's convulsive gesture.

Then, in a moment, May was beside him, such radiance streaming from her that it sent a faint warmth through his numbness, and he straightened himself and smiled into her eyes.

"Dearly beloved, we are gathered together here," the Rector began . . .

The ring was on her hand, the Bishop's benediction had been given, the bridesmaids were a-poise to resume their place in the procession, and the organ was showing preliminary symptoms of breaking out into the Mendelssohn March, without which no newly-wedded couple had ever emerged upon New York.

"Your arm—*I say, give her your arm!*" young Newland nervously hissed; and once more Archer became aware of having been adrift far off in the unknown. What was it that had sent him there, he wondered? Perhaps the glimpse, among the anonymous spectators in the transept, of a dark coil of hair under a hat which, a moment later, revealed itself as belonging to an unknown lady with a long nose, so laughably unlike the person whose image she had evoked that he asked himself if he were becoming subject to hallucinations.

And now he and his wife were pacing slowly down the nave, carried forward on the light Mendelssohn ripples, the spring day beckoning to them through widely opened doors, and Mrs. Welland's chestnuts, with big white favours on their frontlets, curvetting and showing off at the far end of the canvas tunnel.

The footman, who had a still bigger white favour on his lapel, wrapped May's white cloak about her, and Archer jumped into the brougham at her side. She turned to him with a triumphant smile and their hands clasped under her veil.

"Darling!" Archer said—and suddenly the same black abyss yawned before him and he felt himself sinking into it, deeper and deeper, while his voice rambled on smoothly and cheerfully: "Yes, of course I thought I'd lost the ring; no wedding would be complete if the poor devil of a bridegroom didn't go through that. But you *did* keep me waiting, you know! I had time to think of every horror that might possibly happen."

She surprised him by turning, in full Fifth Avenue, and flinging her arms about his neck. "But none ever *can* happen now, can it, Newland, as long as we two are together?"

Every detail of the day had been so carefully thought out that the young couple, after the wedding-breakfast, had ample time to put on their travelling-clothes, descend the wide Mingott stairs between laughing bridesmaids and weeping parents, and get into the brougham under the traditional shower of rice and satin slippers; and there was still half an hour left in which to drive to the station, buy the last weeklies at the bookstall with the air of seasoned travellers, and settle themselves in the reserved compartment in which May's maid had already placed her dove-coloured travelling cloak and glaringly new dressing-bag from London.

The old du Lac aunts at Rhinebeck had put their house at the disposal of the bridal couple, with a readiness inspired by the prospect of spending a week in New York with Mrs. Archer; and Archer, glad to escape the usual "bridal suite" in a Philadelphia or Baltimore hotel, had accepted with an equal alacrity.

May was enchanted at the idea of going to the country, and childishly amused at the vain efforts of the eight bridesmaids to discover where their mysterious retreat was situated. It was thought "very English" to have a country-house lent to one, and the fact gave a last touch of distinction to what was generally conceded to be the most brilliant wedding of the year; but where the house was no one was permitted to know, except the parents of bride and groom, who, when taxed with the knowledge, pursed their lips and said mysteriously: "Ah, they didn't tell us—" which was manifestly true, since there was no need to.

Once they were settled in their compartment, and the train, shaking off the endless wooden suburbs, had pushed out into the pale landscape of spring, talk became easier than Archer had expected. May was still, in look and tone, the simple girl of yesterday, eager to compare notes with him as to the incidents of the wedding, and discussing them as impartially as a bridesmaid talking it all over with an usher. At first Archer had fancied that this detachment was the disguise of an inward tremor; but her clear eyes revealed only the most tranquil unawareness. She was alone for the first time with her husband; but her husband was only the charming comrade of yesterday. There was no one whom she liked as much, no one whom she trusted as completely, and the culminating "lark" of the whole delightful adventure of engagement and marriage was to be off with him alone on a journey, like a grownup person, like a "married woman," in fact.

It was wonderful that—as he had learned in the Mission garden at St. Augustine—such depths of feeling could co-exist with such absence of imagination. But he remembered how, even then, she had surprised him by dropping back to inexpressive girlishness as soon as her conscience had been eased of its burden; and he saw that she would probably go through life dealing to the best of her ability with each experience as it came, but never anticipating any by so much as a stolen glance.

Perhaps that faculty of unawareness was what gave her eyes their transparency, and her face the look of representing a type rather than a person; as if she might have been chosen to pose for a Civic Virtue or a Greek goddess. The blood that ran so close to her fair skin might have been a preserving fluid rather than a ravaging element; yet her look of indestructible youthfulness made her seem neither hard nor dull, but only primitive and pure. In the thick of this meditation Archer suddenly felt himself looking at her with the startled gaze of a stranger, and plunged into a reminiscence of the wedding-breakfast and of Granny Mingott's immense and triumphant pervasion of it.

May settled down to frank enjoyment of the subject. "I was surprised, though—weren't you?—that aunt Medora came after all. Ellen wrote that they were neither of them well enough to take the journey; I do wish it had been she who had recovered! Did you see the exquisite old lace she sent me?"

He had known that the moment must come sooner or later, but he had somewhat imagined that by force of willing he might hold it at bay.

"Yes—I—no: yes, it was beautiful," he said, looking at her blindly, and wondering if, whenever he heard those two syllables, all his carefully built-up world would tumble about him like a house of cards.

"Aren't you tired? It will be good to have some tea when we arrive—I'm sure the aunts have got everything beautifully ready," he rattled on, taking her hand in his; and her mind rushed away instantly to the magnificent tea and coffee service of Baltimore silver which the Beauforts had sent, and which "went" so perfectly with uncle Lovell Mingott's trays and side-dishes.

In the spring twilight the train stopped at the Rhinebeck station, and they walked along the platform to the waiting carriage.

"Ah, how awfully kind of the van der Luydens—they've sent their man over from Skuytercliff to meet us," Archer exclaimed, as a sedate person out of livery approached them and relieved the maid of her bags.

"I'm extremely sorry, sir," said this emissary, "that a little accident has occurred at the Miss du Lacs': a leak in the water-tank. It happened yesterday, and Mr. van der Luyden, who heard of it this morning, sent a house-maid up by the early train to get the Patroon's house ready. It will be quite comfortable, I think you'll find, sir; and the Miss du Lacs have sent their cook over, so that it will be exactly the same as if you'd been at Rhinebeck."

Archer stared at the speaker so blankly that he repeated in

still more apologetic accents: "It'll be exactly the same, sir, I do assure you—" and May's eager voice broke out, covering the embarrassed silence: "The same as Rhinebeck? The Patroon's house? But it will be a hundred thousand times better—won't it, Newland? It's too dear and kind of Mr. van der Luyden to have thought of it."

And as they drove off, with the maid beside the coachman, and their shining bridal bags on the seat before them, she went on excitedly: "Only fancy, I've never been inside it—have you? The van der Luydens show it to so few people. But they opened it for Ellen, it seems, and she told me what a darling little place it was: she says it's the only house she's seen in America that she could imagine being perfectly happy in."

"Well—that's what we're going to be, isn't it?" cried her husband gaily; and she answered with her boyish smile: "Ah, it's just our luck beginning—the wonderful luck we're always going to have together!"

XX

"O F COURSE we must dine with Mrs. Carfry, dearest," Archer said; and his wife looked at him with an anxious frown across the monumental Britannia ware of their lodging house breakfast-table.

In all the rainy desert of autumnal London there were only two people whom the Newland Archers knew; and these two they had sedulously avoided, in conformity with the old New York tradition that it was not "dignified" to force one's self on the notice of one's acquaintances in foreign countries.

Mrs. Archer and Janey, in the course of their visits to Europe, had so unflinchingly lived up to this principle, and met the friendly advances of their fellow-travellers with an air of such impenetrable reserve, that they had almost achieved the record of never having exchanged a word with a "foreigner" other than those employed in hotels and railway-stations. Their own compatriots—save those previously known or properly accredited—they treated with an even more pronounced disdain; so that, unless they ran across a Chivers, a Dagonet or a Mingott, their months abroad were spent in an unbroken *tête-à-tête*. But the utmost precautions are sometimes unavailing; and one night at Botzen one of the two English ladies in the room across the passage (whose names, dress and social situation were already intimately known to Janey) had knocked on the door and asked if Mrs. Archer had a bottle of liniment. The other lady—the intruder's sister, Mrs. Carfry—had been seized with a sudden attack of bronchitis; and Mrs. Archer, who never travelled without a complete family pharmacy, was fortunately able to produce the required remedy.

Mrs. Carfry was very ill, and as she and her sister Miss Harle were travelling alone they were profoundly grateful to the Archer ladies, who supplied them with ingenious comforts and whose efficient maid helped to nurse the invalid back to health.

When the Archers left Botzen they had no idea of ever seeing Mrs. Carfry and Miss Harle again. Nothing, to Mrs. Archer's mind, would have been more "undignified" than to force one's self on the notice of a "foreigner" to whom one had happened to render an accidental service. But Mrs. Carfry and her sister, to whom this point of view was unknown, and who would have found it utterly incomprehensible, felt themselves linked by an eternal gratitude to the "delightful Americans" who had been so kind at Botzen. With touching fidelity they seized every chance of meeting Mrs. Archer and Janey in the course of their continental travels, and displayed a supernatural acuteness in finding out when they were to pass through London on their way to or from the States. The intimacy became indissoluble, and Mrs. Archer and Janey, whenever they alighted at Brown's Hotel, found themselves awaited by two affectionate friends who, like themselves, cultivated ferns in Wardian cases, made macramé lace, read the memoirs of the Baroness Bunsen and had views about the occupants of the leading London pulpits. As Mrs. Archer said, it made "another thing of London" to know Mrs. Carfry and Miss Harle; and by the time that Newland became engaged the tie between the families was so firmly established that it was thought "only right" to send a wedding invitation to the two English ladies, who sent, in return, a pretty bouquet of pressed Alpine flowers under glass. And on the dock, when Newland and his wife sailed for England, Mrs. Archer's last word had been: "You must take May to see Mrs. Carfry."

Newland and his wife had had no idea of obeying this injunction; but Mrs. Carfry, with her usual acuteness, had run them down and sent them an invitation to dine; and it was over this invitation that May Archer was wrinkling her brows across the tea and muffins.

"It's all very well for you, Newland; you *know* them. But I shall feel so shy among a lot of people I've never met. And what shall I wear?"

Newland leaned back in his chair and smiled at her. She looked handsomer and more Diana-like than ever. The moist English air seemed to have deepened the bloom of her cheeks and softened the slight hardness of her virginal features; or else it was simply the inner glow of happiness, shining through like a light under ice.

"Wear, dearest? I thought a trunkful of things had come from Paris last week."

"Yes, of course. I meant to say that I shan't know *which* to wear." She pouted a little. "I've never dined out in London; and I don't want to be ridiculous."

He tried to enter into her perplexity. "But don't English-women dress just like everybody else in the evening?"

"Newland! How can you ask such funny questions? When they go to the theatre in old ball-dresses and bare heads."

"Well, perhaps they wear new ball-dresses at home; but at any rate Mrs. Carfry and Miss Harle won't. They'll wear caps like my mother's—and shawls; very soft shawls."

"Yes; but how will the other women be dressed?"

"Not as well as you, dear," he rejoined, wondering what had suddenly developed in her Janey's morbid interest in clothes.

She pushed back her chair with a sigh. "That's dear of you, Newland; but it doesn't help me much."

He had an inspiration. "Why not wear your wedding-dress? That can't be wrong, can it?"

"Oh, dearest! If I only had it here! But it's gone to Paris to be made over for next winter, and Worth hasn't sent it back."

"Oh, well—" said Archer, getting up. "Look here—the fog's lifting. If we made a dash for the National Gallery we might manage to catch a glimpse of the pictures."

The Newland Archers were on their way home, after a three months' wedding-tour which May, in writing to her girl friends, vaguely summarised as "blissful."

They had not gone to the Italian Lakes: on reflection, Archer had not been able to picture his wife in that particular setting. Her own inclination (after a month with the Paris dressmakers) was for mountaineering in July and swimming in August. This plan they punctually fulfilled, spending July at Interlaken and Grindelwald, and August at a little place called Etretat, on the Normandy coast, which some one had recommended as quaint and quiet. Once or twice, in the mountains, Archer had pointed southward and said: "There's Italy"; and May, her feet in a gentian-bed, had smiled cheerfully, and replied: "It would be lovely to go there next winter, if only you didn't have to be in New York."

But in reality travelling interested her even less than he had expected. She regarded it (once her clothes were ordered) as merely an enlarged opportunity for walking, riding, swimming, and trying her hand at the fascinating new game of lawn tennis; and when they finally got back to London (where they were to spend a fortnight while he ordered *his* clothes) she no longer concealed the eagerness with which she looked forward to sailing.

In London nothing interested her but the theatres and the shops; and she found the theatres less exciting than the Paris *cafés chantants* where, under the blossoming horse-chestnuts of the Champs Élysées, she had had the novel experience of looking down from the restaurant terrace on an audience of "cocottes," and having her husband interpret to her as much of the songs as he thought suitable for bridal ears.

Archer had reverted to all his old inherited ideas about marriage. It was less trouble to conform with the tradition and treat May exactly as all his friends treated their wives than to try to put into practice the theories with which his untrammelled bachelorhood had dallied. There was no use in trying to emancipate a wife who had not the dimmest notion that she was not free; and he had long since discovered that May's only use of the liberty she supposed herself to possess would be to lay it on the altar of her wifely adoration. Her innate dignity would always keep her from making the gift abjectly; and a day might even come (as it once had) when she would find strength to take it altogether back if she thought she were doing it for his own good. But with a conception of marriage so uncomplicated and incurious as hers such a crisis could be brought about only by something visibly outrageous in his own conduct; and the fineness of her feeling for him made that unthinkable. Whatever happened, he knew, she would always be loyal, gallant and unresentful; and that pledged him to the practice of the same virtues.

All this tended to draw him back into his old habits of mind. If her simplicity had been the simplicity of pettiness he would have chafed and rebelled; but since the lines of her character, though so few, were on the same fine mould as her face, she became the tutelary divinity of all his old traditions and reverences.

Such qualities were scarcely of the kind to enliven foreign travel, though they made her so easy and pleasant a companion; but he saw at once how they would fall into place in their proper setting. He had no fear of being oppressed by them, for his artistic and intellectual life would go on, as it always had, outside the domestic circle; and within it there would be nothing small and stifling—coming back to his wife would never be like entering a stuffy room after a tramp in the open. And when they had children the vacant corners in both their lives would be filled.

All these things went through his mind during their long slow drive from Mayfair to South Kensington, where Mrs. Carfry and her sister lived. Archer too would have preferred to escape their friends' hospitality: in conformity with the family tradition he had always travelled as a sight-seer and looker-on, affecting a haughty unconsciousness of the presence of his fellow-beings. Once only, just after Harvard, he had spent a few gay weeks at Florence with a band of queer Europeanised Americans, dancing all night with titled ladies in palaces, and gambling half the day with the rakes and dandies of the fashionable club; but it had all seemed to him, though the greatest fun in the world, as unreal as a carnival. These queer cosmopolitan women, deep in complicated love-affairs which they appeared to feel the need of retailing to every one they met, and the magnificent young officers and elderly dyed wits who were the subjects or the recipients of their confidences, were too different from the people Archer had grown up among, too much like expensive and rather malodorous hot-house exotics, to detain his imagination long. To introduce his wife into such a society was out of the question; and in the course of his travels no other had shown any marked eagerness for his company.

Not long after their arrival in London he had run across the Duke of St. Austrey, and the Duke, instantly and cordially recognising him, had said: "Look me up, won't you?"—but no proper-spirited American would have considered that a suggestion to be acted on, and the meeting was without a sequel. They had even managed to avoid May's English aunt, the banker's wife, who was still in Yorkshire; in fact, they had purposely postponed going to London till the autumn in order that their arrival during the season might not appear pushing and snobbish to these unknown relatives.

"Probably there'll be nobody at Mrs. Carfry's—London's a desert at this season, and you've made yourself much too beautiful," Archer said to May, who sat at his side in the hansom so spotlessly splendid in her sky-blue cloak edged with swansdown that it seemed wicked to expose her to the London grime.

"I don't want them to think that we dress like savages," she replied, with a scorn that Pocahontas might have resented; and he was struck again by the religious reverence of even the most unworldly American women for the social advantages of dress.

"It's their armour," he thought, "their defence against the unknown, and their defiance of it." And he understood for the first time the earnestness with which May, who was incapable of tying a ribbon in her hair to charm him, had gone through the solemn rite of selecting and ordering her extensive wardrobe.

He had been right in expecting the party at Mrs. Carfry's to be a small one. Besides their hostess and her sister, they found, in the long chilly drawing-room, only another shawled lady, a genial Vicar who was her husband, a silent lad whom Mrs. Carfry named as her nephew, and a small dark gentleman with lively eyes whom she introduced as his tutor, pronouncing a French name as she did so.

Into this dimly-lit and dim-featured group May Archer floated like a swan with the sunset on her: she seemed larger, fairer, more voluminously rustling than her husband had ever seen her; and he perceived that the rosiness and rustlingness were the tokens of an extreme and infantile shyness.

"What on earth will they expect me to talk about?" her helpless eyes implored him, at the very moment that her dazzling apparition was calling forth the same anxiety in their own bosoms. But beauty, even when distrustful of itself, awakens confidence in the manly heart; and the Vicar and the French-named tutor were soon manifesting to May their desire to put her at her ease.

In spite of their best efforts, however, the dinner was a languishing affair. Archer noticed that his wife's way of showing herself at her ease with foreigners was to become more uncompromisingly local in her references, so that, though her loveliness was an encouragement to admiration, her conversation was a chill to repartee. The Vicar soon abandoned the struggle; but the tutor, who spoke the most fluent and accomplished English, gallantly continued to pour it out to her until the ladies, to the manifest relief of all concerned, went up to the drawing-room.

The Vicar, after a glass of port, was obliged to hurry away to a meeting, and the shy nephew, who appeared to be an invalid, was packed off to bed. But Archer and the tutor continued to sit over their wine, and suddenly Archer found himself talking as he had not done since his last symposium with Ned Winsett. The Carfry nephew, it turned out, had been threatened with consumption, and had had to leave Harrow for Switzerland, where he had spent two years in the milder air of Lake Leman. Being a bookish youth, he had been entrusted to M. Rivière, who had brought him back to England, and was to remain with him till he went up to Oxford the following spring; and M. Rivière added with simplicity that he should then have to look out for another job.

It seemed impossible, Archer thought, that he should be long without one, so varied were his interests and so many his gifts. He was a man of about thirty, with a thin ugly face (May would certainly have called him common-looking) to which the play of his ideas gave an intense expressiveness; but there was nothing frivolous or cheap in his animation.

His father, who had died young, had filled a small diplomatic post, and it had been intended that the son should follow the same career; but an insatiable taste for letters had thrown the young man into journalism, then into authorship (apparently unsuccessful), and at length—after other experiments and vicissitudes which he spared his listener—into tutoring English youths in Switzerland. Before that, however, he had lived much in Paris, frequented the Goncourt *grenier*, been advised by Maupassant not to attempt to write (even that seemed to Archer a dazzling honour!), and had often talked with Mérimée in his mother's house. He had obviously always been desperately poor and anxious (having a mother and an unmarried sister to provide for), and it was apparent that his literary ambitions had failed. His situation, in fact, seemed, materially speaking, no more brilliant than Ned Winsett's; but he had lived in a world in which, as he said, no one who loved ideas need hunger mentally. As it was precisely of that love that poor Winsett was starving to death, Archer looked with a sort of vicarious envy at this eager impecunious young man who had fared so richly in his poverty.

"You see, Monsieur, it's worth everything, isn't it, to keep one's intellectual liberty, not to enslave one's powers of appreciation, one's critical independence? It was because of that that I abandoned journalism, and took to so much duller work: tutoring and private secretaryship. There is a good deal of drudgery, of course; but one preserves one's moral freedom, what we call in French one's *quant à soi*. And when one hears good talk one can join in it without compromising any opinions but one's own; or one can listen, and answer it inwardly. Ah, good conversation—there's nothing like it, is there? The air of ideas is the only air worth breathing. And so I have never regretted giving up either diplomacy or journalism—two different forms of the same self-abdication." He fixed his vivid eyes on Archer as he lit another cigarette. "*Voyez-vous*, Monsieur, to be able to look life in the face: that's worth living in a garret for, isn't it? But, after all, one must earn enough to pay for the garret; and I confess that to grow old as a private tutor—or a 'private' anything—is almost as chilling to the imagination as a second secretaryship at Bucharest. Sometimes I feel I must make a plunge: an immense plunge. Do you suppose, for instance, there would be any opening for me in America—in New York?"

Archer looked at him with startled eyes. New York, for a young man who had frequented the Goncourts and Flaubert, and who thought the life of ideas the only one worth living! He continued to stare at M. Rivière perplexedly, wondering how to tell him that his very superiorities and advantages would be the surest hindrance to success.

"New York—New York—but must it be especially New York?" he stammered, utterly unable to imagine what lucrative opening his native city could offer to a young man to whom good conversation appeared to be the only necessity.

A sudden flush rose under M. Rivière's sallow skin. "I—I

thought it your metropolis: is not the intellectual life more active there?" he rejoined; then, as if fearing to give his hearer the impression of having asked a favour, he went on hastily: "One throws out random suggestions—more to one's self than to others. In reality, I see no immediate prospect—" and rising from his seat he added, without a trace of constraint: "But Mrs. Carfry will think that I ought to be taking you upstairs."

During the homeward drive Archer pondered deeply on this episode. His hour with M. Rivière had put new air into his lungs, and his first impulse had been to invite him to dine the next day; but he was beginning to understand why married men did not always immediately yield to their first impulses.

"That young tutor is an interesting fellow: we had some awfully good talk after dinner about books and things," he threw out tentatively in the hansom.

May roused herself from one of the dreamy silences into which he had read so many meanings before six months of marriage had given him the key to them.

"The little Frenchman? Wasn't he dreadfully common?" she questioned coldly; and he guessed that she nursed a secret disappointment at having been invited out in London to meet a clergyman and a French tutor. The disappointment was not occasioned by the sentiment ordinarily defined as snobbishness, but by old New York's sense of what was due to it when it risked its dignity in foreign lands. If May's parents had entertained the Carfrys in Fifth Avenue they would have offered them something more substantial than a parson and a schoolmaster.

But Archer was on edge, and took her up.

"Common—common *where*?" he queried; and she returned with unusual readiness: "Why, I should say anywhere but in his school-room. Those people are always awkward in society. But then," she added disarmingly, "I suppose I shouldn't have known if he was clever."

Archer disliked her use of the word "clever" almost as much as her use of the word "common"; but he was beginning to fear his tendency to dwell on the things he disliked in her. After all, her point of view had always been the same. It was that of all the people he had grown up among, and he had always regarded it as necessary but negligible. Until a few months ago he had never known a "nice" woman who looked at life differently; and if a man married it must necessarily be among the nice.

"Ah—then I won't ask him to dine!" he concluded with a laugh; and May echoed, bewildered: "Goodness—ask the Carfrys' tutor?"

"Well, not on the same day with the Carfrys, if you prefer I shouldn't. But I did rather want another talk with him. He's looking for a job in New York."

Her surprise increased with her indifference: he almost fancied that she suspected him of being tainted with "foreignness."

"A job in New York? What sort of a job? People don't have French tutors: what does he want to do?"

"Chiefly to enjoy good conversation, I understand," her husband retorted perversely; and she broke into an appreciative laugh. "Oh, Newland, how funny! Isn't that *French*?"

On the whole, he was glad to have the matter settled for him by her refusing to take seriously his wish to invite M. Rivière. Another after-dinner talk would have made it difficult to avoid the question of New York; and the more Archer considered it the less he was able to fit M. Rivière into any conceivable picture of New York as he knew it.

He perceived with a flash of chilling insight that in future many problems would be thus negatively solved for him; but as he paid the hansom and followed his wife's long train into the house he took refuge in the comforting platitude that the first six months were always the most difficult in marriage. "After that I suppose we shall have pretty nearly finished rubbing off each other's angles," he reflected; but the worst of it was that May's pressure was already bearing on the very angles whose sharpness he most wanted to keep.

XXI

THE SMALL BRIGHT LAWN stretched away smoothly to the big bright sea.

The turf was hemmed with an edge of scarlet geranium and coleus, and cast-iron vases painted in chocolate colour, standing at intervals along the winding path that led to the sea, looped their garlands of petunia and ivy geranium above the neatly raked gravel.

Half way between the edge of the cliff and the square wooden house (which was also chocolate-coloured, but with the tin roof of the verandah striped in yellow and brown to represent an awning) two large targets had been placed against a background of shrubbery. On the other side of the lawn, facing the targets, was pitched a real tent, with benches and garden-seats about it. A number of ladies in summer dresses and gentlemen in grey frock-coats and tall hats stood on the lawn or sat upon the benches; and every now and then a slender girl in starched muslin would step from the tent, bow in hand, and speed her shaft at one of the targets, while the spectators interrupted their talk to watch the result.

Newland Archer, standing on the verandah of the house, looked curiously down upon this scene. On each side of the shiny painted steps was a large blue china flower-pot on a bright yellow china stand. A spiky green plant filled each pot, and below the verandah ran a wide border of blue hydrangeas edged with more red geraniums. Behind him, the French windows of the drawing-rooms through which he had passed gave glimpses, between swaying lace curtains, of glassy parquet floors islanded with chintz *poufs*, dwarf arm-chairs, and velvet tables covered with trifles in silver.

The Newport Archery Club always held its August meeting at the Beauforts'. The sport, which had hitherto known no rival but croquet, was beginning to be discarded in favour of lawn-tennis; but the latter game was still considered too rough and inelegant for social occasions, and as an opportunity to show off pretty dresses and graceful attitudes the bow and arrow held their own.

Archer looked down with wonder at the familiar spectacle.

It surprised him that life should be going on in the old way when his own reactions to it had so completely changed. It was Newport that had first brought home to him the extent of the change. In New York, during the previous winter, after he and May had settled down in the new greenish-yellow house with the bow-window and the Pompeian vestibule, he had dropped back with relief into the old routine of the office, and the renewal of this daily activity had served as a link with his former self. Then there had been the pleasurable excitement of choosing a showy grey stepper for May's brougham (the Wellands had given the carriage), and the abiding occupation and interest of arranging his new library, which, in spite of family doubts and disapprovals, had been carried out as he had dreamed, with a dark embossed paper, Eastlake book-cases and "sincere" arm-chairs and tables. At the Century he had found Winsett again, and at the Knickerbocker the fashionable young men of his own set; and what with the hours dedicated to the law and those given to dining out or entertaining friends at home, with an occasional evening at the Opera or the play, the life he was living had still seemed a fairly real and inevitable sort of business.

But Newport represented the escape from duty into an atmosphere of unmitigated holiday-making. Archer had tried to persuade May to spend the summer on a remote island off the coast of Maine (called, appropriately enough, Mount Desert), where a few hardy Bostonians and Philadelphians were camping in "native" cottages, and whence came reports of enchanting scenery and a wild, almost trapper-like existence amid woods and waters.

But the Wellands always went to Newport, where they owned one of the square boxes on the cliffs, and their son-in-law could adduce no good reason why he and May should not join them there. As Mrs. Welland rather tartly pointed out, it was hardly worth while for May to have worn herself out trying on summer clothes in Paris if she was not to be allowed to wear them; and this argument was of a kind to which Archer had as yet found no answer.

May herself could not understand his obscure reluctance to fall in with so reasonable and pleasant a way of spending the summer. She reminded him that he had always liked Newport in his bachelor days, and as this was indisputable he could only profess that he was sure he was going to like it better than ever now that they were to be there together. But as he stood on the Beaufort verandah and looked out on the brightly peopled lawn it came home to him with a shiver that he was not going to like it at all.

It was not May's fault, poor dear. If, now and then, during their travels, they had fallen slightly out of step, harmony had been restored by their return to the conditions she was used to. He had always foreseen that she would not disappoint him; and he had been right. He had married (as most young men did) because he had met a perfectly charming girl at the moment when a series of rather aimless sentimental adventures were ending in premature disgust; and she had represented peace, stability, comradeship, and the steadying sense of an unescapable duty.

He could not say that he had been mistaken in his choice, for she had fulfilled all that he had expected. It was undoubtedly gratifying to be the husband of one of the handsomest and most popular young married women in New York, especially when she was also one of the sweetest-tempered and most reasonable of wives; and Archer had never been insensible to such advantages. As for the momentary madness which had fallen upon him on the eve of his marriage, he had trained himself to regard it as the last of his discarded experiments. The idea that he could ever, in his senses, have dreamed of marrying the Countess Olenska had become almost unthinkable, and she remained in his memory simply as the most plaintive and poignant of a line of ghosts.

But all these abstractions and eliminations made of his mind a rather empty and echoing place, and he supposed that was one of the reasons why the busy animated people on the Beaufort lawn shocked him as if they had been children playing in a grave-yard.

He heard a murmur of skirts beside him, and the Marchioness Manson fluttered out of the drawing-room window. As usual, she was extraordinarily festooned and bedizened, with a limp Leghorn hat anchored to her head by many windings of faded gauze, and a little black velvet parasol on a carved ivory handle absurdly balanced over her much larger hat-brim.

"My dear Newland, I had no idea that you and May had arrived! You yourself came only yesterday, you say? Ah, business—business—professional duties . . . I understand. Many husbands, I know, find it impossible to join their wives here except for the week-end." She cocked her head on one side and languished at him through screwed-up eyes. "But marriage is one long sacrifice, as I used often to remind my Ellen—"

Archer's heart stopped with the queer jerk which it had given once before, and which seemed suddenly to slam a door between himself and the outer world; but this break of continuity must have been of the briefest, for he presently heard Medora answering a question he had apparently found voice to put.

"No, I am not staying here, but with the Blenkers, in their delicious solitude at Portsmouth. Beaufort was kind enough to send his famous trotters for me this morning, so that I might have at least a glimpse of one of Regina's garden-parties; but this evening I go back to rural life. The Blenkers, dear original beings, have hired a primitive old farm-house at Portsmouth where they gather about them representative people . . ." She drooped slightly beneath her protecting brim, and added with a faint blush: "This week Dr. Agathon Carver is holding a series of Inner Thought meetings there. A contrast indeed to this gay scene of worldly pleasure—but then I have always lived on contrasts! To me the only death is monotony. I always say to Ellen: Beware of monotony; it's the mother of all the deadly sins. But my poor child is going through a phase of exaltation, of abhorrence of the world. You know, I suppose, that she has declined all invitations to stay at Newport, even with her grandmother Mingott? I could hardly persuade her to come with me to the Blenkers', if you will believe it! The life she leads is morbid, unnatural. Ah, if she had only listened to me when it was still possible . . . When the door was still open . . . But shall we go down and watch this absorbing match? I hear your May is one of the competitors."

Strolling toward them from the tent Beaufort advanced

over the lawn, tall, heavy, too tightly buttoned into a London frock-coat, with one of his own orchids in its buttonhole. Archer, who had not seen him for two or three months, was struck by the change in his appearance. In the hot summer light his floridness seemed heavy and bloated, and but for his erect square-shouldered walk he would have looked like an over-fed and over-dressed old man.

There were all sorts of rumours afloat about Beaufort. In the spring he had gone off on a long cruise to the West Indies in his new steam-yacht, and it was reported that, at various points where he had touched, a lady resembling Miss Fanny Ring had been seen in his company. The steam-yacht, built in the Clyde, and fitted with tiled bath-rooms and other un-heard-of luxuries, was said to have cost him half a million; and the pearl necklace which he had presented to his wife on his return was as magnificent as such expiatory offerings are apt to be. Beaufort's fortune was substantial enough to stand the strain; and yet the disquieting rumours persisted, not only in Fifth Avenue but in Wall Street. Some people said he had speculated unfortunately in railways, others that he was being bled by one of the most insatiable members of her profession; and to every report of threatened insolvency Beaufort replied by a fresh extravagance: the building of a new row of orchid-houses, the purchase of a new string of race-horses, or the addition of a new Meissonnier or Cabanel to his picture-gallery.

He advanced toward the Marchioness and Newland with his usual half-sneering smile. "Hullo, Medora! Did the trot-ters do their business? Forty minutes, eh? . . . Well, that's not so bad, considering your nerves had to be spared." He shook hands with Archer, and then, turning back with them, placed himself on Mrs. Manson's other side, and said, in a low voice, a few words which their companion did not catch.

The Marchioness replied by one of her queer foreign jerks, and a *"Que voulez-vous?"* which deepened Beaufort's frown; but he produced a good semblance of a congratulatory smile as he glanced at Archer to say: "You know May's going to carry off the first prize."

"Ah, then it remains in the family," Medora rippled; and at

that moment they reached the tent and Mrs. Beaufort met them in a girlish cloud of mauve muslin and floating veils.

May Welland was just coming out of the tent. In her white dress, with a pale green ribbon about the waist and a wreath of ivy on her hat, she had the same Diana-like aloofness as when she had entered the Beaufort ball-room on the night of her engagement. In the interval not a thought seemed to have passed behind her eyes or a feeling through her heart; and though her husband knew that she had the capacity for both he marvelled afresh at the way in which experience dropped away from her.

She had her bow and arrow in her hand, and placing herself on the chalk-mark traced on the turf she lifted the bow to her shoulder and took aim. The attitude was so full of a classic grace that a murmur of appreciation followed her appearance, and Archer felt the glow of proprietorship that so often cheated him into momentary well-being. Her rivals— Mrs. Reggie Chivers, the Merry girls, and divers rosy Thorleys, Dagonets and Mingotts, stood behind her in a lovely anxious group, brown heads and golden bent above the scores, and pale muslins and flower-wreathed hats mingled in a tender rainbow. All were young and pretty, and bathed in summer bloom; but not one had the nymph-like ease of his wife, when, with tense muscles and happy frown, she bent her soul upon some feat of strength.

"Gad," Archer heard Lawrence Lefferts say, "not one of the lot holds the bow as she does;" and Beaufort retorted: "Yes; but that's the only kind of target she'll ever hit."

Archer felt irrationally angry. His host's contemptuous tribute to May's "niceness" was just what a husband should have wished to hear said of his wife. The fact that a coarse-minded man found her lacking in attraction was simply another proof of her quality; yet the words sent a faint shiver through his heart. What if "niceness" carried to that supreme degree were only a negation, the curtain dropped before an emptiness? As he looked at May, returning flushed and calm from her final bull's-eye, he had the feeling that he had never yet lifted that curtain.

She took the congratulations of her rivals and of the rest of the company with the simplicity that was her crowning grace.

No one could ever be jealous of her triumphs because she managed to give the feeling that she would have been just as serene if she had missed them. But when her eyes met her husband's her face glowed with the pleasure she saw in his.

Mrs. Welland's basket-work poney-carriage was waiting for them, and they drove off among the dispersing carriages, May handling the reins and Archer sitting at her side.

The afternoon sunlight still lingered upon the bright lawns and shrubberies, and up and down Bellevue Avenue rolled a double line of victorias, dog-carts, landaus and "vis-à-vis," carrying well-dressed ladies and gentlemen away from the Beaufort garden-party, or homeward from their daily afternoon turn along the Ocean Drive.

"Shall we go to see Granny?" May suddenly proposed. "I should like to tell her myself that I've won the prize. There's lots of time before dinner."

Archer acquiesced, and she turned the ponies down Narragansett Avenue, crossed Spring Street and drove out toward the rocky moorland beyond. In this unfashionable region Catherine the Great, always indifferent to precedent and thrifty of purse, had built herself in her youth a many-peaked and cross-beamed *cottage-orné* on a bit of cheap land overlooking the bay. Here, in a thicket of stunted oaks, her verandahs spread themselves above the island-dotted waters. A winding drive led up between iron stags and blue glass balls embedded in mounds of geraniums to a front door of highly-varnished walnut under a striped verandah-roof; and behind it ran a narrow hall with a black and yellow star-patterned parquet floor, upon which opened four small square rooms with heavy flock-papers under ceilings on which an Italian house-painter had lavished all the divinities of Olympus. One of these rooms had been turned into a bedroom by Mrs. Mingott when the burden of flesh descended on her, and in the adjoining one she spent her days, enthroned in a large arm-chair between the open door and window, and perpetually waving a palm-leaf fan which the prodigious projection of her bosom kept so far from the rest of her person that the air it set in motion stirred only the fringe of the anti-macassars on the chair-arms.

Since she had been the means of hastening his marriage old

Catherine had shown to Archer the cordiality which a service rendered excites toward the person served. She was persuaded that irrepressible passion was the cause of his impatience; and being an ardent admirer of impulsiveness (when it did not lead to the spending of money) she always received him with a genial twinkle of complicity and a play of allusion to which May seemed fortunately impervious.

She examined and appraised with much interest the diamond-tipped arrow which had been pinned on May's bosom at the conclusion of the match, remarking that in her day a filigree brooch would have been thought enough, but that there was no denying that Beaufort did things handsomely.

"Quite an heirloom, in fact, my dear," the old lady chuckled. "You must leave it in fee to your eldest girl." She pinched May's white arm and watched the colour flood her face. "Well, well, what have I said to make you shake out the red flag? Ain't there going to be any daughters—only boys, eh? Good gracious, look at her blushing again all over her blushes! What—can't I say that either? Mercy me—when my children beg me to have all those gods and goddesses painted out overhead I always say I'm too thankful to have somebody about me that *nothing* can shock!"

Archer burst into a laugh, and May echoed it, crimson to the eyes.

"Well, now tell me all about the party, please, my dears, for I shall never get a straight word about it out of that silly Medora," the ancestress continued; and, as May exclaimed: "Cousin Medora? But I thought she was going back to Portsmouth?" she answered placidly: "So she is—but she's got to come here first to pick up Ellen. Ah—you didn't know Ellen had come to spend the day with me? Such fol-de-rol, her not coming for the summer; but I gave up arguing with young people about fifty years ago. Ellen—*Ellen!*" she cried in her shrill old voice, trying to bend forward far enough to catch a glimpse of the lawn beyond the verandah.

There was no answer, and Mrs. Mingott rapped impatiently with her stick on the shiny floor. A mulatto maid-servant in a bright turban, replying to the summons, informed her mistress that she had seen "Miss Ellen" going down the path to the shore; and Mrs. Mingott turned to Archer.

"Run down and fetch her, like a good grandson; this pretty lady will describe the party to me," she said; and Archer stood up as if in a dream.

He had heard the Countess Olenska's name pronounced often enough during the year and a half since they had last met, and was even familiar with the main incidents of her life in the interval. He knew that she had spent the previous summer at Newport, where she appeared to have gone a great deal into society, but that in the autumn she had suddenly sub-let the "perfect house" which Beaufort had been at such pains to find for her, and decided to establish herself in Washington. There, during the winter, he had heard of her (as one always heard of pretty women in Washington) as shining in the "brilliant diplomatic society" that was supposed to make up for the social short-comings of the Administration. He had listened to these accounts, and to various contradictory reports on her appearance, her conversation, her point of view and her choice of friends, with the detachment with which one listens to reminiscences of some one long since dead; not till Medora suddenly spoke her name at the archery match had Ellen Olenska become a living presence to him again. The Marchioness's foolish lisp had called up a vision of the little fire-lit drawing-room and the sound of the carriage-wheels returning down the deserted street. He thought of a story he had read, of some peasant children in Tuscany lighting a bunch of straw in a wayside cavern, and revealing old silent images in their painted tomb . . .

The way to the shore descended from the bank on which the house was perched to a walk above the water planted with weeping willows. Through their veil Archer caught the glint of the Lime Rock, with its white-washed turret and the tiny house in which the heroic light-house keeper, Ida Lewis, was living her last venerable years. Beyond it lay the flat reaches and ugly government chimneys of Goat Island, the bay spreading northward in a shimmer of gold to Prudence Island with its low growth of oaks, and the shores of Conanicut faint in the sunset haze.

From the willow walk projected a slight wooden pier ending in a sort of pagoda-like summer-house; and in the pagoda a lady stood, leaning against the rail, her back to the shore.

Archer stopped at the sight as if he had waked from sleep. That vision of the past was a dream, and the reality was what awaited him in the house on the bank overhead: was Mrs. Welland's pony-carriage circling around and around the oval at the door, was May sitting under the shameless Olympians and glowing with secret hopes, was the Welland villa at the far end of Bellevue Avenue, and Mr. Welland, already dressed for dinner, and pacing the drawing-room floor, watch in hand, with dyspeptic impatience—for it was one of the houses in which one always knew exactly what is happening at a given hour.

"What am I? A son-in-law—" Archer thought.

The figure at the end of the pier had not moved. For a long moment the young man stood half way down the bank, gazing at the bay furrowed with the coming and going of sail-boats, yacht-launches, fishing-craft and the trailing black coal-barges hauled by noisy tugs. The lady in the summer-house seemed to be held by the same sight. Beyond the grey bastions of Fort Adams a long-drawn sunset was splintering up into a thousand fires, and the radiance caught the sail of a cat-boat as it beat out through the channel between the Lime Rock and the shore. Archer, as he watched, remembered the scene in the Shaughraun, and Montague lifting Ada Dyas's ribbon to his lips without her knowing that he was in the room.

"She doesn't know—she hasn't guessed. Shouldn't I know if she came up behind me, I wonder?" he mused; and suddenly he said to himself: "If she doesn't turn before that sail crosses the Lime Rock light I'll go back."

The boat was gliding out on the receding tide. It slid before the Lime Rock, blotted out Ida Lewis's little house, and passed across the turret in which the light was hung. Archer waited till a wide space of water sparkled between the last reef of the island and the stern of the boat; but still the figure in the summer-house did not move.

He turned and walked up the hill.

"I'm sorry you didn't find Ellen—I should have liked to see her again," May said as they drove home through the dusk. "But perhaps she wouldn't have cared—she seems so changed."

"Changed?" echoed her husband in a colourless voice, his eyes fixed on the ponies' twitching ears.

"So indifferent to her friends, I mean; giving up New York and her house, and spending her time with such queer people. Fancy how hideously uncomfortable she must be at the Blenkers'! She says she does it to keep cousin Medora out of mischief: to prevent her marrying dreadful people. But I sometimes think we've always bored her."

Archer made no answer, and she continued, with a tinge of hardness that he had never before noticed in her frank fresh voice: "After all, I wonder if she wouldn't be happier with her husband."

He burst into a laugh. *"Sancta simplicitas!"* he exclaimed; and as she turned a puzzled frown on him he added: "I don't think I ever heard you say a cruel thing before."

"Cruel?"

"Well—watching the contortions of the damned is supposed to be a favourite sport of the angels; but I believe even they don't think people happier in hell."

"It's a pity she ever married abroad then," said May, in the placid tone with which her mother met Mr. Welland's vagaries; and Archer felt himself gently relegated to the category of unreasonable husbands.

They drove down Bellevue Avenue and turned in between the chamfered wooden gate-posts surmounted by cast-iron lamps which marked the approach to the Welland villa. Lights were already shining through its windows, and Archer, as the carriage stopped, caught a glimpse of his father-in-law, exactly as he had pictured him, pacing the drawing-room, watch in hand and wearing the pained expression that he had long since found to be much more efficacious than anger.

The young man, as he followed his wife into the hall, was conscious of a curious reversal of mood. There was something about the luxury of the Welland house and the density of the Welland atmosphere, so charged with minute observances and exactions, that always stole into his system like a narcotic. The heavy carpets, the watchful servants, the perpetually reminding tick of disciplined clocks, the perpetually renewed stack of cards and invitations on the hall table, the whole chain of tyrannical trifles binding one hour to the next, and each member of the household to all the others, made any less systematised and affluent existence seem unreal and precarious. But now it was the Welland house, and the life he was expected to lead in it, that had become unreal and irrelevant, and the brief scene on the shore, when he had stood irresolute, halfway down the bank, was as close to him as the blood in his veins.

All night he lay awake in the big chintz bedroom at May's side, watching the moonlight slant along the carpet, and thinking of Ellen Olenska driving home across the gleaming beaches behind Beaufort's trotters.

XXII

A PARTY for the Blenkers—the Blenkers?"
    Mr. Welland laid down his knife and fork and looked
anxiously and incredulously across the luncheon-table at his
wife, who, adjusting her gold eye-glasses, read aloud, in the
tone of high comedy: "Professor and Mrs. Emerson Sillerton
request the pleasure of Mr. and Mrs. Welland's company at
the meeting of the Wednesday Afternoon Club on August
25th at 3 o'clock punctually. To meet Mrs. and the Misses
Blenker.

"Red Gables, Catherine Street.   R. S. V. P."

"Good gracious—" Mr. Welland gasped, as if a second
reading had been necessary to bring the monstrous absurdity
of the thing home to him.

"Poor Amy Sillerton—you never can tell what her husband
will do next," Mrs. Welland sighed. "I suppose he's just discovered the Blenkers."

Professor Emerson Sillerton was a thorn in the side of
Newport society; and a thorn that could not be plucked out,
for it grew on a venerable and venerated family tree. He was,
as people said, a man who had had "every advantage." His
father was Sillerton Jackson's uncle, his mother a Pennilow of
Boston; on each side there was wealth and position, and mutual suitability. Nothing—as Mrs. Welland had often remarked—nothing on earth obliged Emerson Sillerton to be
an archæologist, or indeed a Professor of any sort, or to live
in Newport in winter, or do any of the other revolutionary
things that he did. But at least, if he was going to break with
tradition and flout society in the face, he need not have
married poor Amy Dagonet, who had a right to expect
"something different," and money enough to keep her own
carriage.

No one in the Mingott set could understand why Amy Sillerton had submitted so tamely to the eccentricities of a
husband who filled the house with long-haired men and short-
haired women, and, when he travelled, took her to explore
tombs in Yucatan instead of going to Paris or Italy. But there
they were, set in their ways, and apparently unaware that they

were different from other people; and when they gave one of their dreary annual garden-parties every family on the Cliffs, because of the Sillerton-Pennilow-Dagonet connection, had to draw lots and send an unwilling representative.

"It's a wonder," Mrs. Welland remarked, "that they didn't choose the Cup Race day! Do you remember, two years ago, their giving a party for a black man on the day of Julia Mingott's *thé dansant*? Luckily this time there's nothing else going on that I know of—for of course some of us will have to go."

Mr. Welland sighed nervously. " 'Some of us,' my dear— more than one? Three o'clock is such a very awkward hour. I have to be here at half-past three to take my drops: it's really no use trying to follow Bencomb's new treatment if I don't do it systematically; and if I join you later, of course I shall miss my drive." At the thought he laid down his knife and fork again, and a flush of anxiety rose to his finely-wrinkled cheek.

"There's no reason why you should go at all, my dear," his wife answered with a cheerfulness that had become automatic. "I have some cards to leave at the other end of Bellevue Avenue, and I'll drop in at about half-past three and stay long enough to make poor Amy feel that she hasn't been slighted." She glanced hesitatingly at her daughter. "And if Newland's afternoon is provided for perhaps May can drive you out with the ponies, and try their new russet harness."

It was a principle in the Welland family that people's days and hours should be what Mrs. Welland called "provided for." The melancholy possibility of having to "kill time" (especially for those who did not care for whist or solitaire) was a vision that haunted her as the spectre of the unemployed haunts the philanthropist. Another of her principles was that parents should never (at least visibly) interfere with the plans of their married children; and the difficulty of adjusting this respect for May's independence with the exigency of Mr. Welland's claims could be overcome only by the exercise of an ingenuity which left not a second of Mrs. Welland's own time un-provided for.

"Of course I'll drive with Papa—I'm sure Newland will find something to do," May said, in a tone that gently reminded her husband of his lack of response. It was a cause of constant distress to Mrs. Welland that her son-in-law showed so little foresight in planning his days. Often already, during the fortnight that he had passed under her roof, when she enquired how he meant to spend his afternoon, he had answered paradoxically: "Oh, I think for a change I'll just save it instead of spending it—" and once, when she and May had had to go on a long-postponed round of afternoon calls, he had confessed to having lain all the afternoon under a rock on the beach below the house.

"Newland never seems to look ahead," Mrs. Welland once ventured to complain to her daughter; and May answered serenely: "No; but you see it doesn't matter, because when there's nothing particular to do he reads a book."

"Ah, yes—like his father!" Mrs. Welland agreed, as if allowing for an inherited oddity; and after that the question of Newland's unemployment was tacitly dropped.

Nevertheless, as the day for the Sillerton reception approached, May began to show a natural solicitude for his welfare, and to suggest a tennis match at the Chiverses', or a sail on Julius Beaufort's cutter, as a means of atoning for her temporary desertion. "I shall be back by six, you know, dear: Papa never drives later than that—" and she was not reassured till Archer said that he thought of hiring a run-about and driving up the island to a stud-farm to look at a second horse for her brougham. They had been looking for this horse for some time, and the suggestion was so acceptable that May glanced at her mother as if to say: "You see he knows how to plan out his time as well as any of us."

The idea of the stud-farm and the brougham horse had germinated in Archer's mind on the very day when the Emerson Sillerton invitation had first been mentioned; but he had kept it to himself as if there were something clandestine in the plan, and discovery might prevent its execution. He had, however, taken the precaution to engage in advance a run-about with a pair of old livery-stable trotters that could still do their eighteen miles on level roads; and at two o'clock, hastily deserting the luncheon-table, he sprang into the light carriage and drove off.

The day was perfect. A breeze from the north drove little

puffs of white cloud across an ultramarine sky, with a bright sea running under it. Bellevue Avenue was empty at that hour, and after dropping the stable-lad at the corner of Mill Street Archer turned down the Old Beach Road and drove across Eastman's Beach.

He had the feeling of unexplained excitement with which, on half-holidays at school, he used to start off into the unknown. Taking his pair at an easy gait, he counted on reaching the stud-farm, which was not far beyond Paradise Rocks, before three o'clock; so that, after looking over the horse (and trying him if he seemed promising) he would still have four golden hours to dispose of.

As soon as he heard of the Sillerton's party he had said to himself that the Marchioness Manson would certainly come to Newport with the Blenkers, and that Madame Olenska might again take the opportunity of spending the day with her grandmother. At any rate, the Blenker habitation would probably be deserted, and he would be able, without indiscretion, to satisfy a vague curiosity concerning it. He was not sure that he wanted to see the Countess Olenska again; but ever since he had looked at her from the path above the bay he had wanted, irrationally and indescribably, to see the place she was living in, and to follow the movements of her imagined figure as he had watched the real one in the summer-house. The longing was with him day and night, an incessant undefinable craving, like the sudden whim of a sick man for food or drink once tasted and long since forgotten. He could not see beyond the craving, or picture what it might lead to, for he was not conscious of any wish to speak to Madame Olenska or to hear her voice. He simply felt that if he could carry away the vision of the spot of earth she walked on, and the way the sky and sea enclosed it, the rest of the world might seem less empty.

When he reached the stud-farm a glance showed him that the horse was not what he wanted; nevertheless he took a turn behind it in order to prove to himself that he was not in a hurry. But at three o'clock he shook out the reins over the trotters and turned into the by-roads leading to Portsmouth. The wind had dropped and a faint haze on the horizon showed that a fog was waiting to steal up the Saconnet on the turn of the tide; but all about him fields and woods were steeped in golden light.

He drove past grey-shingled farm-houses in orchards, past hay-fields and groves of oak, past villages with white steeples rising sharply into the fading sky; and at last, after stopping to ask the way of some men at work in a field, he turned down a lane between high banks of goldenrod and brambles. At the end of the lane was the blue glimmer of the river; to the left, standing in front of a clump of oaks and maples, he saw a long tumble-down house with white paint peeling from its clapboards.

On the road-side facing the gateway stood one of the open sheds in which the New Englander shelters his farming implements and visitors "hitch" their "teams." Archer, jumping down, led his pair into the shed, and after tying them to a post turned toward the house. The patch of lawn before it had relapsed into a hay-field; but to the left an overgrown box-garden full of dahlias and rusty rose-bushes encircled a ghostly summer-house of trellis-work that had once been white, surmounted by a wooden Cupid who had lost his bow and arrow but continued to take ineffectual aim.

Archer leaned for a while against the gate. No one was in sight, and not a sound came from the open windows of the house: a grizzled Newfoundland dozing before the door seemed as ineffectual a guardian as the arrowless Cupid. It was strange to think that this place of silence and decay was the home of the turbulent Blenkers; yet Archer was sure that he was not mistaken.

For a long time he stood there, content to take in the scene, and gradually falling under its drowsy spell; but at length he roused himself to the sense of the passing time. Should he look his fill and then drive away? He stood irresolute, wishing suddenly to see the inside of the house, so that he might picture the room that Madame Olenska sat in. There was nothing to prevent his walking up to the door and ringing the bell; if, as he supposed, she was away with the rest of the party, he could easily give his name, and ask permission to go into the sitting-room to write a message.

But instead, he crossed the lawn and turned toward the

box-garden. As he entered it he caught sight of something bright-coloured in the summer-house, and presently made it out to be a pink parasol. The parasol drew him like a magnet: he was sure it was hers. He went into the summer-house, and sitting down on the rickety seat picked up the silken thing and looked at its carved handle, which was made of some rare wood that gave out an aromatic scent. Archer lifted the handle to his lips.

He heard a rustle of skirts against the box, and sat motionless, leaning on the parasol handle with clasped hands, and letting the rustle come nearer without lifting his eyes. He had always known that this must happen . . .

"Oh, Mr. Archer!" exclaimed a loud young voice; and looking up he saw before him the youngest and largest of the Blenker girls, blonde and blowsy, in bedraggled muslin. A red blotch on one of her cheeks seemed to show that it had recently been pressed against a pillow, and her half-awakened eyes stared at him hospitably but confusedly.

"Gracious—where did you drop from? I must have been sound asleep in the hammock. Everybody else has gone to Newport. Did you ring?" she incoherently enquired.

Archer's confusion was greater than hers. "I—no—that is, I was just going to. I had to come up the island to see about a horse, and I drove over on a chance of finding Mrs. Blenker and your visitors. But the house seemed empty—so I sat down to wait."

Miss Blenker, shaking off the fumes of sleep, looked at him with increasing interest. "The house *is* empty. Mother's not here, or the Marchioness—or anybody but me." Her glance became faintly reproachful. "Didn't you know that Professor and Mrs. Sillerton are giving a garden-party for mother and all of us this afternoon? It was too unlucky that I couldn't go; but I've had a sore throat, and mother was afraid of the drive home this evening. Did you ever know anything so disappointing? Of course," she added gaily, "I shouldn't have minded half as much if I'd known you were coming."

Symptoms of a lumbering coquetry became visible in her, and Archer found the strength to break in: "But Madame Olenska—has she gone to Newport too?"

Miss Blenker looked at him with surprise. "Madame Olenska—didn't you know she'd been called away?"

"Called away?—"

"Oh, my best parasol! I lent it to that goose of a Katie, because it matched her ribbons, and the careless thing must have dropped it here. We Blenkers are all like that . . . real Bohemians!" Recovering the sunshade with a powerful hand she unfurled it and suspended its rosy dome above her head. "Yes, Ellen was called away yesterday: she lets us call her Ellen, you know. A telegram came from Boston: she said she might be gone for two days. I do *love* the way she does her hair, don't you?" Miss Blenker rambled on.

Archer continued to stare through her as though she had been transparent. All he saw was the trumpery parasol that arched its pinkness above her giggling head.

After a moment he ventured: "You don't happen to know why Madame Olenska went to Boston? I hope it was not on account of bad news?"

Miss Blenker took this with a cheerful incredulity. "Oh, I don't believe so. She didn't tell us what was in the telegram. I think she didn't want the Marchioness to know. She's so romantic-looking, isn't she? Doesn't she remind you of Mrs. Scott-Siddons when she reads 'Lady Geraldine's Courtship'? Did you never hear her?"

Archer was dealing hurriedly with crowding thoughts. His whole future seemed suddenly to be unrolled before him; and passing down its endless emptiness he saw the dwindling figure of a man to whom nothing was ever to happen. He glanced about him at the unpruned garden, the tumble-down house, and the oak-grove under which the dusk was gathering. It had seemed so exactly the place in which he ought to have found Madame Olenska; and she was far away, and even the pink sunshade was not hers . . .

He frowned and hesitated. "You don't know, I suppose—I shall be in Boston tomorrow. If I could manage to see her—"

He felt that Miss Blenker was losing interest in him, though her smile persisted. "Oh, of course; how lovely of you! She's staying at the Parker House; it must be horrible there in this weather."

After that Archer was but intermittently aware of the remarks they exchanged. He could only remember stoutly resisting her entreaty that he should await the returning family and have high tea with them before he drove home. At length, with his hostess still at his side, he passed out of range of the wooden Cupid, unfastened his horses and drove off. At the turn of the lane he saw Miss Blenker standing at the gate and waving the pink parasol.

XXIII

THE NEXT MORNING, when Archer got out of the Fall River train, he emerged upon a steaming midsummer Boston. The streets near the station were full of the smell of beer and coffee and decaying fruit and a shirt-sleeved populace moved through them with the intimate abandon of boarders going down the passage to the bathroom.

Archer found a cab and drove to the Somerset Club for breakfast. Even the fashionable quarters had the air of untidy domesticity to which no excess of heat ever degrades the European cities. Care-takers in calico lounged on the door-steps of the wealthy, and the Common looked like a pleasure-ground on the morrow of a Masonic picnic. If Archer had tried to imagine Ellen Olenska in improbable scenes he could not have called up any into which it was more difficult to fit her than this heat-prostrated and deserted Boston.

He breakfasted with appetite and method, beginning with a slice of melon, and studying a morning paper while he waited for his toast and scrambled eggs. A new sense of energy and activity had possessed him ever since he had announced to May the night before that he had business in Boston, and should take the Fall River boat that night and go on to New York the following evening. It had always been understood that he would return to town early in the week, and when he got back from his expedition to Portsmouth a letter from the office, which fate had conspicuously placed on a corner of the hall table, sufficed to justify his sudden change of plan. He was even ashamed of the ease with which the whole thing had been done: it reminded him, for an uncomfortable moment, of Lawrence Lefferts's masterly contrivances for securing his freedom. But this did not long trouble him, for he was not in an analytic mood.

After breakfast he smoked a cigarette and glanced over the Commercial Advertiser. While he was thus engaged two or three men he knew came in, and the usual greetings were exchanged: it was the same world after all, though he had such a queer sense of having slipped through the meshes of time and space.

He looked at his watch, and finding that it was half-past nine got up and went into the writing-room. There he wrote a few lines, and ordered a messenger to take a cab to the Parker House and wait for the answer. He then sat down behind another newspaper and tried to calculate how long it would take a cab to get to the Parker House.

"The lady was out, sir," he suddenly heard a waiter's voice at his elbow; and he stammered: "Out?—" as if it were a word in a strange language.

He got up and went into the hall. It must be a mistake: she could not be out at that hour. He flushed with anger at his own stupidity: why had he not sent the note as soon as he arrived?

He found his hat and stick and went forth into the street. The city had suddenly become as strange and vast and empty as if he were a traveller from distant lands. For a moment he stood on the door-step hesitating; then he decided to go to the Parker House. What if the messenger had been misinformed, and she were still there?

He started to walk across the Common; and on the first bench, under a tree, he saw her sitting. She had a grey silk sunshade over her head—how could he ever have imagined her with a pink one? As he approached he was struck by her listless attitude: she sat there as if she had nothing else to do. He saw her drooping profile, and the knot of hair fastened low in the neck under her dark hat, and the long wrinkled glove on the hand that held the sunshade. He came a step or two nearer, and she turned and looked at him.

"Oh"—she said; and for the first time he noticed a startled look on her face; but in another moment it gave way to a slow smile of wonder and contentment.

"Oh"—she murmured again, on a different note, as he stood looking down at her; and without rising she made a place for him on the bench.

"I'm here on business—just got here," Archer explained; and, without knowing why, he suddenly began to feign astonishment at seeing her. "But what on earth are *you* doing in this wilderness?" He had really no idea what he was saying: he felt as if he were shouting at her across endless distances, and she might vanish again before he could overtake her.

"I? Oh, I'm here on business too," she answered, turning her head toward him so that they were face to face. The words hardly reached him: he was aware only of her voice, and of the startling fact that not an echo of it had remained in his memory. He had not even remembered that it was low-pitched, with a faint roughness on the consonants.

"You do your hair differently," he said, his heart beating as if he had uttered something irrevocable.

"Differently? No—it's only that I do it as best I can when I'm without Nastasia."

"Nastasia; but isn't she with you?"

"No; I'm alone. For two days it was not worth while to bring her."

"You're alone—at the Parker House?"

She looked at him with a flash of her old malice. "Does it strike you as dangerous?"

"No; not dangerous—"

"But unconventional? I see; I suppose it is." She considered a moment. "I hadn't thought of it, because I've just done something so much more unconventional." The faint tinge of irony lingered in her eyes. "I've just refused to take back a sum of money—that belonged to me."

Archer sprang up and moved a step or two away. She had furled her parasol and sat absently drawing patterns on the gravel. Presently he came back and stood before her.

"Some one—has come here to meet you?"

"Yes."

"With this offer?"

She nodded.

"And you refused—because of the conditions?"

"I refused," she said after a moment.

He sat down by her again. "What were the conditions?"

"Oh, they were not onerous: just to sit at the head of his table now and then."

There was another interval of silence. Archer's heart had slammed itself shut in the queer way it had, and he sat vainly groping for a word.

"He wants you back—at any price?"

"Well—a considerable price. At least the sum is considerable for me."

He paused again, beating about the question he felt he must put.

"It was to meet him here that you came?"

She stared, and then burst into a laugh. "Meet him—my husband? *Here*? At this season he's always at Cowes or Baden."

"He sent some one?"

"Yes."

"With a letter?"

She shook her head. "No; just a message. He never writes. I don't think I've had more than one letter from him." The allusion brought the colour to her cheek, and it reflected itself in Archer's vivid blush.

"Why does he never write?"

"Why should he? What does one have secretaries for?"

The young man's blush deepened. She had pronounced the word as if it had no more significance than any other in her vocabulary. For a moment it was on the tip of his tongue to ask: "Did he send his secretary, then?" But the remembrance of Count Olenski's only letter to his wife was too present to him. He paused again, and then took another plunge.

"And the person?"—

"The emissary? The emissary," Madame Olenska rejoined, still smiling, "might, for all I care, have left already; but he has insisted on waiting till this evening . . . in case . . . on the chance . . ."

"And you came out here to think the chance over?"

"I came out to get a breath of air. The hotel's too stifling. I'm taking the afternoon train back to Portsmouth."

They sat silent, not looking at each other, but straight ahead at the people passing along the path. Finally she turned her eyes again to his face and said: "You're not changed."

He felt like answering: "I was, till I saw you again;" but instead he stood up abruptly and glanced about him at the untidy sweltering park.

"This is horrible. Why shouldn't we go out a little on the bay? There's a breeze, and it will be cooler. We might take the steamboat down to Point Arley." She glanced up at him hesitatingly and he went on: "On a Monday morning there won't be anybody on the boat. My train doesn't leave till evening: I'm going back to New York. Why shouldn't we?" he insisted, looking down at her; and suddenly he broke out: "Haven't we done all we could?"

"Oh"—she murmured again. She stood up and re-opened her sunshade, glancing about her as if to take counsel of the scene, and assure herself of the impossibility of remaining in it. Then her eyes returned to his face. "You mustn't say things like that to me," she said.

"I'll say anything you like; or nothing. I won't open my mouth unless you tell me to. What harm can it do to anybody? All I want is to listen to you," he stammered.

She drew out a little gold-faced watch on an enamelled chain. "Oh, don't calculate," he broke out; "give me the day! I want to get you away from that man. At what time was he coming?"

Her colour rose again. "At eleven."

"Then you must come at once."

"You needn't be afraid—if I don't come."

"Nor you either—if you do. I swear I only want to hear about you, to know what you've been doing. It's a hundred years since we've met—it may be another hundred before we meet again."

She still wavered, her anxious eyes on his face. "Why didn't you come down to the beach to fetch me, the day I was at Granny's?" she asked.

"Because you didn't look round—because you didn't know I was there. I swore I wouldn't unless you looked round." He laughed as the childishness of the confession struck him.

"But I didn't look round on purpose."

"On purpose?"

"I knew you were there; when you drove in I recognised the ponies. So I went down to the beach."

"To get away from me as far as you could?"

She repeated in a low voice: "To get away from you as far as I could."

He laughed out again, this time in boyish satisfaction. "Well, you see it's no use. I may as well tell you," he added, "that the business I came here for was just to find you. But, look here, we must start or we shall miss our boat."

"Our boat?" She frowned perplexedly, and then smiled.

"Oh, but I must go back to the hotel first: I must leave a note—"

"As many notes as you please. You can write here." He drew out a note-case and one of the new stylographic pens. "I've even got an envelope—you see how everything's predestined! There—steady the thing on your knee, and I'll get the pen going in a second. They have to be humoured; wait—" He banged the hand that held the pen against the back of the bench. "It's like jerking down the mercury in a thermometer: just a trick. Now try—"

She laughed, and bending over the sheet of paper which he had laid on his note-case, began to write. Archer walked away a few steps, staring with radiant unseeing eyes at the passers-by, who, in their turn, paused to stare at the unwonted sight of a fashionably-dressed lady writing a note on her knee on a bench in the Common.

Madame Olenska slipped the sheet into the envelope, wrote a name on it, and put it into her pocket. Then she too stood up.

They walked back toward Beacon Street, and near the club Archer caught sight of the plush-lined "herdic" which had carried his note to the Parker House, and whose driver was reposing from this effort by bathing his brow at the corner hydrant.

"I told you everything was predestined! Here's a cab for us. You see!" They laughed, astonished at the miracle of picking up a public conveyance at that hour, and in that unlikely spot, in a city where cab-stands were still a "foreign" novelty.

Archer, looking at his watch, saw that there was time to drive to the Parker House before going to the steamboat landing. They rattled through the hot streets and drew up at the door of the hotel.

Archer held out his hand for the letter. "Shall I take it in?" he asked; but Madame Olenska, shaking her head, sprang out and disappeared through the glazed doors. It was barely half-past ten; but what if the emissary, impatient for her reply, and not knowing how else to employ his time, were already seated among the travellers with cooling drinks at their elbows of whom Archer had caught a glimpse as she went in?

He waited, pacing up and down before the herdic. A

Sicilian youth with eyes like Nastasia's offered to shine his boots, and an Irish matron to sell him peaches; and every few moments the doors opened to let out hot men with straw hats tilted far back, who glanced at him as they went by. He marvelled that the door should open so often, and that all the people it let out should look so like each other, and so like all the other hot men who, at that hour, through the length and breadth of the land, were passing continuously in and out of the swinging doors of hotels.

And then, suddenly, came a face that he could not relate to the other faces. He caught but a flash of it, for his pacings had carried him to the farthest point of his beat, and it was in turning back to the hotel that he saw, in a group of typical countenances—the lank and weary, the round and surprised, the lantern-jawed and mild—this other face that was so many more things at once, and things so different. It was that of a young man, pale too, and half-extinguished by the heat, or worry, or both, but somehow, quicker, vivider, more conscious; or perhaps seeming so because he was so different. Archer hung a moment on a thin thread of memory, but it snapped and floated off with the disappearing face—apparently that of some foreign business man, looking doubly foreign in such a setting. He vanished in the stream of passers-by, and Archer resumed his patrol.

He did not care to be seen watch in hand within view of the hotel, and his unaided reckoning of the lapse of time led him to conclude that, if Madame Olenska was so long in reappearing, it could only be because she had met the emissary and been waylaid by him. At the thought Archer's apprehension rose to anguish.

"If she doesn't come soon I'll go in and find her," he said.

The doors swung open again and she was at his side. They got into the herdic, and as it drove off he took out his watch and saw that she had been absent just three minutes. In the clatter of loose windows that made talk impossible they bumped over the disjointed cobblestones to the wharf.

Seated side by side on a bench of the half-empty boat they found that they had hardly anything to say to each other, or rather that what they had to say communicated itself best in the blessed silence of their release and their isolation.

As the paddle-wheels began to turn, and wharves and shipping to recede through the veil of heat, it seemed to Archer that everything in the old familiar world of habit was receding also. He longed to ask Madame Olenska if she did not have the same feeling: the feeling that they were starting on some long voyage from which they might never return. But he was afraid to say it, or anything else that might disturb the delicate balance of her trust in him. In reality he had no wish to betray that trust. There had been days and nights when the memory of their kiss had burned and burned on his lips; the day before even, on the drive to Portsmouth, the thought of her had run through him like fire; but now that she was beside him, and they were drifting forth into this unknown world, they seemed to have reached the kind of deeper nearness that a touch may sunder.

As the boat left the harbour and turned seaward a breeze stirred about them and the bay broke up into long oily undulations, then into ripples tipped with spray. The fog of sultriness still hung over the city, but ahead lay a fresh world of ruffled waters, and distant promontories with light-houses in the sun. Madame Olenska, leaning back against the boat-rail, drank in the coolness between parted lips. She had wound a long veil about her hat, but it left her face uncovered, and Archer was struck by the tranquil gaiety of her expression. She seemed to take their adventure as a matter of course, and to be neither in fear of unexpected encounters, nor (what was worse) unduly elated by their possibility.

In the bare dining-room of the inn, which he had hoped they would have to themselves, they found a strident party of innocent-looking young men and women—school-teachers on a holiday, the landlord told them—and Archer's heart sank at the idea of having to talk through their noise.

"This is hopeless—I'll ask for a private room," he said; and Madame Olenska, without offering any objection, waited while he went in search of it. The room opened on a long wooden verandah, with the sea coming in at the windows. It was bare and cool, with a table covered with a coarse checkered cloth and adorned by a bottle of pickles and a blueberry pie under a cage. No more guileless-looking *cabinet particulier* ever offered its shelter to a clandestine couple: Archer fancied he saw the sense of its reassurance in the faintly amused smile with which Madame Olenska sat down opposite to him. A woman who had run away from her husband—and reputedly with another man—was likely to have mastered the art of taking things for granted; but something in the quality of her composure took the edge from his irony. By being so quiet, so unsurprised and so simple she had managed to brush away the conventions and make him feel that to seek to be alone was the natural thing for two old friends who had so much to say to each other. . . .

XXIV

T HEY LUNCHED slowly and meditatively, with mute intervals between rushes of talk; for, the spell once broken,
they had much to say, and yet moments when saying became
the mere accompaniment to long duologues of silence. Archer
kept the talk from his own affairs, not with conscious intention but because he did not want to miss a word of her history; and leaning on the table, her chin resting on her clasped
hands, she talked to him of the year and a half since they had
met.

She had grown tired of what people called "society"; New
York was kind, it was almost oppressively hospitable; she
should never forget the way in which it had welcomed her
back; but after the first flush of novelty she had found herself,
as she phrased it, too "different" to care for the things it cared
about—and so she had decided to try Washington, where one
was supposed to meet more varieties of people and of opinion. And on the whole she should probably settle down in
Washington, and make a home there for poor Medora, who
had worn out the patience of all her other relations just at the
time when she most needed looking after and protecting from
matrimonial perils.

"But Dr. Carver—aren't you afraid of Dr. Carver? I hear
he's been staying with you at the Blenkers'."

She smiled. "Oh, the Carver danger is over. Dr. Carver is a
very clever man. He wants a rich wife to finance his plans,
and Medora is simply a good advertisement as a convert."

"A convert to what?"

"To all sorts of new and crazy social schemes. But, do you
know, they interest me more than the blind conformity to
tradition—somebody else's tradition—that I see among our
own friends. It seems stupid to have discovered America only
to make it into a copy of another country." She smiled across
the table. "Do you suppose Christopher Columbus would
have taken all that trouble just to go to the Opera with the
Selfridge Merrys?"

Archer changed colour. "And Beaufort—do you say these
things to Beaufort?" he asked abruptly.

"I haven't seen him for a long time. But I used to; and he understands."

"Ah, it's what I've always told you; you don't like us. And you like Beaufort because he's so unlike us." He looked about the bare room and out at the bare beach and the row of stark white village houses strung along the shore. "We're damnably dull. We've no character, no colour, no variety.—I wonder," he broke out, " why you don't go back?"

Her eyes darkened, and he expected an indignant rejoinder. But she sat silent, as if thinking over what he had said, and he grew frightened lest she should answer that she wondered too.

At length she said: "I believe it's because of you."

It was impossible to make the confession more dispassionately, or in a tone less encouraging to the vanity of the person addressed. Archer reddened to the temples, but dared not move or speak: it was as if her words had been some rare butterfly that the least motion might drive off on startled wings, but that might gather a flock about it if it were left undisturbed.

"At least," she continued, "it was you who made me understand that under the dullness there are things so fine and sensitive and delicate that even those I most cared for in my other life look cheap in comparison. I don't know how to explain myself"—she drew together her troubled brows— "but it seems as if I'd never before understood with how much that is hard and shabby and base the most exquisite pleasures may be paid."

"Exquisite pleasures—it's something to have had them!" he felt like retorting; but the appeal in her eyes kept him silent.

"I want," she went on, "to be perfectly honest with you— and with myself. For a long time I've hoped this chance would come: that I might tell you how you've helped me, what you've made of me—"

Archer sat staring beneath frowning brows. He interrupted her with a laugh. "And what do you make out that you've made of me?"

She paled a little. "Of you?"

"Yes: for I'm of your making much more than you ever

were of mine. I'm the man who married one woman because another one told him to."

Her paleness turned to a fugitive flush. "I thought—you promised—you were not to say such things today."

"Ah—how like a woman! None of you will ever see a bad business through!"

She lowered her voice. "*Is* it a bad business—for May?"

He stood in the window, drumming against the raised sash, and feeling in every fibre the wistful tenderness with which she had spoken her cousin's name.

"For that's the thing we've always got to think of—haven't we—by your own showing?" she insisted.

"My own showing?" he echoed, his blank eyes still on the sea.

"Or if not," she continued, pursuing her own thought with a painful application, "if it's not worth while to have given up, to have missed things, so that others may be saved from disillusionment and misery—then everything I came home for, everything that made my other life seem by contrast so bare and so poor because no one there took account of them—all these things are a sham or a dream—"

He turned around without moving from his place. "And in that case there's no reason on earth why you shouldn't go back?" he concluded for her.

Her eyes were clinging to him desperately. "Oh, *is* there no reason?"

"Not if you staked your all on the success of my marriage. My marriage," he said savagely, "isn't going to be a sight to keep you here." She made no answer, and he went on: "What's the use? You gave me my first glimpse of a real life, and at the same moment you asked me to go on with a sham one. It's beyond human enduring—that's all."

"Oh, don't say that; when I'm enduring it!" she burst out, her eyes filling.

Her arms had dropped along the table, and she sat with her face abandoned to his gaze as if in the recklessness of a desperate peril. The face exposed her as much as if it had been her whole person, with the soul behind it: Archer stood dumb, overwhelmed by what it suddenly told him.

"You too—oh, all this time, you too?"

For answer, she let the tears on her lids overflow and run slowly downward.

Half the width of the room was still between them, and neither made any show of moving. Archer was conscious of a curious indifference to her bodily presence: he would hardly have been aware of it if one of the hands she had flung out on the table had not drawn his gaze as on the occasion when, in the little Twenty-third Street house, he had kept his eye on it in order not to look at her face. Now his imagination spun about the hand as about the edge of a vortex; but still he made no effort to draw nearer. He had known the love that is fed on caresses and feeds them; but this passion that was closer than his bones was not to be superficially satisfied. His one terror was to do anything which might efface the sound and impression of her words; his one thought, that he should never again feel quite alone.

But after a moment the sense of waste and ruin overcame him. There they were, close together and safe and shut in; yet so chained to their separate destinies that they might as well have been half the world apart.

"What's the use—when you will go back?" he broke out, a great hopeless *How on earth can I keep you?* crying out to her beneath his words.

She sat motionless, with lowered lids. "Oh—I shan't go yet!"

"Not yet? Some time, then? Some time that you already foresee?"

At that she raised her clearest eyes. "I promise you: not as long as you hold out. Not as long as we can look straight at each other like this."

He dropped into his chair. What her answer really said was: "If you lift a finger you'll drive me back: back to all the abominations you know of, and all the temptations you half guess." He understood it as clearly as if she had uttered the words, and the thought kept him anchored to his side of the table in a kind of moved and sacred submission.

"What a life for you!—" he groaned.

"Oh—as long as it's a part of yours."

"And mine a part of yours?"

She nodded.

"And that's to be all—for either of us?"

"Well; it *is* all, isn't it?"

At that he sprang up, forgetting everything but the sweetness of her face. She rose too, not as if to meet him or to flee from him, but quietly, as though the worst of the task were done and she had only to wait; so quietly that, as he came close, her outstretched hands acted not as a check but as a guide to him. They fell into his, while her arms, extended but not rigid, kept him far enough off to let her surrendered face say the rest.

They may have stood in that way for a long time, or only for a few moments; but it was long enough for her silence to communicate all she had to say, and for him to feel that only one thing mattered. He must do nothing to make this meeting their last; he must leave their future in her care, asking only that she should keep fast hold of it.

"Don't—don't be unhappy," she said, with a break in her voice, as she drew her hands away; and he answered: "You won't go back—you won't go back?" as if it were the one possibility he could not bear.

"I won't go back," she said; and turning away she opened the door and led the way into the public dining-room.

The strident school-teachers were gathering up their possessions preparatory to a straggling flight to the wharf; across the beach lay the white steam-boat at the pier; and over the sunlit waters Boston loomed in a line of haze.

XXV

ONCE MORE on the boat, and in the presence of others, Archer felt a tranquillity of spirit that surprised as much as it sustained him.

The day, according to any current valuation, had been a rather ridiculous failure; he had not so much as touched Madame Olenska's hand with his lips, or extracted one word from her that gave promise of farther opportunities. Nevertheless, for a man sick with unsatisfied love, and parting for an indefinite period from the object of his passion, he felt himself almost humiliatingly calm and comforted. It was the perfect balance she had held between their loyalty to others and their honesty to themselves that had so stirred and yet tranquillized him; a balance not artfully calculated, as her tears and her falterings showed, but resulting naturally from her unabashed sincerity. It filled him with a tender awe, now the danger was over, and made him thank the fates that no personal vanity, no sense of playing a part before sophisticated witnesses, had tempted him to tempt her. Even after they had clasped hands for good-bye at the Fall River station, and he had turned away alone, the conviction remained with him of having saved out of their meeting much more than he had sacrificed.

He wandered back to the club, and went and sat alone in the deserted library, turning and turning over in his thoughts every separate second of their hours together. It was clear to him, and it grew more clear under closer scrutiny, that if she should finally decide on returning to Europe—returning to her husband—it would not be because her old life tempted her, even on the new terms offered. No: she would go only if she felt herself becoming a temptation to Archer, a temptation to fall away from the standard they had both set up. Her choice would be to stay near him as long as he did not ask her to come nearer; and it depended on himself to keep her just there, safe but secluded.

In the train these thoughts were still with him. They enclosed him in a kind of golden haze, through which the faces about him looked remote and indistinct: he had a feeling that if he spoke to his fellow-travellers they would not understand what he was saying. In this state of abstraction he found himself, the following morning, waking to the reality of a stifling September day in New York. The heat-withered faces in the long train streamed past him, and he continued to stare at them through the same golden blur; but suddenly, as he left the station, one of the faces detached itself, came closer and forced itself upon his consciousness. It was, as he instantly recalled, the face of the young man he had seen, the day before, passing out of the Parker House, and had noted as not conforming to type, as not having an American hotel face.

The same thing struck him now; and again he became aware of a dim stir of former associations. The young man stood looking about him with the dazed air of the foreigner flung upon the harsh mercies of American travel; then he advanced toward Archer, lifted his hat, and said in English: "Surely, Monsieur, we met in London?"

"Ah, to be sure: in London!" Archer grasped his hand with curiosity and sympathy. "So you *did* get here, after all?" he exclaimed, casting a wondering eye on the astute and haggard little countenance of young Carfry's French tutor.

"Oh, I got here—yes," M. Rivière smiled with drawn lips. "But not for long; I return the day after tomorrow." He stood grasping his light valise in one neatly gloved hand, and gazing anxiously, perplexedly, almost appealingly, into Archer's face.

"I wonder, Monsieur, since I've had the good luck to run across you, if I might—"

"I was just going to suggest it: come to luncheon, won't you? Down town, I mean: if you'll look me up in my office I'll take you to a very decent restaurant in that quarter."

M. Rivière was visibly touched and surprised. "You're too kind. But I was only going to ask if you would tell me how to reach some sort of conveyance. There are no porters, and no one here seems to listen—"

"I know: our American stations must surprise you. When you ask for a porter they give you chewing-gum. But if you'll come along I'll extricate you; and you must really lunch with me, you know."

The young man, after a just perceptible hesitation, replied, with profuse thanks, and in a tone that did not carry complete conviction, that he was already engaged; but when they had reached the comparative reassurance of the street he asked if he might call that afternoon.

Archer, at ease in the midsummer leisure of the office, fixed an hour and scribbled his address, which the Frenchman pocketed with reiterated thanks and a wide flourish of his hat. A horse-car received him, and Archer walked away.

Punctually at the hour M. Rivière appeared, shaved, smoothed-out, but still unmistakably drawn and serious. Archer was alone in his office, and the young man, before accepting the seat he proffered, began abruptly: "I believe I saw you, sir, yesterday in Boston."

The statement was insignificant enough, and Archer was about to frame an assent when his words were checked by something mysterious yet illuminating in his visitor's insistent gaze.

"It is extraordinary, very extraordinary," M. Rivière continued, "that we should have met in the circumstances in which I find myself."

"What circumstances?" Archer asked, wondering a little crudely if he needed money.

M. Rivière continued to study him with tentative eyes. "I have come, not to look for employment, as I spoke of doing when we last met, but on a special mission—"

"Ah—!" Archer exclaimed. In a flash the two meetings had connected themselves in his mind. He paused to take in the situation thus suddenly lighted up for him, and M. Rivière also remained silent, as if aware that what he had said was enough.

"A special mission," Archer at length repeated.

The young Frenchman, opening his palms, raised them slightly, and the two men continued to look at each other across the office-desk till Archer roused himself to say: "Do sit down"; whereupon M. Rivière bowed, took a distant chair, and again waited.

"It was about this mission that you wanted to consult me?" Archer finally asked.

M. Rivière bent his head. "Not in my own behalf: on that

score I—I have fully dealt with myself. I should like—if I may—to speak to you about the Countess Olenska."

Archer had known for the last few minutes that the words were coming; but when they came they sent the blood rushing to his temples as if he had been caught by a bent-back branch in a thicket.

"And on whose behalf," he said, "do you wish to do this?"

M. Rivière met the question sturdily. "Well—I might say *hers*, if it did not sound like a liberty. Shall I say instead: on behalf of abstract justice?"

Archer considered him ironically. "In other words: you are Count Olenski's messenger?"

He saw his blush more darkly reflected in M. Rivière's sallow countenance. "Not to *you*, Monsieur. If I come to you, it is on quite other grounds."

"What right have you, in the circumstances, to *be* on any other ground?" Archer retorted. "If you're an emissary you're an emissary."

The young man considered. "My mission is over: as far as the Countess Olenska goes, it has failed."

"I can't help that," Archer rejoined on the same note of irony.

"No: but you can help—" M. Rivière paused, turned his hat about in his still carefully gloved hands, looked into its lining and then back at Archer's face. "You can help, Monsieur, I am convinced, to make it equally a failure with her family."

Archer pushed back his chair and stood up. "Well—and by God I will!" he exclaimed. He stood with his hands in his pockets, staring down wrathfully at the little Frenchman, whose face, though he too had risen, was still an inch or two below the line of Archer's eyes.

M. Rivière paled to his normal hue: paler than that his complexion could hardly turn.

"Why the devil," Archer explosively continued, "should you have thought—since I suppose you're appealing to me on the ground of my relationship to Madame Olenska—that I should take a view contrary to the rest of her family?"

The change of expression in M. Rivière's face was for a

time his only answer. His look passed from timidity to absolute distress: for a young man of his usually resourceful mien it would have been difficult to appear more disarmed and defenceless. "Oh, Monsieur—"

"I can't imagine," Archer continued, " why you should have come to me when there are others so much nearer to the Countess; still less why you thought I should be more accessible to the arguments I suppose you were sent over with."

M. Rivière took this onslaught with a disconcerting humility. "The arguments I want to present to you, Monsieur, are my own and not those I was sent over with."

"Then I see still less reason for listening to them."

M. Rivière again looked into his hat, as if considering whether these last words were not a sufficiently broad hint to put it on and be gone. Then he spoke with sudden decision. "Monsieur—will you tell me one thing? Is it my right to be here that you question? Or do you perhaps believe the whole matter to be already closed?"

His quiet insistence made Archer feel the clumsiness of his own bluster. M. Rivière had succeeded in imposing himself: Archer, reddening slightly, dropped into his chair again, and signed to the young man to be seated.

"I beg your pardon: but why isn't the matter closed?"

M. Rivière gazed back at him with anguish. "You do, then, agree with the rest of the family that, in face of the new proposals I have brought, it is hardly possible for Madame Olenska not to return to her husband?"

"Good God!" Archer exclaimed; and his visitor gave out a low murmur of confirmation.

"Before seeing her, I saw—at Count Olenski's request— Mr. Lovell Mingott, with whom I had several talks before going to Boston. I understand that he represents his mother's view; and that Mrs. Manson Mingott's influence is great throughout her family."

Archer sat silent, with the sense of clinging to the edge of a sliding precipice. The discovery that he had been excluded from a share in these negotiations, and even from the knowledge that they were on foot, caused him a surprise hardly dulled by the acuter wonder of what he was learning. He saw in a flash that if the family had ceased to consult him it was because some deep tribal instinct warned them that he was no longer on their side; and he recalled, with a start of comprehension, a remark of May's during their drive home from Mrs. Manson Mingott's on the day of the Archery Meeting: "Perhaps, after all, Ellen would be happier with her husband."

Even in the tumult of new discoveries Archer remembered his indignant exclamation, and the fact that since then his wife had never named Madame Olenska to him. Her careless allusion had no doubt been the straw held up to see which way the wind blew; the result had been reported to the family, and thereafter Archer had been tacitly omitted from their counsels. He admired the tribal discipline which made May bow to this decision. She would not have done so, he knew, had her conscience protested; but she probably shared the family view that Madame Olenska would be better off as an unhappy wife than as a separated one, and that there was no use in discussing the case with Newland, who had an awkward way of suddenly not seeming to take the most fundamental things for granted.

Archer looked up and met his visitor's anxious gaze. "Don't you know, Monsieur—is it possible you don't know—that the family begin to doubt if they have the right to advise the Countess to refuse her husband's last proposals?"

"The proposals you brought?"

"The proposals I brought."

It was on Archer's lips to exclaim that whatever he knew or did not know was no concern of M. Rivière's; but something in the humble and yet courageous tenacity of M. Rivière's gaze made him reject this conclusion, and he met the young man's question with another. "What is your object in speaking to me of this?"

He had not to wait a moment for the answer. "To beg you, Monsieur—to beg you with all the force I'm capable of—not to let her go back.—Oh, don't let her!" M. Rivière exclaimed.

Archer looked at him with increasing astonishment. There was no mistaking the sincerity of his distress or the strength of his determination: he had evidently resolved to let every-thing go by the board but the supreme need of thus putting himself on record. Archer considered.

"May I ask," he said at length, "if this is the line you took with the Countess Olenska?"

M. Rivière reddened, but his eyes did not falter. "No, Monsieur: I accepted my mission in good faith. I really be-lieved—for reasons I need not trouble you with—that it would be better for Madame Olenska to recover her situation, her fortune, the social consideration that her husband's stand-ing gives her."

"So I supposed: you could hardly have accepted such a mis-sion otherwise."

"I should not have accepted it."

"Well, then—?" Archer paused again, and their eyes met in another protracted scrutiny.

"Ah, Monsieur, after I had seen her, after I had listened to her, I knew she was better off here."

"You knew—?"

"Monsieur, I discharged my mission faithfully: I put the Count's arguments, I stated his offers, without adding any comment of my own. The Countess was good enough to lis-ten patiently; she carried her goodness so far as to see me twice; she considered impartially all I had come to say. And it was in the course of these two talks that I changed my mind, that I came to see things differently."

"May I ask what led to this change?"

"Simply seeing the change in *her*," M. Rivière replied.

"The change in her? Then you knew her before?"

The young man's colour again rose. "I used to see her in her husband's house. I have known Count Olenski for many years. You can imagine that he would not have sent a stranger on such a mission."

Archer's gaze, wandering away to the blank walls of the office, rested on a hanging calendar surmounted by the rug-ged features of the President of the United States. That such a conversation should be going on anywhere within the mil-lions of square miles subject to his rule seemed as strange as anything that the imagination could invent.

"The change—what sort of a change?"

"Ah, Monsieur, if I could tell you!" M. Rivière paused. "*Tenez*—the discovery, I suppose, of what I'd never thought of before: that she's an American. And that if you're an American of *her* kind—of your kind—things that are accepted in certain other societies, or at least put up with as part of a general convenient give-and-take—become unthinkable, simply unthinkable. If Madame Olenska's relations understood what these things were, their opposition to her returning would no doubt be as unconditional as her own; but they seem to regard her husband's wish to have her back as proof of an irresistible longing for domestic life." M. Rivière paused, and then added: "Whereas it's far from being as simple as that."

Archer looked back to the President of the United States, and then down at his desk and at the papers scattered on it. For a second or two he could not trust himself to speak. During this interval he heard M. Rivière's chair pushed back, and was aware that the young man had risen. When he glanced up again he saw that his visitor was as moved as himself.

"Thank you," Archer said simply.

"There's nothing to thank me for, Monsieur: it is I, rather—" M. Rivière broke off, as if speech for him too were difficult. "I should like, though," he continued in a firmer voice, "to add one thing. You asked me if I was in Count Olenski's employ. I am at this moment: I returned to him, a few months ago, for reasons of private necessity such as may happen to any one who has persons, ill and older persons, dependent on him. But from the moment that I have taken the step of coming here to say these things to you I consider myself discharged, and I shall tell him so on my return, and give him the reasons. That's all, Monsieur."

M. Rivière bowed and drew back a step.

"Thank you," Archer said again, as their hands met.

XXVI

EVERY YEAR on the fifteenth of October Fifth Avenue opened its shutters, unrolled its carpets and hung up its triple layer of window-curtains.

By the first of November this household ritual was over, and society had begun to look about and take stock of itself. By the fifteenth the season was in full blast, Opera and theatres were putting forth their new attractions, dinner-engagements were accumulating, and dates for dances being fixed. And punctually at about this time Mrs. Archer always said that New York was very much changed.

Observing it from the lofty stand-point of a non-participant, she was able, with the help of Mr. Sillerton Jackson and Miss Sophy, to trace each new crack in its surface, and all the strange weeds pushing up between the ordered rows of social vegetables. It had been one of the amusements of Archer's youth to wait for this annual pronouncement of his mother's, and to hear her enumerate the minute signs of disintegration that his careless gaze had overlooked. For New York, to Mrs. Archer's mind, never changed without changing for the worse; and in this view Miss Sophy Jackson heartily concurred.

Mr. Sillerton Jackson, as became a man of the world, suspended his judgment and listened with an amused impartiality to the lamentations of the ladies. But even he never denied that New York had changed; and Newland Archer, in the winter of the second year of his marriage, was himself obliged to admit that if it had not actually changed it was certainly changing.

These points had been raised, as usual, at Mrs. Archer's Thanksgiving dinner. At the date when she was officially enjoined to give thanks for the blessings of the year it was her habit to take a mournful though not embittered stock of her world, and wonder what there was to be thankful for. At any rate, not the state of society; society, if it could be said to exist, was rather a spectacle on which to call down Biblical imprecations—and in fact, every one knew what the Reverend Dr. Ashmore meant when he chose a text from Jeremiah (chap. ii., verse 25) for his Thanksgiving sermon. Dr. Ashmore, the new Rector of St. Matthew's, had been chosen because he was very "advanced": his sermons were considered bold in thought and novel in language. When he fulminated against fashionable society he always spoke of its "trend"; and to Mrs. Archer it was terrifying and yet fascinating to feel herself part of a community that was trending.

"There's no doubt that Dr. Ashmore is right: there *is* a marked trend," she said, as if it were something visible and measurable, like a crack in a house.

"It was odd, though, to preach about it on Thanksgiving," Miss Jackson opined; and her hostess drily rejoined: "Oh, he means us to give thanks for what's left."

Archer had been wont to smile at these annual vaticinations of his mother's; but this year even he was obliged to acknowledge, as he listened to an enumeration of the changes, that the "trend" was visible.

"The extravagance in dress—" Miss Jackson began. "Sillerton took me to the first night of the Opera, and I can only tell you that Jane Merry's dress was the only one I recognised from last year; and even that had had the front panel changed. Yet I know she got it out from Worth only two years ago, because my seamstress always goes in to make over her Paris dresses before she wears them."

"Ah, Jane Merry is one of *us*," said Mrs. Archer sighing, as if it were not such an enviable thing to be in an age when ladies were beginning to flaunt abroad their Paris dresses as soon as they were out of the Custom House, instead of letting them mellow under lock and key, in the manner of Mrs. Archer's contemporaries.

"Yes; she's one of the few. In my youth," Miss Jackson rejoined, "it was considered vulgar to dress in the newest fashions; and Amy Sillerton has always told me that in Boston the rule was to put away one's Paris dresses for two years. Old Mrs. Baxter Pennilow, who did everything handsomely, used to import twelve a year, two velvet, two satin, two silk, and the other six of poplin and the finest cashmere. It was a standing order, and as she was ill for two years before she died they found forty-eight Worth dresses that had never been taken out of tissue paper; and when the girls left off their mourning they were able to wear the first lot at the Symphony concerts without looking in advance of the fashion."

"Ah, well, Boston is more conservative than New York; but I always think it's a safe rule for a lady to lay aside her French dresses for one season," Mrs. Archer conceded.

"It was Beaufort who started the new fashion by making his wife clap her new clothes on her back as soon as they arrived: I must say at times it takes all Regina's distinction not to look like . . . like . . ." Miss Jackson glanced around the table, caught Janey's bulging gaze, and took refuge in an unintelligible murmur.

"Like her rivals," said Mr. Sillerton Jackson, with the air of producing an epigram.

"Oh,—" the ladies murmured; and Mrs. Archer added, partly to distract her daughter's attention from forbidden topics: "Poor Regina! Her Thanksgiving hasn't been a very cheerful one, I'm afraid. Have you heard the rumours about Beaufort's speculations, Sillerton?"

Mr. Jackson nodded carelessly. Every one had heard the rumours in question, and he scorned to confirm a tale that was already common property.

A gloomy silence fell upon the party. No one really liked Beaufort, and it was not wholly unpleasant to think the worst of his private life; but the idea of his having brought financial dishonour on his wife's family was too shocking to be enjoyed even by his enemies. Archer's New York tolerated hypocrisy in private relations; but in business matters it exacted a limpid and impeccable honesty. It was a long time since any well-known banker had failed discreditably; but every one remembered the social extinction visited on the heads of the firm when the last event of the kind had happened. It would be the same with the Beauforts, in spite of his power and her popularity; not all the leagued strength of the Dallas connection would save poor Regina if there were any truth in the reports of her husband's unlawful speculations.

The talk took refuge in less ominous topics; but everything they touched on seemed to confirm Mrs. Archer's sense of an accelerated trend.

"Of course, Newland, I know you let dear May go to Mrs. Struthers's Sunday evenings—" she began; and May interposed gaily: "Oh, you know, everybody goes to Mrs. Struthers's now; and she was invited to Granny's last reception."

It was thus, Archer reflected, that New York managed its transitions: conspiring to ignore them till they were well over, and then, in all good faith, imagining that they had taken place in a preceding age. There was always a traitor in the citadel; and after he (or generally she) had surrendered the keys, what was the use of pretending that it was impregnable? Once people had tasted of Mrs. Struthers's easy Sunday hospitality they were not likely to sit at home remembering that her champagne was transmuted Shoe-Polish.

"I know, dear, I know," Mrs. Archer sighed. "Such things have to be, I suppose, as long as *amusement* is what people go out for; but I've never quite forgiven your cousin Madame Olenska for being the first person to countenance Mrs. Struthers."

A sudden blush rose to young Mrs. Archer's face; it surprised her husband as much as the other guests about the table. "Oh, *Ellen*—" she murmured, much in the same accusing and yet deprecating tone in which her parents might have said: "Oh, *the Blenkers*—."

It was the note which the family had taken to sounding on the mention of the Countess Olenska's name, since she had surprised and inconvenienced them by remaining obdurate to her husband's advances; but on May's lips it gave food for thought, and Archer looked at her with the sense of strangeness that sometimes came over him when she was most in the tone of her environment.

His mother, with less than her usual sensitiveness to atmosphere, still insisted: "I've always thought that people like the Countess Olenska, who have lived in aristocratic societies, ought to help us to keep up our social distinctions, instead of ignoring them."

May's blush remained permanently vivid: it seemed to have a significance beyond that implied by the recognition of Madame Olenska's social bad faith.

"I've no doubt we all seem alike to foreigners," said Miss Jackson tartly.

"I don't think Ellen cares for society; but nobody knows

exactly what she does care for," May continued, as if she had been groping for something noncommittal.

"Ah, well—" Mrs. Archer sighed again.

Everybody knew that the Countess Olenska was no longer in the good graces of her family. Even her devoted champion, old Mrs. Manson Mingott, had been unable to defend her refusal to return to her husband. The Mingotts had not proclaimed their disapproval aloud: their sense of solidarity was too strong. They had simply, as Mrs. Welland said, "let poor Ellen find her own level"—and that, mortifyingly and incomprehensibly, was in the dim depths where the Blenkers prevailed, and "people who wrote" celebrated their untidy rites. It was incredible, but it was a fact, that Ellen, in spite of all her opportunities and her privileges, had become simply "Bohemian." The fact enforced the contention that she had made a fatal mistake in not returning to Count Olenski. After all, a young woman's place was under her husband's roof, especially when she had left it in circumstances that . . . well . . . if one had cared to look into them . . .

"Madame Olenska is a great favourite with the gentlemen," said Miss Sophy, with her air of wishing to put forth something conciliatory when she knew that she was planting a dart.

"Ah, that's the danger that a young woman like Madame Olenska is always exposed to," Mrs. Archer mournfully agreed; and the ladies, on this conclusion, gathered up their trains to seek the carcel globes of the drawing-room, while Archer and Mr. Sillerton Jackson withdrew to the Gothic library.

Once established before the grate, and consoling himself for the inadequacy of the dinner by the perfection of his cigar, Mr. Jackson became portentous and communicable.

"If the Beaufort smash comes," he announced, "there are going to be disclosures."

Archer raised his head quickly: he could never hear the name without the sharp vision of Beaufort's heavy figure, opulently furred and shod, advancing through the snow at Skuytercliff.

"There's bound to be," Mr. Jackson continued, "the nastiest kind of a cleaning up. He hasn't spent all his money on Regina."

"Oh, well—that's discounted, isn't it? My belief is he'll pull out yet," said the young man, wanting to change the subject.

"Perhaps—perhaps. I know he was to see some of the influential people today. Of course," Mr. Jackson reluctantly conceded, "it's to be hoped they can tide him over—this time anyhow. I shouldn't like to think of poor Regina's spending the rest of her life in some shabby foreign watering-place for bankrupts."

Archer said nothing. It seemed to him so natural—however tragic—that money ill-gotten should be cruelly expiated, that his mind, hardly lingering over Mrs. Beaufort's doom, wandered back to closer questions. What was the meaning of May's blush when the Countess Olenska had been mentioned?

Four months had passed since the midsummer day that he and Madame Olenska had spent together; and since then he had not seen her. He knew that she had returned to Washington, to the little house which she and Medora Manson had taken there: he had written to her once—a few words, asking when they were to meet again—and she had even more briefly replied: "Not yet."

Since then there had been no farther communication between them, and he had built up within himself a kind of sanctuary in which she throned among his secret thoughts and longings. Little by little it became the scene of his real life, of his only rational activities; thither he brought the books he read, the ideas and feelings which nourished him, his judgments and his visions. Outside it, in the scene of his actual life, he moved with a growing sense of unreality and insufficiency, blundering against familiar prejudices and traditional points of view as an absent-minded man goes on bumping into the furniture of his own room. Absent—that was what he was: so absent from everything most densely real and near to those about him that it sometimes startled him to find they still imagined he was there.

He became aware that Mr. Jackson was clearing his throat preparatory to farther revelations.

"I don't know, of course, how far your wife's family are aware of what people say about—well, about Madame Olenska's refusal to accept her husband's latest offer."

Archer was silent, and Mr. Jackson obliquely continued: "It's a pity—it's certainly a pity—that she refused it."

"A pity? In God's name, why?"

Mr. Jackson looked down his leg to the unwrinkled sock that joined it to a glossy pump.

"Well—to put it on the lowest ground—what's she going to live on now?"

"Now—?"

"If Beaufort—"

Archer sprang up, his fist banging down on the black walnut-edge of the writing-table. The wells of the brass double-inkstand danced in their sockets.

"What the devil do you mean, sir?"

Mr. Jackson, shifting himself slightly in his chair, turned a tranquil gaze on the young man's burning face.

"Well—I have it on pretty good authority—in fact, on old Catherine's herself—that the family reduced Countess Olenska's allowance considerably when she definitely refused to go back to her husband; and as, by this refusal, she also forfeits the money settled on her when she married—which Olenski was ready to make over to her if she returned—why, what the devil do *you* mean, my dear boy, by asking me what *I* mean?" Mr. Jackson good-humouredly retorted.

Archer moved toward the mantelpiece and bent over to knock his ashes into the grate.

"I don't know anything of Madame Olenska's private affairs; but I don't need to, to be certain that what you insinuate—"

"Oh, *I* don't: it's Lefferts, for one," Mr. Jackson interposed.

"Lefferts—who made love to her and got snubbed for it!" Archer broke out contemptuously.

"Ah—*did* he?" snapped the other, as if this were exactly the fact he had been laying a trap for. He still sat sideways from the fire, so that his hard old gaze held Archer's face as if in a spring of steel.

"Well, well: it's a pity she didn't go back before Beaufort's cropper," he repeated. "If she goes *now*, and if he fails, it will only confirm the general impression: which isn't by any means peculiar to Lefferts, by the way."

"Oh, she won't go back now: less than ever!" Archer had no sooner said it than he had once more the feeling that it was exactly what Mr. Jackson had been waiting for.

The old gentleman considered him attentively. "That's your opinion, eh? Well, no doubt you know. But everybody will tell you that the few pennies Medora Manson has left are all in Beaufort's hands; and how the two women are to keep their heads above water unless he does, I can't imagine. Of course, Madame Olenska may still soften old Catherine, who's been the most inexorably opposed to her staying; and old Catherine could make her any allowance she chooses. But we all know that she hates parting with good money; and the rest of the family have no particular interest in keeping Madame Olenska here."

Archer was burning with unavailing wrath: he was exactly in the state when a man is sure to do something stupid, knowing all the while that he is doing it.

He saw that Mr. Jackson had been instantly struck by the fact that Madame Olenska's differences with her grandmother and her other relations were not known to him, and that the old gentleman had drawn his own conclusions as to the reasons for Archer's exclusion from the family councils. This fact warned Archer to go warily; but the insinuations about Beaufort made him reckless. He was mindful, however, if not of his own danger, at least of the fact that Mr. Jackson was under his mother's roof, and consequently his guest. Old New York scrupulously observed the etiquette of hospitality, and no discussion with a guest was ever allowed to degenerate into a disagreement.

"Shall we go up and join my mother?" he suggested curtly, as Mr. Jackson's last cone of ashes dropped into the brass ash-tray at his elbow.

On the drive homeward May remained oddly silent; through the darkness, he still felt her enveloped in her menacing blush. What its menace meant he could not guess: but he was sufficiently warned by the fact that Madame Olenska's name had evoked it.

They went upstairs, and he turned into the library. She usually followed him; but he heard her passing down the passage to her bedroom.

"May!" he called out impatiently; and she came back, with a slight glance of surprise at his tone.

"This lamp is smoking again; I should think the servants might see that it's kept properly trimmed," he grumbled nervously.

"I'm so sorry: it shan't happen again," she answered, in the firm bright tone she had learned from her mother; and it exasperated Archer to feel that she was already beginning to humour him like a younger Mr. Welland. She bent over to lower the wick, and as the light struck up on her white shoulders and the clear curves of her face he thought: "How young she is! For what endless years this life will have to go on!"

He felt, with a kind of horror, his own strong youth and the bounding blood in his veins. "Look here," he said suddenly, "I may have to go to Washington for a few days— soon; next week perhaps."

Her hand remained on the key of the lamp as she turned to him slowly. The heat from its flame had brought back a glow to her face, but it paled as she looked up.

"On business?" she asked, in a tone which implied that there could be no other conceivable reason, and that she had put the question automatically, as if merely to finish his own sentence.

"On business, naturally. There's a patent case coming up before the Supreme Court—" He gave the name of the inventor, and went on furnishing details with all Lawrence Lefferts's practised glibness, while she listened attentively, saying at intervals: "Yes, I see."

"The change will do you good," she said simply, when he had finished; "and you must be sure to go and see Ellen," she added, looking him straight in the eyes with her cloudless smile, and speaking in the tone she might have employed in urging him not to neglect some irksome family duty.

It was the only word that passed between them on the subject; but in the code in which they had both been trained it meant: "Of course you understand that I know all that people have been saying about Ellen, and heartily sympathise with my family in their effort to get her to return to her husband. I also know that, for some reason you have not chosen to tell me, you have advised her against this course, which all the older men of the family, as well as our grandmother, agree in approving; and that it is owing to your encouragement that Ellen defies us all, and exposes herself to the kind of criticism of which Mr. Sillerton Jackson probably gave you, this evening, the hint that has made you so irritable. . . . Hints have indeed not been wanting; but since you appear unwilling to take them from others, I offer you this one myself, in the only form in which well-bred people of our kind can communicate unpleasant things to each other: by letting you understand that I know you mean to see Ellen when you are in Washington, and are perhaps going there expressly for that purpose; and that, since you are sure to see her, I wish you to do so with my full and explicit approval—and to take the opportunity of letting her know what the course of conduct you have encouraged her in is likely to lead to."

Her hand was still on the key of the lamp when the last word of this mute message reached him. She turned the wick down, lifted off the globe, and breathed on the sulky flame.

"They smell less if one blows them out," she explained, with her bright housekeeping air. On the threshold she turned and paused for his kiss.

XXVII

WALL STREET, the next day, had more reassuring reports of Beaufort's situation. They were not definite, but they were hopeful. It was generally understood that he could call on powerful influences in case of emergency, and that he had done so with success; and that evening, when Mrs. Beaufort appeared at the Opera wearing her old smile and a new emerald necklace, society drew a breath of relief.

New York was inexorable in its condemnation of business irregularities. So far there had been no exception to its tacit rule that those who broke the law of probity must pay; and every one was aware that even Beaufort and Beaufort's wife would be offered up unflinchingly to this principle. But to be obliged to offer them up would be not only painful but inconvenient. The disappearance of the Beauforts would leave a considerable void in their compact little circle; and those who were too ignorant or too careless to shudder at the moral catastrophe bewailed in advance the loss of the best ball-room in New York.

Archer had definitely made up his mind to go to Washington. He was waiting only for the opening of the law-suit of which he had spoken to May, so that its date might coincide with that of his visit; but on the following Tuesday he learned from Mr. Letterblair that the case might be postponed for several weeks. Nevertheless, he went home that afternoon determined in any event to leave the next evening. The chances were that May, who knew nothing of his professional life, and had never shown any interest in it, would not learn of the postponement, should it take place, nor remember the names of the litigants if they were mentioned before her; and at any rate he could no longer put off seeing Madame Olenska. There were too many things that he must say to her.

On the Wednesday morning, when he reached his office, Mr. Letterblair met him with a troubled face. Beaufort, after all, had not managed to "tide over"; but by setting afloat the rumour that he had done so he had reassured his depositors, and heavy payments had poured into the bank till the previous evening, when disturbing reports again began to predominate. In consequence, a run on the bank had begun, and its doors were likely to close before the day was over. The ugliest things were being said of Beaufort's dastardly manœuvre, and his failure promised to be one of the most discreditable in the history of Wall Street.

The extent of the calamity left Mr. Letterblair white and incapacitated. "I've seen bad things in my time; but nothing as bad as this. Everybody we know will be hit, one way or another. And what will be done about Mrs. Beaufort? What *can* be done about her? I pity Mrs. Manson Mingott as much as anybody: coming at her age, there's no knowing what effect this affair may have on her. She always believed in Beaufort—she made a friend of him! And there's the whole Dallas connection: poor Mrs. Beaufort is related to every one of you. Her only chance would be to leave her husband—yet how can any one tell her so? Her duty is at his side; and luckily she seems always to have been blind to his private weaknesses."

There was a knock, and Mr. Letterblair turned his head sharply. "What is it? I can't be disturbed."

A clerk brought in a letter for Archer and withdrew. Recognising his wife's hand, the young man opened the envelope and read: "Won't you please come up town as early as you can? Granny had a slight stroke last night. In some mysterious way she found out before any one else this awful news about the bank. Uncle Lovell is away shooting, and the idea of the disgrace has made poor Papa so nervous that he has a temperature and can't leave his room. Mamma needs you dreadfully, and I do hope you can get away at once and go straight to Granny's."

Archer handed the note to his senior partner, and a few minutes later was crawling northward in a crowded horse-car, which he exchanged at Fourteenth Street for one of the high staggering omnibuses of the Fifth Avenue line. It was after twelve o'clock when this laborious vehicle dropped him at old Catherine's. The sitting-room window on the ground floor, where she usually throned, was tenanted by the inadequate figure of her daughter, Mrs. Welland, who signed a haggard welcome as she caught sight of Archer; and at the door he was met by May. The hall wore the unnatural appearance peculiar to well-kept houses suddenly invaded by illness:

wraps and furs lay in heaps on the chairs, a doctor's bag and overcoat were on the table, and beside them letters and cards had already piled up unheeded.

May looked pale but smiling: Dr. Bencomb, who had just come for the second time, took a more hopeful view, and Mrs. Mingott's dauntless determination to live and get well was already having an effect on her family. May led Archer into the old lady's sitting-room, where the sliding doors opening into the bedroom had been drawn shut, and the heavy yellow damask portières dropped over them; and here Mrs. Welland communicated to him in horrified undertones the details of the catastrophe. It appeared that the evening before something dreadful and mysterious had happened. At about eight o'clock, just after Mrs. Mingott had finished the game of solitaire that she always played after dinner, the door-bell had rung, and a lady so thickly veiled that the servants did not immediately recognise her had asked to be received.

The butler, hearing a familiar voice, had thrown open the sitting-room door, announcing: "Mrs. Julius Beaufort"—and had then closed it again on the two ladies. They must have been together, he thought, about an hour. When Mrs. Mingott's bell rang Mrs. Beaufort had already slipped away unseen, and the old lady, white and vast and terrible, sat alone in her great chair, and signed to the butler to help her into her room. She seemed, at that time, though obviously distressed, in complete control of her body and brain. The mulatto maid put her to bed, brought her a cup of tea as usual, laid everything straight in the room, and went away; but at three in the morning the bell rang again, and the two servants, hastening in at this unwonted summons (for old Catherine usually slept like a baby), had found their mistress sitting up against her pillows with a crooked smile on her face and one little hand hanging limp from its huge arm.

The stroke had clearly been a slight one, for she was able to articulate and to make her wishes known; and soon after the doctor's first visit she had begun to regain control of her facial muscles. But the alarm had been great; and proportionately great was the indignation when it was gathered from Mrs. Mingott's fragmentary phrases that Regina Beaufort had come to ask her—incredible effrontery!—to back up her hus-

band, see them through—not to "desert" them, as she called
it—in fact to induce the whole family to cover and condone
their monstrous dishonour.

"I said to her: 'Honour's always been honour, and honesty
honesty, in Manson Mingott's house, and will be till I'm carried out of it feet first,' " the old woman had stammered into
her daughter's ear, in the thick voice of the partly paralysed.
"And when she said: 'But my name, Auntie—my name's
Regina Dallas,' I said: 'It was Beaufort when he covered you
with jewels, and it's got to stay Beaufort now that he's covered you with shame.' "

So much, with tears and gasps of horror, Mrs. Welland imparted, blanched and demolished by the unwonted obligation
of having at last to fix her eyes on the unpleasant and the
discreditable. "If only I could keep it from your father-in-law:
he always says: 'Augusta, for pity's sake, don't destroy my last
illusions'—and how am I to prevent his knowing these horrors?" the poor lady wailed.

"After all, Mamma, he won't have *seen* them," her daughter
suggested; and Mrs. Welland sighed: "Ah, no; thank heaven
he's safe in bed. And Dr. Bencomb has promised to keep him
there till poor Mamma is better, and Regina has been got
away somewhere."

Archer had seated himself near the window and was gazing
out blankly at the deserted thoroughfare. It was evident that
he had been summoned rather for the moral support of the
stricken ladies than because of any specific aid that he could
render. Mr. Lovell Mingott had been telegraphed for, and
messages were being despatched by hand to the members of
the family living in New York; and meanwhile there was
nothing to do but to discuss in hushed tones the consequences of Beaufort's dishonour and of his wife's unjustifiable
action.

Mrs. Lovell Mingott, who had been in another room writing notes, presently reappeared, and added her voice to the
discussion. In *their* day, the elder ladies agreed, the wife of a
man who had done anything disgraceful in business had only
one idea: to efface herself, to disappear with him. "There was
the case of poor Grandmamma Spicer; your great-grandmother, May. Of course," Mrs. Welland hastened to add,

"your great-grandfather's money difficulties were private—losses at cards, or signing a note for somebody—I never quite knew, because Mamma would never speak of it. But she was brought up in the country because her mother had to leave New York after the disgrace, whatever it was: they lived up the Hudson alone, winter and summer, till Mamma was sixteen. It would never have occurred to Grandmamma Spicer to ask the family to 'countenance' her, as I understand Regina calls it; though a private disgrace is nothing compared to the scandal of ruining hundreds of innocent people."

"Yes, it would be more becoming in Regina to hide her own countenance than to talk about other people's," Mrs. Lovell Mingott agreed. "I understand that the emerald necklace she wore at the Opera last Friday had been sent on approval from Ball and Black's in the afternoon. I wonder if they'll ever get it back?"

Archer listened unmoved to the relentless chorus. The idea of absolute financial probity as the first law of a gentleman's code was too deeply ingrained in him for sentimental considerations to weaken it. An adventurer like Lemuel Struthers might build up the millions of his Shoe Polish on any number of shady dealings; but unblemished honesty was the *noblesse oblige* of old financial New York. Nor did Mrs. Beaufort's fate greatly move Archer. He felt, no doubt, more sorry for her than her indignant relatives; but it seemed to him that the tie between husband and wife, even if breakable in prosperity, should be indissoluble in misfortune. As Mr. Letterblair had said, a wife's place was at her husband's side when he was in trouble; but society's place was not at his side, and Mrs. Beaufort's cool assumption that it was seemed almost to make her his accomplice. The mere idea of a woman's appealing to her family to screen her husband's business dishonour was inadmissible, since it was the one thing that the Family, as an institution, could not do.

The mulatto maid called Mrs. Lovell Mingott into the hall, and the latter came back in a moment with a frowning brow.

"She wants me to telegraph for Ellen Olenska. I had written to Ellen, of course, and to Medora; but now it seems that's not enough. I'm to telegraph to her immediately, and to tell her that she's to come alone."

The announcement was received in silence. Mrs. Welland sighed resignedly, and May rose from her seat and went to gather up some newspapers that had been scattered on the floor.

"I suppose it must be done," Mrs. Lovell Mingott continued, as if hoping to be contradicted; and May turned back toward the middle of the room.

"Of course it must be done," she said. "Granny knows what she wants, and we must carry out all her wishes. Shall I write the telegram for you, Auntie? If it goes at once Ellen can probably catch tomorrow morning's train." She pronounced the syllables of the name with a peculiar clearness, as if she had tapped on two silver bells.

"Well, it can't go at once. Jasper and the pantry-boy are both out with notes and telegrams."

May turned to her husband with a smile. "But here's Newland, ready to do anything. Will you take the telegram, Newland? There'll be just time before luncheon."

Archer rose with a murmur of readiness, and she seated herself at old Catherine's rosewood "Bonheur du Jour," and wrote out the message in her large immature hand. When it was written she blotted it neatly and handed it to Archer.

"What a pity," she said, "that you and Ellen will cross each other on the way!—Newland," she added, turning to her mother and aunt, "is obliged to go to Washington about a patent law-suit that is coming up before the Supreme Court. I suppose Uncle Lovell will be back by tomorrow night, and with Granny improving so much it doesn't seem right to ask Newland to give up an important engagement for the firm—does it?"

She paused, as if for an answer, and Mrs. Welland hastily declared: "Oh, of course not, darling. Your Granny would be the last person to wish it." As Archer left the room with the telegram, he heard his mother-in-law add, presumably to Mrs. Lovell Mingott: "But why on earth she should make you telegraph for Ellen Olenska—" and May's clear voice rejoin: "Perhaps it's to urge on her again that after all her duty is with her husband."

The outer door closed on Archer and he walked hastily away toward the telegraph office.

XXVIII

"O L—OL—HOWJER spell it, anyhow?" asked the tart young lady to whom Archer had pushed his wife's telegram across the brass ledge of the Western Union office.

"Olenska—O-len-ska," he repeated, drawing back the message in order to print out the foreign syllables above May's rambling script.

"It's an unlikely name for a New York telegraph office; at least in this quarter," an unexpected voice observed; and turning around Archer saw Lawrence Lefferts at his elbow, pulling an imperturbable moustache and affecting not to glance at the message.

"Hallo, Newland: thought I'd catch you here. I've just heard of old Mrs. Mingott's stroke; and as I was on my way to the house I saw you turning down this street and nipped after you. I suppose you've come from there?"

Archer nodded, and pushed his telegram under the lattice.

"Very bad, eh?" Lefferts continued. "Wiring to the family, I suppose. I gather it *is* bad, if you're including Countess Olenska."

Archer's lips stiffened; he felt a savage impulse to dash his fist into the long vain handsome face at his side.

"Why?" he questioned.

Lefferts, who was known to shrink from discussion, raised his eye-brows with an ironic grimace that warned the other of the watching damsel behind the lattice. Nothing could be worse "form," the look reminded Archer, than any display of temper in a public place.

Archer had never been more indifferent to the requirements of form; but his impulse to do Lawrence Lefferts a physical injury was only momentary. The idea of bandying Ellen Olenska's name with him at such a time, and on whatsoever provocation, was unthinkable. He paid for his telegram, and the two young men went out together into the street. There Archer, having regained his self-control, went on: "Mrs. Mingott is much better: the doctor feels no anxiety whatever"; and Lefferts, with profuse expressions of relief, asked him if

he had heard that there were beastly bad rumours again about
Beaufort. . . .

That afternoon the announcement of the Beaufort failure
was in all the papers. It overshadowed the report of Mrs.
Manson Mingott's stroke, and only the few who had heard
of the mysterious connection between the two events thought
of ascribing old Catherine's illness to anything but the accumulation of flesh and years.

The whole of New York was darkened by the tale of Beaufort's dishonour. There had never, as Mr. Letterblair said,
been a worse case in his memory, nor, for that matter, in the
memory of the far-off Letterblair who had given his name to
the firm. The bank had continued to take in money for a
whole day after its failure was inevitable; and as many of its
clients belonged to one or another of the ruling clans, Beaufort's duplicity seemed doubly cynical. If Mrs. Beaufort had
not taken the tone that such misfortunes (the word was her
own) were "the test of friendship," compassion for her might
have tempered the general indignation against her husband.
As it was—and especially after the object of her nocturnal
visit to Mrs. Manson Mingott had become known—her cyn-
icism was held to exceed his; and she had not the excuse—
nor her detractors the satisfaction—of pleading that she was
"a foreigner." It was some comfort (to those whose securities
were not in jeopardy) to be able to remind themselves that
Beaufort *was*; but, after all, if a Dallas of South Carolina took
his view of the case, and glibly talked of his soon being "on
his feet again," the argument lost its edge, and there was
nothing to do but to accept this awful evidence of the indis-
solubility of marriage. Society must manage to get on without the Beauforts, and there was an end of it—except indeed
for such hapless victims of the disaster as Medora Manson,
the poor old Miss Lannings, and certain other misguided ladies of good family who, if only they had listened to Mr.
Henry van der Luyden . . .

"The best thing the Beauforts can do," said Mrs. Archer,
summing it up as if she were pronouncing a diagnosis and pre-
scribing a course of treatment, "is to go and live at Regina's
little place in North Carolina. Beaufort has always kept a

racing stable, and he had better breed trotting horses. I should say he had all the qualities of a successful horse-dealer." Every one agreed with her, but no one condescended to enquire what the Beauforts really meant to do.

The next day Mrs. Manson Mingott was much better: she recovered her voice sufficiently to give orders that no one should mention the Beauforts to her again, and asked—when Dr. Bencomb appeared—what in the world her family meant by making such a fuss about her health.

"If people of my age *will* eat chicken-salad in the evening what are they to expect?" she enquired; and, the doctor having opportunely modified her dietary, the stroke was transformed into an attack of indigestion. But in spite of her firm tone old Catherine did not wholly recover her former attitude toward life. The growing remoteness of old age, though it had not diminished her curiosity about her neighbours, had blunted her never very lively compassion for their troubles; and she seemed to have no difficulty in putting the Beaufort disaster out of her mind. But for the first time she became absorbed in her own symptoms, and began to take a sentimental interest in certain members of her family to whom she had hitherto been contemptuously indifferent.

Mr. Welland, in particular, had the privilege of attracting her notice. Of her sons-in-law he was the one she had most consistently ignored; and all his wife's efforts to represent him as a man of forceful character and marked intellectual ability (if he had only "chosen") had been met with a derisive chuckle. But his eminence as a valetudinarian now made him an object of engrossing interest, and Mrs. Mingott issued an imperial summons to him to come and compare diets as soon as his temperature permitted; for old Catherine was now the first to recognise that one could not be too careful about temperatures.

Twenty-four hours after Madame Olenska's summons a telegram announced that she would arrive from Washington on the evening of the following day. At the Wellands', where the Newland Archers chanced to be lunching, the question as to who should meet her at Jersey City was immediately raised; and the material difficulties amid which the Welland household struggled as if it had been a frontier outpost, lent animation to the debate. It was agreed that Mrs. Welland could not possibly go to Jersey City because she was to accompany her husband to old Catherine's that afternoon, and the brougham could not be spared, since, if Mr. Welland were "upset" by seeing his mother-in-law for the first time after her attack, he might have to be taken home at a moment's notice. The Welland sons would of course be "down town," Mr. Lovell Mingott would be just hurrying back from his shooting, and the Mingott carriage engaged in meeting him; and one could not ask May, at the close of a winter afternoon, to go alone across the ferry to Jersey City, even in her own carriage. Nevertheless, it might appear inhospitable—and contrary to old Catherine's express wishes—if Madame Olenska were allowed to arrive without any of the family being at the station to receive her. It was just like Ellen, Mrs. Welland's tired voice implied, to place the family in such a dilemma. "It's always one thing after another," the poor lady grieved, in one of her rare revolts against fate; "the only thing that makes me think Mamma must be less well than Dr. Bencomb will admit is this morbid desire to have Ellen come at once, however inconvenient it is to meet her."

The words had been thoughtless, as the utterances of impatience often are; and Mr. Welland was upon them with a pounce.

"Augusta," he said, turning pale and laying down his fork, "have you any other reason for thinking that Bencomb is less to be relied on than he was? Have you noticed that he has been less conscientious than usual in following up my case or your mother's?"

It was Mrs. Welland's turn to grow pale as the endless consequences of her blunder unrolled themselves before her; but she managed to laugh, and take a second helping of scalloped oysters, before she said, struggling back into her old armour of cheerfulness: "My dear, how could you imagine such a thing? I only meant that, after the decided stand Mamma took about its being Ellen's duty to go back to her husband, it seems strange that she should be seized with this sudden whim to see her, when there are half a dozen other grandchildren that she might have asked for. But we must never forget that Mamma, in spite of her wonderful vitality, is a very old woman."

Mr. Welland's brow remained clouded, and it was evident that his perturbed imagination had fastened at once on this last remark. "Yes: your mother's a very old woman; and for all we know Bencomb may not be as successful with very old people. As you say, my dear, it's always one thing after another; and in another ten or fifteen years I suppose I shall have the pleasing duty of looking about for a new doctor. It's always better to make such a change before it's absolutely necessary." And having arrived at this Spartan decision Mr. Welland firmly took up his fork.

"But all the while," Mrs. Welland began again, as she rose from the luncheon-table, and led the way into the wilderness of purple satin and malachite known as the back drawing-room, "I don't see how Ellen's to be got here tomorrow evening; and I do like to have things settled for at least twenty-four hours ahead."

Archer turned from the fascinated contemplation of a small painting representing two Cardinals carousing, in an octagonal ebony frame set with medallions of onyx.

"Shall I fetch her?" he proposed. "I can easily get away from the office in time to meet the brougham at the ferry, if May will send it there." His heart was beating excitedly as he spoke.

Mrs. Welland heaved a sigh of gratitude, and May, who had moved away to the window, turned to shed on him a beam of approval. "So you see, Mamma, everything *will* be settled twenty-four hours in advance," she said, stooping over to kiss her mother's troubled forehead.

May's brougham awaited her at the door, and she was to drive Archer to Union Square, where he could pick up a Broadway car to carry him to the office. As she settled herself in her corner she said: "I didn't want to worry Mamma by raising fresh obstacles; but how can you meet Ellen tomorrow, and bring her back to New York, when you're going to Washington?"

"Oh, I'm not going," Archer answered.

"Not going? Why, what's happened?" Her voice was as clear as a bell, and full of wifely solicitude.

"The case is off—postponed."

"Postponed? How odd! I saw a note this morning from Mr. Letterblair to Mamma saying that he was going to Washington tomorrow for the big patent case that he was to argue before the Supreme Court. You said it was a patent case, didn't you?"

"Well—that's it: the whole office can't go. Letterblair decided to go this morning."

"Then it's *not* postponed?" she continued, with an insistence so unlike her that he felt the blood rising to his face, as if he were blushing for her unwonted lapse from all the traditional delicacies.

"No: but my going is," he answered, cursing the unnecessary explanations that he had given when he had announced his intention of going to Washington, and wondering where he had read that clever liars give details, but that the cleverest do not. It did not hurt him half as much to tell May an untruth as to see her trying to pretend that she had not detected him.

"I'm not going till later on: luckily for the convenience of your family," he continued, taking base refuge in sarcasm. As he spoke he felt that she was looking at him, and he turned his eyes to hers in order not to appear to be avoiding them. Their glances met for a second, and perhaps let them into each other's meanings more deeply than either cared to go.

"Yes; it *is* awfully convenient," May brightly agreed, "that you should be able to meet Ellen after all; you saw how much Mamma appreciated your offering to do it."

"Oh, I'm delighted to do it." The carriage stopped, and as he jumped out she leaned to him and laid her hand on his. "Good-bye, dearest," she said, her eyes so blue that he wondered afterward if they had shone on him through tears.

He turned away and hurried across Union Square, repeating to himself, in a sort of inward chant: "It's all of two hours from Jersey City to old Catherine's. It's all of two hours—and it may be more."

XXIX

H IS WIFE'S dark blue brougham (with the wedding varnish still on it) met Archer at the ferry, and conveyed him luxuriously to the Pennsylvania terminus in Jersey City.

It was a sombre snowy afternoon, and the gas-lamps were lit in the big reverberating station. As he paced the platform, waiting for the Washington express, he remembered that there were people who thought there would one day be a tunnel under the Hudson through which the trains of the Pennsylvania railway would run straight into New York. They were of the brotherhood of visionaries who likewise predicted the building of ships that would cross the Atlantic in five days, the invention of a flying machine, lighting by electricity, telephonic communication without wires, and other Arabian Night marvels.

"I don't care which of their visions comes true," Archer mused, "as long as the tunnel isn't built yet." In his senseless school-boy happiness he pictured Madame Olenska's descent from the train, his discovery of her a long way off, among the throngs of meaningless faces, her clinging to his arm as he guided her to the carriage, their slow approach to the wharf among slipping horses, laden carts, vociferating teamsters, and then the startling quiet of the ferry-boat, where they would sit side by side under the snow, in the motionless carriage, while the earth seemed to glide away under them, rolling to the other side of the sun. It was incredible, the number of things he had to say to her, and in what eloquent order they were forming themselves on his lips . . .

The clanging and groaning of the train came nearer, and it staggered slowly into the station like a prey-laden monster into its lair. Archer pushed forward, elbowing through the crowd, and staring blindly into window after window of the high-hung carriages. And then, suddenly, he saw Madame Olenska's pale and surprised face close at hand, and had again the mortified sensation of having forgotten what she looked like.

They reached each other, their hands met, and he drew her arm through his. "This way—I have the carriage," he said.

After that it all happened as he had dreamed. He helped her into the brougham with her bags, and had afterward the vague recollection of having properly reassured her about her grandmother and given her a summary of the Beaufort situation (he was struck by the softness of her: "Poor Regina!"). Meanwhile the carriage had worked its way out of the coil about the station, and they were crawling down the slippery incline to the wharf, menaced by swaying coal-carts, bewildered horses, dishevelled express-wagons, and an empty hearse—ah, that hearse! She shut her eyes as it passed, and clutched at Archer's hand.

"If only it doesn't mean—poor Granny!"

"Oh, no, no—she's much better—she's all right, really. There—we've passed it!" he exclaimed, as if that made all the difference. Her hand remained in his, and as the carriage lurched across the gang-plank onto the ferry he bent over, unbuttoned her tight brown glove, and kissed her palm as if he had kissed a relic. She disengaged herself with a faint smile, and he said: "You didn't expect me today?"

"Oh, no."

"I meant to go to Washington to see you. I'd made all my arrangements—I very nearly crossed you in the train."

"Oh—" she exclaimed, as if terrified by the narrowness of their escape.

"Do you know—I hardly remembered you?"

"Hardly remembered me?"

"I mean: how shall I explain? I—it's always so. *Each time you happen to me all over again.*"

"Oh, yes: I know! I know!"

"Does it—do I too: to you?" he insisted.

She nodded, looking out of the window.

"Ellen—Ellen—Ellen!"

She made no answer, and he sat in silence, watching her profile grow indistinct against the snow-streaked dusk beyond the window. What had she been doing in all those four long months, he wondered? How little they knew of each other, after all! The precious moments were slipping away, but he had forgotten everything that he had meant to say to her and could only helplessly brood on the mystery of their remoteness and their proximity, which seemed to be symbolised by the fact of their sitting so close to each other, and yet being unable to see each other's faces.

"What a pretty carriage! Is it May's?" she asked, suddenly turning her face from the window.

"Yes."

"It was May who sent you to fetch me, then? How kind of her!"

He made no answer for a moment; then he said explosively: "Your husband's secretary came to see me the day after we met in Boston."

In his brief letter to her he had made no allusion to M. Rivière's visit, and his intention had been to bury the incident in his bosom. But her reminder that they were in his wife's carriage provoked him to an impulse of retaliation. He would see if she liked his reference to Rivière any better than he liked hers to May! As on certain other occasions when he had expected to shake her out of her usual composure, she betrayed no sign of surprise: and at once he concluded: "He writes to her, then."

"M. Rivière went to see you?"

"Yes: didn't you know?"

"No," she answered simply.

"And you're not surprised?"

She hesitated. "Why should I be? He told me in Boston that he knew you; that he'd met you in England I think."

"Ellen—I must ask you one thing."

"Yes."

"I wanted to ask it after I saw him, but I couldn't put it in a letter. It was Rivière who helped you to get away—when you left your husband?"

His heart was beating suffocatingly. Would she meet this question with the same composure?

"Yes: I owe him a great debt," she answered, without the least tremor in her quiet voice.

Her tone was so natural, so almost indifferent, that Archer's turmoil subsided. Once more she had managed, by her sheer simplicity, to make him feel stupidly conventional just when he thought he was flinging convention to the winds.

"I think you're the most honest woman I ever met!" he exclaimed.

"Oh, no—but probably one of the least fussy," she answered, a smile in her voice.

"Call it what you like: you look at things as they are."

"Ah—I've had to. I've had to look at the Gorgon."

"Well—it hasn't blinded you! You've seen that she's just an old bogey like all the others."

"She doesn't blind one; but she dries up one's tears."

The answer checked the pleading on Archer's lips: it seemed to come from depths of experience beyond his reach. The slow advance of the ferry-boat had ceased, and her bows bumped against the piles of the slip with a violence that made the brougham stagger, and flung Archer and Madame Olenska against each other. The young man, trembling, felt the pressure of her shoulder, and passed his arm about her.

"If you're not blind, then, you must see that this can't last."

"What can't?"

"Our being together—and not together."

"No. You ought not to have come today," she said in an altered voice; and suddenly she turned, flung her arms about him and pressed her lips to his. At the same moment the carriage began to move, and a gas-lamp at the head of the slip flashed its light into the window. She drew away, and they sat silent and motionless while the brougham struggled through the congestion of carriages about the ferry-landing. As they gained the street Archer began to speak hurriedly.

"Don't be afraid of me: you needn't squeeze yourself back into your corner like that. A stolen kiss isn't what I want. Look: I'm not even trying to touch the sleeve of your jacket. Don't suppose that I don't understand your reasons for not wanting to let this feeling between us dwindle into an ordinary hole-and-corner love-affair. I couldn't have spoken like this yesterday, because when we've been apart, and I'm looking forward to seeing you, every thought is burnt up in a great flame. But then you come; and you're so much more than I remembered, and what I want of you is so much more than an hour or two every now and then, with wastes of thirsty waiting between, that I can sit perfectly still beside you, like this, with that other vision in my mind, just quietly trusting to it to come true."

For a moment she made no reply; then she asked, hardly

above a whisper: "What do you mean by trusting to it to come true?"

"Why—you know it will, don't you?"

"Your vision of you and me together?" She burst into a sudden hard laugh. "You choose your place well to put it to me!"

"Do you mean because we're in my wife's brougham? Shall we get out and walk, then? I don't suppose you mind a little snow?"

She laughed again, more gently. "No; I shan't get out and walk, because my business is to get to Granny's as quickly as I can. And you'll sit beside me, and we'll look, not at visions, but at realities."

"I don't know what you mean by realities. The only reality to me is this."

She met the words with a long silence, during which the carriage rolled down an obscure side-street and then turned into the searching illumination of Fifth Avenue.

"Is it your idea, then, that I should live with you as your mistress—since I can't be your wife?" she asked.

The crudeness of the question startled him: the word was one that women of his class fought shy of, even when their talk flitted closest about the topic. He noticed that Madame Olenska pronounced it as if it had a recognised place in her vocabulary, and he wondered if it had been used familiarly in her presence in the horrible life she had fled from. Her question pulled him up with a jerk, and he floundered.

"I want—I want somehow to get away with you into a world where words like that—categories like that—won't exist. Where we shall be simply two human beings who love each other, who are the whole of life to each other; and nothing else on earth will matter."

She drew a deep sigh that ended in another laugh. "Oh, my dear—where is that country? Have you ever been there?" she asked; and as he remained sullenly dumb she went on: "I know so many who've tried to find it; and, believe me, they all got out by mistake at wayside stations: at places like Boulogne, or Pisa, or Monte Carlo—and it wasn't at all different from the old world they'd left, but only rather smaller and dingier and more promiscuous."

He had never heard her speak in such a tone, and he remembered the phrase she had used a little while before.

"Yes, the Gorgon *has* dried your tears," he said.

"Well, she opened my eyes too; it's a delusion to say that she blinds people. What she does is just the contrary—she fastens their eyelids open, so that they're never again in the blessed darkness. Isn't there a Chinese torture like that? There ought to be. Ah, believe me, it's a miserable little country!"

The carriage had crossed Forty-second Street: May's sturdy brougham-horse was carrying them northward as if he had been a Kentucky trotter. Archer choked with the sense of wasted minutes and vain words.

"Then what, exactly, is your plan for us?" he asked.

"For *us*? But there's no *us* in that sense! We're near each other only if we stay far from each other. Then we can be ourselves. Otherwise we're only Newland Archer, the husband of Ellen Olenska's cousin, and Ellen Olenska, the cousin of Newland Archer's wife, trying to be happy behind the backs of the people who trust them."

"Ah, I'm beyond that," he groaned.

"No, you're not! You've never been beyond. And *I* have," she said, in a strange voice, "and I know what it looks like there."

He sat silent, dazed with inarticulate pain. Then he groped in the darkness of the carriage for the little bell that signalled orders to the coachman. He remembered that May rang twice when she wished to stop. He pressed the bell, and the carriage drew up beside the curbstone.

"Why are we stopping? This is not Granny's," Madame Olenska exclaimed.

"No: I shall get out here," he stammered, opening the door and jumping to the pavement. By the light of a street-lamp he saw her startled face, and the instinctive motion she made to detain him. He closed the door, and leaned for a moment in the window.

"You're right: I ought not to have come today," he said, lowering his voice so that the coachman should not hear. She bent forward, and seemed about to speak; but he had already called out the order to drive on, and the carriage rolled away while he stood on the corner. The snow was over, and a tingling wind had sprung up, that lashed his face as he stood gazing. Suddenly he felt something stiff and cold on his lashes, and perceived that he had been crying, and that the wind had frozen his tears.

He thrust his hands in his pockets, and walked at a sharp pace down Fifth Avenue to his own house.

XXX

THAT EVENING when Archer came down before dinner he
found the drawing-room empty.

He and May were dining alone, all the family engagements
having been postponed since Mrs. Manson Mingott's illness;
and as May was the more punctual of the two he was surprised that she had not preceded him. He knew that she was
at home, for while he dressed he had heard her moving about
in her room; and he wondered what had delayed her.

He had fallen into the way of dwelling on such conjectures
as a means of tying his thoughts fast to reality. Sometimes he
felt as if he had found the clue to his father-in-law's absorption in trifles; perhaps even Mr. Welland, long ago, had had
escapes and visions, and had conjured up all the hosts of domesticity to defend himself against them.

When May appeared he thought she looked tired. She had
put on the low-necked and tightly-laced dinner-dress which
the Mingott ceremonial exacted on the most informal occasions, and had built her fair hair into its usual accumulated
coils; and her face, in contrast, was wan and almost faded.
But she shone on him with her usual tenderness, and her eyes
had kept the blue dazzle of the day before.

"What became of you, dear?" she asked. "I was waiting at
Granny's, and Ellen came alone, and said she had dropped
you on the way because you had to rush off on business.
There's nothing wrong?"

"Only some letters I'd forgotten, and wanted to get off before dinner."

"Ah—" she said; and a moment afterward: "I'm sorry you
didn't come to Granny's—unless the letters were urgent."

"They were," he rejoined, surprised at her insistence. "Besides, I don't see why I should have gone to your grandmother's. I didn't know you were there."

She turned and moved to the looking-glass above the mantel-piece. As she stood there, lifting her long arm to fasten a
puff that had slipped from its place in her intricate hair,
Archer was struck by something languid and inelastic in her
attitude, and wondered if the deadly monotony of their lives

had laid its weight on her also. Then he remembered that, as he had left the house that morning, she had called over the stairs that she would meet him at her grandmother's so that they might drive home together. He had called back a cheery "Yes!" and then, absorbed in other visions, had forgotten his promise. Now he was smitten with compunction, yet irritated that so trifling an omission should be stored up against him after nearly two years of marriage. He was weary of living in a perpetual tepid honeymoon, without the temperature of passion yet with all its exactions. If May had spoken out her grievances (he suspected her of many) he might have laughed them away; but she was trained to conceal imaginary wounds under a Spartan smile.

To disguise his own annoyance he asked how her grandmother was, and she answered that Mrs. Mingott was still improving, but had been rather disturbed by the last news about the Beauforts.

"What news?"

"It seems they're going to stay in New York. I believe he's going into an insurance business, or something. They're looking about for a small house."

The preposterousness of the case was beyond discussion, and they went in to dinner. During dinner their talk moved in its usual limited circle; but Archer noticed that his wife made no allusion to Madame Olenska, nor to old Catherine's reception of her. He was thankful for the fact, yet felt it to be vaguely ominous.

They went up to the library for coffee, and Archer lit a cigar and took down a volume of Michelet. He had taken to history in the evenings since May had shown a tendency to ask him to read aloud whenever she saw him with a volume of poetry: not that he disliked the sound of his own voice, but because he could always foresee her comments on what he read. In the days of their engagement she had simply (as he now perceived) echoed what he told her; but since he had ceased to provide her with opinions she had begun to hazard her own, with results destructive to his enjoyment of the works commented on.

Seeing that he had chosen history she fetched her work-basket, drew up an arm-chair to the green-shaded student lamp, and uncovered a cushion she was embroidering for his sofa. She was not a clever needle-woman; her large capable hands were made for riding, rowing and open-air activities; but since other wives embroidered cushions for their husbands she did not wish to omit this last link in her devotion.

She was so placed that Archer, by merely raising his eyes, could see her bent above her work-frame, her ruffled elbow-sleeves slipping back from her firm round arms, the betrothal sapphire shining on her left hand above her broad gold wed-ding-ring, and the right hand slowly and laboriously stabbing the canvas. As she sat thus, the lamplight full on her clear brow, he said to himself with a secret dismay that he would always know the thoughts behind it, that never, in all the years to come, would she surprise him by an unexpected mood, by a new idea, a weakness, a cruelty or an emotion. She had spent her poetry and romance on their short court-ing: the function was exhausted because the need was past. Now she was simply ripening into a copy of her mother, and mysteriously, by the very process, trying to turn him into a Mr. Welland. He laid down his book and stood up impa-tiently; and at once she raised her head.

"What's the matter?"

"The room is stifling: I want a little air."

He had insisted that the library curtains should draw back-ward and forward on a rod, so that they might be closed in the evening, instead of remaining nailed to a gilt cornice, and immovably looped up over layers of lace, as in the drawing-room; and he pulled them back and pushed up the sash, lean-ing out into the icy night. The mere fact of not looking at May, seated beside his table, under his lamp, the fact of seeing other houses, roofs, chimneys, of getting the sense of other lives outside his own, other cities beyond New York, and a whole world beyond his world, cleared his brain and made it easier to breathe.

After he had leaned out into the darkness for a few minutes he heard her say: "Newland! Do shut the window. You'll catch your death."

He pulled the sash down and turned back. "Catch my death!" he echoed; and he felt like adding: "But I've caught it already. I *am* dead—I've been dead for months and months."

And suddenly the play of the word flashed up a wild suggestion. What if it were *she* who was dead! If she were going to die—to die soon—and leave him free! The sensation of standing there, in that warm familiar room, and looking at her, and wishing her dead, was so strange, so fascinating and overmastering, that its enormity did not immediately strike him. He simply felt that chance had given him a new possibility to which his sick soul might cling. Yes, May might die—people did: young people, healthy people like herself: she might die, and set him suddenly free.

She glanced up, and he saw by her widening eyes that there must be something strange in his own.

"Newland! Are you ill?"

He shook his head and turned toward his arm-chair. She bent over her work-frame, and as he passed he laid his hand on her hair. "Poor May!" he said.

"Poor? Why poor?" she echoed with a strained laugh.

"Because I shall never be able to open a window without worrying you," he rejoined, laughing also.

For a moment she was silent; then she said very low, her head bowed over her work: "I shall never worry if you're happy."

"Ah, my dear; and I shall never be happy unless I can open the windows!"

"In *this* weather?" she remonstrated; and with a sigh he buried his head in his book.

Six or seven days passed. Archer heard nothing from Madame Olenska, and became aware that her name would not be mentioned in his presence by any member of the family. He did not try to see her; to do so while she was at old Catherine's guarded bedside would have been almost impossible. In the uncertainty of the situation he let himself drift, conscious, somewhere below the surface of his thoughts, of a resolve which had come to him when he had leaned out from his library window into the icy night. The strength of that resolve made it easy to wait and make no sign.

Then one day May told him that Mrs. Manson Mingott

had asked to see him. There was nothing surprising in the
request, for the old lady was steadily recovering, and she had
always openly declared that she preferred Archer to any of her
other grandsons-in-law. May gave the message with evident
pleasure: she was proud of old Catherine's appreciation of her
husband.

There was a moment's pause, and then Archer felt it incumbent on him to say: "All right. Shall we go together this
afternoon?"

His wife's face brightened, but she instantly answered:
"Oh, you'd much better go alone. It bores Granny to see the
same people too often."

Archer's heart was beating violently when he rang old Mrs.
Mingott's bell. He had wanted above all things to go alone,
for he felt sure the visit would give him the chance of saying
a word in private to the Countess Olenska. He had determined to wait till the chance presented itself naturally; and
here it was, and here he was on the doorstep. Behind the
door, behind the curtains of the yellow damask room next to
the hall, she was surely awaiting him; in another moment he
should see her, and be able to speak to her before she led him
to the sick-room.

He wanted only to put one question: after that his course
would be clear. What he wished to ask was simply the date
of her return to Washington; and that question she could
hardly refuse to answer.

But in the yellow sitting-room it was the mulatto maid
who waited. Her white teeth shining like a keyboard, she
pushed back the sliding doors and ushered him into old Catherine's presence.

The old woman sat in a vast throne-like arm-chair near her
bed. Beside her was a mahogany stand bearing a cast bronze
lamp with an engraved globe, over which a green paper shade
had been balanced. There was not a book or a newspaper in
reach, nor any evidence of feminine employment: conversation had always been Mrs. Mingott's sole pursuit, and she
would have scorned to feign an interest in fancywork.

Archer saw no trace of the slight distortion left by her
stroke. She merely looked paler, with darker shadows in the
folds and recesses of her obesity; and, in the fluted mob-cap

tied by a starched bow between her first two chins, and the muslin kerchief crossed over her billowing purple dressing-gown, she seemed like some shrewd and kindly ancestress of her own who might have yielded too freely to the pleasures of the table.

She held out one of the little hands that nestled in a hollow of her huge lap like pet animals, and called to the maid: "Don't let in any one else. If my daughters call, say I'm asleep."

The maid disappeared, and the old lady turned to her grandson.

"My dear, am I perfectly hideous?" she asked gaily, launching out one hand in search of the folds of muslin on her inaccessible bosom. "My daughters tell me it doesn't matter at my age—as if hideousness didn't matter all the more the harder it gets to conceal!"

"My dear, you're handsomer than ever!" Archer rejoined in the same tone; and she threw back her head and laughed.

"Ah, but not as handsome as Ellen!" she jerked out, twinkling at him maliciously; and before he could answer she added: "Was she so awfully handsome the day you drove her up from the ferry?"

He laughed, and she continued: "Was it because you told her so that she had to put you out on the way? In my youth young men didn't desert pretty women unless they were made to!" She gave another chuckle, and interrupted it to say almost querulously: "It's a pity she didn't marry you; I always told her so. It would have spared me all this worry. But who ever thought of sparing their grandmother worry?"

Archer wondered if her illness had blurred her faculties; but suddenly she broke out: "Well, it's settled, anyhow: she's going to stay with me, whatever the rest of the family say! She hadn't been here five minutes before I'd have gone down on my knees to keep her—if only, for the last twenty years, I'd been able to see where the floor was!"

Archer listened in silence, and she went on: "They'd talked me over, as no doubt you know: persuaded me, Lovell, and Letterblair, and Augusta Welland, and all the rest of them, that I must hold out and cut off her allowance, till she was made to see that it was her duty to go back to Olenski. They thought they'd convinced me when the secretary, or whatever he was, came out with the last proposals: handsome proposals I confess they were. After all, marriage is marriage, and money's money—both useful things in their way . . . and I didn't know what to answer—" She broke off and drew a long breath, as if speaking had become an effort. "But the minute I laid eyes on her, I said: 'You sweet bird, you! Shut you up in that cage again? Never!' And now it's settled that she's to stay here and nurse her Granny as long as there's a Granny to nurse. It's not a gay prospect, but she doesn't mind; and of course I've told Letterblair that she's to be given her proper allowance."

The young man heard her with veins aglow; but in his confusion of mind he hardly knew whether her news brought joy or pain. He had so definitely decided on the course he meant to pursue that for the moment he could not readjust his thoughts. But gradually there stole over him the delicious sense of difficulties deferred and opportunities miraculously provided. If Ellen had consented to come and live with her grandmother it must surely be because she had recognised the impossibility of giving him up. This was her answer to his final appeal of the other day: if she would not take the extreme step he had urged, she had at last yielded to half-measures. He sank back into the thought with the involuntary relief of a man who has been ready to risk everything, and suddenly tastes the dangerous sweetness of security.

"She couldn't have gone back—it was impossible!" he exclaimed.

"Ah, my dear, I always knew you were on her side; and that's why I sent for you today, and why I said to your pretty wife, when she proposed to come with you: 'No, my dear, I'm pining to see Newland, and I don't want anybody to share our transports.' For you see, my dear—" she drew her head back as far as its tethering chins permitted, and looked him full in the eyes—"you see, we shall have a fight yet. The family don't want her here, and they'll say it's because I've been ill, because I'm a weak old woman, that she's persuaded me. I'm not well enough yet to fight them one by one, and you've got to do it for me."

"I?" he stammered.

"You. Why not?" she jerked back at him, her round eyes suddenly as sharp as pen-knives. Her hand fluttered from its chair-arm and lit on his with a clutch of little pale nails like bird-claws. "Why not?" she searchingly repeated.

Archer, under the exposure of her gaze, had recovered his self-possession.

"Oh, I don't count—I'm too insignificant."

"Well, you're Letterblair's partner, ain't you? You've got to get at them through Letterblair. Unless you've got a reason," she insisted.

"Oh, my dear, I back you to hold your own against them all without my help; but you shall have it if you need it," he reassured her.

"Then we're safe!" she sighed; and smiling on him with all her ancient cunning she added, as she settled her head among the cushions: "I always knew you'd back us up, because they never quote you when they talk about its being her duty to go home."

He winced a little at her terrifying perspicacity, and longed to ask: "And May—do they quote her?" But he judged it safer to turn the question.

"And Madame Olenska? When am I to see her?" he said.

The old lady chuckled, crumpled her lids, and went through the pantomime of archness. "Not today. One at a time, please. Madame Olenska's gone out."

He flushed with disappointment, and she went on: "She's gone out, my child: gone in my carriage to see Regina Beaufort."

She paused for this announcement to produce its effect. "That's what she's reduced me to already. The day after she got here she put on her best bonnet, and told me, as cool as a cucumber, that she was going to call on Regina Beaufort. 'I don't know her; who is she?' says I. 'She's your grand-niece, and a most unhappy woman,' she says. 'She's the wife of a scoundrel,' I answered. 'Well,' she says, 'and so am I, and yet all my family want me to go back to him.' Well, that floored me, and I let her go; and finally one day she said it was raining too hard to go out on foot, and she wanted me to lend her my carriage. 'What for?' I asked her; and she said: 'To go and see cousin Regina'—*cousin!* Now, my dear, I looked out of the window, and saw it wasn't raining a drop; but I understood her, and I let her have the carriage . . . After all, Regina's a brave woman, and so is she; and I've always liked courage above everything."

Archer bent down and pressed his lips on the little hand that still lay on his.

"Eh—eh—eh! Whose hand did you think you were kissing, young man—your wife's, I hope?" the old lady snapped out with her mocking cackle; and as he rose to go she called out after him: "Give her her Granny's love; but you'd better not say anything about our talk."

XXXI

ARCHER HAD been stunned by old Catherine's news. It was only natural that Madame Olenska should have hastened from Washington in response to her grandmother's summons; but that she should have decided to remain under her roof—especially now that Mrs. Mingott had almost regained her health—was less easy to explain.

Archer was sure that Madame Olenska's decision had not been influenced by the change in her financial situation. He knew the exact figure of the small income which her husband had allowed her at their separation. Without the addition of her grandmother's allowance it was hardly enough to live on, in any sense known to the Mingott vocabulary; and now that Medora Manson, who shared her life, had been ruined, such a pittance would barely keep the two women clothed and fed. Yet Archer was convinced that Madame Olenska had not accepted her grandmother's offer from interested motives.

She had the heedless generosity and the spasmodic extravagance of persons used to large fortunes, and indifferent to money; but she could go without many things which her relations considered indispensable, and Mrs. Lovell Mingott and Mrs. Welland had often been heard to deplore that any one who had enjoyed the cosmopolitan luxuries of Count Olenski's establishments should care so little about "how things were done." Moreover, as Archer knew, several months had passed since her allowance had been cut off; yet in the interval she had made no effort to regain her grandmother's favour. Therefore if she had changed her course it must be for a different reason.

He did not have far to seek for that reason. On the way from the ferry she had told him that he and she must remain apart; but she had said it with her head on his breast. He knew that there was no calculated coquetry in her words; she was fighting her fate as he had fought his, and clinging desperately to her resolve that they should not break faith with the people who trusted them. But during the ten days which had elapsed since her return to New York she had perhaps guessed from his silence, and from the fact of his making no attempt to see her, that he was meditating a decisive step, a step from which there was no turning back. At the thought, a sudden fear of her own weakness might have seized her, and she might have felt that, after all, it was better to accept the compromise usual in such cases, and follow the line of least resistance.

An hour earlier, when he had rung Mrs. Mingott's bell, Archer had fancied that his path was clear before him. He had meant to have a word alone with Madame Olenska, and failing that, to learn from her grandmother on what day, and by which train, she was returning to Washington. In that train he intended to join her, and travel with her to Washington, or as much farther as she was willing to go. His own fancy inclined to Japan. At any rate she would understand at once that, wherever she went, he was going. He meant to leave a note for May that should cut off any other alternative.

He had fancied himself not only nerved for this plunge but eager to take it; yet his first feeling on hearing that the course of events was changed had been one of relief. Now, however, as he walked home from Mrs. Mingott's, he was conscious of a growing distaste for what lay before him. There was nothing unknown or unfamiliar in the path he was presumably to tread; but when he had trodden it before it was as a free man, who was accountable to no one for his actions, and could lend himself with an amused detachment to the game of precautions and prevarications, concealments and compliances, that the part required. This procedure was called "protecting a woman's honour"; and the best fiction, combined with the after-dinner talk of his elders, had long since initiated him into every detail of its code.

Now he saw the matter in a new light, and his part in it seemed singularly diminished. It was, in fact, that which, with a secret fatuity, he had watched Mrs. Thorley Rushworth play toward a fond and unperceiving husband: a smiling, bantering, humouring, watchful and incessant lie. A lie by day, a lie by night, a lie in every touch and every look; a lie in every caress and every quarrel; a lie in every word and in every silence.

It was easier, and less dastardly on the whole, for a wife to play such a part toward her husband. A woman's standard of truthfulness was tacitly held to be lower: she was the subject creature, and versed in the arts of the enslaved. Then she could always plead moods and nerves, and the right not to be held too strictly to account; and even in the most strait-laced societies the laugh was always against the husband.

But in Archer's little world no one laughed at a wife deceived, and a certain measure of contempt was attached to men who continued their philandering after marriage. In the rotation of crops there was a recognised season for wild oats; but they were not to be sown more than once.

Archer had always shared this view: in his heart he thought Lefferts despicable. But to love Ellen Olenska was not to become a man like Lefferts: for the first time Archer found himself face to face with the dread argument of the individual case. Ellen Olenska was like no other woman, he was like no other man: their situation, therefore, resembled no one else's, and they were answerable to no tribunal but that of their own judgment.

Yes, but in ten minutes more he would be mounting his own doorstep; and there were May, and habit, and honour, and all the old decencies that he and his people had always believed in . . .

At his corner he hesitated, and then walked on down Fifth Avenue.

Ahead of him, in the winter night, loomed a big unlit house. As he drew near he thought how often he had seen it blazing with lights, its steps awninged and carpeted, and carriages waiting in double line to draw up at the curbstone. It was in the conservatory that stretched its dead-black bulk down the side street that he had taken his first kiss from May; it was under the myriad candles of the ball-room that he had seen her appear, tall and silver-shining as a young Diana.

Now the house was as dark as the grave, except for a faint flare of gas in the basement, and a light in one upstairs room where the blind had not been lowered. As Archer reached the corner he saw that the carriage standing at the door was Mrs. Manson Mingott's. What an opportunity for Sillerton Jackson, if he should chance to pass! Archer had been greatly moved by old Catherine's account of Madame Olenska's attitude toward Mrs. Beaufort; it made the righteous reprobation of New York seem like a passing by on the other side. But he knew well enough what construction the clubs and drawing-rooms would put on Ellen Olenska's visits to her cousin.

He paused and looked up at the lighted window. No doubt the two women were sitting together in that room: Beaufort had probably sought consolation elsewhere. There were even rumours that he had left New York with Fanny Ring; but Mrs. Beaufort's attitude made the report seem improbable.

Archer had the nocturnal perspective of Fifth Avenue almost to himself. At that hour most people were indoors, dressing for dinner; and he was secretly glad that Ellen's exit was likely to be unobserved. As the thought passed through his mind the door opened, and she came out. Behind her was a faint light, such as might have been carried down the stairs to show her the way. She turned to say a word to some one; then the door closed, and she came down the steps.

"Ellen," he said in a low voice, as she reached the pavement.

She stopped with a slight start, and just then he saw two young men of fashionable cut approaching. There was a familiar air about their overcoats and the way their smart silk mufflers were folded over their white ties; and he wondered how youths of their quality happened to be dining out so early. Then he remembered that the Reggie Chiverses, whose house was a few doors above, were taking a large party that evening to see Adelaide Neilson in Romeo and Juliet, and guessed that the two were of the number. They passed under a lamp, and he recognised Lawrence Lefferts and a young Chivers.

A mean desire not to have Madame Olenska seen at the Beauforts' door vanished as he felt the penetrating warmth of her hand.

"I shall see you now—we shall be together," he broke out, hardly knowing what he said.

"Ah," she answered, "Granny has told you?"

While he watched her he was aware that Lefferts and Chivers, on reaching the farther side of the street corner, had discreetly struck away across Fifth Avenue. It was the kind of masculine solidarity that he himself often practised; now he sickened at their connivance. Did she really imagine that he and she could live like this? And if not, what else did she imagine?

"Tomorrow I must see you—somewhere where we can be alone," he said, in a voice that sounded almost angry to his own ears.

She wavered, and moved toward the carriage.

"But I shall be at Granny's—for the present that is," she added, as if conscious that her change of plans required some explanation.

"Somewhere where we can be alone," he insisted.

She gave a faint laugh that grated on him.

"In New York? But there are no churches . . . no monuments."

"There's the Art Museum—in the Park," he explained, as she looked puzzled. "At half-past two. I shall be at the door . . ."

She turned away without answering and got quickly into the carriage. As it drove off she leaned forward, and he thought she waved her hand in the obscurity. He stared after her in a turmoil of contradictory feelings. It seemed to him that he had been speaking not to the woman he loved but to another, a woman he was indebted to for pleasures already wearied of: it was hateful to find himself the prisoner of this hackneyed vocabulary.

"She'll come!" he said to himself, almost contemptuously.

Avoiding the popular "Wolfe collection," whose anecdotic canvases filled one of the main galleries of the queer wilderness of cast-iron and encaustic tiles known as the Metropolitan Museum, they had wandered down a passage to the room where the "Cesnola antiquities" mouldered in unvisited loneliness.

They had this melancholy retreat to themselves, and seated on the divan enclosing the central steam-radiator, they were staring silently at the glass cabinets mounted in ebonised wood which contained the recovered fragments of Ilium.

"It's odd," Madame Olenska said, "I never came here before."

"Ah, well—. Some day, I suppose, it will be a great Museum."

"Yes," she assented absently.

She stood up and wandered across the room. Archer, remaining seated, watched the light movements of her figure, so girlish even under its heavy furs, the cleverly planted heron wing in her fur cap, and the way a dark curl lay like a flattened vine spiral on each cheek above the ear. His mind, as always when they first met, was wholly absorbed in the delicious details that made her herself and no other. Presently he rose and approached the case before which she stood. Its glass shelves were crowded with small broken objects—hardly recognisable domestic utensils, ornaments and personal trifles—made of glass, of clay, of discoloured bronze and other time-blurred substances.

"It seems cruel," she said, "that after a while nothing matters . . . any more than these little things, that used to be necessary and important to forgotten people, and now have to be guessed at under a magnifying glass and labelled: 'Use unknown.' "

"Yes; but meanwhile—"

"Ah, meanwhile—"

As she stood there, in her long sealskin coat, her hands thrust in a small round muff, her veil drawn down like a transparent mask to the tip of her nose, and the bunch of violets he had brought her stirring with her quickly-taken breath, it seemed incredible that this pure harmony of line and colour should ever suffer the stupid law of change.

"Meanwhile everything matters—that concerns you," he said.

She looked at him thoughtfully, and turned back to the divan. He sat down beside her and waited; but suddenly he heard a step echoing far off down the empty rooms, and felt the pressure of the minutes.

"What is it you wanted to tell me?" she asked, as if she had received the same warning.

"What I wanted to tell you?" he rejoined. "Why, that I believe you came to New York because you were afraid."

"Afraid?"

"Of my coming to Washington."

She looked down at her muff, and he saw her hands stir in it uneasily.

"Well—?"

"Well—yes," she said.

"You *were* afraid? You knew—?"

"Yes: I knew . . ."

"Well, then?" he insisted.

"Well, then: this is better, isn't it?" she returned with a long questioning sigh.

"Better—?"

"We shall hurt others less. Isn't it, after all, what you always wanted?"

"To have you here, you mean—in reach and yet out of reach? To meet you in this way, on the sly? It's the very reverse of what I want. I told you the other day what I wanted."

She hesitated. "And you still think this—worse?"

"A thousand times!" He paused. "It would be easy to lie to you; but the truth is I think it detestable."

"Oh, so do I!" she cried with a deep breath of relief.

He sprang up impatiently. "Well, then—it's my turn to ask: what is it, in God's name, that you think better?"

She hung her head and continued to clasp and unclasp her hands in her muff. The step drew nearer, and a guardian in a braided cap walked listlessly through the room like a ghost stalking through a necropolis. They fixed their eyes simultaneously on the case opposite them, and when the official figure had vanished down a vista of mummies and sarcophagi Archer spoke again.

"What do you think better?"

Instead of answering she murmured: "I promised Granny to stay with her because it seemed to me that here I should be safer."

"From me?"

She bent her head slightly, without looking at him.

"Safer from loving me?"

Her profile did not stir, but he saw a tear overflow on her lashes and hang in a mesh of her veil.

"Safer from doing irreparable harm. Don't let us be like all the others!" she protested.

"What others? I don't profess to be different from my kind. I'm consumed by the same wants and the same longings."

She glanced at him with a kind of terror, and he saw a faint colour steal into her cheeks.

"Shall I—once come to you; and then go home?" she suddenly hazarded in a low clear voice.

The blood rushed to the young man's forehead. "Dearest!" he said, without moving. It seemed as if he held his heart in his hands, like a full cup that the least motion might overbrim.

Then her last phrase struck his ear and his face clouded. "Go home? What do you mean by going home?"

"Home to my husband."

"And you expect me to say yes to that?"

She raised her troubled eyes to his. "What else is there? I can't stay here and lie to the people who've been good to me."

"But that's the very reason why I ask you to come away!"

"And destroy their lives, when they've helped me to remake mine?"

Archer sprang to his feet and stood looking down on her in inarticulate despair. It would have been easy to say: "Yes, come; come once." He knew the power she would put in his hands if she consented; there would be no difficulty then in persuading her not to go back to her husband.

But something silenced the word on his lips. A sort of passionate honesty in her made it inconceivable that he should try to draw her into that familiar trap. "If I were to let her come," he said to himself, "I should have to let her go again." And that was not to be imagined.

But he saw the shadow of the lashes on her wet cheek, and wavered.

"After all," he began again, " we have lives of our own. . . . There's no use attempting the impossible. You're so unprejudiced about some things, so used, as you say, to looking at the Gorgon, that I don't know why you're afraid to face our case, and see it as it really is—unless you think the sacrifice is not worth making."

She stood up also, her lips tightening under a rapid frown.

"Call it that, then—I must go," she said, drawing her little watch from her bosom.

She turned away, and he followed and caught her by the wrist. "Well, then: come to me once," he said, his head turning suddenly at the thought of losing her; and for a second or two they looked at each other almost like enemies.

"When?" he insisted. "Tomorrow?"

She hesitated. "The day after."

"Dearest—!" he said again.

She had disengaged her wrist; but for a moment they continued to hold each other's eyes, and he saw that her face, which had grown very pale, was flooded with a deep inner radiance. His heart beat with awe: he felt that he had never before beheld love visible.

"Oh, I shall be late—good-bye. No, don't come any farther than this," she cried, walking hurriedly away down the long room, as if the reflected radiance in his eyes had frightened her. When she reached the door she turned for a moment to wave a quick farewell.

Archer walked home alone. Darkness was falling when he let himself into his house, and he looked about at the familiar objects in the hall as if he viewed them from the other side of the grave.

The parlour-maid, hearing his step, ran up the stairs to light the gas on the upper landing.

"Is Mrs. Archer in?"

"No, sir; Mrs. Archer went out in the carriage after luncheon, and hasn't come back."

With a sense of relief he entered the library and flung himself down in his armchair. The parlour-maid followed, bringing the student lamp and shaking some coals onto the dying fire. When she left he continued to sit motionless, his elbows on his knees, his chin on his clasped hands, his eyes fixed on the red grate.

He sat there without conscious thoughts, without sense of the lapse of time, in a deep and grave amazement that seemed to suspend life rather than quicken it. "This was what had to be, then . . . this was what had to be," he kept repeating to himself, as if he hung in the clutch of doom. What he had dreamed of had been so different that there was a mortal chill in his rapture.

The door opened and May came in.

"I'm dreadfully late—you weren't worried, were you?" she asked, laying her hand on his shoulder with one of her rare caresses.

He looked up astonished. "Is it late?"

"After seven. I believe you've been asleep!" She laughed, and drawing out her hat pins tossed her velvet hat on the sofa. She looked paler than usual, but sparkling with an unwonted animation.

"I went to see Granny, and just as I was going away Ellen came in from a walk; so I stayed and had a long talk with her. It was ages since we'd had a real talk. . . ." She had dropped into her usual armchair, facing his, and was running her fingers through her rumpled hair. He fancied she expected him to speak.

"A really good talk," she went on, smiling with what seemed to Archer an unnatural vividness. "She was so dear—just like the old Ellen. I'm afraid I haven't been fair to her lately. I've sometimes thought—"

Archer stood up and leaned against the mantelpiece, out of the radius of the lamp.

"Yes, you've thought—?" he echoed as she paused.

"Well, perhaps I haven't judged her fairly. She's so different—at least on the surface. She takes up such odd people—she seems to like to make herself conspicuous. I suppose it's the life she's led in that fast European society; no doubt we seem dreadfully dull to her. But I don't want to judge her unfairly."

She paused again, a little breathless with the unwonted length of her speech, and sat with her lips slightly parted and a deep blush on her cheeks.

Archer, as he looked at her, was reminded of the glow which had suffused her face in the Mission Garden at St. Augustine. He became aware of the same obscure effort in her, the same reaching out toward something beyond the usual range of her vision.

"She hates Ellen," he thought, "and she's trying to overcome the feeling, and to get me to help her to overcome it."

The thought moved him, and for a moment he was on the point of breaking the silence between them, and throwing himself on her mercy.

"You understand, don't you," she went on, " why the family have sometimes been annoyed? We all did what we could for her at first; but she never seemed to understand. And now this idea of going to see Mrs. Beaufort, of going there in Granny's carriage! I'm afraid she's quite alienated the van der Luydens . . ."

"Ah," said Archer with an impatient laugh. The open door had closed between them again.

"It's time to dress; we're dining out, aren't we?" he asked, moving from the fire.

She rose also, but lingered near the hearth. As he walked past her she moved forward impulsively, as though to detain him: their eyes met, and he saw that hers were of the same swimming blue as when he had left her to drive to Jersey City.

She flung her arms about his neck and pressed her cheek to his.

"You haven't kissed me today," she said in a whisper; and he felt her tremble in his arms.

XXXII

AT THE COURT of the Tuileries," said Mr. Sillerton Jackson with his reminiscent smile, "such things were pretty openly tolerated."

The scene was the van der Luydens' black walnut dining-room in Madison Avenue, and the time the evening after Newland Archer's visit to the Museum of Art. Mr. and Mrs. van der Luyden had come to town for a few days from Skuytercliff, whither they had precipitately fled at the announcement of Beaufort's failure. It had been represented to them that the disarray into which society had been thrown by this deplorable affair made their presence in town more necessary than ever. It was one of the occasions when, as Mrs. Archer put it, they "owed it to society" to show themselves at the Opera, and even to open their own doors.

"It will never do, my dear Louisa, to let people like Mrs. Lemuel Struthers think they can step into Regina's shoes. It is just at such times that new people push in and get a footing. It was owing to the epidemic of chicken-pox in New York the winter Mrs. Struthers first appeared that the married men slipped away to her house while their wives were in the nursery. You and dear Henry, Louisa, must stand in the breach as you always have."

Mr. and Mrs. van der Luyden could not remain deaf to such a call, and reluctantly but heroically they had come to town, unmuffled the house, and sent out invitations for two dinners and an evening reception.

On this particular evening they had invited Sillerton Jackson, Mrs. Archer and Newland and his wife to go with them to the Opera, where Faust was being sung for the first time that winter. Nothing was done without ceremony under the van der Luyden roof, and though there were but four guests the repast had begun at seven punctually, so that the proper sequence of courses might be served without haste before the gentlemen settled down to their cigars.

Archer had not seen his wife since the evening before. He had left early for the office, where he had plunged into an accumulation of unimportant business. In the afternoon one of the senior partners had made an unexpected call on his time; and he had reached home so late that May had preceded him to the van der Luydens', and sent back the carriage.

Now, across the Skuytercliff carnations and the massive plate, she struck him as pale and languid; but her eyes shone, and she talked with exaggerated animation.

The subject which had called forth Mr. Sillerton Jackson's favourite allusion had been brought up (Archer fancied not without intention) by their hostess. The Beaufort failure, or rather the Beaufort attitude since the failure, was still a fruitful theme for the drawing-room moralist; and after it had been thoroughly examined and condemned Mrs. van der Luyden had turned her scrupulous eyes on May Archer.

"Is it possible, dear, that what I hear is true? I was told your grandmother Mingott's carriage was seen standing at Mrs. Beaufort's door." It was noticeable that she no longer called the offending lady by her Christian name.

May's colour rose, and Mrs. Archer put in hastily: "If it was, I'm convinced it was there without Mrs. Mingott's knowledge."

"Ah, you think—?" Mrs. van der Luyden paused, sighed, and glanced at her husband.

"I'm afraid," Mr. van der Luyden said, "that Madame Olenska's kind heart may have led her into the imprudence of calling on Mrs. Beaufort."

"Or her taste for peculiar people," put in Mrs. Archer in a dry tone, while her eyes dwelt innocently on her son's.

"I'm sorry to think it of Madame Olenska," said Mrs. van der Luyden; and Mrs. Archer murmured: "Ah, my dear—and after you'd had her twice at Skuytercliff!"

It was at this point that Mr. Jackson seized the chance to place his favourite allusion.

"At the Tuileries," he repeated, seeing the eyes of the company expectantly turned on him, "the standard was excessively lax in some respects; and if you'd asked where Morny's money came from—! Or who paid the debts of some of the Court beauties . . ."

"I hope, dear Sillerton," said Mrs. Archer, "you are not suggesting that we should adopt such standards?"

"I never suggest," returned Mr. Jackson imperturbably.

"But Madame Olenska's foreign bringing-up may make her less particular—"

"Ah," the two elder ladies sighed.

"Still, to have kept her grandmother's carriage at a defaulter's door!" Mr. van der Luyden protested; and Archer guessed that he was remembering, and resenting, the hampers of carnations he had sent to the little house in Twenty-third Street.

"Of course I've always said that she looks at things quite differently," Mrs. Archer summed up.

A flush rose to May's forehead. She looked across the table at her husband, and said precipitately: "I'm sure Ellen meant it kindly."

"Imprudent people are often kind," said Mrs. Archer, as if the fact were scarcely an extenuation; and Mrs. van der Luyden murmured: "If only she had consulted some one—"

"Ah, that she never did!" Mrs. Archer rejoined.

At this point Mr. van der Luyden glanced at his wife, who bent her head slightly in the direction of Mrs. Archer; and the glimmering trains of the three ladies swept out of the door while the gentlemen settled down to their cigars. Mr. van der Luyden supplied short ones on Opera nights; but they were so good that they made his guests deplore his inexorable punctuality.

Archer, after the first act, had detached himself from the party and made his way to the back of the club box. From there he watched, over various Chivers, Mingott and Rushworth shoulders, the same scene that he had looked at, two years previously, on the night of his first meeting with Ellen Olenska. He had half-expected her to appear again in old Mrs. Mingott's box, but it remained empty; and he sat motionless, his eyes fastened on it, till suddenly Madame Nilsson's pure soprano broke out into *"M'ama, non m'ama . . ."*

Archer turned to the stage, where, in the familiar setting of giant roses and pen-wiper pansies, the same large blonde victim was succumbing to the same small brown seducer.

From the stage his eyes wandered to the point of the horseshoe where May sat between two older ladies, just as, on that former evening, she had sat between Mrs. Lovell Mingott and her newly-arrived "foreign" cousin. As on that evening, she was all in white; and Archer, who had not noticed what she wore, recognised the blue-white satin and old lace of her wedding dress.

It was the custom, in old New York, for brides to appear in this costly garment during the first year or two of marriage: his mother, he knew, kept hers in tissue paper in the hope that Janey might some day wear it, though poor Janey was reaching the age when pearl grey poplin and no bridesmaids would be thought more "appropriate."

It struck Archer that May, since their return from Europe, had seldom worn her bridal satin, and the surprise of seeing her in it made him compare her appearance with that of the young girl he had watched with such blissful anticipations two years earlier.

Though May's outline was slightly heavier, as her goddess-like build had foretold, her athletic erectness of carriage, and the girlish transparency of her expression, remained unchanged: but for the slight languor that Archer had lately noticed in her she would have been the exact image of the girl playing with the bouquet of lilies-of-the-valley on her betrothal evening. The fact seemed an additional appeal to his pity: such innocence was as moving as the trustful clasp of a child. Then he remembered the passionate generosity latent under that incurious calm. He recalled her glance of understanding when he had urged that their engagement should be announced at the Beaufort ball; he heard the voice in which she had said, in the Mission garden: "I couldn't have my happiness made out of a wrong—a wrong to some one else;" and an uncontrollable longing seized him to tell her the truth, to throw himself on her generosity, and ask for the freedom he had once refused.

Newland Archer was a quiet and self-controlled young man. Conformity to the discipline of a small society had become almost his second nature. It was deeply distasteful to him to do anything melodramatic and conspicuous, anything Mr. van der Luyden would have deprecated and the club box condemned as bad form. But he had become suddenly unconscious of the club box, of Mr. van der Luyden, of all that had so long enclosed him in the warm shelter of habit. He walked along the semi-circular passage at the back of the house, and opened the door of Mrs. van der Luyden's box as if it had been a gate into the unknown.

"*M'ama!*" thrilled out the triumphant Marguerite; and the occupants of the box looked up in surprise at Archer's entrance. He had already broken one of the rules of his world, which forbade the entering of a box during a solo.

Slipping between Mr. van der Luyden and Sillerton Jackson, he leaned over his wife.

"I've got a beastly headache; don't tell any one, but come home, won't you?" he whispered.

May gave him a glance of comprehension, and he saw her whisper to his mother, who nodded sympathetically; then she murmured an excuse to Mrs. van der Luyden, and rose from her seat just as Marguerite fell into Faust's arms. Archer, while he helped her on with her Opera cloak, noticed the exchange of a significant smile between the older ladies.

As they drove away May laid her hand shyly on his. "I'm so sorry you don't feel well. I'm afraid they've been overworking you again at the office."

"No—it's not that: do you mind if I open the window?" he returned confusedly, letting down the pane on his side. He sat staring out into the street, feeling his wife beside him as a silent watchful interrogation, and keeping his eyes steadily fixed on the passing houses. At their door she caught her skirt in the step of the carriage, and fell against him.

"Did you hurt yourself?" he asked, steadying her with his arm.

"No; but my poor dress—see how I've torn it!" she exclaimed. She bent to gather up a mud-stained breadth, and followed him up the steps into the hall. The servants had not expected them so early, and there was only a glimmer of gas on the upper landing.

Archer mounted the stairs, turned up the light, and put a match to the brackets on each side of the library mantelpiece. The curtains were drawn, and the warm friendly aspect of the room smote him like that of a familiar face met during an unavowable errand.

He noticed that his wife was very pale, and asked if he should get her some brandy.

"Oh, no," she exclaimed with a momentary flush, as she took off her cloak. "But hadn't you better go to bed at once?" she added, as he opened a silver box on the table and took out a cigarette.

Archer threw down the cigarette and walked to his usual place by the fire.

"No; my head is not as bad as that." He paused. "And there's something I want to say; something important—that I must tell you at once."

She had dropped into an armchair, and raised her head as he spoke. "Yes, dear?" she rejoined, so gently that he wondered at the lack of wonder with which she received this preamble.

"May—" he began, standing a few feet from her chair, and looking over at her as if the slight distance between them were an unbridgeable abyss. The sound of his voice echoed uncannily through the homelike hush, and he repeated: "There is something I've got to tell you . . . about myself . . ."

She sat silent, without a movement or a tremor of her lashes. She was still extremely pale, but her face had a curious tranquillity of expression that seemed drawn from some secret inner source.

Archer checked the conventional phrases of self-accusal that were crowding to his lips. He was determined to put the case baldly, without vain recrimination or excuse.

"Madame Olenska—" he said; but at the name his wife raised her hand as if to silence him. As she did so the gas-light struck on the gold of her wedding-ring.

"Oh, why should we talk about Ellen tonight?" she asked, with a slight pout of impatience.

"Because I ought to have spoken before."

Her face remained calm. "Is it really worth while, dear? I know I've been unfair to her at times—perhaps we all have. You've understood her, no doubt, better than we did: you've always been kind to her. But what does it matter, now it's all over?"

Archer looked at her blankly. Could it be possible that the sense of unreality in which he felt himself imprisoned had communicated itself to his wife?

"All over—what do you mean?" he asked in an indistinct stammer.

May still looked at him with transparent eyes. "Why—since she's going back to Europe so soon; since Granny approves and understands, and has arranged to make her independent of her husband—"

She broke off, and Archer, grasping the corner of the mantelpiece in one convulsed hand, and steadying himself against it, made a vain effort to extend the same control to his reeling thoughts.

"I supposed," he heard his wife's even voice go on, "that you had been kept at the office this evening about the business arrangements. It was settled this morning, I believe." She lowered her eyes under his unseeing stare, and another fugitive flush passed over her face.

He understood that his own eyes must be unbearable, and turning away, rested his elbows on the mantel-shelf and covered his face. Something drummed and clanged furiously in his ears; he could not tell if it were the blood in his veins, or the tick of the clock on the mantel.

May sat without moving or speaking while the clock slowly measured out five minutes. A lump of coal fell forward in the grate, and hearing her rise to push it back, Archer at length turned and faced her.

"It's impossible," he exclaimed.

"Impossible—?"

"How do you know—what you've just told me?"

"I saw Ellen yesterday—I told you I'd seen her at Granny's."

"It wasn't then that she told you?"

"No; I had a note from her this afternoon.—Do you want to see it?"

He could not find his voice, and she went out of the room, and came back almost immediately.

"I thought you knew," she said simply.

She laid a sheet of paper on the table, and Archer put out his hand and took it up. The letter contained only a few lines.

"May dear, I have at last made Granny understand that my visit to her could be no more than a visit; and she has been as kind and generous as ever. She sees now that if I return to

Europe I must live by myself, or rather with poor Aunt Medora, who is coming with me. I am hurrying back to Washington to pack up, and we sail next week. You must be very good to Granny when I'm gone—as good as you've always been to me. Ellen.

"If any of my friends wish to urge me to change my mind, please tell them it would be utterly useless."

Archer read the letter over two or three times; then he flung it down and burst out laughing.

The sound of his laugh startled him. It recalled Janey's midnight fright when she had caught him rocking with incomprehensible mirth over May's telegram announcing that the date of their marriage had been advanced.

"Why did she write this?" he asked, checking his laugh with a supreme effort.

May met the question with her unshaken candour. "I suppose because we talked things over yesterday—"

"What things?"

"I told her I was afraid I hadn't been fair to her—hadn't always understood how hard it must have been for her here, alone among so many people who were relations and yet strangers; who felt the right to criticise, and yet didn't always know the circumstances." She paused. "I knew you'd been the one friend she could always count on; and I wanted her to know that you and I were the same—in all our feelings."

She hesitated, as if waiting for him to speak, and then added slowly: "She understood my wishing to tell her this. I think she understands everything."

She went up to Archer, and taking one of his cold hands pressed it quickly against her cheek.

"My head aches too; good-night, dear," she said, and turned to the door, her torn and muddy wedding-dress dragging after her across the room.

IT WAS, as Mrs. Archer smilingly said to Mrs. Welland, a great event for a young couple to give their first big dinner.

The Newland Archers, since they had set up their household, had received a good deal of company in an informal way. Archer was fond of having three or four friends to dine, and May welcomed them with the beaming readiness of which her mother had set her the example in conjugal affairs. Her husband questioned whether, if left to herself, she would ever have asked any one to the house; but he had long given up trying to disengage her real self from the shape into which tradition and training had moulded her. It was expected that well-off young couples in New York should do a good deal of informal entertaining, and a Welland married to an Archer was doubly pledged to the tradition.

But a big dinner, with a hired *chef* and two borrowed footmen, with Roman punch, roses from Henderson's, and *menus* on gilt-edged cards, was a different affair, and not to be lightly undertaken. As Mrs. Archer remarked, the Roman punch made all the difference; not in itself but by its manifold implications—since it signified either canvas-backs or terrapin, two soups, a hot and a cold sweet, full *décolletage* with short sleeves, and guests of a proportionate importance.

It was always an interesting occasion when a young pair launched their first invitations in the third person, and their summons was seldom refused even by the seasoned and sought-after. Still, it was admittedly a triumph that the van der Luydens, at May's request, should have stayed over in order to be present at her farewell dinner for the Countess Olenska.

The two mothers-in-law sat in May's drawing-room on the afternoon of the great day, Mrs. Archer writing out the *menus* on Tiffany's thickest gilt-edged bristol, while Mrs. Welland superintended the placing of the palms and standard lamps.

Archer, arriving late from his office, found them still there. Mrs. Archer had turned her attention to the name-cards for the table, and Mrs. Welland was considering the effect of bringing forward the large gilt sofa, so that another "corner" might be created between the piano and the window.

May, they told him, was in the dining-room inspecting the mound of Jacqueminot roses and maidenhair in the centre of the long table, and the placing of the Maillard bonbons in openwork silver baskets between the candelabra. On the piano stood a large basket of orchids which Mr. van der Luyden had had sent from Skuytercliff. Everything was, in short, as it should be on the approach of so considerable an event.

Mrs. Archer ran thoughtfully over the list, checking off each name with her sharp gold pen.

"Henry van der Luyden—Louisa—the Lovell Mingotts—the Reggie Chiverses—Lawrence Lefferts and Gertrude—(yes, I suppose May was right to have them)—the Selfridge Merrys, Sillerton Jackson, Van Newland and his wife. (How time passes! It seems only yesterday that he was your best man, Newland)—and Countess Olenska—yes, I think that's all. . . ."

Mrs. Welland surveyed her son-in-law affectionately. "No one can say, Newland, that you and May are not giving Ellen a handsome send-off."

"Ah, well," said Mrs. Archer, "I understand May's wanting her cousin to tell people abroad that we're not quite barbarians."

"I'm sure Ellen will appreciate it. She was to arrive this morning, I believe. It will make a most charming last impression. The evening before sailing is usually so dreary," Mrs. Welland cheerfully continued.

Archer turned toward the door, and his mother-in-law called to him: "Do go in and have a peep at the table. And don't let May tire herself too much." But he affected not to hear, and sprang up the stairs to his library. The room looked at him like an alien countenance composed into a polite grimace; and he perceived that it had been ruthlessly "tidied," and prepared, by a judicious distribution of ash-trays and cedar-wood boxes, for the gentlemen to smoke in.

"Ah, well," he thought, "it's not for long—" and he went on to his dressing-room.

*   *   *

Ten days had passed since Madame Olenska's departure from New York. During those ten days Archer had had no sign from her but that conveyed by the return of a key wrapped in tissue paper, and sent to his office in a sealed envelope addressed in her hand. This retort to his last appeal might have been interpreted as a classic move in a familiar game; but the young man chose to give it a different meaning. She was still fighting against her fate; but she was going to Europe, and she was not returning to her husband. Nothing, therefore, was to prevent his following her; and once he had taken the irrevocable step, and had proved to her that it was irrevocable, he believed she would not send him away.

This confidence in the future had steadied him to play his part in the present. It had kept him from writing to her, or betraying, by any sign or act, his misery and mortification. It seemed to him that in the deadly silent game between them the trumps were still in his hands; and he waited.

There had been, nevertheless, moments sufficiently difficult to pass; as when Mr. Letterblair, the day after Madame Olenska's departure, had sent for him to go over the details of the trust which Mrs. Manson Mingott wished to create for her granddaughter. For a couple of hours Archer had examined the terms of the deed with his senior, all the while obscurely feeling that if he had been consulted it was for some reason other than the obvious one of his cousinship; and that the close of the conference would reveal it.

"Well, the lady can't deny that it's a handsome arrangement," Mr. Letterblair had summed up, after mumbling over a summary of the settlement. "In fact I'm bound to say she's been treated pretty handsomely all round."

"All round?" Archer echoed with a touch of derision. "Do you refer to her husband's proposal to give her back her own money?"

Mr. Letterblair's bushy eyebrows went up a fraction of an inch. "My dear sir, the law's the law; and your wife's cousin was married under the French law. It's to be presumed she knew what that meant."

"Even if she did, what happened subsequently—." But Archer paused. Mr. Letterblair had laid his pen-handle against his big corrugated nose, and was looking down it with the expression assumed by virtuous elderly gentlemen when they wish their youngers to understand that virtue is not synonymous with ignorance.

"My dear sir, I've no wish to extenuate the Count's transgressions; but—but on the other side . . . I wouldn't put my hand in the fire . . . well, that there hadn't been tit for tat . . . with the young champion. . . ." Mr. Letterblair unlocked a drawer and pushed a folded paper toward Archer. "This report, the result of discreet enquiries . . ." And then, as Archer made no effort to glance at the paper or to repudiate the suggestion, the lawyer somewhat flatly continued: "I don't say it's conclusive, you observe; far from it. But straws show . . . and on the whole it's eminently satisfactory for all parties that this dignified solution has been reached."

"Oh, eminently," Archer assented, pushing back the paper.

A day or two later, on responding to a summons from Mrs. Manson Mingott, his soul had been more deeply tried.

He had found the old lady depressed and querulous.

"You know she's deserted me?" she began at once; and without waiting for his reply: "Oh, don't ask me why! She gave so many reasons that I've forgotten them all. My private belief is that she couldn't face the boredom. At any rate that's what Augusta and my daughters-in-law think. And I don't know that I altogether blame her. Olenski's a finished scoundrel; but life with him must have been a good deal gayer than it is in Fifth Avenue. Not that the family would admit that: they think Fifth Avenue is Heaven with the rue de la Paix thrown in. And poor Ellen, of course, has no idea of going back to her husband. She held out as firmly as ever against that. So she's to settle down in Paris with that fool Medora. . . . Well, Paris is Paris; and you can keep a carriage there on next to nothing. But she was as gay as a bird, and I shall miss her." Two tears, the parched tears of the old, rolled down her puffy cheeks and vanished in the abysses of her bosom.

"All I ask is," she concluded, "that they shouldn't bother me any more. I must really be allowed to digest my gruel. . . ." And she twinkled a little wistfully at Archer.

It was that evening, on his return home, that May announced her intention of giving a farewell dinner to her cousin. Madame Olenska's name had not been pronounced between them since the night of her flight to Washington; and Archer looked at his wife with surprise.

"A dinner—why?" he interrogated.

Her colour rose. "But you like Ellen—I thought you'd be pleased."

"It's awfully nice—your putting it in that way. But I really don't see—"

"I mean to do it, Newland," she said, quietly rising and going to her desk. "Here are the invitations all written. Mother helped me—she agrees that we ought to." She paused, embarrassed and yet smiling, and Archer suddenly saw before him the embodied image of the Family.

"Oh, all right," he said, staring with unseeing eyes at the list of guests that she had put in his hand.

When he entered the drawing-room before dinner May was stooping over the fire and trying to coax the logs to burn in their unaccustomed setting of immaculate tiles.

The tall lamps were all lit, and Mr. van der Luyden's orchids had been conspicuously disposed in various receptacles of modern porcelain and knobby silver. Mrs. Newland Archer's drawing-room was generally thought a great success. A gilt bamboo *jardinière*, in which the primulas and cinerarias were punctually renewed, blocked the access to the bay window (where the old-fashioned would have preferred a bronze reduction of the Venus of Milo); the sofas and arm-chairs of pale brocade were cleverly grouped about little plush tables densely covered with silver toys, porcelain animals and efflorescent photograph frames; and tall rosy-shaded lamps shot up like tropical flowers among the palms.

"I don't think Ellen has ever seen this room lighted up," said May, rising flushed from her struggle, and sending about her a glance of pardonable pride. The brass tongs which she had propped against the side of the chimney fell with a crash that drowned her husband's answer; and before he could restore them Mr. and Mrs. van der Luyden were announced.

The other guests quickly followed, for it was known that the van der Luydens liked to dine punctually. The room was nearly full, and Archer was engaged in showing to Mrs.

Selfridge Merry a small highly-varnished Verbeckhoven "Study of Sheep," which Mr. Welland had given May for Christmas, when he found Madame Olenska at his side.

She was excessively pale, and her pallor made her dark hair seem denser and heavier than ever. Perhaps that, or the fact that she had wound several rows of amber beads about her neck, reminded him suddenly of the little Ellen Mingott he had danced with at children's parties, when Medora Manson had first brought her to New York.

The amber beads were trying to her complexion, or her dress was perhaps unbecoming: her face looked lustreless and almost ugly, and he had never loved it as he did at that minute. Their hands met, and he thought he heard her say: "Yes, we're sailing tomorrow in the Russia—"; then there was an unmeaning noise of opening doors, and after an interval May's voice: "Newland! Dinner's been announced. Won't you please take Ellen in?"

Madame Olenska put her hand on his arm, and he noticed that the hand was ungloved, and remembered how he had kept his eyes fixed on it the evening that he had sat with her in the little Twenty-third Street drawing-room. All the beauty that had forsaken her face seemed to have taken refuge in the long pale fingers and faintly dimpled knuckles on his sleeve, and he said to himself: "If it were only to see her hand again I should have to follow her—."

It was only at an entertainment ostensibly offered to a "foreign visitor" that Mrs. van der Luyden could suffer the diminution of being placed on her host's left. The fact of Madame Olenska's "foreignness" could hardly have been more adroitly emphasised than by this farewell tribute; and Mrs. van der Luyden accepted her displacement with an affability which left no doubt as to her approval. There were certain things that had to be done, and if done at all, done handsomely and thoroughly; and one of these, in the old New York code, was the tribal rally around a kinswoman about to be eliminated from the tribe. There was nothing on earth that the Wellands and Mingotts would not have done to proclaim their unalterable affection for the Countess Olenska now that her passage for Europe was engaged; and Archer, at the head of his table, sat marvelling at the silent

untiring activity with which her popularity had been re-
trieved, grievances against her silenced, her past counte-
nanced, and her present irradiated by the family approval.
Mrs. van der Luyden shone on her with the dim benevolence
which was her nearest approach to cordiality, and Mr. van der
Luyden, from his seat at May's right, cast down the table
glances plainly intended to justify all the carnations he had
sent from Skuytercliff.

Archer, who seemed to be assisting at the scene in a state
of odd imponderability, as if he floated somewhere between
chandelier and ceiling, wondered at nothing so much as his
own share in the proceedings. As his glance travelled from
one placid well-fed face to another he saw all the harmless-
looking people engaged upon May's canvas-backs as a band
of dumb conspirators, and himself and the pale woman on his
right as the centre of their conspiracy. And then it came over
him, in a vast flash made up of many broken gleams, that to
all of them he and Madame Olenska were lovers, lovers in the
extreme sense peculiar to "foreign" vocabularies. He guessed
himself to have been, for months, the centre of countless silently observing eyes and patiently listening ears, he understood that, by means as yet unknown to him, the separation
between himself and the partner of his guilt had been
achieved, and that now the whole tribe had rallied about his
wife on the tacit assumption that nobody knew anything, or
had ever imagined anything, and that the occasion of the entertainment was simply May Archer's natural desire to take an
affectionate leave of her friend and cousin.

It was the old New York way of taking life " without effusion of blood": the way of people who dreaded scandal more
than disease, who placed decency above courage, and who
considered that nothing was more ill-bred than "scenes," except the behaviour of those who gave rise to them.

As these thoughts succeeded each other in his mind Archer
felt like a prisoner in the centre of an armed camp. He looked
about the table, and guessed at the inexorableness of his cap-
tors from the tone in which, over the asparagus from Florida,
they were dealing with Beaufort and his wife. "It's to show
me," he thought, " what would happen to *me*—" and a
deathly sense of the superiority of implication and analogy

over direct action, and of silence over rash words, closed in on him like the doors of the family vault.

He laughed, and met Mrs. van der Luyden's startled eyes.

"You think it laughable?" she said with a pinched smile. "Of course poor Regina's idea of remaining in New York has its ridiculous side, I suppose;" and Archer muttered: "Of course."

At this point, he became conscious that Madame Olenska's other neighbour had been engaged for some time with the lady on his right. At the same moment he saw that May, serenely enthroned between Mr. van der Luyden and Mr. Selfridge Merry, had cast a quick glance down the table. It was evident that the host and the lady on his right could not sit through the whole meal in silence. He turned to Madame Olenska, and her pale smile met him. "Oh, do let's see it through," it seemed to say.

"Did you find the journey tiring?" he asked in a voice that surprised him by its naturalness; and she answered that, on the contrary, she had seldom travelled with fewer discomforts.

"Except, you know, the dreadful heat in the train," she added; and he remarked that she would not suffer from that particular hardship in the country she was going to.

"I never," he declared with intensity, " was more nearly frozen than once, in April, in the train between Calais and Paris."

She said she did not wonder, but remarked that, after all, one could always carry an extra rug, and that every form of travel had its hardships; to which he abruptly returned that he thought them all of no account compared with the blessedness of getting away. She changed colour, and he added, his voice suddenly rising in pitch: "I mean to do a lot of travelling myself before long." A tremor crossed her face, and leaning over to Reggie Chivers, he cried out: "I say, Reggie, what do you say to a trip round the world: now, next month, I mean? I'm game if you are—" at which Mrs. Reggie piped up that she could not think of letting Reggie go till after the Martha Washington Ball she was getting up for the Blind Asylum in Easter week; and her husband placidly observed that by that time he would have to be practising for the International Polo match.

But Mr. Selfridge Merry had caught the phrase "round the world," and having once circled the globe in his steam-yacht, he seized the opportunity to send down the table several striking items concerning the shallowness of the Mediterranean ports. Though, after all, he added, it didn't matter; for when you'd seen Athens and Smyrna and Constantinople, what else was there? And Mrs. Merry said she could never be too grateful to Dr. Bencomb for having made them promise not to go to Naples on account of the fever.

"But you must have three weeks to do India properly," her husband conceded, anxious to have it understood that he was no frivolous globe-trotter.

And at this point the ladies went up to the drawing-room.

In the library, in spite of weightier presences, Lawrence Lefferts predominated.

The talk, as usual, had veered around to the Beauforts, and even Mr. van der Luyden and Mr. Selfridge Merry, installed in the honorary arm-chairs tacitly reserved for them, paused to listen to the younger man's philippic.

Never had Lefferts so abounded in the sentiments that adorn Christian manhood and exalt the sanctity of the home. Indignation lent him a scathing eloquence, and it was clear that if others had followed his example, and acted as he talked, society would never have been weak enough to receive a foreign upstart like Beaufort—no, sir, not even if he'd married a van der Luyden or a Lanning instead of a Dallas. And what chance would there have been, Lefferts wrathfully questioned, of his marrying into such a family as the Dallases, if he had not already wormed his way into certain houses, as people like Mrs. Lemuel Struthers had managed to worm theirs in his wake? If society chose to open its doors to vulgar women the harm was not great, though the gain was doubtful; but once it got in the way of tolerating men of obscure origin and tainted wealth the end was total disintegration—and at no distant date.

"If things go on at this pace," Lefferts thundered, looking like a young prophet dressed by Poole, and who had not yet been stoned, "we shall see our children fighting for invitations to swindlers' houses, and marrying Beaufort's bastards."

"Oh, I say—draw it mild!" Reggie Chivers and young Newland protested, while Mr. Selfridge Merry looked genuinely alarmed, and an expression of pain and disgust settled on Mr. van der Luyden's sensitive face.

"Has he got any?" cried Mr. Sillerton Jackson, pricking up his ears; and while Lefferts tried to turn the question with a laugh, the old gentleman twittered into Archer's ear: "Queer, those fellows who are always wanting to set things right. The people who have the worst cooks are always telling you they're poisoned when they dine out. But I hear there are pressing reasons for our friend Lawrence's diatribe:—type-writer this time, I understand. . . ."

The talk swept past Archer like some senseless river running and running because it did not know enough to stop. He saw, on the faces about him, expressions of interest, amusement and even mirth. He listened to the younger men's laughter, and to the praise of the Archer Madeira, which Mr. van der Luyden and Mr. Merry were thoughtfully celebrating. Through it all he was dimly aware of a general attitude of friendliness toward himself, as if the guard of the prisoner he felt himself to be were trying to soften his captivity; and the perception increased his passionate determination to be free.

In the drawing-room, where they presently joined the ladies, he met May's triumphant eyes, and read in them the conviction that everything had "gone off" beautifully. She rose from Madame Olenska's side, and immediately Mrs. van der Luyden beckoned the latter to a seat on the gilt sofa where she throned. Mrs. Selfridge Merry bore across the room to join them, and it became clear to Archer that here also a conspiracy of rehabilitation and obliteration was going on. The silent organisation which held his little world together was determined to put itself on record as never for a moment having questioned the propriety of Madame Olenska's conduct, or the completeness of Archer's domestic felicity. All these amiable and inexorable persons were resolutely engaged in pretending to each other that they had never heard of, suspected, or even conceived possible, the least hint to the contrary; and from this tissue of elaborate mutual dissimulation Archer once more disengaged the fact that New York believed him to be Madame Olenska's lover. He caught the glitter of victory in his wife's eyes, and for the first time understood that she shared the belief. The discovery roused a laughter of inner devils that reverberated through all his efforts to discuss the Martha Washington ball with Mrs. Reggie Chivers and little Mrs. Newland; and so the evening swept on, running and running like a senseless river that did not know how to stop.

At length he saw that Madame Olenska had risen and was saying good-bye. He understood that in a moment she would be gone, and tried to remember what he had said to her at dinner; but he could not recall a single word they had exchanged.

She went up to May, the rest of the company making a circle about her as she advanced. The two young women clasped hands; then May bent forward and kissed her cousin.

"Certainly our hostess is much the handsomer of the two," Archer heard Reggie Chivers say in an undertone to young Mrs. Newland; and he remembered Beaufort's coarse sneer at May's ineffectual beauty.

A moment later he was in the hall, putting Madame Olenska's cloak about her shoulders.

Through all his confusion of mind he had held fast to the resolve to say nothing that might startle or disturb her. Convinced that no power could now turn him from his purpose he had found strength to let events shape themselves as they would. But as he followed Madame Olenska into the hall he thought with a sudden hunger of being for a moment alone with her at the door of her carriage.

"Is your carriage here?" he asked; and at that moment Mrs. van der Luyden, who was being majestically inserted into her sables, said gently: "We are driving dear Ellen home."

Archer's heart gave a jerk, and Madame Olenska, clasping her cloak and fan with one hand, held out the other to him. "Good-bye," she said.

"Good-bye—but I shall see you soon in Paris," he answered aloud—it seemed to him that he had shouted it.

"Oh," she murmured, "if you and May could come—!"

Mr. van der Luyden advanced to give her his arm, and Archer turned to Mrs. van der Luyden. For a moment, in the billowy darkness inside the big landau, he caught the dim oval of a face, eyes shining steadily—and she was gone.

As he went up the steps he crossed Lawrence Lefferts coming down with his wife. Lefferts caught his host by the sleeve, drawing back to let Gertrude pass.

"I say, old chap: do you mind just letting it be understood that I'm dining with you at the club tomorrow night? Thanks so much, you old brick! Good-night."

"It *did* go off beautifully, didn't it?" May questioned from the threshold of the library.

Archer roused himself with a start. As soon as the last carriage had driven away, he had come up to the library and shut himself in, with the hope that his wife, who still lingered below, would go straight to her room. But there she stood, pale and drawn, yet radiating the factitious energy of one who has passed beyond fatigue.

"May I come and talk it over?" she asked.

"Of course, if you like. But you must be awfully sleepy—"

"No, I'm not sleepy. I should like to sit with you a little."

"Very well," he said, pushing her chair near the fire.

She sat down and he resumed his seat; but neither spoke for a long time. At length Archer began abruptly: "Since you're not tired, and want to talk, there's something I must tell you. I tried to the other night—."

She looked at him quickly. "Yes, dear. Something about yourself?"

"About myself. You say you're not tired: well, I am. Horribly tired . . ."

In an instant she was all tender anxiety. "Oh, I've seen it coming on, Newland! You've been so wickedly over-worked—"

"Perhaps it's that. Anyhow, I want to make a break—"

"A break? To give up the law?"

"To go away, at any rate—at once. On a long trip, ever so far off—away from everything—"

He paused, conscious that he had failed in his attempt to speak with the indifference of a man who longs for a change, and is yet too weary to welcome it. Do what he would, the chord of eagerness vibrated. "Away from everything—" he repeated.

"Ever so far? Where, for instance?" she asked.

"Oh, I don't know. India—or Japan."

She stood up, and as he sat with bent head, his chin propped on his hands, he felt her warmly and fragrantly hovering over him.

"As far as that? But I'm afraid you can't, dear . . ." she said in an unsteady voice. "Not unless you'll take me with you." And then, as he was silent, she went on, in tones so clear and evenly-pitched that each separate syllable tapped like a little hammer on his brain: "That is, if the doctors will let me go . . . but I'm afraid they won't. For you see, Newland, I've been sure since this morning of something I've been so longing and hoping for—"

He looked up at her with a sick stare, and she sank down, all dew and roses, and hid her face against his knee.

"Oh, my dear," he said, holding her to him while his cold hand stroked her hair.

There was a long pause, which the inner devils filled with strident laughter; then May freed herself from his arms and stood up.

"You didn't guess—?"

"Yes—I; no. That is, of course I hoped—"

They looked at each other for an instant and again fell silent; then, turning his eyes from hers, he asked abruptly: "Have you told any one else?"

"Only Mamma and your mother." She paused, and then added hurriedly, the blood flushing up to her forehead: "That is—and Ellen. You know I told you we'd had a long talk one afternoon—and how dear she was to me."

"Ah—" said Archer, his heart stopping.

He felt that his wife was watching him intently. "Did you *mind* my telling her first, Newland?"

"Mind? Why should I?" He made a last effort to collect himself. "But that was a fortnight ago, wasn't it? I thought you said you weren't sure till today."

Her colour burned deeper, but she held his gaze. "No; I wasn't sure then—but I told her I was. And you see I was right!" she exclaimed, her blue eyes wet with victory.

XXXIV

NEWLAND ARCHER sat at the writing-table in his library in East Thirty-ninth Street.

He had just got back from a big official reception for the inauguration of the new galleries at the Metropolitan Museum, and the spectacle of those great spaces crowded with the spoils of the ages, where the throng of fashion circulated through a series of scientifically catalogued treasures, had suddenly pressed on a rusted spring of memory.

"Why, this used to be one of the old Cesnola rooms," he heard some one say; and instantly everything about him vanished, and he was sitting alone on a hard leather divan against a radiator, while a slight figure in a long sealskin cloak moved away down the meagrely-fitted vista of the old Museum.

The vision had roused a host of other associations, and he sat looking with new eyes at the library which, for over thirty years, had been the scene of his solitary musings and of all the family confabulations.

It was the room in which most of the real things of his life had happened. There his wife, nearly twenty-six years ago, had broken to him, with a blushing circumlocution that would have caused the young women of the new generation to smile, the news that she was to have a child; and there their eldest boy, Dallas, too delicate to be taken to church in midwinter, had been christened by their old friend the Bishop of New York, the ample magnificent irreplaceable Bishop, so long the pride and ornament of his diocese. There Dallas had first staggered across the floor shouting "Dad," while May and the nurse laughed behind the door; there their second child, Mary (who was so like her mother), had announced her engagement to the dullest and most reliable of Reggie Chivers's many sons; and there Archer had kissed her through her wedding veil before they went down to the motor which was to carry them to Grace Church—for in a world where all else had reeled on its foundations the "Grace Church wedding" remained an unchanged institution.

It was in the library that he and May had always discussed the future of the children: the studies of Dallas and his young

brother Bill, Mary's incurable indifference to "accomplish-
ments," and passion for sport and philanthropy, and the vague
leanings toward "art" which had finally landed the restless
and curious Dallas in the office of a rising New York architect.

The young men nowadays were emancipating themselves
from the law and business and taking up all sorts of new
things. If they were not absorbed in state politics or municipal reform, the chances were that they were going in for
Central American archæology, for architecture or landscape-
engineering; taking a keen and learned interest in the pre-
revolutionary buildings of their own country, studying and
adapting Georgian types, and protesting at the meaningless
use of the word "Colonial." Nobody nowadays had "Colonial" houses except the millionaire grocers of the suburbs.

But above all—sometimes Archer put it above all—it was
in that library that the Governor of New York, coming down
from Albany one evening to dine and spend the night, had
turned to his host, and said, banging his clenched fist on the
table and gnashing his eye-glasses: "Hang the professional
politician! You're the kind of man the country wants, Archer.
If the stable's ever to be cleaned out, men like you have got
to lend a hand in the cleaning."

"Men like you—" how Archer had glowed at the phrase!
How eagerly he had risen up at the call! It was an echo of Ned
Winsett's old appeal to roll his sleeves up and get down into
the muck; but spoken by a man who set the example of the
gesture, and whose summons to follow him was irresistible.

Archer, as he looked back, was not sure that men like himself *were* what his country needed, at least in the active service
to which Theodore Roosevelt had pointed; in fact, there was
reason to think it did not, for after a year in the State Assem-
bly he had not been re-elected, and had dropped back thankfully into obscure if useful municipal work, and from that
again to the writing of occasional articles in one of the reforming weeklies that were trying to shake the country out of
its apathy. It was little enough to look back on; but when he
remembered to what the young men of his generation and his
set had looked forward—the narrow groove of money-
making, sport and society to which their vision had been limited—even his small contribution to the new state of things

seemed to count, as each brick counts in a well-built wall. He had done little in public life; he would always be by nature a contemplative and a dilettante; but he had had high things to contemplate, great things to delight in; and one great man's friendship to be his strength and pride.

He had been, in short, what people were beginning to call "a good citizen." In New York, for many years past, every new movement, philanthropic, municipal or artistic, had taken account of his opinion and wanted his name. People said: "Ask Archer" when there was a question of starting the first school for crippled children, reorganising the Museum of Art, founding the Grolier Club, inaugurating the new Library, or getting up a new society of chamber music. His days were full, and they were filled decently. He supposed it was all a man ought to ask.

Something he knew he had missed: the flower of life. But he thought of it now as a thing so unattainable and improbable that to have repined would have been like despairing because one had not drawn the first prize in a lottery. There were a hundred million tickets in *his* lottery, and there was only one prize; the chances had been too decidedly against him. When he thought of Ellen Olenska it was abstractly, serenely, as one might think of some imaginary beloved in a book or a picture: she had become the composite vision of all that he had missed. That vision, faint and tenuous as it was, had kept him from thinking of other women. He had been what was called a faithful husband; and when May had suddenly died—carried off by the infectious pneumonia through which she had nursed their youngest child—he had honestly mourned her. Their long years together had shown him that it did not so much matter if marriage was a dull duty, as long as it kept the dignity of a duty: lapsing from that, it became a mere battle of ugly appetites. Looking about him, he honoured his own past, and mourned for it. After all, there was good in the old ways.

His eyes, making the round of the room—done over by Dallas with English mezzotints, Chippendale cabinets, bits of chosen blue-and-white and pleasantly shaded electric lamps—came back to the old Eastlake writing-table that he had never been willing to banish, and to his first photograph of May, which still kept its place beside his inkstand.

There she was, tall, round-bosomed and willowy, in her starched muslin and flapping Leghorn, as he had seen her under the orange-trees in the Mission garden. And as he had seen her that day, so she had remained; never quite at the same height, yet never far below it: generous, faithful, unwearied; but so lacking in imagination, so incapable of growth, that the world of her youth had fallen into pieces and rebuilt itself without her ever being conscious of the change. This hard bright blindness had kept her immediate horizon apparently unaltered. Her incapacity to recognise change made her children conceal their views from her as Archer concealed his; there had been, from the first, a joint pretence of sameness, a kind of innocent family hypocrisy, in which father and children had unconsciously collaborated. And she had died thinking the world a good place, full of loving and harmonious households like her own, and resigned to leave it because she was convinced that, whatever happened, Newland would continue to inculcate in Dallas the same principles and prejudices which had shaped his parents' lives, and that Dallas in turn (when Newland followed her) would transmit the sacred trust to little Bill. And of Mary she was sure as of her own self. So, having snatched little Bill from the grave, and given her life in the effort, she went contentedly to her place in the Archer vault in St. Mark's, where Mrs. Archer already lay safe from the terrifying "trend" which her daughter-in-law had never even become aware of.

Opposite May's portrait stood one of her daughter. Mary Chivers was as tall and fair as her mother, but large-waisted, flat-chested and slightly slouching, as the altered fashion required. Mary Chivers's mighty feats of athleticism could not have been performed with the twenty-inch waist that May Archer's azure sash so easily spanned. And the difference seemed symbolic; the mother's life had been as closely girt as her figure. Mary, who was no less conventional, and no more intelligent, yet led a larger life and held more tolerant views. There was good in the new order too.

The telephone clicked, and Archer, turning from the photographs, unhooked the transmitter at his elbow. How far they were from the days when the legs of the brass-buttoned messenger boy had been New York's only means of quick communication!

"Chicago wants you."

Ah—it must be a long-distance from Dallas, who had been sent to Chicago by his firm to talk over the plan of the Lakeside palace they were to build for a young millionaire with ideas. The firm always sent Dallas on such errands.

"Hallo, Dad—Yes: Dallas. I say—how do you feel about sailing on Wednesday? Mauretania: Yes, next Wednesday as ever is. Our client wants me to look at some Italian gardens before we settle anything, and has asked me to nip over on the next boat. I've got to be back on the first of June—" the voice broke into a joyful conscious laugh—"so we must look alive. I say, Dad, I want your help: do come."

Dallas seemed to be speaking in the room: the voice was as near by and natural as if he had been lounging in his favourite arm-chair by the fire. The fact would not ordinarily have surprised Archer, for long-distance telephoning had become as much a matter of course as electric lighting and five-day Atlantic voyages. But the laugh did startle him; it still seemed wonderful that across all those miles and miles of country—forest, river, mountain, prairie, roaring cities and busy indifferent millions—Dallas's laugh should be able to say: "Of course, whatever happens, I must get back on the first, because Fanny Beaufort and I are to be married on the fifth."

The voice began again: "Think it over? No, sir: not a minute. You've got to say yes now. Why not, I'd like to know? If you can allege a single reason—No; I knew it. Then it's a go, eh? Because I count on you to ring up the Cunard office first thing tomorrow; and you'd better book a return on a boat from Marseilles. I say, Dad; it'll be our last time together, in this kind of way—. Oh, good! I knew you would."

Chicago rang off, and Archer rose and began to pace up and down the room.

It would be their last time together in this kind of way: the boy was right. They would have lots of other "times" after Dallas's marriage, his father was sure; for the two were born comrades, and Fanny Beaufort, whatever one might think of her, did not seem likely to interfere with their intimacy. On the contrary, from what he had seen of her, he thought she would be naturally included in it. Still, change was change, and differences were differences, and much as he felt himself drawn toward his future daughter-in-law, it was tempting to seize this last chance of being alone with his boy.

There was no reason why he should not seize it, except the profound one that he had lost the habit of travel. May had disliked to move except for valid reasons, such as taking the children to the sea or in the mountains: she could imagine no other motive for leaving the house in Thirty-ninth Street or their comfortable quarters at the Wellands' in Newport. After Dallas had taken his degree she had thought it her duty to travel for six months; and the whole family had made the old-fashioned tour through England, Switzerland and Italy. Their time being limited (no one knew why) they had omitted France. Archer remembered Dallas's wrath at being asked to contemplate Mont Blanc instead of Rheims and Chartres. But Mary and Bill wanted mountain-climbing, and had already yawned their way in Dallas's wake through the English cathedrals; and May, always fair to her children, had insisted on holding the balance evenly between their athletic and artistic proclivities. She had indeed proposed that her husband should go to Paris for a fortnight, and join them on the Italian lakes after they had "done" Switzerland; but Archer had declined. "We'll stick together," he said; and May's face had brightened at his setting such a good example to Dallas.

Since her death, nearly two years before, there had been no reason for his continuing in the same routine. His children had urged him to travel: Mary Chivers had felt sure it would do him good to go abroad and "see the galleries." The very mysteriousness of such a cure made her the more confident of its efficacy. But Archer had found himself held fast by habit, by memories, by a sudden startled shrinking from new things.

Now, as he reviewed his past, he saw into what a deep rut he had sunk. The worst of doing one's duty was that it apparently unfitted one for doing anything else. At least that was the view that the men of his generation had taken. The trenchant divisions between right and wrong, honest and dishonest, respectable and the reverse, had left so little scope for the unforeseen. There are moments when a man's imagination, so easily subdued to what it lives in, suddenly rises above its daily level, and surveys the long windings of destiny. Archer hung there and wondered. . . .

What was left of the little world he had grown up in, and whose standards had bent and bound him? He remembered a sneering prophecy of poor Lawrence Lefferts's, uttered years ago in that very room: "If things go on at this rate, our children will be marrying Beaufort's bastards."

It was just what Archer's eldest son, the pride of his life, was doing; and nobody wondered or reproved. Even the boy's Aunt Janey, who still looked so exactly as she used to in her elderly youth, had taken her mother's emeralds and seed-pearls out of their pink cotton-wool, and carried them with her own twitching hands to the future bride; and Fanny Beaufort, instead of looking disappointed at not receiving a "set" from a Paris jeweller, had exclaimed at their old-fashioned beauty, and declared that when she wore them she should feel like an Isabey miniature.

Fanny Beaufort, who had appeared in New York at eighteen, after the death of her parents, had won its heart much as Madame Olenska had won it thirty years earlier; only instead of being distrustful and afraid of her, society took her joyfully for granted. She was pretty, amusing and accomplished: what more did any one want? Nobody was narrow-minded enough to rake up against her the half-forgotten facts of her father's past and her own origin. Only the older people remembered so obscure an incident in the business life of New York as Beaufort's failure, or the fact that after his wife's death he had been quietly married to the notorious Fanny Ring, and had left the country with his new wife, and a little girl who inherited her beauty. He was subsequently heard of in Constantinople, then in Russia; and a dozen years later American travellers were handsomely entertained by him in Buenos Ayres, where he represented a large insurance agency. He and his wife died there in the odour of prosperity; and one day their orphaned daughter had appeared in New York in charge of May Archer's sister-in-law, Mrs. Jack Welland, whose husband had been appointed the girl's guardian. The fact threw her into almost cousinly relationship with Newland Archer's children, and nobody was surprised when Dallas's engagement was announced.

Nothing could more clearly give the measure of the distance that the world had travelled. People nowadays were too busy—busy with reforms and "movements," with fads and fetishes and frivolities—to bother much about their neighbours. And of what account was anybody's past, in the huge kaleidoscope where all the social atoms spun around on the same plane?

Newland Archer, looking out of his hotel window at the stately gaiety of the Paris streets, felt his heart beating with the confusion and eagerness of youth.

It was long since it had thus plunged and reared under his widening waistcoat, leaving him, the next minute, with an empty breast and hot temples. He wondered if it was thus that his son's conducted itself in the presence of Miss Fanny Beaufort—and decided that it was not. "It functions as actively, no doubt, but the rhythm is different," he reflected, recalling the cool composure with which the young man had announced his engagement, and taken for granted that his family would approve.

"The difference is that these young people take it for granted that they're going to get whatever they want, and that we almost always took it for granted that we shouldn't. Only, I wonder—the thing one's so certain of in advance: can it ever make one's heart beat as wildly?"

It was the day after their arrival in Paris, and the spring sunshine held Archer in his open window, above the wide silvery prospect of the Place Vendôme. One of the things he had stipulated—almost the only one—when he had agreed to come abroad with Dallas, was that, in Paris, he shouldn't be made to go to one of the new-fangled "palaces."

"Oh, all right—of course," Dallas good-naturedly agreed. "I'll take you to some jolly old-fashioned place—the Bristol say—" leaving his father speechless at hearing that the century-long home of kings and emperors was now spoken of as an old-fashioned inn, where one went for its quaint inconveniences and lingering local colour.

Archer had pictured often enough, in the first impatient years, the scene of his return to Paris; then the personal vision had faded, and he had simply tried to see the city as the setting of Madame Olenska's life. Sitting alone at night in his library, after the household had gone to bed, he had evoked the radiant outbreak of spring down the avenues of horse-chestnuts, the flowers and statues in the public gardens, the whiff of lilacs from the flower-carts, the majestic roll of the river under the great bridges, and the life of art and study and pleasure that filled each mighty artery to bursting. Now the spectacle was before him in its glory, and as he looked out on it he felt shy, old-fashioned, inadequate: a mere grey speck of a man compared with the ruthless magnificent fellow he had dreamed of being. . . .

Dallas's hand came down cheerily on his shoulder. "Hullo, father: this is something like, isn't it?" They stood for a while looking out in silence, and then the young man continued: "By the way, I've got a message for you: the Countess Olenska expects us both at half-past five."

He said it lightly, carelessly, as he might have imparted any casual item of information, such as the hour at which their train was to leave for Florence the next evening. Archer looked at him, and thought he saw in his gay young eyes a gleam of his great-grandmother Mingott's malice.

"Oh, didn't I tell you?" Dallas pursued. "Fanny made me swear to do three things while I was in Paris: get her the score of the last Debussy songs, go to the Grand-Guignol and see Madame Olenska. You know she was awfully good to Fanny when Mr. Beaufort sent her over from Buenos Ayres to the Assomption. Fanny hadn't any friends in Paris, and Madame Olenska used to be kind to her and trot her about on holidays. I believe she was a great friend of the first Mrs. Beaufort's. And she's our cousin, of course. So I rang her up this morning, before I went out, and told her you and I were here for two days and wanted to see her."

Archer continued to stare at him. "You told her I was here?"

"Of course—why not?" Dallas's eye brows went up whimsically. Then, getting no answer, he slipped his arm through his father's with a confidential pressure.

"I say, father: what was she like?"

Archer felt his colour rise under his son's unabashed gaze. "Come, own up: you and she were great pals, weren't you? Wasn't she most awfully lovely?"

"Lovely? I don't know. She was different."

"Ah—there you have it! That's what it always comes to,

doesn't it? When she comes, *she's different*—and one doesn't know why. It's exactly what I feel about Fanny."

His father drew back a step, releasing his arm. "About Fanny? But, my dear fellow—I should hope so! Only I don't see—"

"Dash it, Dad, don't be prehistoric! Wasn't she—once— your Fanny?"

Dallas belonged body and soul to the new generation. He was the first-born of Newland and May Archer, yet it had never been possible to inculcate in him even the rudiments of reserve. "What's the use of making mysteries? It only makes people want to nose 'em out," he always objected when enjoined to discretion. But Archer, meeting his eyes, saw the filial light under their banter.

"My Fanny—?"

"Well, the woman you'd have chucked everything for: only you didn't," continued his surprising son.

"I didn't," echoed Archer with a kind of solemnity.

"No: you date, you see, dear old boy. But mother said—"

"Your mother?"

"Yes: the day before she died. It was when she sent for me alone—you remember? She said she knew we were safe with you, and always would be, because once, when she asked you to, you'd given up the thing you most wanted."

Archer received this strange communication in silence. His eyes remained unseeingly fixed on the thronged sunlit square below the window. At length he said in a low voice: "She never asked me."

"No. I forgot. You never did ask each other anything, did you? And you never told each other anything. You just sat and watched each other, and guessed at what was going on underneath. A deaf-and-dumb asylum, in fact! Well, I back your generation for knowing more about each other's private thoughts than we ever have time to find out about our own.—I say, Dad," Dallas broke off, "you're not angry with me? If you are, let's make it up and go and lunch at Henri's. I've got to rush out to Versailles afterward."

Archer did not accompany his son to Versailles. He preferred to spend the afternoon in solitary roamings through

Paris. He had to deal all at once with the packed regrets and stifled memories of an inarticulate lifetime.

After a little while he did not regret Dallas's indiscretion. It seemed to take an iron band from his heart to know that, after all, some one had guessed and pitied. . . . And that it should have been his wife moved him indescribably. Dallas, for all his affectionate insight, would not have understood that. To the boy, no doubt, the episode was only a pathetic instance of vain frustration, of wasted forces. But was it really no more? For a long time Archer sat on a bench in the Champs Elysées and wondered, while the stream of life rolled by. . . .

A few streets away, a few hours away, Ellen Olenska waited. She had never gone back to her husband, and when he had died, some years before, she had made no change in her way of living. There was nothing now to keep her and Archer apart—and that afternoon he was to see her.

He got up and walked across the Place de la Concorde and the Tuileries gardens to the Louvre. She had once told him that she often went there, and he had a fancy to spend the intervening time in a place where he could think of her as perhaps having lately been. For an hour or more he wandered from gallery to gallery through the dazzle of afternoon light, and one by one the pictures burst on him in their half-forgotten splendour, filling his soul with the long echoes of beauty. After all, his life had been too starved. . . .

Suddenly, before an effulgent Titian, he found himself saying: "But I'm only fifty-seven—" and then he turned away. For such summer dreams it was too late; but surely not for a quiet harvest of friendship, of comradeship, in the blessed hush of her nearness.

He went back to the hotel, where he and Dallas were to meet; and together they walked again across the Place de la Concorde and over the bridge that leads to the Chamber of Deputies.

Dallas, unconscious of what was going on in his father's mind, was talking excitedly and abundantly of Versailles. He had had but one previous glimpse of it, during a holiday trip in which he had tried to pack all the sights he had been deprived of when he had had to go with the family to Switzerland; and tumultuous enthusiasm and cock-sure criticism tripped each other up on his lips.

As Archer listened, his sense of inadequacy and inexpressiveness increased. The boy was not insensitive, he knew; but he had the facility and self-confidence that came of looking at fate not as a master but as an equal. "That's it: they feel equal to things—they know their way about," he mused, thinking of his son as the spokesman of the new generation which had swept away all the old landmarks, and with them the sign-posts and the danger-signal.

Suddenly Dallas stopped short, grasping his father's arm. "Oh, by Jove," he exclaimed.

They had come out into the great tree-planted space before the Invalides. The dome of Mansart floated ethereally above the budding trees and the long grey front of the building: drawing up into itself all the rays of afternoon light, it hung there like the visible symbol of the race's glory.

Archer knew that Madame Olenska lived in a square near one of the avenues radiating from the Invalides; and he had pictured the quarter as quiet and almost obscure, forgetting the central splendour that lit it up. Now, by some queer process of association, that golden light became for him the pervading illumination in which she lived. For nearly thirty years, her life—of which he knew so strangely little—had been spent in this rich atmosphere that he already felt to be too dense and yet too stimulating for his lungs. He thought of the theatres she must have been to, the pictures she must have looked at, the sober and splendid old houses she must have frequented, the people she must have talked with, the incessant stir of ideas, curiosities, images and associations thrown out by an intensely social race in a setting of immemorial manners; and suddenly he remembered the young Frenchman who had once said to him: "Ah, good conversation—there is nothing like it, is there?"

Archer had not seen M. Rivière, or heard of him, for nearly thirty years; and that fact gave the measure of his ignorance of Madame Olenska's existence. More than half a lifetime divided them, and she had spent the long interval among people he did not know, in a society he but faintly guessed at, in conditions he would never wholly understand. During that time he had been living with his youthful memory of her; but she had doubtless had other and more tangible companionship. Perhaps she too had kept her memory of him as something apart; but if she had, it must have been like a relic in a small dim chapel, where there was not time to pray every day. . . .

They had crossed the Place des Invalides, and were walking down one of the thoroughfares flanking the building. It was a quiet quarter, after all, in spite of its splendour and its history; and the fact gave one an idea of the riches Paris had to draw on, since such scenes as this were left to the few and the indifferent.

The day was fading into a soft sun-shot haze, pricked here and there by a yellow electric light, and passers were rare in the little square into which they had turned. Dallas stopped again, and looked up.

"It must be here," he said, slipping his arm through his father's with a movement from which Archer's shyness did not shrink; and they stood together looking up at the house.

It was a modern building, without distinctive character, but many-windowed, and pleasantly balconied up its wide cream-coloured front. On one of the upper balconies, which hung well above the rounded tops of the horse-chestnuts in the square, the awnings were still lowered, as though the sun had just left it.

"I wonder which floor—?" Dallas conjectured; and moving toward the *porte-cochère* he put his head into the porter's lodge, and came back to say: "The fifth. It must be the one with the awnings."

Archer remained motionless, gazing at the upper windows as if the end of their pilgrimage had been attained.

"I say, you know, it's nearly six," his son at length reminded him.

The father glanced away at an empty bench under the trees. "I believe I'll sit there a moment," he said.

"Why—aren't you well?" his son exclaimed.

"Oh, perfectly. But I should like you, please, to go up without me."

Dallas paused before him, visibly bewildered. "But, I say, Dad: do you mean you won't come up at all?"

"I don't know," said Archer slowly.

"If you don't she won't understand."

"Go, my boy; perhaps I shall follow you."

Dallas gave him a long look through the twilight.

"But what on earth shall I say?"

"My dear fellow, don't you always know what to say?" his father rejoined with a smile.

"Very well. I shall say you're old-fashioned, and prefer walking up the five flights because you don't like lifts."

His father smiled again. "Say I'm old-fashioned: that's enough."

Dallas looked at him again, and then, with an incredulous gesture, passed out of sight under the vaulted doorway.

Archer sat down on the bench and continued to gaze at the awninged balcony. He calculated the time it would take his son to be carried up in the lift to the fifth floor, to ring the bell, and be admitted to the hall, and then ushered into the drawing-room. He pictured Dallas entering that room with his quick assured step and his delightful smile, and wondered if the people were right who said that his boy "took after him."

Then he tried to see the persons already in the room—for probably at that sociable hour there would be more than one—and among them a dark lady, pale and dark, who would look up quickly, half rise, and hold out a long thin hand with three rings on it. . . . He thought she would be sitting in a sofa-corner near the fire, with azaleas banked behind her on a table.

"It's more real to me here than if I went up," he suddenly heard himself say; and the fear lest that last shadow of reality should lose its edge kept him rooted to his seat as the minutes succeeded each other.

He sat for a long time on the bench in the thickening dusk, his eyes never turning from the balcony. At length a light shone through the windows, and a moment later a man-servant came out on the balcony, drew up the awnings, and closed the shutters.

At that, as if it had been the signal he waited for, Newland Archer got up slowly and walked back alone to his hotel.

THE END.

Chronology

1862   Born January 24 at 80 East 21st Street, New York City, and baptized Edith Newbold Jones; third and last child of George Frederic Jones and Lucretia Rhinelander (brothers are Frederic, b. 1846, and Henry, b. 1850). Parents belong to long-established, socially prominent New York families. Father's income based on Manhattan landholdings.

1865   Receives gift of spitz puppy, beginning a lifelong passion for small dogs.

1866   Family moves to Europe in November for prolonged residence due to post-Civil War depression in real estate market. Sails to England with parents, nurse Hannah Doyle ("Doyley"), and brother Henry, who begins law studies at Trinity Hall College, Cambridge.

1867   Family spends year in Rome.

1868   Family travels through Spain and settles in Paris. Taught to read by father; recites Tennyson for visiting maternal grandmother. Begins "making up," inventing stories using parents and their friends as characters.

1870–71 Stays at Wildbad, a spa in Württemberg, while mother takes water cure. Studies New Testament in German, takes walks in Black Forest. Suffers severe attack of typhoid fever (later remembers convalescence as beginning of recurrent apprehension of "some dark undefinable menace forever dogging my steps, lurking and threatening"). Family settles in Florence at end of 1870.

1872–75 Family returns to the United States, dividing year between three-story brownstone on West 23rd Street, New York, and Pencraig, their summer home in Newport, Rhode Island. At Pencraig rides pony, swims in cove, watches archery contests, visits neighboring family of astronomer Lewis Rutherfurd. Studies French, medieval and romantic German poetry with Rutherfurd family governess, Anna Bahlmann (who later becomes the Joneses' governess). Begins lifelong friendship with sister-in-law Mary Cadwalader Jones, wife (later divorced) of brother Frederic. In father's eight-hundred-volume New York library finds histories (including Plutarch, Macaulay, Carlyle, Parkman), diaries and correspondence (Pepys, Cowper, Madame de Sévigné), criticism (Sainte-Beuve), art history and archaeology (Ruskin, Schliemann), poetry (Homer and Dante in translation, most English poets, some French), and a few novels (Scott, Irving). Mother forbids the reading of contemporary fiction. Later remembers reading as "a secret ecstasy of communion." Summer 1875, forms close friendship with Emelyn, daughter of Edward Abiel Washburn, rector of Calvary Church, New York.

1876–77   Begins *Fast and Loose*, 30,000-word novella about trials of ill-starred young lovers, autumn 1876. Keeps enterprise secret from everyone except Emelyn Washburn. Finished January 1877, manuscript includes mock hostile reviews ("every character is a failure, the plot a vacuum").

1878–79   *Verses*, volume of twenty-nine poems, printed in Newport, arranged and paid for by mother. Summer 1879, Newport neighbor Allen Thorndike Rice shows some of the poems to Henry Wadsworth Longfellow, who recommends them to William Dean Howells. Howells publishes one in *Atlantic Monthly*. Makes social debut at end of year.

1880–81   Two poems appear in the New York *World*. Courted in New York, Newport, and Bar Harbor, Maine, by Henry Leyden Stevens, twenty-one-year-old son of prominent social figure, Mrs. Paran Stevens. November 1880, goes to southern France with mother and ailing father. Henry Stevens joins them September 1881.

1882   Father, age sixty-one, dies in Cannes in March. Inherits over $20,000 in trust fund. August, engagement to Henry Stevens announced in Newport, with marriage scheduled for autumn. Engagement is broken off in October, apparently at insistence of Mrs. Stevens. Travels with mother to Paris.

1883   Spends summer at Bar Harbor. Meets Walter Van Rensselaer Berry, twenty-four-year-old Harvard graduate studying for admission to the District of Columbia bar.

They become close, but Berry leaves without proposing marriage. In August, Edward Robbins ("Teddy") Wharton, friend of brother Henry, arrives in Bar Harbor and begins courtship. A thirty-three-year-old Harvard graduate interested mainly in camping, hunting, fishing, and riding, he lives with his family in Boston and receives a $2,000 annuity from them.

1884   Hires Catherine Gross, Alsatian immigrant, as personal attendant (she will be Wharton's companion and housekeeper for over four decades).

1885–88   Marries Edward Wharton April 29, 1885, at Trinity Chapel, New York City. Henry Stevens dies of tuberculosis, July 18, 1885. Whartons move into Pencraig Cottage, small house on mother's Newport estate, leaving every February for four months of European travel, mostly in Italy. Introduced by Egerton Winthrop, wealthy New York art collector and their occasional traveling companion, to contemporary French literature and works of Darwin, Huxley, Spencer, Haeckel, and other writers on evolution. Whartons spend a year's income (about $10,000) on four-month Aegean cruise, 1888. Learns in Athens that she has inherited $120,000 from reclusive New York cousin Joshua Jones.

1889   Rents small house on Madison Avenue, New York City. Four poems accepted for publication by *Scribner's Magazine*, *Harper's Monthly*, and *Century Illustrated Monthly Magazine*.

1890–92   Suffers intermittently from inexplicable nausea and fatigue. Short story, "Mrs. Manstey's View," accepted by *Scribner's* May 1890, published July 1891. November 1891, purchases narrow house on Fourth Avenue near 78th Street (eventually 884 Park Avenue) for $19,670. (A few years later acquires its adjoining twin at 882 Park for the household staff to live in.) Works on novella, *Bunner Sisters*. It is rejected by *Scribner's*, December 1892.

1893   Buys Land's End, Newport estate overlooking the Atlantic, for $80,000 in March. Works with Boston architect Ogden Codman on decoration of its interior. French novelist Paul Bourget and his wife are guests. Three stories, "That Good May Come," "The Fullness of Life," and "The Lamp of Psyche," accepted by *Scribner's*, whose editor, Edward Burlingame, proposes a short-story volume for Charles Scribner's Sons. Wharton agrees, suggesting inclusion of *Bunner Sisters*. Sails for Europe in December.

1894–95   Burlingame rejects "Something Exquisite." Writes to him from Florence, expressing gratitude for his criticism and doubt about her own abilities. Travels through Tuscany. Visits Violet Paget ("Vernon Lee"), English novelist and historian of eighteenth-century Italy. After research at monastery of San Vivaldo and in Florence museums, identifies group of terra-cotta sculptures, previously thought to date from the seventeenth century, as work of Giovanni della Robbia (1469–1529). Writes article for *Scribner's* on her findings and surrounding Tuscan landscape. Notifies Burlingame in July 1894 that short-story volume will need another six months to prepare. Suffering from intense exhaustion, nausea, and melancholia, breaks off correspondence with Burlingame for sixteen months. Mother moves to Paris (brothers Frederic and Henry both live in Europe); meetings and correspondence with her become infrequent. Writes "The Valley of Childish Things, and Other Emblems," collection of ten short fables, and sends it in December 1895 to Burlingame, who rejects it.

1896–97   Partially recovered, writes, with architect Ogden Codman, *The Decoration of Houses*, study of interior arrangements and furnishings in upper-class city homes. Shows incomplete manuscript to Burlingame, who gives it to William Brownell, senior editor at Scribner's. Summer 1897, resumes friendship with Walter Berry, who stays for a month at Land's End, assisting Wharton in the revision of *The Decoration of Houses* (Codman is incapacitated by sunstroke). Wharton persuades Brownell to increase the number of halftone plates and makes extensive recommendations concerning the book's design. Published by Scribner's December 1897; sales are unexpectedly good.

1898   Writes and revises seven stories between March and July, despite recurring illness. In letter to Burlingame, discusses her earliest stories: "I regard them as the excesses of youth. They were all written at the top of my voice, and 'The Fullness of Life' is one long shriek. I may not write any better, but at least I hope that I write in a lower key." Suffers mental and physical breakdown in August. Goes to Philadelphia in October to take the "rest cure" invented by Dr. S. Weir Mitchell and is treated as an outpatient under Mitchell's supervision. Therapy involves massage, electrical stimulation of the muscles, abundant eating, and near total isolation.

1899   January, settles with Edward for four-month stay in house at 1329 K Street in Washington, found for them by Walter Berry, who becomes close literary adviser and supporter. *The Greater Inclination*, long delayed collection of short stories, published by Scribner's in March to enthusiastic reviews; sales exceed 3,000 copies. Protests to Scribner's that book has been insufficiently advertised. Begins extensive correspondence with Sara Norton, daughter of Harvard professor Charles Eliot Norton. Summer, travels in Europe, joined by the Bourgets in Switzerland; tours northern Italy with them, through Bergamo and Val Camonica. Returns to Land's End in September. Seeking escape from Newport climate, visits Lenox, Massachusetts, in fall.

1900   Novella, *The Touchstone* (in England, *A Gift from the Grave*), appears in the March and April *Scribner's*; published by Scribner's in April, selling 5,000 copies by year's end. Travels in England, Paris, and northern Italy, again accompanied by the Bourgets. Spends summer and fall at inn in Lenox while Edward goes on yachting trip. Begins concerted work on novel *The Valley of Decision*. Sends Henry James copy of "The Line of Least Resistance"; he responds with praise and detailed criticism, encouraging further effort. Wharton removes story from volume being prepared.

1901   February to June, negotiates purchase for $40,600 of 113-acre Lenox property extending into the village of Lee. After breaking with Codman over his fee, hires architect Francis V. L. Hoppin to design house modeled on Christopher Wren's Belton House in Lincolnshire, England. Oversees landscaping and gardening. *Crucial Instances*, second volume of stories, published by Scribner's in April.

Mother dies in Paris, age seventy-six, on June 28. Her will leaves large sums outright to Frederic and Henry but creates a trust fund for Edith's share of the remainder of the estate. Trust eventually amounts to $90,000; total annual private income about $22,000. Wharton goes to London and Paris to see her brothers and persuades them to make husband Edward co-trustee with brother Henry. Works on play *The Man of Genius* (never finished) and on dramatization of Prosper Mérimée's *Manon Lescaut* (never produced).

1902   *The Valley of Decision*, historical novel set in eighteenth-century Italy, published by Scribner's in February. Wharton criticizes its design while it is being prepared. Suffers collapse (nausea, depression, fatigue) after publication. Reviews are generally enthusiastic and sales are good. Begins *Disintegration*, novel set in contemporary New York society, but does not finish it. Writes travel articles, poetry, theatrical reviews, and literary criticism, including essays on Gabriele D'Annunzio and George Eliot. Translates Hermann Sudermann's play *Es Lebe das Leben* as *The Joy of Living* (it runs briefly on Broadway and sells in book form for a number of years). Henry James writes Wharton in August that *The Valley of Decision* is "accomplished, pondered, saturated" and "brilliant and interesting from a literary point of view," but urges her to abandon historical subject matter "in favour of the American subject. There it is round you. Don't pass it by—the immediate, the real, the only, the yours, the novelist's that it waits for. Take hold of it and keep hold and let it pull you where it will . . . *Do New York!* The 1st-hand account is precious." Meets Theodore Roosevelt in Newport at christening of his godchild, beginning a long friendship. Moves into Lenox house, named "The Mount" after Long Island home of Revolutionary War ancestor Ebenezer Stevens. Edward suffers first of series of nervous collapses.

1903   January, sails for Italy with ailing husband. Travels slowly north from Rome through Tuscany, the Veneto, and Lombardy, inspecting ancient estates for series of articles commissioned by R. W. Gilder for *Century*. Visits Violet Paget at Villa Pomerino outside of Florence. Meets art expert Bernhard Berenson, who strongly dislikes her. Goes to Salsomaggiore, west of Parma, for treatment of her asthma. Summer and fall spent at The Mount, with interval at Newport. Sells Land's End for $122,500, June 13. Begins *The House of Mirth*. *Sanctuary*, novella, published by Scribner's in October. Sails for England, early December. First conversations with Henry James, who comes up from Rye to London in mid-December.

1904   Purchases her first automobile, a Panhard-Levassor. With Edward driving, travels south to Hyères for a stay with the Bourgets, then to Cannes and Monte Carlo and back across France. In England, visits Henry James in Rye and tours Sussex with him. Returns to Lenox in late spring. Enthusiastic about motor travel, hires a permanent chauffeur. *The Descent of Man*, collection of stories, published by Scribner's in April. After reading reviews, writes Brownell that "the continued cry that I am an echo of Mr. James (whose books of the last ten years I can't read, much as I delight in the man) . . . makes me feel rather hopeless." Hires Anna Bahlmann as secretary and literary assistant. Agrees with Burlingame in August to begin serialization of *The House of Mirth* in January 1905 *Scribner's*; undertakes schedule of intense work (usually writing in the morning) to meet deadline. (Finishes in March 1905; serialized Jan.–Nov.) House guests at The Mount include Brooks Adams and his wife, George Cabot Lodge (son of Senator Henry Cabot Lodge), Walter Berry, and Gaillard Lapsley, American-born don of medieval history at Trinity College, Cambridge. Henry James arrives in October with his friend Howard Sturgis, "the kindest and strangest of men." *Italian Villas and Their Gardens*, based on magazine articles, published by The Century Company in November. Returns to New York just before Christmas.

1905   Henry James visits at 884 Park Avenue for a few days in January. Whartons dine at the White House with President Roosevelt in March. *Italian Backgrounds*, sketches written since 1894, published by Scribner's in March. After European trip in spring, including visit to Salsomaggiore for asthma treatment, returns to The Mount. House guests include printer Berkeley Updike, illustrator Moncure Robinson, publisher Walter Maynard, Robert Grant, novelist and judge of the probate court in Boston, and Henry James. Visits Sara and Charles Eliot Norton. *The House of Mirth* published by Scribner's, October 14, in first printing of 40,000; 140,000 copies in print by the end of the year, "the most rapid sale of any book ever published by Scribner," according to Brownell. Literary earnings for year exceed $20,000. Henry James writes Wharton that the novel is an "altogether superior thing" but "better written than composed." Reviews generally favorable. December, undertakes collaboration on stage version with playwright Clyde Fitch.

1906   Sails for France, March 17. Through Paul Bourget, enters intellectual and social circles of Paris, especially those of the Faubourg St. Germain. Among new acquaintances are poet Comtesse Anna de Noailles, historian Gustave Schlumberger, and his close friend, Comtesse Charlotte de Cossé-Brissac. Charles du Bos, young follower of Bourget, translates *The House of Mirth* as *La Demeure de liesse*, published in the *Revue de Paris*. Novella *Madame de Treymes* appears in the August *Scribner's*; published by Scribner's in February 1907. Goes to England at the end of April. Whartons and Henry James make short motor tour of England. Visits Queen's Acre, Howard Sturgis's home in Windsor, for the first time (it soon becomes the center of her English social life). Meets Percy Lubbock, young writer and disciple of Henry James. Returns to France and takes motor tour with brother Henry, visiting cathedrals at Amiens and Beauvais, and Nohant, home of George Sand. Returns to Lenox in June. Works on novel *Justine Brent* (later retitled *The Fruit of the Tree*). September, goes to Detroit with Edward and Walter Berry to see first performance of stage version of *The House of Mirth*. October opening in New York is a critical and commercial failure; Wharton calls the experience "instructive." Edward is away from Lenox, hunting and fishing, during much of the fall. Literary earnings for the year total almost $32,000.

1907   Returns to Paris in January and rents the apartment of the George Vanderbilts at 58 Rue de Varenne, in the heart of the Faubourg St. Germain. *The Fruit of the Tree* serialized in *Scribner's*, January–November. March, takes a "motorflight" through France with Edward and Henry James, visiting Nohant and touring southern France. Invites James to stay for another month, and organizes a second automobile excursion. Engages instructor to teach her contemporary French; for a lesson exercise, writes a precursor sketch of *Ethan Frome*. April, sees much of William Morton Fullerton, forty-two-year-old Paris correspondent for the London *Times*, former student of Charles Eliot Norton, and disciple of Henry James. Spends summer at The Mount completing *The Fruit of the Tree*, which is published by Scribner's in October; sales reach 60,000. Reviews are good. Fullerton arrives at The Mount in October for a visit of several days. Wharton begins a journal addressed to him. Returns to Paris in December.

1908   January–February, Edward afflicted by "nervous depression." Wharton leads active social life, seeing linguist Vicomte Robert d'Humières, American ambassador Henry White, watercolorist Walter Gay and his wife, Matilda, James Van Alen, Fullerton, Comtesse Rosa de Fitz-James, Bourget, playwright Paul Hervieu, Charles du Bos, and others. February, spends time with Fullerton while Edward is away. March 21, Edward, suffering from depression and pervasive pain, leaves for spa at Hot Springs, Arkansas. Wharton writes Brownell that Edward's illness has prevented her from making much progress on new novel, *The Custom of the Country*, and doubts that it will be ready for serial publication by January 1909. April, moves to brother Henry's townhouse on Place des Etats-Unis. Egerton Winthrop visits. When Henry James visits for two weeks in late April, arranges to have Jacques Emile Blanche paint portrait that she considers the best ever done of him. May, has first significant meetings with Henry Adams. Wharton and Fullerton begin an affair. Meditates in her journal on the propriety of her behavior; writes series of love sonnets. May 22, gives Fullerton journal addressed to him; he returns it the following day as she leaves for America. On fifth day of crossing, writes story "The Choice"; resumes work on *The Custom of the Country*. In Lenox, has difficulty breathing for six weeks. Scribner's publishes *The Hermit and the Wild Woman*, fourth collection of stories, in September, *A Motor-Flight Through France*, travel account, in October. Writes poetry, reads Nietzsche. Leaves for Europe, October 30. Meets aging George Meredith at Box Hill, near London, goes with James Barrie to see performance of his play *What Every Woman Knows*. At Stanway, Gloucestershire home of Lady Mary Elcho, meets two young Englishmen who become close friends: Robert Norton, a landscape painter, and John Hugh Smith, a banker expert in Anglo-Russian financial affairs. Sees much of Henry James, who soon professes exhaustion from her visits, referring to her as "the Angel of Devastation." Crosses to France with Howard Sturgis for Christmas at Rue de Varenne. Literary earnings for year are about $15,000.

1909   January, Edward arrives in Paris, suffering from insomnia and inexplicable pain in his face and limbs. Work on *The Custom of the Country* again interrupted. Edward returns to Lenox in mid-April. *Artemis to Actaeon*, book of poetry, published by Scribner's in late April. Continues to write poetry, including "Ogrin the Hermit," long narrative based on a portion of the Tristan and Iseult legend. When lease on 58 Rue de Varenne expires, moves to large suite in Hotel Crillon, Place de la Concorde, April. June, goes to London with Fullerton; they spend the night at the Charing Cross Hotel. After Fullerton leaves for America, writes "Terminus," fifty-two-line love poem. Stays in England until mid-July, visiting with Sturgis, Lapsley, and James. When Fullerton returns, they spend night in Rye at James's Lamb House. Involves Henry James and Frederick Macmillan, Fullerton's publisher, in complicated scheme to conceal gift of money to Fullerton to meet blackmail demands of his ex-mistress, Henrietta Mirecourt. September, Henry Adams arranges another meeting between Wharton and Bernhard Berenson. Friendship develops. Edward arrives in Paris with his sister Nancy in November; soon confesses to Wharton that during the summer he sold some of her holdings, bought property in Boston, and lived there with his mistress. Edward returns to Boston. Later admits to embezzling $50,000 from Wharton's trust funds; makes restitution by drawing upon $67,000 recently inherited from his mother.

1910   Moves into apartment at 53 Rue de Varenne, January. Writes stories "The Eyes" and "The Triumph of Night." Sells New York houses. Edward returns to Paris, agrees to enter Swiss sanatorium for treatment of his depression. Walter Berry moves to Paris, stays in Whartons' guest suite for several months. July 3, sees Nijinsky dance in *L'Oiseau de Feu*. Affair with Fullerton ends. Visits Henry and William James at Lamb House in August. Sails in

September to New York with Edward. October, Edward departs on trip around the world; Wharton returns to Paris, ill and exhausted. *Tales of Men and Ghosts* published by Scribner's in October; sells about 4,000 copies. December, begins short story that becomes novel *Ethan Frome*.

1911   January, confesses to Hugh Smith that "my writing tires and preoccupies me more than it used to." Tries unsuccessfully with William Dean Howells and Edmund Gosse to secure the Nobel Prize for Henry James. May, at Salsomaggiore for hay fever; begins concerted work on novel *The Reef*. Returns to Lenox at end of June. Has Henry James, Hugh Smith, and Lapsley as guests. Wharton and Edward agree to formal separation, then reverse decision. Returns to Europe in September after entrusting Edward with power to sell The Mount. *Ethan Frome* serialized in *Scribner's* from August through October, published by Scribner's in September. Reviewers in America and England call it one of her finest achievements. Disappointed with sales (4,000 copies by mid-November), Wharton protests to Scribner's, citing lack of advertising, poor distribution, and bad typesetting. Tours central Italy and visits Berenson for the first time at his home, Villa I Tatti, near Florence.

1912   Edward arrives in February at Rue de Varenne and stays until May. Relations remain distant and strained. Visits La Verna, monastery in Tuscany, with Berry. Sale of The Mount for undisclosed sum completed in June. Offers to live with Edward in United States, but he refuses. Summer, sees much of Henry James during visits to England. Arranges with Charles Scribner for $8,000 of her royalties to be given to James under the guise of an advance for his novel-in-progress, *The Ivory Tower*. (James receives $3,600 in 1913; the novel is never completed.) *The Reef* published by D. Appleton and Company, which had given her $15,000 advance. Reviews are relatively poor; sales reach 7,000. Resumes work on *The Custom of the Country*.

1913   *The Custom of the Country* appears in *Scribner's*, January–November. Receives unexpected letter from brother Henry denouncing her for coldness toward Countess Tecla, his mistress and intended wife. Sues Edward for divorce on grounds of adultery; Paris tribunal grants decree, April 16. Initiates effort to raise gift of money for Henry James's seventieth birthday; effort abandoned when James discovers and angrily rejects it. Drives across Sicily with Berry. Friendship develops with Geoffrey Scott, author of *The Architecture of Humanism*. Favorably impressed by premiere of Igor Stravinsky's ballet *Le Sacre du Printemps* in Paris, May 29. Considers buying house outside of London, but eventually decides against it. August, finishes *The Custom of the Country*. Travels with Berenson through Luxembourg and Germany, stopping at Cologne, Dresden, and Berlin. Begins novel *Literature*, never completed. *The Custom of the Country* published by Scribner's in October; sales reach nearly 60,000. December, attends wedding of niece, landscape gardener Beatrix Jones (daughter of brother Frederic and Mary Cadwalader), in New York. Finds New York "queer, rootless" and "overwhelming."

1914   Returns to Paris in January. Sends Henry James copy of Marcel Proust's recently published *Du Côté de chez Swann*. March, sails from Marseilles to Algiers with Percy Lubbock and Anna Bahlmann. Drives through northern Algeria and through Tunisia, "an unexpurgated page of the Arabian nights." July, tours Spain with Berry for three weeks, viewing cave paintings at Altamira. Returns to Paris July 31, three days before outbreak of war between France and Germany. August, establishes workroom near Rue de Varenne for seamstresses and other women thrown out of work by economic disruption of general mobilization. Collects funds, selects supervisory staff, arranges for supply of work orders, free lunches, and coal allotments. Late August, goes to Stocks, English country house rented from novelist Mrs. Humphry Ward, a trip planned before the war. Sees Henry James at Rye. After learning of battle of the Marne, makes arrangements, with great difficulty, to return to Paris; succeeds by end of September. November, establishes and directs American Hostels for Refugees. Selects Elisina Tyler, friend since 1912, as administrative deputy; raises $100,000 in first twelve months. (Hostels assist 9,330 refugees by end of 1915, providing free or low-cost food, clothing, coal, housing, medical and child care, and assistance in finding work.)

1915 February, visits the front in the Argonne and Verdun. Tours hospitals, investigating need for blankets and clothing; watches French assault on village of Vauquois. Makes five more visits to front in next six months, including tour of forward trenches in the Vosges; describes them in articles for *Scribner's* (collected in *Fighting France, from Dunkerque to Belfort*, published by Scribner's in November). April, organizes Children of Flanders Rescue Committee with Tyler, establishing six homes between Paris and the Normandy coast. Committee sets up classes in lacemaking for girls, industrial training for boys, French for Flemish speakers. Nearly 750 Flemish children, many of them tubercular, cared for in 1915. Increasingly concentrates on fund-raising and creation of sponsoring committees in France and the United States, delegating daily administration to Tyler. Arranges benefit concerts and an art exhibition. Edits *The Book of the Homeless* (published by Scribner's early in 1916), with introductions by Marshal Joffre and Theodore Roosevelt. Contributors of poetry, essays, art, fiction, and musical scores include Cocteau, Conrad, Howells, Anna de Noailles, Hardy, Yeats, Eleanora Duse, Sarah Bernhardt, Henry James, Max Beerbohm, Paul Claudel, Edmond Rostand, Monet, Leon Bakst, and Stravinsky. Wharton does most of the translations. Proceeds (approximately $8,000 from the book, $7,000 from the sale of art and manuscripts) go to Hostels and Rescue Committee. Friendship with André Gide, who serves on a Hostels committee. Secretary and former governess Anna Bahlmann dies in autumn. October, makes short visit to England. Learns in December that Henry James is dying; writes Lapsley: "His friendship was the pride and honour of my life."

1916 Henry James dies February 28. Spring, helps establish treatment program for tubercular French soldiers. Informs Charles Scribner that she is working on novel *The Glimpses of the Moon* and a novella "of the dimensions of *Ethan Frome*. It deals with the same kind of life in a midsummer landscape." Offers the latter for serial publication, but Charles Scribner declines, having already scheduled her 1892 novella *Bunner Sisters* for fall; accepts offer from Appleton for book and from *McClure's* for serial. Feels financial pressure due to expense of refugee work, reduced literary earnings, and effects of American income tax. Made

Chevalier of the Legion of Honor, April 8. Mourns death of Egerton Winthrop (tells Berenson that Winthrop and Henry James "made up the sum of the best I have known in human nature"). *Xingu and Other Stories* (mostly prewar work) published in October by Scribner's.

1917   Novella *Summer*, companion piece to *Ethan Frome*, serialized in *McClure's* for $7,000, February–August; published by Appleton. Grows fond of Ronald Simmons, young American officer and painter. After tuberculosis treatment centers are taken over by the Red Cross, establishes four convalescent homes for tubercular civilians. September, makes month-long tour of French Morocco with Walter Berry. Witnesses self-lacerative ritual dances and visits harem, noting its air of "somewhat melancholy respectability."

1918   Inspired by success of American troops, gives public lecture on American life. Summer, brother Frederic dies; Wharton, long estranged from him, writes sadly of her brother Henry's failure to contact her. Deeply grieved by death of Ronald Simmons, August 12. Finds Paris increasingly noisy. After long negotiation, purchases Pavillon Colombe, house in village of St. Brice-sous-Fôret, outside of Paris. Novel *The Marne* published by Appleton.

1919   Leases Ste. Claire du Vieux Château in Hyères, overlooking Mediterranean. Summer, moves into Pavillon Colombe. Rising expenses, support of financially troubled former sister-in-law Mary Cadwalader Jones, establishment of trust fund for three Belgian children, together with changing New York real estate market and effects of American income tax, create financial pressure. Accepts offer of $18,000 from *The Pictorial Review* for serial rights to her next novel. Unable to finish *The Glimpses of the Moon*, suggests *A Son at the Front*, but both magazine and book editors feel that the public is tired of war material. Proposes novel *Old New York* (later retitled *The Age of Innocence*), set in 1875. Magazine accepts, and Appleton advances $15,000 against royalties. *French Ways and Their Meaning*, collection of magazine articles, published by Appleton. "Beatrice Palmato" outline and fragment, explicit treatment of father-daughter incest, probably written at this time (the story is never finished).

1920   Howard Sturgis dies early in year; end of Queen's Acre gatherings. *In Morocco*, travel account, published by Scribner's in October. *The Age of Innocence*, serialized in *The Pictorial Review* July–October, published by Appleton in October, sells 66,000 copies in six months (by 1922 it earns Wharton nearly $70,000). December, moves to Hyères for several months.

1921   Resumes work on *The Glimpses of the Moon*. Writes *The Old Maid*, novella about out-of-wedlock birth (rejected by *Ladies' Home Journal* for being "a bit too vigorous for us"). Begins long friendship with Philomène de la Forest-Divonne, future journalist and novelist writing under the name Claude Sylve. *The Age of Innocence* awarded Pulitzer Prize in May. Later learns that the jury had originally voted for Sinclair Lewis's *Main Street*, but had been overruled by the trustees of Columbia University, who thought it too controversial. Writes to Lewis in August of her "disgust" at the action and invites him to St. Brice (he makes the first of several visits in October). *The Old Maid* bought by *Red Book* for $2,250 (serialized Feb.–April 1922). September, finishes *The Glimpses of the Moon*. Goes to Hyères in mid-December.

1922   At Hyères until late May; June to mid-December at St. Brice. Summer, long-time friend and correspondent Sara Norton dies. When estranged brother Henry dies Wharton writes Berenson that "he was the dearest of brothers to all my youth." *The Glimpses of the Moon* serialized in *The Pictorial Review*; published by Appleton in August, sells more than 100,000 copies in America and Britain in six months. Earns $60,000 from various rights and royalties.

1923   Film version of *The Glimpses of the Moon*, with dialogue titles by F. Scott Fitzgerald, released in April. (Six other films were made from Wharton's works between 1918 and 1934; she had no involvement in any of the productions.) Invited by Yale University to receive honorary Doctor of Letters degree. Although reluctant to attend, decides she needs to see United States if she is to continue writing about it. Accepts degree (the first to be awarded to a woman by Yale) at commencement in New Haven, June 20. Returns to France after eleven-day visit, her first since 1913 and her last. Novel *A Son at the Front* published by

Scribner's in September, fulfilling promise made a decade earlier to give Scribner's another novel after *The Custom of the Country*. Works on novel *The Mother's Recompense*.

1924   *Old New York*, collection of four novellas, published by Appleton in May in boxed sets of four volumes. Titles are *False Dawn (The 'Forties)*, *The Old Maid (The 'Fifties)*, *The Spark (The 'Sixties)*, *New Year's Day (The 'Seventies)*. About 26,000 sets sold in six months, with another 3,000 volumes sold individually. Awarded Gold Medal for "distinguished service" by National Institute of Arts and Letters.

1925   *The Mother's Recompense* published by Appleton in April after serialization in *The Pictorial Review* October 1924–February 1925. Sales are good. June, receives inscribed copy of *The Great Gatsby* from F. Scott Fitzgerald. Sends Fitzgerald a critique he finds helpful. July, Fitzgerald visits St. Brice; the encounter is strained and awkward. *The Writing of Fiction*, collection of five essays, including long appreciation of Proust, published by Scribner's in the late summer.

1926   Charters 360-ton steam yacht *Osprey* for ten-week cruise with guests through the Mediterranean and Aegean, March–June. *Here and Beyond*, collection of short stories, published by Appleton in summer. *Twelve Poems* published in London by The Medici Society. Elected to the National Institute of Arts and Letters. September, travels with Berry through northern Italy.

1927   January, Berry suffers mild stroke; convalesces at Hyères for two months, depressed and irritable. Wharton buys Ste. Claire, Hyères home, for $40,000. Finishes novel *Twilight Sleep*. *The Pictorial Review* pays $40,000 for serial rights to novel *The Children* after *Delineator* offers $42,000; promises *Delineator* the novel *The Keys of Heaven*. *Twilight Sleep* published by Appleton in June; sells well. Walter Berry suffers second stroke in Paris, October 2. Wharton visits him on his deathbed; he dies October 12. Writes Lapsley: "No words can tell of my desolation. He had been to me in turn all that one being can be to another, in love, in friendship, in understanding."

1928   January, finishes *The Children*. Serialized in *The Pictorial Review* April–July, published by Appleton in September; earns $95,000 from sales and film rights. Edward Wharton dies in New York, February 7. Begins novel *Hudson River Bracketed* after abandoning *The Keys of Heaven*. Friendship develops with Desmond MacCarthy, British writer and editor. December, *The Age of Innocence*, dramatized by Margaret Ayer Barnes, opens on Broadway, runs until June 1929, then tours for four months, earning $23,500.

1929   Severe winter storms devastate Ste. Claire gardens; describes effect as "torture." February, learns that *Delineator* began serialization of *Hudson River Bracketed* in September 1928, six months ahead of schedule. Contracts severe pneumonia and nearly dies. Recovers by midsummer. August, death of Geoffrey Scott. October, finishes *Hudson River Bracketed* (published by Appleton in Nov.) and begins restoration of Ste. Claire gardens. Awarded Gold Medal for "special distinction in literature" by American Academy of Arts and Letters.

1930–31 Elected to the American Academy of Arts and Letters. *Certain People*, collection of short stories, published by Appleton in summer 1930. Autumn, meets art critic and historian Kenneth Clark while traveling in Tuscany; deep friendship develops. December, meets Aldous Huxley, who introduces her to anthropologist Bronislaw Malinowski.

1932   January, finishes novel *The Gods Arrive*, sequel to *Hudson River Bracketed*. Rejected for serial publication by *The Saturday Evening Post*, *Liberty*, and *Collier's* because it features an unmarried couple living together. Sold to *Delineator* for $50,000 despite Wharton's anger over handling of *Hudson River Bracketed*, appearing February–August. Published by Appleton later in year, it sells poorly. Begins autobiography, *A Backward Glance*. Effects of the Depression begin to be felt in greatly diminished literary earnings; magazine offers for short stories fall drastically. May, visits Rome, attends several Roman Catholic services there. Reads histories of religious orders and lives of saints. Becomes godmother to Kenneth Clark's son Colin.

1933   Catherine Gross, Wharton's companion since 1884, falls
        into paranoid dementia in April, dies in October. *Human
        Nature*, collection of short stories, published by Appleton.
        By threat of legal action, forces *Ladies' Home Journal* to
        honor pre-Depression agreement to pay $25,000 for her
        autobiography; installments appear October 1933–April
        1934. Begins novel *The Buccaneers* (never finished, but
        published by Appleton-Century in 1938 with Wharton's
        long outline of the remainder of the story and an after-
        word by Gaillard Lapsley).

1934   Visits Amsterdam, then tours England and Scotland.
        Guided through National Gallery in London by Kenneth
        Clark. *A Backward Glance* published by Appleton-Century.
        Breaks with Appleton editor Rutger Jewett, who had
        acted as her agent without commission for over a decade,
        blaming him for decreased literary earnings; engages
        James Pinker as new agent.

1935   April, suffers mild stroke, with temporary loss of sight in
        left eye. September, Mary Cadwalader Jones dies. *The Old
        Maid*, dramatized by Zoë Akins, opens in New York for
        successful run.

1936   *Ethan Frome*, dramatized by Owen and Donald Davis,
        tours United States after successful New York run. Income
        from both plays is about $130,000, ending financial worry.
        The World Over, collection of short stories, published by
        Appleton-Century.

1937   Sends last completed short story, "All Souls," to her
        agent, February. Suffers stroke, June 3. Dies at St. Brice
        on the evening of August 11. Buried near Walter Berry in
        the Cimetière des Gonards, Versailles, August 14.

Note on the Texts

A letter from Edith Wharton to Edward Burlingame of *Scribner's* about a manuscript in preparation offers a description of her writing habits: "You must wonder why I don't have duplicate typewritten copy, but the truth is that I revise so much that by the time I have corrected my final copy I haven't patience left to correct the duplicate; if I do, I always make new changes." Wharton revised her writing thoroughly, and often. A novel typically went through several stages of composition and revision: a handwritten version, itself revised and sometimes pasted over with new sheets; two typescripts, each corrected by hand and sometimes pasted over; and some reworking of the proofs. In fact, since most of her works were published first in periodical and then in book form, there was often revision on the proofs of both. Wharton's concern for accuracy of detail was not limited to verbal changes, or what she once called her "wholesale slaughter of adjectives." In another letter to her editor concerning a different novel, not as accurately proofread as her work usually was, she wrote, "If there is another printing . . . do please let me know in time, so that I can revise the punctuation with my own hand."

Wharton closely supervised the publication of her works in this way her entire life, except during World War I when she was overseas and found it impossible to do so. From the evidence of her extensive correspondence with editors at Charles Scribner's Sons, she was fortunate in finding a publisher as eager to carry out her intentions as she was meticulous. This combination of circumstances establishes the authority of the first book publication of many of her works.

The four novels printed in this volume—*The House of Mirth*, *The Reef*, *The Custom of the Country*, and *The Age of Innocence*—were commercial successes, each seeing numerous printings in Wharton's lifetime. Because Wharton continually and closely revised the proofs of her books, and because she rarely revised a work after the book was published, the selection of the best text of each work is straightforward. For *The Reef*, for example, the only authoritative text is that of the first

American edition, published in New York by D. Appleton and Company in 1912. It is the only text Wharton published, and the plates of the Appleton edition were used for all later printings. For each of the other three novels, discussed below, Wharton revised a magazine version for publication as a book. These authorially revised texts are the clear choice for reprinting here.

The House of Mirth first appeared in eleven issues of *Scribner's* from January to November 1905. Wharton's work on the novel had been intermittent and desultory until Burlingame requested delivery of the opening chapters to fill a spot in the magazine left by another novel that would not be ready in time. The first installments would have to be published before Wharton had decided how to bring about the climax, and the whole novel had to be completed in four or five months. Wharton tied herself for the first time to the discipline of daily writing, and the experience, she later wrote, turned her "from a drifting amateur into a professional."

The periodical version was thus produced hurriedly, on a tight schedule, and Wharton wrote often to William Brownell, her editor at Scribner's, with revisions. Charles Scribner's Sons published the book edition in October 1905, before serialization was complete, and the same month saw Canadian and British publication of the Scribner text. Wharton thus read and revised proofs twice within a short period of time, for the magazine and for the book. The latter reading resulted in several revisions; only the last installment of the magazine text is identical to that of the book, since revision of the book had by this point caught up with the magazine. Changes in the book version are often toward greater economy of expression or more precise description, frequently involving the substitution of a verb or an adjective. Judging from its relative freedom from typographical errors, the text of the book version was proofread closely, and it accurately reflects Wharton's final decisions concerning the wording and pointing of her novel. (One error that was not caught is corrected in the present edition. The name of the character called Bertie Van Osburgh in early drafts is changed in the first edition to Freddy, except in two instances; "Bertie" has been corrected to "Freddy" at 277.26 and 277.29.)

The Custom of the Country ran in *Scribner's* from January to November 1913, despite Wharton and Burlingame's initial agreement that the novel would do better if issued first in book form. As with *The House of Mirth*, Scribner's brought out the book edition one month before the serialization was complete, in October 1913. *The Custom of the Country* was also published simultaneously in Canada and Britain, but again only the New York publisher received manuscript and the corrected proofs. Wharton revised *The Custom of the Country* much more heavily between serial and book versions than she did *The House of Mirth*. Some of the revisions serve to mute the language of action, as when "glance up sharply" becomes "glance up at her" (629.40), or "darting out into the passage" becomes "opening her door" (636.31). Others prune the wording of the periodical text: at 640.21, for example, "At the farther end of the room she saw Mr. Spragg standing" was shortened to "Mr. Spragg was standing". The numerous revisions, as well as the minimal errors, reflect the detailed attention Wharton gave to this revised text, and it is the one reprinted here.

The Age of Innocence appeared in *The Pictorial Review* in four large installments, from July/August to November 1920. In this form the novel had no chapter divisions. As a book, it was first published the same year by D. Appleton and Company in New York and in London. As was the case with her other books, Wharton extensively revised the magazine text of *The Age of Innocence*. Differences between serial and book involve not only stylistic changes similar to the revisions of *The House of Mirth* and *The Custom of the Country* but numerous changes in punctuation and spelling as well. *The Pictorial Review* was not a literary magazine of the order of *Scribner's* or *Harper's*, and its editorial style differed considerably from Appleton's and, almost certainly, from Wharton's.

The many subsequent printings of the novel during Wharton's lifetime all used the plates of the Appleton edition, which, however, received important corrections after two impressions had already been run off. In the earlier volumes, the representation of Agathon Carver's greeting card on page 159 (1142.20–22 in the present volume) is set in roman type. Later printings correctly set it in "gothic" type, as indicated in the accompanying text. Another change occurs on page 186 of the first edition (1162.20 of the present volume). In the first two impressions, the Rector who marries Newland Archer and May Welland commences the wedding with the first words of the burial service: "Forasmuch as it hath pleased Almighty God—"; later, the words were corrected to: "Dearly beloved, we are gathered together here,". This change of one line involved no resetting of the rest of the page. A third change (at 1125.24) altered a reference to "Guy de Maupassant's incomparable tales" to one to "the prolific Alphonse Daudet's brilliant tales". These changes and approximately thirty others were surely made at Wharton's request. The text reprinted here is that of the sixth impression of the first edition, which incorporates the last set of extensive revisions which are obviously authorial.

This volume is concerned only with presenting the texts of these editions; it does not attempt to reproduce features of the typographic design—such as the display capitalization of chapter openings. The texts are reproduced without change, except for the correction of obvious typographical errors. Spelling, punctuation, and capitalization often are expressive features, and they are not altered, even when inconsistent or irregular. The following is a list of the typographical errors, cited by page and line number: 60.29, drive,; 73.23, universe.; 113.12, Sévres; 113.28, ormulu; 117.19, instincts.; 277.26, Bertie; 277.29, Bertie; 290.19, Lily'; 317.7–8, artifically; 431.3, "Oh, (no indent); 496.15, her . .; 520.39, pallour; 637.15, Oh,; 686.3, possiblities; 794.39, case,; 810.24, chateau; 980.36, 'Is; 990.8, apart is; 1030.11, Chiverses; 1034.39, this; 1091.26, that that's; 1204.31, themselves.; 1207.1, see; 1262.29, you."; 1290.10–11, landscape—engineering. Errors corrected second printing: 407.10–11, had had (*LOA*); 739.40, vulgarist; 1069.10, delapidated (*LOA*); 1235.27, "form".

Notes

For references to other studies and further biographical background than is provided in the Chronology, see R.W.B. Lewis, *Edith Wharton: A Biography* (New York: Harper & Row, 1975). In the notes below, the reference numbers denote page and line of the present volume (the line count includes chapter headings).

THE HOUSE OF MIRTH

1.1   THE HOUSE OF MIRTH]   The first title for the novel was *A Moment's Ornament*. This was followed by *The Year of the Rose*. This title comes from Ecclesiastes 7:4: "The heart of the wise is in the house of mourning; but the heart of fools is in the house of mirth."

6.8   *The Benedick*]   The apartment house for bachelors is named after the spirited bachelor Benedick in *Much Ado About Nothing*.

17.10   *oubliettes*]   Originally dungeons for persons condemned to perpetual imprisonment or to perish in secret.

32.21–22   *chaufroix*]   *Chaudfroid*. Jellied preparation of fowl or game cooked but served cold.

37.4   vulgar . . . Quirinal]   The vulgar throngs on the Quirinal Hill in Rome, an enormous tourist attraction at the turn of the century because of its palaces, papal stables, and the casino housing the paintings of the then very popular Guido Reni.

72.10–11   *jeune . . . marier*]   Young girl on the lookout for a husband.

113.37–38   *point de Milan*]   A kind of lace.

142.32–33   go . . . Miranda]   As though to ask Caliban, Prospero's "deformed slave" in *The Tempest*, for a judgment on Prospero's beautiful daughter, Miranda.

156.22–25   the *Eumenides* . . . repose.]   Aeschylus, *Eumenides*, lines 66 ff.

193.24–25   the Condamine *gargote*]   A cheap restaurant named Condamine.

208.8–9   *salon-lit*]   A compartment in a sleeping car.

308.25   *disjecta membra*]   Scattered remains.

THE REEF

373.17   Cerdine]   Popular French actress of the day.

373.29   'L'Ami Fritz'] A three-act play about a patriotic French Alsatian, written by the pseudonymous pair who signed themselves Erckmann-Chatrian and derived from their novel of the same name. First produced in 1864.

373.30–31   'Le Vertige'] A four-act comedy by Legros Langeron. It had its premiere in April 1901.

384.35   *baignoire*] A theater box that could be shielded from the public by a grate.

386.14   *consommateurs*] Patrons.

386.21   *Oedipe*] Presumably a French translation of Sophocles' *Oedipus Tyrannus*.

448.23   *passementerie*] A kind of embroidery used to decorate women's dresses.

THE CUSTOM OF THE COUNTRY

635.22   Indiana Frusk] When Edith Wharton was challenged about this name and that of Undine Spragg, she replied that anyone could find them, with others like Lurline Spreckels and Florida Yurlee, in the daily register of the Paris *Herald-Tribune*.

645.31–32   "When . . . Stop,"] A title invented by Edith Wharton, and taken from Robert Browning's "A Toccata of Galuppi's" (XIV: "As for Venice and its people, merely born to droop and drop . . . What of soul was left, I wonder, when the kissing had to stop?").

645.34   "Oolaloo"] A title invented by Edith Wharton, probably to suggest the French exclamation "Ooh la la!" and perhaps as an echo of Poe's "Ulalume."

645.35   Ned . . . Fountain,"] Both actor and title are inventions of Edith Wharton. The title comes from the well-known hobo song, "The Big Rock Candy Mountain," which circulated in the 1900s.

645.40–646.2   Sarah . . . "Fade"] Two roles of the actress Sarah Bernhardt. The first is *L'Aiglon*, a six-act verse drama by Edmond Rostand, dating from 1900; it portrays the son of Napoleon pursuing vain dreams of glory. The second is *Phèdre* by Racine.

649.6   'Cavaleeria,'] Enrico Caruso as Turiddu in Mascagni's *Cavalleria Rusticana*.

674.14   *divers et ondoyant*] "Diverse and ever in motion." Preceded by the phrase "marvelously vain," this is Montaigne's definition of man, toward the end of Chapter One in *Essays*, Book I.

716.19   "You . . . now,"] Undine was a female water sprite.

811.3   inaccessible "Faubourg"]   Faubourg St. Germain, a section of Paris
on the Left Bank, containing the town seats of many of the French nobility
and several of the most brilliant of the Paris salons.

877.40   *cachottière*]   Secretive.

938.24   Hôtel de Chelles]   In this context, "Hôtel" means a townhouse.

948.5   *faire valoir*]   To get a good revenue.

958.29   *Journal des Débats*]   One of the great daily newspapers in Paris;
originally a record of parliamentary debates and actions.

1009.10   Pitti Palace]   Brunelleschi's Palazzo Pitti is one of the most monumental buildings in Europe.

THE AGE OF INNOCENCE

1017.3–4   Christine . . . Faust]   The Swedish soprano sang the role of
Marguerite in Gounod's *Faust* on November 1, 1871, and at various times
later.

1032.1   Jewel Song]   "Air des Bijoux," the Jewel Song, occurs at mid-
point in *Faust*, in the middle of Act III.

1032.21   *bouton d'or*]   The flower known in English as "bachelor's button." The reference is to the yellow and gold color scheme of the drawing
room.

1037.32   "Monsieur de Camors"]   A novel by Octave Feuillet, published
in 1867. In a manner somewhat reminiscent of the Marquis de Sade, it tells
of an utterly unprincipled French aristocrat and his entanglement with several
women, one of whom, his beautiful cousin, is as naturally depraved as he is.
The English translation (*Camors: or, Life Under the New Empire*) was reviewed
by Henry James, not without admiration, in the July 30, 1868, issue of *The
Nation*.

1061.12–13   Patti . . . Sonnambula]   Adelina Patti sang the soprano role
of Amina in Vincenzo Bellini's opera *La Sonnambula* in 1859 and 1860 in New
York, but did not appear again in New York for twenty years.

1083.25   "Contes Drôlatiques,"]   *Droll Stories* by Honoré de Balzac.

1097.10   poet . . . Fay."]   The American poet Joseph Rodman Drake's
600-line work of 1835 recounts the tale of a love affair between a mortal maid
and an errant fairy.

1098.4–5   the Century]   A men's club devoted to literature and the arts,
founded in 1847.

1117.16   "Le Voyage de M. Perrichon,"]   The famous and still popular
five-act comedy by Eugène Labiche, first produced in 1860. In the course of

the action, the archetypical bourgeois M. Perrichon is rescued from a Swiss glacier by a suitor of his young daughter. When the other suitor notices that M. Perrichon is not properly affected by the exploit, he arranges that he himself shall be rescued by M. Perrichon, who is thereafter devoted to his interests.

1125.33   "The House of Life."]   A poetical sequence by Dante Gabriel Rossetti. The version Newland Archer is reading is presumably *Sonnets and Songs, towards a work to be called "The House of Life,"* published in England in 1870. The 1881 version of *The House of Life* consisted entirely of 101 sonnets, 53 of which had been added since 1870.

1140.39   cousin]   In some later printings of the novel, "cousin" was changed to "nephew" by either Edith Wharton or an editor.

1167.22   Botzen]   The German name, usually spelled Bozen, for what is now Bolzano, in the South Tyrol.

1173.35   the Goncourt *grenier*]   Literally "garret" or "loft," *grenier* here refers to the den established by the Goncourt brothers in the 1880s on the top floor of their house in Auteil, near the Bois de Boulogne in Paris. It served as a workroom and a salon for literary visitors.

1195.22–23   Mrs. Scott-Siddons . . . Courtship']   Mary Frances Scott-Siddons (1844–96), an English actress, was the niece of the actress Fanny Kemble and the granddaughter of the famous Sarah Siddons. She appeared in America frequently, performing in several Shakespearian roles and giving readings from Victorian poetry. "Lady Geraldine's Courtship," a romantic ballad by Elizabeth Barrett Browning (in *Poems*, 1844), was famous chiefly for bringing about the first meeting with Robert Browning.

1281.1–2   Verbeckhoven . . . Sheep,"]   The Flemish painter Eugène Joseph Verboeckhoven (1798–1881) was known especially for paintings of animals in landscape. He was extremely popular with American picture-buyers.

CATALOGING INFORMATION

Wharton, Edith, 1862–1937.
  Novels: The house of mirth; The reef;
  The custom of the country; The age of innocence.
  Ed. by R.W.B. Lewis.

  (The Library of America ; 30)
I. Title. II. The house of mirth. III. The reef.
IV. The custom of the country. V. The age of innocence.
VI. Series.
PS3545.H16A6   1985   813'.52
ISBN 0-940450-31-3

For a list of titles in The Library of America, write to:
The Library of America
14 East 60th Street
New York, NY 10022

This book is set in 10 point Linotron Galliard,
a face designed for photocomposition by Matthew Carter
and based on the sixteenth-century face Granjon. The paper
is acid-free Ecusta Nyalite and meets the requirements for perma-
nence of the American National Standards Institute. The binding
material is Brillianta, a 100% woven rayon cloth made by
Van Heek-Scholco Textielfabrieken, Holland. The com-
position is by Haddon Craftsmen, Inc., and The
Clarinda Company. Printing and binding
by R. R. Donnelley & Sons Company.
Designed by Bruce Campbell.

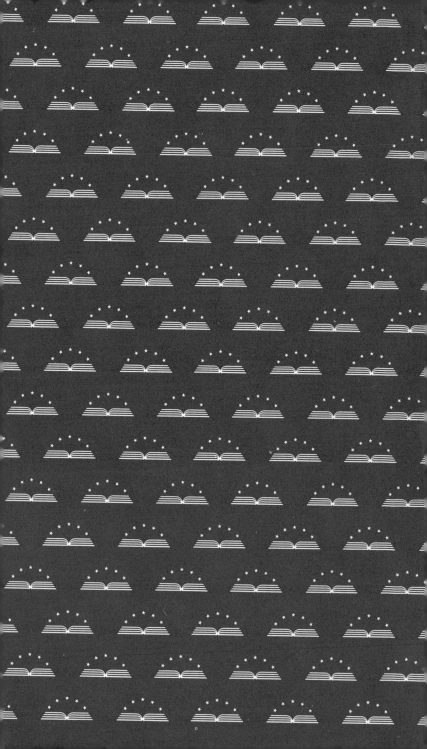